THE BABY-SITTERS CLUB

KRISTY'S GREAT IDEA

**DON'T MISS THE OTHER
BABY-SITTERS CLUB GRAPHIC NOVELS!**

THE TRUTH ABOUT STACEY

MARY ANNE SAVES THE DAY

CLAUDIA AND MEAN JANINE

DAWN AND THE IMPOSSIBLE THREE

ANN M. MARTIN

THE BABY-SITTERS CLUB

KRISTY'S GREAT IDEA

A GRAPHIC NOVEL BY
RAINA TELGEMEIER
WITH COLOR BY BRADEN LAMB

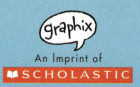

An Imprint of
SCHOLASTIC

Text copyright © 2006, 2015 by Ann M. Martin
Art copyright © 2006, 2015 by Raina Telgemeier

All rights reserved. Published by Graphix, an imprint of Scholastic Inc., *Publishers since 1920*. SCHOLASTIC, GRAPHIX, THE BABY-SITTERS CLUB, and associated logos are trademarks and/or registered trademarks of Scholastic Inc.

The publisher does not have any control over and does not assume any responsibility for author or third-party websites or their content.

No part of this publication may be reproduced, stored in a retrieval system, or transmitted in any form or by any means, electronic, mechanical, photocopying, recording, or otherwise, without written permission of the publisher. For information regarding permission, write to Scholastic Inc., Attention: Permissions Department, 557 Broadway, New York, NY 10012.

This book is a work of fiction. Names, characters, places, and incidents are either the product of the author's imagination or are used fictitiously, and any resemblance to actual persons, living or dead, business establishments, events, or locales is entirely coincidental.

Library of Congress Control Number: 2014945626

ISBN 978-0-545-81386-0 (hardcover)
ISBN 978-1-338-88823-2 (paperback)

10 9 8 7 6 5   24 25 26 27

Printed in China   62
This edition first printing, April 2023

Lettering by Comicraft
Edited by Cassandra Pelham Fulton, Janna Morishima, and David Levithan
Book design by Phil Falco
Creative Director: David Saylor

This book is for Beth McKeever Perkins, my old baby-sitting buddy.
With Love (and years of memories)
A. M. M.

Thanks to my family and friends, KC Witherell, Marisa Bulzone, Jason Little,
Ellie Berger, Jean Feiwel, David Saylor, David Levithan, Janna Morishima,
Cassandra Pelham, Phil Falco, Braden Lamb, my fellow cartoonists,
and A. M. M. for being an inspiration!
R. T.

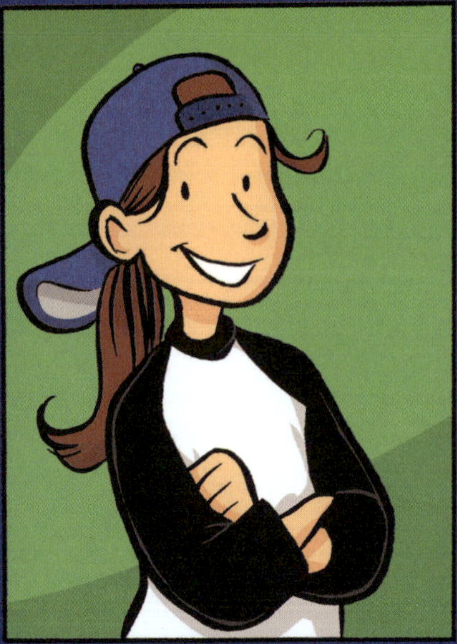

KRISTY THOMAS
PRESIDENT

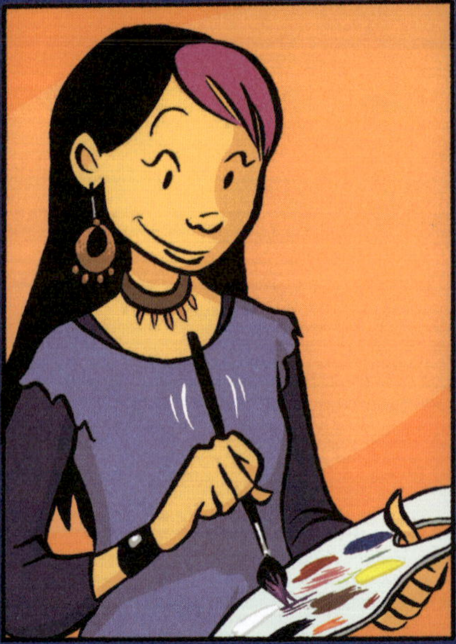

CLAUDIA KISHI
VICE PRESIDENT

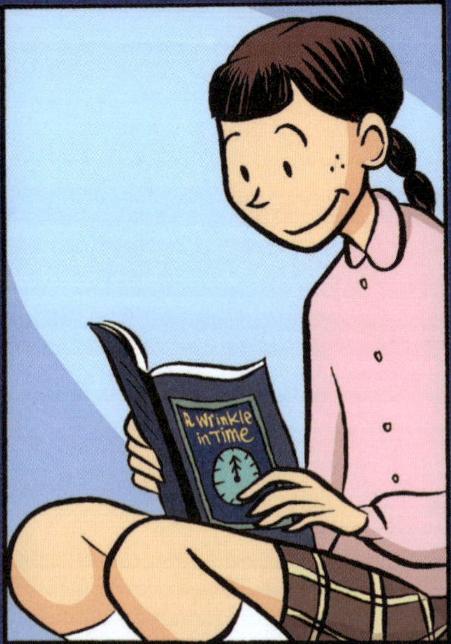
A Wrinkle in Time

MARY ANNE SPIER
SECRETARY

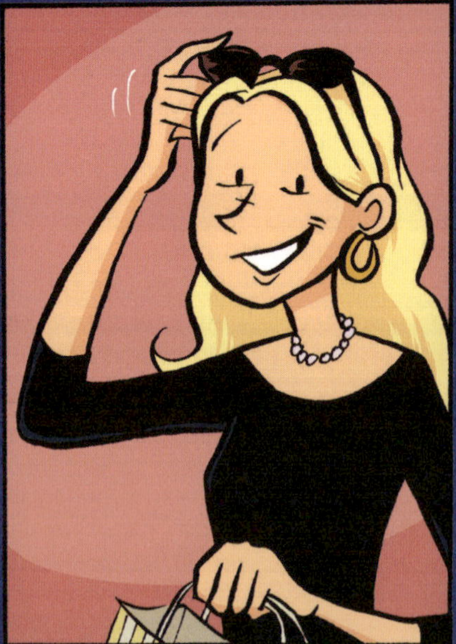

STACEY MCGILL
TREASURER

CHAPTER 1

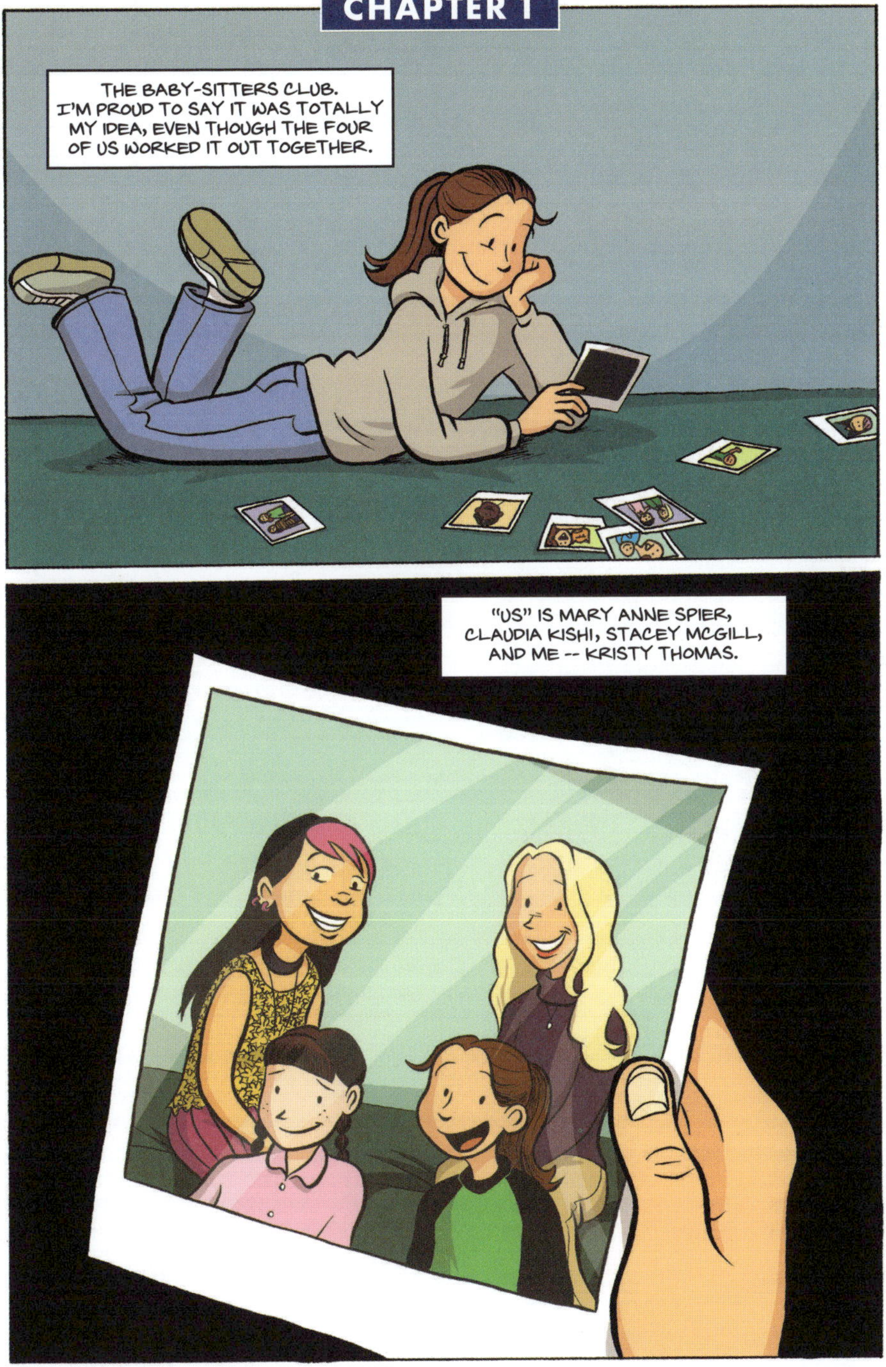
THE BABY-SITTERS CLUB. I'M PROUD TO SAY IT WAS TOTALLY MY IDEA, EVEN THOUGH THE FOUR OF US WORKED IT OUT TOGETHER.
"US" IS MARY ANNE SPIER, CLAUDIA KISHI, STACEY MCGILL, AND ME -- KRISTY THOMAS.

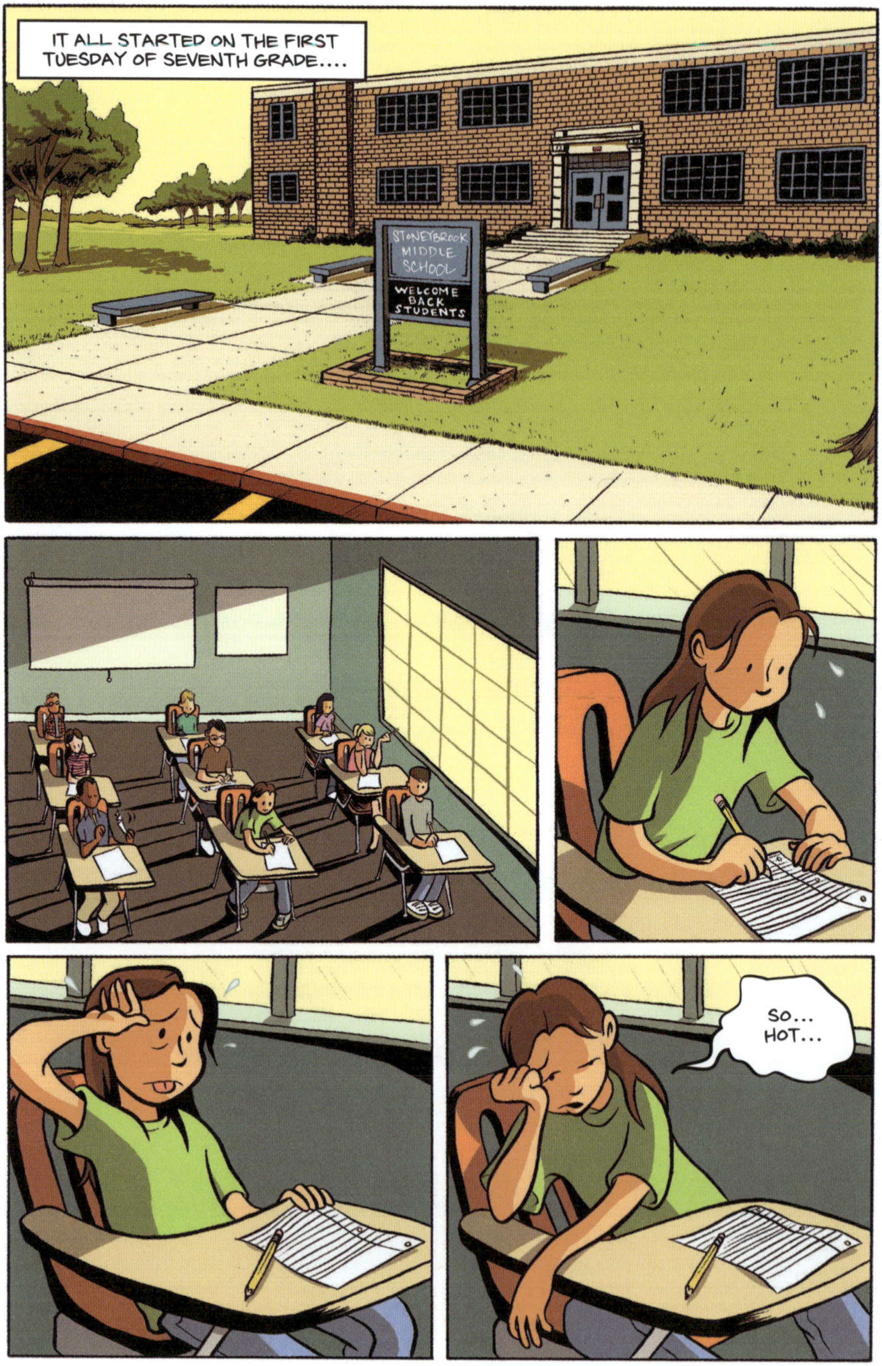
IT ALL STARTED ON THE FIRST TUESDAY OF SEVENTH GRADE....
STONEYBROOK MIDDLE SCHOOL
WELCOME BACK STUDENTS
SO... HOT...

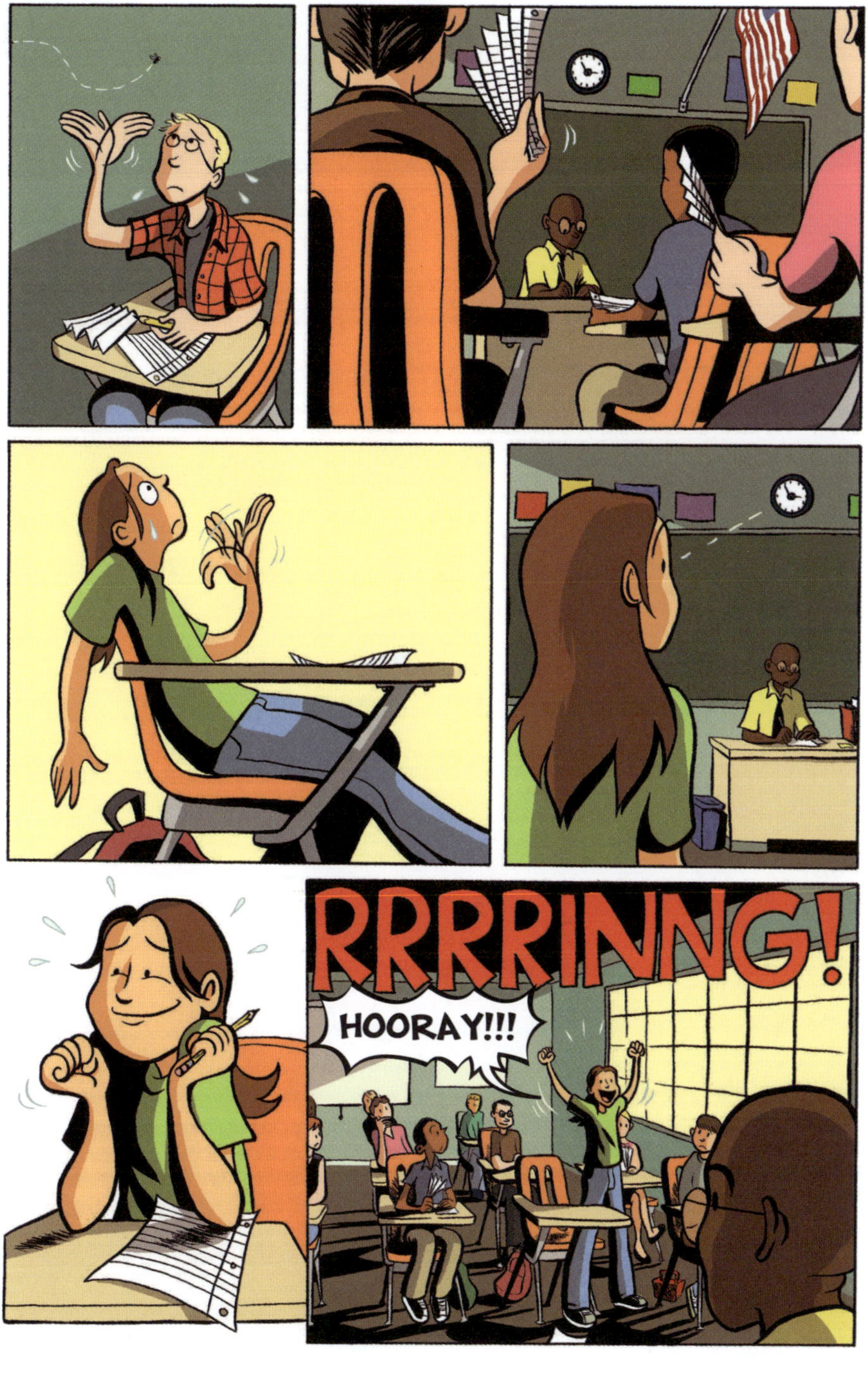
RRRRINNG!
HOORAY!!!

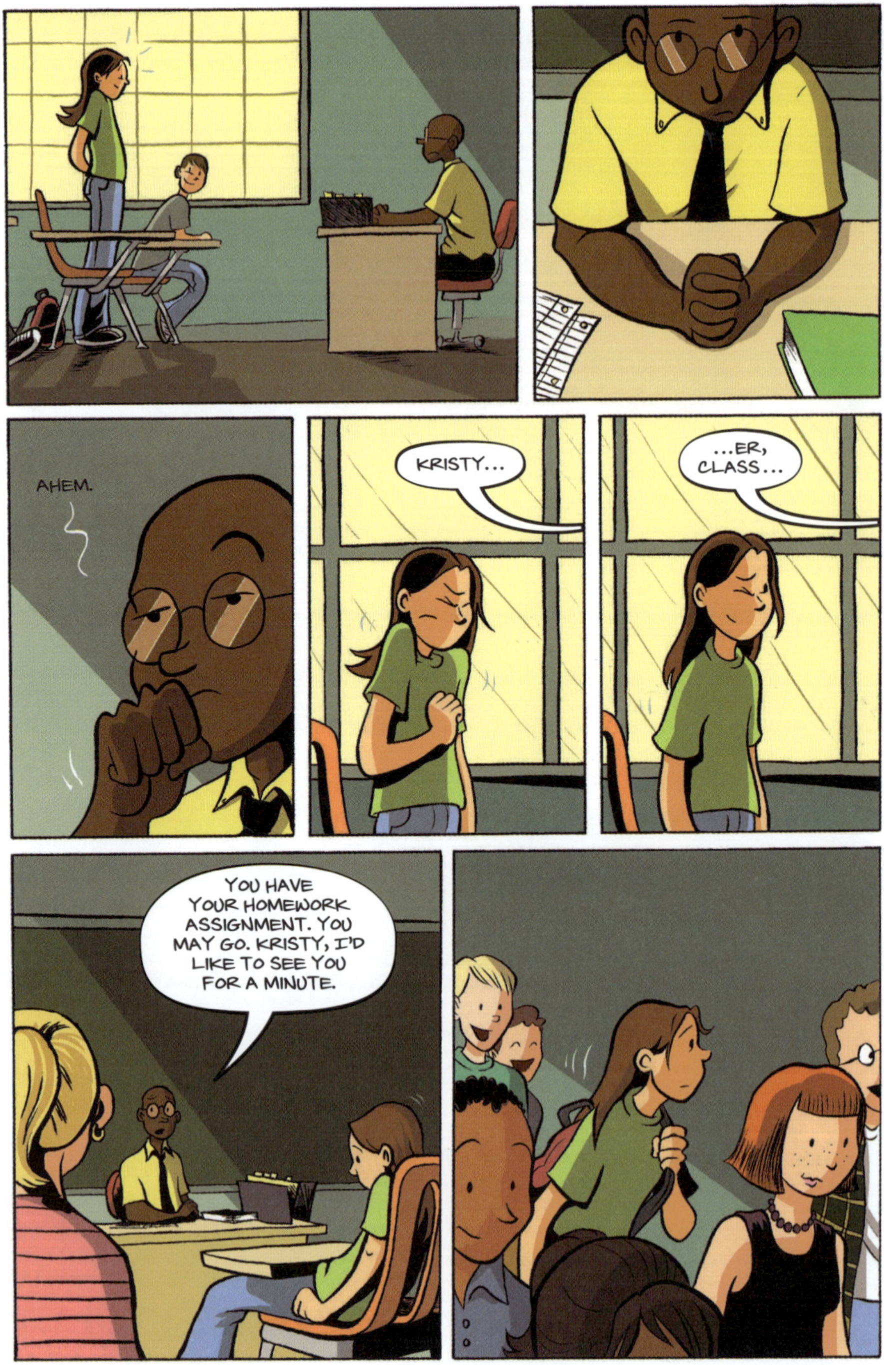
AHEM.
KRISTY...
...ER, CLASS...
YOU HAVE YOUR HOMEWORK ASSIGNMENT. YOU MAY GO. KRISTY, I'D LIKE TO SEE YOU FOR A MINUTE.

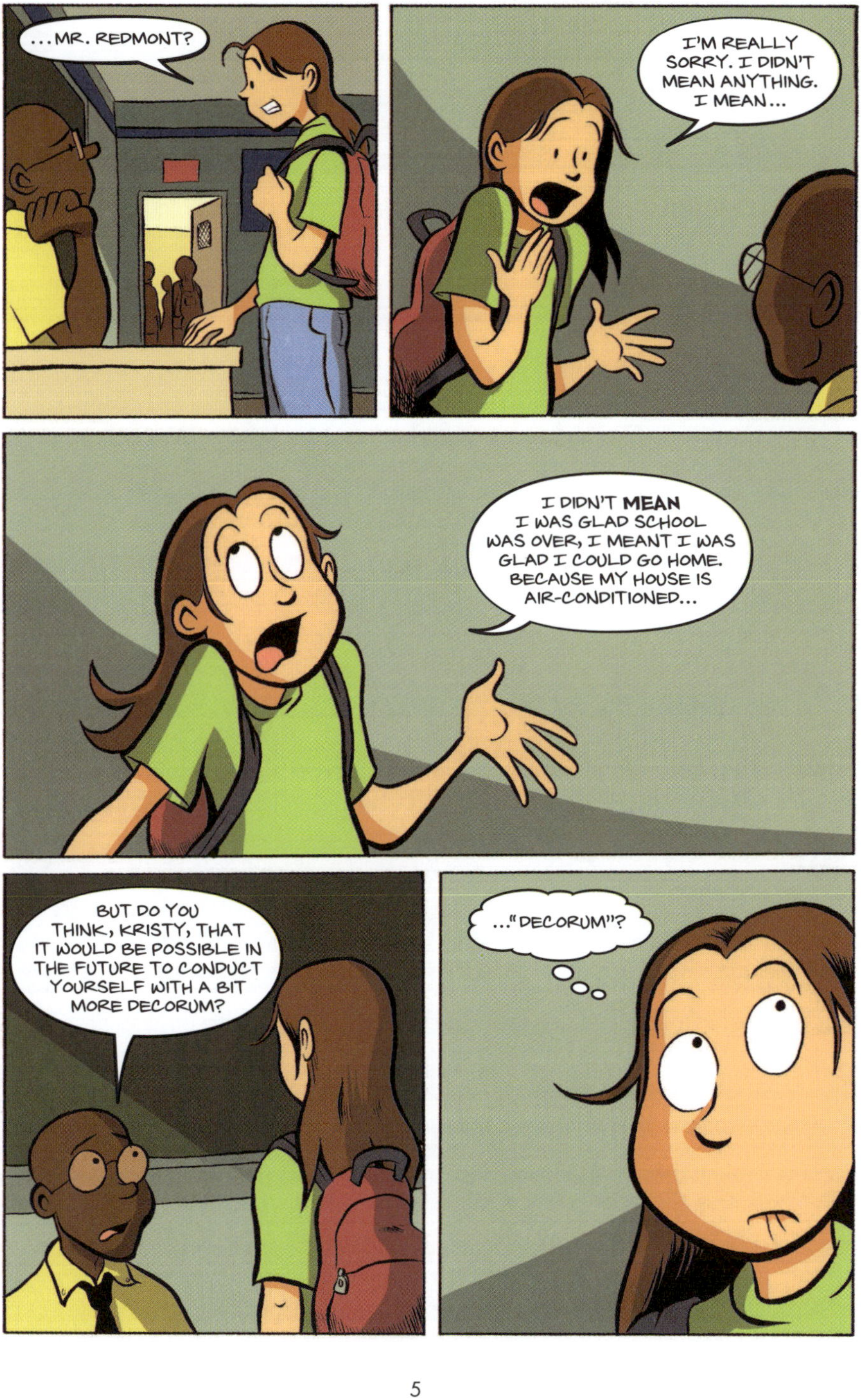
...MR. REDMONT?
I'M REALLY SORRY. I DIDN'T MEAN ANYTHING. I MEAN...
I DIDN'T **MEAN** I WAS GLAD SCHOOL WAS OVER, I MEANT I WAS GLAD I COULD GO HOME. BECAUSE MY HOUSE IS AIR-CONDITIONED...
BUT DO YOU THINK, KRISTY, THAT IT WOULD BE POSSIBLE IN THE FUTURE TO CONDUCT YOURSELF WITH A BIT MORE DECORUM?
..."DECORUM"?

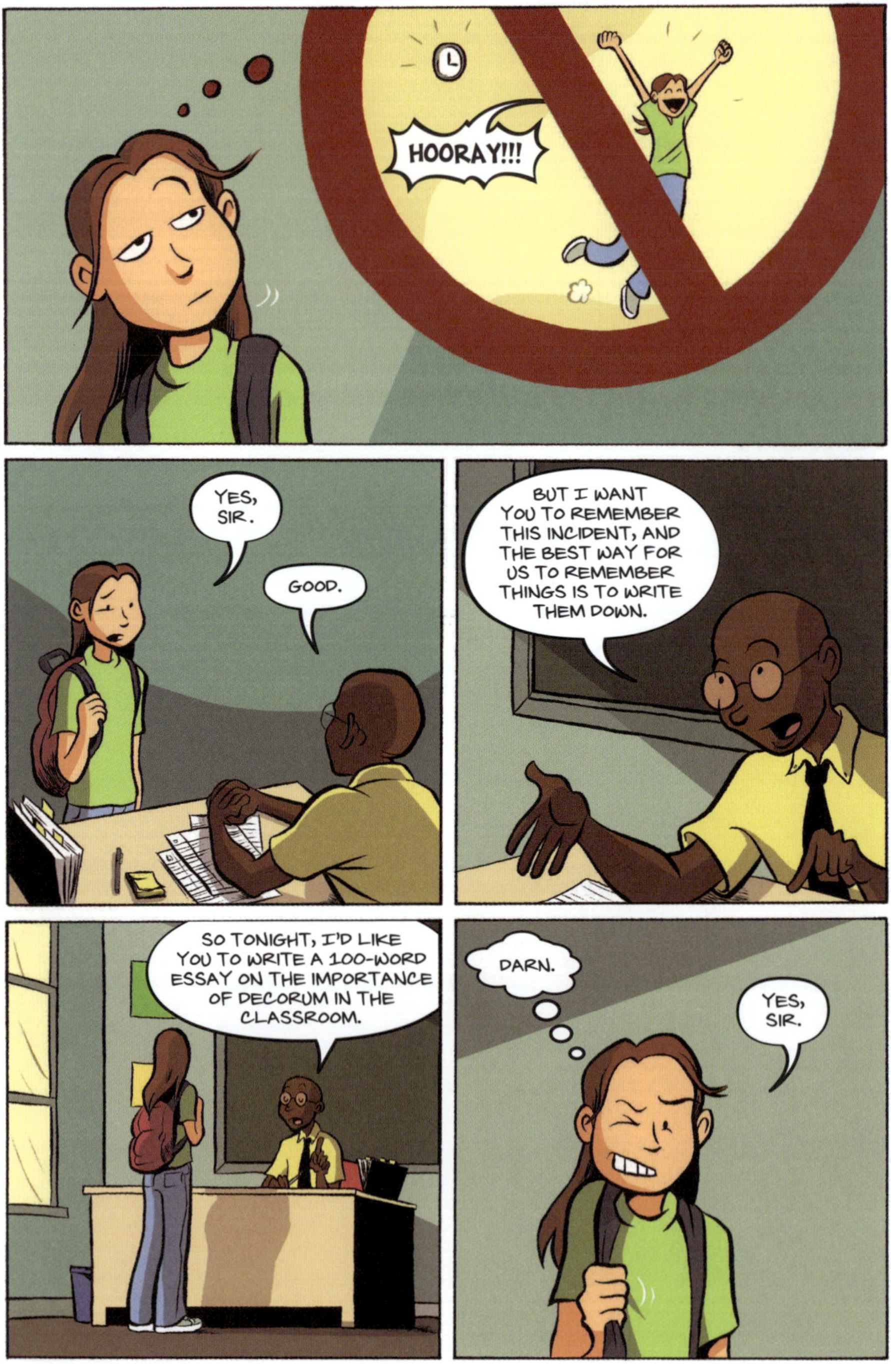
HOORAY!!!
YES, SIR.
GOOD.
BUT I WANT YOU TO REMEMBER THIS INCIDENT, AND THE BEST WAY FOR US TO REMEMBER THINGS IS TO WRITE THEM DOWN.
SO TONIGHT, I'D LIKE YOU TO WRITE A 100-WORD ESSAY ON THE IMPORTANCE OF DECORUM IN THE CLASSROOM.
DARN.
YES, SIR.

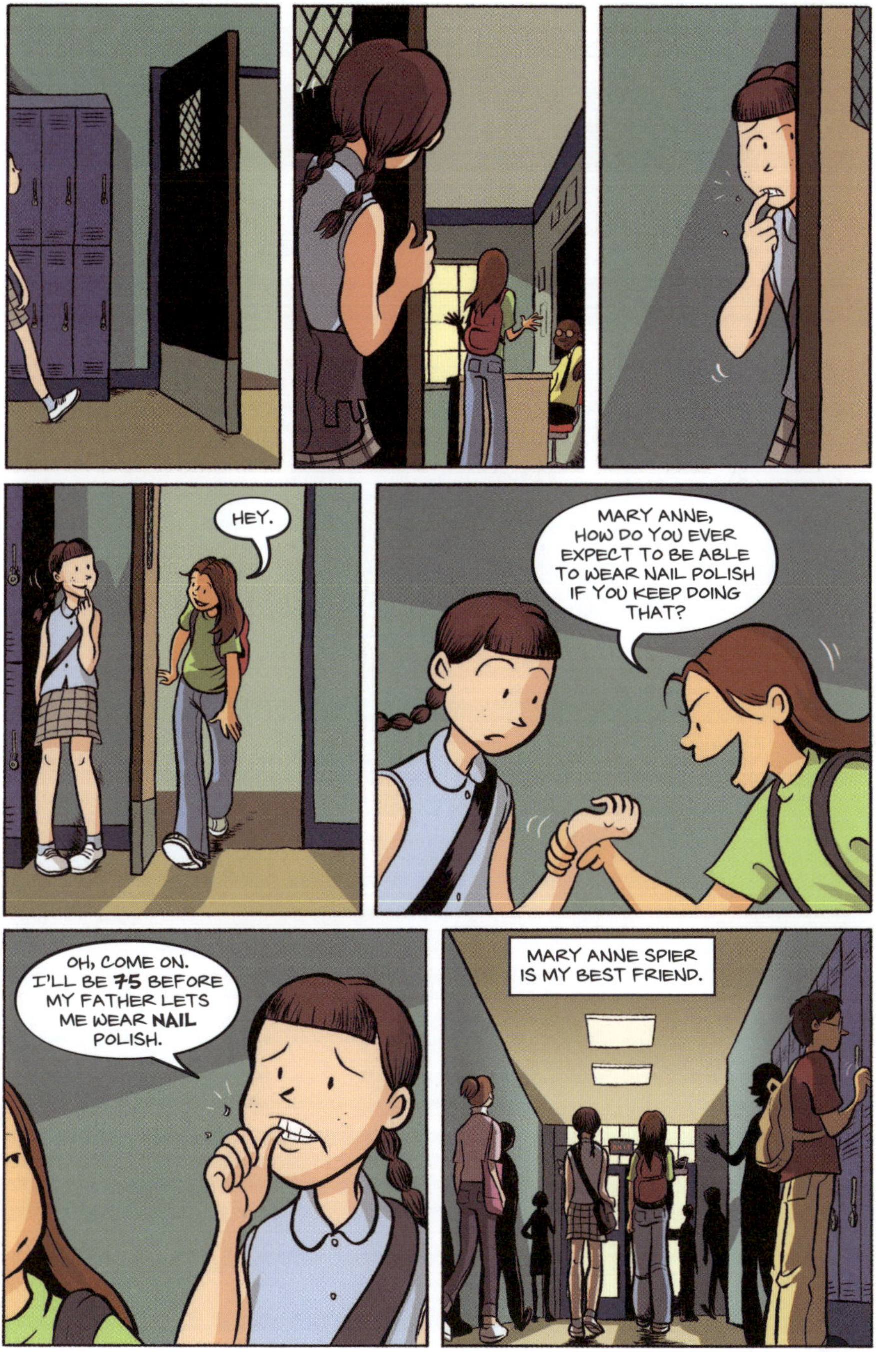
HEY.
MARY ANNE, HOW DO YOU EVER EXPECT TO BE ABLE TO WEAR NAIL POLISH IF YOU KEEP DOING THAT?
OH, COME ON. I'LL BE 75 BEFORE MY FATHER LETS ME WEAR NAIL POLISH.
MARY ANNE SPIER IS MY BEST FRIEND.

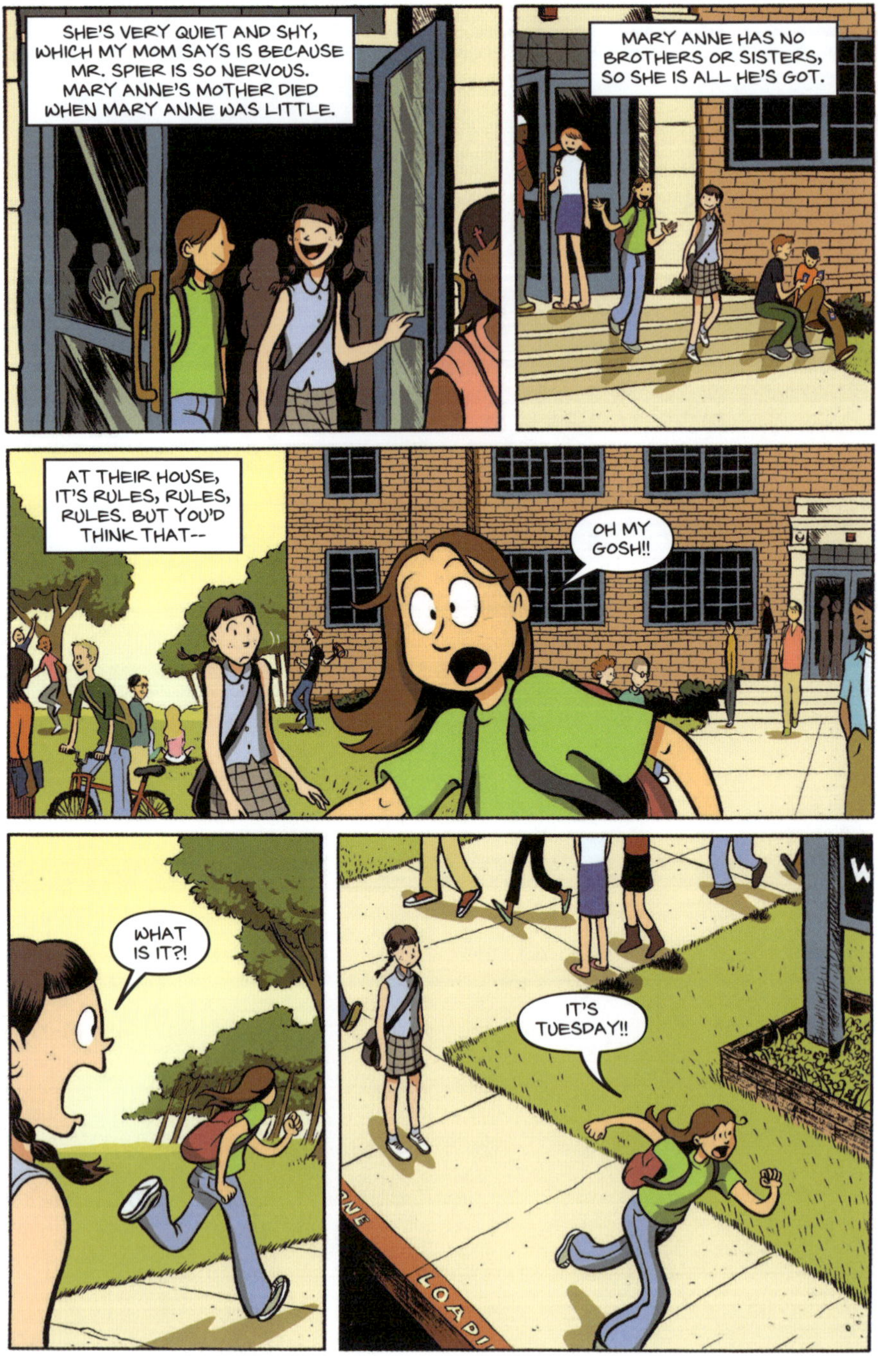
SHE'S VERY QUIET AND SHY, WHICH MY MOM SAYS IS BECAUSE MR. SPIER IS SO NERVOUS. MARY ANNE'S MOTHER DIED WHEN MARY ANNE WAS LITTLE.
MARY ANNE HAS NO BROTHERS OR SISTERS, SO SHE IS ALL HE'S GOT.
AT THEIR HOUSE, IT'S RULES, RULES, RULES. BUT YOU'D THINK THAT--
OH MY GOSH!!
WHAT IS IT?!
IT'S TUESDAY!!

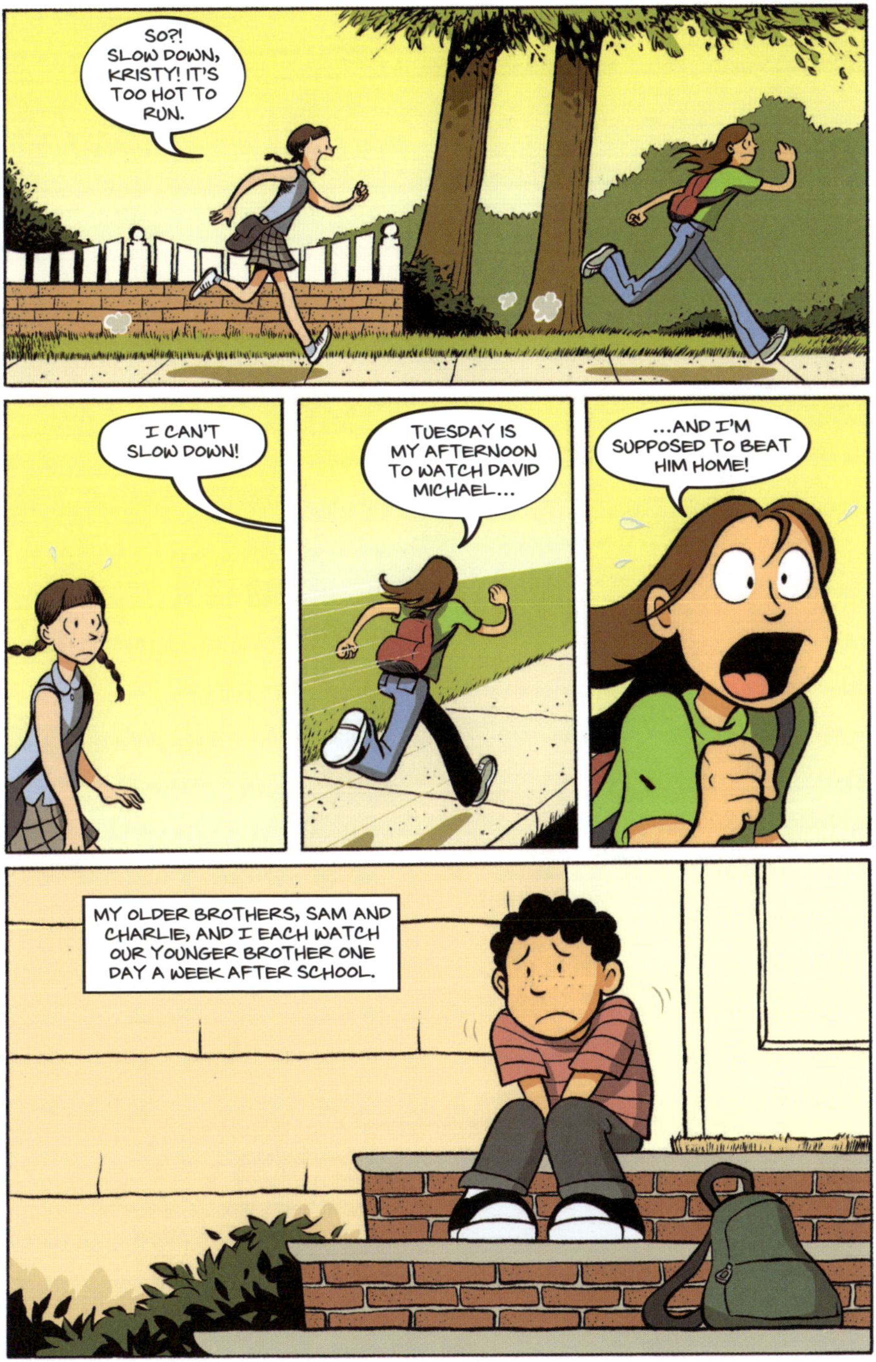
SO?! SLOW DOWN, KRISTY! IT'S TOO HOT TO RUN.
I CAN'T SLOW DOWN!
TUESDAY IS MY AFTERNOON TO WATCH DAVID MICHAEL...
...AND I'M SUPPOSED TO BEAT HIM HOME!
MY OLDER BROTHERS, SAM AND CHARLIE, AND I EACH WATCH OUR YOUNGER BROTHER ONE DAY A WEEK AFTER SCHOOL.

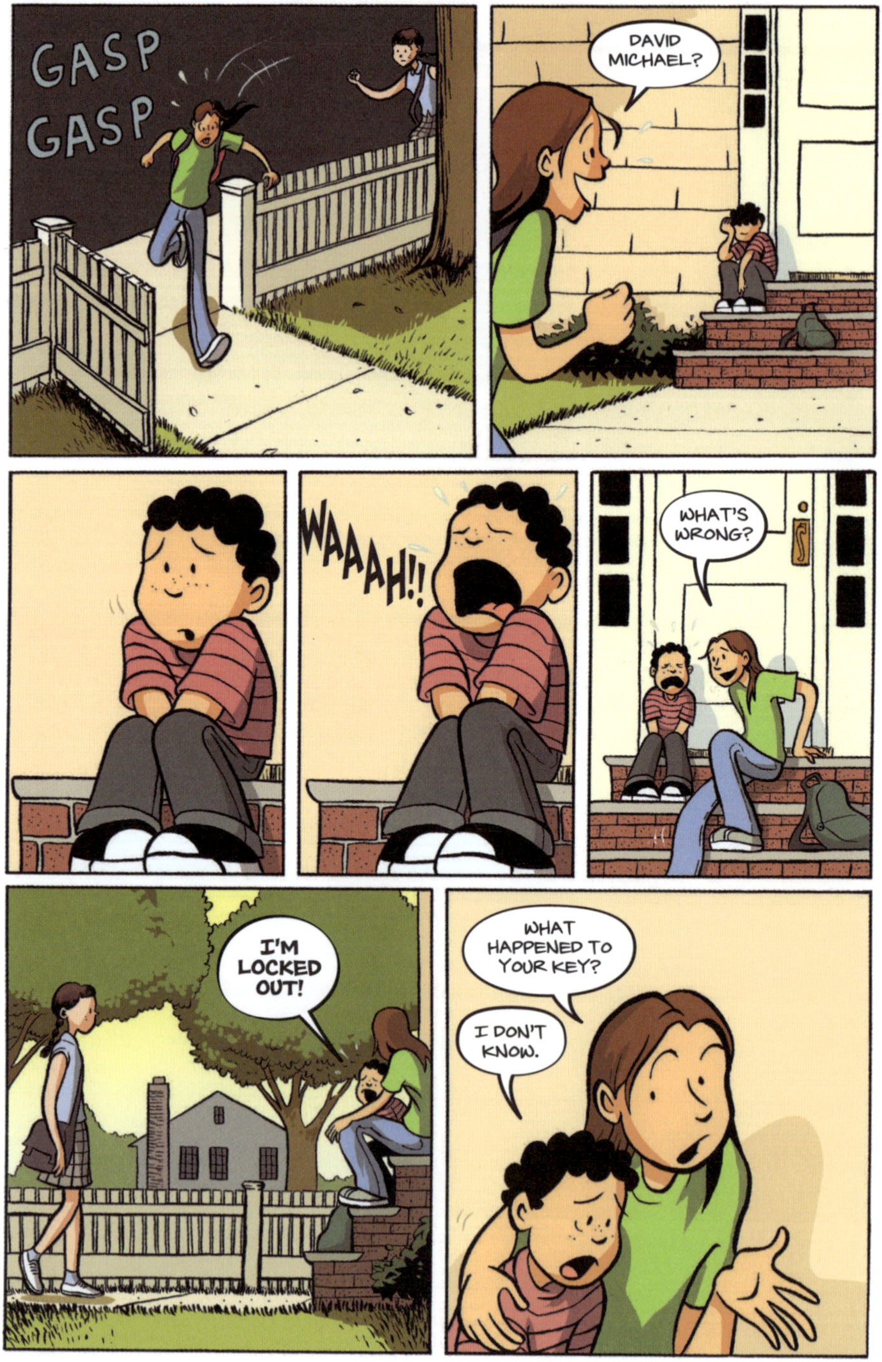
GASP
GASP
DAVID MICHAEL?
WAAAH!!
WHAT'S WRONG?
I'M LOCKED OUT!
WHAT HAPPENED TO YOUR KEY?
I DON'T KNOW.

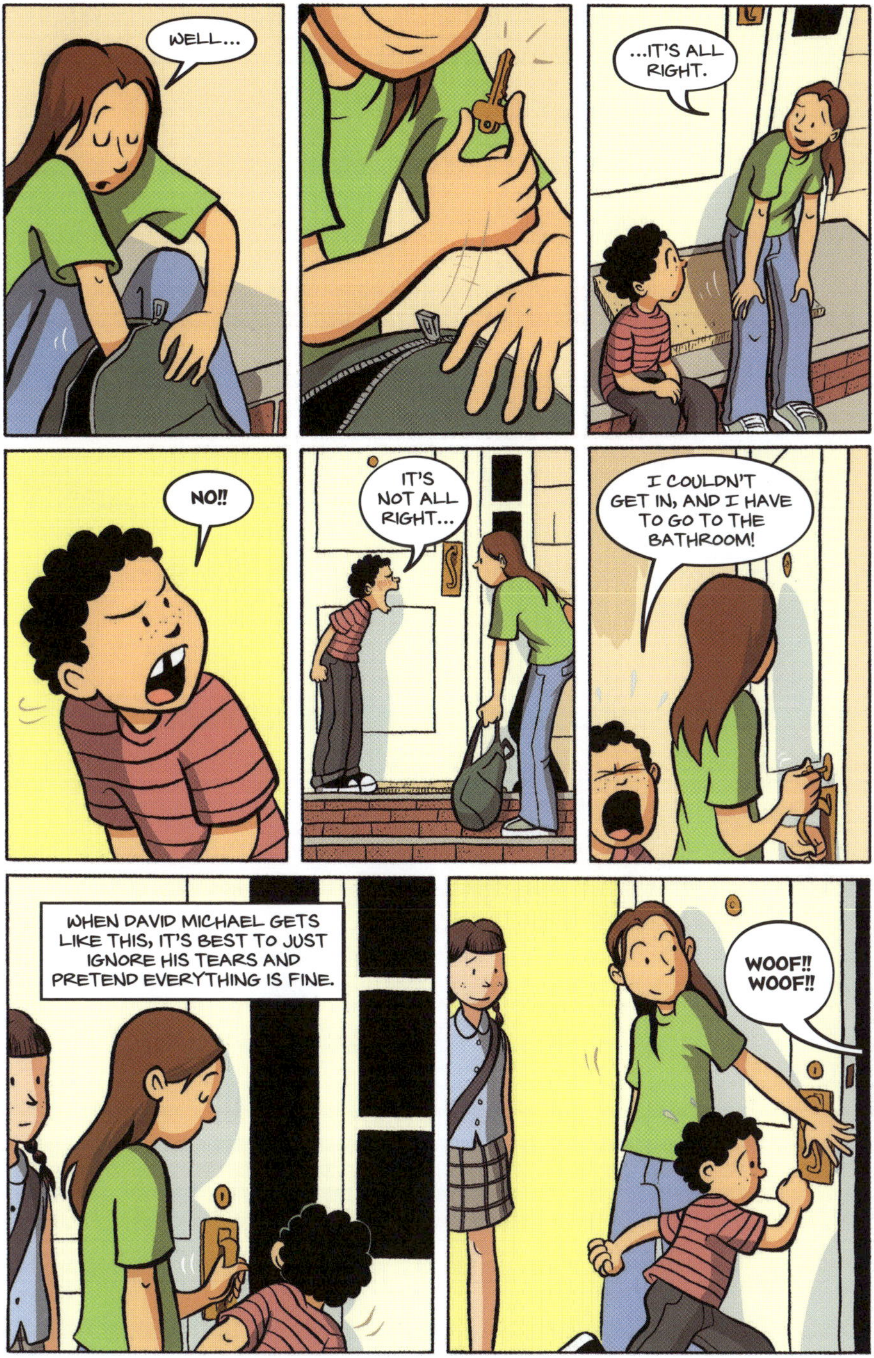
WELL...
...IT'S ALL RIGHT.
NO!!
IT'S NOT ALL RIGHT...
I COULDN'T GET IN, AND I HAVE TO GO TO THE BATHROOM!
WHEN DAVID MICHAEL GETS LIKE THIS, IT'S BEST TO JUST IGNORE HIS TEARS AND PRETEND EVERYTHING IS FINE.
WOOF!! WOOF!!

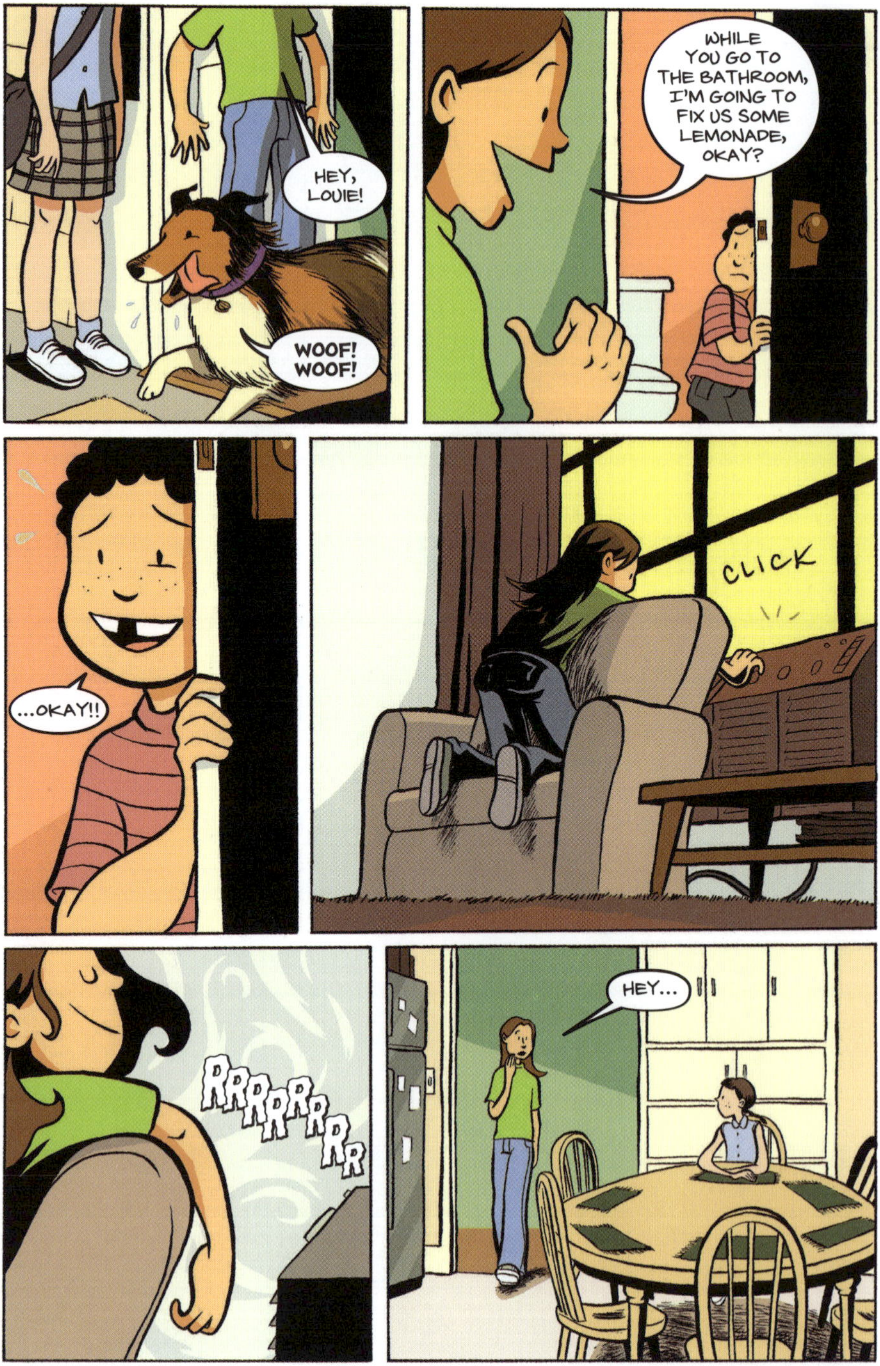
HEY, LOUIE!
WOOF! WOOF!
WHILE YOU GO TO THE BATHROOM, I'M GOING TO FIX US SOME LEMONADE, OKAY?
...OKAY!!
CLICK
RRRRRRRRRR
HEY...

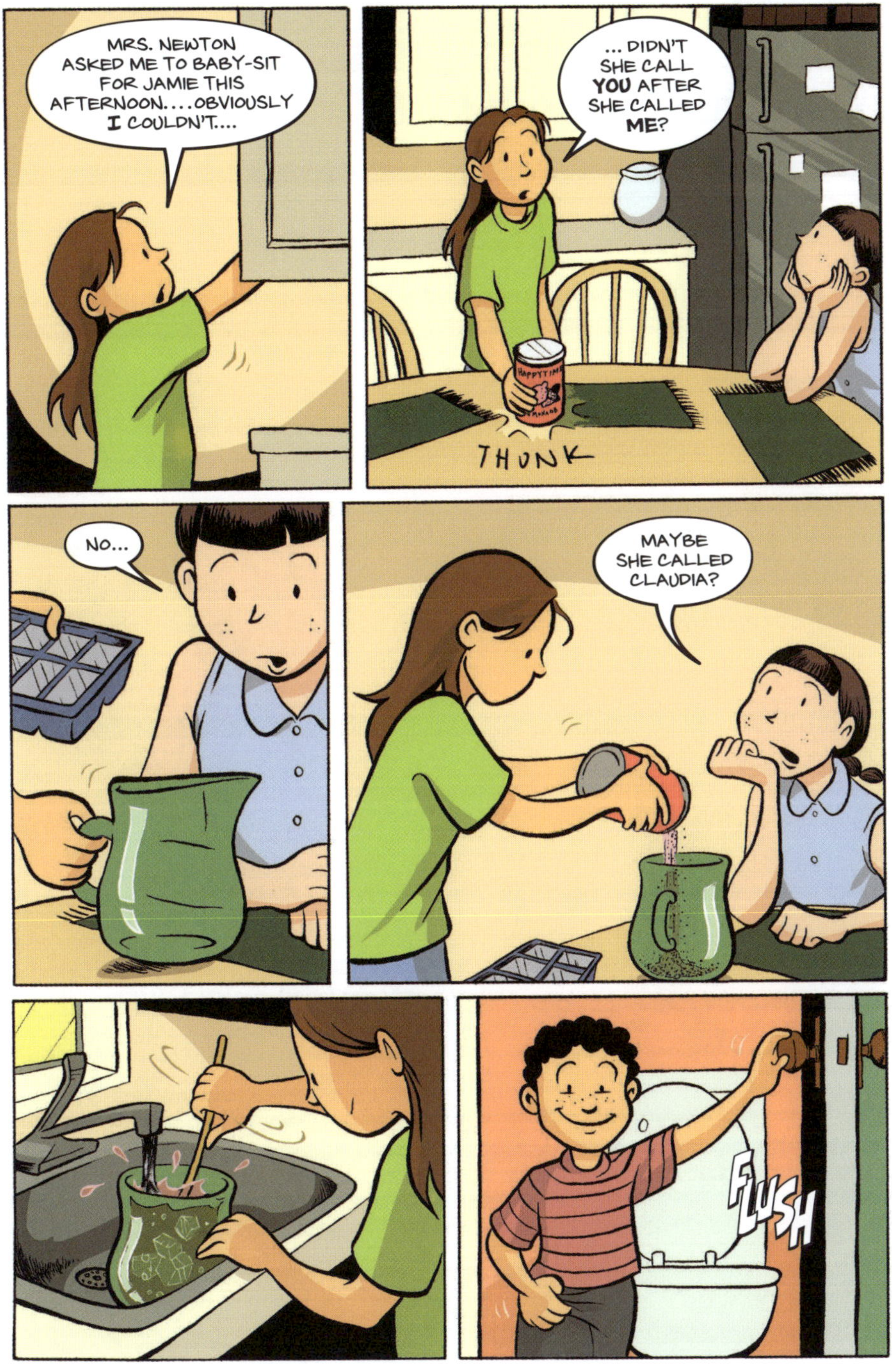
MRS. NEWTON ASKED ME TO BABY-SIT FOR JAMIE THIS AFTERNOON....OBVIOUSLY I COULDN'T....
...DIDN'T SHE CALL YOU AFTER SHE CALLED ME?
THUNK
NO...
MAYBE SHE CALLED CLAUDIA?
FLUSH

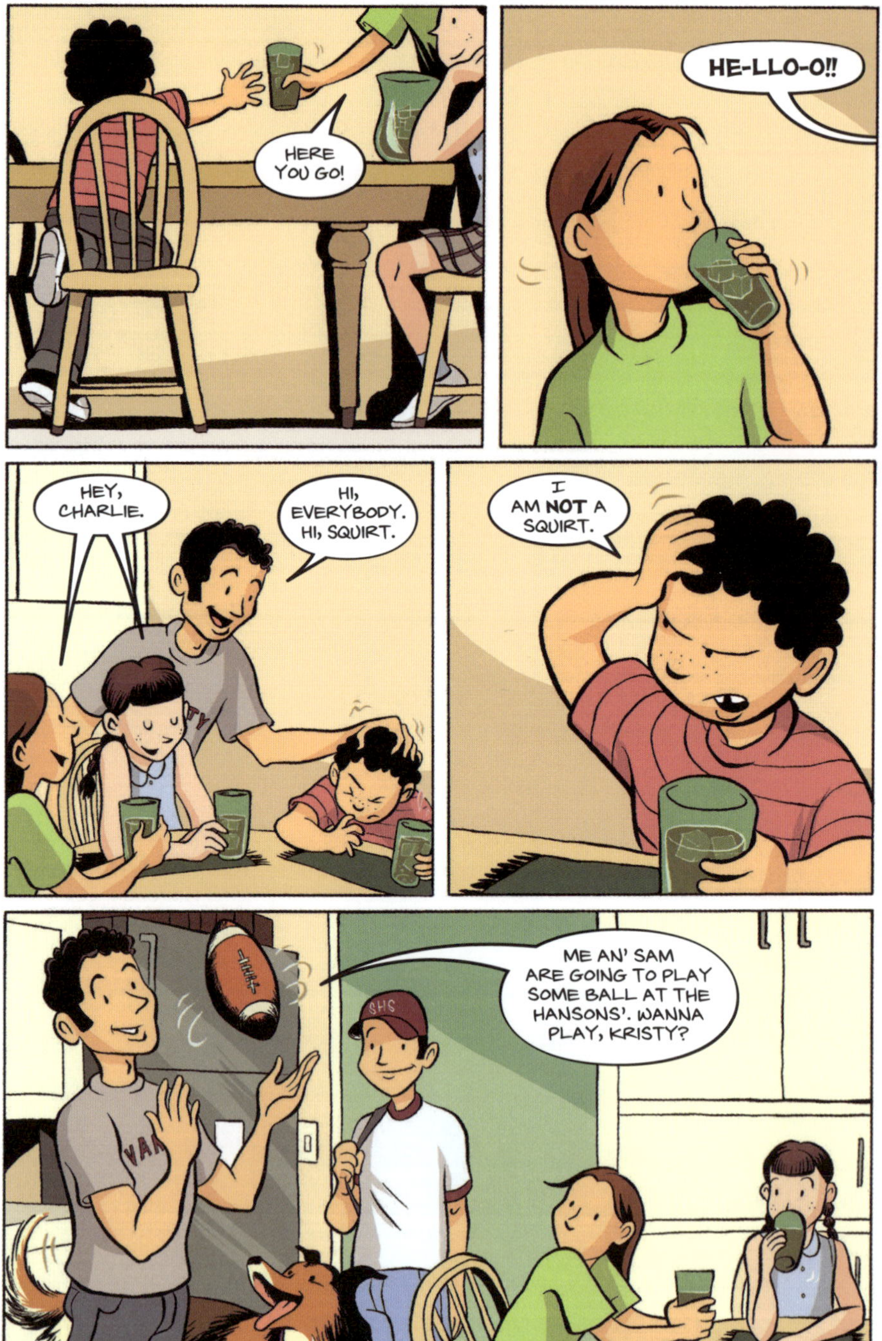
HERE YOU GO!
HE-LLO-O!!
HEY, CHARLIE.
HI, EVERYBODY. HI, SQUIRT.
I AM **NOT** A SQUIRT.
ME AN' SAM ARE GOING TO PLAY SOME BALL AT THE HANSONS'. WANNA PLAY, KRISTY?

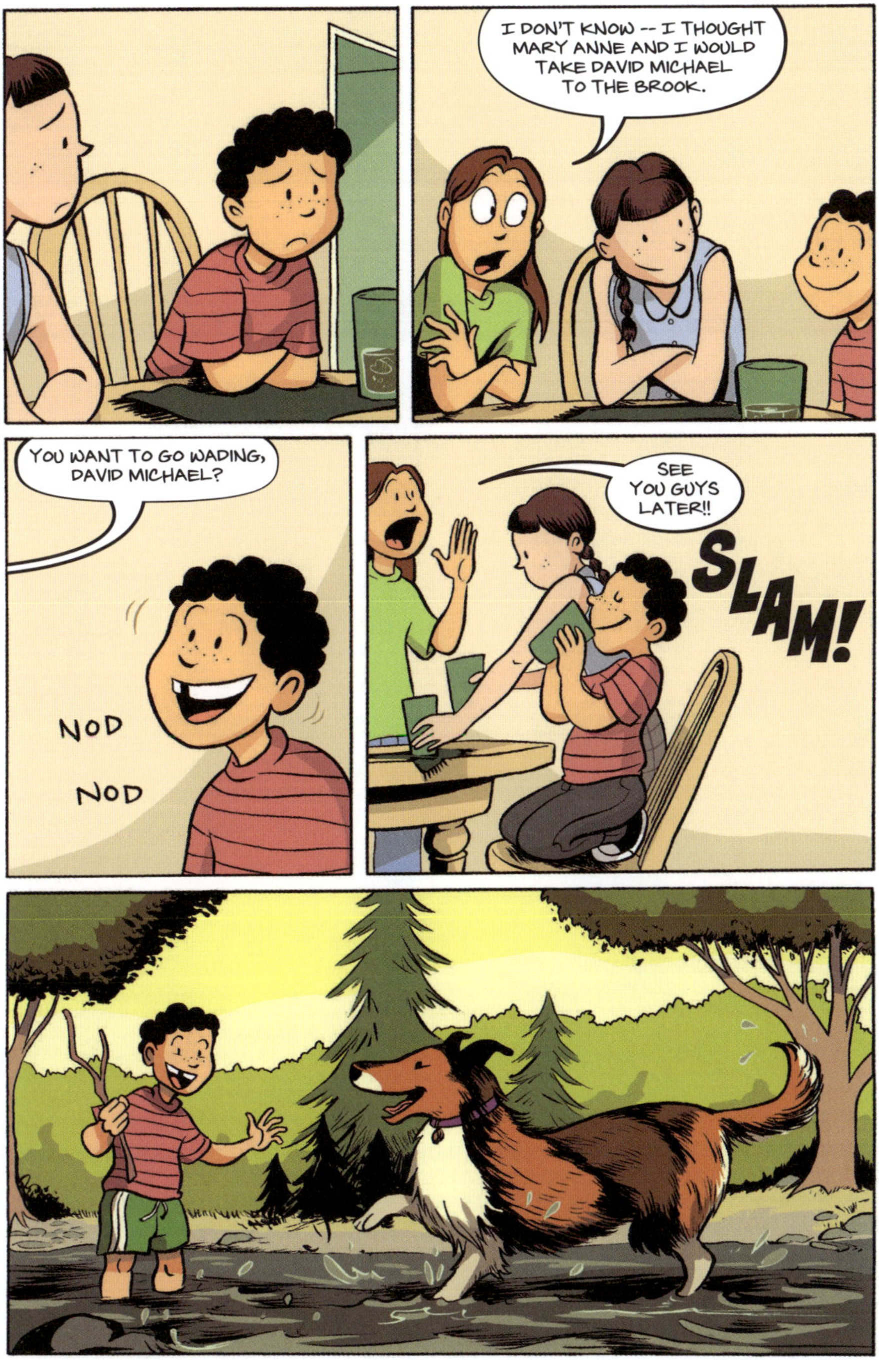
I DON'T KNOW -- I THOUGHT MARY ANNE AND I WOULD TAKE DAVID MICHAEL TO THE BROOK.
YOU WANT TO GO WADING, DAVID MICHAEL?
NOD
NOD
SEE YOU GUYS LATER!!
SLAM!

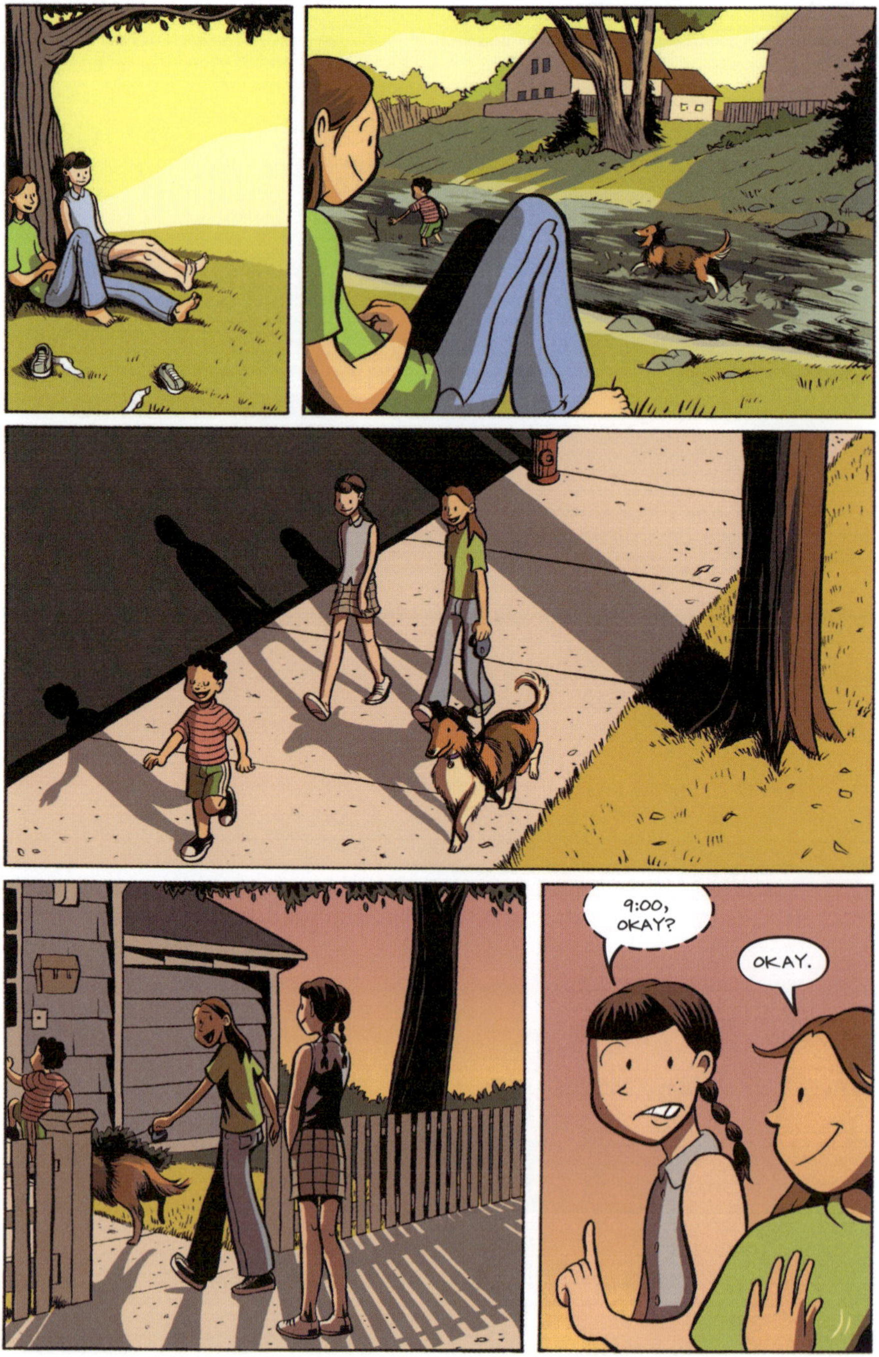
9:00, OKAY?
OKAY.

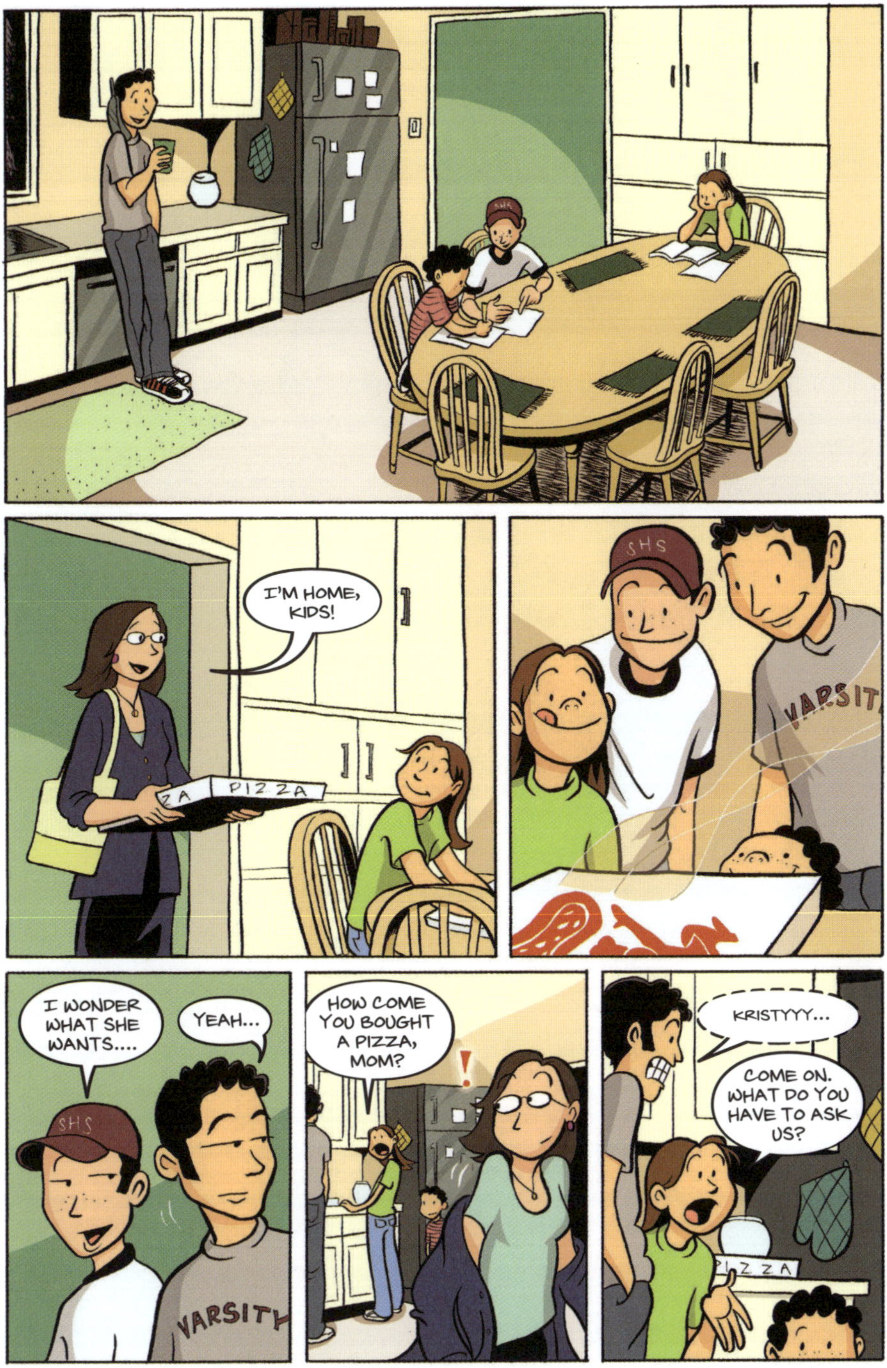
I'M HOME, KIDS!
PIZZA
VARSITY
I WONDER WHAT SHE WANTS....
YEAH...
HOW COME YOU BOUGHT A PIZZA, MOM?
!
KRISTYYY...
COME ON. WHAT DO YOU HAVE TO ASK US?

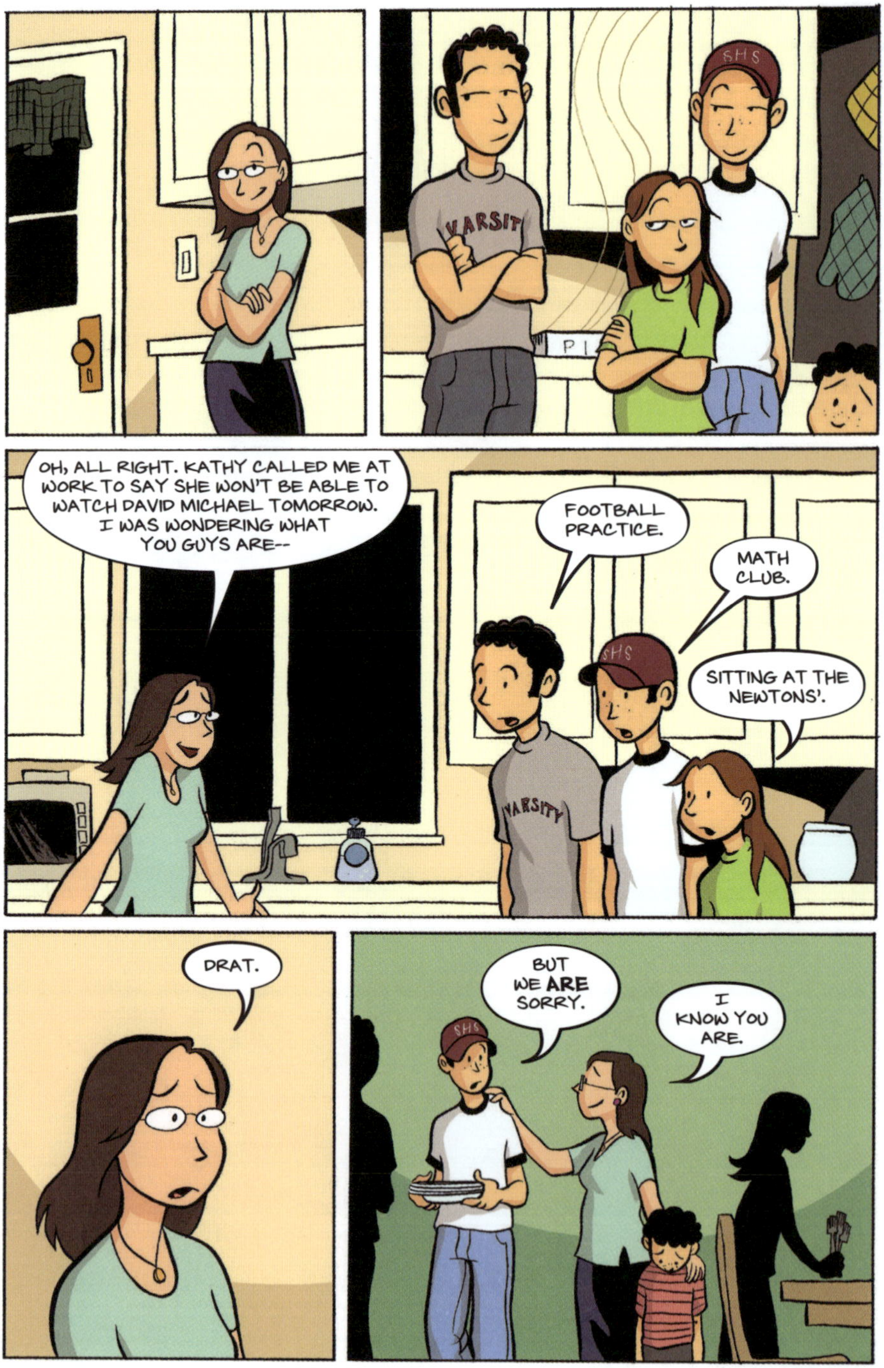
OH, ALL RIGHT. KATHY CALLED ME AT WORK TO SAY SHE WON'T BE ABLE TO WATCH DAVID MICHAEL TOMORROW. I WAS WONDERING WHAT YOU GUYS ARE--
FOOTBALL PRACTICE.
MATH CLUB.
SITTING AT THE NEWTONS'.
DRAT.
BUT WE **ARE** SORRY.
I KNOW YOU ARE.

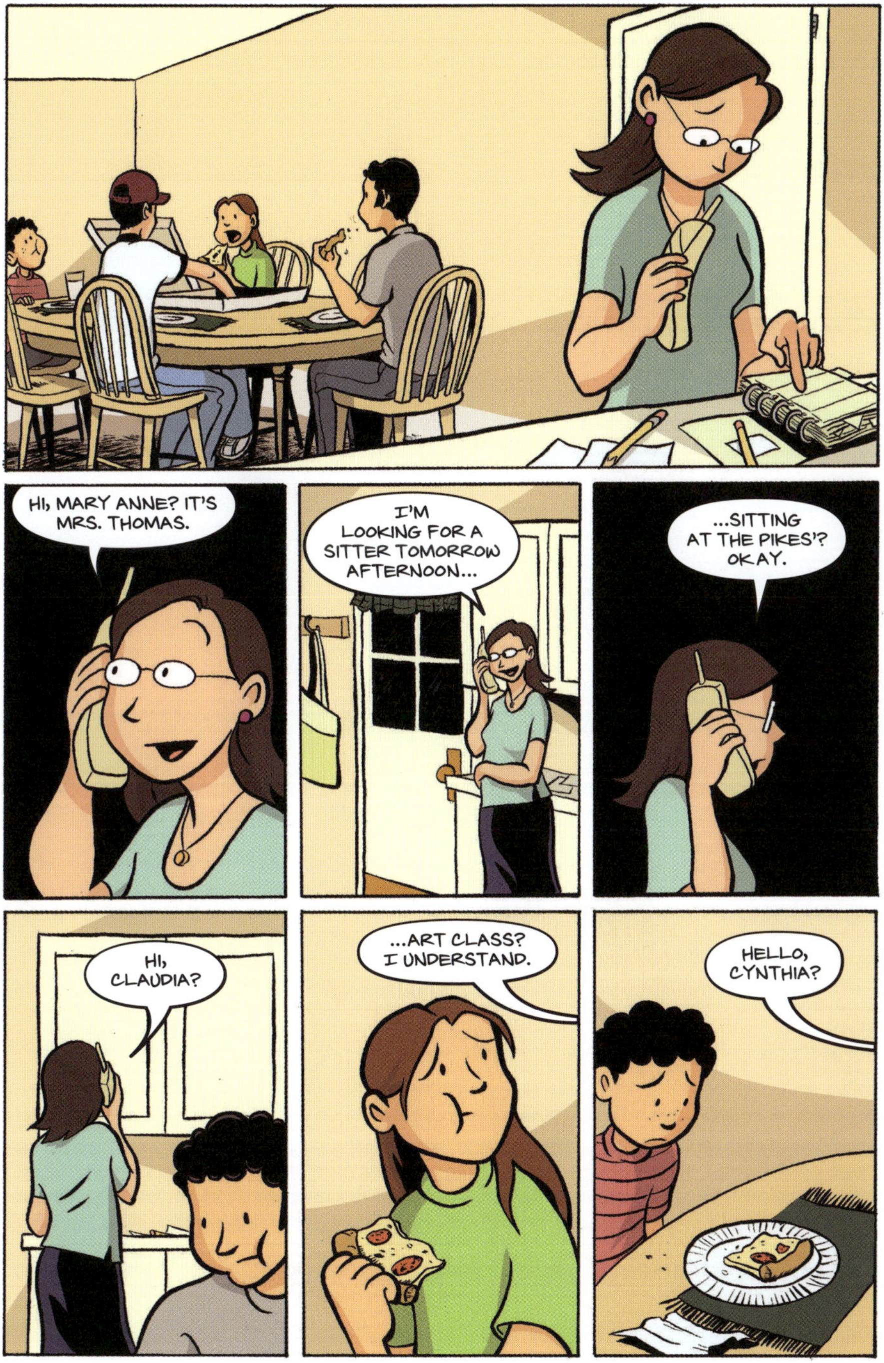
HI, MARY ANNE? IT'S MRS. THOMAS.
I'M LOOKING FOR A SITTER TOMORROW AFTERNOON...
...SITTING AT THE PIKES'? OKAY.
HI, CLAUDIA?
...ART CLASS? I UNDERSTAND.
HELLO, CYNTHIA?

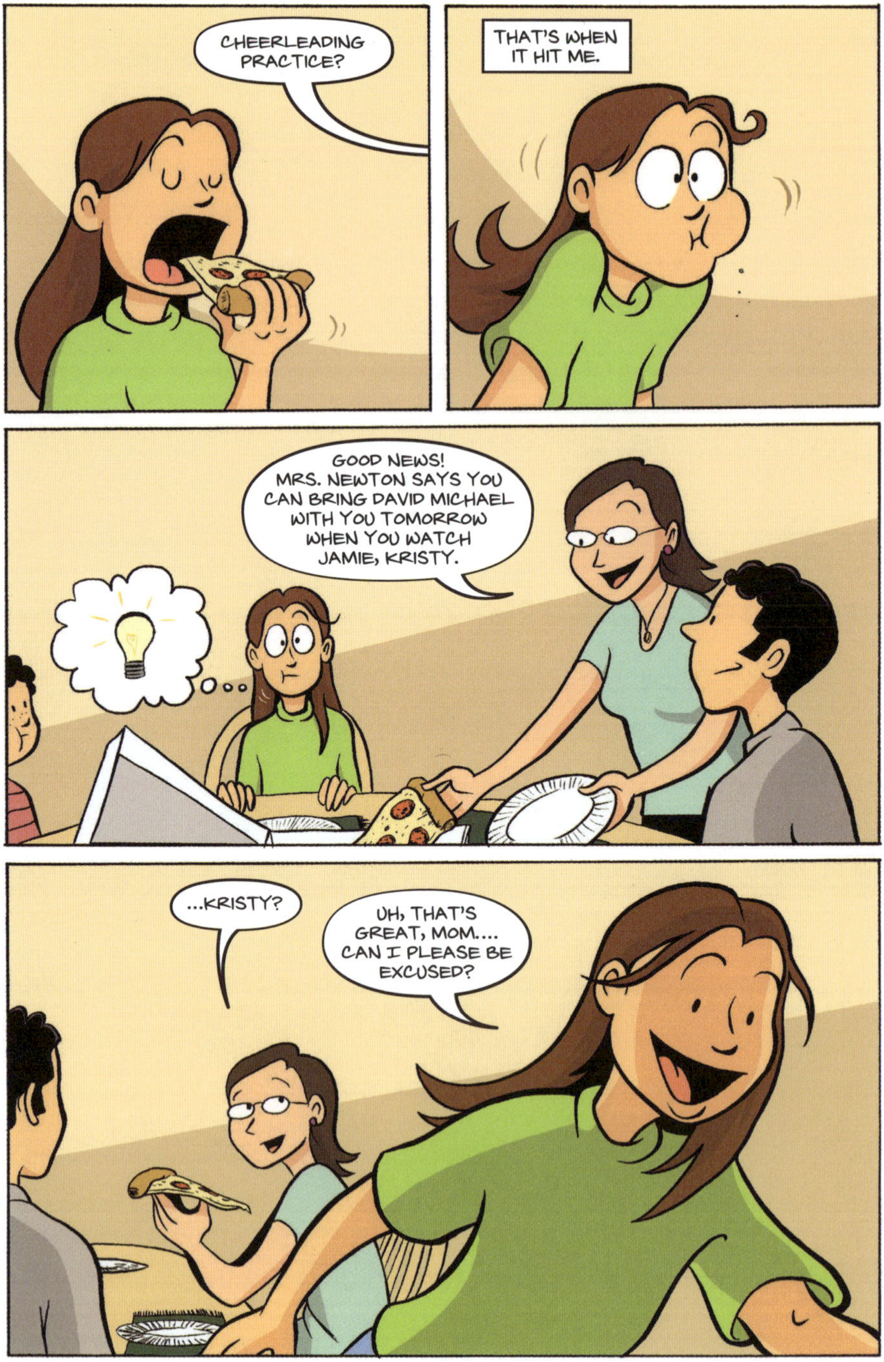

CHEERLEADING PRACTICE?
THAT'S WHEN IT HIT ME.
GOOD NEWS! MRS. NEWTON SAYS YOU CAN BRING DAVID MICHAEL WITH YOU TOMORROW WHEN YOU WATCH JAMIE, KRISTY.
...KRISTY?
UH, THAT'S GREAT, MOM.... CAN I PLEASE BE EXCUSED?

CHAPTER 2

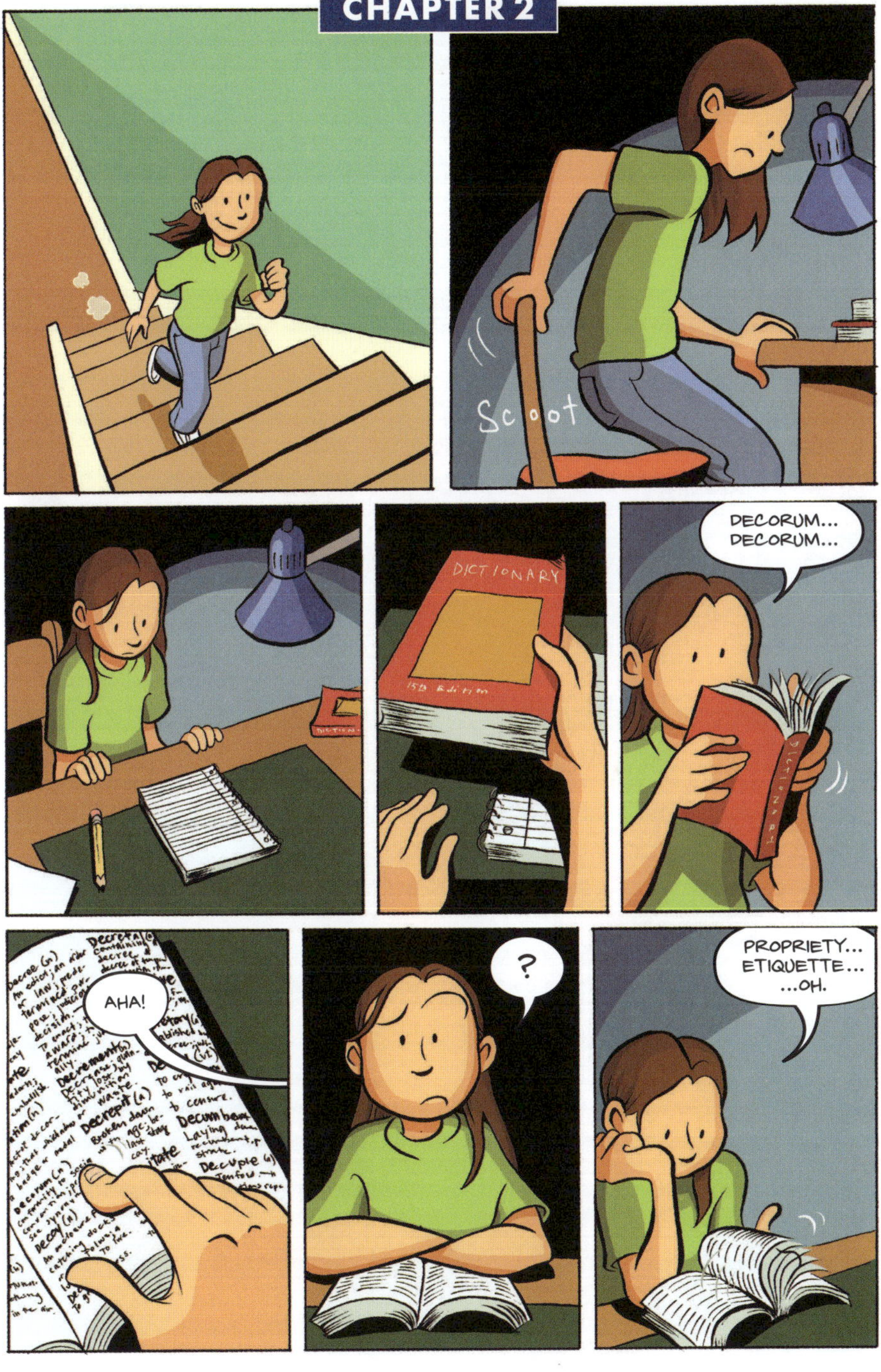
Scoot
DICTIONARY
DECORUM... DECORUM...
AHA!
?
PROPRIETY... ETIQUETTE... ...OH.

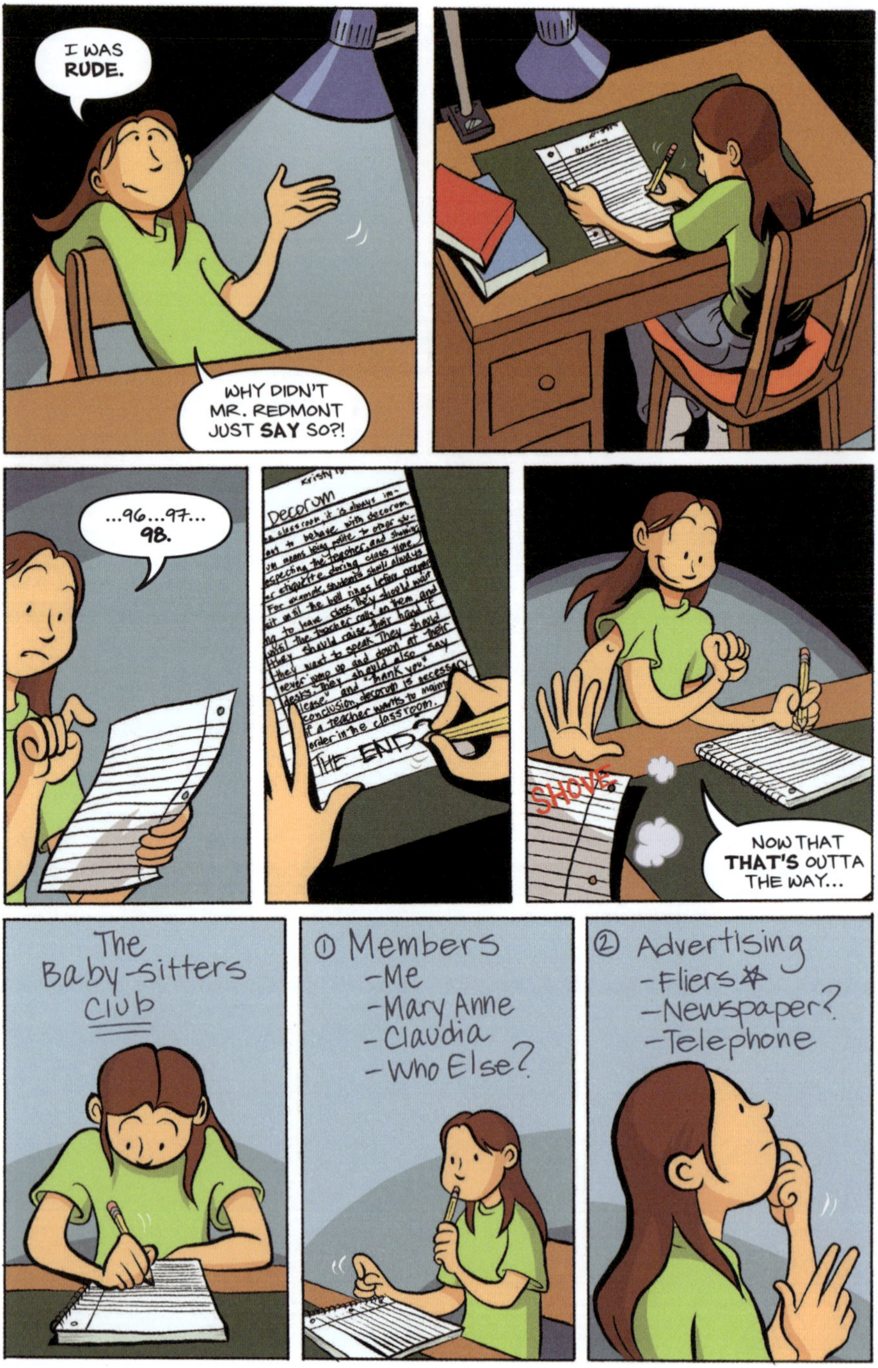
I WAS RUDE.
WHY DIDN'T MR. REDMONT JUST SAY SO?!
...96...97... 98.
Decorum
THE END
SHOVE
NOW THAT THAT'S OUTTA THE WAY...
The Baby-sitters Club
① Members
-Me
-Mary Anne
-Claudia
-Who Else?
② Advertising
-Fliers
-Newspaper?
-Telephone

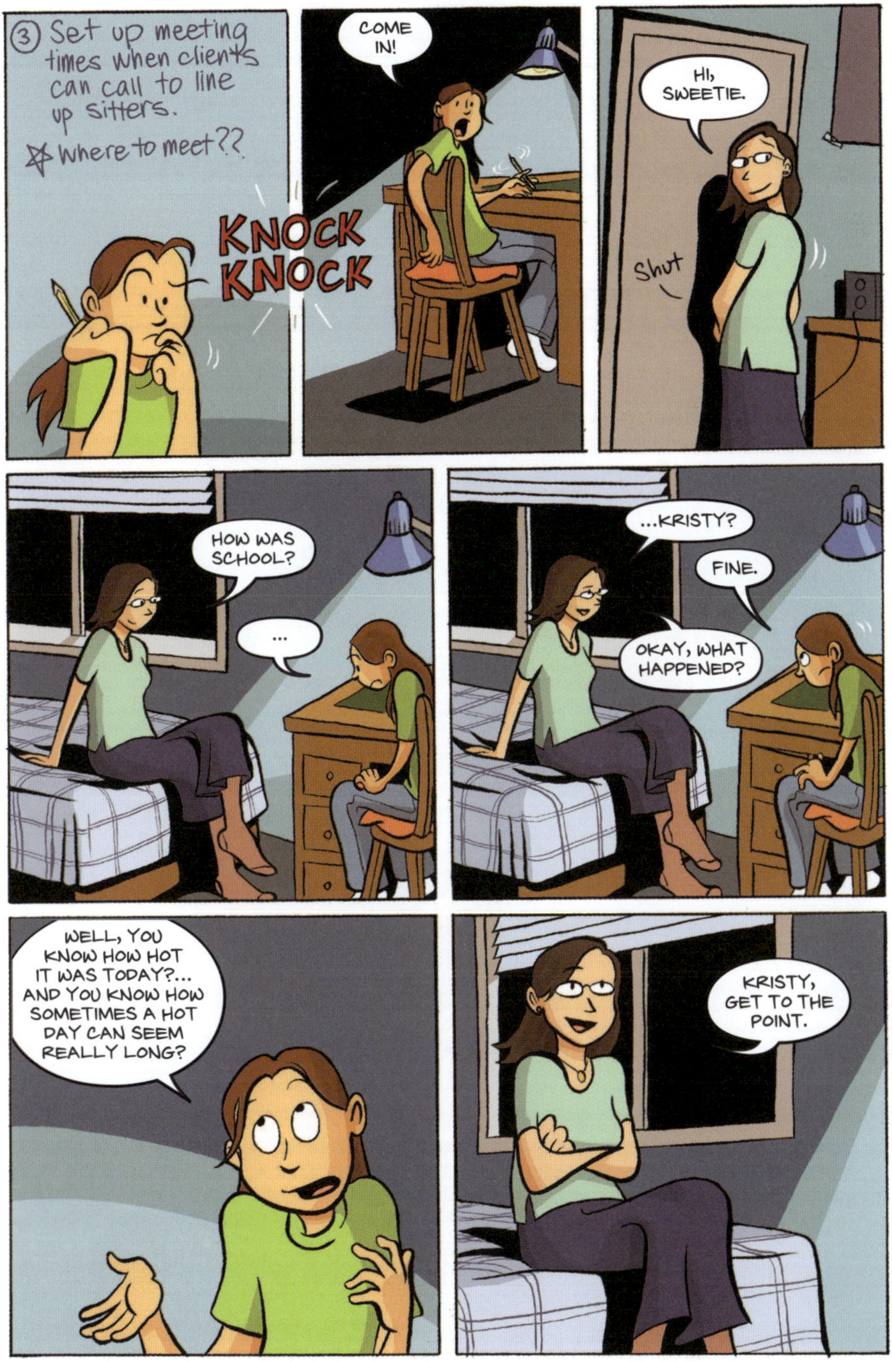
3 Set up meeting times when clients can call to line up sitters.
Where to meet??
KNOCK KNOCK
COME IN!
HI, SWEETIE.
Shut
HOW WAS SCHOOL?
...
...KRISTY?
FINE.
OKAY, WHAT HAPPENED?
WELL, YOU KNOW HOW HOT IT WAS TODAY?... AND YOU KNOW HOW SOMETIMES A HOT DAY CAN SEEM REALLY LONG?
KRISTY, GET TO THE POINT.

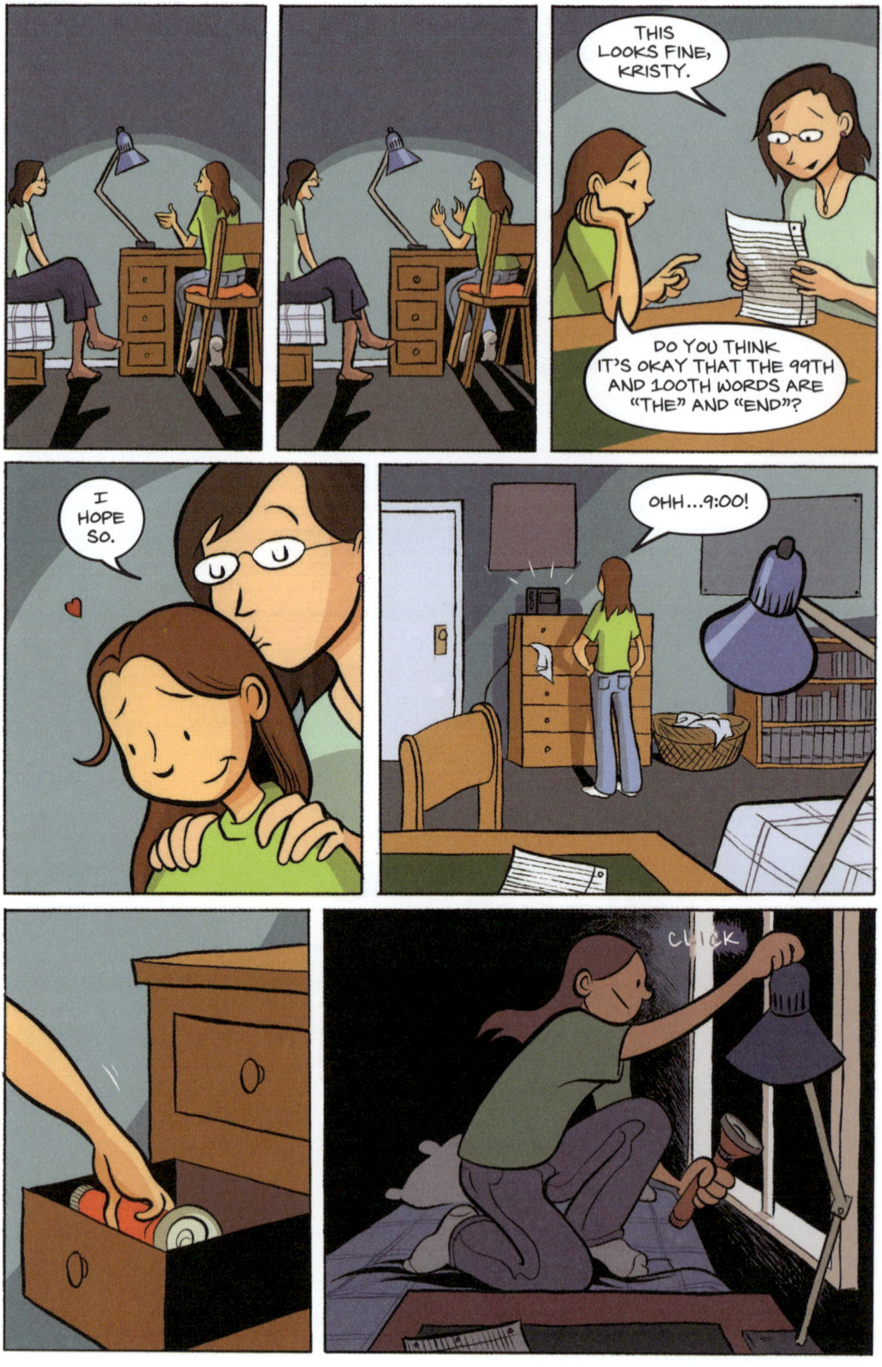
THIS LOOKS FINE, KRISTY.
DO YOU THINK IT'S OKAY THAT THE 99TH AND 100TH WORDS ARE "THE" AND "END"?
I HOPE SO.
OHH...9:00!
CLICK

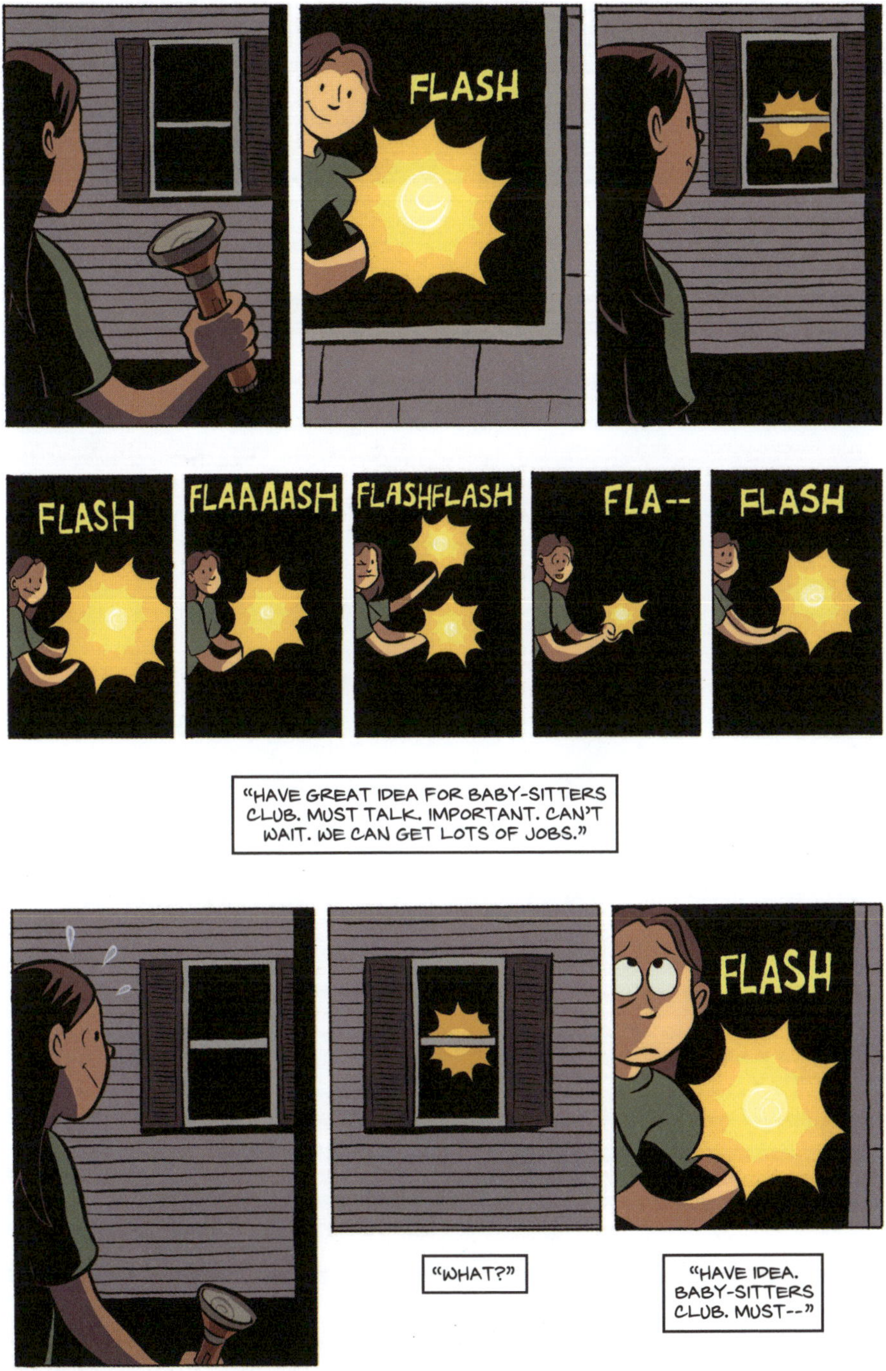
FLASH
FLASH
FLAAAASH
FLASHFLASH
FLA--
FLASH
"HAVE GREAT IDEA FOR BABY-SITTERS CLUB. MUST TALK. IMPORTANT. CAN'T WAIT. WE CAN GET LOTS OF JOBS."
FLASH
"WHAT?"
"HAVE IDEA. BABY-SITTERS CLUB. MUST--"

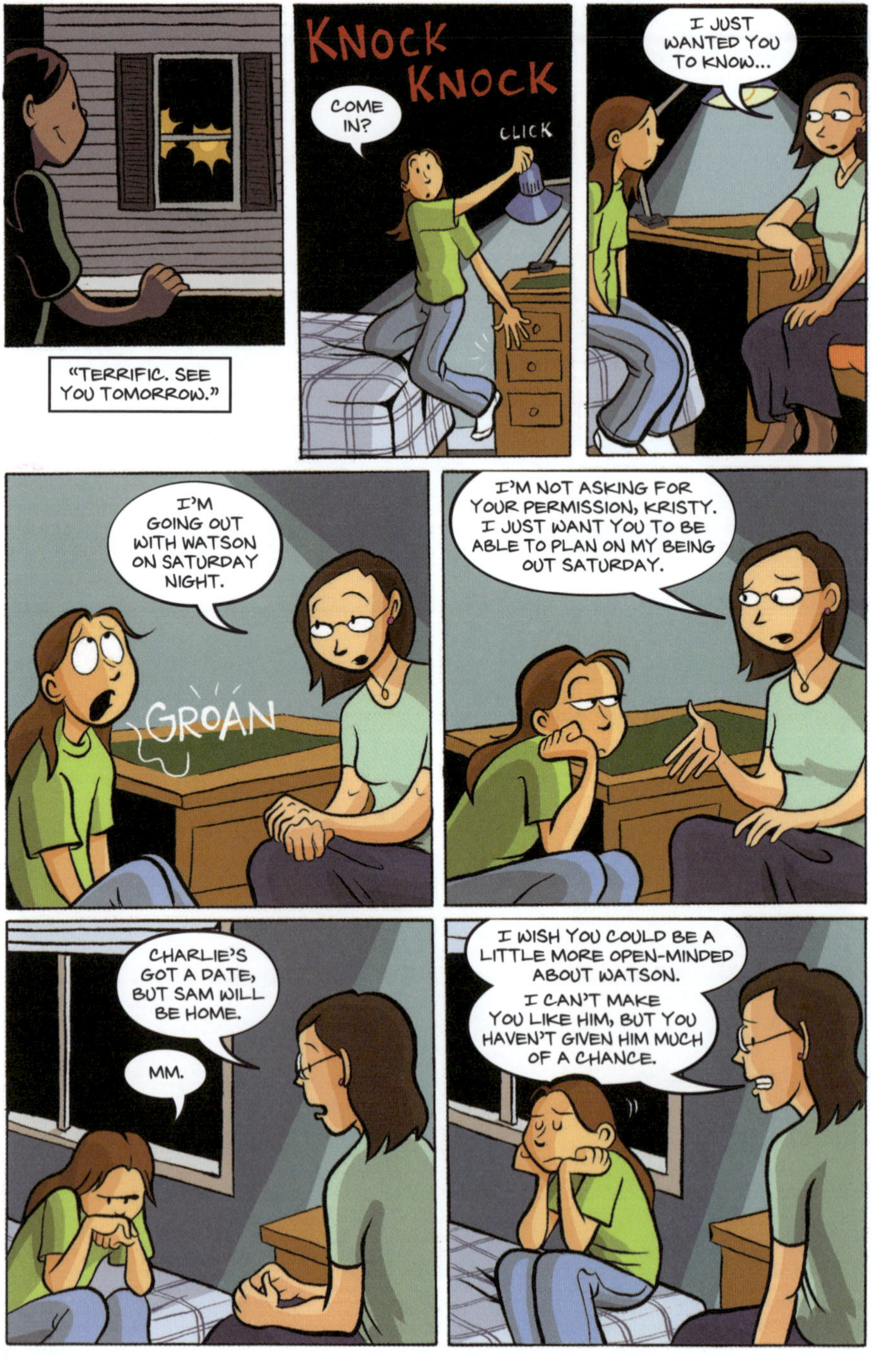
"TERRIFIC. SEE YOU TOMORROW."
KNOCK KNOCK
COME IN?
CLICK
I JUST WANTED YOU TO KNOW...
I'M GOING OUT WITH WATSON ON SATURDAY NIGHT.
GROAN
I'M NOT ASKING FOR YOUR PERMISSION, KRISTY. I JUST WANT YOU TO BE ABLE TO PLAN ON MY BEING OUT SATURDAY.
CHARLIE'S GOT A DATE, BUT SAM WILL BE HOME.
MM.
I WISH YOU COULD BE A LITTLE MORE OPEN-MINDED ABOUT WATSON.
I CAN'T MAKE YOU LIKE HIM, BUT YOU HAVEN'T GIVEN HIM MUCH OF A CHANCE.

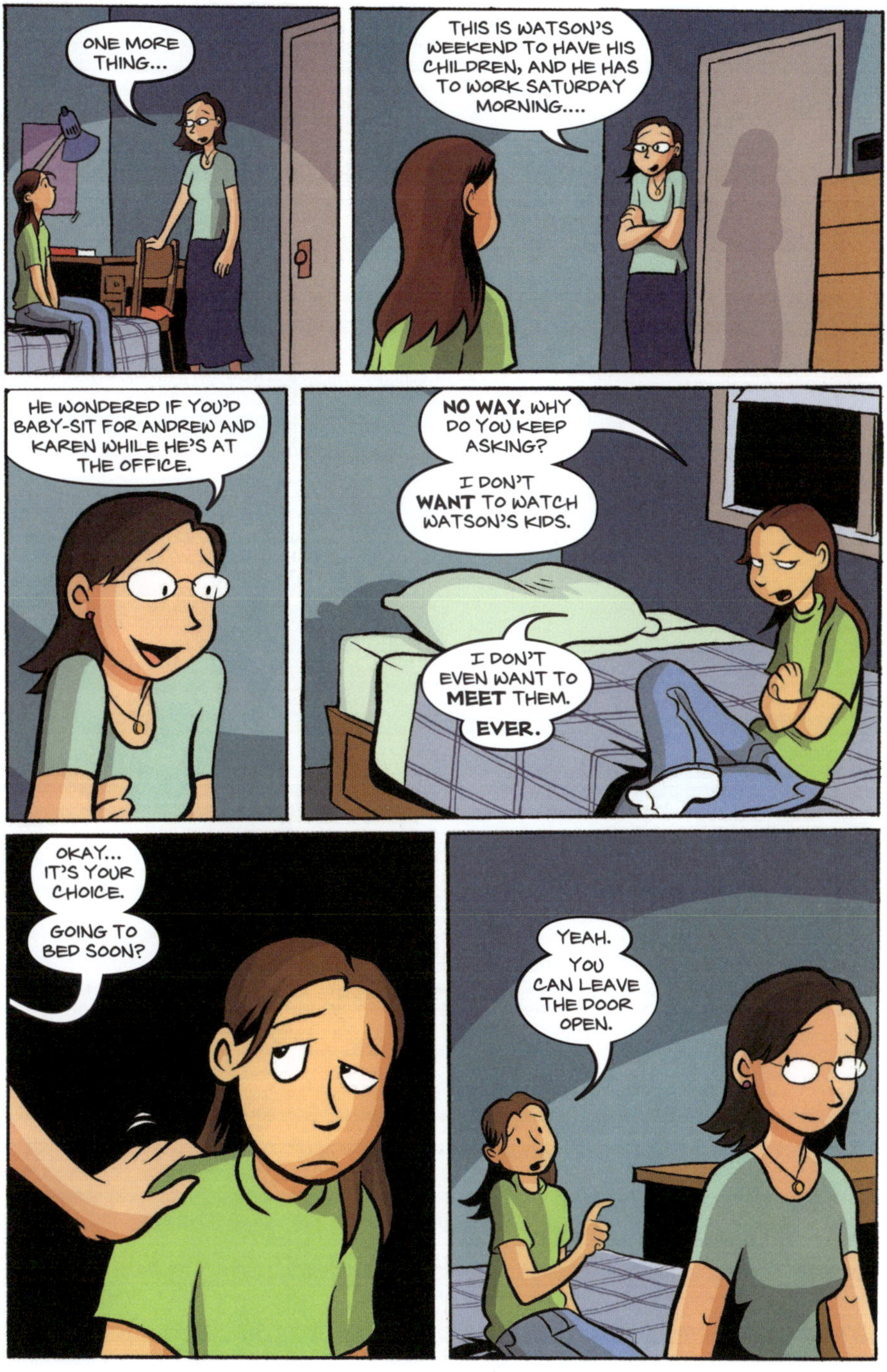
ONE MORE THING...
THIS IS WATSON'S WEEKEND TO HAVE HIS CHILDREN, AND HE HAS TO WORK SATURDAY MORNING....
HE WONDERED IF YOU'D BABY-SIT FOR ANDREW AND KAREN WHILE HE'S AT THE OFFICE.
NO WAY. WHY DO YOU KEEP ASKING?
I DON'T **WANT** TO WATCH WATSON'S KIDS.
I DON'T EVEN WANT TO **MEET** THEM.
EVER.
OKAY... IT'S YOUR CHOICE.
GOING TO BED SOON?
YEAH.
YOU CAN LEAVE THE DOOR OPEN.

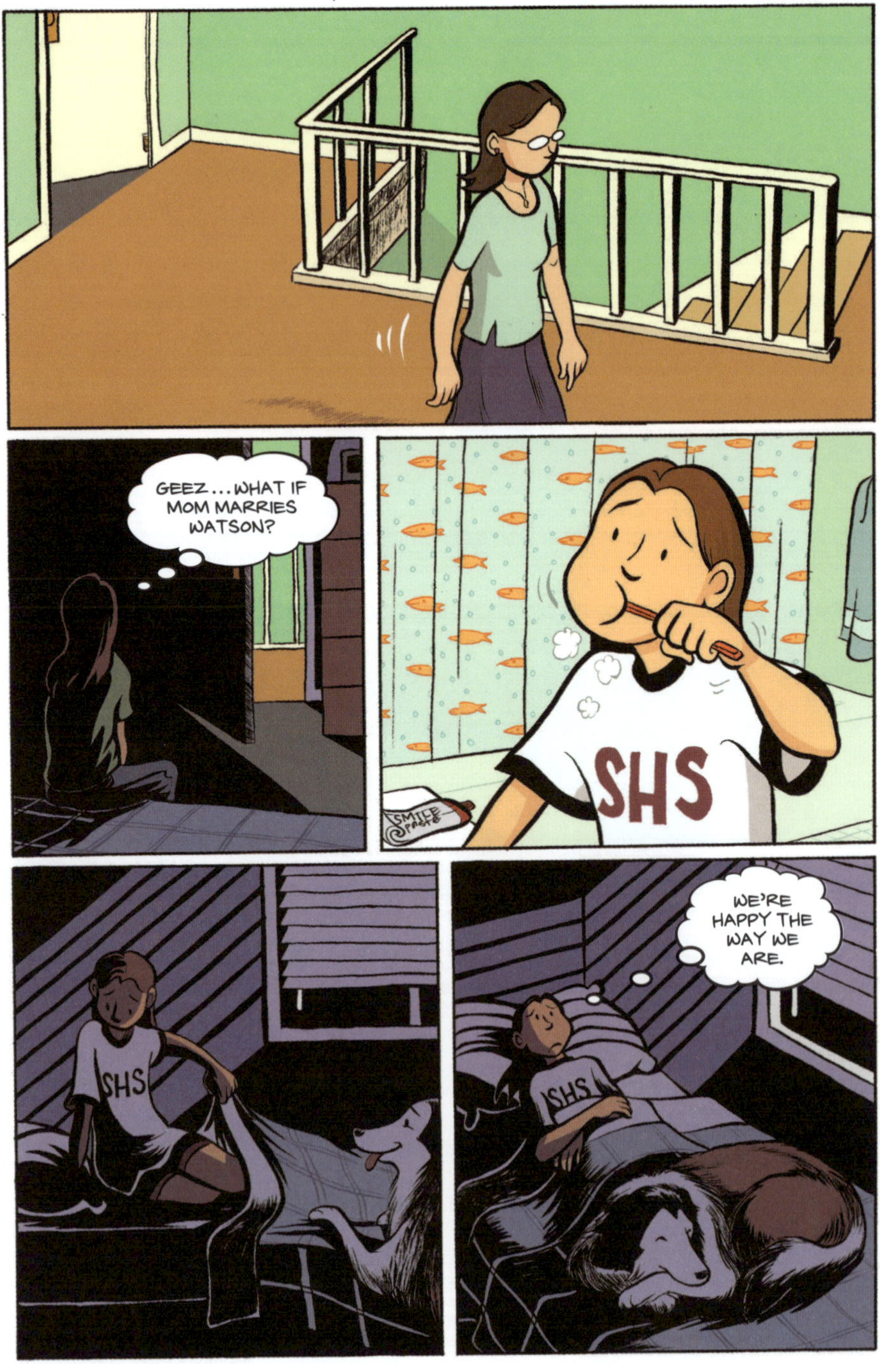
GEEZ... WHAT IF MOM MARRIES WATSON?
SMILE PASTE
SHS
WE'RE HAPPY THE WAY WE ARE.

CHAPTER 3

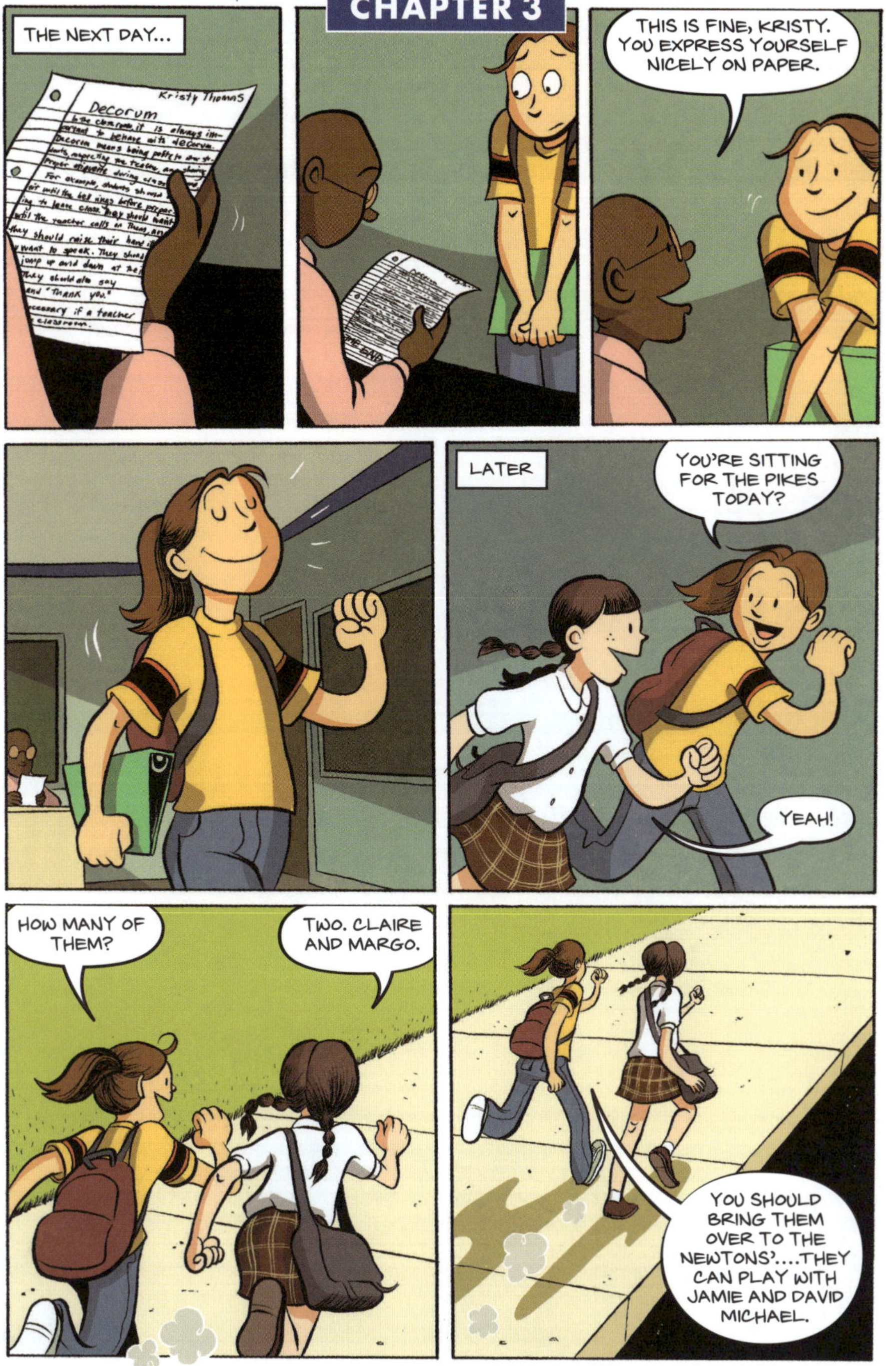
THE NEXT DAY...
Kristy Thomas
Decorum
THIS IS FINE, KRISTY. YOU EXPRESS YOURSELF NICELY ON PAPER.
LATER
YOU'RE SITTING FOR THE PIKES TODAY?
YEAH!
HOW MANY OF THEM?
TWO. CLAIRE AND MARGO.
YOU SHOULD BRING THEM OVER TO THE NEWTONS'....THEY CAN PLAY WITH JAMIE AND DAVID MICHAEL.

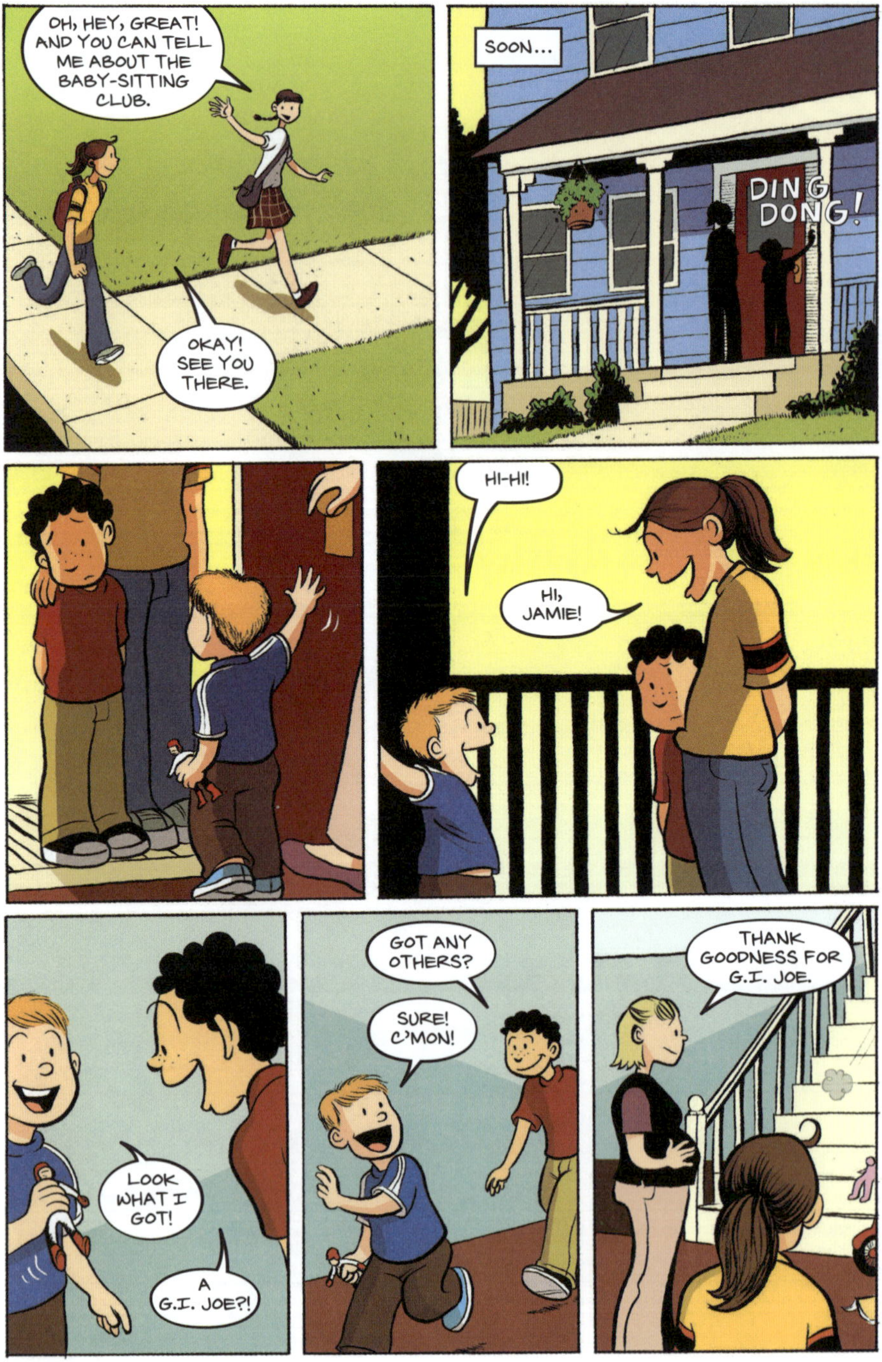
OH, HEY, GREAT! AND YOU CAN TELL ME ABOUT THE BABY-SITTING CLUB.
OKAY! SEE YOU THERE.
SOON...
DING DONG!
HI-HI!
HI, JAMIE!
LOOK WHAT I GOT!
A G.I. JOE?!
GOT ANY OTHERS?
SURE! C'MON!
THANK GOODNESS FOR G.I. JOE.

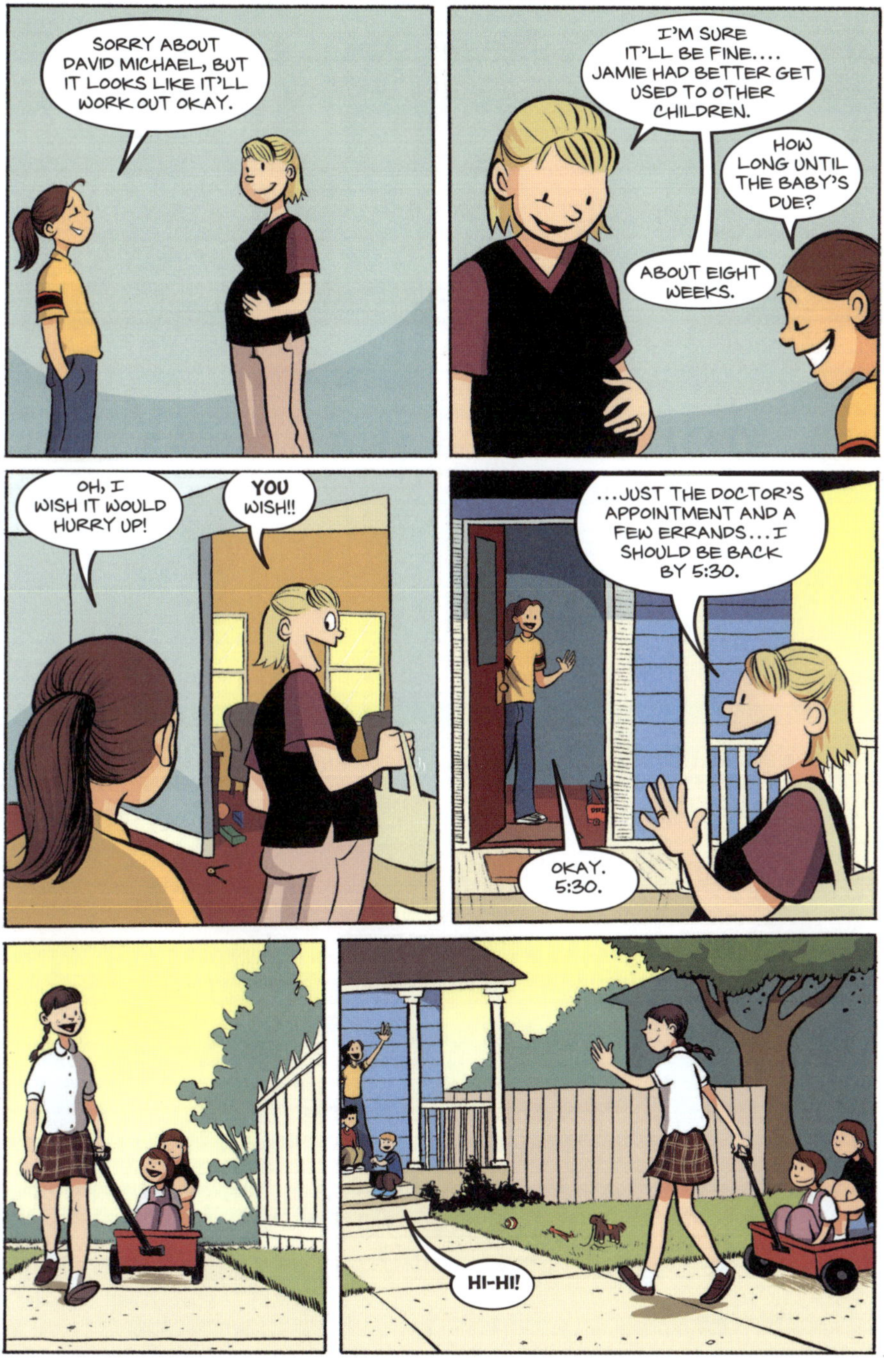
SORRY ABOUT DAVID MICHAEL, BUT IT LOOKS LIKE IT'LL WORK OUT OKAY.
I'M SURE IT'LL BE FINE.... JAMIE HAD BETTER GET USED TO OTHER CHILDREN.
HOW LONG UNTIL THE BABY'S DUE?
ABOUT EIGHT WEEKS.
OH, I WISH IT WOULD HURRY UP!
YOU WISH!!
...JUST THE DOCTOR'S APPOINTMENT AND A FEW ERRANDS...I SHOULD BE BACK BY 5:30.
OKAY. 5:30.
HI-HI!

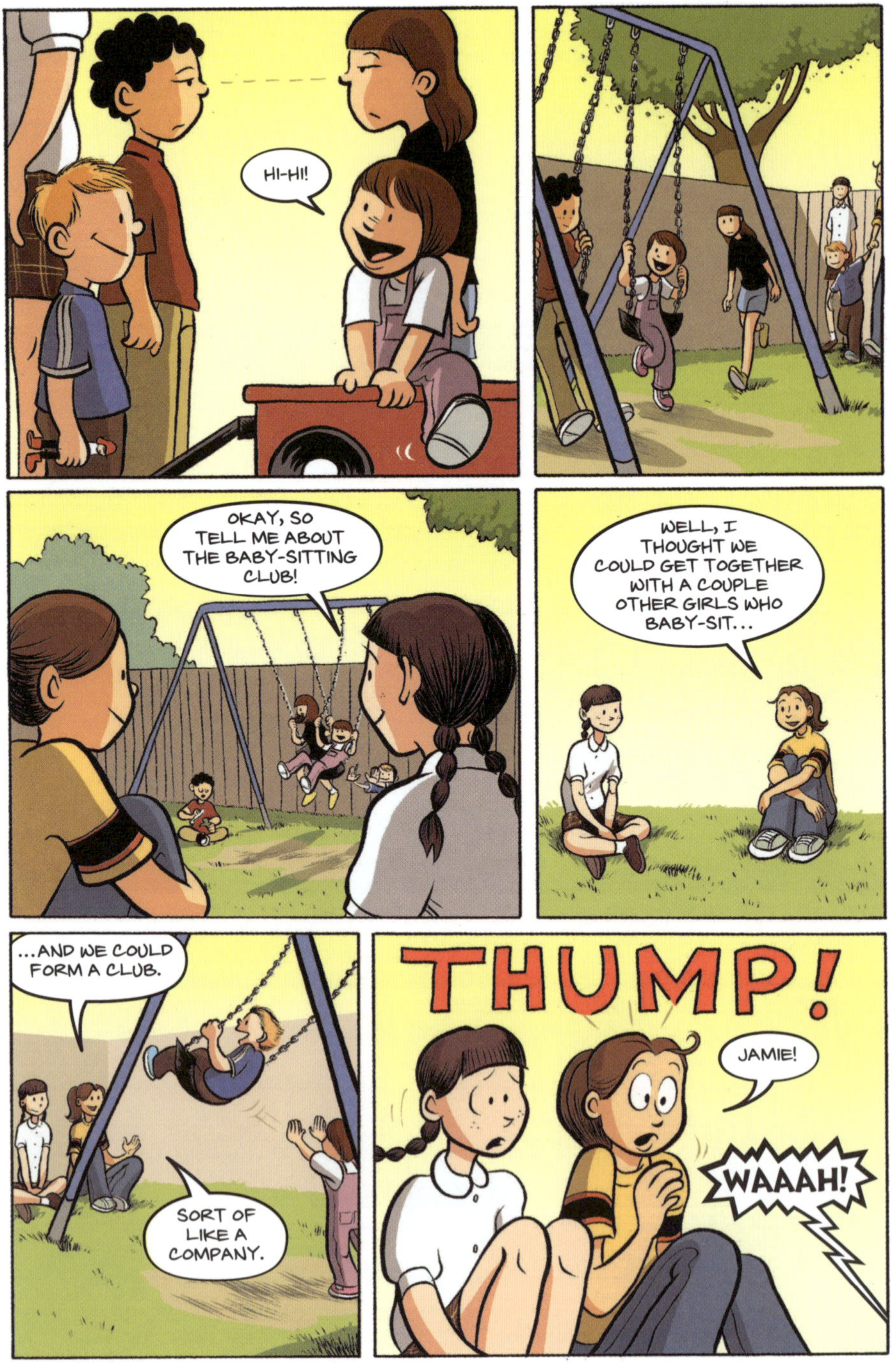
HI-HI!
OKAY, SO TELL ME ABOUT THE BABY-SITTING CLUB!
WELL, I THOUGHT WE COULD GET TOGETHER WITH A COUPLE OTHER GIRLS WHO BABY-SIT...
...AND WE COULD FORM A CLUB.
SORT OF LIKE A COMPANY.
THUMP!
JAMIE!
WAAAH!

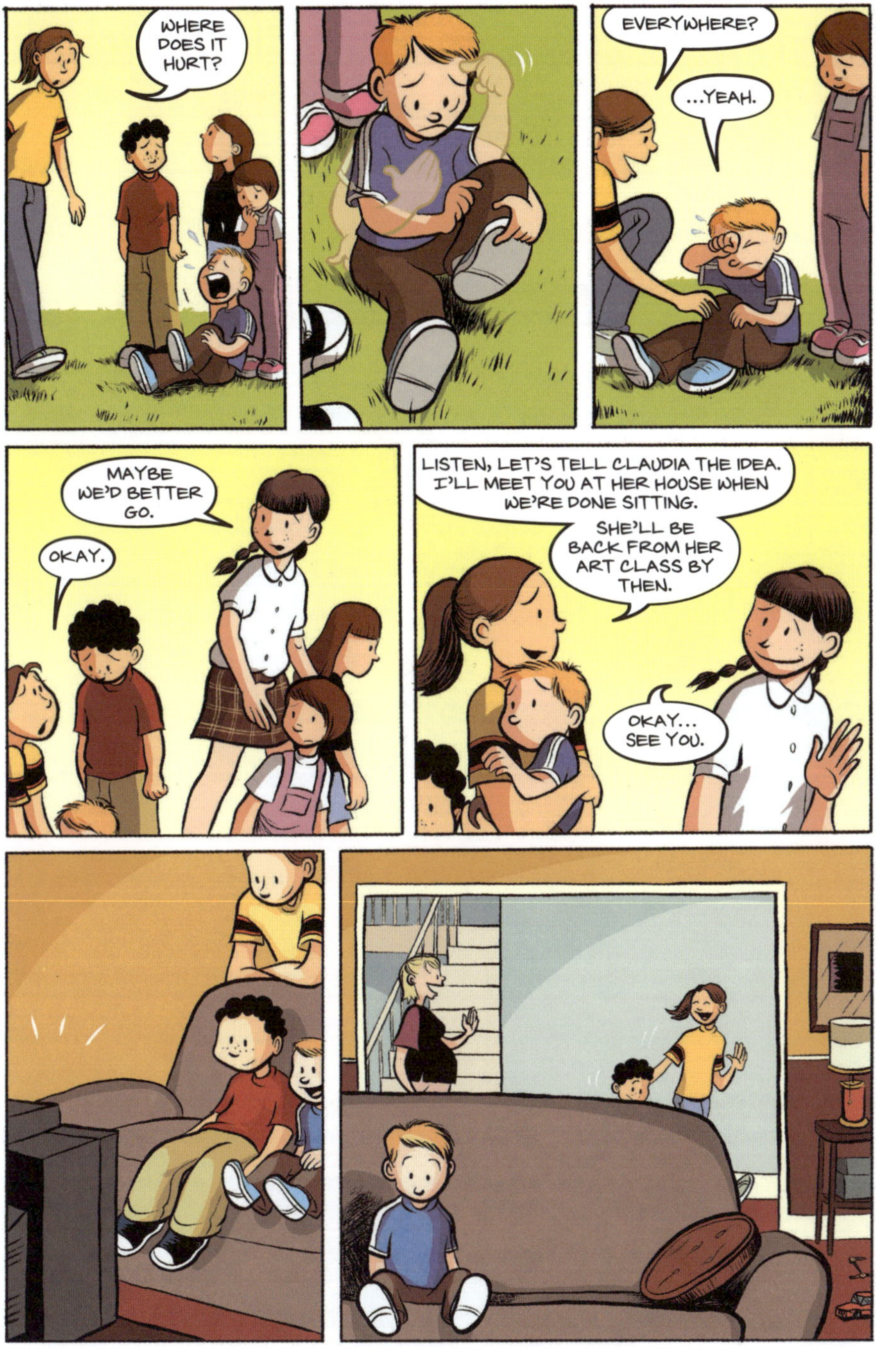
WHERE DOES IT HURT?
EVERYWHERE?
...YEAH.
MAYBE WE'D BETTER GO.
OKAY.
LISTEN, LET'S TELL CLAUDIA THE IDEA. I'LL MEET YOU AT HER HOUSE WHEN WE'RE DONE SITTING.
SHE'LL BE BACK FROM HER ART CLASS BY THEN.
OKAY... SEE YOU.

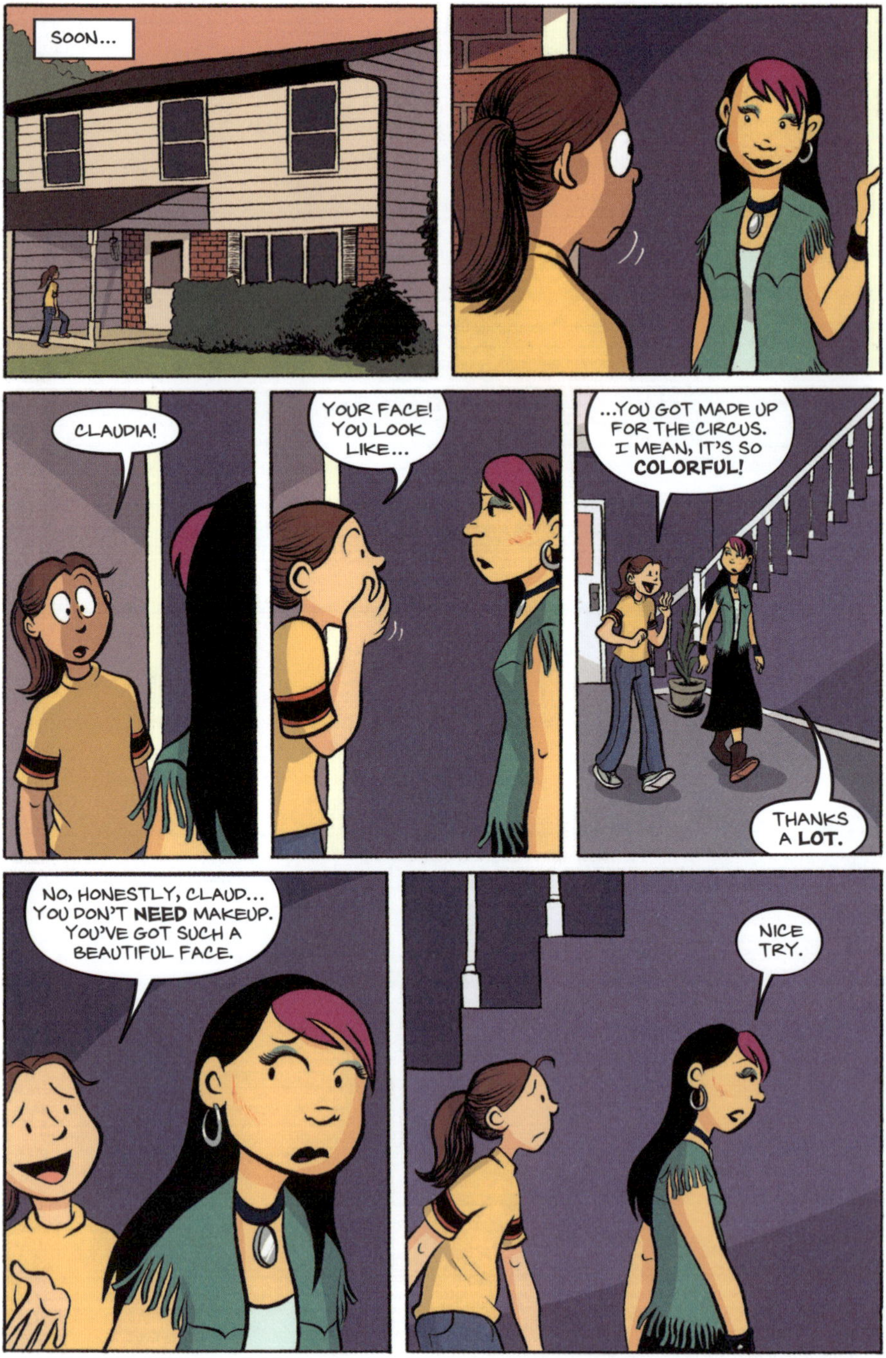
SOON...
CLAUDIA!
YOUR FACE! YOU LOOK LIKE...
...YOU GOT MADE UP FOR THE CIRCUS. I MEAN, IT'S SO **COLORFUL!**
THANKS A **LOT.**
NO, HONESTLY, CLAUD... YOU DON'T **NEED** MAKEUP. YOU'VE GOT SUCH A BEAUTIFUL FACE.
NICE TRY.

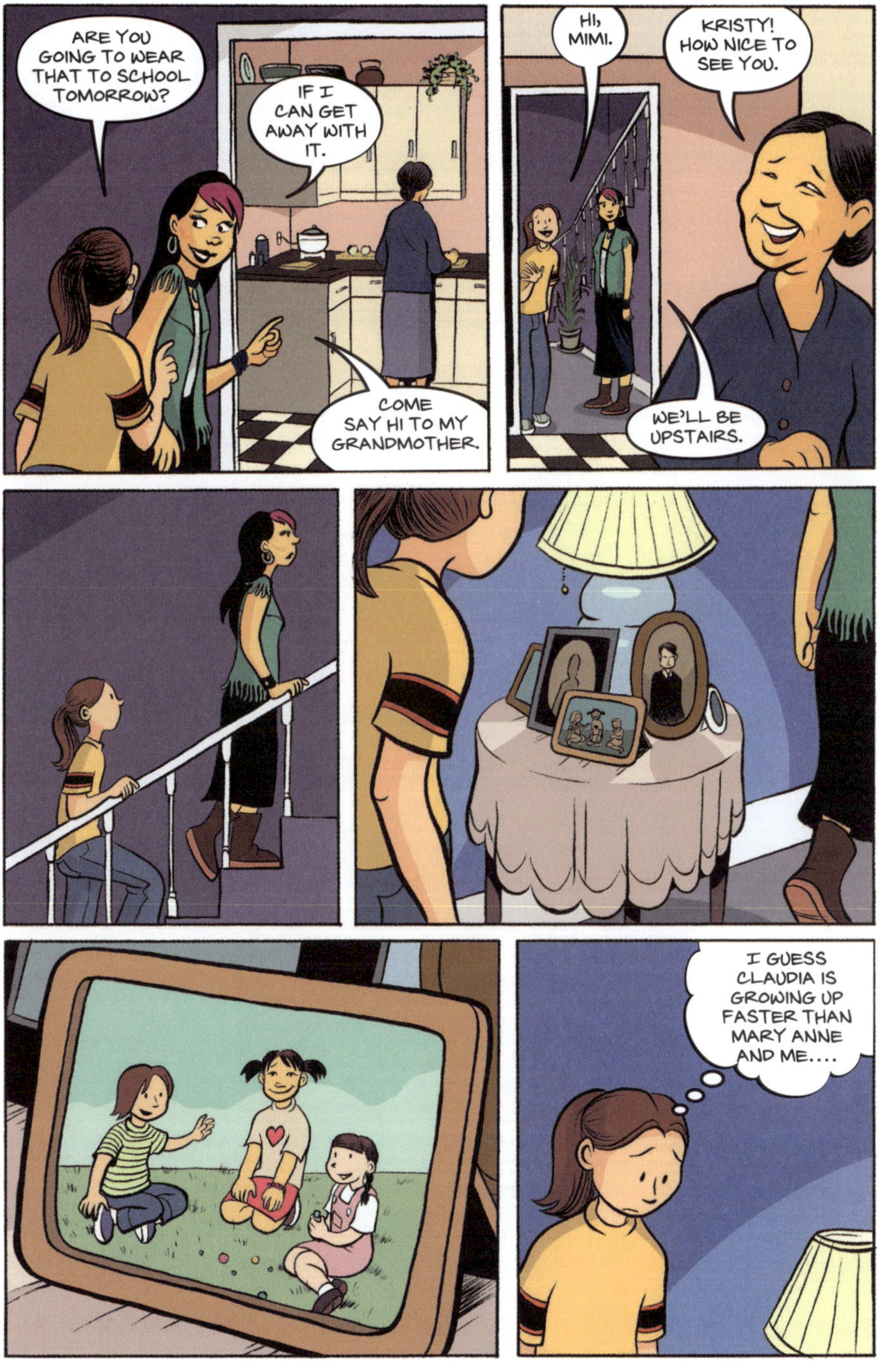
ARE YOU GOING TO WEAR THAT TO SCHOOL TOMORROW?
IF I CAN GET AWAY WITH IT.
COME SAY HI TO MY GRANDMOTHER.
HI, MIMI.
KRISTY! HOW NICE TO SEE YOU.
WE'LL BE UPSTAIRS.
I GUESS CLAUDIA IS GROWING UP FASTER THAN MARY ANNE AND ME....

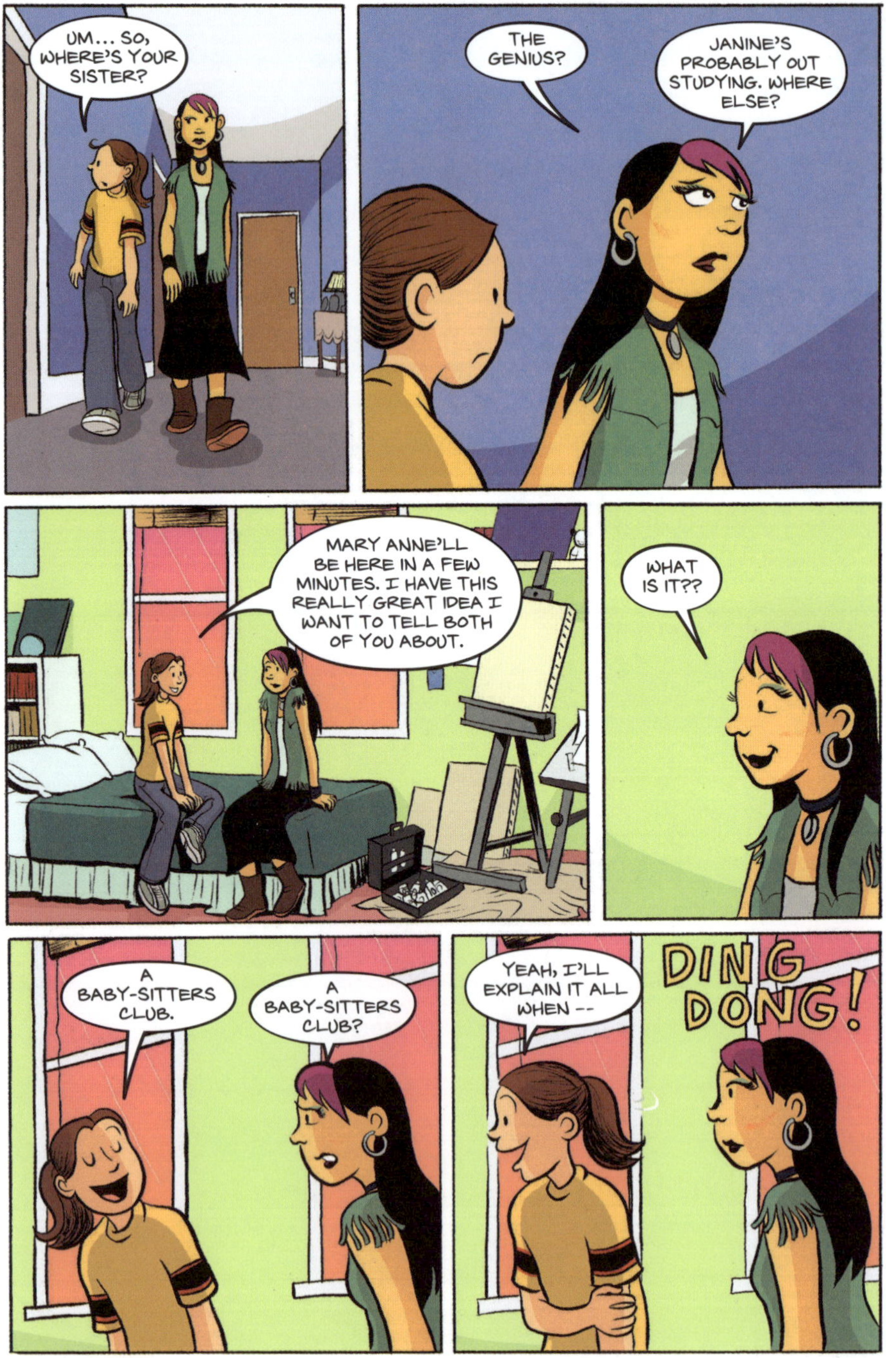
UM... SO, WHERE'S YOUR SISTER?
THE GENIUS?
JANINE'S PROBABLY OUT STUDYING. WHERE ELSE?
MARY ANNE'LL BE HERE IN A FEW MINUTES. I HAVE THIS REALLY GREAT IDEA I WANT TO TELL BOTH OF YOU ABOUT.
WHAT IS IT??
A BABY-SITTERS CLUB.
A BABY-SITTERS CLUB?
YEAH, I'LL EXPLAIN IT ALL WHEN --
DING DONG!

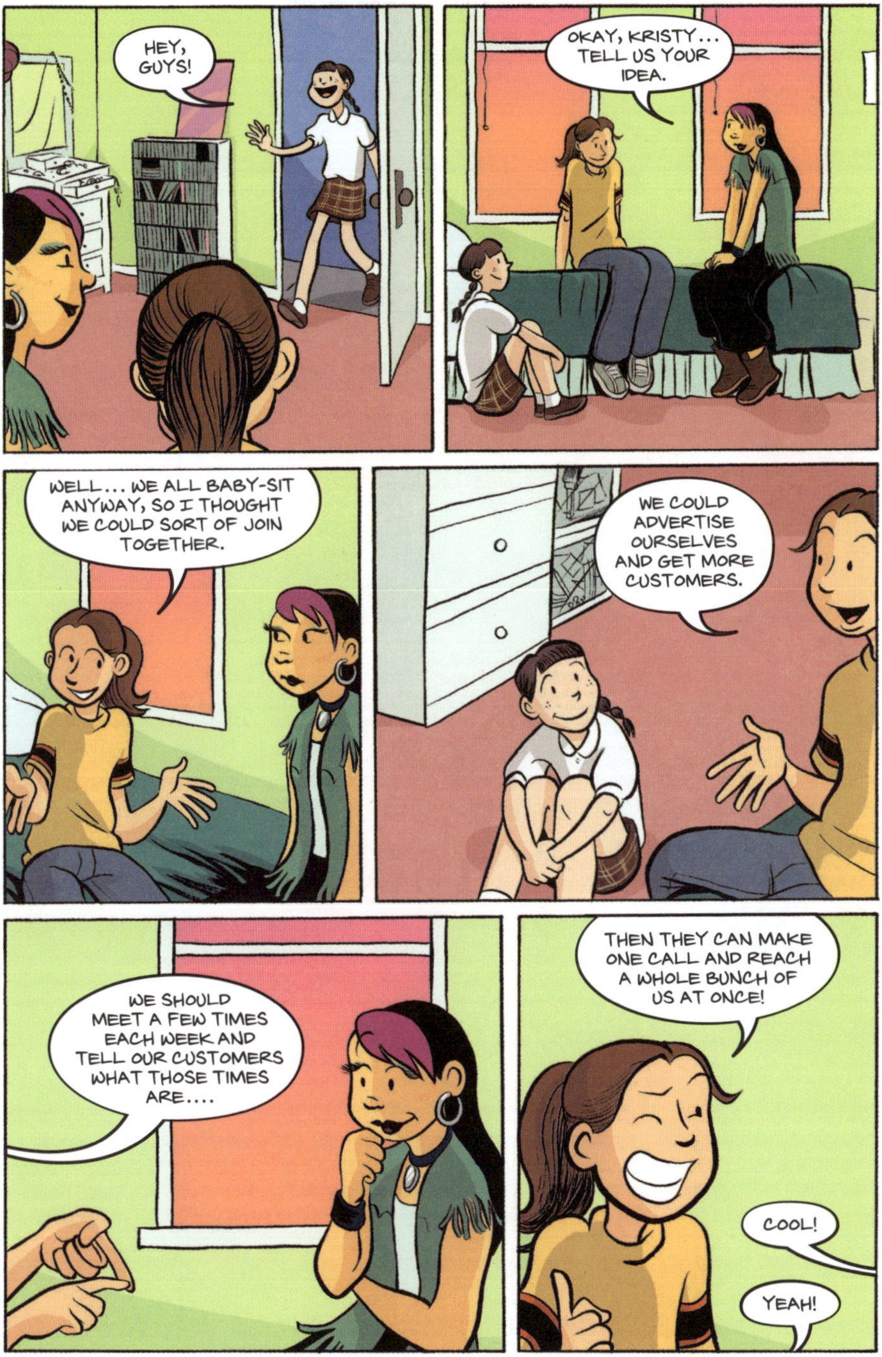
HEY, GUYS!
OKAY, KRISTY... TELL US YOUR IDEA.
WELL... WE ALL BABY-SIT ANYWAY, SO I THOUGHT WE COULD SORT OF JOIN TOGETHER.
WE COULD ADVERTISE OURSELVES AND GET MORE CUSTOMERS.
WE SHOULD MEET A FEW TIMES EACH WEEK AND TELL OUR CUSTOMERS WHAT THOSE TIMES ARE....
THEN THEY CAN MAKE ONE CALL AND REACH A WHOLE BUNCH OF US AT ONCE!
COOL!
YEAH!

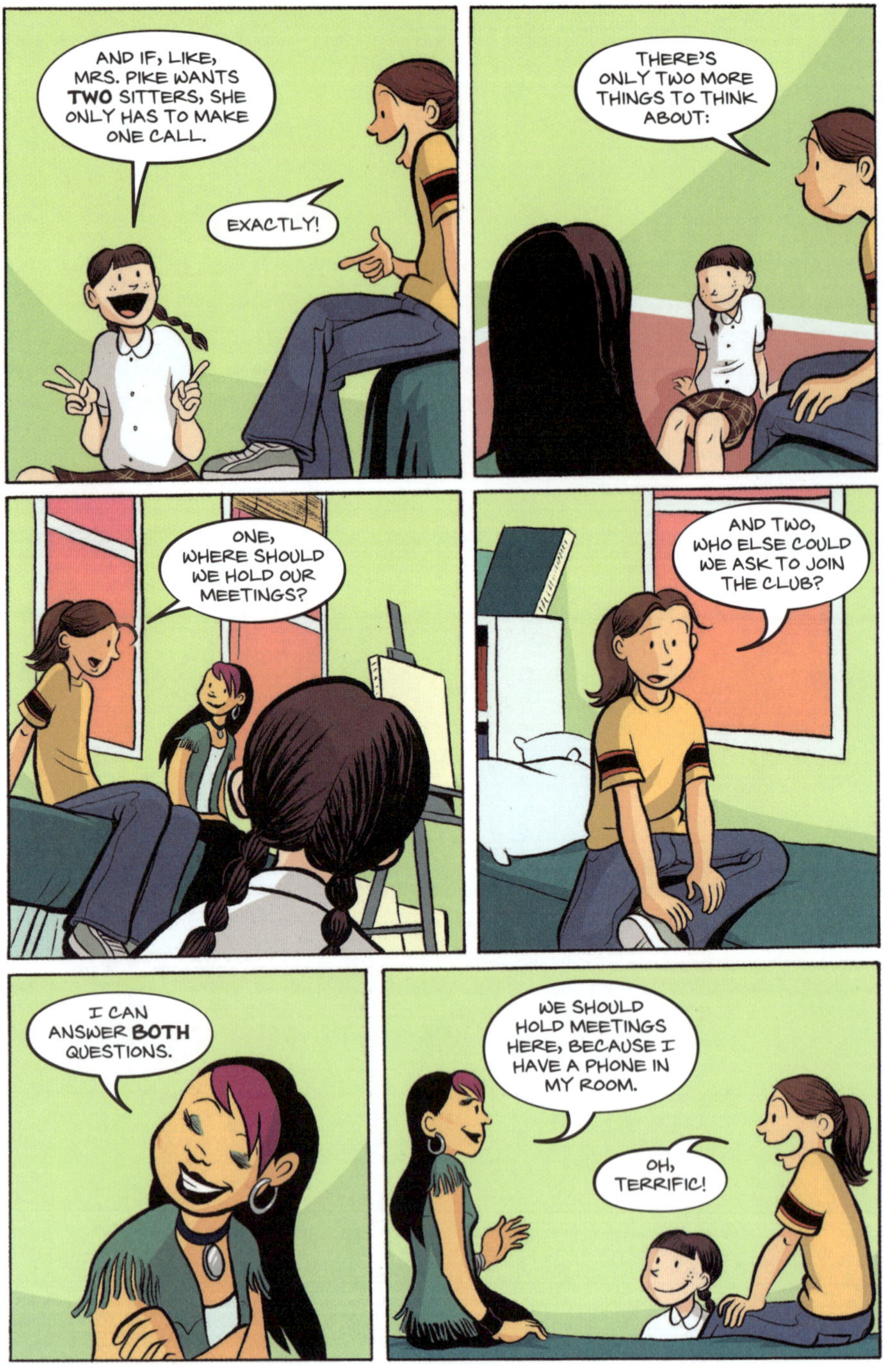
AND IF, LIKE, MRS. PIKE WANTS **TWO** SITTERS, SHE ONLY HAS TO MAKE ONE CALL.
EXACTLY!
THERE'S ONLY TWO MORE THINGS TO THINK ABOUT:
ONE, WHERE SHOULD WE HOLD OUR MEETINGS?
AND TWO, WHO ELSE COULD WE ASK TO JOIN THE CLUB?
I CAN ANSWER **BOTH** QUESTIONS.
WE SHOULD HOLD MEETINGS HERE, BECAUSE I HAVE A PHONE IN MY ROOM.
OH, TERRIFIC!

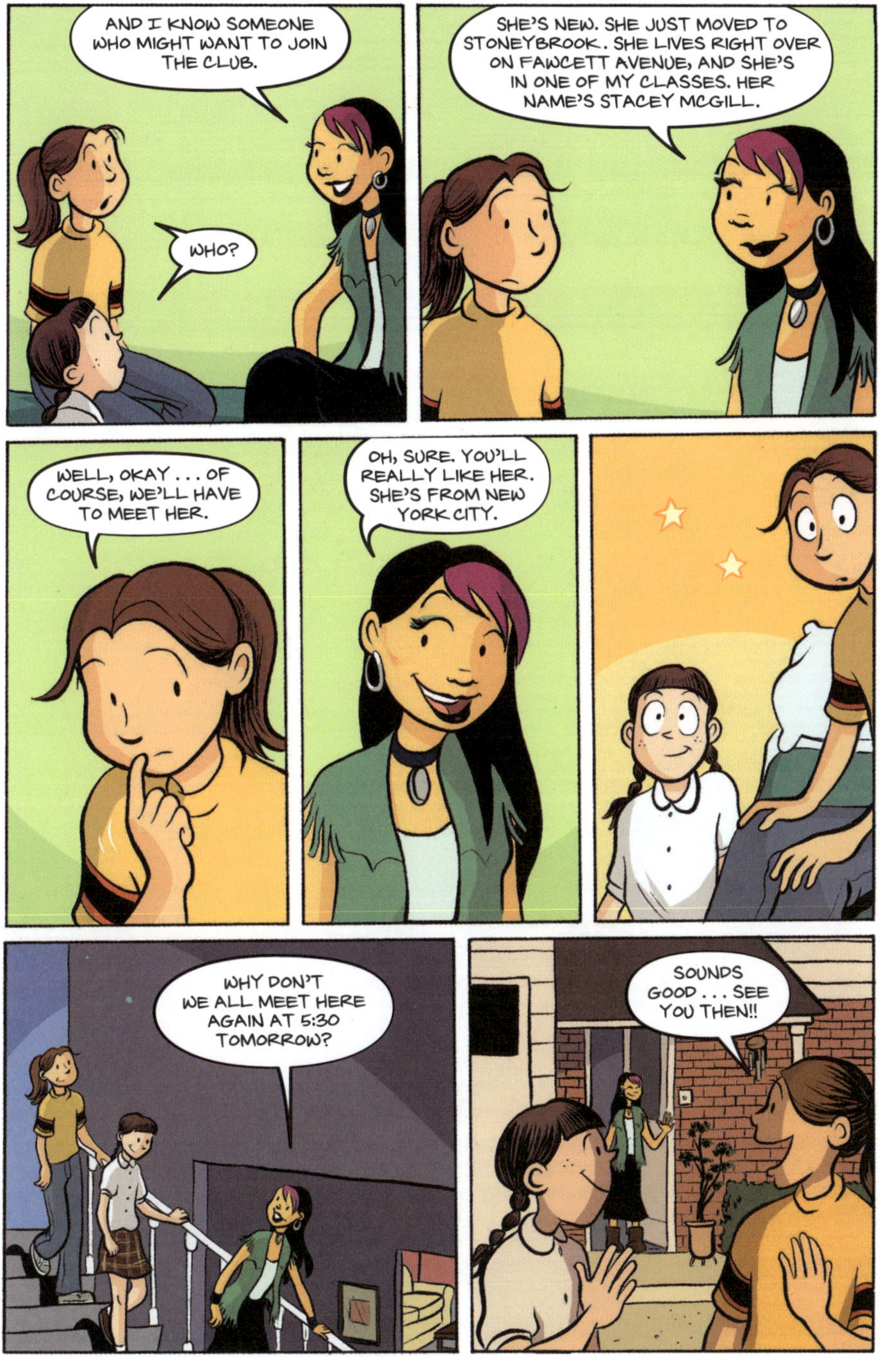
AND I KNOW SOMEONE WHO MIGHT WANT TO JOIN THE CLUB.
WHO?
SHE'S NEW. SHE JUST MOVED TO STONEYBROOK. SHE LIVES RIGHT OVER ON FAWCETT AVENUE, AND SHE'S IN ONE OF MY CLASSES. HER NAME'S STACEY MCGILL.
WELL, OKAY . . . OF COURSE, WE'LL HAVE TO MEET HER.
OH, SURE. YOU'LL REALLY LIKE HER. SHE'S FROM NEW YORK CITY.
WHY DON'T WE ALL MEET HERE AGAIN AT 5:30 TOMORROW?
SOUNDS GOOD . . . SEE YOU THEN!!

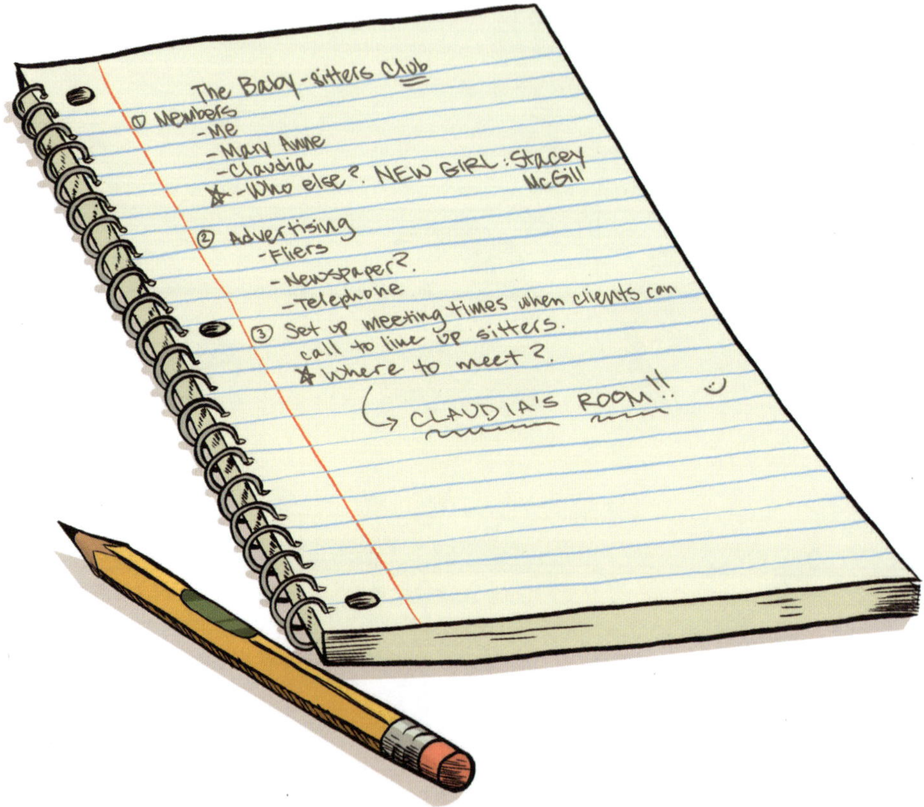
The Baby-sitters Club
① Members
-Me
-Mary Anne
-Claudia
-Who else?. NEW GIRL: Stacey McGill
② Advertising
-Fliers
-Newspaper?.
-Telephone
③ Set up meeting times when clients can call to line up sitters.
Where to meet?
CLAUDIA'S ROOM!!

CHAPTER 4

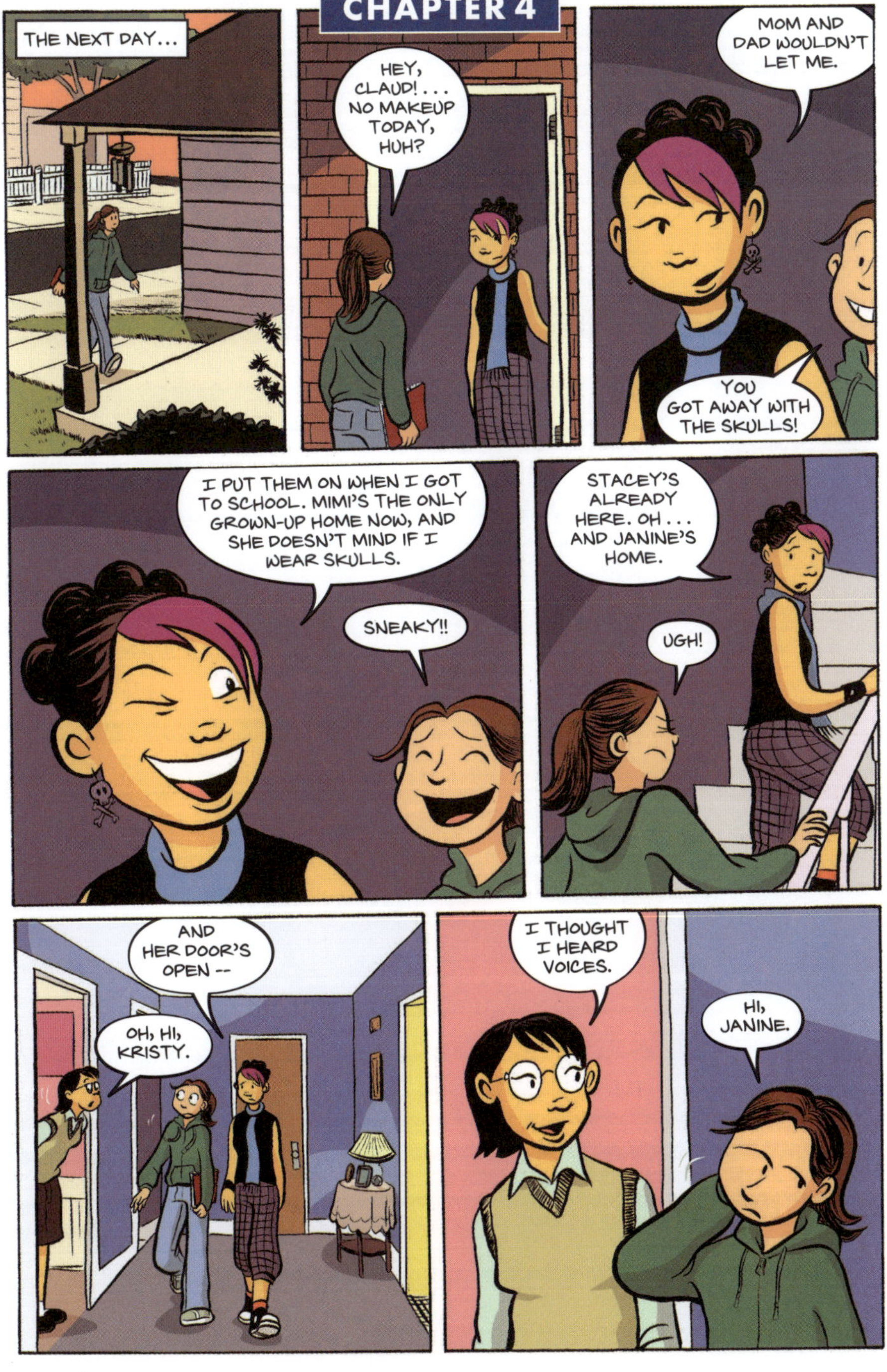

THE NEXT DAY...
HEY, CLAUD! . . . NO MAKEUP TODAY, HUH?
MOM AND DAD WOULDN'T LET ME.
YOU GOT AWAY WITH THE SKULLS!
I PUT THEM ON WHEN I GOT TO SCHOOL. MIMI'S THE ONLY GROWN-UP HOME NOW, AND SHE DOESN'T MIND IF I WEAR SKULLS.
SNEAKY!!
STACEY'S ALREADY HERE. OH . . . AND JANINE'S HOME.
UGH!
AND HER DOOR'S OPEN --
OH, HI, KRISTY.
I THOUGHT I HEARD VOICES.
HI, JANINE.

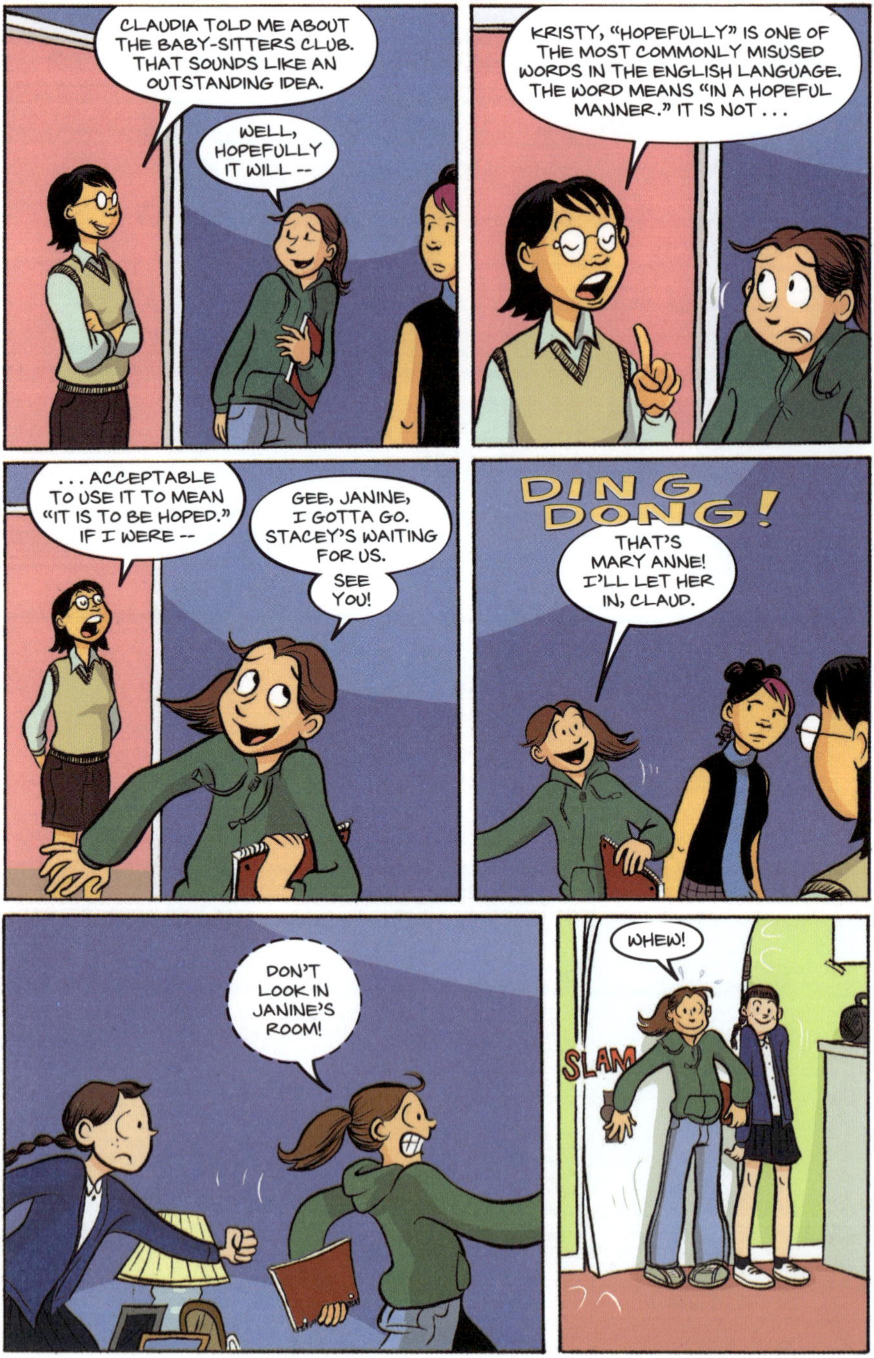
CLAUDIA TOLD ME ABOUT THE BABY-SITTERS CLUB. THAT SOUNDS LIKE AN OUTSTANDING IDEA.
WELL, HOPEFULLY IT WILL --
KRISTY, "HOPEFULLY" IS ONE OF THE MOST COMMONLY MISUSED WORDS IN THE ENGLISH LANGUAGE. THE WORD MEANS "IN A HOPEFUL MANNER." IT IS NOT . . .
. . . ACCEPTABLE TO USE IT TO MEAN "IT IS TO BE HOPED." IF I WERE --
GEE, JANINE, I GOTTA GO. STACEY'S WAITING FOR US.
SEE YOU!
DING DONG!
THAT'S MARY ANNE! I'LL LET HER IN, CLAUD.
DON'T LOOK IN JANINE'S ROOM!
WHEW!
SLAM

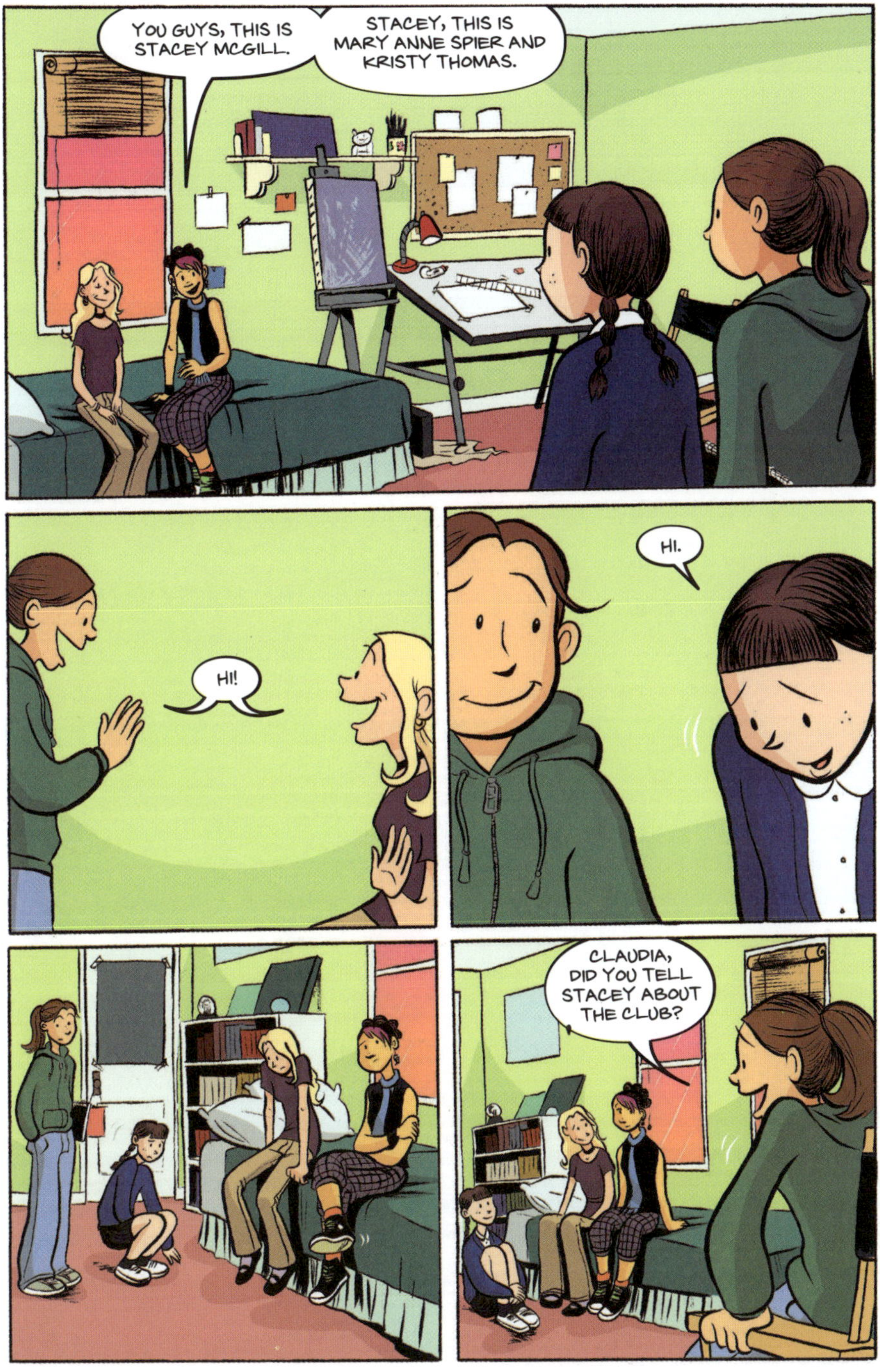
YOU GUYS, THIS IS STACEY MCGILL.
STACEY, THIS IS MARY ANNE SPIER AND KRISTY THOMAS.
HI!
HI.
CLAUDIA, DID YOU TELL STACEY ABOUT THE CLUB?

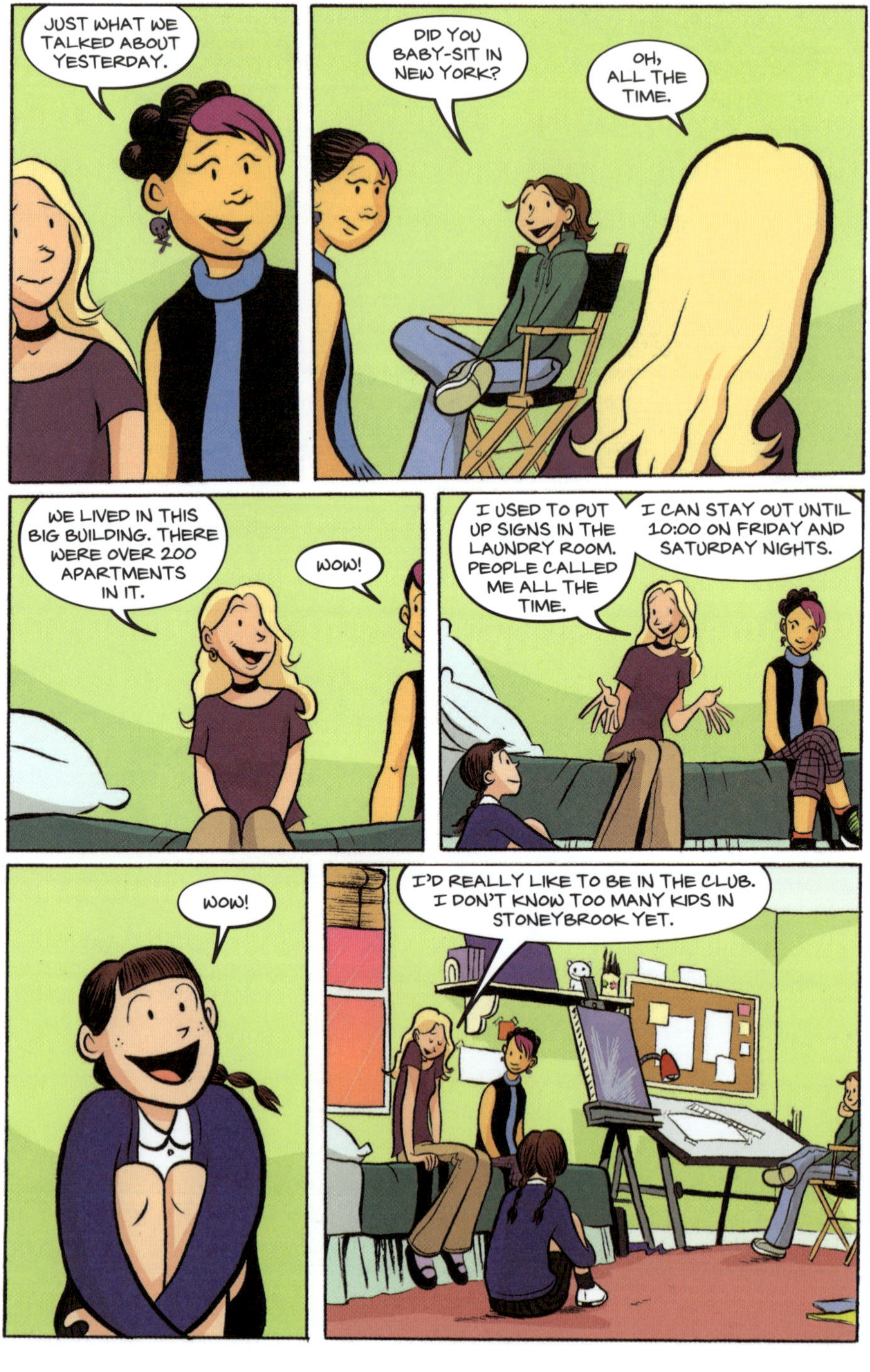
JUST WHAT WE TALKED ABOUT YESTERDAY.
DID YOU BABY-SIT IN NEW YORK?
OH, ALL THE TIME.
WE LIVED IN THIS BIG BUILDING. THERE WERE OVER 200 APARTMENTS IN IT.
WOW!
I USED TO PUT UP SIGNS IN THE LAUNDRY ROOM. PEOPLE CALLED ME ALL THE TIME.
I CAN STAY OUT UNTIL 10:00 ON FRIDAY AND SATURDAY NIGHTS.
WOW!
I'D REALLY LIKE TO BE IN THE CLUB. I DON'T KNOW TOO MANY KIDS IN STONEYBROOK YET.

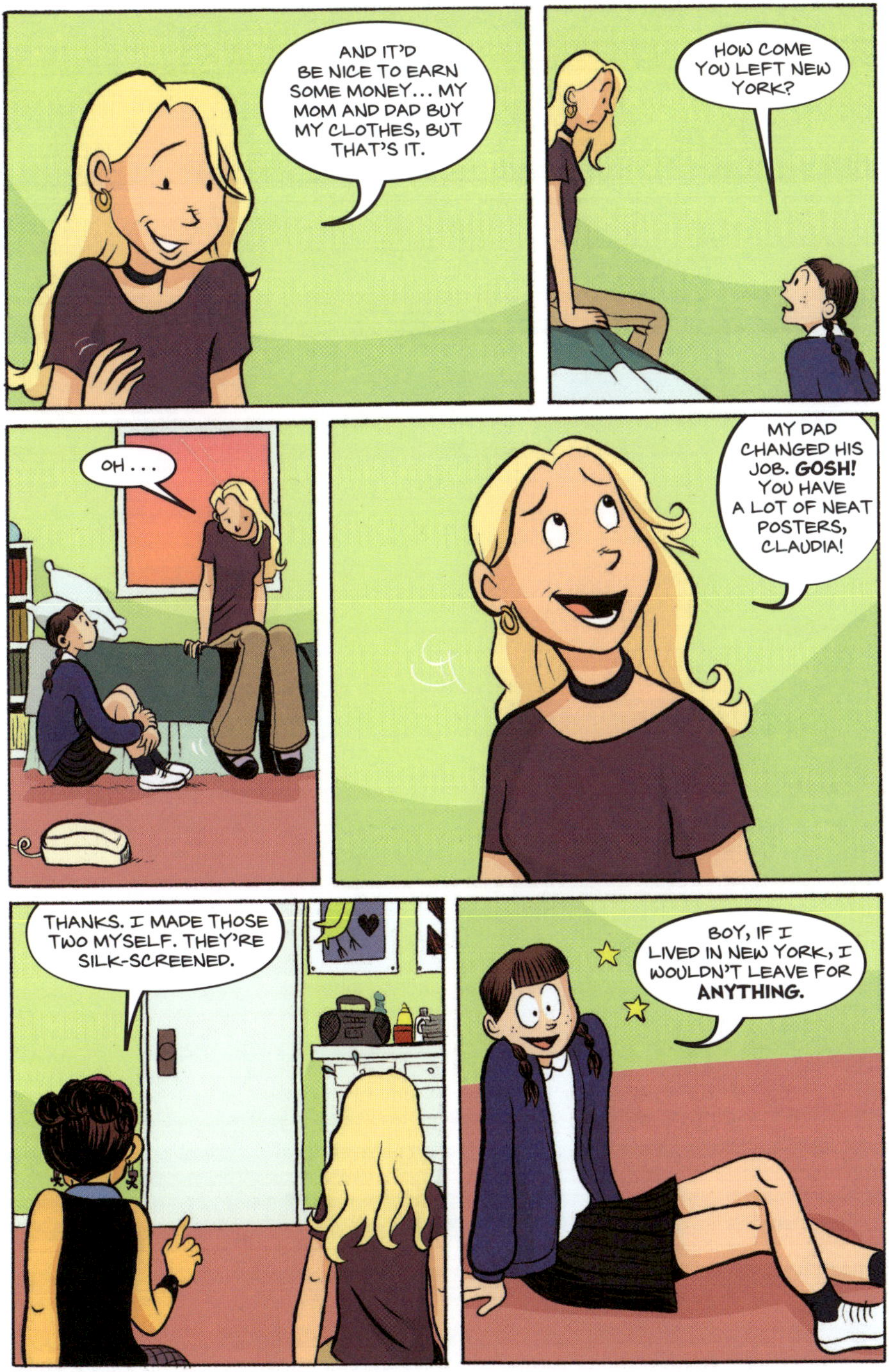
AND IT'D BE NICE TO EARN SOME MONEY... MY MOM AND DAD BUY MY CLOTHES, BUT THAT'S IT.
HOW COME YOU LEFT NEW YORK?
OH...
MY DAD CHANGED HIS JOB. **GOSH!** YOU HAVE A LOT OF NEAT POSTERS, CLAUDIA!
THANKS. I MADE THOSE TWO MYSELF. THEY'RE SILK-SCREENED.
BOY, IF I LIVED IN NEW YORK, I WOULDN'T LEAVE FOR **ANYTHING.**

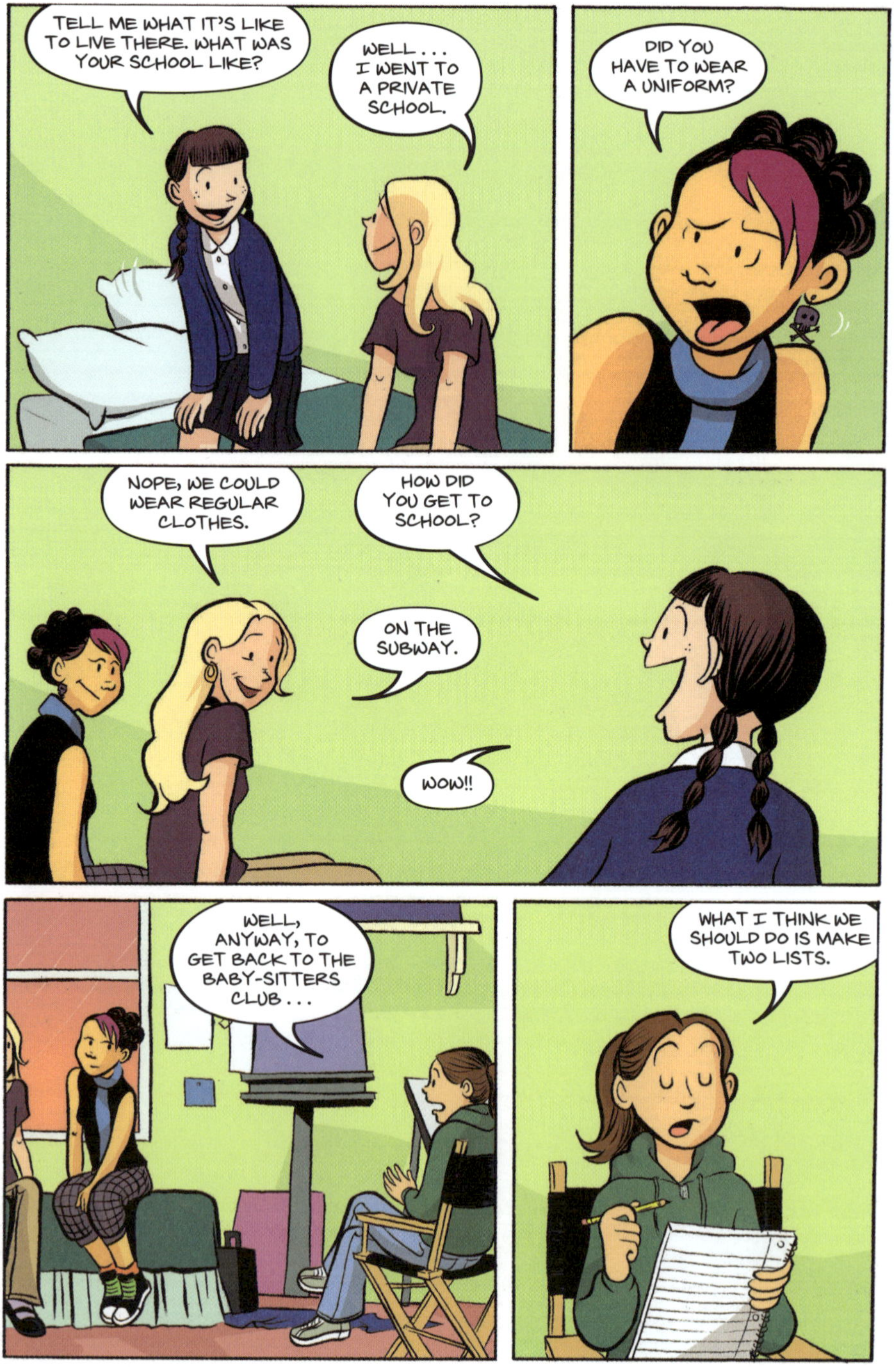
TELL ME WHAT IT'S LIKE TO LIVE THERE. WHAT WAS YOUR SCHOOL LIKE?
WELL . . . I WENT TO A PRIVATE SCHOOL.
DID YOU HAVE TO WEAR A UNIFORM?
NOPE, WE COULD WEAR REGULAR CLOTHES.
HOW DID YOU GET TO SCHOOL?
ON THE SUBWAY.
WOW!!
WELL, ANYWAY, TO GET BACK TO THE BABY-SITTERS CLUB . . .
WHAT I THINK WE SHOULD DO IS MAKE TWO LISTS.

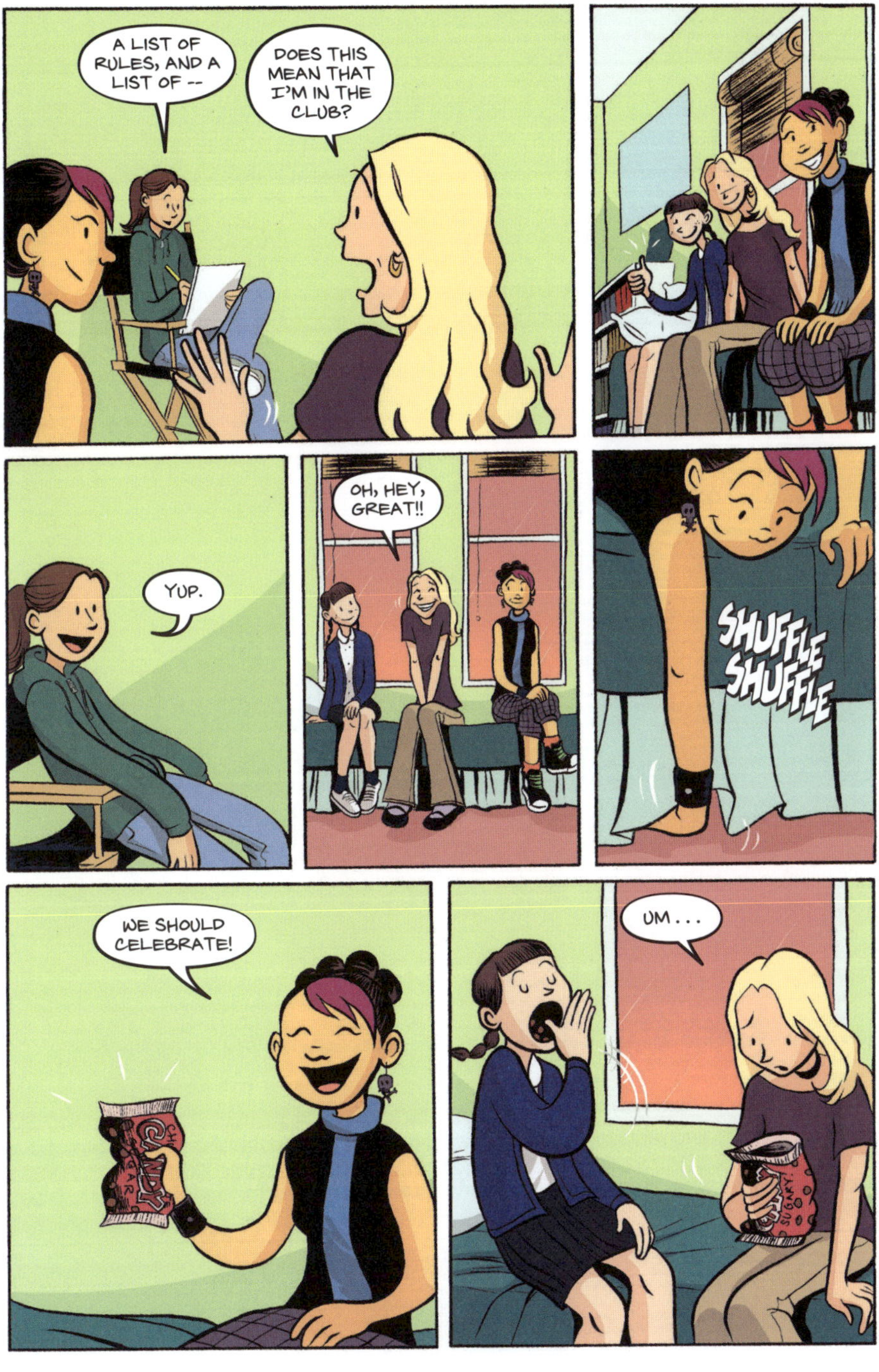
A LIST OF RULES, AND A LIST OF --
DOES THIS MEAN THAT I'M IN THE CLUB?
YUP.
OH, HEY, GREAT!!
SHUFFLE SHUFFLE
WE SHOULD CELEBRATE!
CANDY
UM . . .
SUGARY

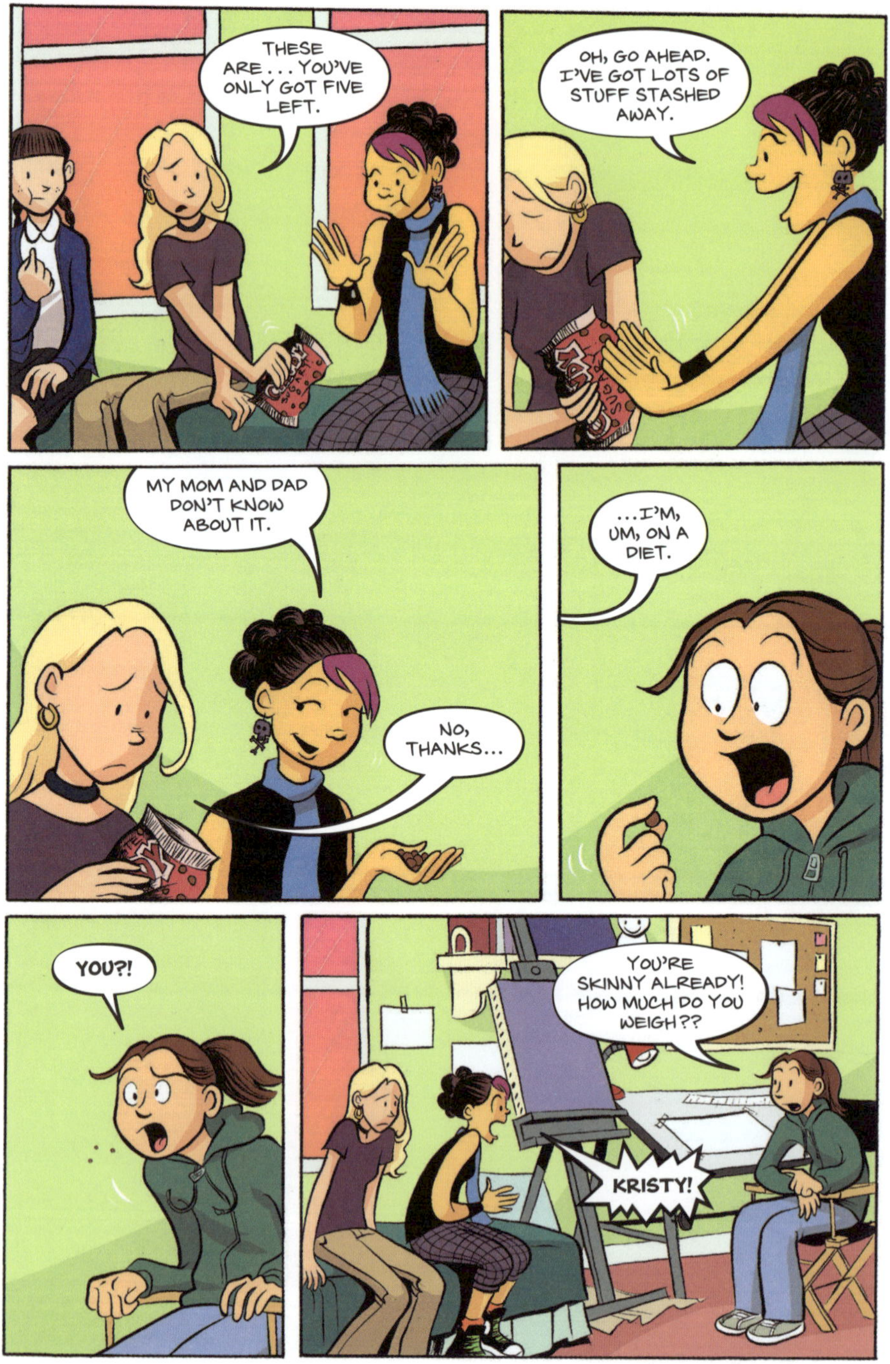
THESE ARE . . . YOU'VE ONLY GOT FIVE LEFT.
OH, GO AHEAD. I'VE GOT LOTS OF STUFF STASHED AWAY.
MY MOM AND DAD DON'T KNOW ABOUT IT.
NO, THANKS...
...I'M, UM, ON A DIET.
YOU?!
YOU'RE SKINNY ALREADY! HOW MUCH DO YOU WEIGH??
KRISTY!

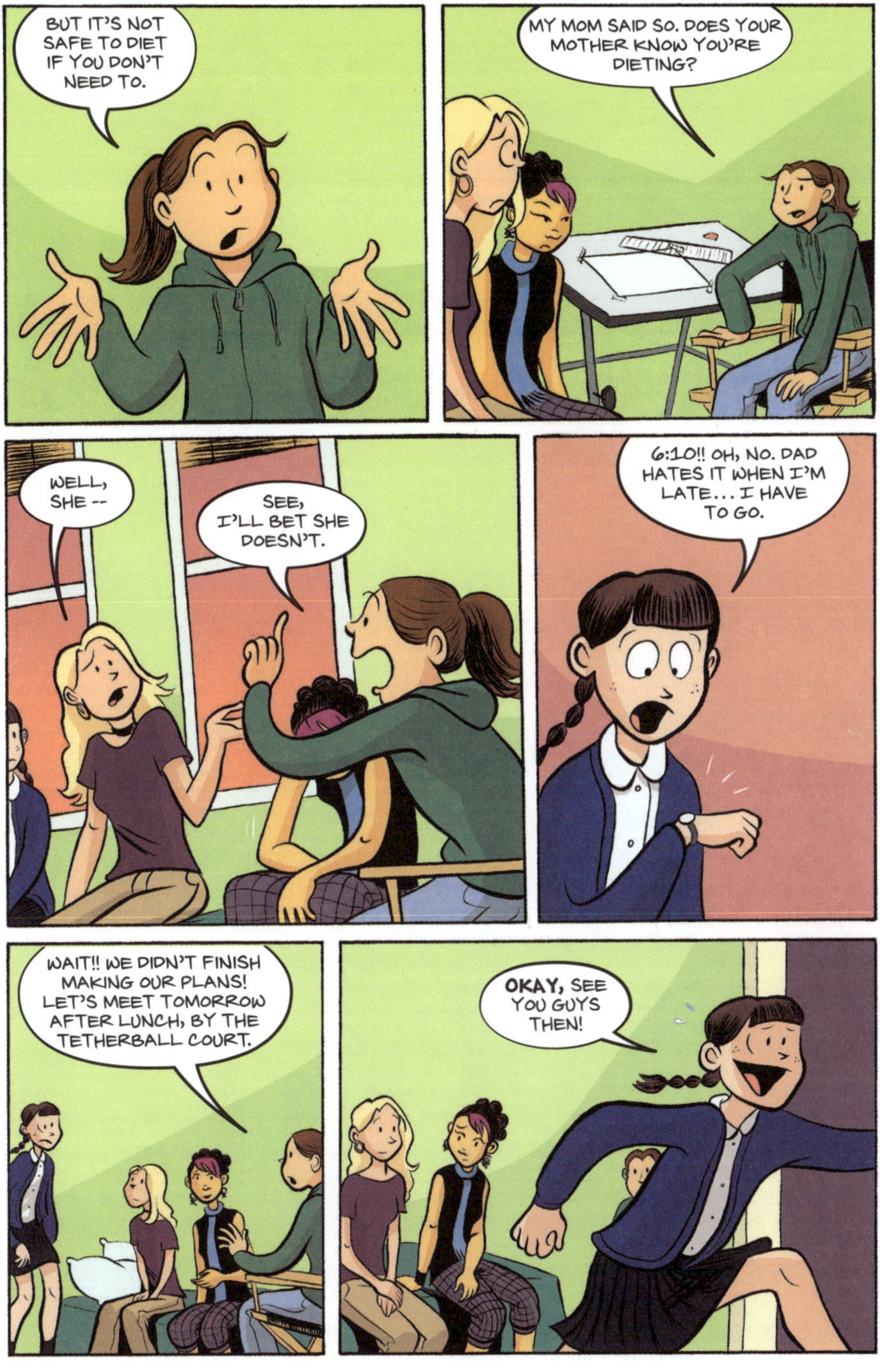
BUT IT'S NOT SAFE TO DIET IF YOU DON'T NEED TO.
MY MOM SAID SO. DOES YOUR MOTHER KNOW YOU'RE DIETING?
WELL, SHE --
SEE, I'LL BET SHE DOESN'T.
6:10!! OH, NO. DAD HATES IT WHEN I'M LATE... I HAVE TO GO.
WAIT!! WE DIDN'T FINISH MAKING OUR PLANS! LET'S MEET TOMORROW AFTER LUNCH, BY THE TETHERBALL COURT.
OKAY, SEE YOU GUYS THEN!

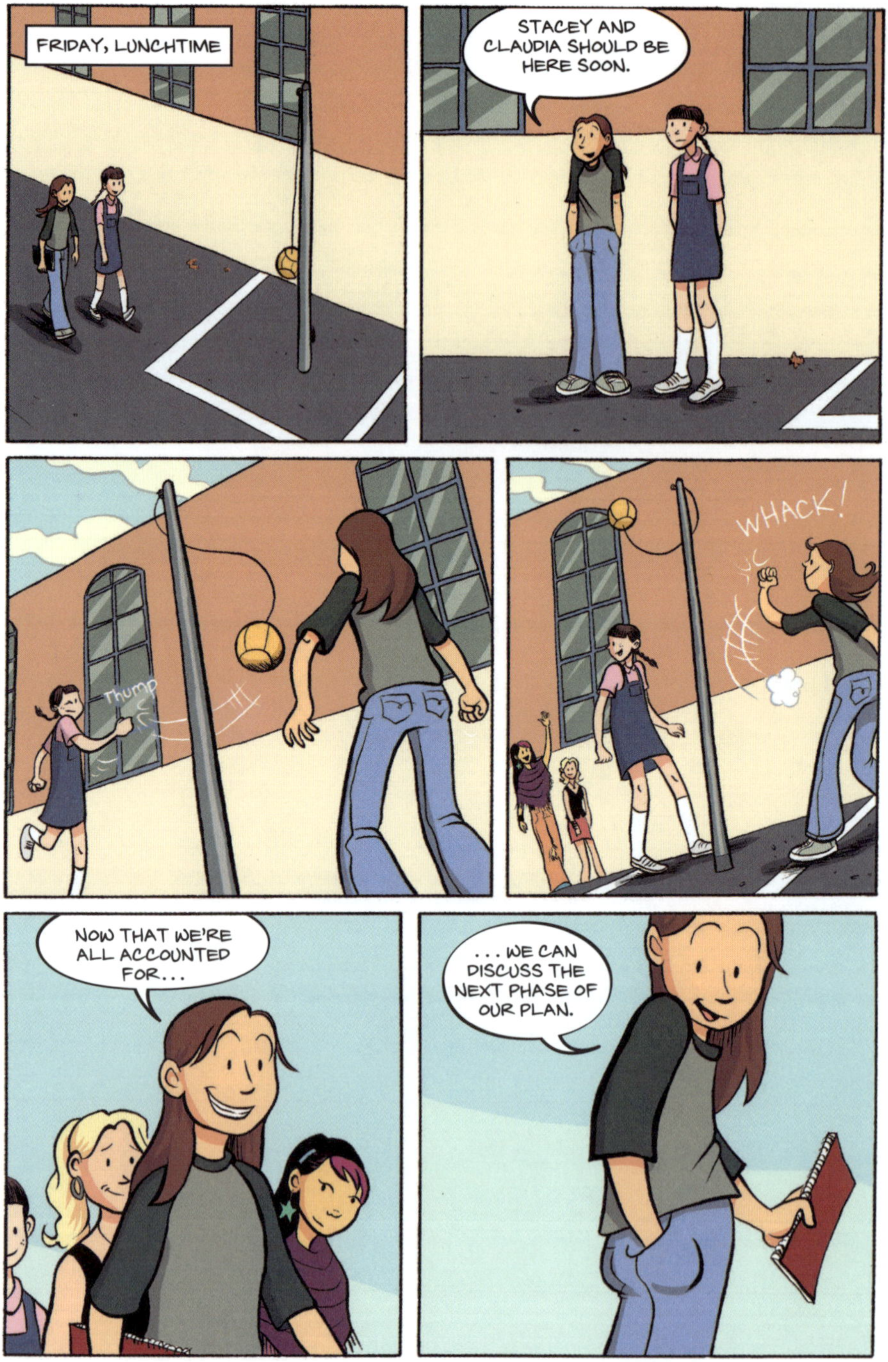
FRIDAY, LUNCHTIME
STACEY AND CLAUDIA SHOULD BE HERE SOON.
Thump
WHACK!
NOW THAT WE'RE ALL ACCOUNTED FOR...
...WE CAN DISCUSS THE NEXT PHASE OF OUR PLAN.

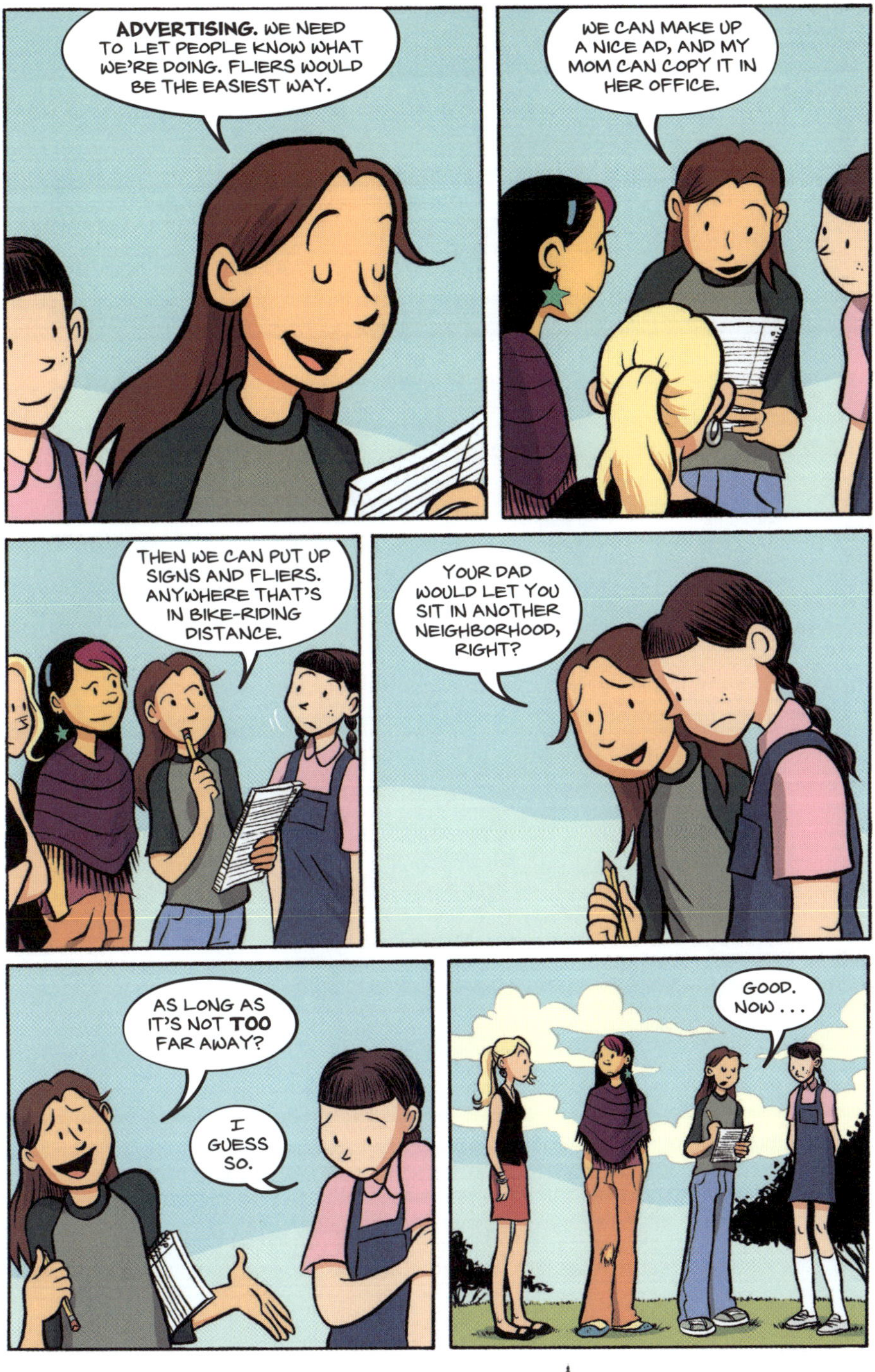
ADVERTISING. WE NEED TO LET PEOPLE KNOW WHAT WE'RE DOING. FLIERS WOULD BE THE EASIEST WAY.
WE CAN MAKE UP A NICE AD, AND MY MOM CAN COPY IT IN HER OFFICE.
THEN WE CAN PUT UP SIGNS AND FLIERS. ANYWHERE THAT'S IN BIKE-RIDING DISTANCE.
YOUR DAD WOULD LET YOU SIT IN ANOTHER NEIGHBORHOOD, RIGHT?
AS LONG AS IT'S NOT TOO FAR AWAY?
I GUESS SO.
GOOD. NOW . . .

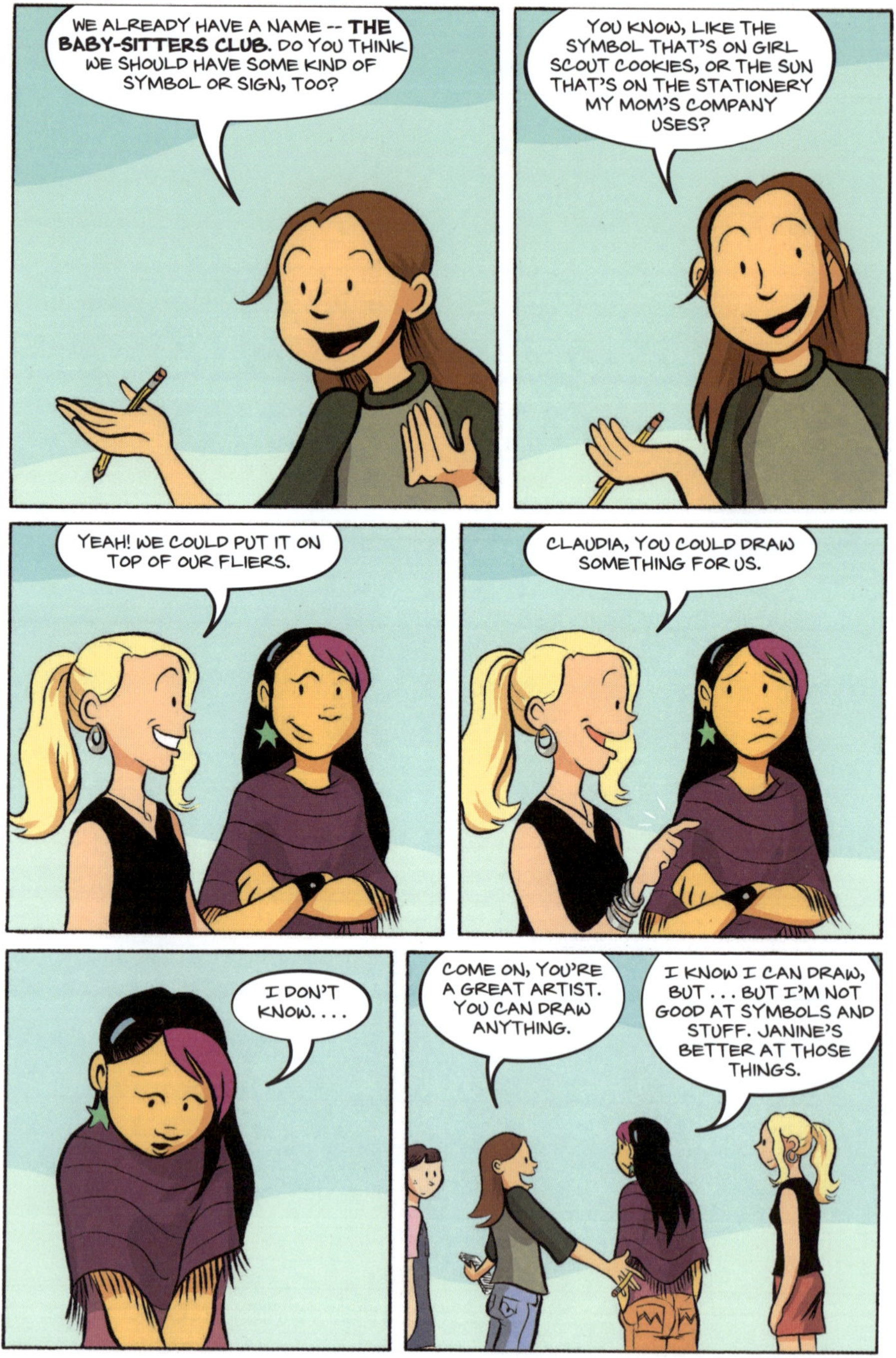
WE ALREADY HAVE A NAME -- THE BABY-SITTERS CLUB. DO YOU THINK WE SHOULD HAVE SOME KIND OF SYMBOL OR SIGN, TOO?
YOU KNOW, LIKE THE SYMBOL THAT'S ON GIRL SCOUT COOKIES, OR THE SUN THAT'S ON THE STATIONERY MY MOM'S COMPANY USES?
YEAH! WE COULD PUT IT ON TOP OF OUR FLIERS.
CLAUDIA, YOU COULD DRAW SOMETHING FOR US.
I DON'T KNOW. . . .
COME ON, YOU'RE A GREAT ARTIST. YOU CAN DRAW ANYTHING.
I KNOW I CAN DRAW, BUT . . . BUT I'M NOT GOOD AT SYMBOLS AND STUFF. JANINE'S BETTER AT THOSE THINGS.

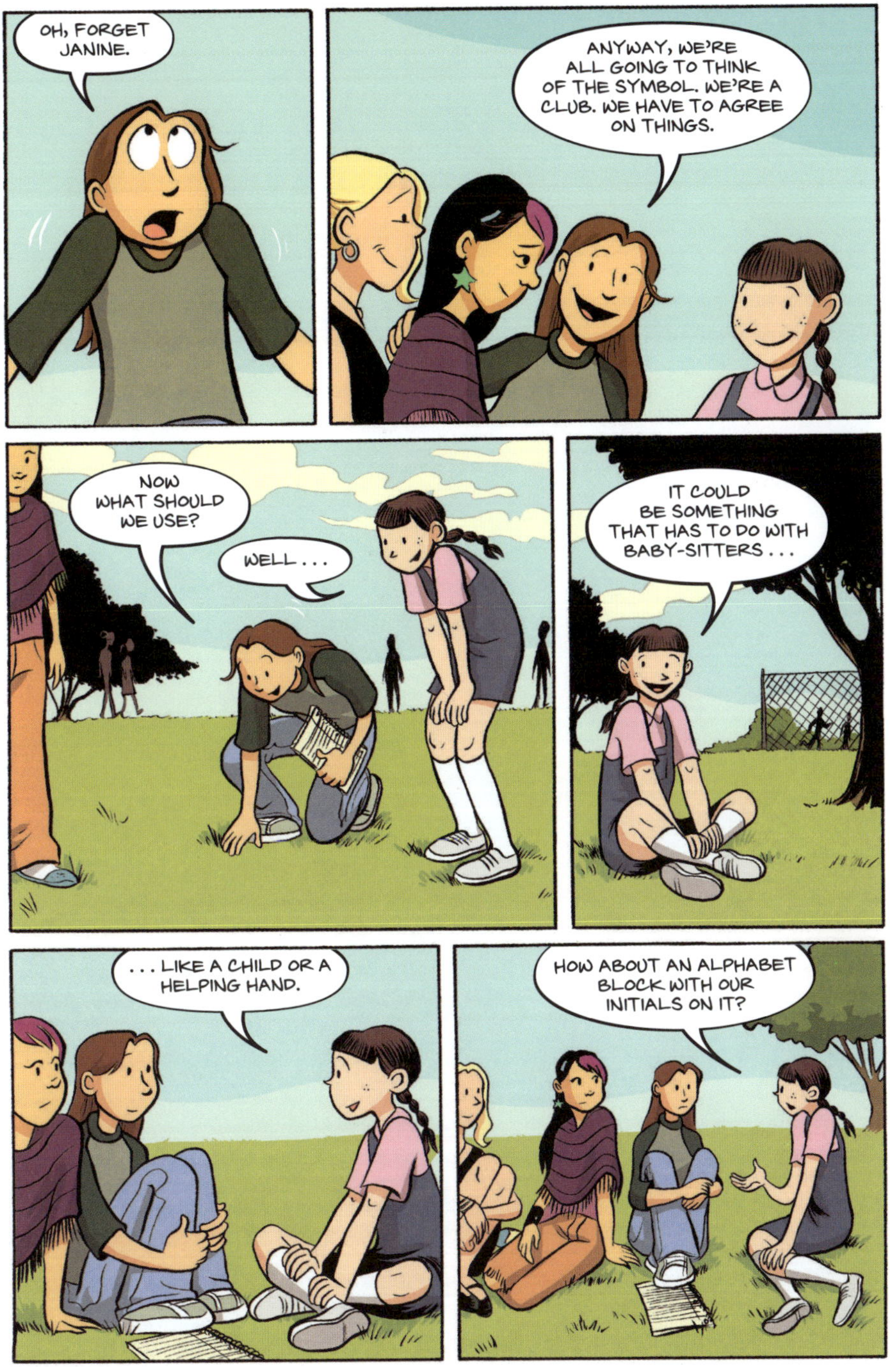
OH, FORGET JANINE.
ANYWAY, WE'RE ALL GOING TO THINK OF THE SYMBOL. WE'RE A CLUB. WE HAVE TO AGREE ON THINGS.
NOW WHAT SHOULD WE USE?
WELL . . .
IT COULD BE SOMETHING THAT HAS TO DO WITH BABY-SITTERS . . .
. . . LIKE A CHILD OR A HELPING HAND.
HOW ABOUT AN ALPHABET BLOCK WITH OUR INITIALS ON IT?

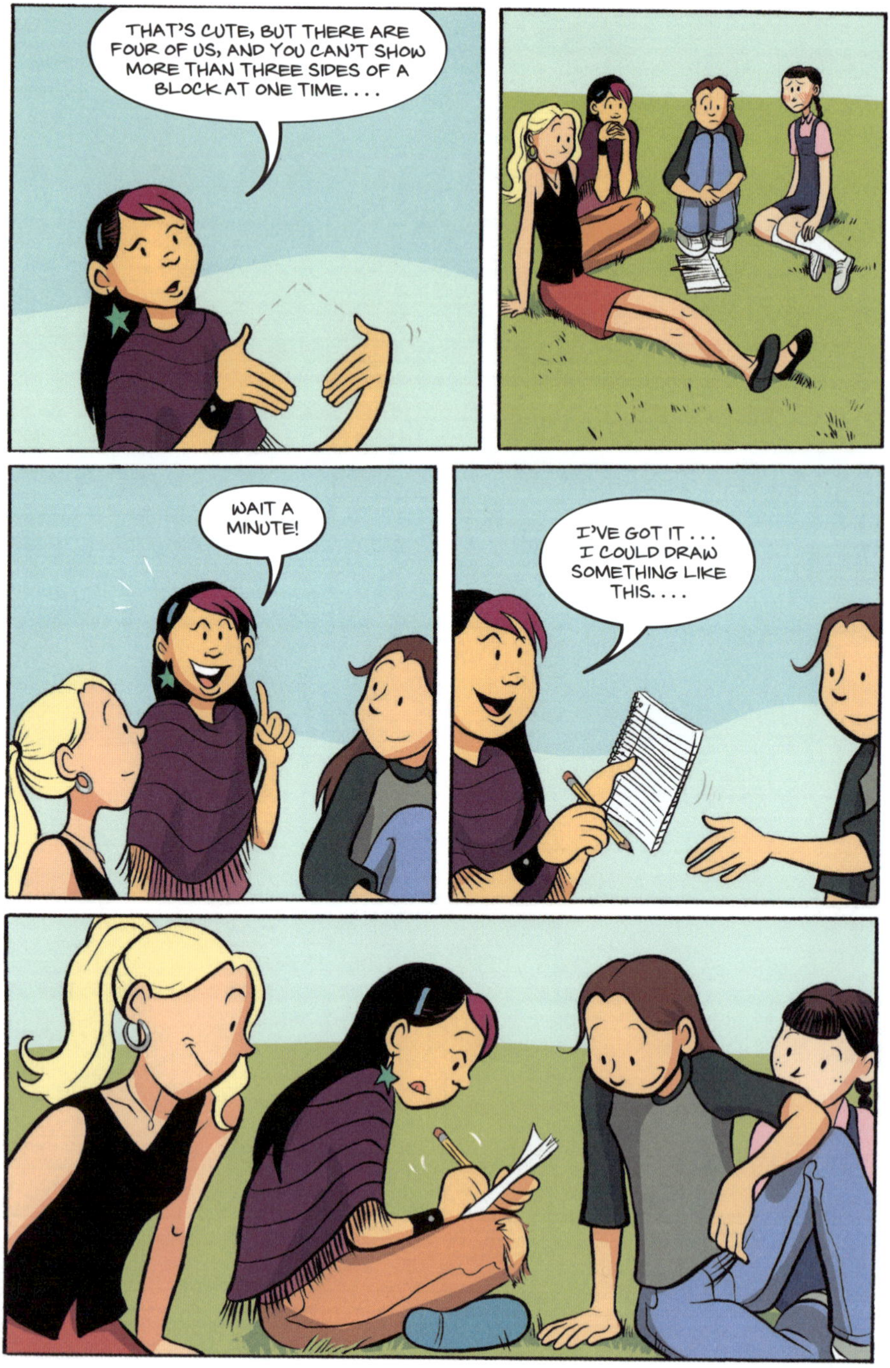
THAT'S CUTE, BUT THERE ARE FOUR OF US, AND YOU CAN'T SHOW MORE THAN THREE SIDES OF A BLOCK AT ONE TIME. . . .
WAIT A MINUTE!
I'VE GOT IT . . . I COULD DRAW SOMETHING LIKE THIS. . . .

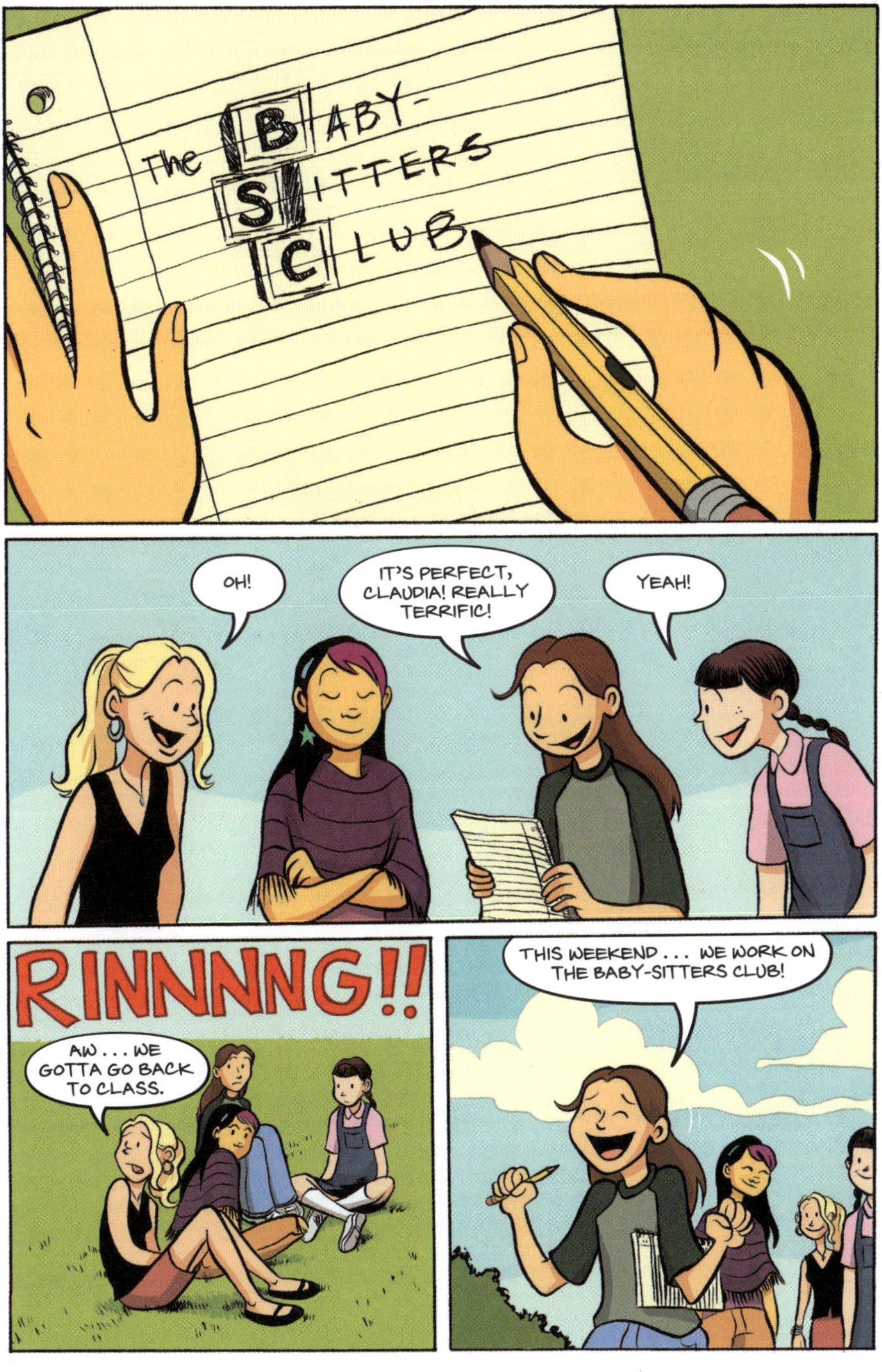
The BABY-SITTERS CLUB
OH!
IT'S PERFECT, CLAUDIA! REALLY TERRIFIC!
YEAH!
RINNNNG!!
AW... WE GOTTA GO BACK TO CLASS.
THIS WEEKEND... WE WORK ON THE BABY-SITTERS CLUB!

CHAPTER 5

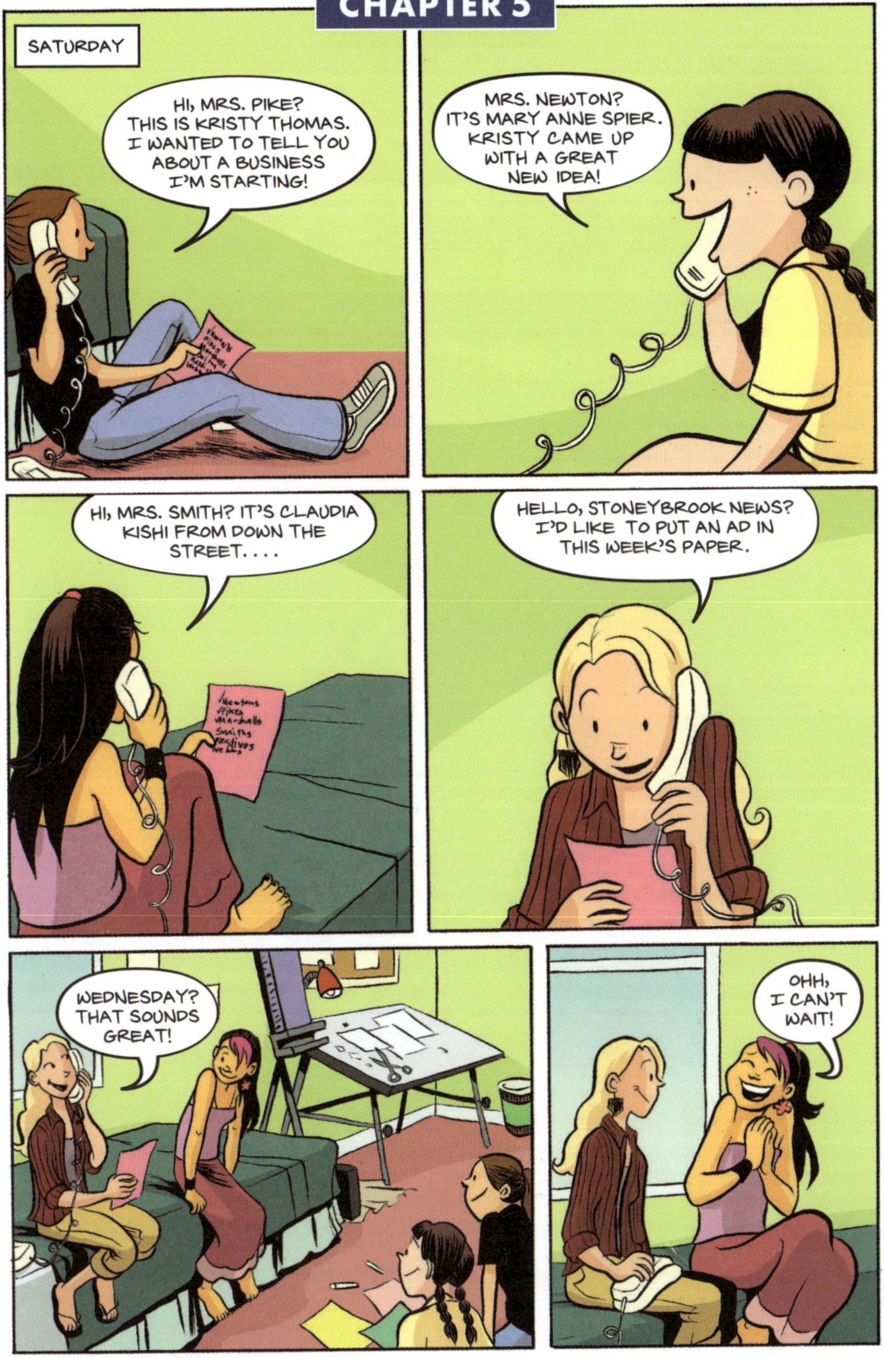
SATURDAY
HI, MRS. PIKE? THIS IS KRISTY THOMAS. I WANTED TO TELL YOU ABOUT A BUSINESS I'M STARTING!
MRS. NEWTON? IT'S MARY ANNE SPIER. KRISTY CAME UP WITH A GREAT NEW IDEA!
HI, MRS. SMITH? IT'S CLAUDIA KISHI FROM DOWN THE STREET. . . .
HELLO, STONEYBROOK NEWS? I'D LIKE TO PUT AN AD IN THIS WEEK'S PAPER.
WEDNESDAY? THAT SOUNDS GREAT!
OHH, I CAN'T WAIT!

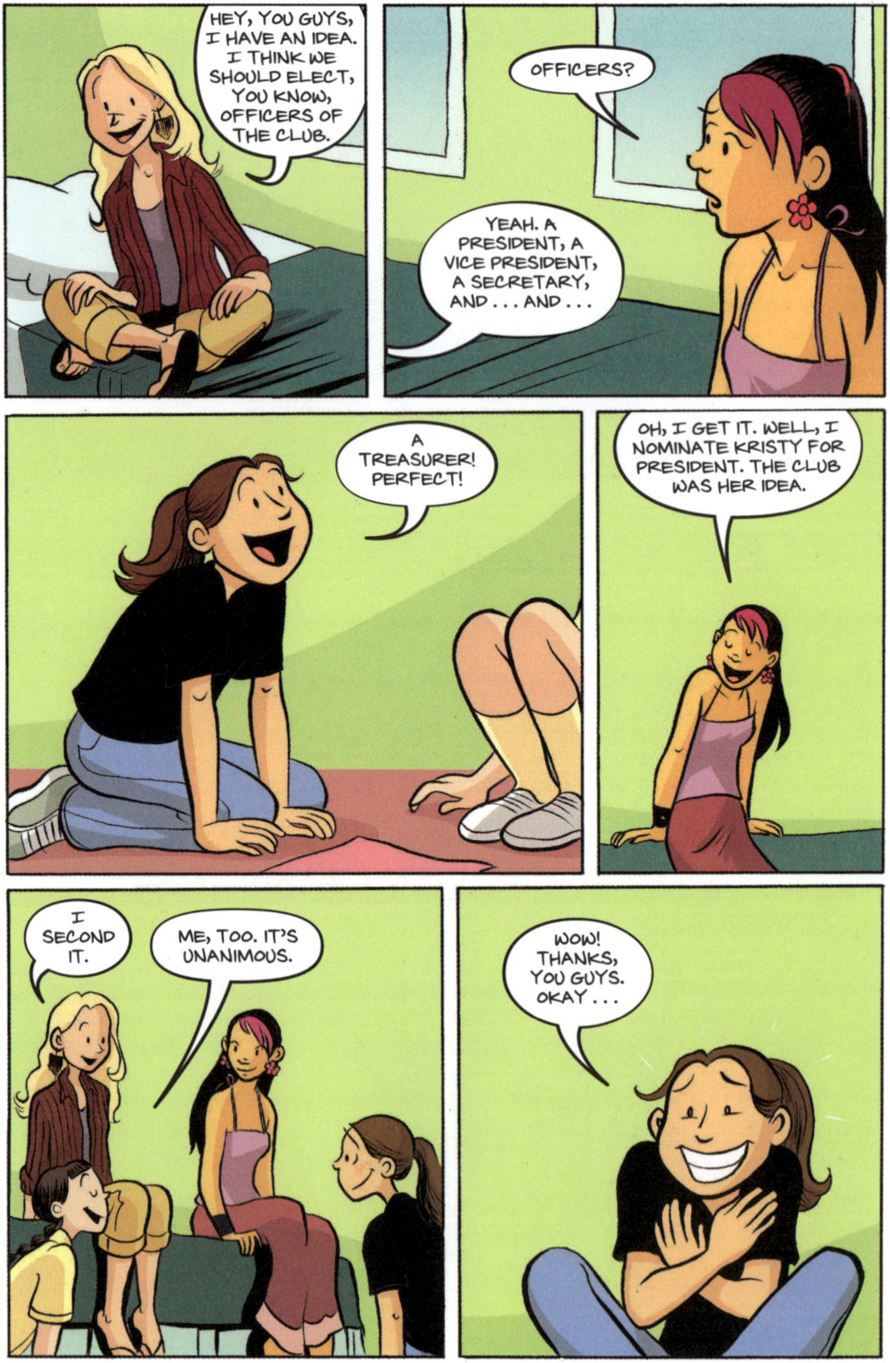
HEY, YOU GUYS, I HAVE AN IDEA. I THINK WE SHOULD ELECT, YOU KNOW, OFFICERS OF THE CLUB.
OFFICERS?
YEAH. A PRESIDENT, A VICE PRESIDENT, A SECRETARY, AND . . . AND . . .
A TREASURER! PERFECT!
OH, I GET IT. WELL, I NOMINATE KRISTY FOR PRESIDENT. THE CLUB WAS HER IDEA.
I SECOND IT.
ME, TOO. IT'S UNANIMOUS.
WOW! THANKS, YOU GUYS. OKAY . . .

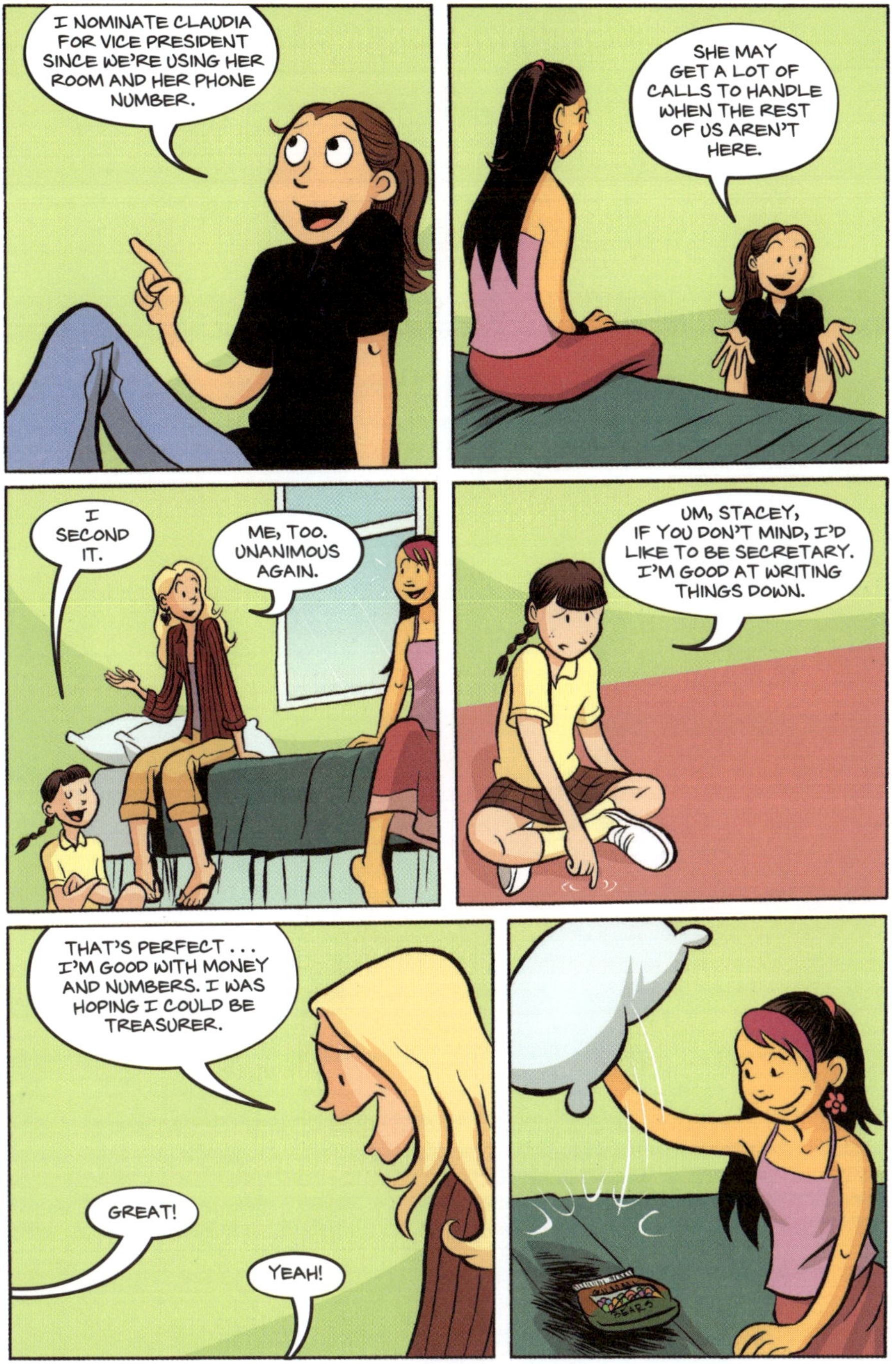
I NOMINATE CLAUDIA FOR VICE PRESIDENT SINCE WE'RE USING HER ROOM AND HER PHONE NUMBER.
SHE MAY GET A LOT OF CALLS TO HANDLE WHEN THE REST OF US AREN'T HERE.
I SECOND IT.
ME, TOO. UNANIMOUS AGAIN.
UM, STACEY, IF YOU DON'T MIND, I'D LIKE TO BE SECRETARY. I'M GOOD AT WRITING THINGS DOWN.
THAT'S PERFECT . . . I'M GOOD WITH MONEY AND NUMBERS. I WAS HOPING I COULD BE TREASURER.
GREAT!
YEAH!

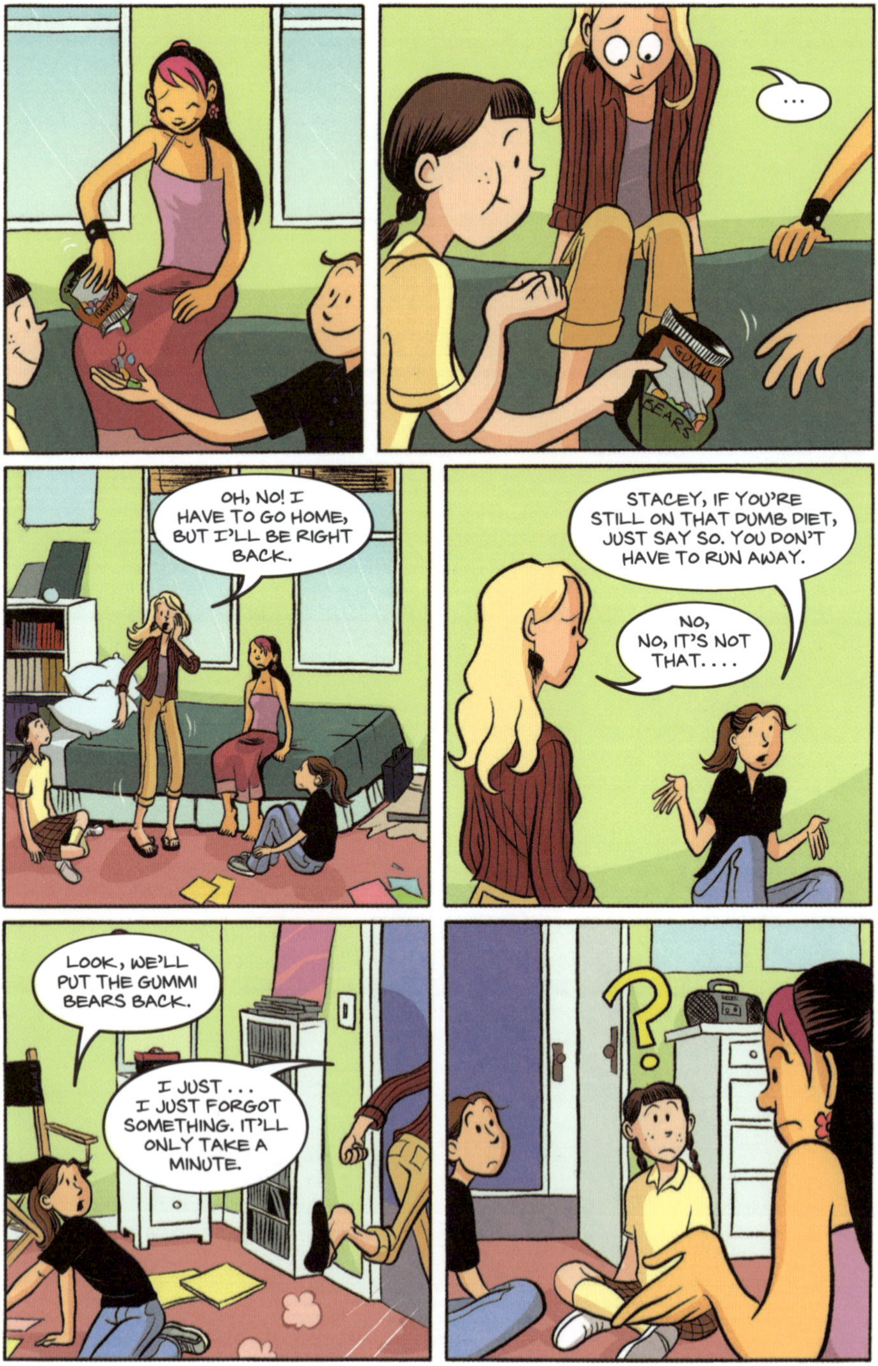

...
GUMMI BEARS
OH, NO! I HAVE TO GO HOME, BUT I'LL BE RIGHT BACK.
STACEY, IF YOU'RE STILL ON THAT DUMB DIET, JUST SAY SO. YOU DON'T HAVE TO RUN AWAY.
NO, NO, IT'S NOT THAT. . . .
LOOK, WE'LL PUT THE GUMMI BEARS BACK.
I JUST . . . I JUST FORGOT SOMETHING. IT'LL ONLY TAKE A MINUTE.
?

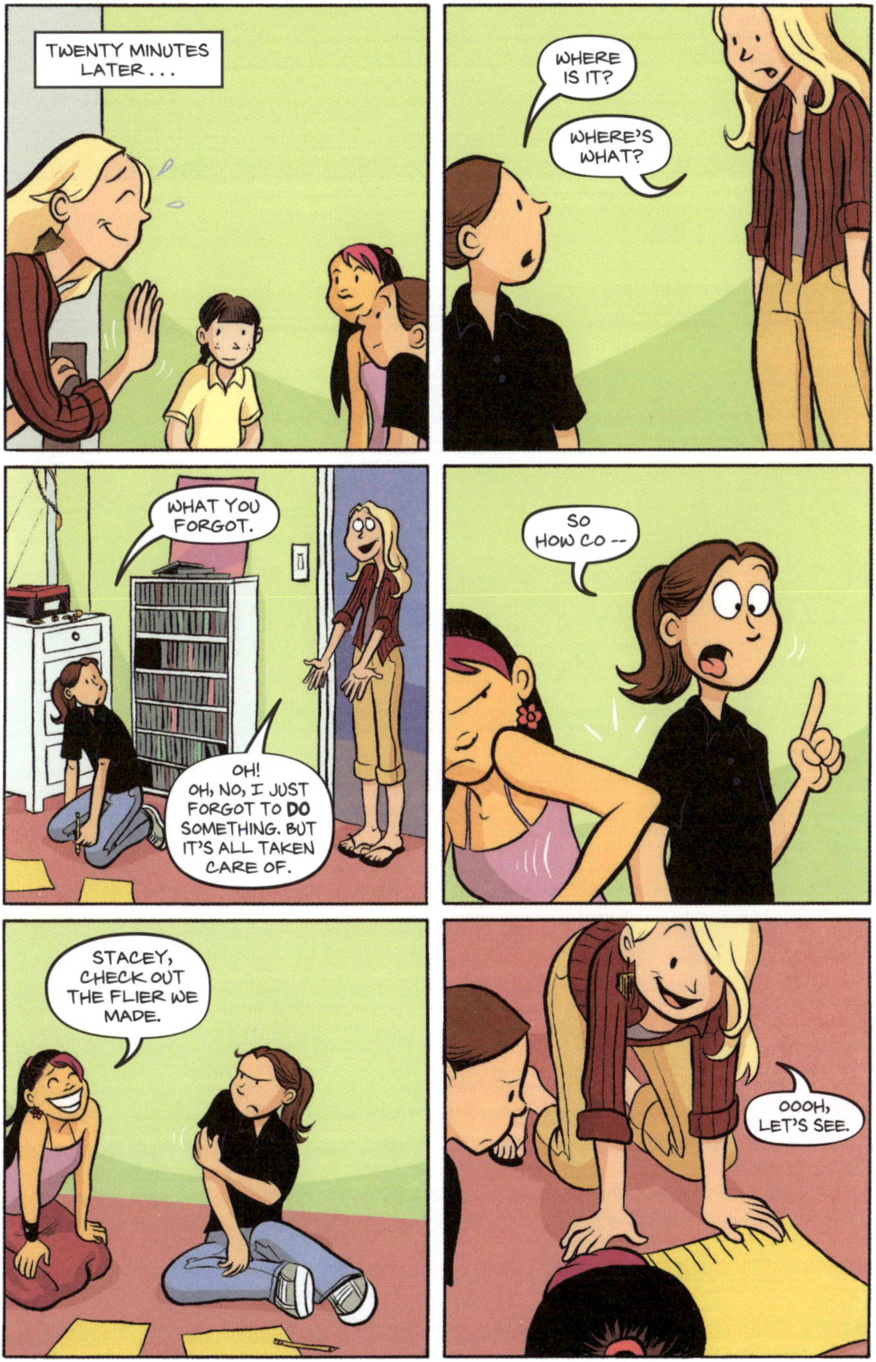

TWENTY MINUTES LATER . . .
WHERE IS IT?
WHERE'S WHAT?
WHAT YOU FORGOT.
OH! OH, NO, I JUST FORGOT TO **DO** SOMETHING. BUT IT'S ALL TAKEN CARE OF.
SO HOW CO --
STACEY, CHECK OUT THE FLIER WE MADE.
OOOH, LET'S SEE.

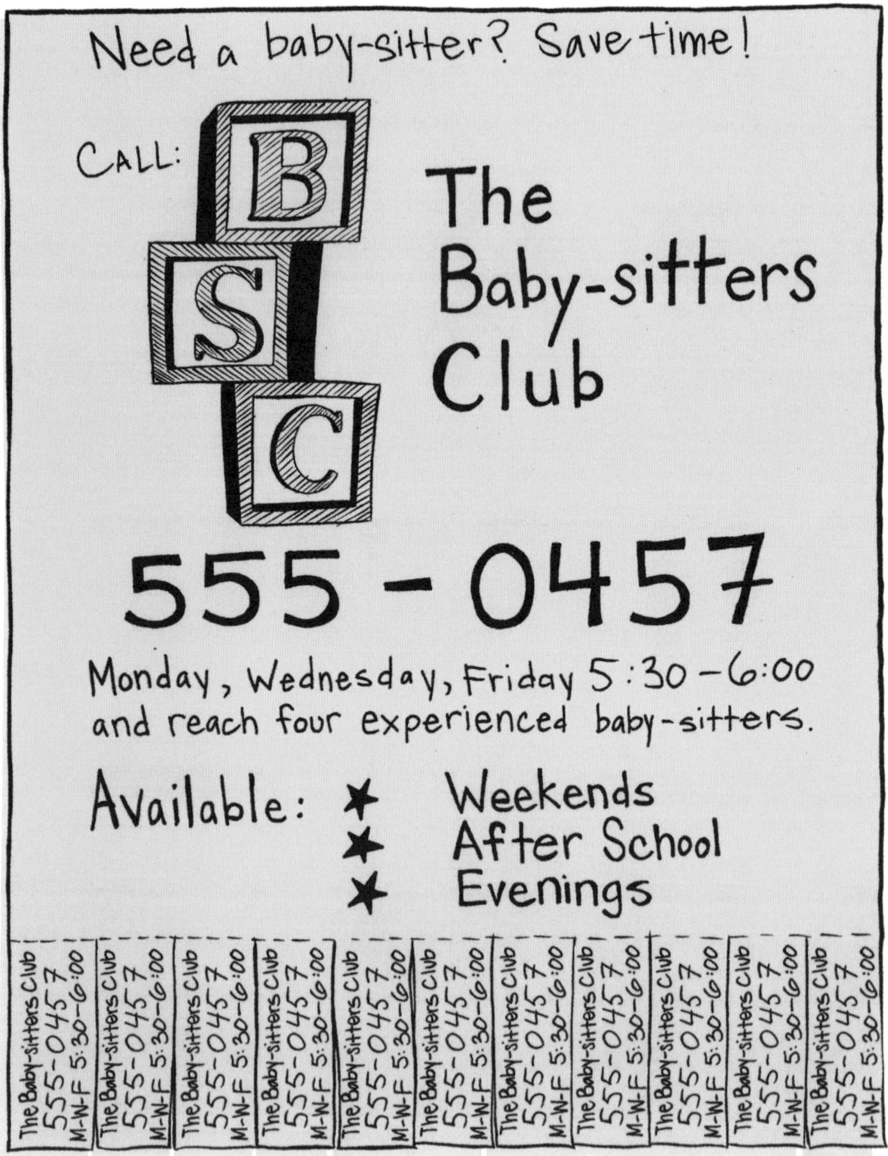
Need a baby-sitter? Save time!
CALL:
BSC
The Baby-sitters Club
555-0457
Monday, Wednesday, Friday 5:30-6:00
and reach four experienced baby-sitters.
Available: ★ Weekends ★ After School ★ Evenings
The Baby-sitters Club 555-0457 M-W-F 5:30-6:00
The Baby-sitters Club 555-0457 M-W-F 5:30-6:00
The Baby-sitters Club 555-0457 M-W-F 5:30-6:00
The Baby-sitters Club 555-0457 M-W-F 5:30-6:00
The Baby-sitters Club 555-0457 M-W-F 5:30-6:00
The Baby-sitters Club 555-0457 M-W-F 5:30-6:00
The Baby-sitters Club 555-0457 M-W-F 5:30-6:00
The Baby-sitters Club 555-0457 M-W-F 5:30-6:00
The Baby-sitters Club 555-0457 M-W-F 5:30-6:00
The Baby-sitters Club 555-0457 M-W-F 5:30-6:00
The Baby-sitters Club 555-0457 M-W-F 5:30-6:00

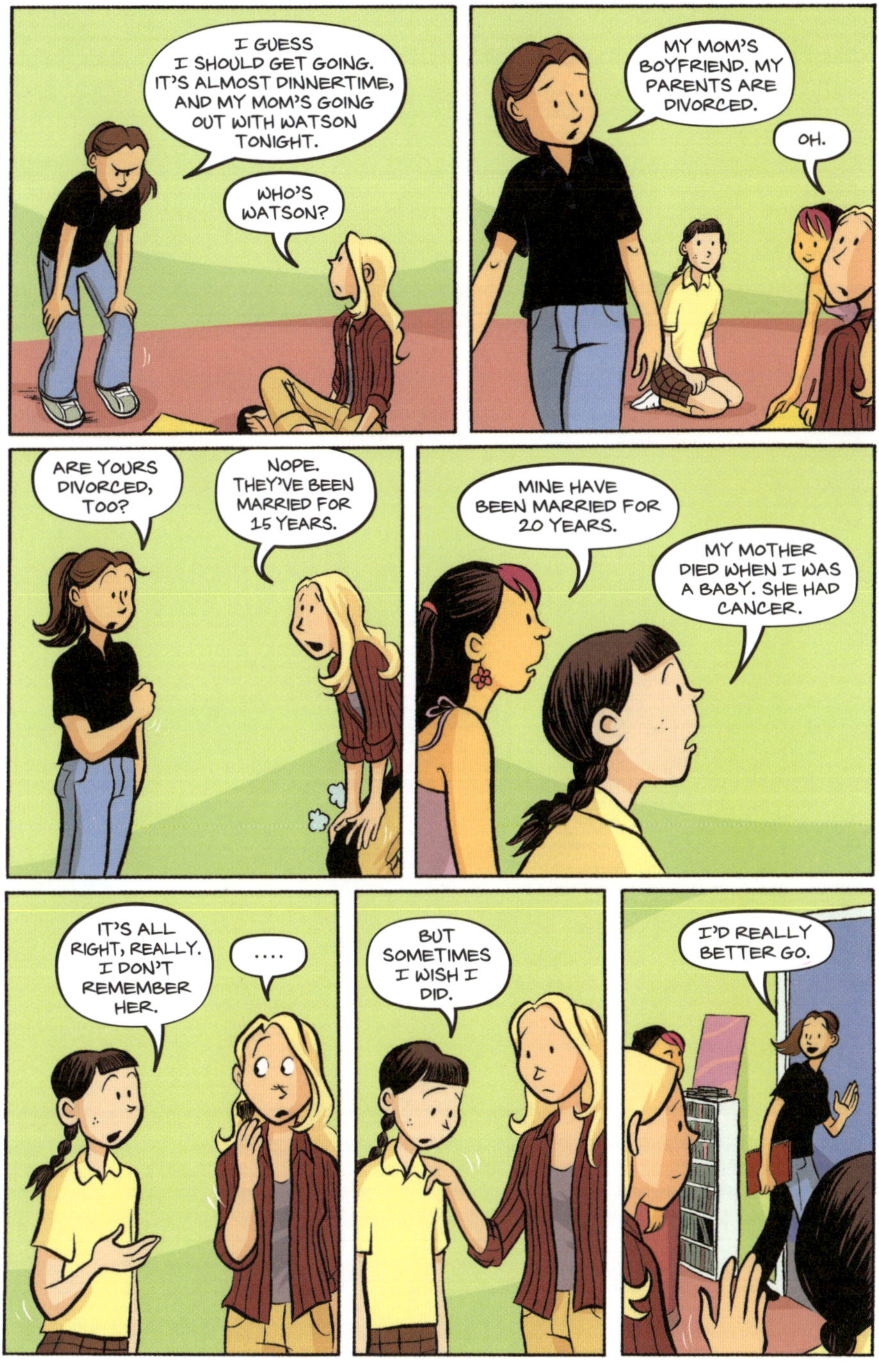
I GUESS I SHOULD GET GOING. IT'S ALMOST DINNERTIME, AND MY MOM'S GOING OUT WITH WATSON TONIGHT.
WHO'S WATSON?
MY MOM'S BOYFRIEND. MY PARENTS ARE DIVORCED.
OH.
ARE YOURS DIVORCED, TOO?
NOPE. THEY'VE BEEN MARRIED FOR 15 YEARS.
MINE HAVE BEEN MARRIED FOR 20 YEARS.
MY MOTHER DIED WHEN I WAS A BABY. SHE HAD CANCER.
IT'S ALL RIGHT, REALLY. I DON'T REMEMBER HER.
....
BUT SOMETIMES I WISH I DID.
I'D REALLY BETTER GO.

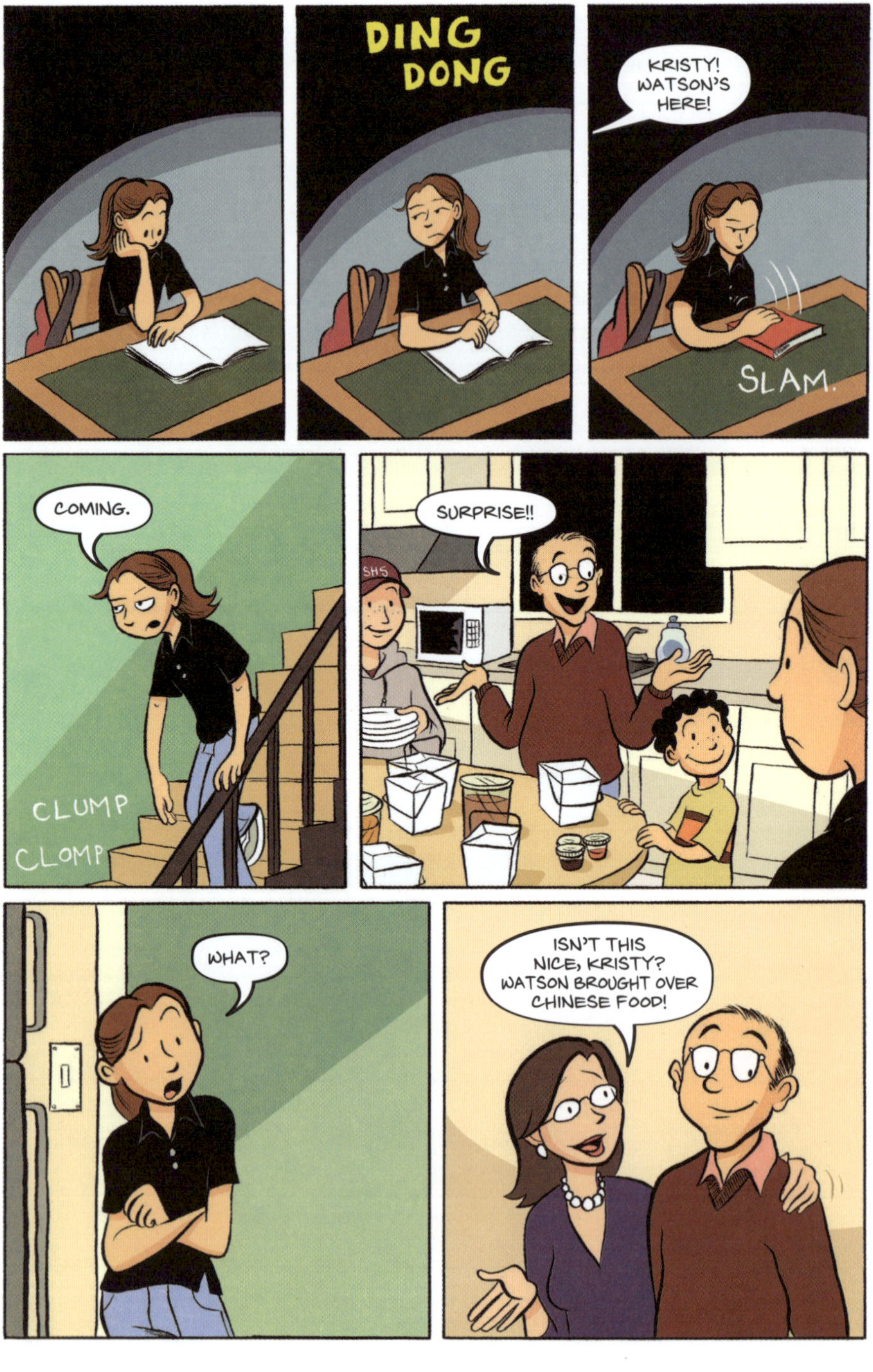
DING DONG
KRISTY! WATSON'S HERE!
SLAM.
COMING.
CLUMP
CLOMP
SURPRISE!!
SHS
WHAT?
ISN'T THIS NICE, KRISTY? WATSON BROUGHT OVER CHINESE FOOD!

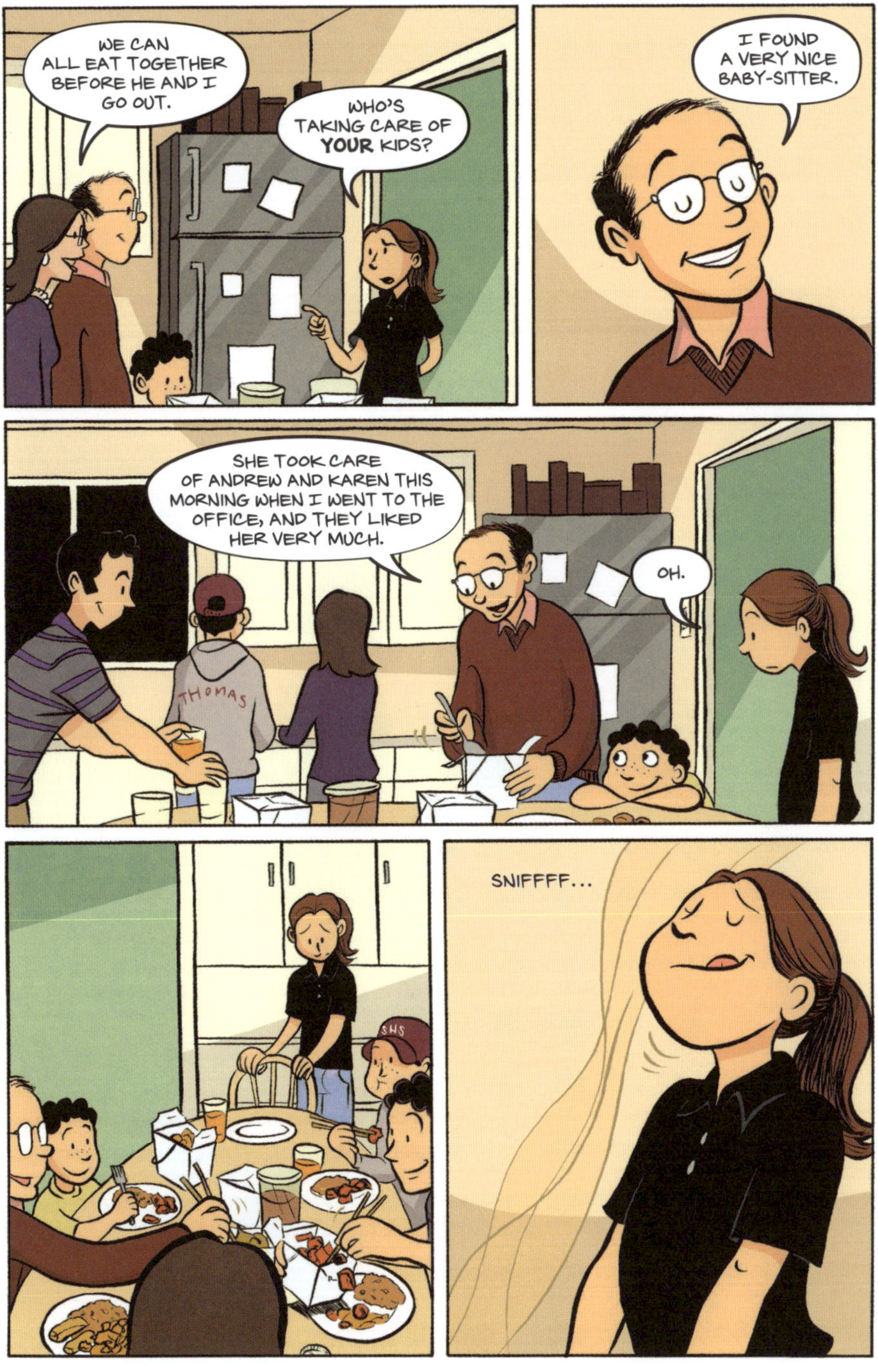
WE CAN ALL EAT TOGETHER BEFORE HE AND I GO OUT.
WHO'S TAKING CARE OF **YOUR** KIDS?
I FOUND A VERY NICE BABY-SITTER.
SHE TOOK CARE OF ANDREW AND KAREN THIS MORNING WHEN I WENT TO THE OFFICE, AND THEY LIKED HER VERY MUCH.
OH.
THOMAS
SHS
SNIFFFF...

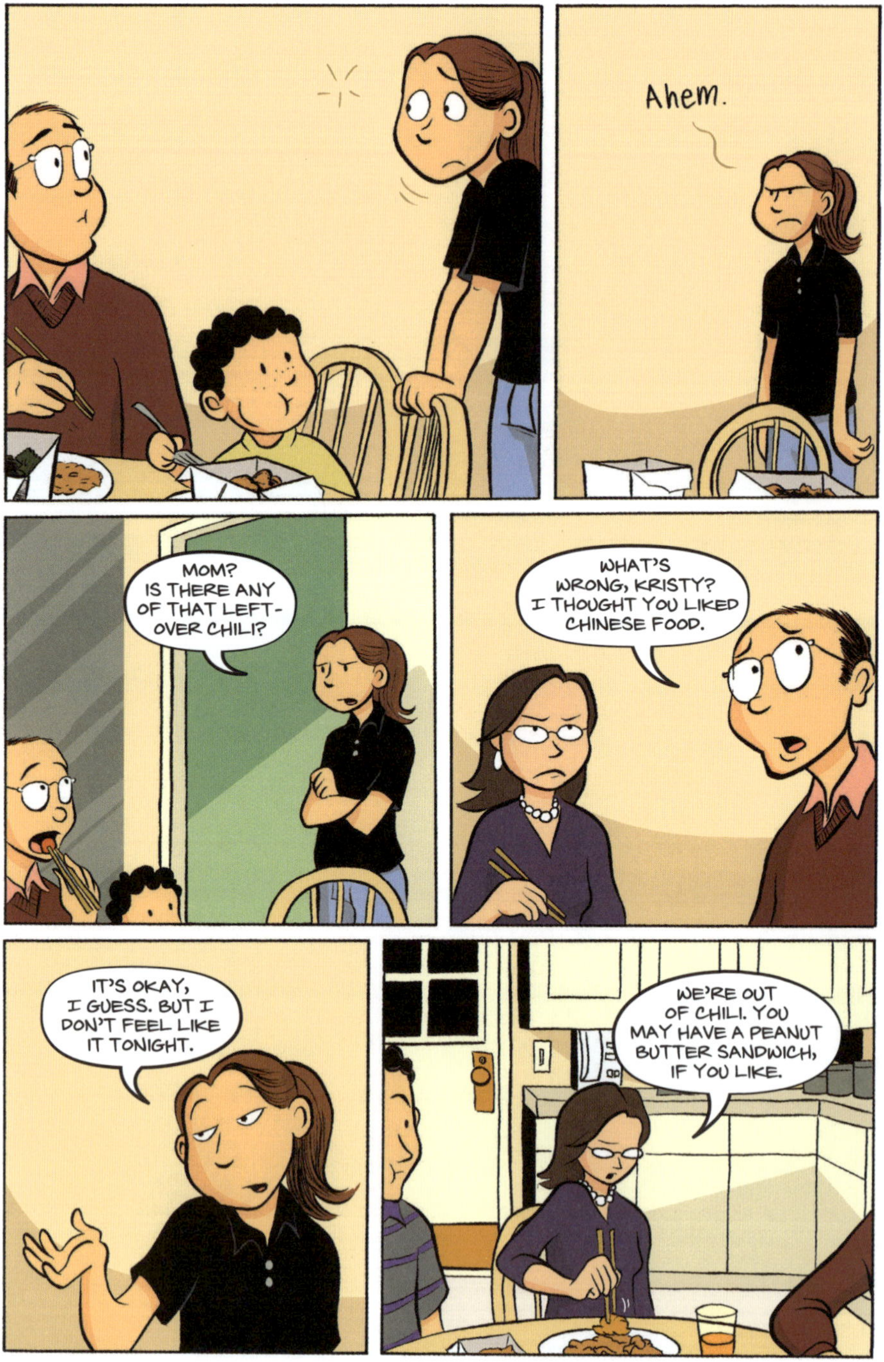
Ahem.
MOM? IS THERE ANY OF THAT LEFT-OVER CHILI?
WHAT'S WRONG, KRISTY? I THOUGHT YOU LIKED CHINESE FOOD.
IT'S OKAY, I GUESS. BUT I DON'T FEEL LIKE IT TONIGHT.
WE'RE OUT OF CHILI. YOU MAY HAVE A PEANUT BUTTER SANDWICH, IF YOU LIKE.

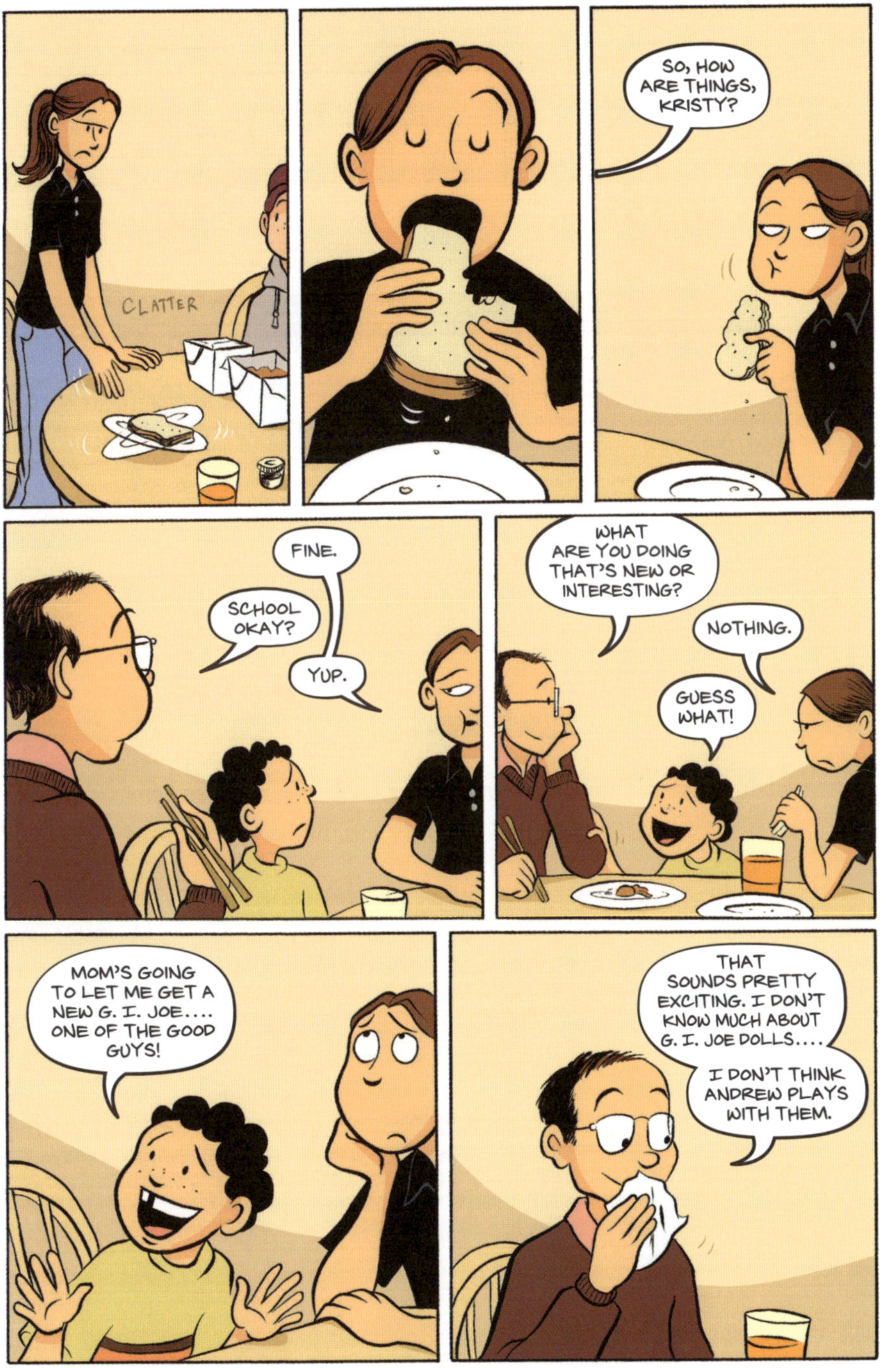
CLATTER
SO, HOW ARE THINGS, KRISTY?
FINE.
SCHOOL OKAY?
YUP.
WHAT ARE YOU DOING THAT'S NEW OR INTERESTING?
NOTHING.
GUESS WHAT!
MOM'S GOING TO LET ME GET A NEW G. I. JOE.... ONE OF THE GOOD GUYS!
THAT SOUNDS PRETTY EXCITING. I DON'T KNOW MUCH ABOUT G. I. JOE DOLLS....
I DON'T THINK ANDREW PLAYS WITH THEM.

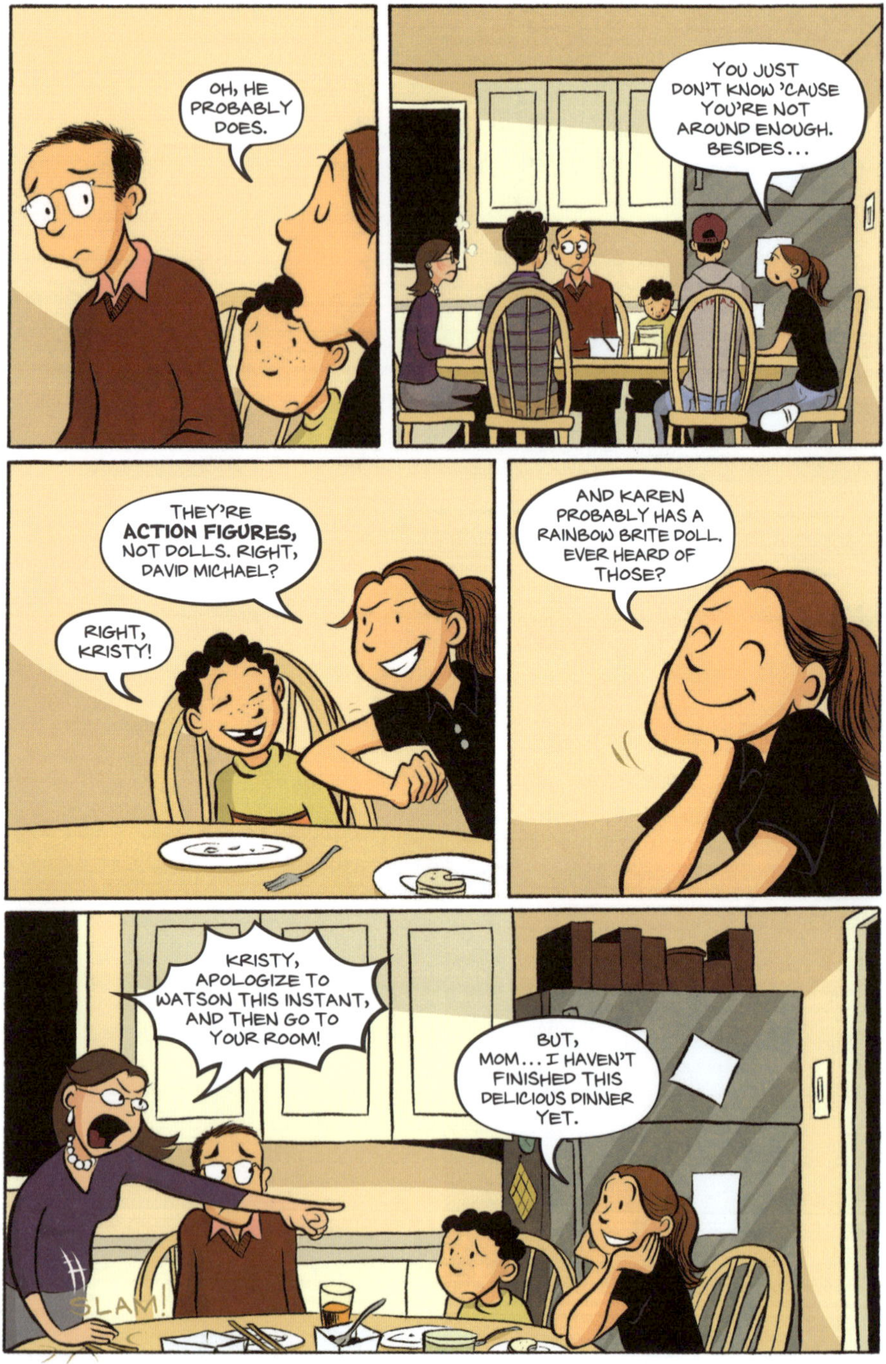

OH, HE PROBABLY DOES.
YOU JUST DON'T KNOW 'CAUSE YOU'RE NOT AROUND ENOUGH. BESIDES...
THEY'RE **ACTION FIGURES,** NOT DOLLS. RIGHT, DAVID MICHAEL?
RIGHT, KRISTY!
AND KAREN PROBABLY HAS A RAINBOW BRITE DOLL. EVER HEARD OF THOSE?
KRISTY, APOLOGIZE TO WATSON THIS INSTANT, AND THEN GO TO YOUR ROOM!
SLAM!
BUT, MOM... I HAVEN'T FINISHED THIS DELICIOUS DINNER YET.

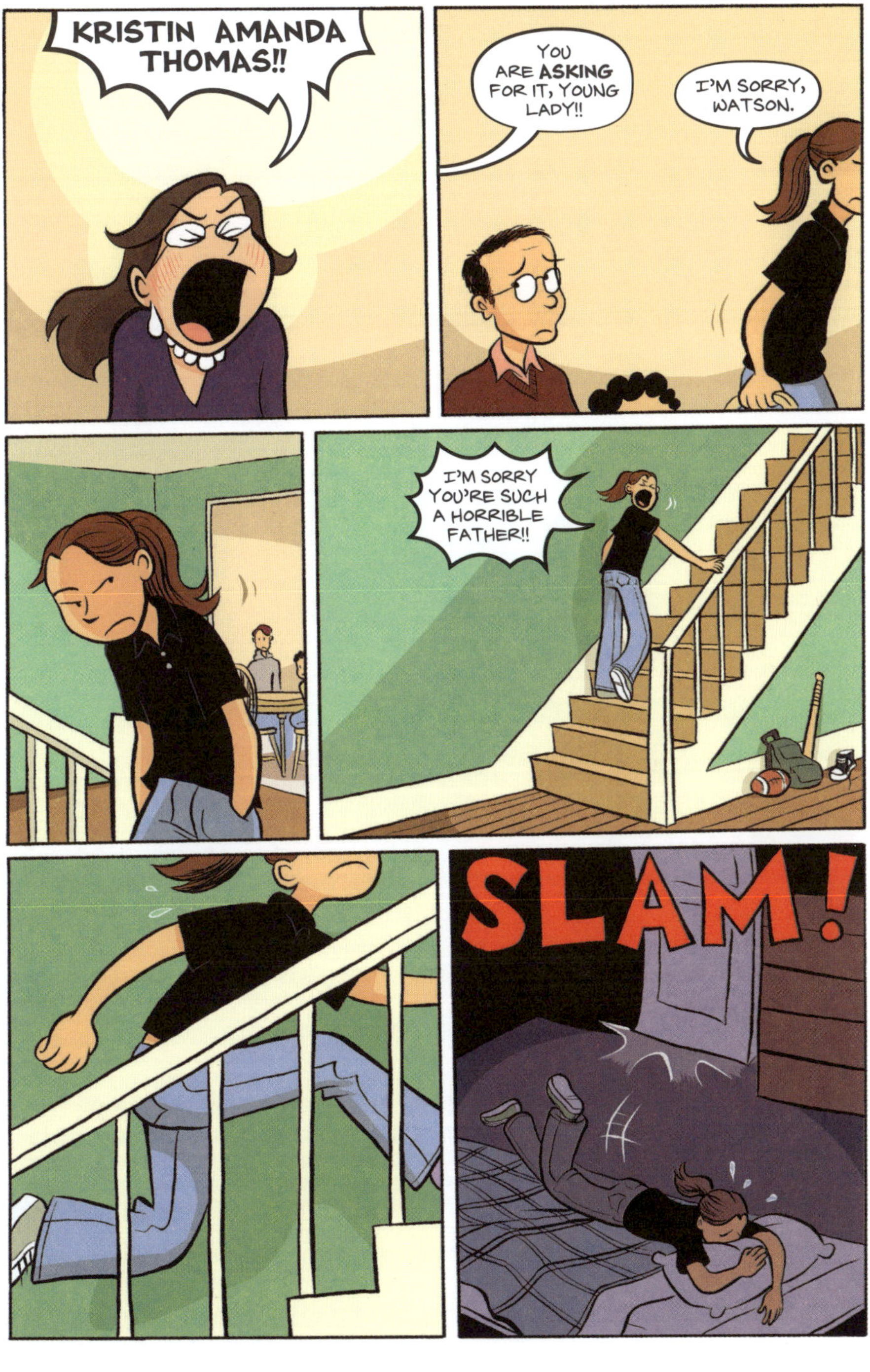
KRISTIN AMANDA THOMAS!!
YOU ARE ASKING FOR IT, YOUNG LADY!!
I'M SORRY, WATSON.
I'M SORRY YOU'RE SUCH A HORRIBLE FATHER!!
SLAM!

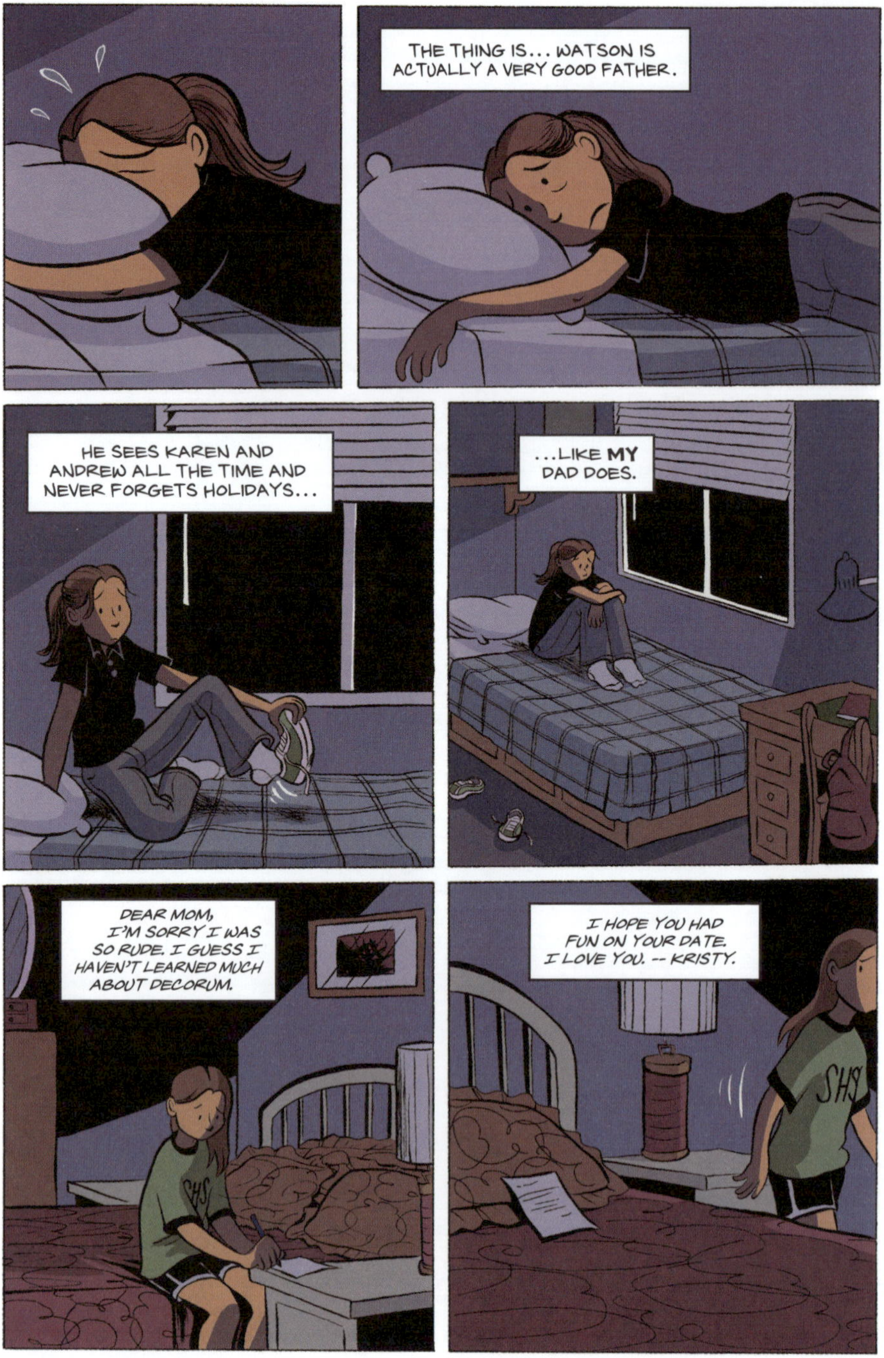
THE THING IS... WATSON IS ACTUALLY A VERY GOOD FATHER.
HE SEES KAREN AND ANDREW ALL THE TIME AND NEVER FORGETS HOLIDAYS...
...LIKE MY DAD DOES.
DEAR MOM, I'M SORRY I WAS SO RUDE. I GUESS I HAVEN'T LEARNED MUCH ABOUT DECORUM.
I HOPE YOU HAD FUN ON YOUR DATE. I LOVE YOU. -- KRISTY.
SHS

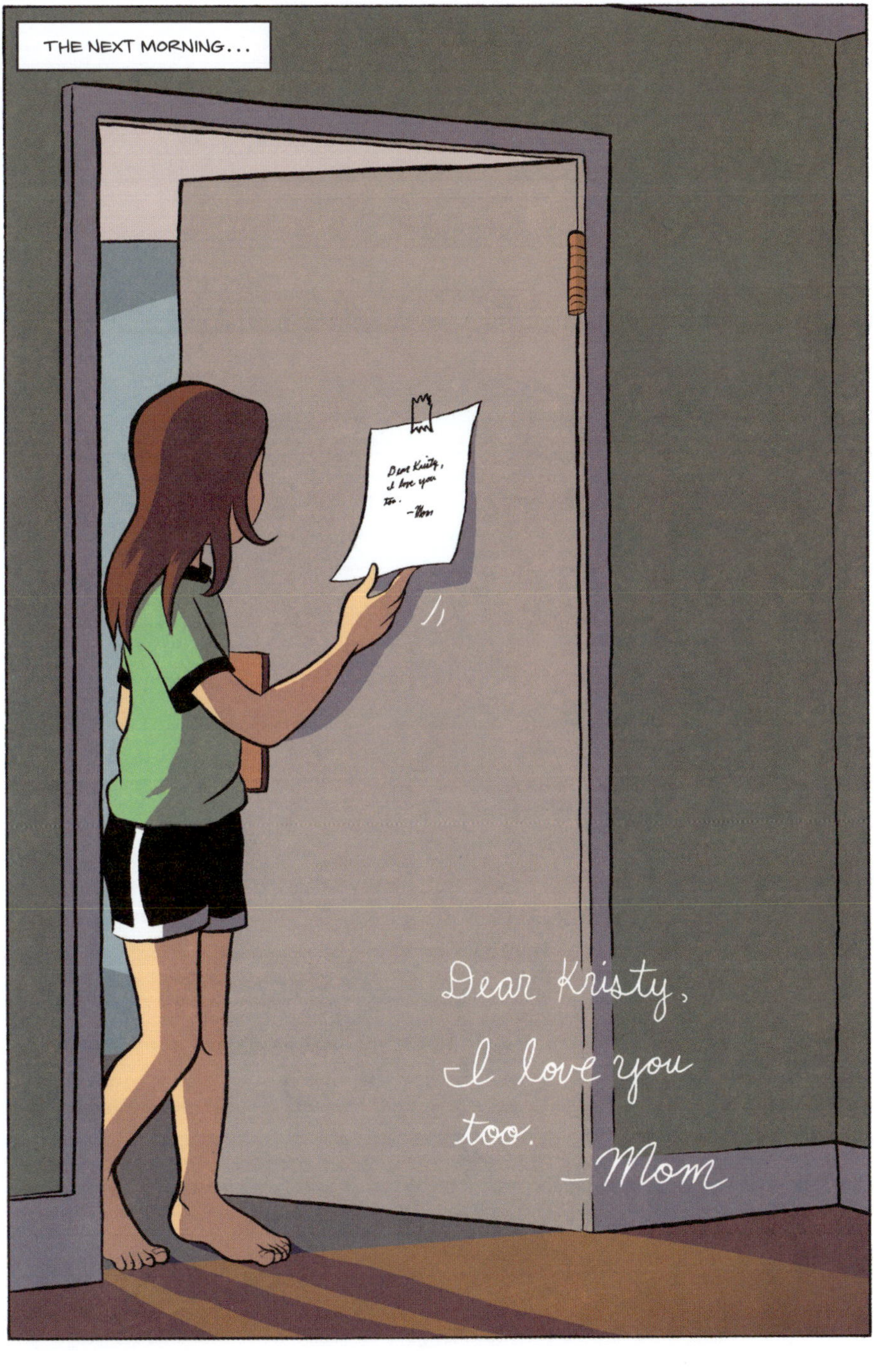
THE NEXT MORNING...
Dear Kristy,
I love you
too.
—Mom

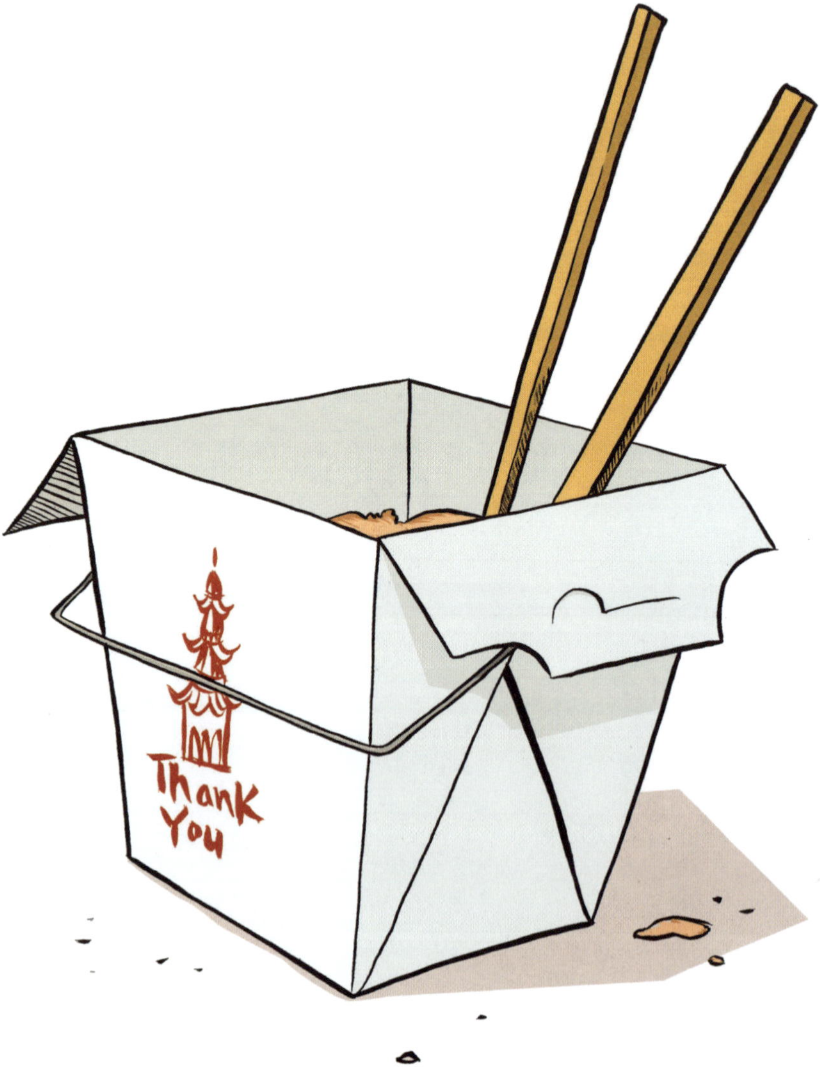
Thank
You

CHAPTER 6

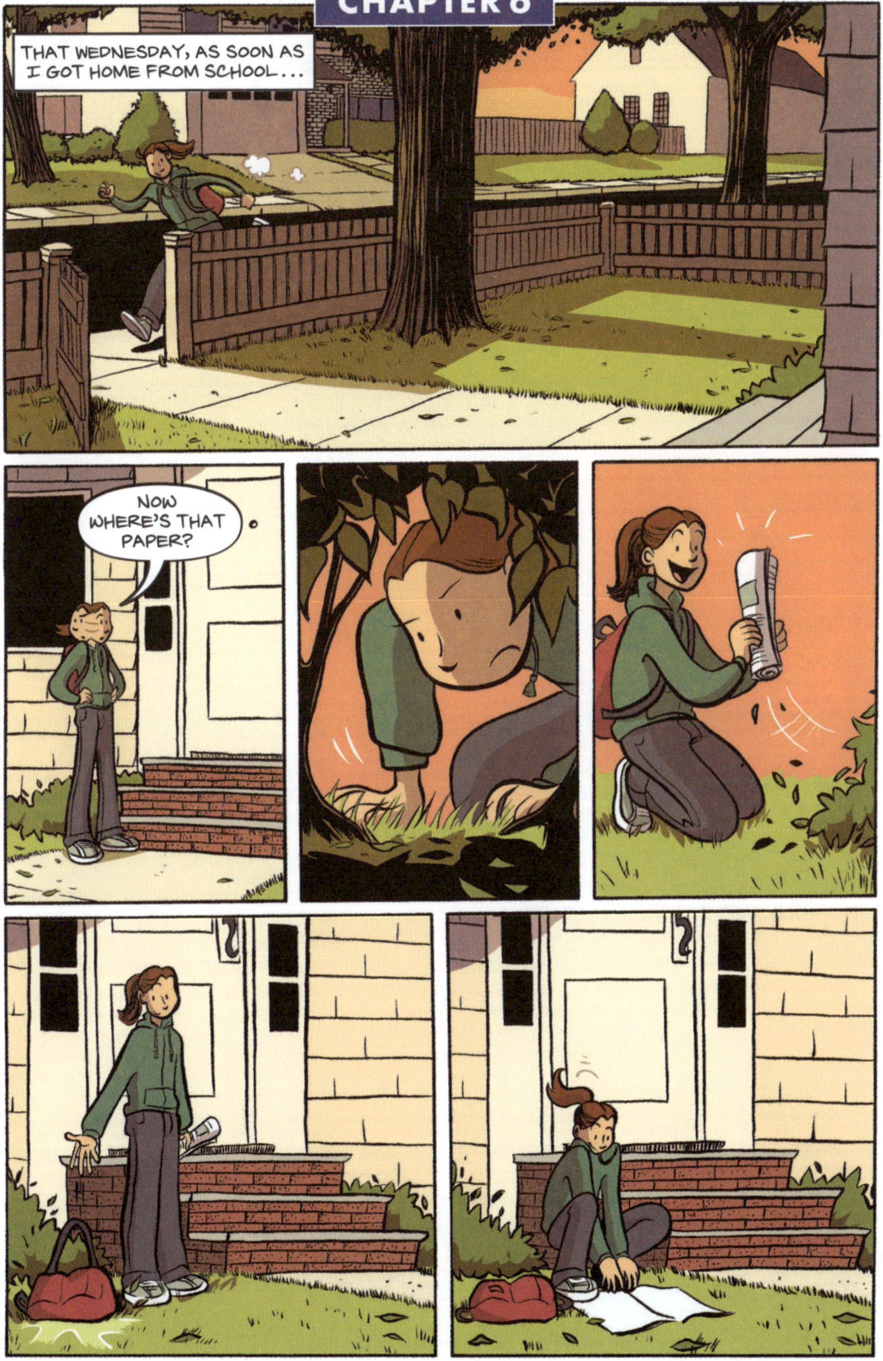
THAT WEDNESDAY, AS SOON AS I GOT HOME FROM SCHOOL . . .
NOW WHERE'S THAT PAPER?

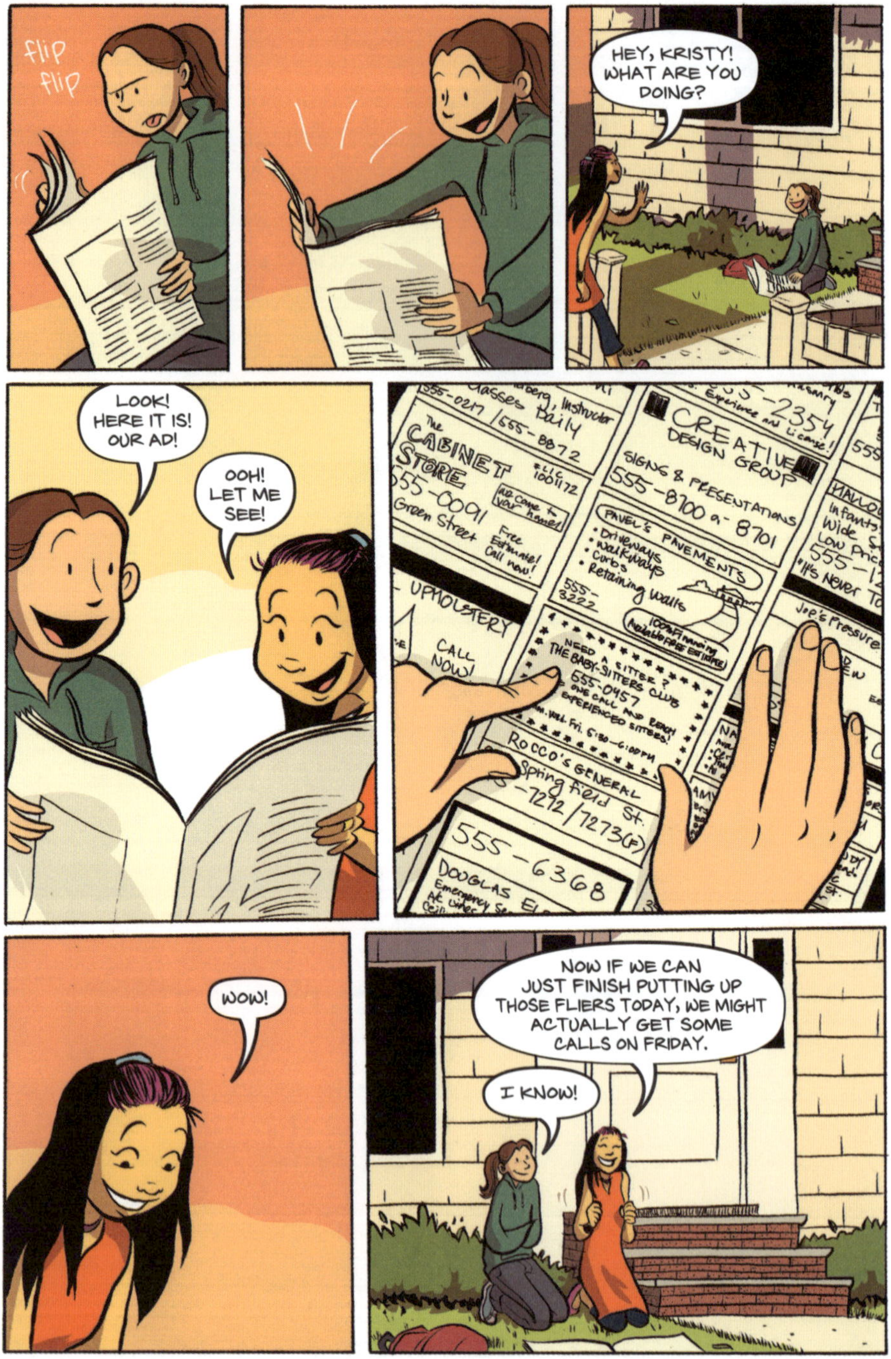
flip
flip
HEY, KRISTY! WHAT ARE YOU DOING?
LOOK! HERE IT IS! OUR AD!
OOH! LET ME SEE!
CREATIVE DESIGN GROUP
SIGNS & PRESENTATIONS
555-8700 or 8701
PAVEL'S PAVEMENTS
• Driveways • Walkways • Curbs • Retaining Walls
The CABINET STORE
555-0091
Green Street
Free Estimate! Call now!
UPHOLSTERY
CALL NOW!
NEED A SITTER? THE BABY-SITTERS CLUB
555-0457
ROCCO'S GENERAL
Spring field St.
555-6368
DOUGLAS
WOW!
NOW IF WE CAN JUST FINISH PUTTING UP THOSE FLIERS TODAY, WE MIGHT ACTUALLY GET SOME CALLS ON FRIDAY.
I KNOW!

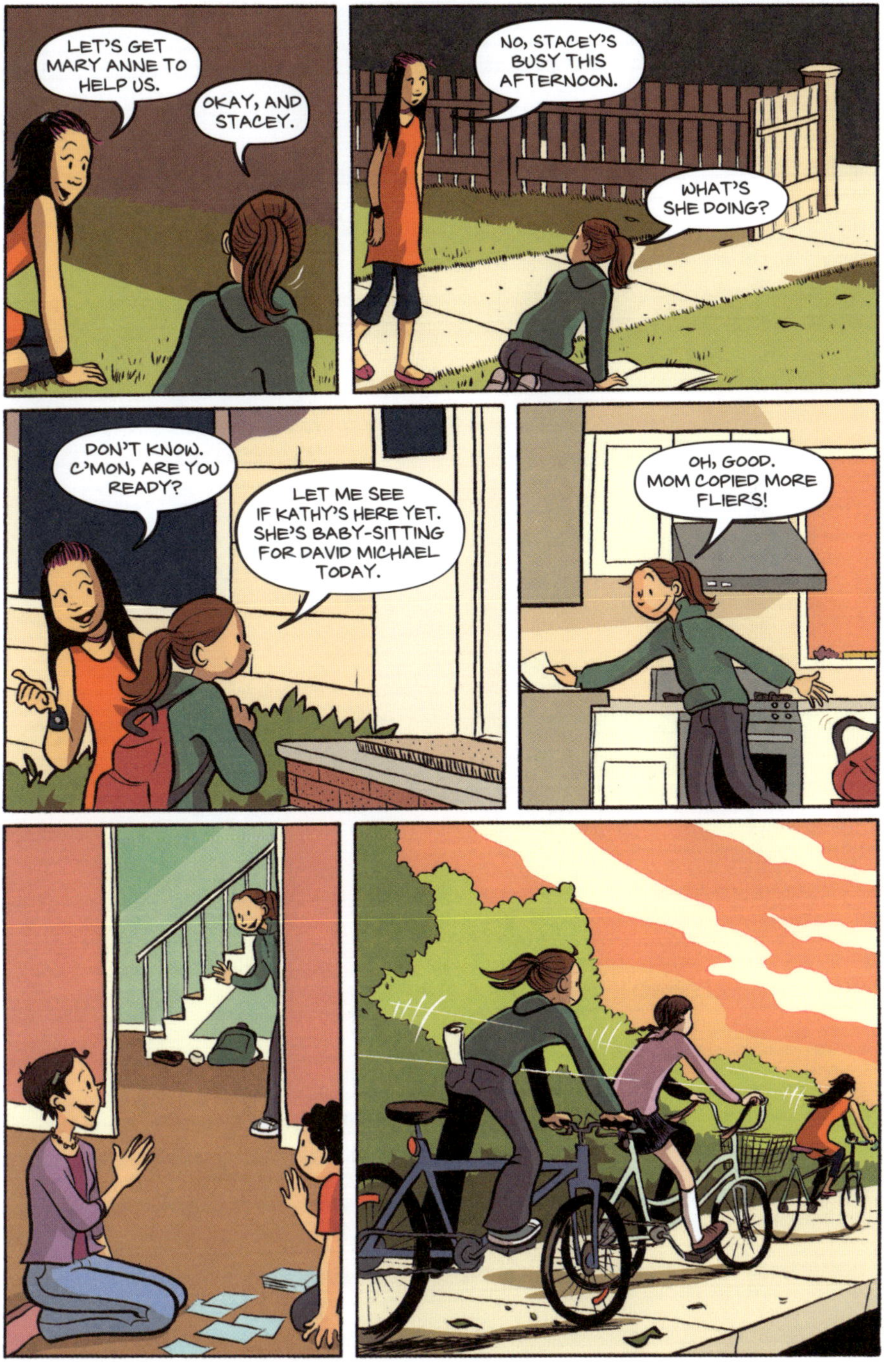
LET'S GET MARY ANNE TO HELP US.
OKAY, AND STACEY.
NO, STACEY'S BUSY THIS AFTERNOON.
WHAT'S SHE DOING?
DON'T KNOW. C'MON, ARE YOU READY?
LET ME SEE IF KATHY'S HERE YET. SHE'S BABY-SITTING FOR DAVID MICHAEL TODAY.
OH, GOOD. MOM COPIED MORE FLIERS!

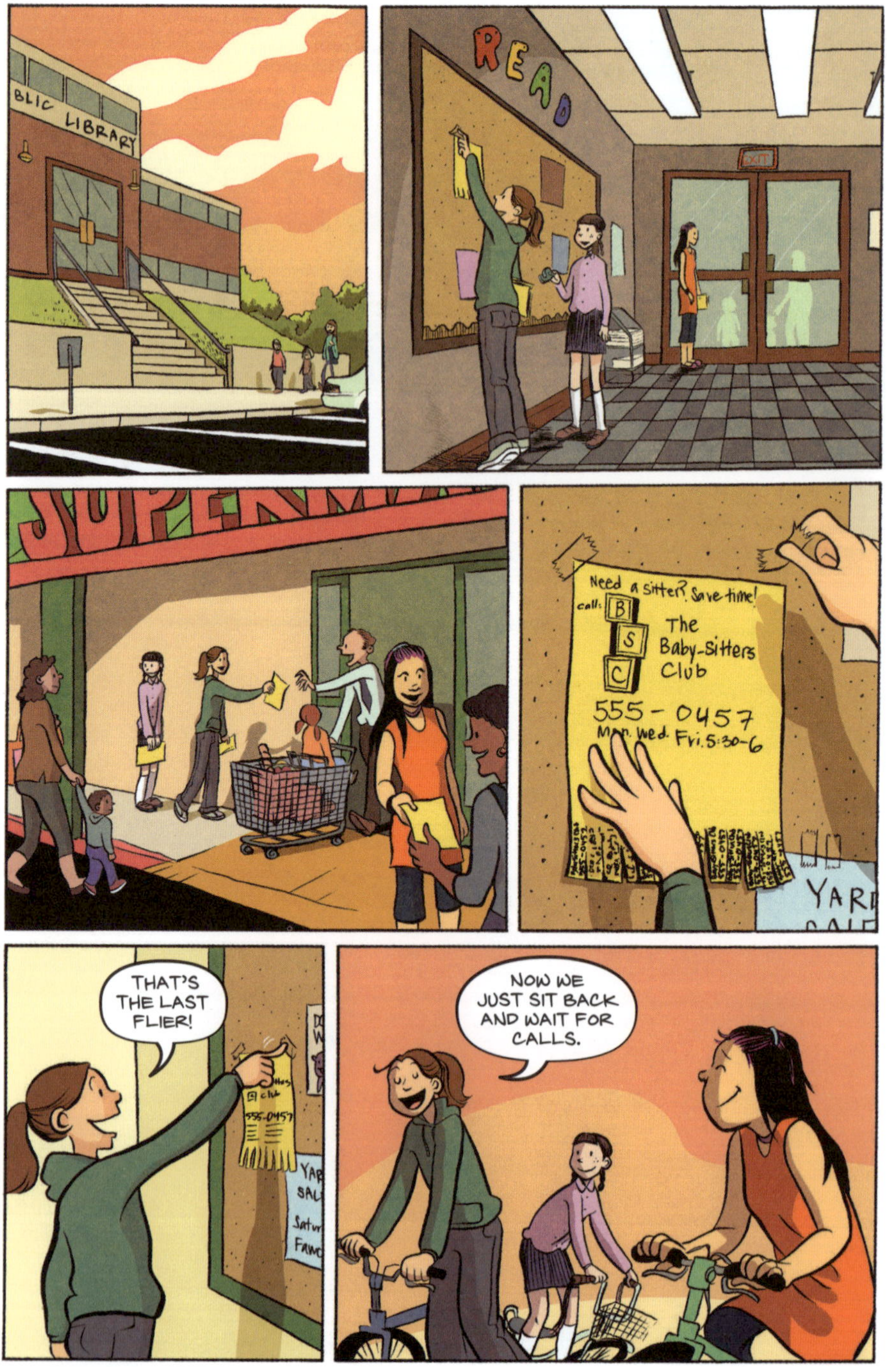
BLIC LIBRARY
READ
EXIT
Need a sitter? Save time!
call: B S C
The Baby-Sitters Club
555-0457
Mon. Wed. Fri. 5:30-6
THAT'S THE LAST FLIER!
NOW WE JUST SIT BACK AND WAIT FOR CALLS.

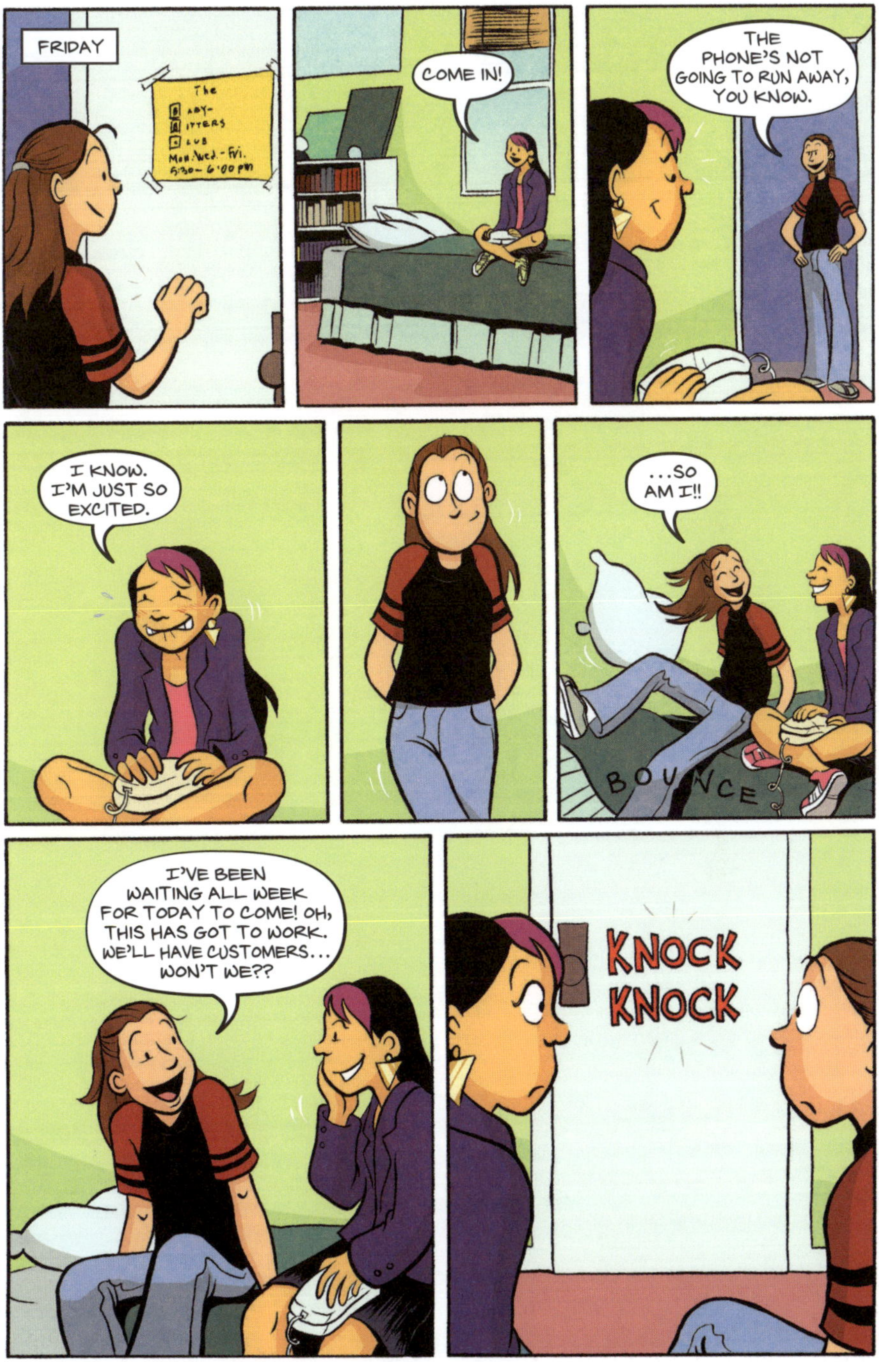
FRIDAY
The Baby-sitters Club Mon. Wed. - Fri. 5:30 - 6:00 pm
COME IN!
THE PHONE'S NOT GOING TO RUN AWAY, YOU KNOW.
I KNOW. I'M JUST SO EXCITED.
...SO AM I!!
BOUNCE
I'VE BEEN WAITING ALL WEEK FOR TODAY TO COME! OH, THIS HAS GOT TO WORK. WE'LL HAVE CUSTOMERS... WON'T WE??
KNOCK KNOCK

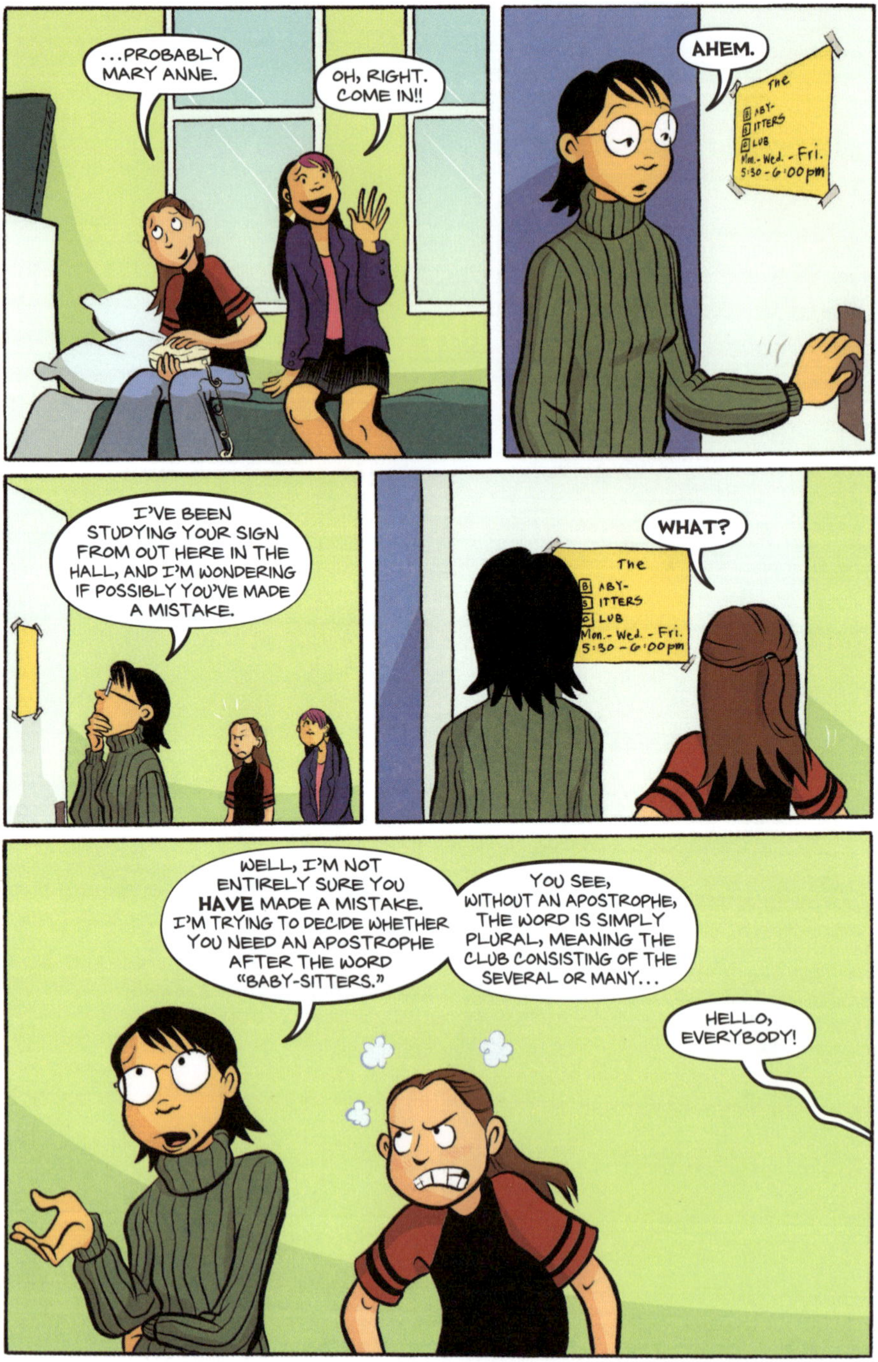
...PROBABLY MARY ANNE.
OH, RIGHT. COME IN!!
AHEM.
The
B ABY-
S ITTERS
C LUB
Mon.- Wed. - Fri.
5:30 - 6:00 pm
I'VE BEEN STUDYING YOUR SIGN FROM OUT HERE IN THE HALL, AND I'M WONDERING IF POSSIBLY YOU'VE MADE A MISTAKE.
WHAT?
WELL, I'M NOT ENTIRELY SURE YOU HAVE MADE A MISTAKE. I'M TRYING TO DECIDE WHETHER YOU NEED AN APOSTROPHE AFTER THE WORD "BABY-SITTERS."
YOU SEE, WITHOUT AN APOSTROPHE, THE WORD IS SIMPLY PLURAL, MEANING THE CLUB CONSISTING OF THE SEVERAL OR MANY...
HELLO, EVERYBODY!

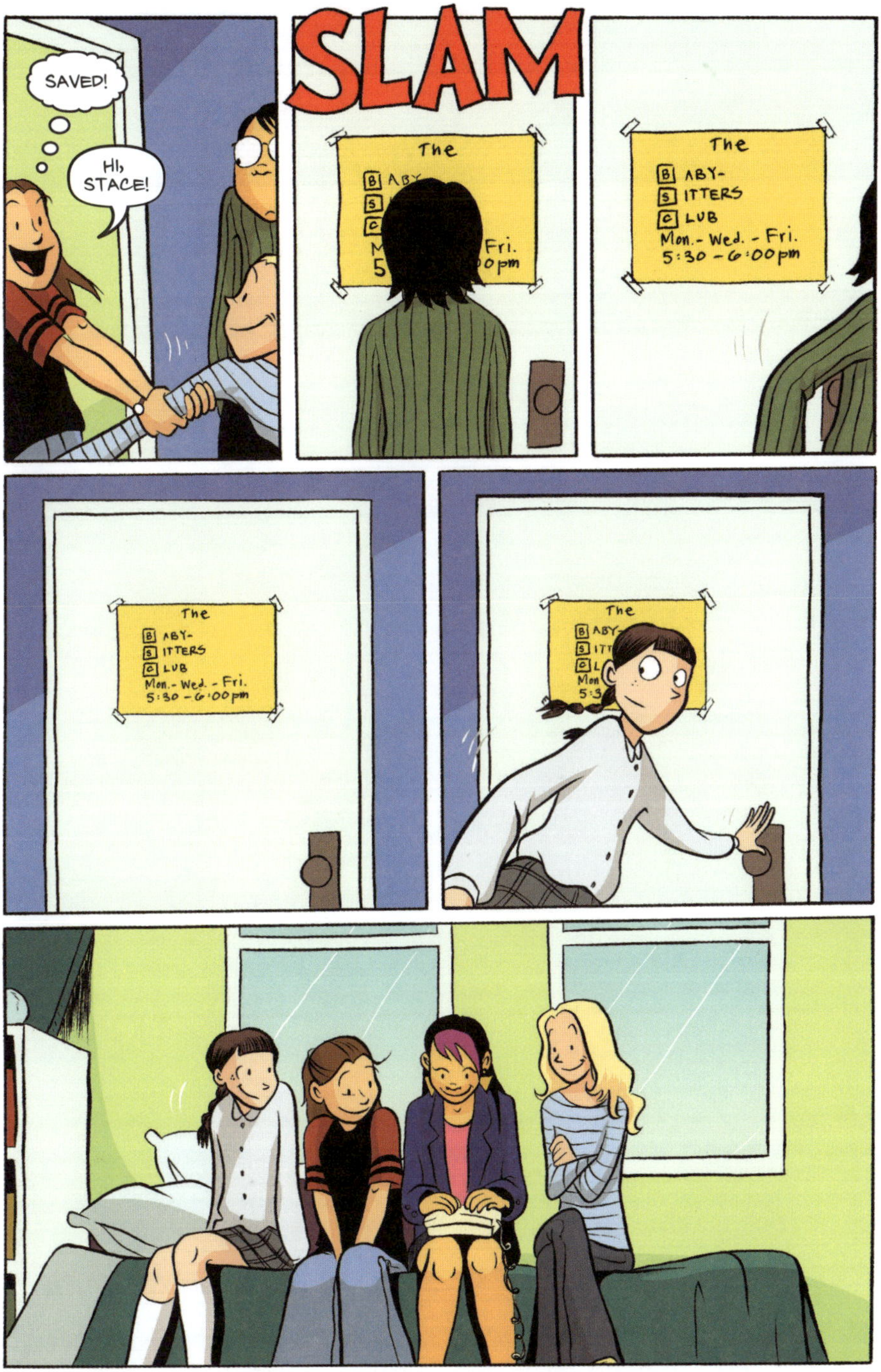
SAVED!
HI, STACE!
SLAM
The
B ABY-
S ITTERS
C LUB
Mon.- Wed. - Fri.
5:30 - 6:00pm

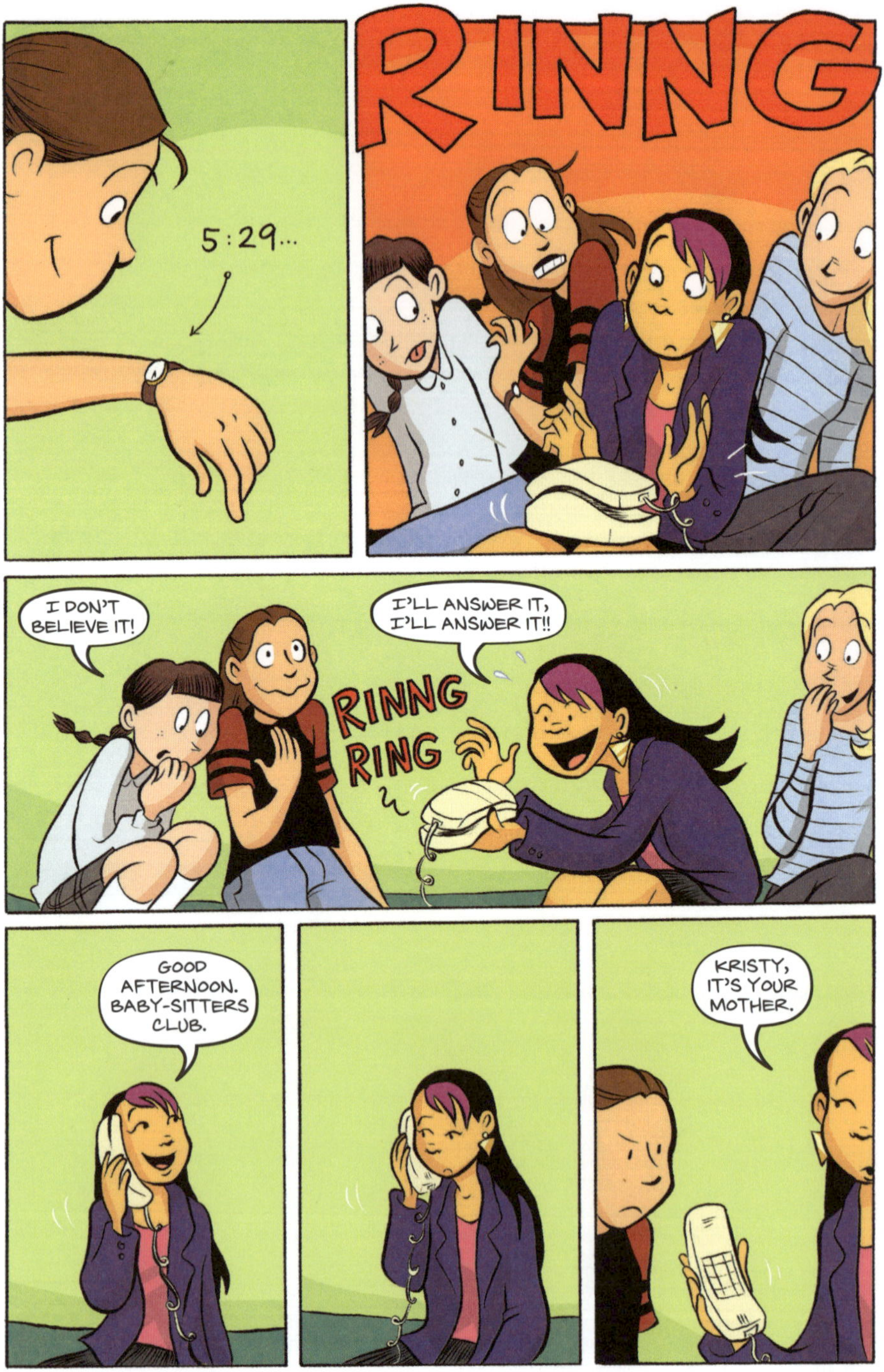
5:29...
RINNG
I DON'T BELIEVE IT!
I'LL ANSWER IT, I'LL ANSWER IT!!
RINNG RING
GOOD AFTERNOON. BABY-SITTERS CLUB.
KRISTY, IT'S YOUR MOTHER.

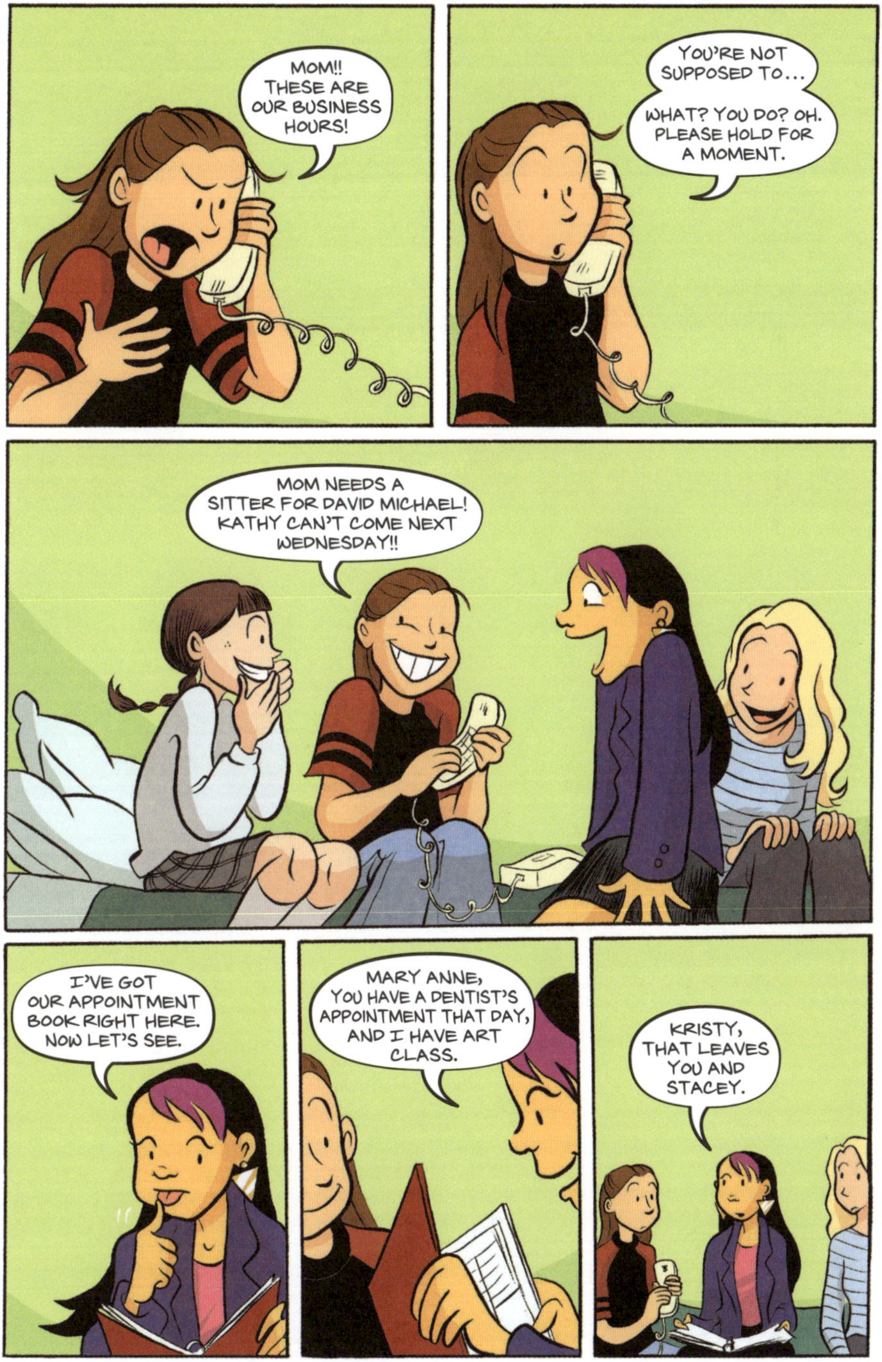
MOM!! THESE ARE OUR BUSINESS HOURS!
YOU'RE NOT SUPPOSED TO...
WHAT? YOU DO? OH. PLEASE HOLD FOR A MOMENT.
MOM NEEDS A SITTER FOR DAVID MICHAEL! KATHY CAN'T COME NEXT WEDNESDAY!!
I'VE GOT OUR APPOINTMENT BOOK RIGHT HERE. NOW LET'S SEE.
MARY ANNE, YOU HAVE A DENTIST'S APPOINTMENT THAT DAY, AND I HAVE ART CLASS.
KRISTY, THAT LEAVES YOU AND STACEY.

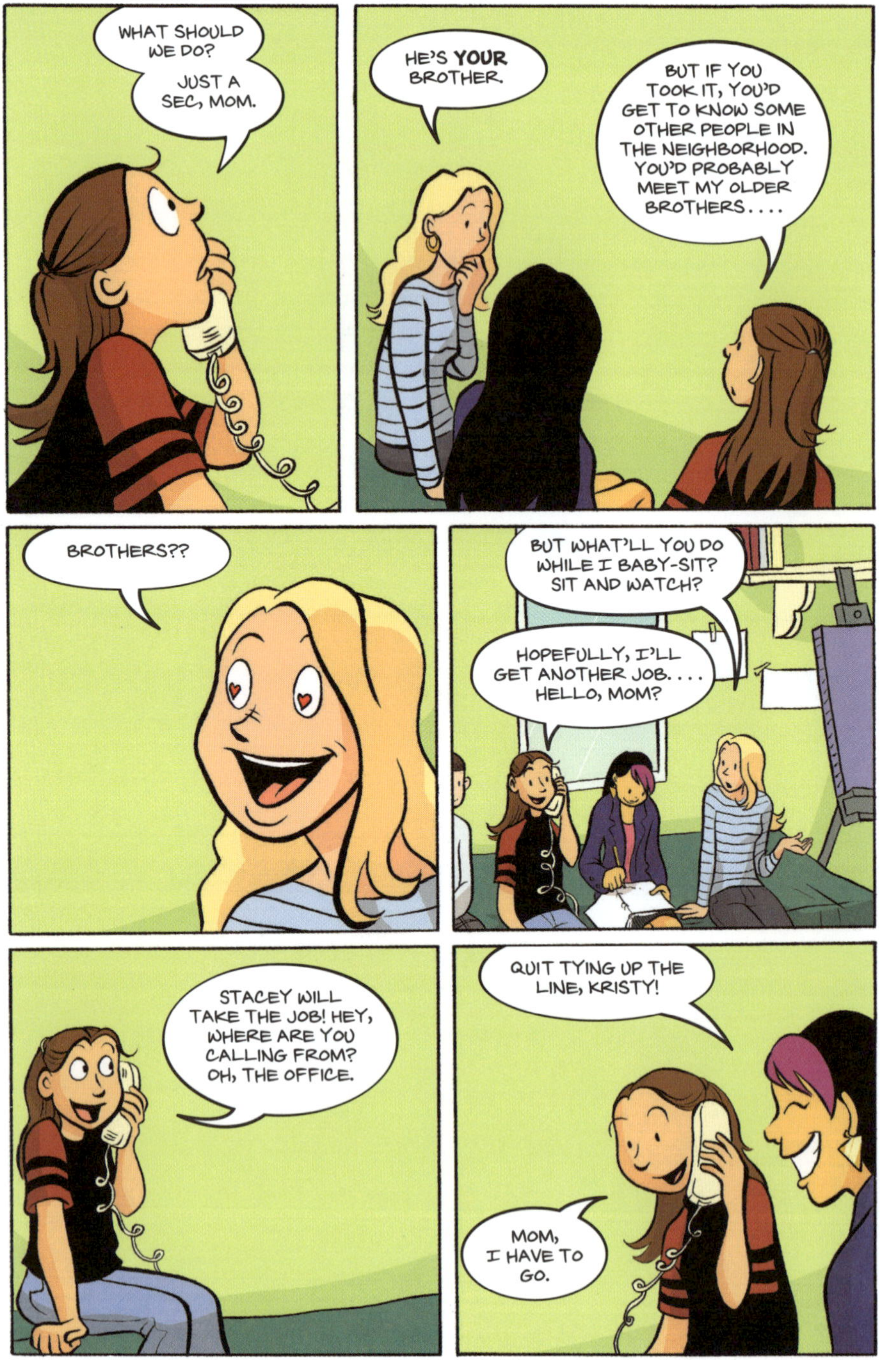
WHAT SHOULD WE DO?
JUST A SEC, MOM.
HE'S **YOUR** BROTHER.
BUT IF YOU TOOK IT, YOU'D GET TO KNOW SOME OTHER PEOPLE IN THE NEIGHBORHOOD. YOU'D PROBABLY MEET MY OLDER BROTHERS....
BROTHERS??
BUT WHAT'LL YOU DO WHILE I BABY-SIT? SIT AND WATCH?
HOPEFULLY, I'LL GET ANOTHER JOB.... HELLO, MOM?
STACEY WILL TAKE THE JOB! HEY, WHERE ARE YOU CALLING FROM? OH, THE OFFICE.
QUIT TYING UP THE LINE, KRISTY!
MOM, I HAVE TO GO.

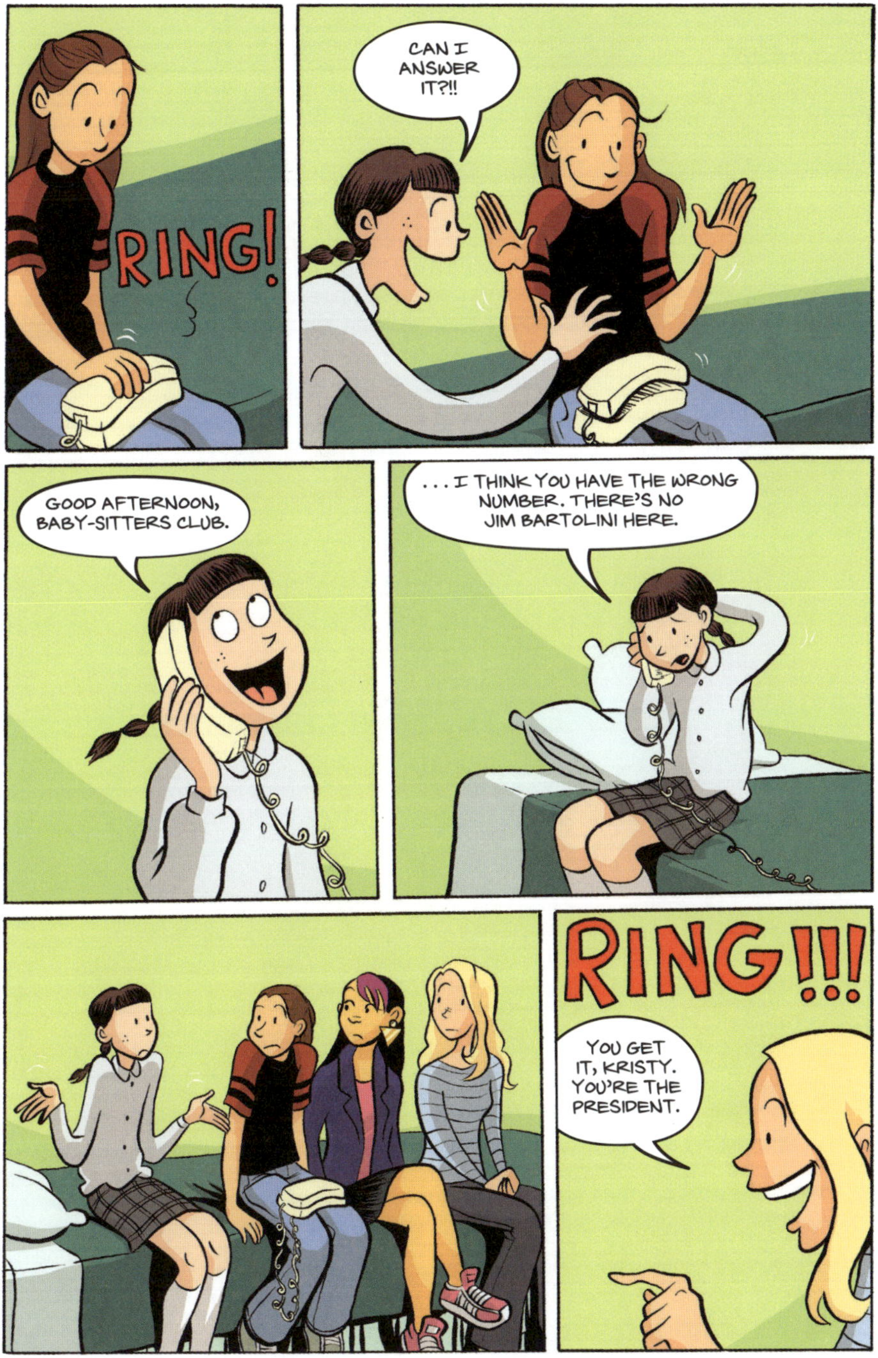
RING!
CAN I ANSWER IT?!!
GOOD AFTERNOON, BABY-SITTERS CLUB.
. . . I THINK YOU HAVE THE WRONG NUMBER. THERE'S NO JIM BARTOLINI HERE.
RING!!!
YOU GET IT, KRISTY. YOU'RE THE PRESIDENT.

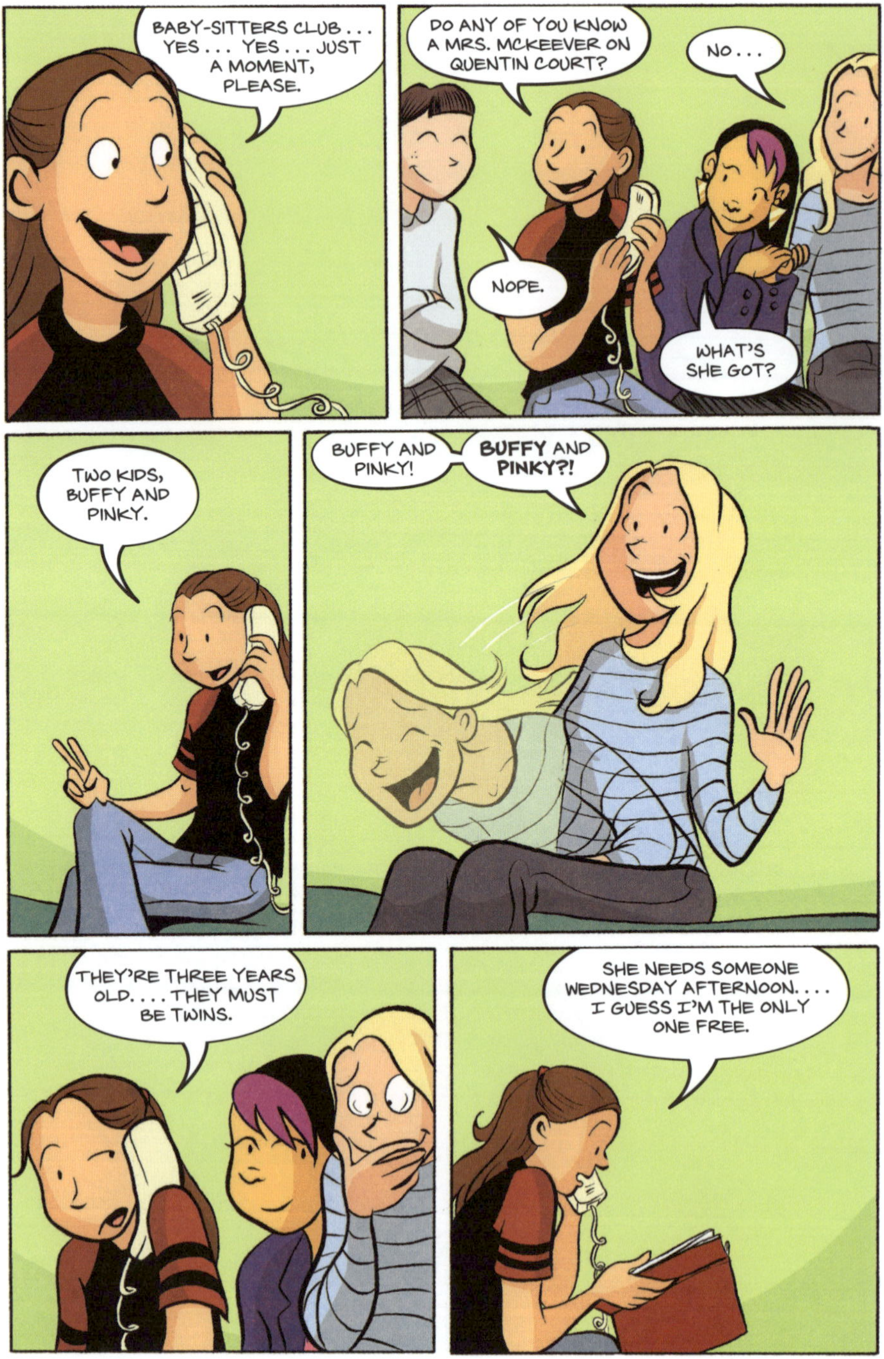
BABY-SITTERS CLUB . . . YES . . . YES . . . JUST A MOMENT, PLEASE.
DO ANY OF YOU KNOW A MRS. MCKEEVER ON QUENTIN COURT?
NO . . .
NOPE.
WHAT'S SHE GOT?
TWO KIDS, BUFFY AND PINKY.
BUFFY AND PINKY!
BUFFY AND **PINKY?!**
THEY'RE THREE YEARS OLD. . . . THEY MUST BE TWINS.
SHE NEEDS SOMEONE WEDNESDAY AFTERNOON. . . . I GUESS I'M THE ONLY ONE FREE.

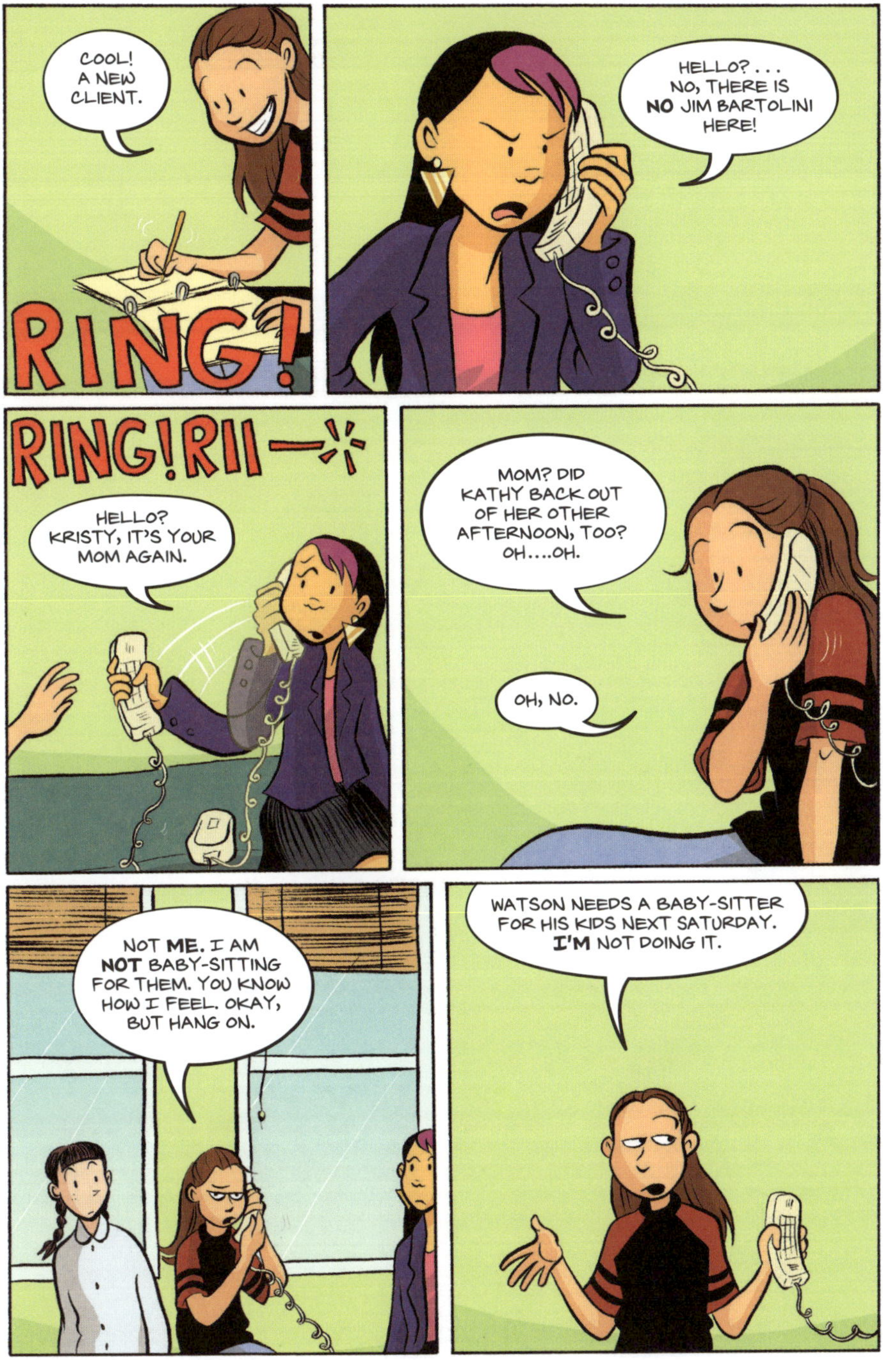
COOL! A NEW CLIENT.
RING!
HELLO? . . . NO, THERE IS **NO** JIM BARTOLINI HERE!
RING!RII—
HELLO? KRISTY, IT'S YOUR MOM AGAIN.
MOM? DID KATHY BACK OUT OF HER OTHER AFTERNOON, TOO? OH....OH.
OH, NO.
NOT **ME.** I AM **NOT** BABY-SITTING FOR THEM. YOU KNOW HOW I FEEL. OKAY, BUT HANG ON.
WATSON NEEDS A BABY-SITTER FOR HIS KIDS NEXT SATURDAY. **I'M** NOT DOING IT.

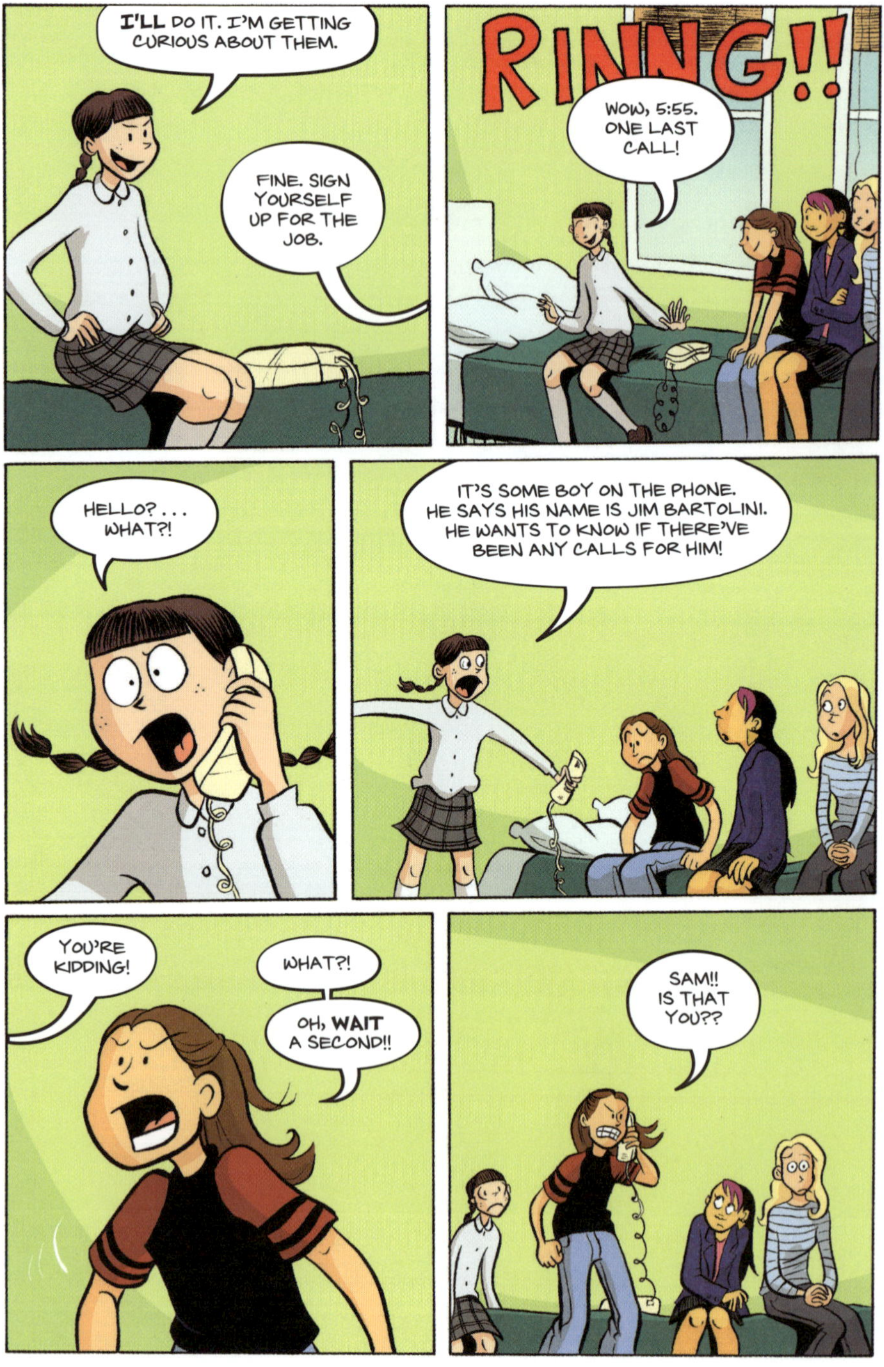
I'LL DO IT. I'M GETTING CURIOUS ABOUT THEM.
FINE. SIGN YOURSELF UP FOR THE JOB.
RINNG!!
WOW, 5:55. ONE LAST CALL!
HELLO? . . . WHAT?!
IT'S SOME BOY ON THE PHONE. HE SAYS HIS NAME IS JIM BARTOLINI. HE WANTS TO KNOW IF THERE'VE BEEN ANY CALLS FOR HIM!
YOU'RE KIDDING!
WHAT?!
OH, WAIT A SECOND!!
SAM!! IS THAT YOU??

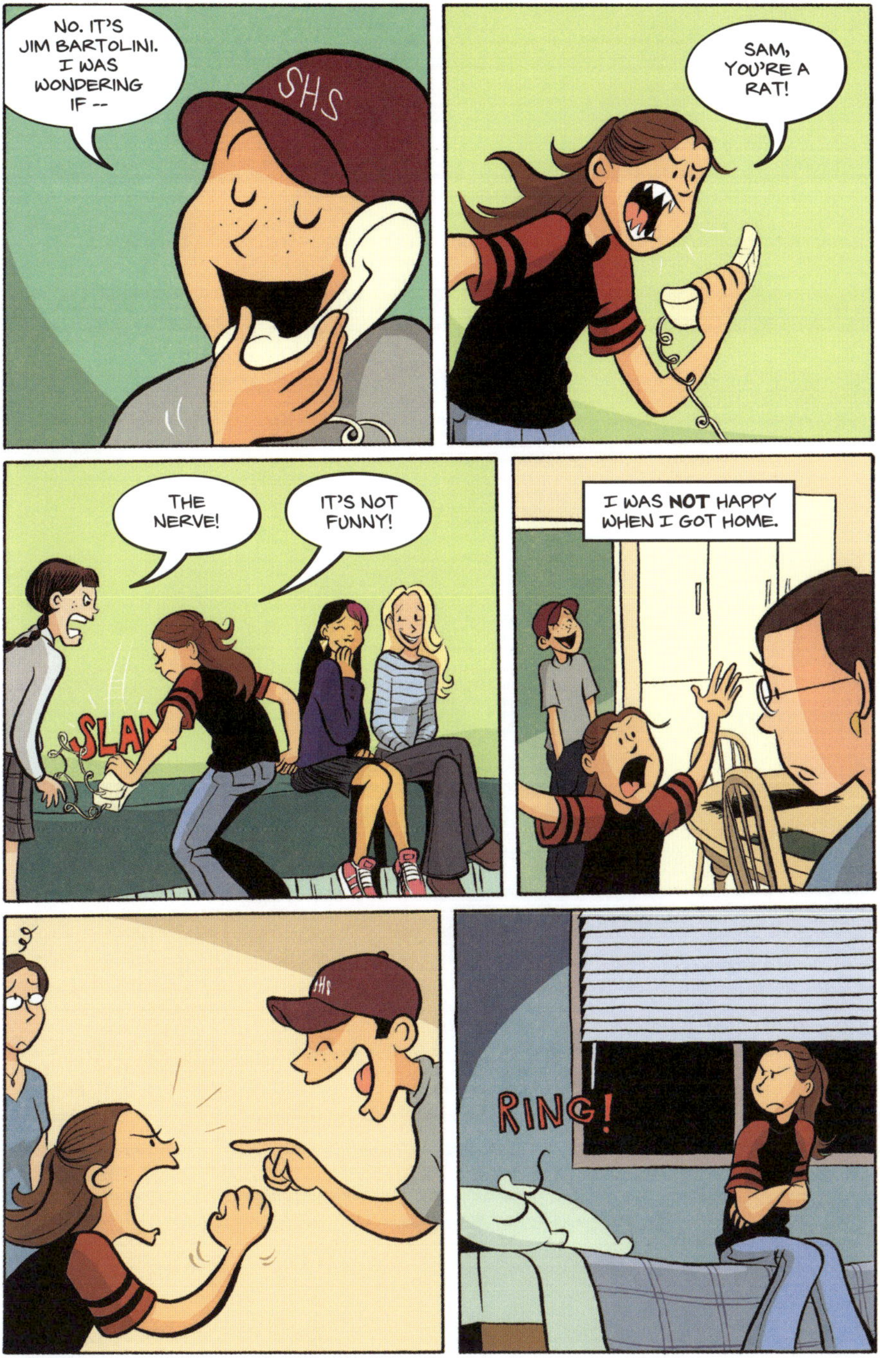
NO. IT'S JIM BARTOLINI. I WAS WONDERING IF --
SHS
SAM, YOU'RE A RAT!
THE NERVE!
IT'S NOT FUNNY!
SLAM
I WAS **NOT** HAPPY WHEN I GOT HOME.
SHS
RING!

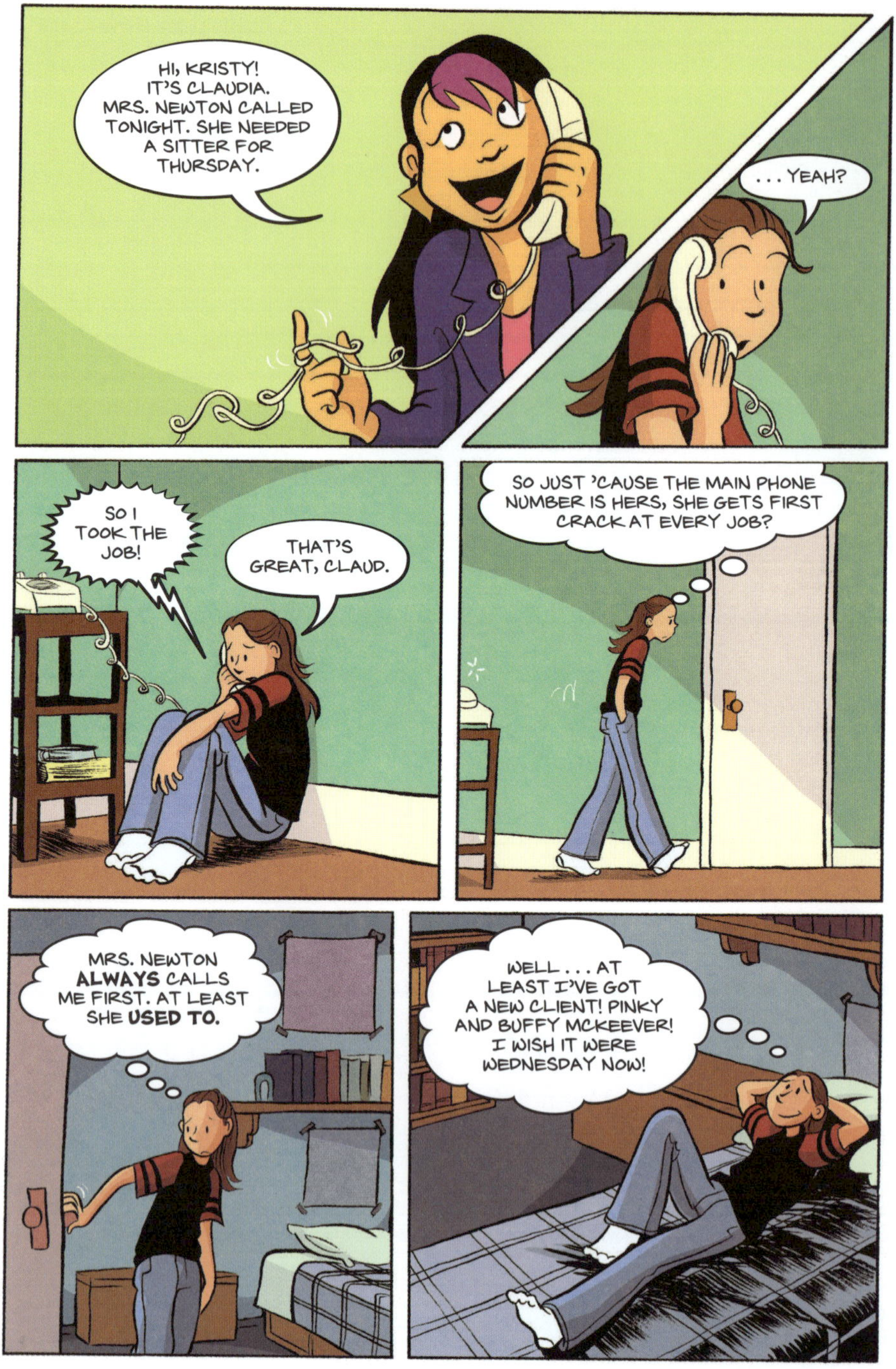
HI, KRISTY! IT'S CLAUDIA. MRS. NEWTON CALLED TONIGHT. SHE NEEDED A SITTER FOR THURSDAY.
. . . YEAH?
SO I TOOK THE JOB!
THAT'S GREAT, CLAUD.
SO JUST 'CAUSE THE MAIN PHONE NUMBER IS HERS, SHE GETS FIRST CRACK AT EVERY JOB?
MRS. NEWTON **ALWAYS** CALLS ME FIRST. AT LEAST SHE **USED TO.**
WELL . . . AT LEAST I'VE GOT A NEW CLIENT! PINKY AND BUFFY MCKEEVER! I WISH IT WERE WEDNESDAY NOW!

CHAPTER 7

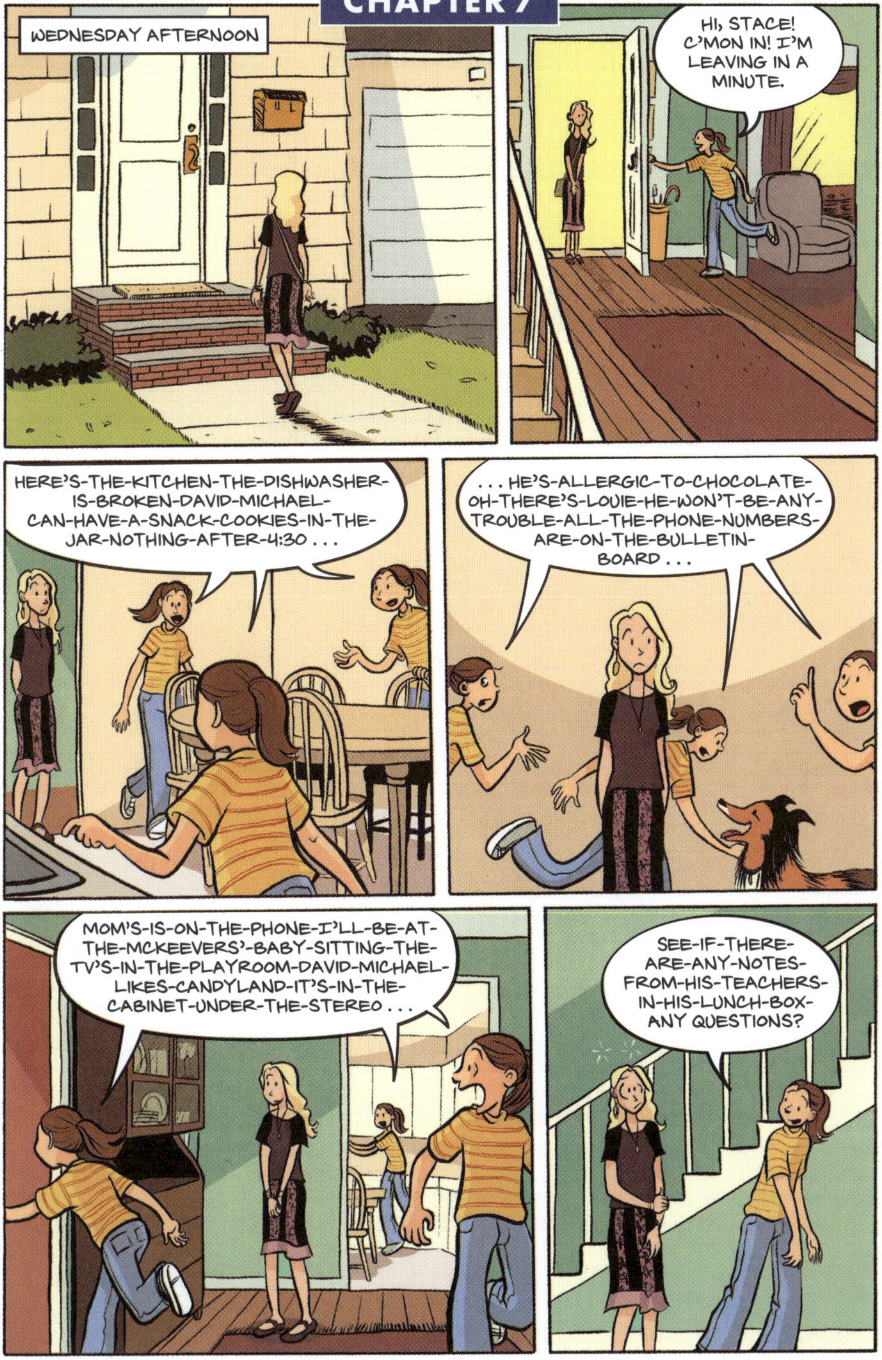
WEDNESDAY AFTERNOON
HI, STACE! C'MON IN! I'M LEAVING IN A MINUTE.
HERE'S-THE-KITCHEN-THE-DISHWASHER-IS-BROKEN-DAVID-MICHAEL-CAN-HAVE-A-SNACK-COOKIES-IN-THE-JAR-NOTHING-AFTER-4:30 . . .
. . . HE'S-ALLERGIC-TO-CHOCOLATE-OH-THERE'S-LOUIE-HE-WON'T-BE-ANY-TROUBLE-ALL-THE-PHONE-NUMBERS-ARE-ON-THE-BULLETIN-BOARD . . .
MOM'S-IS-ON-THE-PHONE-I'LL-BE-AT-THE-MCKEEVERS'-BABY-SITTING-THE-TV'S-IN-THE-PLAYROOM-DAVID-MICHAEL-LIKES-CANDYLAND-IT'S-IN-THE-CABINET-UNDER-THE-STEREO . . .
SEE-IF-THERE-ARE-ANY-NOTES-FROM-HIS-TEACHERS-IN-HIS-LUNCH-BOX-ANY QUESTIONS?

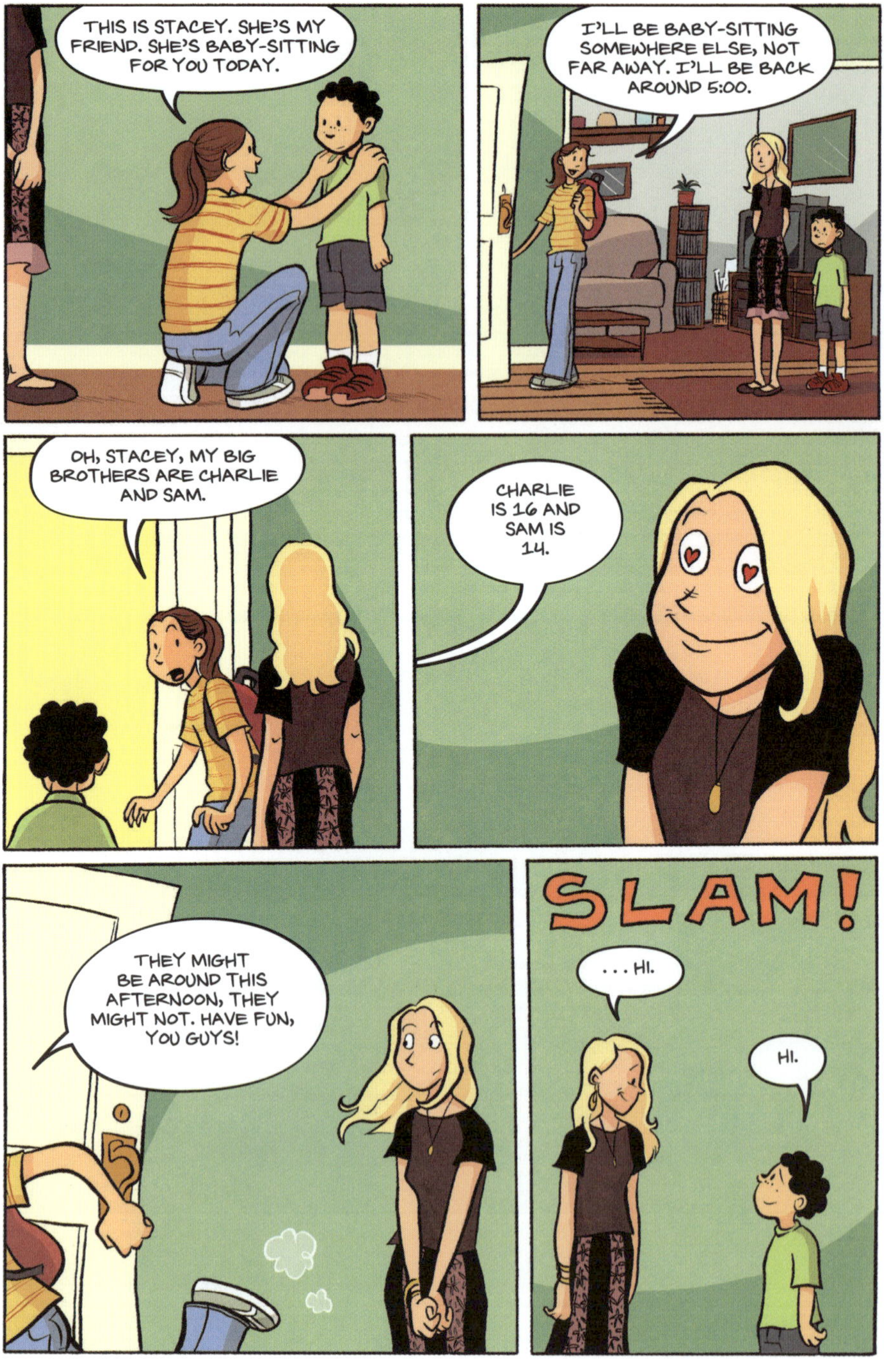
THIS IS STACEY. SHE'S MY FRIEND. SHE'S BABY-SITTING FOR YOU TODAY.
I'LL BE BABY-SITTING SOMEWHERE ELSE, NOT FAR AWAY. I'LL BE BACK AROUND 5:00.
OH, STACEY, MY BIG BROTHERS ARE CHARLIE AND SAM.
CHARLIE IS 16 AND SAM IS 14.
THEY MIGHT BE AROUND THIS AFTERNOON, THEY MIGHT NOT. HAVE FUN, YOU GUYS!
SLAM!
. . . HI.
HI.

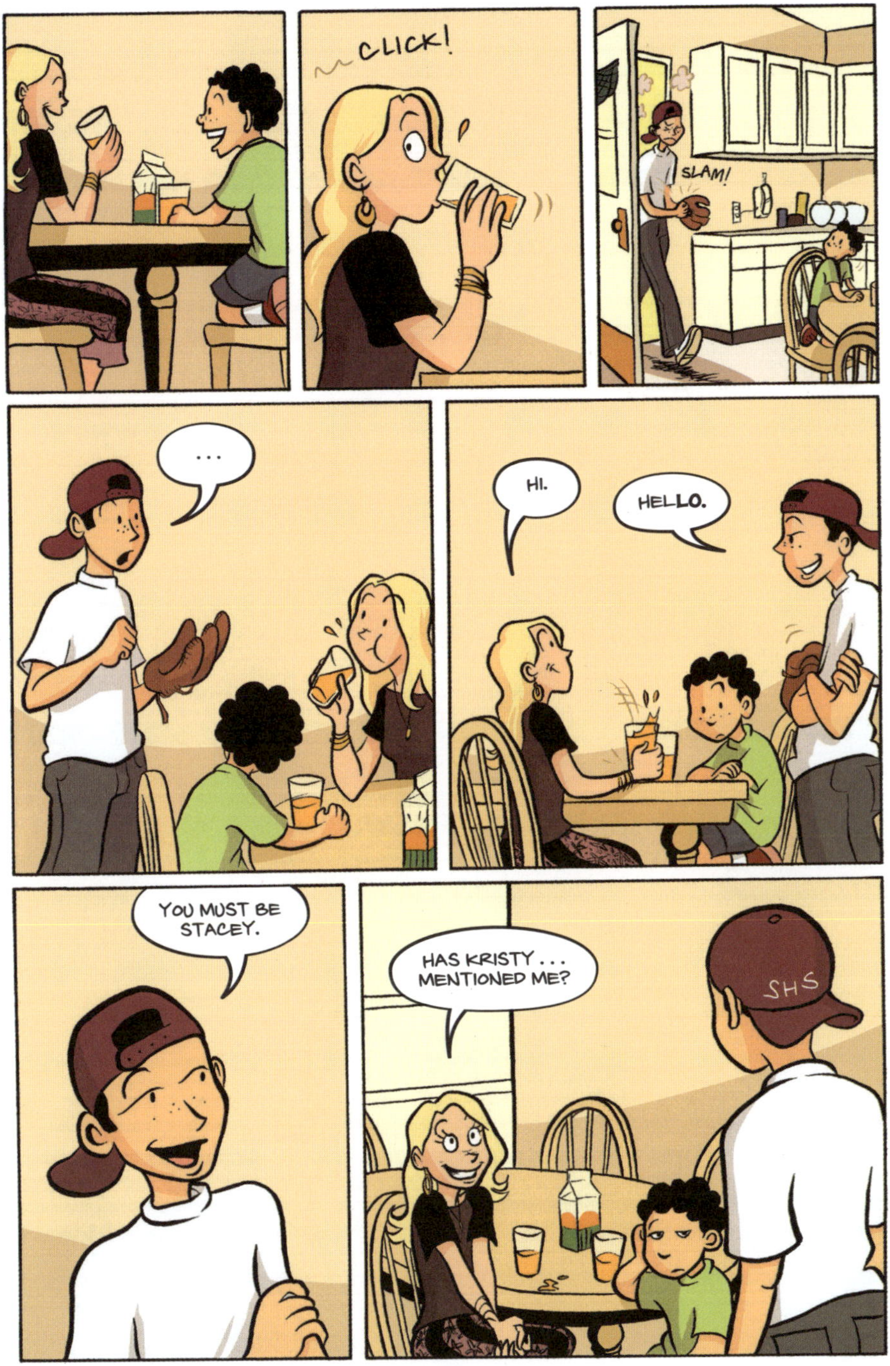
CLICK!
SLAM!
...
HI.
HELLO.
YOU MUST BE STACEY.
HAS KRISTY . . . MENTIONED ME?
SHS

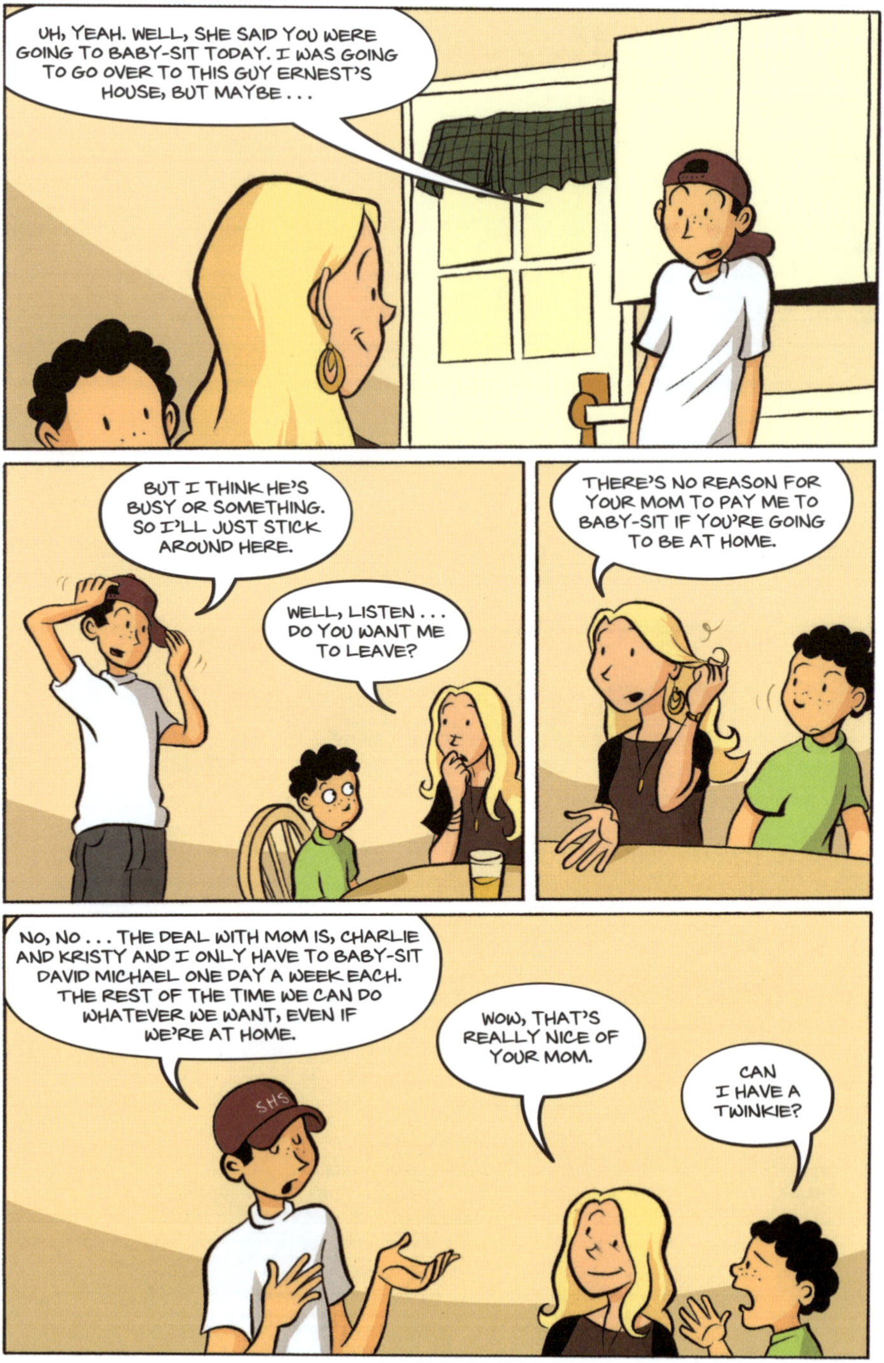
UH, YEAH. WELL, SHE SAID YOU WERE GOING TO BABY-SIT TODAY. I WAS GOING TO GO OVER TO THIS GUY ERNEST'S HOUSE, BUT MAYBE . . .
BUT I THINK HE'S BUSY OR SOMETHING. SO I'LL JUST STICK AROUND HERE.
WELL, LISTEN . . . DO YOU WANT ME TO LEAVE?
THERE'S NO REASON FOR YOUR MOM TO PAY ME TO BABY-SIT IF YOU'RE GOING TO BE AT HOME.
NO, NO . . . THE DEAL WITH MOM IS, CHARLIE AND KRISTY AND I ONLY HAVE TO BABY-SIT DAVID MICHAEL ONE DAY A WEEK EACH. THE REST OF THE TIME WE CAN DO WHATEVER WE WANT, EVEN IF WE'RE AT HOME.
SHS
WOW, THAT'S REALLY NICE OF YOUR MOM.
CAN I HAVE A TWINKIE?

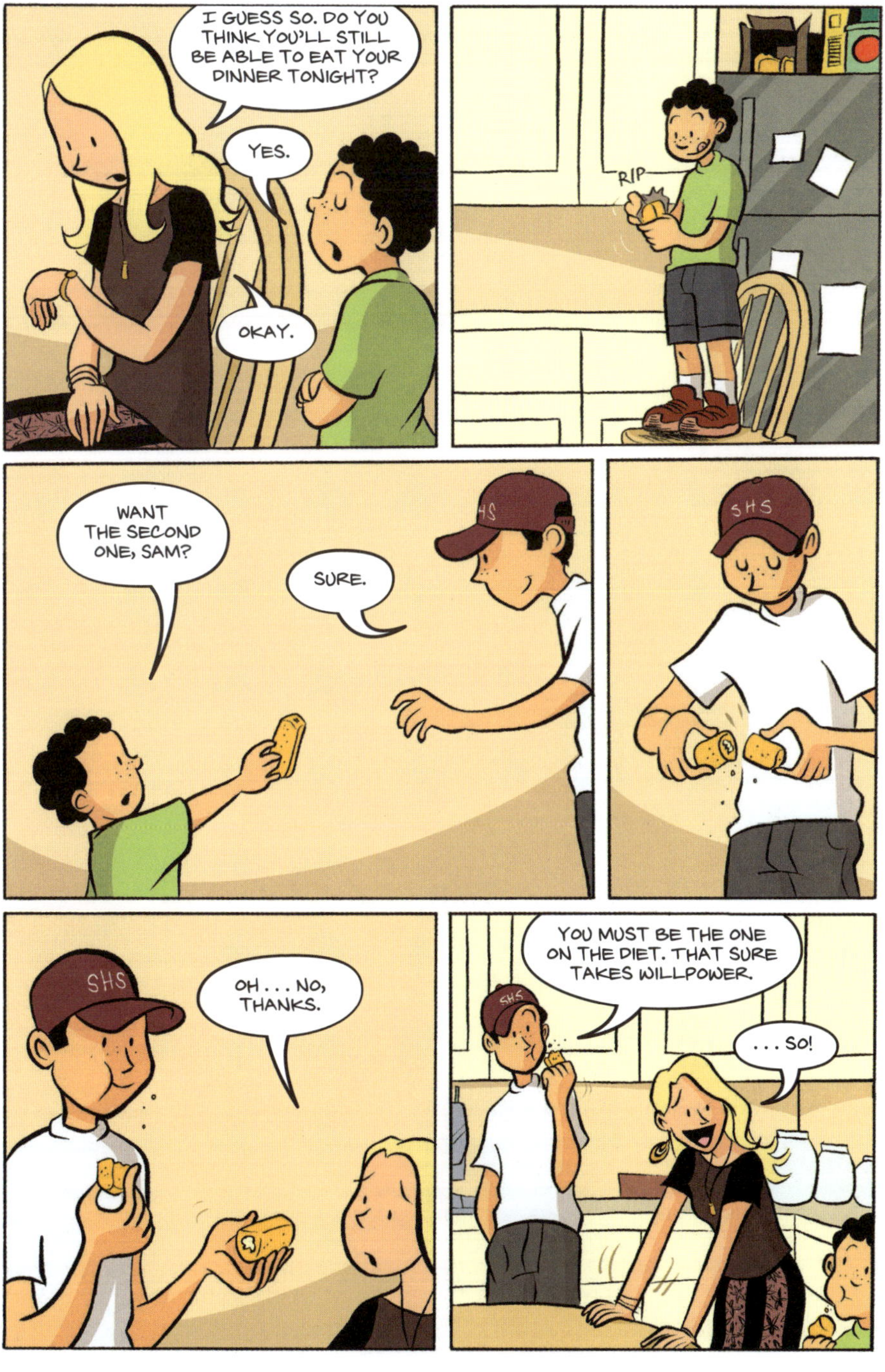
I GUESS SO. DO YOU THINK YOU'LL STILL BE ABLE TO EAT YOUR DINNER TONIGHT?
YES.
OKAY.
RIP
WANT THE SECOND ONE, SAM?
SURE.
SHS
SHS
SHS
OH . . . NO, THANKS.
YOU MUST BE THE ONE ON THE DIET. THAT SURE TAKES WILLPOWER.
SHS
. . . SO!

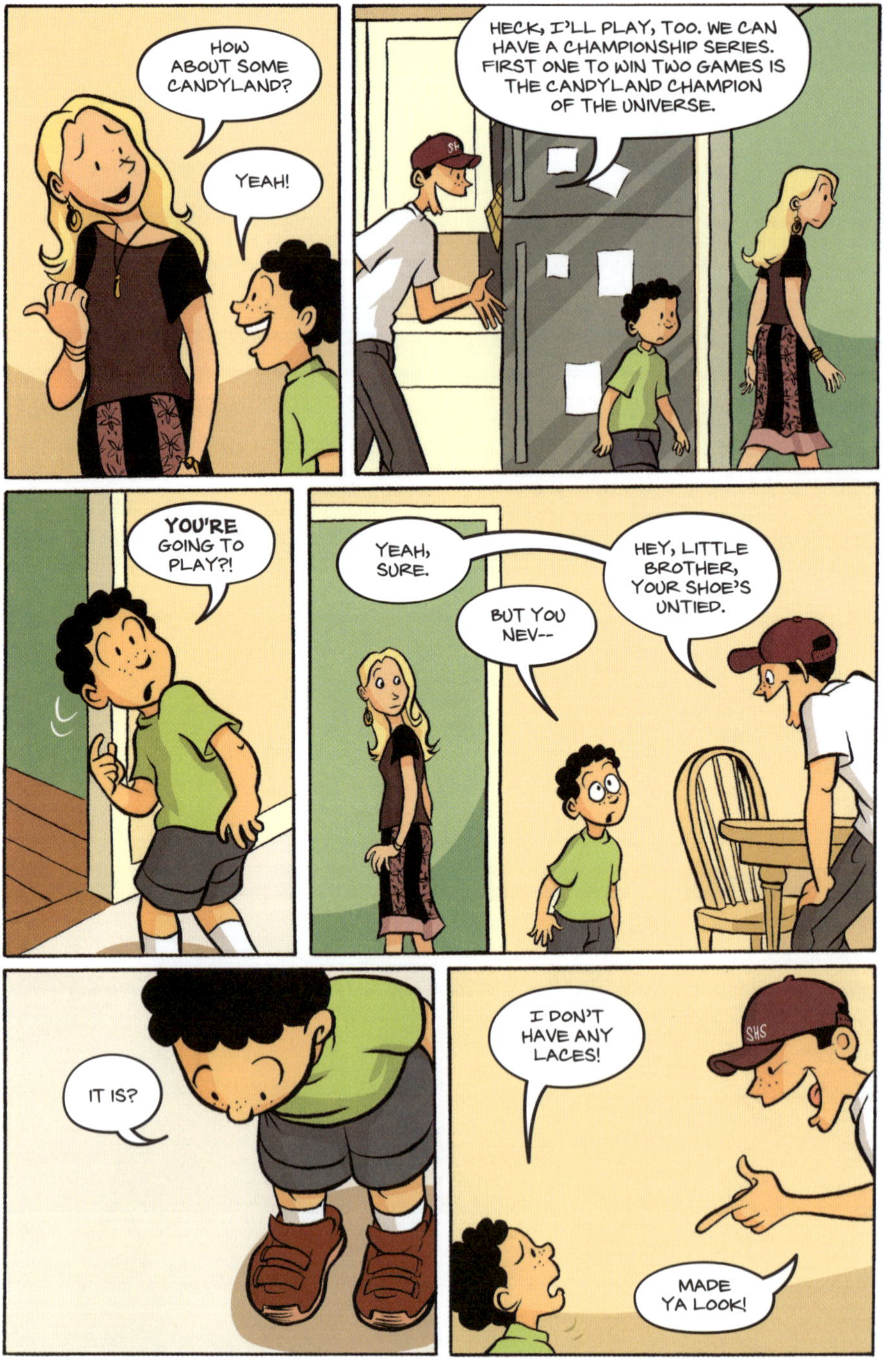
HOW ABOUT SOME CANDYLAND?
YEAH!
HECK, I'LL PLAY, TOO. WE CAN HAVE A CHAMPIONSHIP SERIES. FIRST ONE TO WIN TWO GAMES IS THE CANDYLAND CHAMPION OF THE UNIVERSE.
SHS
YOU'RE GOING TO PLAY?!
YEAH, SURE.
BUT YOU NEV--
HEY, LITTLE BROTHER, YOUR SHOE'S UNTIED.
IT IS?
I DON'T HAVE ANY LACES!
SHS
MADE YA LOOK!

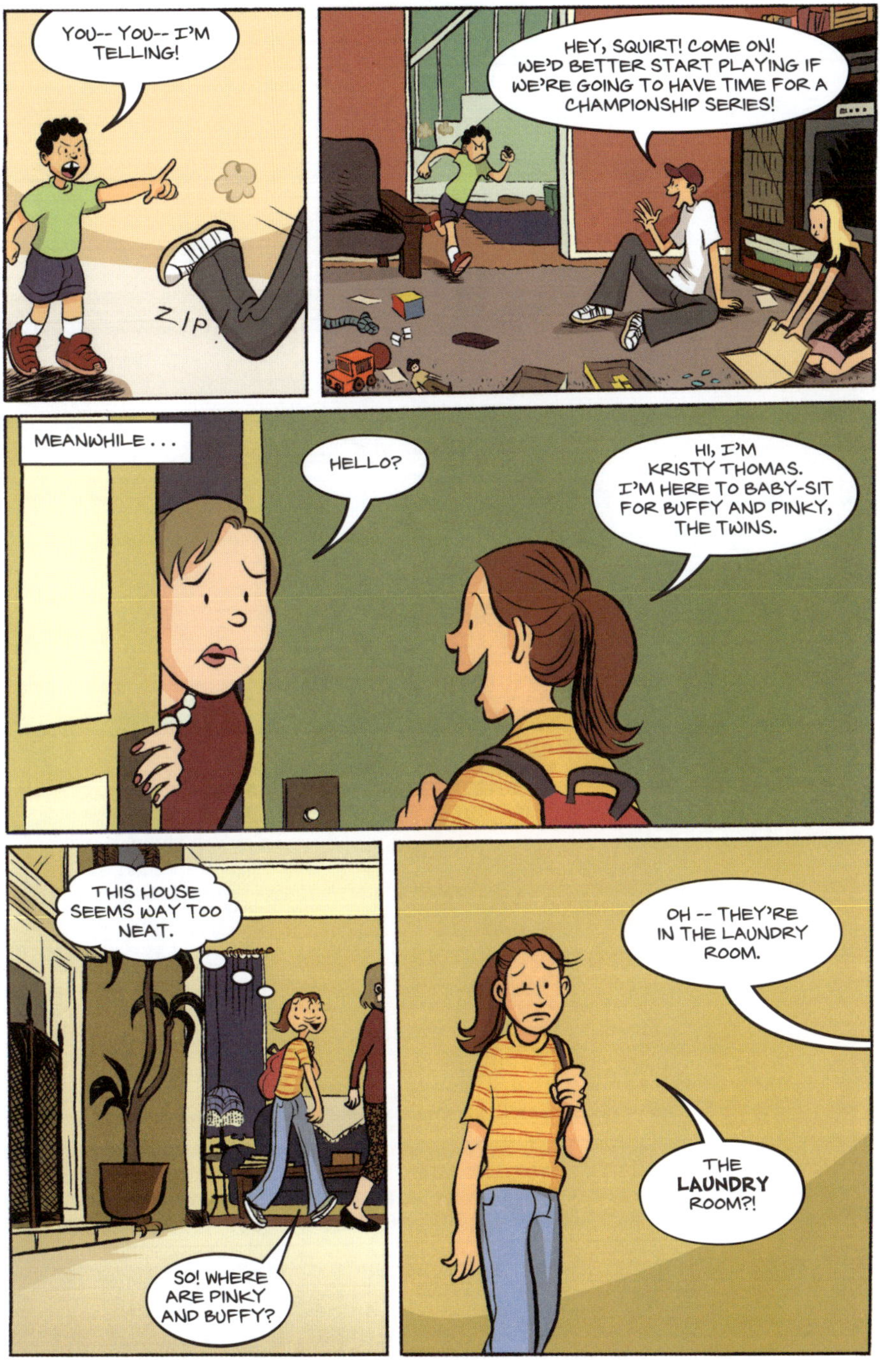
YOU-- YOU-- I'M TELLING!
ZIP!
HEY, SQUIRT! COME ON! WE'D BETTER START PLAYING IF WE'RE GOING TO HAVE TIME FOR A CHAMPIONSHIP SERIES!
MEANWHILE . . .
HELLO?
HI, I'M KRISTY THOMAS. I'M HERE TO BABY-SIT FOR BUFFY AND PINKY, THE TWINS.
THIS HOUSE SEEMS WAY TOO NEAT.
SO! WHERE ARE PINKY AND BUFFY?
OH -- THEY'RE IN THE LAUNDRY ROOM.
THE **LAUNDRY** ROOM?!

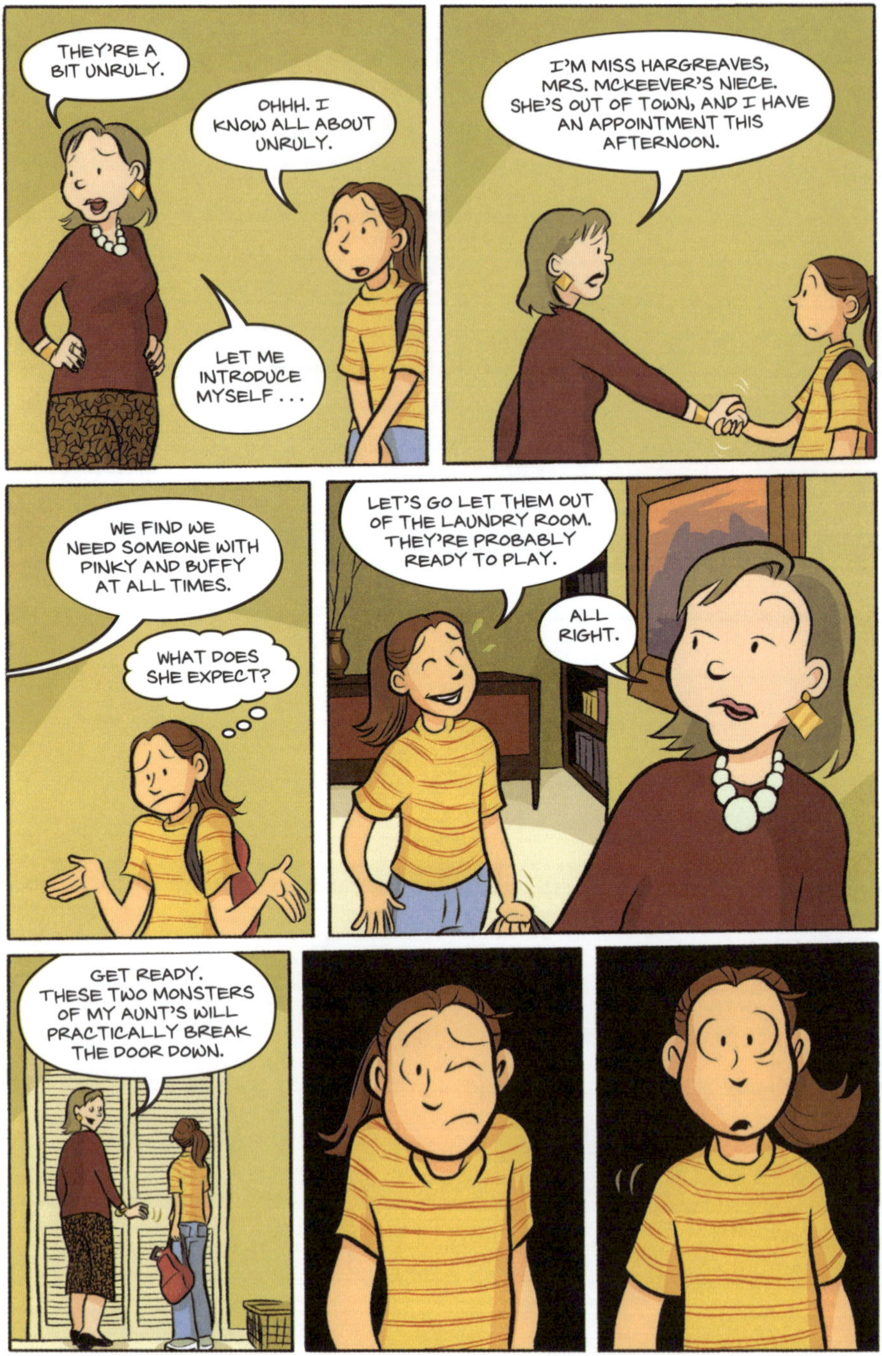
THEY'RE A BIT UNRULY.
OHHH. I KNOW ALL ABOUT UNRULY.
LET ME INTRODUCE MYSELF . . .
I'M MISS HARGREAVES, MRS. MCKEEVER'S NIECE. SHE'S OUT OF TOWN, AND I HAVE AN APPOINTMENT THIS AFTERNOON.
WE FIND WE NEED SOMEONE WITH PINKY AND BUFFY AT ALL TIMES.
WHAT DOES SHE EXPECT?
LET'S GO LET THEM OUT OF THE LAUNDRY ROOM. THEY'RE PROBABLY READY TO PLAY.
ALL RIGHT.
GET READY. THESE TWO MONSTERS OF MY AUNT'S WILL PRACTICALLY BREAK THE DOOR DOWN.

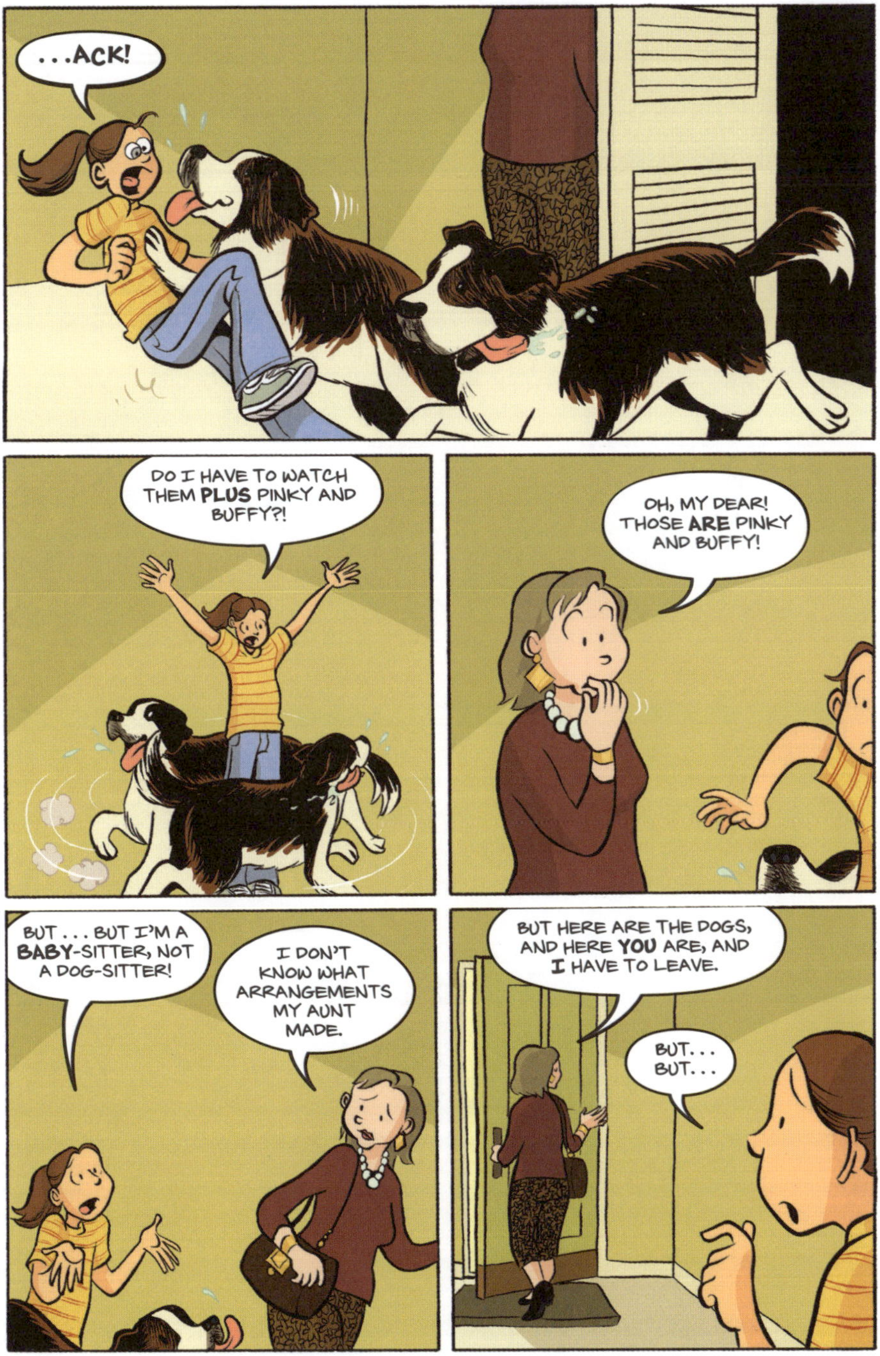
. . .ACK!
DO I HAVE TO WATCH THEM PLUS PINKY AND BUFFY?!
OH, MY DEAR! THOSE ARE PINKY AND BUFFY!
BUT . . . BUT I'M A BABY-SITTER, NOT A DOG-SITTER!
I DON'T KNOW WHAT ARRANGEMENTS MY AUNT MADE.
BUT HERE ARE THE DOGS, AND HERE YOU ARE, AND I HAVE TO LEAVE.
BUT. . . BUT. . .

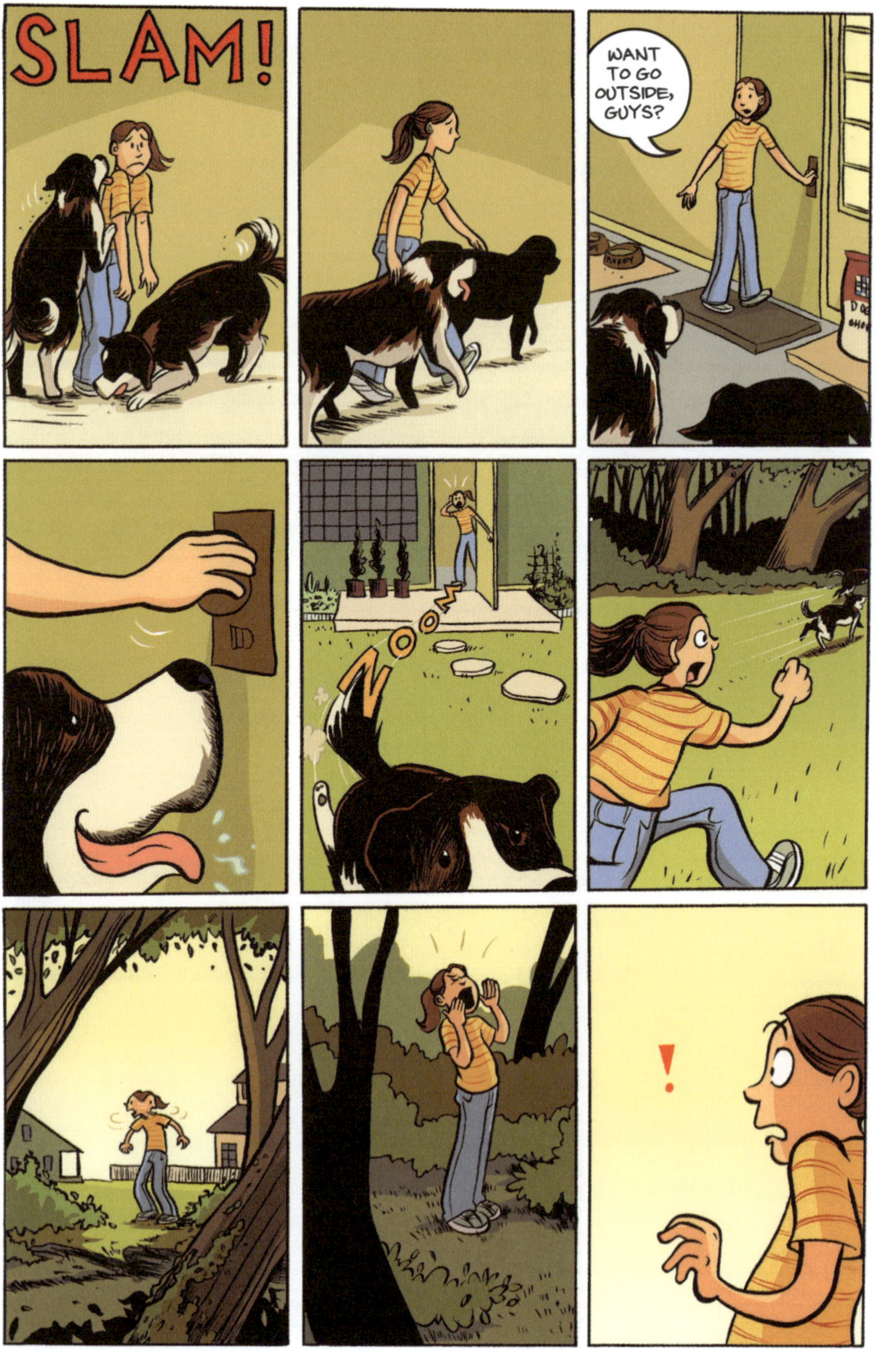
SLAM!
WANT TO GO OUTSIDE, GUYS?
ZOOM
!

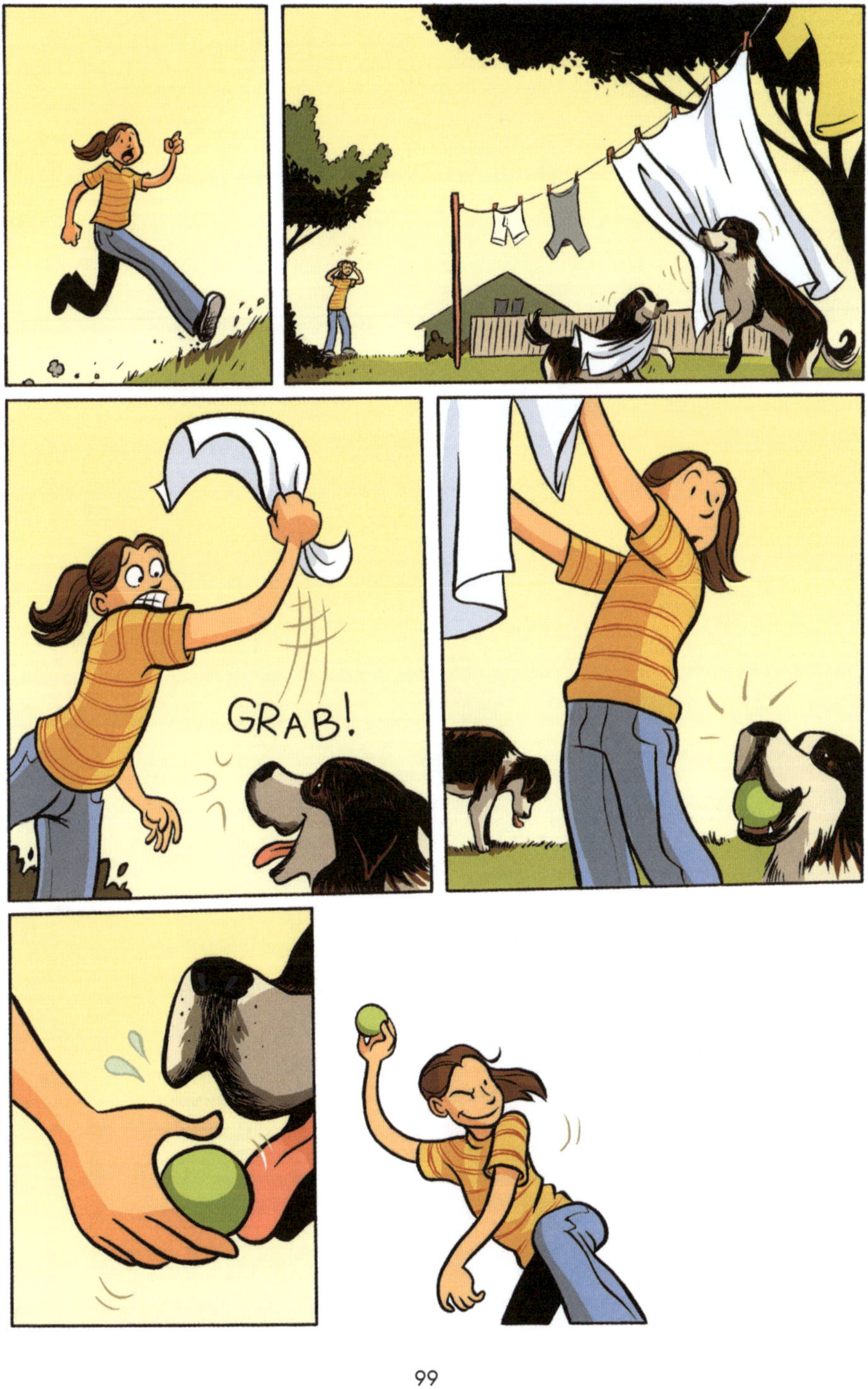
GRAB!

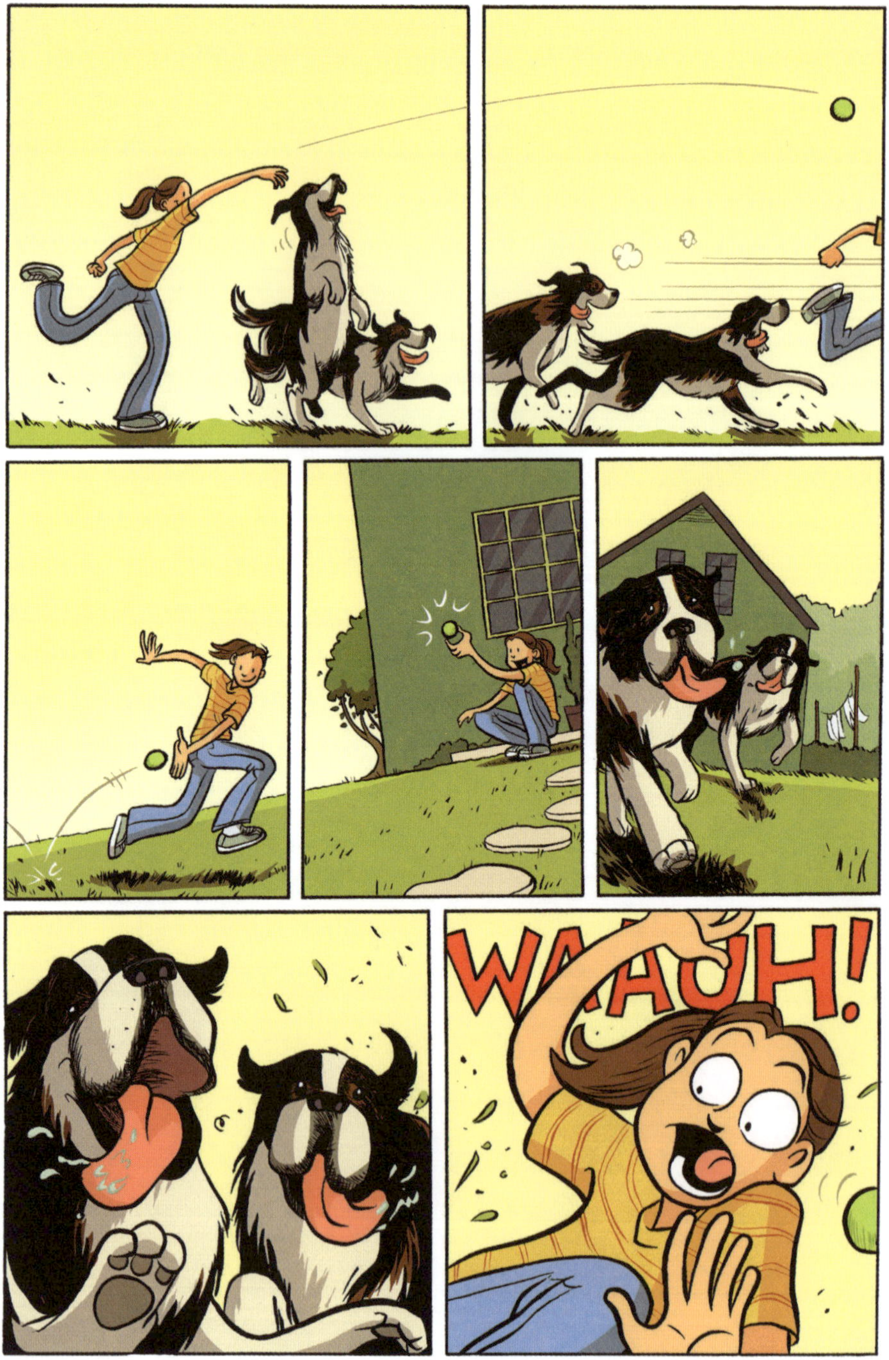
WAAUH!

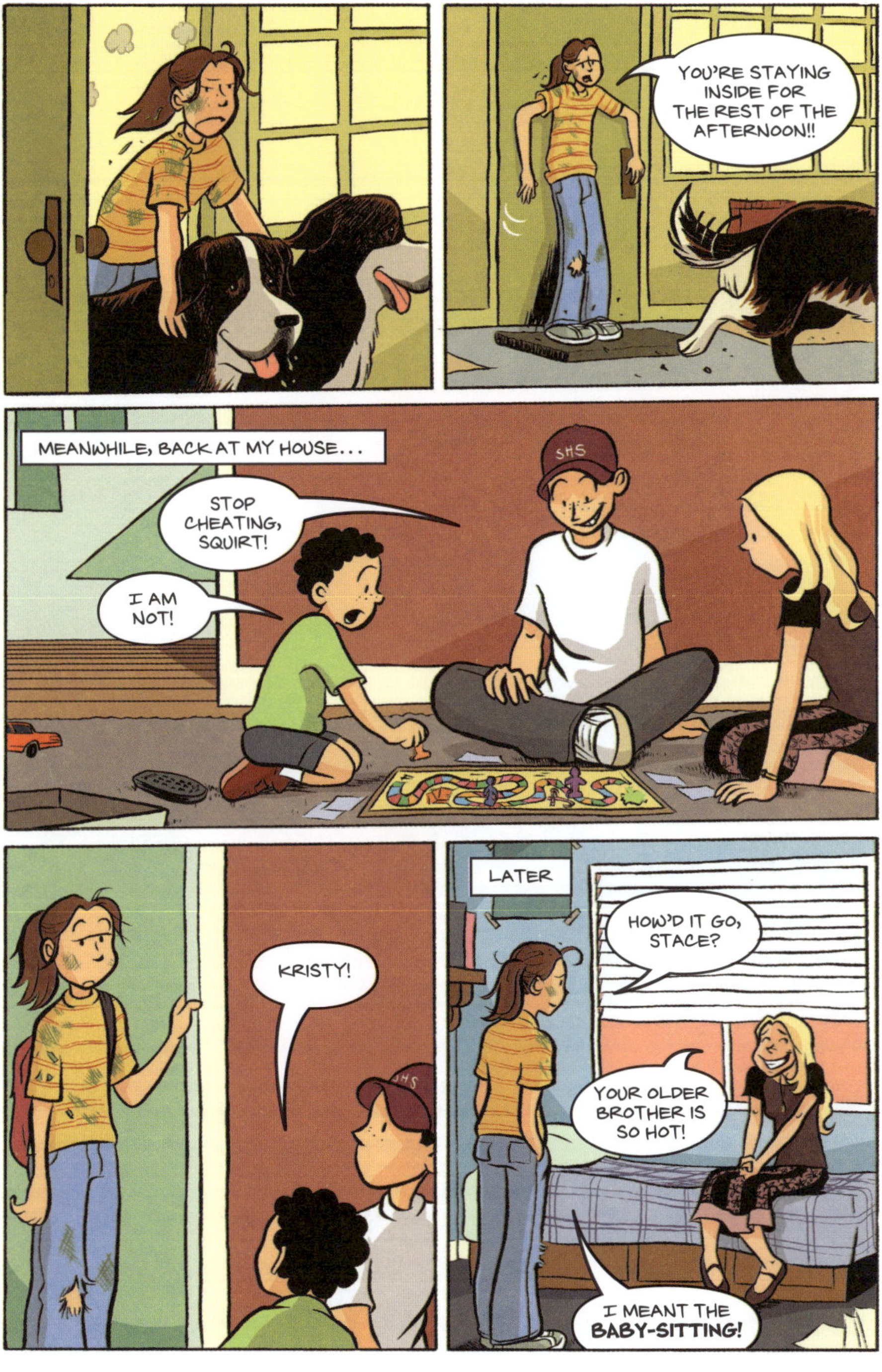

YOU'RE STAYING INSIDE FOR THE REST OF THE AFTERNOON!!
MEANWHILE, BACK AT MY HOUSE...
STOP CHEATING, SQUIRT!
I AM NOT!
KRISTY!
LATER
HOW'D IT GO, STACE?
YOUR OLDER BROTHER IS SO HOT!
I MEANT THE **BABY-SITTING!**

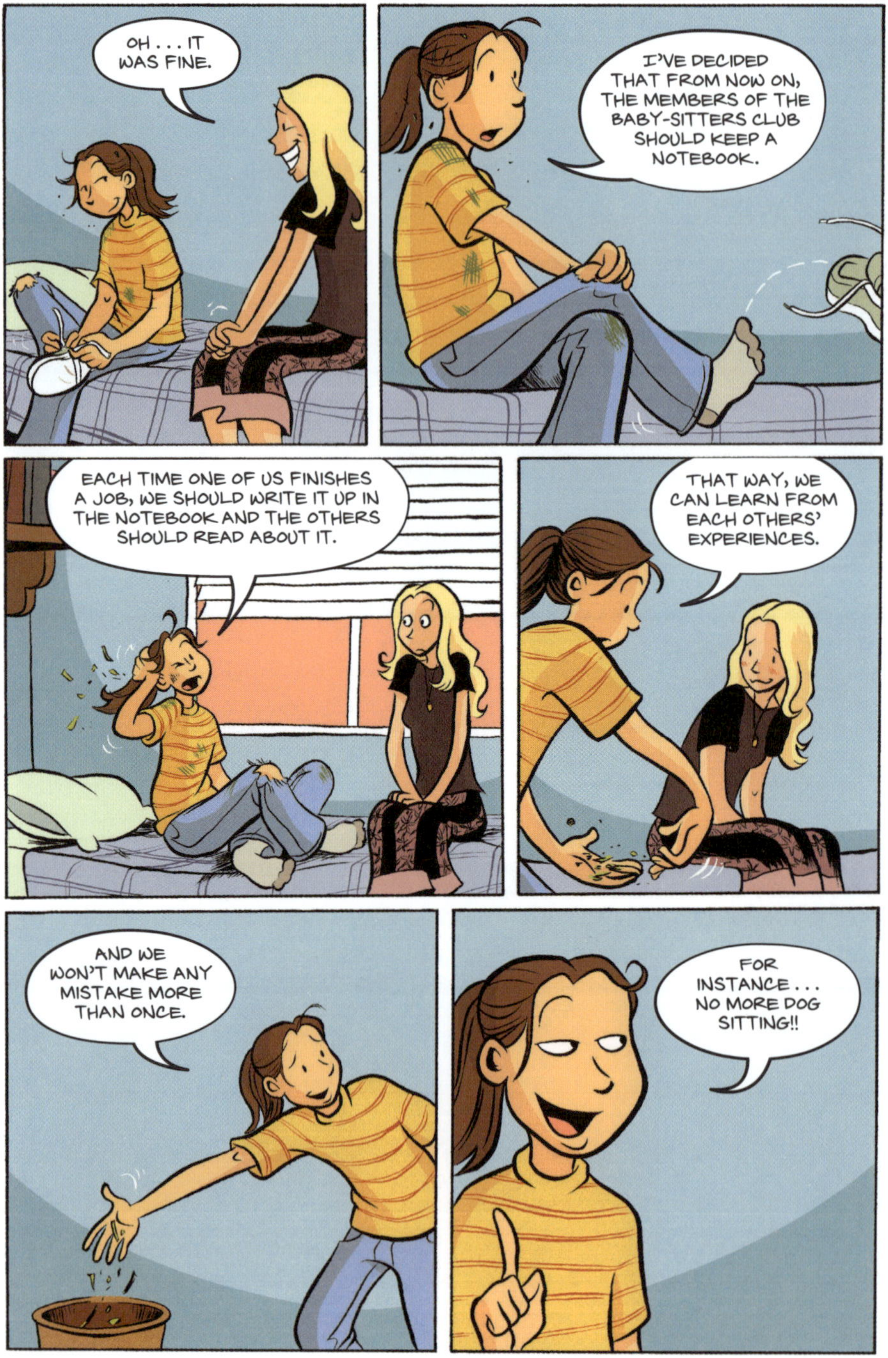
OH . . . IT WAS FINE.
I'VE DECIDED THAT FROM NOW ON, THE MEMBERS OF THE BABY-SITTERS CLUB SHOULD KEEP A NOTEBOOK.
EACH TIME ONE OF US FINISHES A JOB, WE SHOULD WRITE IT UP IN THE NOTEBOOK AND THE OTHERS SHOULD READ ABOUT IT.
THAT WAY, WE CAN LEARN FROM EACH OTHERS' EXPERIENCES.
AND WE WON'T MAKE ANY MISTAKE MORE THAN ONCE.
FOR INSTANCE . . . NO MORE DOG SITTING!!

Friday, September 26th

Kristy says we have to keep a record of every baby-sitting job we do in this book. My first job thrugh the Baby-siters Club was yesterday. I was sitting for Jamie Newton, only it wasn't just for Jamie it was for Jamie and his three cusins. And boy were they WILD!

* Claudia *

CHAPTER 8

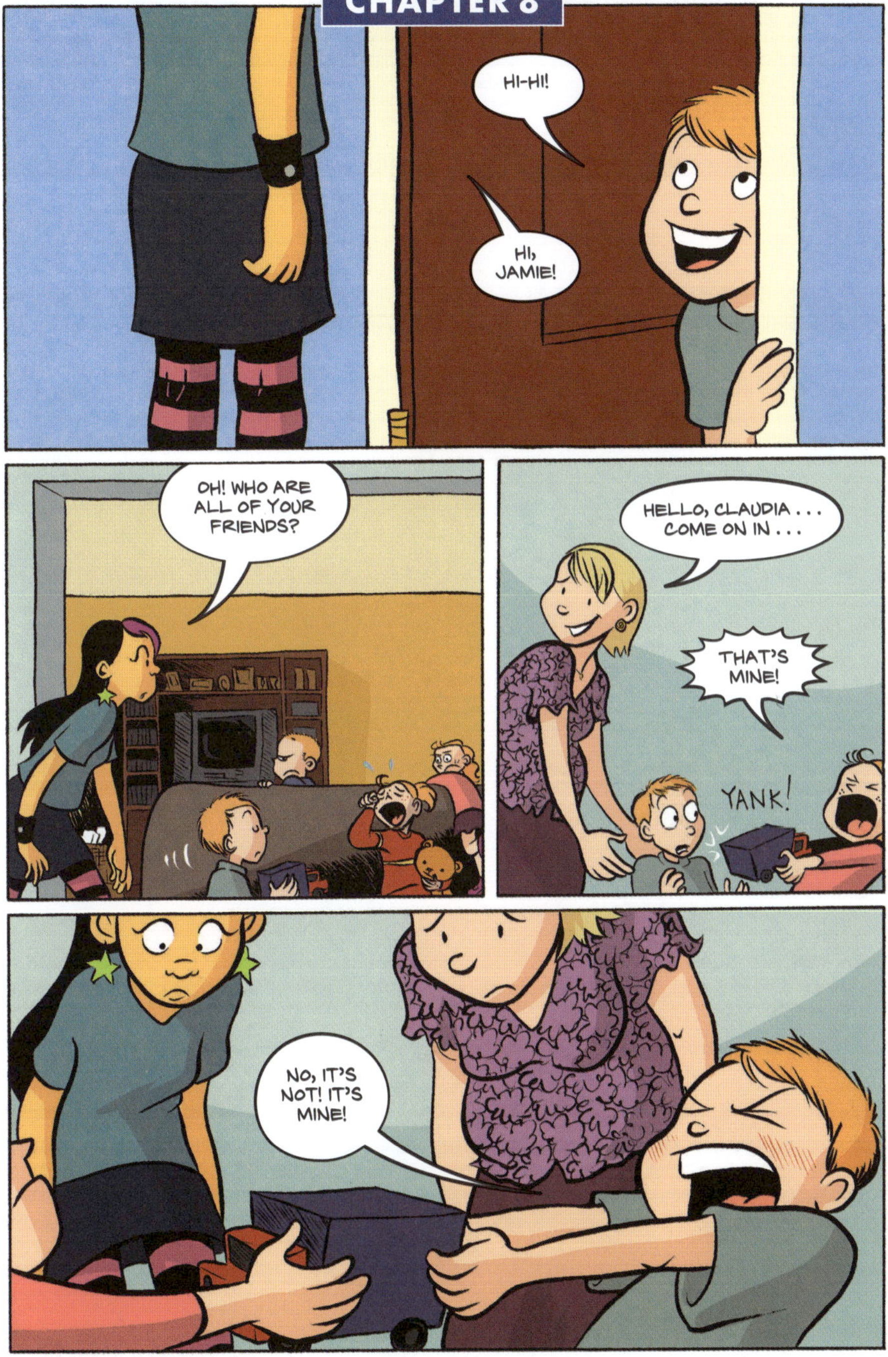
HI-HI!
HI, JAMIE!
OH! WHO ARE ALL OF YOUR FRIENDS?
HELLO, CLAUDIA . . . COME ON IN . . .
THAT'S MINE!
YANK!
NO, IT'S NOT! IT'S MINE!

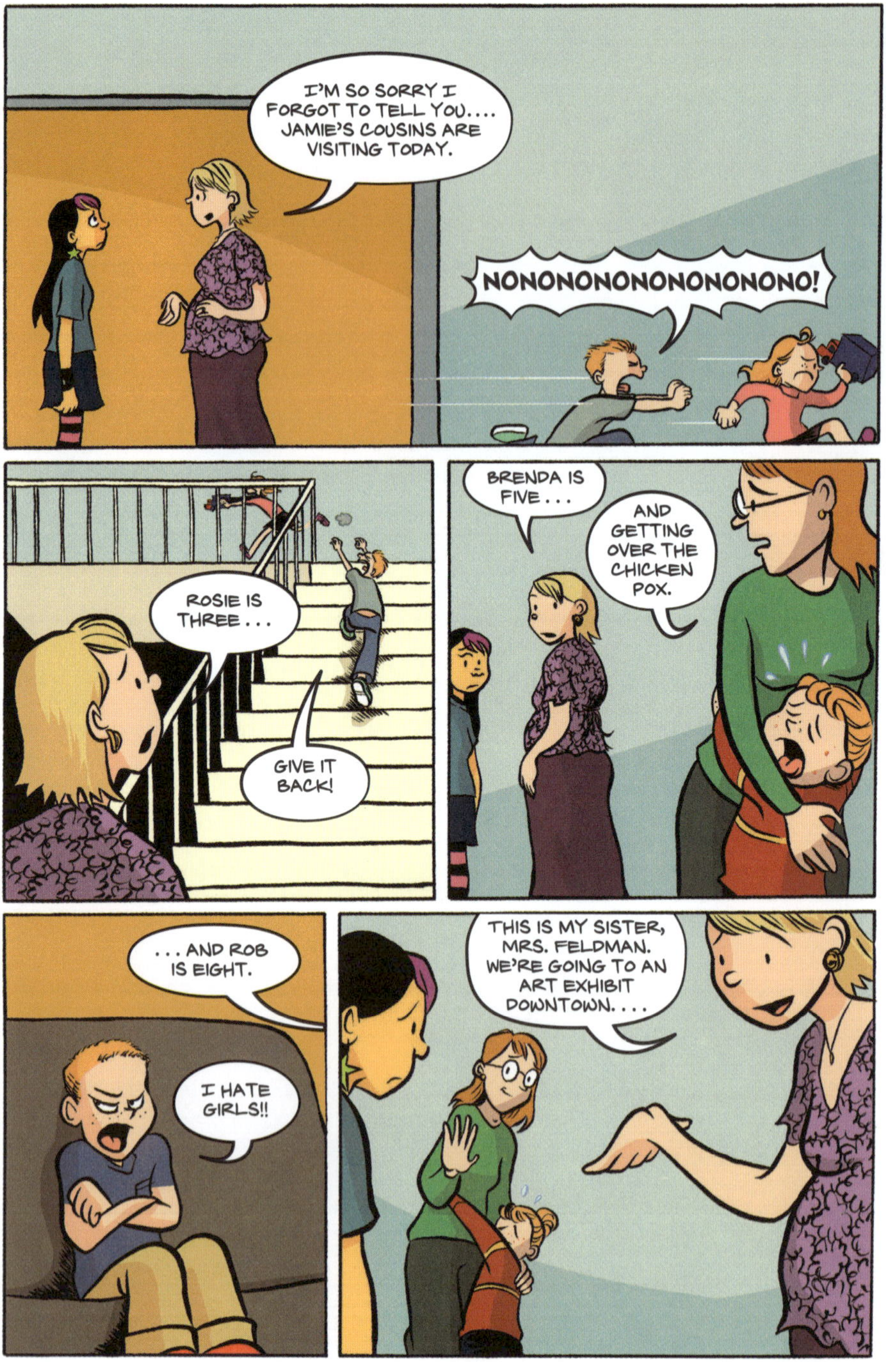
I'M SO SORRY I FORGOT TO TELL YOU.... JAMIE'S COUSINS ARE VISITING TODAY.
NONONONONONONONONO!
ROSIE IS THREE...
GIVE IT BACK!
BRENDA IS FIVE...
AND GETTING OVER THE CHICKEN POX.
...AND ROB IS EIGHT.
I HATE GIRLS!!
THIS IS MY SISTER, MRS. FELDMAN. WE'RE GOING TO AN ART EXHIBIT DOWNTOWN....

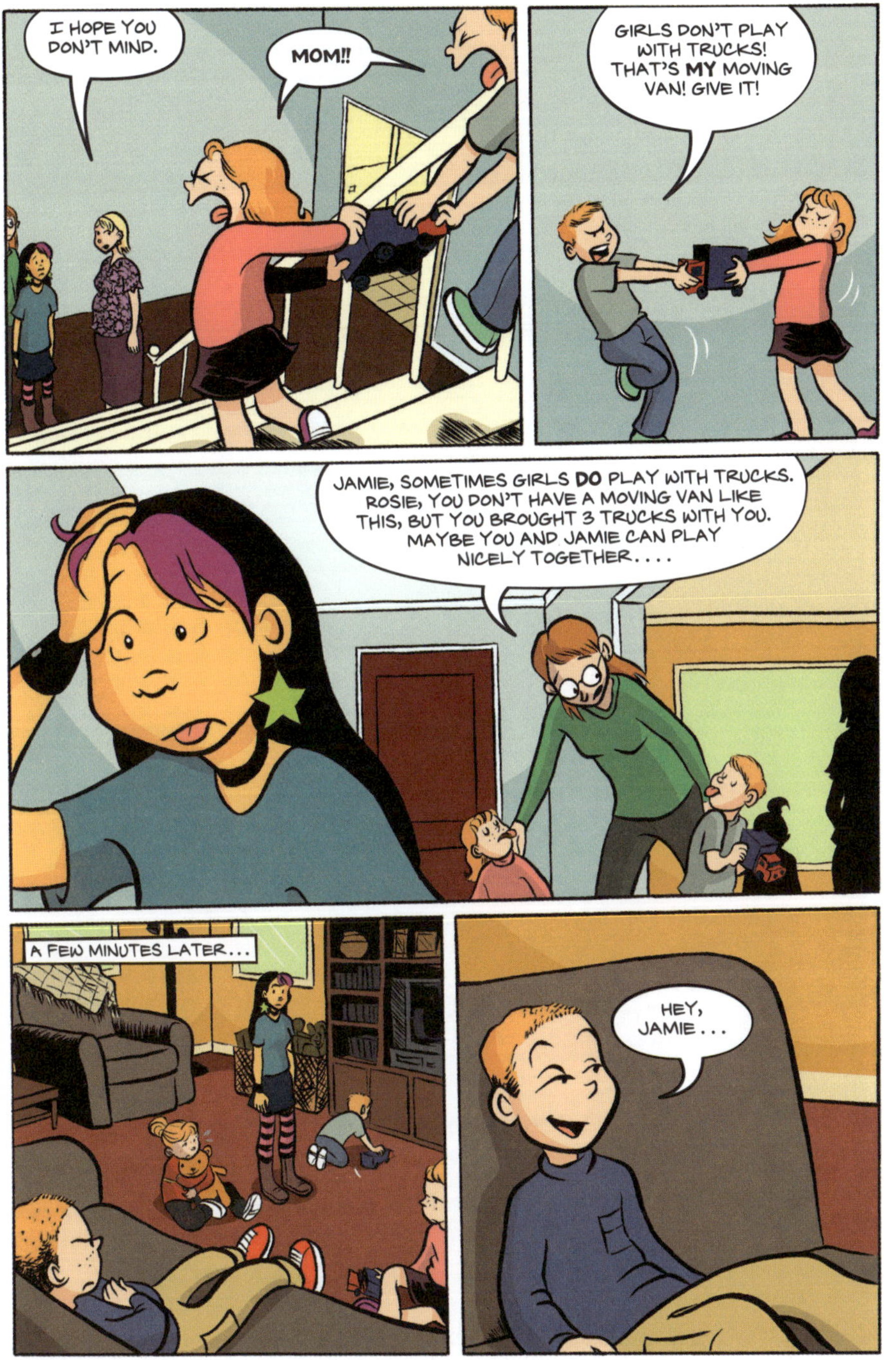
I HOPE YOU DON'T MIND.
MOM!!
GIRLS DON'T PLAY WITH TRUCKS! THAT'S **MY** MOVING VAN! GIVE IT!
JAMIE, SOMETIMES GIRLS **DO** PLAY WITH TRUCKS. ROSIE, YOU DON'T HAVE A MOVING VAN LIKE THIS, BUT YOU BROUGHT 3 TRUCKS WITH YOU. MAYBE YOU AND JAMIE CAN PLAY NICELY TOGETHER. . . .
A FEW MINUTES LATER. . .
HEY, JAMIE. . .

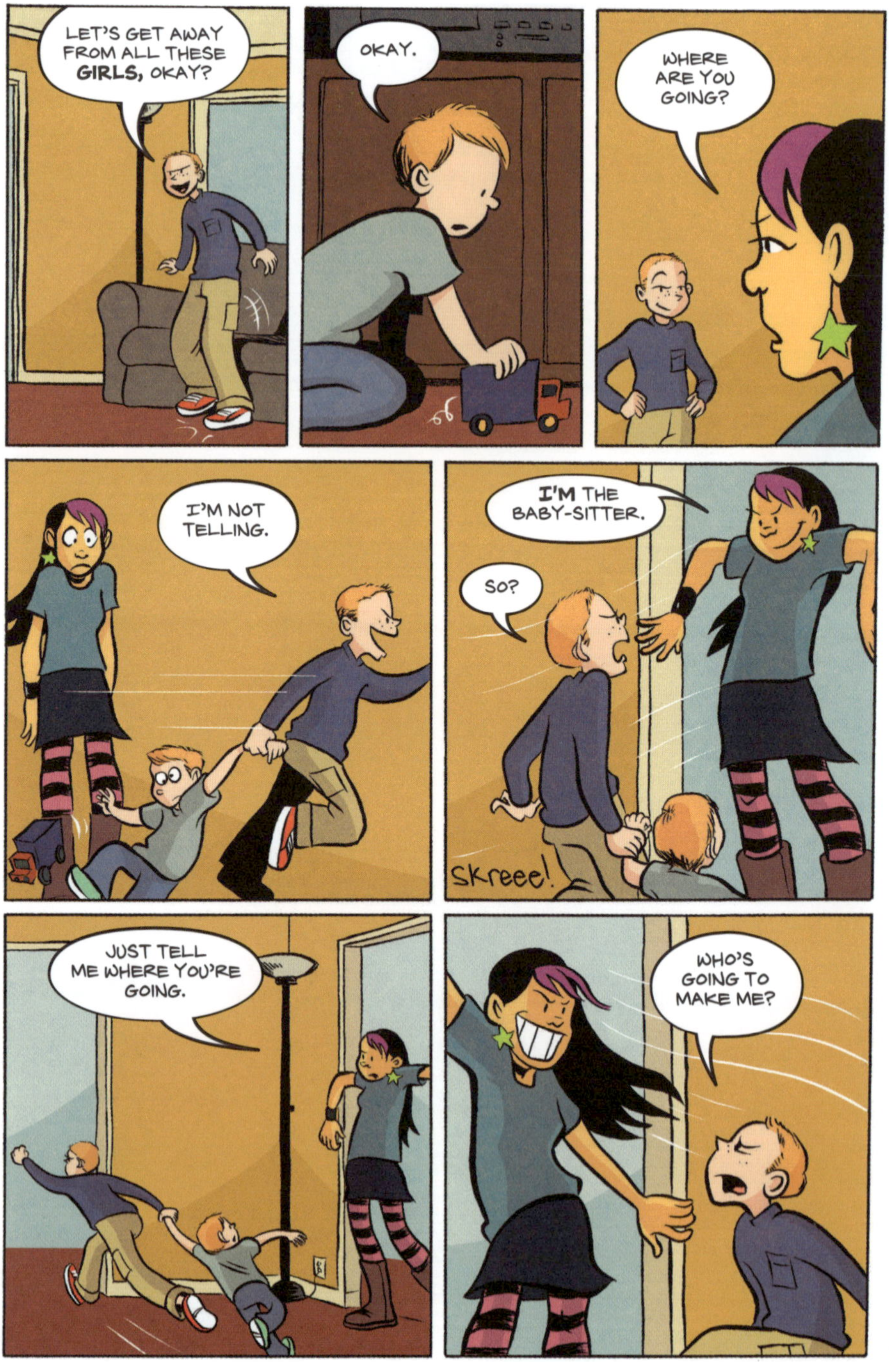
LET'S GET AWAY FROM ALL THESE GIRLS, OKAY?
OKAY.
WHERE ARE YOU GOING?
I'M NOT TELLING.
I'M THE BABY-SITTER.
SO?
SKREEE!
JUST TELL ME WHERE YOU'RE GOING.
WHO'S GOING TO MAKE ME?

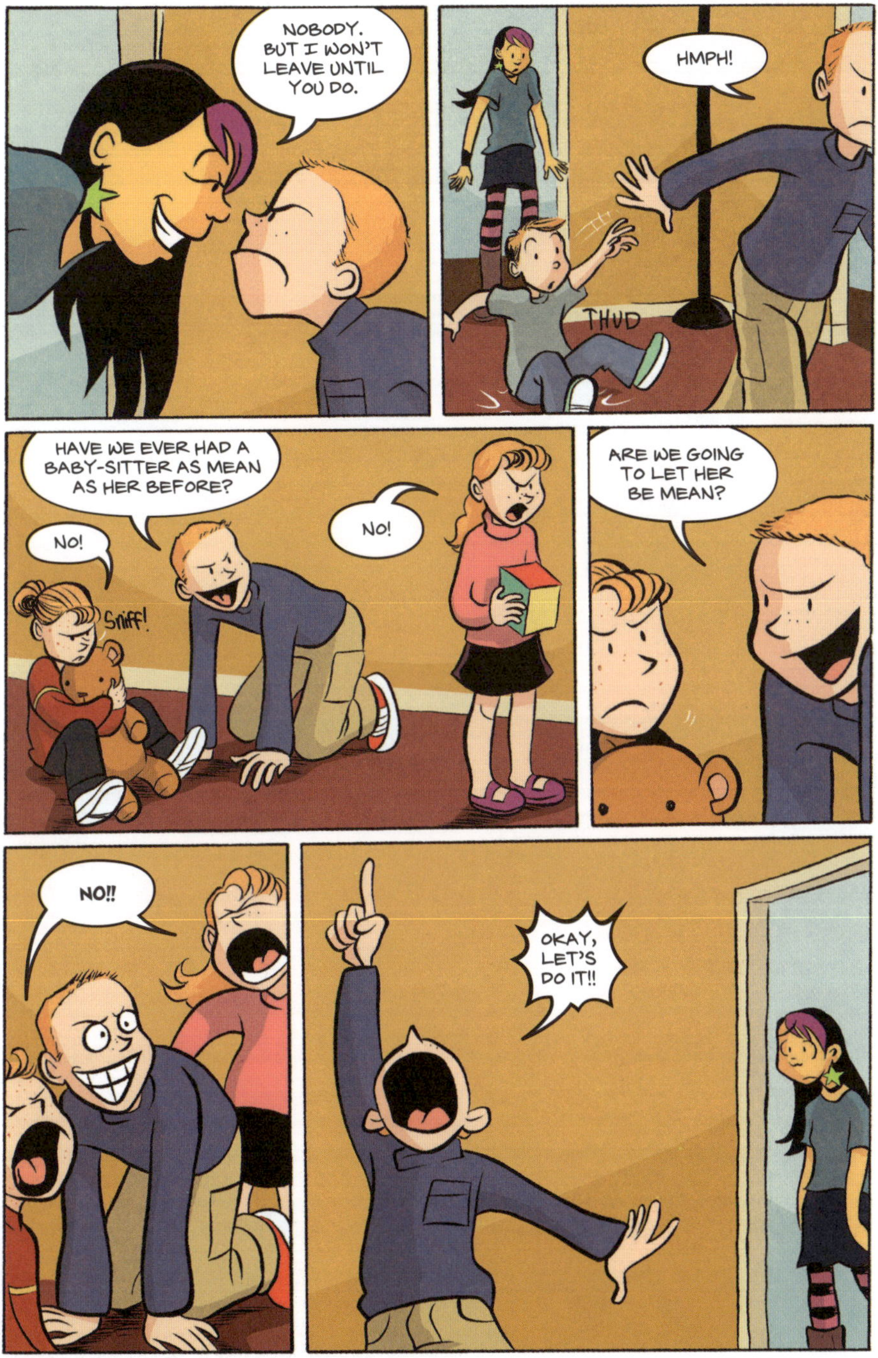
NOBODY. BUT I WON'T LEAVE UNTIL YOU DO.
HMPH!
THUD
HAVE WE EVER HAD A BABY-SITTER AS MEAN AS HER BEFORE?
NO!
Sniff!
NO!
ARE WE GOING TO LET HER BE MEAN?
NO!!
OKAY, LET'S DO IT!!

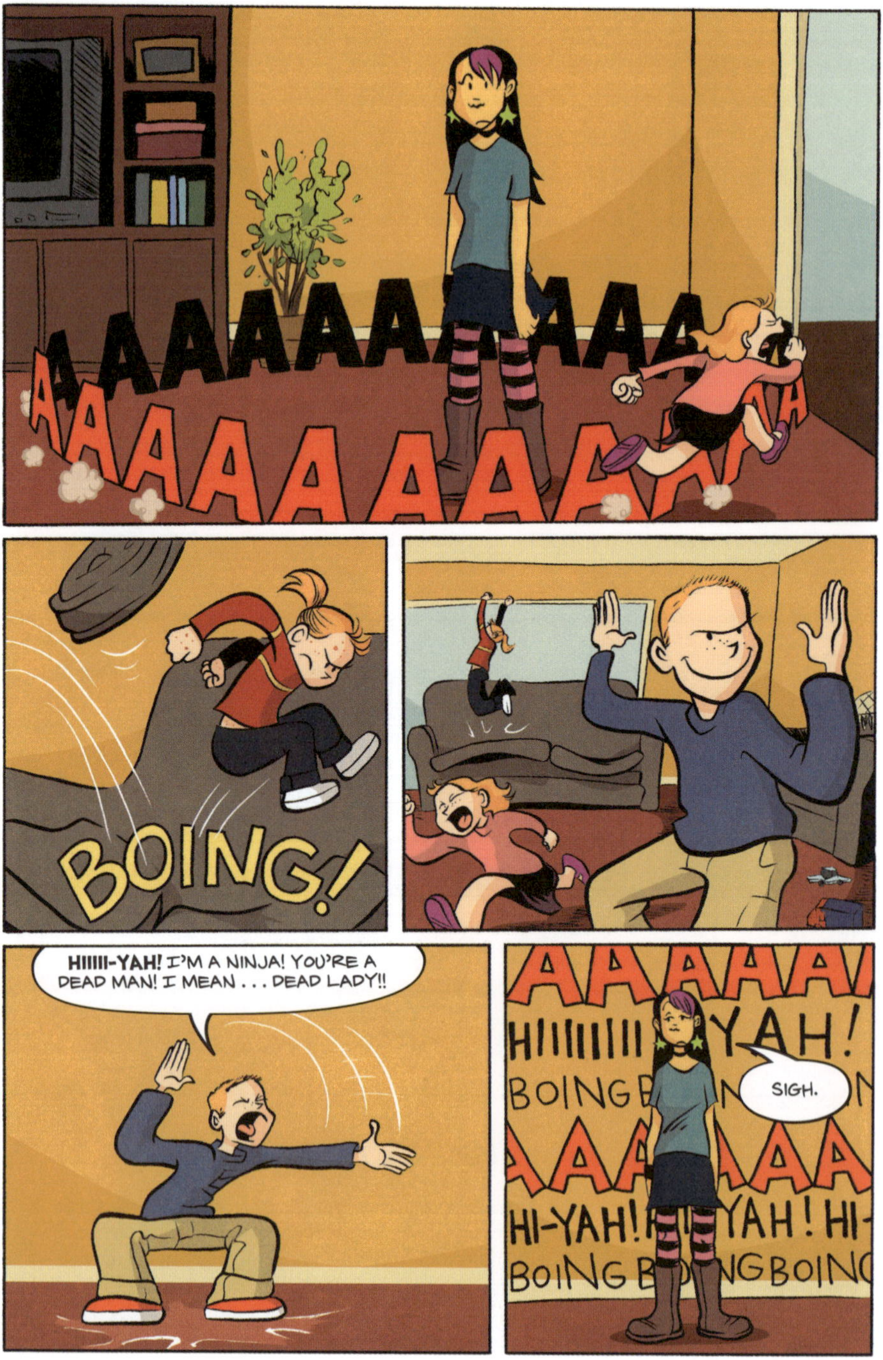
AAAAAAAAAAA
AAAAAAAAAAAA
BOING!
HIIIII-YAH! I'M A NINJA! YOU'RE A DEAD MAN! I MEAN . . . DEAD LADY!!
SIGH.

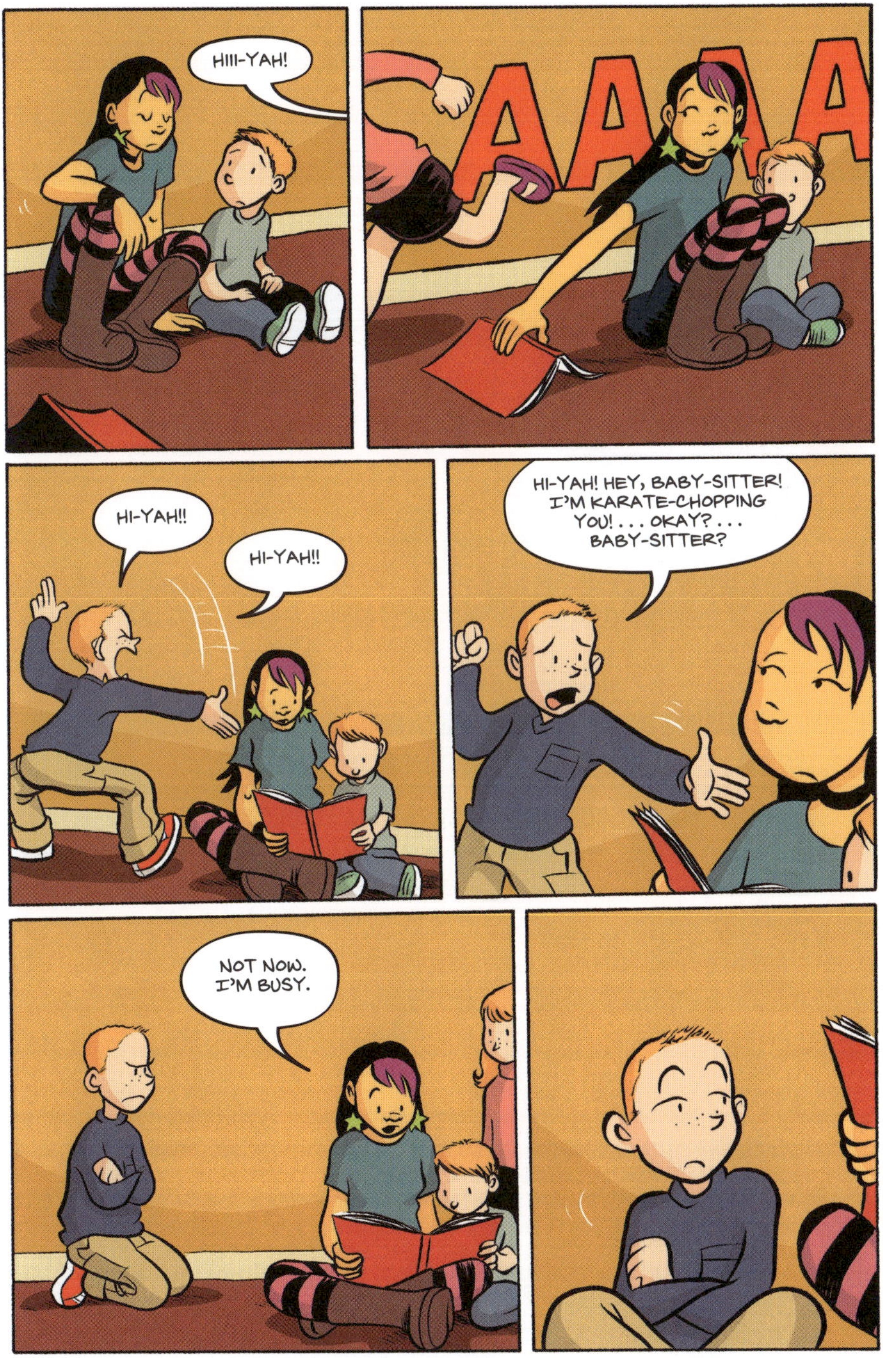
HIII-YAH!
HI-YAH!!
HI-YAH!!
HI-YAH! HEY, BABY-SITTER! I'M KARATE-CHOPPING YOU! . . . OKAY? . . . BABY-SITTER?
NOT NOW. I'M BUSY.

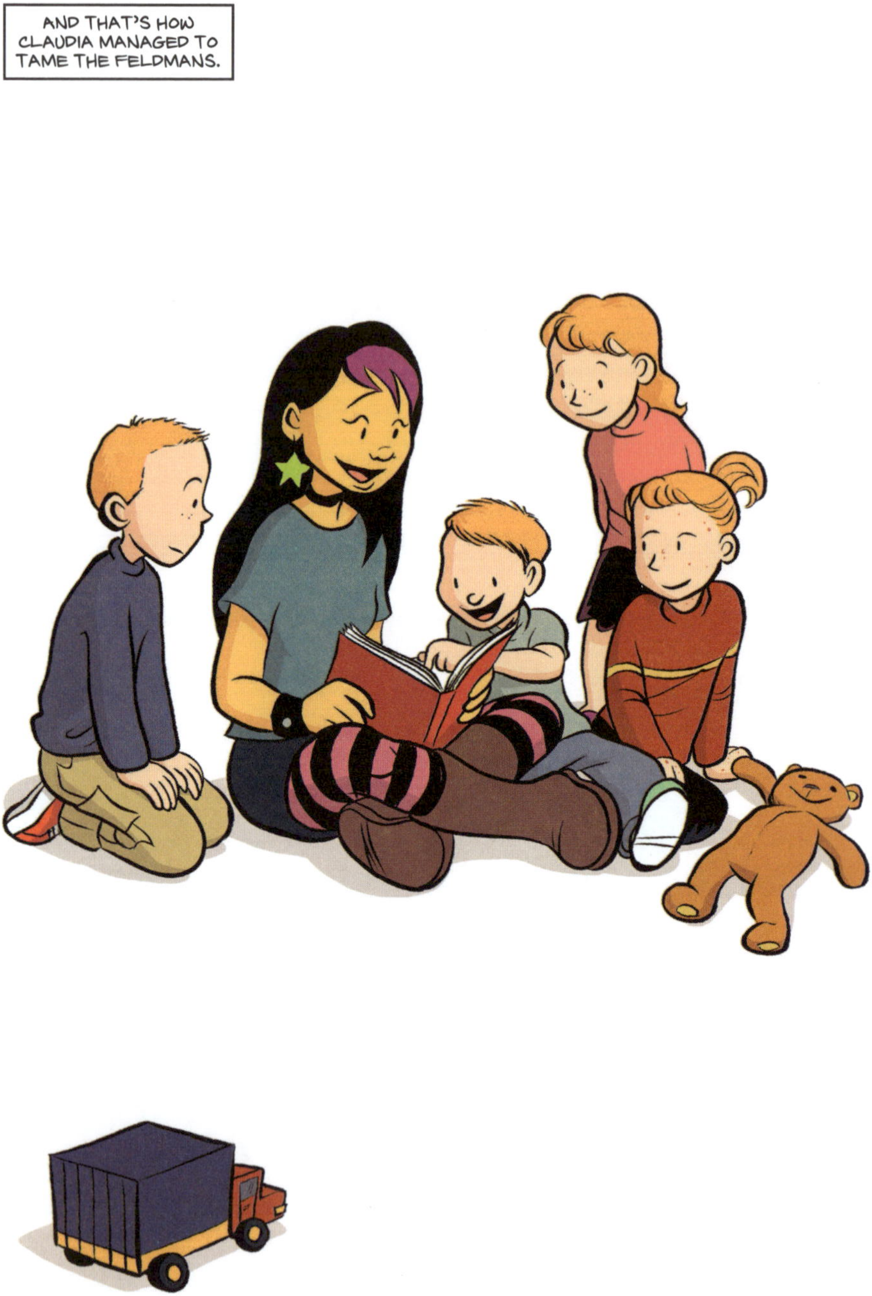
AND THAT'S HOW CLAUDIA MANAGED TO TAME THE FELDMANS.

Saturday, September 27

   I don't know what Kristy always makes such a fuss about. Watson's kids are cute. I think Kristy would like them if she ever baby-sat for them. Are you reading this, Kristy? I hope so. Well, this notebook is for us to write our experiences and our problems in, especially our problems.
   And there were a few problems at Watson's house...

                           Mary Anne

CHAPTER 9

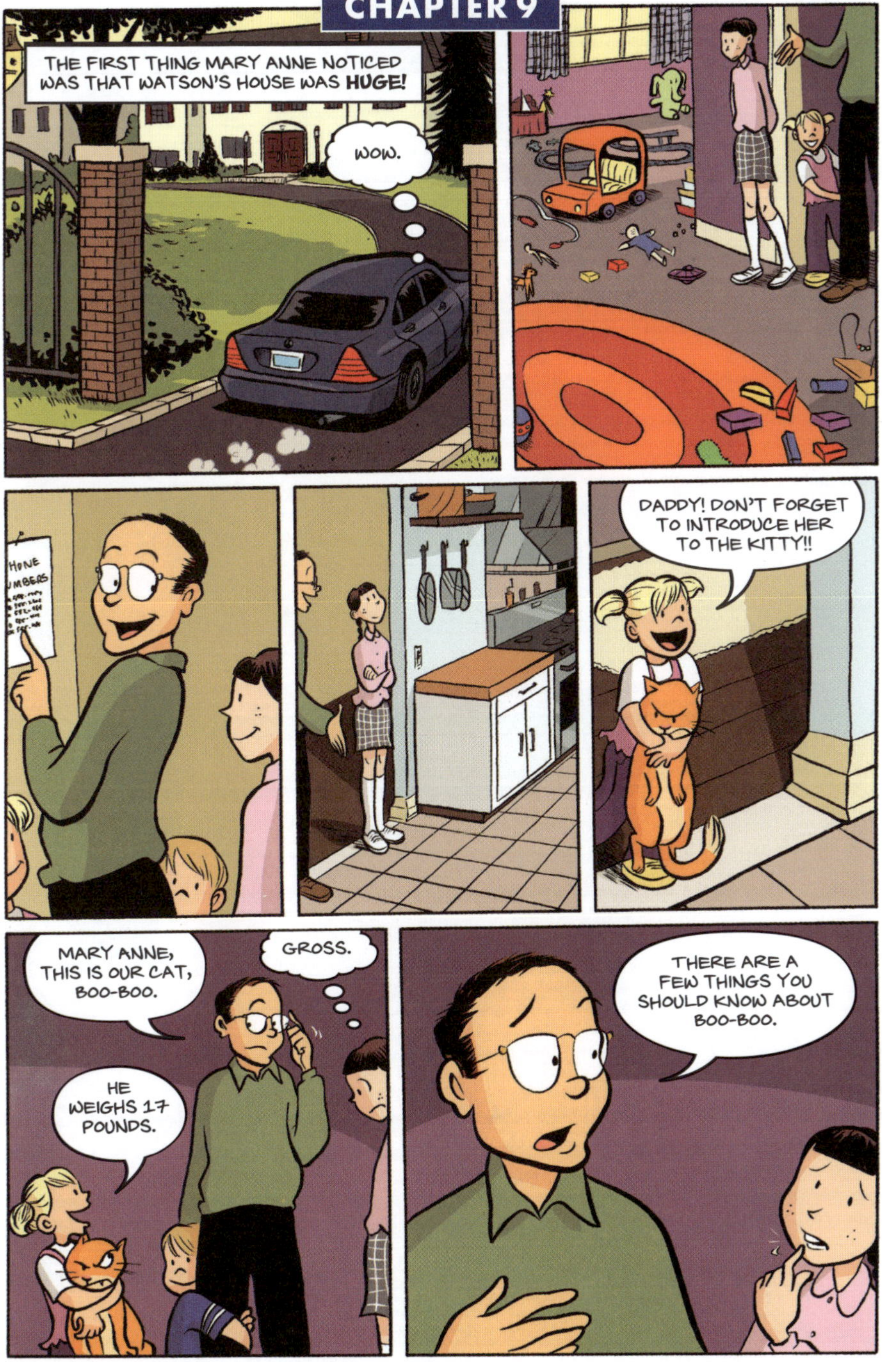
THE FIRST THING MARY ANNE NOTICED WAS THAT WATSON'S HOUSE WAS **HUGE!**
WOW.
DADDY! DON'T FORGET TO INTRODUCE HER TO THE KITTY!!
MARY ANNE, THIS IS OUR CAT, BOO-BOO.
GROSS.
HE WEIGHS 17 POUNDS.
THERE ARE A FEW THINGS YOU SHOULD KNOW ABOUT BOO-BOO.

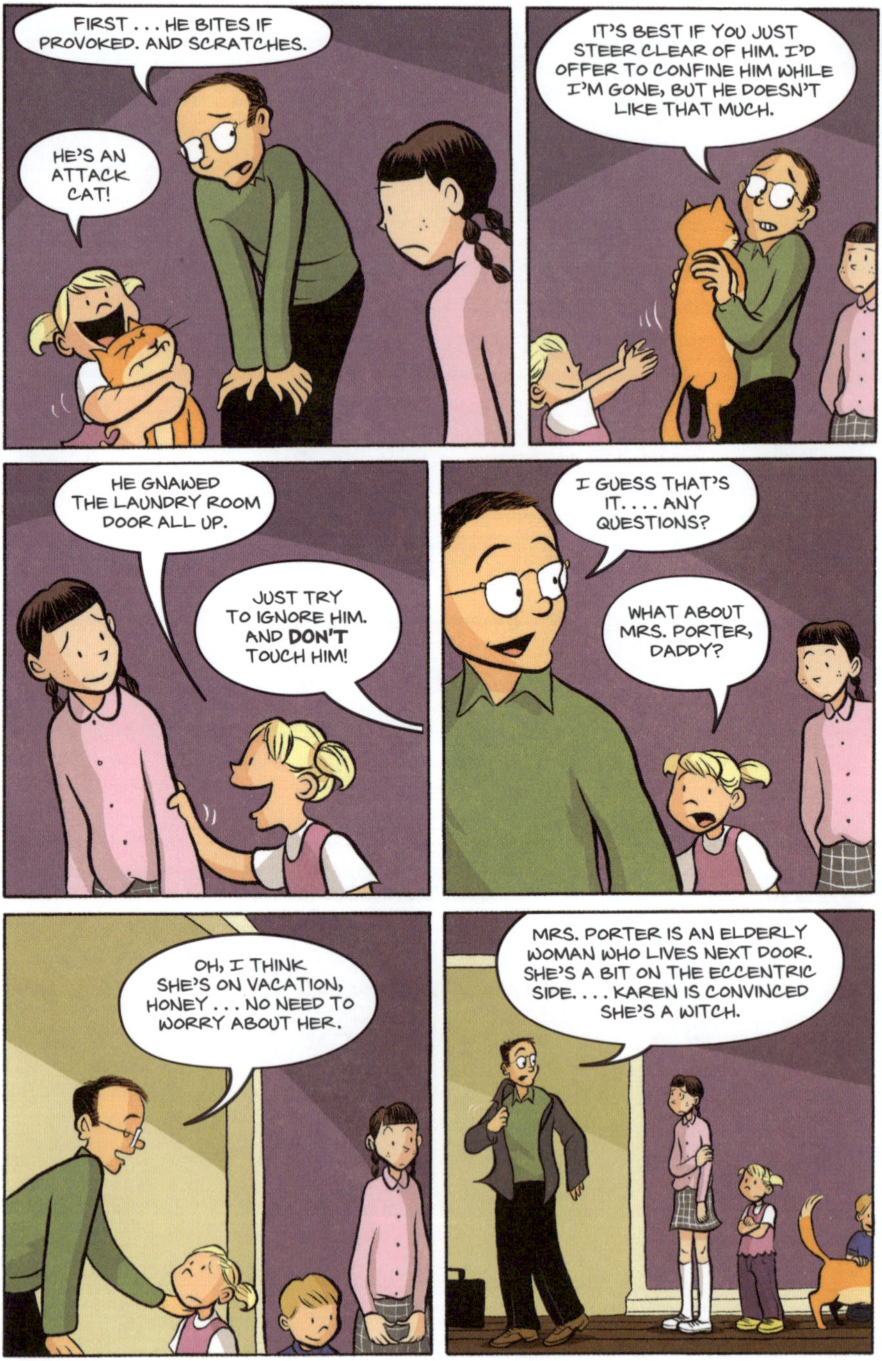
FIRST . . . HE BITES IF PROVOKED. AND SCRATCHES.
HE'S AN ATTACK CAT!
IT'S BEST IF YOU JUST STEER CLEAR OF HIM. I'D OFFER TO CONFINE HIM WHILE I'M GONE, BUT HE DOESN'T LIKE THAT MUCH.
HE GNAWED THE LAUNDRY ROOM DOOR ALL UP.
JUST TRY TO IGNORE HIM. AND **DON'T** TOUCH HIM!
I GUESS THAT'S IT. . . . ANY QUESTIONS?
WHAT ABOUT MRS. PORTER, DADDY?
OH, I THINK SHE'S ON VACATION, HONEY . . . NO NEED TO WORRY ABOUT HER.
MRS. PORTER IS AN ELDERLY WOMAN WHO LIVES NEXT DOOR. SHE'S A BIT ON THE ECCENTRIC SIDE. . . . KAREN IS CONVINCED SHE'S A WITCH.

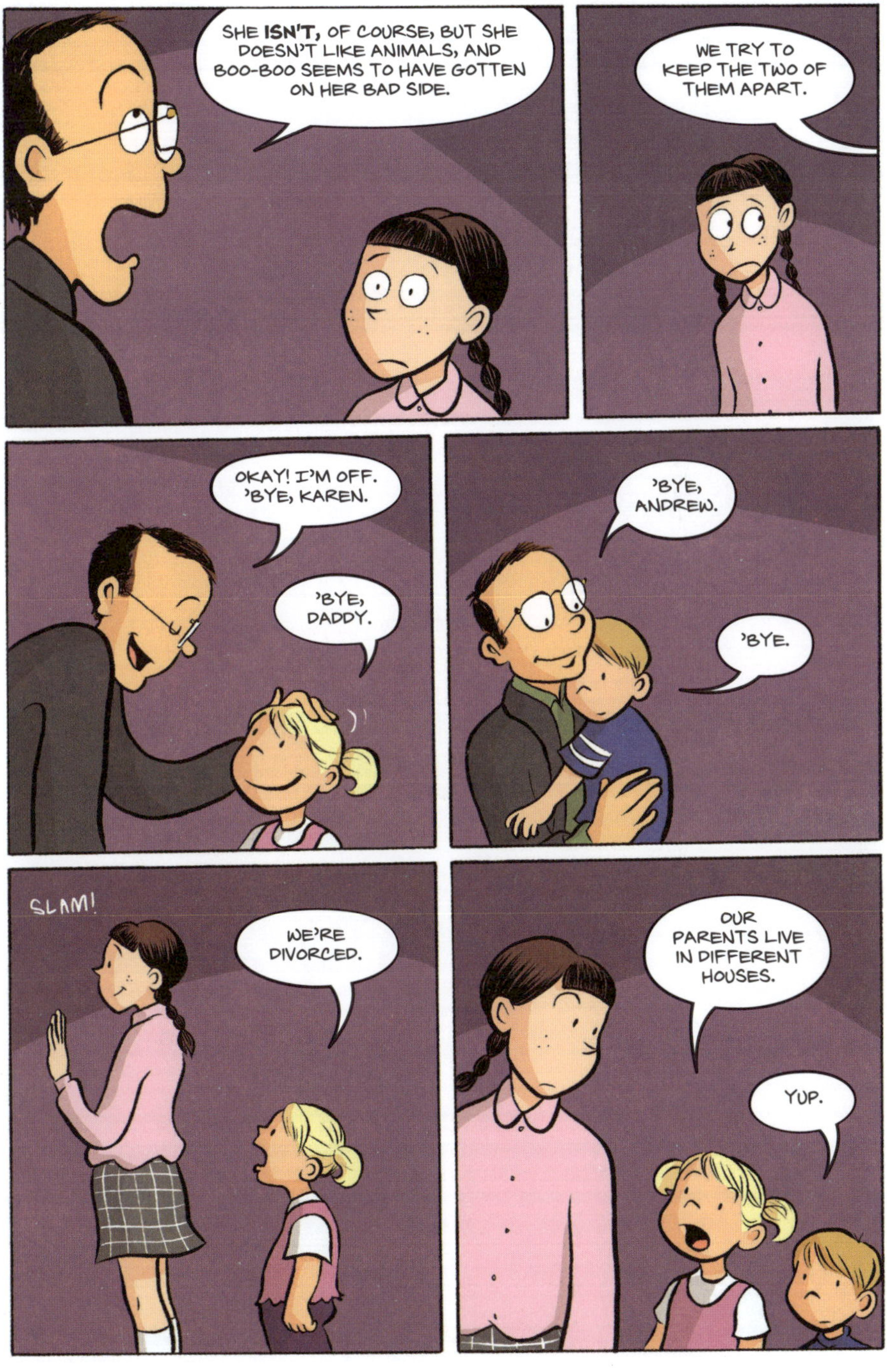
SHE **ISN'T,** OF COURSE, BUT SHE DOESN'T LIKE ANIMALS, AND BOO-BOO SEEMS TO HAVE GOTTEN ON HER BAD SIDE.
WE TRY TO KEEP THE TWO OF THEM APART.
OKAY! I'M OFF. 'BYE, KAREN.
'BYE, DADDY.
'BYE, ANDREW.
'BYE.
SLAM!
WE'RE DIVORCED.
OUR PARENTS LIVE IN DIFFERENT HOUSES.
YUP.

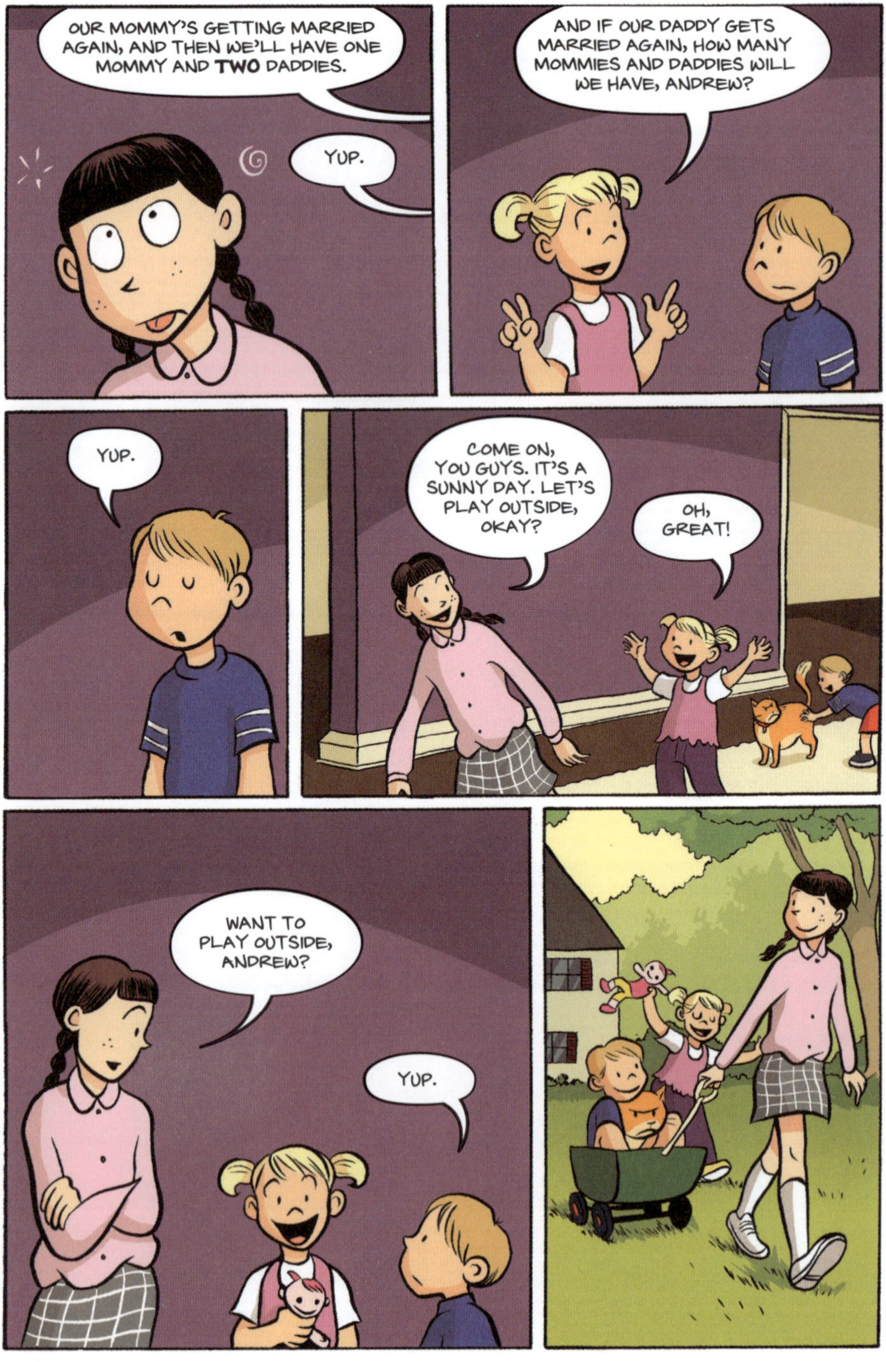
OUR MOMMY'S GETTING MARRIED AGAIN, AND THEN WE'LL HAVE ONE MOMMY AND TWO DADDIES.
YUP.
AND IF OUR DADDY GETS MARRIED AGAIN, HOW MANY MOMMIES AND DADDIES WILL WE HAVE, ANDREW?
YUP.
COME ON, YOU GUYS. IT'S A SUNNY DAY. LET'S PLAY OUTSIDE, OKAY?
OH, GREAT!
WANT TO PLAY OUTSIDE, ANDREW?
YUP.

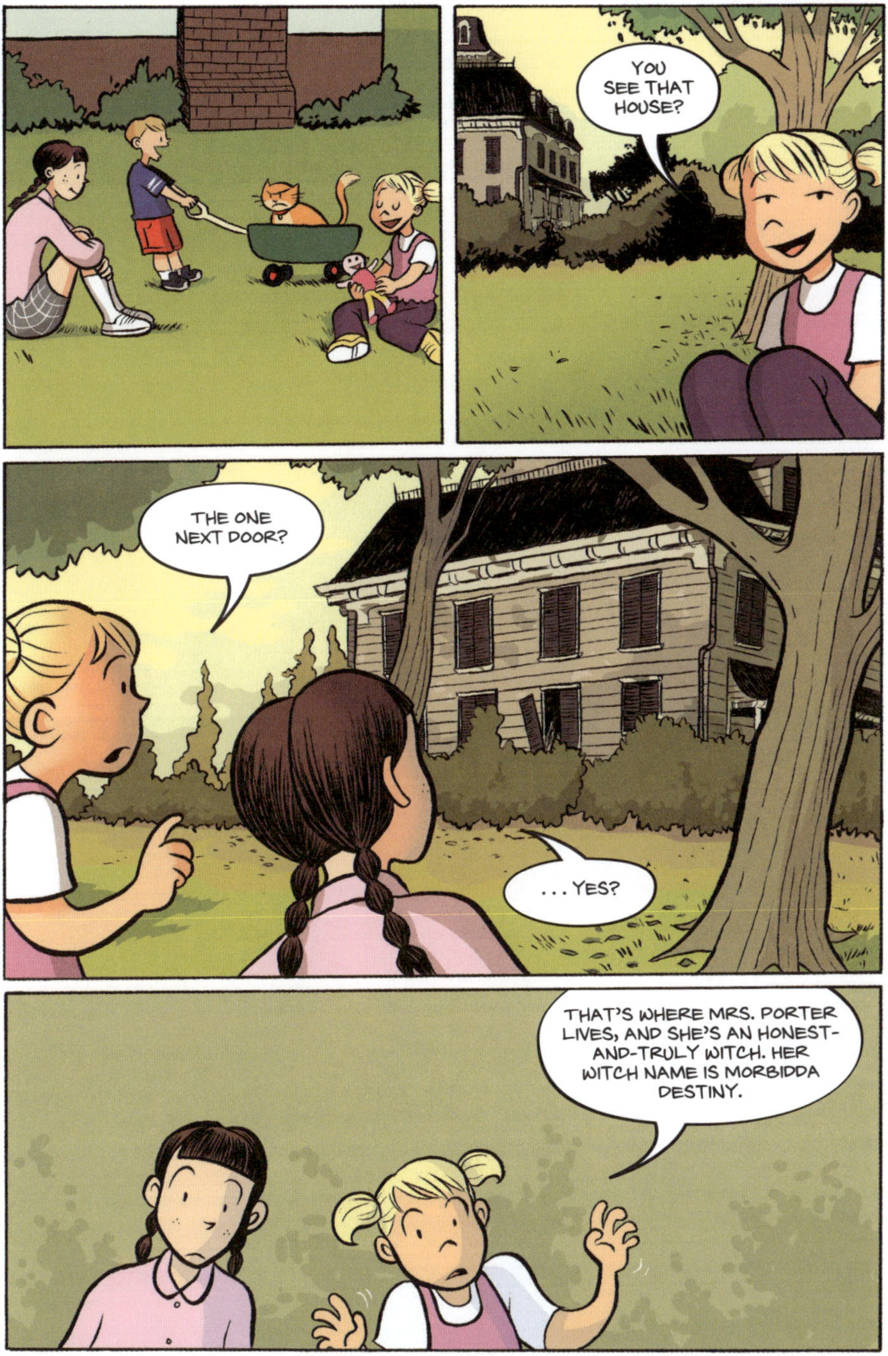
YOU SEE THAT HOUSE?
THE ONE NEXT DOOR?
. . . YES?
THAT'S WHERE MRS. PORTER LIVES, AND SHE'S AN HONEST-AND-TRULY WITCH. HER WITCH NAME IS MORBIDDA DESTINY.

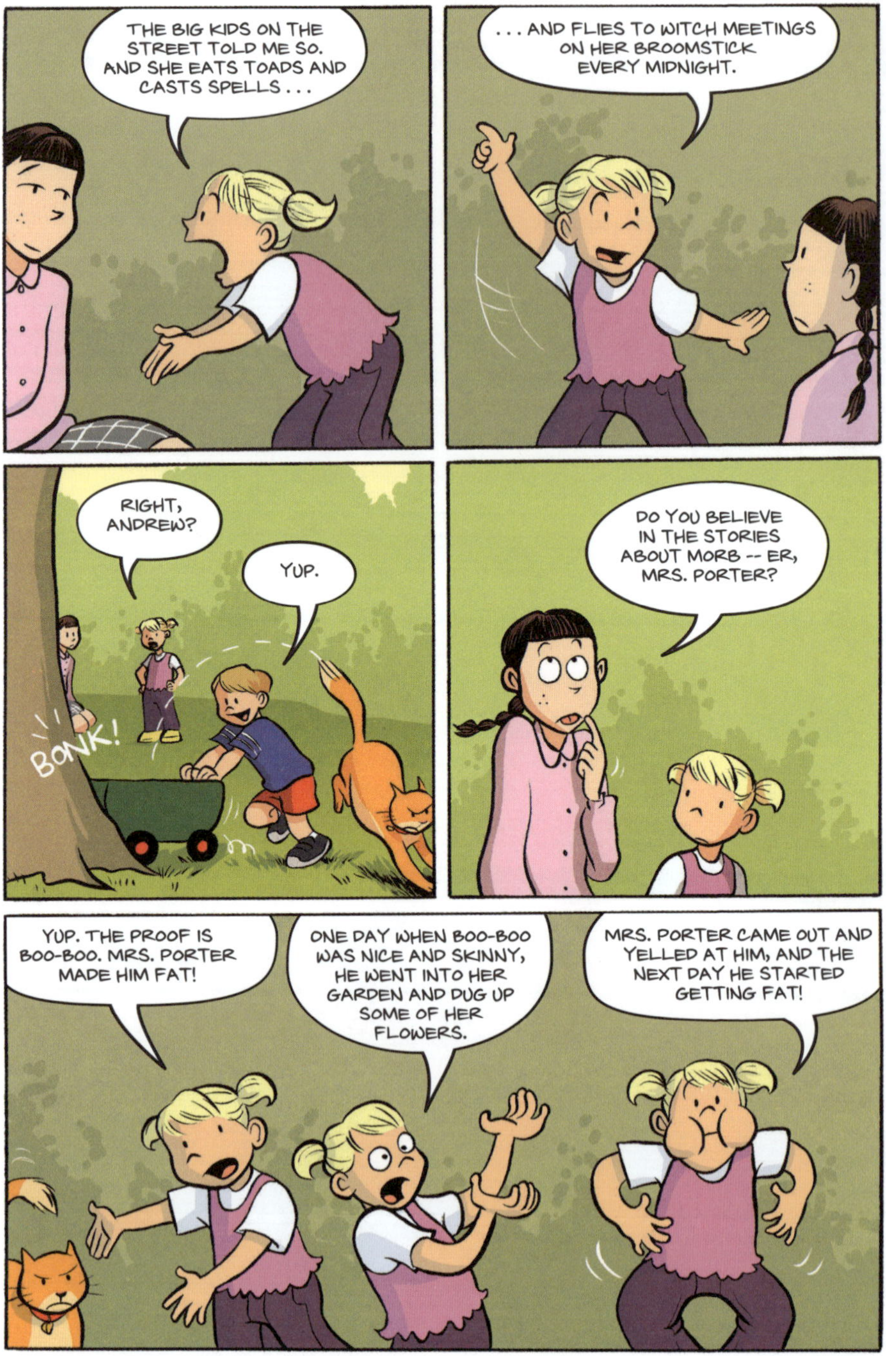
THE BIG KIDS ON THE STREET TOLD ME SO. AND SHE EATS TOADS AND CASTS SPELLS . . .
. . . AND FLIES TO WITCH MEETINGS ON HER BROOMSTICK EVERY MIDNIGHT.
RIGHT, ANDREW?
YUP.
BONK!
DO YOU BELIEVE IN THE STORIES ABOUT MORB -- ER, MRS. PORTER?
YUP. THE PROOF IS BOO-BOO. MRS. PORTER MADE HIM FAT!
ONE DAY WHEN BOO-BOO WAS NICE AND SKINNY, HE WENT INTO HER GARDEN AND DUG UP SOME OF HER FLOWERS.
MRS. PORTER CAME OUT AND YELLED AT HIM, AND THE NEXT DAY HE STARTED GETTING FAT!

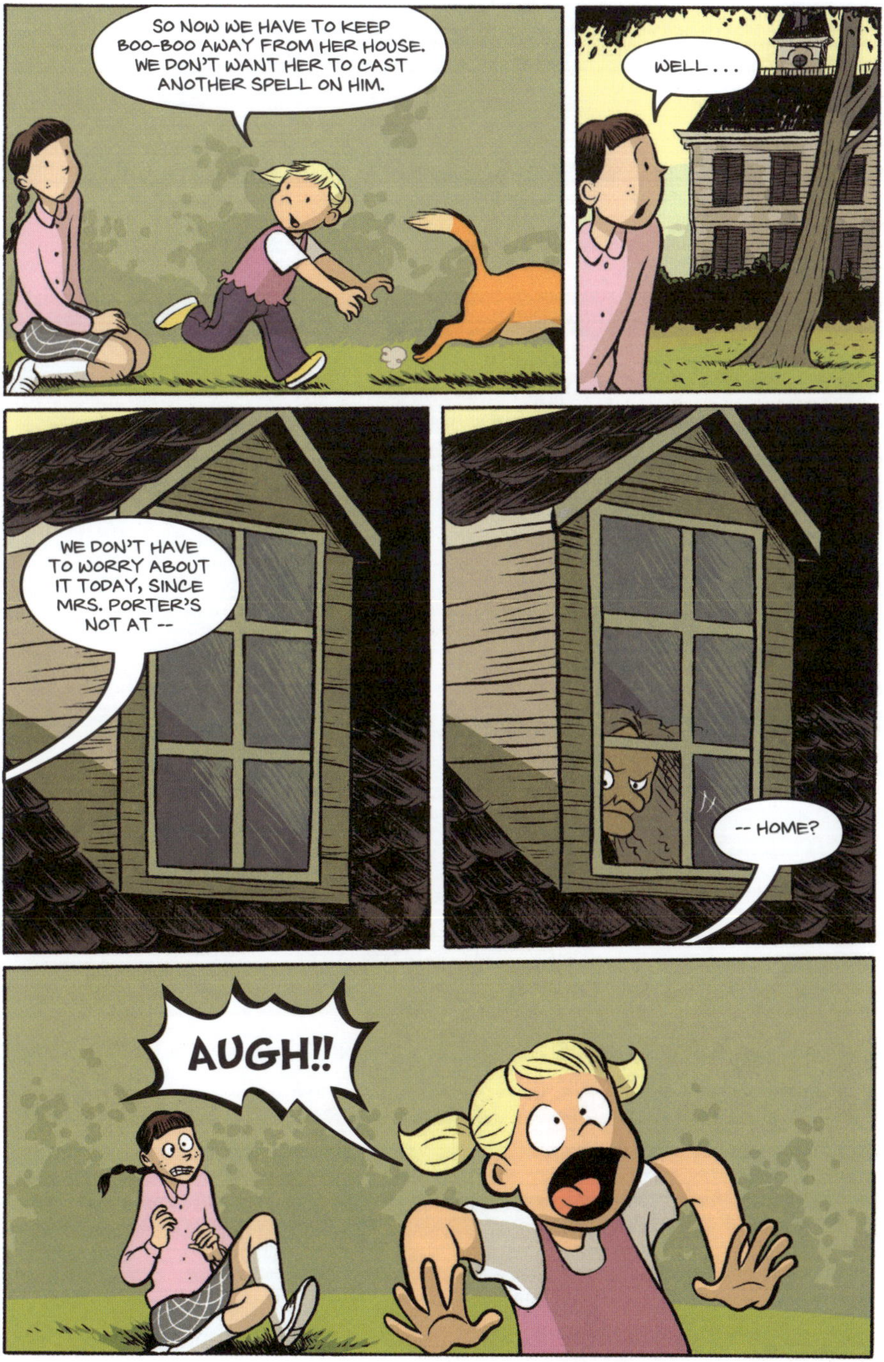
SO NOW WE HAVE TO KEEP BOO-BOO AWAY FROM HER HOUSE. WE DON'T WANT HER TO CAST ANOTHER SPELL ON HIM.
WELL . . .
WE DON'T HAVE TO WORRY ABOUT IT TODAY, SINCE MRS. PORTER'S NOT AT --
-- HOME?
AUGH!!

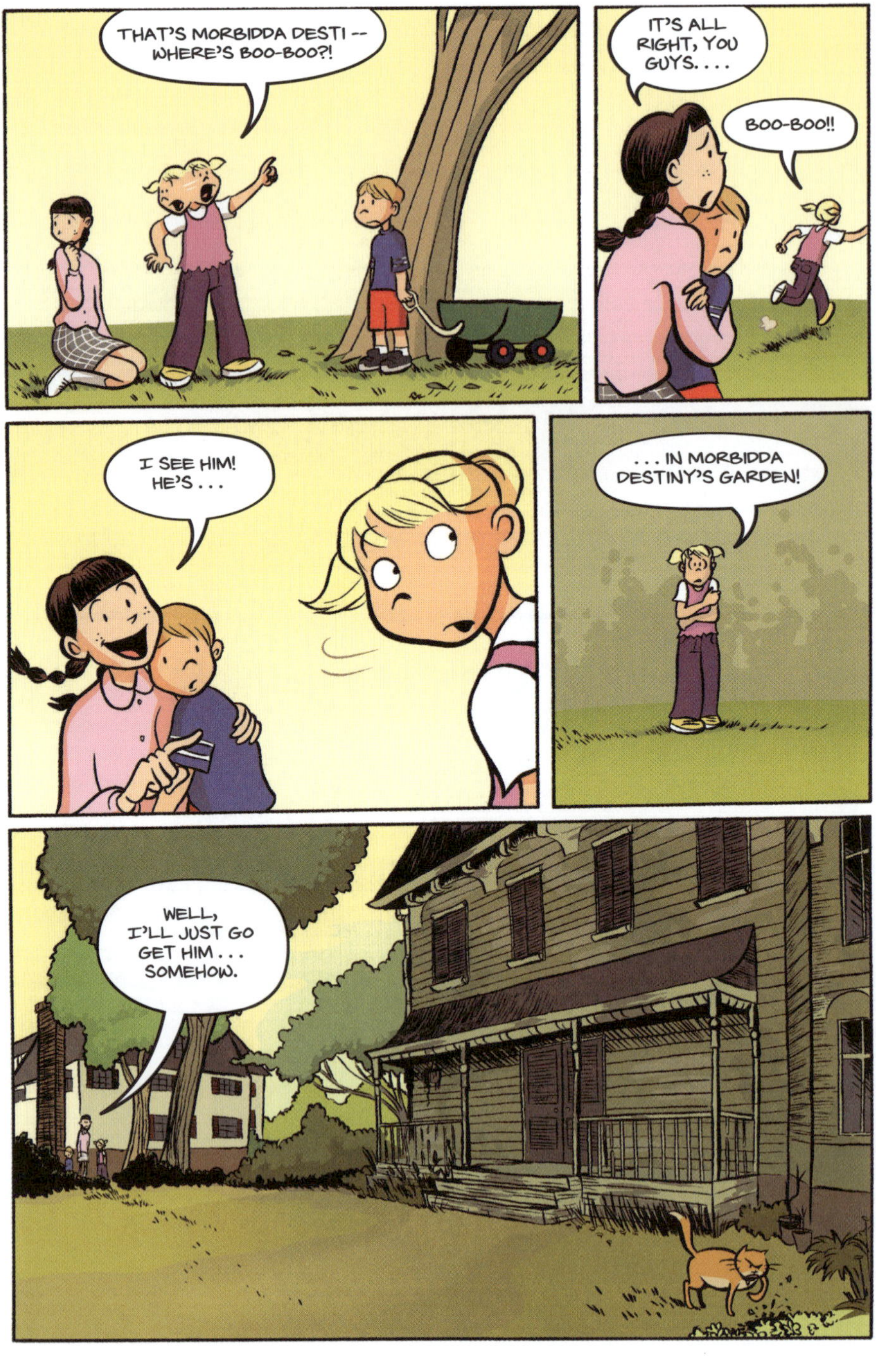
THAT'S MORBIDDA DESTI -- WHERE'S BOO-BOO?!
IT'S ALL RIGHT, YOU GUYS. . . .
BOO-BOO!!
I SEE HIM! HE'S . . .
. . . IN MORBIDDA DESTINY'S GARDEN!
WELL, I'LL JUST GO GET HIM . . . SOMEHOW.

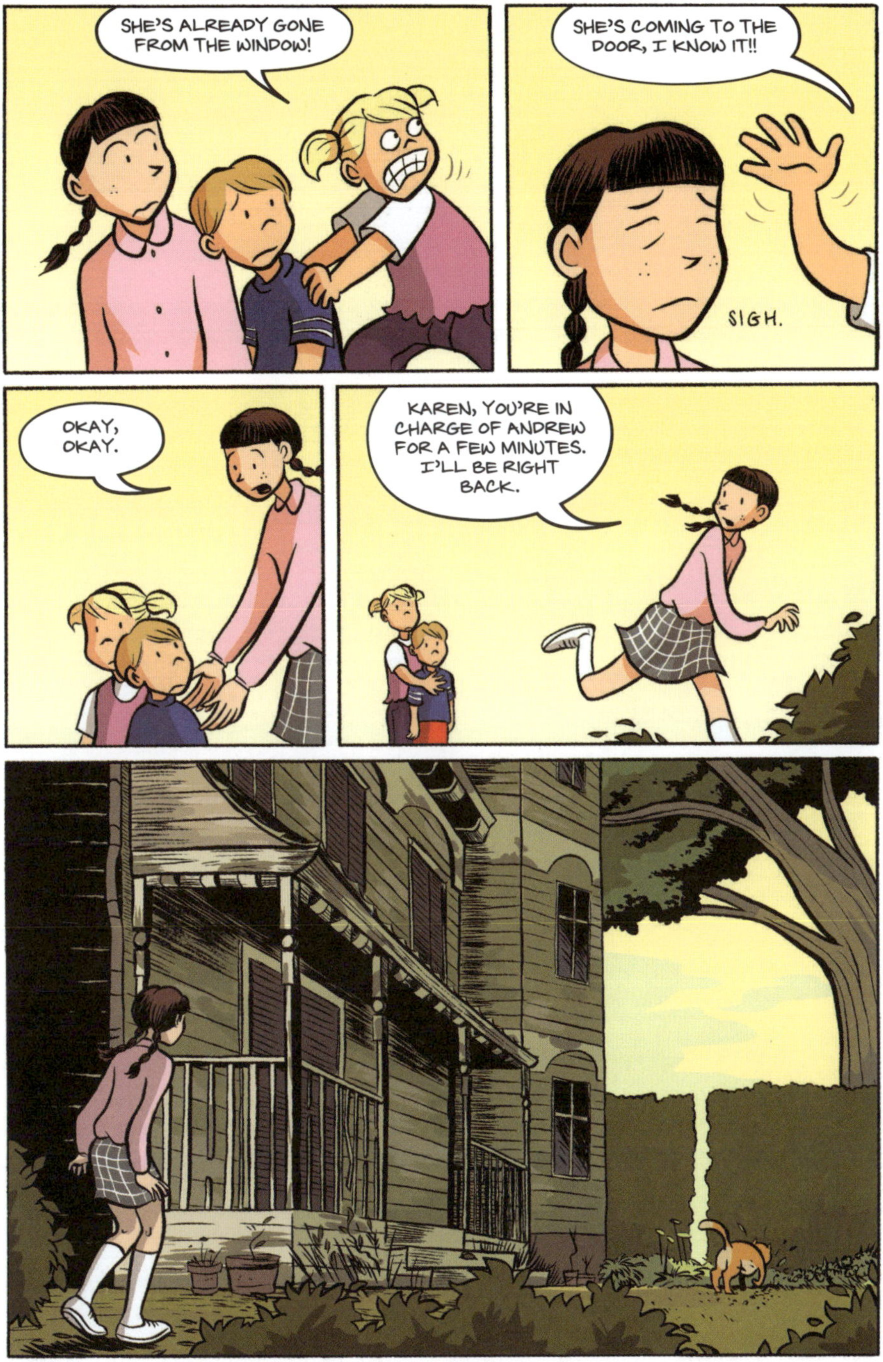
SHE'S ALREADY GONE FROM THE WINDOW!
SHE'S COMING TO THE DOOR, I KNOW IT!!
SIGH.
OKAY, OKAY.
KAREN, YOU'RE IN CHARGE OF ANDREW FOR A FEW MINUTES. I'LL BE RIGHT BACK.

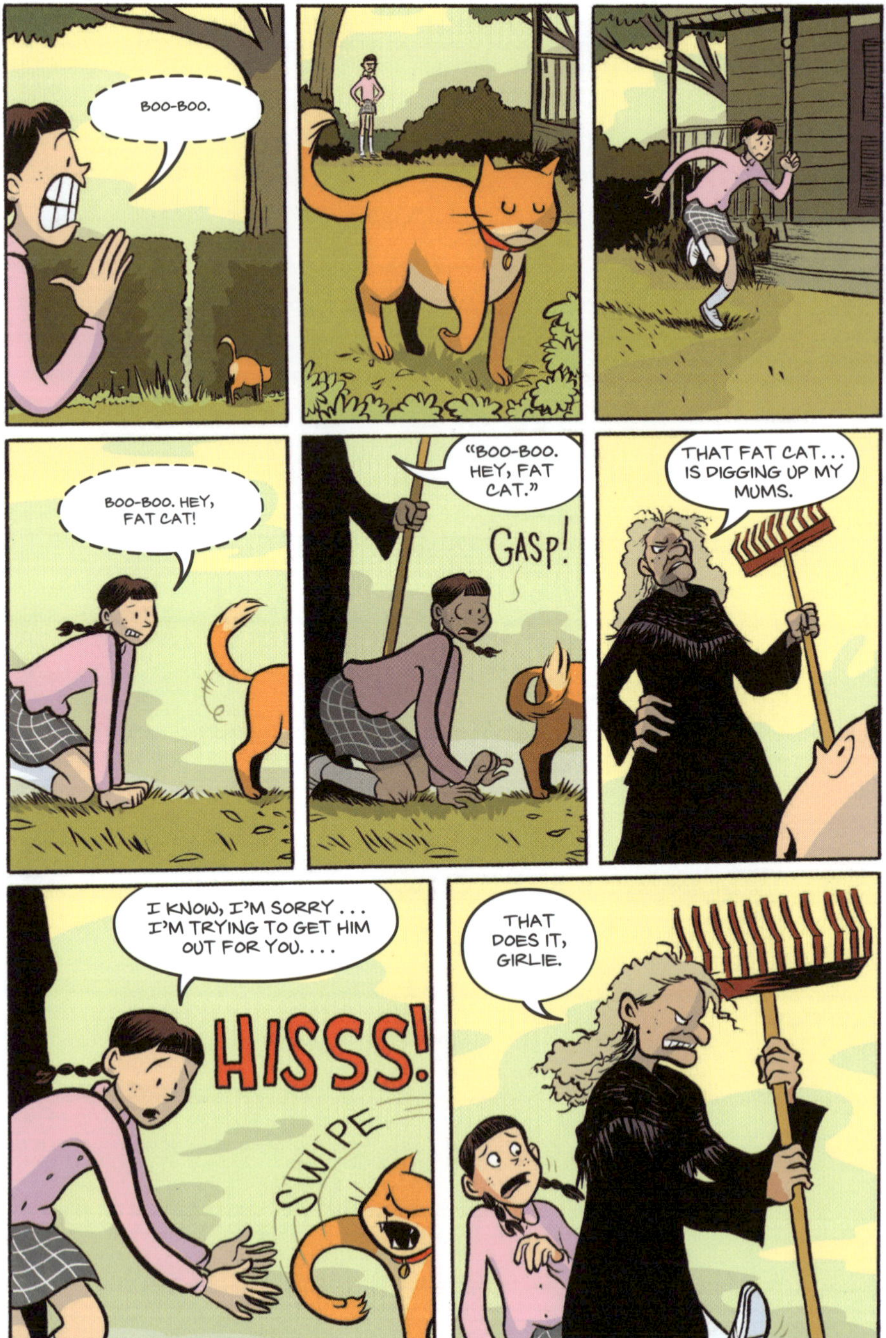
BOO-BOO.
BOO-BOO. HEY, FAT CAT!
"BOO-BOO. HEY, FAT CAT."
GASP!
THAT FAT CAT... IS DIGGING UP MY MUMS.
I KNOW, I'M SORRY . . . I'M TRYING TO GET HIM OUT FOR YOU. . . .
HISSS!
SWIPE
THAT DOES IT, GIRLIE.

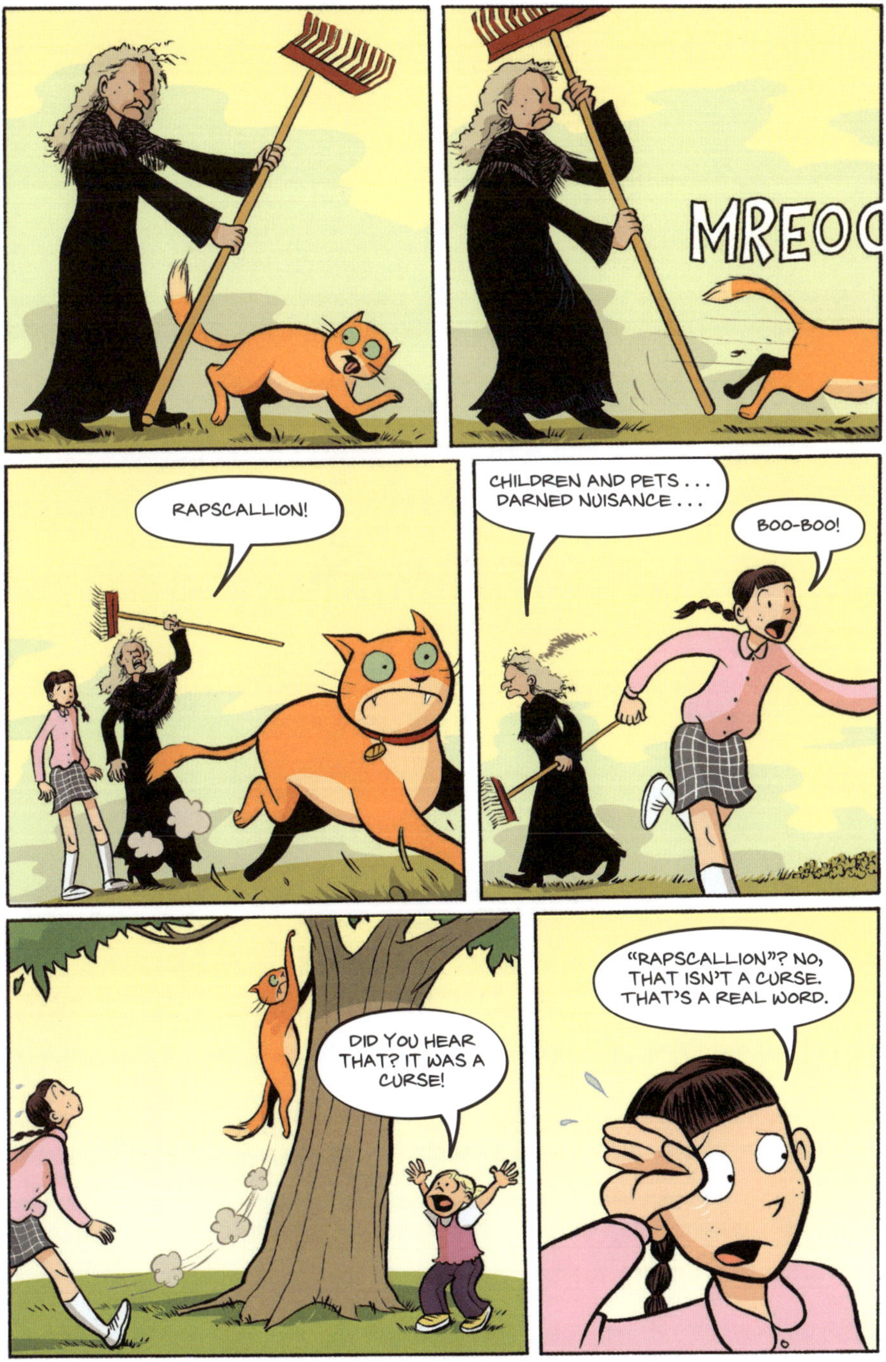
MREOO
RAPSCALLION!
CHILDREN AND PETS . . .
DARNED NUISANCE . . .
BOO-BOO!
DID YOU HEAR THAT? IT WAS A CURSE!
"RAPSCALLION"? NO, THAT ISN'T A CURSE. THAT'S A REAL WORD.

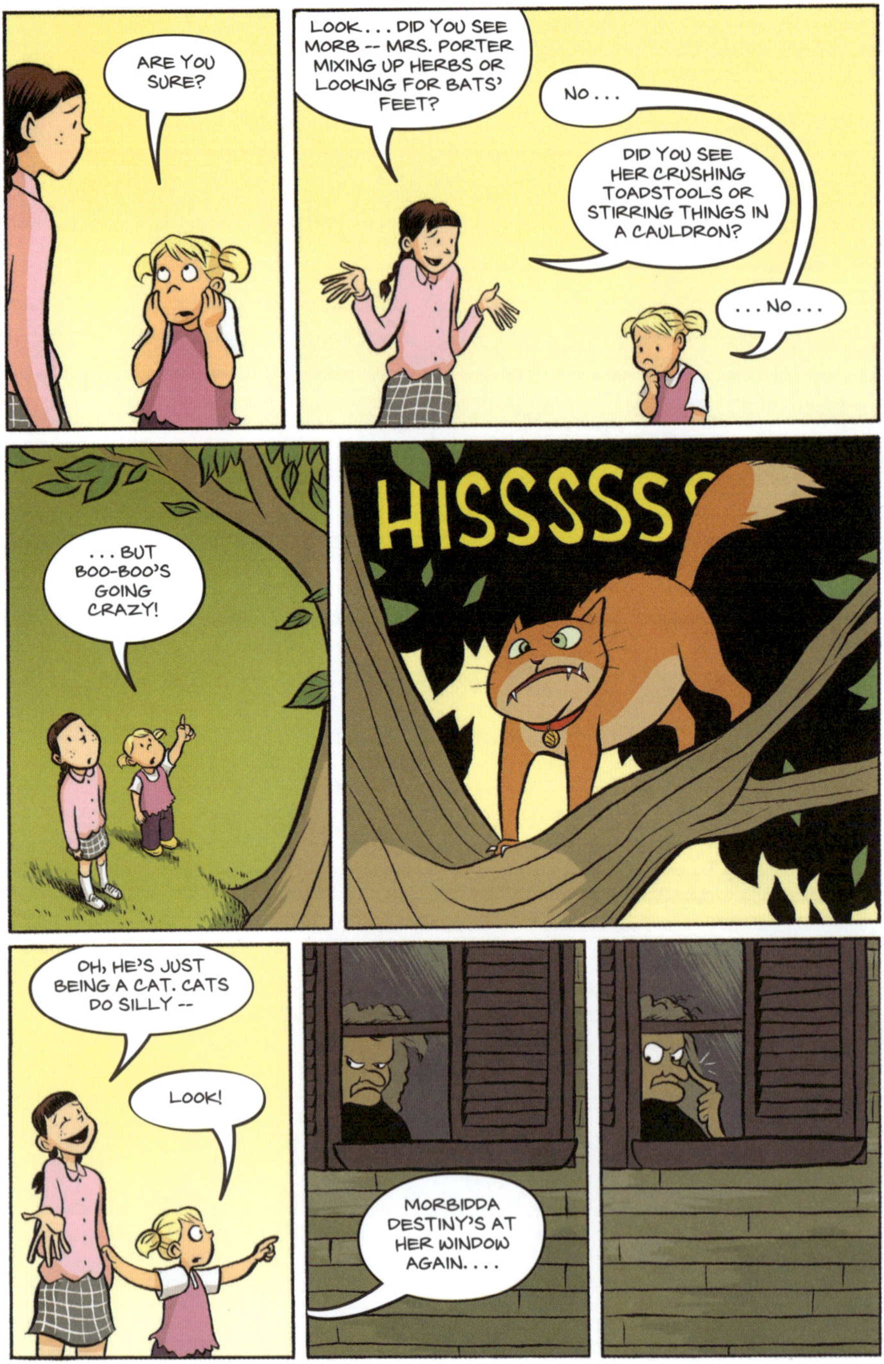
ARE YOU SURE?
LOOK . . . DID YOU SEE MORB -- MRS. PORTER MIXING UP HERBS OR LOOKING FOR BATS' FEET?
NO . . .
DID YOU SEE HER CRUSHING TOADSTOOLS OR STIRRING THINGS IN A CAULDRON?
. . . NO . . .
. . . BUT BOO-BOO'S GOING CRAZY!
HISSSSS
OH, HE'S JUST BEING A CAT. CATS DO SILLY --
LOOK!
MORBIDDA DESTINY'S AT HER WINDOW AGAIN. . . .

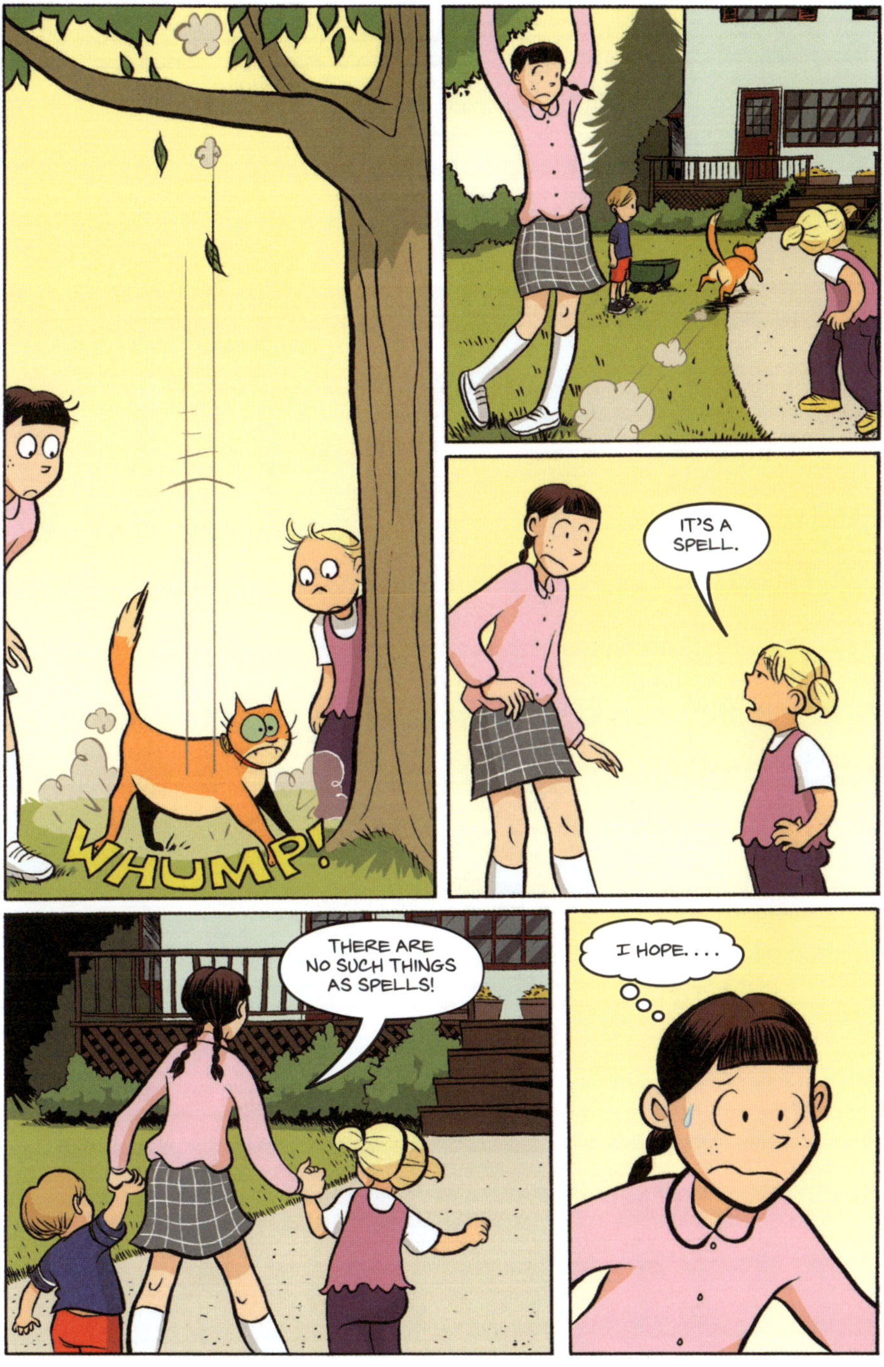
WHUMP!
IT'S A SPELL.
THERE ARE NO SUCH THINGS AS SPELLS!
I HOPE. . . .

CHAPTER 10

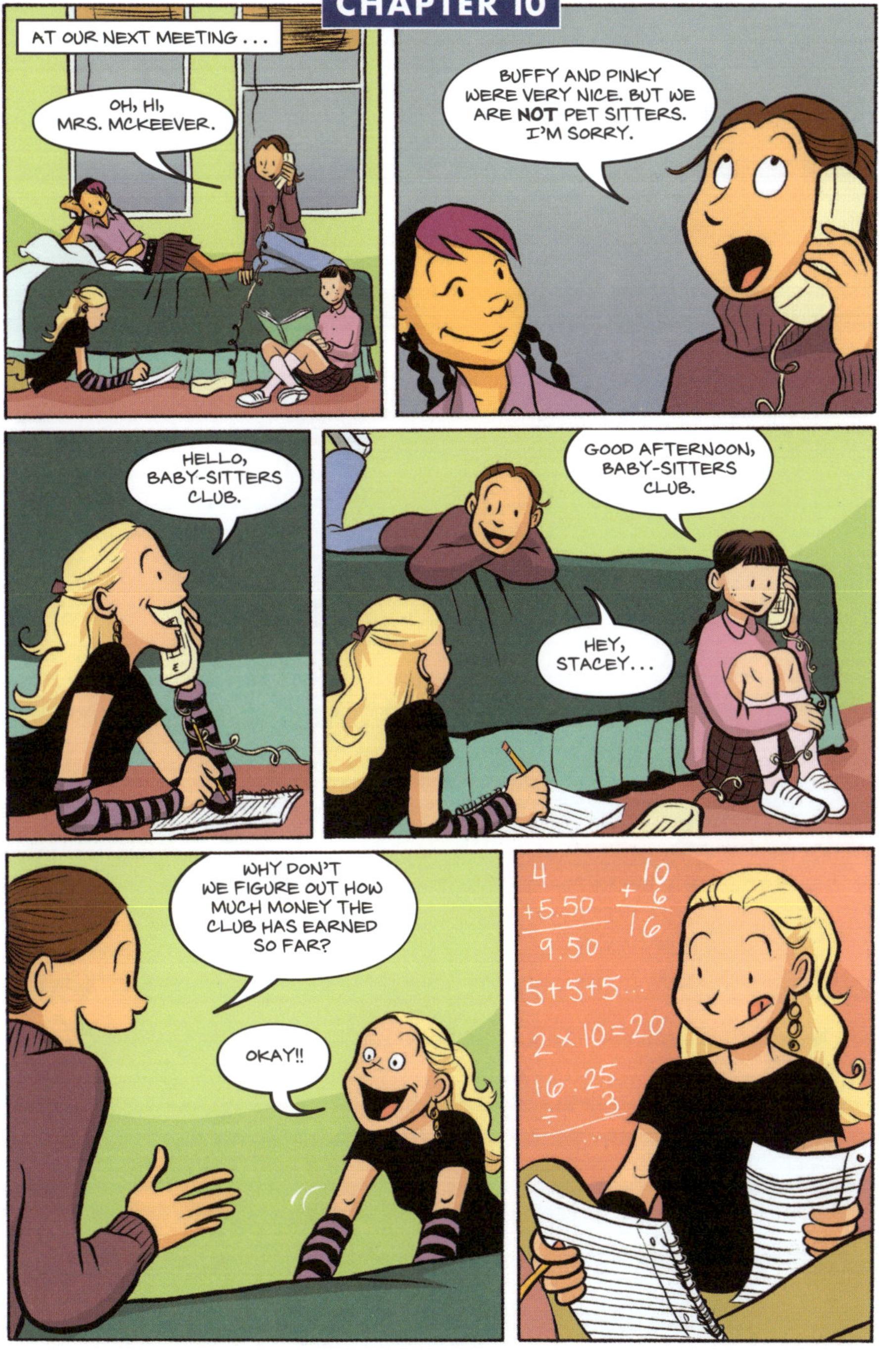

AT OUR NEXT MEETING . . .
OH, HI, MRS. MCKEEVER.
BUFFY AND PINKY WERE VERY NICE. BUT WE ARE NOT PET SITTERS. I'M SORRY.
HELLO, BABY-SITTERS CLUB.
GOOD AFTERNOON, BABY-SITTERS CLUB.
HEY, STACEY...
WHY DON'T WE FIGURE OUT HOW MUCH MONEY THE CLUB HAS EARNED SO FAR?
OKAY!!
4
+5.50
9.50
10
+6
16
5+5+5...
2×10=20
16.25
÷ 3

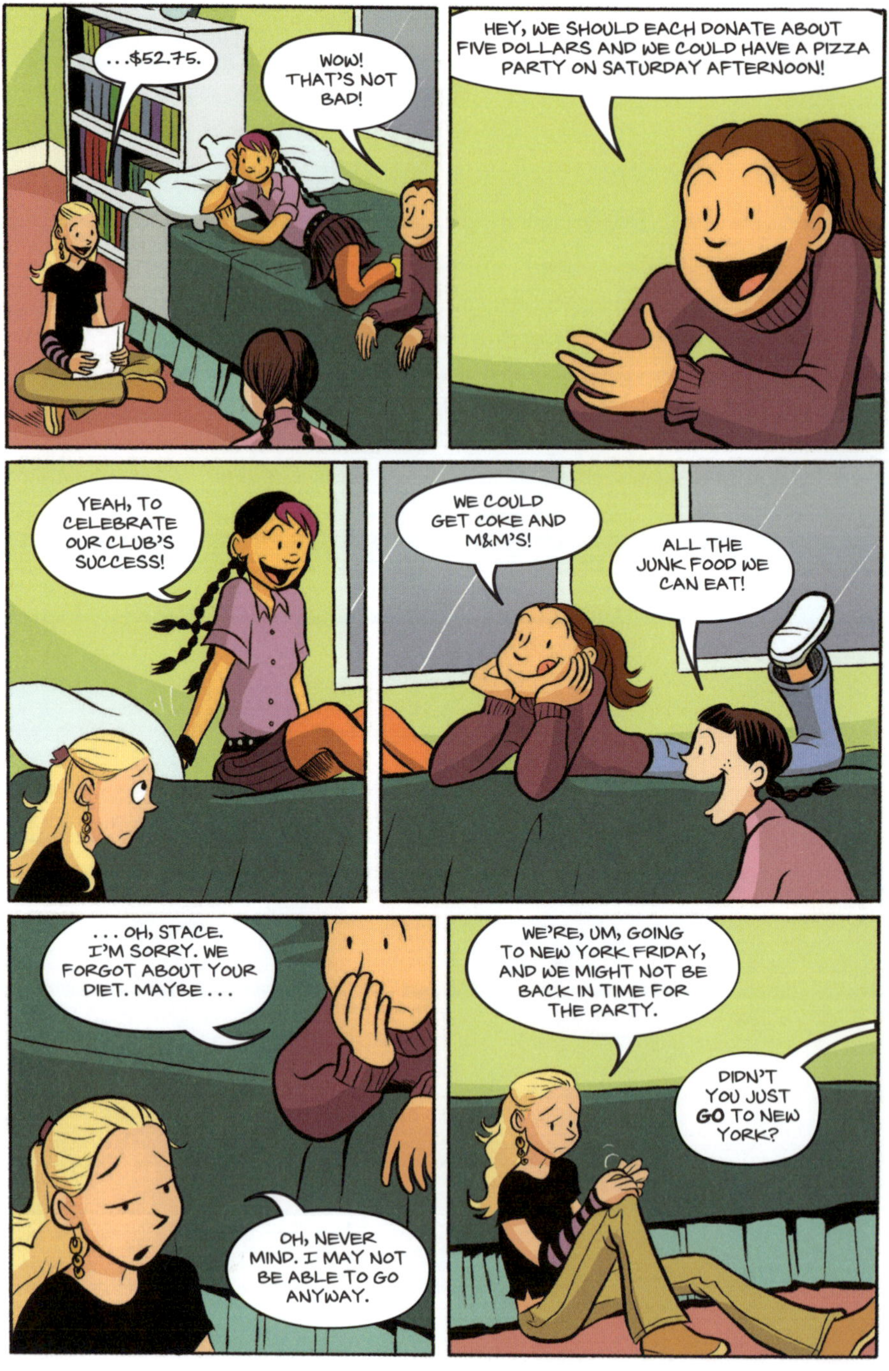

. . . $52.75.
WOW! THAT'S NOT BAD!
HEY, WE SHOULD EACH DONATE ABOUT FIVE DOLLARS AND WE COULD HAVE A PIZZA PARTY ON SATURDAY AFTERNOON!
YEAH, TO CELEBRATE OUR CLUB'S SUCCESS!
WE COULD GET COKE AND M&M'S!
ALL THE JUNK FOOD WE CAN EAT!
. . . OH, STACE. I'M SORRY. WE FORGOT ABOUT YOUR DIET. MAYBE . . .
OH, NEVER MIND. I MAY NOT BE ABLE TO GO ANYWAY.
WE'RE, UM, GOING TO NEW YORK FRIDAY, AND WE MIGHT NOT BE BACK IN TIME FOR THE PARTY.
DIDN'T YOU JUST **GO** TO NEW YORK?

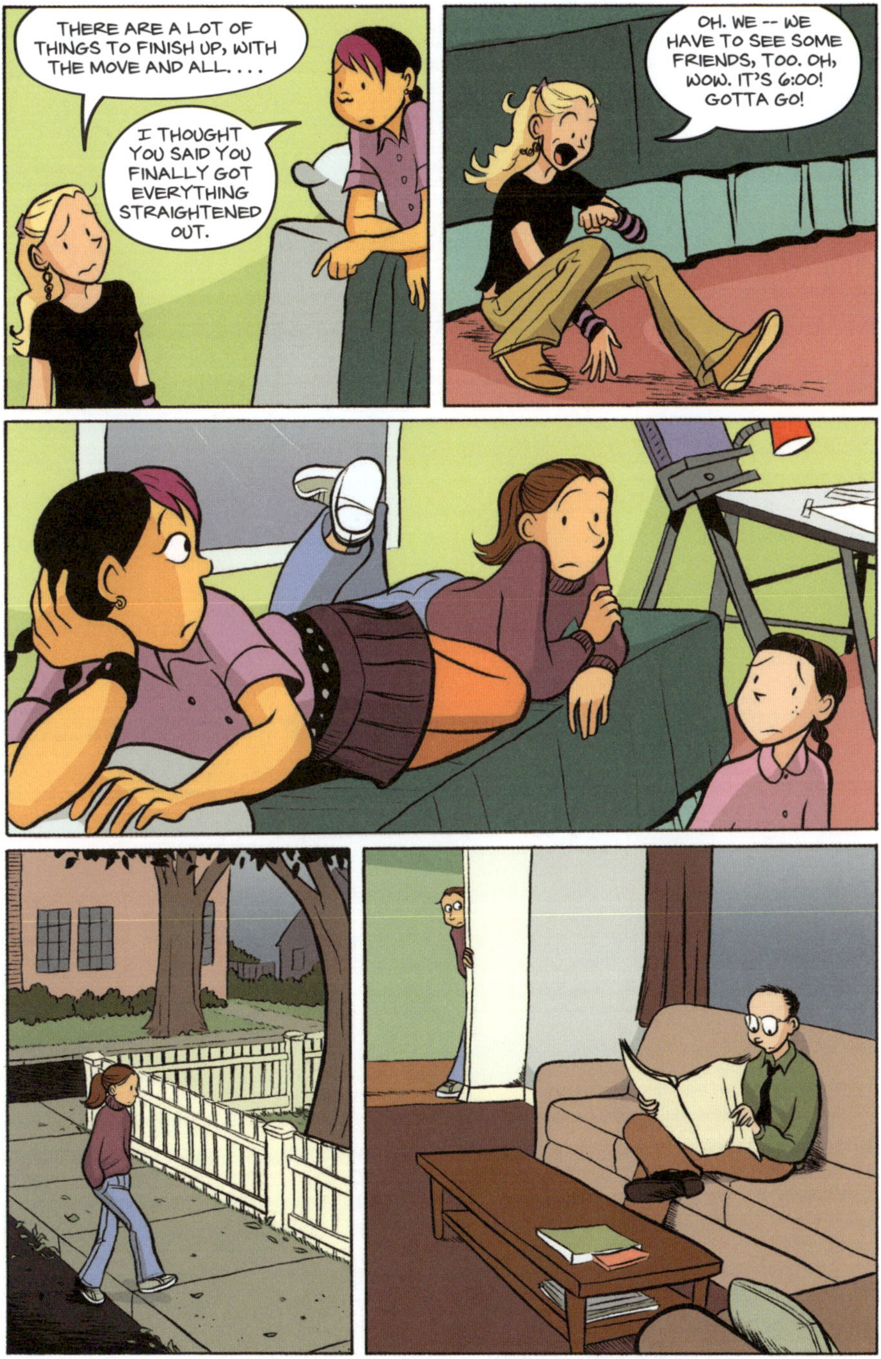
THERE ARE A LOT OF THINGS TO FINISH UP, WITH THE MOVE AND ALL. . . .
I THOUGHT YOU SAID YOU FINALLY GOT EVERYTHING STRAIGHTENED OUT.
OH. WE -- WE HAVE TO SEE SOME FRIENDS, TOO. OH, WOW. IT'S 6:00! GOTTA GO!

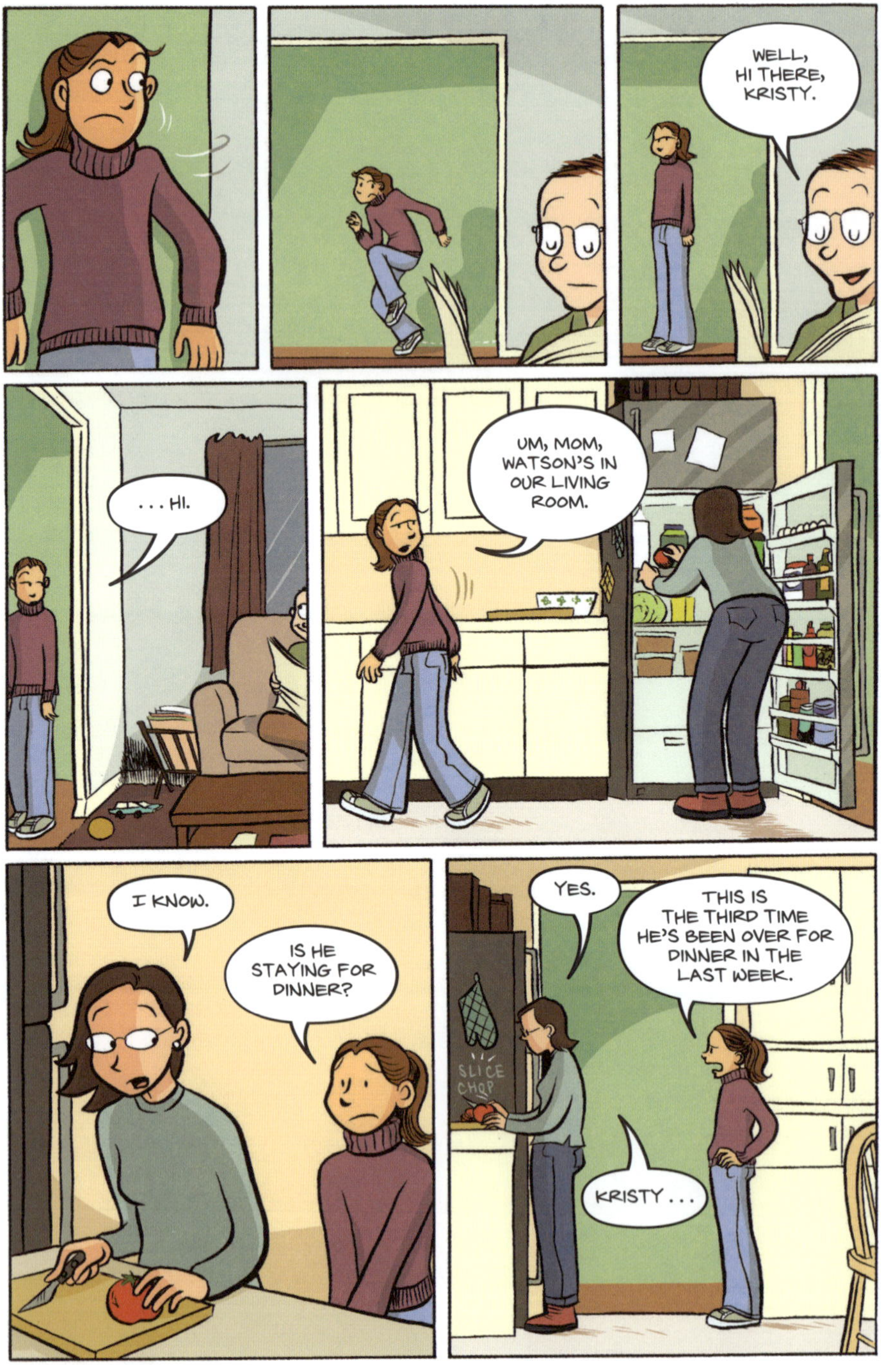
WELL, HI THERE, KRISTY.
. . . HI.
UM, MOM, WATSON'S IN OUR LIVING ROOM.
I KNOW.
IS HE STAYING FOR DINNER?
YES.
THIS IS THE THIRD TIME HE'S BEEN OVER FOR DINNER IN THE LAST WEEK.
KRISTY . . .
SLICE CHOP

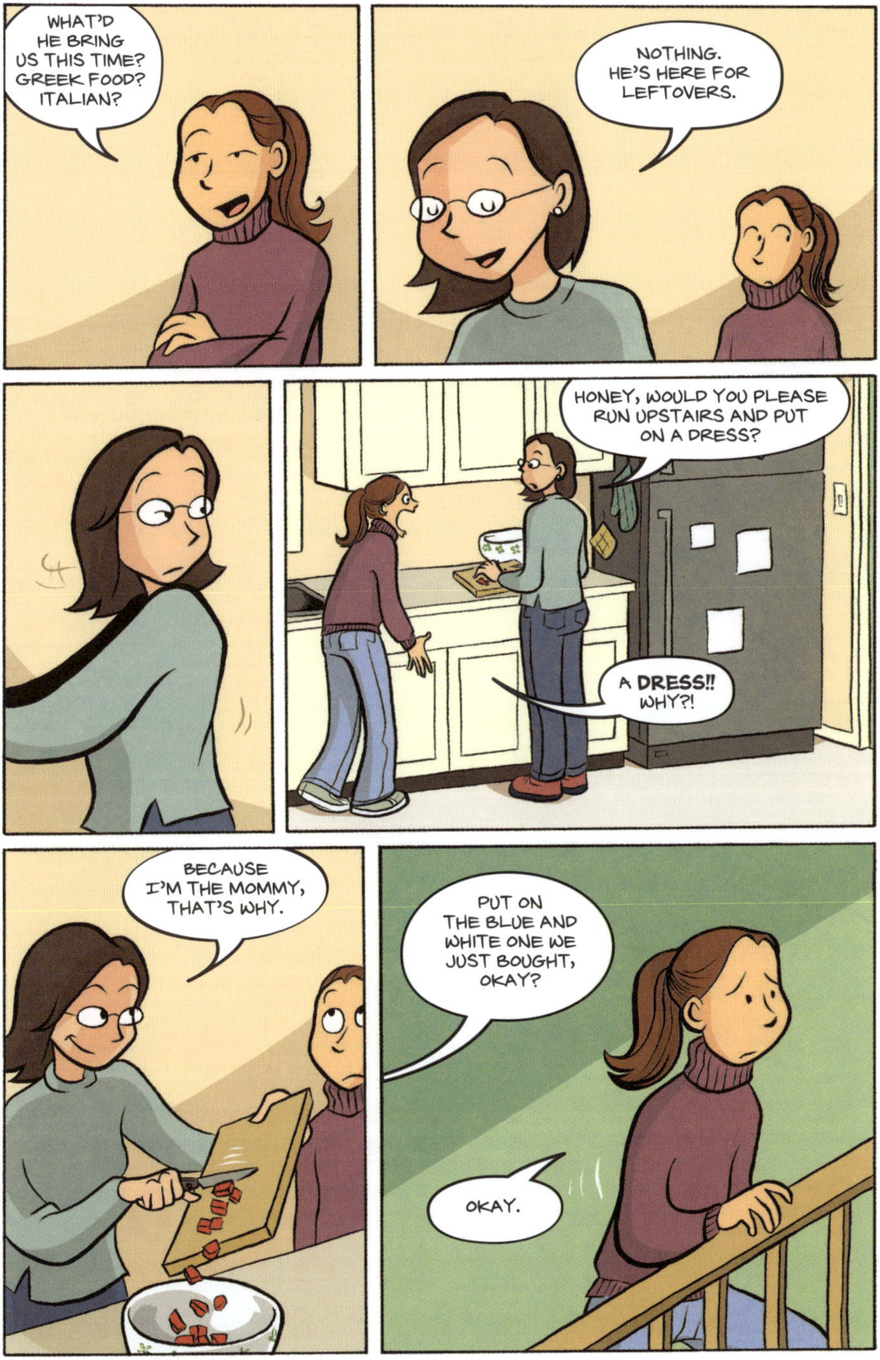
WHAT'D HE BRING US THIS TIME? GREEK FOOD? ITALIAN?
NOTHING. HE'S HERE FOR LEFTOVERS.
HONEY, WOULD YOU PLEASE RUN UPSTAIRS AND PUT ON A DRESS?
A **DRESS!!** WHY?!
BECAUSE I'M THE MOMMY, THAT'S WHY.
PUT ON THE BLUE AND WHITE ONE WE JUST BOUGHT, OKAY?
OKAY.

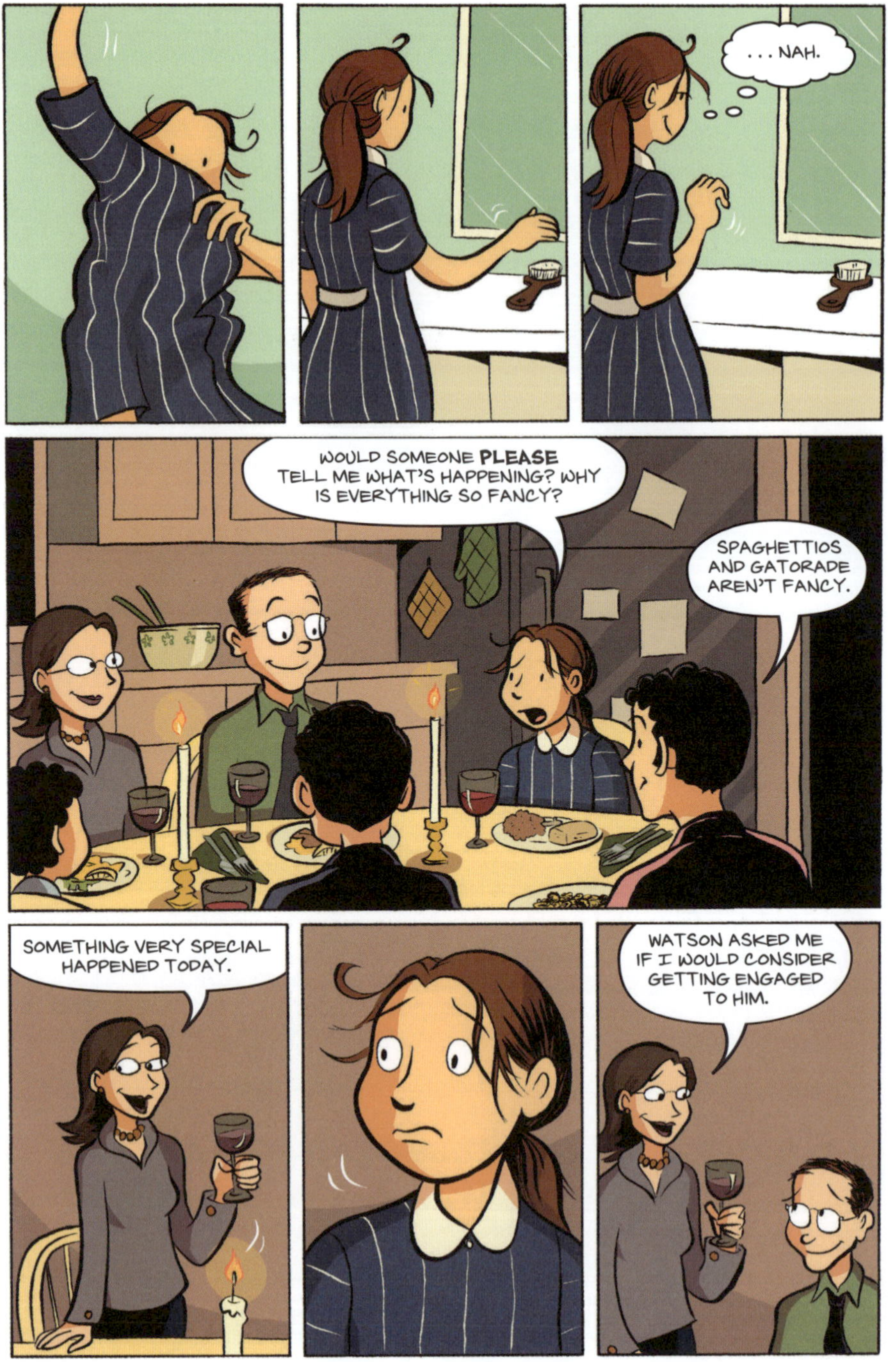
. . . NAH.
WOULD SOMEONE **PLEASE** TELL ME WHAT'S HAPPENING? WHY IS EVERYTHING SO FANCY?
SPAGHETTIOS AND GATORADE AREN'T FANCY.
SOMETHING VERY SPECIAL HAPPENED TODAY.
WATSON ASKED ME IF I WOULD CONSIDER GETTING ENGAGED TO HIM.

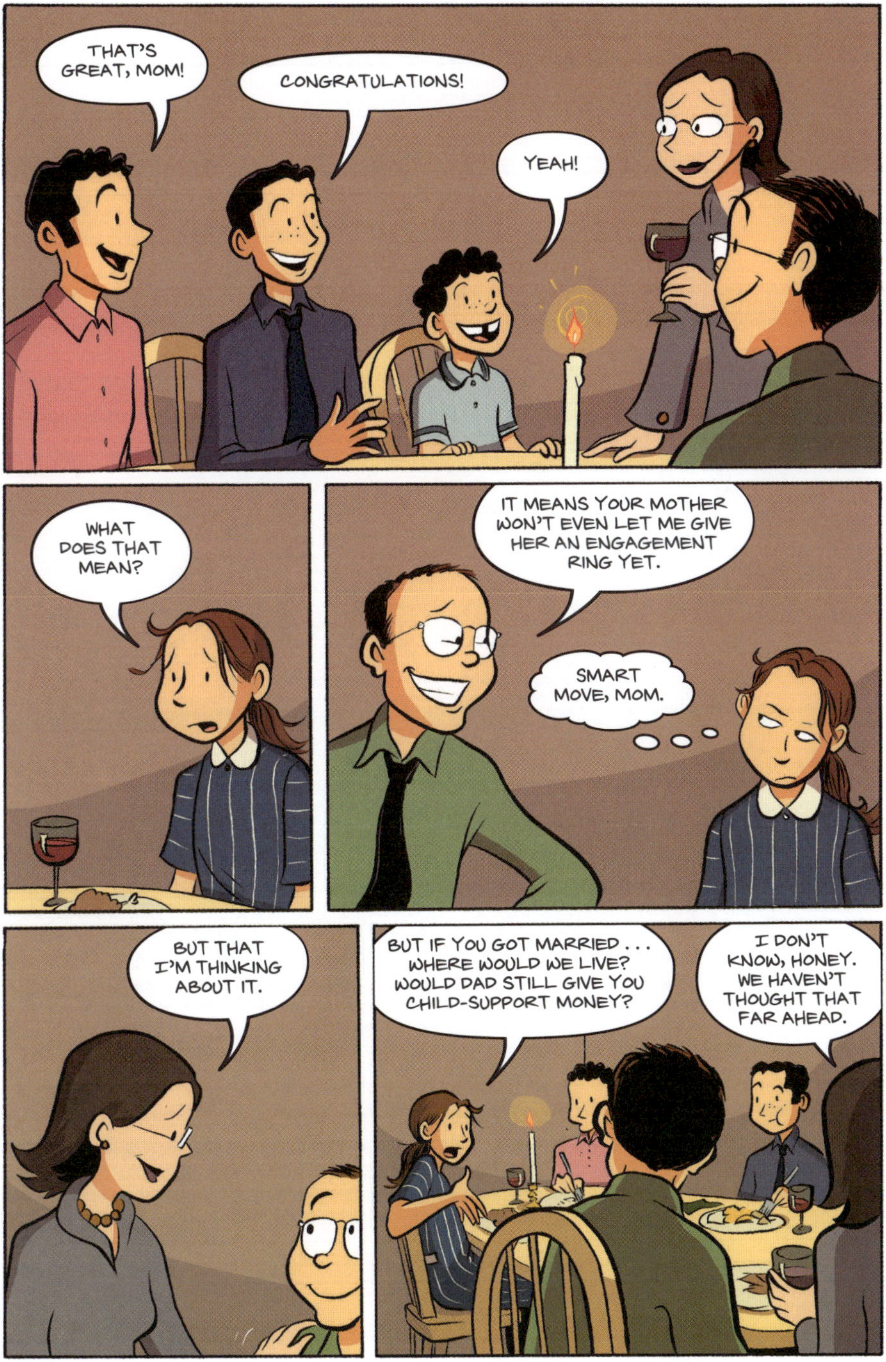

THAT'S GREAT, MOM!
CONGRATULATIONS!
YEAH!
WHAT DOES THAT MEAN?
IT MEANS YOUR MOTHER WON'T EVEN LET ME GIVE HER AN ENGAGEMENT RING YET.
SMART MOVE, MOM.
BUT THAT I'M THINKING ABOUT IT.
BUT IF YOU GOT MARRIED . . . WHERE WOULD WE LIVE? WOULD DAD STILL GIVE YOU CHILD-SUPPORT MONEY?
I DON'T KNOW, HONEY. WE HAVEN'T THOUGHT THAT FAR AHEAD.

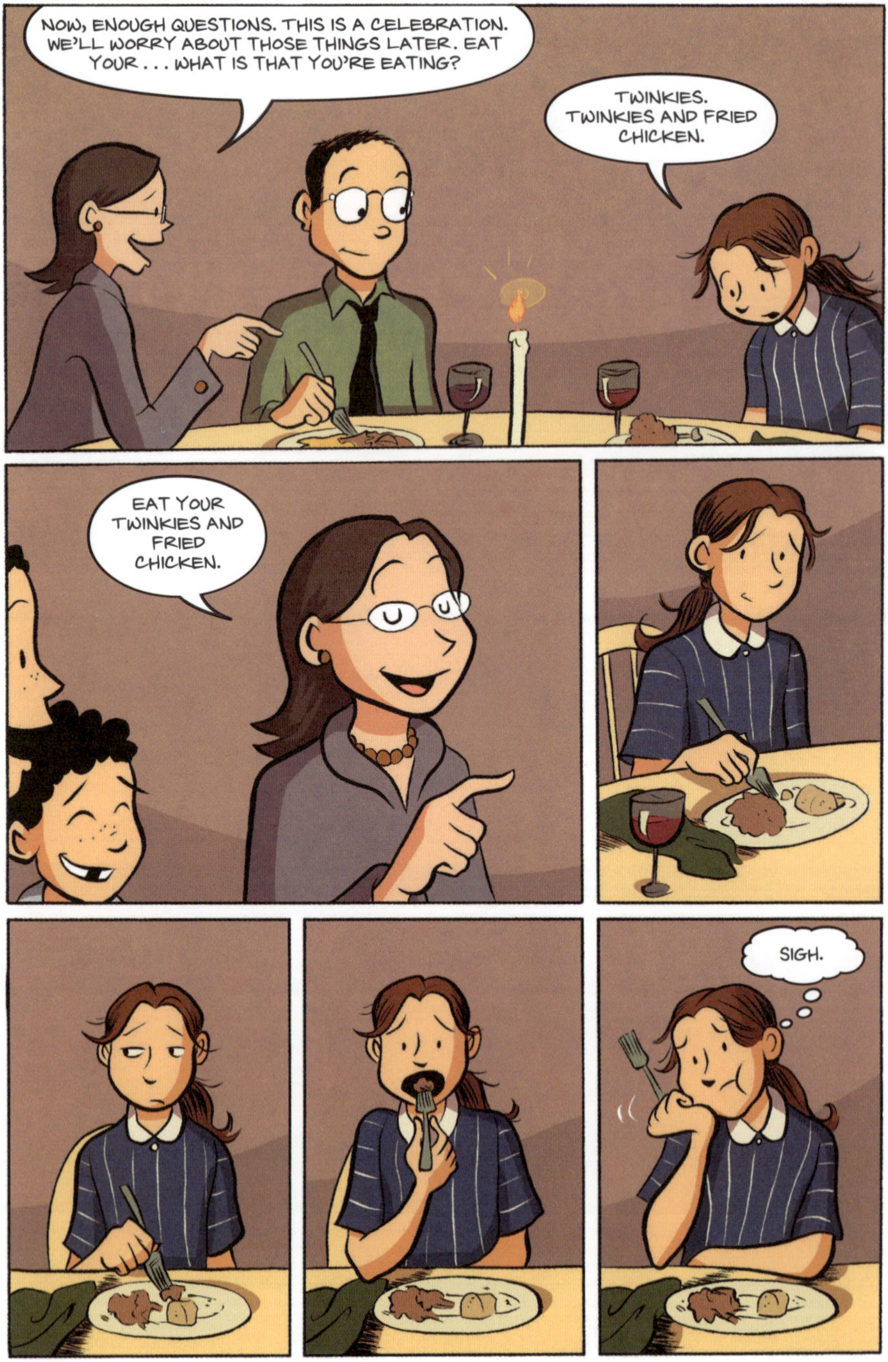
NOW, ENOUGH QUESTIONS. THIS IS A CELEBRATION. WE'LL WORRY ABOUT THOSE THINGS LATER. EAT YOUR . . . WHAT IS THAT YOU'RE EATING?
TWINKIES. TWINKIES AND FRIED CHICKEN.
EAT YOUR TWINKIES AND FRIED CHICKEN.
SIGH.

CHAPTER 11

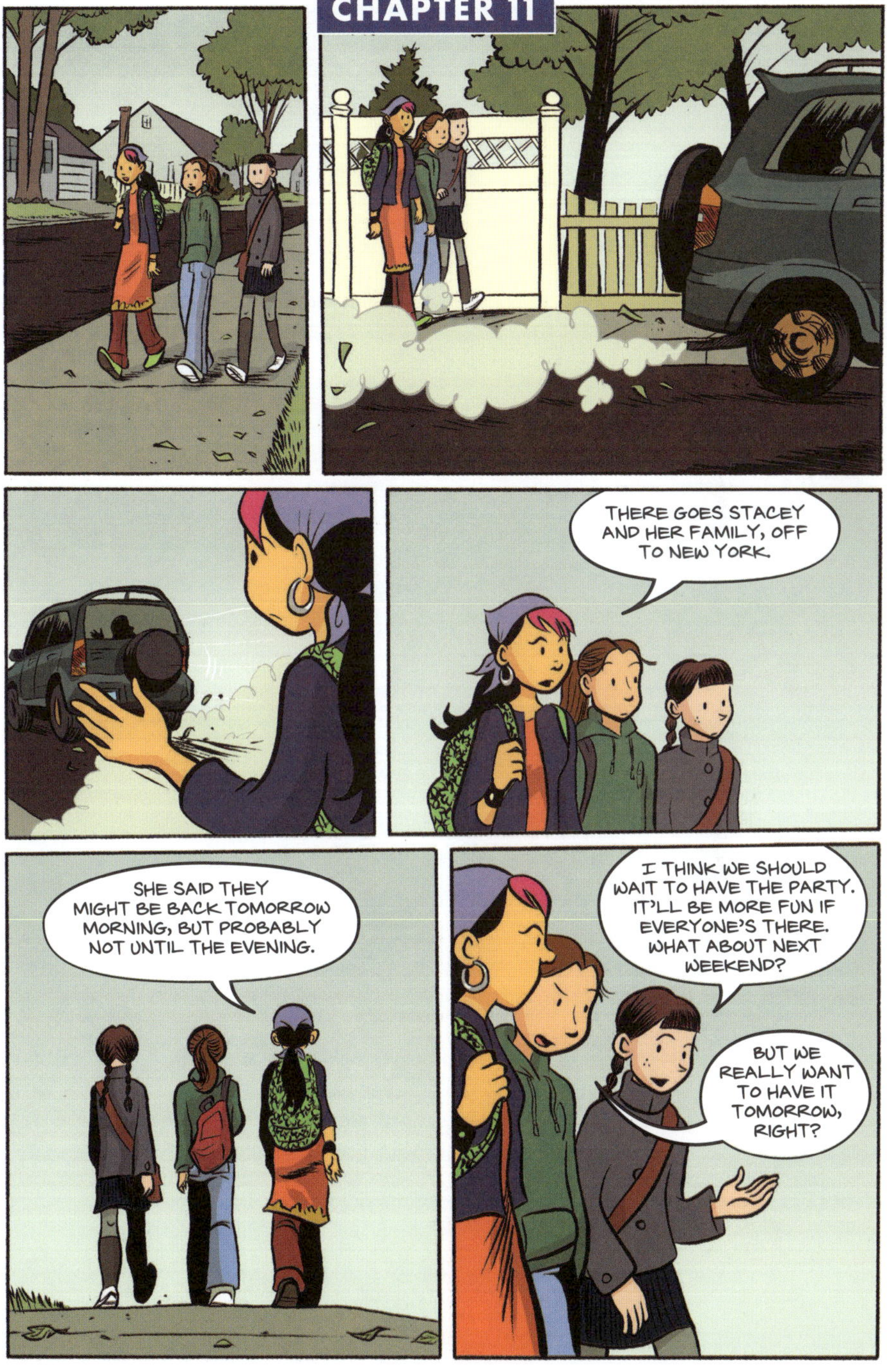
THERE GOES STACEY AND HER FAMILY, OFF TO NEW YORK.
SHE SAID THEY MIGHT BE BACK TOMORROW MORNING, BUT PROBABLY NOT UNTIL THE EVENING.
I THINK WE SHOULD WAIT TO HAVE THE PARTY. IT'LL BE MORE FUN IF EVERYONE'S THERE. WHAT ABOUT NEXT WEEKEND?
BUT WE REALLY WANT TO HAVE IT TOMORROW, RIGHT?

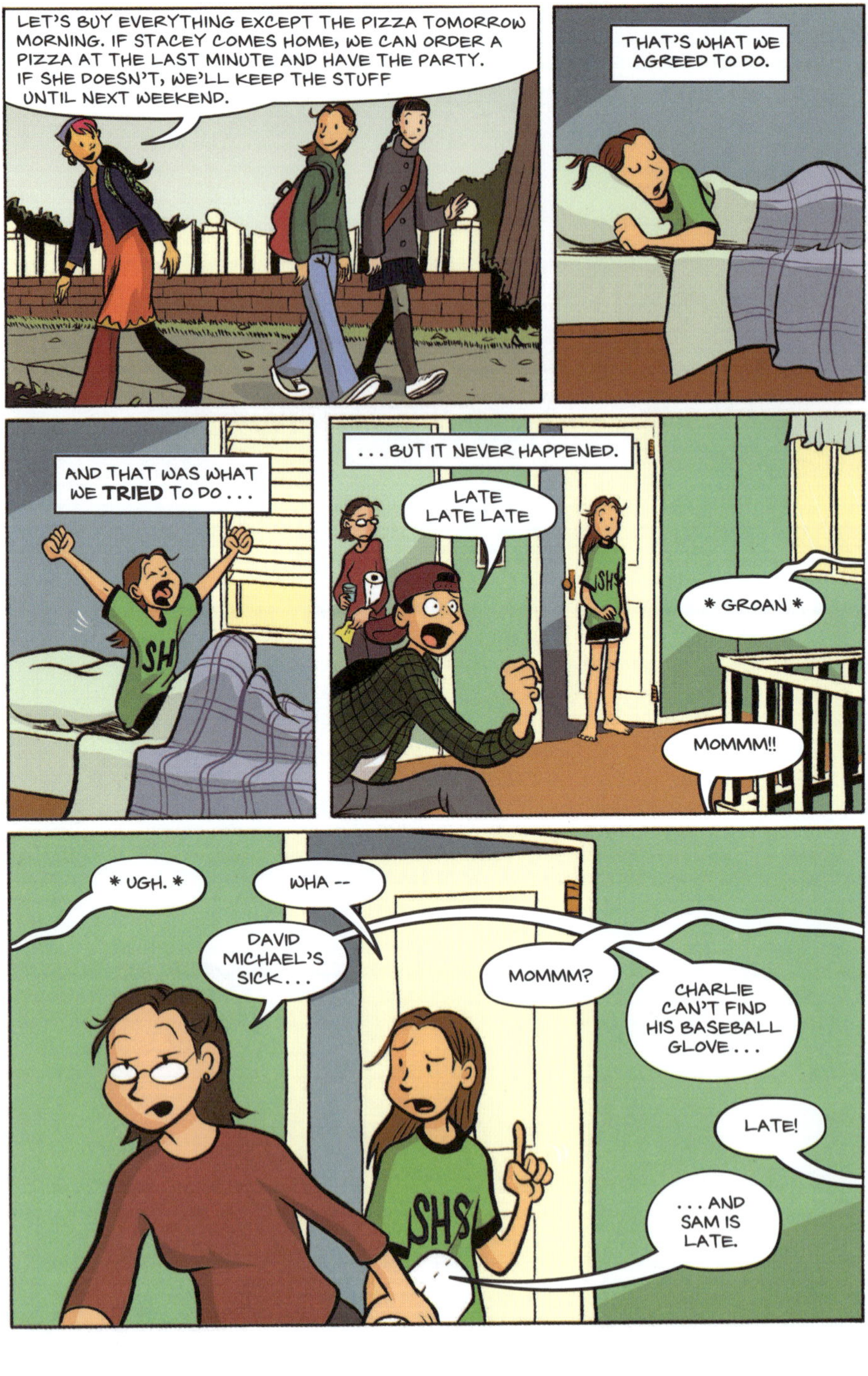
LET'S BUY EVERYTHING EXCEPT THE PIZZA TOMORROW MORNING. IF STACEY COMES HOME, WE CAN ORDER A PIZZA AT THE LAST MINUTE AND HAVE THE PARTY. IF SHE DOESN'T, WE'LL KEEP THE STUFF UNTIL NEXT WEEKEND.
THAT'S WHAT WE AGREED TO DO.
AND THAT WAS WHAT WE **TRIED** TO DO . . .
. . . BUT IT NEVER HAPPENED.
LATE LATE LATE
* GROAN *
MOMMM!!
* UGH. *
WHA --
DAVID MICHAEL'S SICK . . .
MOMMM?
CHARLIE CAN'T FIND HIS BASEBALL GLOVE . . .
LATE!
. . . AND SAM IS LATE.

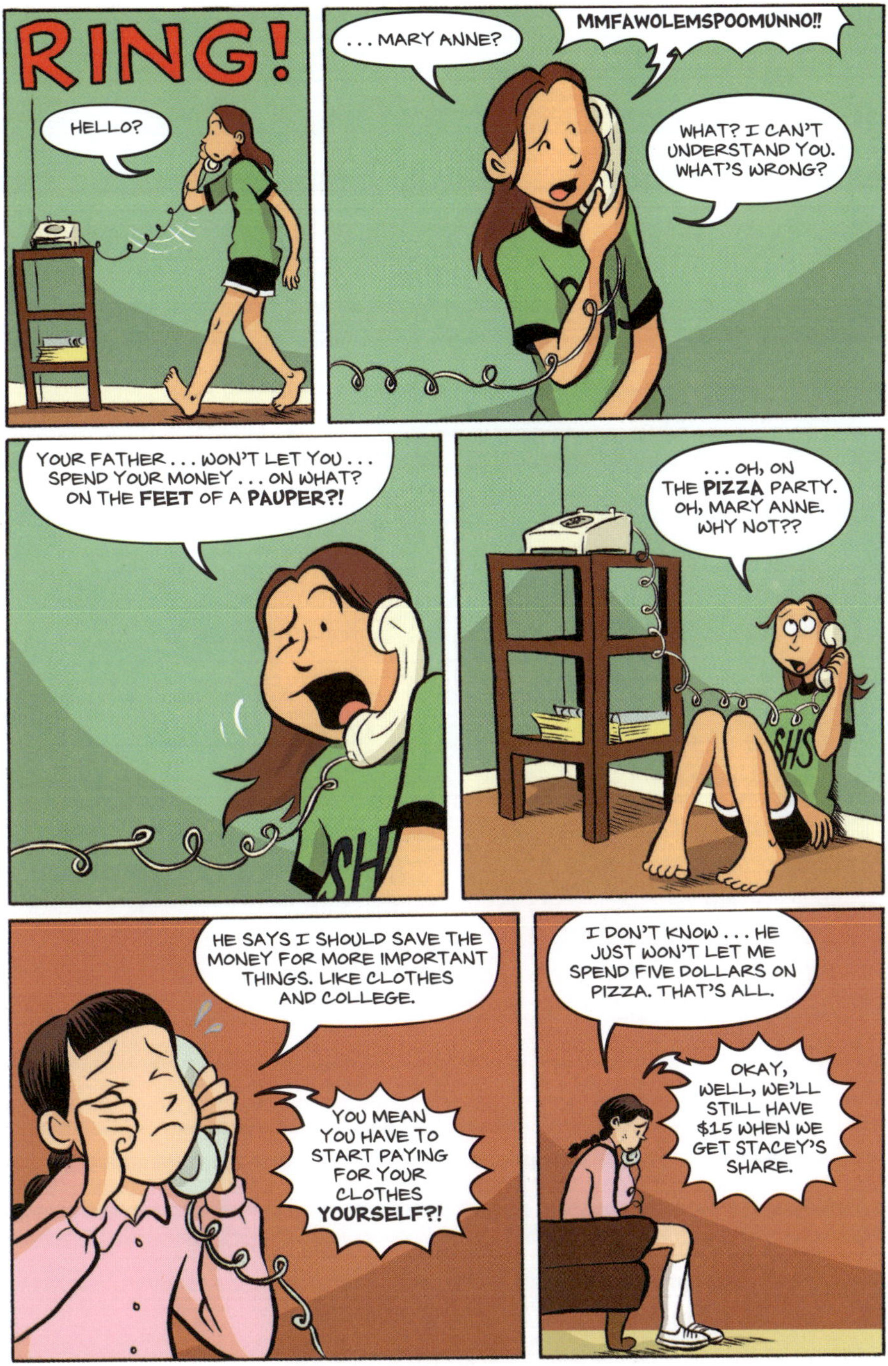
RING!
HELLO?
. . . MARY ANNE?
MMFAWOLEMSPOOMUNNO!!
WHAT? I CAN'T UNDERSTAND YOU. WHAT'S WRONG?
YOUR FATHER . . . WON'T LET YOU . . . SPEND YOUR MONEY . . . ON WHAT? ON THE **FEET** OF A **PAUPER?!**
. . . OH, ON THE **PIZZA** PARTY. OH, MARY ANNE. WHY NOT??
HE SAYS I SHOULD SAVE THE MONEY FOR MORE IMPORTANT THINGS. LIKE CLOTHES AND COLLEGE.
YOU MEAN YOU HAVE TO START PAYING FOR YOUR CLOTHES **YOURSELF?!**
I DON'T KNOW . . . HE JUST WON'T LET ME SPEND FIVE DOLLARS ON PIZZA. THAT'S ALL.
OKAY, WELL, WE'LL STILL HAVE $15 WHEN WE GET STACEY'S SHARE.

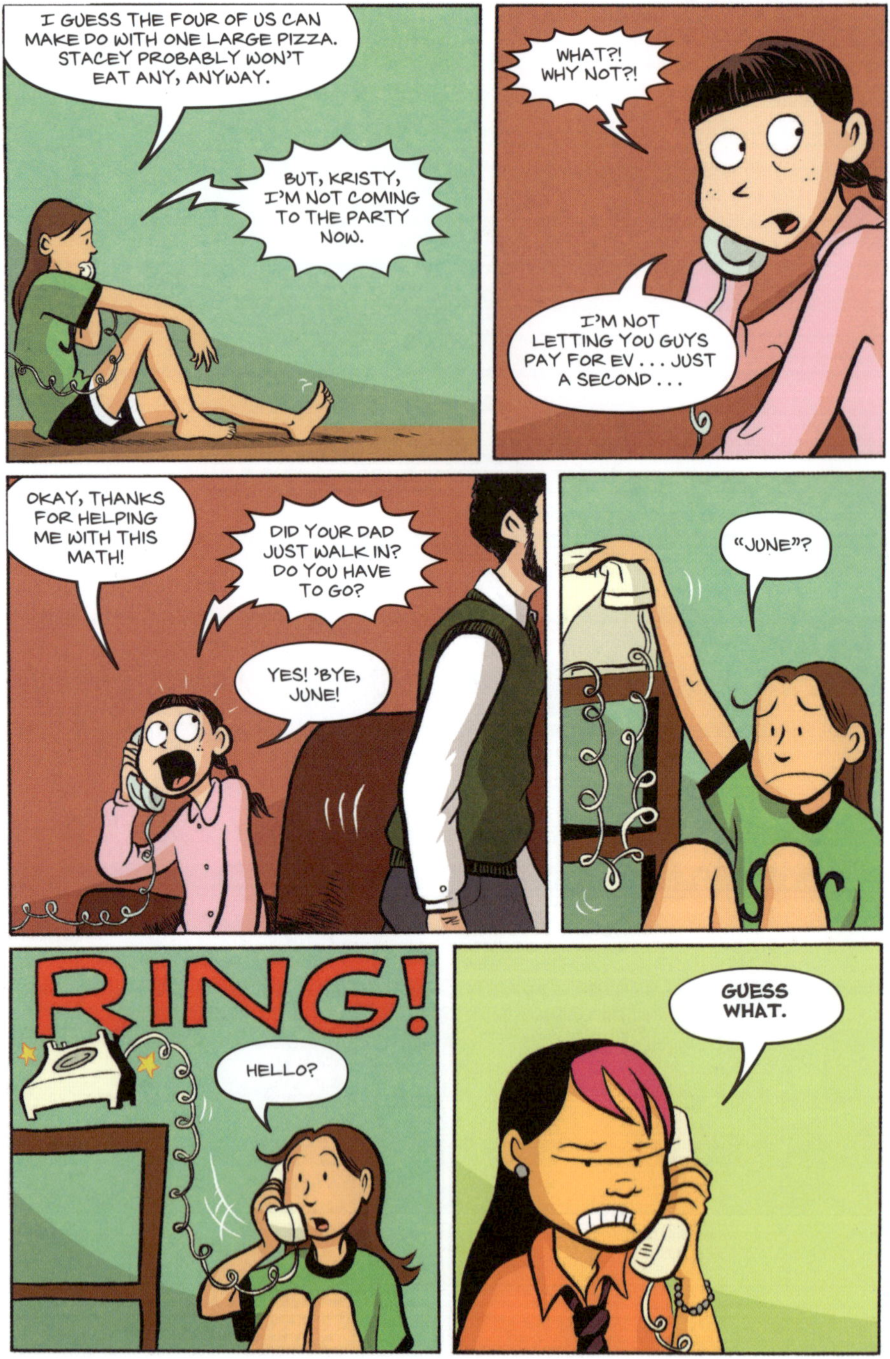
I GUESS THE FOUR OF US CAN MAKE DO WITH ONE LARGE PIZZA. STACEY PROBABLY WON'T EAT ANY, ANYWAY.
BUT, KRISTY, I'M NOT COMING TO THE PARTY NOW.
WHAT?! WHY NOT?!
I'M NOT LETTING YOU GUYS PAY FOR EV . . . JUST A SECOND . . .
OKAY, THANKS FOR HELPING ME WITH THIS MATH!
DID YOUR DAD JUST WALK IN? DO YOU HAVE TO GO?
YES! 'BYE, JUNE!
"JUNE"?
RING!
HELLO?
GUESS WHAT.

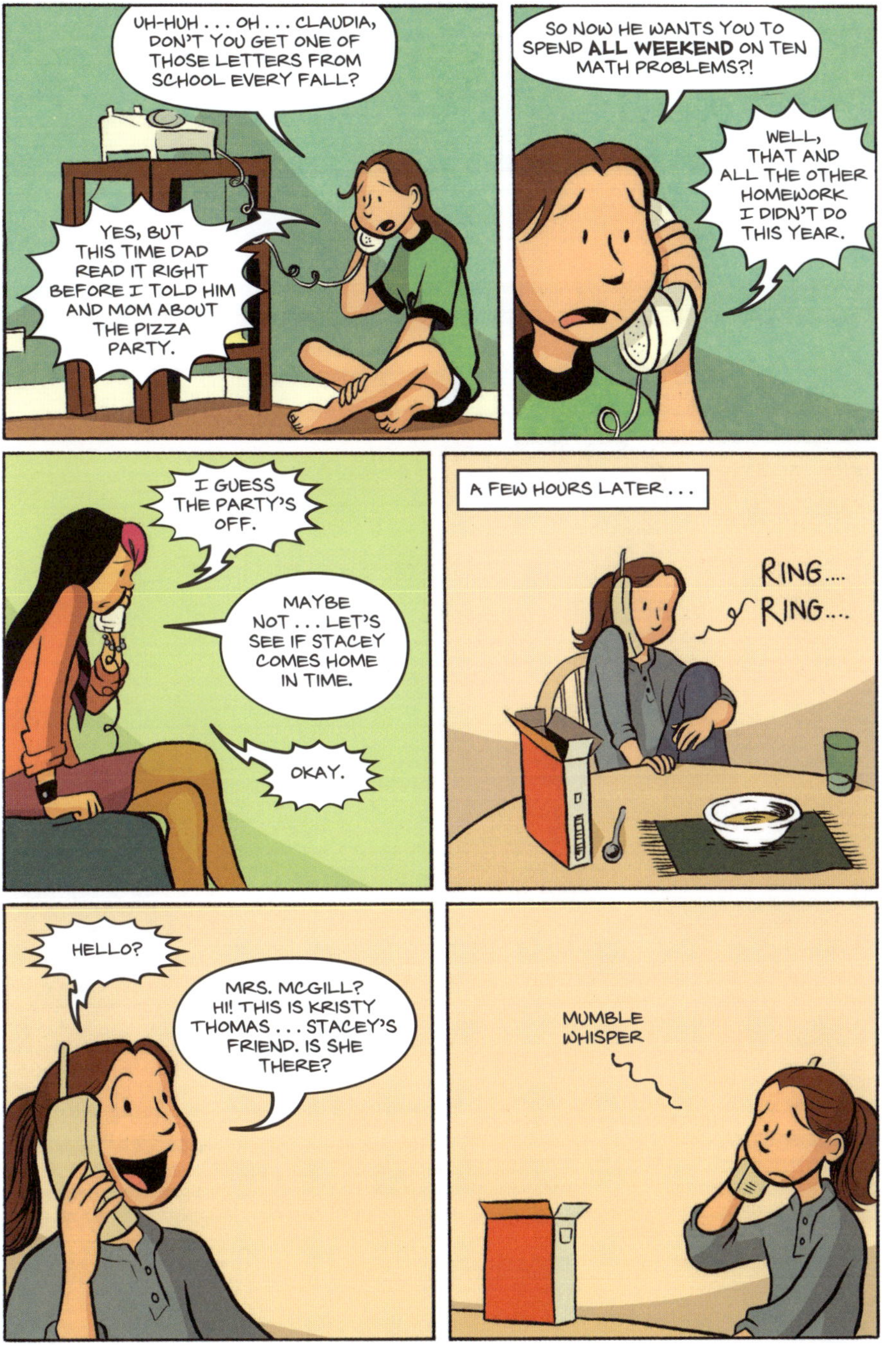
UH-HUH . . . OH . . . CLAUDIA, DON'T YOU GET ONE OF THOSE LETTERS FROM SCHOOL EVERY FALL?
YES, BUT THIS TIME DAD READ IT RIGHT BEFORE I TOLD HIM AND MOM ABOUT THE PIZZA PARTY.
SO NOW HE WANTS YOU TO SPEND **ALL WEEKEND** ON TEN MATH PROBLEMS?!
WELL, THAT AND ALL THE OTHER HOMEWORK I DIDN'T DO THIS YEAR.
I GUESS THE PARTY'S OFF.
MAYBE NOT . . . LET'S SEE IF STACEY COMES HOME IN TIME.
OKAY.
A FEW HOURS LATER . . .
RING....
RING....
HELLO?
MRS. MCGILL? HI! THIS IS KRISTY THOMAS . . . STACEY'S FRIEND. IS SHE THERE?
MUMBLE WHISPER

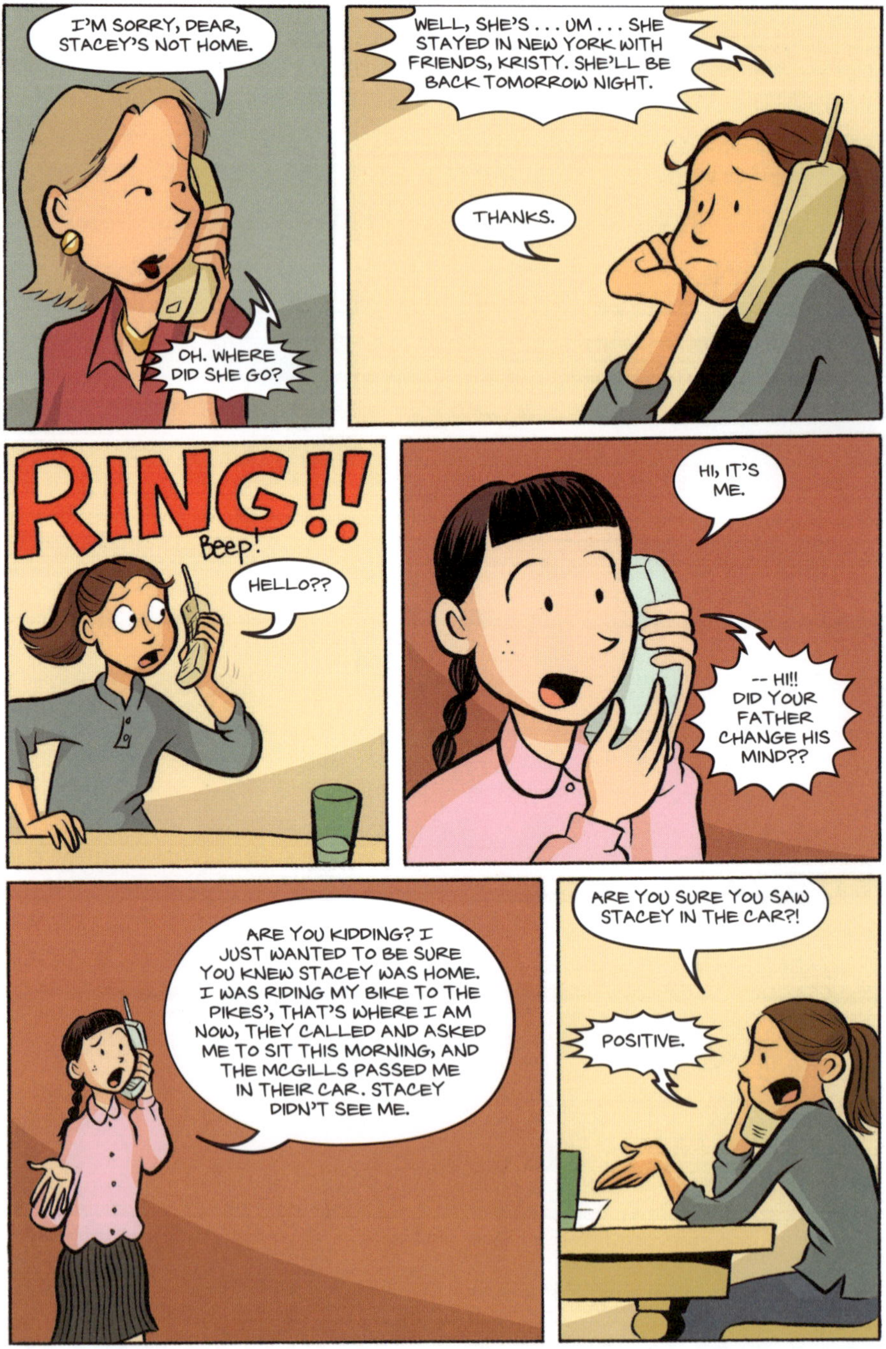
I'M SORRY, DEAR, STACEY'S NOT HOME.
OH. WHERE DID SHE GO?
WELL, SHE'S . . . UM . . . SHE STAYED IN NEW YORK WITH FRIENDS, KRISTY. SHE'LL BE BACK TOMORROW NIGHT.
THANKS.
RING!!
Beep!
HELLO??
HI, IT'S ME.
-- HI!! DID YOUR FATHER CHANGE HIS MIND??
ARE YOU KIDDING? I JUST WANTED TO BE SURE YOU KNEW STACEY WAS HOME. I WAS RIDING MY BIKE TO THE PIKES', THAT'S WHERE I AM NOW, THEY CALLED AND ASKED ME TO SIT THIS MORNING, AND THE MCGILLS PASSED ME IN THEIR CAR. STACEY DIDN'T SEE ME.
ARE YOU SURE YOU SAW STACEY IN THE CAR?!
POSITIVE.

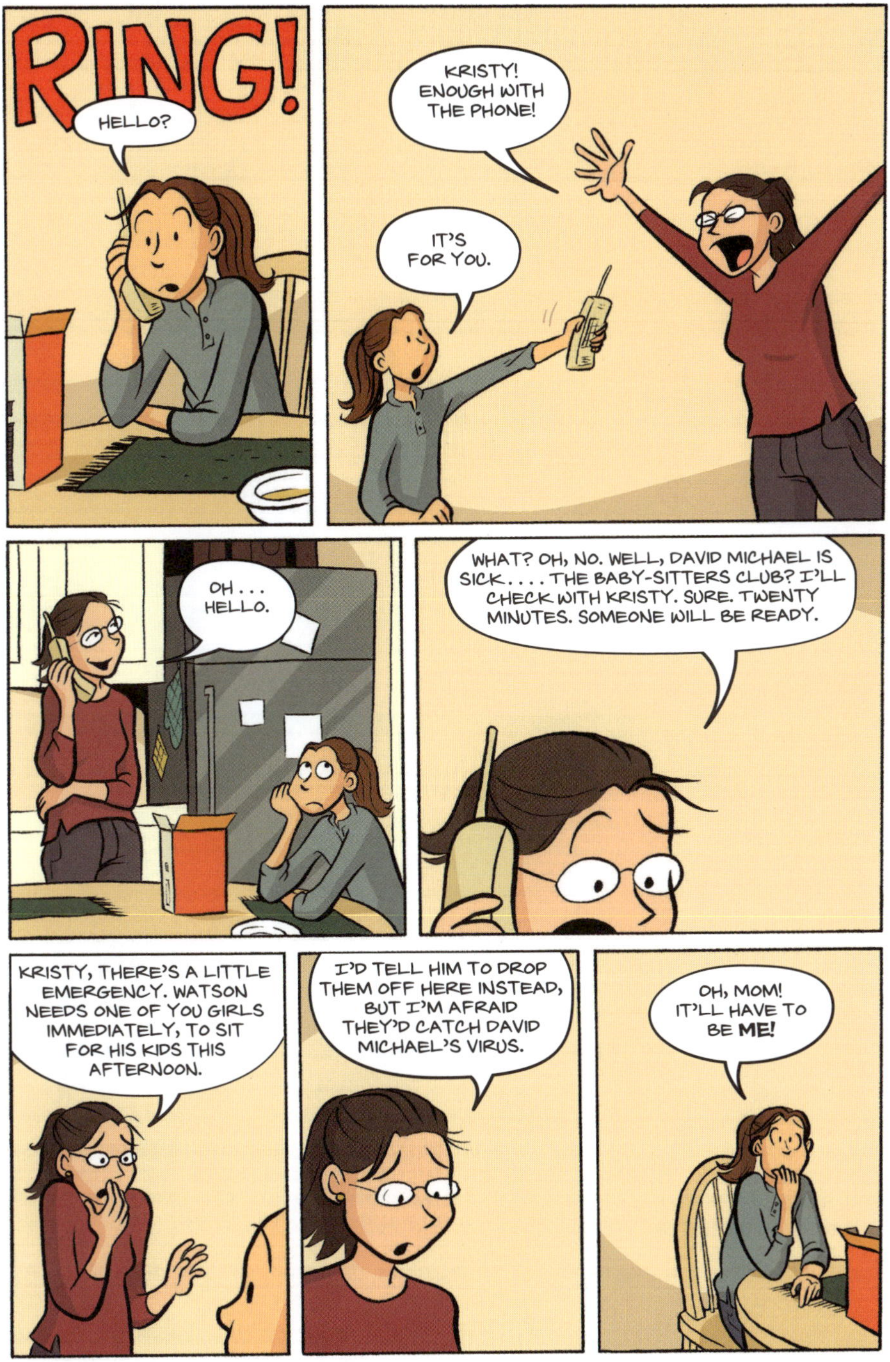
RING!
HELLO?
KRISTY! ENOUGH WITH THE PHONE!
IT'S FOR YOU.
OH . . . HELLO.
WHAT? OH, NO. WELL, DAVID MICHAEL IS SICK. . . . THE BABY-SITTERS CLUB? I'LL CHECK WITH KRISTY. SURE. TWENTY MINUTES. SOMEONE WILL BE READY.
KRISTY, THERE'S A LITTLE EMERGENCY. WATSON NEEDS ONE OF YOU GIRLS IMMEDIATELY, TO SIT FOR HIS KIDS THIS AFTERNOON.
I'D TELL HIM TO DROP THEM OFF HERE INSTEAD, BUT I'M AFRAID THEY'D CATCH DAVID MICHAEL'S VIRUS.
OH, MOM! IT'LL HAVE TO BE **ME!**

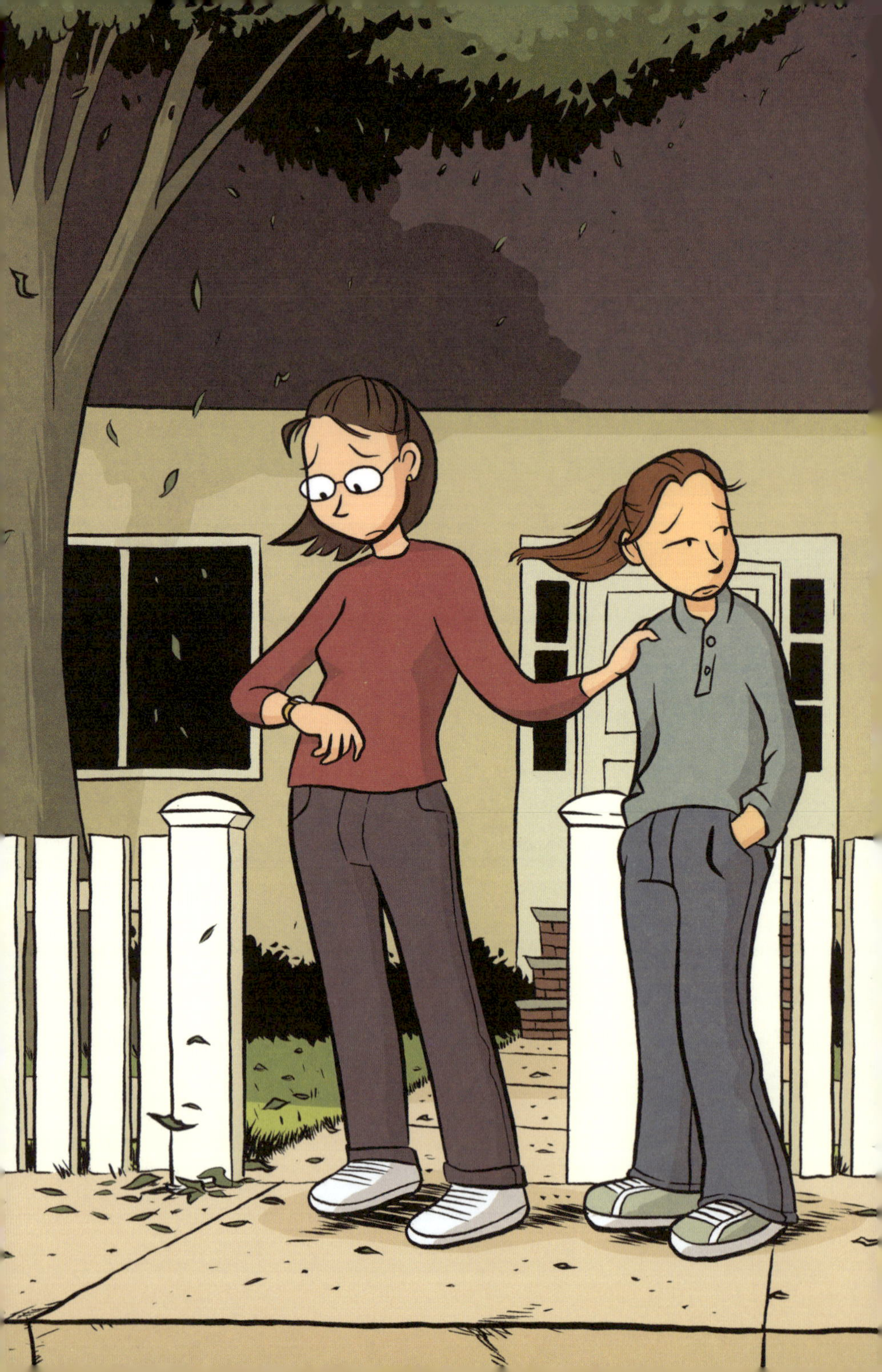

CHAPTER 12

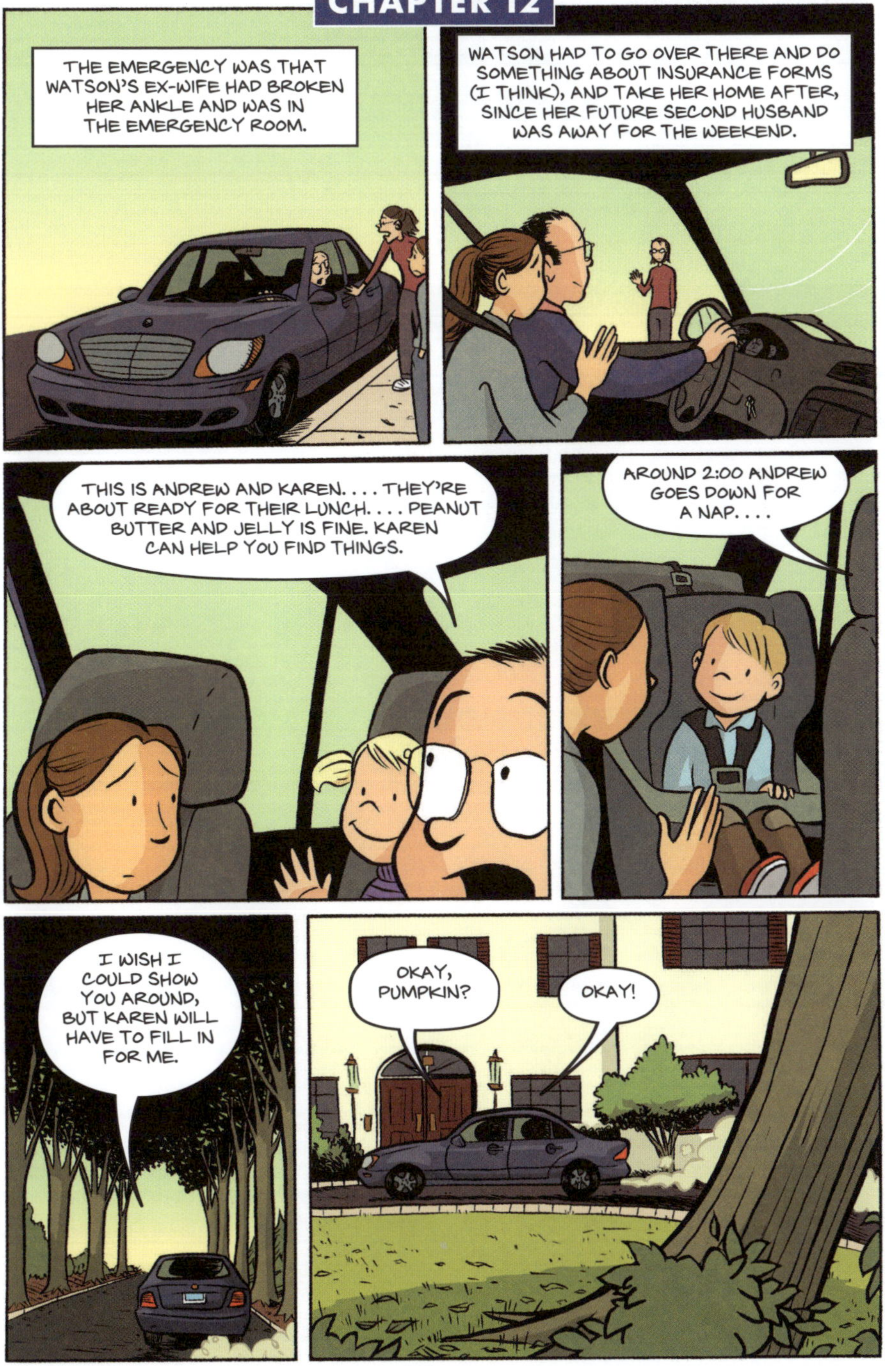
THE EMERGENCY WAS THAT WATSON'S EX-WIFE HAD BROKEN HER ANKLE AND WAS IN THE EMERGENCY ROOM.
WATSON HAD TO GO OVER THERE AND DO SOMETHING ABOUT INSURANCE FORMS (I THINK), AND TAKE HER HOME AFTER, SINCE HER FUTURE SECOND HUSBAND WAS AWAY FOR THE WEEKEND.
THIS IS ANDREW AND KAREN. . . . THEY'RE ABOUT READY FOR THEIR LUNCH. . . . PEANUT BUTTER AND JELLY IS FINE. KAREN CAN HELP YOU FIND THINGS.
AROUND 2:00 ANDREW GOES DOWN FOR A NAP. . . .
I WISH I COULD SHOW YOU AROUND, BUT KAREN WILL HAVE TO FILL IN FOR ME.
OKAY, PUMPKIN?
OKAY!

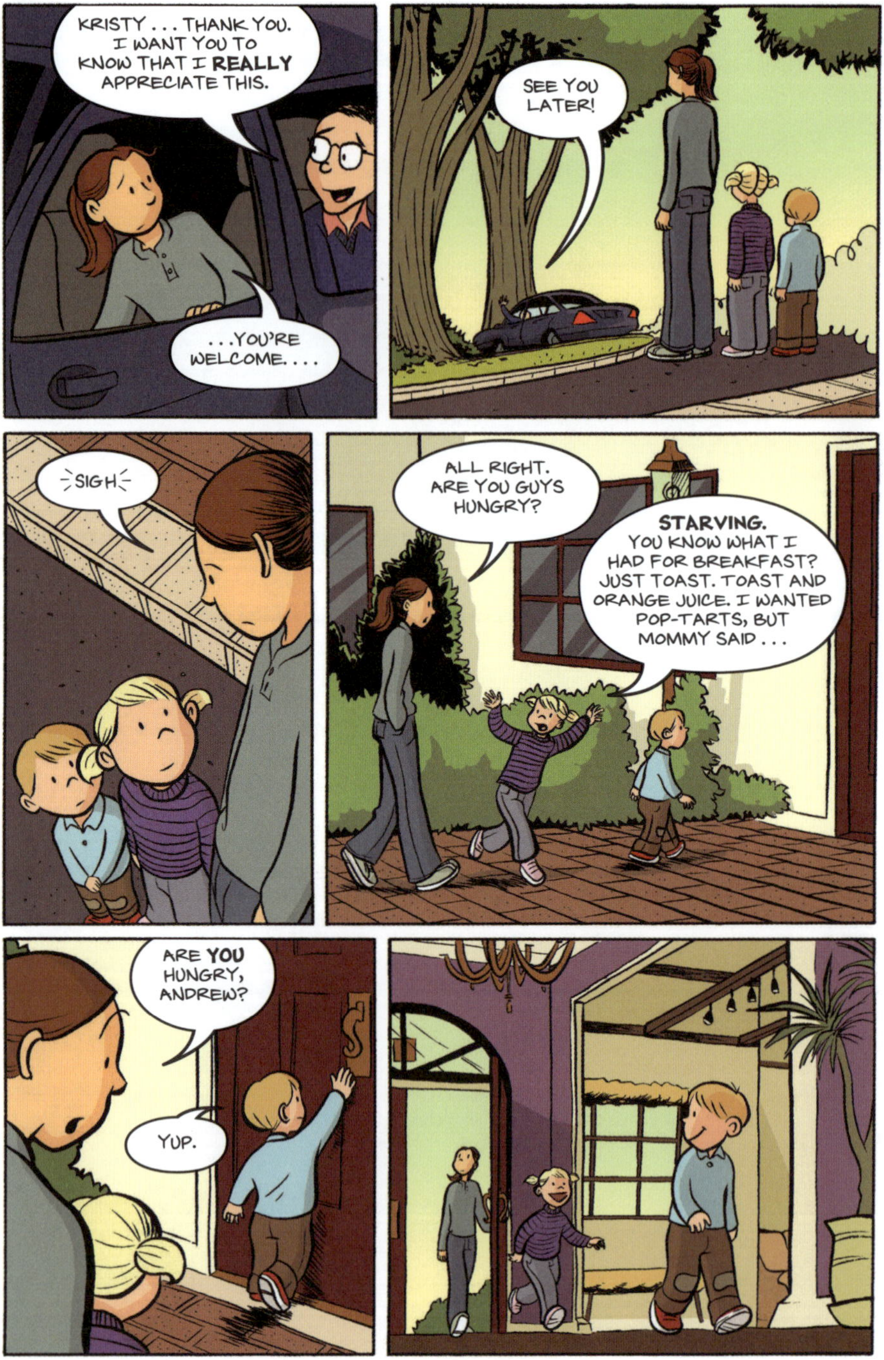
KRISTY . . . THANK YOU. I WANT YOU TO KNOW THAT I **REALLY** APPRECIATE THIS.
. . .YOU'RE WELCOME. . . .
SEE YOU LATER!
SIGH
ALL RIGHT. ARE YOU GUYS HUNGRY?
STARVING. YOU KNOW WHAT I HAD FOR BREAKFAST? JUST TOAST. TOAST AND ORANGE JUICE. I WANTED POP-TARTS, BUT MOMMY SAID . . .
ARE **YOU** HUNGRY, ANDREW?
YUP.

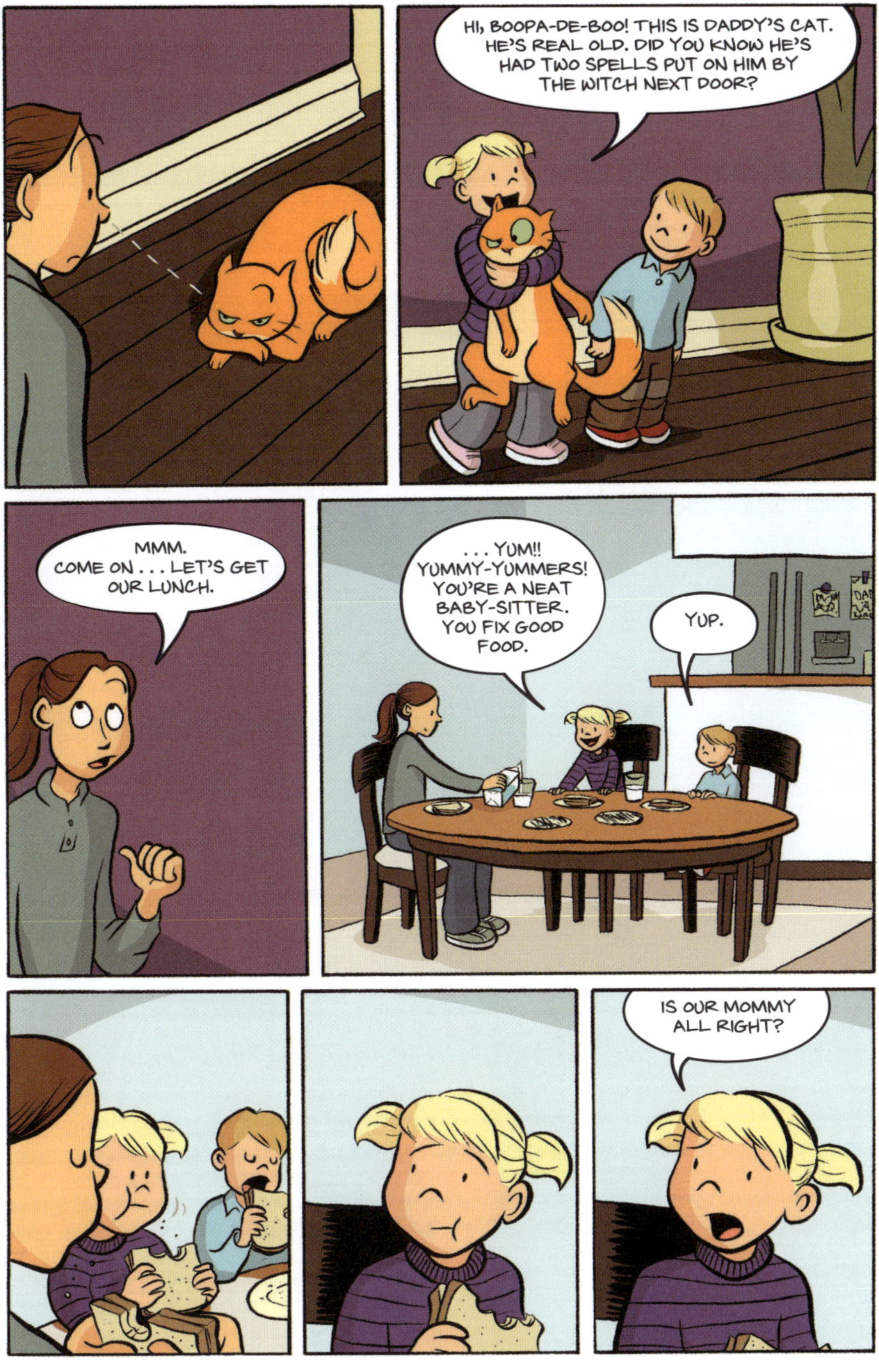
HI, BOOPA-DE-BOO! THIS IS DADDY'S CAT. HE'S REAL OLD. DID YOU KNOW HE'S HAD TWO SPELLS PUT ON HIM BY THE WITCH NEXT DOOR?
MMM. COME ON . . . LET'S GET OUR LUNCH.
. . . YUM!! YUMMY-YUMMERS! YOU'RE A NEAT BABY-SITTER. YOU FIX GOOD FOOD.
YUP.
IS OUR MOMMY ALL RIGHT?

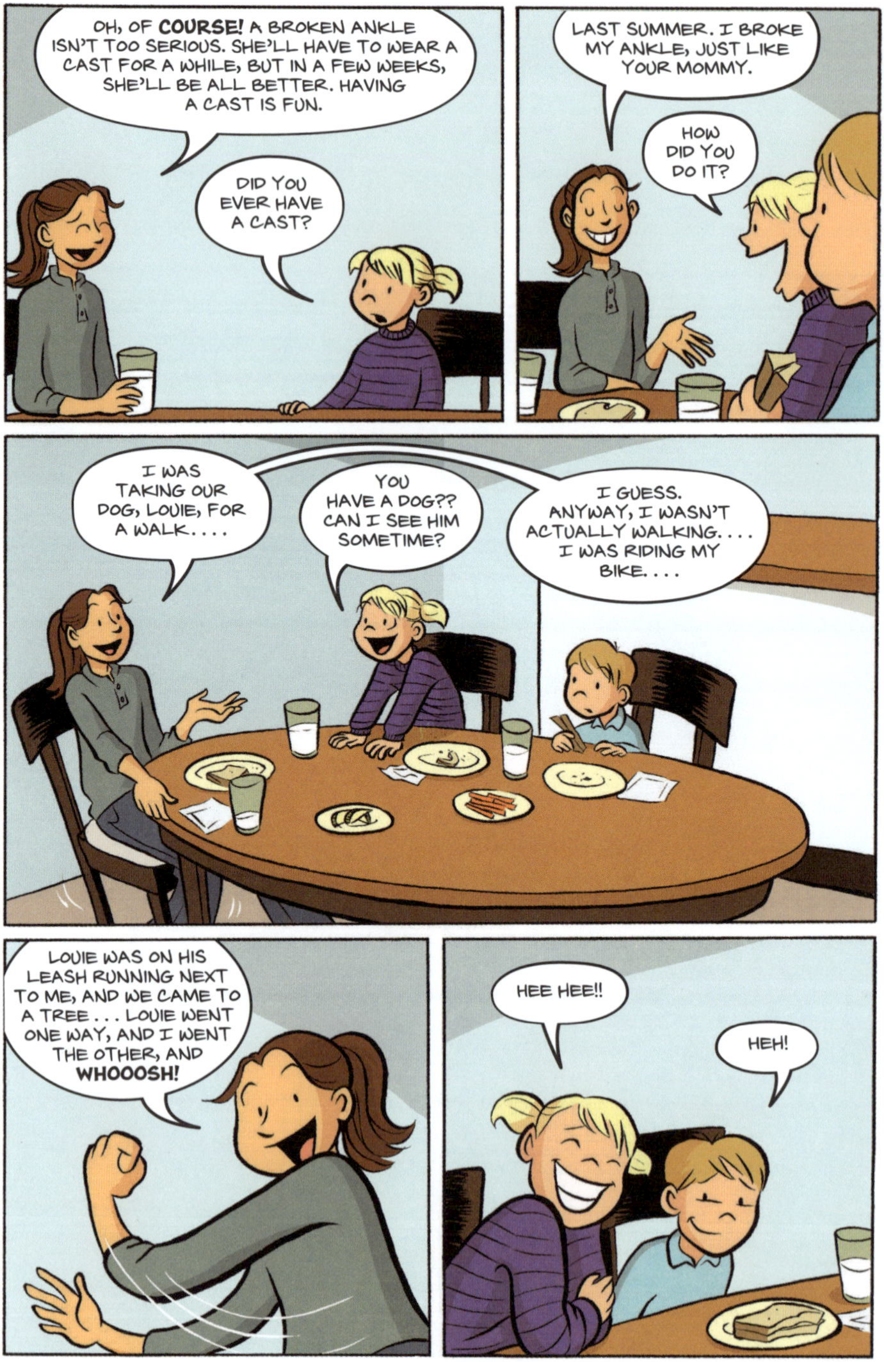
OH, OF COURSE! A BROKEN ANKLE ISN'T TOO SERIOUS. SHE'LL HAVE TO WEAR A CAST FOR A WHILE, BUT IN A FEW WEEKS, SHE'LL BE ALL BETTER. HAVING A CAST IS FUN.
DID YOU EVER HAVE A CAST?
LAST SUMMER. I BROKE MY ANKLE, JUST LIKE YOUR MOMMY.
HOW DID YOU DO IT?
I WAS TAKING OUR DOG, LOUIE, FOR A WALK. . . .
YOU HAVE A DOG?? CAN I SEE HIM SOMETIME?
I GUESS. ANYWAY, I WASN'T ACTUALLY WALKING. . . . I WAS RIDING MY BIKE. . . .
LOUIE WAS ON HIS LEASH RUNNING NEXT TO ME, AND WE CAME TO A TREE . . . LOUIE WENT ONE WAY, AND I WENT THE OTHER, AND WHOOOSH!
HEE HEE!!
HEH!

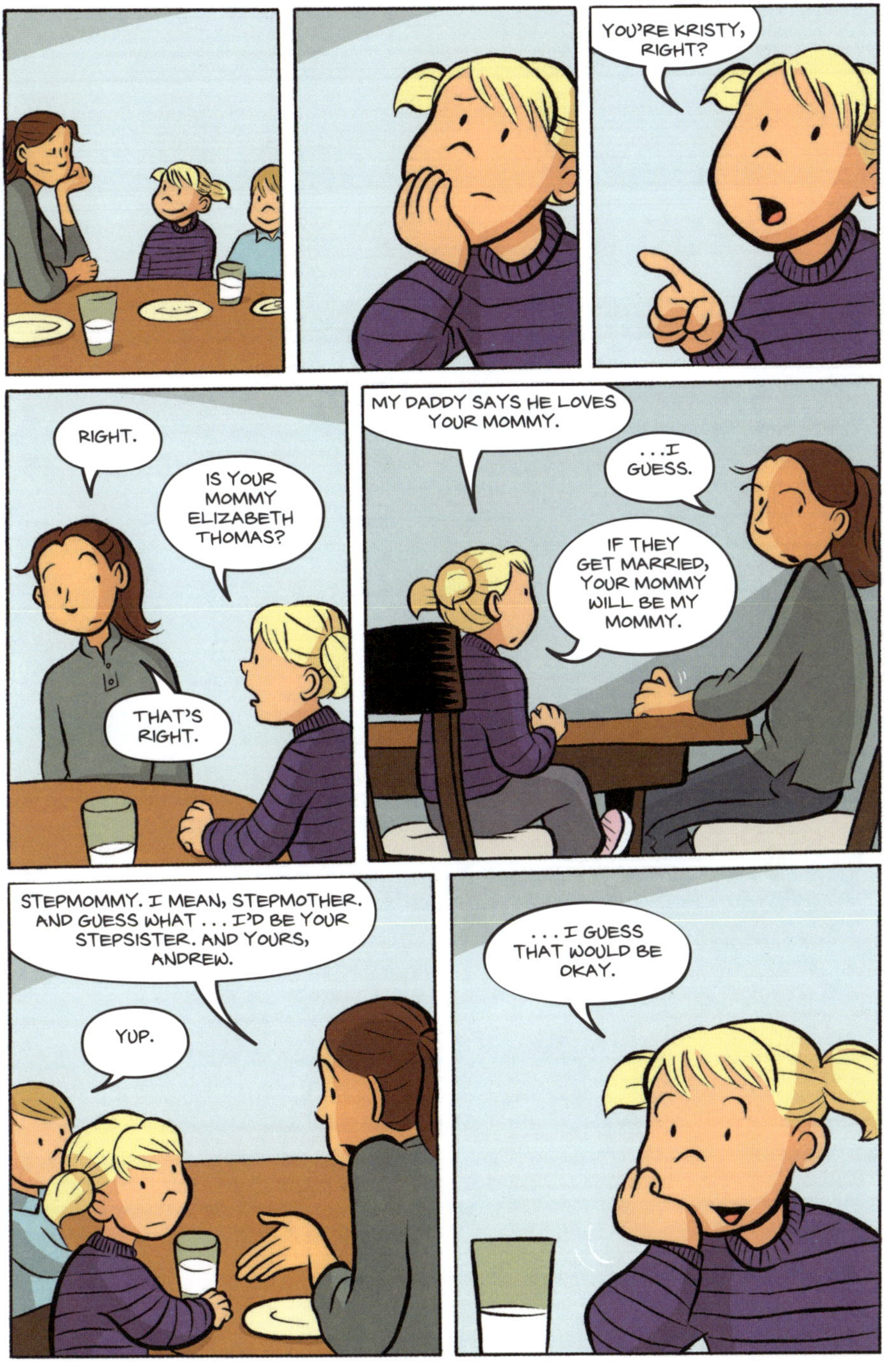
YOU'RE KRISTY, RIGHT?
RIGHT.
IS YOUR MOMMY ELIZABETH THOMAS?
THAT'S RIGHT.
MY DADDY SAYS HE LOVES YOUR MOMMY.
. . . I GUESS.
IF THEY GET MARRIED, YOUR MOMMY WILL BE MY MOMMY.
STEPMOMMY. I MEAN, STEPMOTHER. AND GUESS WHAT . . . I'D BE YOUR STEPSISTER. AND YOURS, ANDREW.
YUP.
. . . I GUESS THAT WOULD BE OKAY.

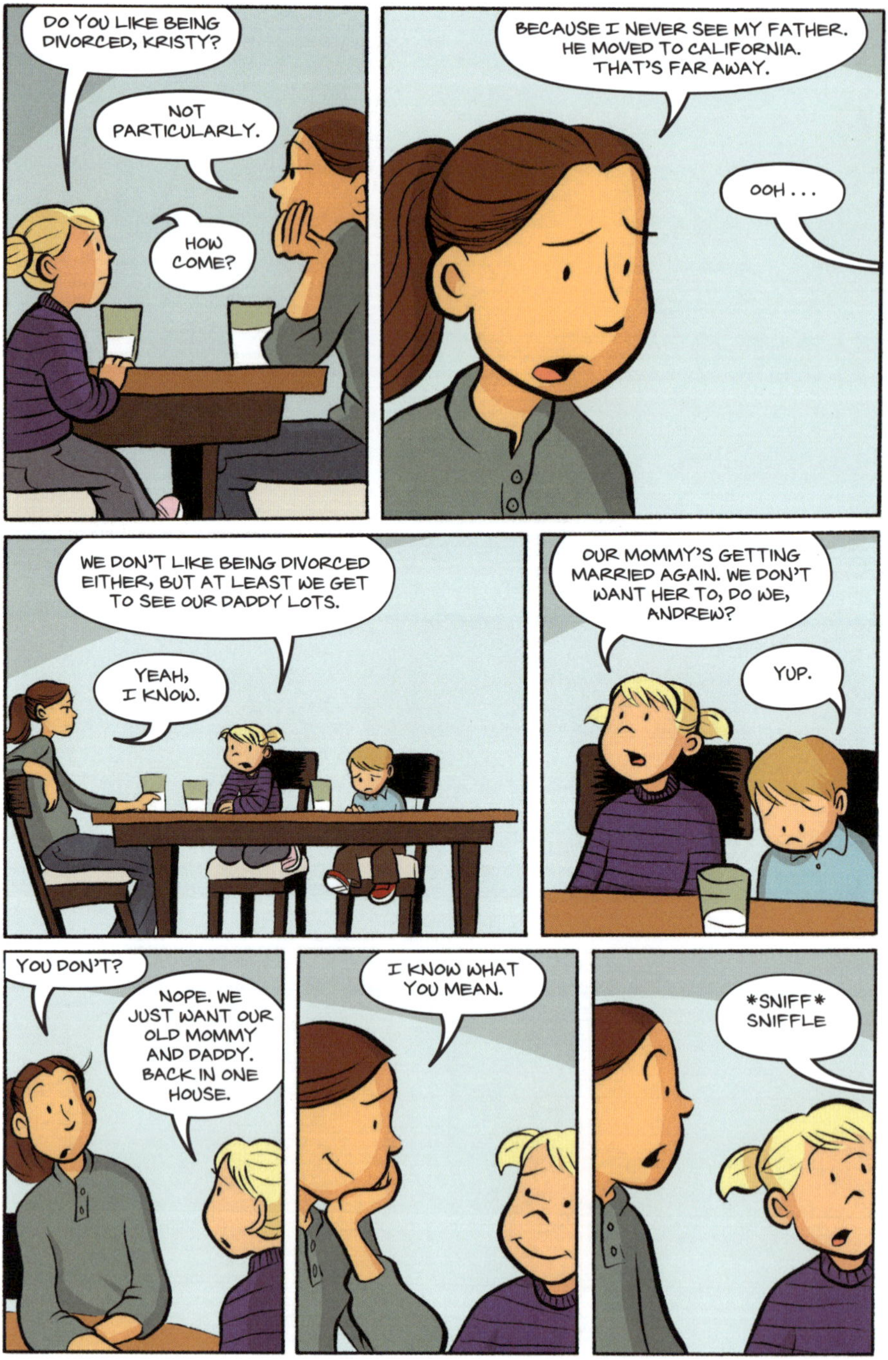
DO YOU LIKE BEING DIVORCED, KRISTY?
NOT PARTICULARLY.
HOW COME?
BECAUSE I NEVER SEE MY FATHER. HE MOVED TO CALIFORNIA. THAT'S FAR AWAY.
OOH . . .
WE DON'T LIKE BEING DIVORCED EITHER, BUT AT LEAST WE GET TO SEE OUR DADDY LOTS.
YEAH, I KNOW.
OUR MOMMY'S GETTING MARRIED AGAIN. WE DON'T WANT HER TO, DO WE, ANDREW?
YUP.
YOU DON'T?
NOPE. WE JUST WANT OUR OLD MOMMY AND DADDY. BACK IN ONE HOUSE.
I KNOW WHAT YOU MEAN.
SNIFF SNIFFLE

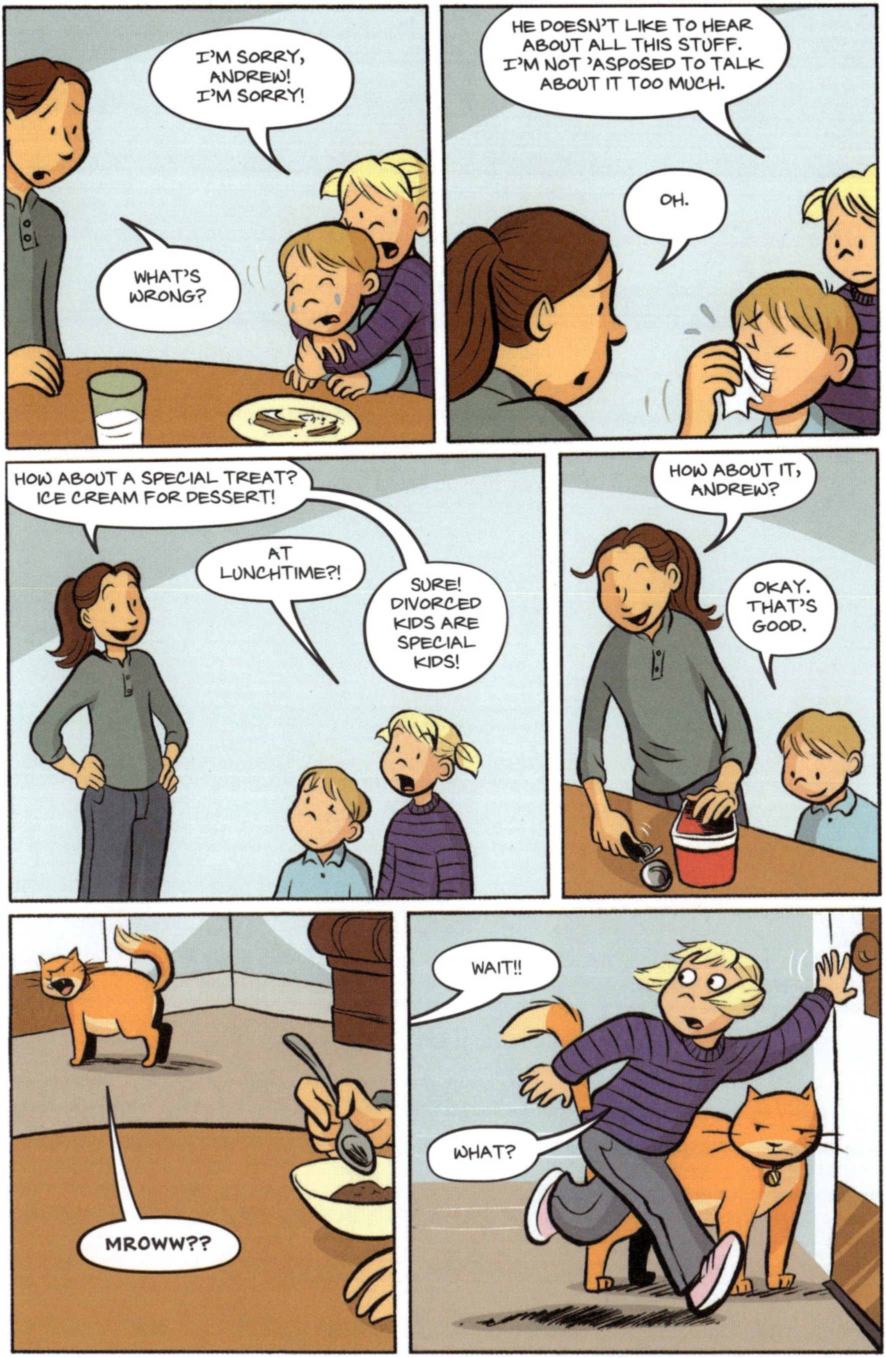
I'M SORRY, ANDREW! I'M SORRY!
WHAT'S WRONG?
HE DOESN'T LIKE TO HEAR ABOUT ALL THIS STUFF. I'M NOT 'ASPOSED TO TALK ABOUT IT TOO MUCH.
OH.
HOW ABOUT A SPECIAL TREAT? ICE CREAM FOR DESSERT!
AT LUNCHTIME?!
SURE! DIVORCED KIDS ARE SPECIAL KIDS!
HOW ABOUT IT, ANDREW?
OKAY. THAT'S GOOD.
MROWW??
WAIT!!
WHAT?

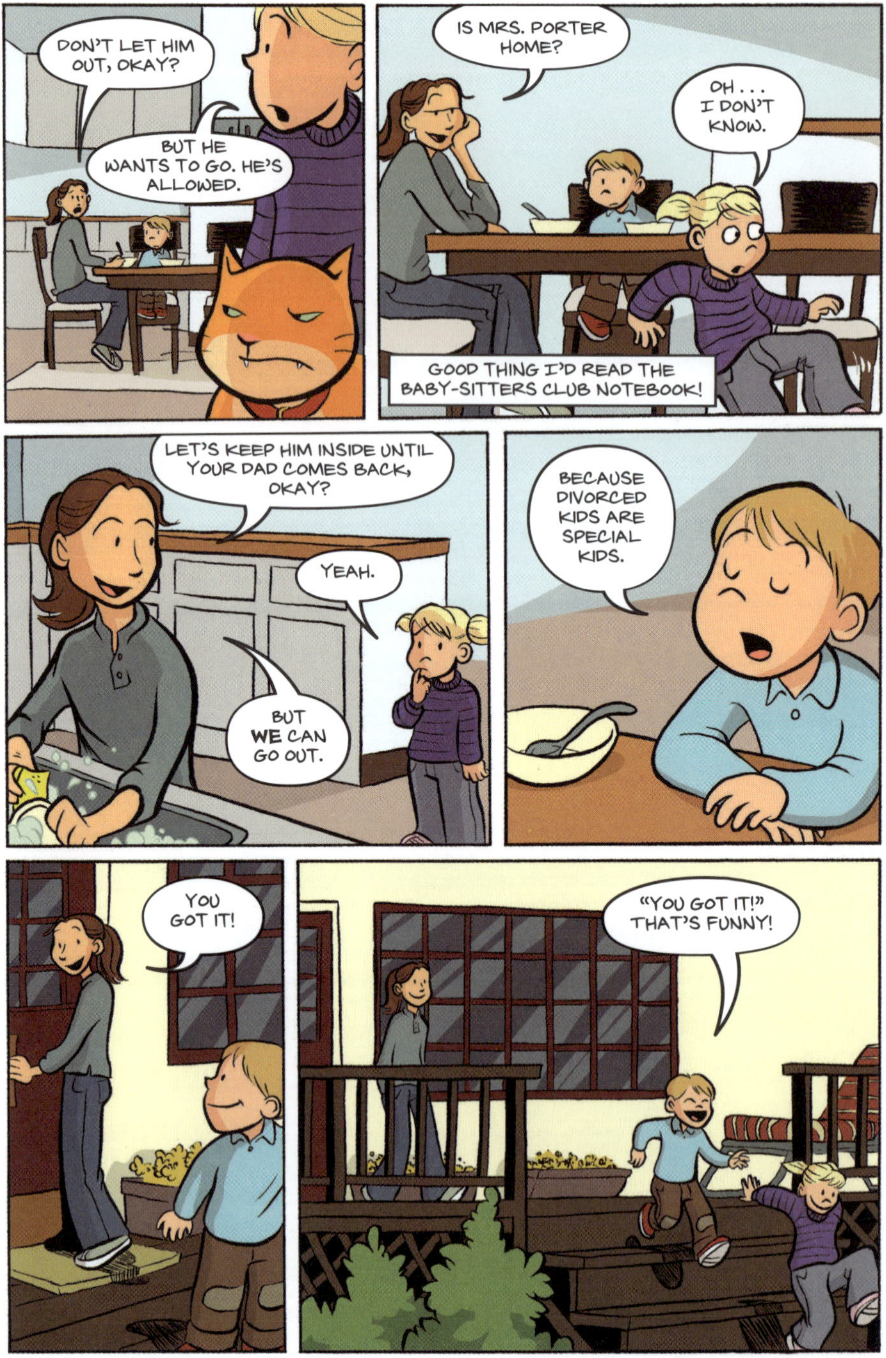
DON'T LET HIM OUT, OKAY?
BUT HE WANTS TO GO. HE'S ALLOWED.
IS MRS. PORTER HOME?
OH . . . I DON'T KNOW.
GOOD THING I'D READ THE BABY-SITTERS CLUB NOTEBOOK!
LET'S KEEP HIM INSIDE UNTIL YOUR DAD COMES BACK, OKAY?
YEAH.
BUT WE CAN GO OUT.
BECAUSE DIVORCED KIDS ARE SPECIAL KIDS.
YOU GOT IT!
"YOU GOT IT!" THAT'S FUNNY!

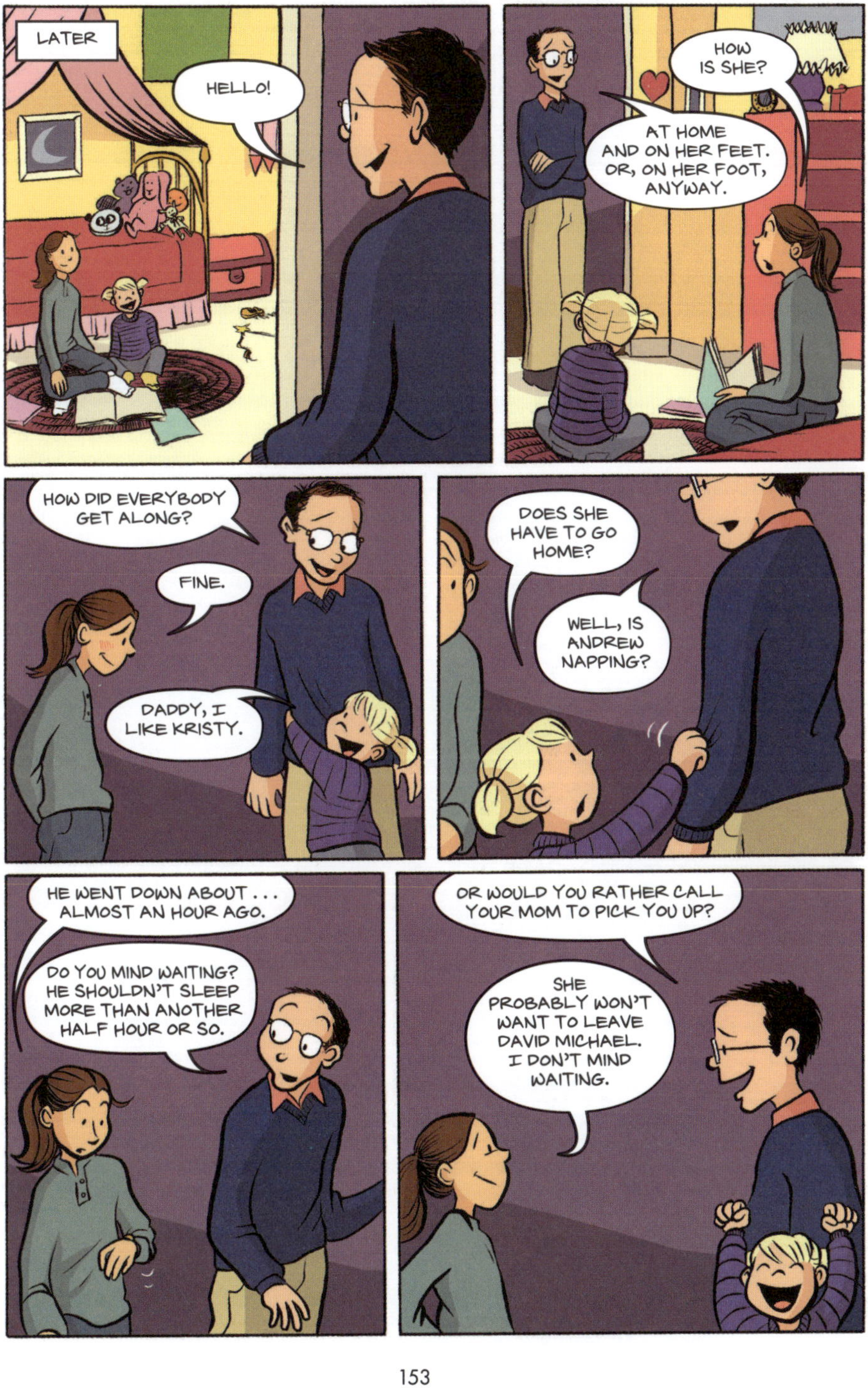
LATER
HELLO!
HOW IS SHE?
AT HOME AND ON HER FEET. OR, ON HER FOOT, ANYWAY.
HOW DID EVERYBODY GET ALONG?
FINE.
DADDY, I LIKE KRISTY.
DOES SHE HAVE TO GO HOME?
WELL, IS ANDREW NAPPING?
HE WENT DOWN ABOUT . . . ALMOST AN HOUR AGO.
DO YOU MIND WAITING? HE SHOULDN'T SLEEP MORE THAN ANOTHER HALF HOUR OR SO.
OR WOULD YOU RATHER CALL YOUR MOM TO PICK YOU UP?
SHE PROBABLY WON'T WANT TO LEAVE DAVID MICHAEL. I DON'T MIND WAITING.

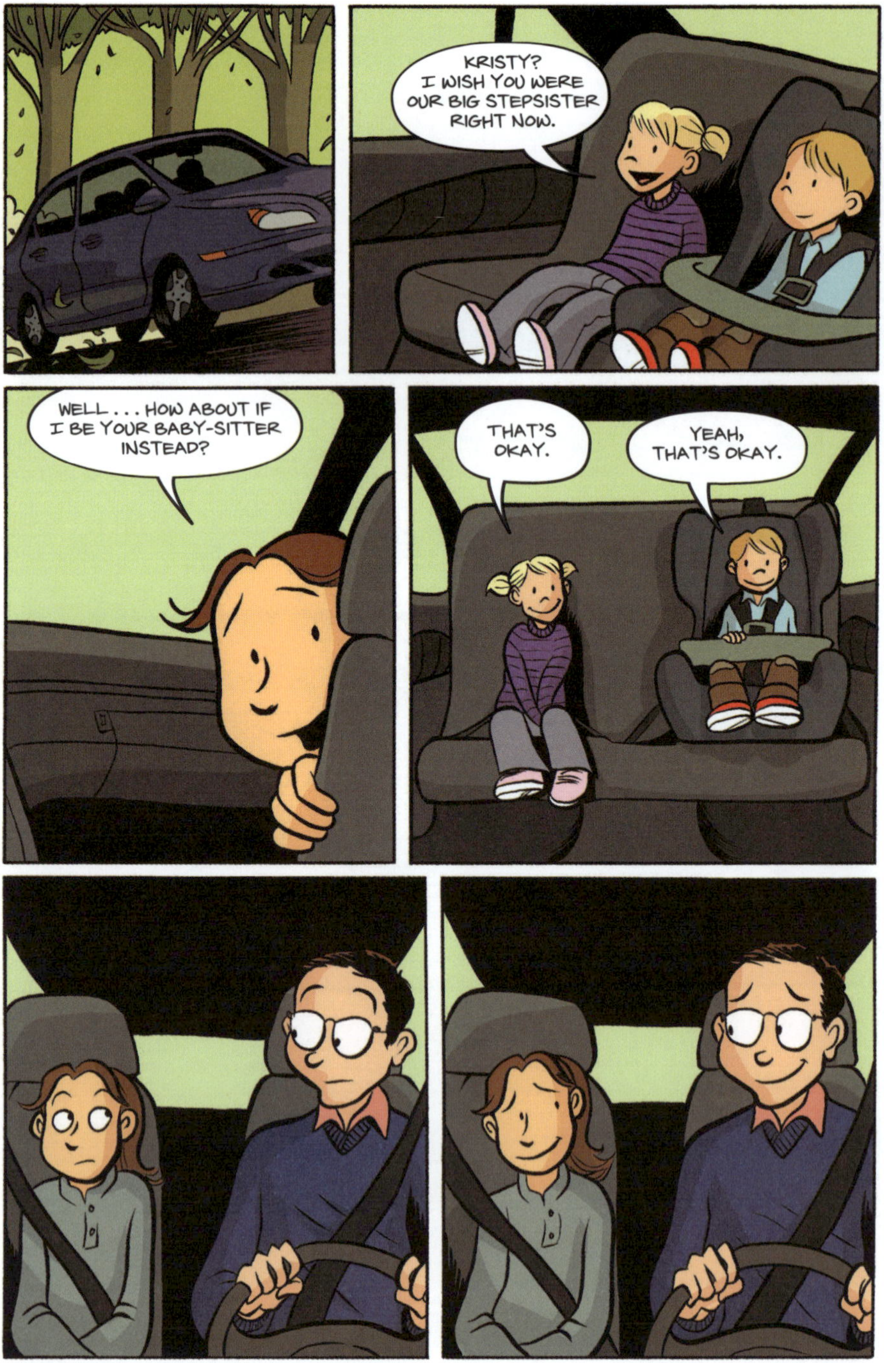
KRISTY? I WISH YOU WERE OUR BIG STEPSISTER RIGHT NOW.
WELL . . . HOW ABOUT IF I BE YOUR BABY-SITTER INSTEAD?
THAT'S OKAY.
YEAH, THAT'S OKAY.

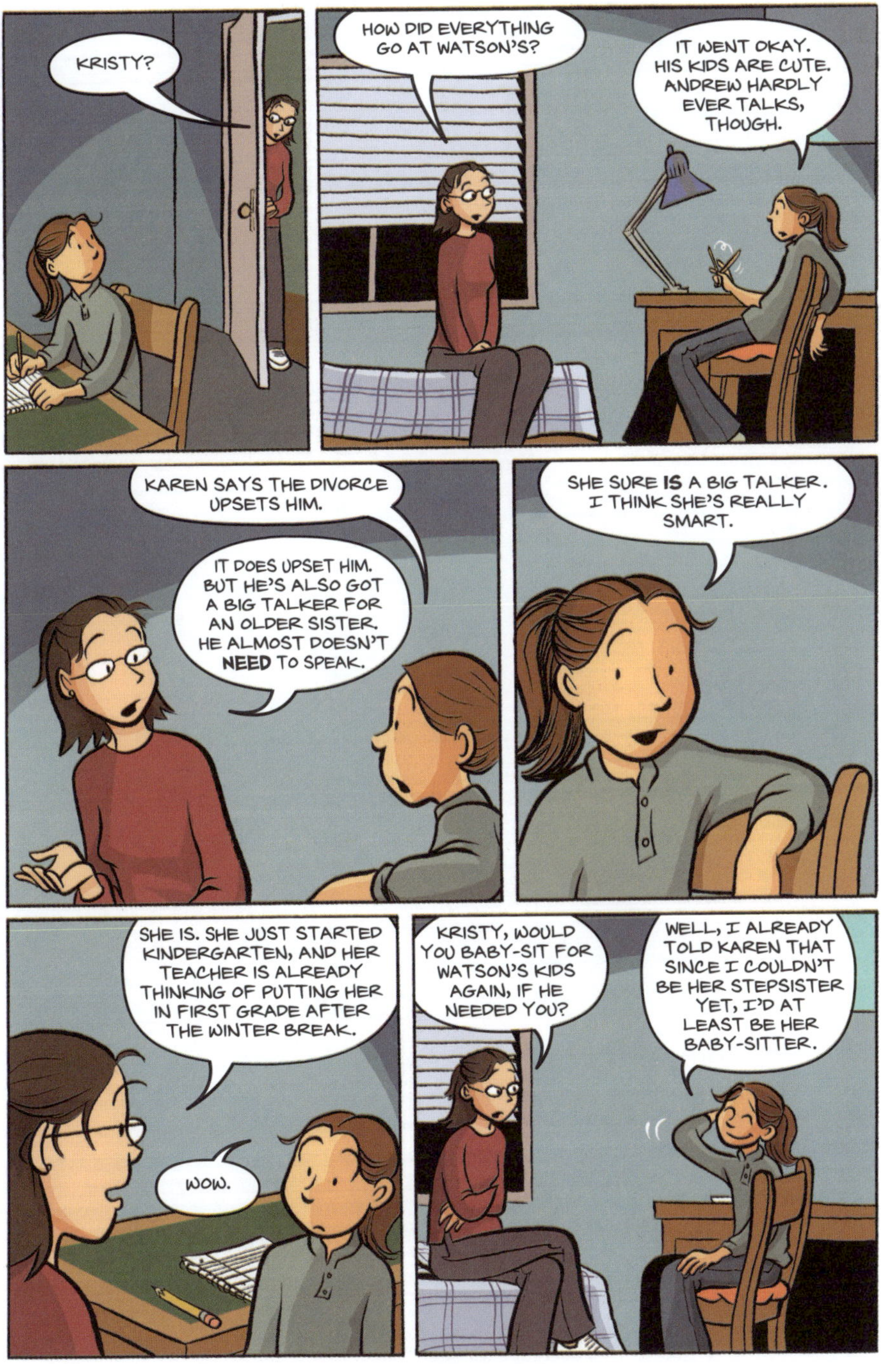
KRISTY?
HOW DID EVERYTHING GO AT WATSON'S?
IT WENT OKAY. HIS KIDS ARE CUTE. ANDREW HARDLY EVER TALKS, THOUGH.
KAREN SAYS THE DIVORCE UPSETS HIM.
IT DOES UPSET HIM. BUT HE'S ALSO GOT A BIG TALKER FOR AN OLDER SISTER. HE ALMOST DOESN'T **NEED** TO SPEAK.
SHE SURE **IS** A BIG TALKER. I THINK SHE'S REALLY SMART.
SHE IS. SHE JUST STARTED KINDERGARTEN, AND HER TEACHER IS ALREADY THINKING OF PUTTING HER IN FIRST GRADE AFTER THE WINTER BREAK.
WOW.
KRISTY, WOULD YOU BABY-SIT FOR WATSON'S KIDS AGAIN, IF HE NEEDED YOU?
WELL, I ALREADY TOLD KAREN THAT SINCE I COULDN'T BE HER STEPSISTER YET, I'D AT LEAST BE HER BABY-SITTER.

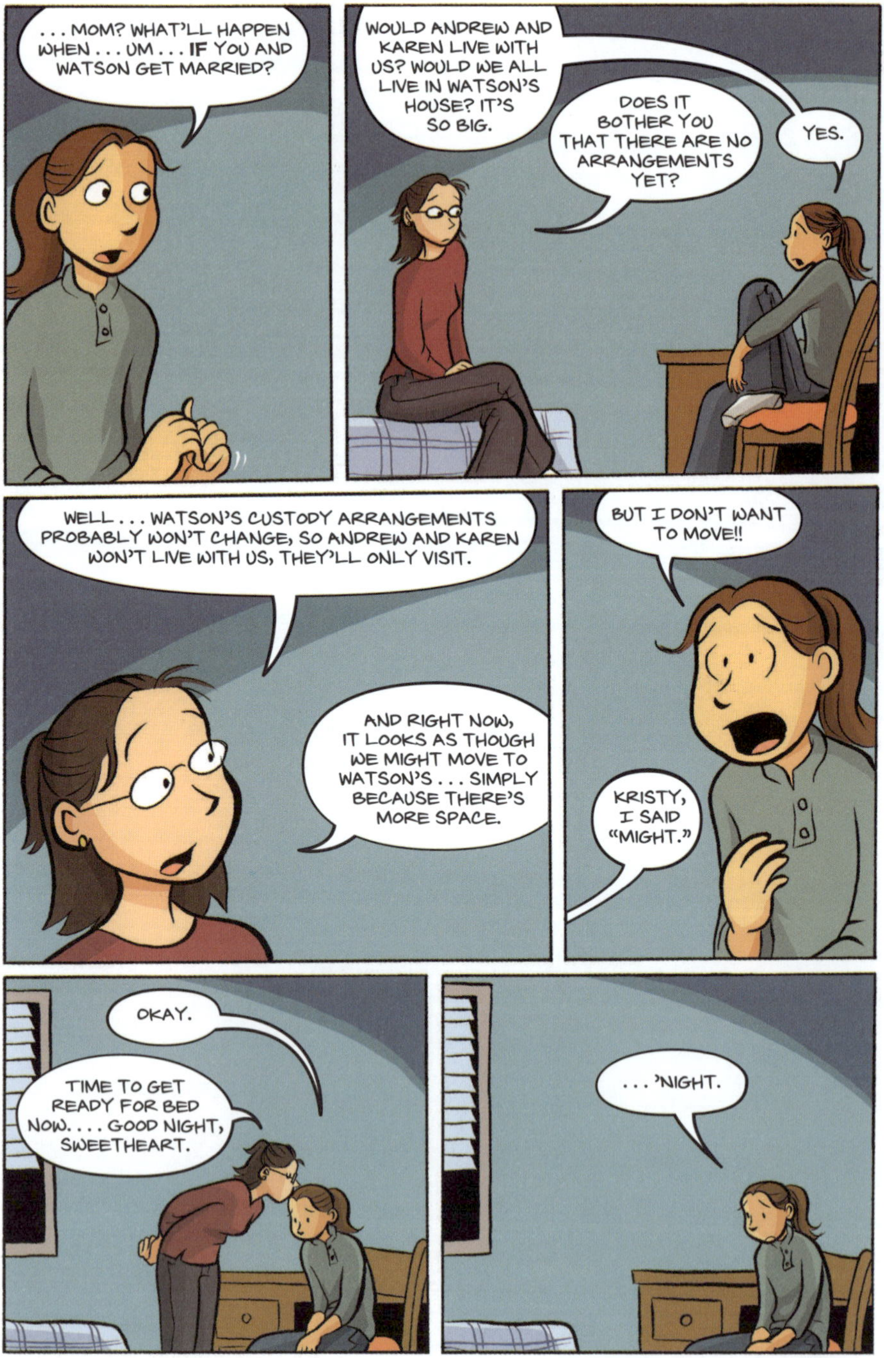
. . . MOM? WHAT'LL HAPPEN WHEN . . . UM . . . IF YOU AND WATSON GET MARRIED?
WOULD ANDREW AND KAREN LIVE WITH US? WOULD WE ALL LIVE IN WATSON'S HOUSE? IT'S SO BIG.
DOES IT BOTHER YOU THAT THERE ARE NO ARRANGEMENTS YET?
YES.
WELL . . . WATSON'S CUSTODY ARRANGEMENTS PROBABLY WON'T CHANGE, SO ANDREW AND KAREN WON'T LIVE WITH US, THEY'LL ONLY VISIT.
AND RIGHT NOW, IT LOOKS AS THOUGH WE MIGHT MOVE TO WATSON'S . . . SIMPLY BECAUSE THERE'S MORE SPACE.
BUT I DON'T WANT TO MOVE!!
KRISTY, I SAID "MIGHT."
TIME TO GET READY FOR BED NOW. . . . GOOD NIGHT, SWEETHEART.
OKAY.
. . . 'NIGHT.

CHAPTER 13

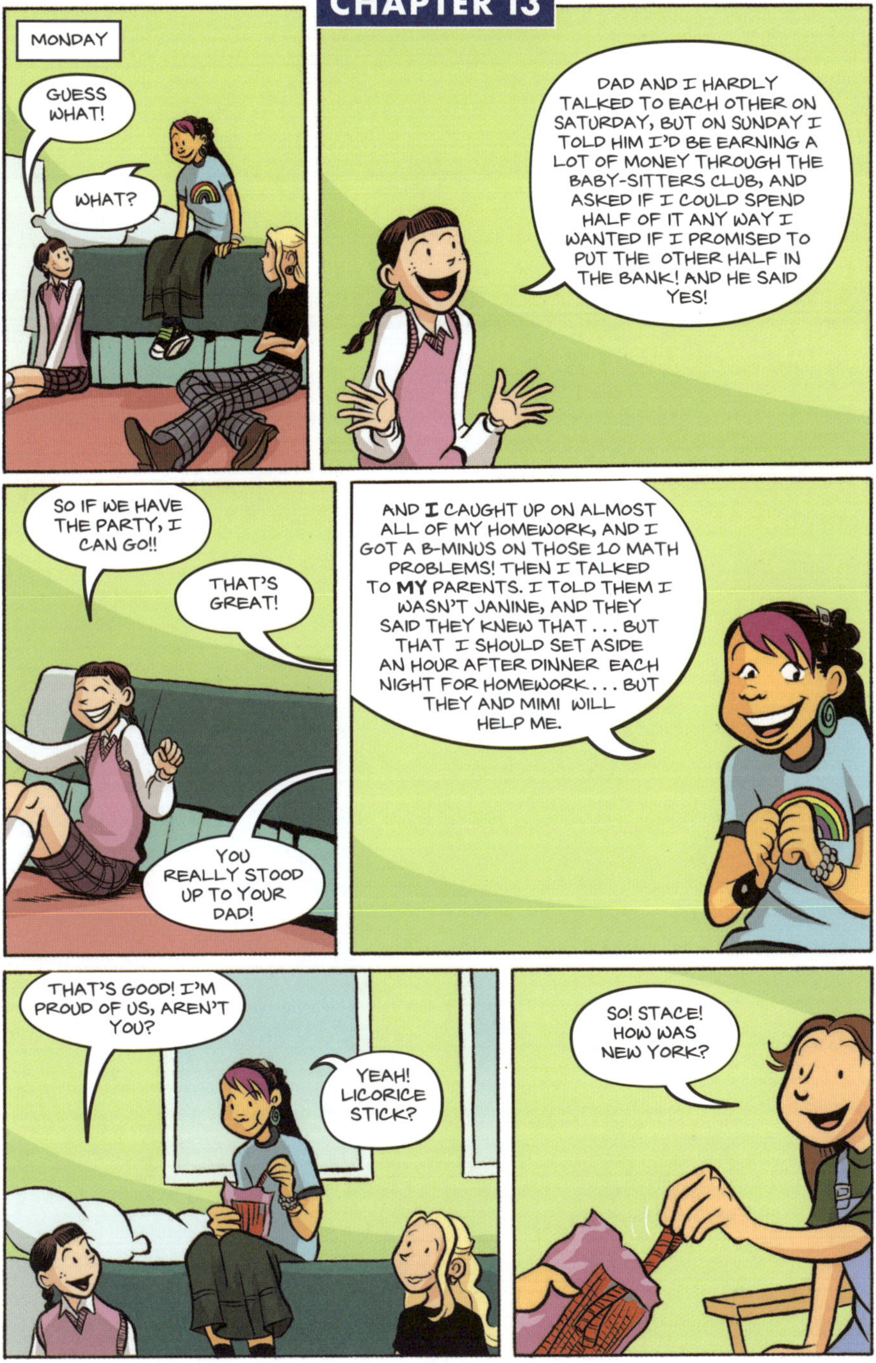
MONDAY
GUESS WHAT!
WHAT?
DAD AND I HARDLY TALKED TO EACH OTHER ON SATURDAY, BUT ON SUNDAY I TOLD HIM I'D BE EARNING A LOT OF MONEY THROUGH THE BABY-SITTERS CLUB, AND ASKED IF I COULD SPEND HALF OF IT ANY WAY I WANTED IF I PROMISED TO PUT THE OTHER HALF IN THE BANK! AND HE SAID YES!
SO IF WE HAVE THE PARTY, I CAN GO!!
THAT'S GREAT!
YOU REALLY STOOD UP TO YOUR DAD!
AND I CAUGHT UP ON ALMOST ALL OF MY HOMEWORK, AND I GOT A B-MINUS ON THOSE 10 MATH PROBLEMS! THEN I TALKED TO MY PARENTS. I TOLD THEM I WASN'T JANINE, AND THEY SAID THEY KNEW THAT . . . BUT THAT I SHOULD SET ASIDE AN HOUR AFTER DINNER EACH NIGHT FOR HOMEWORK . . . BUT THEY AND MIMI WILL HELP ME.
THAT'S GOOD! I'M PROUD OF US, AREN'T YOU?
YEAH! LICORICE STICK?
SO! STACE! HOW WAS NEW YORK?

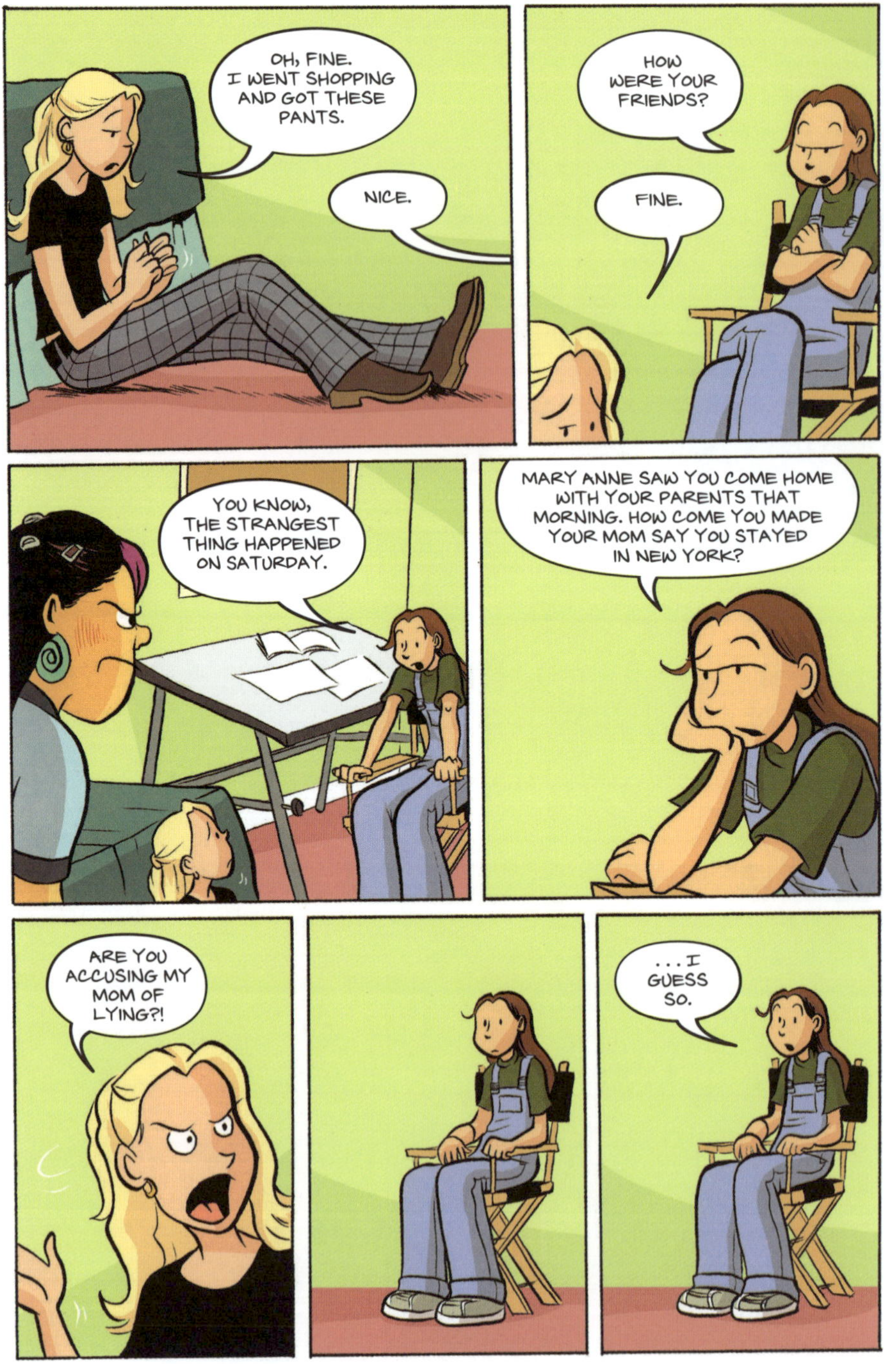
OH, FINE. I WENT SHOPPING AND GOT THESE PANTS.
NICE.
HOW WERE YOUR FRIENDS?
FINE.
YOU KNOW, THE STRANGEST THING HAPPENED ON SATURDAY.
MARY ANNE SAW YOU COME HOME WITH YOUR PARENTS THAT MORNING. HOW COME YOU MADE YOUR MOM SAY YOU STAYED IN NEW YORK?
ARE YOU ACCUSING MY MOM OF LYING?!
...I GUESS SO.

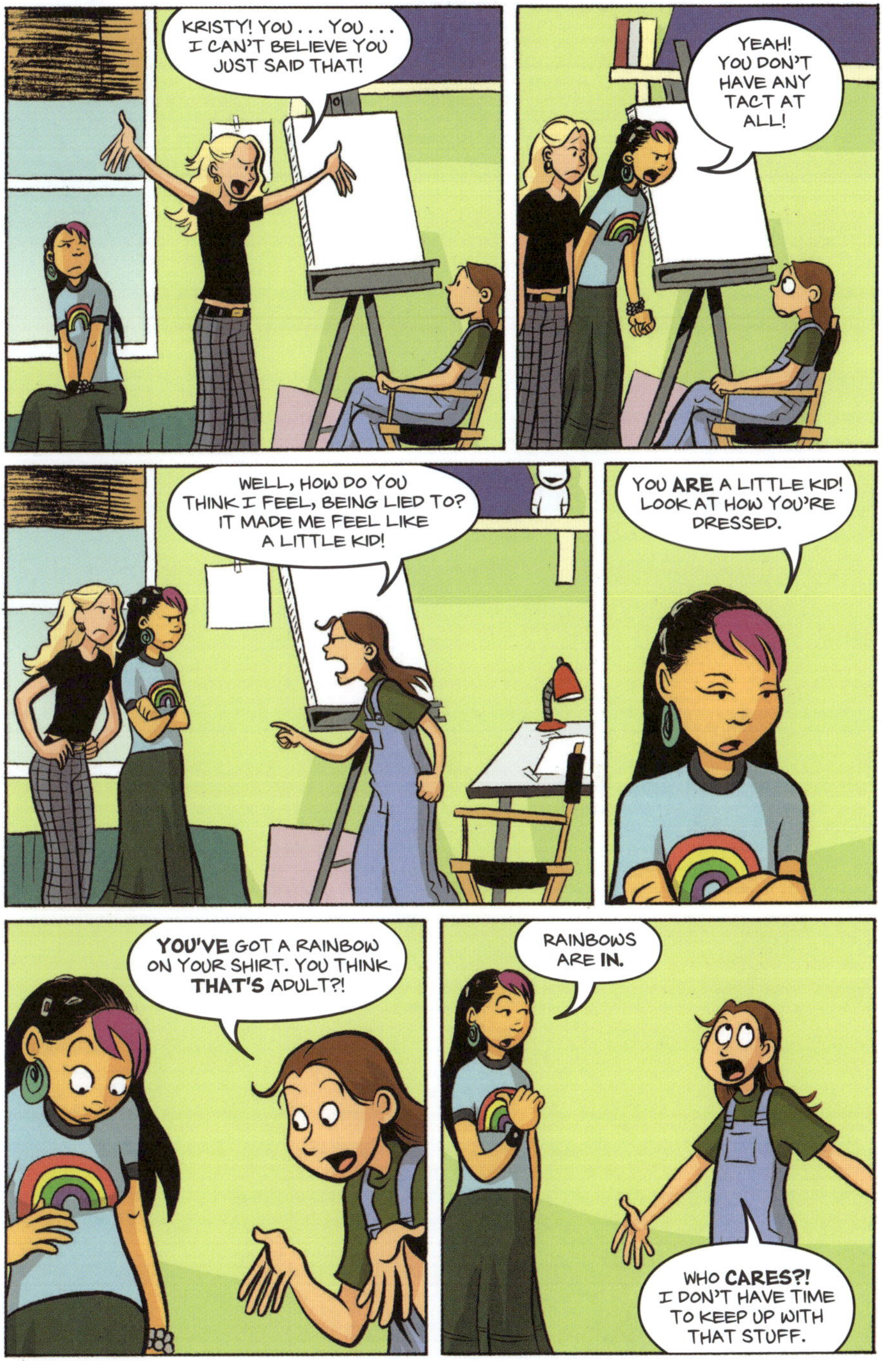
KRISTY! YOU . . . YOU . . . I CAN'T BELIEVE YOU JUST SAID THAT!
YEAH! YOU DON'T HAVE ANY TACT AT ALL!
WELL, HOW DO YOU THINK I FEEL, BEING LIED TO? IT MADE ME FEEL LIKE A LITTLE KID!
YOU **ARE** A LITTLE KID! LOOK AT HOW YOU'RE DRESSED.
YOU'VE GOT A RAINBOW ON YOUR SHIRT. YOU THINK **THAT'S** ADULT?!
RAINBOWS ARE **IN.**
WHO **CARES?!** I DON'T HAVE TIME TO KEEP UP WITH THAT STUFF.

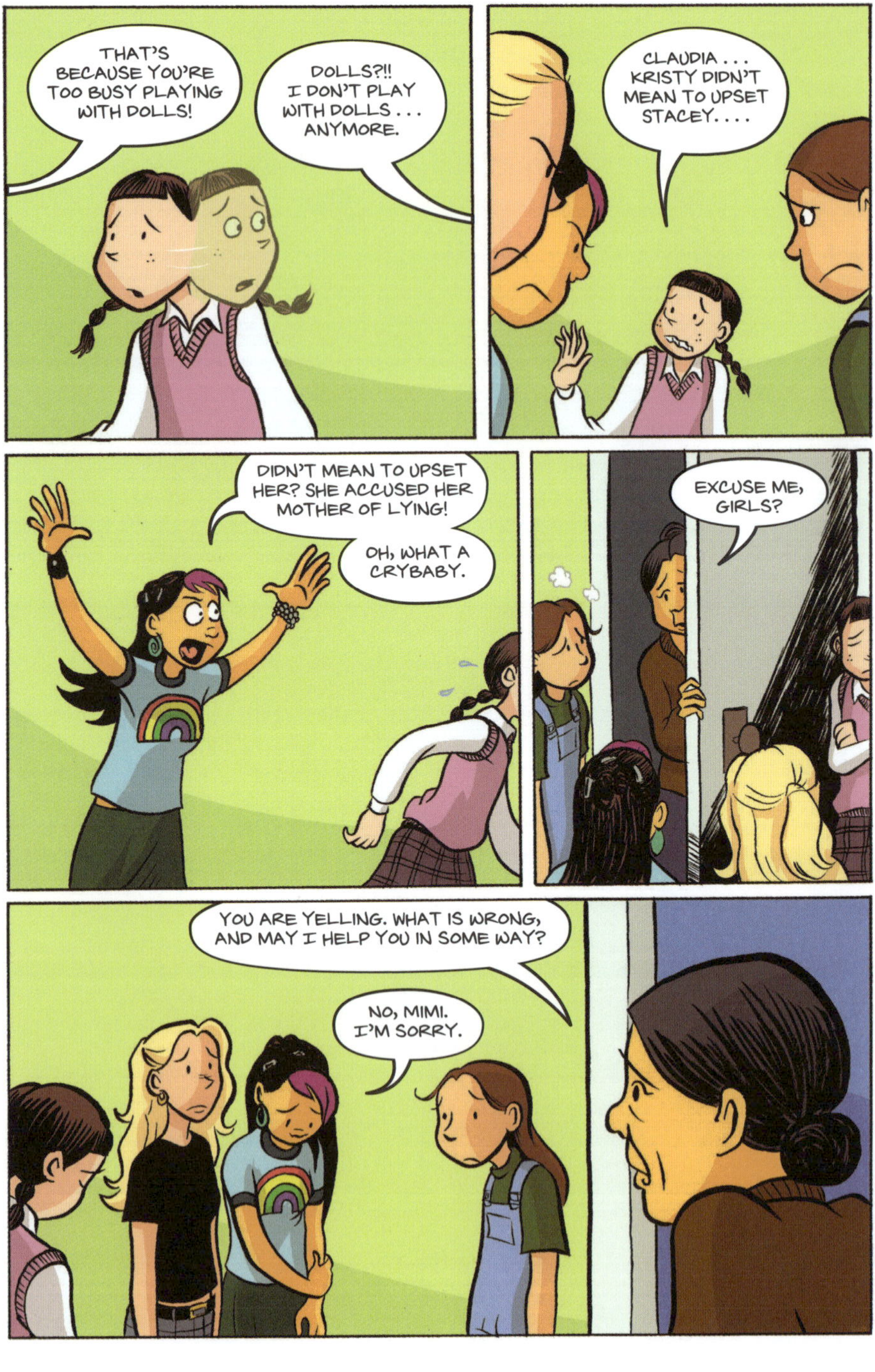
THAT'S BECAUSE YOU'RE TOO BUSY PLAYING WITH DOLLS!
DOLLS?!! I DON'T PLAY WITH DOLLS . . . ANYMORE.
CLAUDIA . . . KRISTY DIDN'T MEAN TO UPSET STACEY. . . .
DIDN'T MEAN TO UPSET HER? SHE ACCUSED HER MOTHER OF LYING!
OH, WHAT A CRYBABY.
EXCUSE ME, GIRLS?
YOU ARE YELLING. WHAT IS WRONG, AND MAY I HELP YOU IN SOME WAY?
NO, MIMI. I'M SORRY.

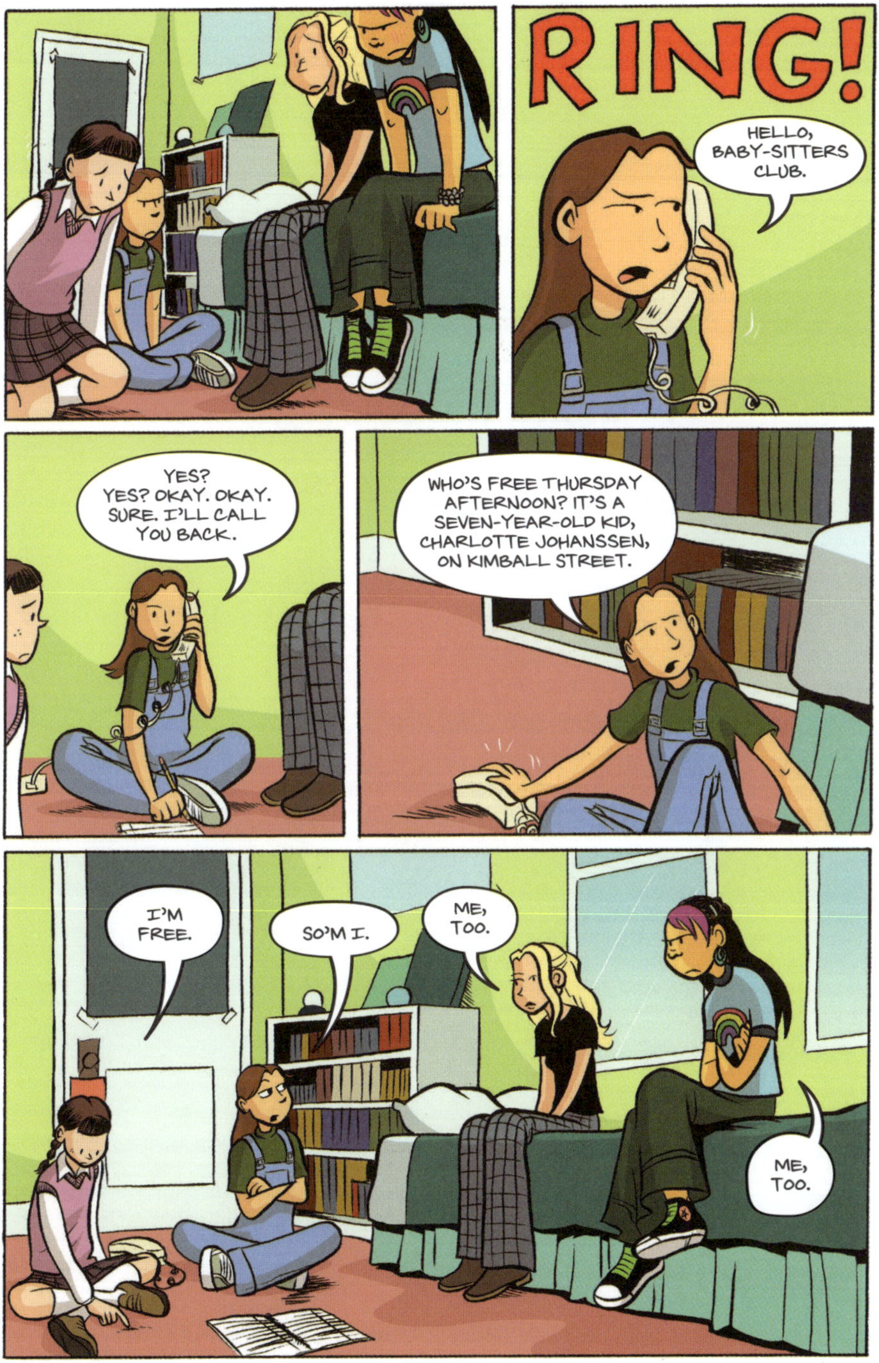
RING!
HELLO, BABY-SITTERS CLUB.
YES? YES? OKAY. OKAY. SURE. I'LL CALL YOU BACK.
WHO'S FREE THURSDAY AFTERNOON? IT'S A SEVEN-YEAR-OLD KID, CHARLOTTE JOHANSSEN, ON KIMBALL STREET.
I'M FREE.
SO'M I.
ME, TOO.
ME, TOO.

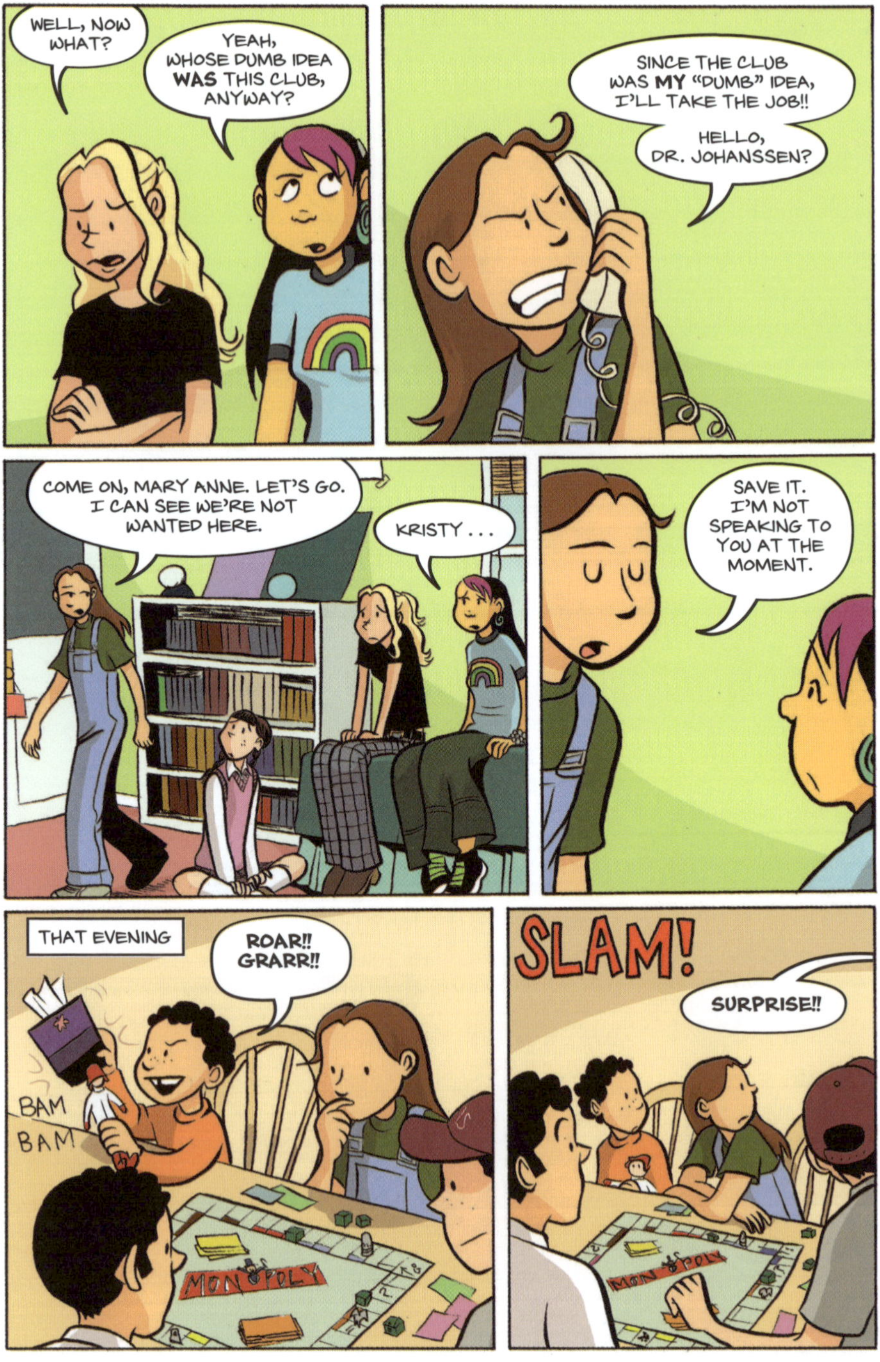

WELL, NOW WHAT?
YEAH, WHOSE DUMB IDEA **WAS** THIS CLUB, ANYWAY?
SINCE THE CLUB WAS **MY** "DUMB" IDEA, I'LL TAKE THE JOB!!
HELLO, DR. JOHANSSEN?
COME ON, MARY ANNE. LET'S GO. I CAN SEE WE'RE NOT WANTED HERE.
KRISTY . . .
SAVE IT. I'M NOT SPEAKING TO YOU AT THE MOMENT.
THAT EVENING
ROAR!! GRARR!!
BAM BAM
SLAM!
SURPRISE!!

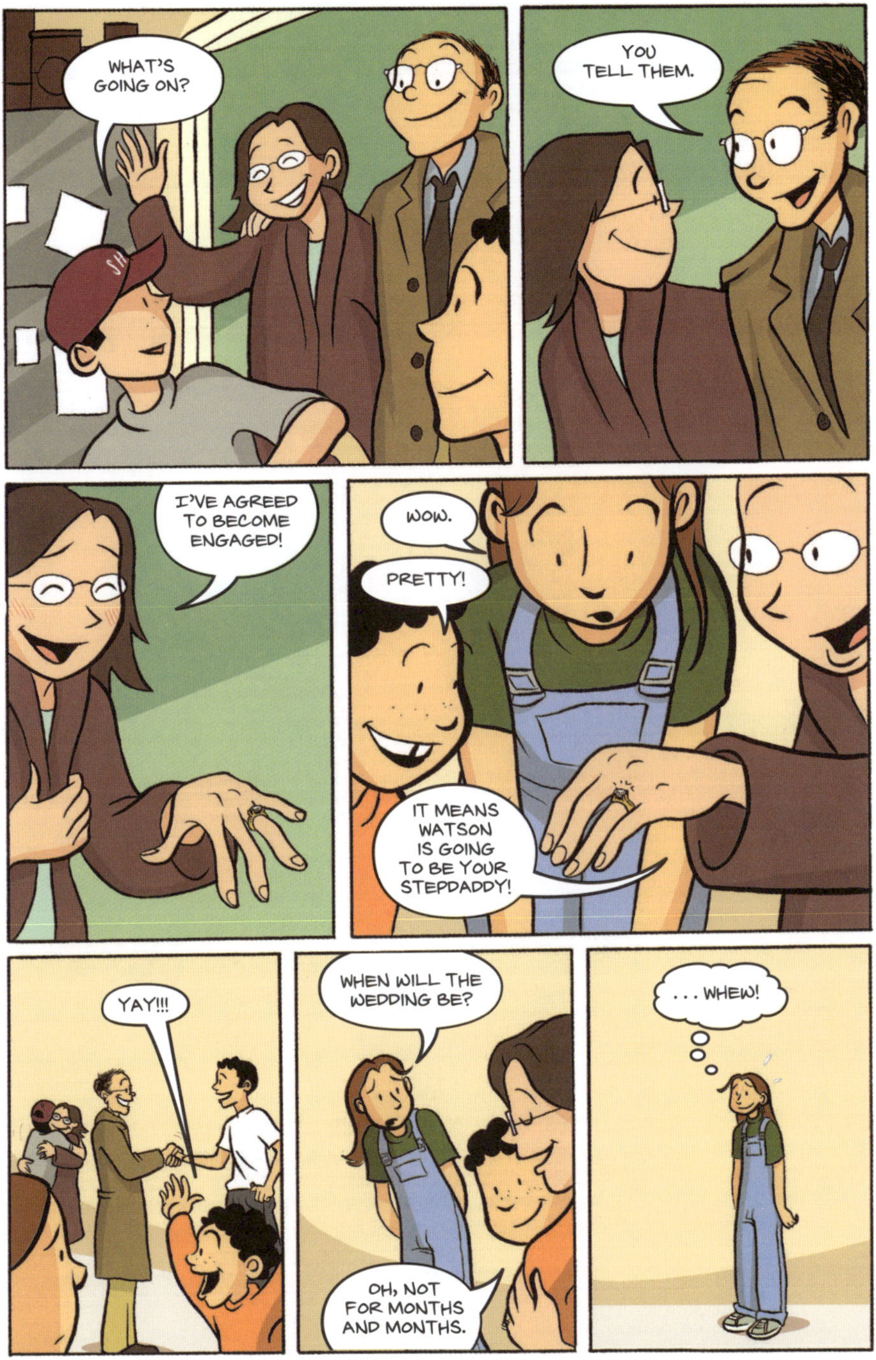
WHAT'S GOING ON?
YOU TELL THEM.
I'VE AGREED TO BECOME ENGAGED!
WOW.
PRETTY!
IT MEANS WATSON IS GOING TO BE YOUR STEPDADDY!
YAY!!!
WHEN WILL THE WEDDING BE?
OH, NOT FOR MONTHS AND MONTHS.
. . . WHEW!

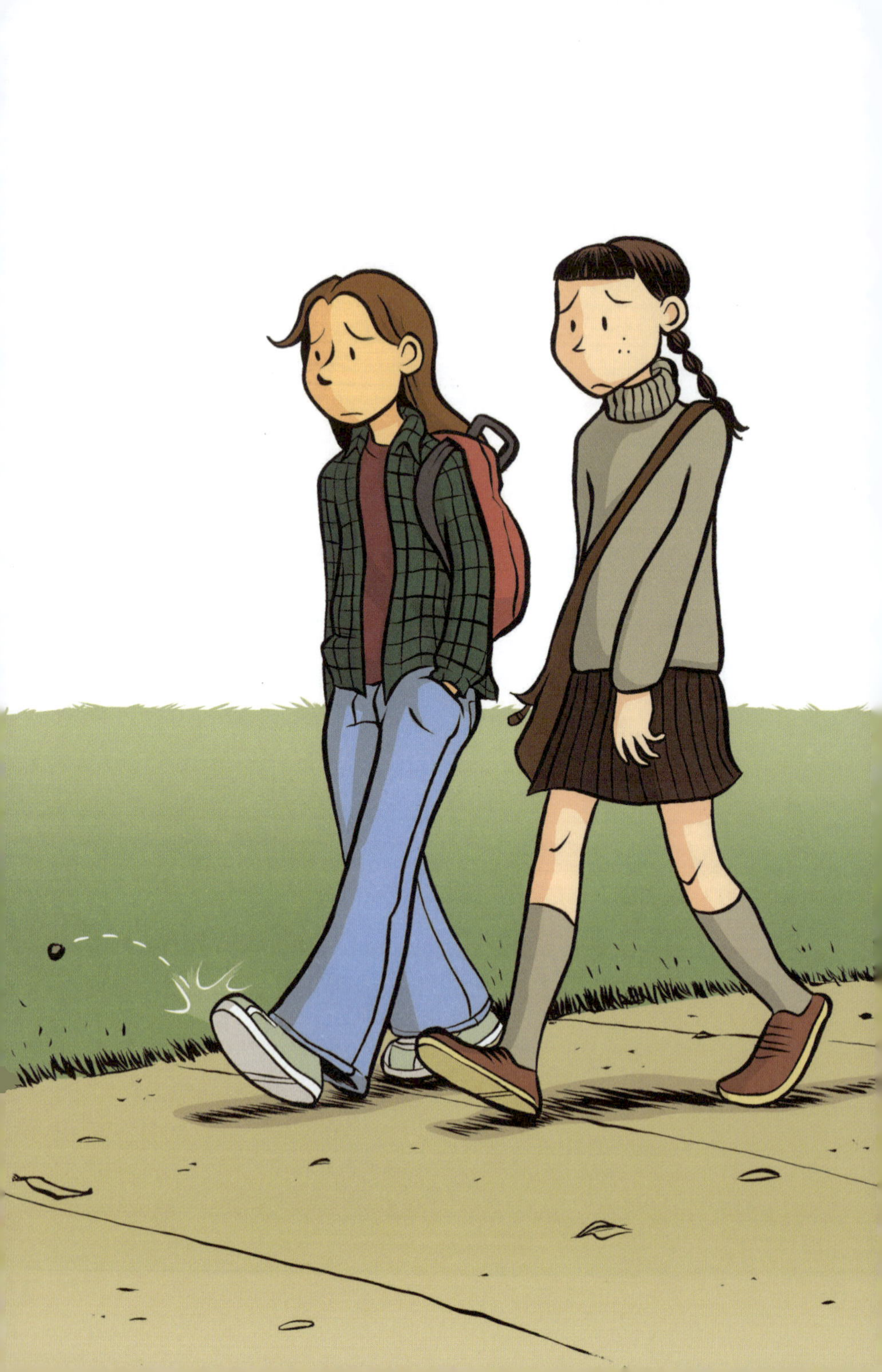

CHAPTER 14

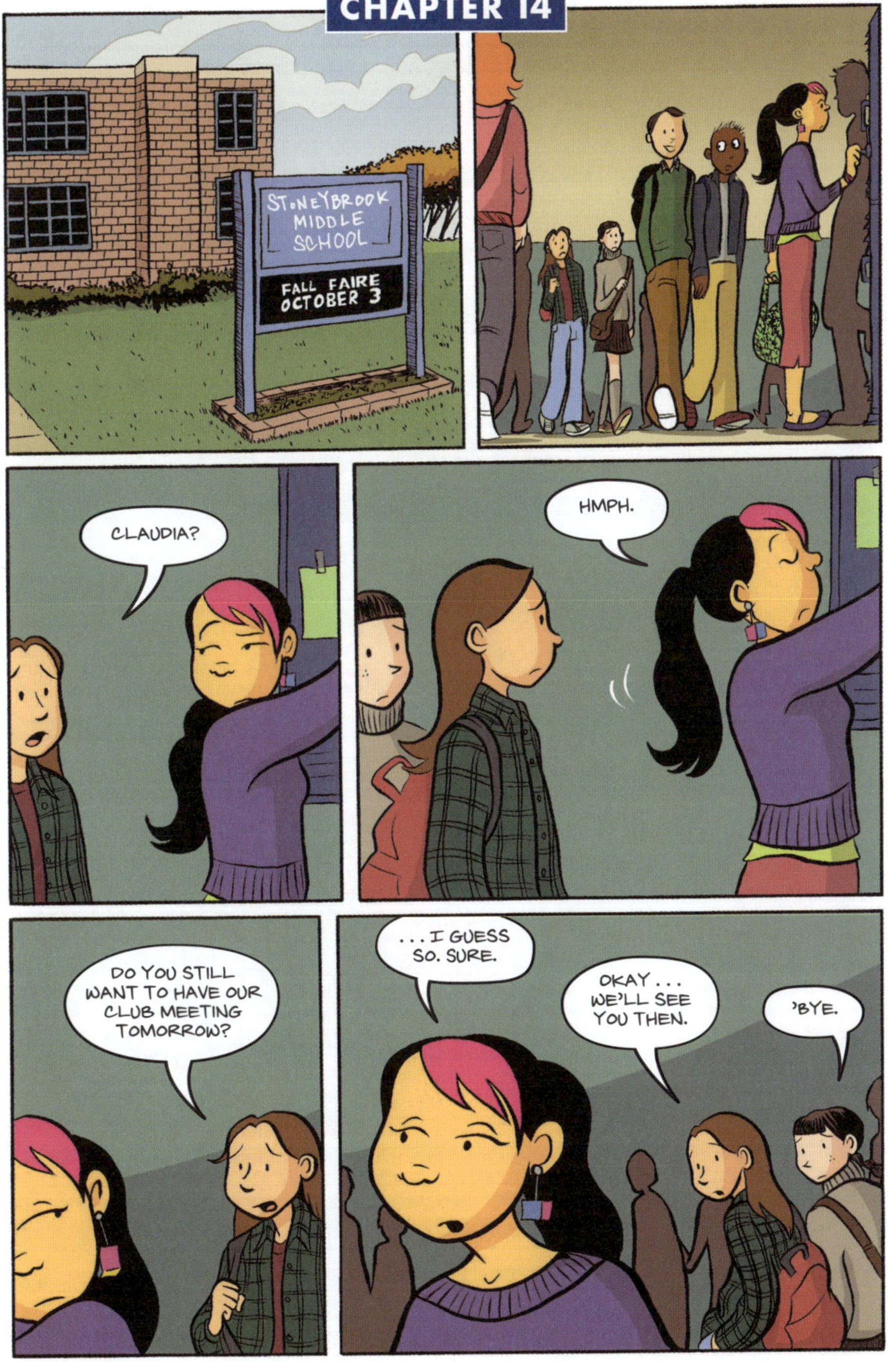
STONEYBROOK MIDDLE SCHOOL
FALL FAIRE OCTOBER 3
CLAUDIA?
HMPH.
DO YOU STILL WANT TO HAVE OUR CLUB MEETING TOMORROW?
...I GUESS SO. SURE.
OKAY... WE'LL SEE YOU THEN.
'BYE.

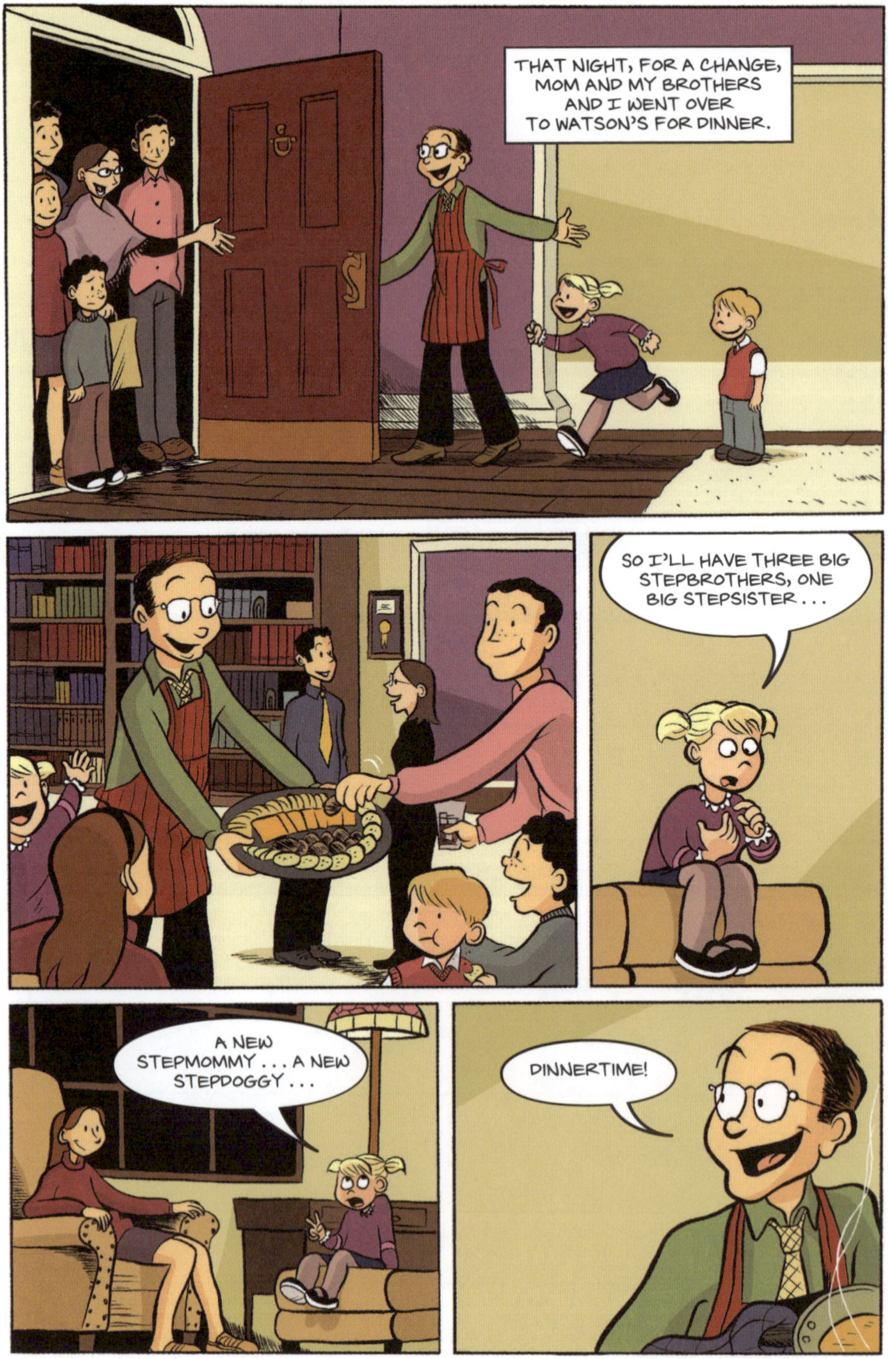
THAT NIGHT, FOR A CHANGE, MOM AND MY BROTHERS AND I WENT OVER TO WATSON'S FOR DINNER.
SO I'LL HAVE THREE BIG STEPBROTHERS, ONE BIG STEPSISTER . . .
A NEW STEPMOMMY . . . A NEW STEPDOGGY . . .
DINNERTIME!

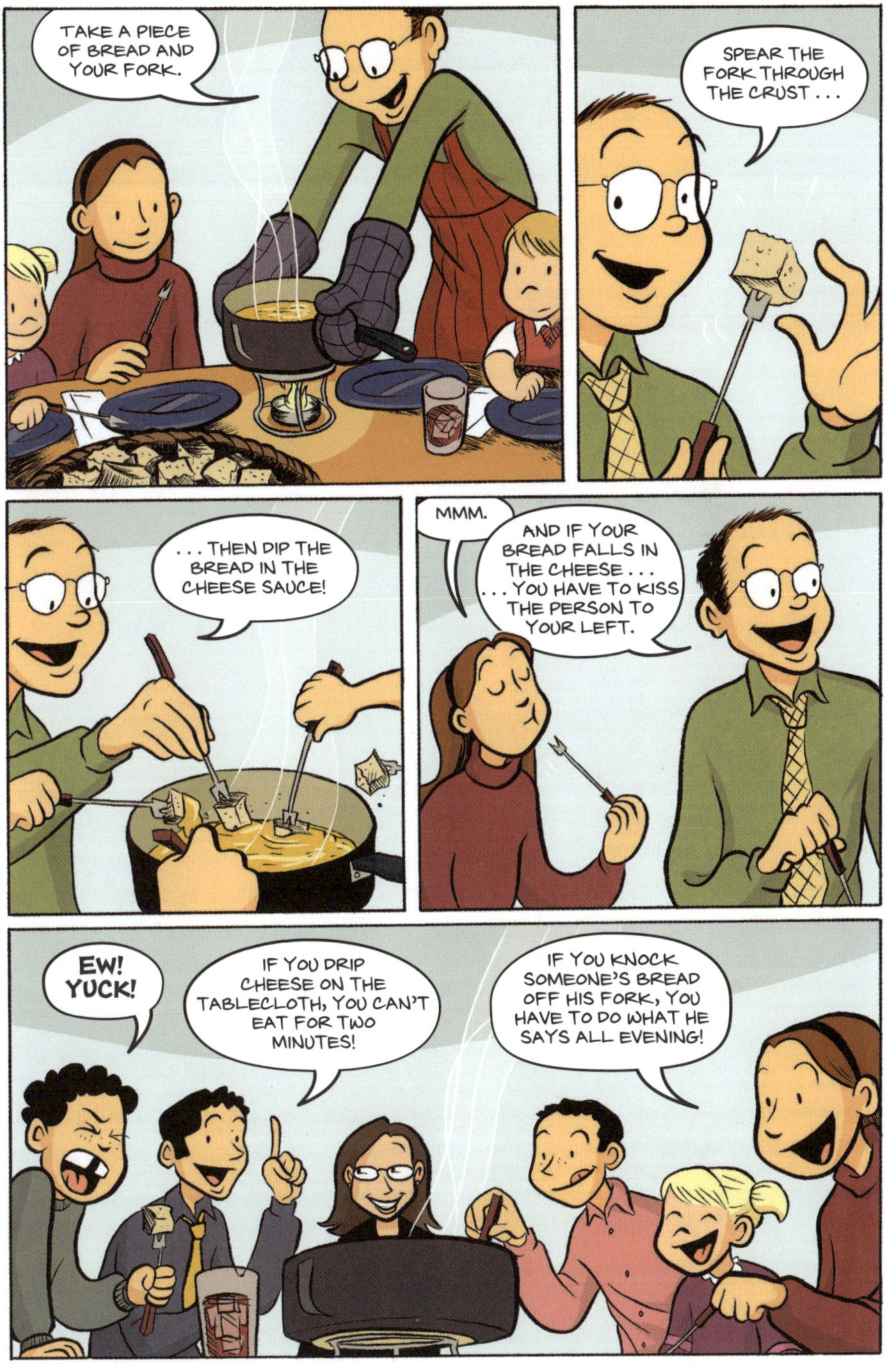
TAKE A PIECE OF BREAD AND YOUR FORK.
SPEAR THE FORK THROUGH THE CRUST . . .
. . . THEN DIP THE BREAD IN THE CHEESE SAUCE!
MMM.
AND IF YOUR BREAD FALLS IN THE CHEESE . . .
. . . YOU HAVE TO KISS THE PERSON TO YOUR LEFT.
EW! YUCK!
IF YOU DRIP CHEESE ON THE TABLECLOTH, YOU CAN'T EAT FOR TWO MINUTES!
IF YOU KNOCK SOMEONE'S BREAD OFF HIS FORK, YOU HAVE TO DO WHAT HE SAYS ALL EVENING!

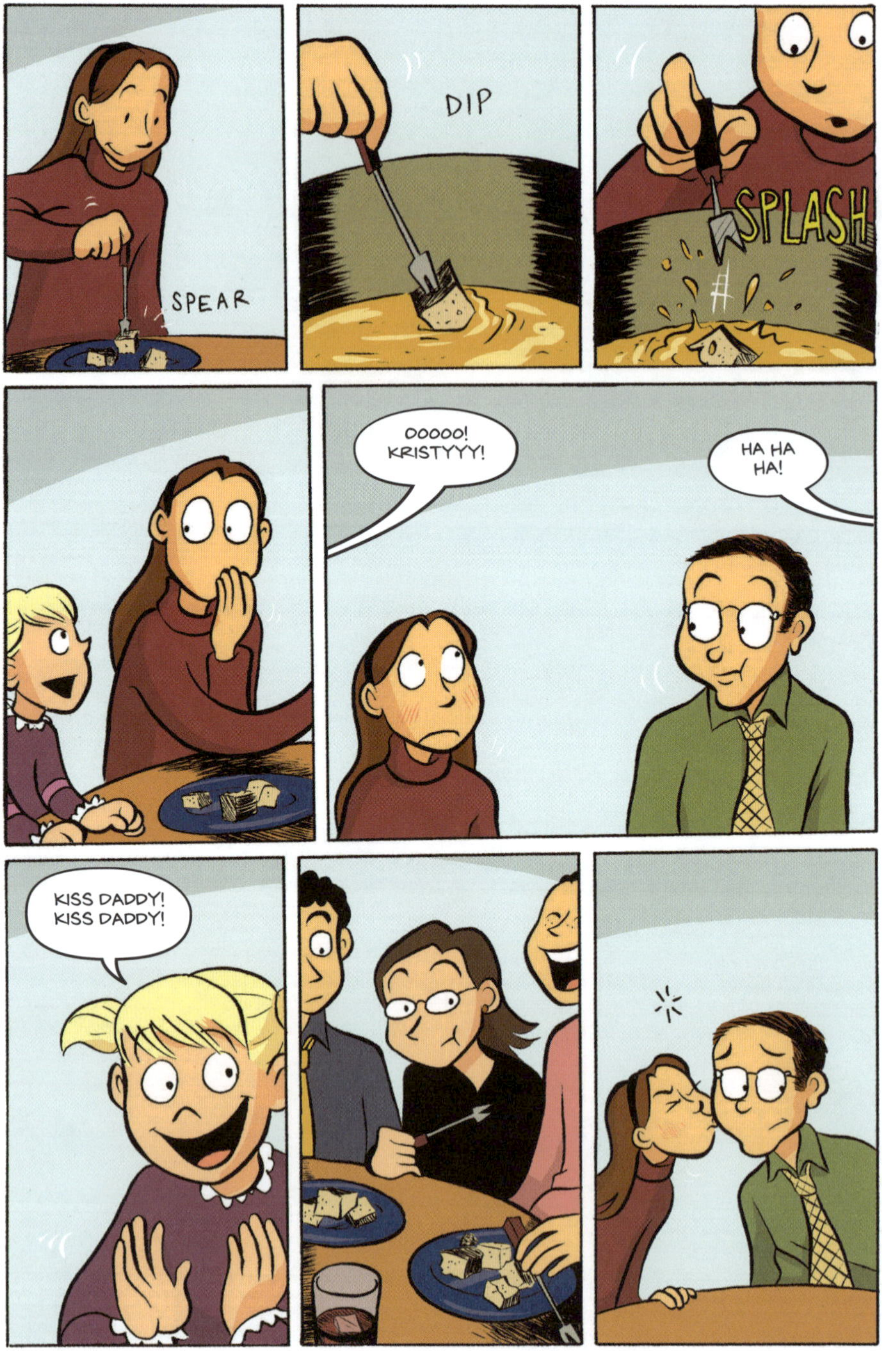
SPEAR
DIP
SPLASH
OOOOO! KRISTYYY!
HA HA HA!
KISS DADDY! KISS DADDY!

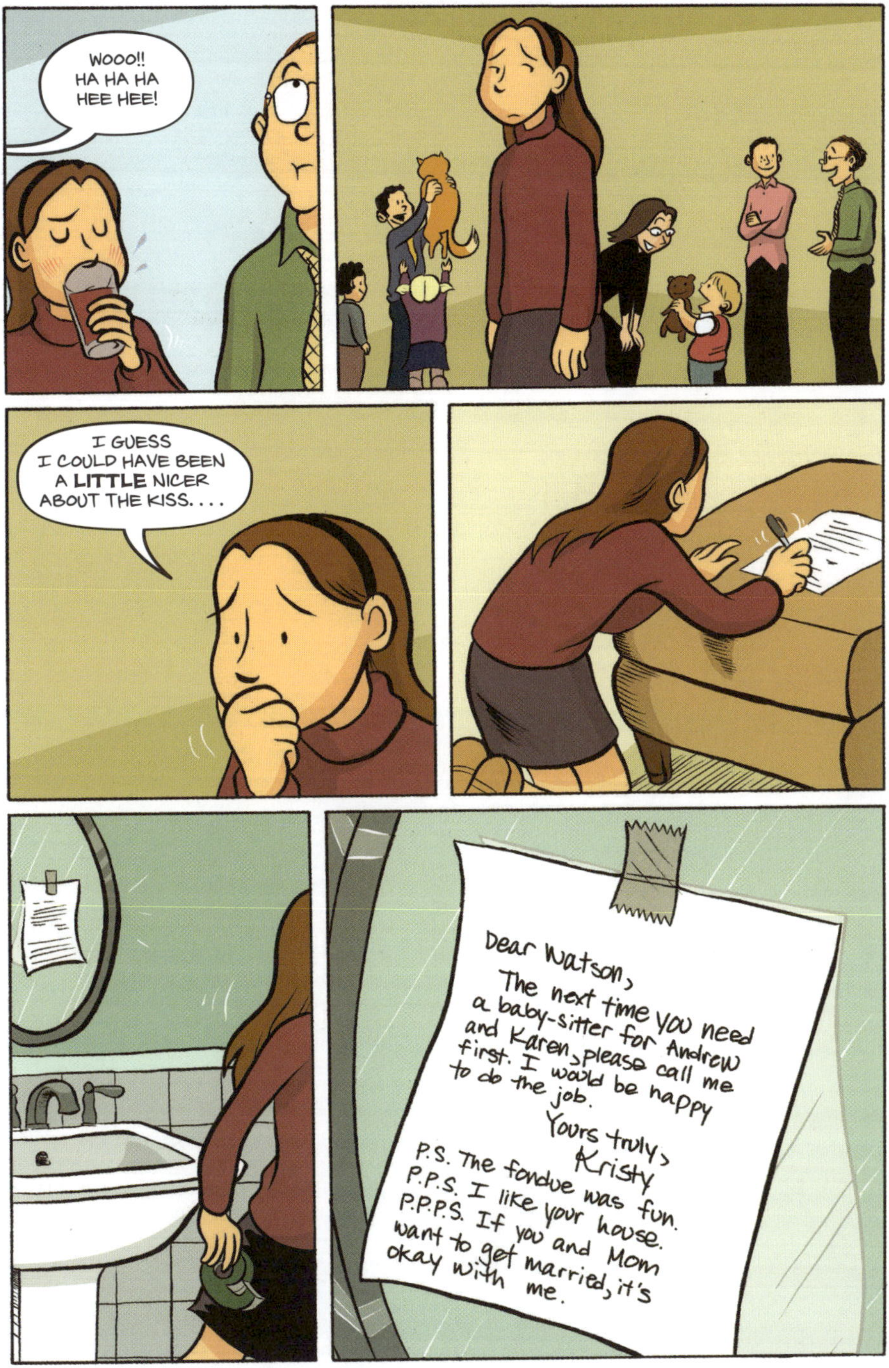
WOOO!! HA HA HA HEE HEE!
I GUESS I COULD HAVE BEEN A **LITTLE** NICER ABOUT THE KISS. . . .
Dear Watson,
The next time you need a baby-sitter for Andrew and Karen, please call me first. I would be happy to do the job.
Yours truly,
Kristy
P.S. The fondue was fun.
P.P.S. I like your house.
P.P.P.S. If you and Mom want to get married, it's okay with me.

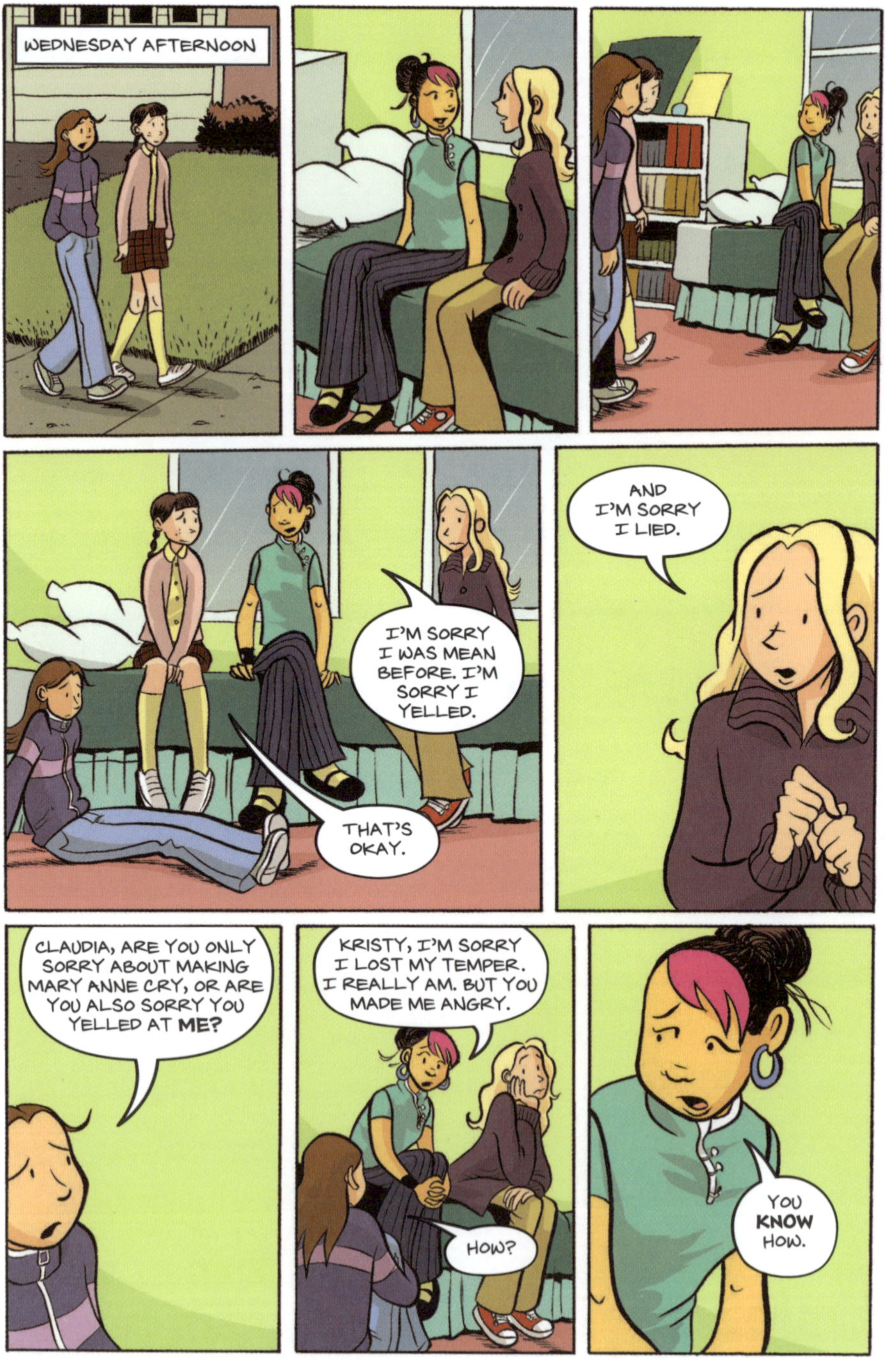
WEDNESDAY AFTERNOON
I'M SORRY I WAS MEAN BEFORE. I'M SORRY I YELLED.
THAT'S OKAY.
AND I'M SORRY I LIED.
CLAUDIA, ARE YOU ONLY SORRY ABOUT MAKING MARY ANNE CRY, OR ARE YOU ALSO SORRY YOU YELLED AT **ME?**
KRISTY, I'M SORRY I LOST MY TEMPER. I REALLY AM. BUT YOU MADE ME ANGRY.
HOW?
YOU **KNOW** HOW.

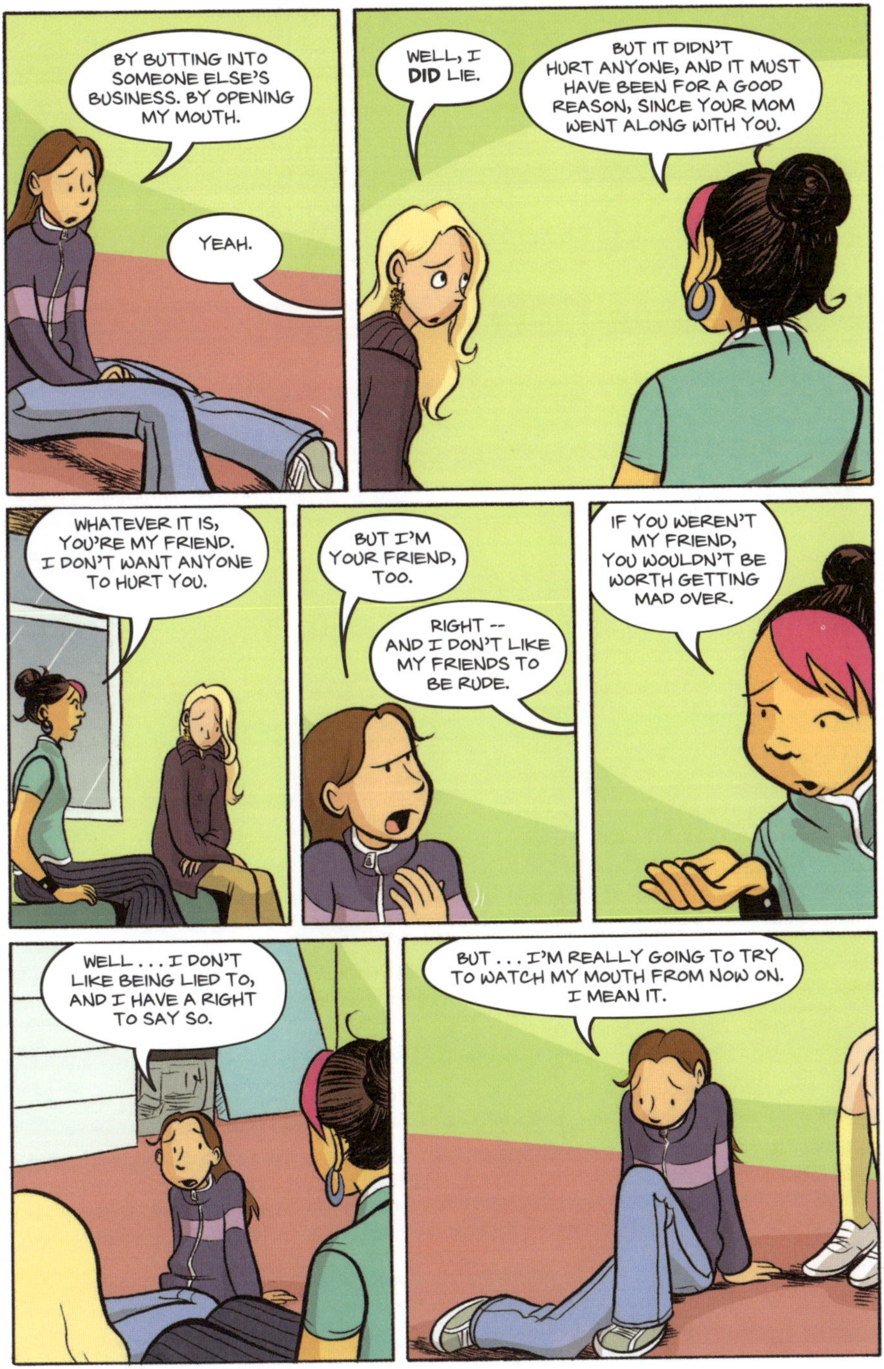
BY BUTTING INTO SOMEONE ELSE'S BUSINESS. BY OPENING MY MOUTH.
YEAH.
WELL, I **DID** LIE.
BUT IT DIDN'T HURT ANYONE, AND IT MUST HAVE BEEN FOR A GOOD REASON, SINCE YOUR MOM WENT ALONG WITH YOU.
WHATEVER IT IS, YOU'RE MY FRIEND. I DON'T WANT ANYONE TO HURT YOU.
BUT I'M YOUR FRIEND, TOO.
RIGHT -- AND I DON'T LIKE MY FRIENDS TO BE RUDE.
IF YOU WEREN'T MY FRIEND, YOU WOULDN'T BE WORTH GETTING MAD OVER.
WELL . . . I DON'T LIKE BEING LIED TO, AND I HAVE A RIGHT TO SAY SO.
BUT . . . I'M REALLY GOING TO TRY TO WATCH MY MOUTH FROM NOW ON. I MEAN IT.

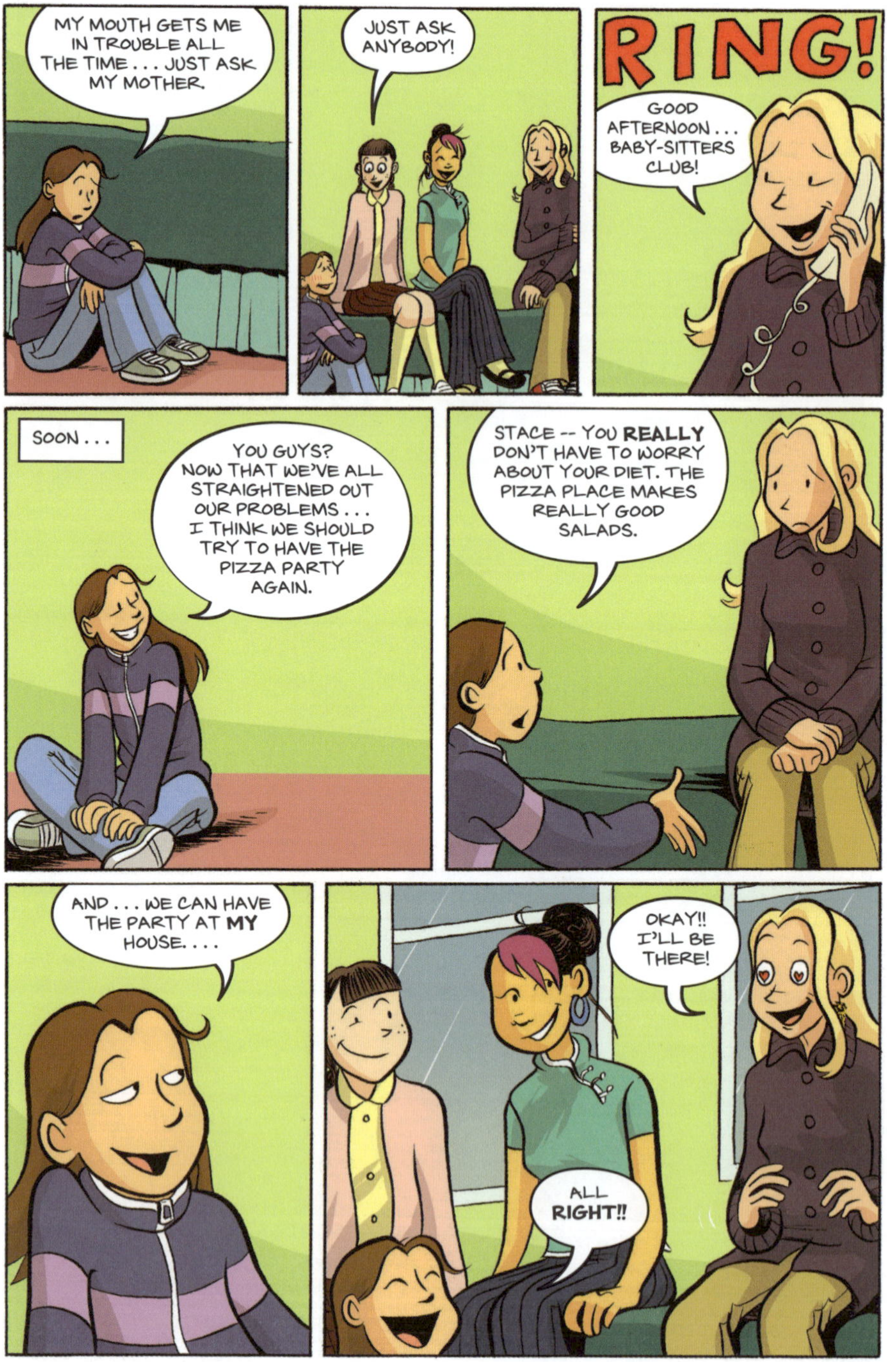
MY MOUTH GETS ME IN TROUBLE ALL THE TIME . . . JUST ASK MY MOTHER.
JUST ASK ANYBODY!
RING!
GOOD AFTERNOON . . . BABY-SITTERS CLUB!
SOON . . .
YOU GUYS? NOW THAT WE'VE ALL STRAIGHTENED OUT OUR PROBLEMS . . . I THINK WE SHOULD TRY TO HAVE THE PIZZA PARTY AGAIN.
STACE -- YOU **REALLY** DON'T HAVE TO WORRY ABOUT YOUR DIET. THE PIZZA PLACE MAKES REALLY GOOD SALADS.
AND . . . WE CAN HAVE THE PARTY AT **MY** HOUSE. . . .
OKAY!! I'LL BE THERE!
ALL **RIGHT!!**

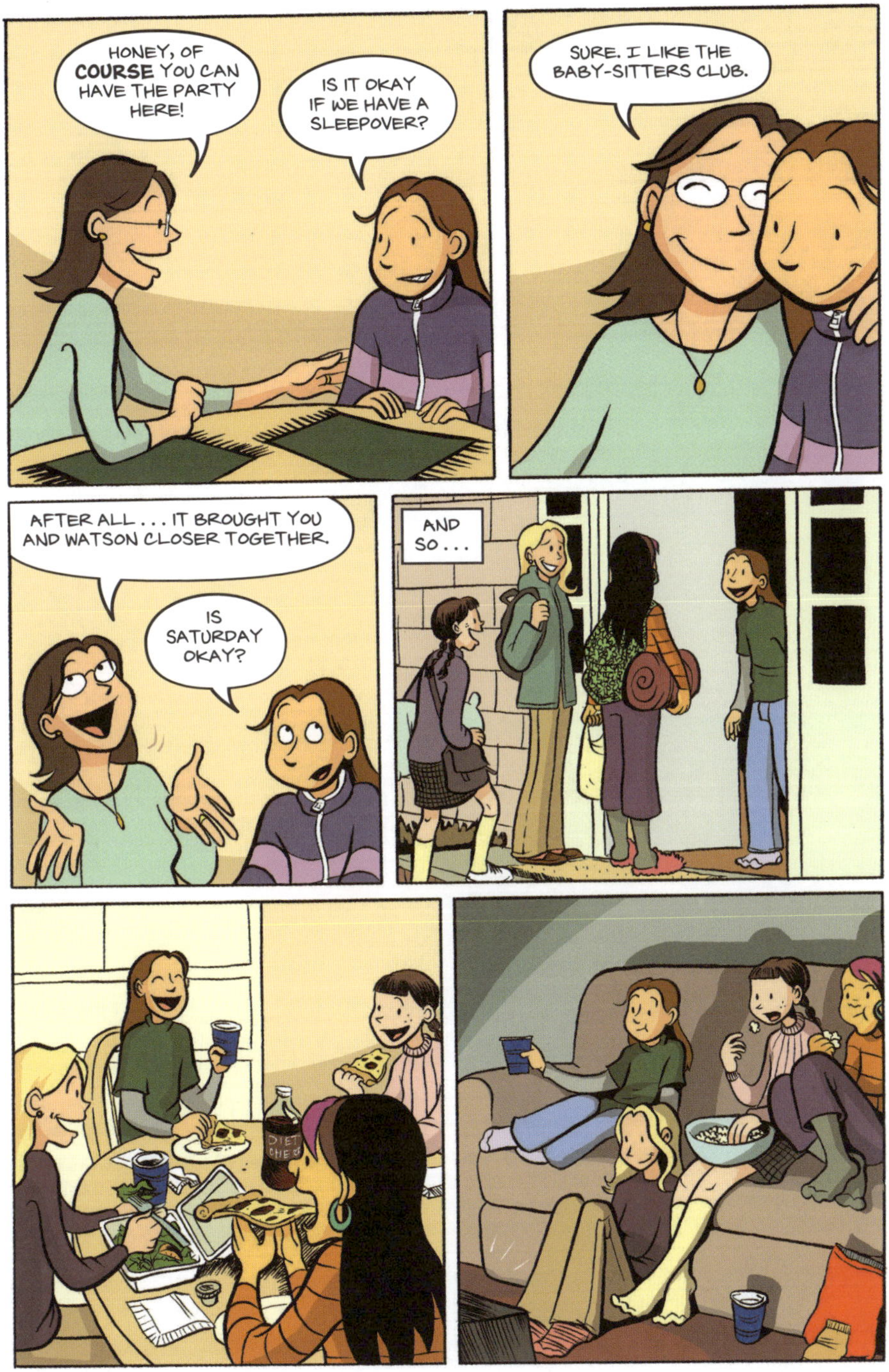
HONEY, OF COURSE YOU CAN HAVE THE PARTY HERE!
IS IT OKAY IF WE HAVE A SLEEPOVER?
SURE. I LIKE THE BABY-SITTERS CLUB.
AFTER ALL . . . IT BROUGHT YOU AND WATSON CLOSER TOGETHER.
IS SATURDAY OKAY?
AND SO . . .

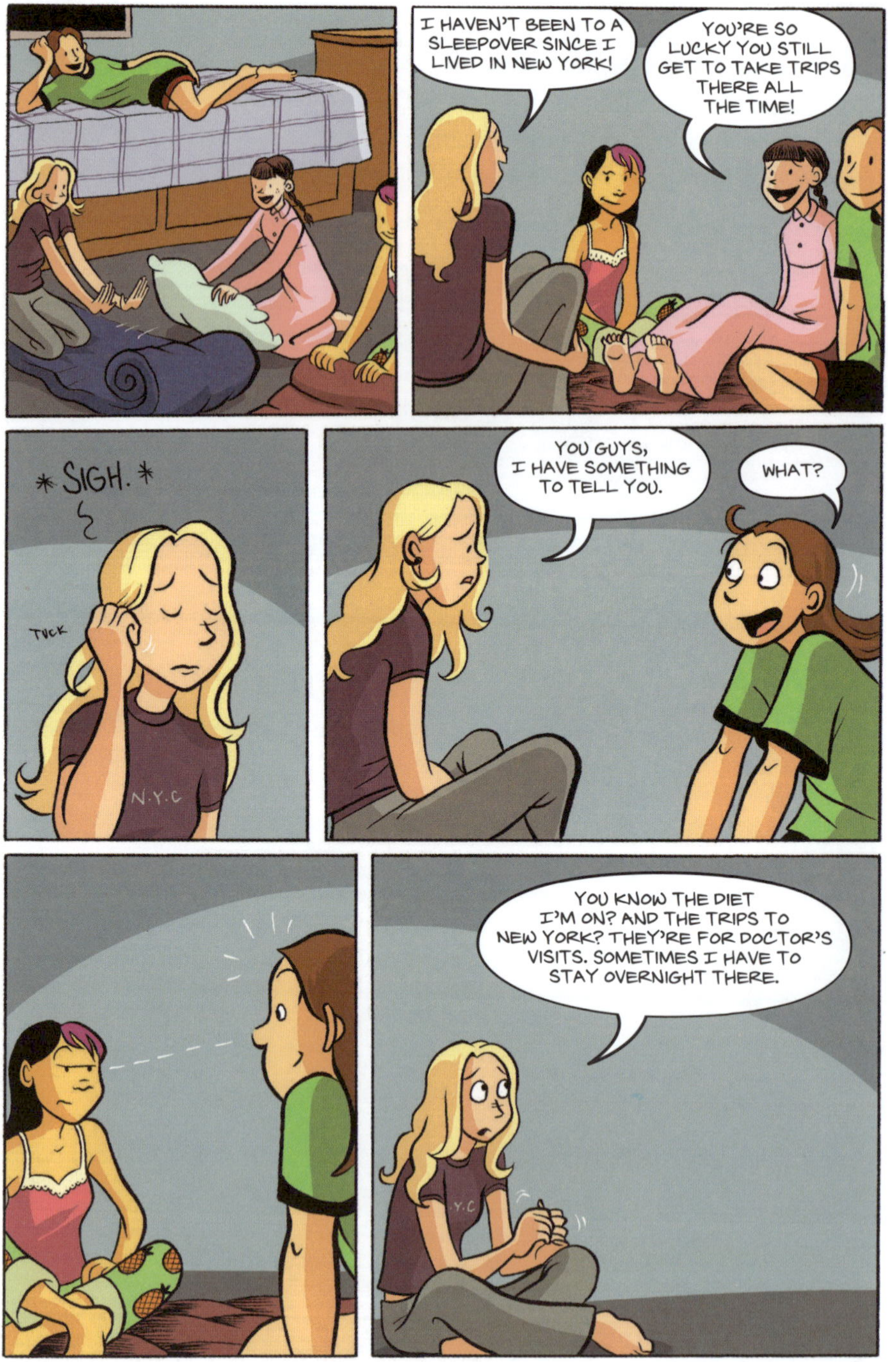
I HAVEN'T BEEN TO A SLEEPOVER SINCE I LIVED IN NEW YORK!
YOU'RE SO LUCKY YOU STILL GET TO TAKE TRIPS THERE ALL THE TIME!
SIGH.
TUCK
N.Y.C
YOU GUYS, I HAVE SOMETHING TO TELL YOU.
WHAT?
YOU KNOW THE DIET I'M ON? AND THE TRIPS TO NEW YORK? THEY'RE FOR DOCTOR'S VISITS. SOMETIMES I HAVE TO STAY OVERNIGHT THERE.

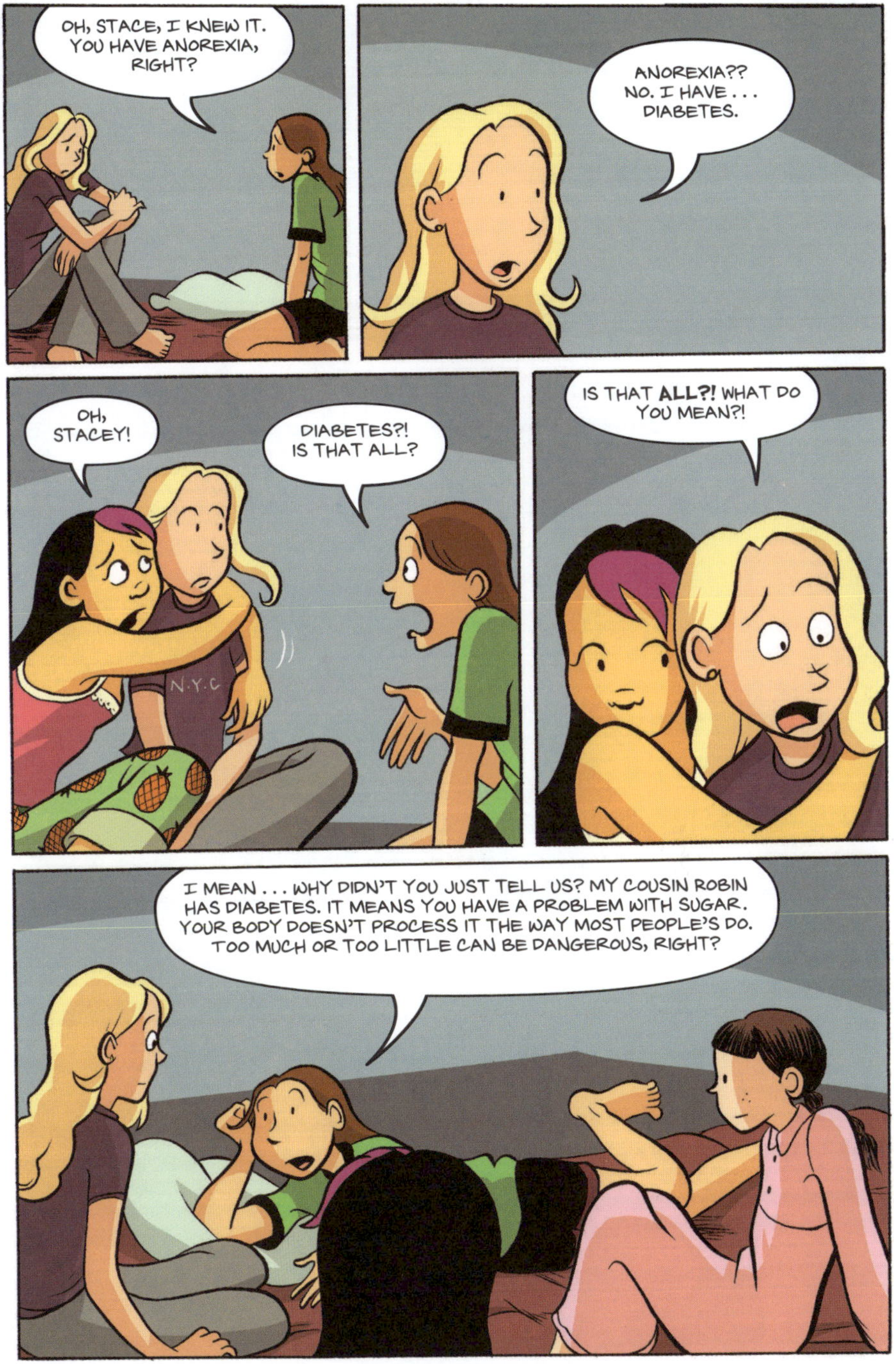
OH, STACE, I KNEW IT. YOU HAVE ANOREXIA, RIGHT?
ANOREXIA?? NO. I HAVE . . . DIABETES.
OH, STACEY!
DIABETES?! IS THAT ALL?
IS THAT **ALL?!** WHAT DO YOU MEAN?!
N.Y.C
I MEAN . . . WHY DIDN'T YOU JUST TELL US? MY COUSIN ROBIN HAS DIABETES. IT MEANS YOU HAVE A PROBLEM WITH SUGAR. YOUR BODY DOESN'T PROCESS IT THE WAY MOST PEOPLE'S DO. TOO MUCH OR TOO LITTLE CAN BE DANGEROUS, RIGHT?

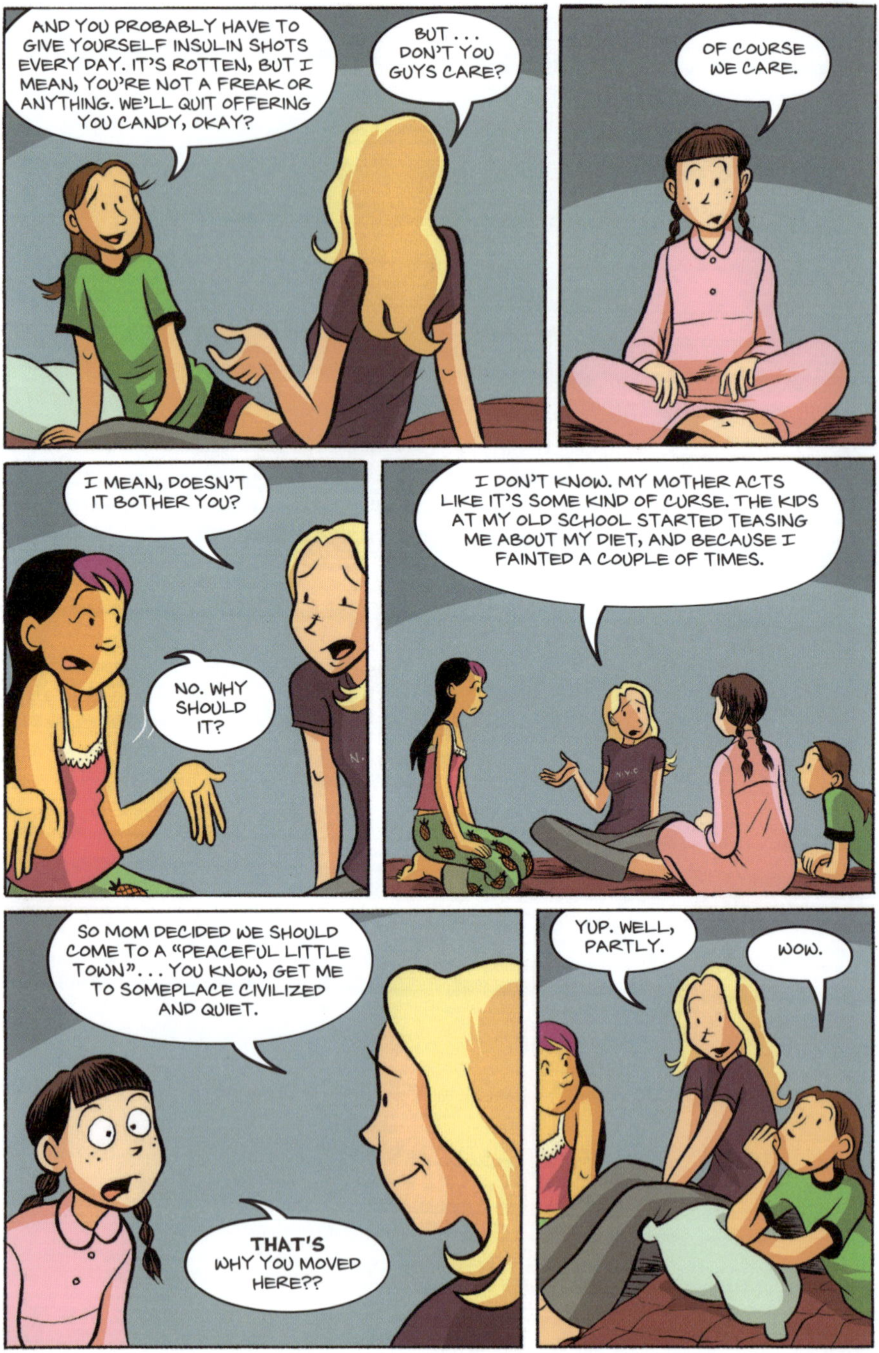
AND YOU PROBABLY HAVE TO GIVE YOURSELF INSULIN SHOTS EVERY DAY. IT'S ROTTEN, BUT I MEAN, YOU'RE NOT A FREAK OR ANYTHING. WE'LL QUIT OFFERING YOU CANDY, OKAY?
BUT . . . DON'T YOU GUYS CARE?
OF COURSE WE CARE.
I MEAN, DOESN'T IT BOTHER YOU?
NO. WHY SHOULD IT?
I DON'T KNOW. MY MOTHER ACTS LIKE IT'S SOME KIND OF CURSE. THE KIDS AT MY OLD SCHOOL STARTED TEASING ME ABOUT MY DIET, AND BECAUSE I FAINTED A COUPLE OF TIMES.
SO MOM DECIDED WE SHOULD COME TO A "PEACEFUL LITTLE TOWN" . . . YOU KNOW, GET ME TO SOMEPLACE CIVILIZED AND QUIET.
THAT'S WHY YOU MOVED HERE??
YUP. WELL, PARTLY.
WOW.

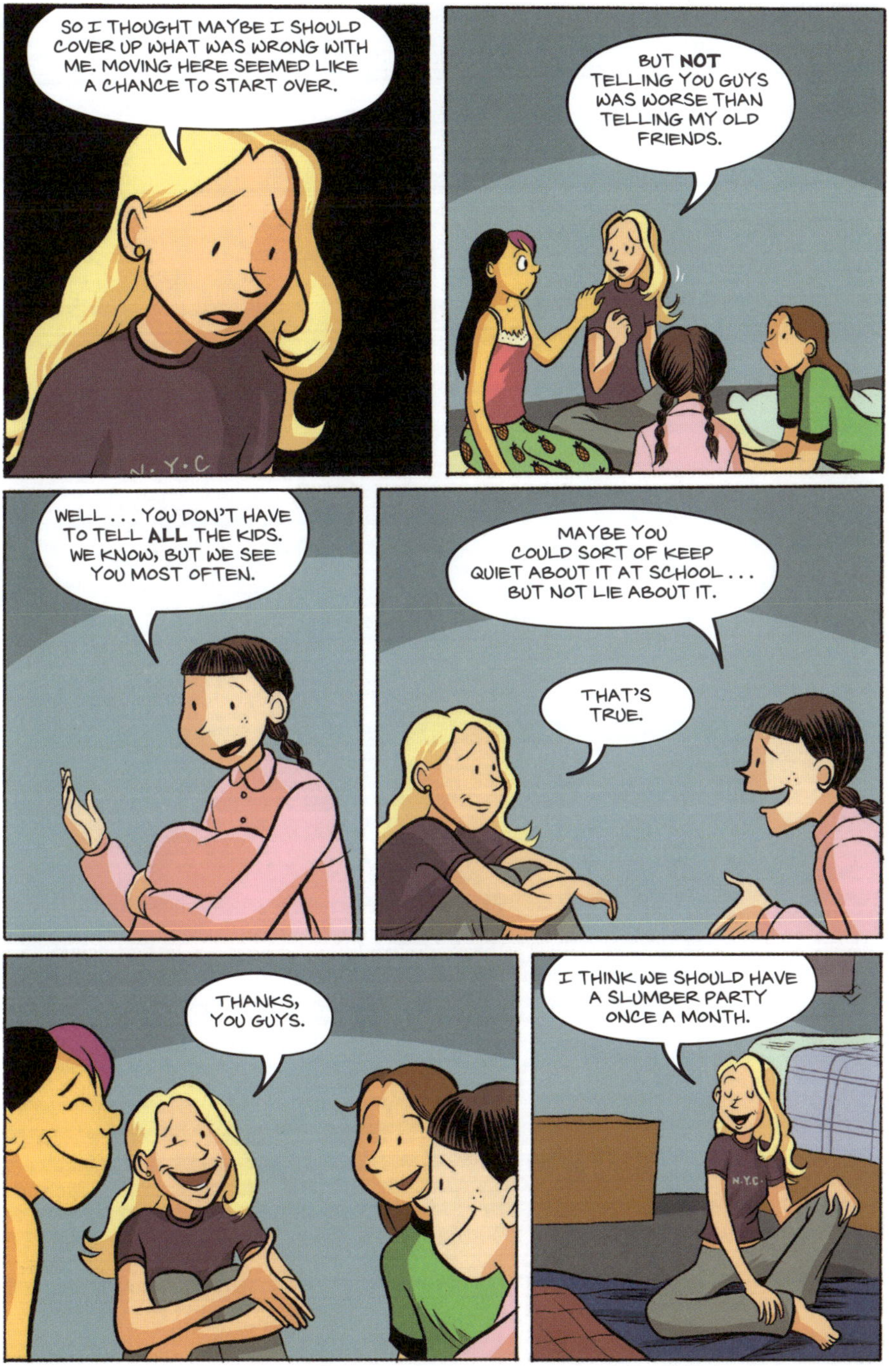
SO I THOUGHT MAYBE I SHOULD COVER UP WHAT WAS WRONG WITH ME. MOVING HERE SEEMED LIKE A CHANCE TO START OVER.
BUT **NOT** TELLING YOU GUYS WAS WORSE THAN TELLING MY OLD FRIENDS.
N.Y.C
WELL . . . YOU DON'T HAVE TO TELL **ALL** THE KIDS. WE KNOW, BUT WE SEE YOU MOST OFTEN.
MAYBE YOU COULD SORT OF KEEP QUIET ABOUT IT AT SCHOOL . . . BUT NOT LIE ABOUT IT.
THAT'S TRUE.
THANKS, YOU GUYS.
I THINK WE SHOULD HAVE A SLUMBER PARTY ONCE A MONTH.
N.Y.C.

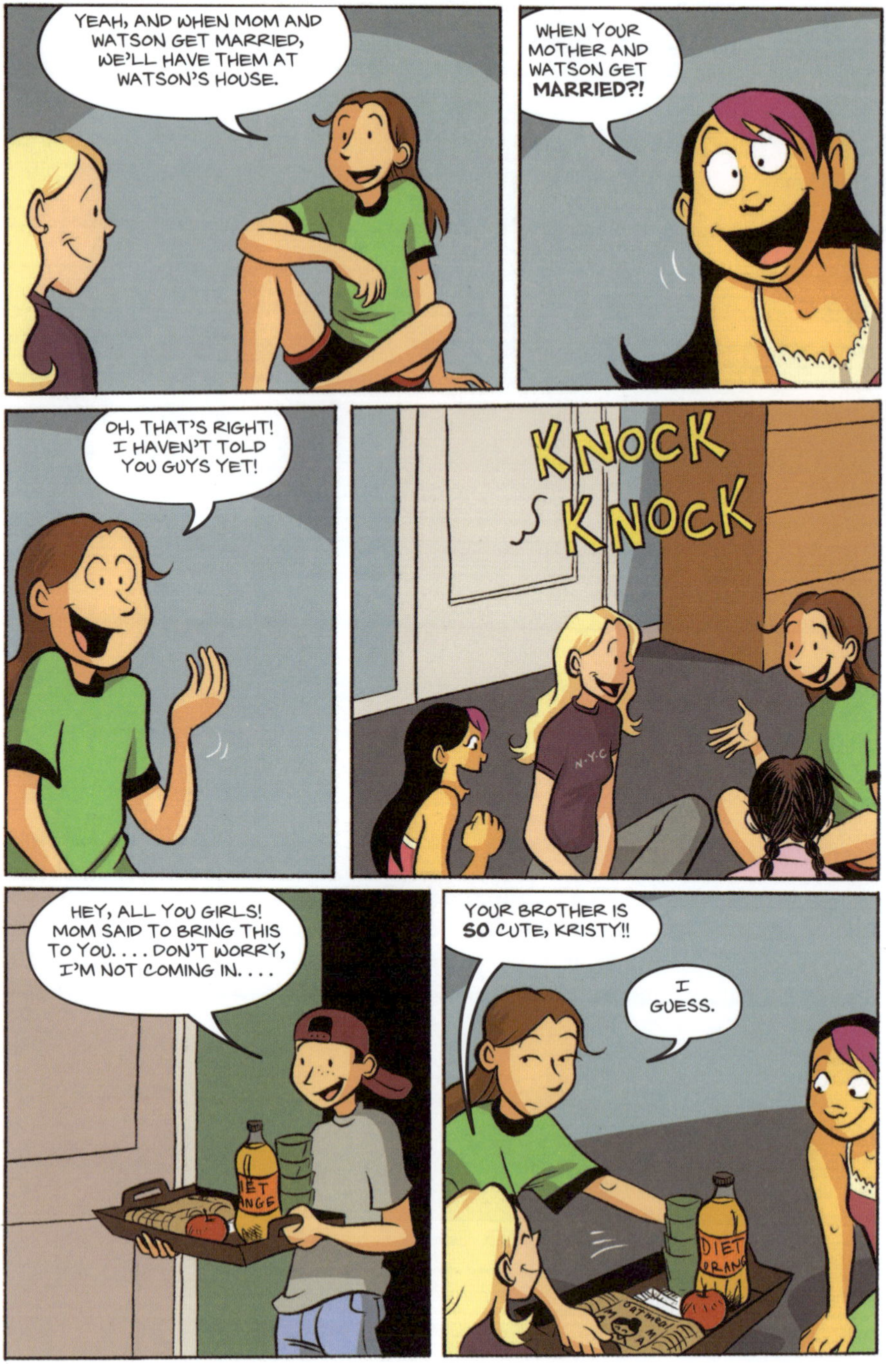
YEAH, AND WHEN MOM AND WATSON GET MARRIED, WE'LL HAVE THEM AT WATSON'S HOUSE.
WHEN YOUR MOTHER AND WATSON GET **MARRIED?!**
OH, THAT'S RIGHT! I HAVEN'T TOLD YOU GUYS YET!
KNOCK KNOCK
HEY, ALL YOU GIRLS! MOM SAID TO BRING THIS TO YOU. . . . DON'T WORRY, I'M NOT COMING IN. . . .
YOUR BROTHER IS **SO** CUTE, KRISTY!!
I GUESS.

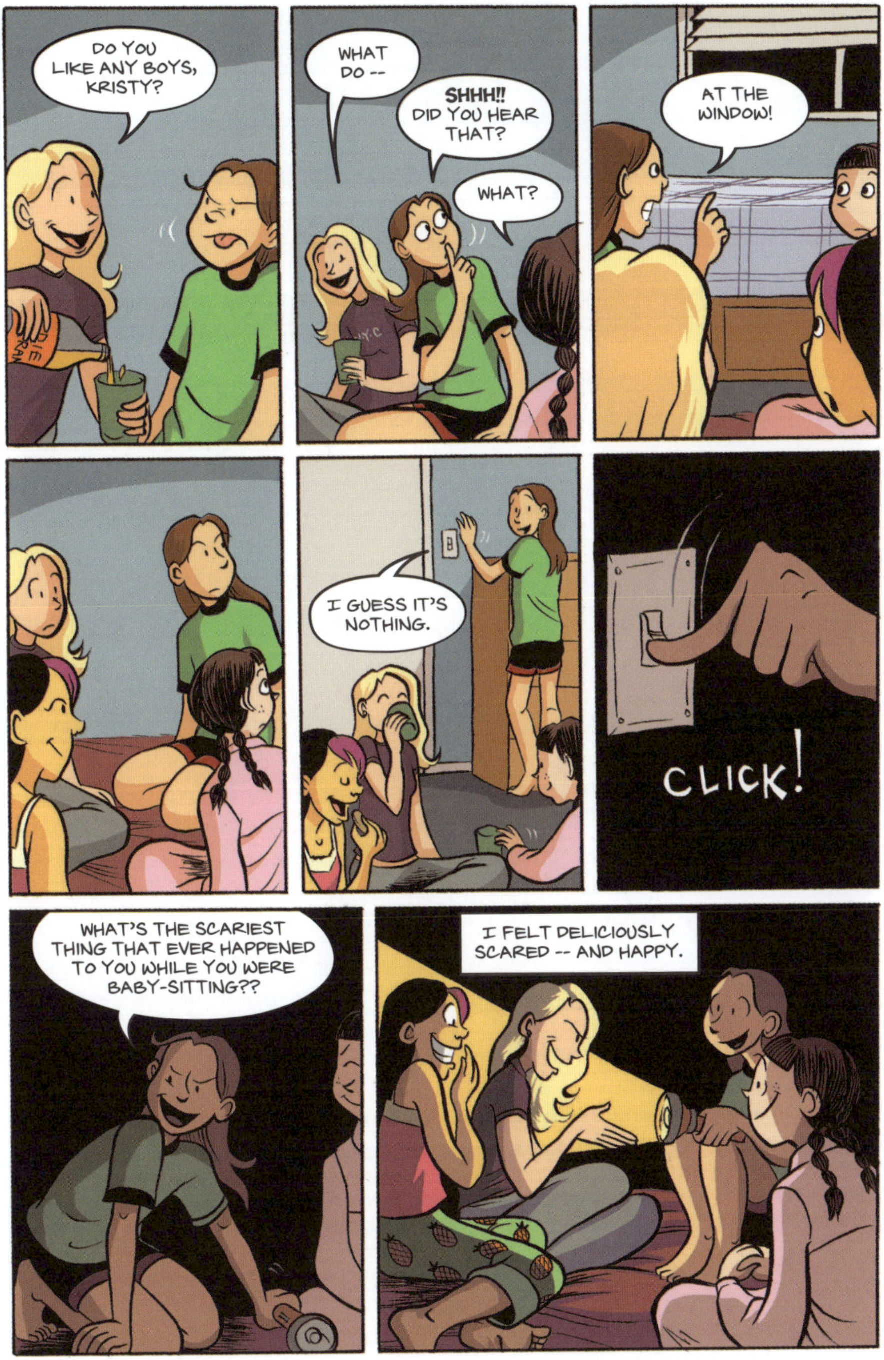
DO YOU LIKE ANY BOYS, KRISTY?
WHAT DO --
SHHH!! DID YOU HEAR THAT?
WHAT?
AT THE WINDOW!
I GUESS IT'S NOTHING.
CLICK!
WHAT'S THE SCARIEST THING THAT EVER HAPPENED TO YOU WHILE YOU WERE BABY-SITTING??
I FELT DELICIOUSLY SCARED -- AND HAPPY.

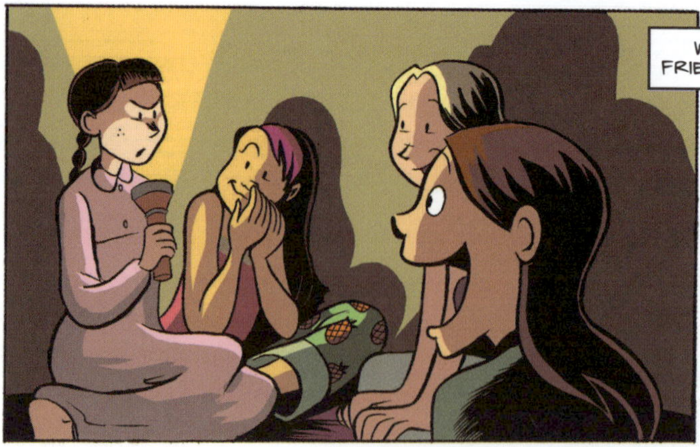
WE WERE FRIENDS AGAIN.

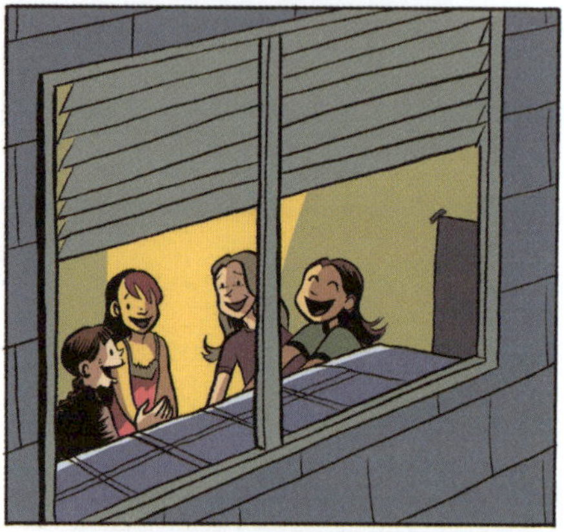
OUR CLUB WAS A SUCCESS, AND I, KRISTY THOMAS, HAD MADE IT WORK . . . OR, HELPED TO MAKE IT WORK.

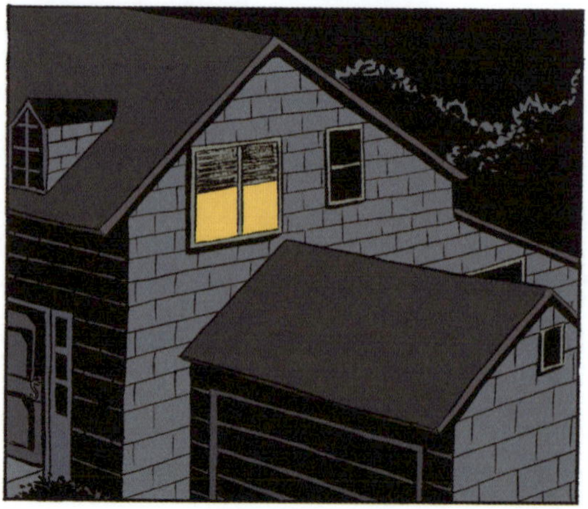
I HOPED THAT MARY ANNE, CLAUDIA, STACEY, AND I -- THE BABY-SITTERS CLUB -- WOULD STAY TOGETHER FOR A LONG TIME.

ANN M. MARTIN'S The Baby-sitters Club is one of the most popular series in the history of publishing — with more than 190 million books in print worldwide — and inspired a generation of young readers. Her novels include *Belle Teal*, *A Corner of the Universe* (a Newbery Honor book), *Here Today*, *A Dog's Life*, and *On Christmas Eve*, as well as the much-loved collaborations, *P.S. Longer Letter Later* and *Snail Mail No More*, with Paula Danziger, and *The Doll People* and *The Meanest Doll in the World*, written with Laura Godwin and illustrated by Brian Selznick. Ann lives in upstate New York.

RAINA TELGEMEIER is the #1 *New York Times* bestselling, multiple Eisner Award–winning creator of *Smile*, *Sisters*, and *Guts*, which are all graphic memoirs based on her childhood. She is also the creator of *Drama* and *Ghosts*, and is the adapter and illustrator of the first four Baby-sitters Club graphic novels. Raina lives in the San Francisco Bay Area. To learn more, visit her online at goraina.com.

DON'T MISS THE OTHER BABY-SITTERS CLUB GRAPHIC NOVELS!

RAINA TELGEMEIER
THE BABY-SITTERS CLUB
KRISTY'S GREAT IDEA
ANN M. MARTIN
RAINA TELGEMEIER
THE BABY-SITTERS CLUB
THE TRUTH ABOUT STACEY
BASED ON THE NOVEL BY
ANN M. MARTIN
RAINA TELGEMEIER
THE BABY-SITTERS CLUB
MARY ANNE SAVES THE DAY
ANN M. MARTIN
RAINA TELGEMEIER
THE BABY-SITTERS CLUB
CLAUDIA AND MEAN JANINE
ANN M. MARTIN
GALE GALLIGAN
THE BABY-SITTERS CLUB
DAWN AND THE IMPOSSIBLE THREE
ANN M. MARTIN
GALE GALLIGAN
THE BABY-SITTERS CLUB
KRISTY'S BIG DAY
ANN M. MARTIN
GALE GALLIGAN
THE BABY-SITTERS CLUB
BOY-CRAZY STACEY
ANN M. MARTIN
GALE GALLIGAN
THE BABY-SITTERS CLUB
LOGAN LIKES MARY ANNE!
ANN M. MARTIN
GABRIELA EPSTEIN
THE BABY-SITTERS CLUB
CLAUDIA AND THE NEW GIRL
ANN M. MARTIN
CHAN CHAU
THE BABY-SITTERS CLUB
KRISTY AND THE SNOBS
ANN M. MARTIN
GABRIELA EPSTEIN
THE BABY-SITTERS CLUB
GOOD-BYE STACEY, GOOD-BYE
ANN M. MARTIN
CHAN CHAU
THE BABY-SITTERS CLUB
JESSI'S SECRET LANGUAGE
ANN M. MARTIN

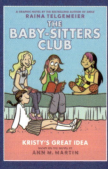

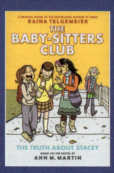

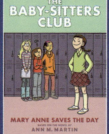

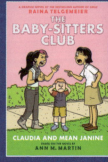

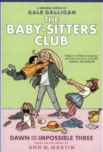

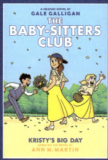

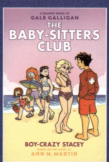

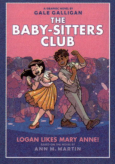

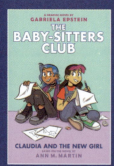

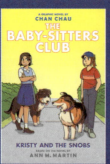

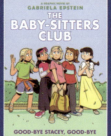

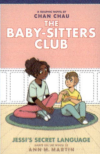

ANN M. MARTIN

THE BABY-SITTERS CLUB

THE TRUTH ABOUT STACEY

A GRAPHIC NOVEL BY
RAINA TELGEMEIER
WITH COLOR BY BRADEN LAMB

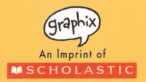

An Imprint of
SCHOLASTIC

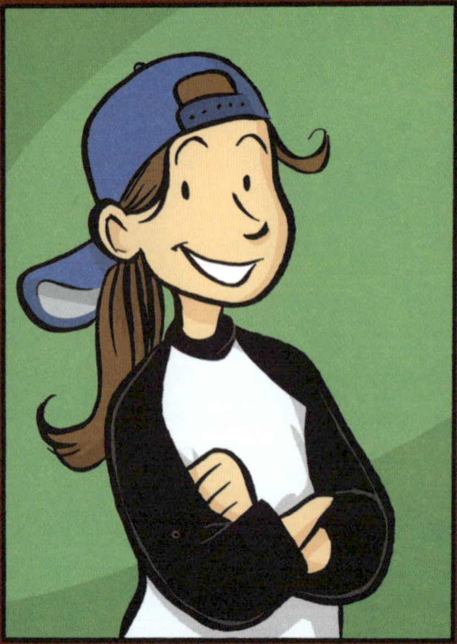

KRISTY THOMAS
PRESIDENT

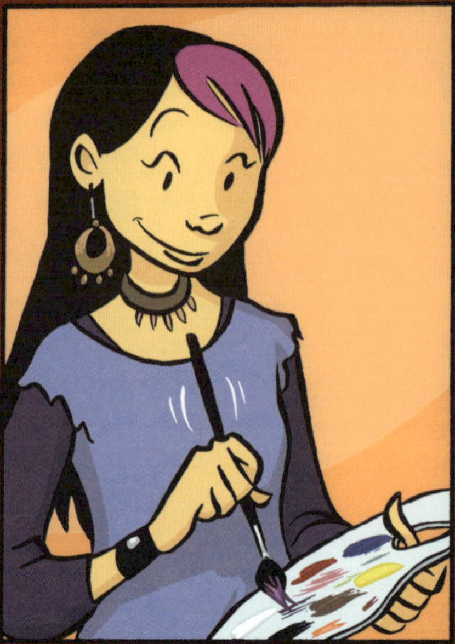

CLAUDIA KISHI
VICE PRESIDENT

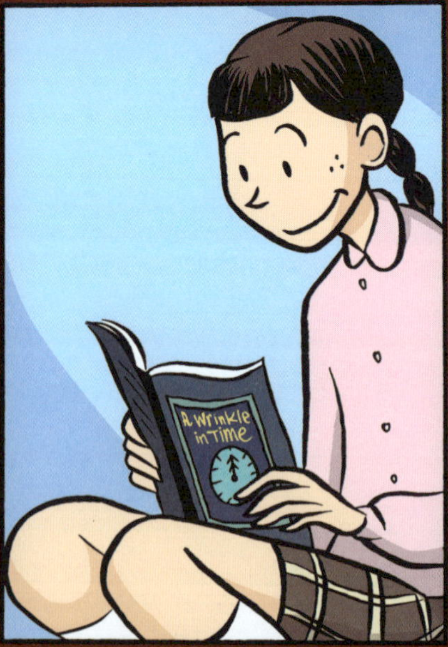
A Wrinkle in Time

MARY ANNE SPIER
SECRETARY

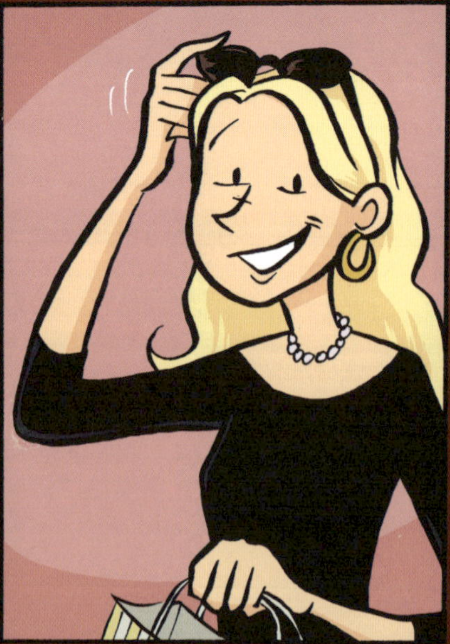

STACEY MCGILL
TREASURER

CHAPTER 1

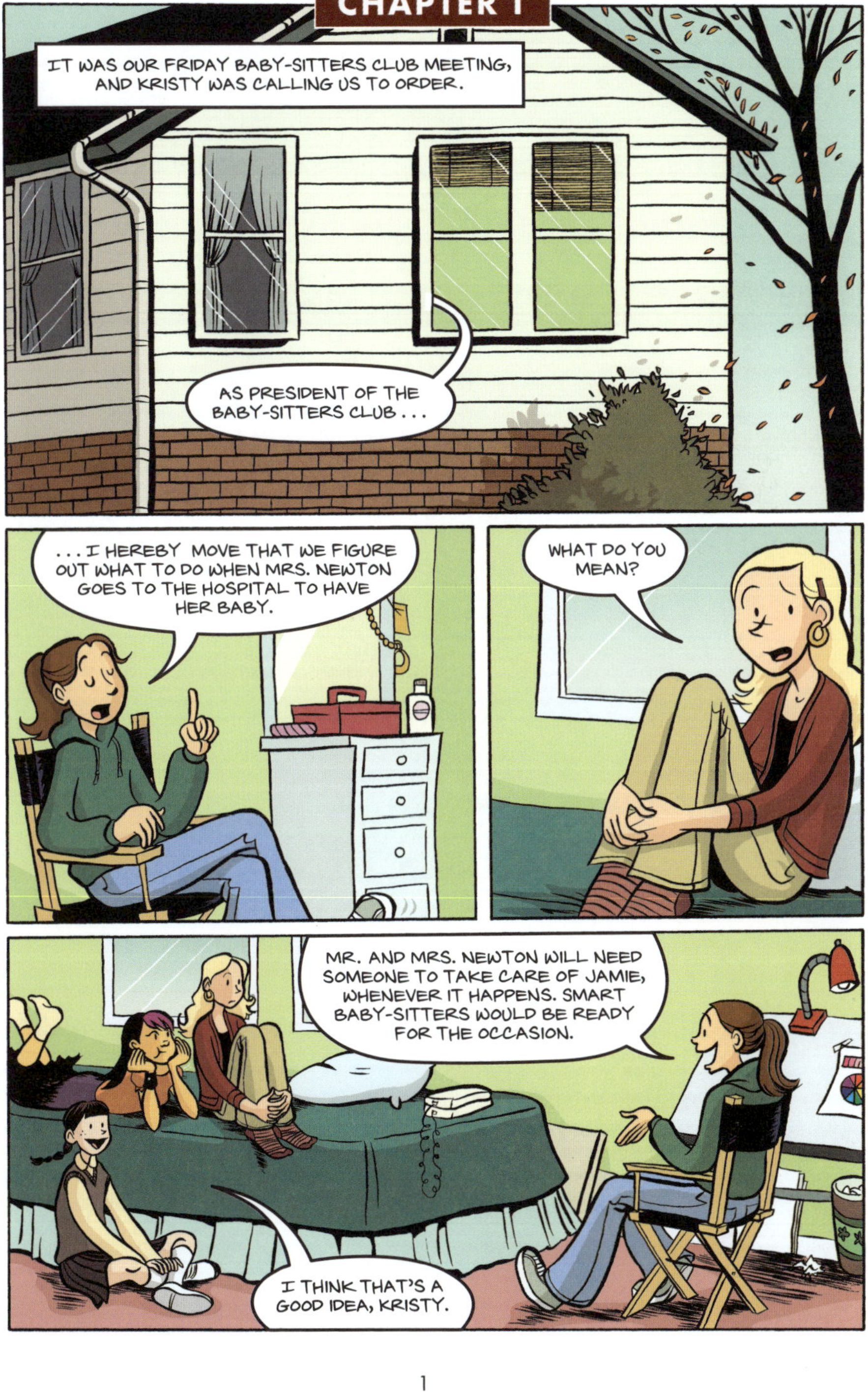

IT WAS OUR FRIDAY BABY-SITTERS CLUB MEETING, AND KRISTY WAS CALLING US TO ORDER.
AS PRESIDENT OF THE BABY-SITTERS CLUB . . .
. . . I HEREBY MOVE THAT WE FIGURE OUT WHAT TO DO WHEN MRS. NEWTON GOES TO THE HOSPITAL TO HAVE HER BABY.
WHAT DO YOU MEAN?
MR. AND MRS. NEWTON WILL NEED SOMEONE TO TAKE CARE OF JAMIE, WHENEVER IT HAPPENS. SMART BABY-SITTERS WOULD BE READY FOR THE OCCASION.
I THINK THAT'S A GOOD IDEA, KRISTY.

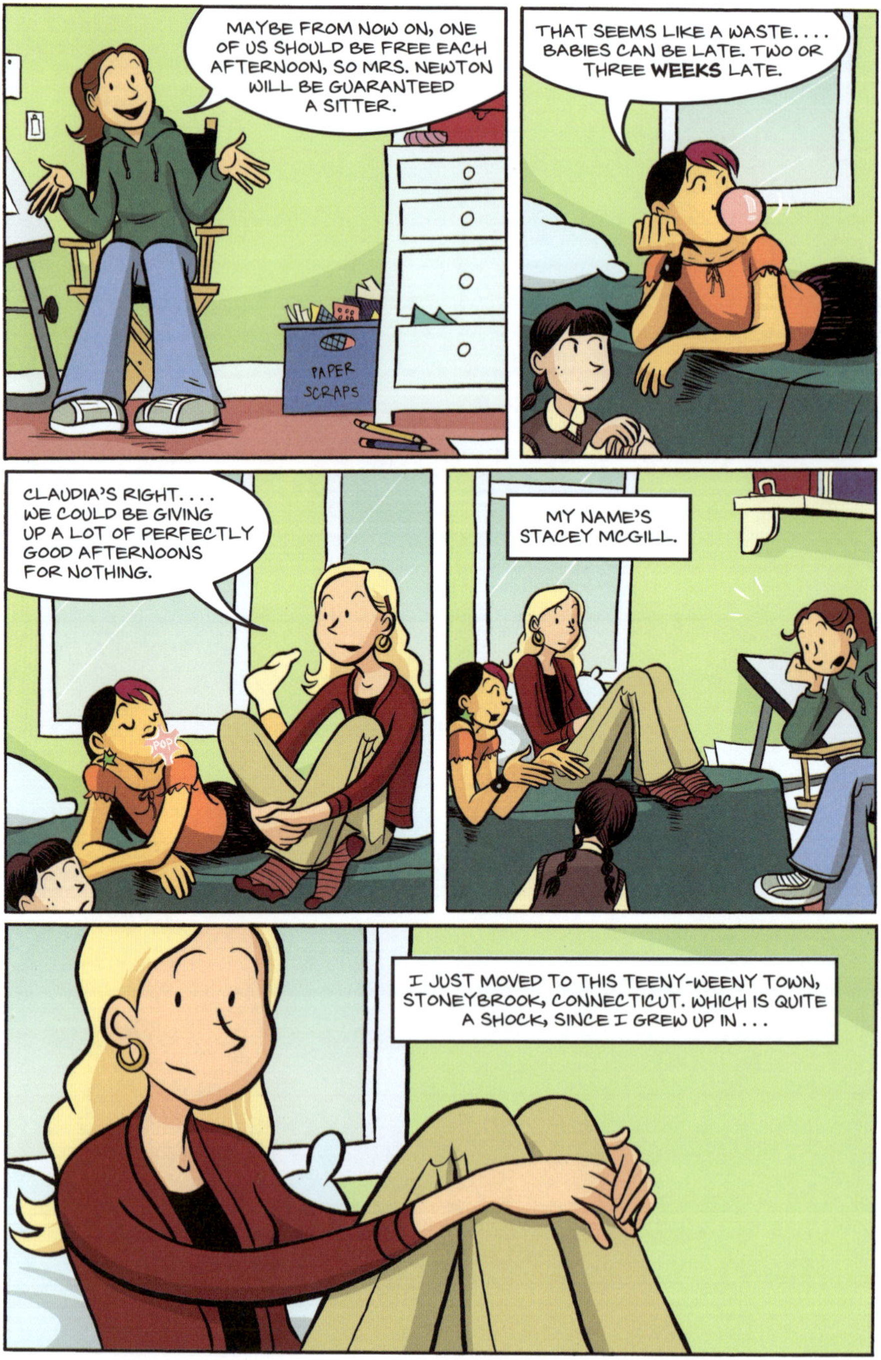
MAYBE FROM NOW ON, ONE OF US SHOULD BE FREE EACH AFTERNOON, SO MRS. NEWTON WILL BE GUARANTEED A SITTER.
PAPER SCRAPS
THAT SEEMS LIKE A WASTE. . . . BABIES CAN BE LATE. TWO OR THREE **WEEKS** LATE.
CLAUDIA'S RIGHT. . . . WE COULD BE GIVING UP A LOT OF PERFECTLY GOOD AFTERNOONS FOR NOTHING.
POP
MY NAME'S STACEY MCGILL.
I JUST MOVED TO THIS TEENY-WEENY TOWN, STONEYBROOK, CONNECTICUT. WHICH IS QUITE A SHOCK, SINCE I GREW UP IN . . .

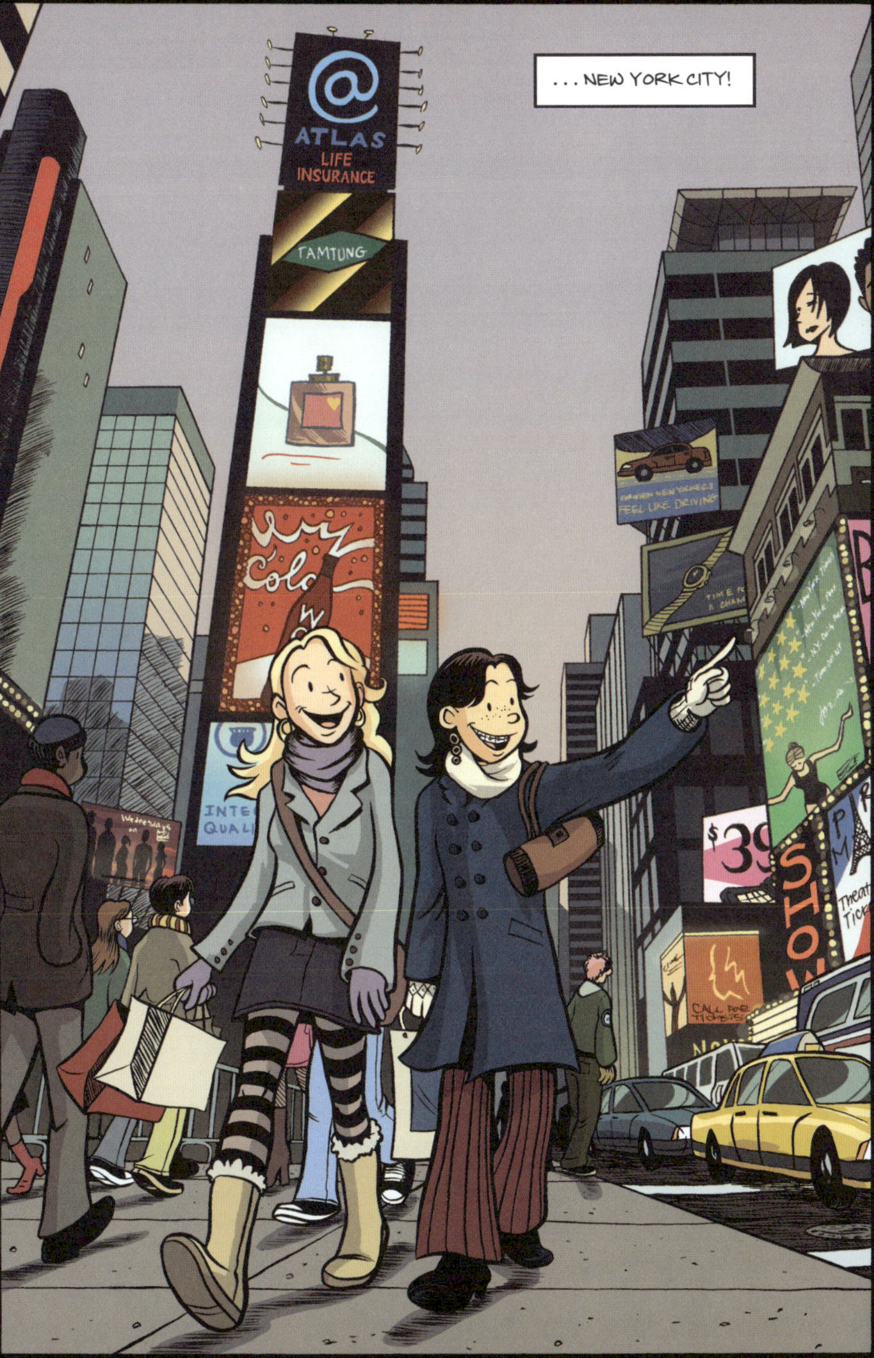
. . . NEW YORK CITY!
@
ATLAS
LIFE
INSURANCE
TAMTUNG
FEEL LIKE DRIVING
$39
SHOW
CALL FOR TICKETS

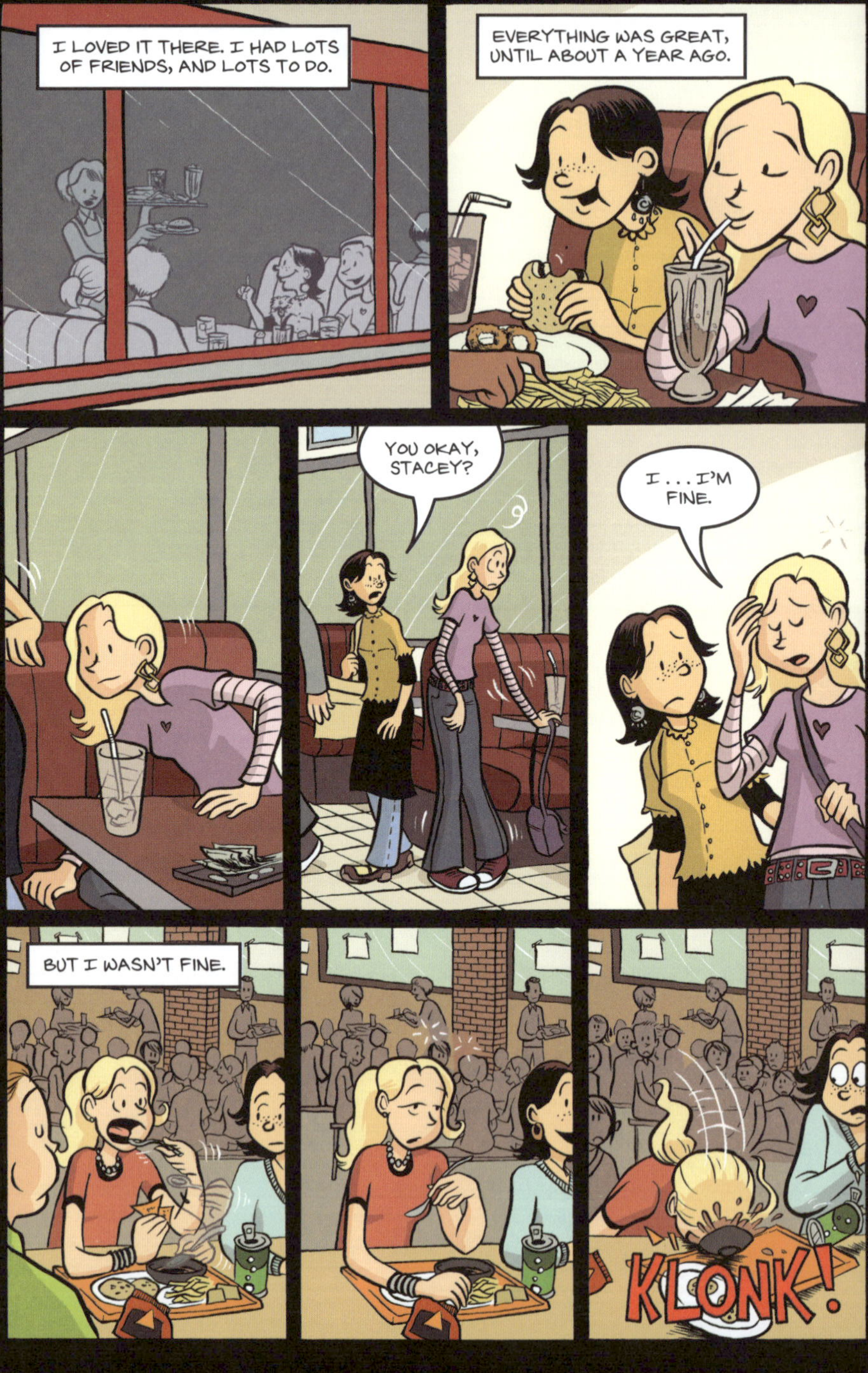
I LOVED IT THERE. I HAD LOTS OF FRIENDS, AND LOTS TO DO.
EVERYTHING WAS GREAT, UNTIL ABOUT A YEAR AGO.
YOU OKAY, STACEY?
I . . . I'M FINE.
BUT I WASN'T FINE.
KLONK!

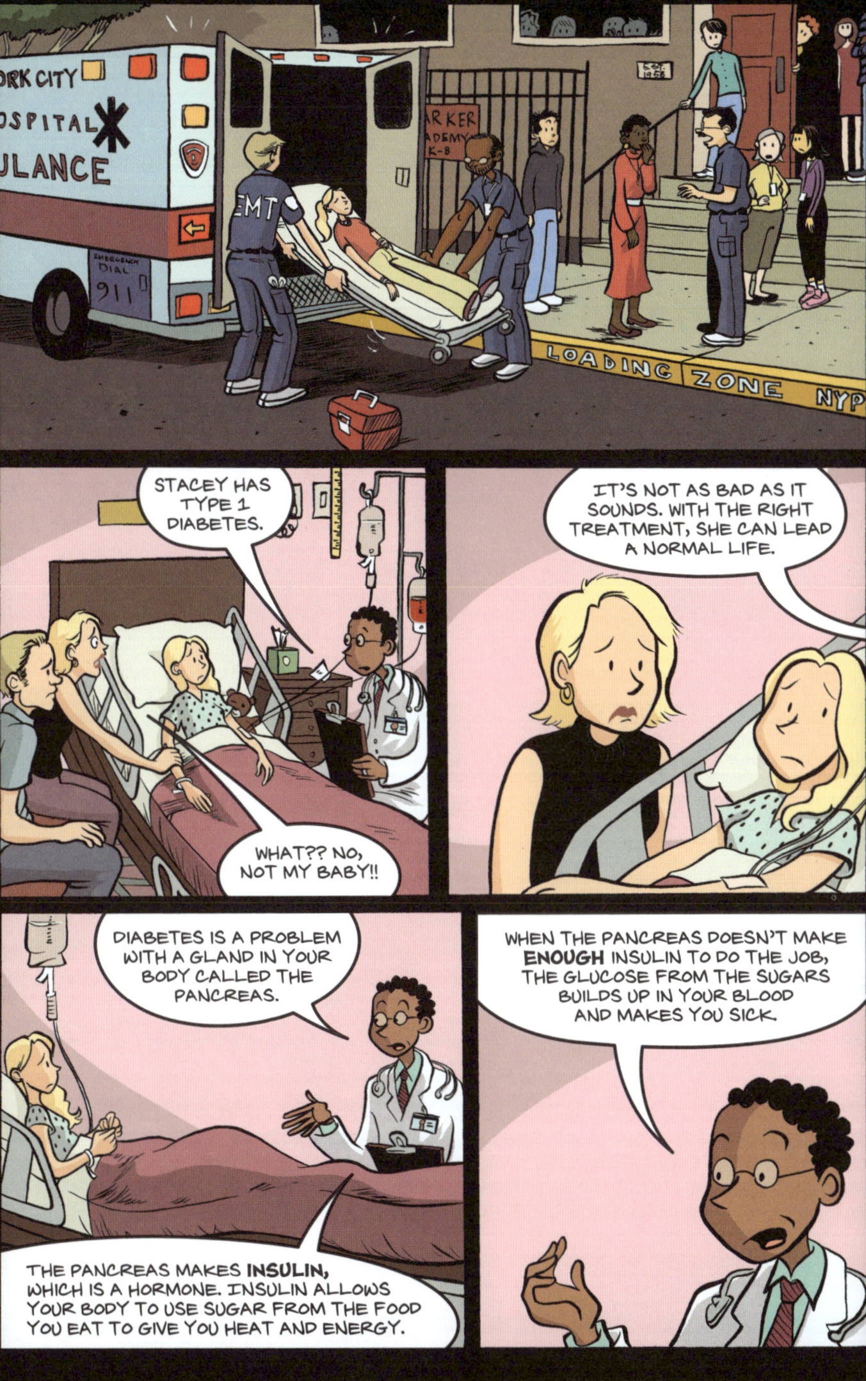
ORK CITY
OSPITAL
ULANCE
EMT
EMERGENCY DIAL 911
ARKER
ADEMY
K-8
LOADING ZONE NYP
STACEY HAS TYPE 1 DIABETES.
WHAT?? NO, NOT MY BABY!!
IT'S NOT AS BAD AS IT SOUNDS. WITH THE RIGHT TREATMENT, SHE CAN LEAD A NORMAL LIFE.
DIABETES IS A PROBLEM WITH A GLAND IN YOUR BODY CALLED THE PANCREAS.
THE PANCREAS MAKES **INSULIN,** WHICH IS A HORMONE. INSULIN ALLOWS YOUR BODY TO USE SUGAR FROM THE FOOD YOU EAT TO GIVE YOU HEAT AND ENERGY.
WHEN THE PANCREAS DOESN'T MAKE **ENOUGH** INSULIN TO DO THE JOB, THE GLUCOSE FROM THE SUGARS BUILDS UP IN YOUR BLOOD AND MAKES YOU SICK.

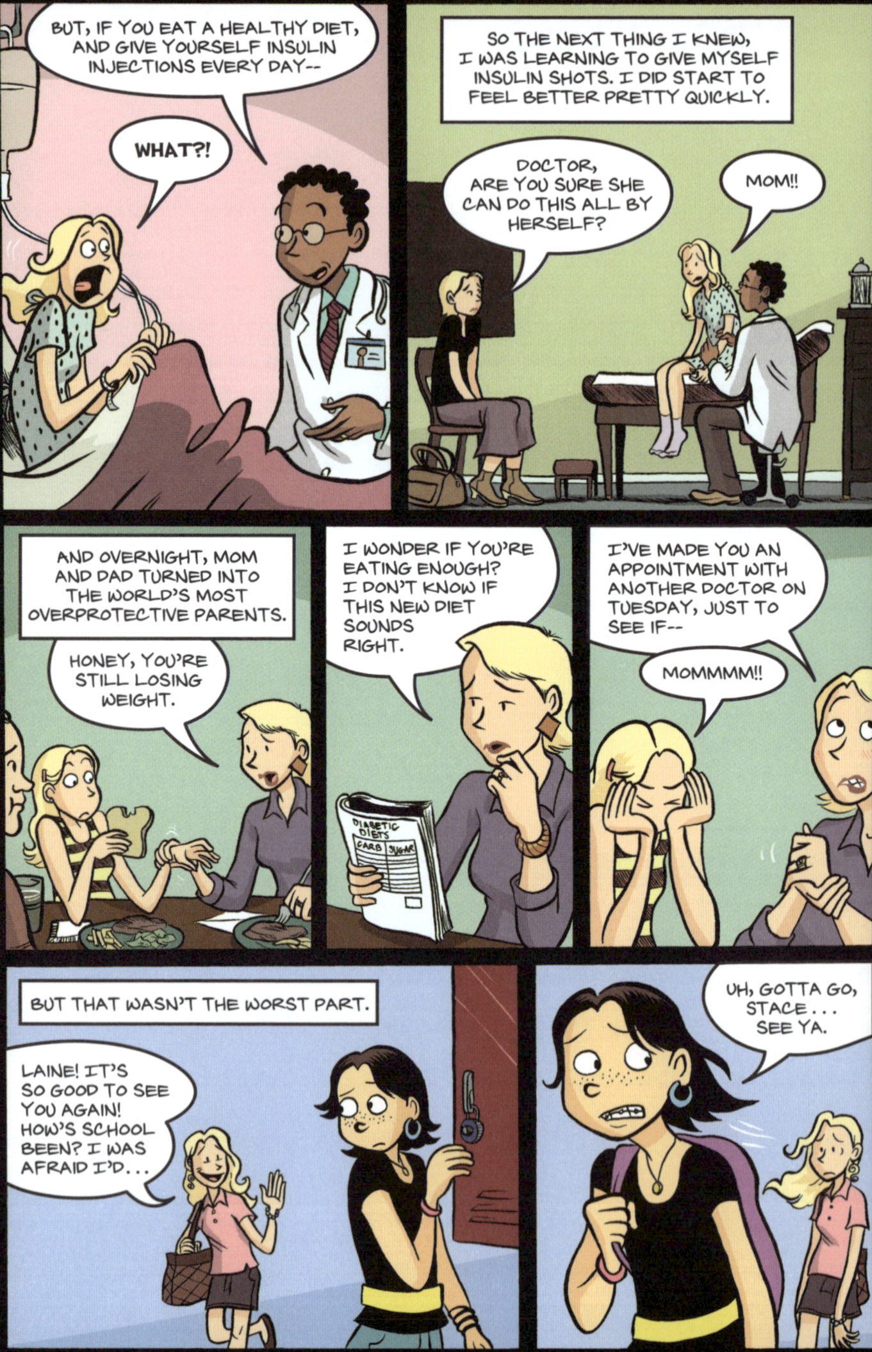
BUT, IF YOU EAT A HEALTHY DIET, AND GIVE YOURSELF INSULIN INJECTIONS EVERY DAY--
WHAT?!
SO THE NEXT THING I KNEW, I WAS LEARNING TO GIVE MYSELF INSULIN SHOTS. I DID START TO FEEL BETTER PRETTY QUICKLY.
DOCTOR, ARE YOU SURE SHE CAN DO THIS ALL BY HERSELF?
MOM!!
AND OVERNIGHT, MOM AND DAD TURNED INTO THE WORLD'S MOST OVERPROTECTIVE PARENTS.
HONEY, YOU'RE STILL LOSING WEIGHT.
I WONDER IF YOU'RE EATING ENOUGH? I DON'T KNOW IF THIS NEW DIET SOUNDS RIGHT.
DIABETIC DIETS
CARB
SUGAR
I'VE MADE YOU AN APPOINTMENT WITH ANOTHER DOCTOR ON TUESDAY, JUST TO SEE IF--
MOMMMM!!
BUT THAT WASN'T THE WORST PART.
LAINE! IT'S SO GOOD TO SEE YOU AGAIN! HOW'S SCHOOL BEEN? I WAS AFRAID I'D . . .
UH, GOTTA GO, STACE . . . SEE YA.

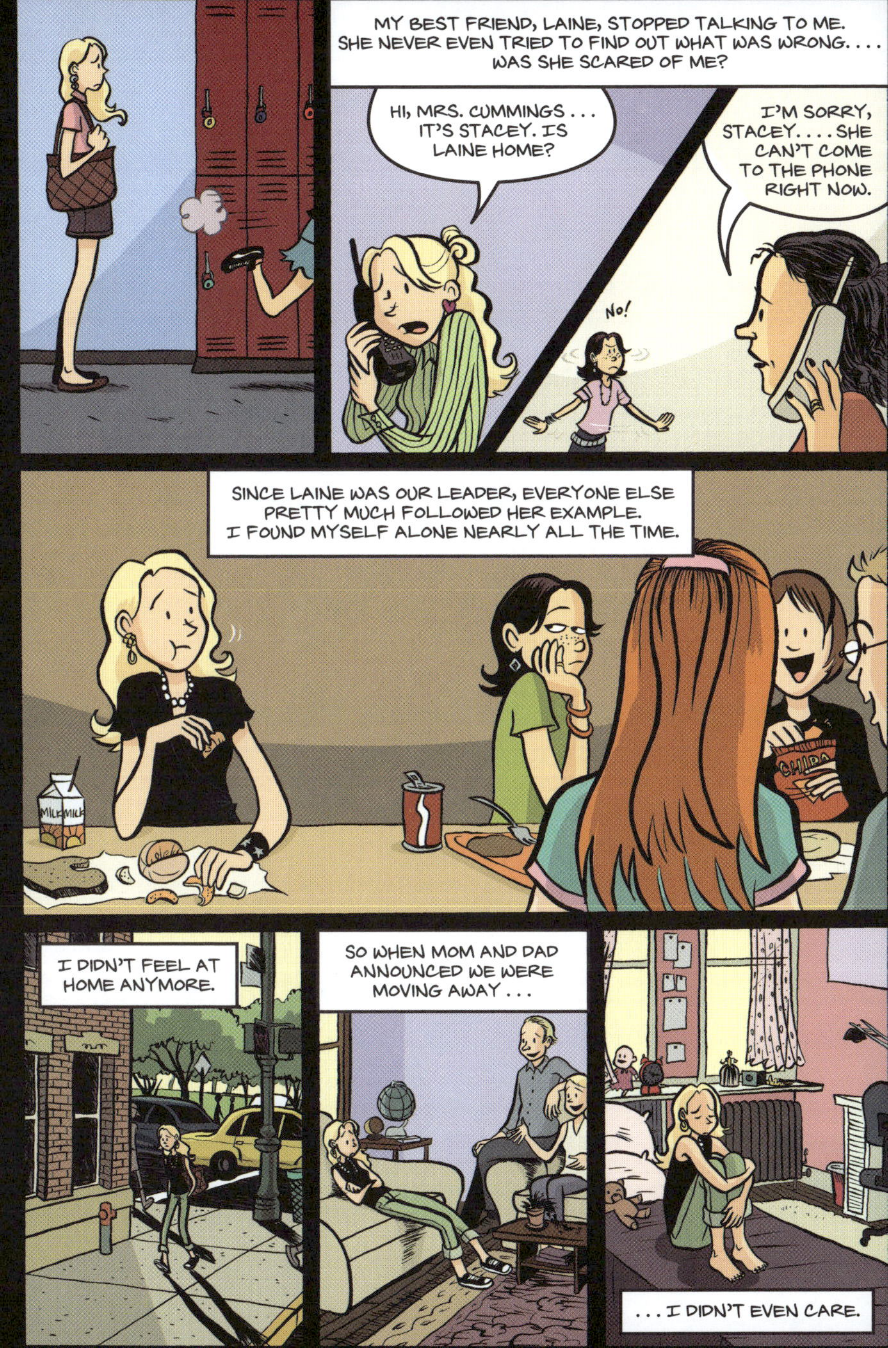
MY BEST FRIEND, LAINE, STOPPED TALKING TO ME. SHE NEVER EVEN TRIED TO FIND OUT WHAT WAS WRONG. . . . WAS SHE SCARED OF ME?
HI, MRS. CUMMINGS . . . IT'S STACEY. IS LAINE HOME?
NO!
I'M SORRY, STACEY. . . . SHE CAN'T COME TO THE PHONE RIGHT NOW.
SINCE LAINE WAS OUR LEADER, EVERYONE ELSE PRETTY MUCH FOLLOWED HER EXAMPLE. I FOUND MYSELF ALONE NEARLY ALL THE TIME.
MILK MILK
CHIPS
I DIDN'T FEEL AT HOME ANYMORE.
SO WHEN MOM AND DAD ANNOUNCED WE WERE MOVING AWAY . . .
. . . I DIDN'T EVEN CARE.

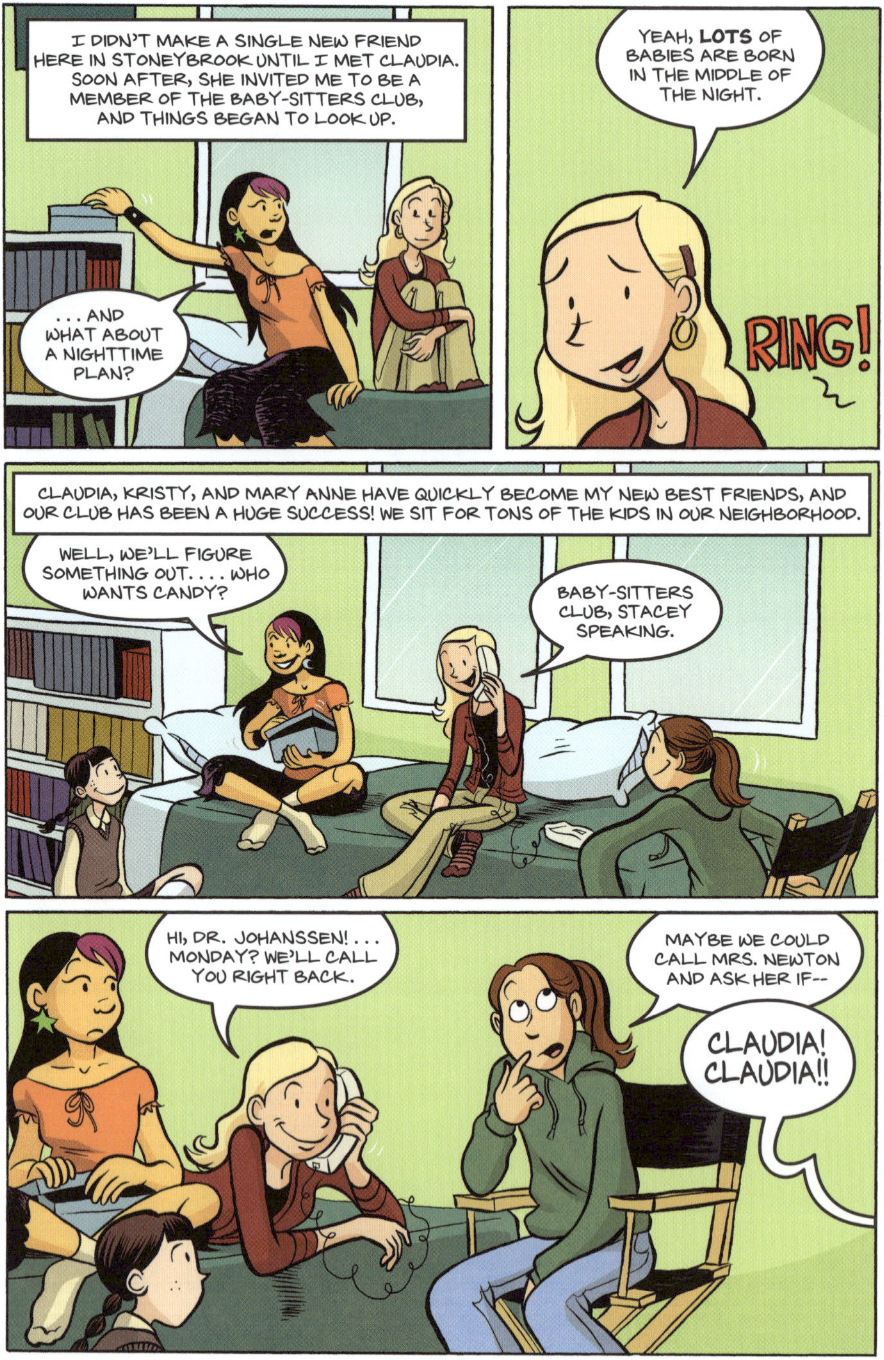
I DIDN'T MAKE A SINGLE NEW FRIEND HERE IN STONEYBROOK UNTIL I MET CLAUDIA. SOON AFTER, SHE INVITED ME TO BE A MEMBER OF THE BABY-SITTERS CLUB, AND THINGS BEGAN TO LOOK UP.
. . . AND WHAT ABOUT A NIGHTTIME PLAN?
YEAH, **LOTS** OF BABIES ARE BORN IN THE MIDDLE OF THE NIGHT.
RING!
CLAUDIA, KRISTY, AND MARY ANNE HAVE QUICKLY BECOME MY NEW BEST FRIENDS, AND OUR CLUB HAS BEEN A HUGE SUCCESS! WE SIT FOR TONS OF THE KIDS IN OUR NEIGHBORHOOD.
WELL, WE'LL FIGURE SOMETHING OUT. . . . WHO WANTS CANDY?
BABY-SITTERS CLUB, STACEY SPEAKING.
HI, DR. JOHANSSEN! . . . MONDAY? WE'LL CALL YOU RIGHT BACK.
MAYBE WE COULD CALL MRS. NEWTON AND ASK HER IF--
CLAUDIA! CLAUDIA!!

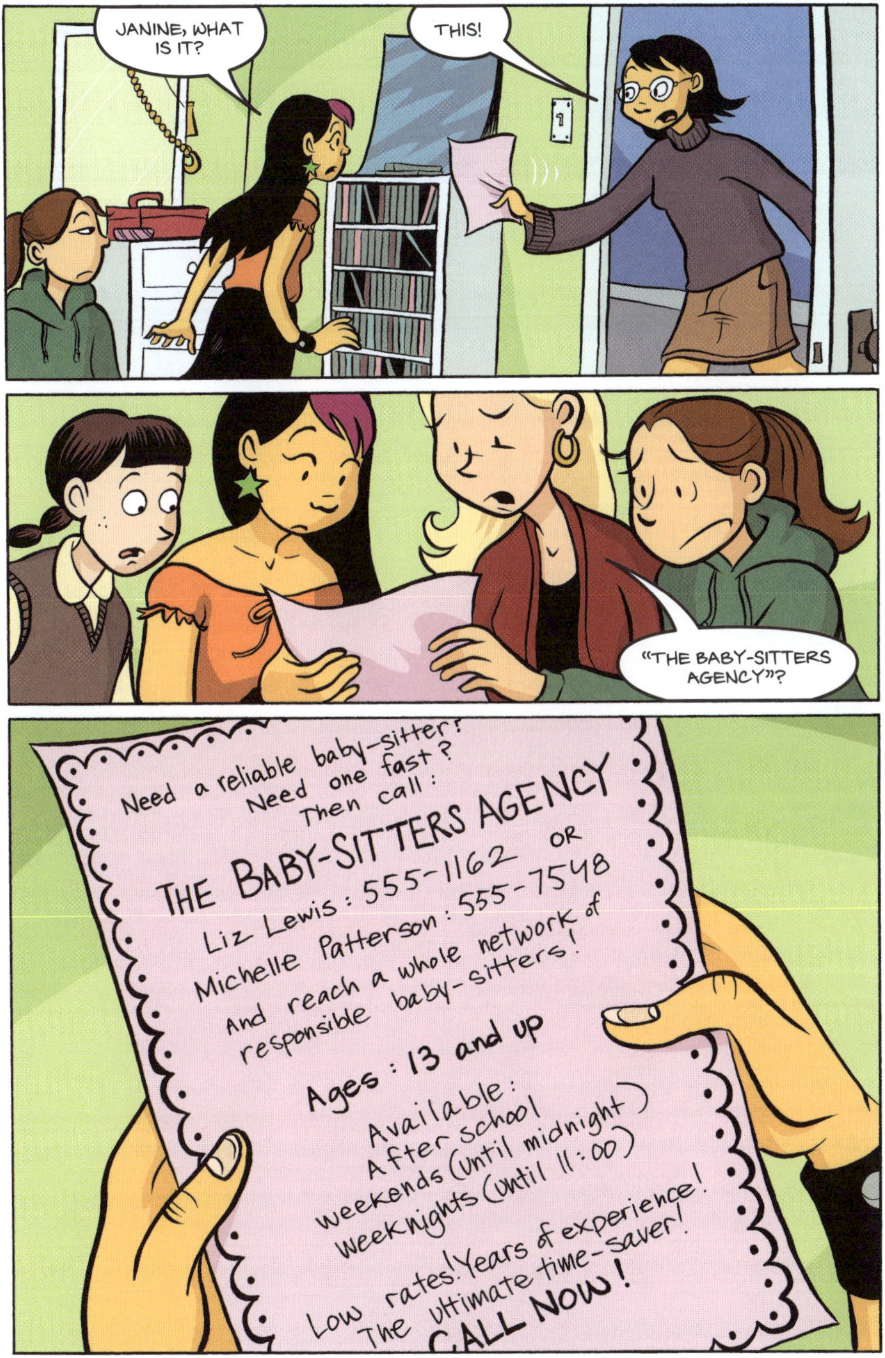
JANINE, WHAT IS IT?
THIS!
"THE BABY-SITTERS AGENCY"?
Need a reliable baby-sitter? Need one fast? Then call:
THE BABY-SITTERS AGENCY
Liz Lewis: 555-1162 OR
Michelle Patterson: 555-7548
And reach a whole network of responsible baby-sitters!
Ages: 13 and up
Available:
After school
weekends (until midnight)
weeknights (until 11:00)
Low rates! Years of experience!
The ultimate time-saver!
CALL NOW!

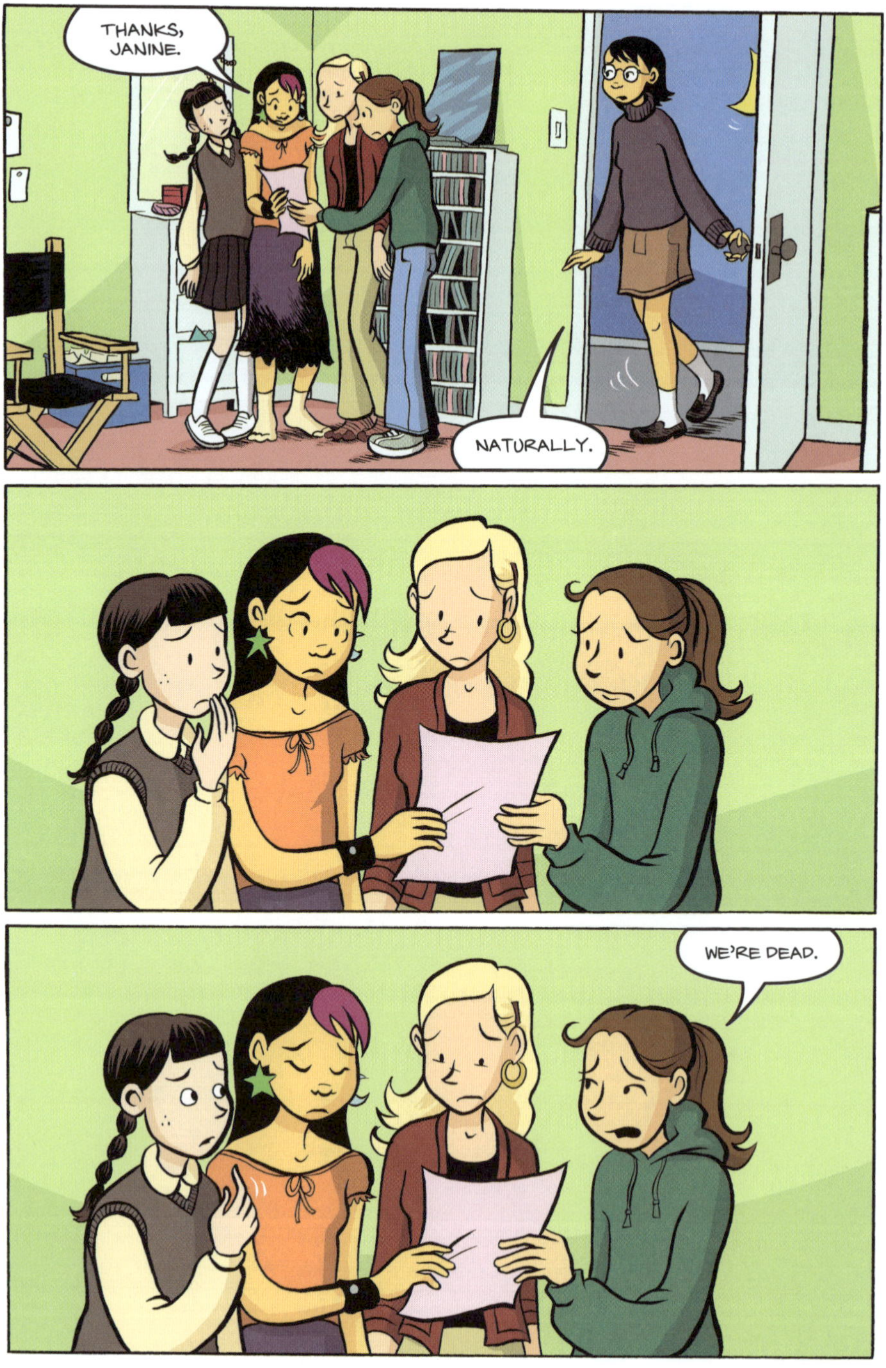
THANKS, JANINE.
NATURALLY.
WE'RE DEAD.

CHAPTER 2

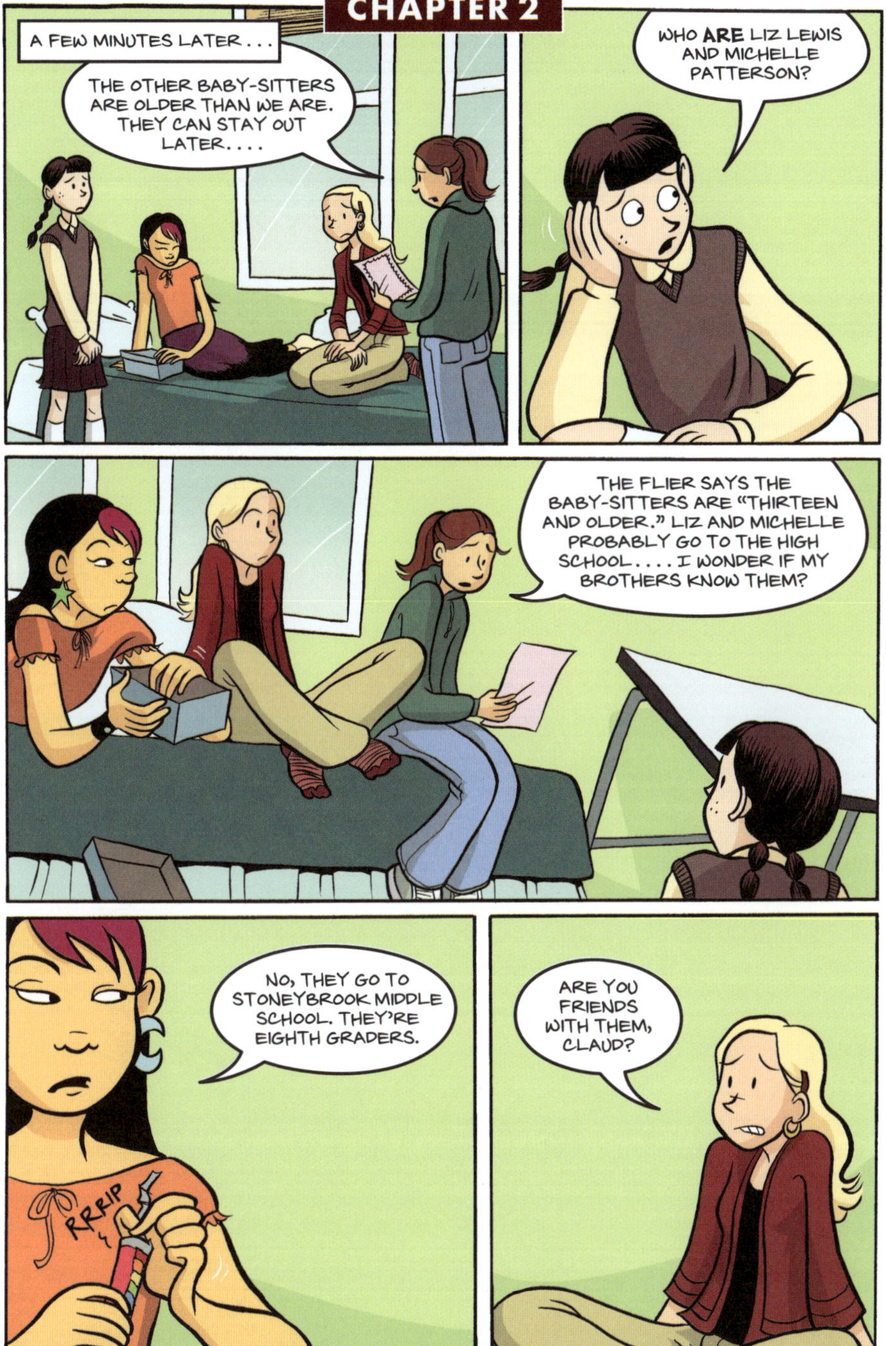
A FEW MINUTES LATER . . .
THE OTHER BABY-SITTERS ARE OLDER THAN WE ARE. THEY CAN STAY OUT LATER. . . .
WHO **ARE** LIZ LEWIS AND MICHELLE PATTERSON?
THE FLIER SAYS THE BABY-SITTERS ARE "THIRTEEN AND OLDER." LIZ AND MICHELLE PROBABLY GO TO THE HIGH SCHOOL. . . . I WONDER IF MY BROTHERS KNOW THEM?
NO, THEY GO TO STONEYBROOK MIDDLE SCHOOL. THEY'RE EIGHTH GRADERS.
RRRIP
ARE YOU FRIENDS WITH THEM, CLAUD?

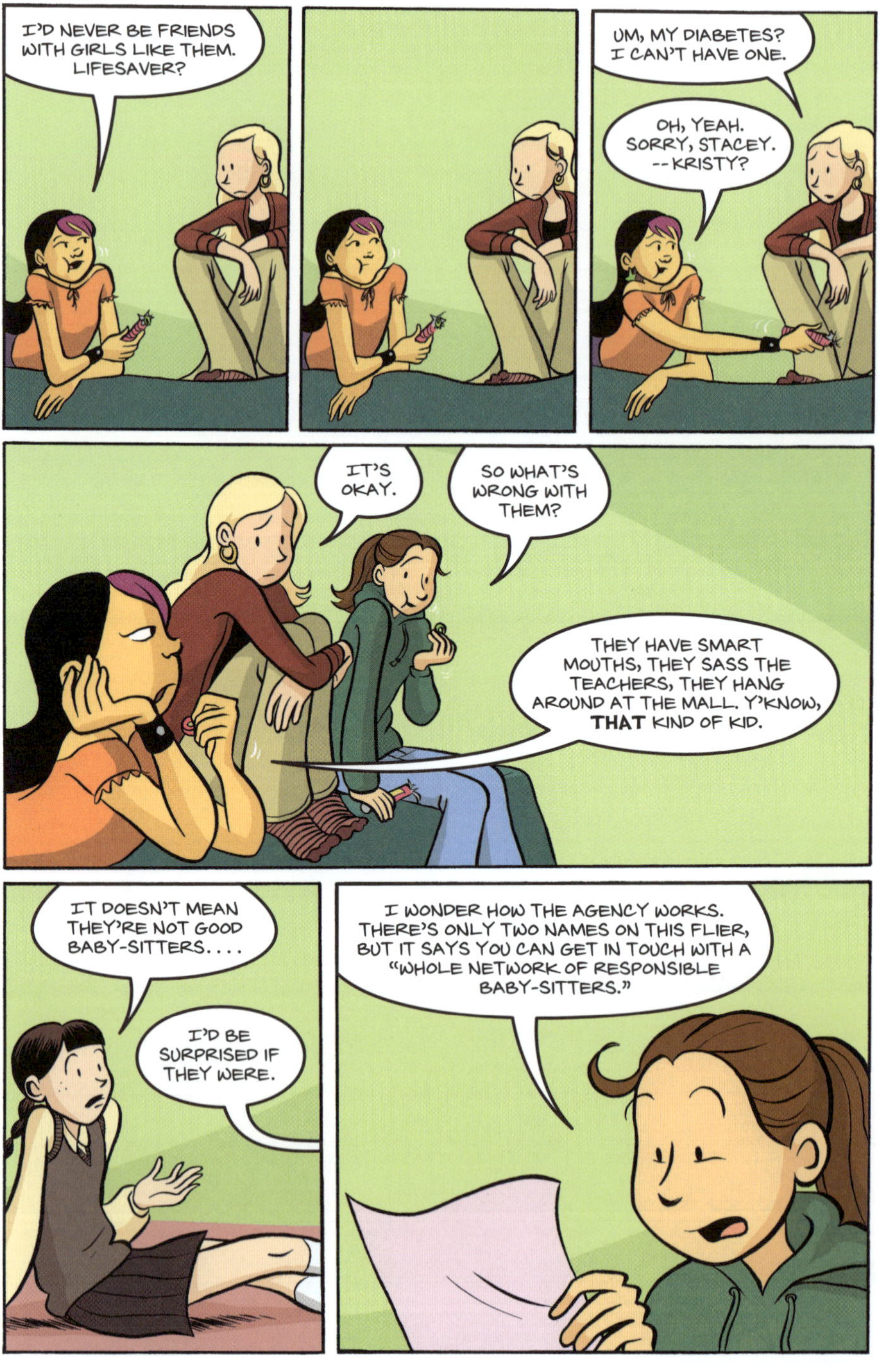
I'D NEVER BE FRIENDS WITH GIRLS LIKE THEM. LIFESAVER?
UM, MY DIABETES? I CAN'T HAVE ONE.
OH, YEAH. SORRY, STACEY. --KRISTY?
IT'S OKAY.
SO WHAT'S WRONG WITH THEM?
THEY HAVE SMART MOUTHS, THEY SASS THE TEACHERS, THEY HANG AROUND AT THE MALL. Y'KNOW, **THAT** KIND OF KID.
IT DOESN'T MEAN THEY'RE NOT GOOD BABY-SITTERS. . . .
I'D BE SURPRISED IF THEY WERE.
I WONDER HOW THE AGENCY WORKS. THERE'S ONLY TWO NAMES ON THIS FLIER, BUT IT SAYS YOU CAN GET IN TOUCH WITH A "WHOLE NETWORK OF RESPONSIBLE BABY-SITTERS."

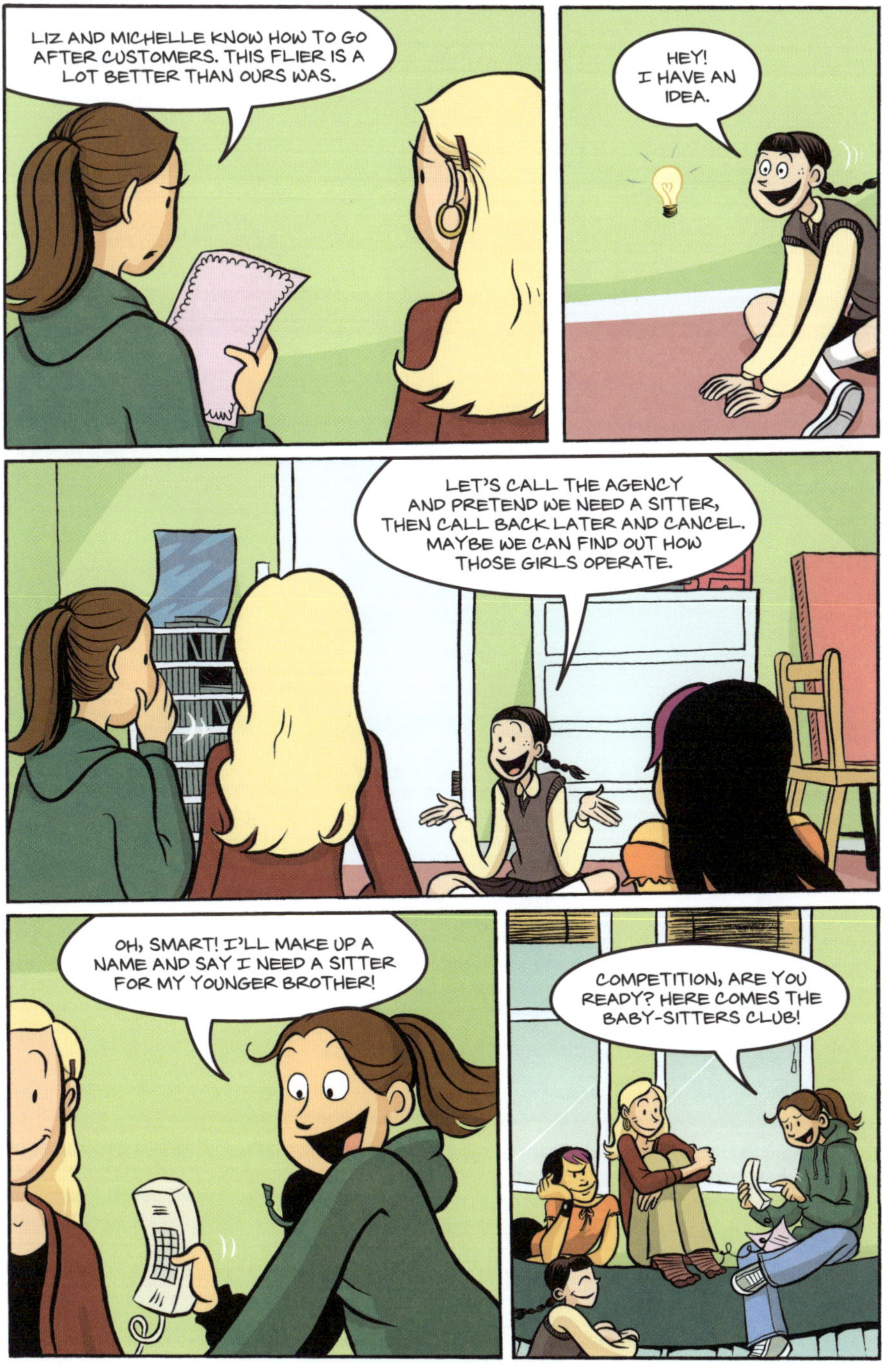
LIZ AND MICHELLE KNOW HOW TO GO AFTER CUSTOMERS. THIS FLIER IS A LOT BETTER THAN OURS WAS.
HEY! I HAVE AN IDEA.
LET'S CALL THE AGENCY AND PRETEND WE NEED A SITTER, THEN CALL BACK LATER AND CANCEL. MAYBE WE CAN FIND OUT HOW THOSE GIRLS OPERATE.
OH, SMART! I'LL MAKE UP A NAME AND SAY I NEED A SITTER FOR MY YOUNGER BROTHER!
COMPETITION, ARE YOU READY? HERE COMES THE BABY-SITTERS CLUB!

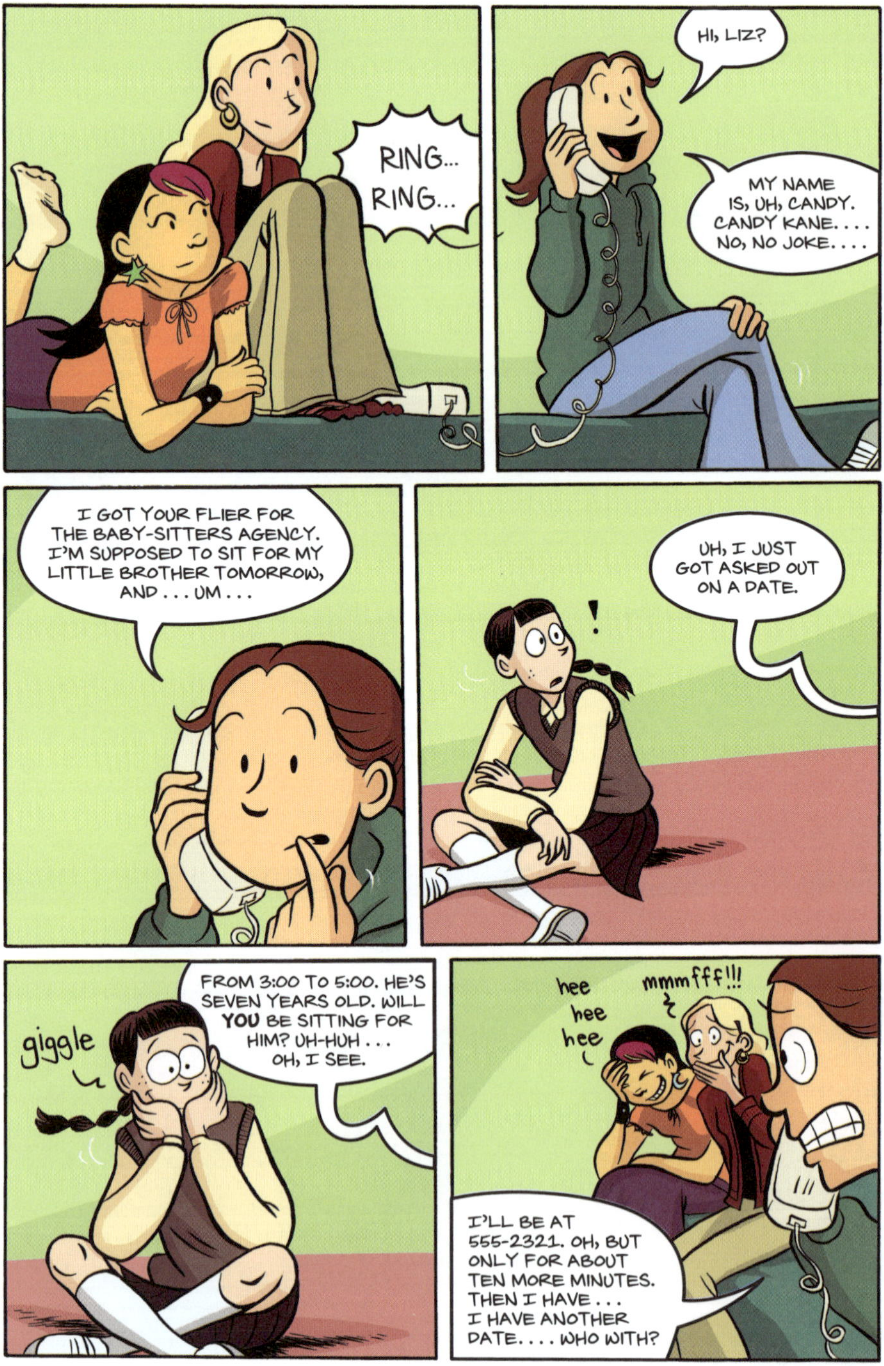
RING... RING...
HI, LIZ?
MY NAME IS, UH, CANDY. CANDY KANE. . . . NO, NO JOKE. . . .
I GOT YOUR FLIER FOR THE BABY-SITTERS AGENCY. I'M SUPPOSED TO SIT FOR MY LITTLE BROTHER TOMORROW, AND . . . UM . . .
UH, I JUST GOT ASKED OUT ON A DATE.
!
FROM 3:00 TO 5:00. HE'S SEVEN YEARS OLD. WILL **YOU** BE SITTING FOR HIM? UH-HUH . . . OH, I SEE.
giggle
hee hee hee
mmmfff!!!
I'LL BE AT 555-2321. OH, BUT ONLY FOR ABOUT TEN MORE MINUTES. THEN I HAVE . . . I HAVE ANOTHER DATE. . . . WHO WITH?

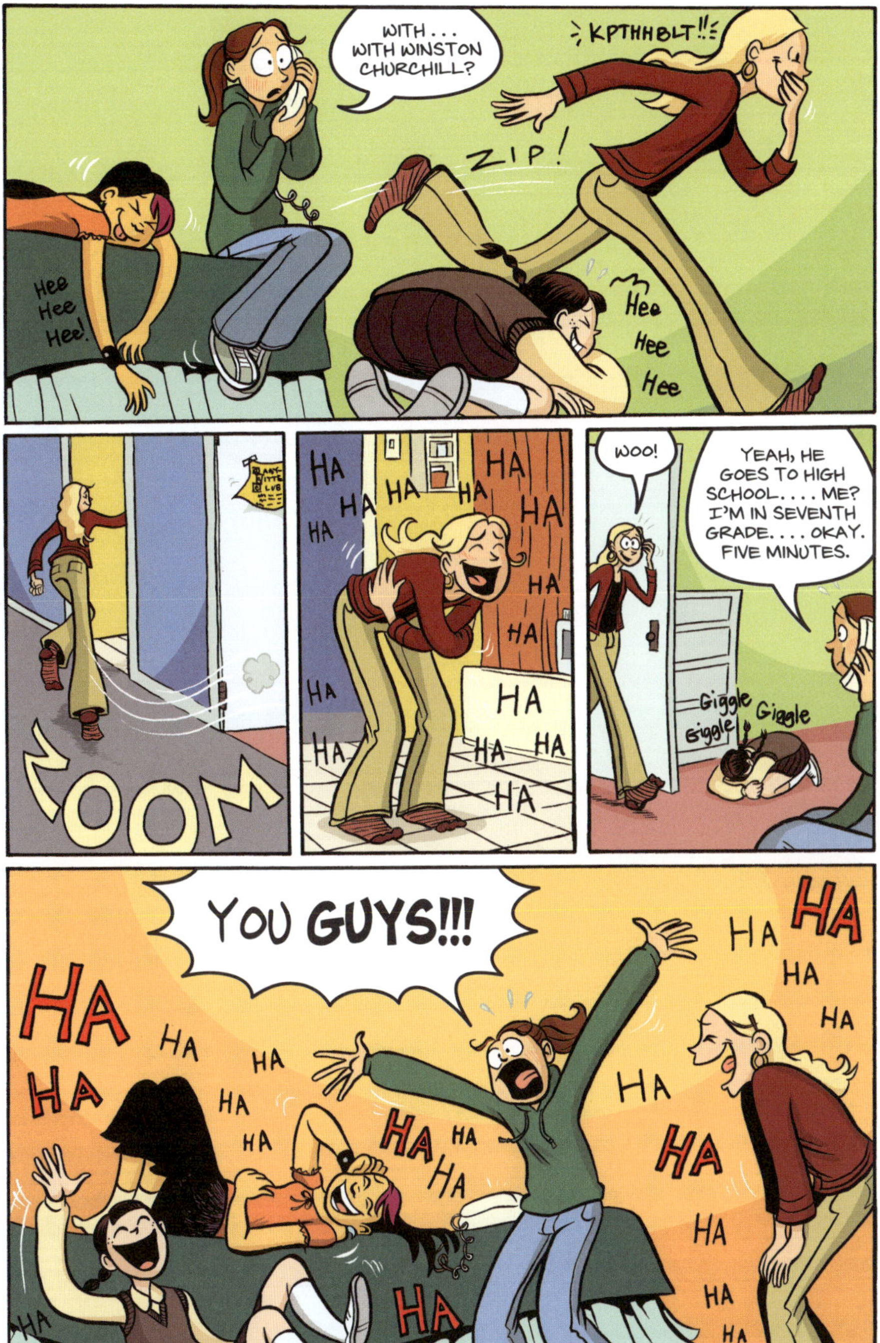
WITH . . . WITH WINSTON CHURCHILL?
KPTHHBLT!!
ZIP!
Hee Hee Hee!
Hee Hee Hee
ZOOM
HA HA HA HA HA HA HA HA HA HA HA HA HA HA HA
WOO!
YEAH, HE GOES TO HIGH SCHOOL. . . . ME? I'M IN SEVENTH GRADE. . . . OKAY. FIVE MINUTES.
Giggle Giggle Giggle
YOU GUYS!!!
HA HA HA HA HA HA HA HA HA HA HA HA HA HA HA HA HA HA HA HA HA HA HA

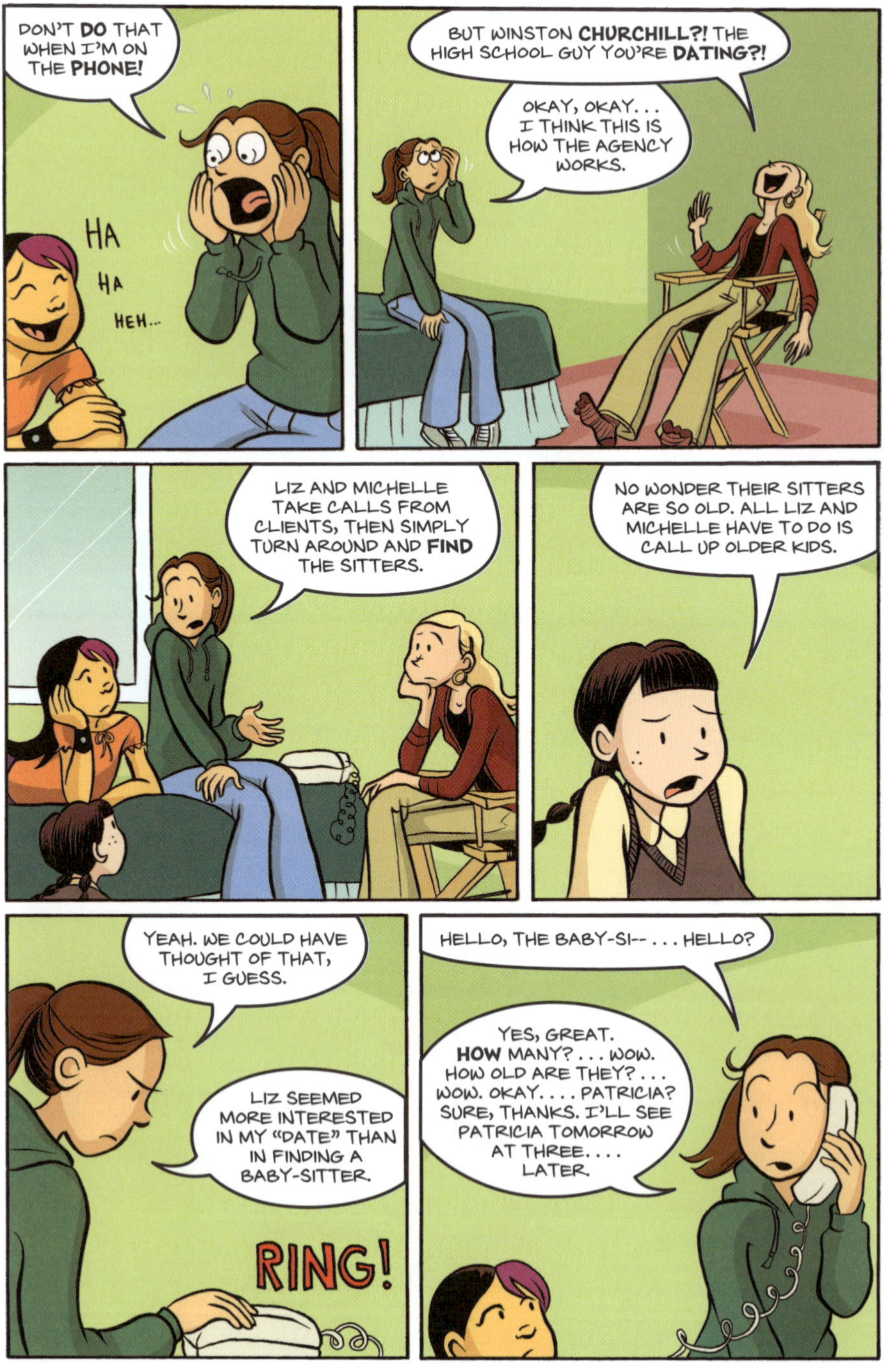
DON'T **DO** THAT WHEN I'M ON THE **PHONE!**
HA
HA
HEH...
BUT WINSTON **CHURCHILL?!** THE HIGH SCHOOL GUY YOU'RE **DATING?!**
OKAY, OKAY... I THINK THIS IS HOW THE AGENCY WORKS.
LIZ AND MICHELLE TAKE CALLS FROM CLIENTS, THEN SIMPLY TURN AROUND AND **FIND** THE SITTERS.
NO WONDER THEIR SITTERS ARE SO OLD. ALL LIZ AND MICHELLE HAVE TO DO IS CALL UP OLDER KIDS.
YEAH. WE COULD HAVE THOUGHT OF THAT, I GUESS.
LIZ SEEMED MORE INTERESTED IN MY "DATE" THAN IN FINDING A BABY-SITTER.
RING!
HELLO, THE BABY-SI-- ... HELLO?
YES, GREAT. **HOW** MANY? ... WOW. HOW OLD ARE THEY? ... WOW. OKAY.... PATRICIA? SURE, THANKS. I'LL SEE PATRICIA TOMORROW AT THREE.... LATER.

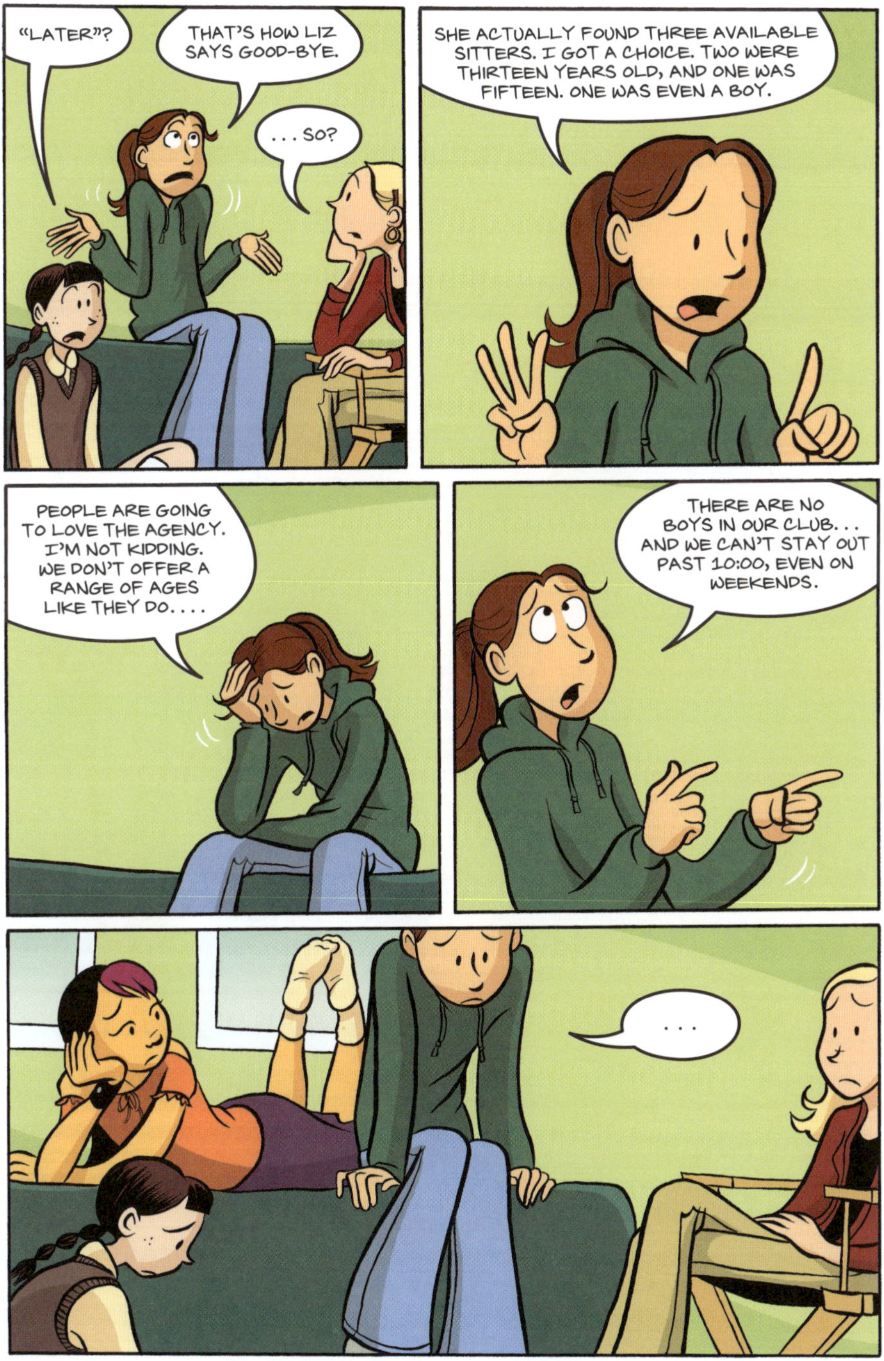
"LATER"?
THAT'S HOW LIZ SAYS GOOD-BYE.
. . . SO?
SHE ACTUALLY FOUND THREE AVAILABLE SITTERS. I GOT A CHOICE. TWO WERE THIRTEEN YEARS OLD, AND ONE WAS FIFTEEN. ONE WAS EVEN A BOY.
PEOPLE ARE GOING TO LOVE THE AGENCY. I'M NOT KIDDING. WE DON'T OFFER A RANGE OF AGES LIKE THEY DO. . . .
THERE ARE NO BOYS IN OUR CLUB. . . AND WE CAN'T STAY OUT PAST 10:00, EVEN ON WEEKENDS.
. . .

STACEY'S DINNER PLATE:

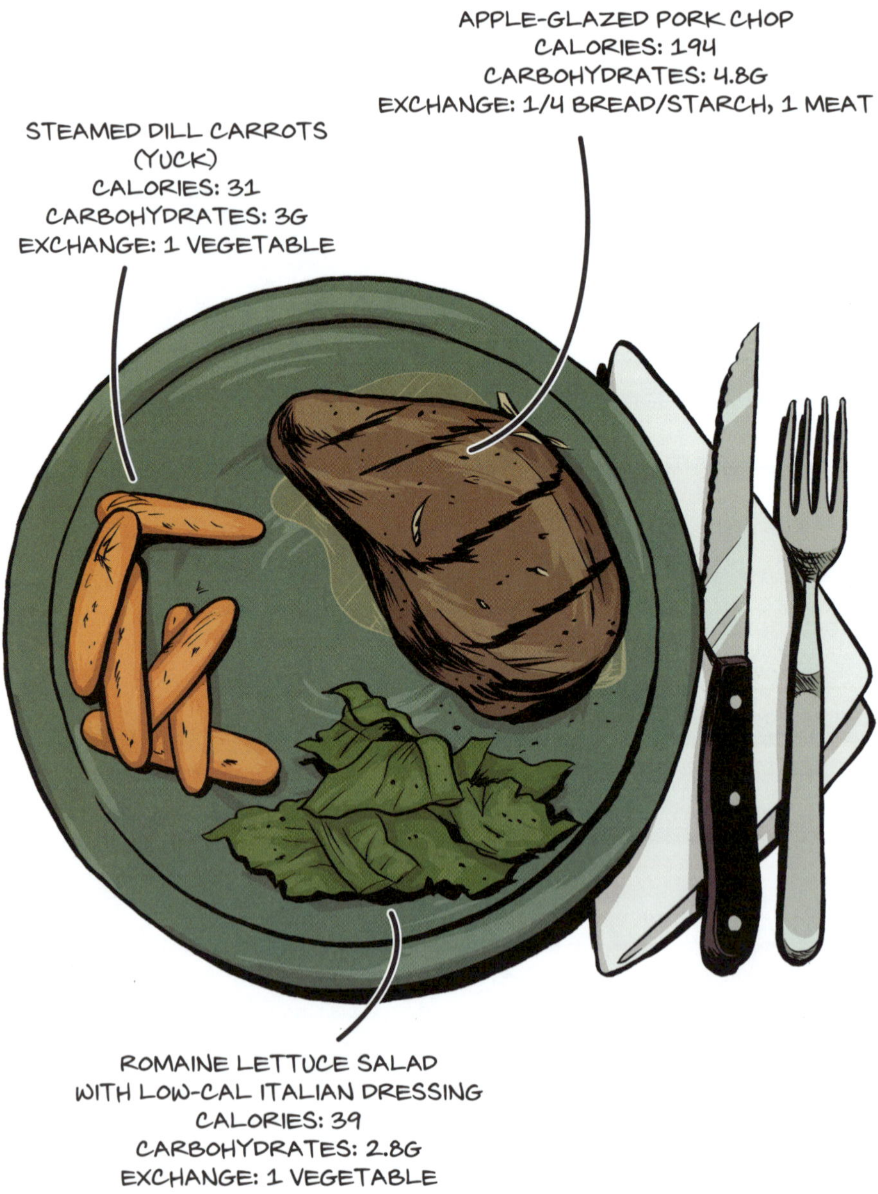
APPLE-GLAZED PORK CHOP
CALORIES: 194
CARBOHYDRATES: 4.8G
EXCHANGE: 1/4 BREAD/STARCH, 1 MEAT
STEAMED DILL CARROTS
(YUCK)
CALORIES: 31
CARBOHYDRATES: 3G
EXCHANGE: 1 VEGETABLE
ROMAINE LETTUCE SALAD
WITH LOW-CAL ITALIAN DRESSING
CALORIES: 39
CARBOHYDRATES: 2.8G
EXCHANGE: 1 VEGETABLE

CHAPTER 3

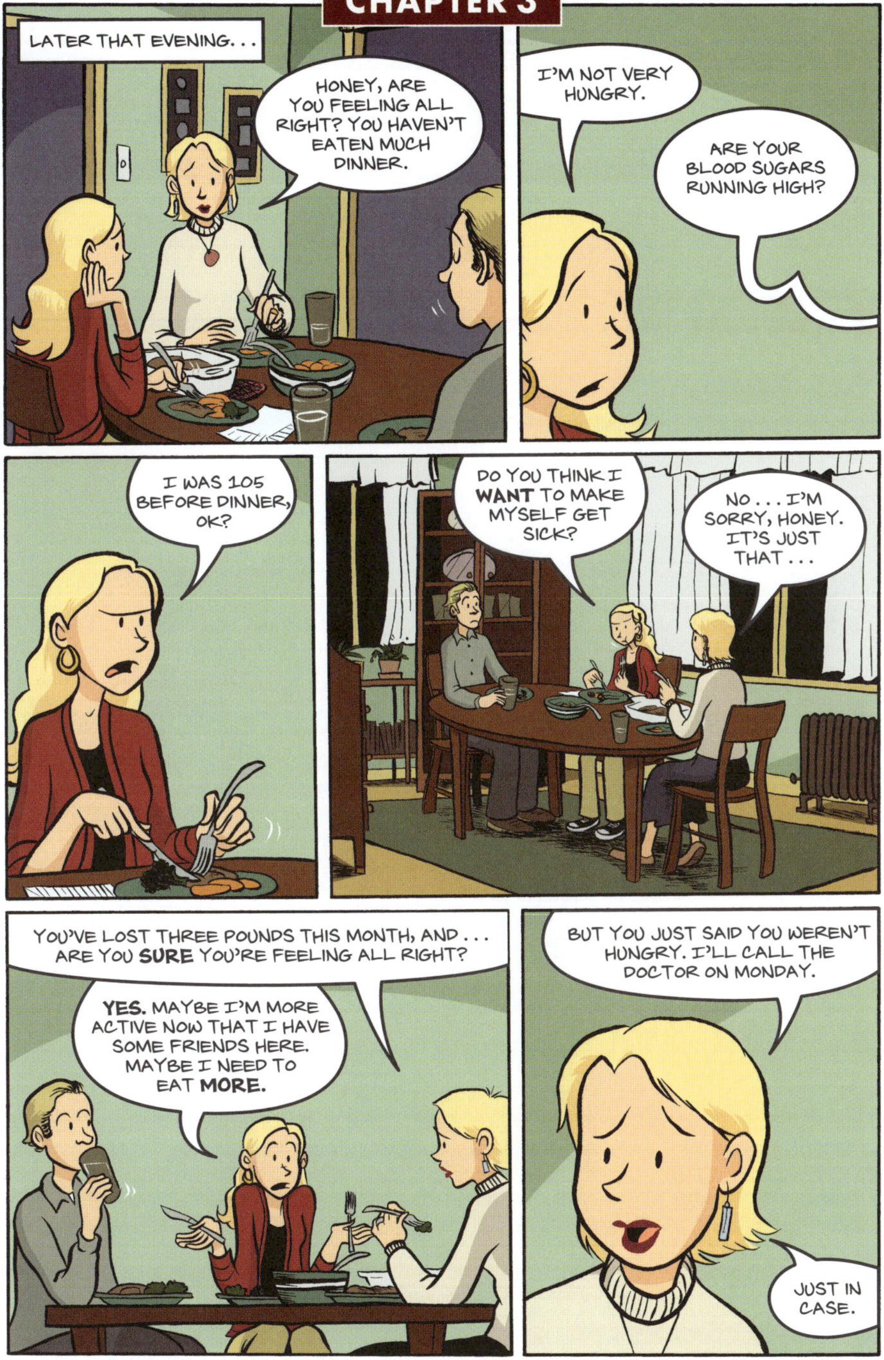
LATER THAT EVENING...
HONEY, ARE YOU FEELING ALL RIGHT? YOU HAVEN'T EATEN MUCH DINNER.
I'M NOT VERY HUNGRY.
ARE YOUR BLOOD SUGARS RUNNING HIGH?
I WAS 105 BEFORE DINNER, OK?
DO YOU THINK I **WANT** TO MAKE MYSELF GET SICK?
NO... I'M SORRY, HONEY. IT'S JUST THAT...
YOU'VE LOST THREE POUNDS THIS MONTH, AND... ARE YOU **SURE** YOU'RE FEELING ALL RIGHT?
YES. MAYBE I'M MORE ACTIVE NOW THAT I HAVE SOME FRIENDS HERE. MAYBE I NEED TO EAT **MORE.**
BUT YOU JUST SAID YOU WEREN'T HUNGRY. I'LL CALL THE DOCTOR ON MONDAY.
JUST IN CASE.

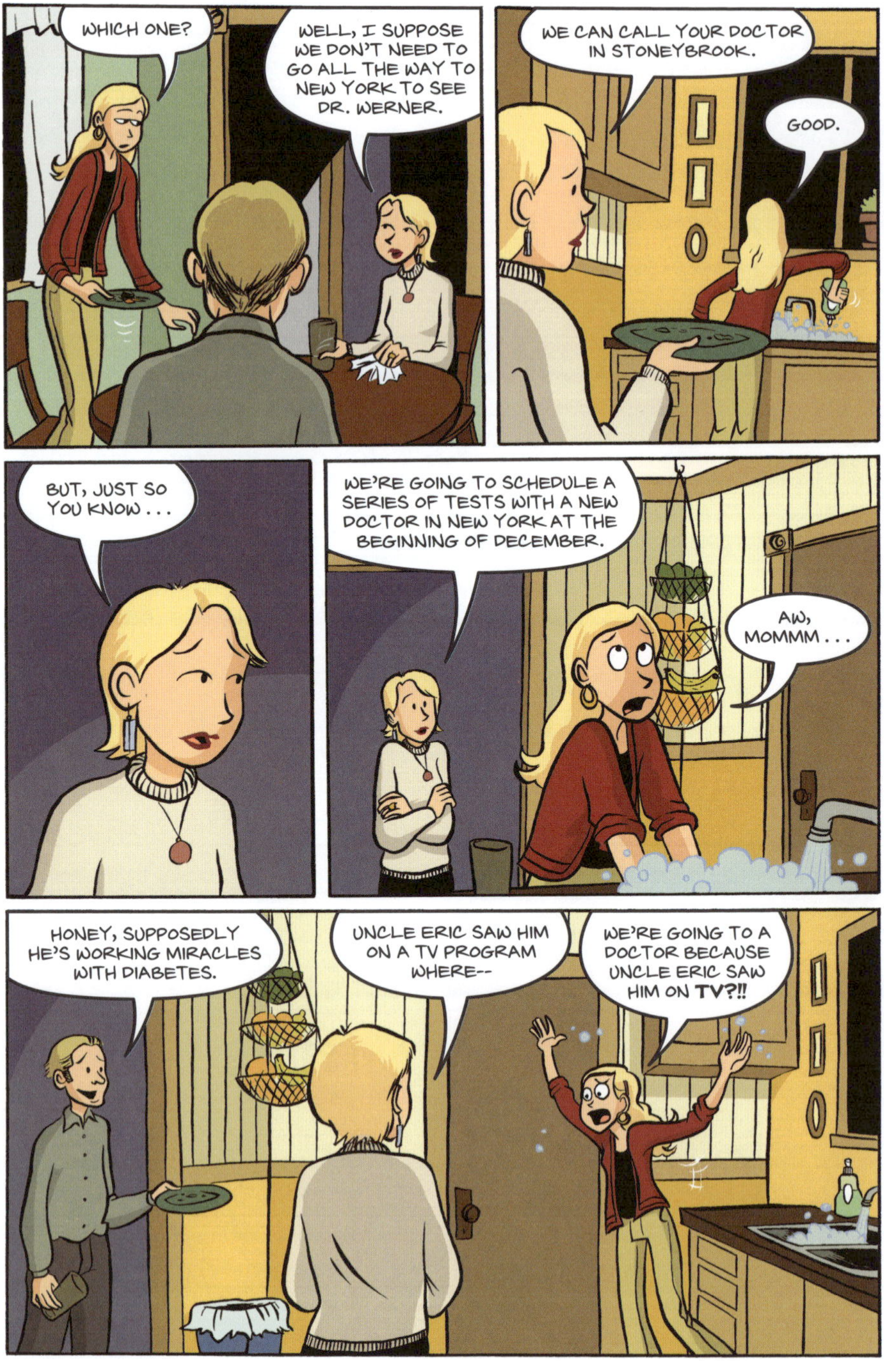
WHICH ONE?
WELL, I SUPPOSE WE DON'T NEED TO GO ALL THE WAY TO NEW YORK TO SEE DR. WERNER.
WE CAN CALL YOUR DOCTOR IN STONEYBROOK.
GOOD.
BUT, JUST SO YOU KNOW . . .
WE'RE GOING TO SCHEDULE A SERIES OF TESTS WITH A NEW DOCTOR IN NEW YORK AT THE BEGINNING OF DECEMBER.
AW, MOMMM . . .
HONEY, SUPPOSEDLY HE'S WORKING MIRACLES WITH DIABETES.
UNCLE ERIC SAW HIM ON A TV PROGRAM WHERE--
WE'RE GOING TO A DOCTOR BECAUSE UNCLE ERIC SAW HIM ON **TV?!!**

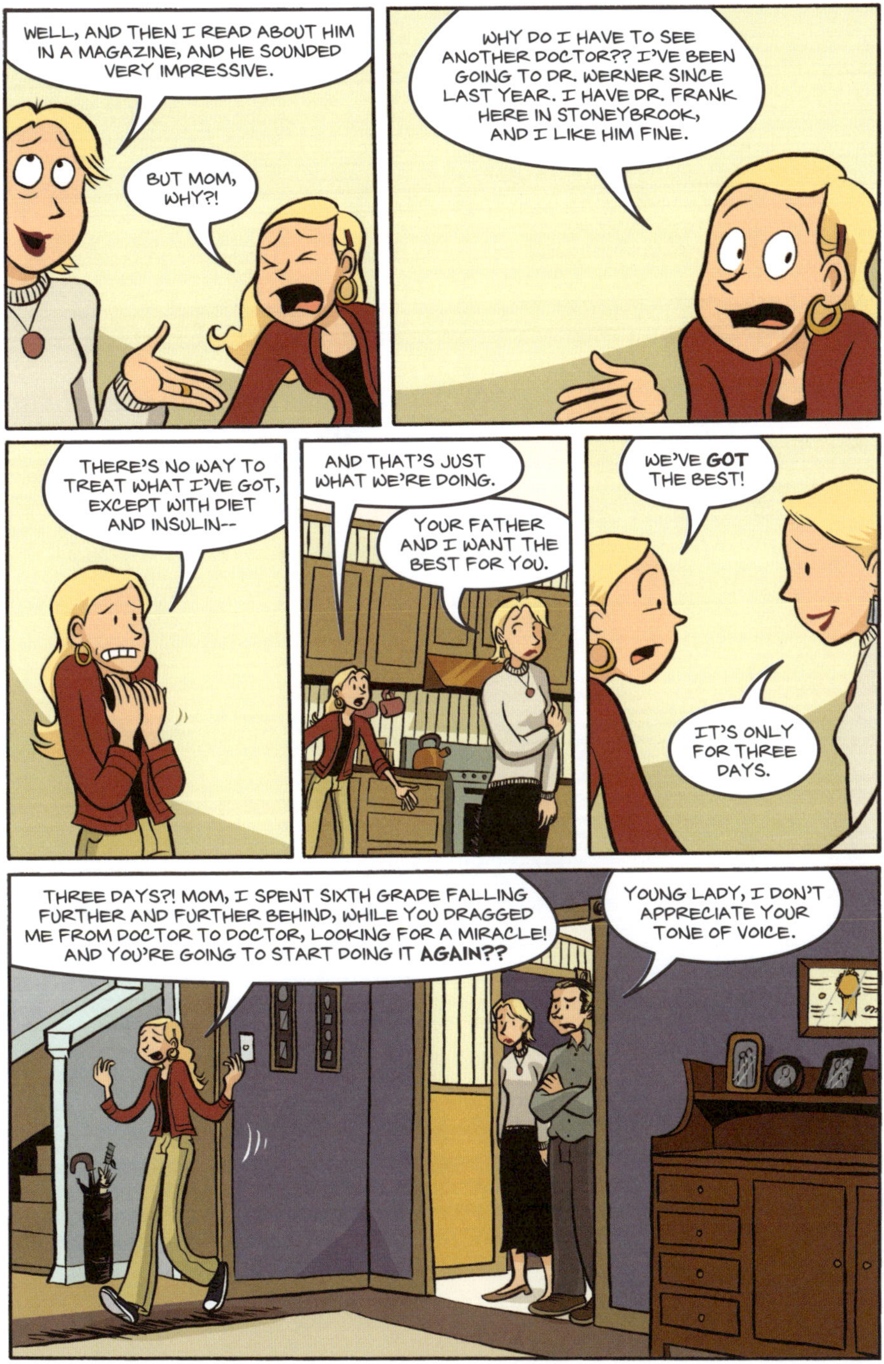
WELL, AND THEN I READ ABOUT HIM IN A MAGAZINE, AND HE SOUNDED VERY IMPRESSIVE.
BUT MOM, WHY?!
WHY DO I HAVE TO SEE ANOTHER DOCTOR?? I'VE BEEN GOING TO DR. WERNER SINCE LAST YEAR. I HAVE DR. FRANK HERE IN STONEYBROOK, AND I LIKE HIM FINE.
THERE'S NO WAY TO TREAT WHAT I'VE GOT, EXCEPT WITH DIET AND INSULIN--
AND THAT'S JUST WHAT WE'RE DOING.
YOUR FATHER AND I WANT THE BEST FOR YOU.
WE'VE **GOT** THE BEST!
IT'S ONLY FOR THREE DAYS.
THREE DAYS?! MOM, I SPENT SIXTH GRADE FALLING FURTHER AND FURTHER BEHIND, WHILE YOU DRAGGED ME FROM DOCTOR TO DOCTOR, LOOKING FOR A MIRACLE! AND YOU'RE GOING TO START DOING IT **AGAIN??**
YOUNG LADY, I DON'T APPRECIATE YOUR TONE OF VOICE.

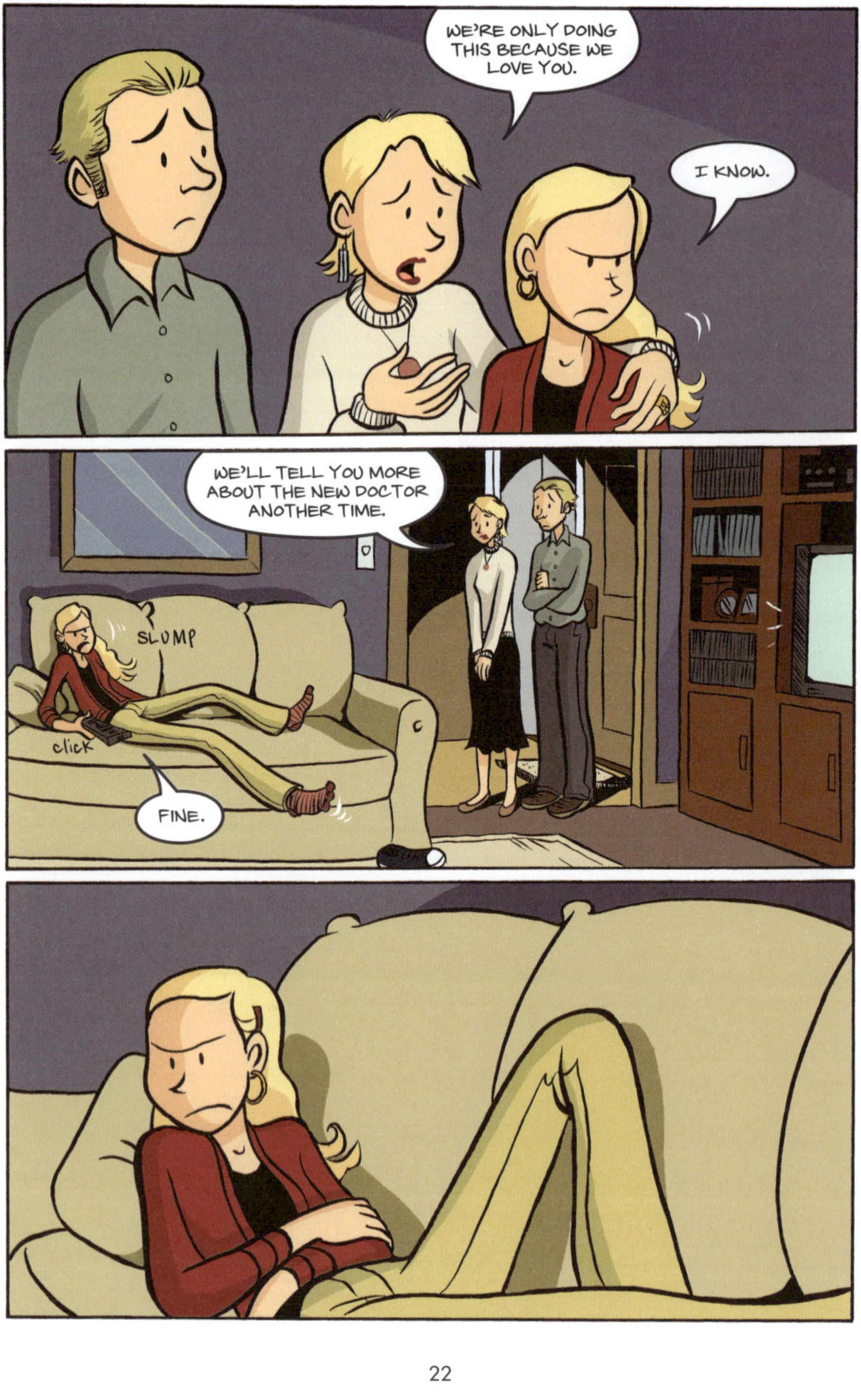
WE'RE ONLY DOING THIS BECAUSE WE LOVE YOU.
I KNOW.
WE'LL TELL YOU MORE ABOUT THE NEW DOCTOR ANOTHER TIME.
SLUMP
click
FINE.

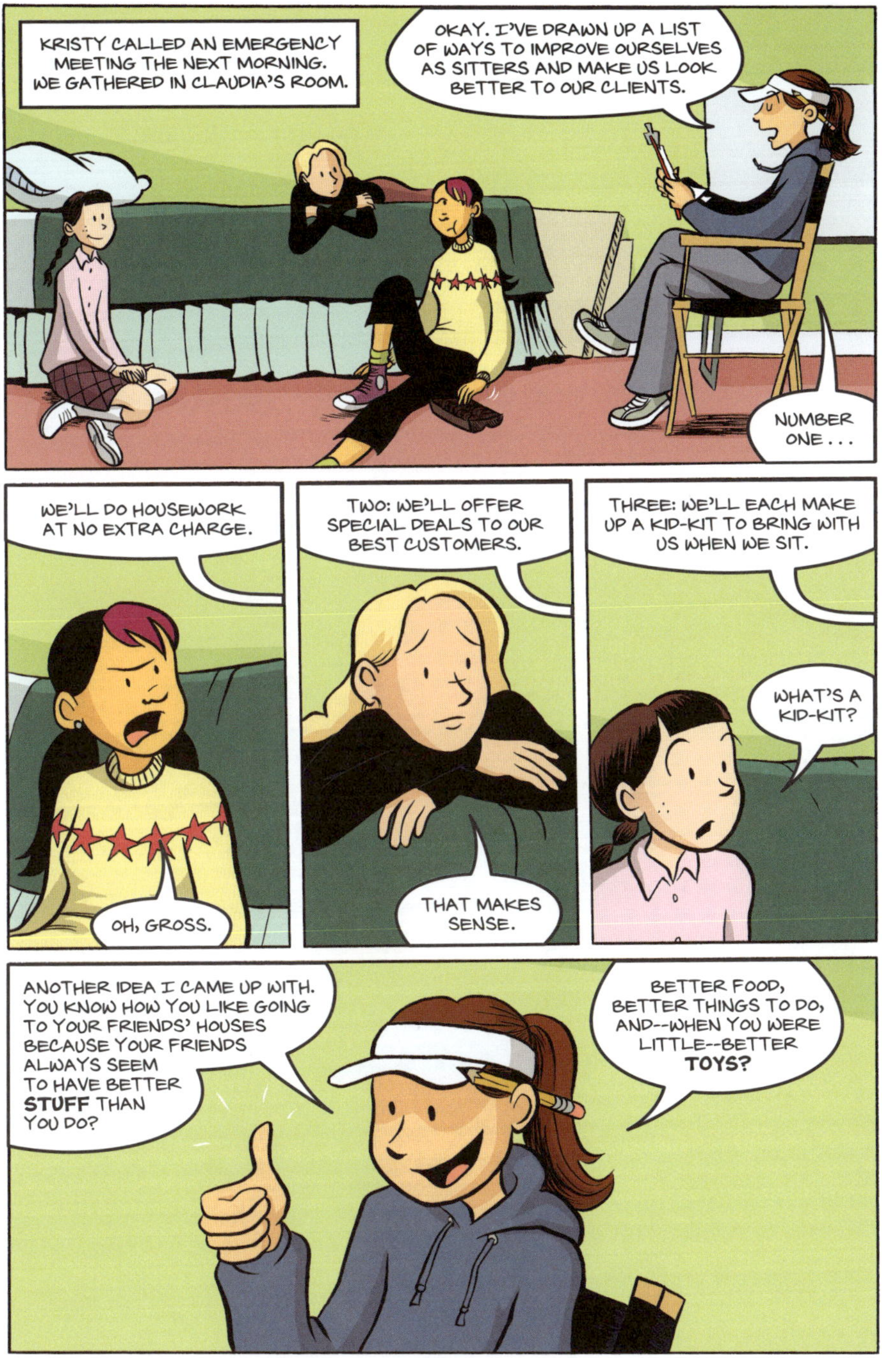
KRISTY CALLED AN EMERGENCY MEETING THE NEXT MORNING. WE GATHERED IN CLAUDIA'S ROOM.
OKAY. I'VE DRAWN UP A LIST OF WAYS TO IMPROVE OURSELVES AS SITTERS AND MAKE US LOOK BETTER TO OUR CLIENTS.
NUMBER ONE . . .
WE'LL DO HOUSEWORK AT NO EXTRA CHARGE.
OH, GROSS.
TWO: WE'LL OFFER SPECIAL DEALS TO OUR BEST CUSTOMERS.
THAT MAKES SENSE.
THREE: WE'LL EACH MAKE UP A KID-KIT TO BRING WITH US WHEN WE SIT.
WHAT'S A KID-KIT?
ANOTHER IDEA I CAME UP WITH. YOU KNOW HOW YOU LIKE GOING TO YOUR FRIENDS' HOUSES BECAUSE YOUR FRIENDS ALWAYS SEEM TO HAVE BETTER **STUFF** THAN YOU DO?
BETTER FOOD, BETTER THINGS TO DO, AND--WHEN YOU WERE LITTLE--BETTER **TOYS?**

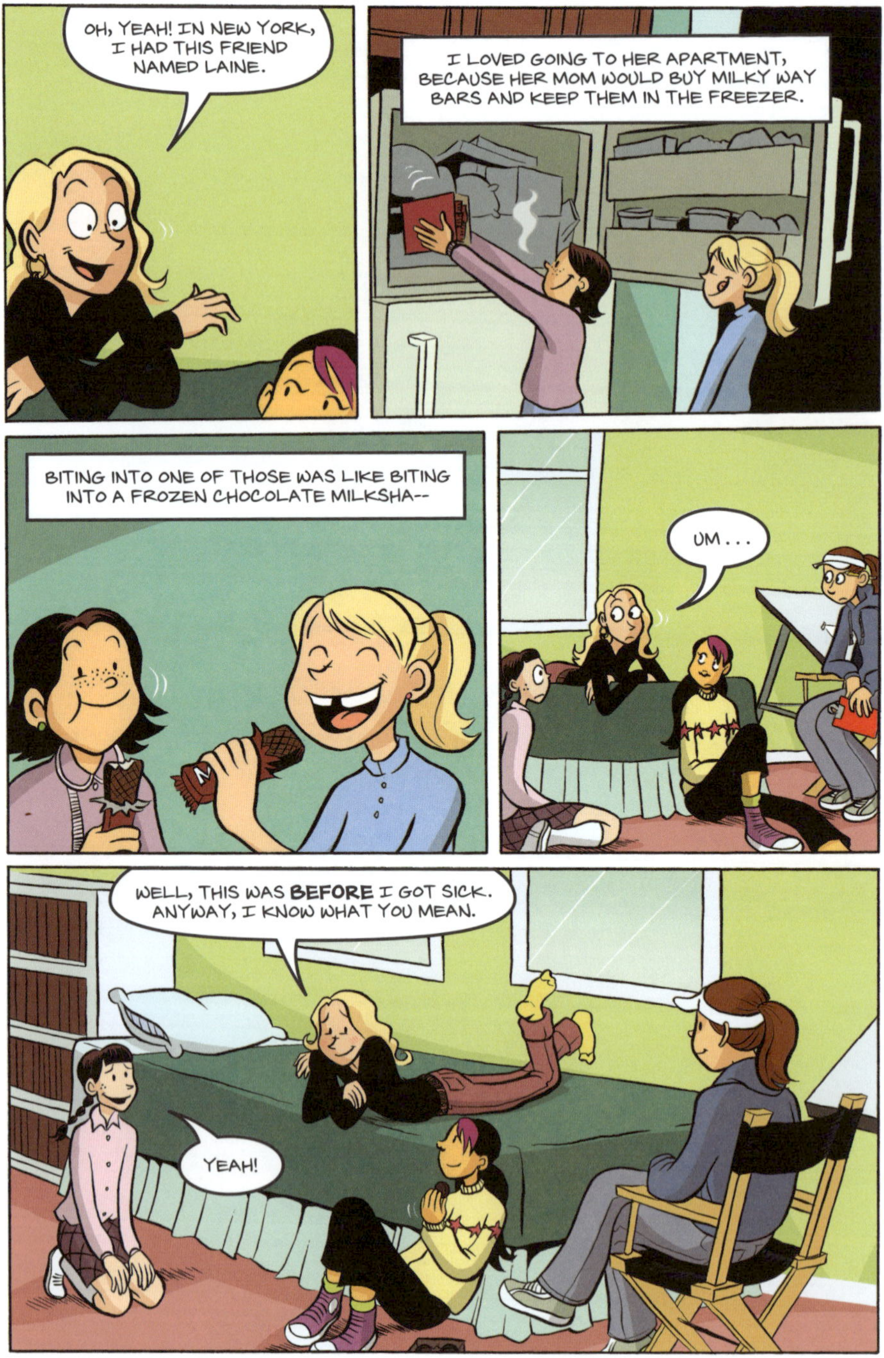
OH, YEAH! IN NEW YORK, I HAD THIS FRIEND NAMED LAINE.
I LOVED GOING TO HER APARTMENT, BECAUSE HER MOM WOULD BUY MILKY WAY BARS AND KEEP THEM IN THE FREEZER.
BITING INTO ONE OF THOSE WAS LIKE BITING INTO A FROZEN CHOCOLATE MILKSHA--
UM . . .
WELL, THIS WAS **BEFORE** I GOT SICK. ANYWAY, I KNOW WHAT YOU MEAN.
YEAH!

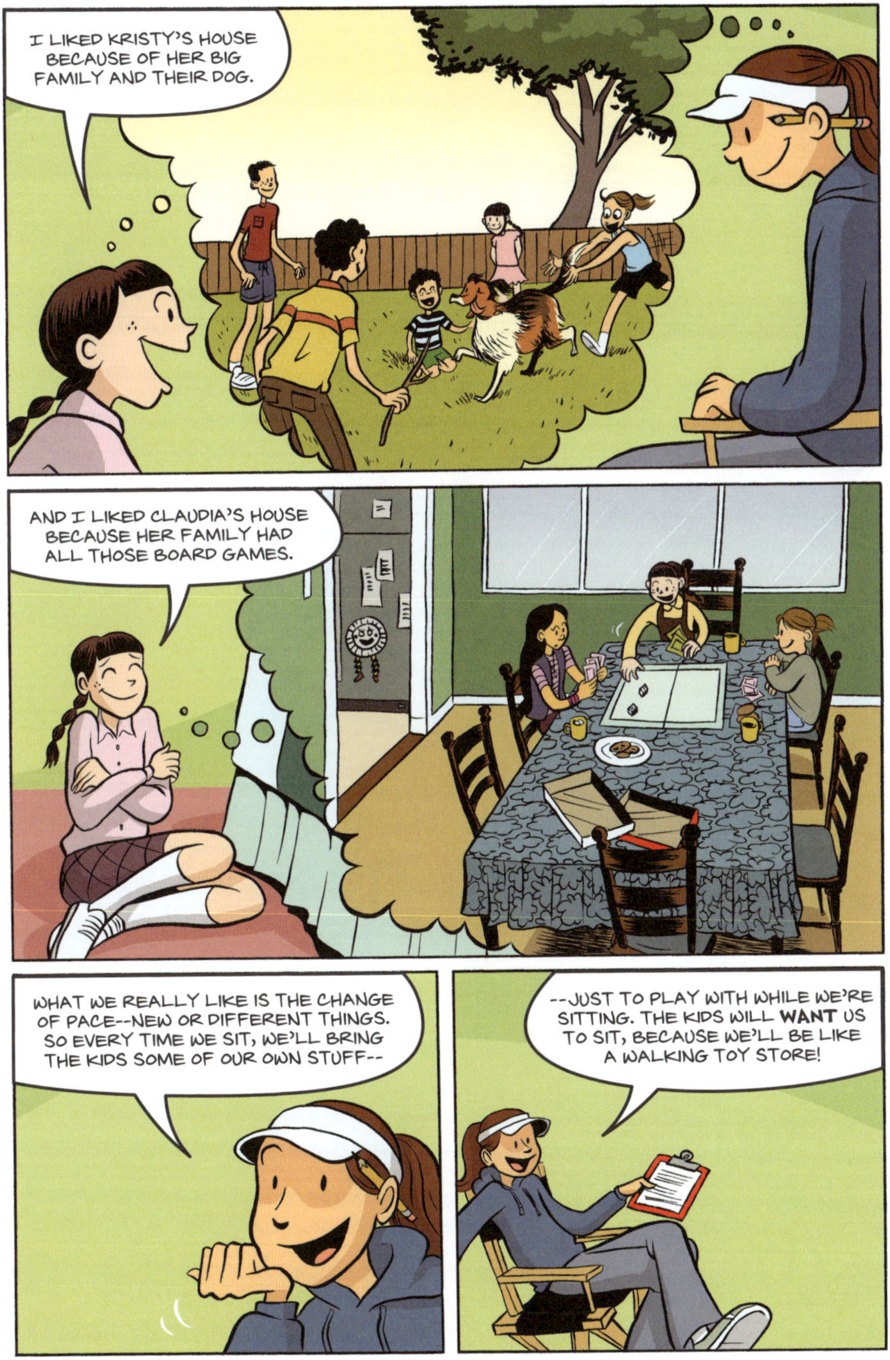
I LIKED KRISTY'S HOUSE BECAUSE OF HER BIG FAMILY AND THEIR DOG.
AND I LIKED CLAUDIA'S HOUSE BECAUSE HER FAMILY HAD ALL THOSE BOARD GAMES.
WHAT WE REALLY LIKE IS THE CHANGE OF PACE--NEW OR DIFFERENT THINGS. SO EVERY TIME WE SIT, WE'LL BRING THE KIDS SOME OF OUR OWN STUFF--
--JUST TO PLAY WITH WHILE WE'RE SITTING. THE KIDS WILL **WANT** US TO SIT, BECAUSE WE'LL BE LIKE A WALKING TOY STORE!

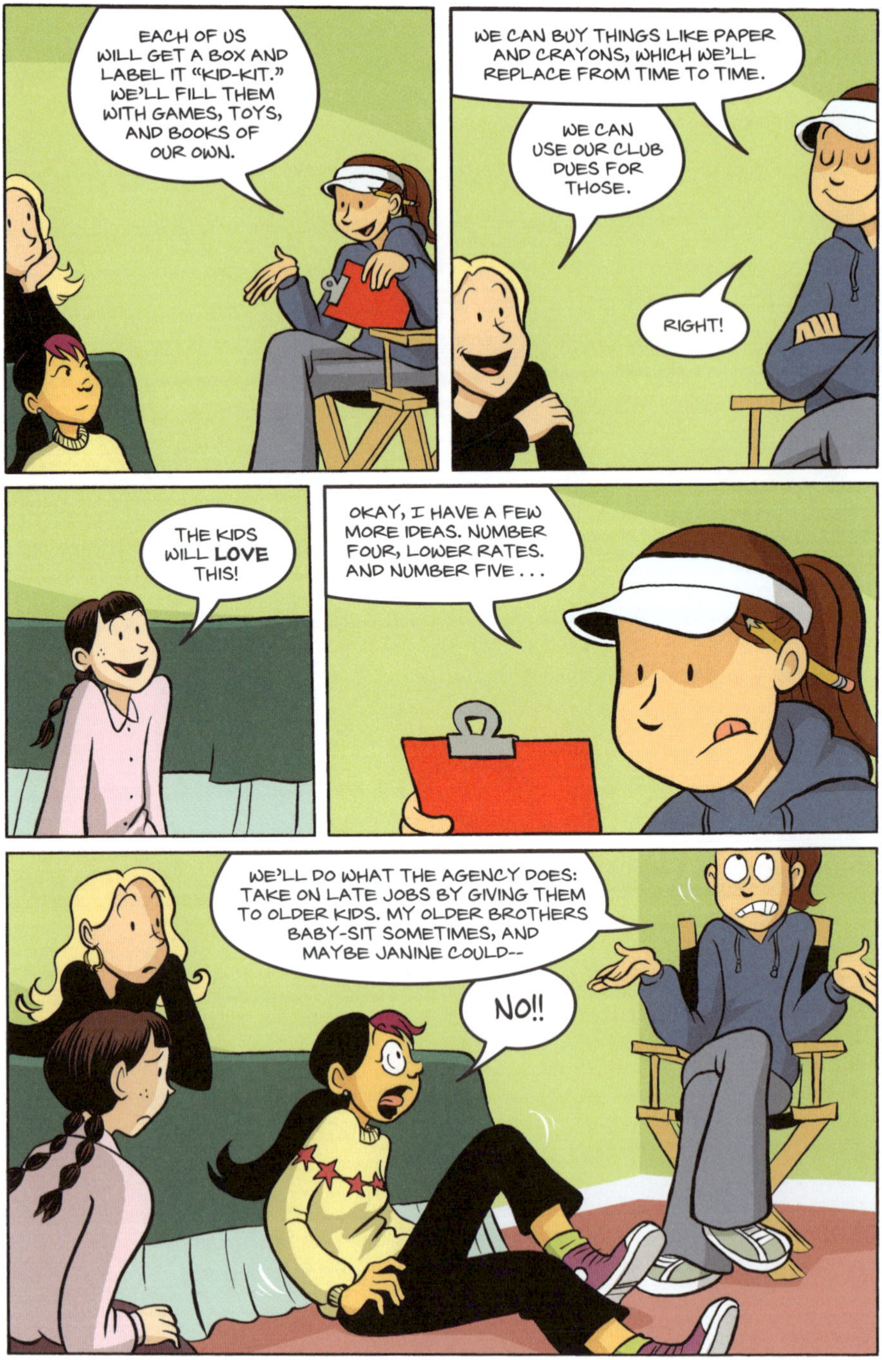
EACH OF US WILL GET A BOX AND LABEL IT "KID-KIT." WE'LL FILL THEM WITH GAMES, TOYS, AND BOOKS OF OUR OWN.
WE CAN BUY THINGS LIKE PAPER AND CRAYONS, WHICH WE'LL REPLACE FROM TIME TO TIME.
WE CAN USE OUR CLUB DUES FOR THOSE.
RIGHT!
THE KIDS WILL **LOVE** THIS!
OKAY, I HAVE A FEW MORE IDEAS. NUMBER FOUR, LOWER RATES. AND NUMBER FIVE . . .
WE'LL DO WHAT THE AGENCY DOES: TAKE ON LATE JOBS BY GIVING THEM TO OLDER KIDS. MY OLDER BROTHERS BABY-SIT SOMETIMES, AND MAYBE JANINE COULD--
NO!!

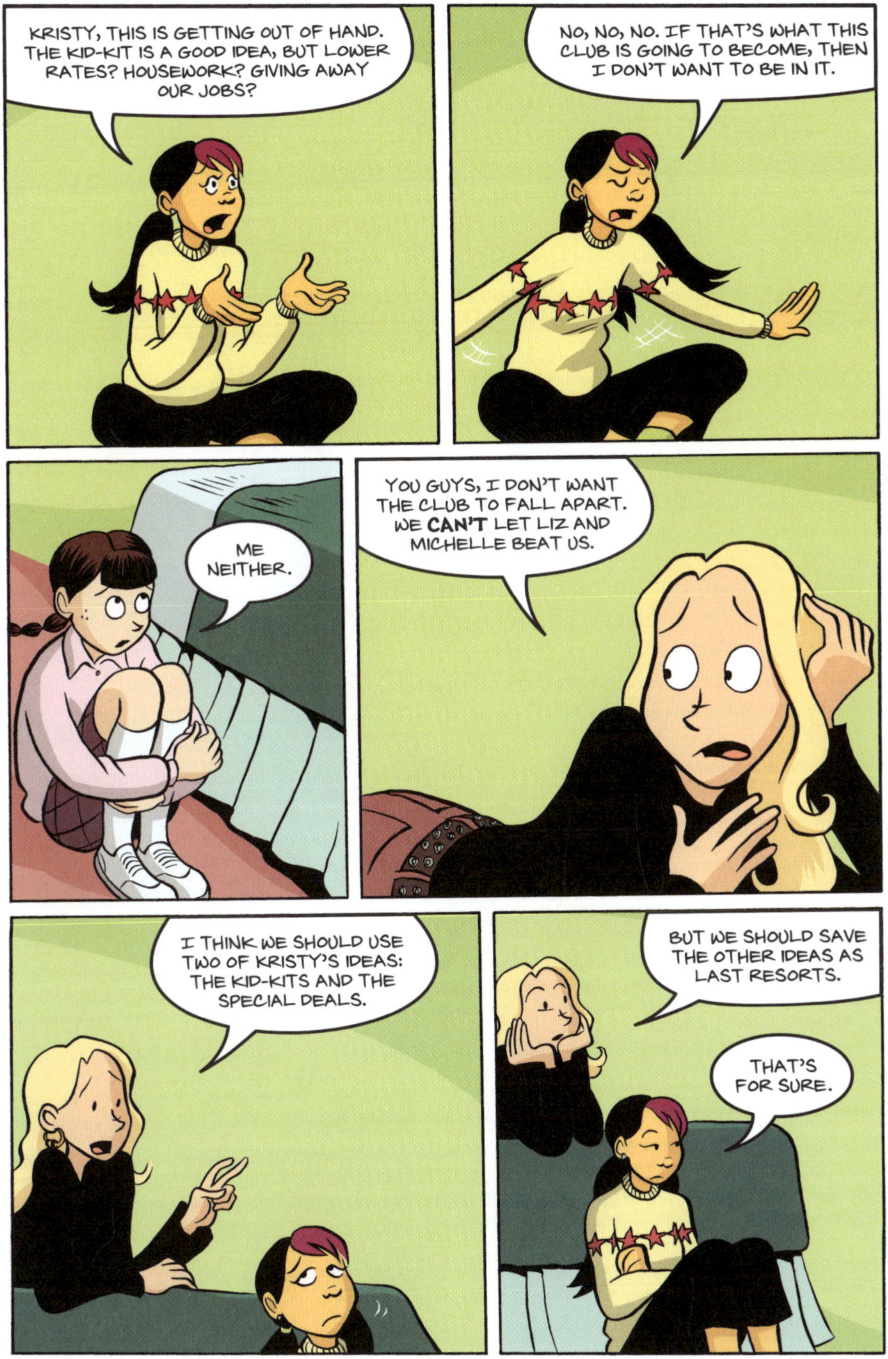
KRISTY, THIS IS GETTING OUT OF HAND. THE KID-KIT IS A GOOD IDEA, BUT LOWER RATES? HOUSEWORK? GIVING AWAY OUR JOBS?
NO, NO, NO. IF THAT'S WHAT THIS CLUB IS GOING TO BECOME, THEN I DON'T WANT TO BE IN IT.
ME NEITHER.
YOU GUYS, I DON'T WANT THE CLUB TO FALL APART. WE **CAN'T** LET LIZ AND MICHELLE BEAT US.
I THINK WE SHOULD USE TWO OF KRISTY'S IDEAS: THE KID-KITS AND THE SPECIAL DEALS.
BUT WE SHOULD SAVE THE OTHER IDEAS AS LAST RESORTS.
THAT'S FOR SURE.

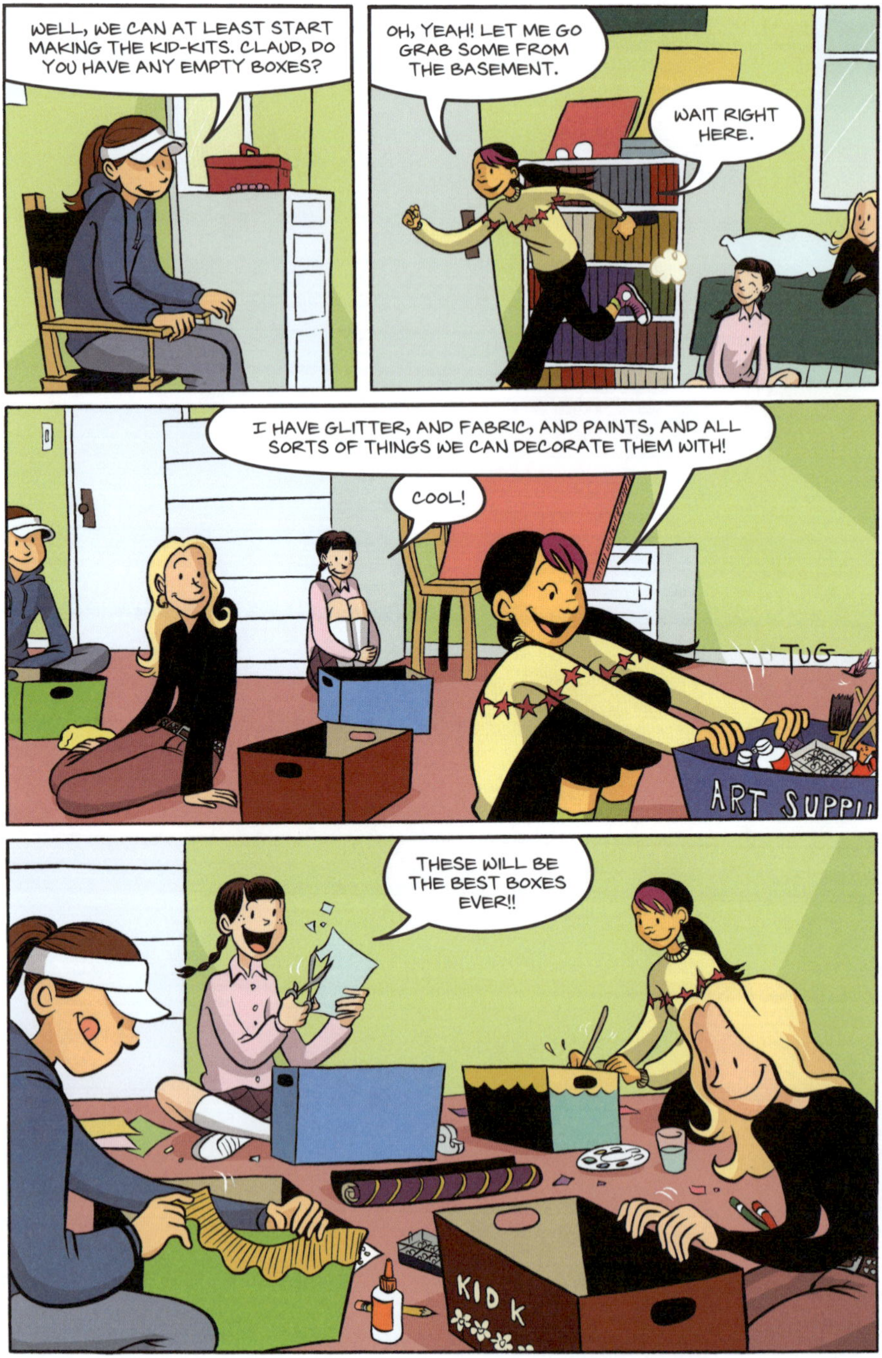
WELL, WE CAN AT LEAST START MAKING THE KID-KITS. CLAUD, DO YOU HAVE ANY EMPTY BOXES?
OH, YEAH! LET ME GO GRAB SOME FROM THE BASEMENT.
WAIT RIGHT HERE.
I HAVE GLITTER, AND FABRIC, AND PAINTS, AND ALL SORTS OF THINGS WE CAN DECORATE THEM WITH!
COOL!
TUG
ART SUPPLI
THESE WILL BE THE BEST BOXES EVER!!
KID K

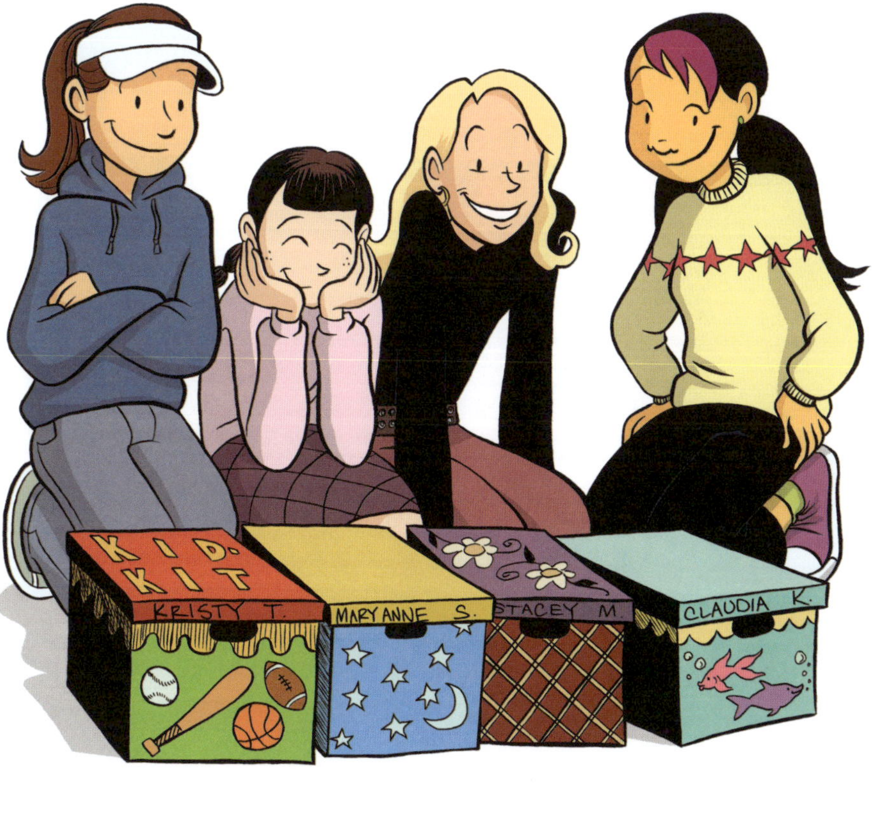
KID-KIT
KRISTY T.
MARY ANNE S.
STACEY M.
CLAUDIA K.

November 10

   Monday I had a sitting job for Charlotte Johanssen. I love sitting for Charlotte, she's one of my very favorite kids. And her mother, Dr. Johanssen, is a Doctor at Stoneybrook Medical Center, so I like talking to her — she always asks me how I'm doing and how I feel about my treatments. Today was no different, except for what happened near the end of the afternoon...

                                      Stacey

CHAPTER 4

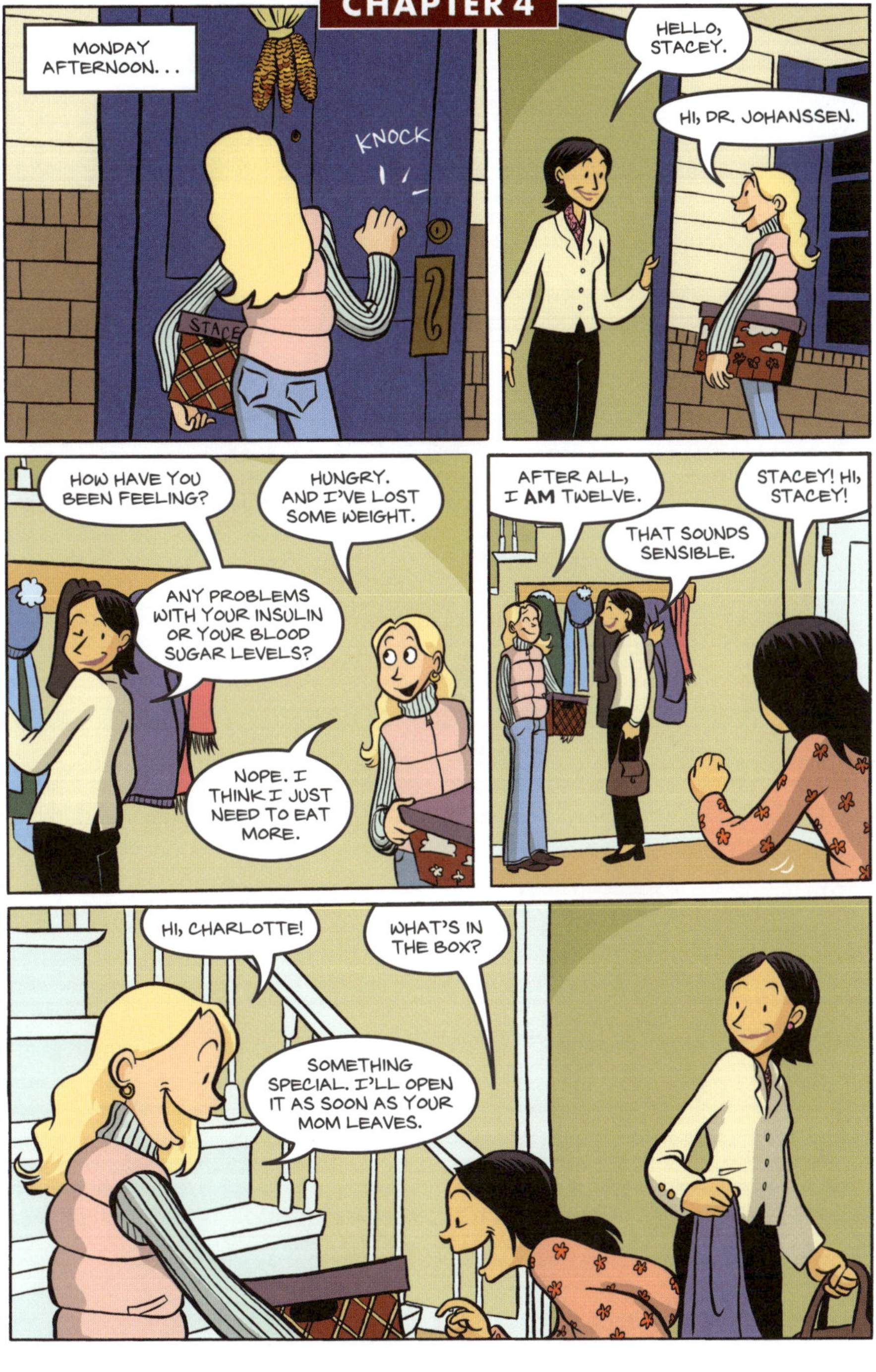
MONDAY AFTERNOON. . .
KNOCK
STACE
HELLO, STACEY.
HI, DR. JOHANSSEN.
HOW HAVE YOU BEEN FEELING?
HUNGRY. AND I'VE LOST SOME WEIGHT.
ANY PROBLEMS WITH YOUR INSULIN OR YOUR BLOOD SUGAR LEVELS?
NOPE. I THINK I JUST NEED TO EAT MORE.
AFTER ALL, I **AM** TWELVE.
THAT SOUNDS SENSIBLE.
STACEY! HI, STACEY!
HI, CHARLOTTE!
WHAT'S IN THE BOX?
SOMETHING SPECIAL. I'LL OPEN IT AS SOON AS YOUR MOM LEAVES.

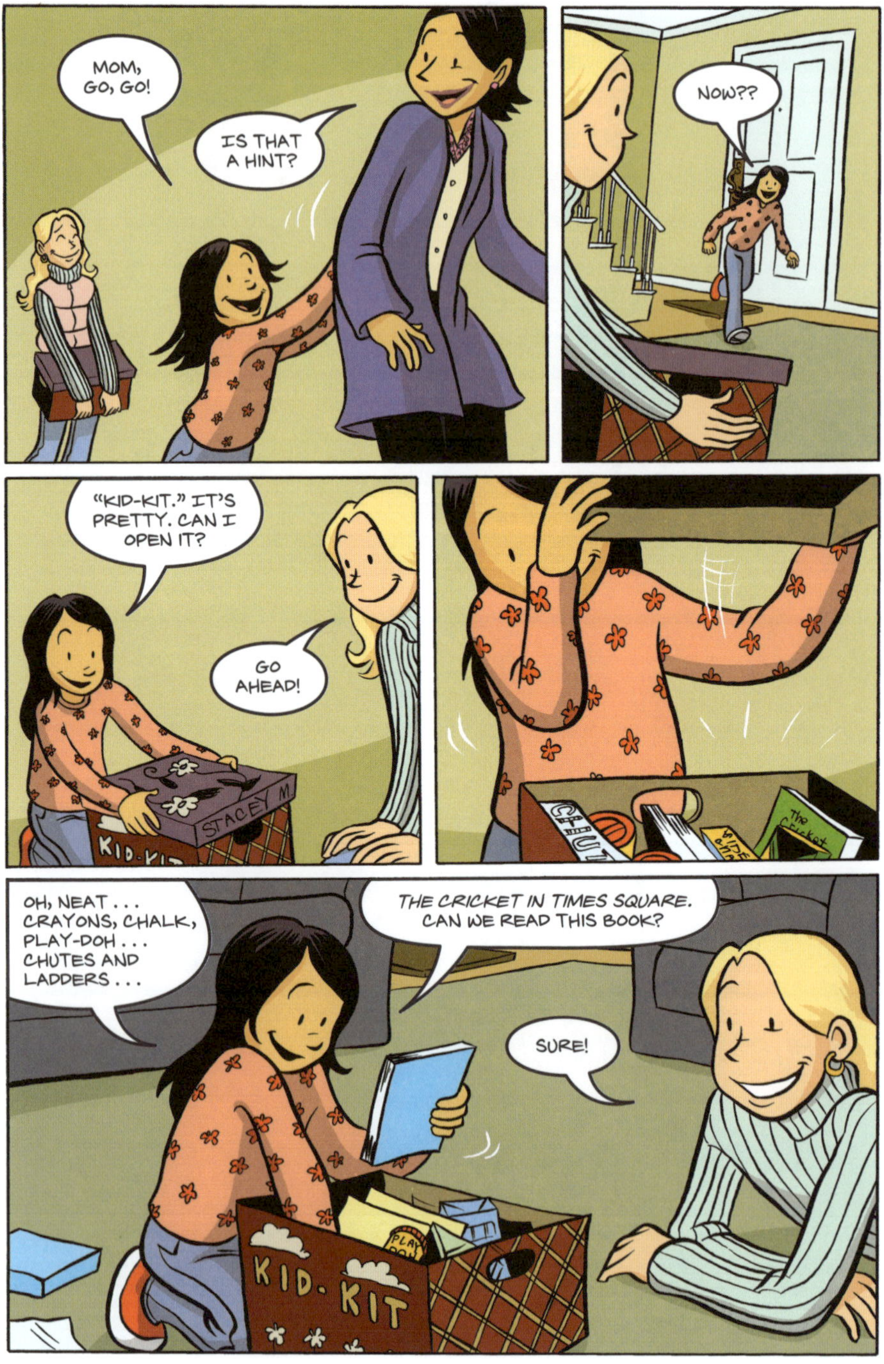
MOM, GO, GO!
IS THAT A HINT?
NOW??
"KID-KIT." IT'S PRETTY. CAN I OPEN IT?
GO AHEAD!
STACEY M
KID-KIT
OH, NEAT . . . CRAYONS, CHALK, PLAY-DOH . . . CHUTES AND LADDERS . . .
THE CRICKET IN TIMES SQUARE. CAN WE READ THIS BOOK?
SURE!
KID-KIT

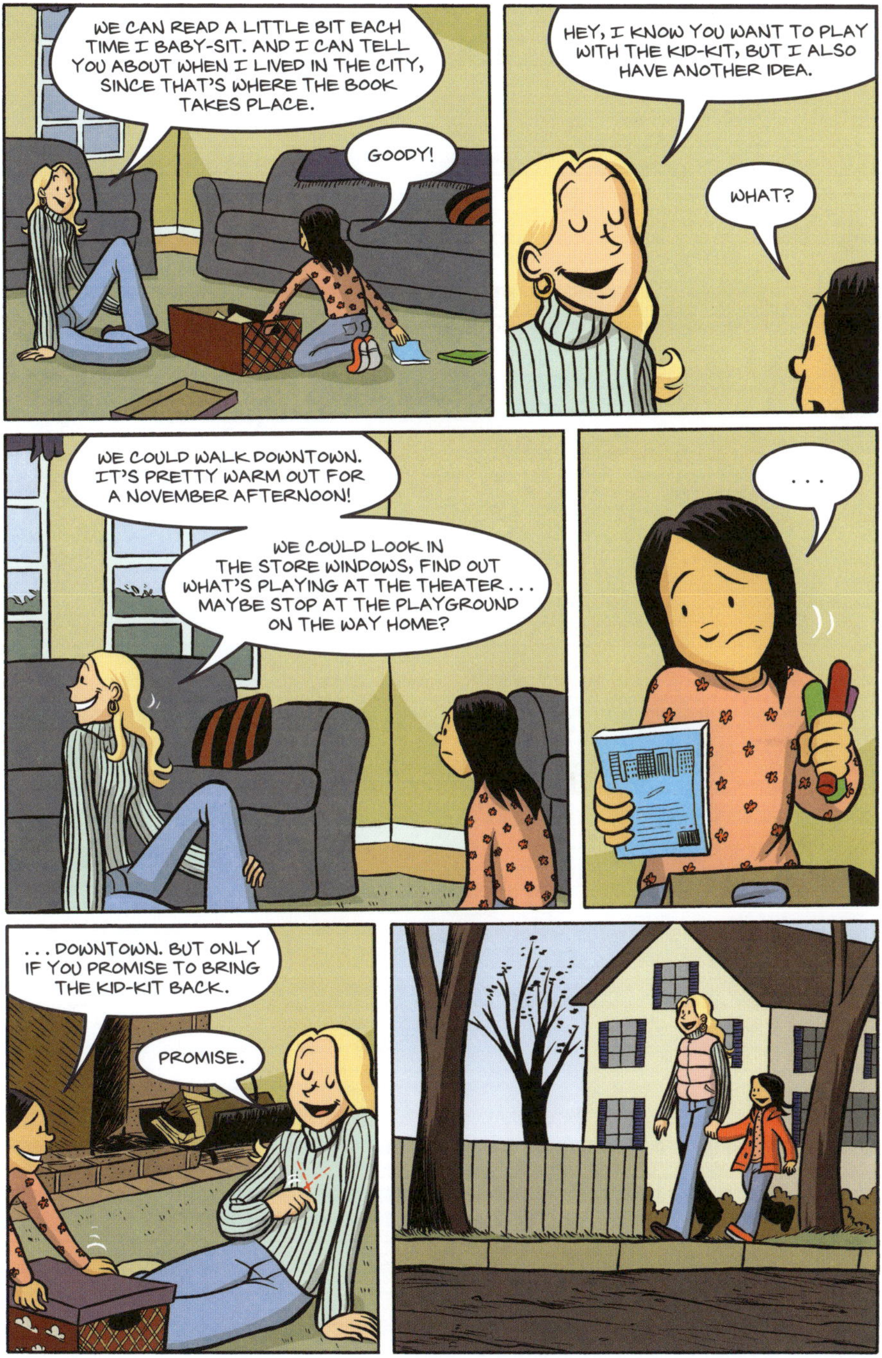
WE CAN READ A LITTLE BIT EACH TIME I BABY-SIT. AND I CAN TELL YOU ABOUT WHEN I LIVED IN THE CITY, SINCE THAT'S WHERE THE BOOK TAKES PLACE.
GOODY!
HEY, I KNOW YOU WANT TO PLAY WITH THE KID-KIT, BUT I ALSO HAVE ANOTHER IDEA.
WHAT?
WE COULD WALK DOWNTOWN. IT'S PRETTY WARM OUT FOR A NOVEMBER AFTERNOON!
WE COULD LOOK IN THE STORE WINDOWS, FIND OUT WHAT'S PLAYING AT THE THEATER . . . MAYBE STOP AT THE PLAYGROUND ON THE WAY HOME?
. . .
. . . DOWNTOWN. BUT ONLY IF YOU PROMISE TO BRING THE KID-KIT BACK.
PROMISE.

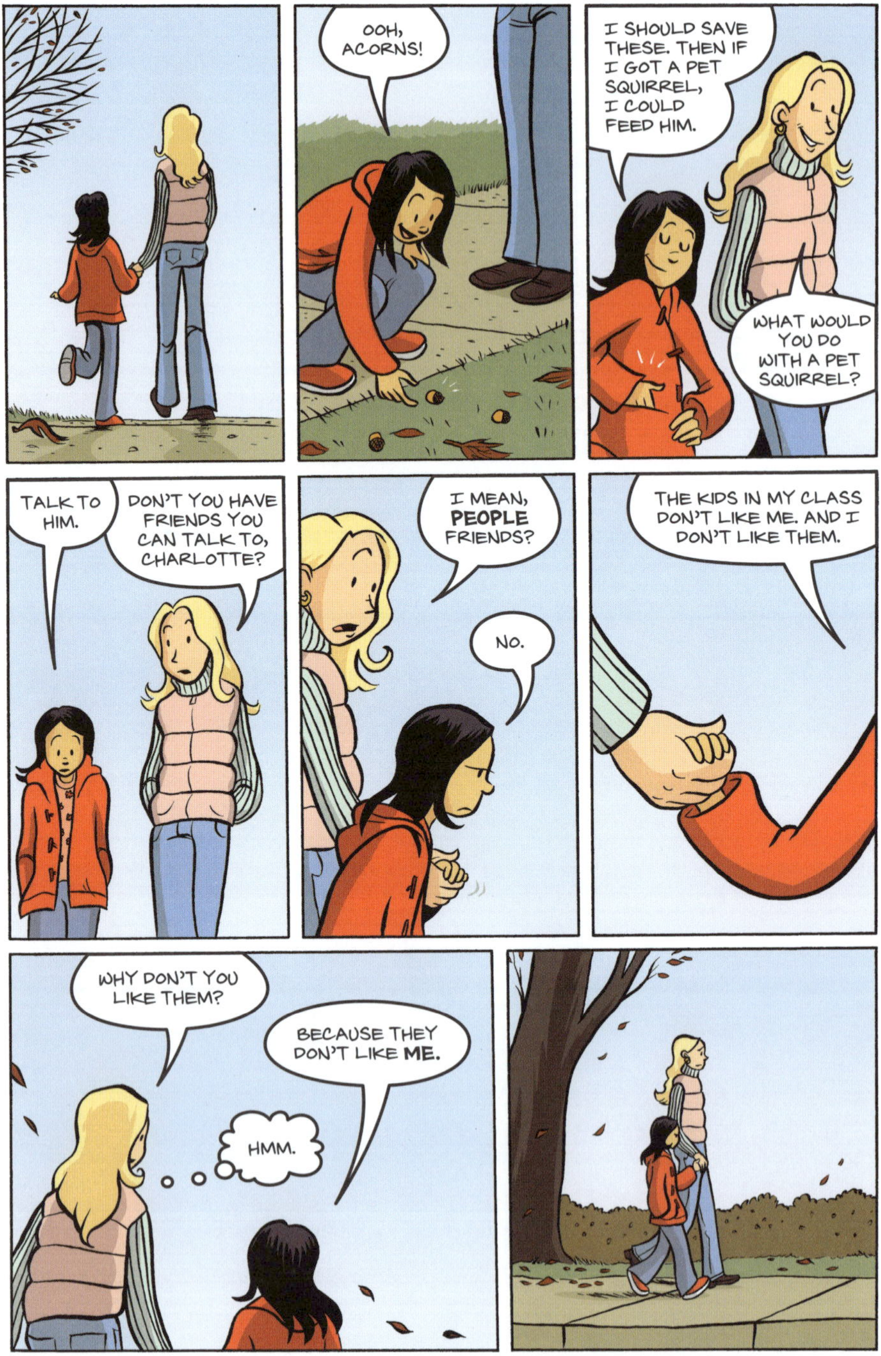
OOH, ACORNS!
I SHOULD SAVE THESE. THEN IF I GOT A PET SQUIRREL, I COULD FEED HIM.
WHAT WOULD YOU DO WITH A PET SQUIRREL?
TALK TO HIM.
DON'T YOU HAVE FRIENDS YOU CAN TALK TO, CHARLOTTE?
I MEAN, **PEOPLE** FRIENDS?
NO.
THE KIDS IN MY CLASS DON'T LIKE ME. AND I DON'T LIKE THEM.
WHY DON'T YOU LIKE THEM?
BECAUSE THEY DON'T LIKE **ME.**
HMM.

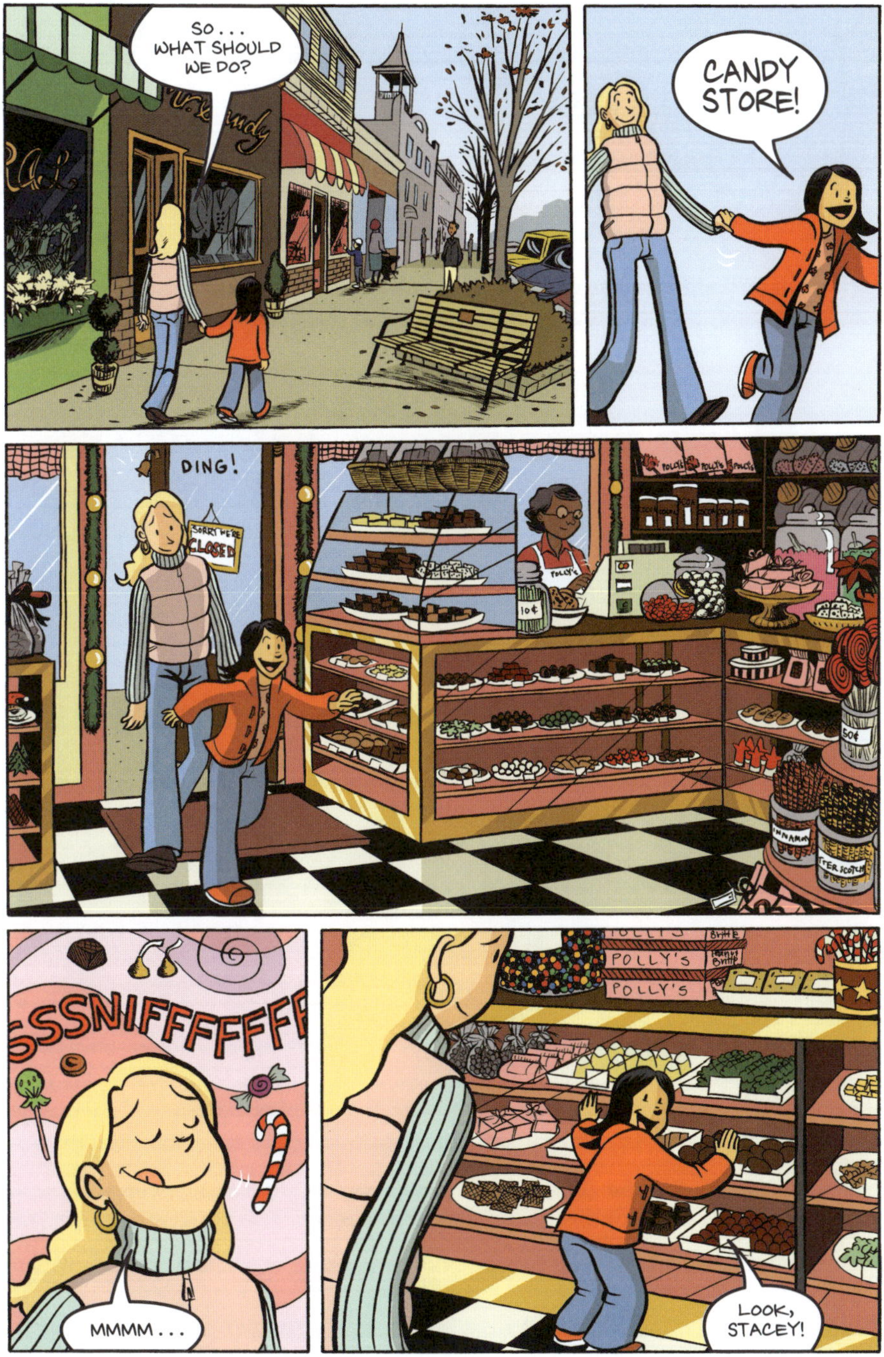
SO... WHAT SHOULD WE DO?
CANDY STORE!
DING!
SORRY WE'RE CLOSED
POLLY'S
10¢
50¢
SSSNIFFFFFFF
MMMM...
POLLY'S
POLLY'S
LOOK, STACEY!

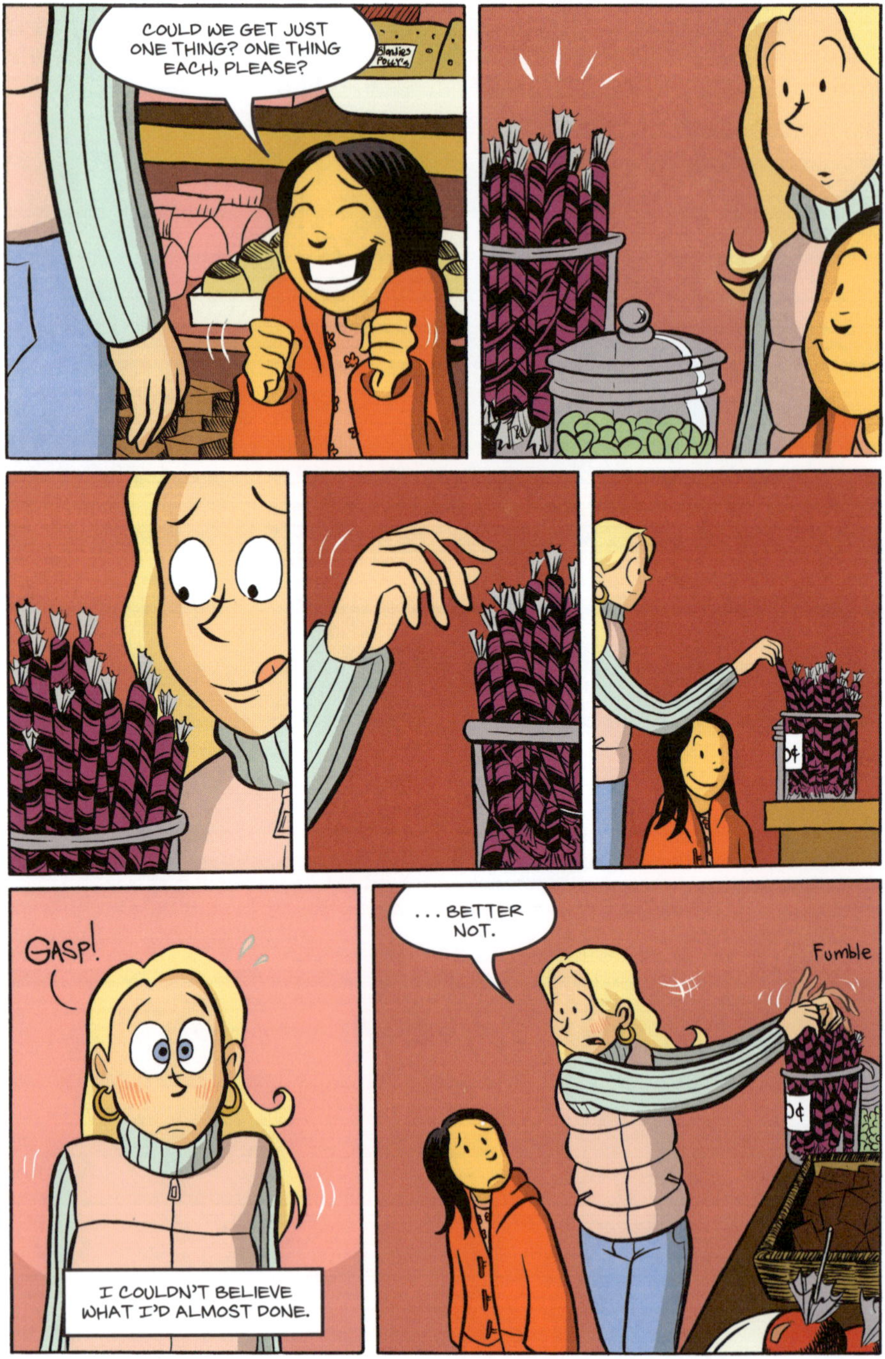
COULD WE GET JUST ONE THING? ONE THING EACH, PLEASE?
GASP!
I COULDN'T BELIEVE WHAT I'D ALMOST DONE.
. . . BETTER NOT.
Fumble

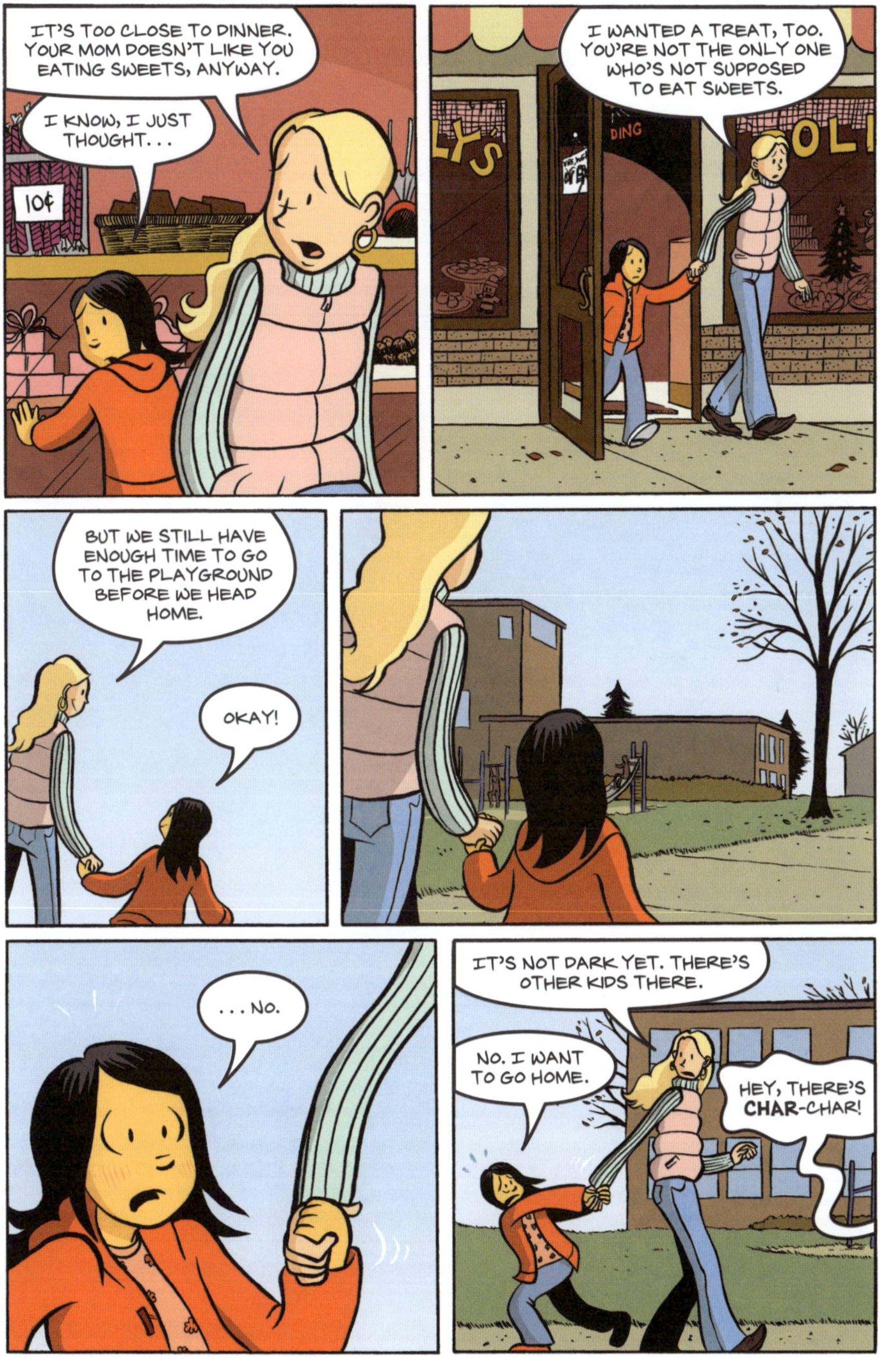
IT'S TOO CLOSE TO DINNER. YOUR MOM DOESN'T LIKE YOU EATING SWEETS, ANYWAY.
I KNOW, I JUST THOUGHT. . .
10¢
I WANTED A TREAT, TOO. YOU'RE NOT THE ONLY ONE WHO'S NOT SUPPOSED TO EAT SWEETS.
DING
BUT WE STILL HAVE ENOUGH TIME TO GO TO THE PLAYGROUND BEFORE WE HEAD HOME.
OKAY!
. . . NO.
IT'S NOT DARK YET. THERE'S OTHER KIDS THERE.
NO. I WANT TO GO HOME.
HEY, THERE'S **CHAR**-CHAR!

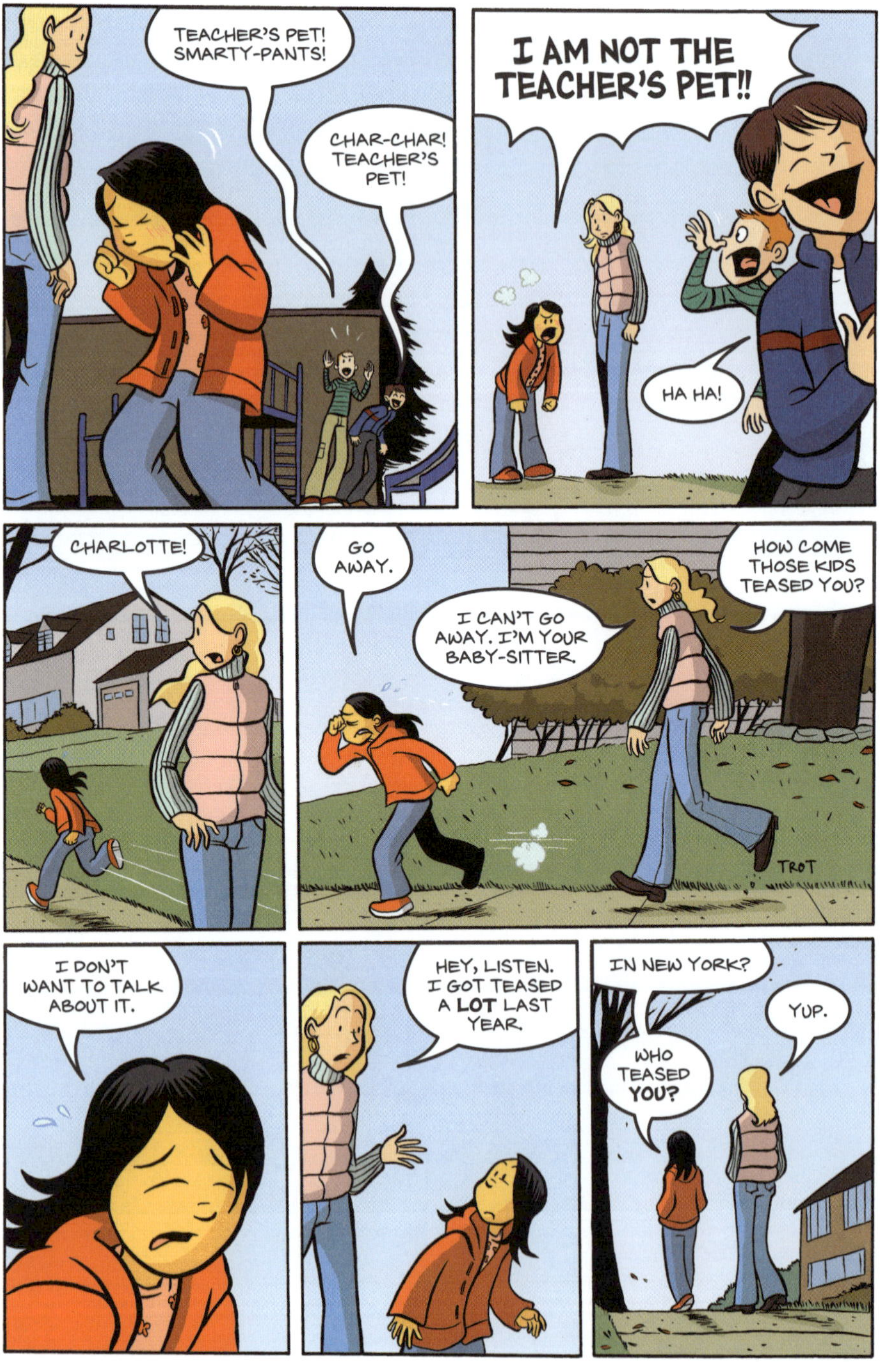
TEACHER'S PET! SMARTY-PANTS!
CHAR-CHAR! TEACHER'S PET!
I AM NOT THE TEACHER'S PET!!
HA HA!
CHARLOTTE!
GO AWAY.
I CAN'T GO AWAY. I'M YOUR BABY-SITTER.
HOW COME THOSE KIDS TEASED YOU?
TROT
I DON'T WANT TO TALK ABOUT IT.
HEY, LISTEN. I GOT TEASED A **LOT** LAST YEAR.
IN NEW YORK?
YUP.
WHO TEASED **YOU?**

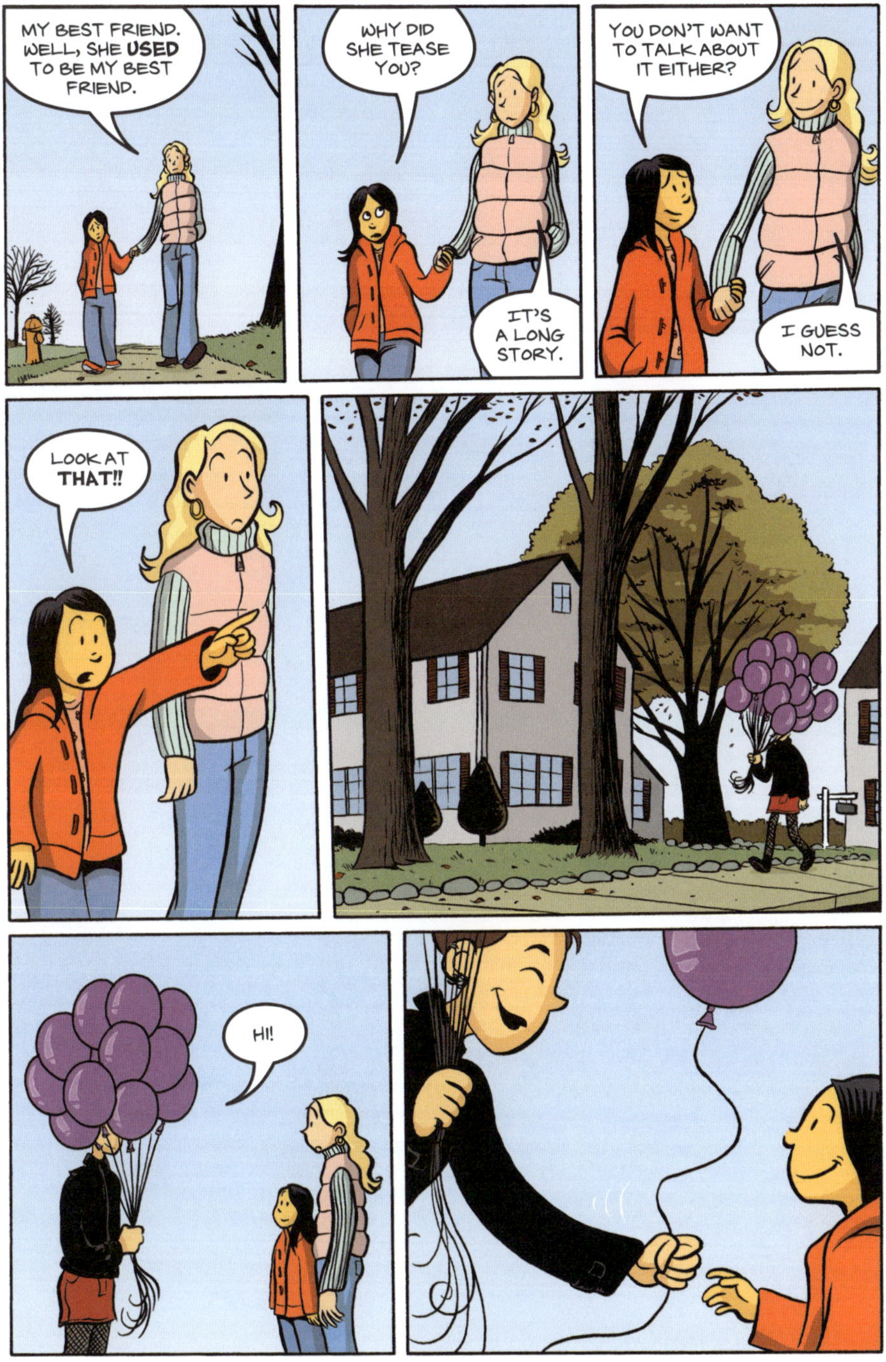
MY BEST FRIEND. WELL, SHE **USED** TO BE MY BEST FRIEND.
WHY DID SHE TEASE YOU?
IT'S A LONG STORY.
YOU DON'T WANT TO TALK ABOUT IT EITHER?
I GUESS NOT.
LOOK AT **THAT!!**
HI!

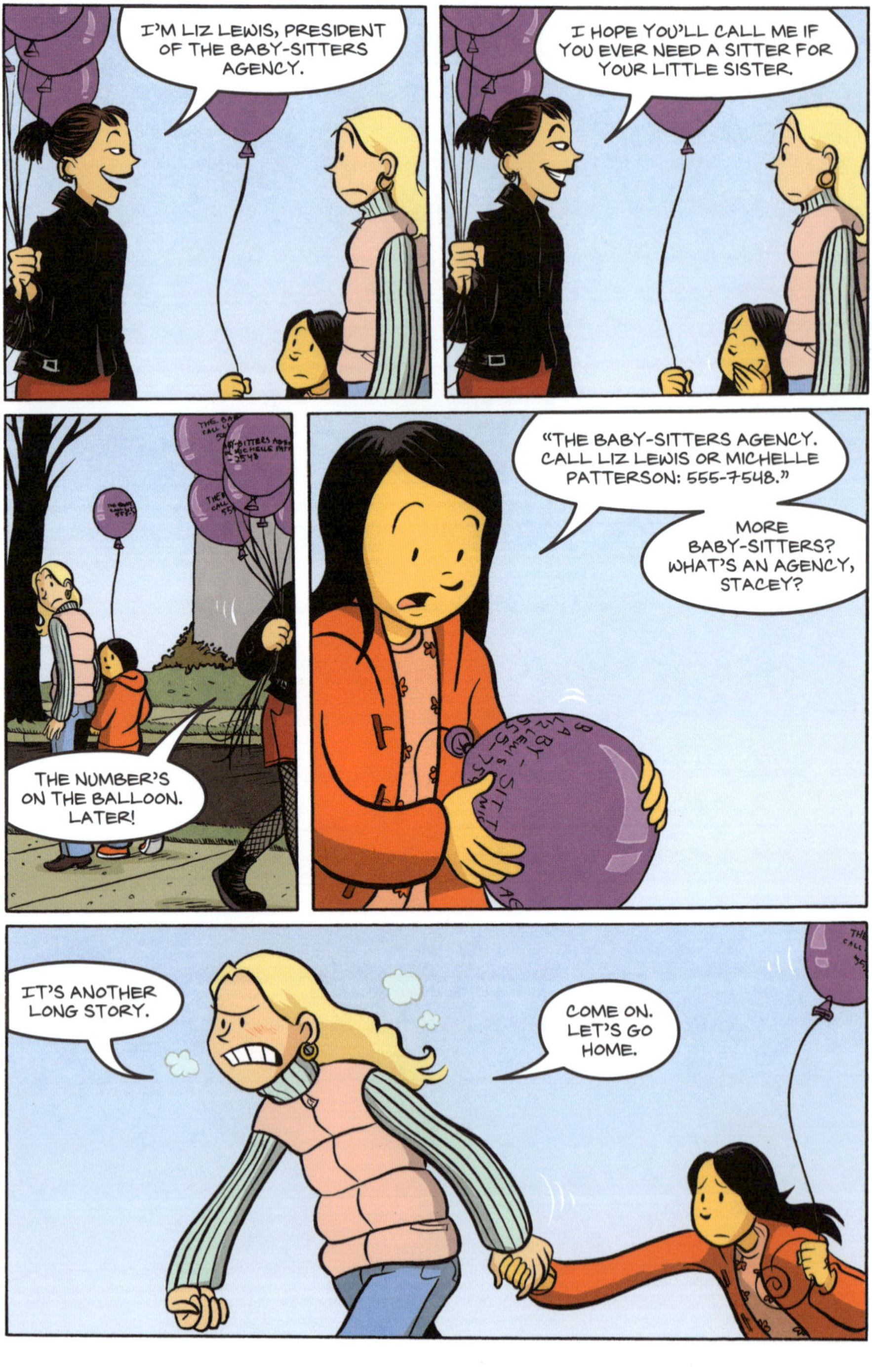
I'M LIZ LEWIS, PRESIDENT OF THE BABY-SITTERS AGENCY.
I HOPE YOU'LL CALL ME IF YOU EVER NEED A SITTER FOR YOUR LITTLE SISTER.
THE NUMBER'S ON THE BALLOON. LATER!
"THE BABY-SITTERS AGENCY. CALL LIZ LEWIS OR MICHELLE PATTERSON: 555-7548."
MORE BABY-SITTERS? WHAT'S AN AGENCY, STACEY?
IT'S ANOTHER LONG STORY.
COME ON. LET'S GO HOME.

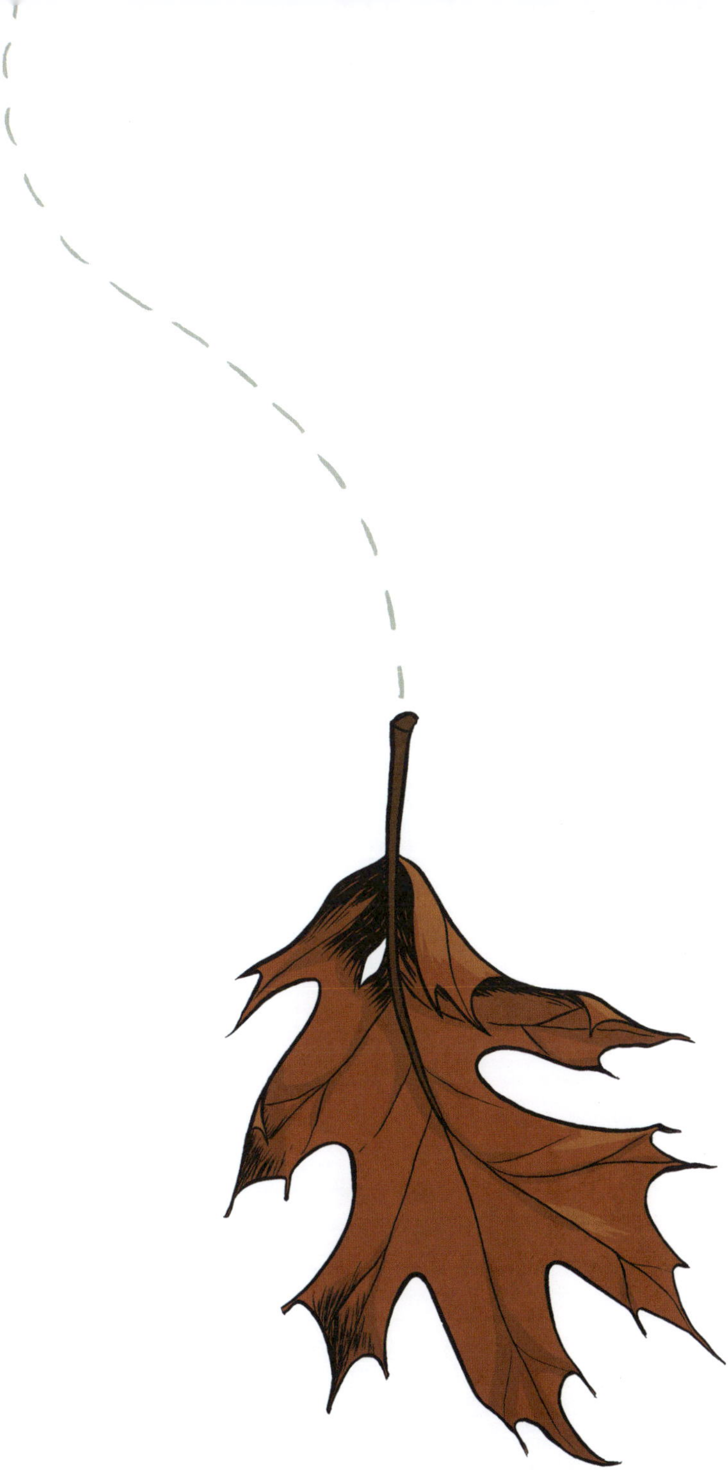

Sunday, November 23

   It is just one week since Liz Lewis and Michelle Patterson sent around their fliers. Usually, our club gets about fourteen or fifteen jobs a week. Since last Monday, we've had <u>SEVEN</u>. That's why I'm writing in our notebook. This book is supposed to be a diary of our baby-sitting jobs, so each of us can write up our problems and experiences for the other club members to read. But the Baby-sitters Agency is the biggest problem we've ever had, and I plan to keep track of it in our notebook.

We better do something fast.

                                — Kristy

CHAPTER 5

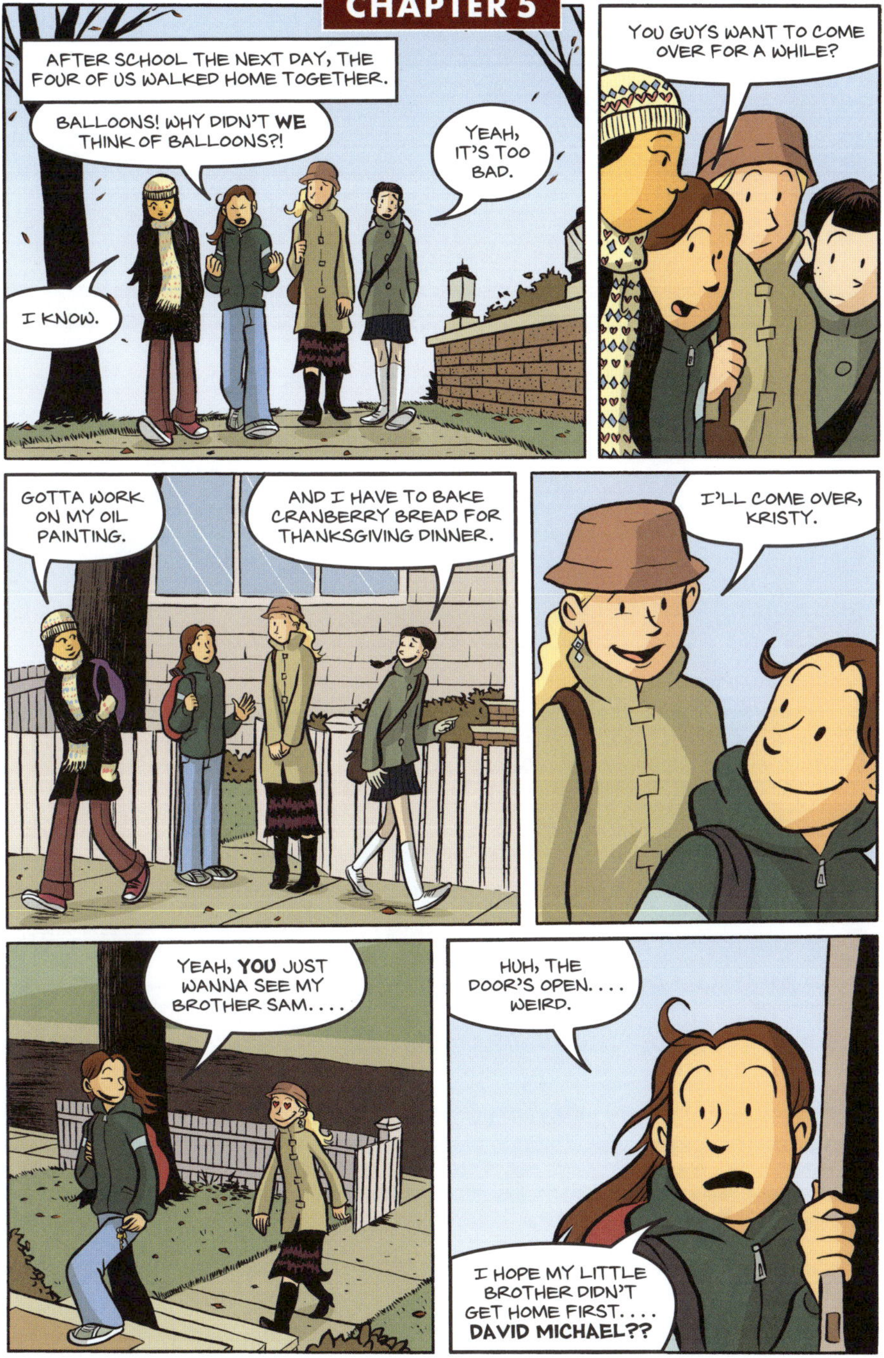
AFTER SCHOOL THE NEXT DAY, THE FOUR OF US WALKED HOME TOGETHER.
BALLOONS! WHY DIDN'T **WE** THINK OF BALLOONS?!
YEAH, IT'S TOO BAD.
I KNOW.
YOU GUYS WANT TO COME OVER FOR A WHILE?
GOTTA WORK ON MY OIL PAINTING.
AND I HAVE TO BAKE CRANBERRY BREAD FOR THANKSGIVING DINNER.
I'LL COME OVER, KRISTY.
YEAH, **YOU** JUST WANNA SEE MY BROTHER SAM....
HUH, THE DOOR'S OPEN.... WEIRD.
I HOPE MY LITTLE BROTHER DIDN'T GET HOME FIRST.... **DAVID MICHAEL??**

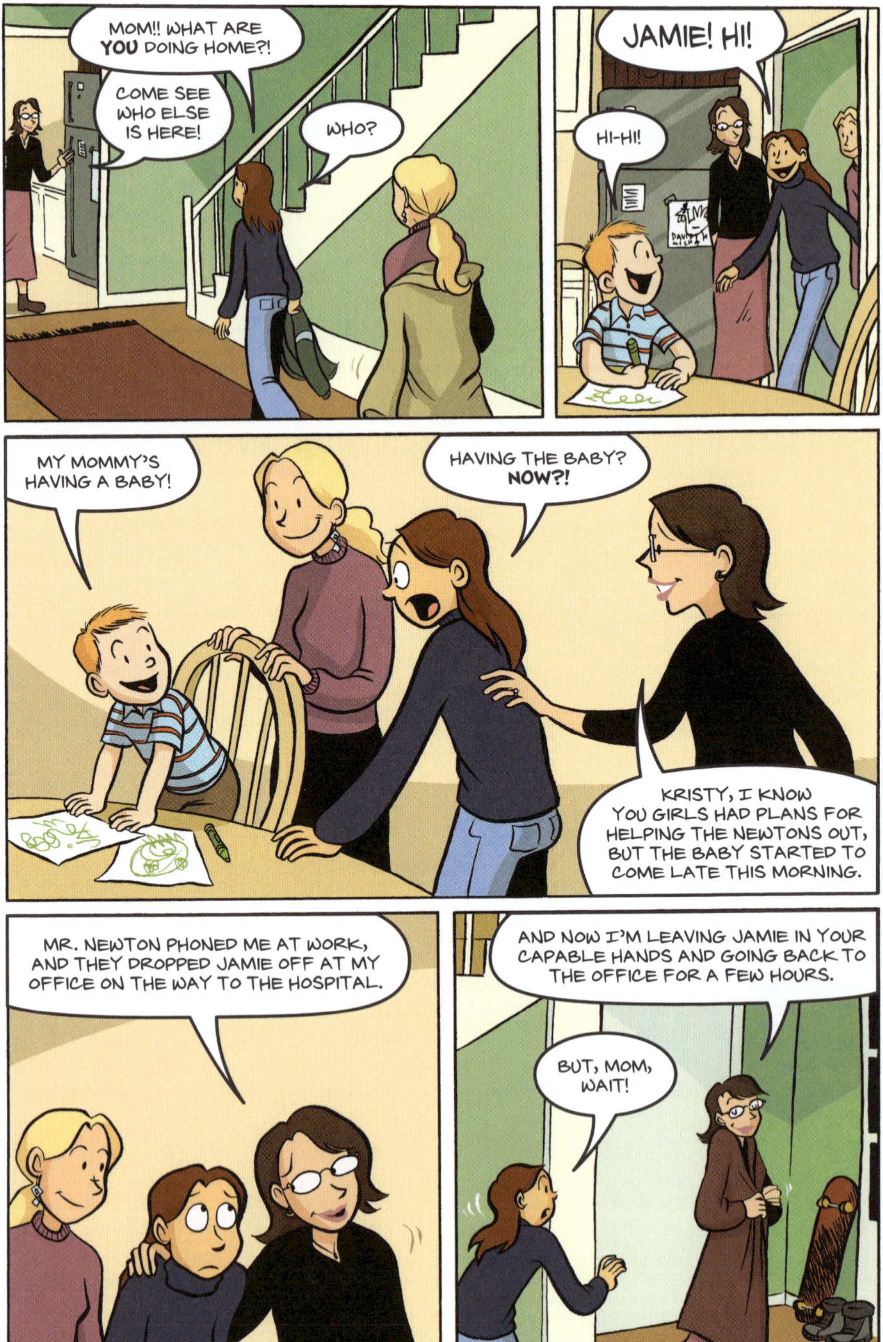
MOM!! WHAT ARE **YOU** DOING HOME?!
COME SEE WHO ELSE IS HERE!
WHO?
JAMIE! HI!
HI-HI!
MY MOMMY'S HAVING A BABY!
HAVING THE BABY? **NOW?!**
KRISTY, I KNOW YOU GIRLS HAD PLANS FOR HELPING THE NEWTONS OUT, BUT THE BABY STARTED TO COME LATE THIS MORNING.
MR. NEWTON PHONED ME AT WORK, AND THEY DROPPED JAMIE OFF AT MY OFFICE ON THE WAY TO THE HOSPITAL.
AND NOW I'M LEAVING JAMIE IN YOUR CAPABLE HANDS AND GOING BACK TO THE OFFICE FOR A FEW HOURS.
BUT, MOM, WAIT!

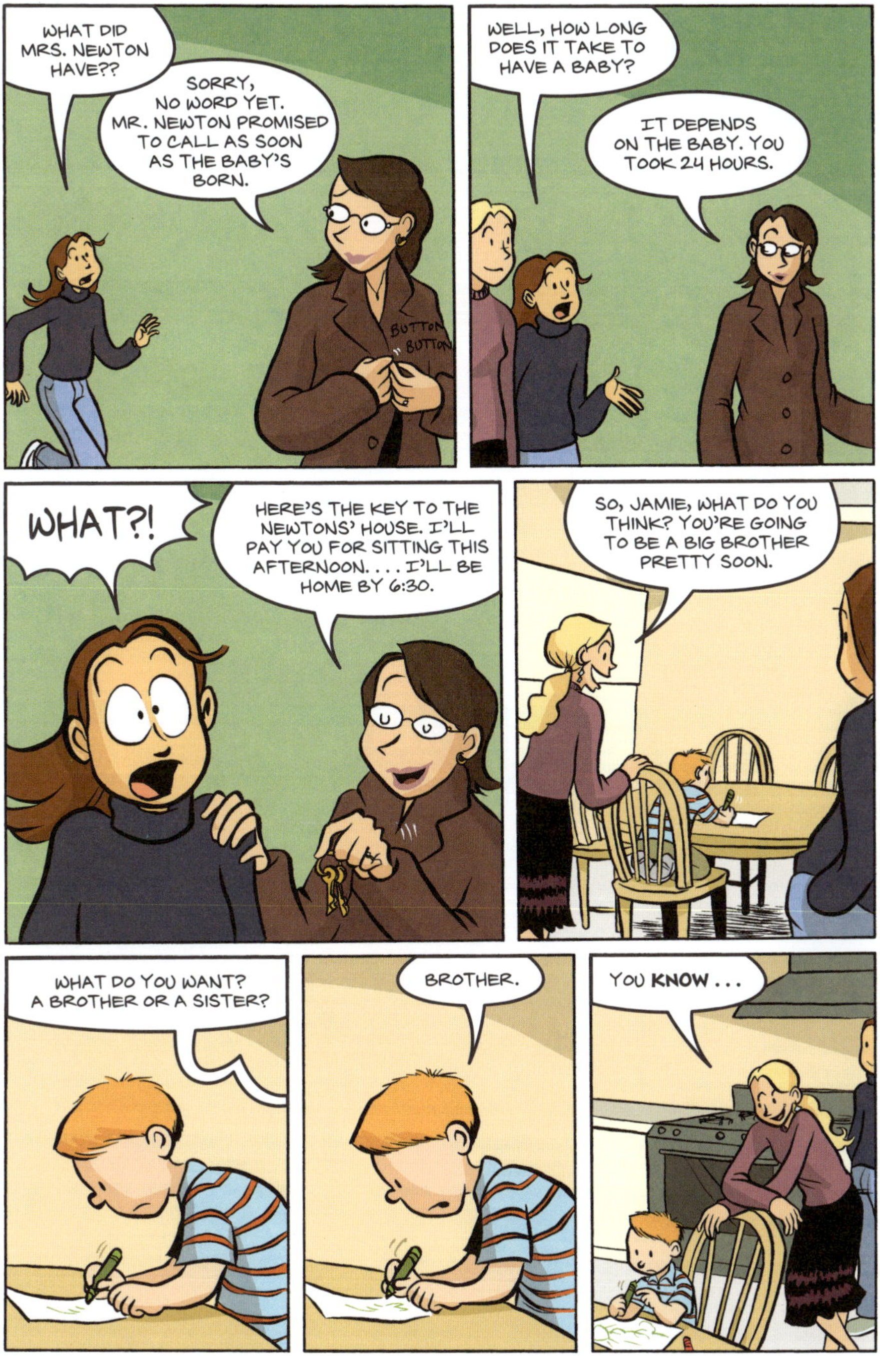
WHAT DID MRS. NEWTON HAVE??
SORRY, NO WORD YET. MR. NEWTON PROMISED TO CALL AS SOON AS THE BABY'S BORN.
BUTTON BUTTON
WELL, HOW LONG DOES IT TAKE TO HAVE A BABY?
IT DEPENDS ON THE BABY. YOU TOOK 24 HOURS.
WHAT?!
HERE'S THE KEY TO THE NEWTONS' HOUSE. I'LL PAY YOU FOR SITTING THIS AFTERNOON. . . . I'LL BE HOME BY 6:30.
SO, JAMIE, WHAT DO YOU THINK? YOU'RE GOING TO BE A BIG BROTHER PRETTY SOON.
WHAT DO YOU WANT? A BROTHER OR A SISTER?
BROTHER.
YOU **KNOW** . . .

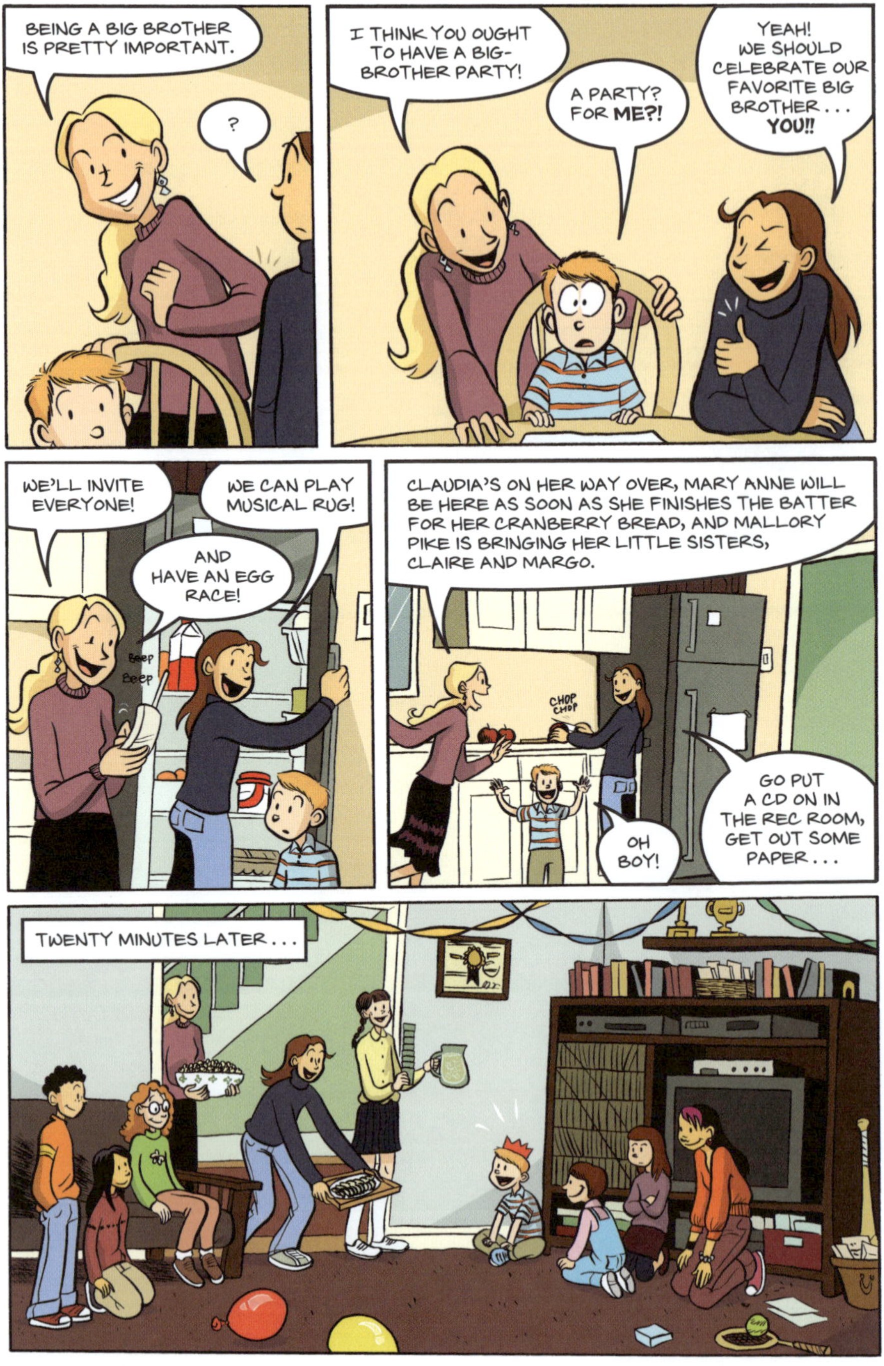
BEING A BIG BROTHER IS PRETTY IMPORTANT.
?
I THINK YOU OUGHT TO HAVE A BIG-BROTHER PARTY!
A PARTY? FOR **ME?!**
YEAH! WE SHOULD CELEBRATE OUR FAVORITE BIG BROTHER . . . **YOU!!**
WE'LL INVITE EVERYONE!
WE CAN PLAY MUSICAL RUG!
AND HAVE AN EGG RACE!
BEEP BEEP
CLAUDIA'S ON HER WAY OVER, MARY ANNE WILL BE HERE AS SOON AS SHE FINISHES THE BATTER FOR HER CRANBERRY BREAD, AND MALLORY PIKE IS BRINGING HER LITTLE SISTERS, CLAIRE AND MARGO.
CHOP CHOP
OH BOY!
GO PUT A CD ON IN THE REC ROOM, GET OUT SOME PAPER . . .
TWENTY MINUTES LATER . . .

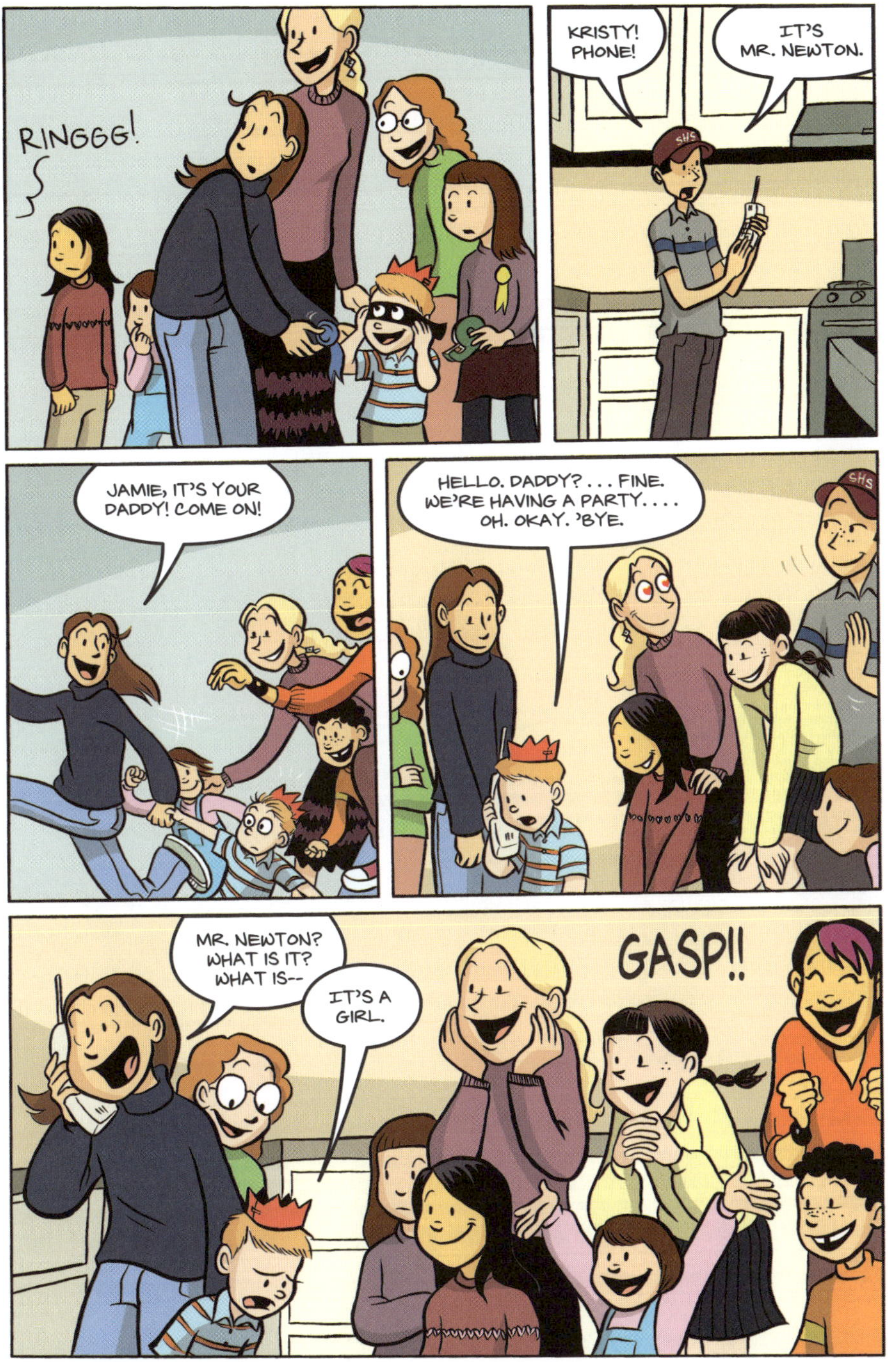
RINGGG!
KRISTY! PHONE!
IT'S MR. NEWTON.
SHS
JAMIE, IT'S YOUR DADDY! COME ON!
HELLO. DADDY? . . . FINE. WE'RE HAVING A PARTY. . . . OH. OKAY. 'BYE.
SHS
MR. NEWTON? WHAT IS IT? WHAT IS--
IT'S A GIRL.
GASP!!

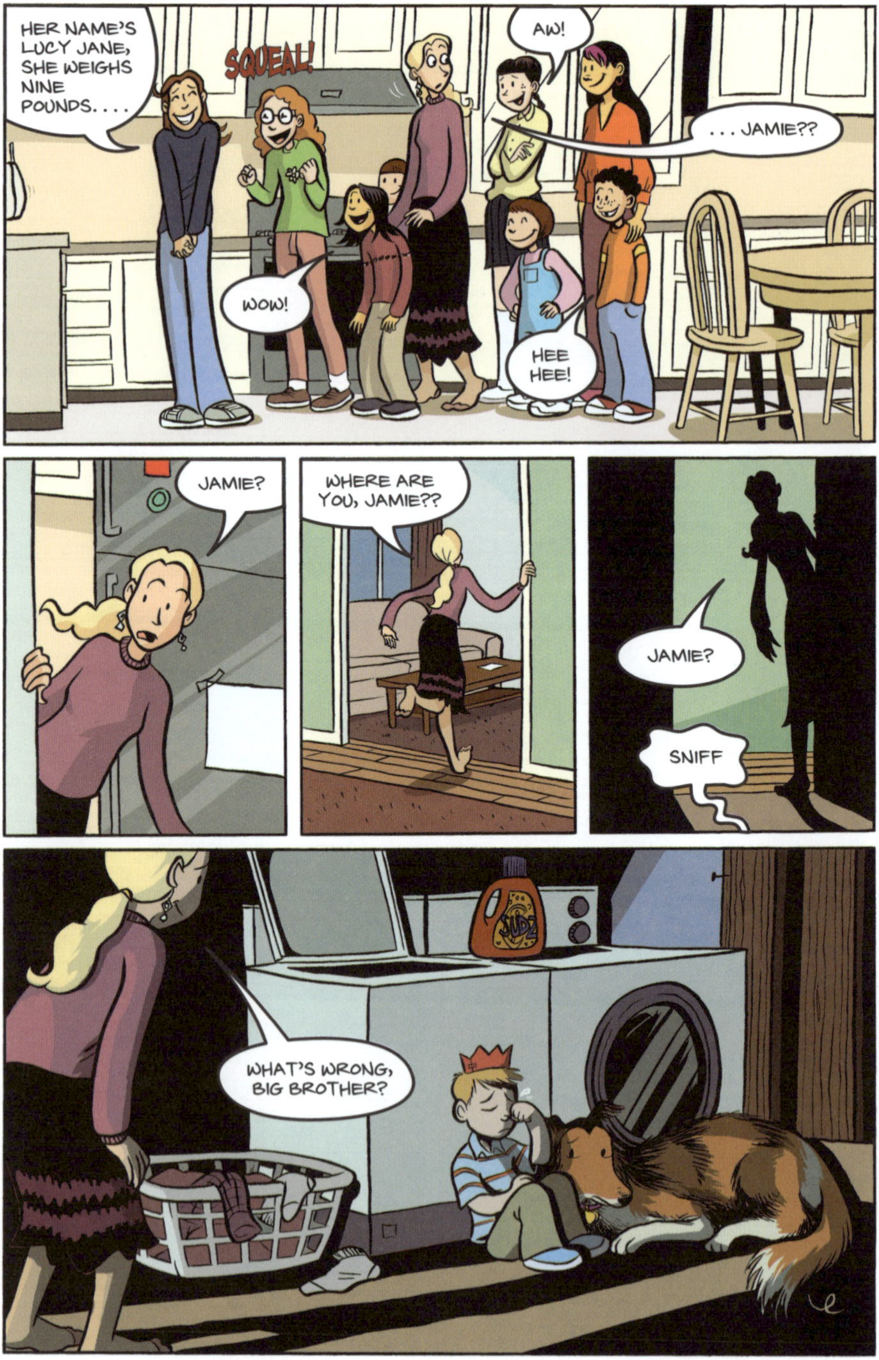
HER NAME'S LUCY JANE, SHE WEIGHS NINE POUNDS. . . .
SQUEAL!
AW!
. . . JAMIE??
WOW!
HEE HEE!
JAMIE?
WHERE ARE YOU, JAMIE??
JAMIE?
SNIFF
SUDZ
WHAT'S WRONG, BIG BROTHER?

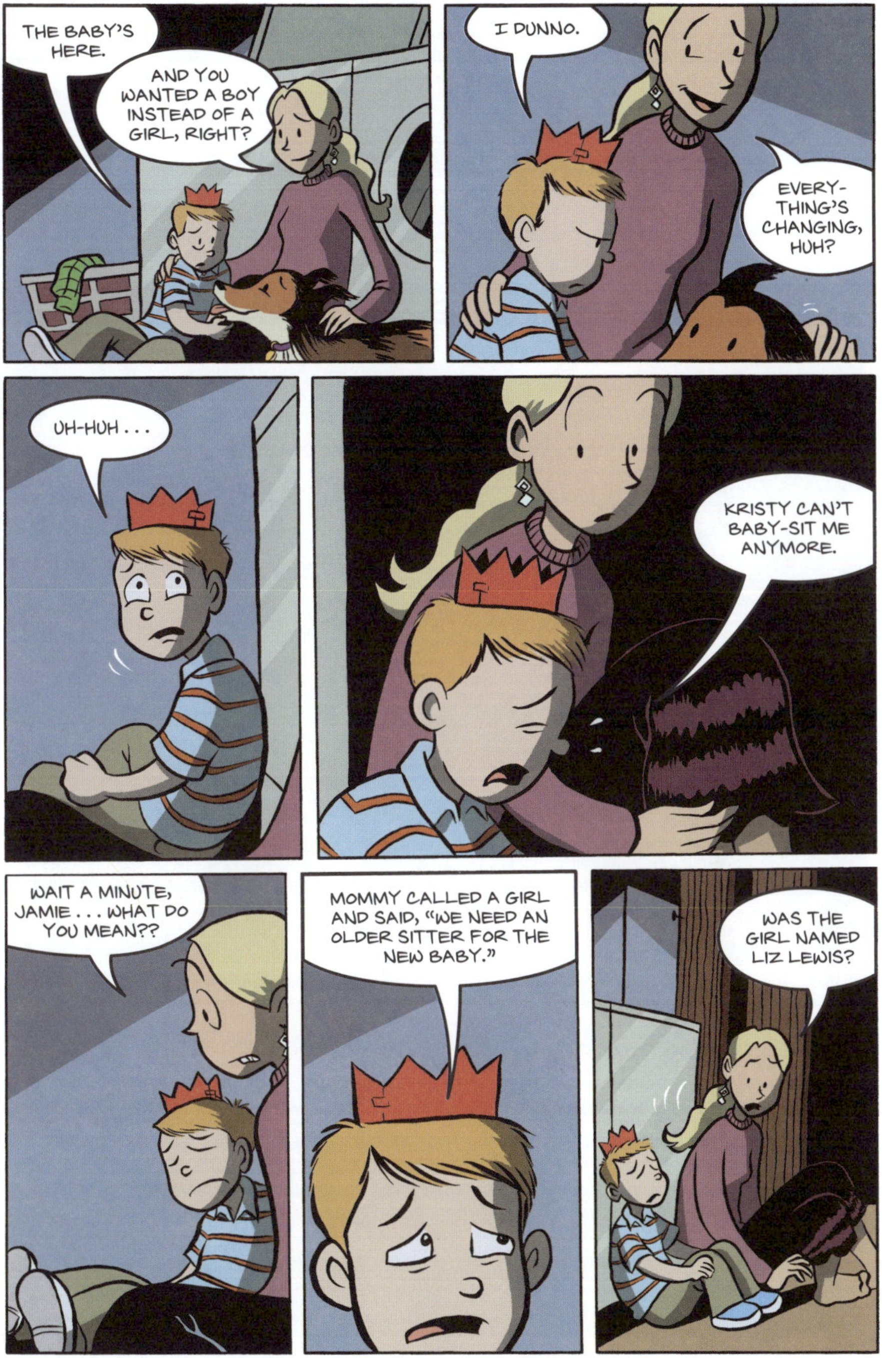
THE BABY'S HERE.
AND YOU WANTED A BOY INSTEAD OF A GIRL, RIGHT?
I DUNNO.
EVERY-THING'S CHANGING, HUH?
UH-HUH . . .
KRISTY CAN'T BABY-SIT ME ANYMORE.
WAIT A MINUTE, JAMIE . . . WHAT DO YOU MEAN??
MOMMY CALLED A GIRL AND SAID, "WE NEED AN OLDER SITTER FOR THE NEW BABY."
WAS THE GIRL NAMED LIZ LEWIS?

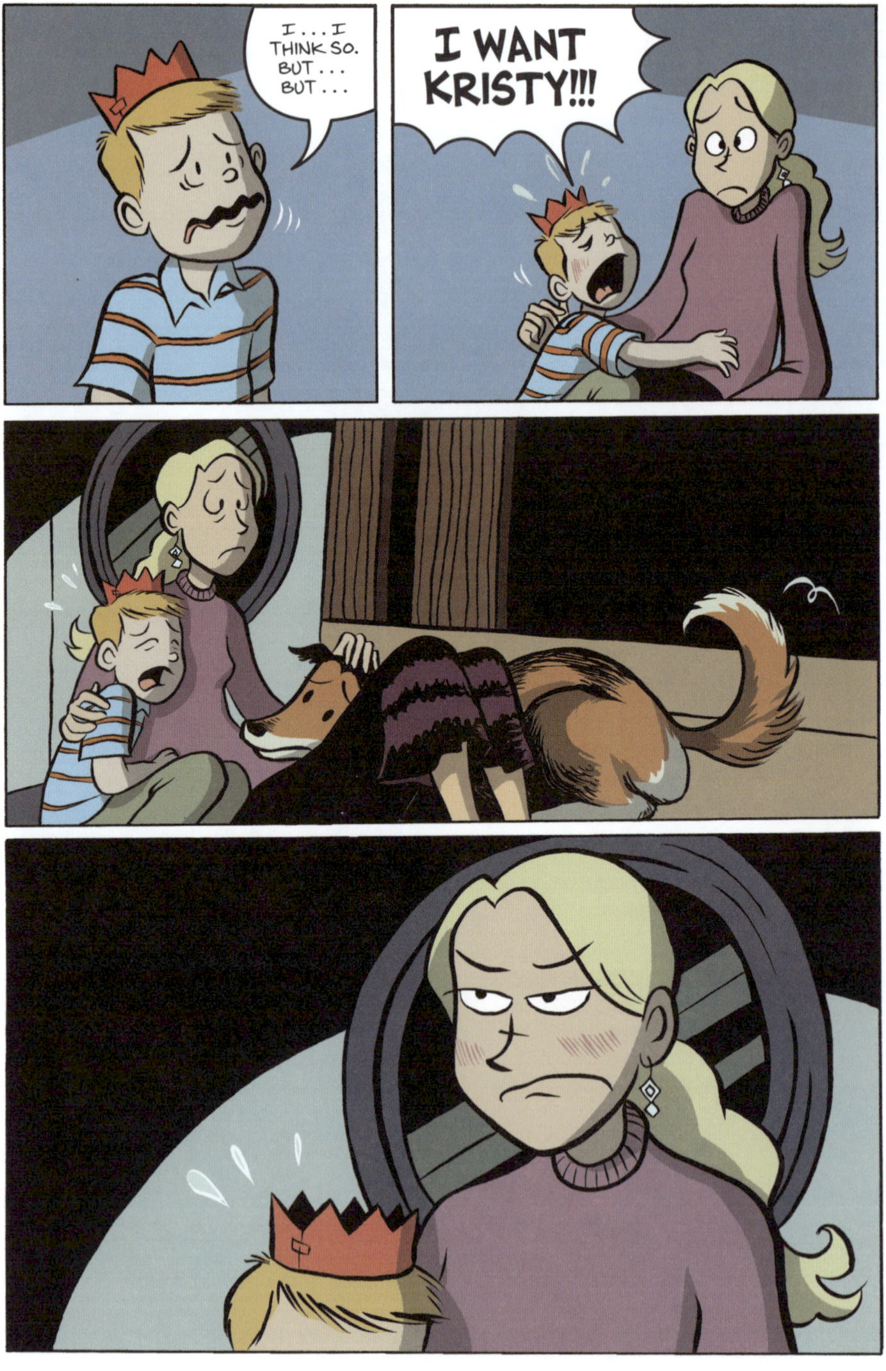
I... I THINK SO. BUT... BUT...
I WANT KRISTY!!!

CHAPTER 6

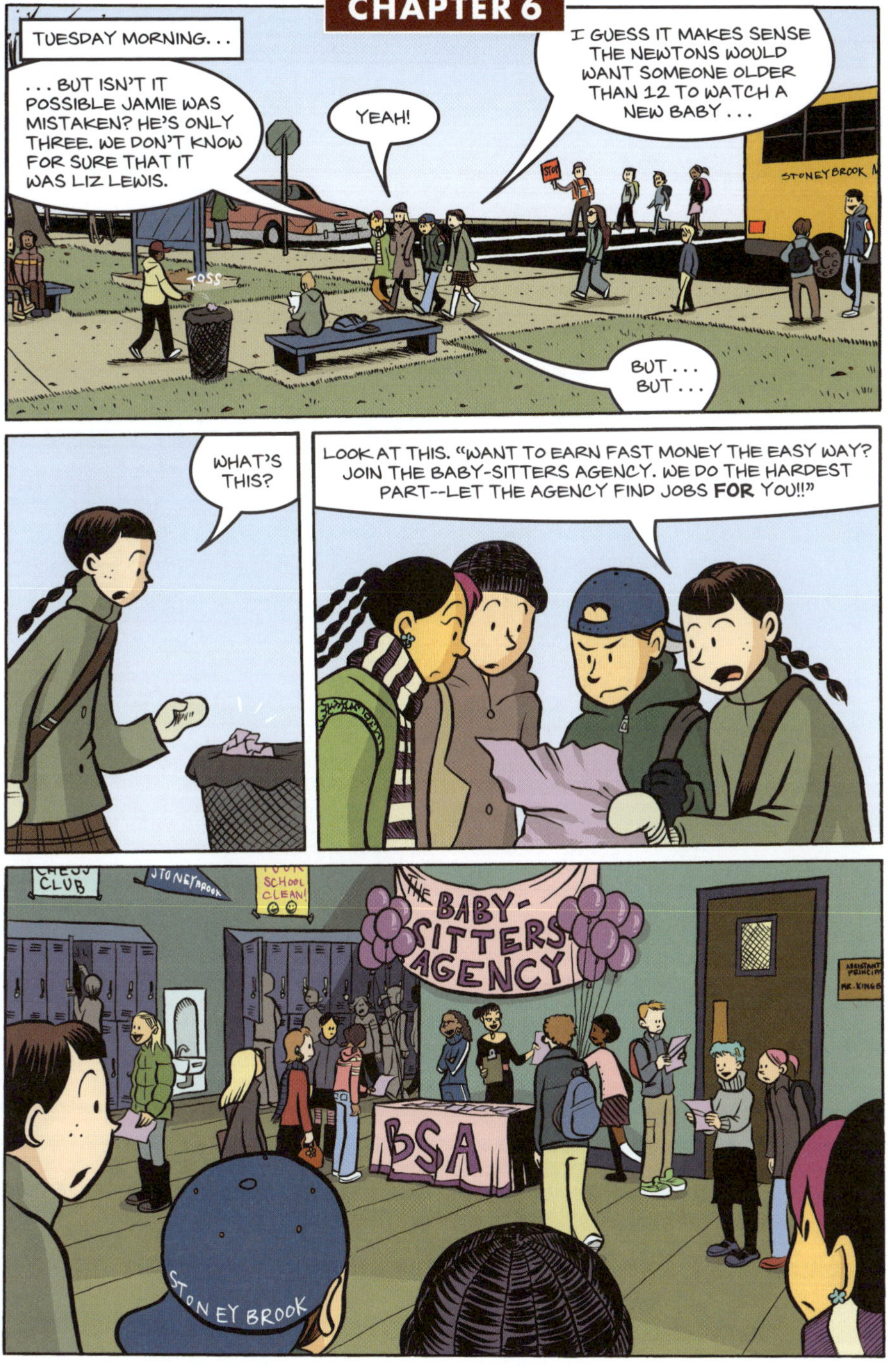

TUESDAY MORNING...
... BUT ISN'T IT POSSIBLE JAMIE WAS MISTAKEN? HE'S ONLY THREE. WE DON'T KNOW FOR SURE THAT IT WAS LIZ LEWIS.
YEAH!
I GUESS IT MAKES SENSE THE NEWTONS WOULD WANT SOMEONE OLDER THAN 12 TO WATCH A NEW BABY...
TOSS
STOP
BUT... BUT...
WHAT'S THIS?
LOOK AT THIS. "WANT TO EARN FAST MONEY THE EASY WAY? JOIN THE BABY-SITTERS AGENCY. WE DO THE HARDEST PART--LET THE AGENCY FIND JOBS FOR YOU!!"
CHESS CLUB
STONEYBROOK
SCHOOL CLEAN!
THE BABY-SITTERS AGENCY
BSA
STONEY BROOK

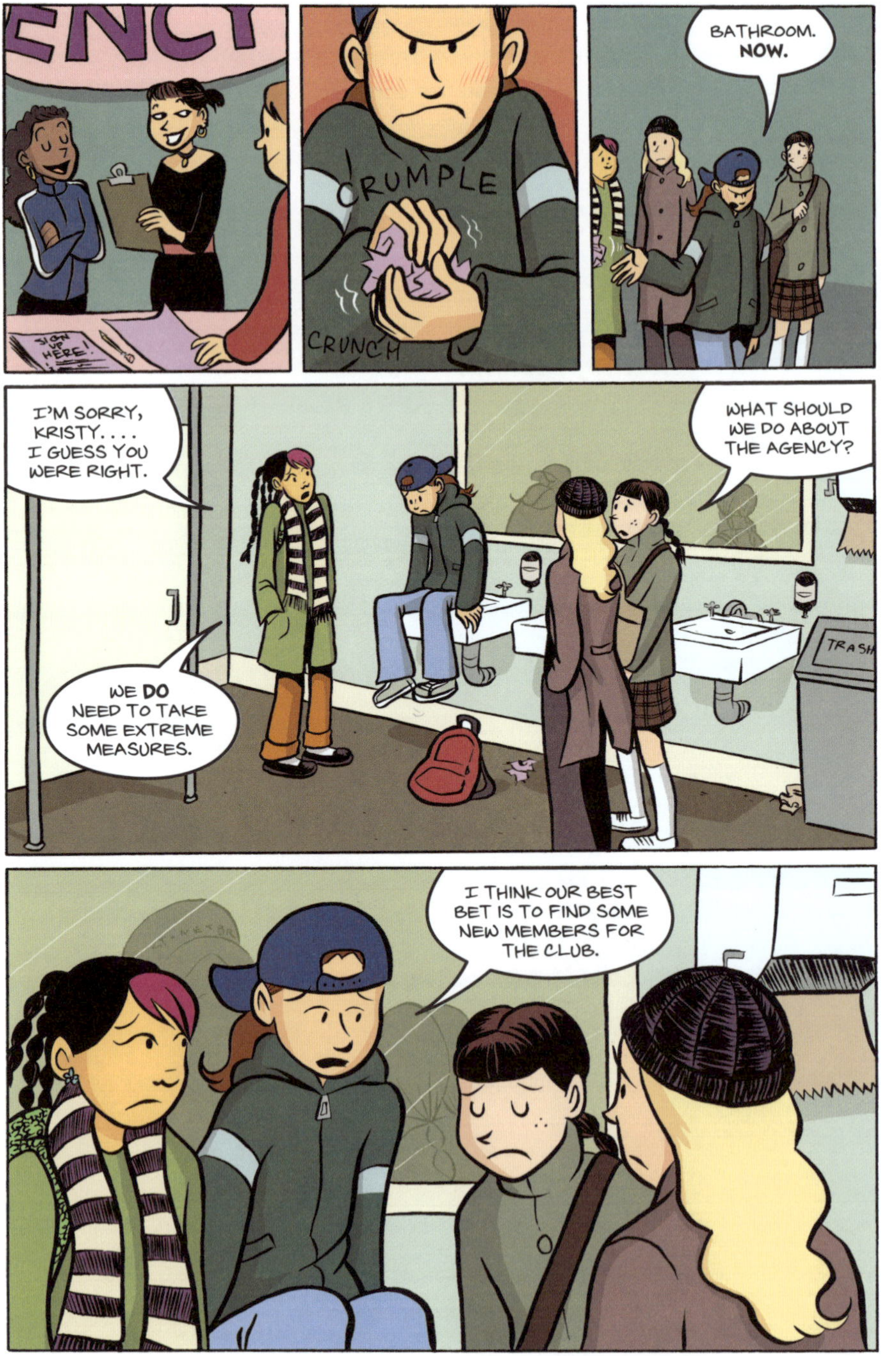
ENCY
SIGN UP HERE!
CRUMPLE
CRUNCH
BATHROOM. **NOW.**
I'M SORRY, KRISTY. . . . I GUESS YOU WERE RIGHT.
WHAT SHOULD WE DO ABOUT THE AGENCY?
WE **DO** NEED TO TAKE SOME EXTREME MEASURES.
TRASH
I THINK OUR BEST BET IS TO FIND SOME NEW MEMBERS FOR THE CLUB.

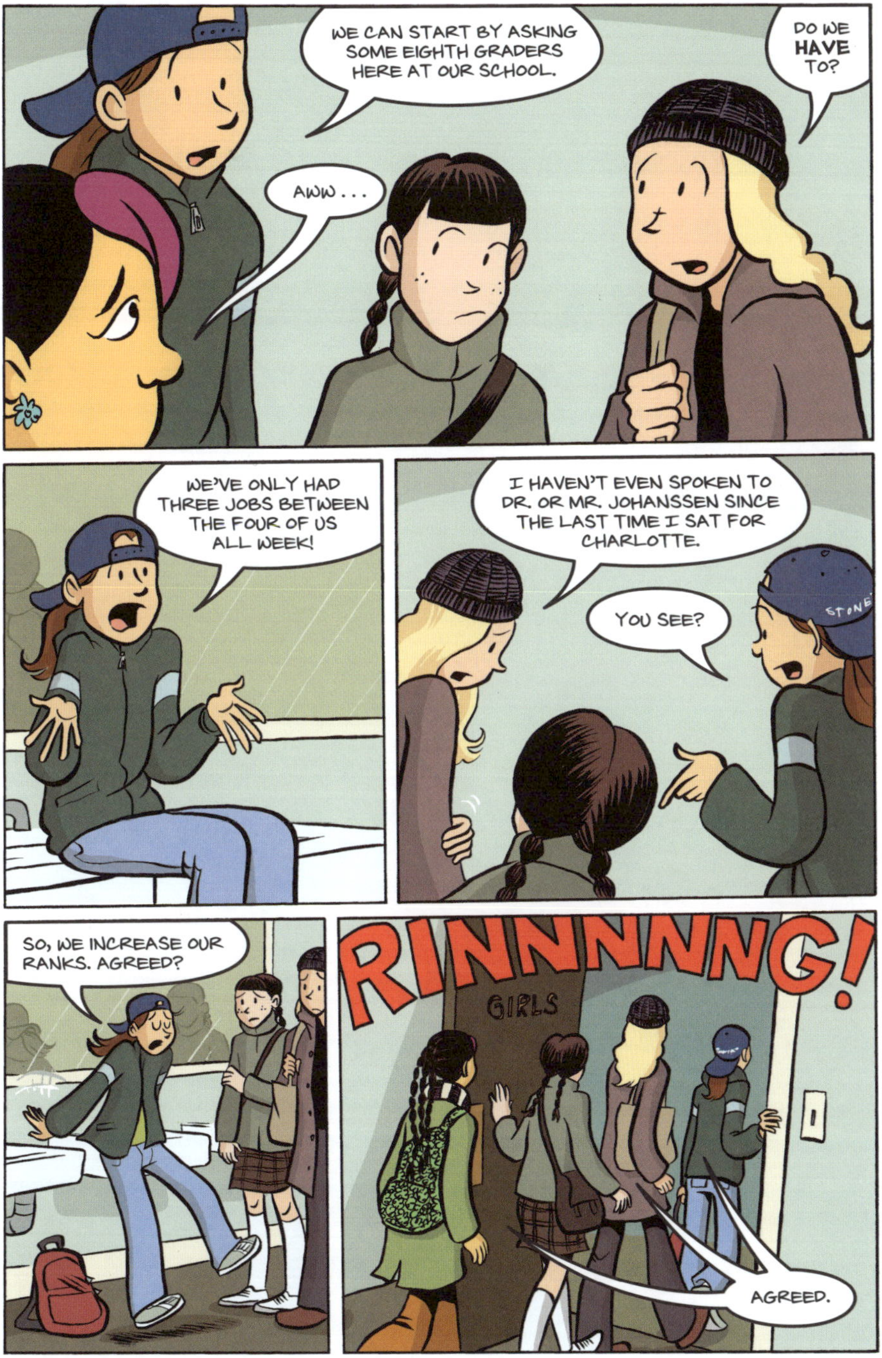
WE CAN START BY ASKING SOME EIGHTH GRADERS HERE AT OUR SCHOOL.
DO WE HAVE TO?
AWW . . .
WE'VE ONLY HAD THREE JOBS BETWEEN THE FOUR OF US ALL WEEK!
I HAVEN'T EVEN SPOKEN TO DR. OR MR. JOHANSSEN SINCE THE LAST TIME I SAT FOR CHARLOTTE.
YOU SEE?
STONE
SO, WE INCREASE OUR RANKS. AGREED?
RINNNNNG!
GIRLS
AGREED.

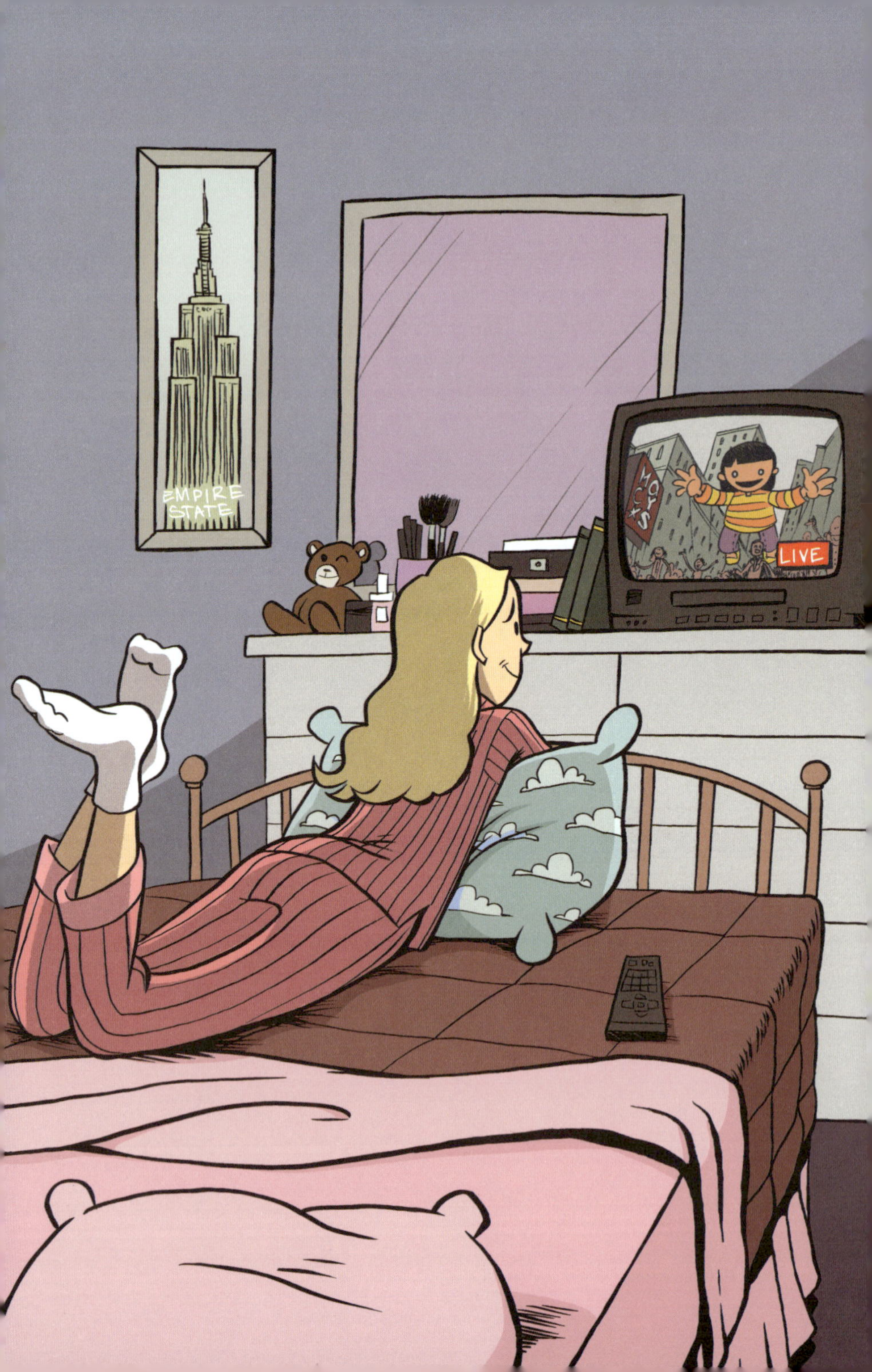
EMPIRE
STATE
MACY★S
LIVE

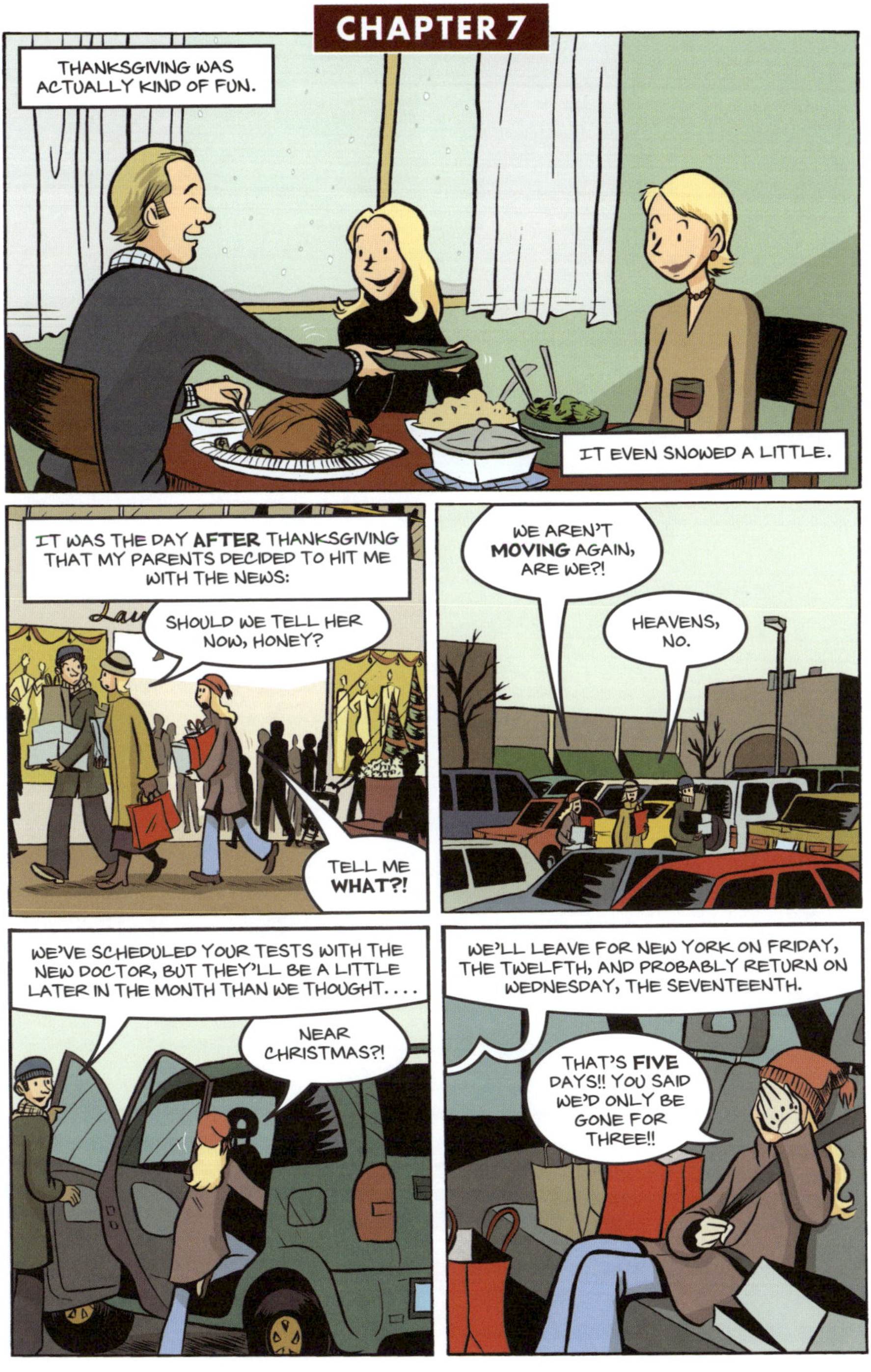
CHAPTER 7
THANKSGIVING WAS ACTUALLY KIND OF FUN.
IT EVEN SNOWED A LITTLE.
IT WAS THE DAY AFTER THANKSGIVING THAT MY PARENTS DECIDED TO HIT ME WITH THE NEWS:
SHOULD WE TELL HER NOW, HONEY?
TELL ME WHAT?!
WE AREN'T MOVING AGAIN, ARE WE?!
HEAVENS, NO.
WE'VE SCHEDULED YOUR TESTS WITH THE NEW DOCTOR, BUT THEY'LL BE A LITTLE LATER IN THE MONTH THAN WE THOUGHT....
NEAR CHRISTMAS?!
WE'LL LEAVE FOR NEW YORK ON FRIDAY, THE TWELFTH, AND PROBABLY RETURN ON WEDNESDAY, THE SEVENTEENTH.
THAT'S FIVE DAYS!! YOU SAID WE'D ONLY BE GONE FOR THREE!!

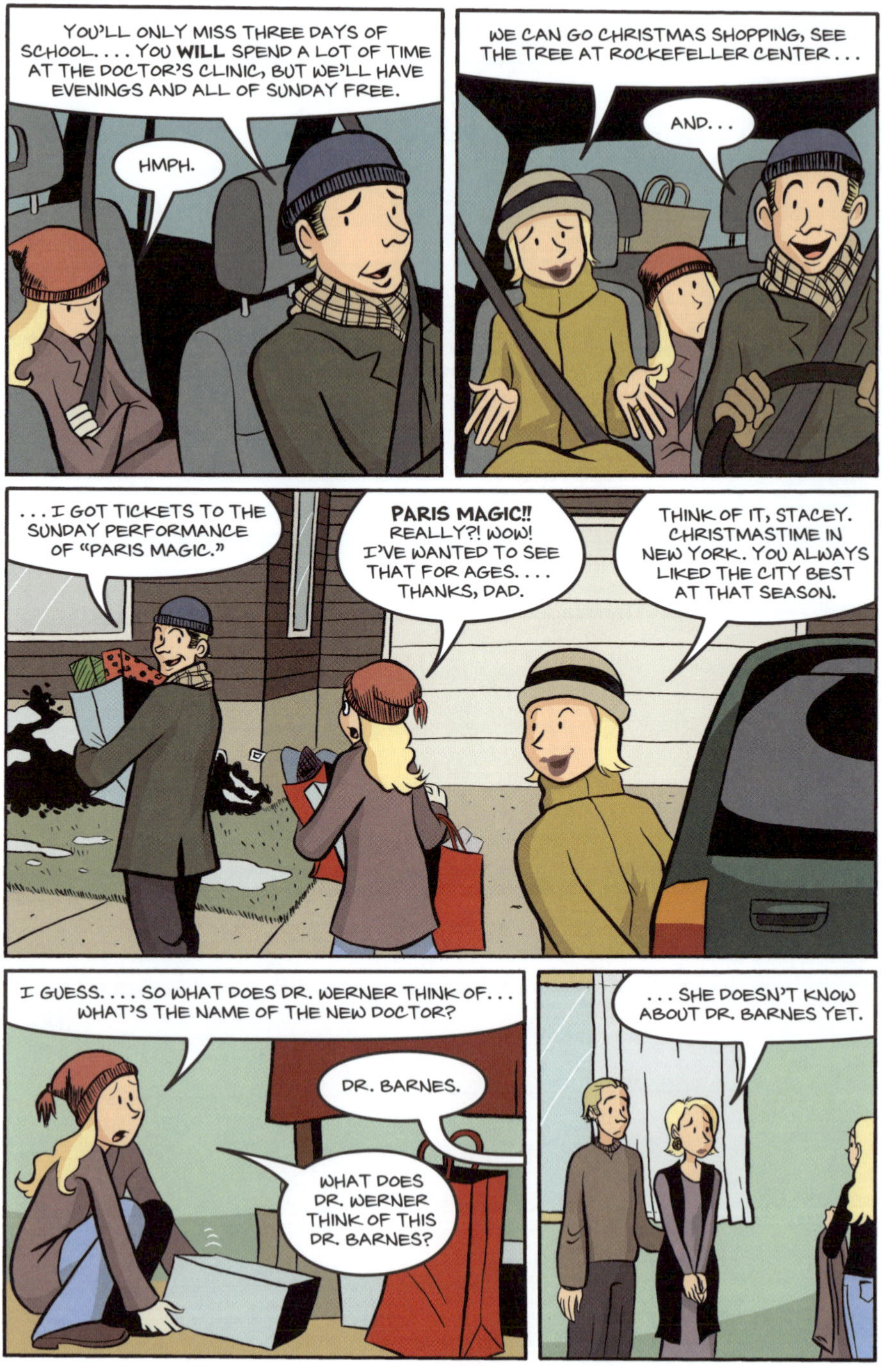
YOU'LL ONLY MISS THREE DAYS OF SCHOOL. . . . YOU **WILL** SPEND A LOT OF TIME AT THE DOCTOR'S CLINIC, BUT WE'LL HAVE EVENINGS AND ALL OF SUNDAY FREE.
HMPH.
WE CAN GO CHRISTMAS SHOPPING, SEE THE TREE AT ROCKEFELLER CENTER . . .
AND. . .
. . . I GOT TICKETS TO THE SUNDAY PERFORMANCE OF "PARIS MAGIC."
PARIS MAGIC!! REALLY?! WOW! I'VE WANTED TO SEE THAT FOR AGES. . . . THANKS, DAD.
THINK OF IT, STACEY. CHRISTMASTIME IN NEW YORK. YOU ALWAYS LIKED THE CITY BEST AT THAT SEASON.
I GUESS. . . . SO WHAT DOES DR. WERNER THINK OF. . . WHAT'S THE NAME OF THE NEW DOCTOR?
DR. BARNES.
WHAT DOES DR. WERNER THINK OF THIS DR. BARNES?
. . . SHE DOESN'T KNOW ABOUT DR. BARNES YET.

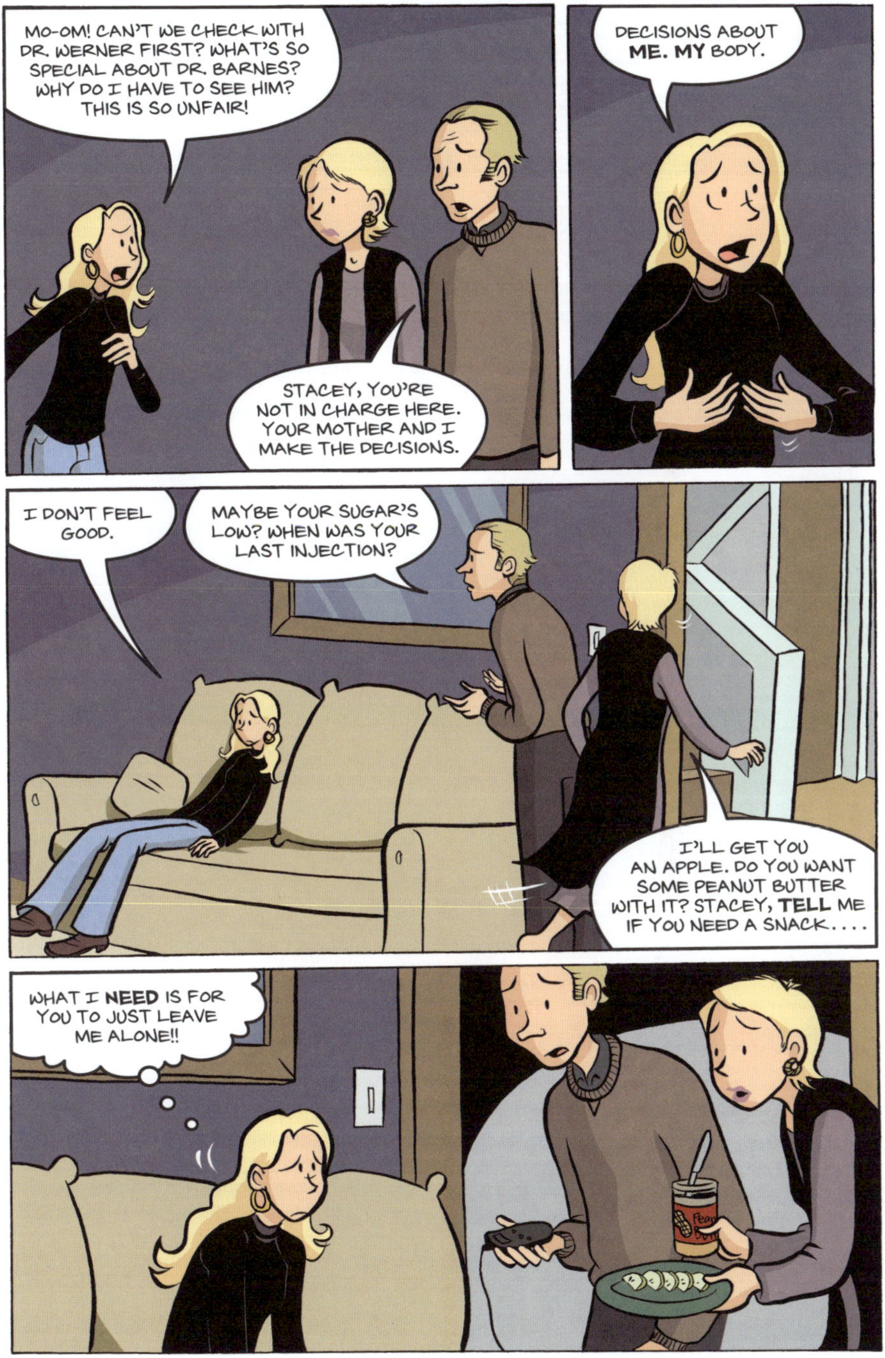
MO-OM! CAN'T WE CHECK WITH DR. WERNER FIRST? WHAT'S SO SPECIAL ABOUT DR. BARNES? WHY DO I HAVE TO SEE HIM? THIS IS SO UNFAIR!
STACEY, YOU'RE NOT IN CHARGE HERE. YOUR MOTHER AND I MAKE THE DECISIONS.
DECISIONS ABOUT **ME. MY** BODY.
I DON'T FEEL GOOD.
MAYBE YOUR SUGAR'S LOW? WHEN WAS YOUR LAST INJECTION?
I'LL GET YOU AN APPLE. DO YOU WANT SOME PEANUT BUTTER WITH IT? STACEY, **TELL** ME IF YOU NEED A SNACK....
WHAT I **NEED** IS FOR YOU TO JUST LEAVE ME ALONE!!

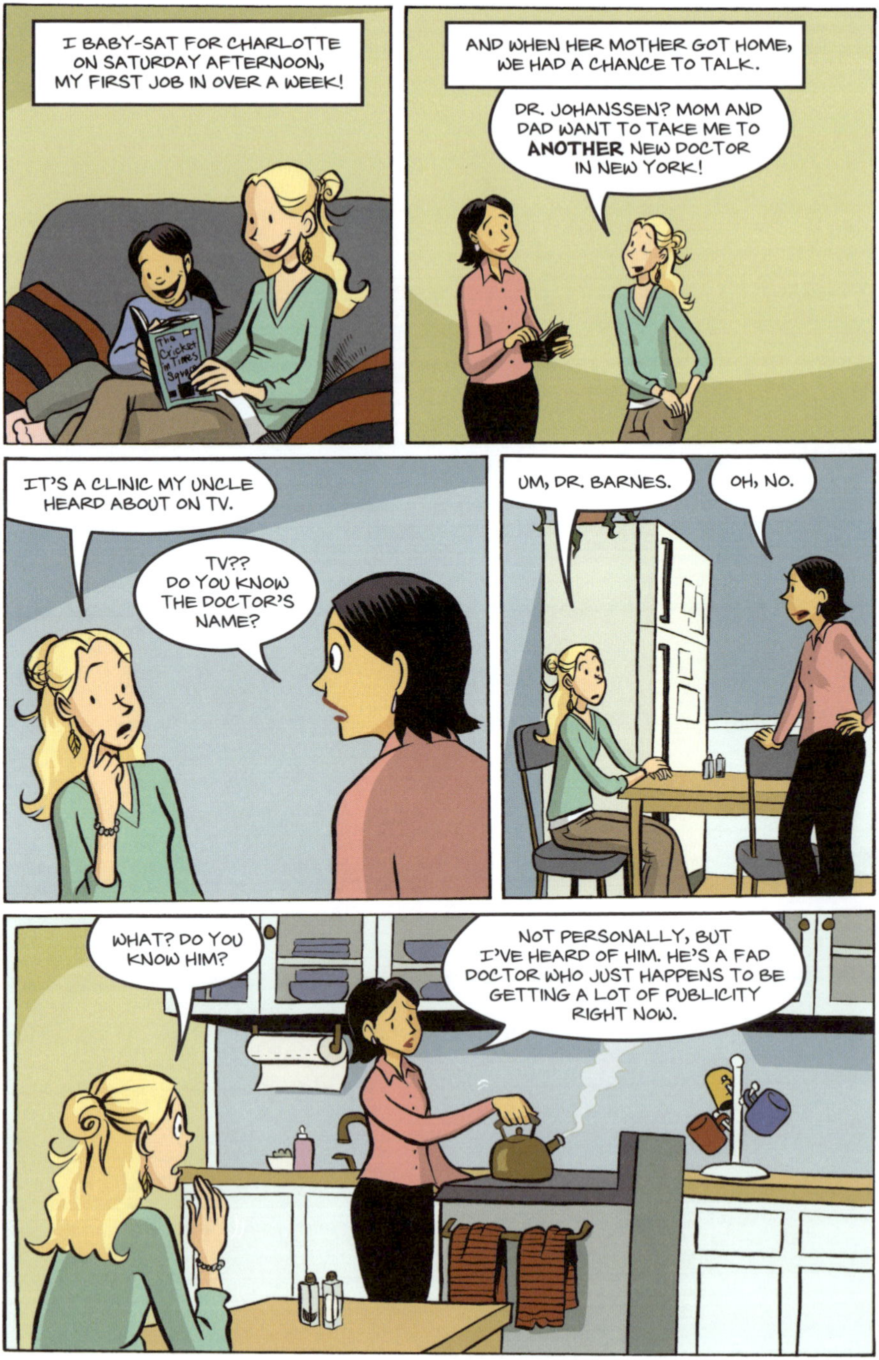
I BABY-SAT FOR CHARLOTTE ON SATURDAY AFTERNOON, MY FIRST JOB IN OVER A WEEK!
AND WHEN HER MOTHER GOT HOME, WE HAD A CHANCE TO TALK.
DR. JOHANSSEN? MOM AND DAD WANT TO TAKE ME TO **ANOTHER** NEW DOCTOR IN NEW YORK!
IT'S A CLINIC MY UNCLE HEARD ABOUT ON TV.
TV?? DO YOU KNOW THE DOCTOR'S NAME?
UM, DR. BARNES.
OH, NO.
WHAT? DO YOU KNOW HIM?
NOT PERSONALLY, BUT I'VE HEARD OF HIM. HE'S A FAD DOCTOR WHO JUST HAPPENS TO BE GETTING A LOT OF PUBLICITY RIGHT NOW.

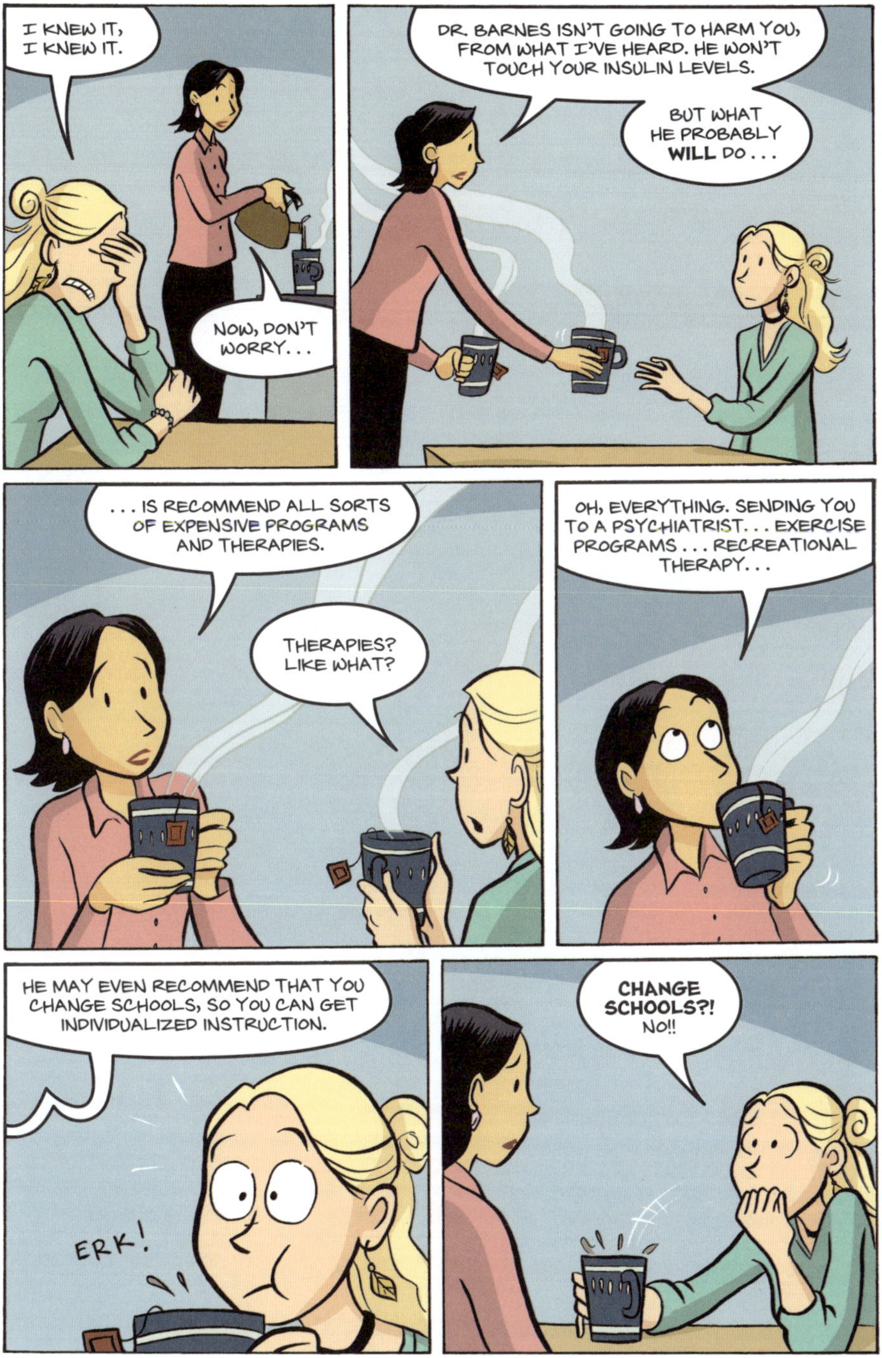

I KNEW IT, I KNEW IT.
NOW, DON'T WORRY...
DR. BARNES ISN'T GOING TO HARM YOU, FROM WHAT I'VE HEARD. HE WON'T TOUCH YOUR INSULIN LEVELS.
BUT WHAT HE PROBABLY **WILL** DO...
...IS RECOMMEND ALL SORTS OF EXPENSIVE PROGRAMS AND THERAPIES.
THERAPIES? LIKE WHAT?
OH, EVERYTHING. SENDING YOU TO A PSYCHIATRIST... EXERCISE PROGRAMS... RECREATIONAL THERAPY...
HE MAY EVEN RECOMMEND THAT YOU CHANGE SCHOOLS, SO YOU CAN GET INDIVIDUALIZED INSTRUCTION.
ERK!
CHANGE SCHOOLS?! NO!!

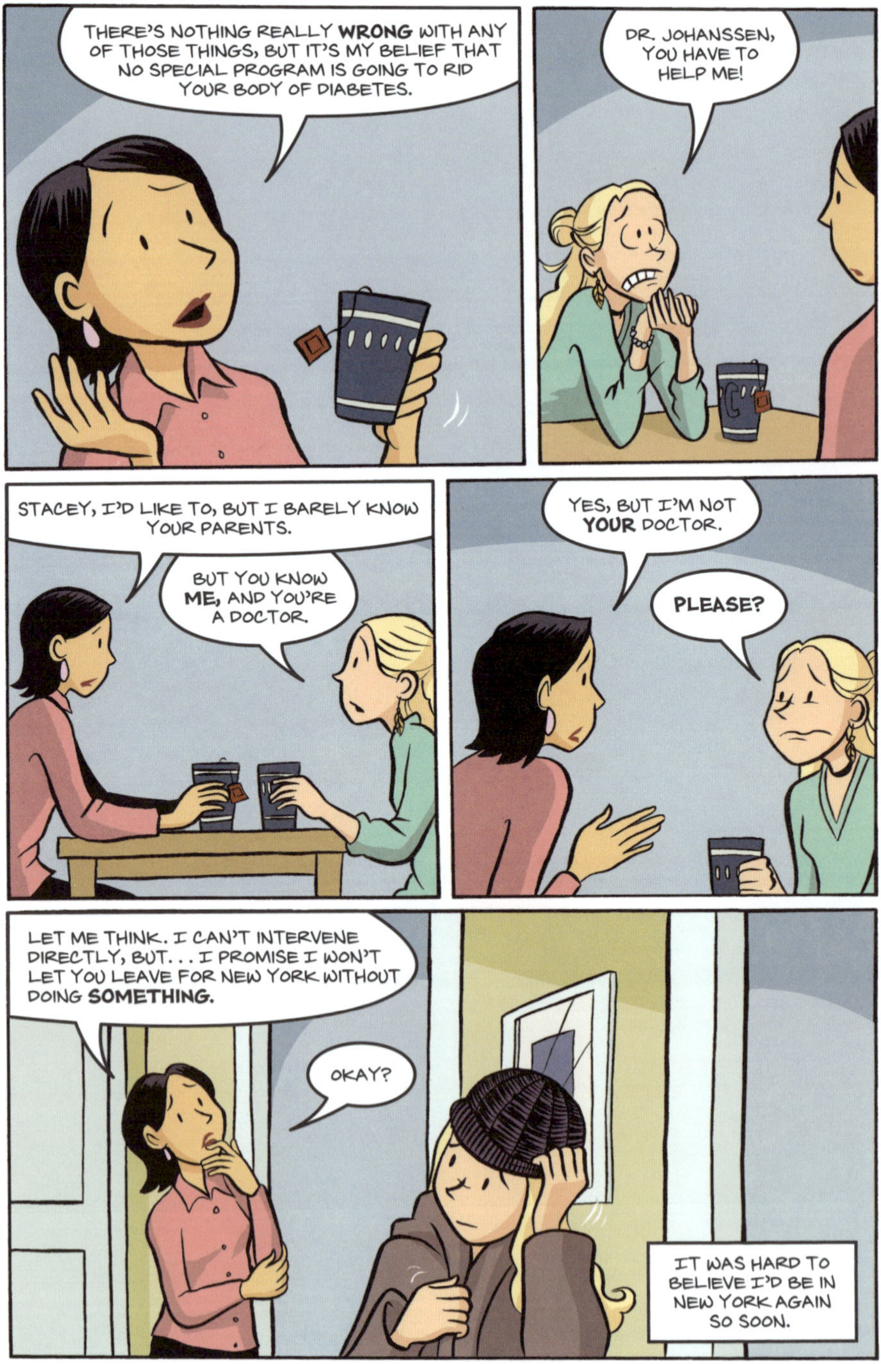
THERE'S NOTHING REALLY **WRONG** WITH ANY OF THOSE THINGS, BUT IT'S MY BELIEF THAT NO SPECIAL PROGRAM IS GOING TO RID YOUR BODY OF DIABETES.
DR. JOHANSSEN, YOU HAVE TO HELP ME!
STACEY, I'D LIKE TO, BUT I BARELY KNOW YOUR PARENTS.
BUT YOU KNOW **ME,** AND YOU'RE A DOCTOR.
YES, BUT I'M NOT **YOUR** DOCTOR.
PLEASE?
LET ME THINK. I CAN'T INTERVENE DIRECTLY, BUT. . . I PROMISE I WON'T LET YOU LEAVE FOR NEW YORK WITHOUT DOING **SOMETHING.**
OKAY?
IT WAS HARD TO BELIEVE I'D BE IN NEW YORK AGAIN SO SOON.

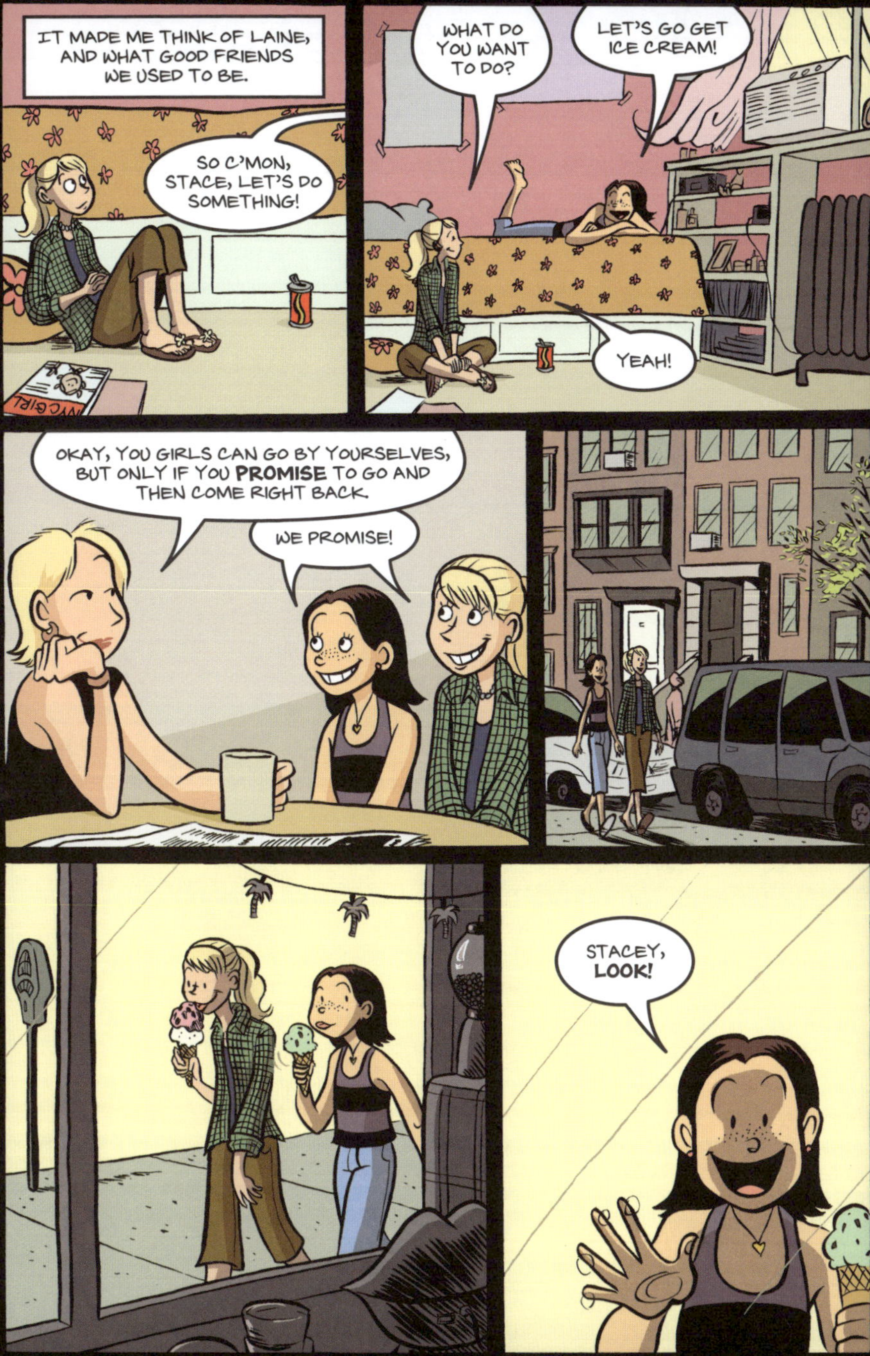
IT MADE ME THINK OF LAINE, AND WHAT GOOD FRIENDS WE USED TO BE.
SO C'MON, STACE, LET'S DO SOMETHING!
NYC GIRL
WHAT DO YOU WANT TO DO?
LET'S GO GET ICE CREAM!
YEAH!
OKAY, YOU GIRLS CAN GO BY YOURSELVES, BUT ONLY IF YOU **PROMISE** TO GO AND THEN COME RIGHT BACK.
WE PROMISE!
STACEY, **LOOK!**

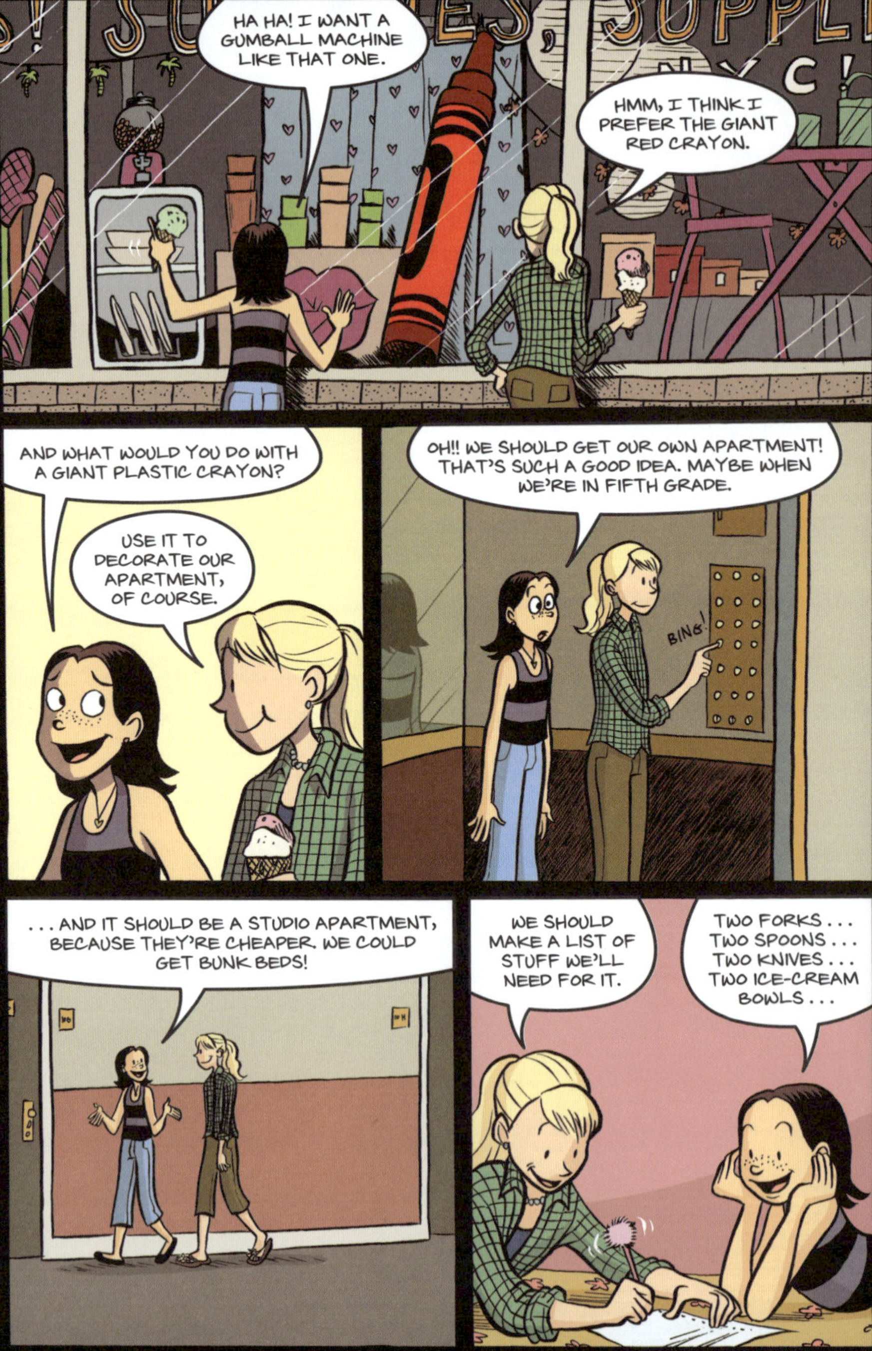
HA HA! I WANT A GUMBALL MACHINE LIKE THAT ONE.
HMM, I THINK I PREFER THE GIANT RED CRAYON.
AND WHAT WOULD YOU DO WITH A GIANT PLASTIC CRAYON?
USE IT TO DECORATE OUR APARTMENT, OF COURSE.
OH!! WE SHOULD GET OUR OWN APARTMENT! THAT'S SUCH A GOOD IDEA. MAYBE WHEN WE'RE IN FIFTH GRADE.
BING!
. . . AND IT SHOULD BE A STUDIO APARTMENT, BECAUSE THEY'RE CHEAPER. WE COULD GET BUNK BEDS!
WE SHOULD MAKE A LIST OF STUFF WE'LL NEED FOR IT.
TWO FORKS . . . TWO SPOONS . . . TWO KNIVES . . . TWO ICE-CREAM BOWLS . . .

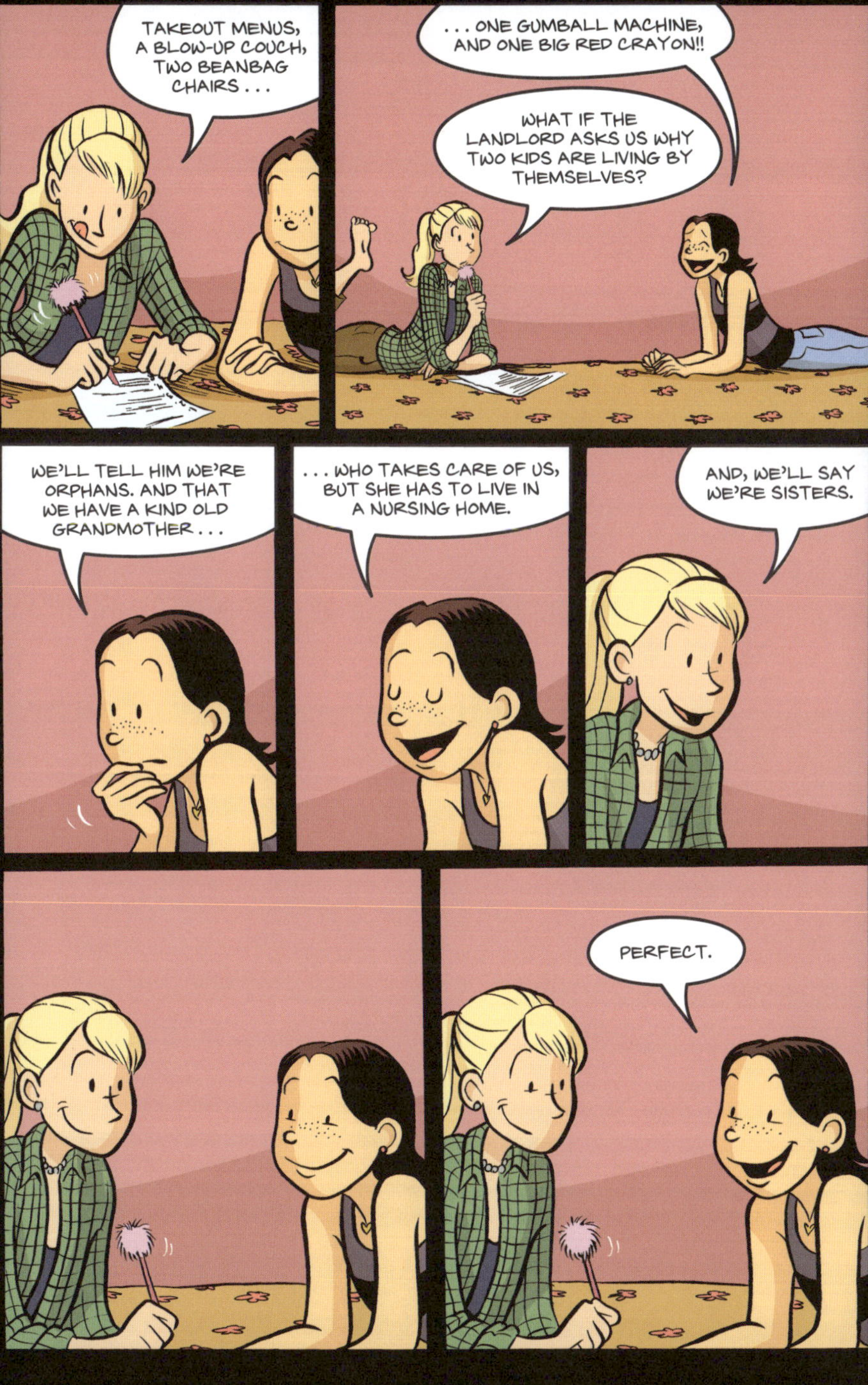

TAKEOUT MENUS, A BLOW-UP COUCH, TWO BEANBAG CHAIRS . . .
. . . ONE GUMBALL MACHINE, AND ONE BIG RED CRAYON!!
WHAT IF THE LANDLORD ASKS US WHY TWO KIDS ARE LIVING BY THEMSELVES?
WE'LL TELL HIM WE'RE ORPHANS. AND THAT WE HAVE A KIND OLD GRANDMOTHER . . .
. . . WHO TAKES CARE OF US, BUT SHE HAS TO LIVE IN A NURSING HOME.
AND, WE'LL SAY WE'RE SISTERS.
PERFECT.

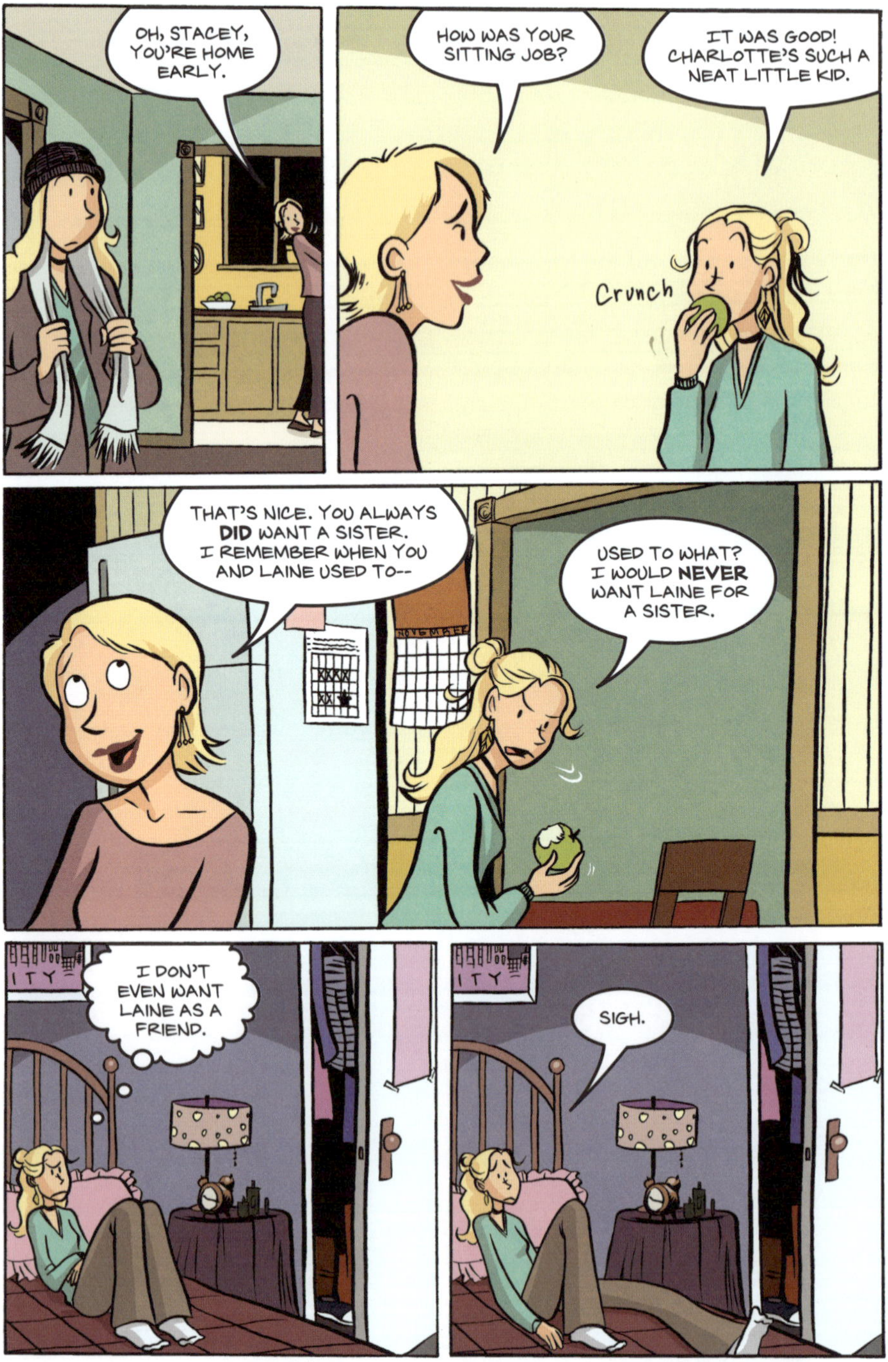
OH, STACEY, YOU'RE HOME EARLY.
HOW WAS YOUR SITTING JOB?
IT WAS GOOD! CHARLOTTE'S SUCH A NEAT LITTLE KID.
Crunch
THAT'S NICE. YOU ALWAYS **DID** WANT A SISTER. I REMEMBER WHEN YOU AND LAINE USED TO--
USED TO WHAT? I WOULD **NEVER** WANT LAINE FOR A SISTER.
I DON'T EVEN WANT LAINE AS A FRIEND.
SIGH.

CHAPTER 8

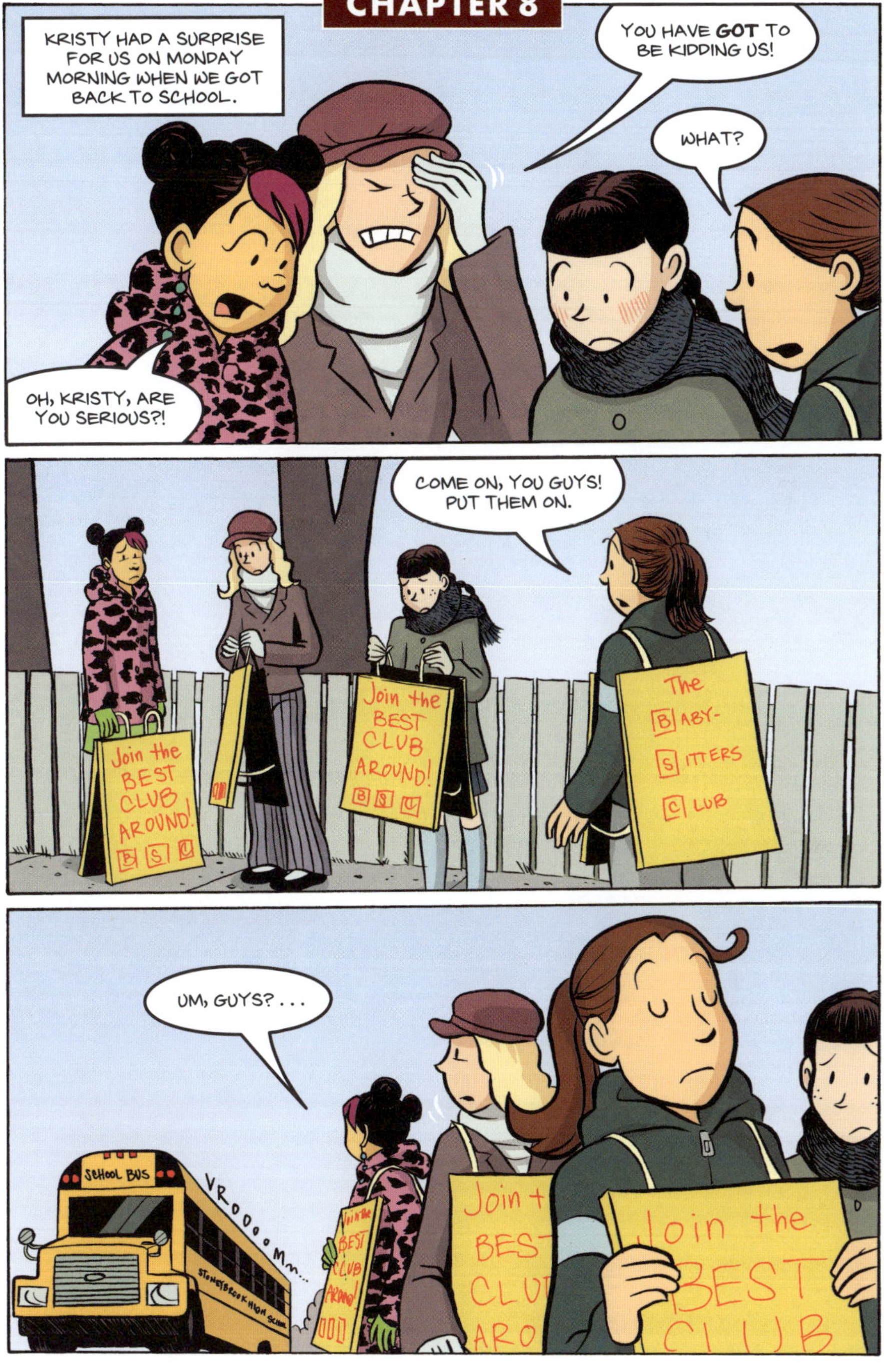

KRISTY HAD A SURPRISE FOR US ON MONDAY MORNING WHEN WE GOT BACK TO SCHOOL.
YOU HAVE **GOT** TO BE KIDDING US!
WHAT?
OH, KRISTY, ARE YOU SERIOUS?!
COME ON, YOU GUYS! PUT THEM ON.
Join the BEST CLUB AROUND! BSC
Join the BEST CLUB AROUND! BSC
The Baby-Sitters Club
UM, GUYS? . . .
SCHOOL BUS
VROooomm...
Join the BEST CLUB

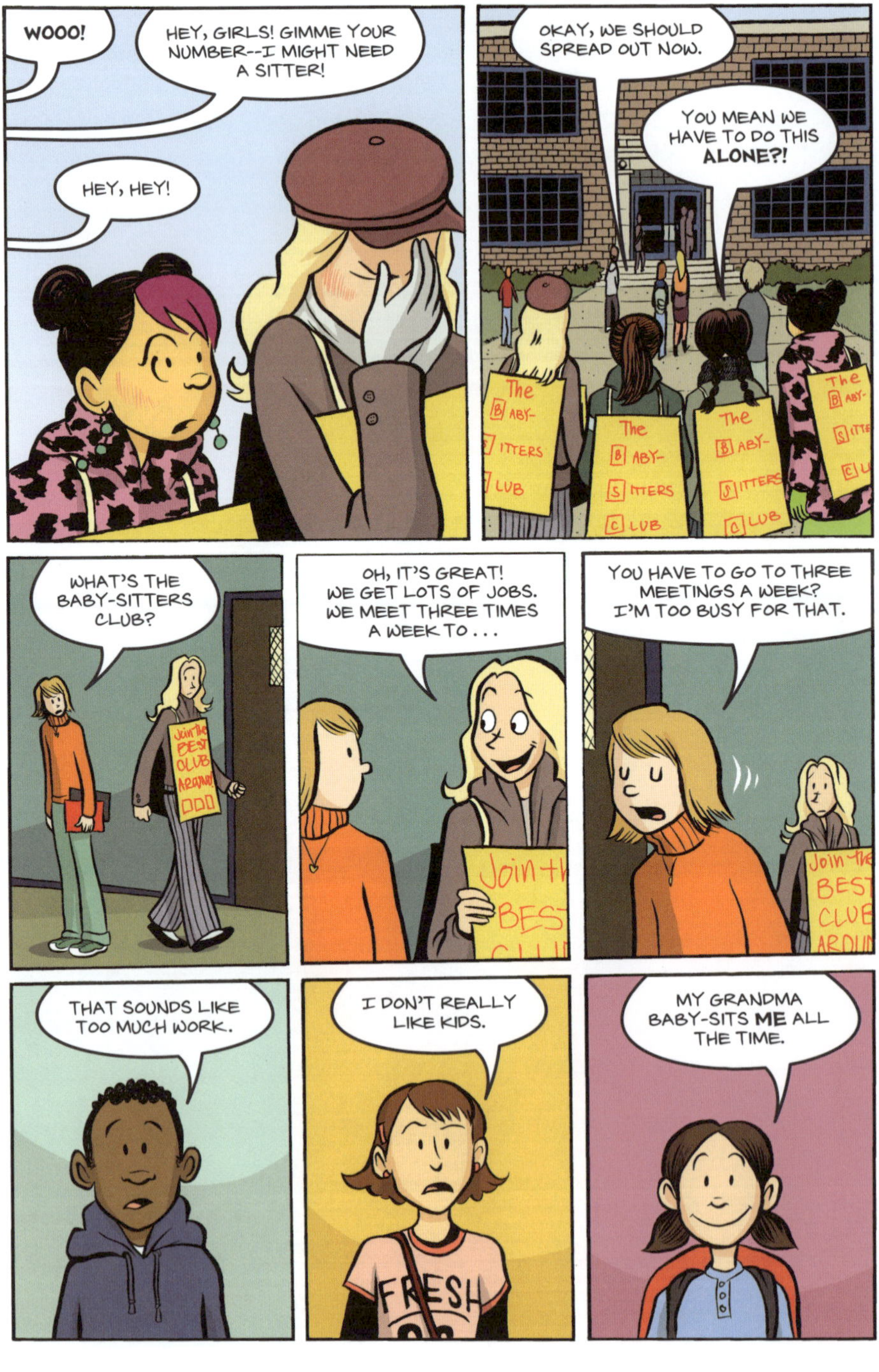
WOOO!
HEY, GIRLS! GIMME YOUR NUMBER--I MIGHT NEED A SITTER!
HEY, HEY!
OKAY, WE SHOULD SPREAD OUT NOW.
YOU MEAN WE HAVE TO DO THIS **ALONE?!**
The BABY-SITTERS CLUB
WHAT'S THE BABY-SITTERS CLUB?
Join the BEST CLUB AROUND
OH, IT'S GREAT! WE GET LOTS OF JOBS. WE MEET THREE TIMES A WEEK TO . . .
YOU HAVE TO GO TO THREE MEETINGS A WEEK? I'M TOO BUSY FOR THAT.
THAT SOUNDS LIKE TOO MUCH WORK.
I DON'T REALLY LIKE KIDS.
FRESH
MY GRANDMA BABY-SITS **ME** ALL THE TIME.

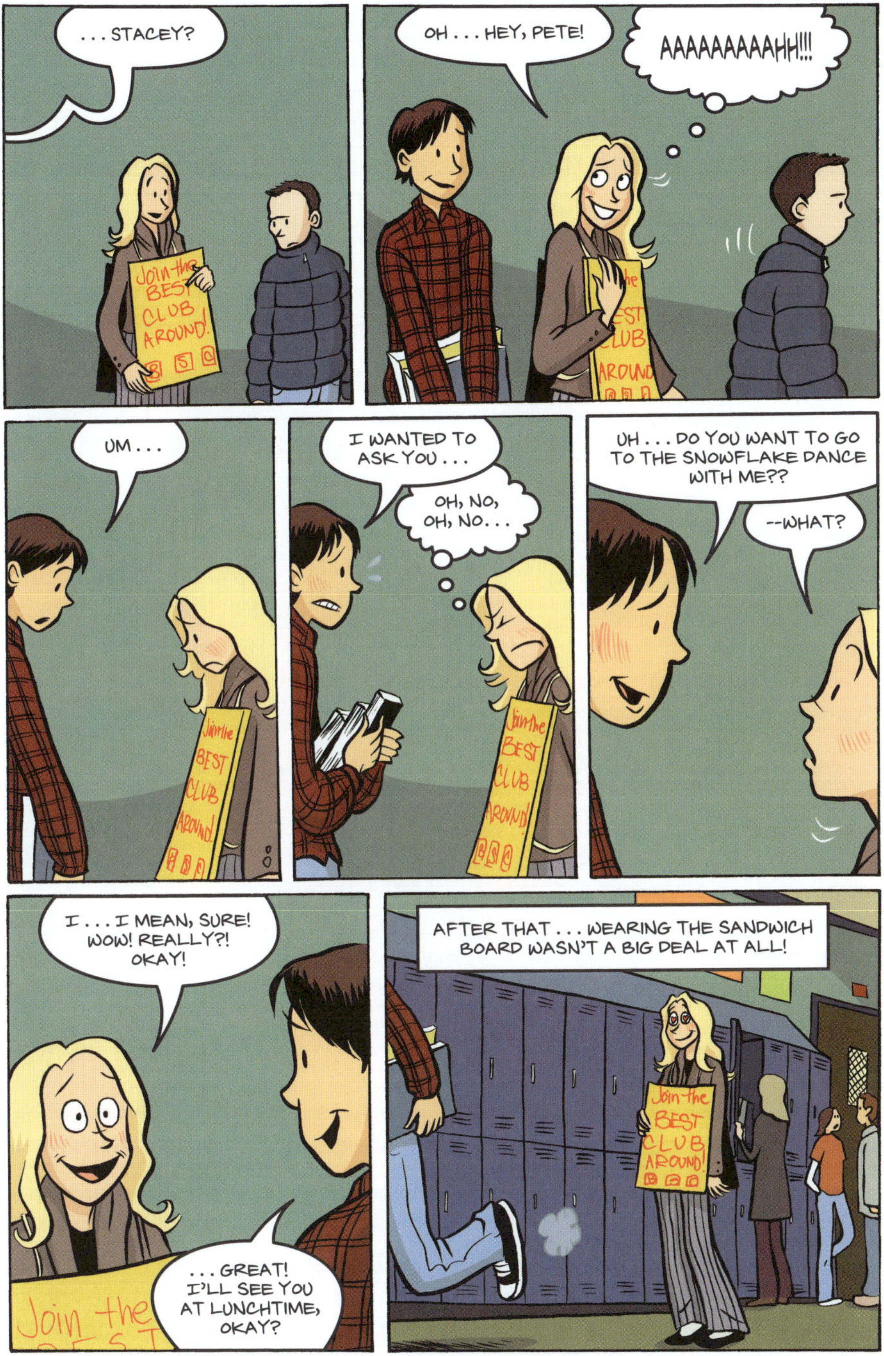
...STACEY?
OH... HEY, PETE!
AAAAAAAAAHH!!!
Join the BEST CLUB AROUND!
UM...
I WANTED TO ASK YOU...
OH, NO, OH, NO...
UH... DO YOU WANT TO GO TO THE SNOWFLAKE DANCE WITH ME??
--WHAT?
I... I MEAN, SURE! WOW! REALLY?! OKAY!
...GREAT! I'LL SEE YOU AT LUNCHTIME, OKAY?
AFTER THAT... WEARING THE SANDWICH BOARD WASN'T A BIG DEAL AT ALL!

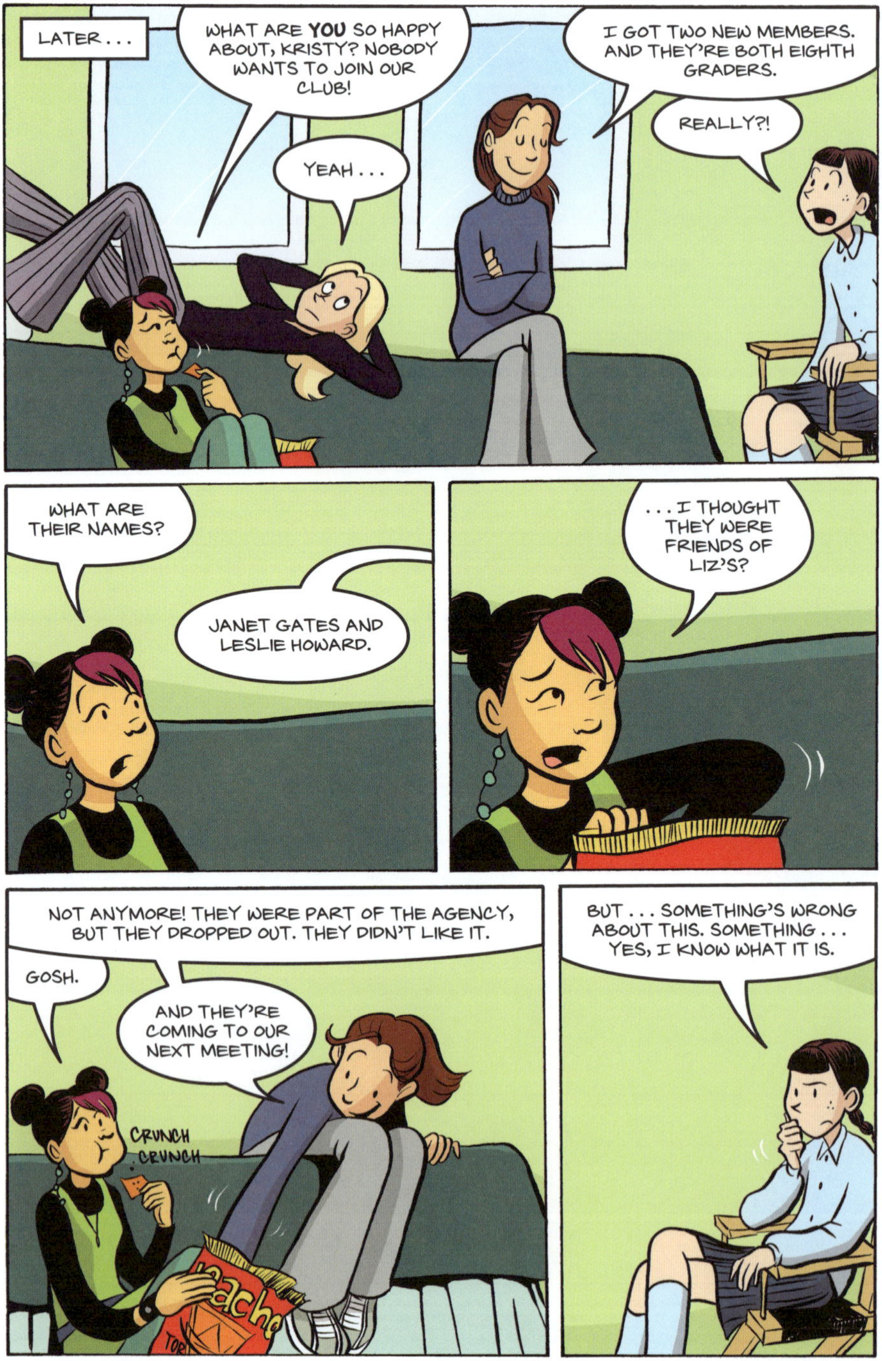
LATER . . .
WHAT ARE **YOU** SO HAPPY ABOUT, KRISTY? NOBODY WANTS TO JOIN OUR CLUB!
YEAH . . .
I GOT TWO NEW MEMBERS. AND THEY'RE BOTH EIGHTH GRADERS.
REALLY?!
WHAT ARE THEIR NAMES?
JANET GATES AND LESLIE HOWARD.
. . . I THOUGHT THEY WERE FRIENDS OF LIZ'S?
NOT ANYMORE! THEY WERE PART OF THE AGENCY, BUT THEY DROPPED OUT. THEY DIDN'T LIKE IT.
GOSH.
AND THEY'RE COMING TO OUR NEXT MEETING!
CRUNCH
CRUNCH
BUT . . . SOMETHING'S WRONG ABOUT THIS. SOMETHING . . . YES, I KNOW WHAT IT IS.

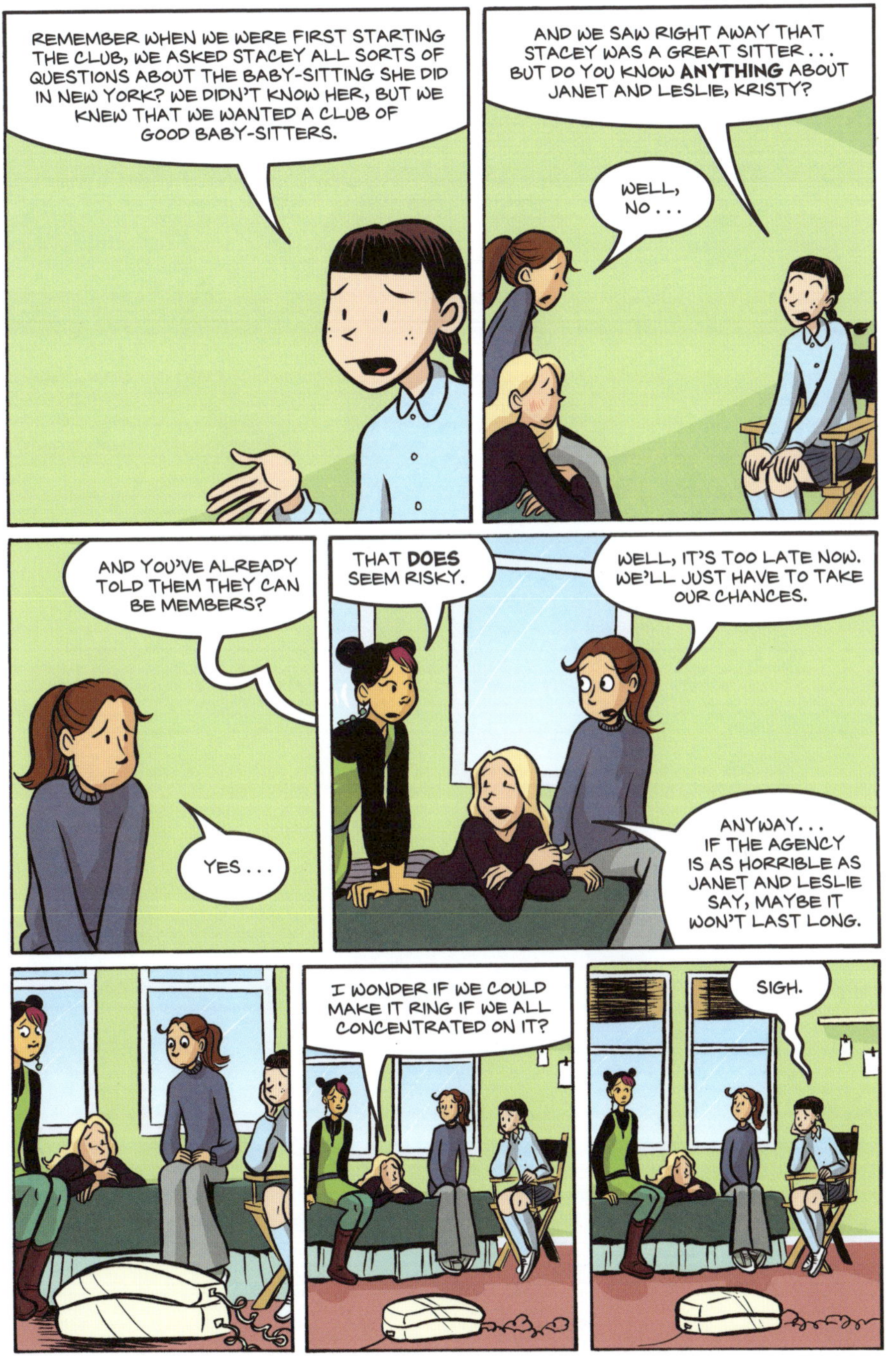
REMEMBER WHEN WE WERE FIRST STARTING THE CLUB, WE ASKED STACEY ALL SORTS OF QUESTIONS ABOUT THE BABY-SITTING SHE DID IN NEW YORK? WE DIDN'T KNOW HER, BUT WE KNEW THAT WE WANTED A CLUB OF GOOD BABY-SITTERS.
AND WE SAW RIGHT AWAY THAT STACEY WAS A GREAT SITTER . . . BUT DO YOU KNOW **ANYTHING** ABOUT JANET AND LESLIE, KRISTY?
WELL, NO . . .
AND YOU'VE ALREADY TOLD THEM THEY CAN BE MEMBERS?
YES . . .
THAT **DOES** SEEM RISKY.
WELL, IT'S TOO LATE NOW. WE'LL JUST HAVE TO TAKE OUR CHANCES.
ANYWAY . . . IF THE AGENCY IS AS HORRIBLE AS JANET AND LESLIE SAY, MAYBE IT WON'T LAST LONG.
I WONDER IF WE COULD MAKE IT RING IF WE ALL CONCENTRATED ON IT?
SIGH.

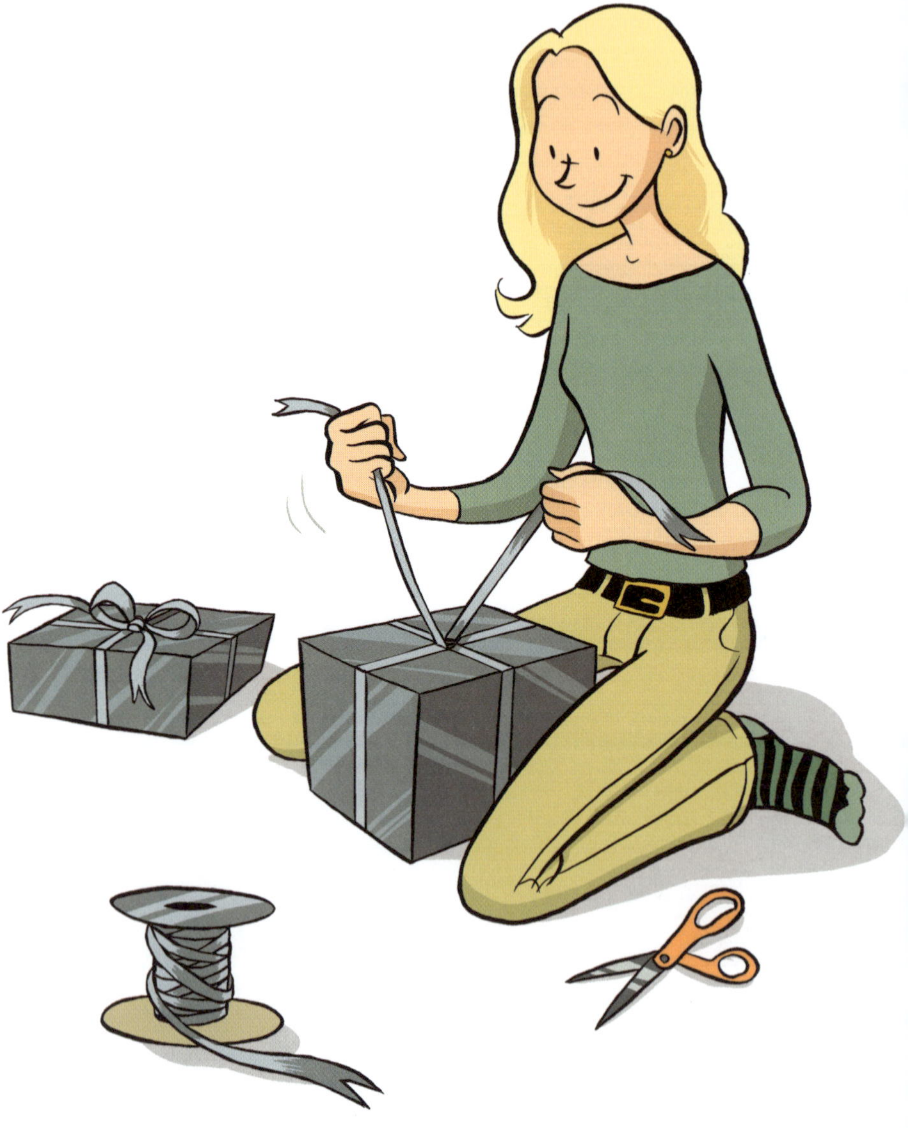

CHAPTER 9

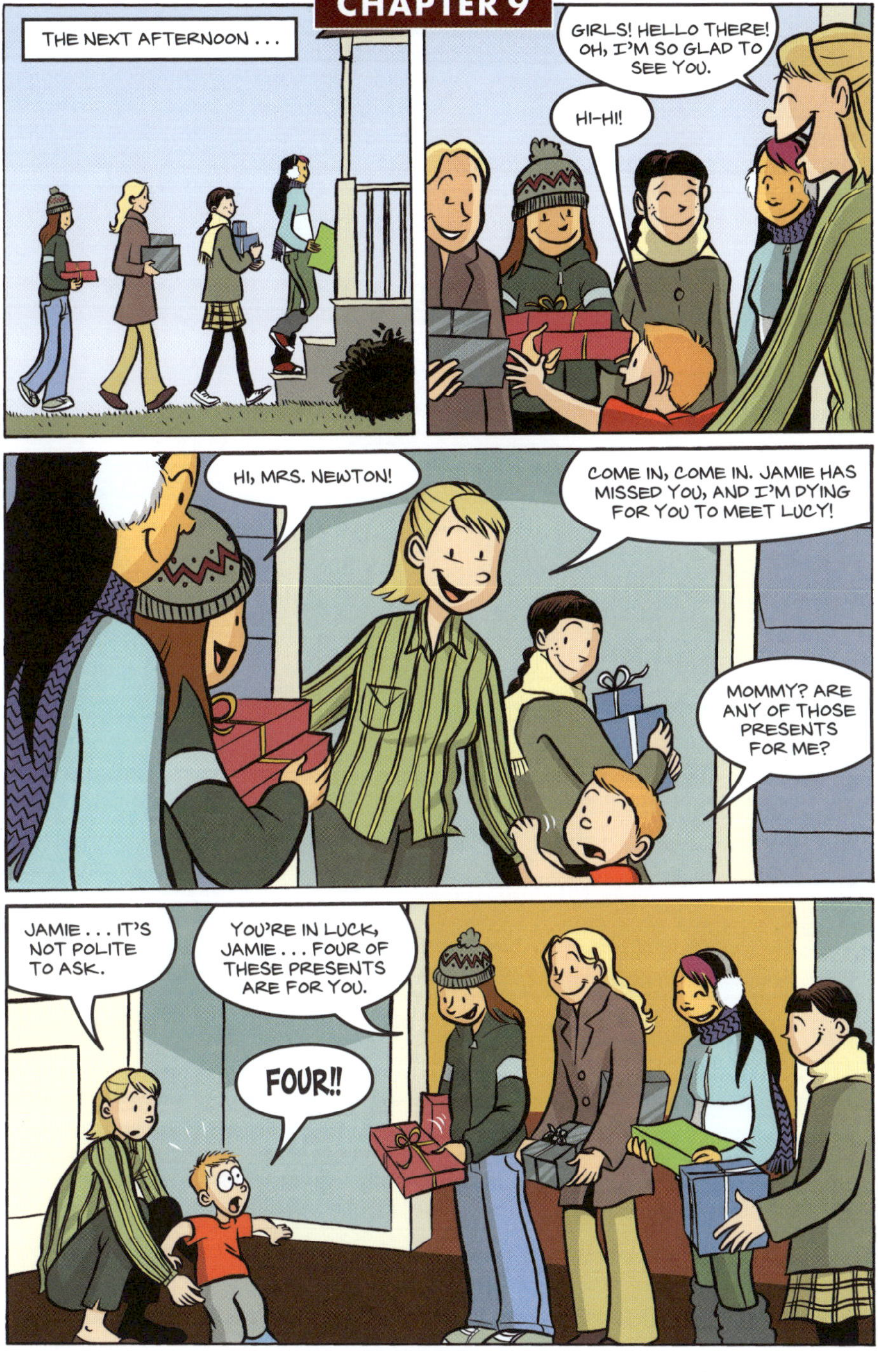
THE NEXT AFTERNOON . . .
GIRLS! HELLO THERE! OH, I'M SO GLAD TO SEE YOU.
HI-HI!
HI, MRS. NEWTON!
COME IN, COME IN. JAMIE HAS MISSED YOU, AND I'M DYING FOR YOU TO MEET LUCY!
MOMMY? ARE ANY OF THOSE PRESENTS FOR ME?
JAMIE . . . IT'S NOT POLITE TO ASK.
YOU'RE IN LUCK, JAMIE . . . FOUR OF THESE PRESENTS ARE FOR YOU.
FOUR!!

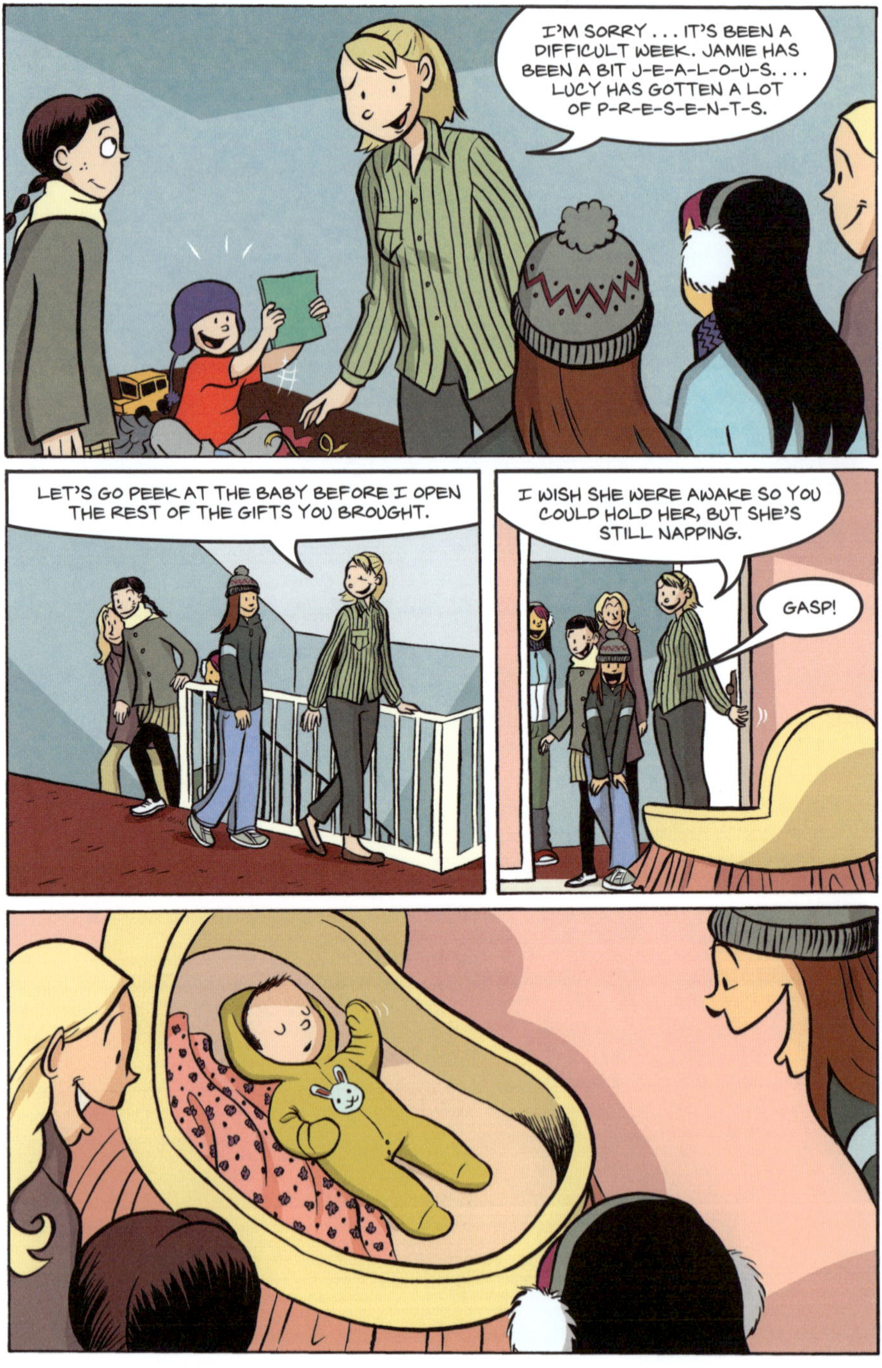
I'M SORRY . . . IT'S BEEN A DIFFICULT WEEK. JAMIE HAS BEEN A BIT J-E-A-L-O-U-S. . . . LUCY HAS GOTTEN A LOT OF P-R-E-S-E-N-T-S.
LET'S GO PEEK AT THE BABY BEFORE I OPEN THE REST OF THE GIFTS YOU BROUGHT.
I WISH SHE WERE AWAKE SO YOU COULD HOLD HER, BUT SHE'S STILL NAPPING.
GASP!

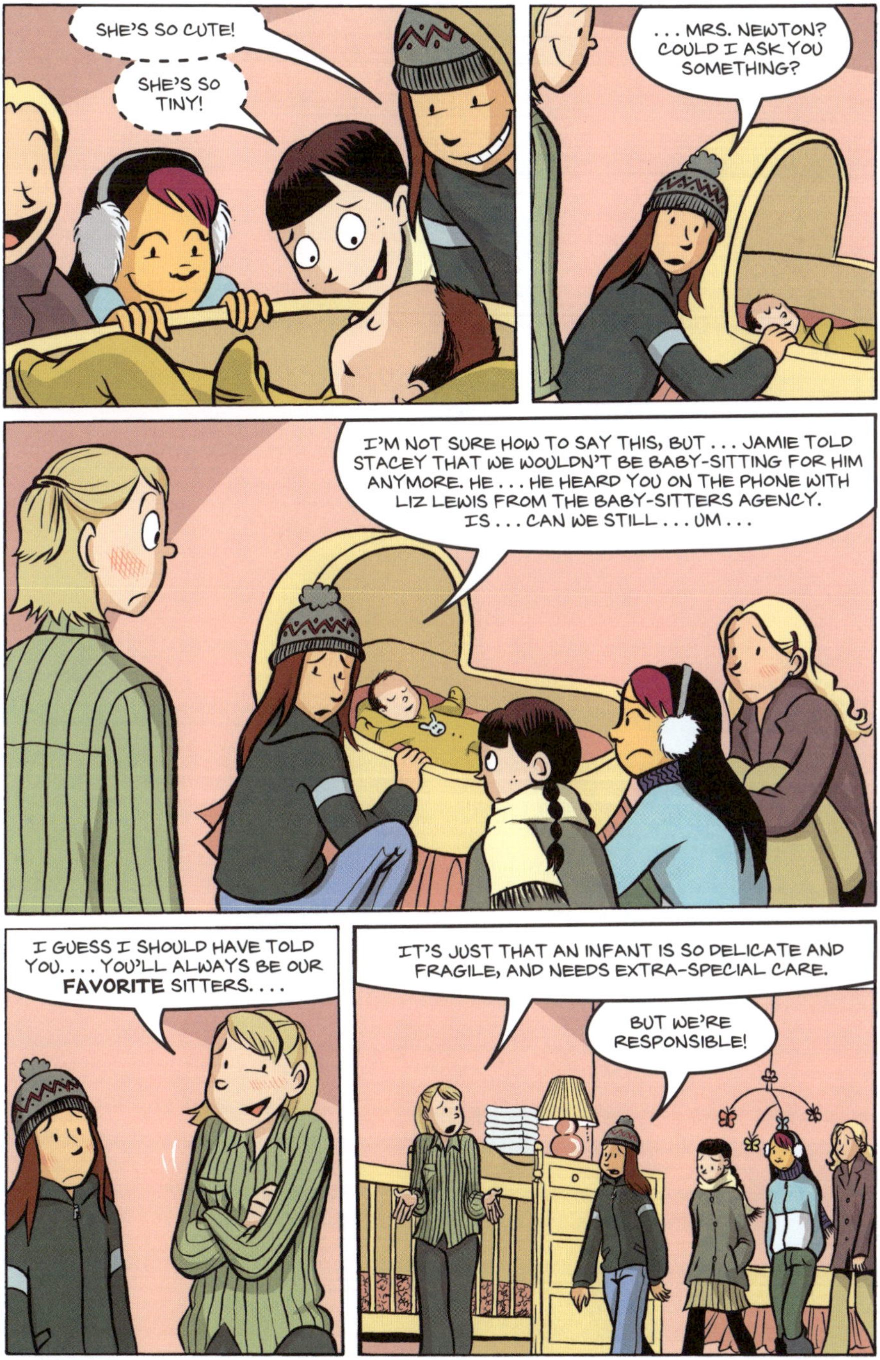
SHE'S SO CUTE!
SHE'S SO TINY!
. . . MRS. NEWTON? COULD I ASK YOU SOMETHING?
I'M NOT SURE HOW TO SAY THIS, BUT . . . JAMIE TOLD STACEY THAT WE WOULDN'T BE BABY-SITTING FOR HIM ANYMORE. HE . . . HE HEARD YOU ON THE PHONE WITH LIZ LEWIS FROM THE BABY-SITTERS AGENCY. IS . . . CAN WE STILL . . . UM . . .
I GUESS I SHOULD HAVE TOLD YOU. . . . YOU'LL ALWAYS BE OUR **FAVORITE** SITTERS. . . .
IT'S JUST THAT AN INFANT IS SO DELICATE AND FRAGILE, AND NEEDS EXTRA-SPECIAL CARE.
BUT WE'RE RESPONSIBLE!

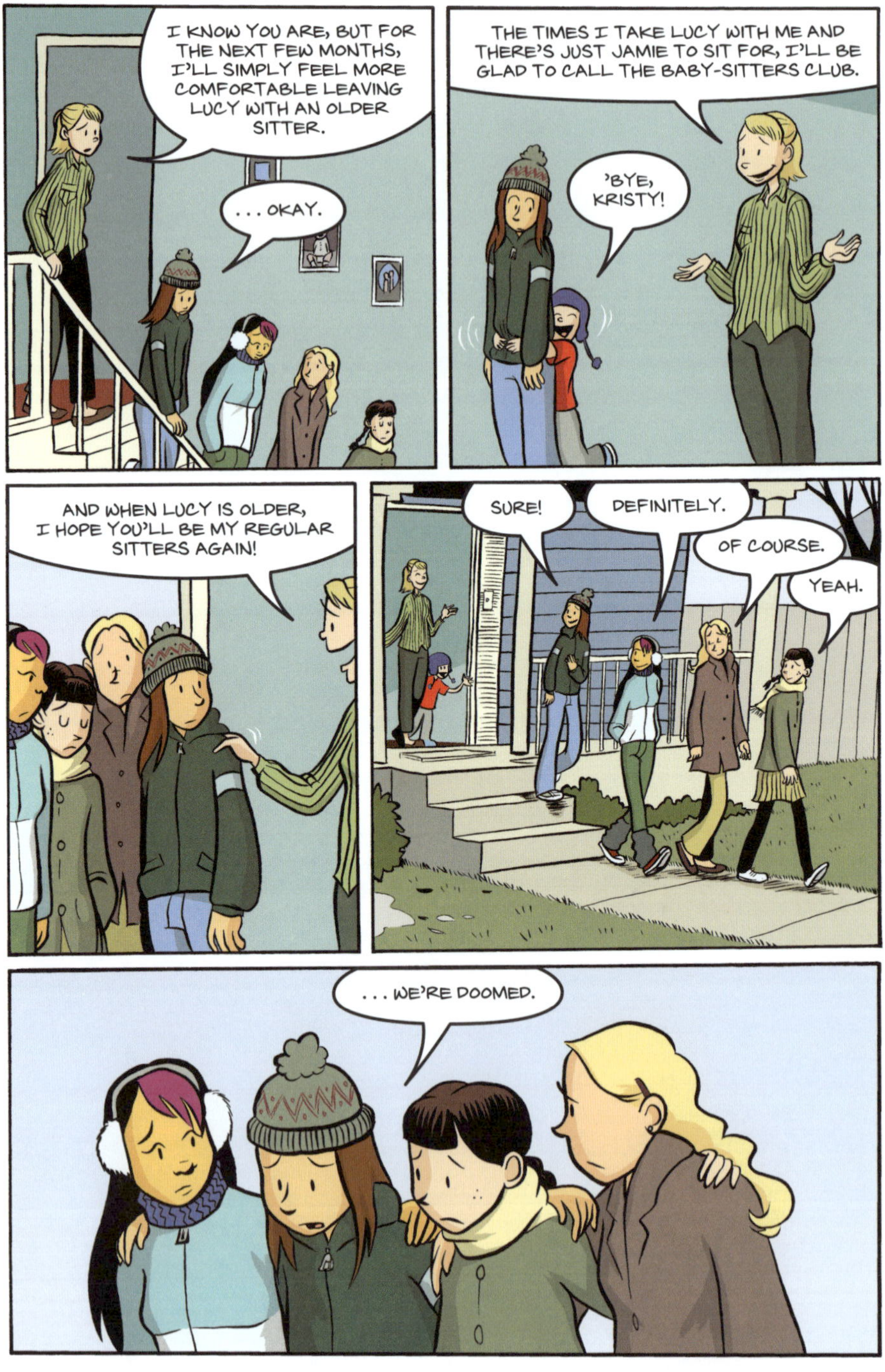
I KNOW YOU ARE, BUT FOR THE NEXT FEW MONTHS, I'LL SIMPLY FEEL MORE COMFORTABLE LEAVING LUCY WITH AN OLDER SITTER.
. . . OKAY.
THE TIMES I TAKE LUCY WITH ME AND THERE'S JUST JAMIE TO SIT FOR, I'LL BE GLAD TO CALL THE BABY-SITTERS CLUB.
'BYE, KRISTY!
AND WHEN LUCY IS OLDER, I HOPE YOU'LL BE MY REGULAR SITTERS AGAIN!
SURE!
DEFINITELY.
OF COURSE.
YEAH.
. . . WE'RE DOOMED.

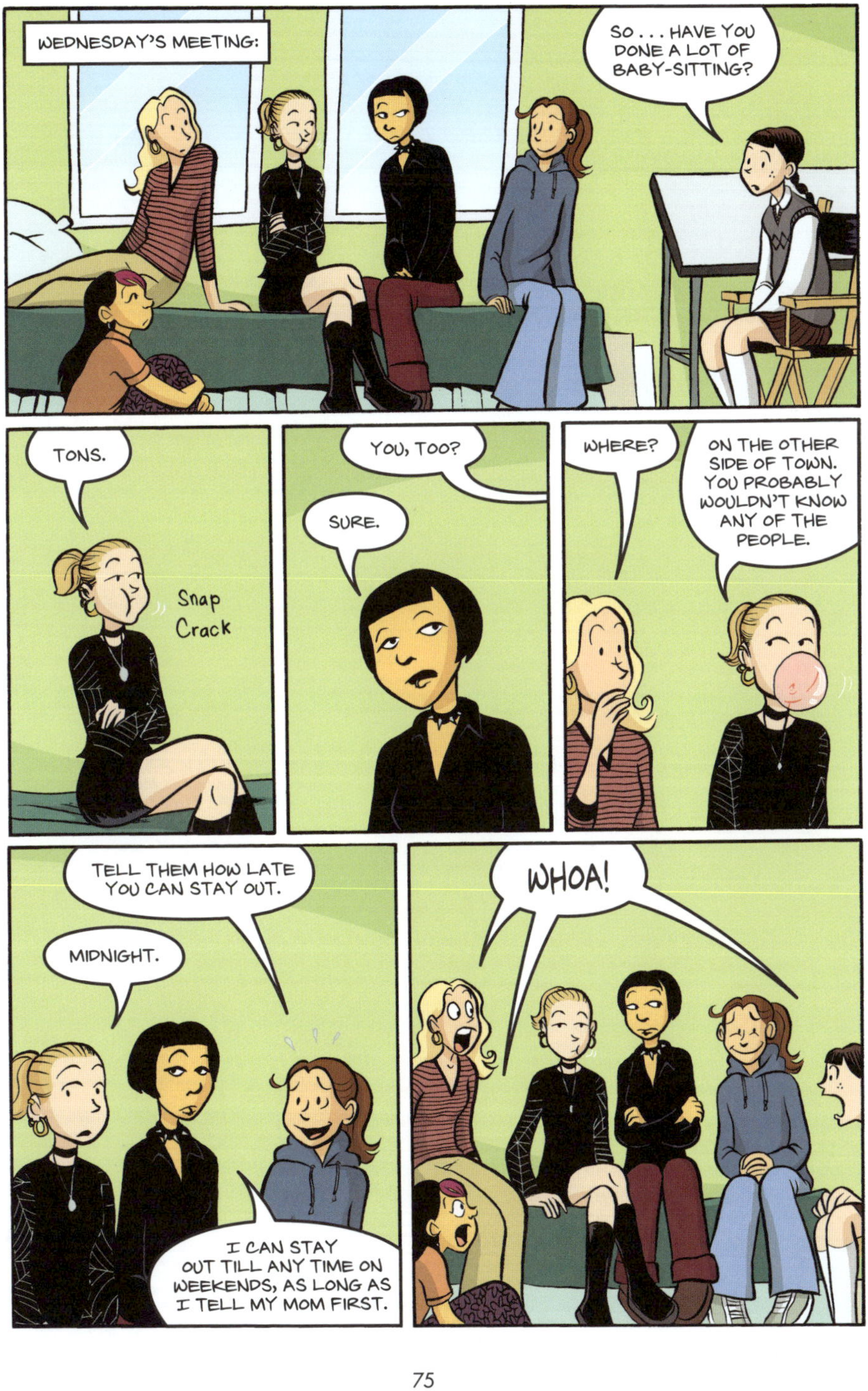
WEDNESDAY'S MEETING:
SO . . . HAVE YOU DONE A LOT OF BABY-SITTING?
TONS.
Snap
Crack
YOU, TOO?
SURE.
WHERE?
ON THE OTHER SIDE OF TOWN. YOU PROBABLY WOULDN'T KNOW ANY OF THE PEOPLE.
TELL THEM HOW LATE YOU CAN STAY OUT.
MIDNIGHT.
I CAN STAY OUT TILL ANY TIME ON WEEKENDS, AS LONG AS I TELL MY MOM FIRST.
WHOA!

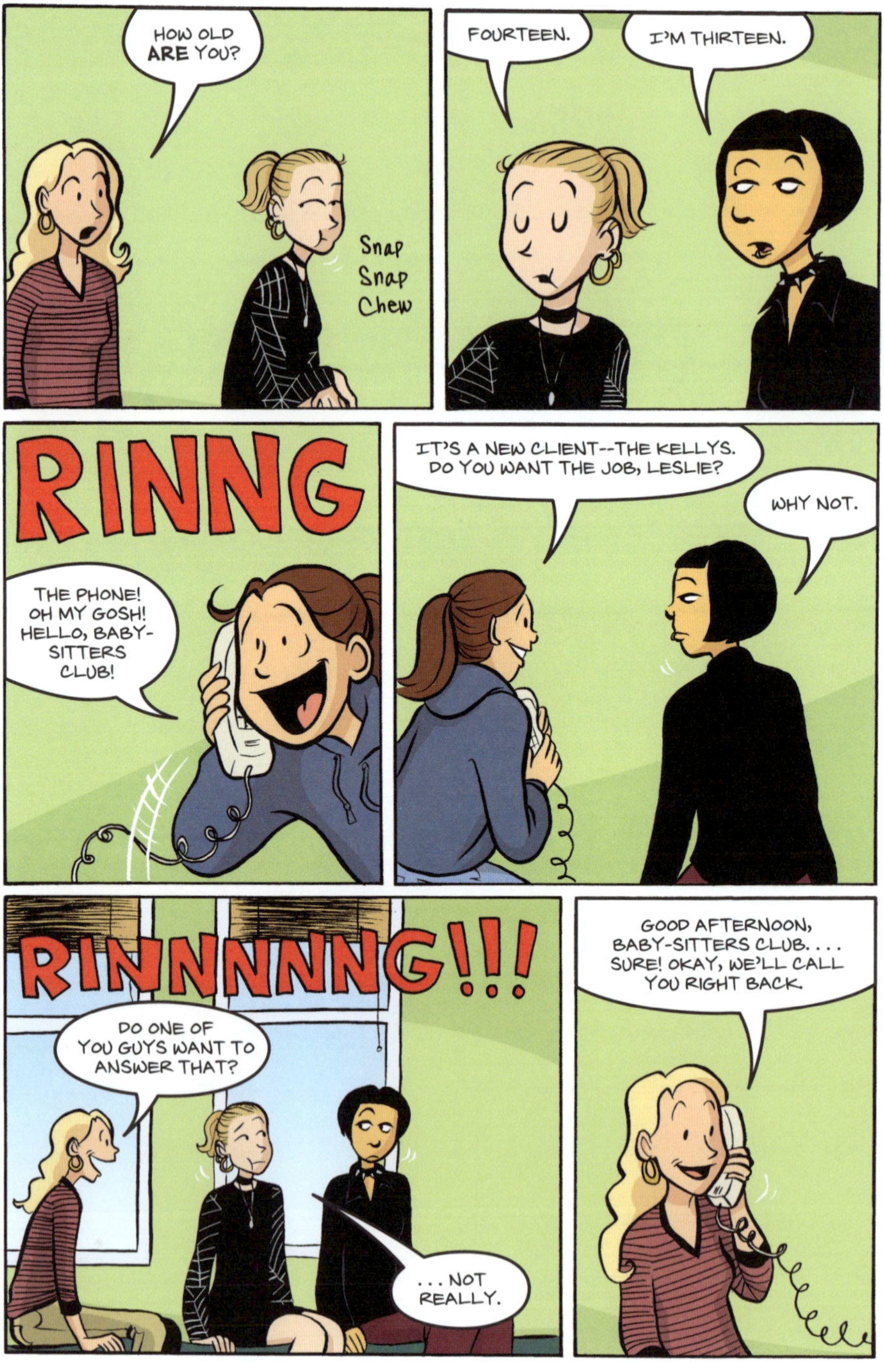
HOW OLD ARE YOU?
Snap Snap Chew
FOURTEEN.
I'M THIRTEEN.
RINNG
THE PHONE! OH MY GOSH! HELLO, BABY-SITTERS CLUB!
IT'S A NEW CLIENT--THE KELLYS. DO YOU WANT THE JOB, LESLIE?
WHY NOT.
RINNNNNG!!!
DO ONE OF YOU GUYS WANT TO ANSWER THAT?
. . . NOT REALLY.
GOOD AFTERNOON, BABY-SITTERS CLUB. . . . SURE! OKAY, WE'LL CALL YOU RIGHT BACK.

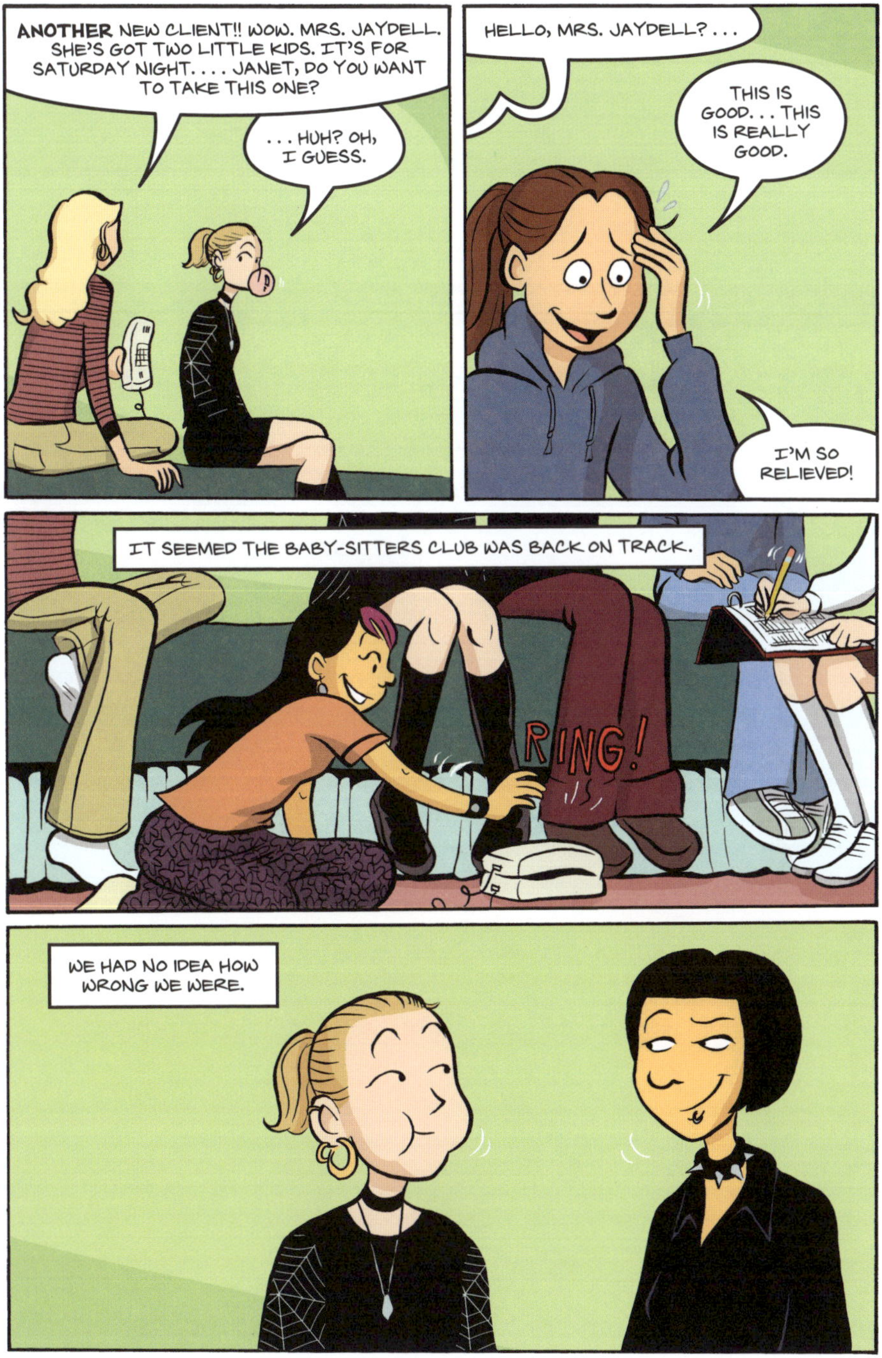
ANOTHER NEW CLIENT!! WOW. MRS. JAYDELL. SHE'S GOT TWO LITTLE KIDS. IT'S FOR SATURDAY NIGHT. . . . JANET, DO YOU WANT TO TAKE THIS ONE?
. . . HUH? OH, I GUESS.
HELLO, MRS. JAYDELL? . . .
THIS IS GOOD. . . THIS IS REALLY GOOD.
I'M SO RELIEVED!
IT SEEMED THE BABY-SITTERS CLUB WAS BACK ON TRACK.
RING!
WE HAD NO IDEA HOW WRONG WE WERE.

Monday, December 8

Today Kristy, Stacey + Mary Anne all arived early for our baby-sitters club meeting. We were all realy excited to find out how Janet and Leslie's siting jobs had gone on ~~Soo~~ Saturday.

When it was 5:30 we kept expecting the doorbell to ring any seconde. But it didnt. Soon it was 5:50. Where were they. Krist was getting worried. ~~Writ~~ Write this down in our notebook, somebody, she said. Somethings wrong.

Claudia

CHAPTER 10

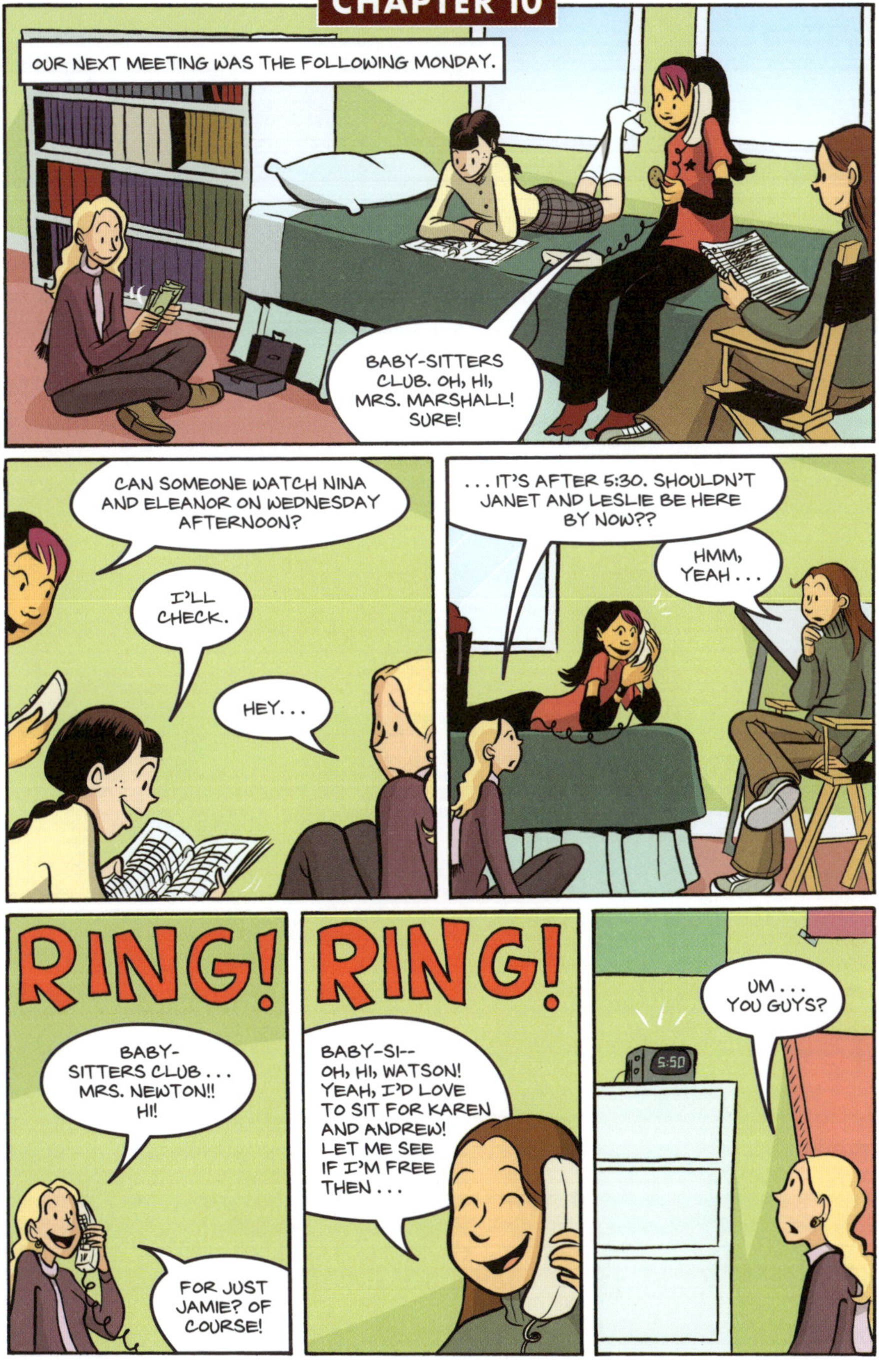

OUR NEXT MEETING WAS THE FOLLOWING MONDAY.
BABY-SITTERS CLUB. OH, HI, MRS. MARSHALL! SURE!
CAN SOMEONE WATCH NINA AND ELEANOR ON WEDNESDAY AFTERNOON?
I'LL CHECK.
HEY...
...IT'S AFTER 5:30. SHOULDN'T JANET AND LESLIE BE HERE BY NOW??
HMM, YEAH...
RING!
BABY-SITTERS CLUB... MRS. NEWTON!! HI!
FOR JUST JAMIE? OF COURSE!
RING!
BABY-SI-- OH, HI, WATSON! YEAH, I'D LOVE TO SIT FOR KAREN AND ANDREW! LET ME SEE IF I'M FREE THEN...
5:50
UM... YOU GUYS?

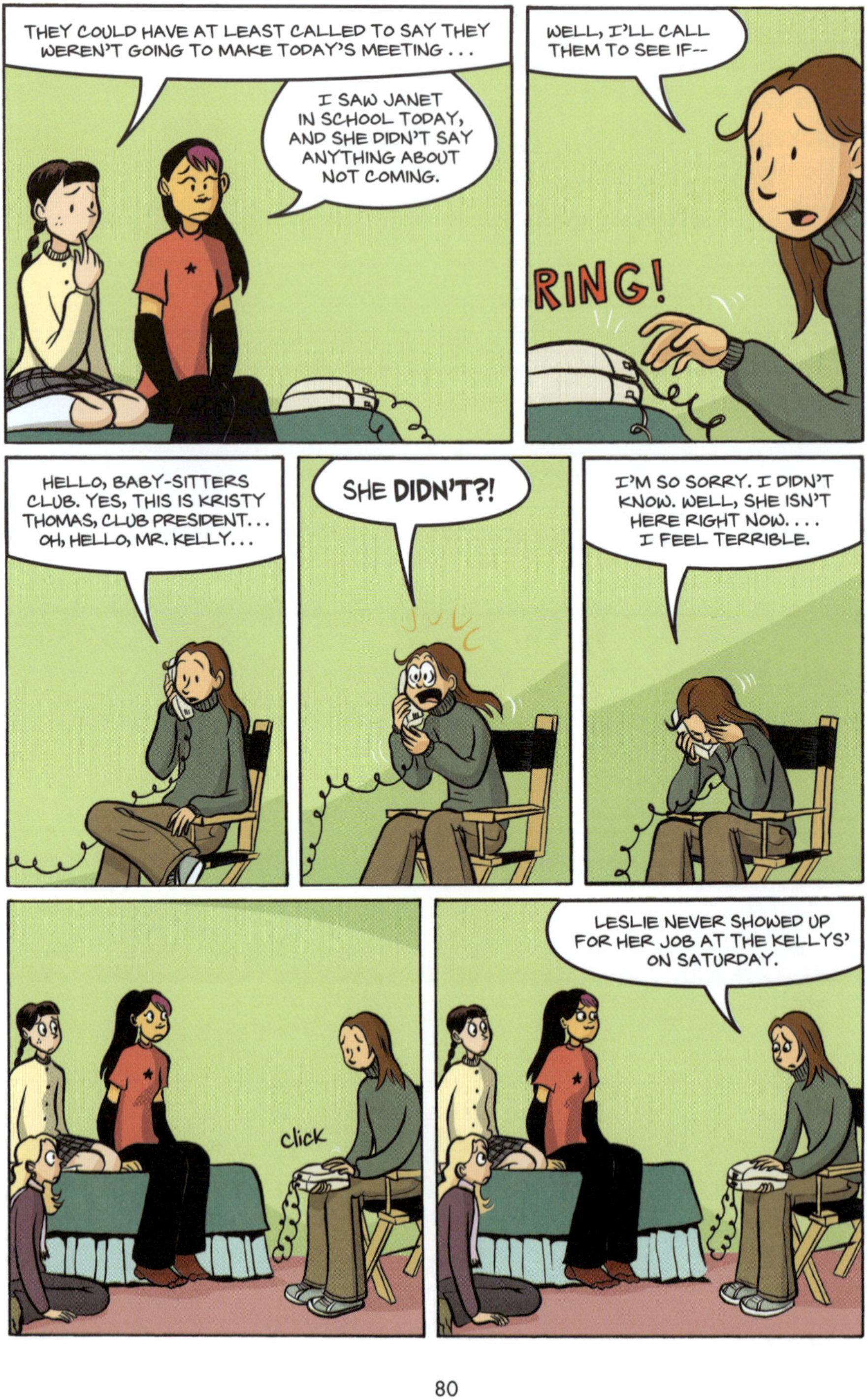
THEY COULD HAVE AT LEAST CALLED TO SAY THEY WEREN'T GOING TO MAKE TODAY'S MEETING . . .
I SAW JANET IN SCHOOL TODAY, AND SHE DIDN'T SAY ANYTHING ABOUT NOT COMING.
WELL, I'LL CALL THEM TO SEE IF--
RING!
HELLO, BABY-SITTERS CLUB. YES, THIS IS KRISTY THOMAS, CLUB PRESIDENT. . . OH, HELLO, MR. KELLY. . .
SHE DIDN'T?!
I'M SO SORRY. I DIDN'T KNOW. WELL, SHE ISN'T HERE RIGHT NOW. . . . I FEEL TERRIBLE.
click
LESLIE NEVER SHOWED UP FOR HER JOB AT THE KELLYS' ON SATURDAY.

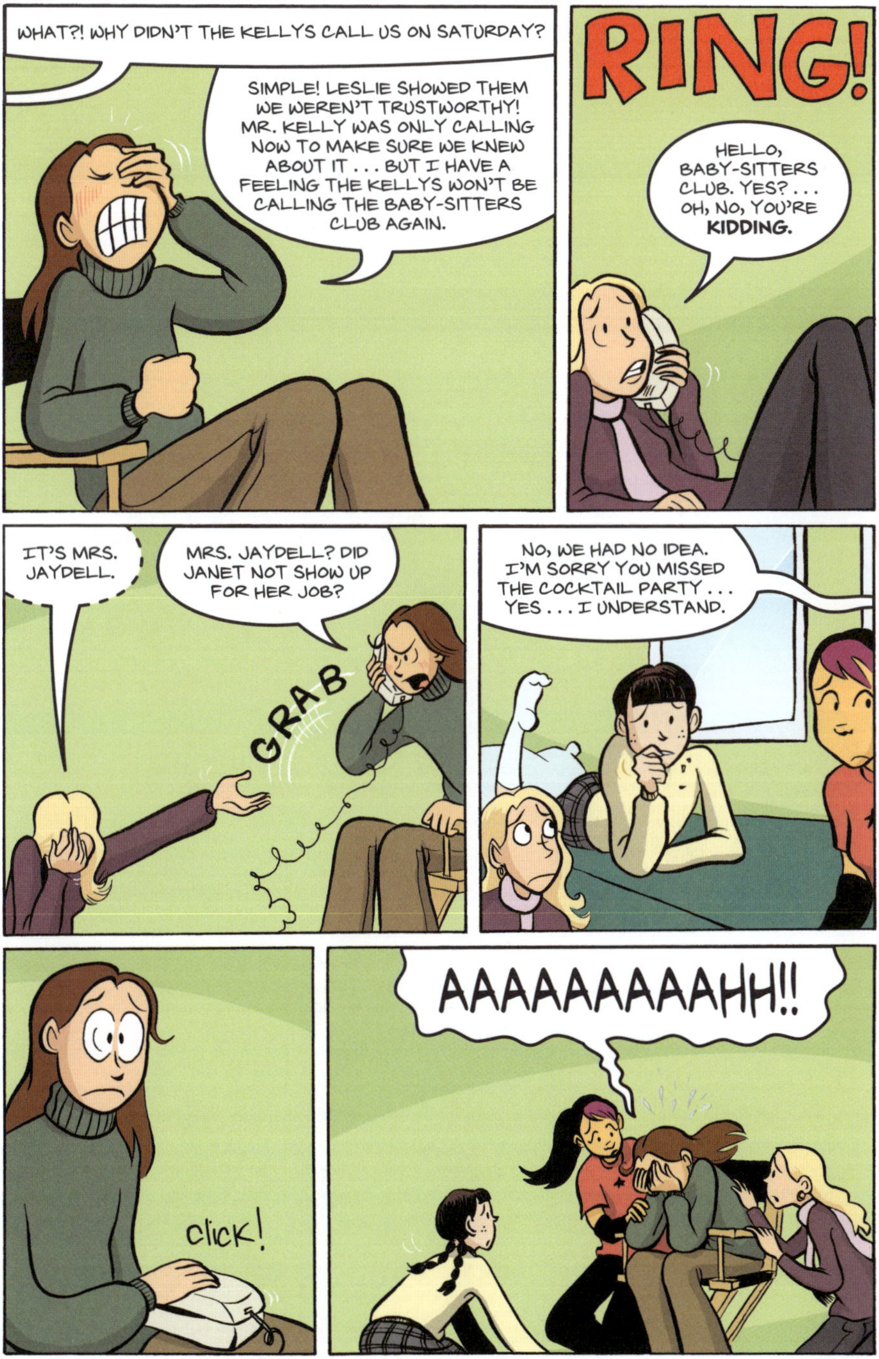
WHAT?! WHY DIDN'T THE KELLYS CALL US ON SATURDAY?
SIMPLE! LESLIE SHOWED THEM WE WEREN'T TRUSTWORTHY! MR. KELLY WAS ONLY CALLING NOW TO MAKE SURE WE KNEW ABOUT IT . . . BUT I HAVE A FEELING THE KELLYS WON'T BE CALLING THE BABY-SITTERS CLUB AGAIN.
RING!
HELLO, BABY-SITTERS CLUB. YES? . . . OH, NO, YOU'RE **KIDDING.**
IT'S MRS. JAYDELL.
MRS. JAYDELL? DID JANET NOT SHOW UP FOR HER JOB?
GRAB
NO, WE HAD NO IDEA. I'M SORRY YOU MISSED THE COCKTAIL PARTY . . . YES . . . I UNDERSTAND.
CLICK!
AAAAAAAAAHH!!

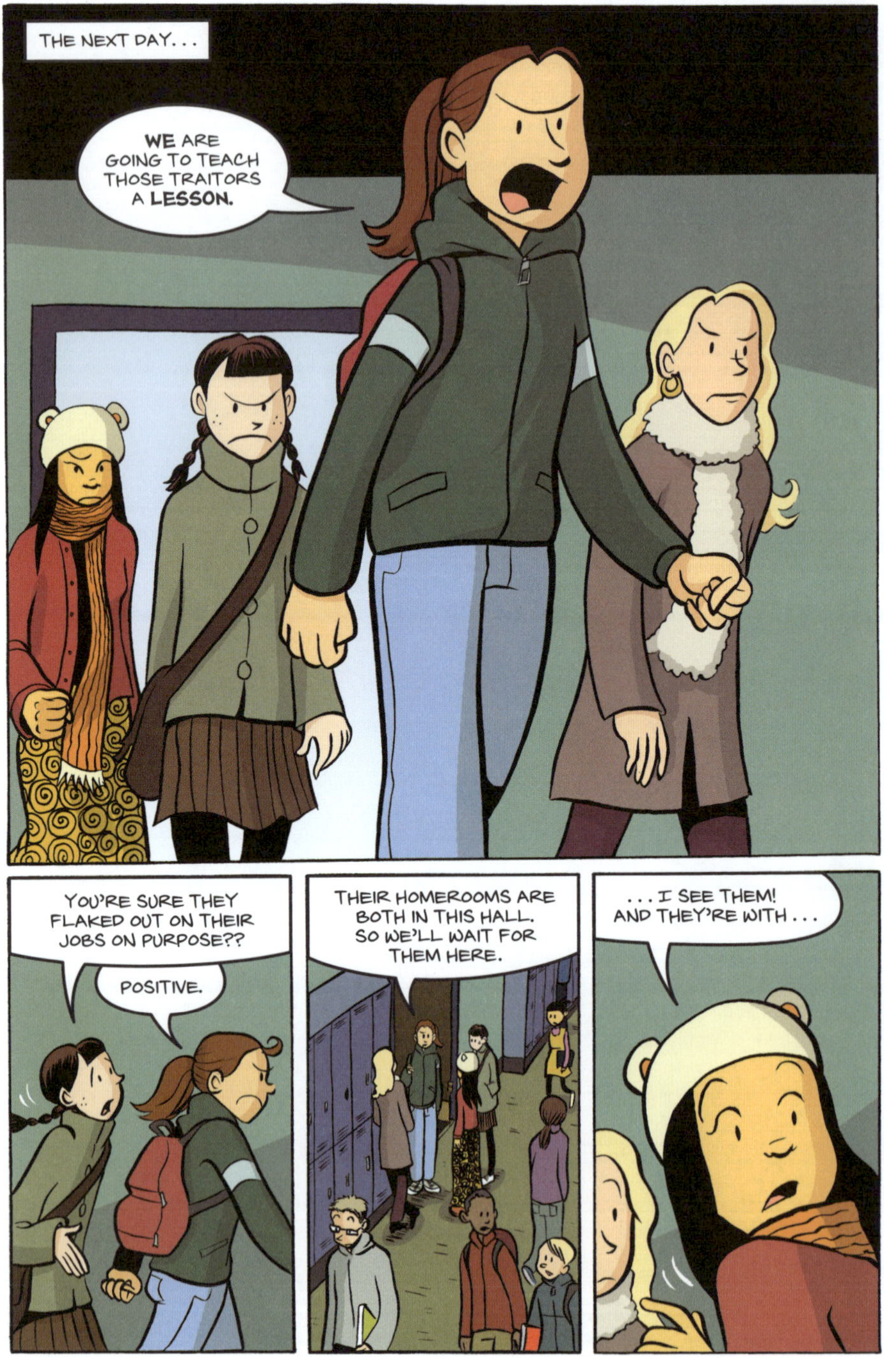
THE NEXT DAY...
WE ARE GOING TO TEACH THOSE TRAITORS A LESSON.
YOU'RE SURE THEY FLAKED OUT ON THEIR JOBS ON PURPOSE??
POSITIVE.
THEIR HOMEROOMS ARE BOTH IN THIS HALL. SO WE'LL WAIT FOR THEM HERE.
...I SEE THEM! AND THEY'RE WITH...

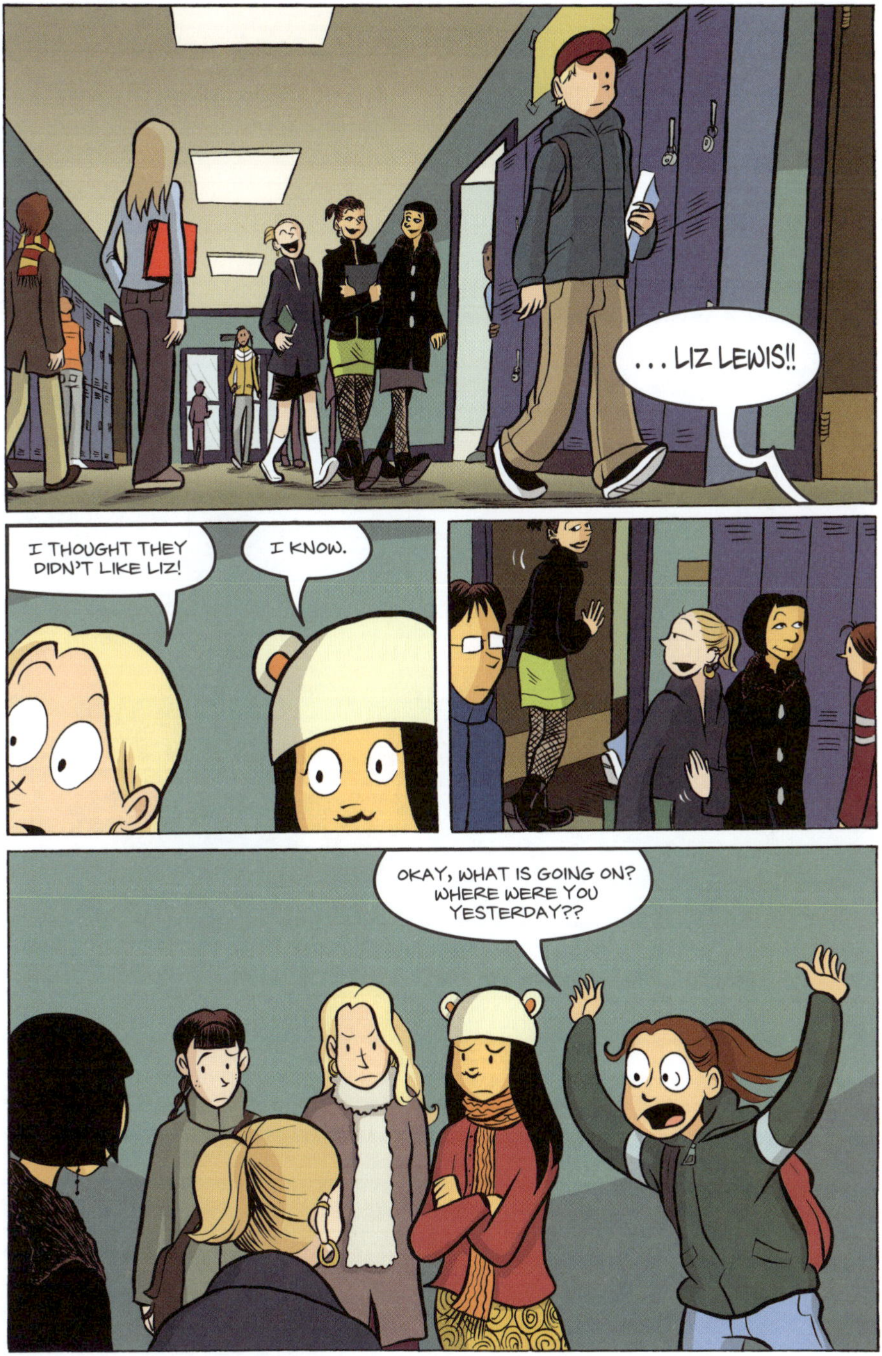
. . . LIZ LEWIS!!
I THOUGHT THEY DIDN'T LIKE LIZ!
I KNOW.
OKAY, WHAT IS GOING ON? WHERE WERE YOU YESTERDAY??

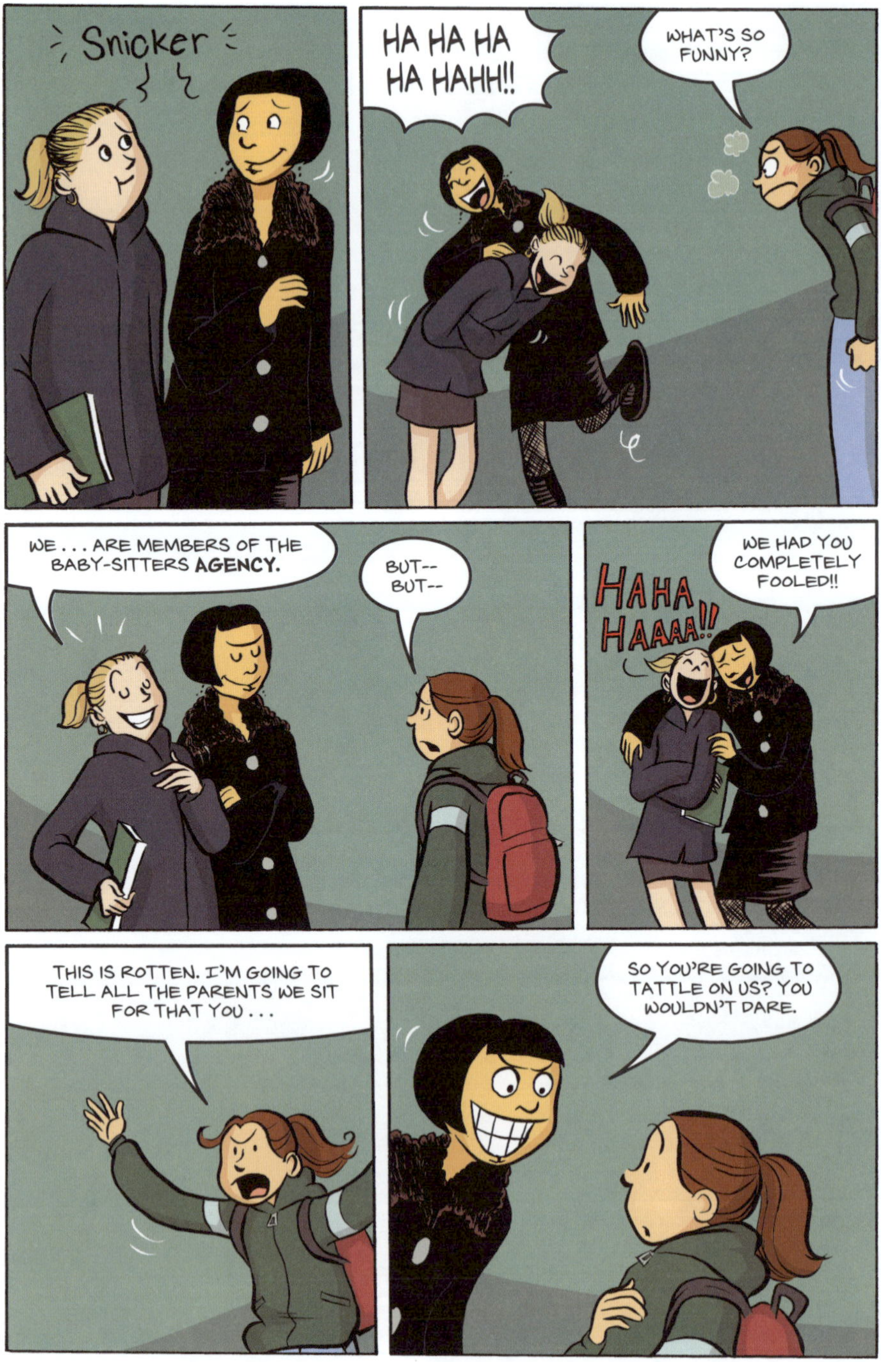
Snicker
HA HA HA HA HAHH!!
WHAT'S SO FUNNY?
WE . . . ARE MEMBERS OF THE BABY-SITTERS **AGENCY.**
BUT-- BUT--
HAHA HAAAA!!
WE HAD YOU COMPLETELY FOOLED!!
THIS IS ROTTEN. I'M GOING TO TELL ALL THE PARENTS WE SIT FOR THAT YOU . . .
SO YOU'RE GOING TO TATTLE ON US? YOU WOULDN'T DARE.

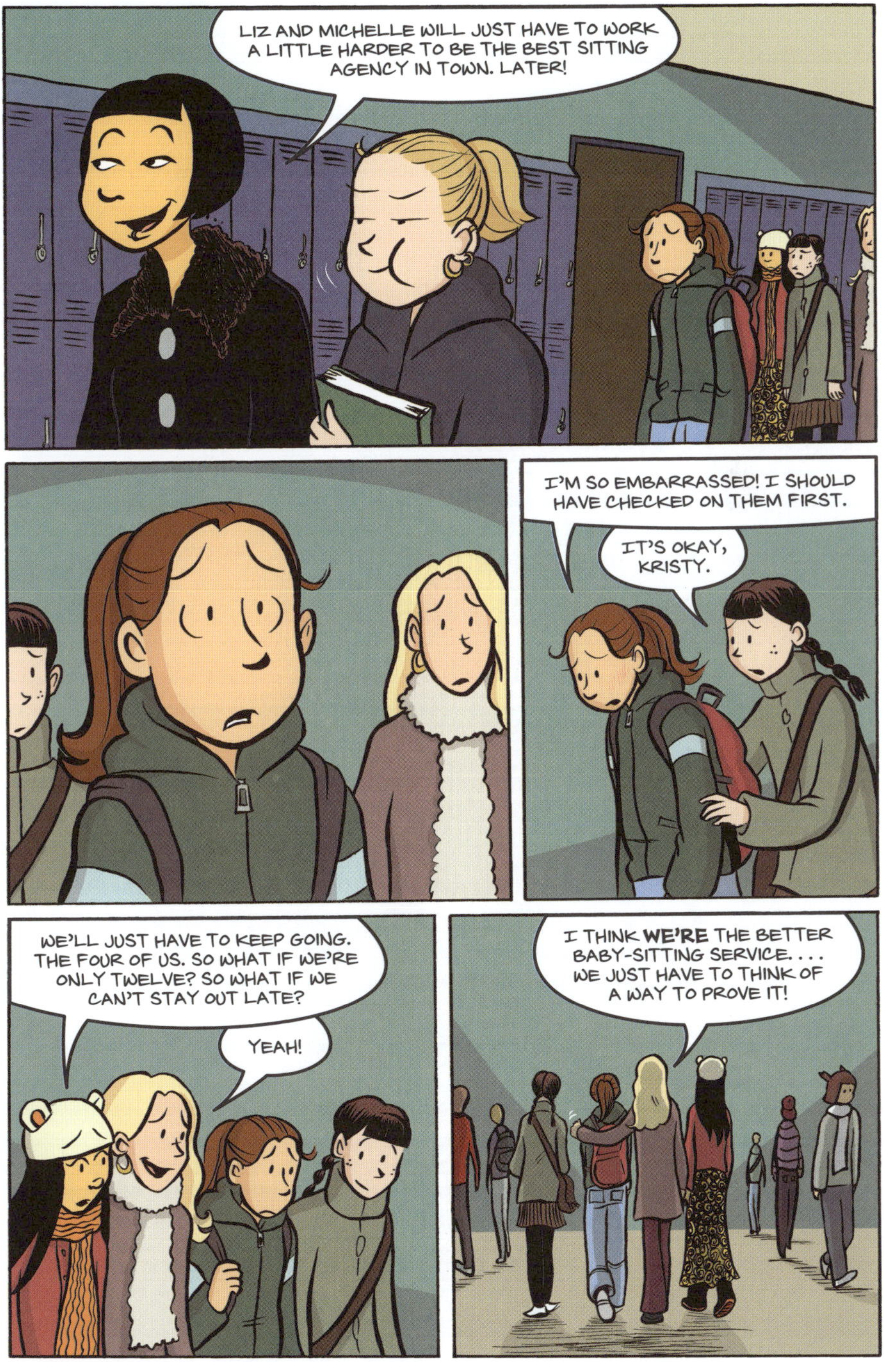
LIZ AND MICHELLE WILL JUST HAVE TO WORK A LITTLE HARDER TO BE THE BEST SITTING AGENCY IN TOWN. LATER!
I'M SO EMBARRASSED! I SHOULD HAVE CHECKED ON THEM FIRST.
IT'S OKAY, KRISTY.
WE'LL JUST HAVE TO KEEP GOING. THE FOUR OF US. SO WHAT IF WE'RE ONLY TWELVE? SO WHAT IF WE CAN'T STAY OUT LATE?
YEAH!
I THINK **WE'RE** THE BETTER BABY-SITTING SERVICE. . . . WE JUST HAVE TO THINK OF A WAY TO PROVE IT!

Wednesday, December 10th

Earlier this afternoon, I baby-sat for Jamie while Mrs. Newton took Lucy to a doctor's appointment. Something was bothering him. He moped around as if he'd lost his best friend. He greeted me cheerfully enough when I arrived, but as soon as Mrs. Newton carried a bundled-up Lucy out the back door, his face fell....

       Mary Anne

CHAPTER 11

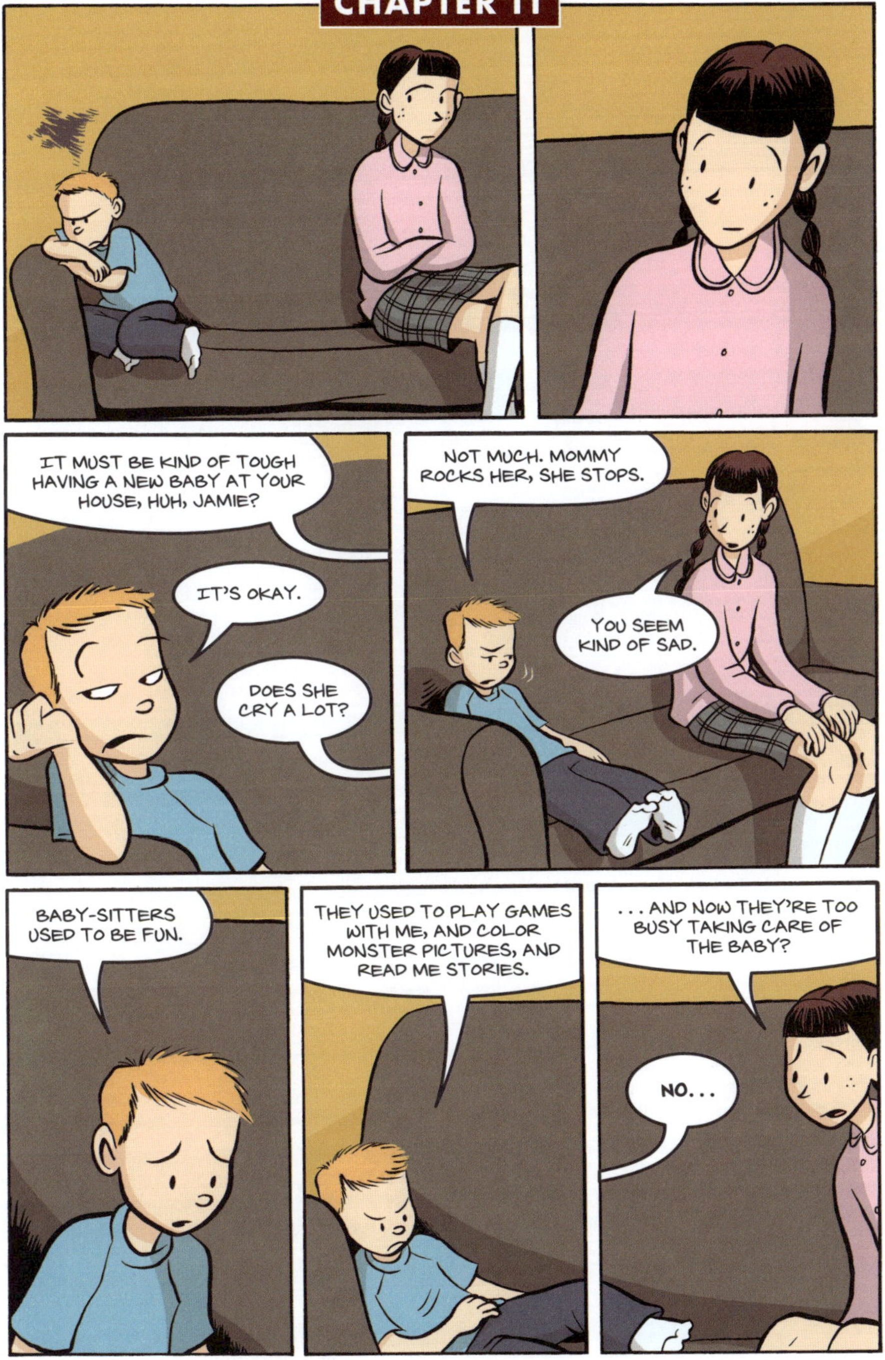
IT MUST BE KIND OF TOUGH HAVING A NEW BABY AT YOUR HOUSE, HUH, JAMIE?
IT'S OKAY.
DOES SHE CRY A LOT?
NOT MUCH. MOMMY ROCKS HER, SHE STOPS.
YOU SEEM KIND OF SAD.
BABY-SITTERS USED TO BE FUN.
THEY USED TO PLAY GAMES WITH ME, AND COLOR MONSTER PICTURES, AND READ ME STORIES.
. . . AND NOW THEY'RE TOO BUSY TAKING CARE OF THE BABY?
NO. . .

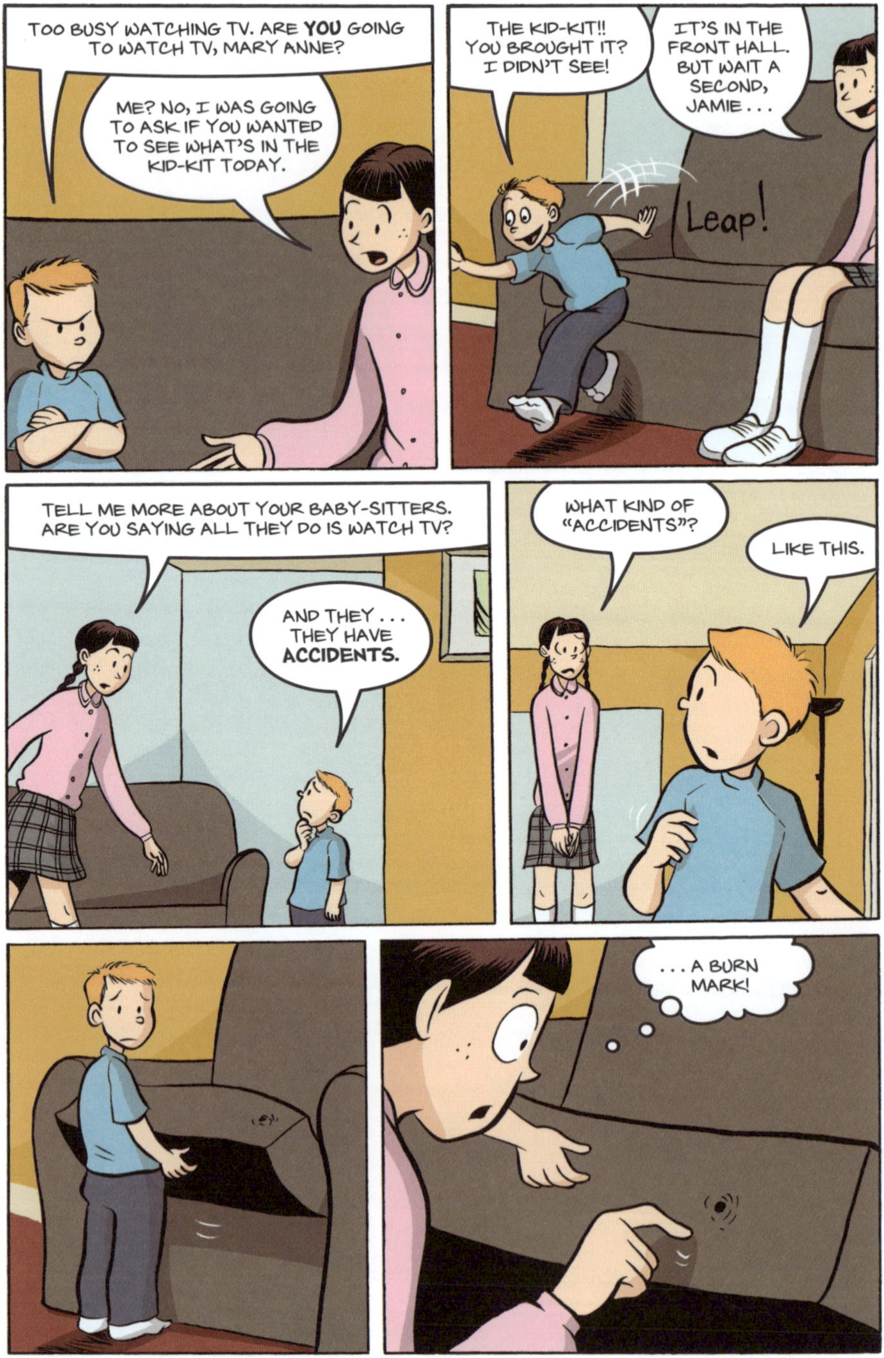
TOO BUSY WATCHING TV. ARE **YOU** GOING TO WATCH TV, MARY ANNE?
ME? NO, I WAS GOING TO ASK IF YOU WANTED TO SEE WHAT'S IN THE KID-KIT TODAY.
THE KID-KIT!! YOU BROUGHT IT? I DIDN'T SEE!
IT'S IN THE FRONT HALL. BUT WAIT A SECOND, JAMIE . . .
Leap!
TELL ME MORE ABOUT YOUR BABY-SITTERS. ARE YOU SAYING ALL THEY DO IS WATCH TV?
AND THEY . . . THEY HAVE **ACCIDENTS.**
WHAT KIND OF "ACCIDENTS"?
LIKE THIS.
. . . A BURN MARK!

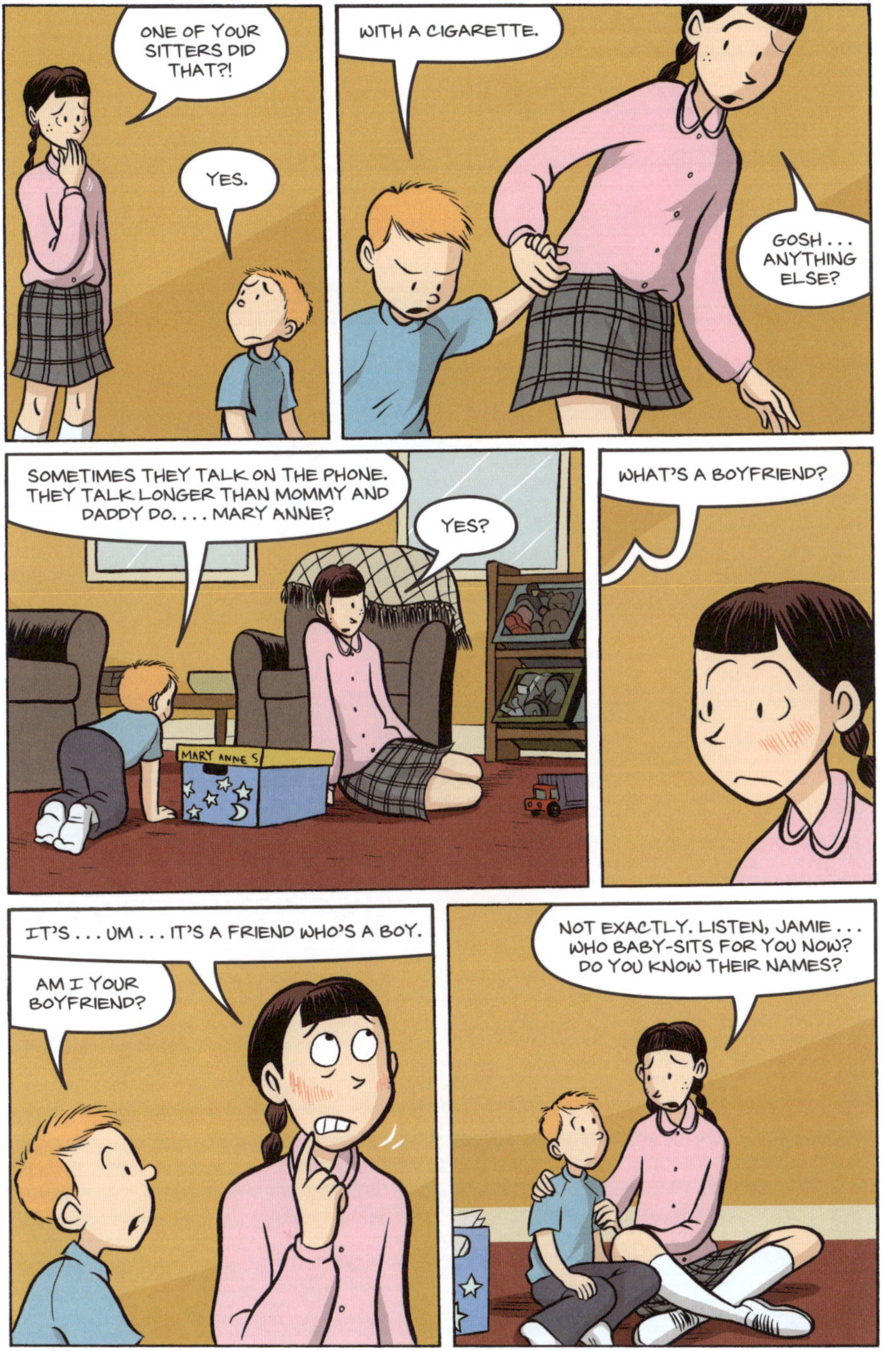
ONE OF YOUR SITTERS DID THAT?!
YES.
WITH A CIGARETTE.
GOSH . . . ANYTHING ELSE?
SOMETIMES THEY TALK ON THE PHONE. THEY TALK LONGER THAN MOMMY AND DADDY DO. . . . MARY ANNE?
YES?
MARY ANNE'S
WHAT'S A BOYFRIEND?
IT'S . . . UM . . . IT'S A FRIEND WHO'S A BOY.
AM I YOUR BOYFRIEND?
NOT EXACTLY. LISTEN, JAMIE . . . WHO BABY-SITS FOR YOU NOW? DO YOU KNOW THEIR NAMES?

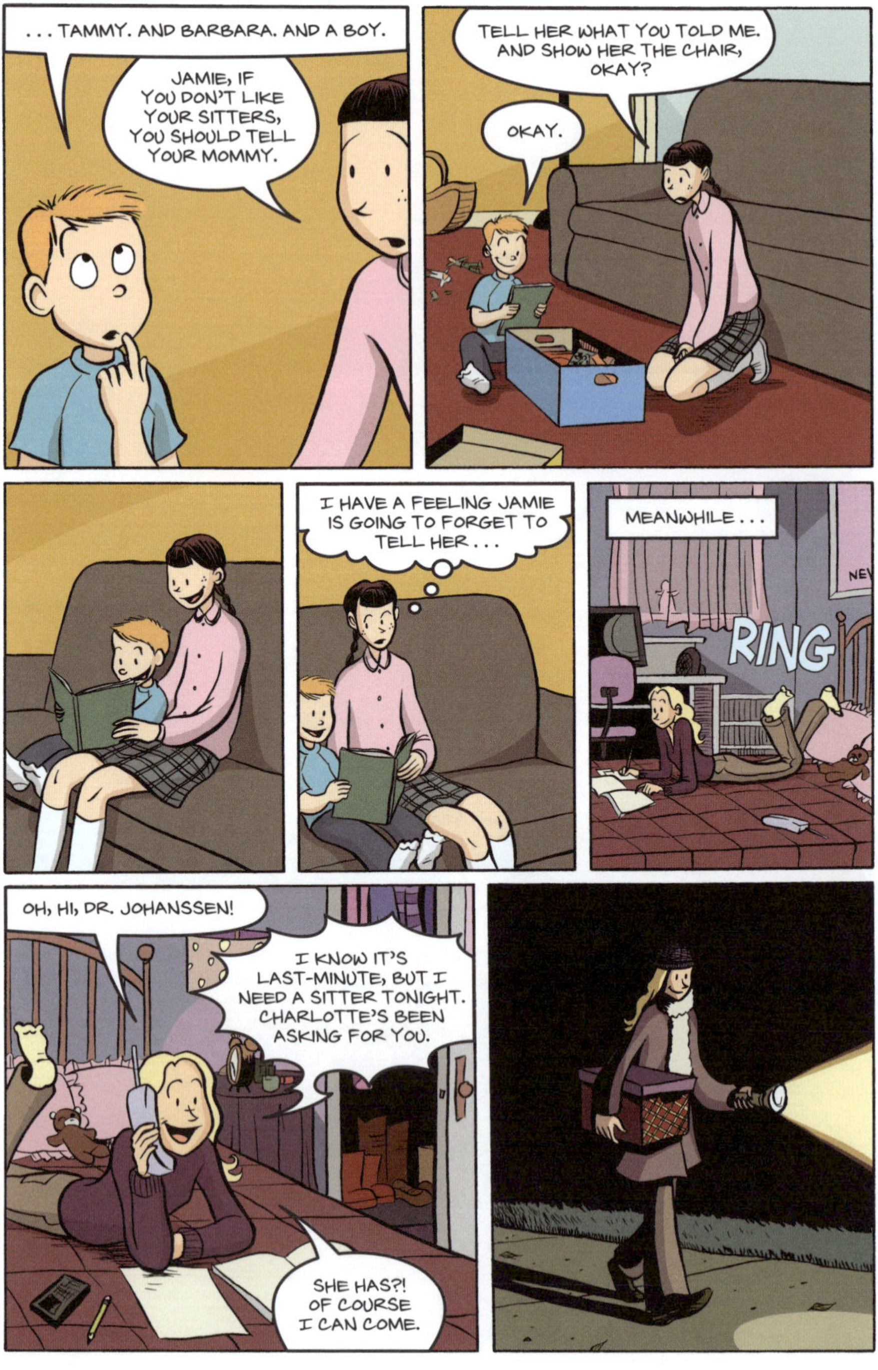

. . . TAMMY. AND BARBARA. AND A BOY.
JAMIE, IF YOU DON'T LIKE YOUR SITTERS, YOU SHOULD TELL YOUR MOMMY.
TELL HER WHAT YOU TOLD ME. AND SHOW HER THE CHAIR, OKAY?
OKAY.
I HAVE A FEELING JAMIE IS GOING TO FORGET TO TELL HER . . .
MEANWHILE . . .
RING
OH, HI, DR. JOHANSSEN!
I KNOW IT'S LAST-MINUTE, BUT I NEED A SITTER TONIGHT. CHARLOTTE'S BEEN ASKING FOR YOU.
SHE HAS?! OF COURSE I CAN COME.

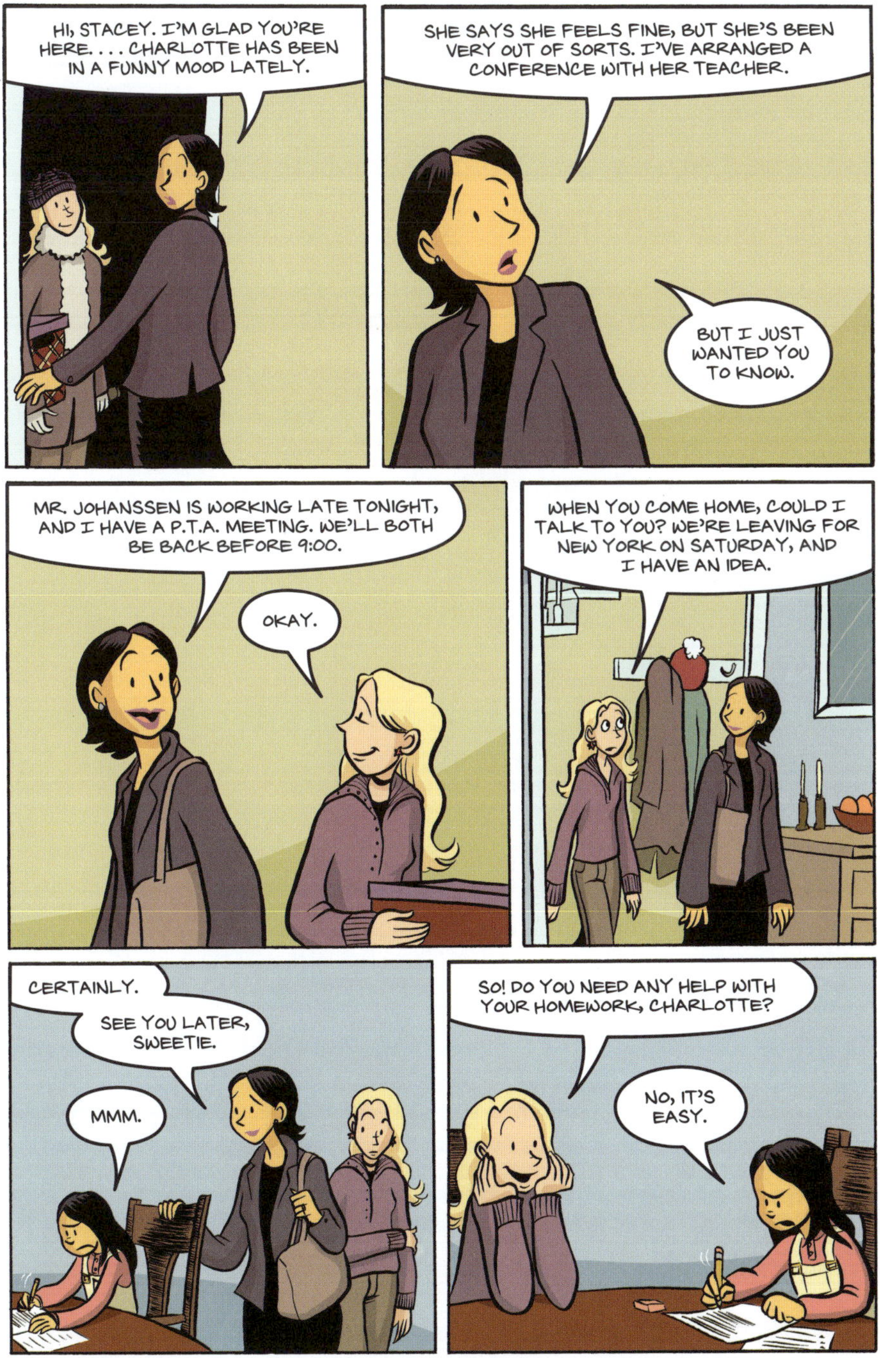
HI, STACEY. I'M GLAD YOU'RE HERE. . . . CHARLOTTE HAS BEEN IN A FUNNY MOOD LATELY.
SHE SAYS SHE FEELS FINE, BUT SHE'S BEEN VERY OUT OF SORTS. I'VE ARRANGED A CONFERENCE WITH HER TEACHER.
BUT I JUST WANTED YOU TO KNOW.
MR. JOHANSSEN IS WORKING LATE TONIGHT, AND I HAVE A P.T.A. MEETING. WE'LL BOTH BE BACK BEFORE 9:00.
OKAY.
WHEN YOU COME HOME, COULD I TALK TO YOU? WE'RE LEAVING FOR NEW YORK ON SATURDAY, AND I HAVE AN IDEA.
CERTAINLY.
SEE YOU LATER, SWEETIE.
MMM.
SO! DO YOU NEED ANY HELP WITH YOUR HOMEWORK, CHARLOTTE?
NO, IT'S EASY.

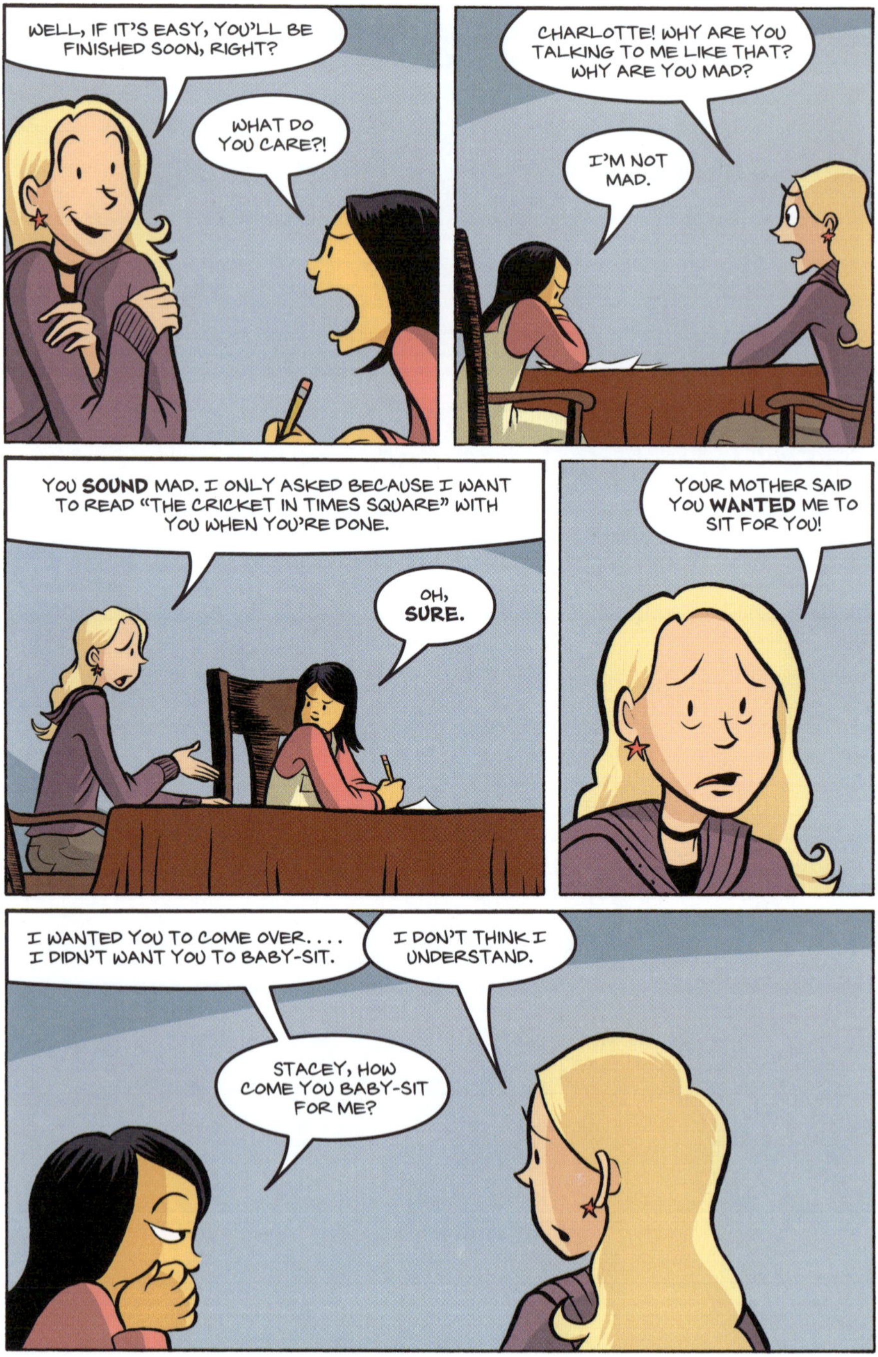
WELL, IF IT'S EASY, YOU'LL BE FINISHED SOON, RIGHT?
WHAT DO YOU CARE?!
CHARLOTTE! WHY ARE YOU TALKING TO ME LIKE THAT? WHY ARE YOU MAD?
I'M NOT MAD.
YOU **SOUND** MAD. I ONLY ASKED BECAUSE I WANT TO READ "THE CRICKET IN TIMES SQUARE" WITH YOU WHEN YOU'RE DONE.
OH, **SURE.**
YOUR MOTHER SAID YOU **WANTED** ME TO SIT FOR YOU!
I WANTED YOU TO COME OVER. . . . I DIDN'T WANT YOU TO BABY-SIT.
I DON'T THINK I UNDERSTAND.
STACEY, HOW COME YOU BABY-SIT FOR ME?

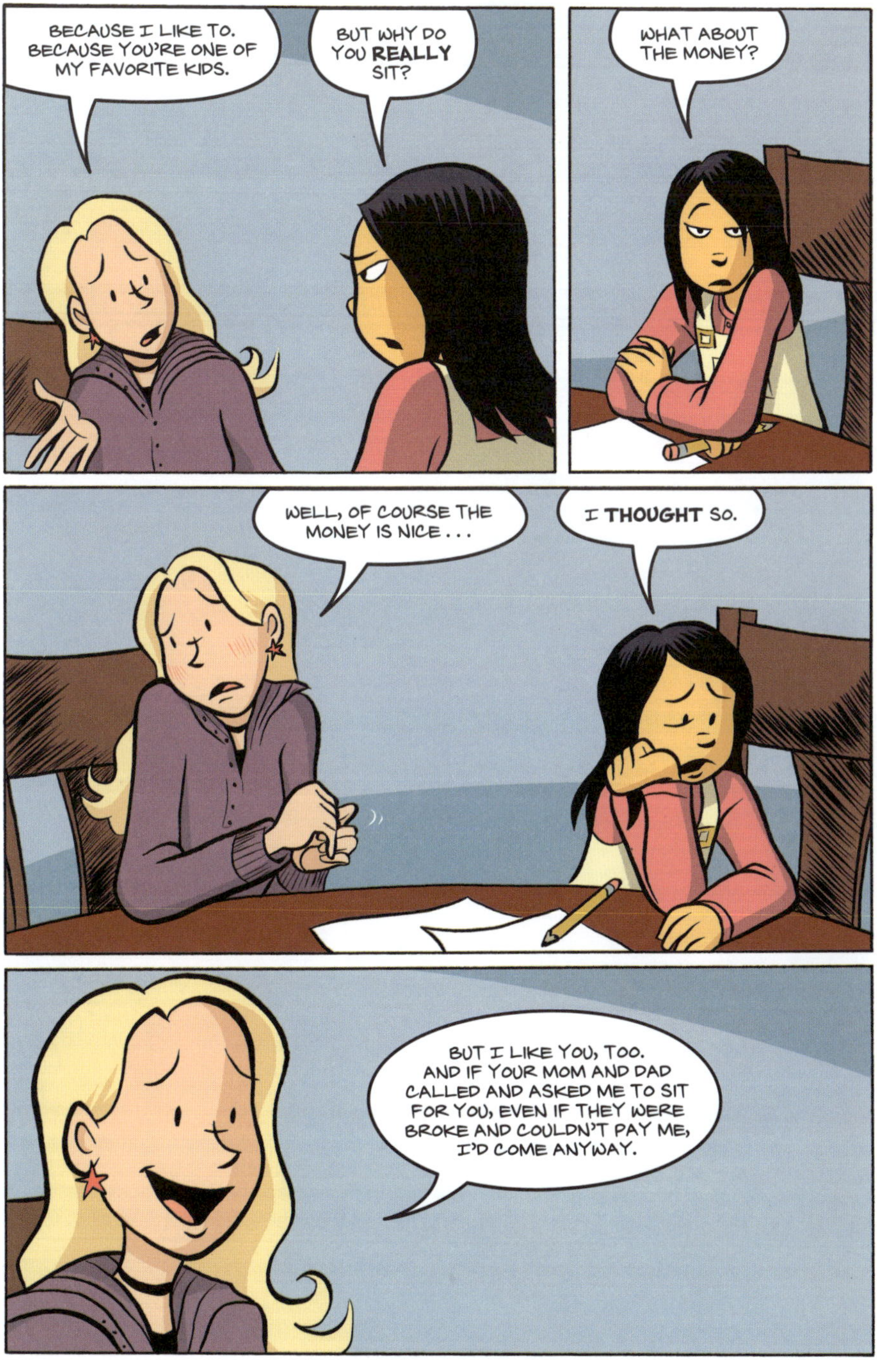
BECAUSE I LIKE TO. BECAUSE YOU'RE ONE OF MY FAVORITE KIDS.
BUT WHY DO YOU **REALLY** SIT?
WHAT ABOUT THE MONEY?
WELL, OF COURSE THE MONEY IS NICE . . .
I **THOUGHT** SO.
BUT I LIKE YOU, TOO. AND IF YOUR MOM AND DAD CALLED AND ASKED ME TO SIT FOR YOU, EVEN IF THEY WERE BROKE AND COULDN'T PAY ME, I'D COME ANYWAY.

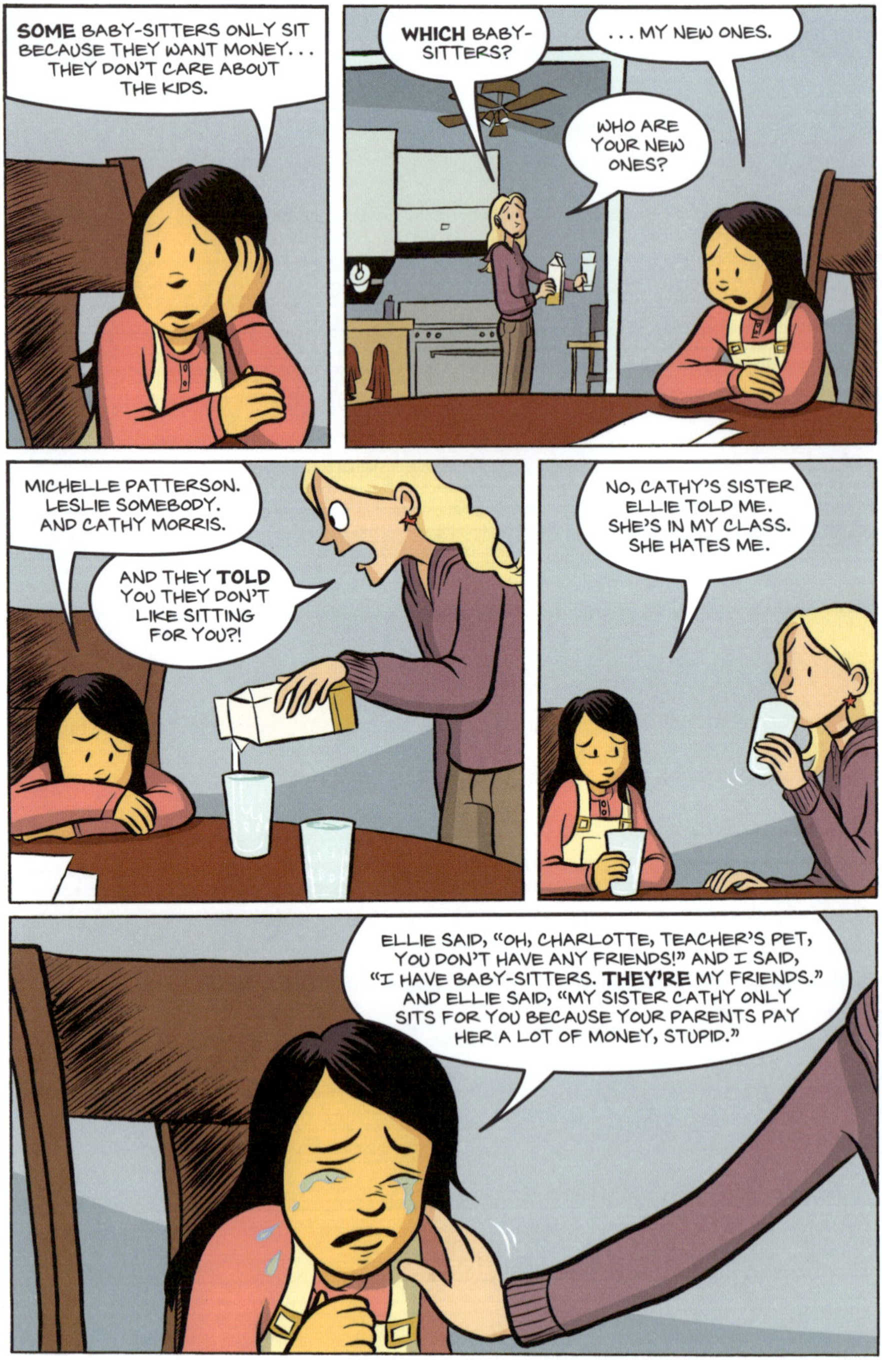

SOME BABY-SITTERS ONLY SIT BECAUSE THEY WANT MONEY... THEY DON'T CARE ABOUT THE KIDS.
WHICH BABY-SITTERS?
... MY NEW ONES.
WHO ARE YOUR NEW ONES?
MICHELLE PATTERSON. LESLIE SOMEBODY. AND CATHY MORRIS.
AND THEY TOLD YOU THEY DON'T LIKE SITTING FOR YOU?!
NO, CATHY'S SISTER ELLIE TOLD ME. SHE'S IN MY CLASS. SHE HATES ME.
ELLIE SAID, "OH, CHARLOTTE, TEACHER'S PET, YOU DON'T HAVE ANY FRIENDS!" AND I SAID, "I HAVE BABY-SITTERS. THEY'RE MY FRIENDS." AND ELLIE SAID, "MY SISTER CATHY ONLY SITS FOR YOU BECAUSE YOUR PARENTS PAY HER A LOT OF MONEY, STUPID."

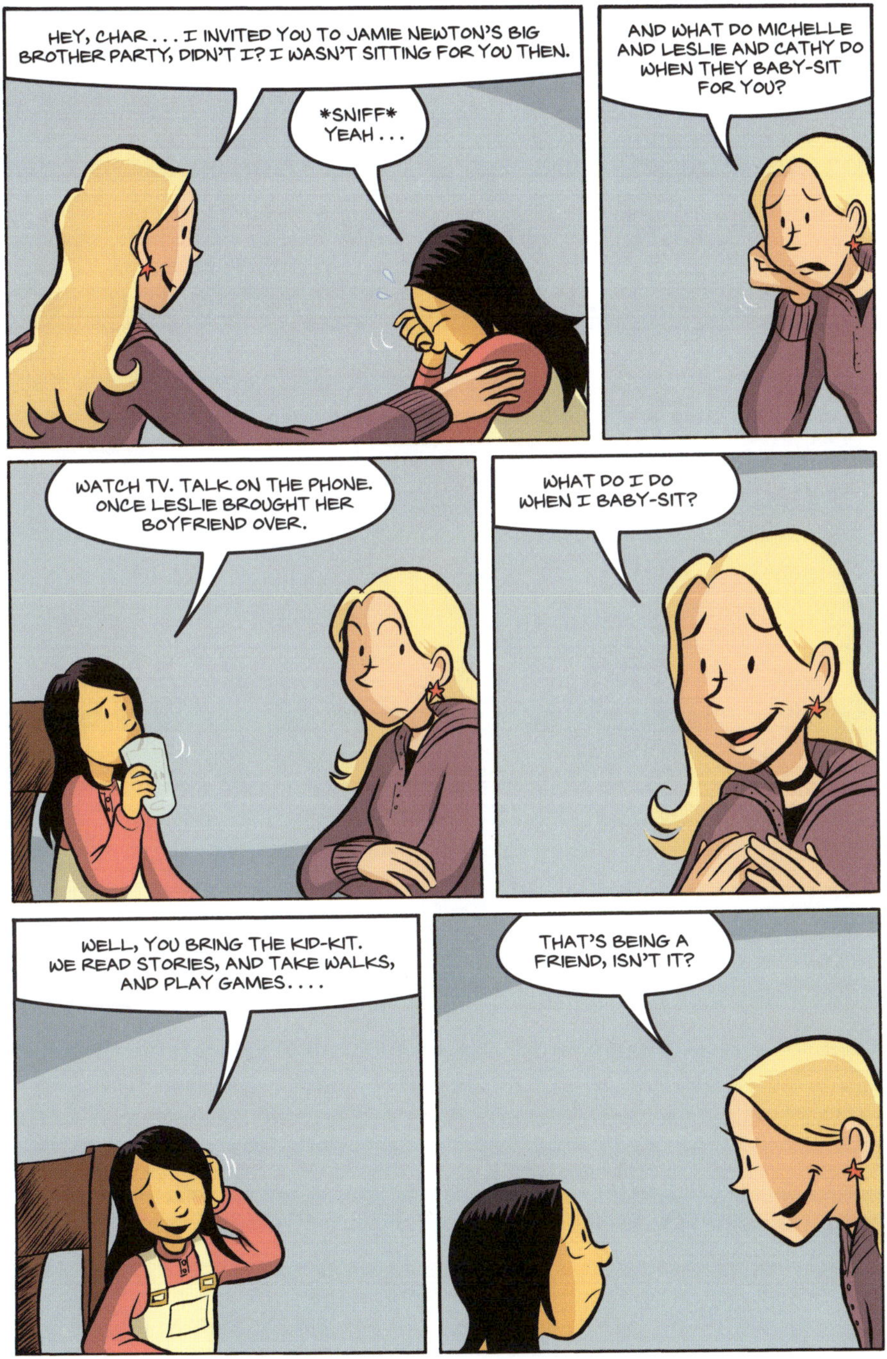
HEY, CHAR . . . I INVITED YOU TO JAMIE NEWTON'S BIG BROTHER PARTY, DIDN'T I? I WASN'T SITTING FOR YOU THEN.
SNIFF YEAH . . .
AND WHAT DO MICHELLE AND LESLIE AND CATHY DO WHEN THEY BABY-SIT FOR YOU?
WATCH TV. TALK ON THE PHONE. ONCE LESLIE BROUGHT HER BOYFRIEND OVER.
WHAT DO I DO WHEN I BABY-SIT?
WELL, YOU BRING THE KID-KIT. WE READ STORIES, AND TAKE WALKS, AND PLAY GAMES. . . .
THAT'S BEING A FRIEND, ISN'T IT?

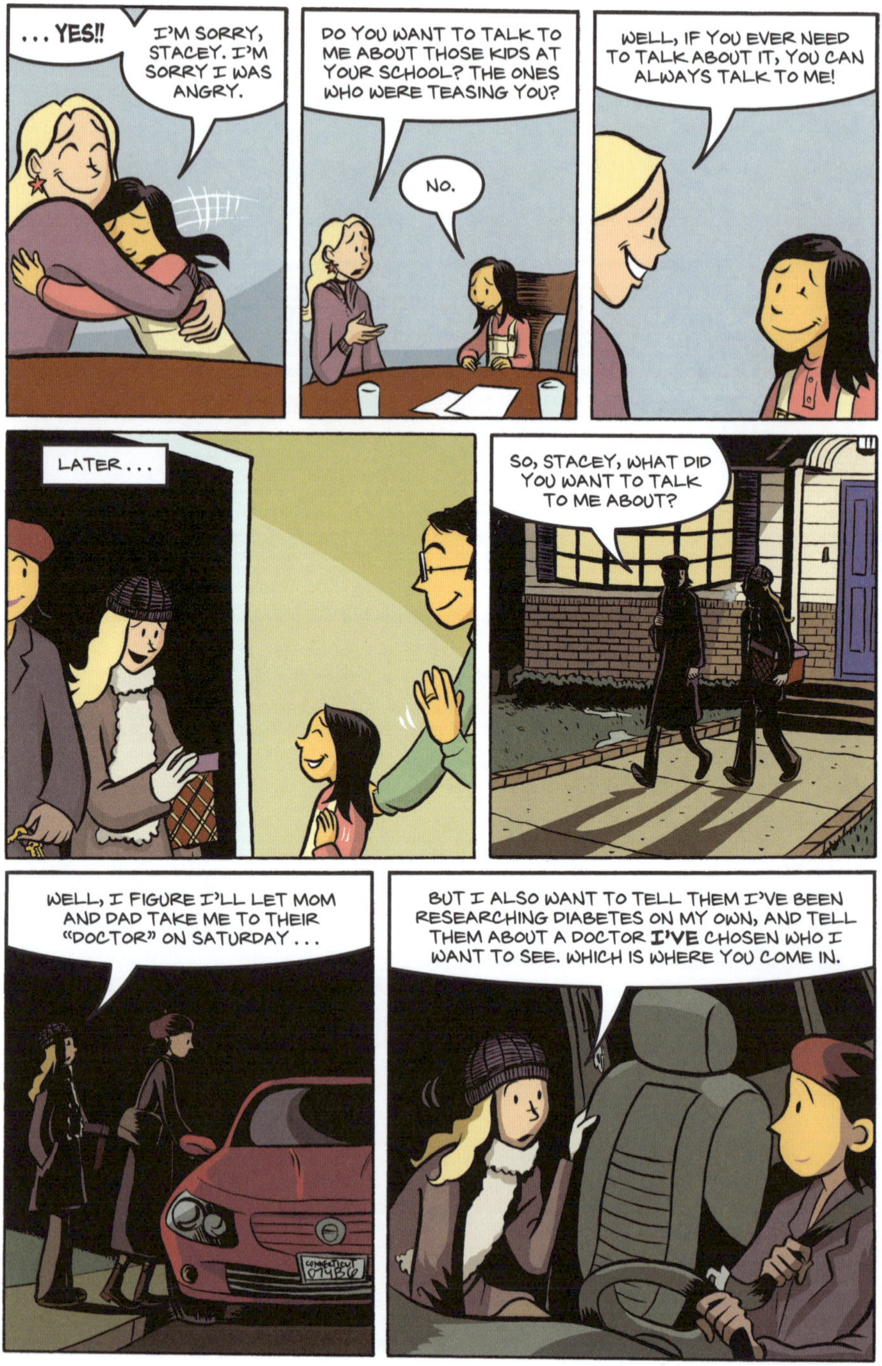

. . . YES!!
I'M SORRY, STACEY. I'M SORRY I WAS ANGRY.
DO YOU WANT TO TALK TO ME ABOUT THOSE KIDS AT YOUR SCHOOL? THE ONES WHO WERE TEASING YOU?
NO.
WELL, IF YOU EVER NEED TO TALK ABOUT IT, YOU CAN ALWAYS TALK TO ME!
LATER . . .
SO, STACEY, WHAT DID YOU WANT TO TALK TO ME ABOUT?
WELL, I FIGURE I'LL LET MOM AND DAD TAKE ME TO THEIR "DOCTOR" ON SATURDAY . . .
BUT I ALSO WANT TO TELL THEM I'VE BEEN RESEARCHING DIABETES ON MY OWN, AND TELL THEM ABOUT A DOCTOR **I'VE** CHOSEN WHO I WANT TO SEE. WHICH IS WHERE YOU COME IN.

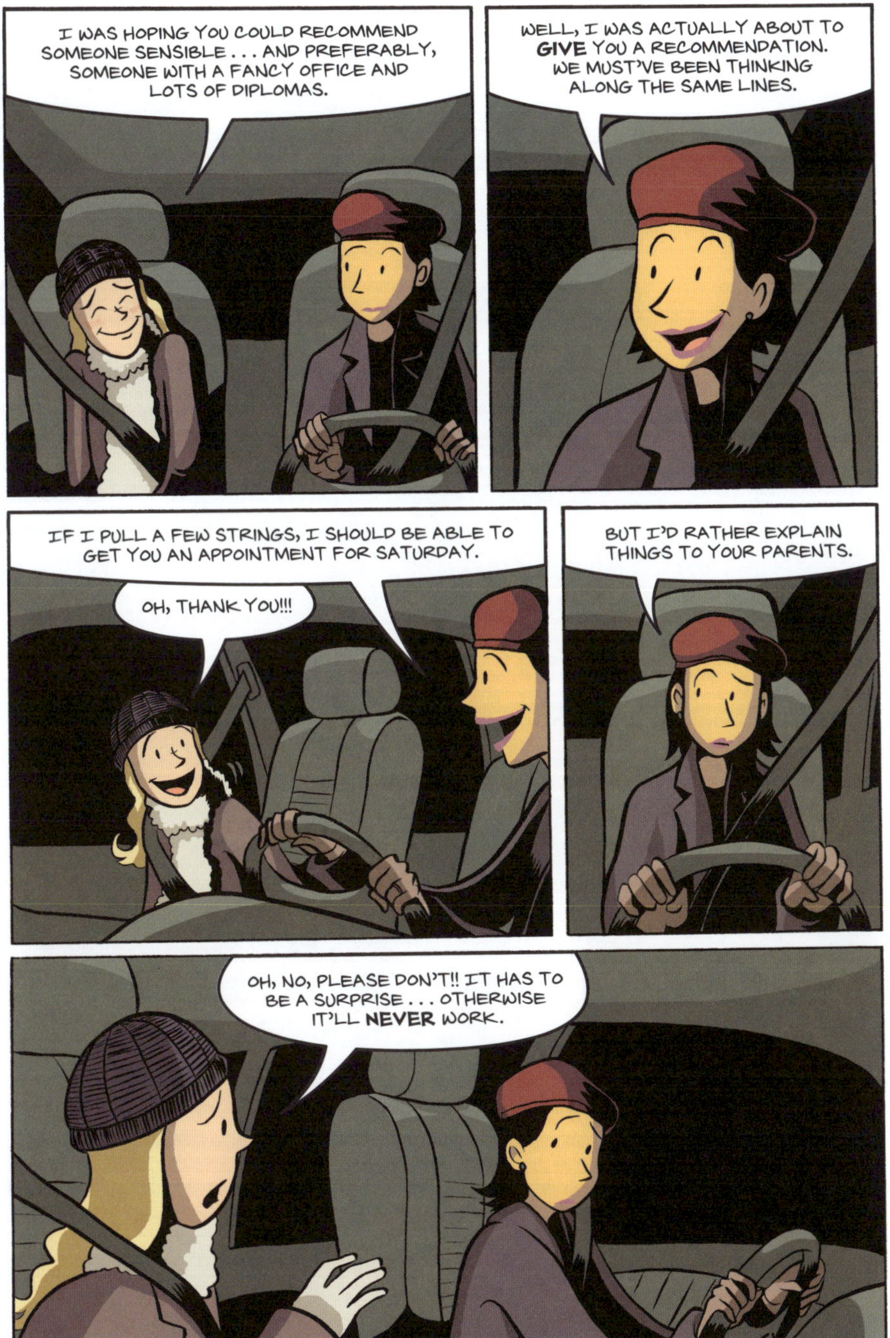
I WAS HOPING YOU COULD RECOMMEND SOMEONE SENSIBLE . . . AND PREFERABLY, SOMEONE WITH A FANCY OFFICE AND LOTS OF DIPLOMAS.
WELL, I WAS ACTUALLY ABOUT TO **GIVE** YOU A RECOMMENDATION. WE MUST'VE BEEN THINKING ALONG THE SAME LINES.
IF I PULL A FEW STRINGS, I SHOULD BE ABLE TO GET YOU AN APPOINTMENT FOR SATURDAY.
OH, THANK YOU!!!
BUT I'D RATHER EXPLAIN THINGS TO YOUR PARENTS.
OH, NO, PLEASE DON'T!! IT HAS TO BE A SURPRISE . . . OTHERWISE IT'LL **NEVER** WORK.

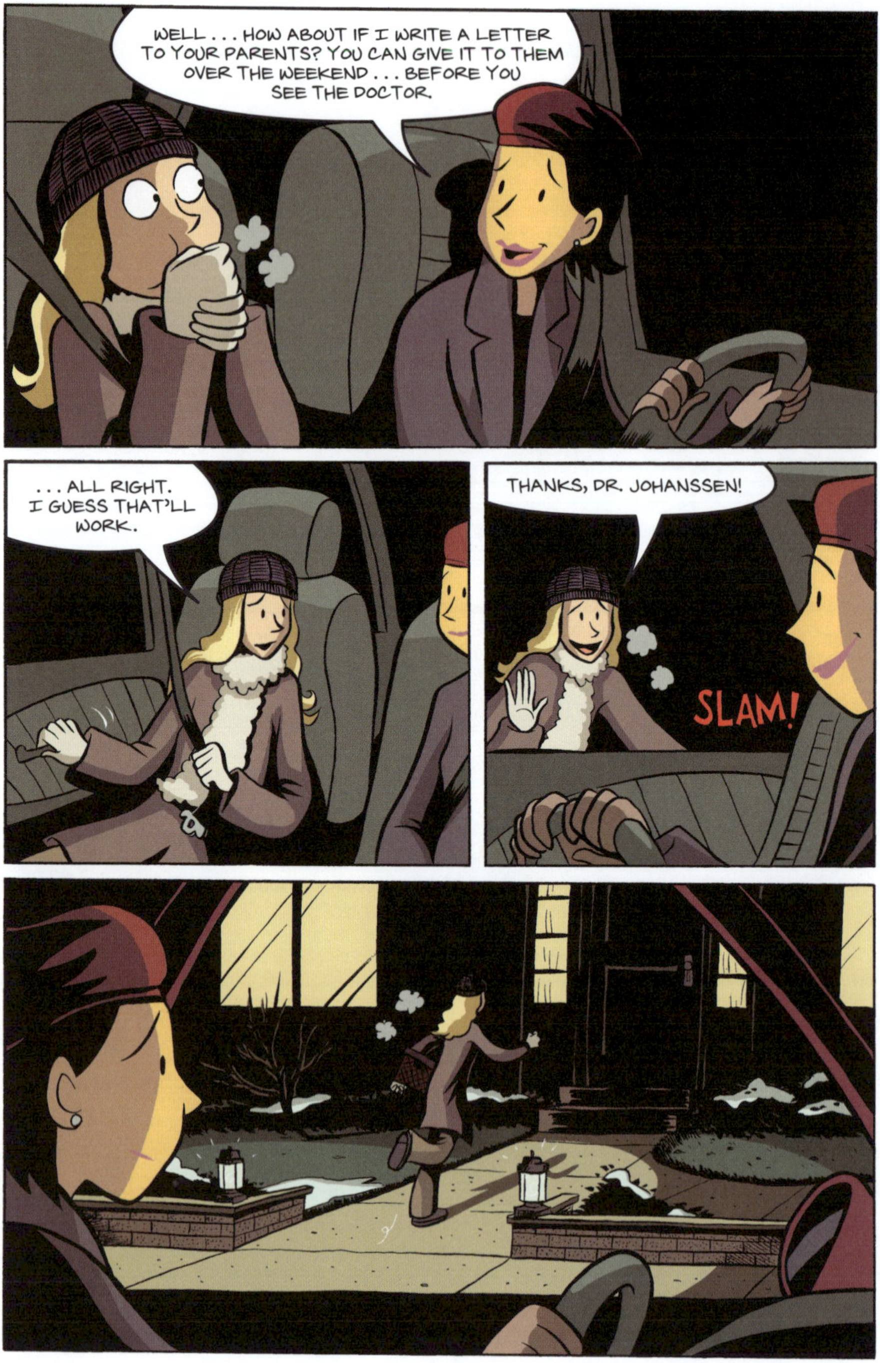
WELL . . . HOW ABOUT IF I WRITE A LETTER TO YOUR PARENTS? YOU CAN GIVE IT TO THEM OVER THE WEEKEND . . . BEFORE YOU SEE THE DOCTOR.
. . . ALL RIGHT. I GUESS THAT'LL WORK.
THANKS, DR. JOHANSSEN!
SLAM!

CHAPTER 12

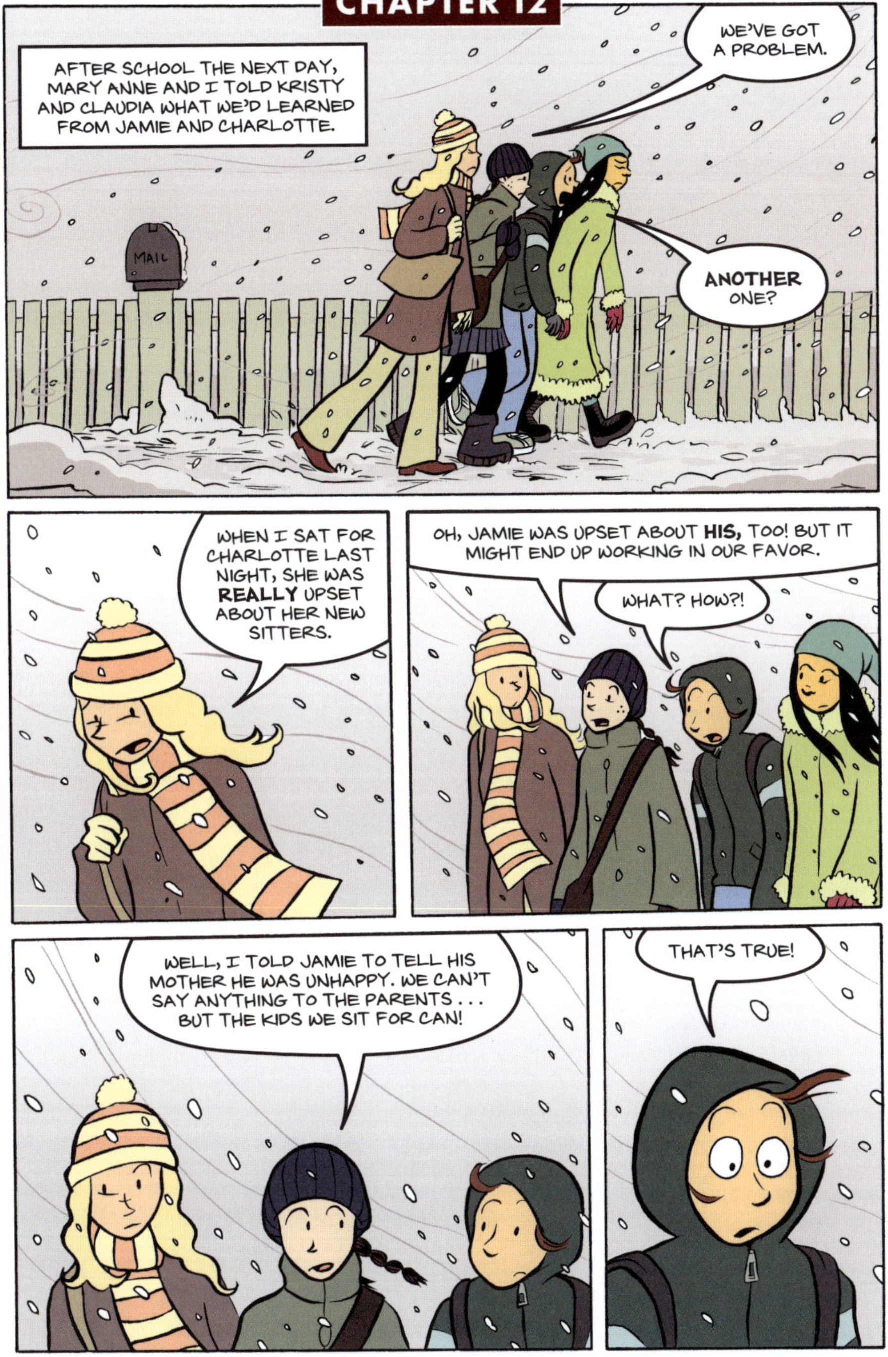
AFTER SCHOOL THE NEXT DAY, MARY ANNE AND I TOLD KRISTY AND CLAUDIA WHAT WE'D LEARNED FROM JAMIE AND CHARLOTTE.
WE'VE GOT A PROBLEM.
ANOTHER ONE?
WHEN I SAT FOR CHARLOTTE LAST NIGHT, SHE WAS REALLY UPSET ABOUT HER NEW SITTERS.
OH, JAMIE WAS UPSET ABOUT HIS, TOO! BUT IT MIGHT END UP WORKING IN OUR FAVOR.
WHAT? HOW?!
WELL, I TOLD JAMIE TO TELL HIS MOTHER HE WAS UNHAPPY. WE CAN'T SAY ANYTHING TO THE PARENTS . . . BUT THE KIDS WE SIT FOR CAN!
THAT'S TRUE!
MAIL

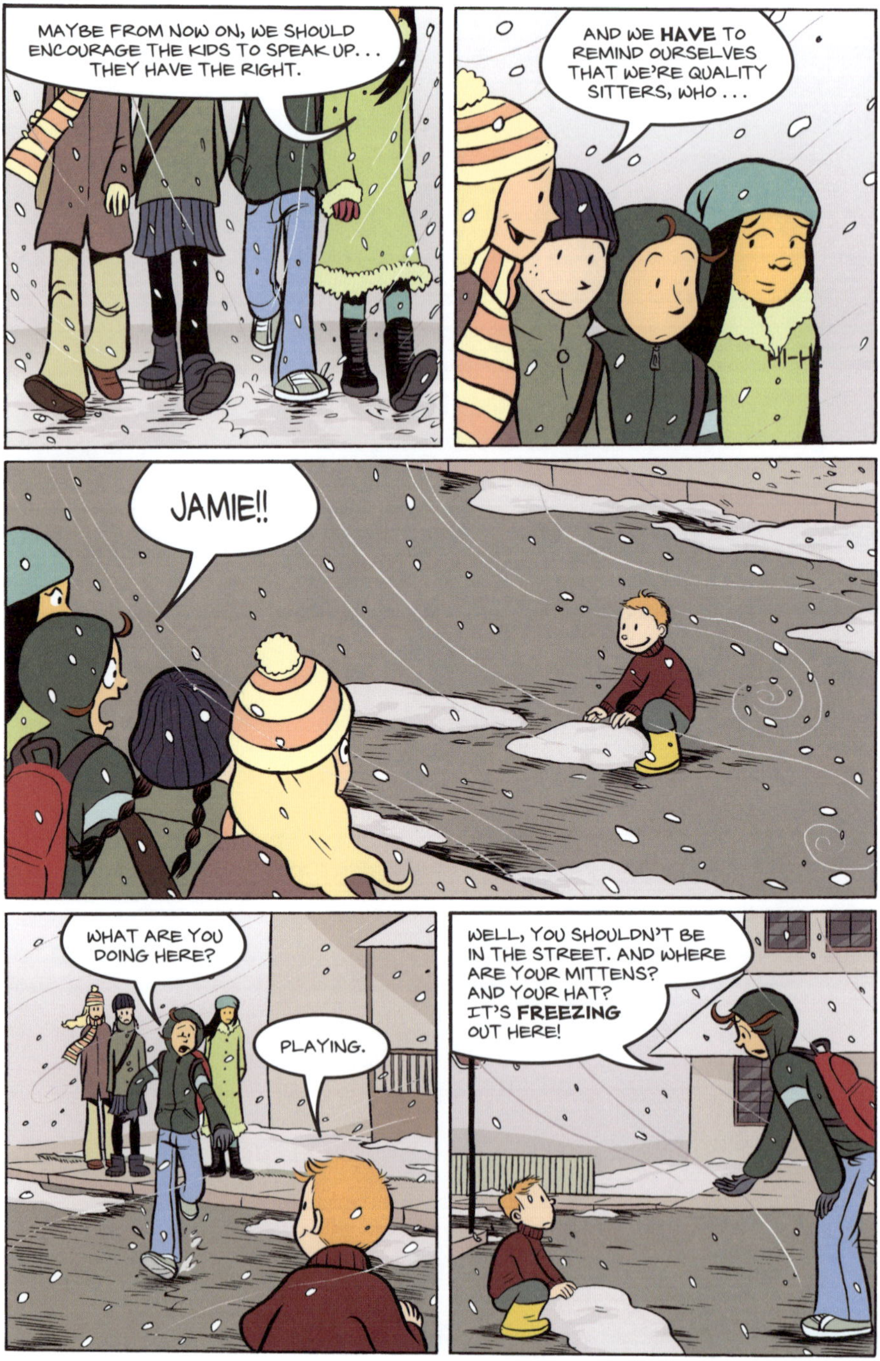
MAYBE FROM NOW ON, WE SHOULD ENCOURAGE THE KIDS TO SPEAK UP... THEY HAVE THE RIGHT.
AND WE **HAVE** TO REMIND OURSELVES THAT WE'RE QUALITY SITTERS, WHO...
HI-HI!
JAMIE!!
WHAT ARE YOU DOING HERE?
PLAYING.
WELL, YOU SHOULDN'T BE IN THE STREET. AND WHERE ARE YOUR MITTENS? AND YOUR HAT? IT'S **FREEZING** OUT HERE!

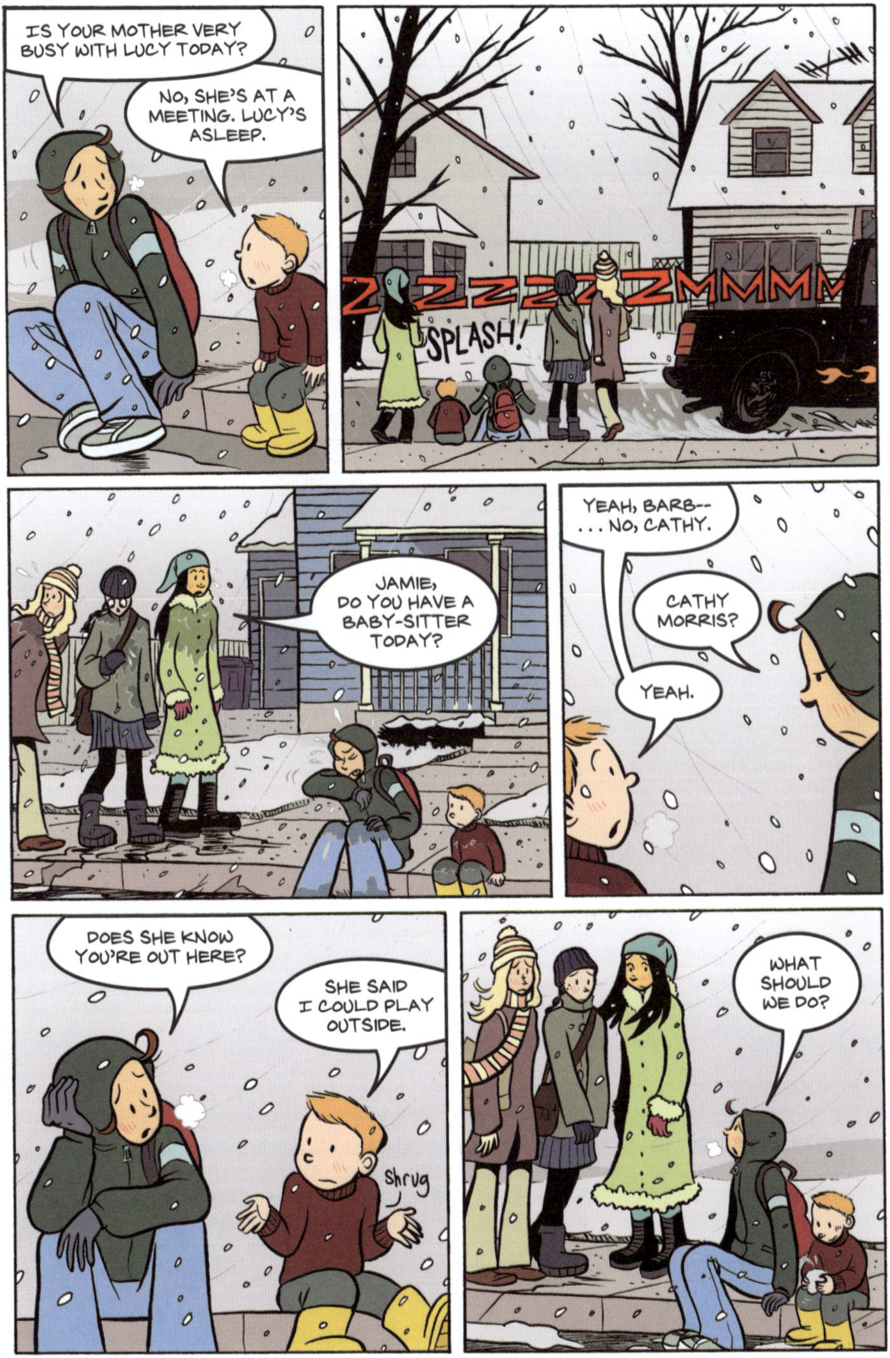
IS YOUR MOTHER VERY BUSY WITH LUCY TODAY?
NO, SHE'S AT A MEETING. LUCY'S ASLEEP.
ZZZZZZZMMMMM
SPLASH!
JAMIE, DO YOU HAVE A BABY-SITTER TODAY?
YEAH, BARB-- . . . NO, CATHY.
CATHY MORRIS?
YEAH.
DOES SHE KNOW YOU'RE OUT HERE?
SHE SAID I COULD PLAY OUTSIDE.
shrug
WHAT SHOULD WE DO?

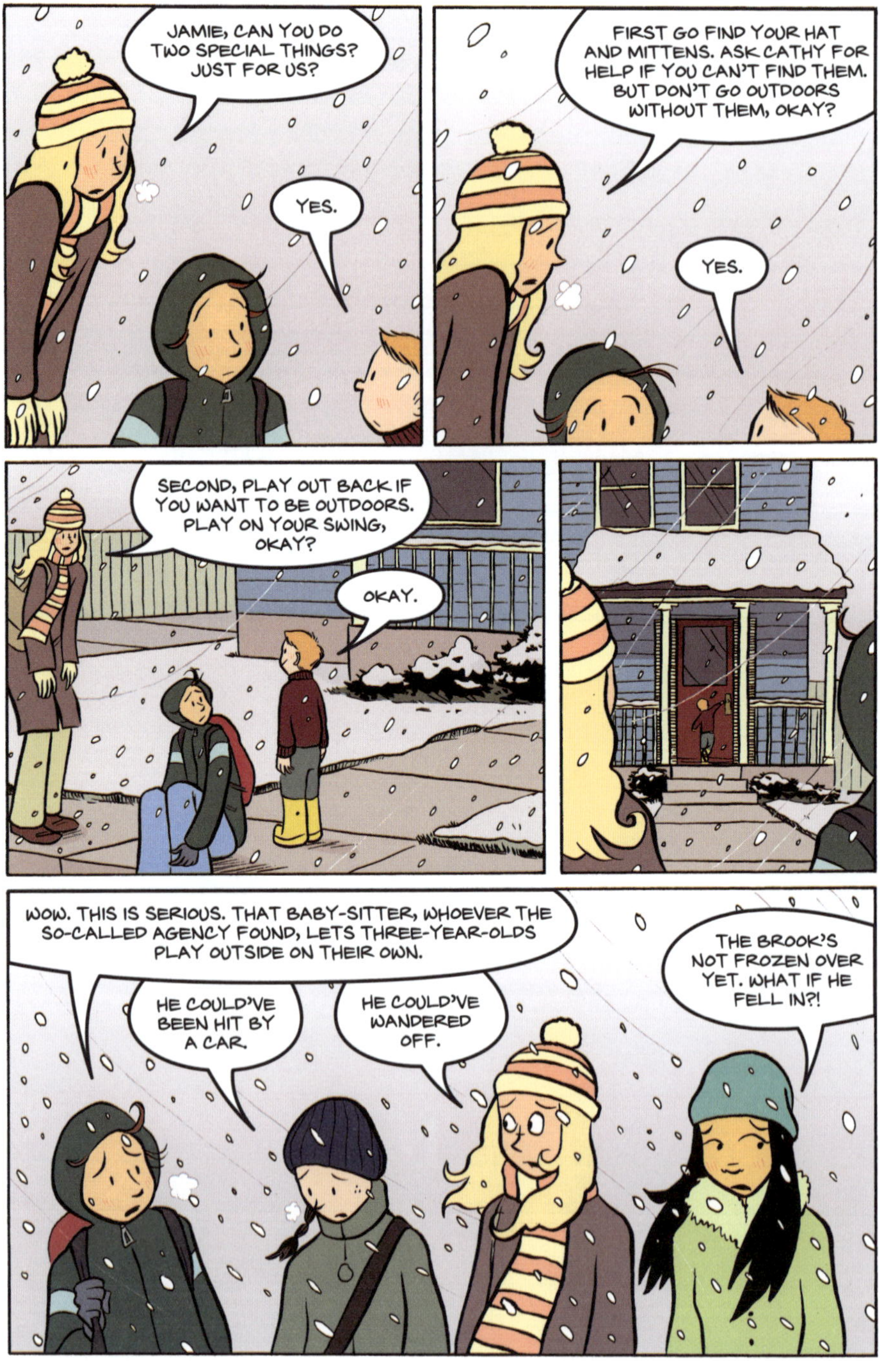
JAMIE, CAN YOU DO TWO SPECIAL THINGS? JUST FOR US?
YES.
FIRST GO FIND YOUR HAT AND MITTENS. ASK CATHY FOR HELP IF YOU CAN'T FIND THEM. BUT DON'T GO OUTDOORS WITHOUT THEM, OKAY?
YES.
SECOND, PLAY OUT BACK IF YOU WANT TO BE OUTDOORS. PLAY ON YOUR SWING, OKAY?
OKAY.
WOW. THIS IS SERIOUS. THAT BABY-SITTER, WHOEVER THE SO-CALLED AGENCY FOUND, LETS THREE-YEAR-OLDS PLAY OUTSIDE ON THEIR OWN.
HE COULD'VE BEEN HIT BY A CAR.
HE COULD'VE WANDERED OFF.
THE BROOK'S NOT FROZEN OVER YET. WHAT IF HE FELL IN?!

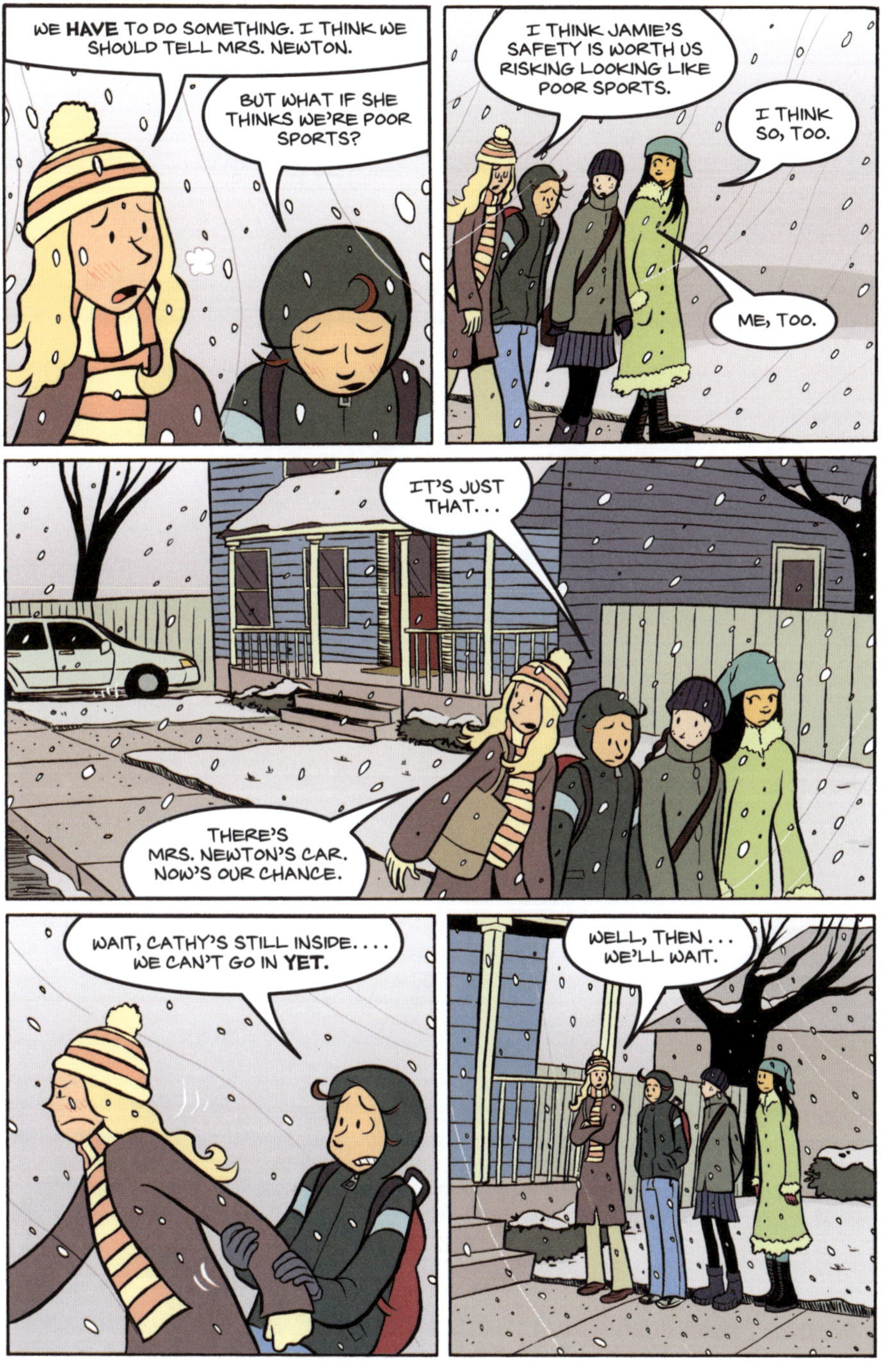
WE HAVE TO DO SOMETHING. I THINK WE SHOULD TELL MRS. NEWTON.
BUT WHAT IF SHE THINKS WE'RE POOR SPORTS?
I THINK JAMIE'S SAFETY IS WORTH US RISKING LOOKING LIKE POOR SPORTS.
I THINK SO, TOO.
ME, TOO.
IT'S JUST THAT. . .
THERE'S MRS. NEWTON'S CAR. NOW'S OUR CHANCE.
WAIT, CATHY'S STILL INSIDE. . . . WE CAN'T GO IN YET.
WELL, THEN . . . WE'LL WAIT.

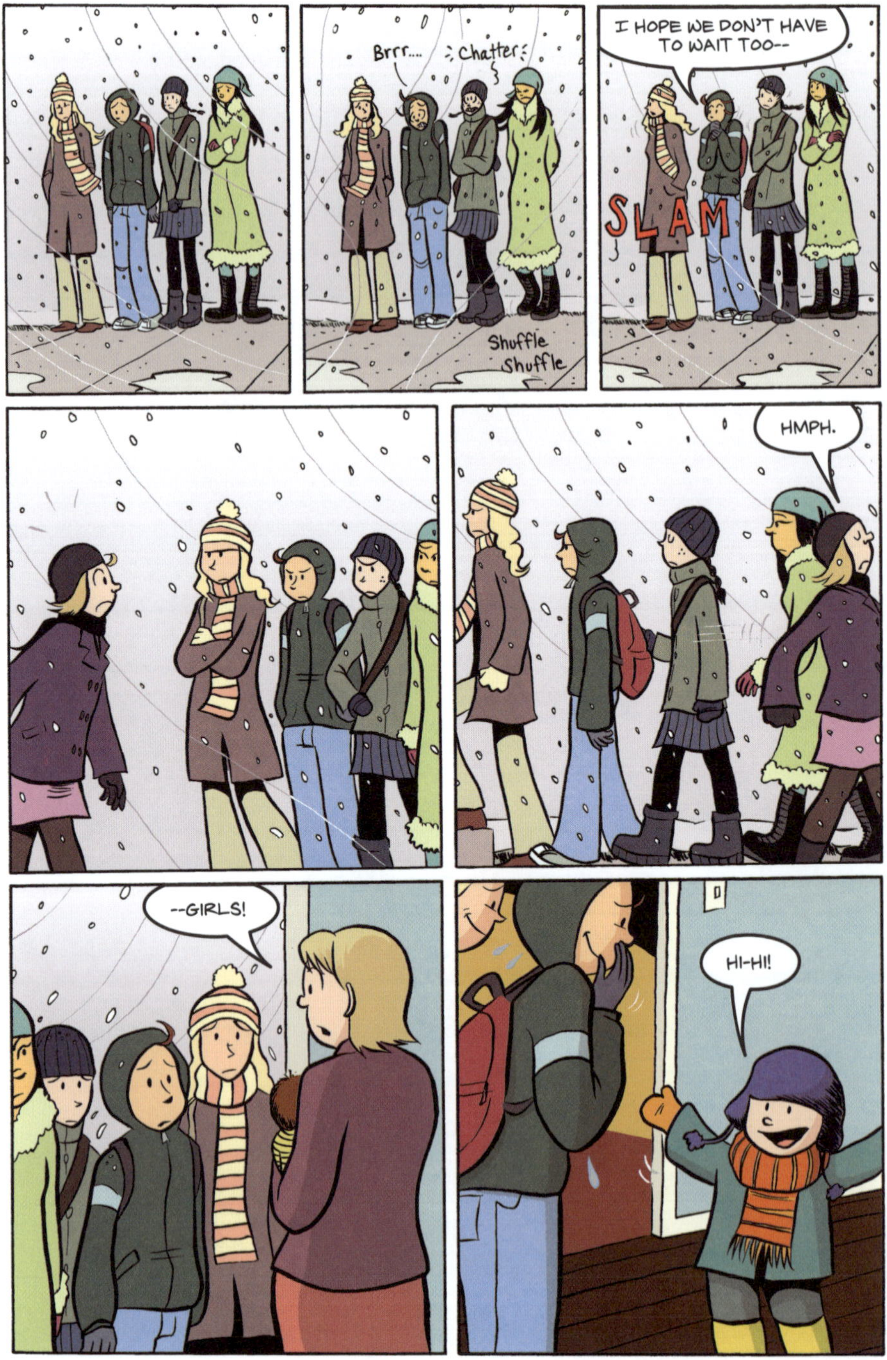
Brrr....
Chatter
Shuffle
Shuffle
I HOPE WE DON'T HAVE TO WAIT TOO--
SLAM
HMPH.
--GIRLS!
HI-HI!

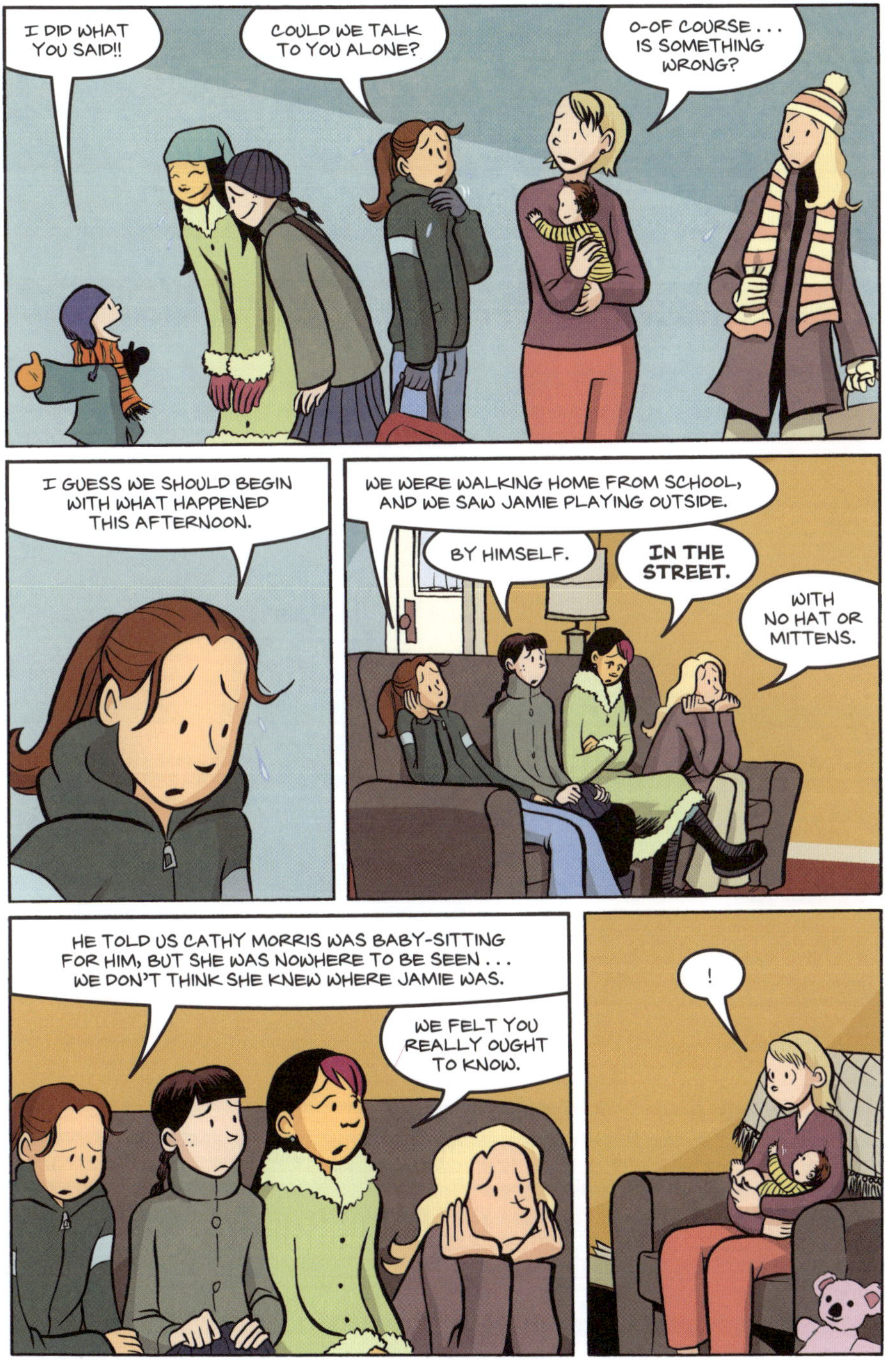
I DID WHAT YOU SAID!!
COULD WE TALK TO YOU ALONE?
O-OF COURSE . . . IS SOMETHING WRONG?
I GUESS WE SHOULD BEGIN WITH WHAT HAPPENED THIS AFTERNOON.
WE WERE WALKING HOME FROM SCHOOL, AND WE SAW JAMIE PLAYING OUTSIDE.
BY HIMSELF.
IN THE STREET.
WITH NO HAT OR MITTENS.
HE TOLD US CATHY MORRIS WAS BABY-SITTING FOR HIM, BUT SHE WAS NOWHERE TO BE SEEN . . . WE DON'T THINK SHE KNEW WHERE JAMIE WAS.
WE FELT YOU REALLY OUGHT TO KNOW.
!

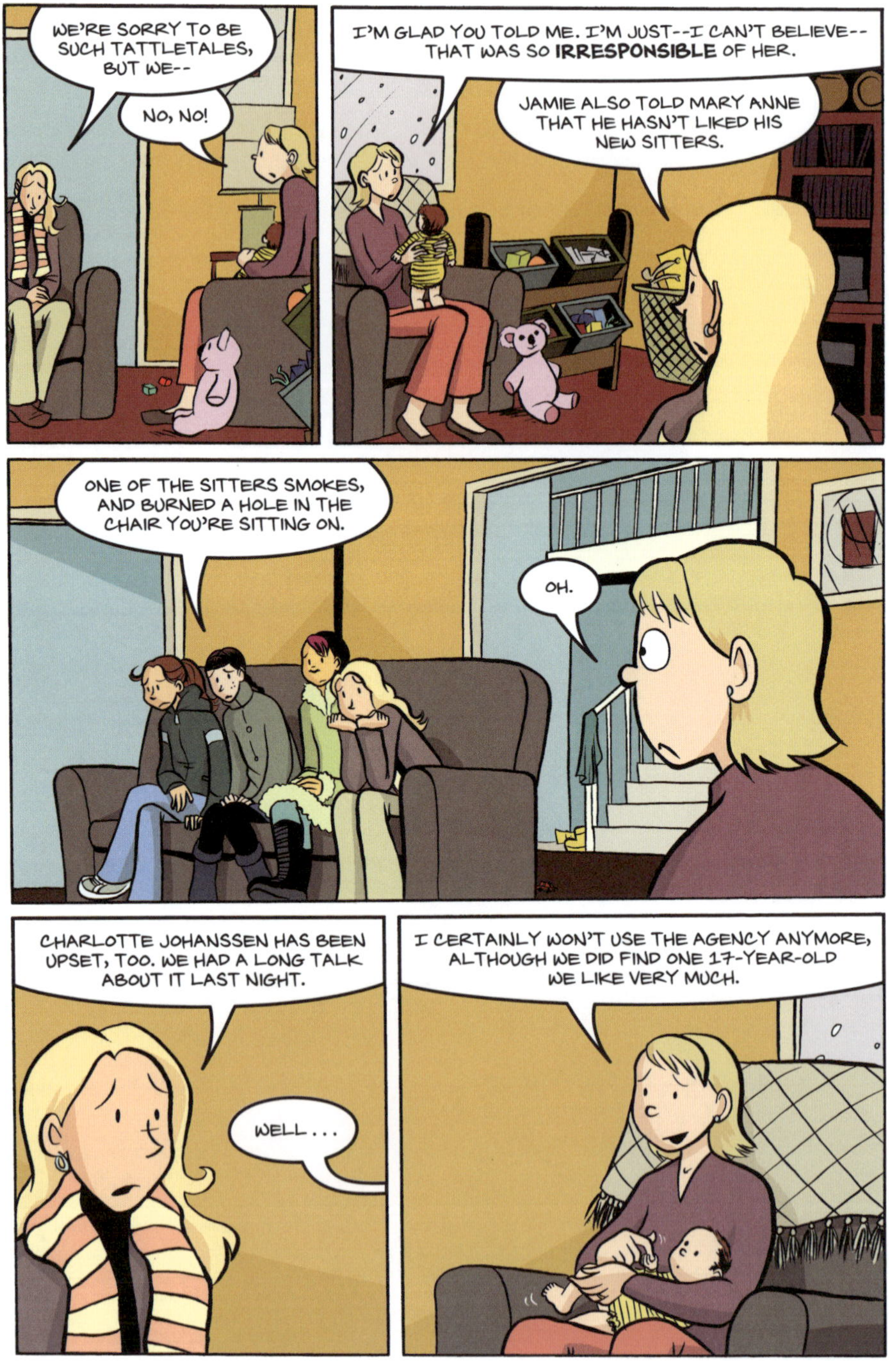
WE'RE SORRY TO BE SUCH TATTLETALES, BUT WE--
NO, NO!
I'M GLAD YOU TOLD ME. I'M JUST--I CAN'T BELIEVE--THAT WAS SO **IRRESPONSIBLE** OF HER.
JAMIE ALSO TOLD MARY ANNE THAT HE HASN'T LIKED HIS NEW SITTERS.
ONE OF THE SITTERS SMOKES, AND BURNED A HOLE IN THE CHAIR YOU'RE SITTING ON.
OH.
CHARLOTTE JOHANSSEN HAS BEEN UPSET, TOO. WE HAD A LONG TALK ABOUT IT LAST NIGHT.
WELL . . .
I CERTAINLY WON'T USE THE AGENCY ANYMORE, ALTHOUGH WE DID FIND ONE 17-YEAR-OLD WE LIKE VERY MUCH.

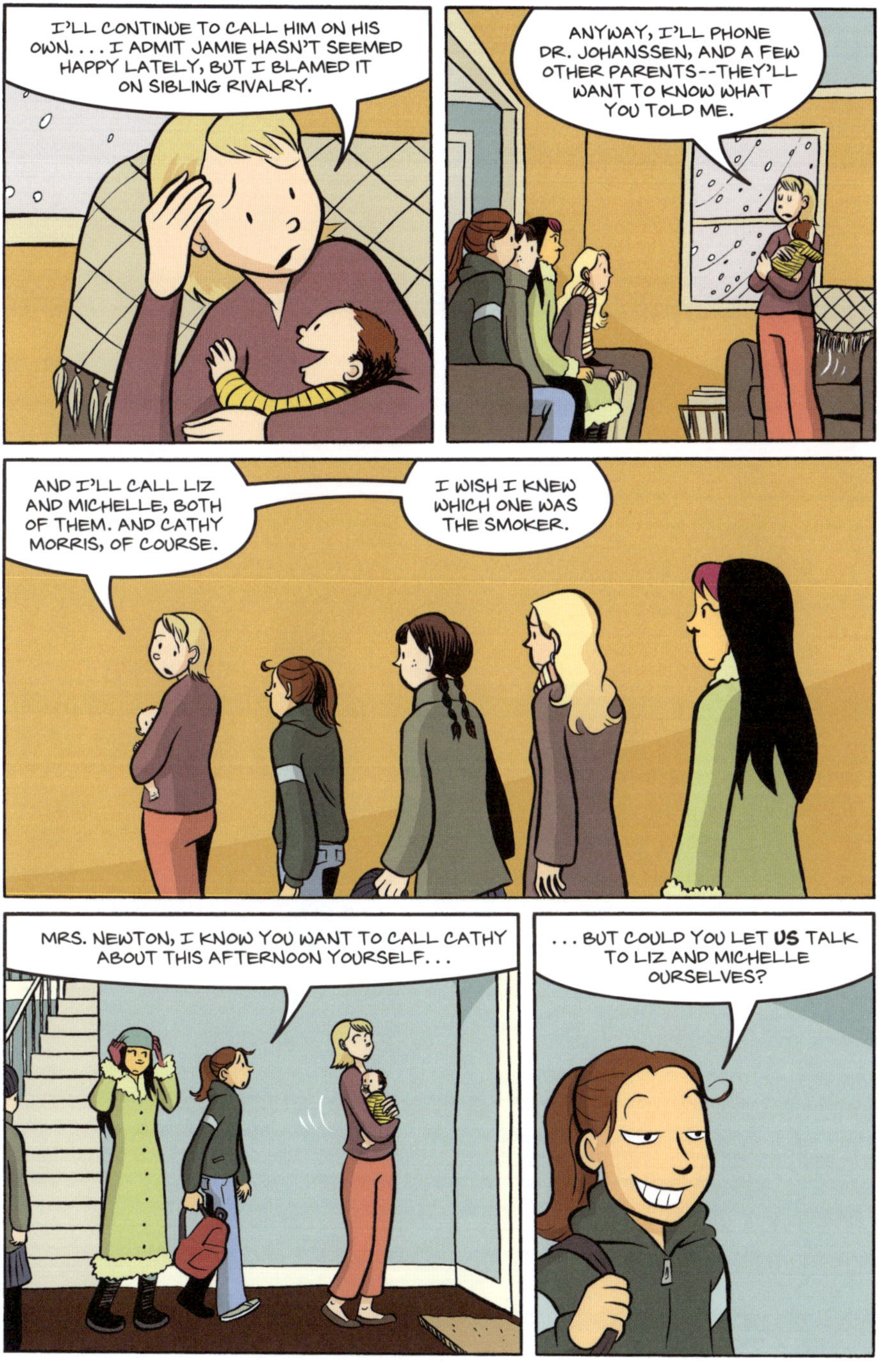
I'LL CONTINUE TO CALL HIM ON HIS OWN. . . . I ADMIT JAMIE HASN'T SEEMED HAPPY LATELY, BUT I BLAMED IT ON SIBLING RIVALRY.
ANYWAY, I'LL PHONE DR. JOHANSSEN, AND A FEW OTHER PARENTS--THEY'LL WANT TO KNOW WHAT YOU TOLD ME.
AND I'LL CALL LIZ AND MICHELLE, BOTH OF THEM. AND CATHY MORRIS, OF COURSE.
I WISH I KNEW WHICH ONE WAS THE SMOKER.
MRS. NEWTON, I KNOW YOU WANT TO CALL CATHY ABOUT THIS AFTERNOON YOURSELF. . .
. . . BUT COULD YOU LET **US** TALK TO LIZ AND MICHELLE OURSELVES?

CHAPTER 13

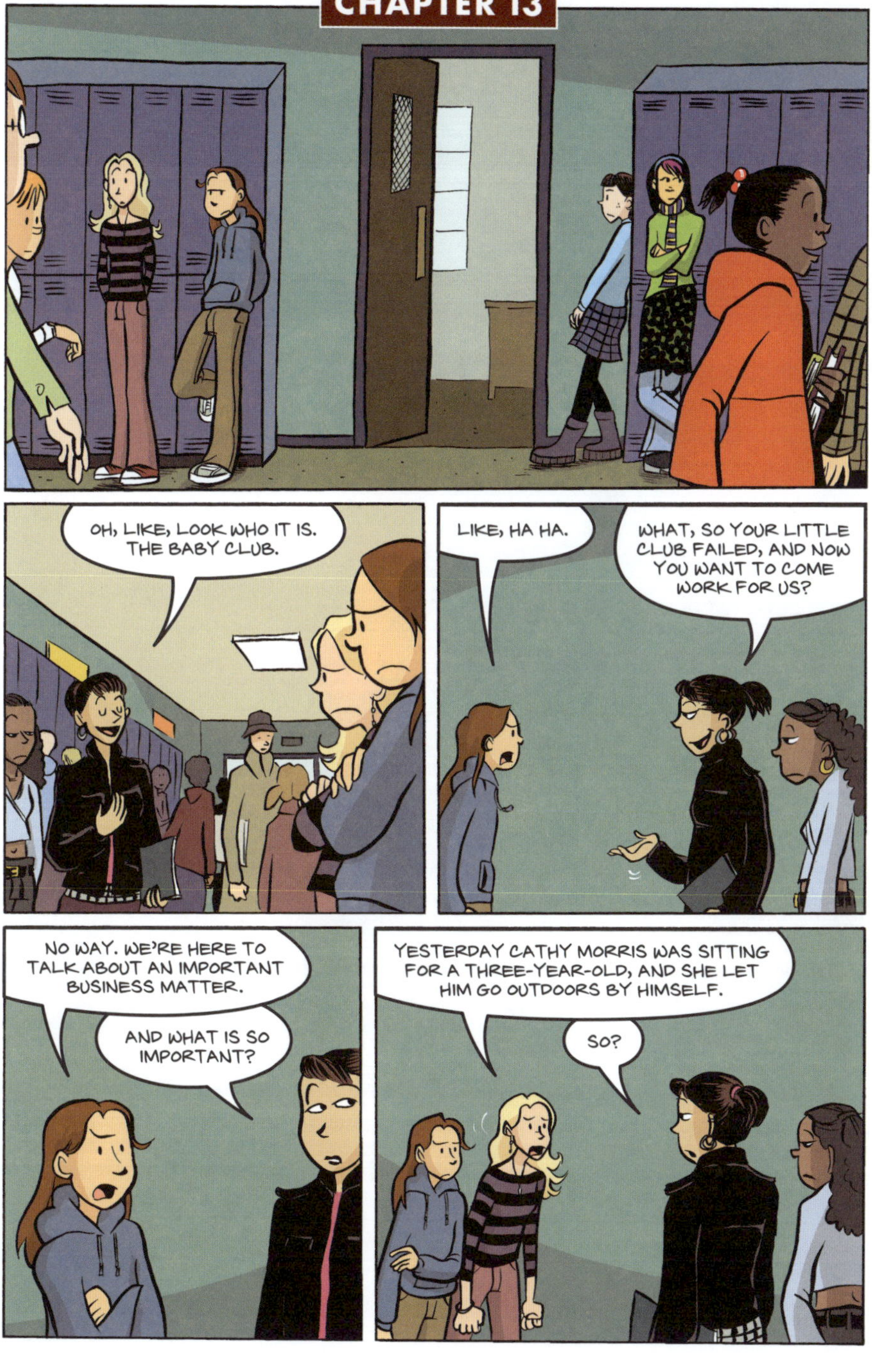

OH, LIKE, LOOK WHO IT IS. THE BABY CLUB.
LIKE, HA HA.
WHAT, SO YOUR LITTLE CLUB FAILED, AND NOW YOU WANT TO COME WORK FOR US?
NO WAY. WE'RE HERE TO TALK ABOUT AN IMPORTANT BUSINESS MATTER.
AND WHAT IS SO IMPORTANT?
YESTERDAY CATHY MORRIS WAS SITTING FOR A THREE-YEAR-OLD, AND SHE LET HIM GO OUTDOORS BY HIMSELF.
SO?

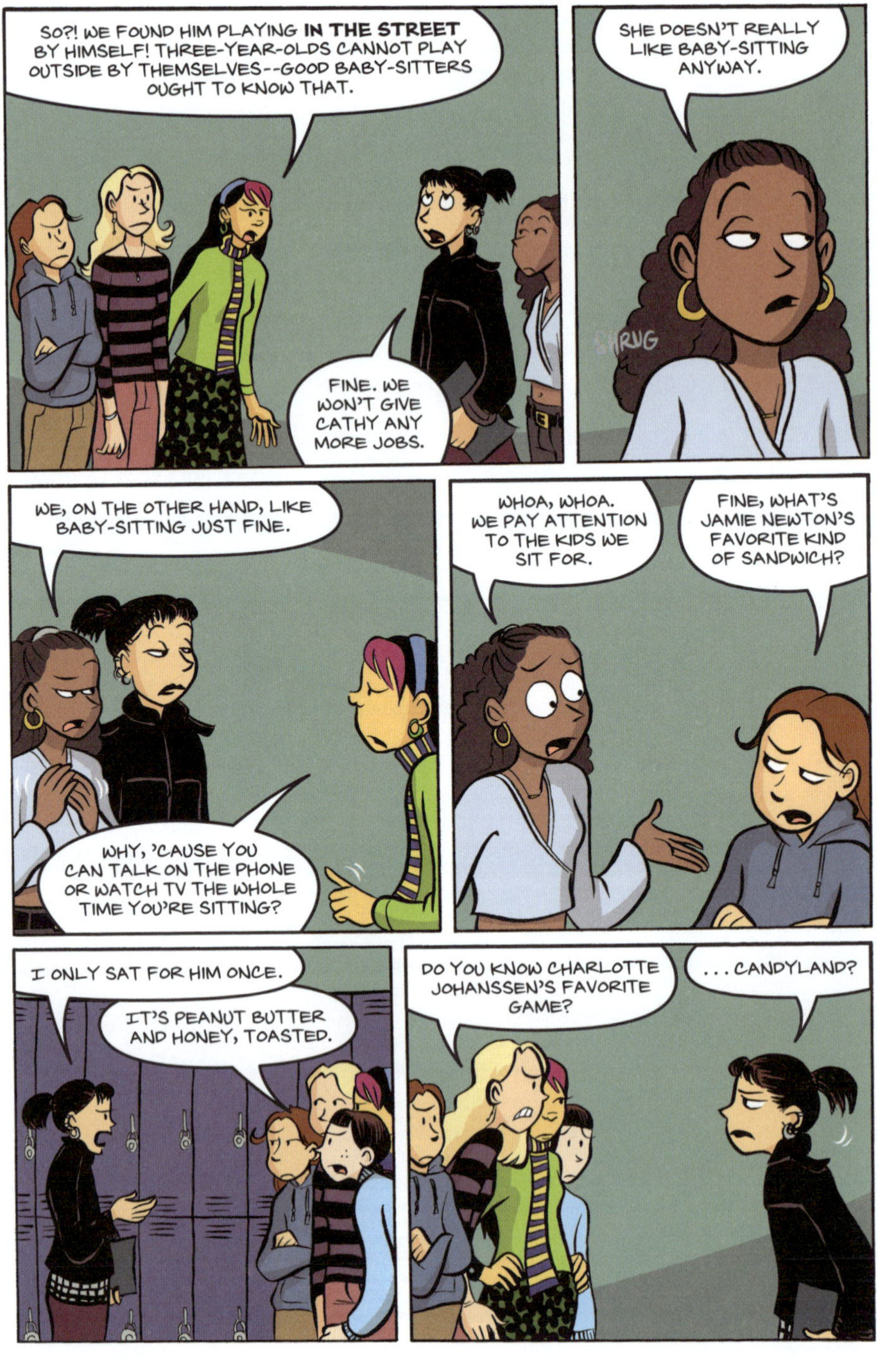
SO?! WE FOUND HIM PLAYING **IN THE STREET** BY HIMSELF! THREE-YEAR-OLDS CANNOT PLAY OUTSIDE BY THEMSELVES--GOOD BABY-SITTERS OUGHT TO KNOW THAT.
FINE. WE WON'T GIVE CATHY ANY MORE JOBS.
SHE DOESN'T REALLY LIKE BABY-SITTING ANYWAY.
SHRUG
WE, ON THE OTHER HAND, LIKE BABY-SITTING JUST FINE.
WHY, 'CAUSE YOU CAN TALK ON THE PHONE OR WATCH TV THE WHOLE TIME YOU'RE SITTING?
WHOA, WHOA. WE PAY ATTENTION TO THE KIDS WE SIT FOR.
FINE, WHAT'S JAMIE NEWTON'S FAVORITE KIND OF SANDWICH?
I ONLY SAT FOR HIM ONCE.
IT'S PEANUT BUTTER AND HONEY, TOASTED.
DO YOU KNOW CHARLOTTE JOHANSSEN'S FAVORITE GAME?
. . . CANDYLAND?

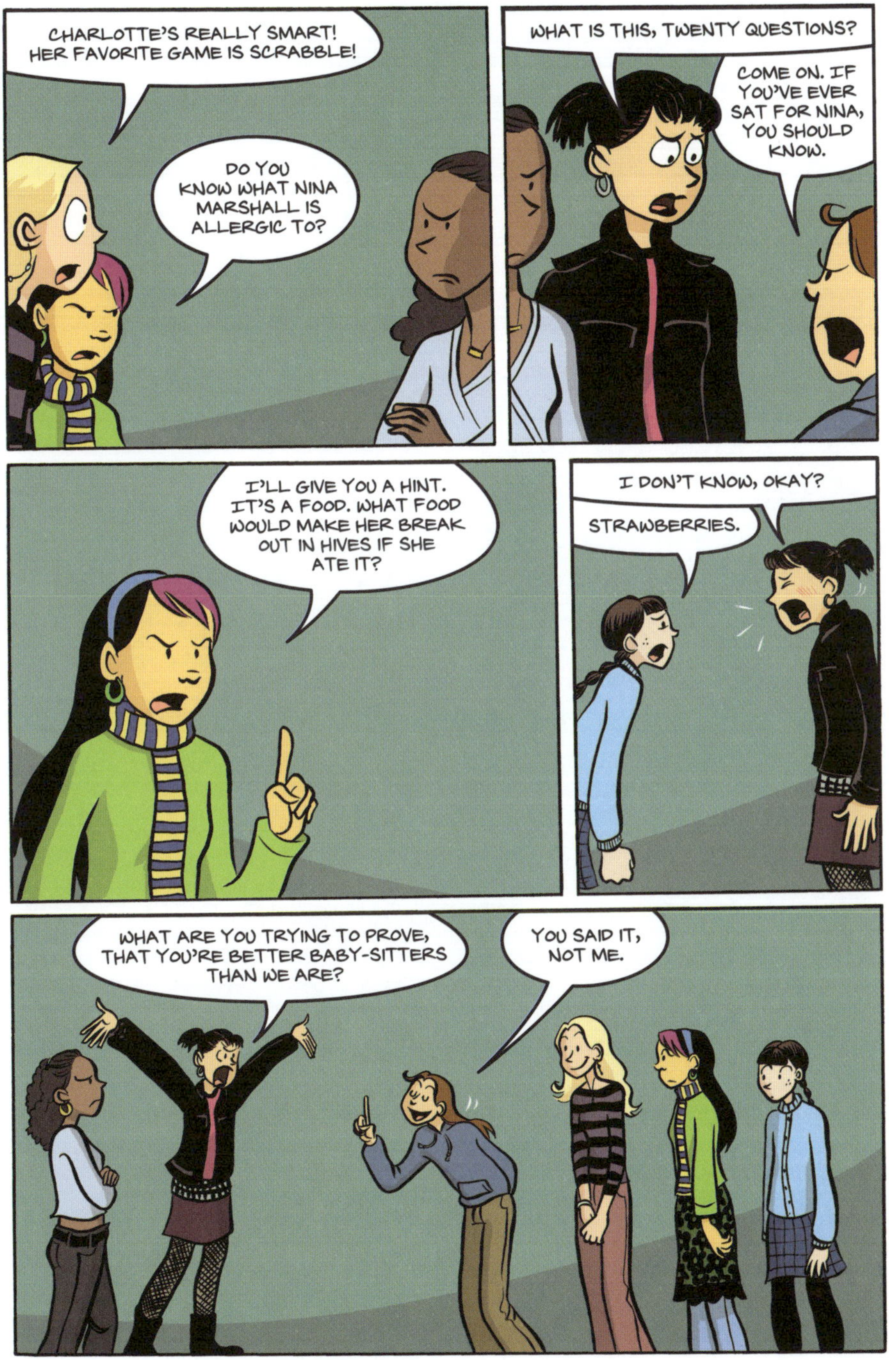
CHARLOTTE'S REALLY SMART! HER FAVORITE GAME IS SCRABBLE!
DO YOU KNOW WHAT NINA MARSHALL IS ALLERGIC TO?
WHAT IS THIS, TWENTY QUESTIONS?
COME ON. IF YOU'VE EVER SAT FOR NINA, YOU SHOULD KNOW.
I'LL GIVE YOU A HINT. IT'S A FOOD. WHAT FOOD WOULD MAKE HER BREAK OUT IN HIVES IF SHE ATE IT?
I DON'T KNOW, OKAY?
STRAWBERRIES.
WHAT ARE YOU TRYING TO PROVE, THAT YOU'RE BETTER BABY-SITTERS THAN WE ARE?
YOU SAID IT, NOT ME.

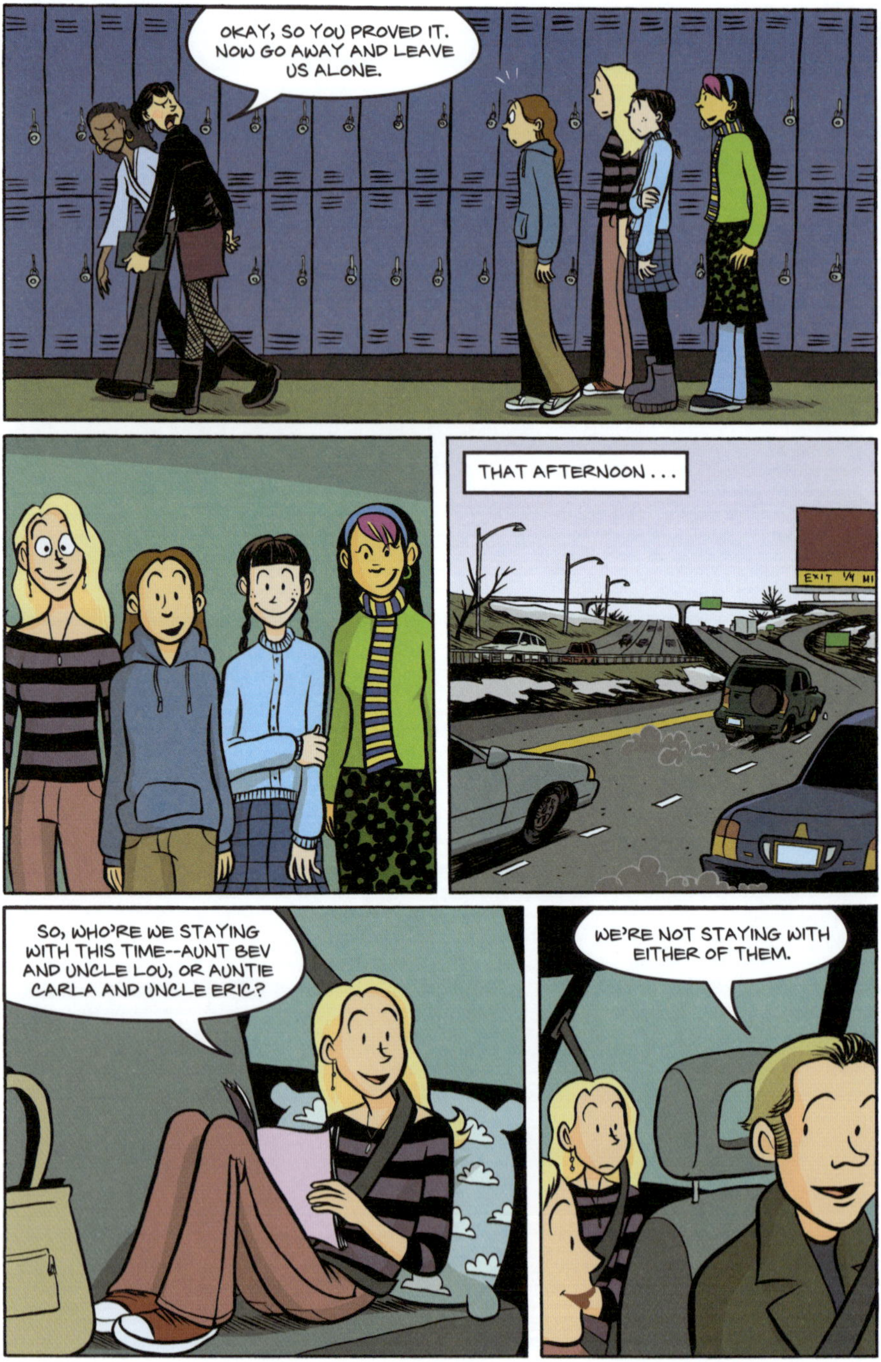
OKAY, SO YOU PROVED IT. NOW GO AWAY AND LEAVE US ALONE.
THAT AFTERNOON . . .
EXIT 1/4 MI
SO, WHO'RE WE STAYING WITH THIS TIME--AUNT BEV AND UNCLE LOU, OR AUNTIE CARLA AND UNCLE ERIC?
WE'RE NOT STAYING WITH EITHER OF THEM.

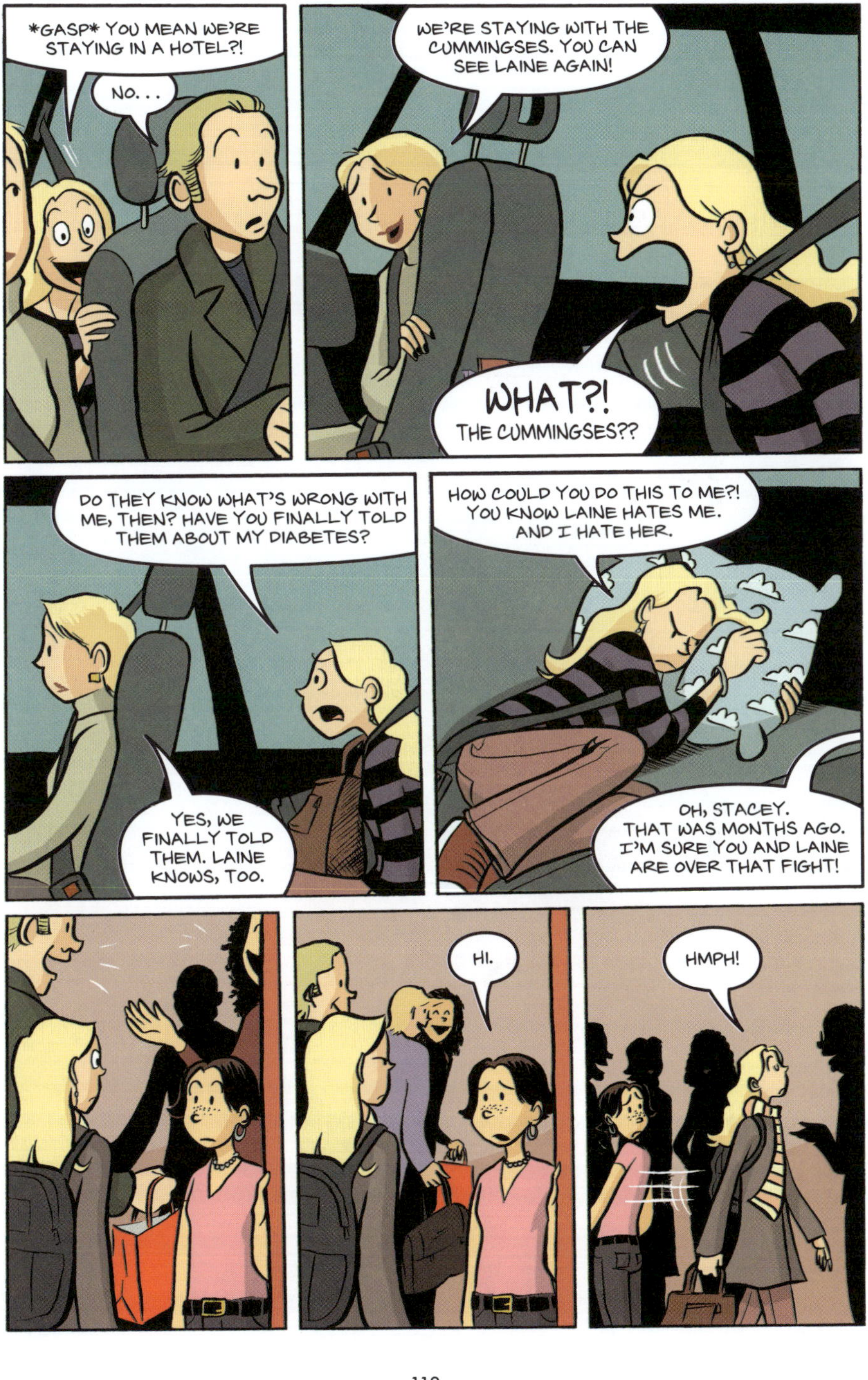
GASP YOU MEAN WE'RE STAYING IN A HOTEL?!
NO. . .
WE'RE STAYING WITH THE CUMMINGSES. YOU CAN SEE LAINE AGAIN!
WHAT?! THE CUMMINGSES??
DO THEY KNOW WHAT'S WRONG WITH ME, THEN? HAVE YOU FINALLY TOLD THEM ABOUT MY DIABETES?
YES, WE FINALLY TOLD THEM. LAINE KNOWS, TOO.
HOW COULD YOU DO THIS TO ME?! YOU KNOW LAINE HATES ME. AND I HATE HER.
OH, STACEY. THAT WAS MONTHS AGO. I'M SURE YOU AND LAINE ARE OVER THAT FIGHT!
HI.
HMPH!

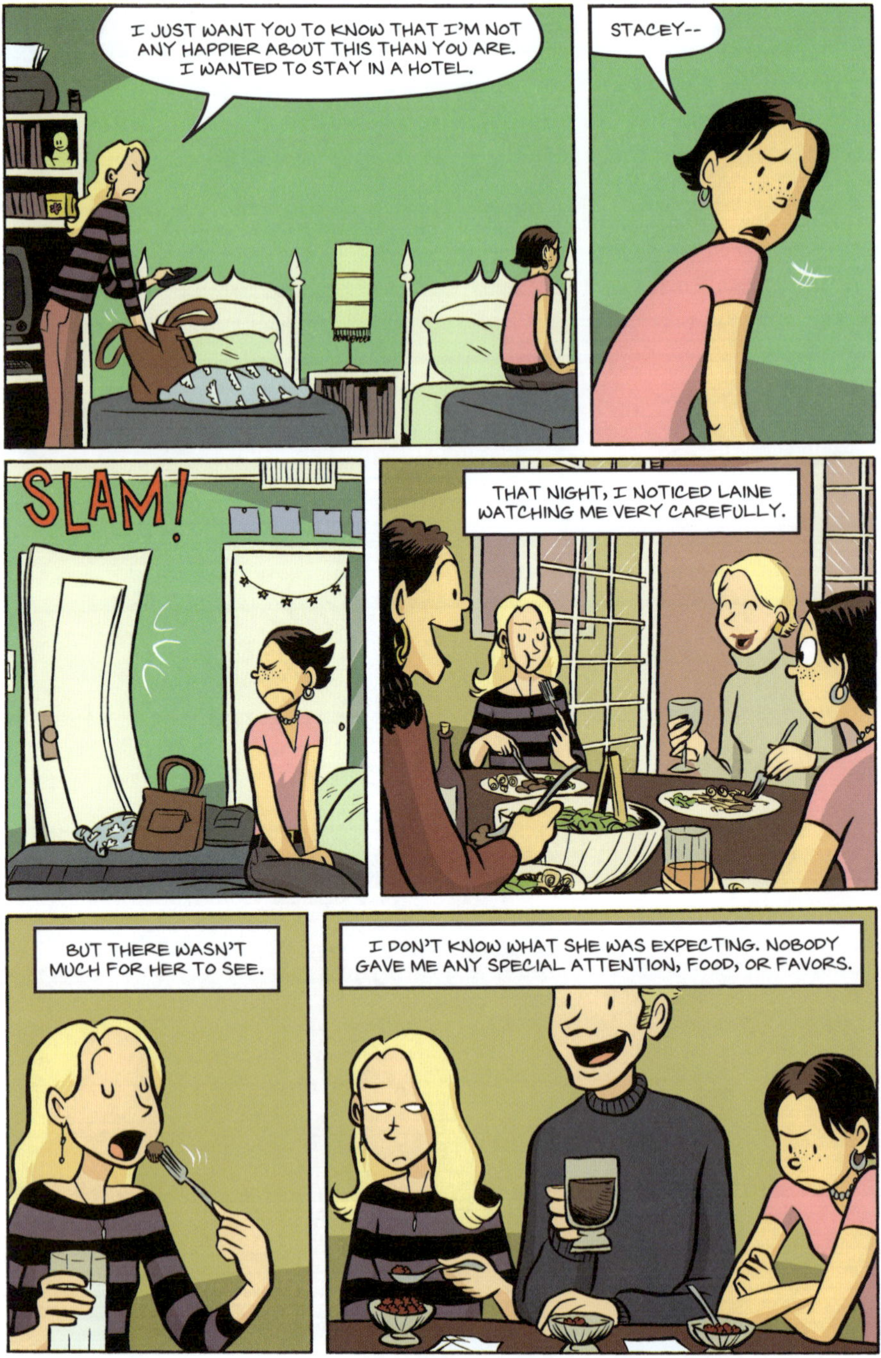
I JUST WANT YOU TO KNOW THAT I'M NOT ANY HAPPIER ABOUT THIS THAN YOU ARE. I WANTED TO STAY IN A HOTEL.
STACEY--
SLAM!
THAT NIGHT, I NOTICED LAINE WATCHING ME VERY CAREFULLY.
BUT THERE WASN'T MUCH FOR HER TO SEE.
I DON'T KNOW WHAT SHE WAS EXPECTING. NOBODY GAVE ME ANY SPECIAL ATTENTION, FOOD, OR FAVORS.

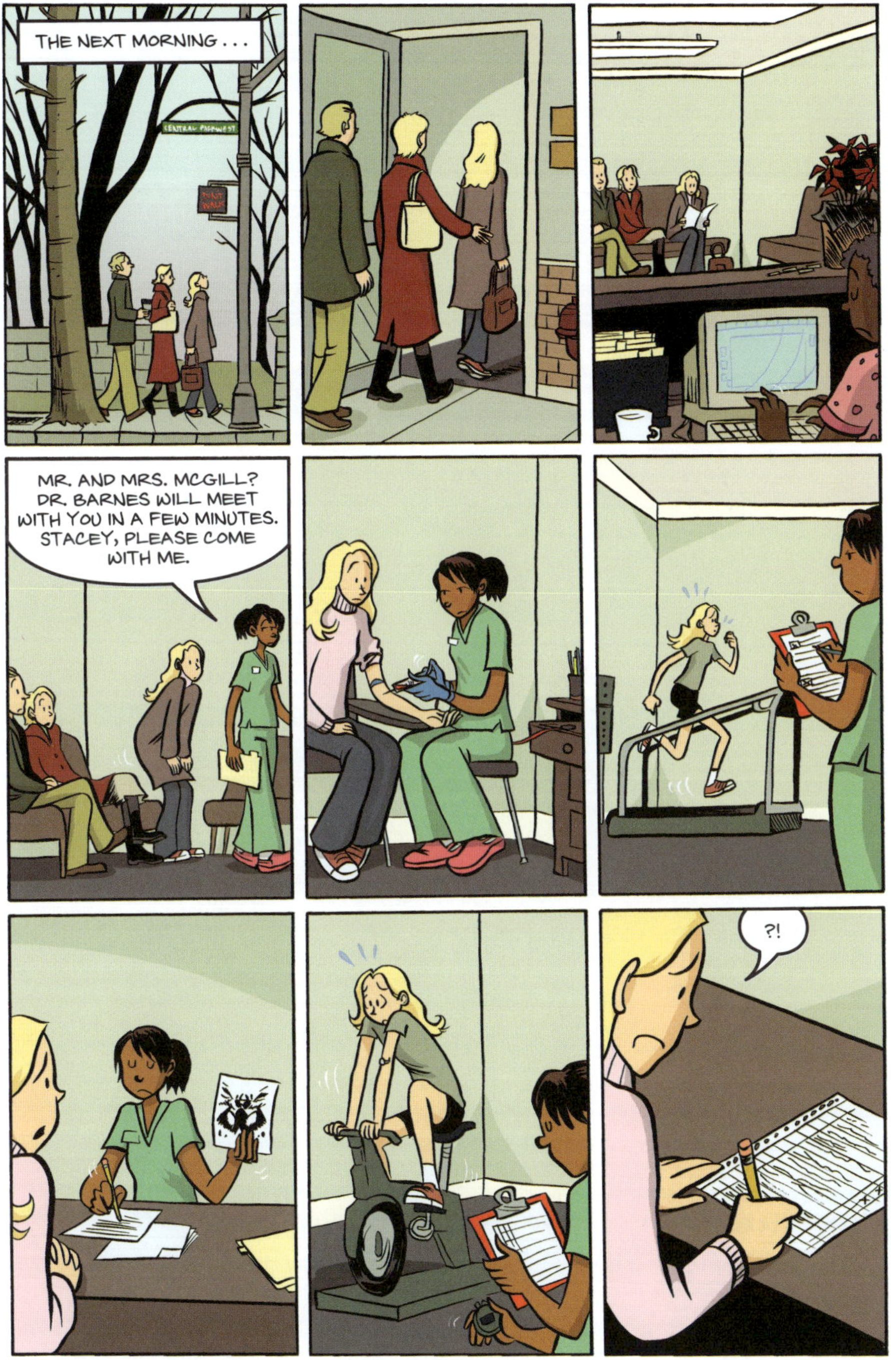
THE NEXT MORNING . . .
CENTRAL PARKWEST
MR. AND MRS. MCGILL? DR. BARNES WILL MEET WITH YOU IN A FEW MINUTES. STACEY, PLEASE COME WITH ME.
?!

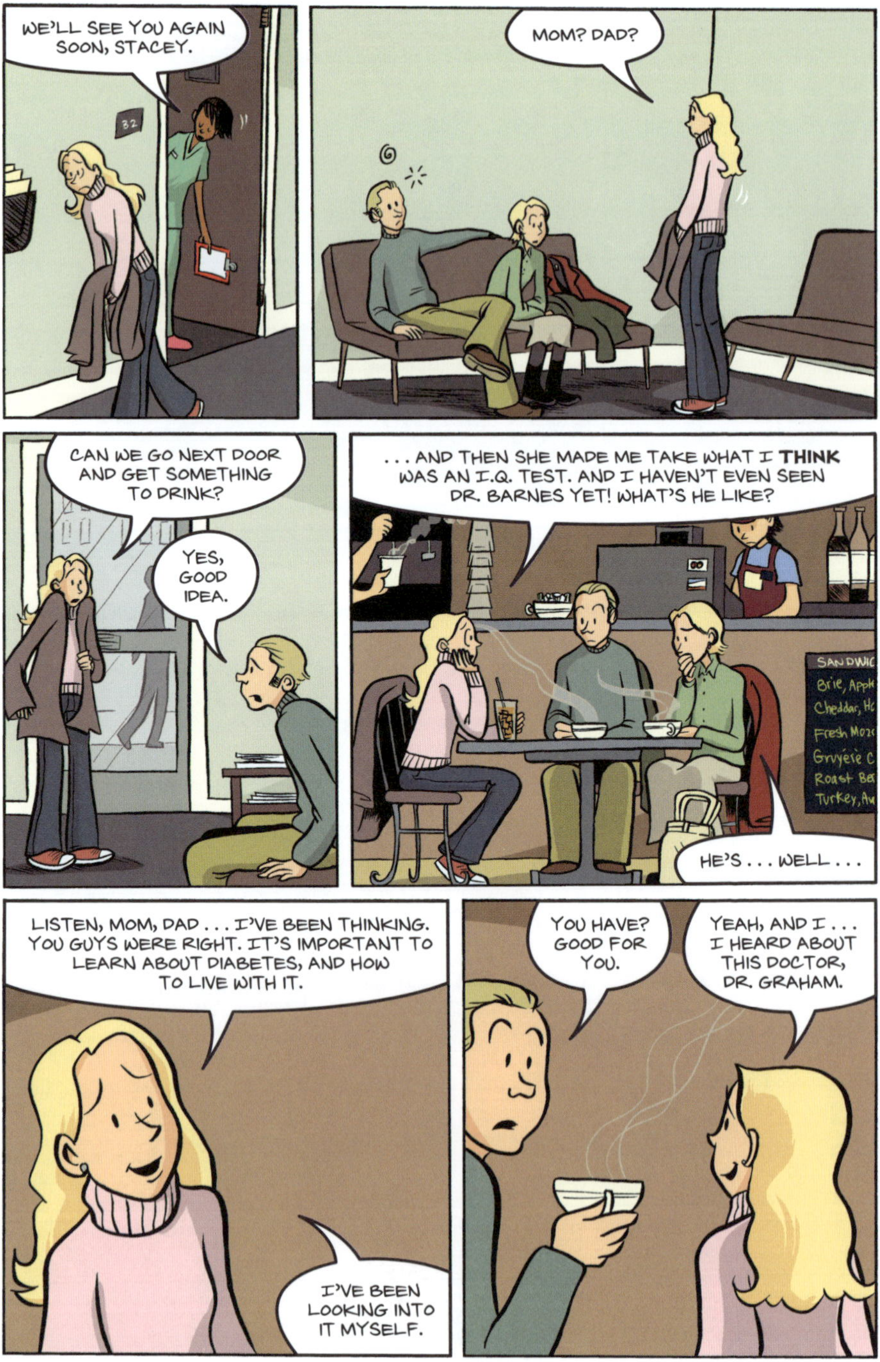
WE'LL SEE YOU AGAIN SOON, STACEY.
32
MOM? DAD?
CAN WE GO NEXT DOOR AND GET SOMETHING TO DRINK?
YES, GOOD IDEA.
. . . AND THEN SHE MADE ME TAKE WHAT I **THINK** WAS AN I.Q. TEST. AND I HAVEN'T EVEN SEEN DR. BARNES YET! WHAT'S HE LIKE?
HE'S . . . WELL . . .
LISTEN, MOM, DAD . . . I'VE BEEN THINKING. YOU GUYS WERE RIGHT. IT'S IMPORTANT TO LEARN ABOUT DIABETES, AND HOW TO LIVE WITH IT.
I'VE BEEN LOOKING INTO IT MYSELF.
YOU HAVE? GOOD FOR YOU.
YEAH, AND I . . . I HEARD ABOUT THIS DOCTOR, DR. GRAHAM.

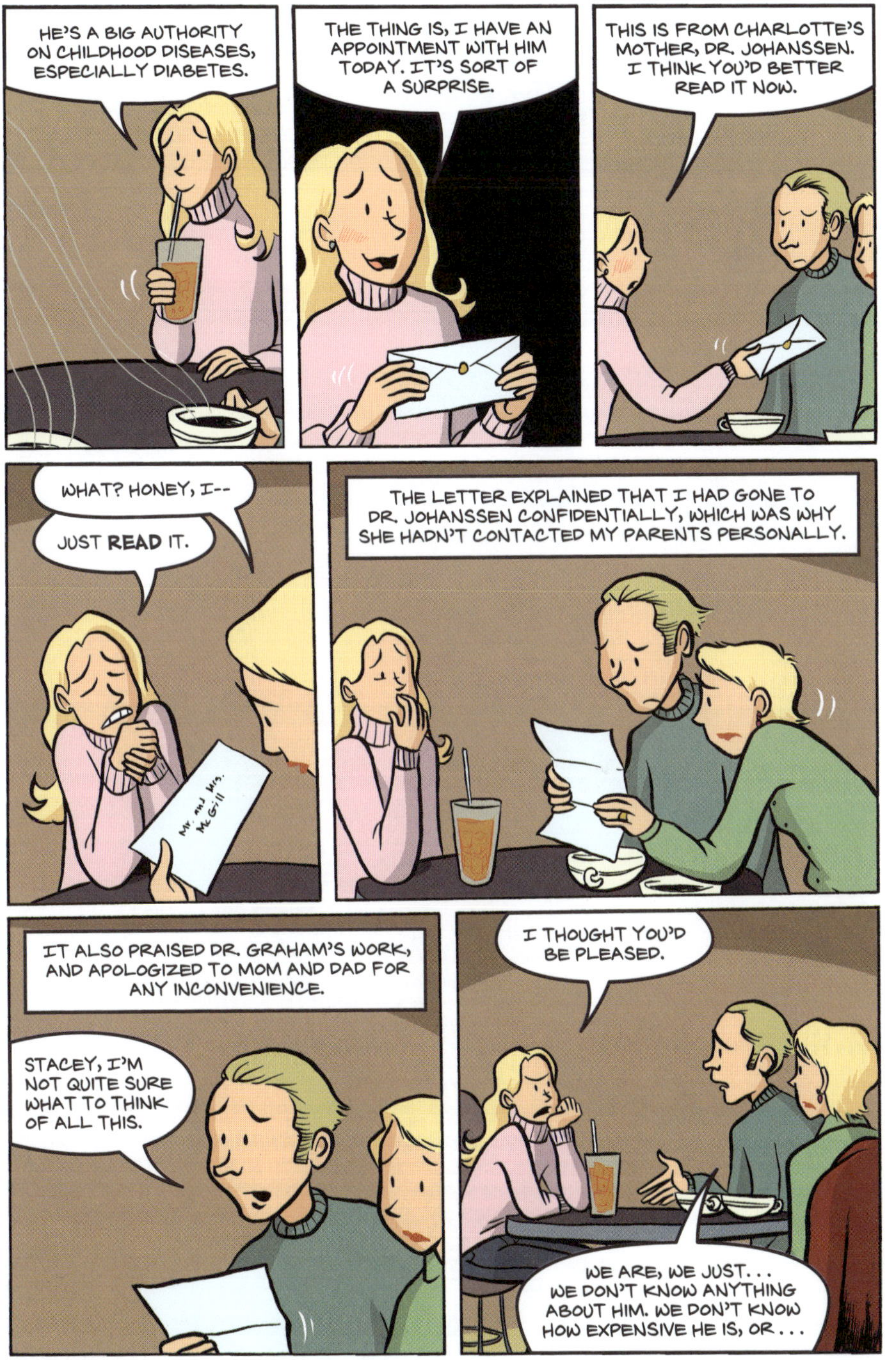
HE'S A BIG AUTHORITY ON CHILDHOOD DISEASES, ESPECIALLY DIABETES.
THE THING IS, I HAVE AN APPOINTMENT WITH HIM TODAY. IT'S SORT OF A SURPRISE.
THIS IS FROM CHARLOTTE'S MOTHER, DR. JOHANSSEN. I THINK YOU'D BETTER READ IT NOW.
WHAT? HONEY, I--
JUST **READ** IT.
Mr. and Mrs. McGill
THE LETTER EXPLAINED THAT I HAD GONE TO DR. JOHANSSEN CONFIDENTIALLY, WHICH WAS WHY SHE HADN'T CONTACTED MY PARENTS PERSONALLY.
IT ALSO PRAISED DR. GRAHAM'S WORK, AND APOLOGIZED TO MOM AND DAD FOR ANY INCONVENIENCE.
STACEY, I'M NOT QUITE SURE WHAT TO THINK OF ALL THIS.
I THOUGHT YOU'D BE PLEASED.
WE ARE, WE JUST... WE DON'T KNOW ANYTHING ABOUT HIM. WE DON'T KNOW HOW EXPENSIVE HE IS, OR...

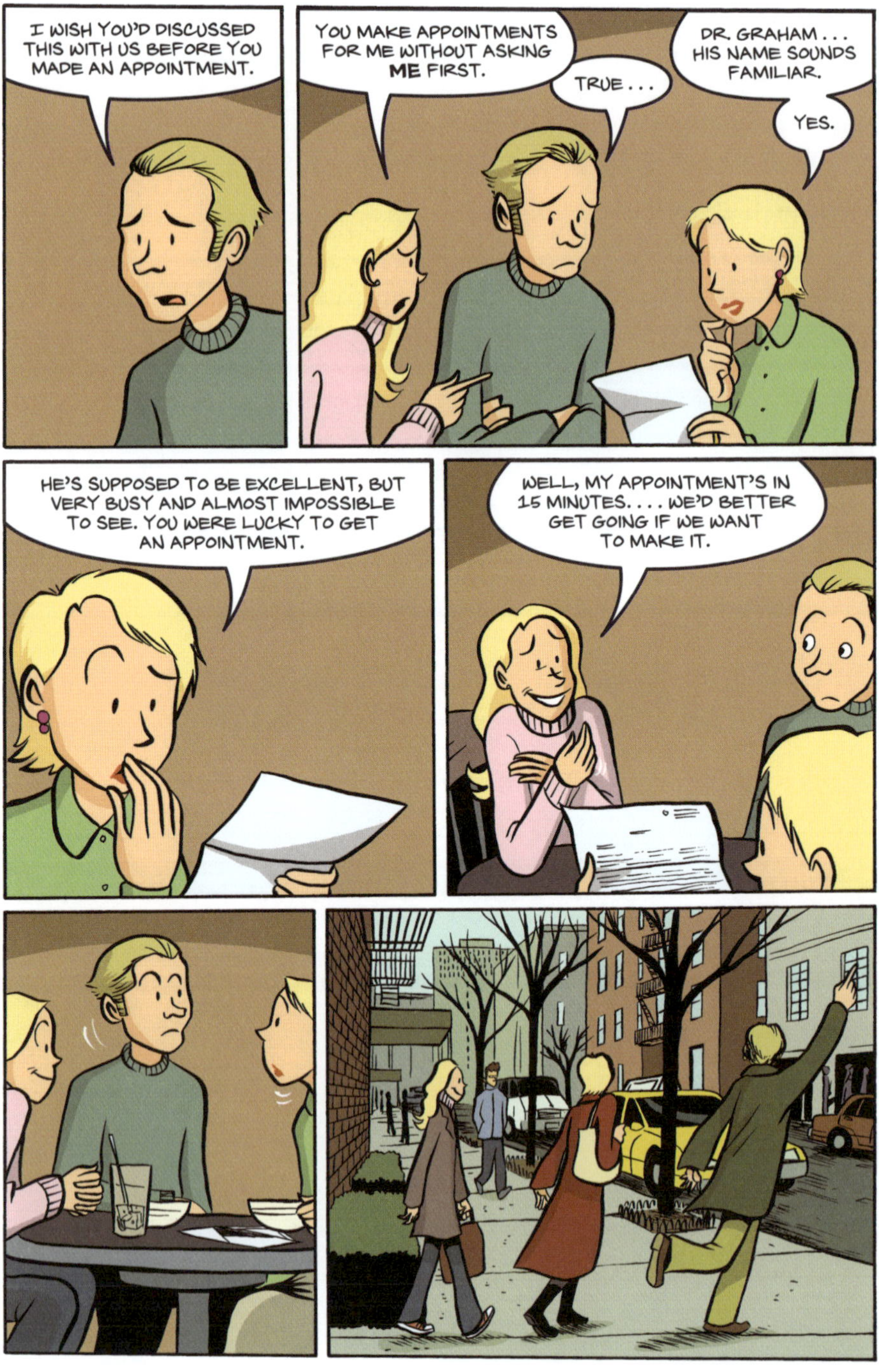
I WISH YOU'D DISCUSSED THIS WITH US BEFORE YOU MADE AN APPOINTMENT.
YOU MAKE APPOINTMENTS FOR ME WITHOUT ASKING **ME** FIRST.
TRUE . . .
DR. GRAHAM . . . HIS NAME SOUNDS FAMILIAR.
YES.
HE'S SUPPOSED TO BE EXCELLENT, BUT VERY BUSY AND ALMOST IMPOSSIBLE TO SEE. YOU WERE LUCKY TO GET AN APPOINTMENT.
WELL, MY APPOINTMENT'S IN 15 MINUTES. . . . WE'D BETTER GET GOING IF WE WANT TO MAKE IT.

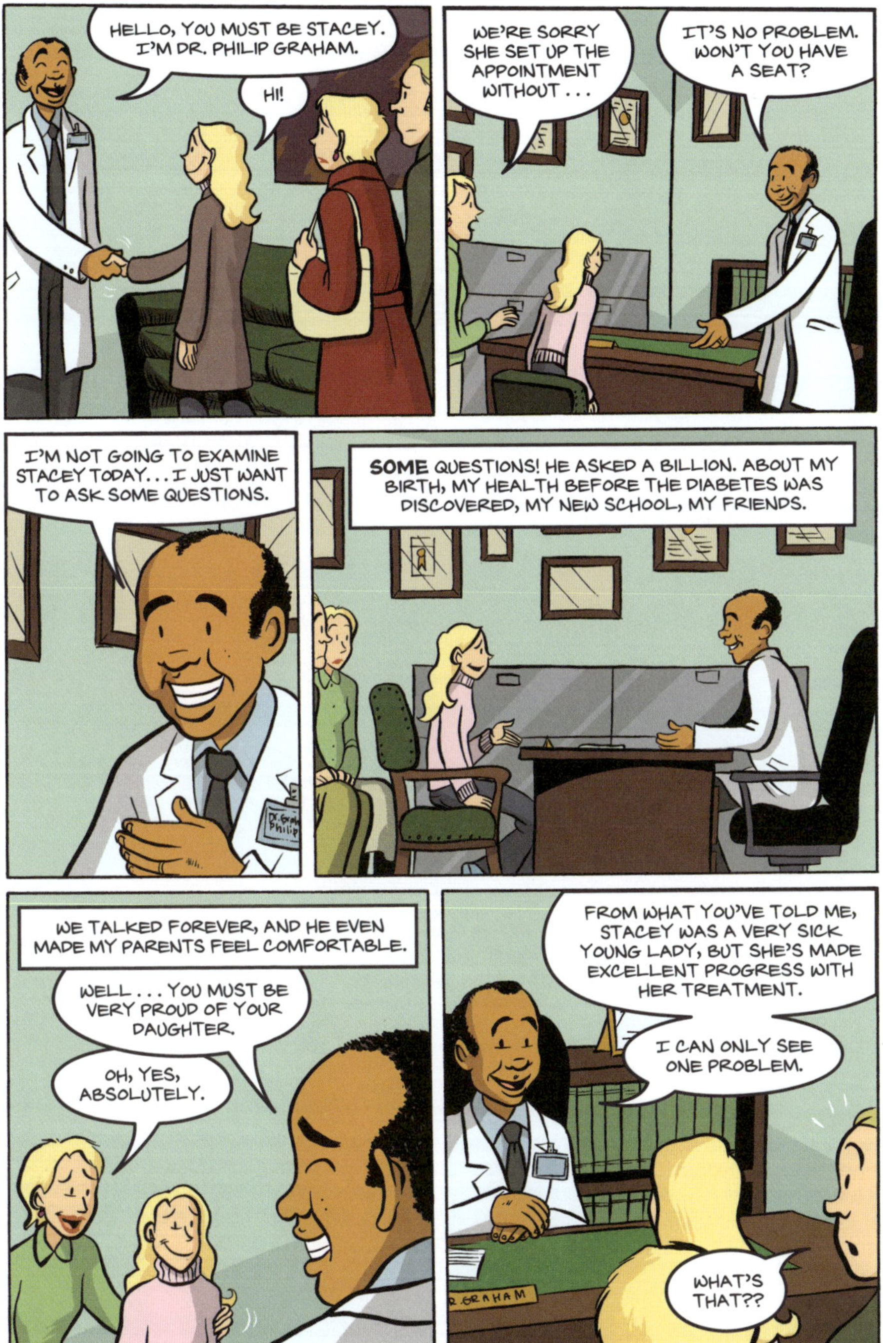
HELLO, YOU MUST BE STACEY. I'M DR. PHILIP GRAHAM.
HI!
WE'RE SORRY SHE SET UP THE APPOINTMENT WITHOUT . . .
IT'S NO PROBLEM. WON'T YOU HAVE A SEAT?
I'M NOT GOING TO EXAMINE STACEY TODAY. . . I JUST WANT TO ASK SOME QUESTIONS.
SOME QUESTIONS! HE ASKED A BILLION. ABOUT MY BIRTH, MY HEALTH BEFORE THE DIABETES WAS DISCOVERED, MY NEW SCHOOL, MY FRIENDS.
WE TALKED FOREVER, AND HE EVEN MADE MY PARENTS FEEL COMFORTABLE.
WELL . . . YOU MUST BE VERY PROUD OF YOUR DAUGHTER.
OH, YES, ABSOLUTELY.
FROM WHAT YOU'VE TOLD ME, STACEY WAS A VERY SICK YOUNG LADY, BUT SHE'S MADE EXCELLENT PROGRESS WITH HER TREATMENT.
I CAN ONLY SEE ONE PROBLEM.
R GRAHAM
WHAT'S THAT??

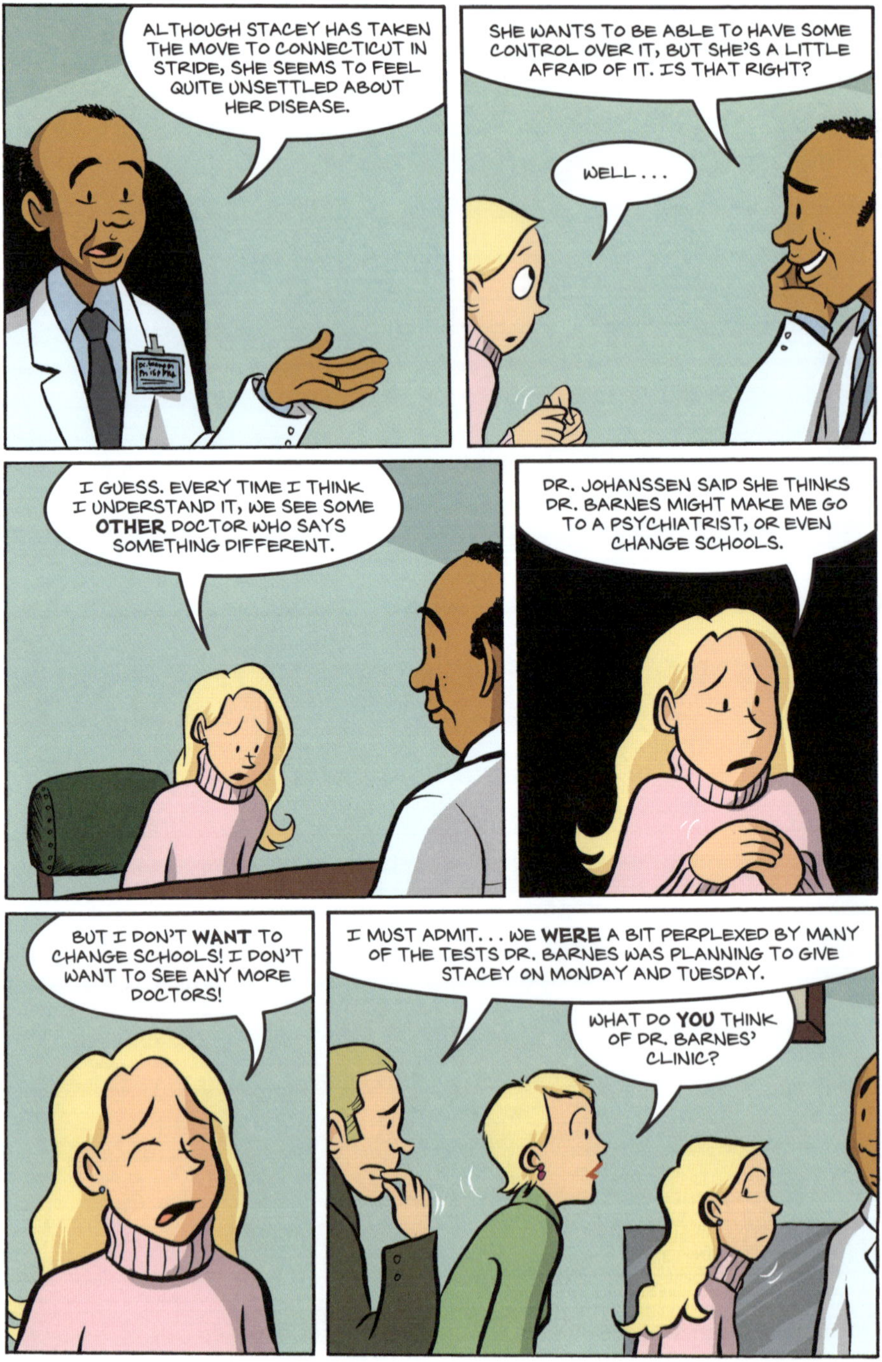
ALTHOUGH STACEY HAS TAKEN THE MOVE TO CONNECTICUT IN STRIDE, SHE SEEMS TO FEEL QUITE UNSETTLED ABOUT HER DISEASE.
SHE WANTS TO BE ABLE TO HAVE SOME CONTROL OVER IT, BUT SHE'S A LITTLE AFRAID OF IT. IS THAT RIGHT?
WELL . . .
I GUESS. EVERY TIME I THINK I UNDERSTAND IT, WE SEE SOME **OTHER** DOCTOR WHO SAYS SOMETHING DIFFERENT.
DR. JOHANSSEN SAID SHE THINKS DR. BARNES MIGHT MAKE ME GO TO A PSYCHIATRIST, OR EVEN CHANGE SCHOOLS.
BUT I DON'T **WANT** TO CHANGE SCHOOLS! I DON'T WANT TO SEE ANY MORE DOCTORS!
I MUST ADMIT. . . WE **WERE** A BIT PERPLEXED BY MANY OF THE TESTS DR. BARNES WAS PLANNING TO GIVE STACEY ON MONDAY AND TUESDAY.
WHAT DO **YOU** THINK OF DR. BARNES' CLINIC?

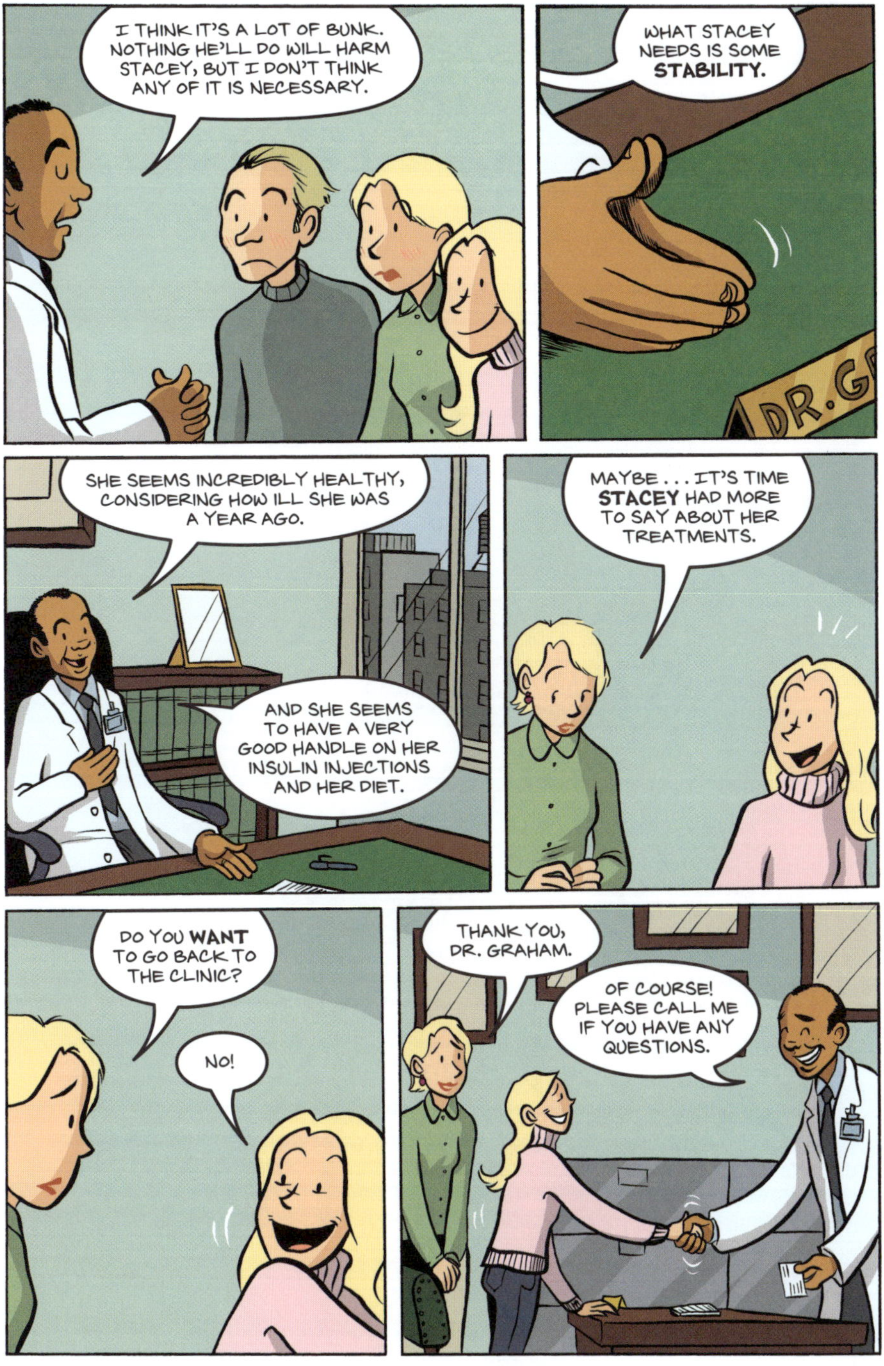
I THINK IT'S A LOT OF BUNK. NOTHING HE'LL DO WILL HARM STACEY, BUT I DON'T THINK ANY OF IT IS NECESSARY.
WHAT STACEY NEEDS IS SOME STABILITY.
DR. GR
SHE SEEMS INCREDIBLY HEALTHY, CONSIDERING HOW ILL SHE WAS A YEAR AGO.
AND SHE SEEMS TO HAVE A VERY GOOD HANDLE ON HER INSULIN INJECTIONS AND HER DIET.
MAYBE . . . IT'S TIME STACEY HAD MORE TO SAY ABOUT HER TREATMENTS.
DO YOU WANT TO GO BACK TO THE CLINIC?
NO!
THANK YOU, DR. GRAHAM.
OF COURSE! PLEASE CALL ME IF YOU HAVE ANY QUESTIONS.

CHAPTER 14

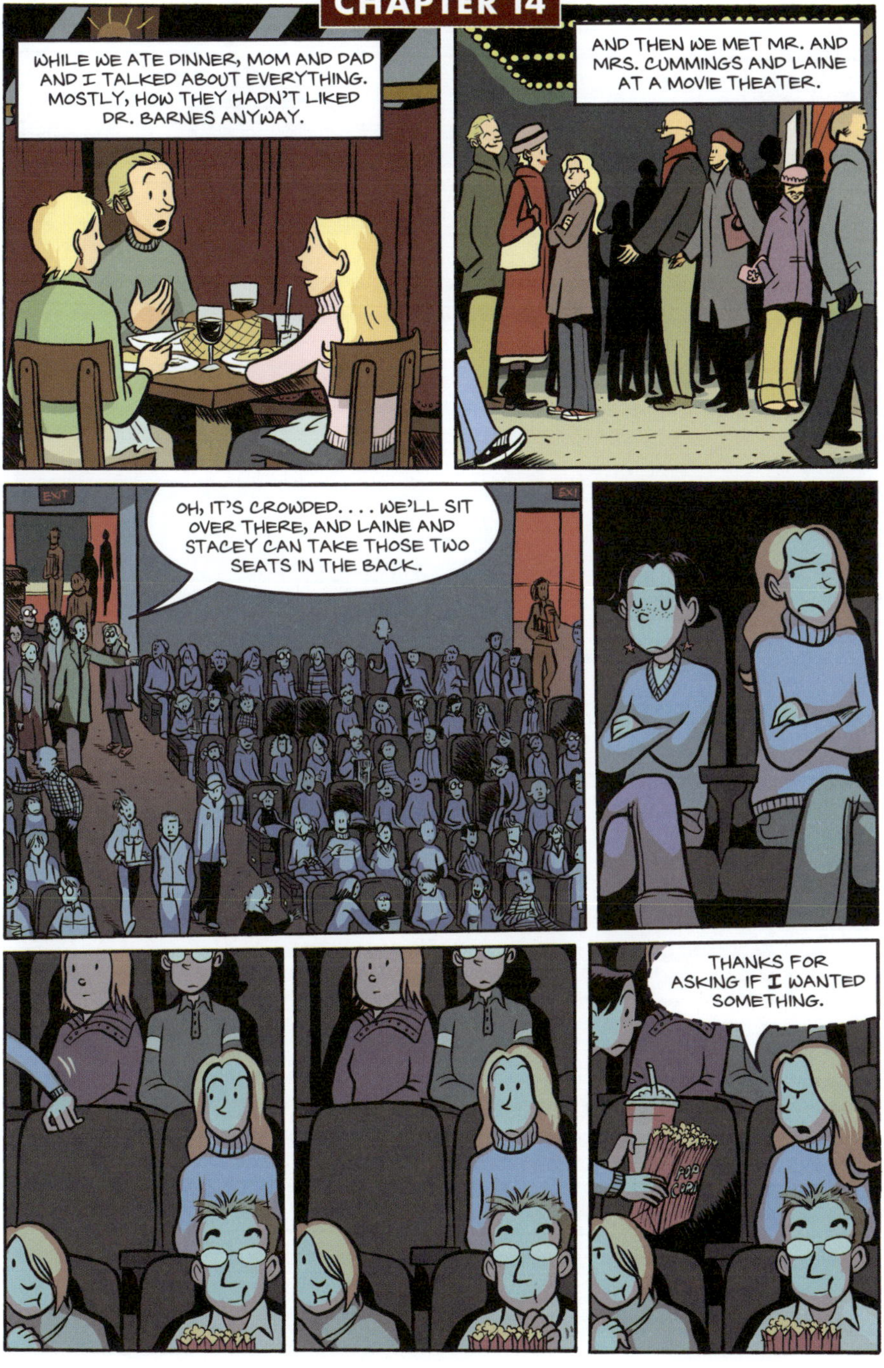
WHILE WE ATE DINNER, MOM AND DAD AND I TALKED ABOUT EVERYTHING. MOSTLY, HOW THEY HADN'T LIKED DR. BARNES ANYWAY.
AND THEN WE MET MR. AND MRS. CUMMINGS AND LAINE AT A MOVIE THEATER.
EXIT
OH, IT'S CROWDED. . . . WE'LL SIT OVER THERE, AND LAINE AND STACEY CAN TAKE THOSE TWO SEATS IN THE BACK.
THANKS FOR ASKING IF I WANTED SOMETHING.
POP CORN

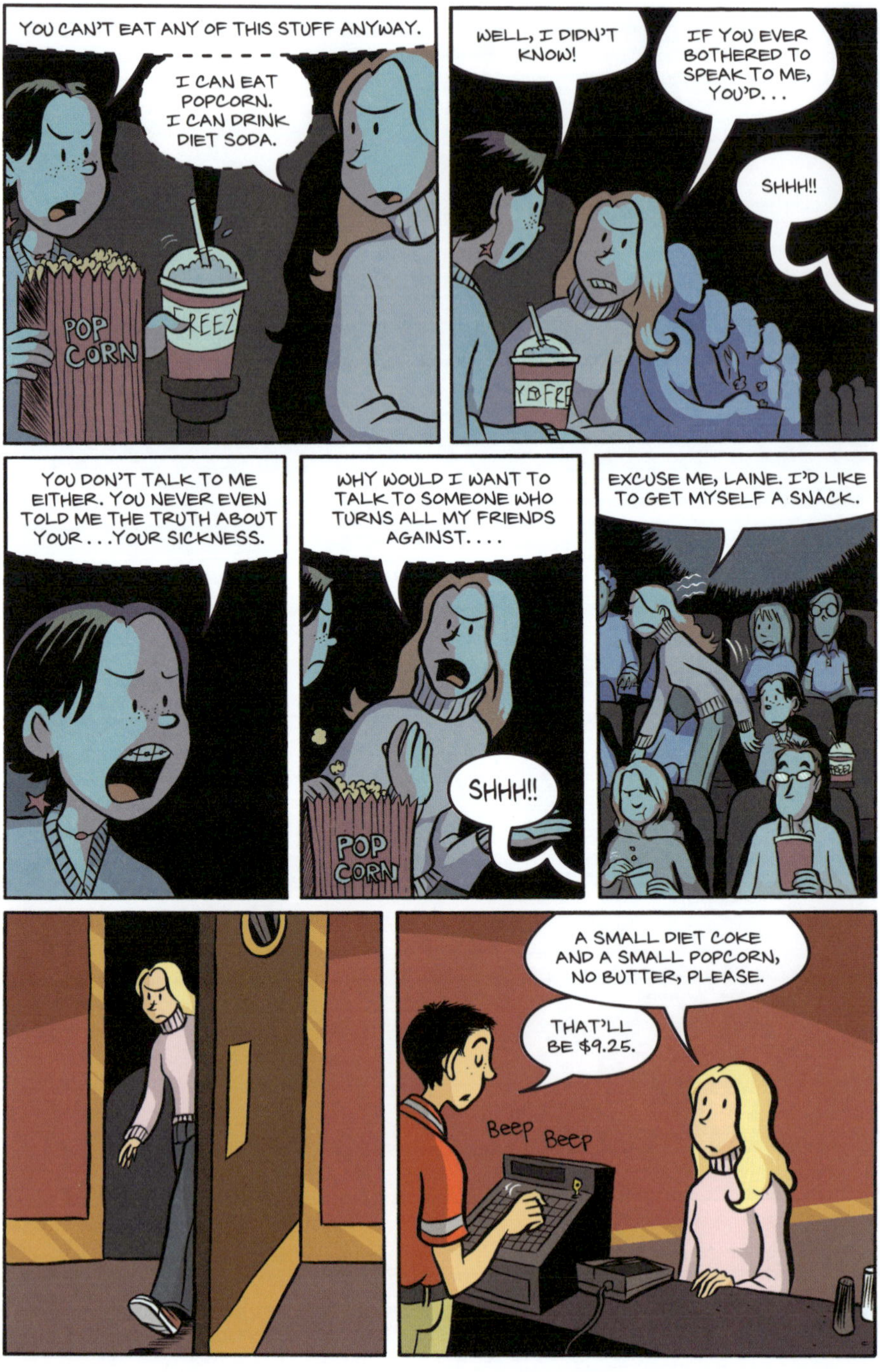
YOU CAN'T EAT ANY OF THIS STUFF ANYWAY.
I CAN EAT POPCORN. I CAN DRINK DIET SODA.
POP CORN
FREEZ
WELL, I DIDN'T KNOW!
IF YOU EVER BOTHERED TO SPEAK TO ME, YOU'D. . .
SHHH!!
YOU DON'T TALK TO ME EITHER. YOU NEVER EVEN TOLD ME THE TRUTH ABOUT YOUR . . . YOUR SICKNESS.
WHY WOULD I WANT TO TALK TO SOMEONE WHO TURNS ALL MY FRIENDS AGAINST. . . .
SHHH!!
POP CORN
EXCUSE ME, LAINE. I'D LIKE TO GET MYSELF A SNACK.
A SMALL DIET COKE AND A SMALL POPCORN, NO BUTTER, PLEASE.
THAT'LL BE $9.25.
Beep Beep

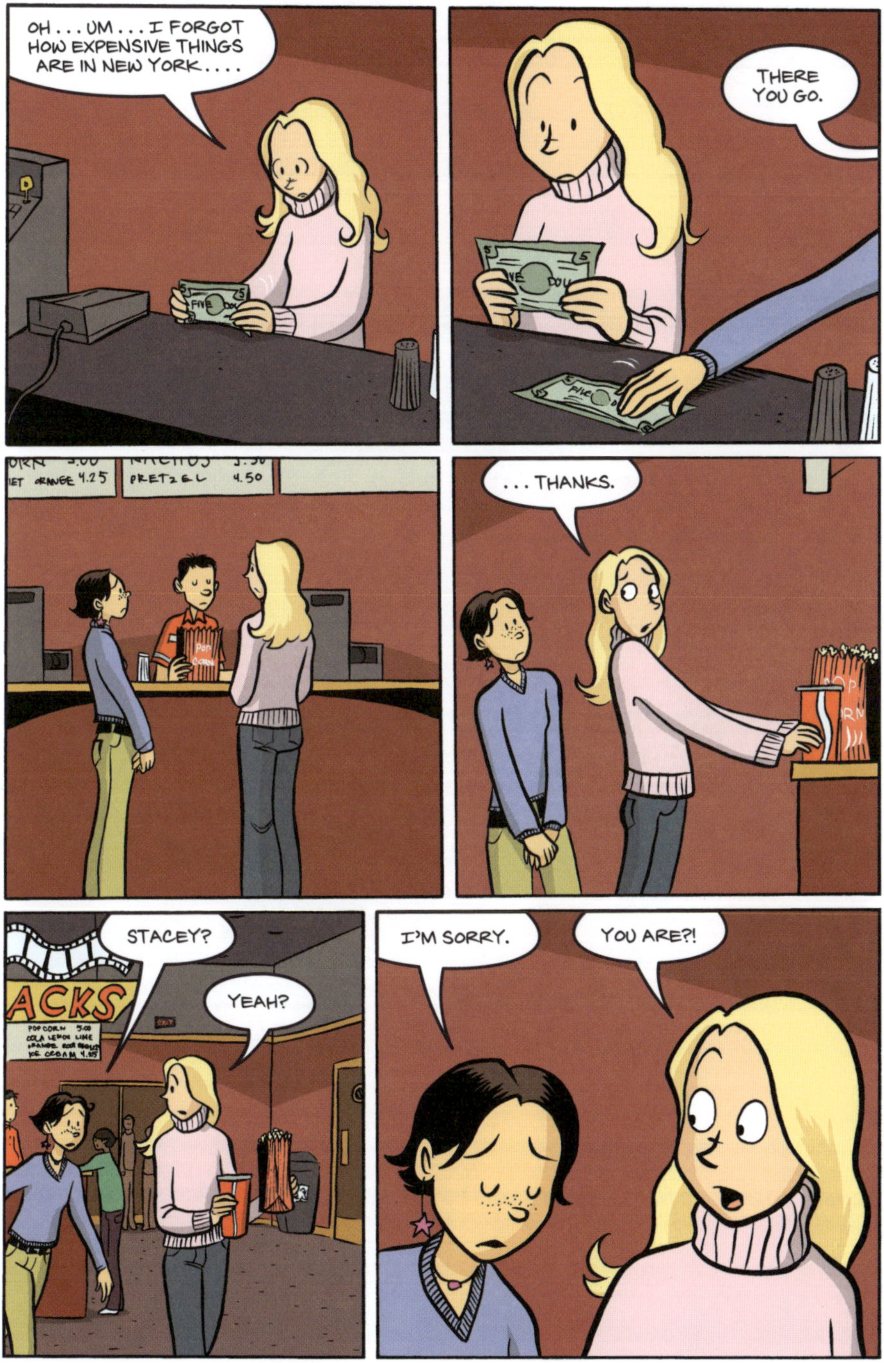
OH . . . UM . . . I FORGOT HOW EXPENSIVE THINGS ARE IN NEW YORK . . . .
THERE YOU GO.
PRETZEL 4.50
. . . THANKS.
STACEY?
YEAH?
I'M SORRY.
YOU ARE?!

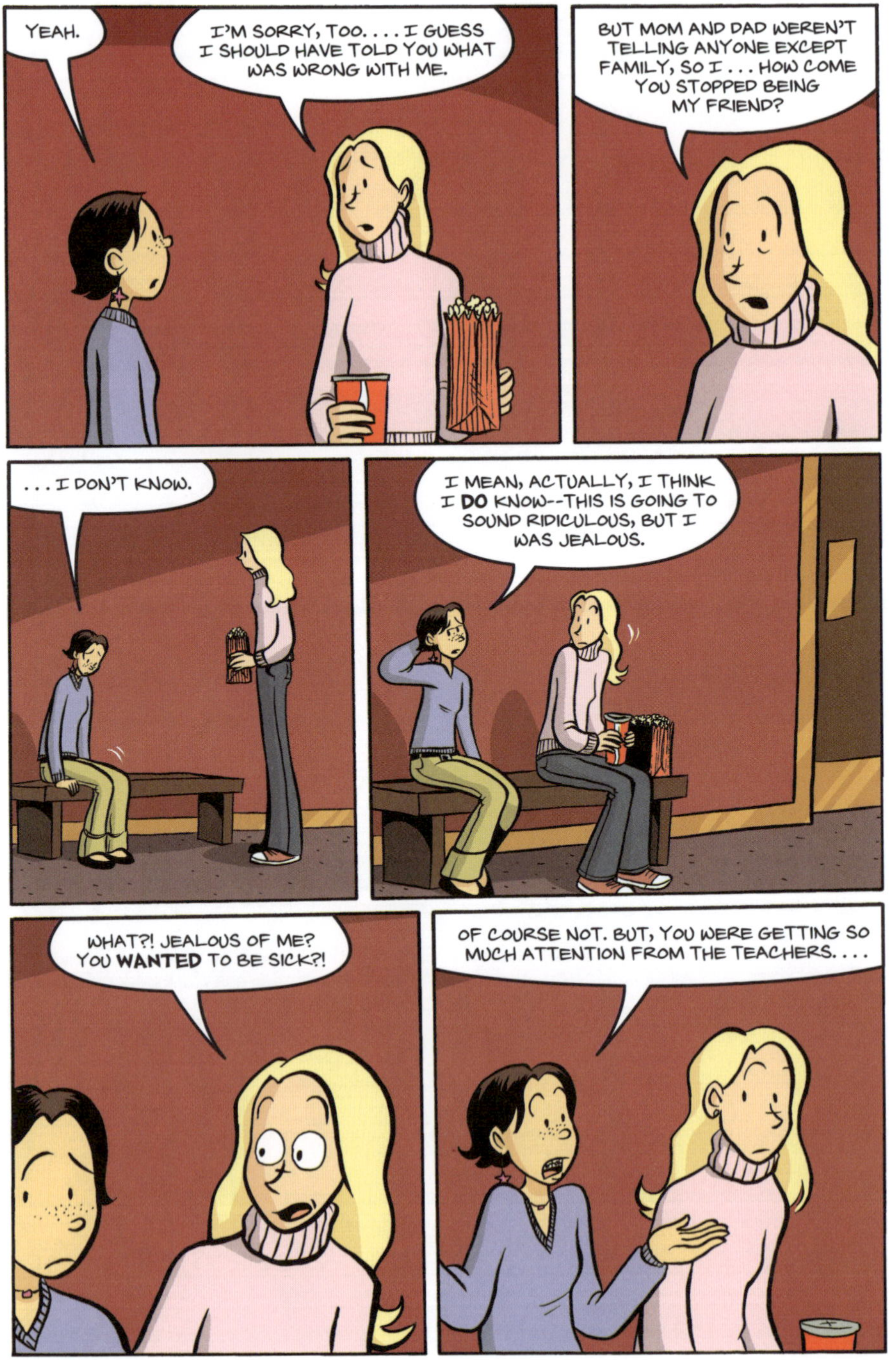
YEAH.
I'M SORRY, TOO. . . . I GUESS I SHOULD HAVE TOLD YOU WHAT WAS WRONG WITH ME.
BUT MOM AND DAD WEREN'T TELLING ANYONE EXCEPT FAMILY, SO I . . . HOW COME YOU STOPPED BEING MY FRIEND?
. . . I DON'T KNOW.
I MEAN, ACTUALLY, I THINK I **DO** KNOW--THIS IS GOING TO SOUND RIDICULOUS, BUT I WAS JEALOUS.
WHAT?! JEALOUS OF ME? YOU **WANTED** TO BE SICK?!
OF COURSE NOT. BUT, YOU WERE GETTING SO MUCH ATTENTION FROM THE TEACHERS. . . .

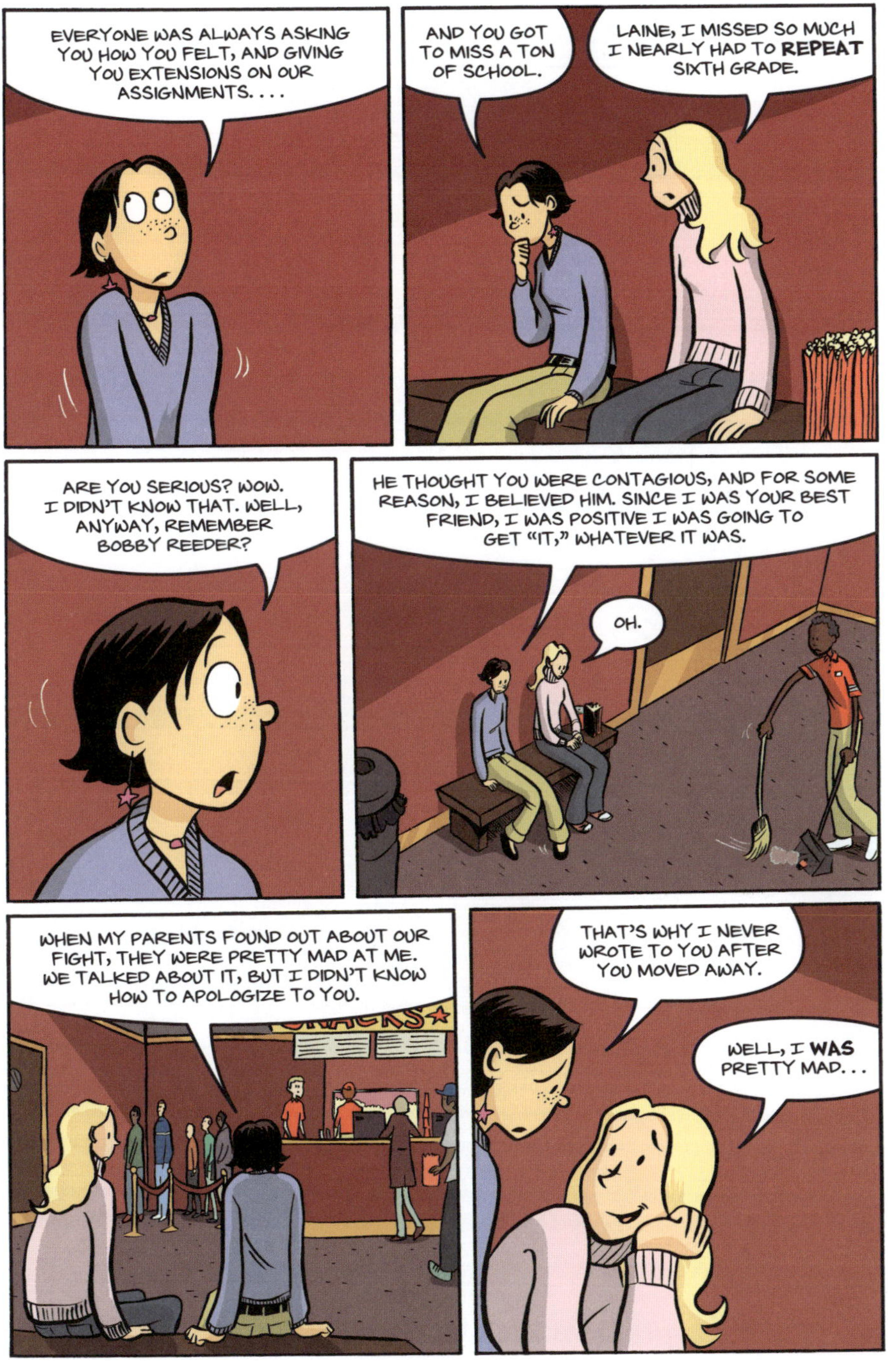
EVERYONE WAS ALWAYS ASKING YOU HOW YOU FELT, AND GIVING YOU EXTENSIONS ON OUR ASSIGNMENTS. . . .
AND YOU GOT TO MISS A TON OF SCHOOL.
LAINE, I MISSED SO MUCH I NEARLY HAD TO **REPEAT** SIXTH GRADE.
ARE YOU SERIOUS? WOW. I DIDN'T KNOW THAT. WELL, ANYWAY, REMEMBER BOBBY REEDER?
HE THOUGHT YOU WERE CONTAGIOUS, AND FOR SOME REASON, I BELIEVED HIM. SINCE I WAS YOUR BEST FRIEND, I WAS POSITIVE I WAS GOING TO GET "IT," WHATEVER IT WAS.
OH.
WHEN MY PARENTS FOUND OUT ABOUT OUR FIGHT, THEY WERE PRETTY MAD AT ME. WE TALKED ABOUT IT, BUT I DIDN'T KNOW HOW TO APOLOGIZE TO YOU.
THAT'S WHY I NEVER WROTE TO YOU AFTER YOU MOVED AWAY.
WELL, I **WAS** PRETTY MAD. . .

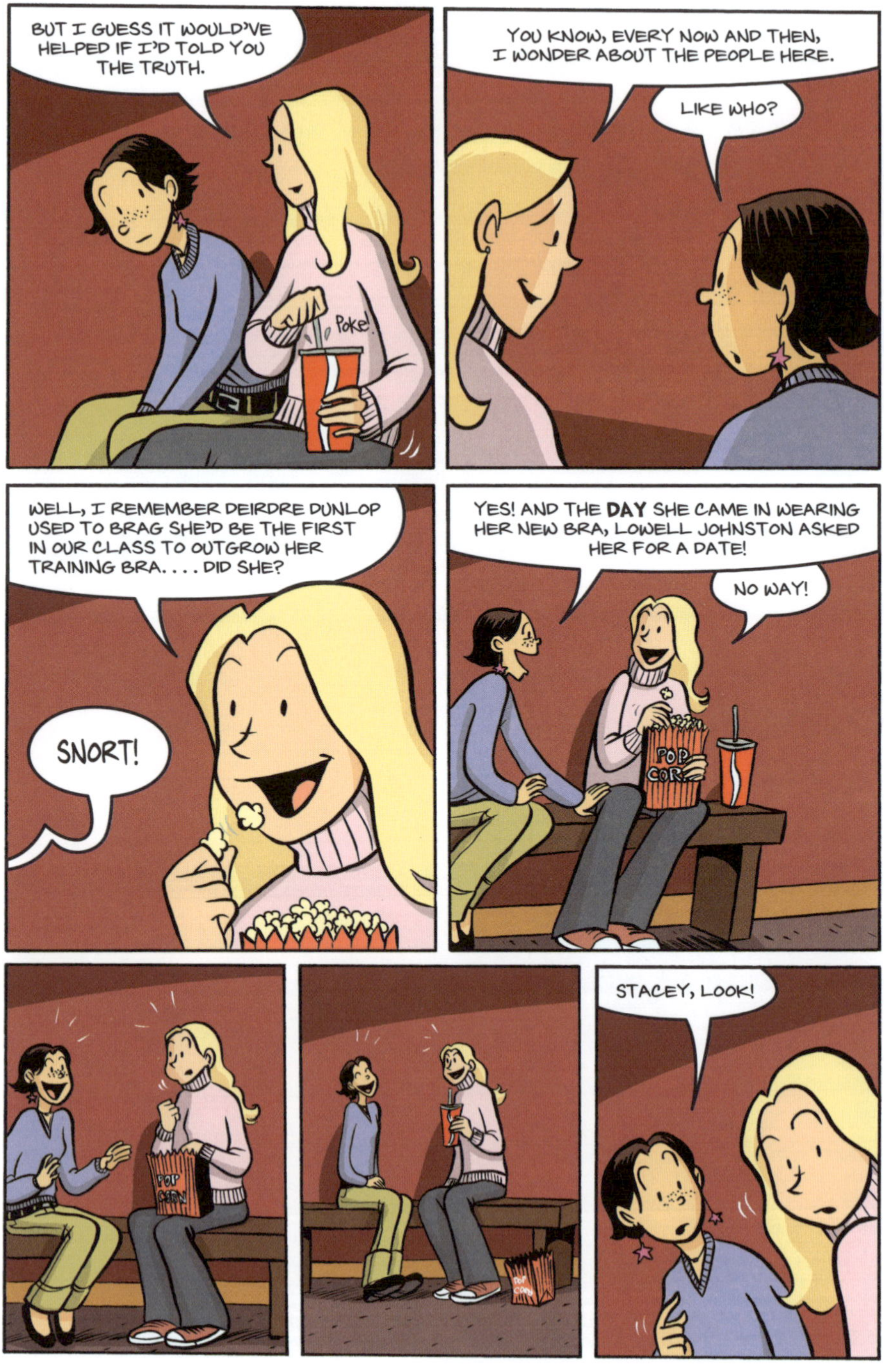
BUT I GUESS IT WOULD'VE HELPED IF I'D TOLD YOU THE TRUTH.
Poke!
YOU KNOW, EVERY NOW AND THEN, I WONDER ABOUT THE PEOPLE HERE.
LIKE WHO?
WELL, I REMEMBER DEIRDRE DUNLOP USED TO BRAG SHE'D BE THE FIRST IN OUR CLASS TO OUTGROW HER TRAINING BRA. . . . DID SHE?
SNORT!
YES! AND THE **DAY** SHE CAME IN WEARING HER NEW BRA, LOWELL JOHNSTON ASKED HER FOR A DATE!
NO WAY!
POP CORN
STACEY, LOOK!

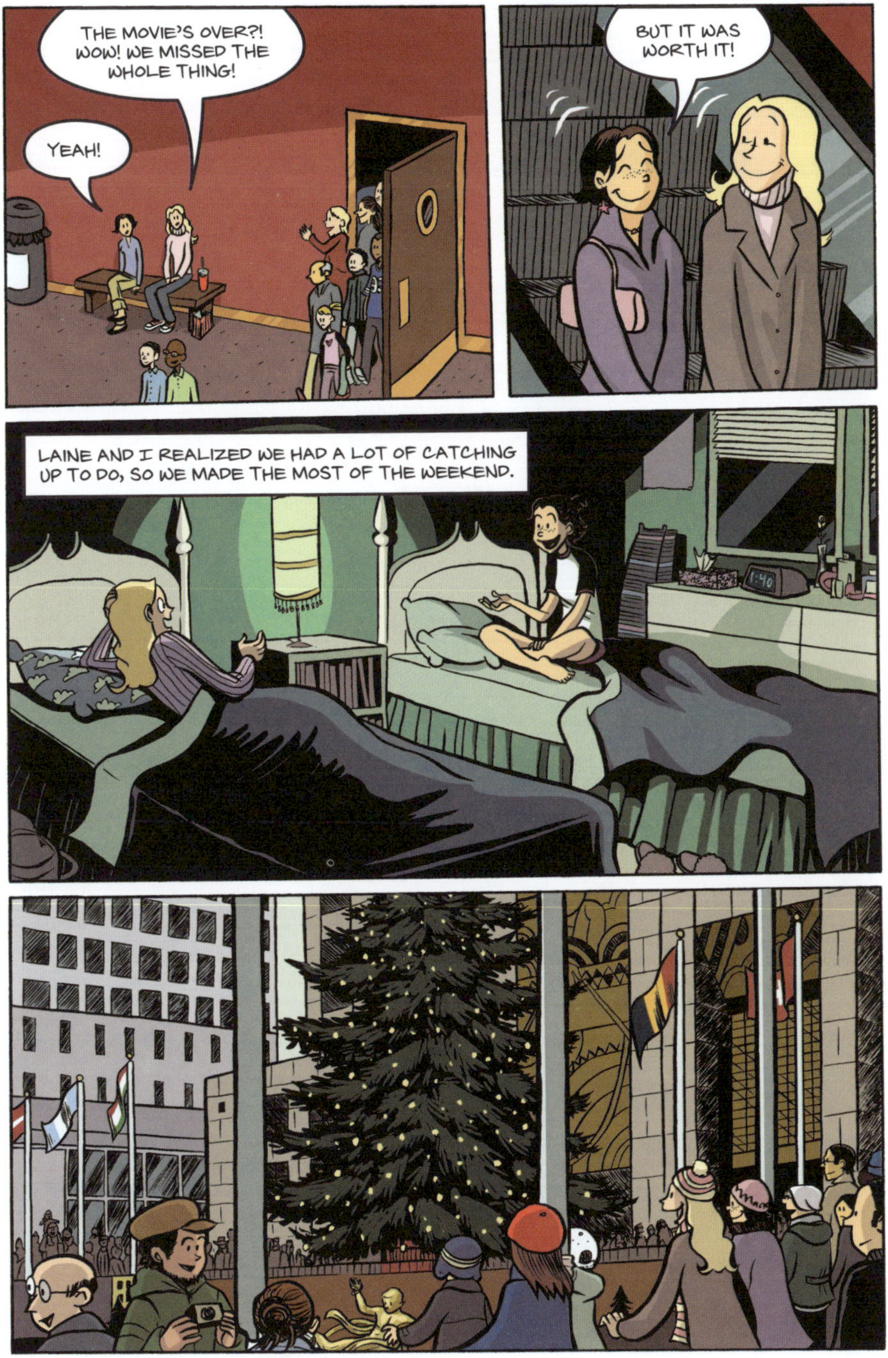
THE MOVIE'S OVER?! WOW! WE MISSED THE WHOLE THING!
YEAH!
BUT IT WAS WORTH IT!
LAINE AND I REALIZED WE HAD A LOT OF CATCHING UP TO DO, SO WE MADE THE MOST OF THE WEEKEND.
1:40

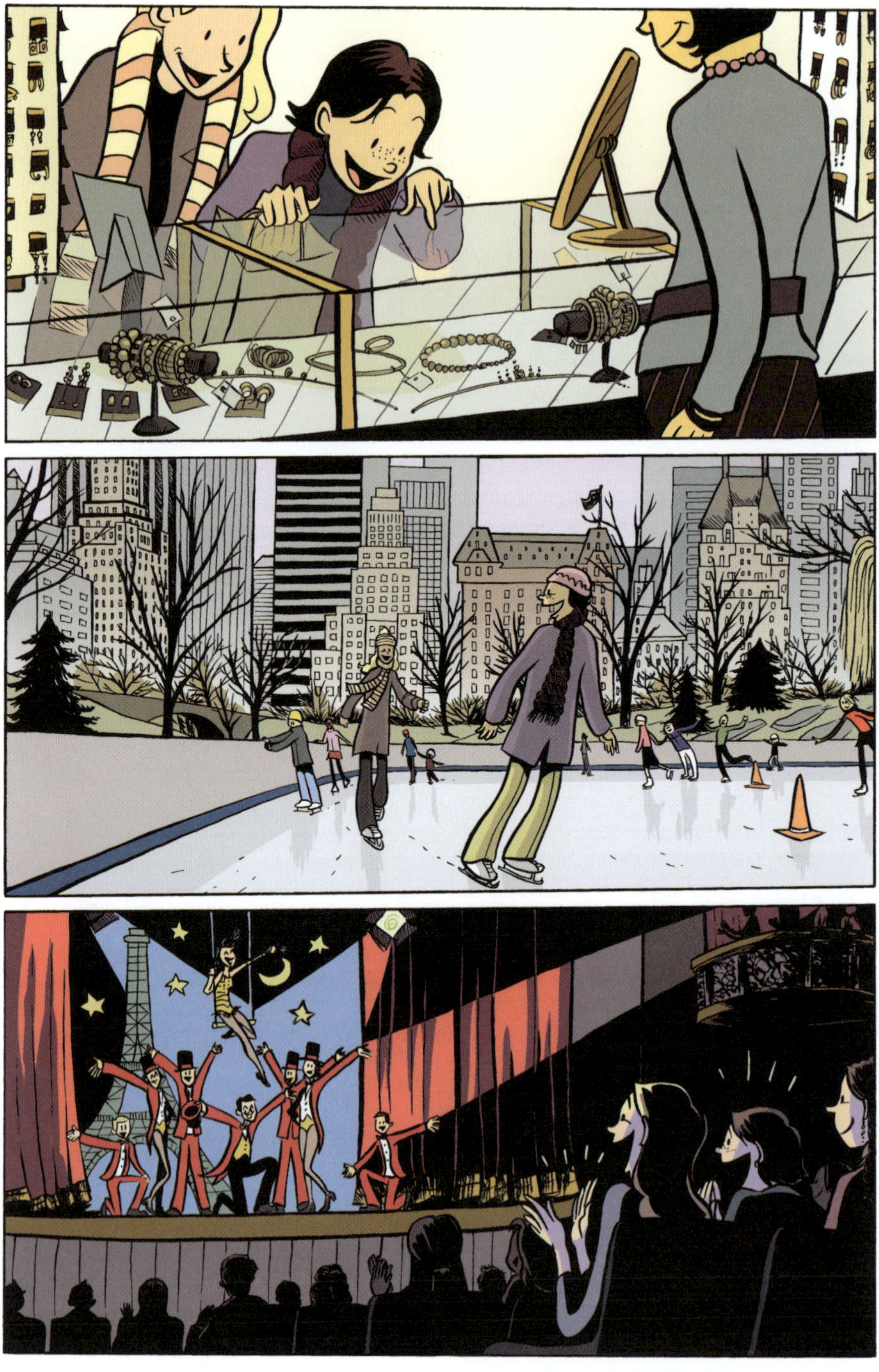

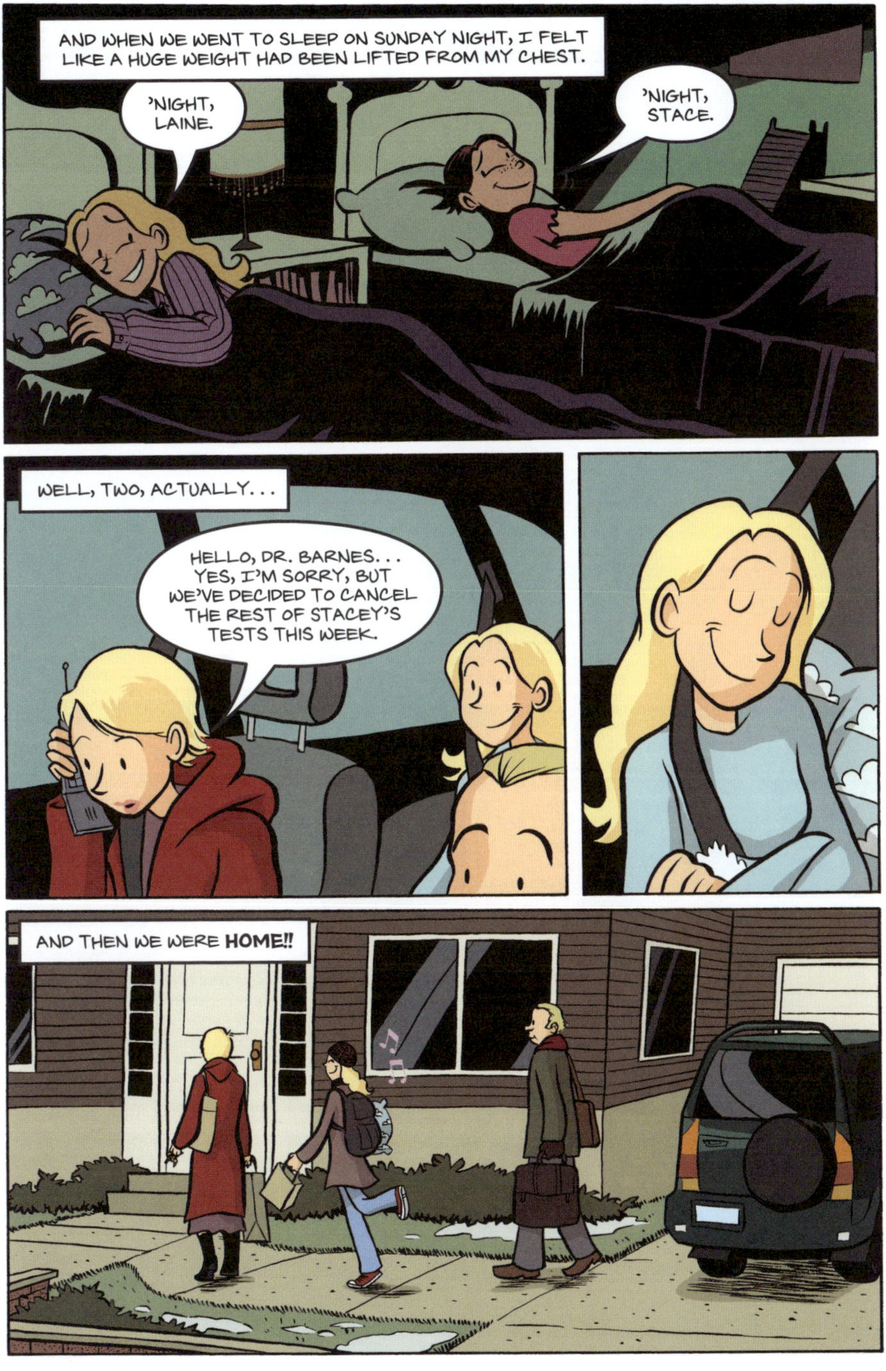
AND WHEN WE WENT TO SLEEP ON SUNDAY NIGHT, I FELT LIKE A HUGE WEIGHT HAD BEEN LIFTED FROM MY CHEST.
'NIGHT, LAINE.
'NIGHT, STACE.
WELL, TWO, ACTUALLY...
HELLO, DR. BARNES... YES, I'M SORRY, BUT WE'VE DECIDED TO CANCEL THE REST OF STACEY'S TESTS THIS WEEK.
AND THEN WE WERE **HOME!!**

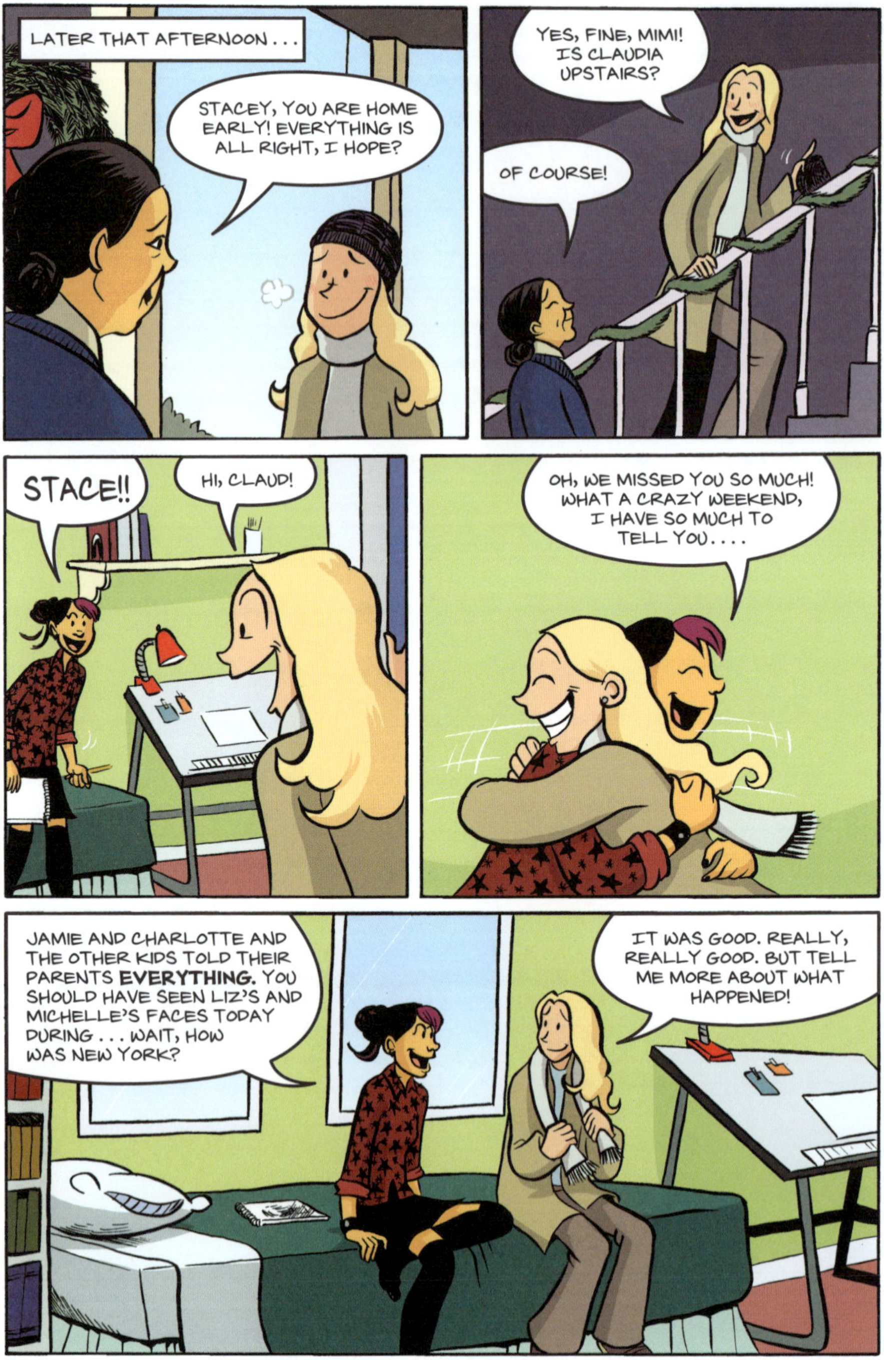
LATER THAT AFTERNOON . . .
STACEY, YOU ARE HOME EARLY! EVERYTHING IS ALL RIGHT, I HOPE?
YES, FINE, MIMI! IS CLAUDIA UPSTAIRS?
OF COURSE!
STACE!!
HI, CLAUD!
OH, WE MISSED YOU SO MUCH! WHAT A CRAZY WEEKEND, I HAVE SO MUCH TO TELL YOU. . . .
JAMIE AND CHARLOTTE AND THE OTHER KIDS TOLD THEIR PARENTS EVERYTHING. YOU SHOULD HAVE SEEN LIZ'S AND MICHELLE'S FACES TODAY DURING . . . WAIT, HOW WAS NEW YORK?
IT WAS GOOD. REALLY, REALLY GOOD. BUT TELL ME MORE ABOUT WHAT HAPPENED!

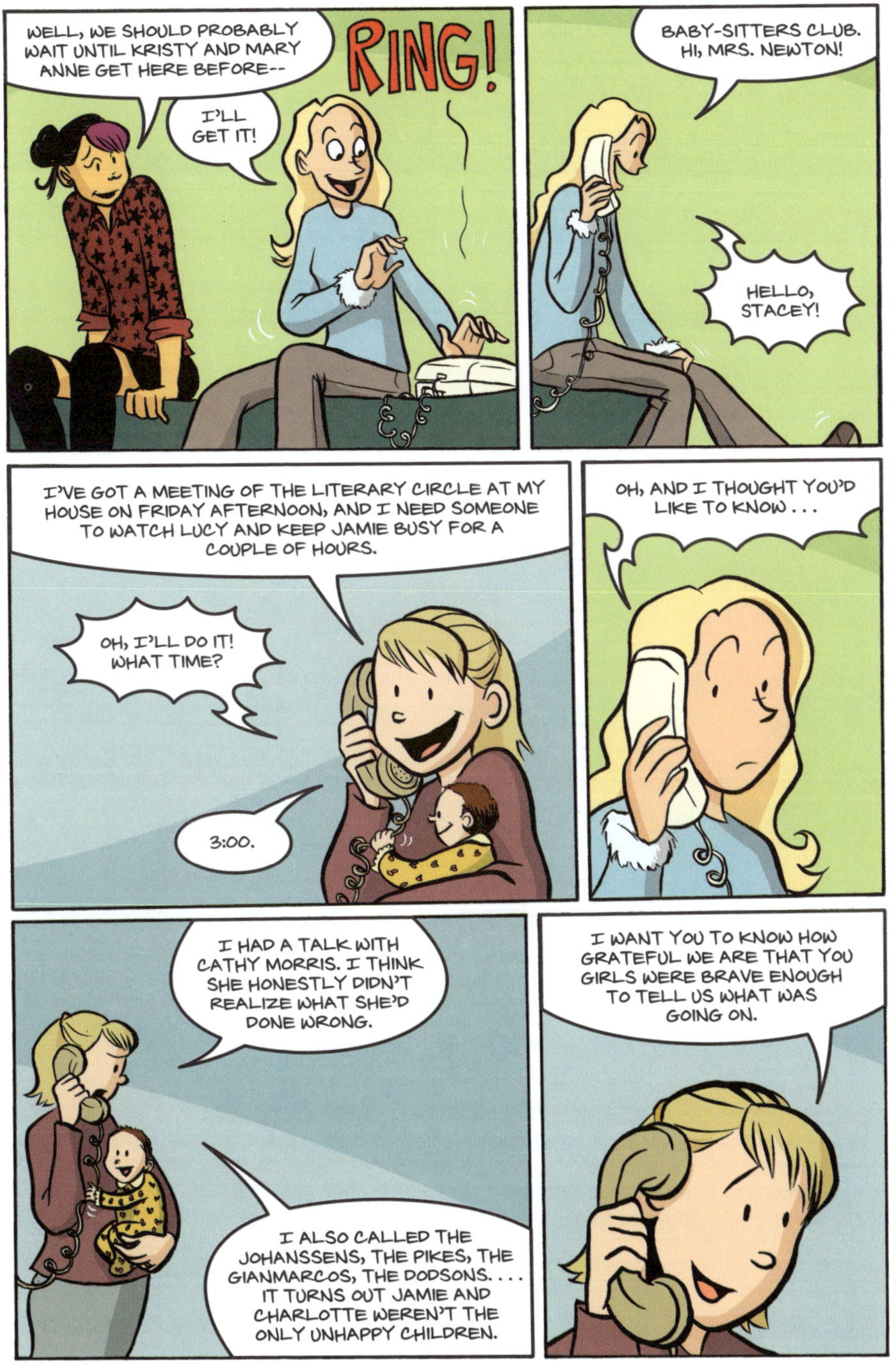
WELL, WE SHOULD PROBABLY WAIT UNTIL KRISTY AND MARY ANNE GET HERE BEFORE--
RING!
I'LL GET IT!
BABY-SITTERS CLUB. HI, MRS. NEWTON!
HELLO, STACEY!
I'VE GOT A MEETING OF THE LITERARY CIRCLE AT MY HOUSE ON FRIDAY AFTERNOON, AND I NEED SOMEONE TO WATCH LUCY AND KEEP JAMIE BUSY FOR A COUPLE OF HOURS.
OH, I'LL DO IT! WHAT TIME?
3:00.
OH, AND I THOUGHT YOU'D LIKE TO KNOW . . .
I HAD A TALK WITH CATHY MORRIS. I THINK SHE HONESTLY DIDN'T REALIZE WHAT SHE'D DONE WRONG.
I ALSO CALLED THE JOHANSSENS, THE PIKES, THE GIANMARCOS, THE DODSONS. . . . IT TURNS OUT JAMIE AND CHARLOTTE WEREN'T THE ONLY UNHAPPY CHILDREN.
I WANT YOU TO KNOW HOW GRATEFUL WE ARE THAT YOU GIRLS WERE BRAVE ENOUGH TO TELL US WHAT WAS GOING ON.

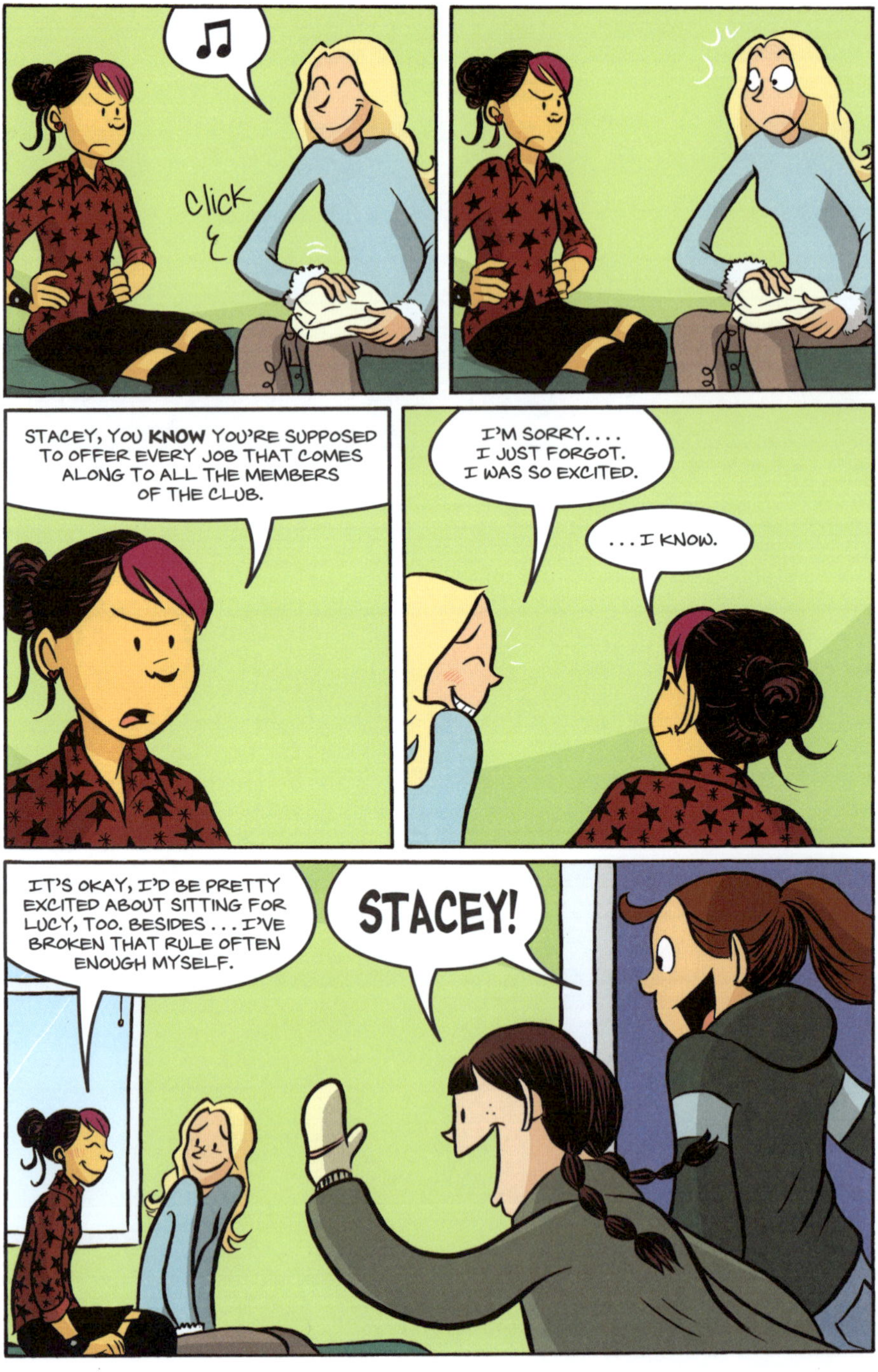
♫
CLICK
STACEY, YOU KNOW YOU'RE SUPPOSED TO OFFER EVERY JOB THAT COMES ALONG TO ALL THE MEMBERS OF THE CLUB.
I'M SORRY.... I JUST FORGOT. I WAS SO EXCITED.
...I KNOW.
IT'S OKAY, I'D BE PRETTY EXCITED ABOUT SITTING FOR LUCY, TOO. BESIDES... I'VE BROKEN THAT RULE OFTEN ENOUGH MYSELF.
STACEY!

CHAPTER 15

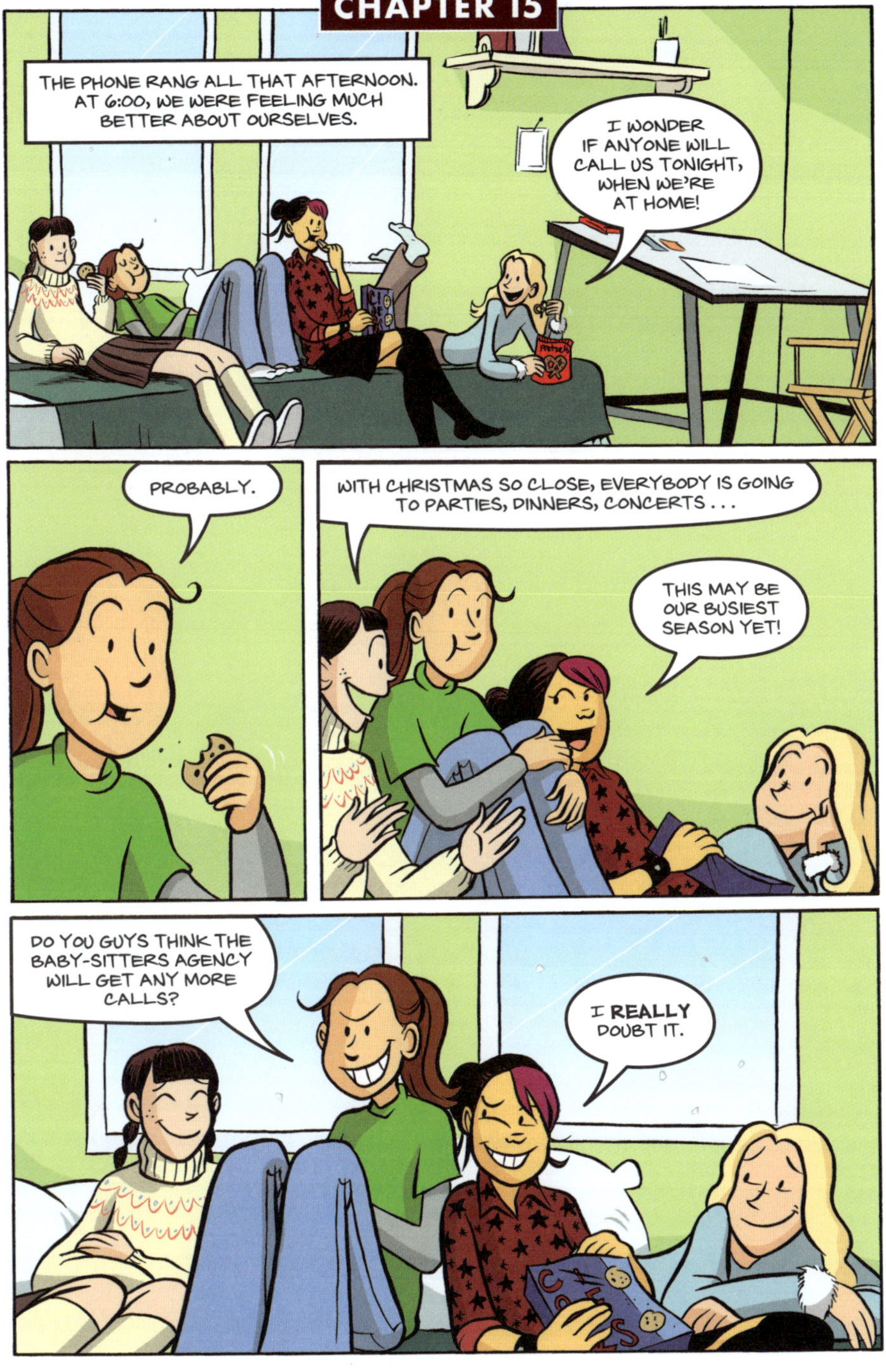
THE PHONE RANG ALL THAT AFTERNOON. AT 6:00, WE WERE FEELING MUCH BETTER ABOUT OURSELVES.
I WONDER IF ANYONE WILL CALL US TONIGHT, WHEN WE'RE AT HOME!
PROBABLY.
WITH CHRISTMAS SO CLOSE, EVERYBODY IS GOING TO PARTIES, DINNERS, CONCERTS . . .
THIS MAY BE OUR BUSIEST SEASON YET!
DO YOU GUYS THINK THE BABY-SITTERS AGENCY WILL GET ANY MORE CALLS?
I **REALLY** DOUBT IT.

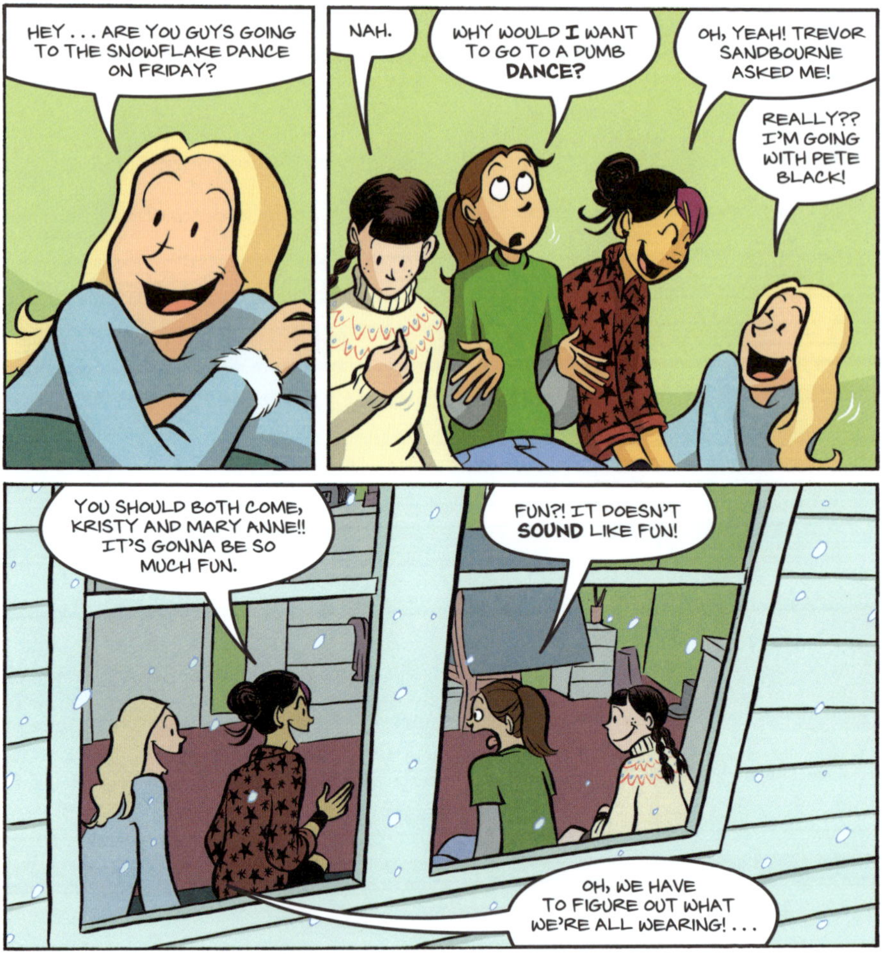
HEY . . . ARE YOU GUYS GOING TO THE SNOWFLAKE DANCE ON FRIDAY?
NAH.
WHY WOULD **I** WANT TO GO TO A DUMB **DANCE?**
OH, YEAH! TREVOR SANDBOURNE ASKED ME!
REALLY?? I'M GOING WITH PETE BLACK!
YOU SHOULD BOTH COME, KRISTY AND MARY ANNE!! IT'S GONNA BE SO MUCH FUN.
FUN?! IT DOESN'T **SOUND** LIKE FUN!
OH, WE HAVE TO FIGURE OUT WHAT WE'RE ALL WEARING! . . .

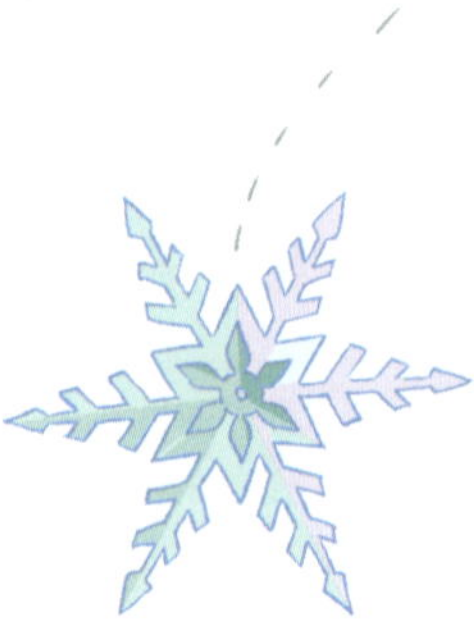

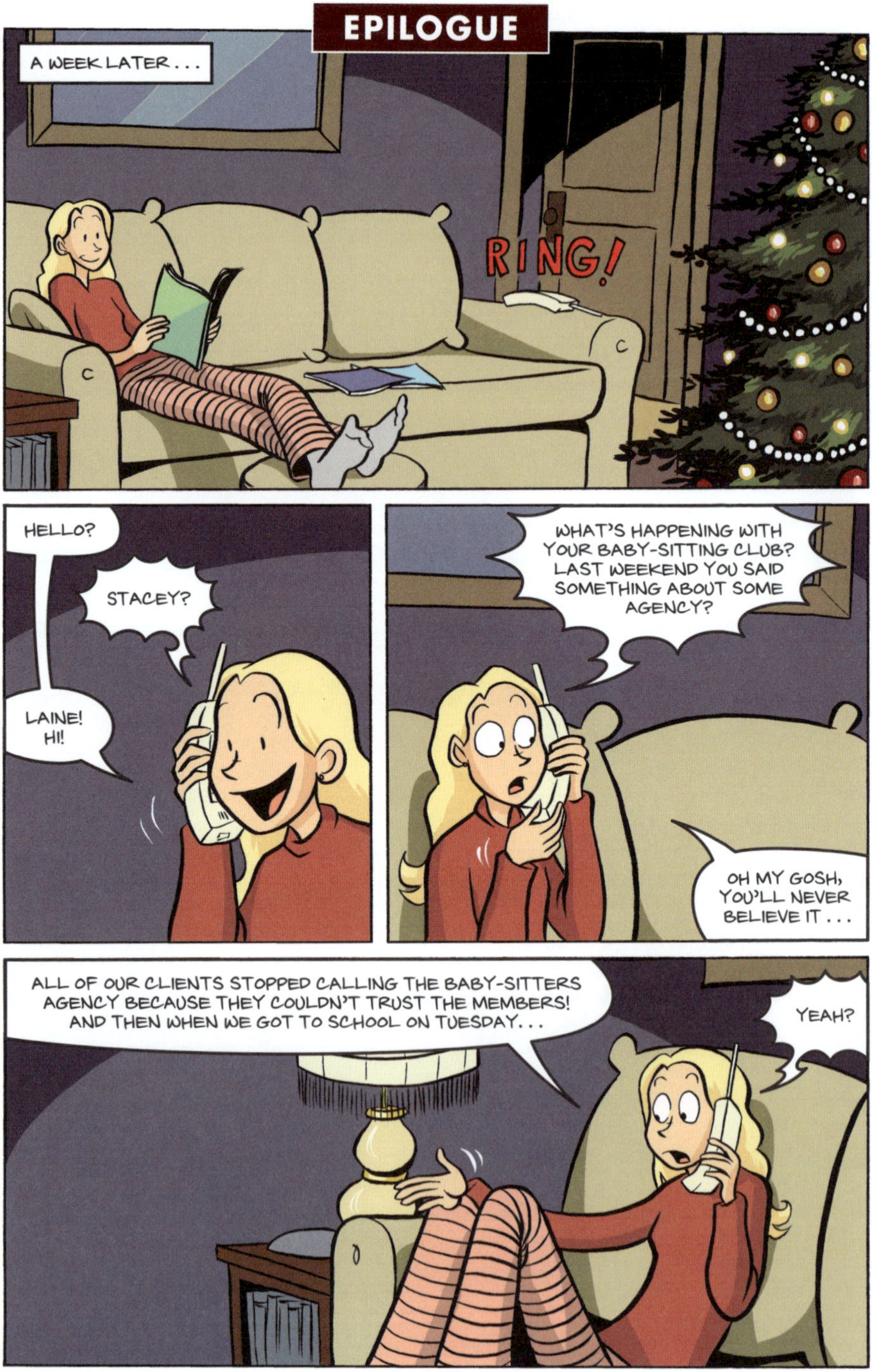
EPILOGUE
A WEEK LATER . . .
RING!
HELLO?
STACEY?
LAINE! HI!
WHAT'S HAPPENING WITH YOUR BABY-SITTING CLUB? LAST WEEKEND YOU SAID SOMETHING ABOUT SOME AGENCY?
OH MY GOSH, YOU'LL NEVER BELIEVE IT . . .
ALL OF OUR CLIENTS STOPPED CALLING THE BABY-SITTERS AGENCY BECAUSE THEY COULDN'T TRUST THE MEMBERS! AND THEN WHEN WE GOT TO SCHOOL ON TUESDAY. . .
YEAH?

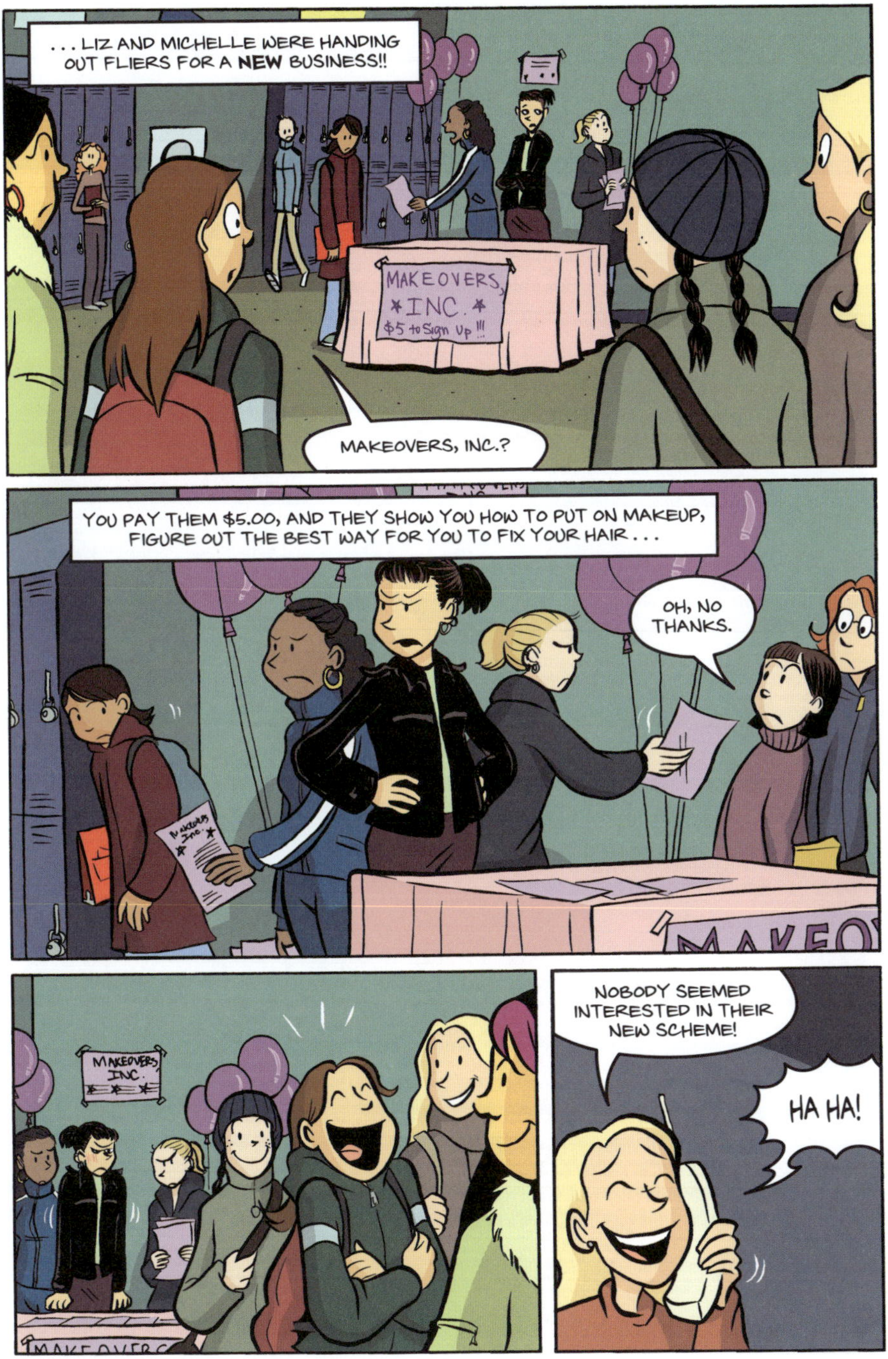
. . . LIZ AND MICHELLE WERE HANDING OUT FLIERS FOR A **NEW** BUSINESS!!
MAKEOVERS, INC. $5 to Sign Up!!!
MAKEOVERS, INC.?
YOU PAY THEM $5.00, AND THEY SHOW YOU HOW TO PUT ON MAKEUP, FIGURE OUT THE BEST WAY FOR YOU TO FIX YOUR HAIR . . .
Makeovers Inc.
OH, NO THANKS.
MAKEOVERS, INC.
NOBODY SEEMED INTERESTED IN THEIR NEW SCHEME!
HA HA!

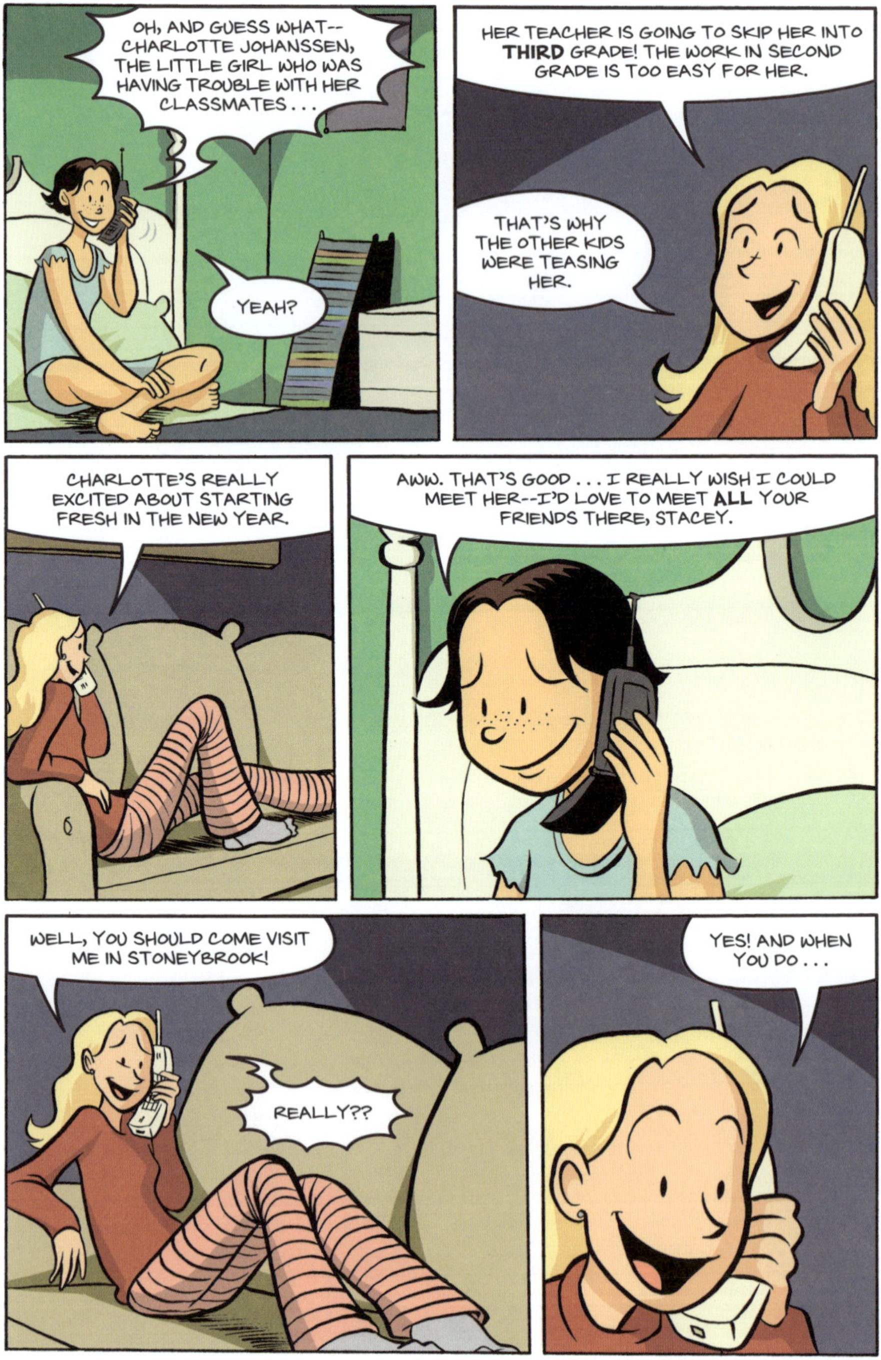
OH, AND GUESS WHAT-- CHARLOTTE JOHANSSEN, THE LITTLE GIRL WHO WAS HAVING TROUBLE WITH HER CLASSMATES . . .
YEAH?
HER TEACHER IS GOING TO SKIP HER INTO THIRD GRADE! THE WORK IN SECOND GRADE IS TOO EASY FOR HER.
THAT'S WHY THE OTHER KIDS WERE TEASING HER.
CHARLOTTE'S REALLY EXCITED ABOUT STARTING FRESH IN THE NEW YEAR.
AWW. THAT'S GOOD . . . I REALLY WISH I COULD MEET HER--I'D LOVE TO MEET ALL YOUR FRIENDS THERE, STACEY.
WELL, YOU SHOULD COME VISIT ME IN STONEYBROOK!
REALLY??
YES! AND WHEN YOU DO . . .

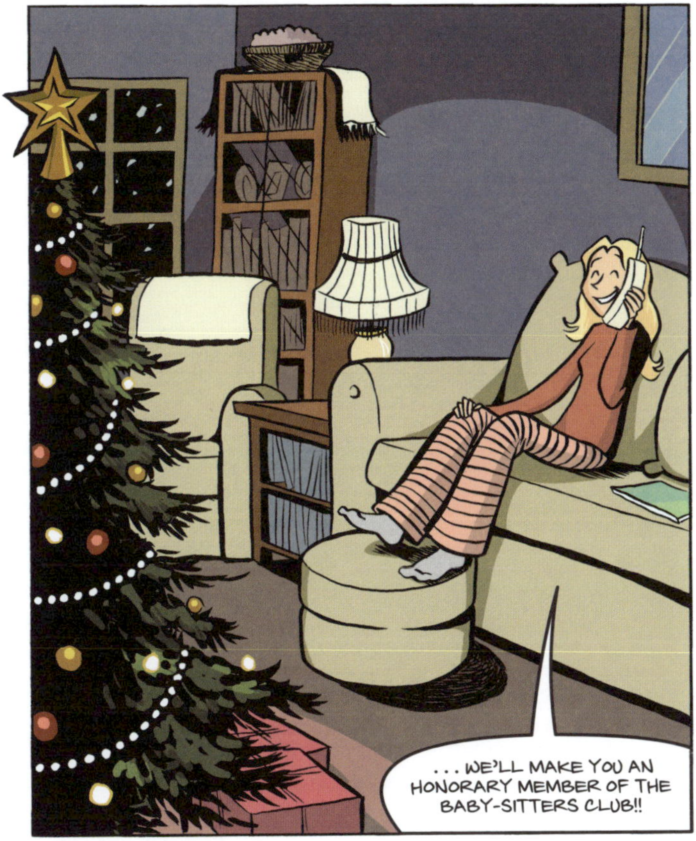
. . . WE'LL MAKE YOU AN HONORARY MEMBER OF THE BABY-SITTERS CLUB!!

This book is for my old pal, Claudia Werner
A. M. M.

Thanks to Marion Vitus, Adam Girardet, Duane Ballanger, Lisa Jonte, Arthur Levine, and Braden Lamb. As always, a huge thank-you to my family, my friends, and especially, Dave.
R. T.

Text copyright © 2006, 2015 by Ann M. Martin
Art copyright © 2006, 2015 by Raina Telgemeier

All rights reserved. Published by Graphix, an imprint of Scholastic Inc., *Publishers since 1920*. SCHOLASTIC, GRAPHIX, THE BABY-SITTERS CLUB, and associated logos are trademarks and/or registered trademarks of Scholastic Inc.

The publisher does not have any control over and does not assume any responsibility for author or third-party websites or their content.

No part of this publication may be reproduced, stored in a retrieval system, or transmitted in any form or by any means, electronic, mechanical, photocopying, recording, or otherwise, without written permission of the publisher. For information regarding permission, write to Scholastic Inc., Attention: Permissions Department, 557 Broadway, New York, NY 10012.

This book is a work of fiction. Names, characters, places, and incidents are either the product of the author's imagination or are used fictitiously, and any resemblance to actual persons, living or dead, business establishments, events, or locales is entirely coincidental.

Library of Congress Control Number: 2014945627

ISBN 978-0-545-81388-4 (hardcover)
ISBN 978-1-338-88824-9 (paperback)

10 9 8 7 6 5 4   24 25 26 27

Printed in China   62
This edition first printing, April 2023

Lettering by John Green
Edited by Cassandra Pelham Fulton, Janna Morishima, and David Levithan
Book design by Phil Falco
Creative Director: David Saylor

ANN M. MARTIN

THE BABY-SITTERS CLUB

MARY ANNE SAVES THE DAY

A GRAPHIC NOVEL BY
RAINA TELGEMEIER
WITH COLOR BY BRADEN LAMB

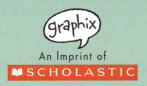

An Imprint of
SCHOLASTIC

Text copyright © 2007, 2015 by Ann M. Martin
Art copyright © 2007, 2015 by Raina Telgemeier

All rights reserved. Published by Graphix, an imprint of Scholastic Inc., *Publishers since 1920.* SCHOLASTIC, GRAPHIX, THE BABY-SITTERS CLUB, and associated logos are trademarks and/or registered trademarks of Scholastic Inc.

The publisher does not have any control over and does not assume any responsibility for author or third-party websites or their content.

No part of this publication may be reproduced, stored in a retrieval system, or transmitted in any form or by any means, electronic, mechanical, photocopying, recording, or otherwise, without written permission of the publisher. For information regarding permission, write to Scholastic Inc., Attention: Permissions Department, 557 Broadway, New York, NY 10012.

This book is a work of fiction. Names, characters, places, and incidents are either the product of the author's imagination or are used fictitiously, and any resemblance to actual persons, living or dead, business establishments, events, or locales is entirely coincidental.

Library of Congress Control Number: 2015935841

ISBN 978-0-545-88617-8 (hardcover)
ISBN 978-1-338-88825-6 (paperback)

10 9 8 7 6 5 4 3 2   23 24 25 26 27

Printed in China   62
This edition first printing, April 2023

Lettering by John Green
Edited by Cassandra Pelham Fulton, Sheila Keenan, and David Levithan
Book design by Phil Falco
Creative Director: David Saylor

This book is for the real Claire and Margo: Claire DuBois Gordon
and Margo Méndez-Peñate, Class of 2006

A. M. M.

Thanks to David Saylor, Cassandra Pelham, Ellie Berger,
Marion Vitus, Alisa Harris, Ben Wilgus, Zack Giallongo, Steve Flack,
Phil Falco, Braden Lamb, and John Green. And of course, thanks to
Dave Roman, for always encouraging me to do my best.

R. T.

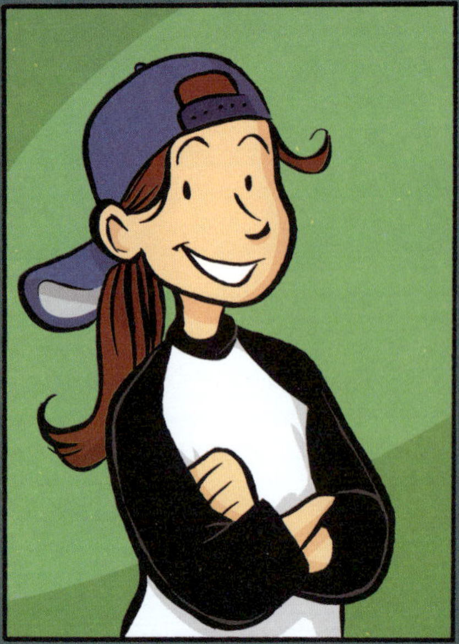

KRISTY THOMAS
PRESIDENT

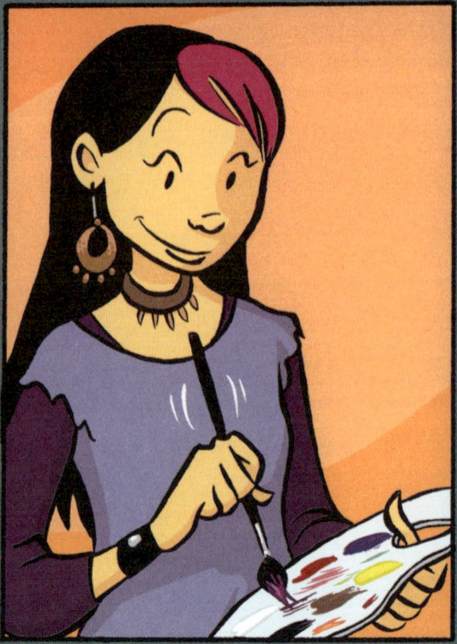

CLAUDIA KISHI
VICE PRESIDENT

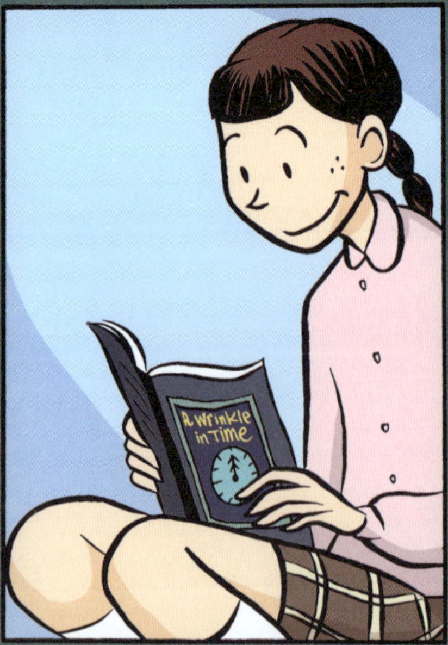
A Wrinkle in Time

MARY ANNE SPIER
SECRETARY

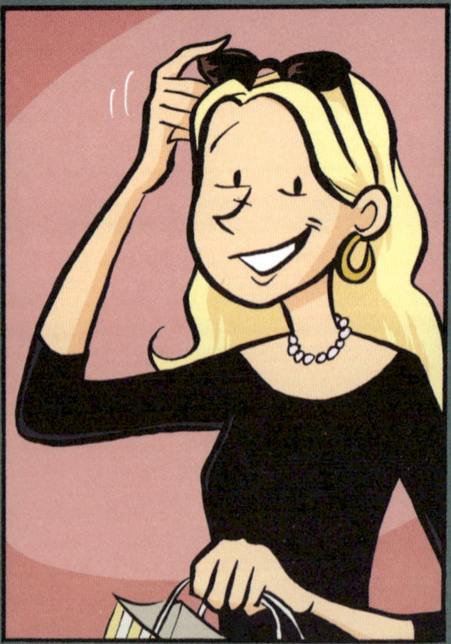

STACEY MCGILL
TREASURER

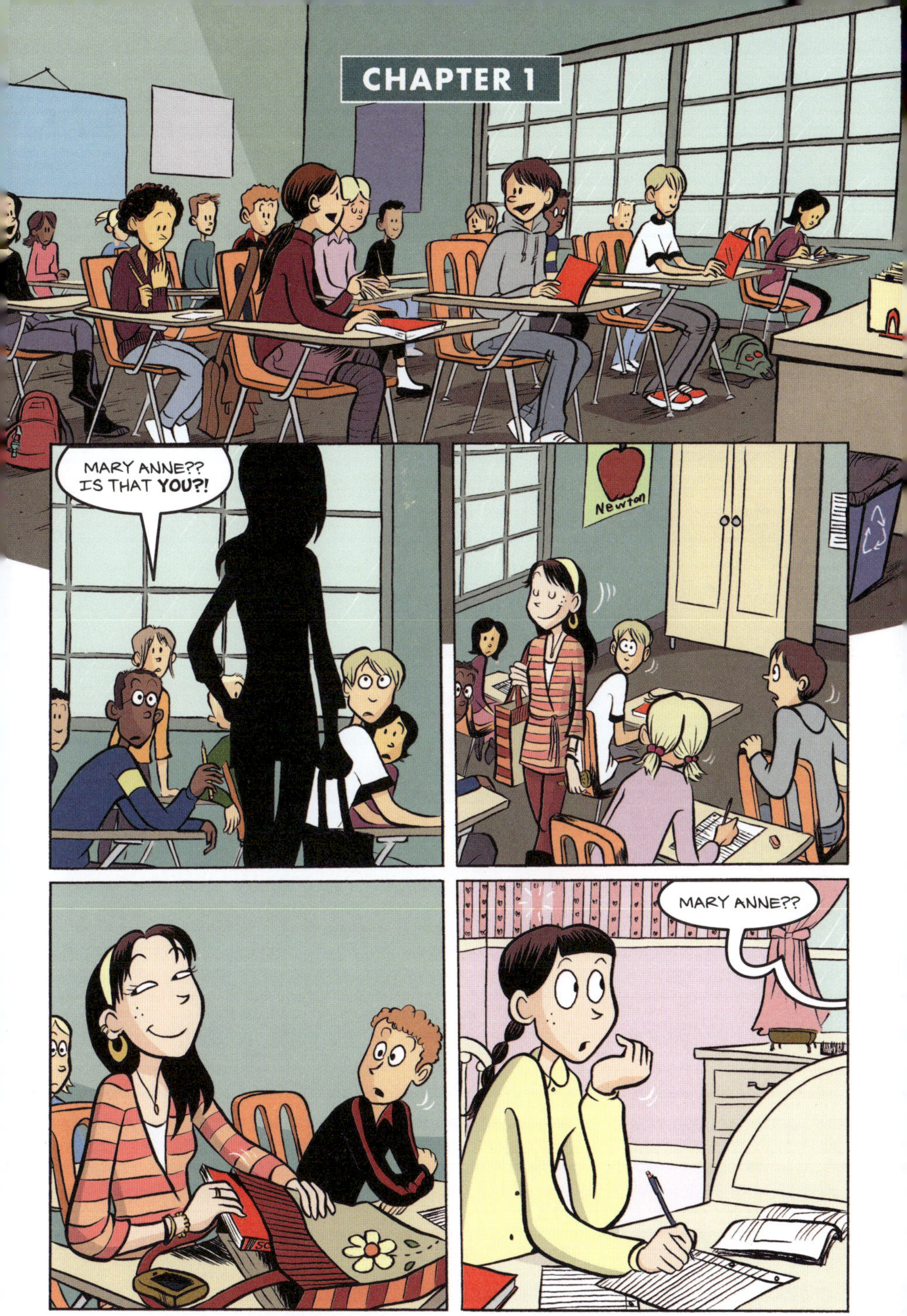
CHAPTER 1
MARY ANNE??
IS THAT YOU?!
Newton
MARY ANNE??

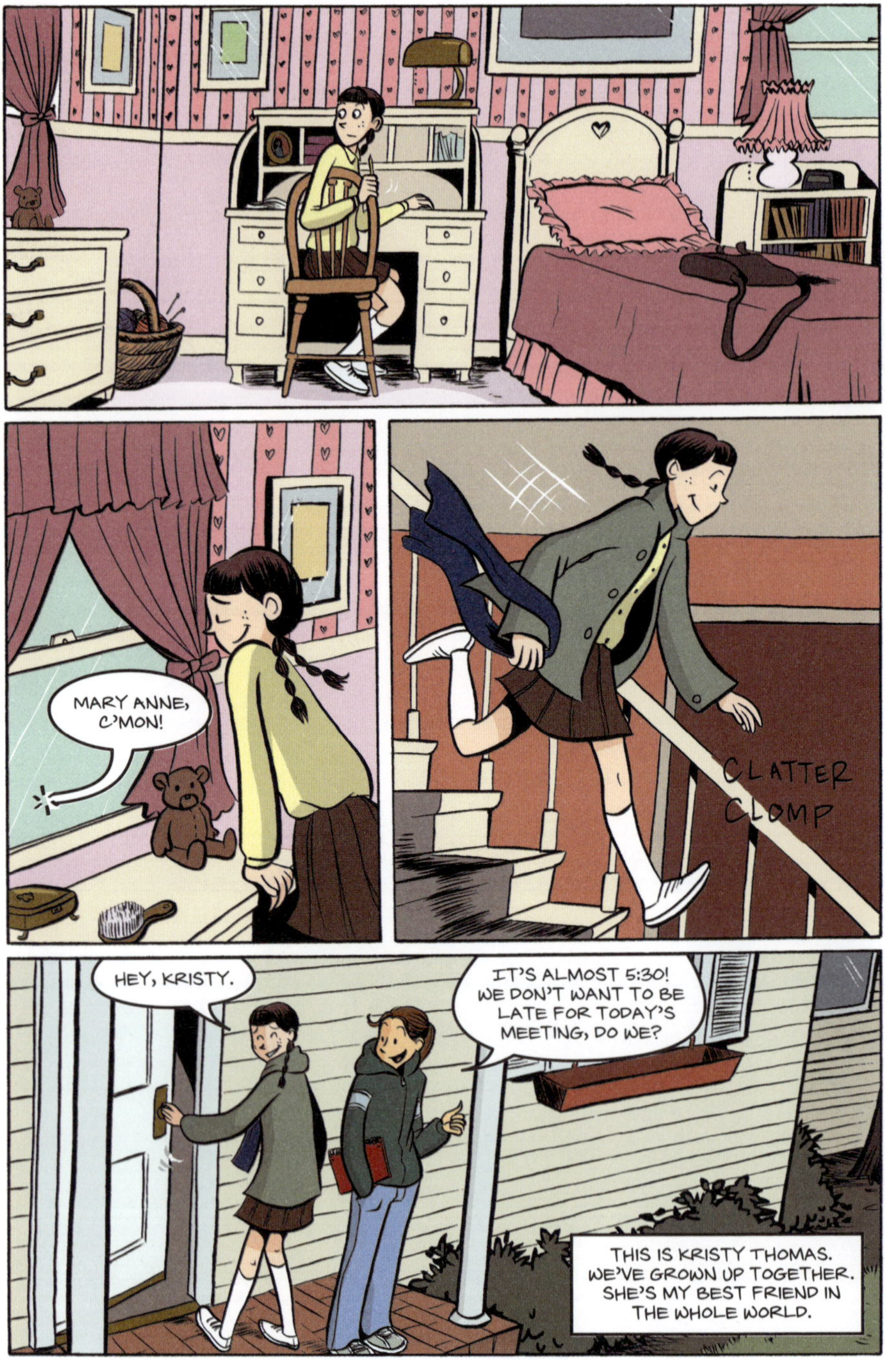
MARY ANNE, C'MON!
CLATTER
CLOMP
HEY, KRISTY.
IT'S ALMOST 5:30! WE DON'T WANT TO BE LATE FOR TODAY'S MEETING, DO WE?
THIS IS KRISTY THOMAS. WE'VE GROWN UP TOGETHER. SHE'S MY BEST FRIEND IN THE WHOLE WORLD.

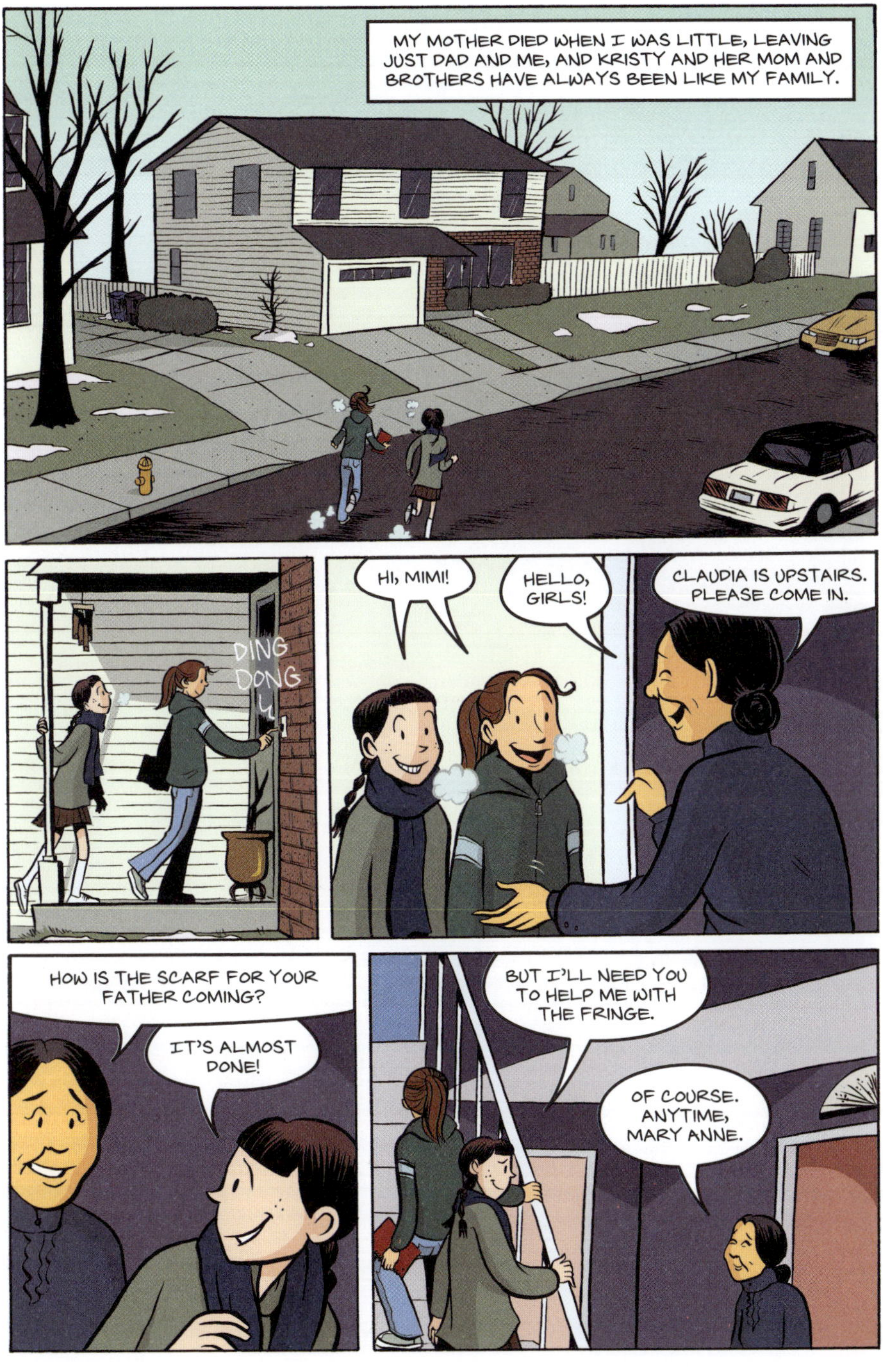

MY MOTHER DIED WHEN I WAS LITTLE, LEAVING JUST DAD AND ME, AND KRISTY AND HER MOM AND BROTHERS HAVE ALWAYS BEEN LIKE MY FAMILY.
DING DONG
HI, MIMI!
HELLO, GIRLS!
CLAUDIA IS UPSTAIRS. PLEASE COME IN.
HOW IS THE SCARF FOR YOUR FATHER COMING?
IT'S ALMOST DONE!
BUT I'LL NEED YOU TO HELP ME WITH THE FRINGE.
OF COURSE. ANYTIME, MARY ANNE.

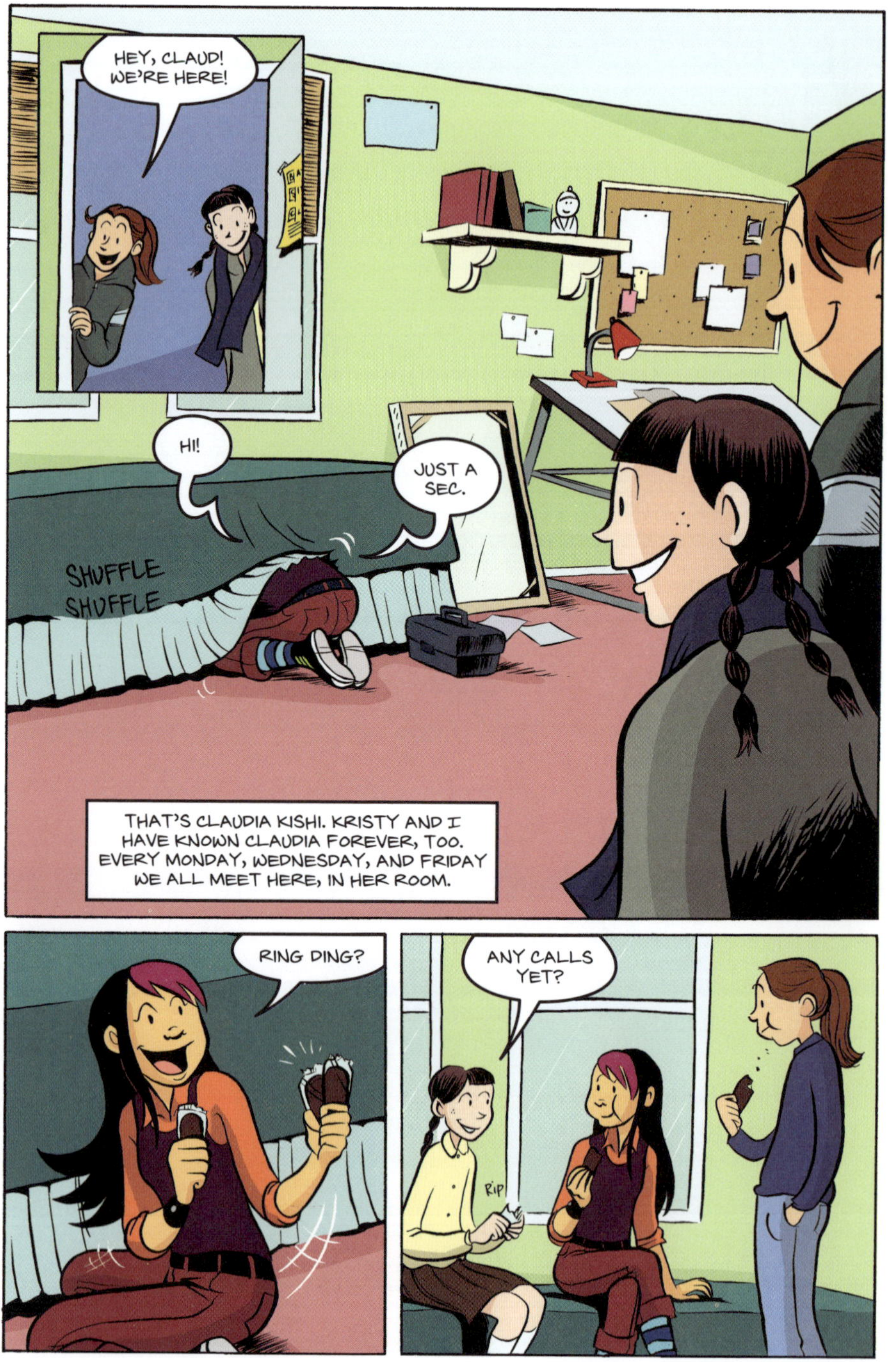
HEY, CLAUD! WE'RE HERE!
HI!
JUST A SEC.
SHUFFLE SHUFFLE
THAT'S CLAUDIA KISHI. KRISTY AND I HAVE KNOWN CLAUDIA FOREVER, TOO. EVERY MONDAY, WEDNESDAY, AND FRIDAY WE ALL MEET HERE, IN HER ROOM.
RING DING?
ANY CALLS YET?
RIP

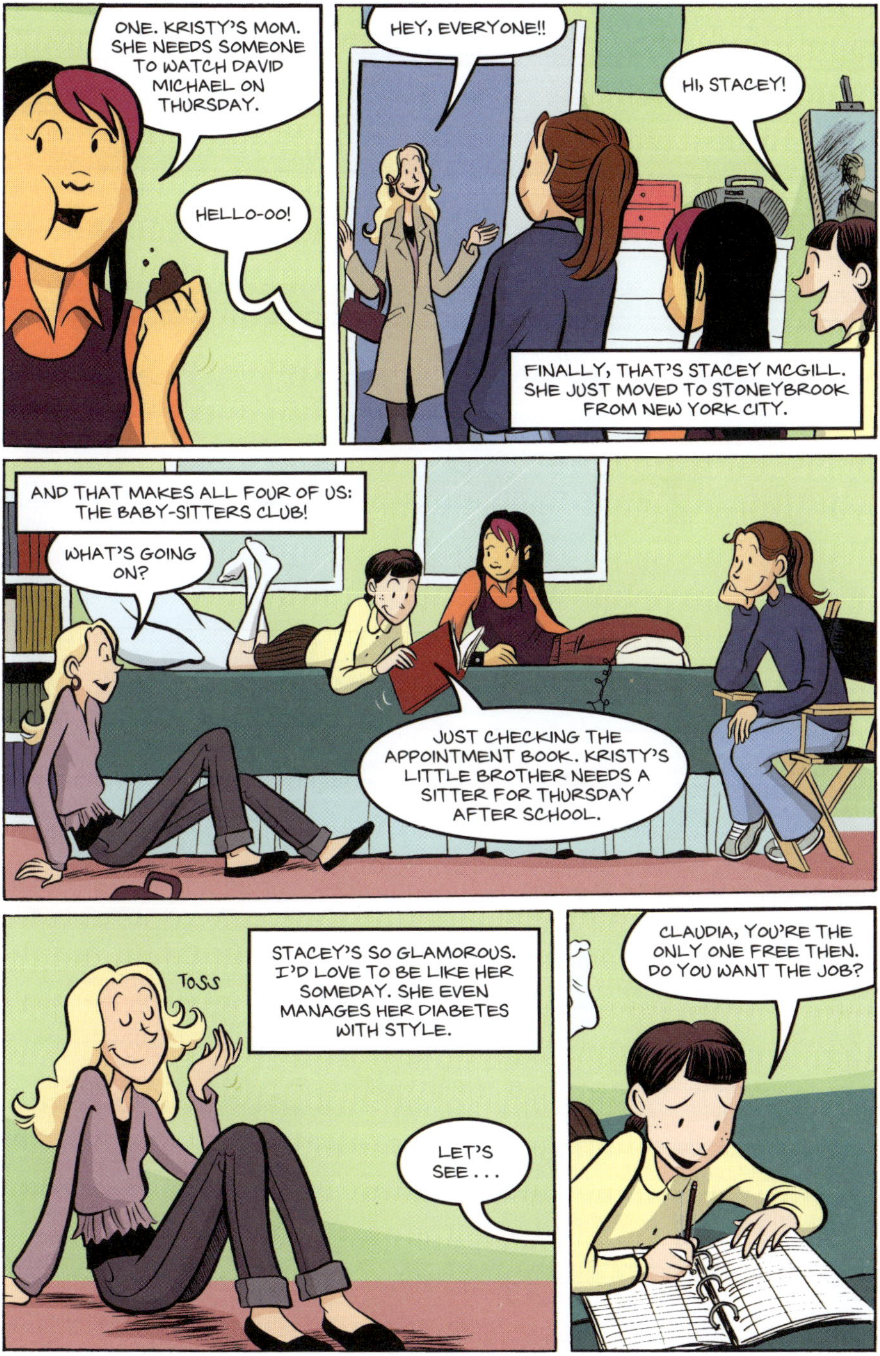
ONE. KRISTY'S MOM. SHE NEEDS SOMEONE TO WATCH DAVID MICHAEL ON THURSDAY.
HELLO-OO!
HEY, EVERYONE!!
HI, STACEY!
FINALLY, THAT'S STACEY MCGILL. SHE JUST MOVED TO STONEYBROOK FROM NEW YORK CITY.
AND THAT MAKES ALL FOUR OF US: THE BABY-SITTERS CLUB!
WHAT'S GOING ON?
JUST CHECKING THE APPOINTMENT BOOK. KRISTY'S LITTLE BROTHER NEEDS A SITTER FOR THURSDAY AFTER SCHOOL.
TOSS
STACEY'S SO GLAMOROUS. I'D LOVE TO BE LIKE HER SOMEDAY. SHE EVEN MANAGES HER DIABETES WITH STYLE.
LET'S SEE . . .
CLAUDIA, YOU'RE THE ONLY ONE FREE THEN. DO YOU WANT THE JOB?

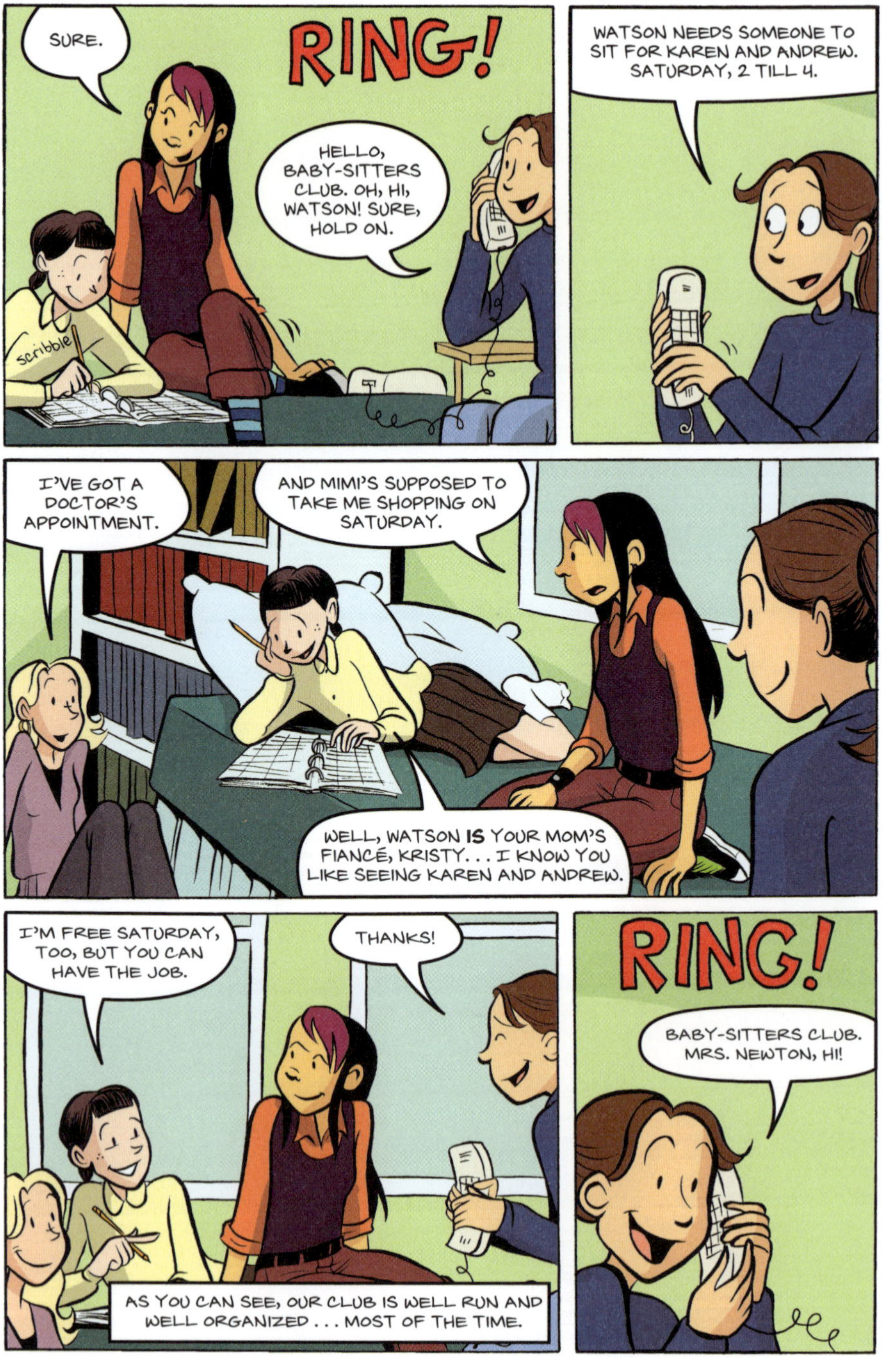
SURE.
RING!
HELLO, BABY-SITTERS CLUB. OH, HI, WATSON! SURE, HOLD ON.
WATSON NEEDS SOMEONE TO SIT FOR KAREN AND ANDREW. SATURDAY, 2 TILL 4.
I'VE GOT A DOCTOR'S APPOINTMENT.
AND MIMI'S SUPPOSED TO TAKE ME SHOPPING ON SATURDAY.
WELL, WATSON IS YOUR MOM'S FIANCÉ, KRISTY. . . I KNOW YOU LIKE SEEING KAREN AND ANDREW.
I'M FREE SATURDAY, TOO, BUT YOU CAN HAVE THE JOB.
THANKS!
AS YOU CAN SEE, OUR CLUB IS WELL RUN AND WELL ORGANIZED . . . MOST OF THE TIME.
RING!
BABY-SITTERS CLUB. MRS. NEWTON, HI!

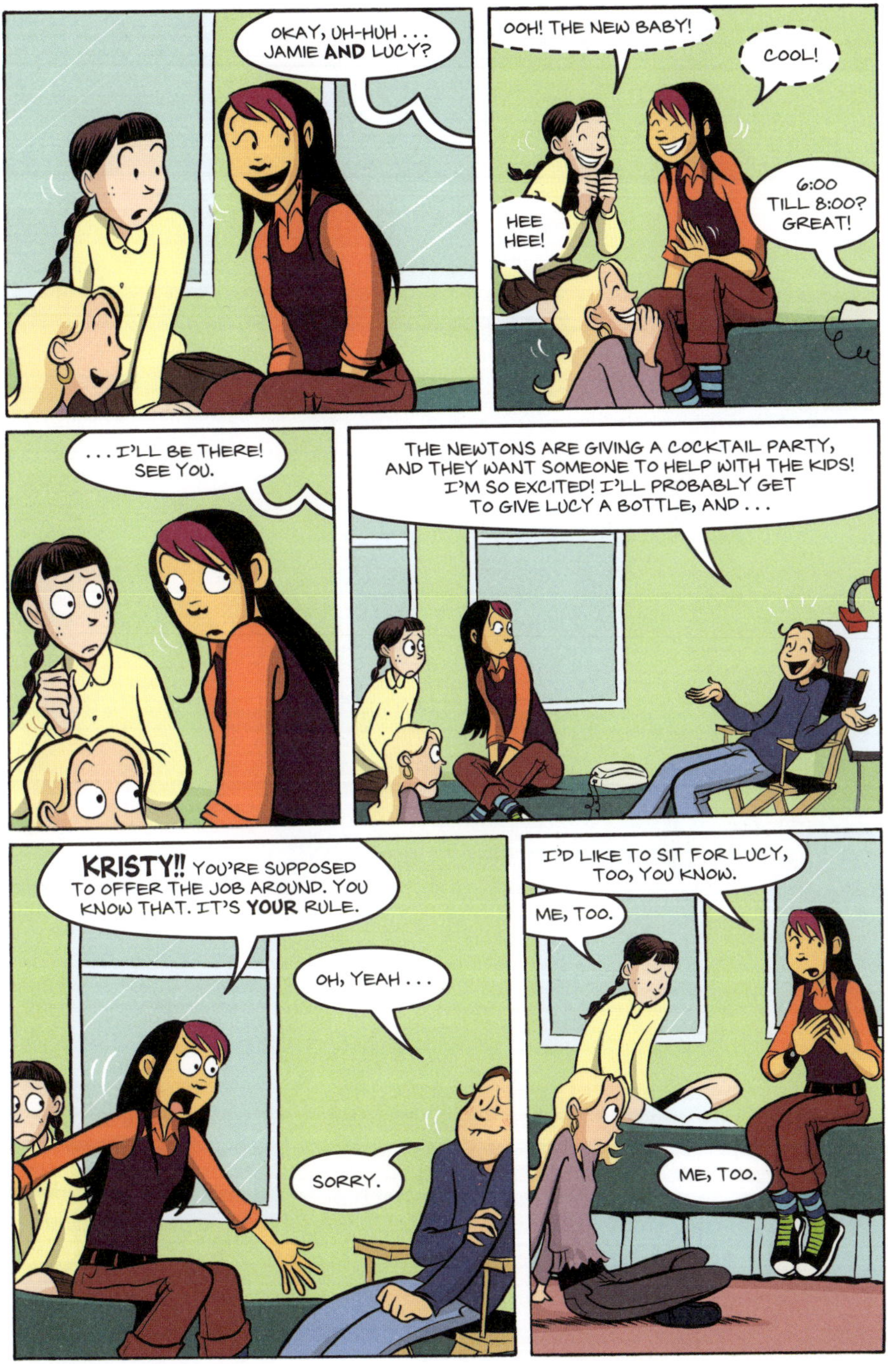
OKAY, UH-HUH . . .
JAMIE AND LUCY?
OOH! THE NEW BABY!
COOL!
HEE HEE!
6:00 TILL 8:00? GREAT!
. . . I'LL BE THERE! SEE YOU.
THE NEWTONS ARE GIVING A COCKTAIL PARTY, AND THEY WANT SOMEONE TO HELP WITH THE KIDS! I'M SO EXCITED! I'LL PROBABLY GET TO GIVE LUCY A BOTTLE, AND . . .
KRISTY!! YOU'RE SUPPOSED TO OFFER THE JOB AROUND. YOU KNOW THAT. IT'S YOUR RULE.
OH, YEAH . . .
SORRY.
I'D LIKE TO SIT FOR LUCY, TOO, YOU KNOW.
ME, TOO.
ME, TOO.

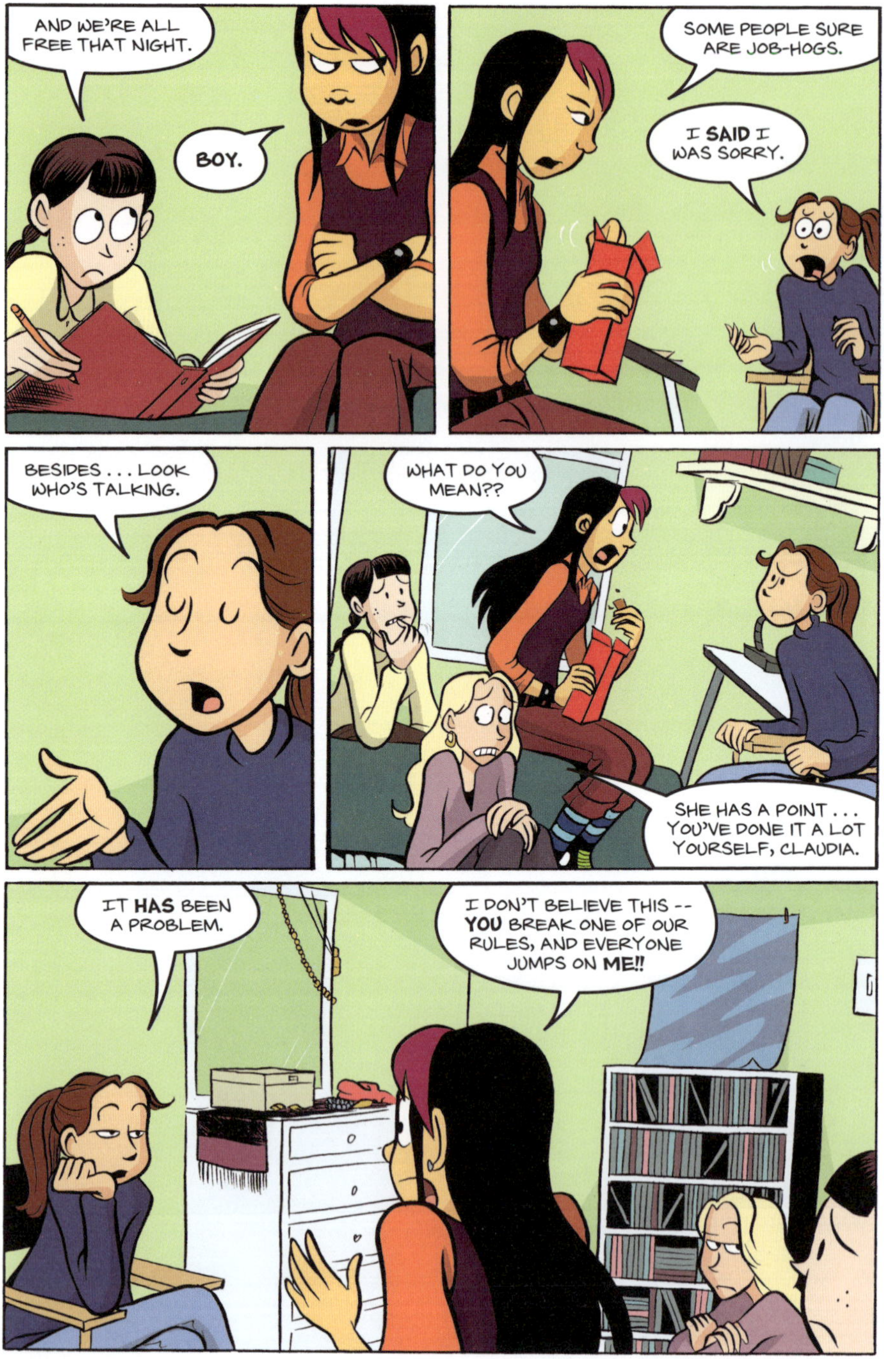
AND WE'RE ALL FREE THAT NIGHT.
BOY.
SOME PEOPLE SURE ARE JOB-HOGS.
I **SAID** I WAS SORRY.
BESIDES . . . LOOK WHO'S TALKING.
WHAT DO YOU MEAN??
SHE HAS A POINT . . . YOU'VE DONE IT A LOT YOURSELF, CLAUDIA.
IT **HAS** BEEN A PROBLEM.
I DON'T BELIEVE THIS -- **YOU** BREAK ONE OF OUR RULES, AND EVERYONE JUMPS ON **ME!!**

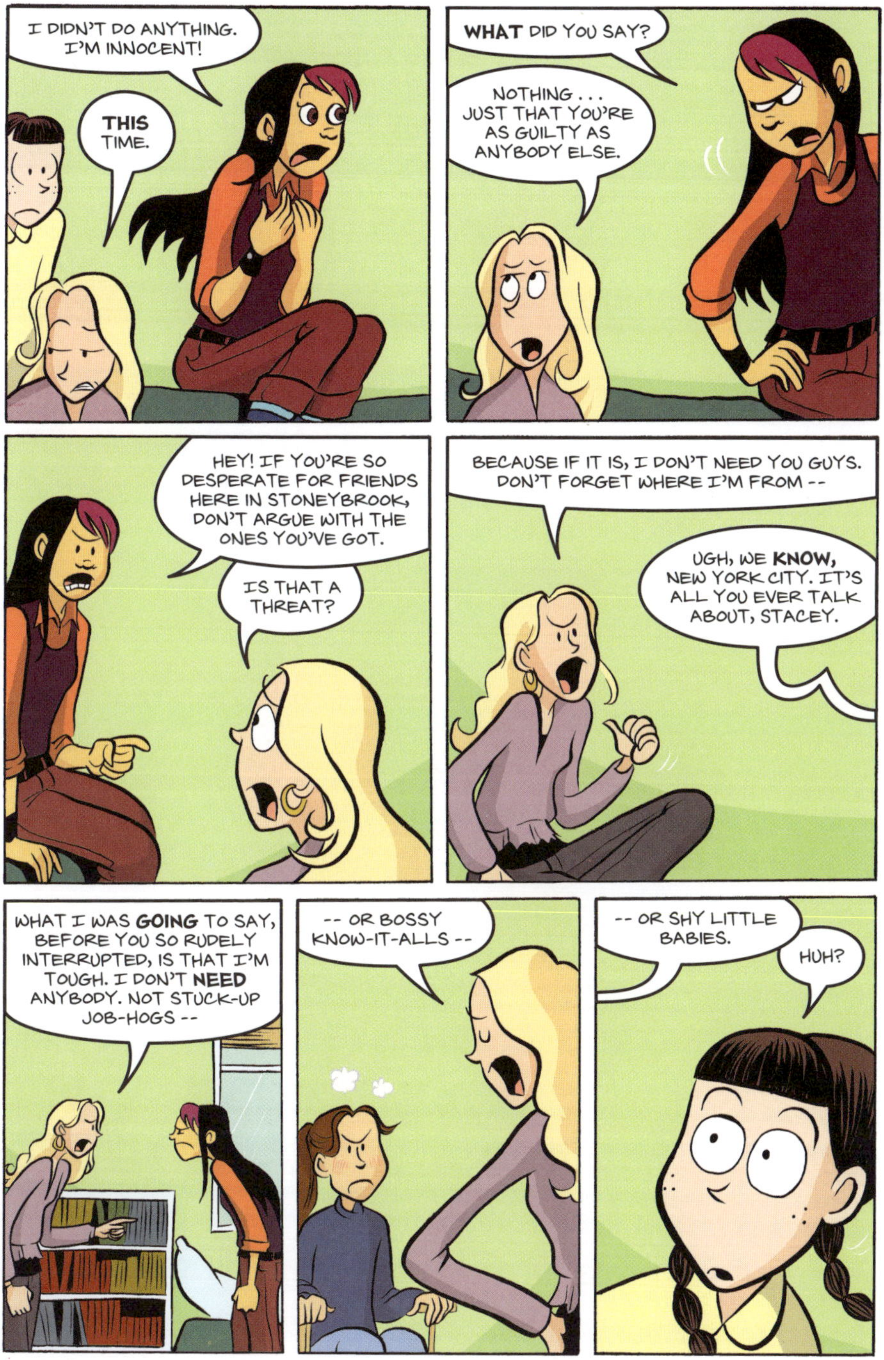
I DIDN'T DO ANYTHING. I'M INNOCENT!
THIS TIME.
WHAT DID YOU SAY?
NOTHING . . . JUST THAT YOU'RE AS GUILTY AS ANYBODY ELSE.
HEY! IF YOU'RE SO DESPERATE FOR FRIENDS HERE IN STONEYBROOK, DON'T ARGUE WITH THE ONES YOU'VE GOT.
IS THAT A THREAT?
BECAUSE IF IT IS, I DON'T NEED YOU GUYS. DON'T FORGET WHERE I'M FROM --
UGH, WE **KNOW,** NEW YORK CITY. IT'S ALL YOU EVER TALK ABOUT, STACEY.
WHAT I WAS **GOING** TO SAY, BEFORE YOU SO RUDELY INTERRUPTED, IS THAT I'M TOUGH. I DON'T **NEED** ANYBODY. NOT STUCK-UP JOB-HOGS --
-- OR BOSSY KNOW-IT-ALLS --
-- OR SHY LITTLE BABIES.
HUH?

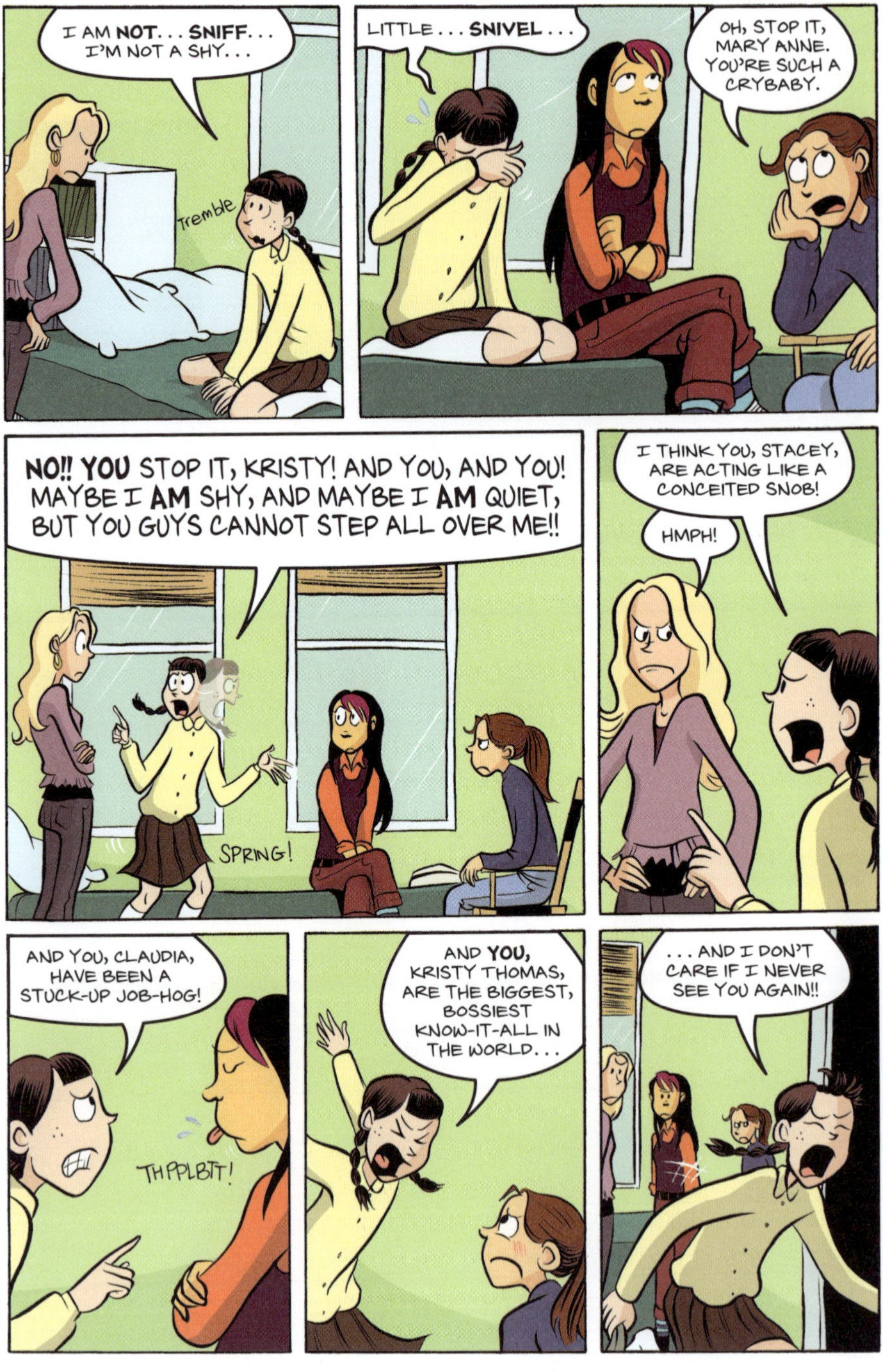
I AM **NOT**. . . **SNIFF**. . . I'M NOT A SHY. . .
Tremble
LITTLE . . . **SNIVEL** . . .
OH, STOP IT, MARY ANNE. YOU'RE SUCH A CRYBABY.
NO!! YOU STOP IT, KRISTY! AND YOU, AND YOU! MAYBE I **AM** SHY, AND MAYBE I **AM** QUIET, BUT YOU GUYS CANNOT STEP ALL OVER ME!!
SPRING!
I THINK YOU, STACEY, ARE ACTING LIKE A CONCEITED SNOB!
HMPH!
AND YOU, CLAUDIA, HAVE BEEN A STUCK-UP JOB-HOG!
THPPLBTT!
AND **YOU,** KRISTY THOMAS, ARE THE BIGGEST, BOSSIEST KNOW-IT-ALL IN THE WORLD. . .
. . . AND I DON'T CARE IF I NEVER SEE YOU AGAIN!!

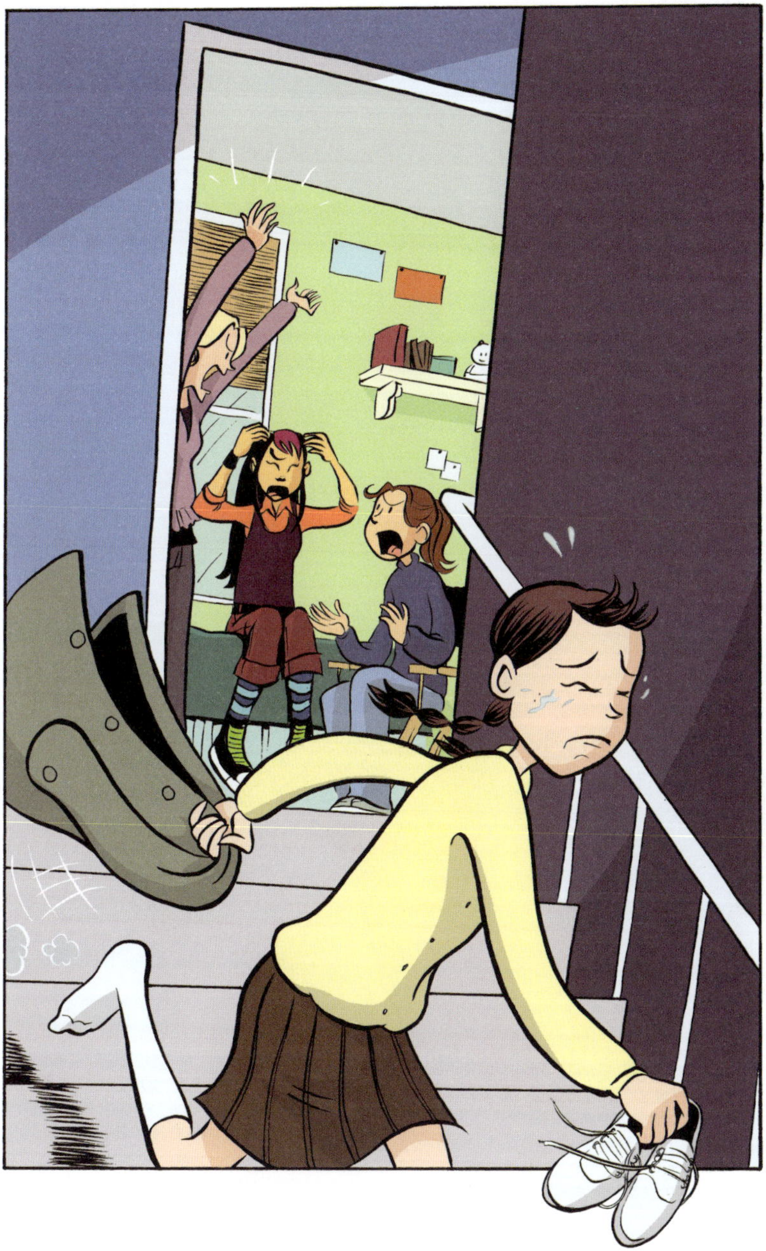

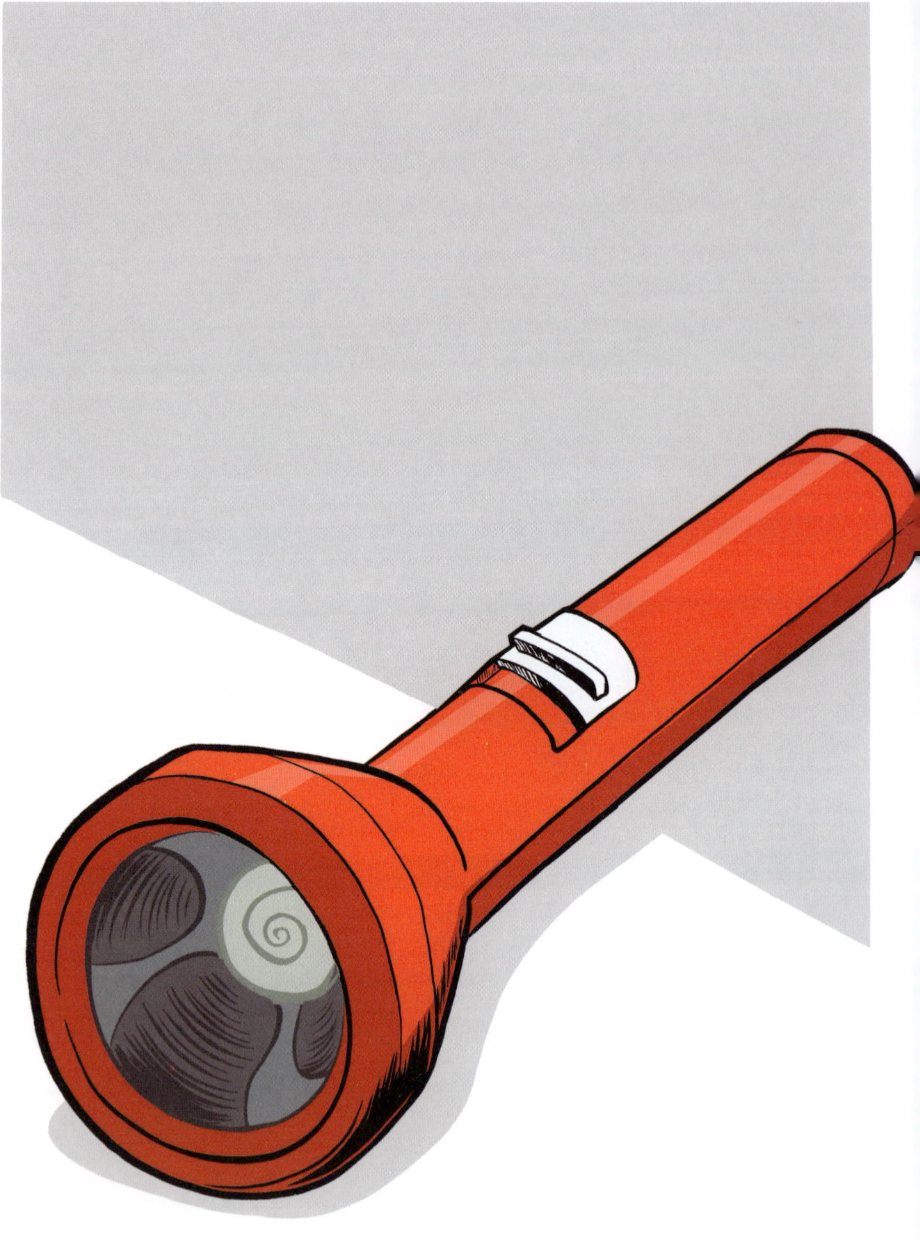

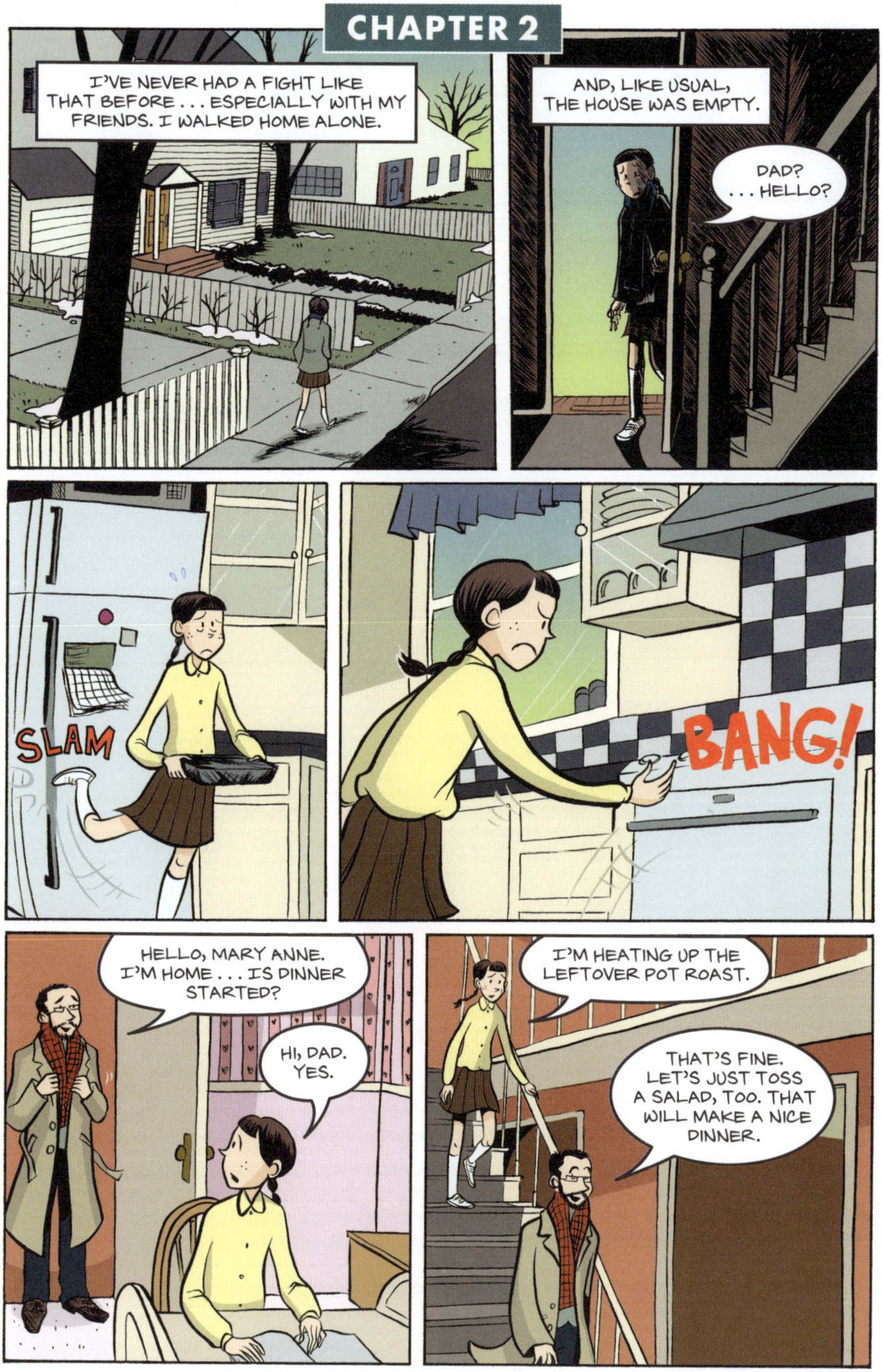
CHAPTER 2
I'VE NEVER HAD A FIGHT LIKE THAT BEFORE . . . ESPECIALLY WITH MY FRIENDS. I WALKED HOME ALONE.
AND, LIKE USUAL, THE HOUSE WAS EMPTY.
DAD? . . . HELLO?
SLAM
BANG!
HELLO, MARY ANNE. I'M HOME . . . IS DINNER STARTED?
HI, DAD. YES.
I'M HEATING UP THE LEFTOVER POT ROAST.
THAT'S FINE. LET'S JUST TOSS A SALAD, TOO. THAT WILL MAKE A NICE DINNER.

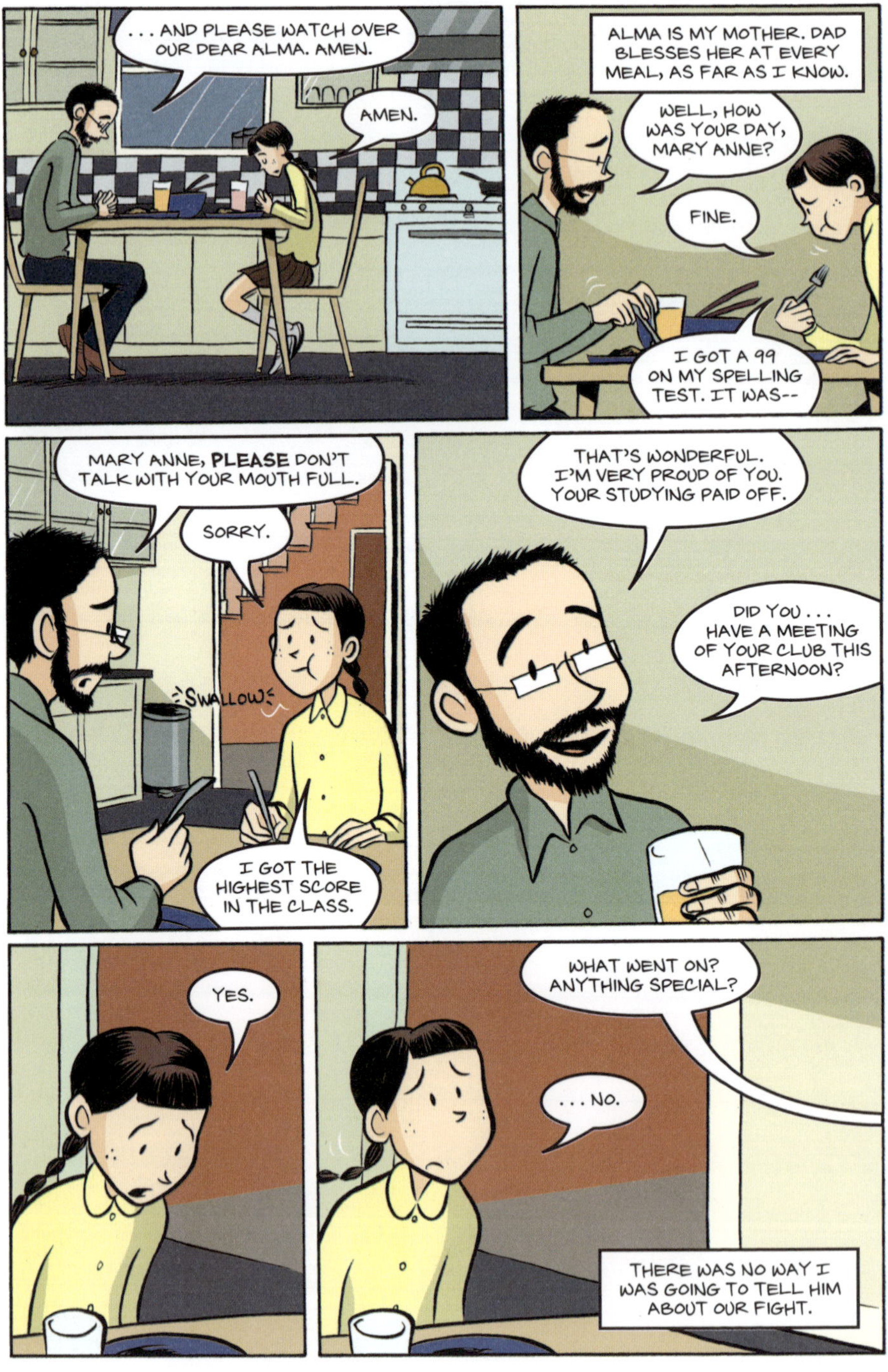
. . . AND PLEASE WATCH OVER OUR DEAR ALMA. AMEN.
AMEN.
ALMA IS MY MOTHER. DAD BLESSES HER AT EVERY MEAL, AS FAR AS I KNOW.
WELL, HOW WAS YOUR DAY, MARY ANNE?
FINE.
I GOT A 99 ON MY SPELLING TEST. IT WAS--
MARY ANNE, **PLEASE** DON'T TALK WITH YOUR MOUTH FULL.
SORRY.
SWALLOW
I GOT THE HIGHEST SCORE IN THE CLASS.
THAT'S WONDERFUL. I'M VERY PROUD OF YOU. YOUR STUDYING PAID OFF.
DID YOU . . . HAVE A MEETING OF YOUR CLUB THIS AFTERNOON?
YES.
WHAT WENT ON? ANYTHING SPECIAL?
. . . NO.
THERE WAS NO WAY I WAS GOING TO TELL HIM ABOUT OUR FIGHT.

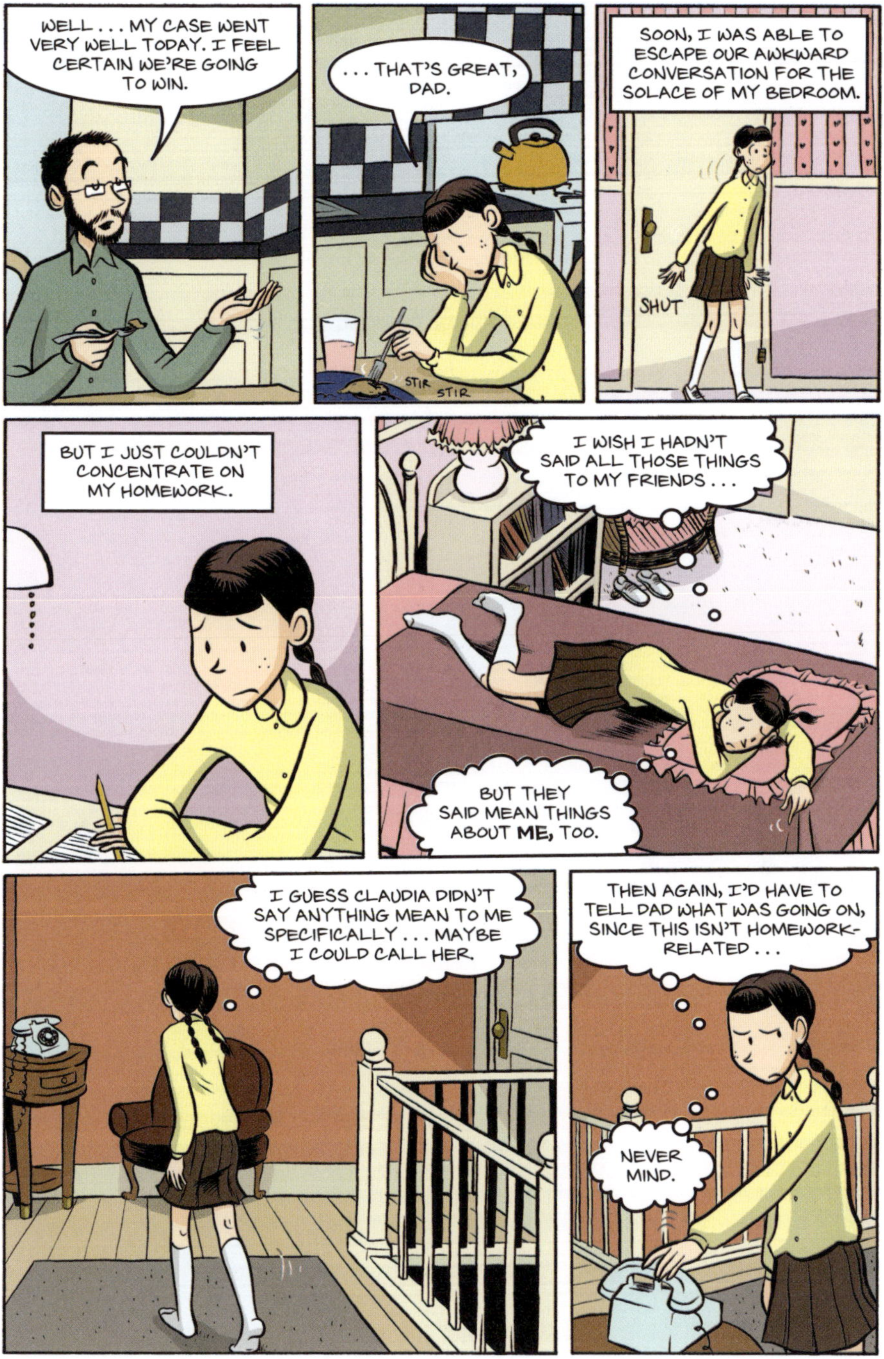
WELL . . . MY CASE WENT VERY WELL TODAY. I FEEL CERTAIN WE'RE GOING TO WIN.
. . . THAT'S GREAT, DAD.
STIR STIR
SOON, I WAS ABLE TO ESCAPE OUR AWKWARD CONVERSATION FOR THE SOLACE OF MY BEDROOM.
SHUT
BUT I JUST COULDN'T CONCENTRATE ON MY HOMEWORK.
I WISH I HADN'T SAID ALL THOSE THINGS TO MY FRIENDS . . .
BUT THEY SAID MEAN THINGS ABOUT **ME**, TOO.
I GUESS CLAUDIA DIDN'T SAY ANYTHING MEAN TO ME SPECIFICALLY . . . MAYBE I COULD CALL HER.
THEN AGAIN, I'D HAVE TO TELL DAD WHAT WAS GOING ON, SINCE THIS ISN'T HOMEWORK-RELATED . . .
NEVER MIND.

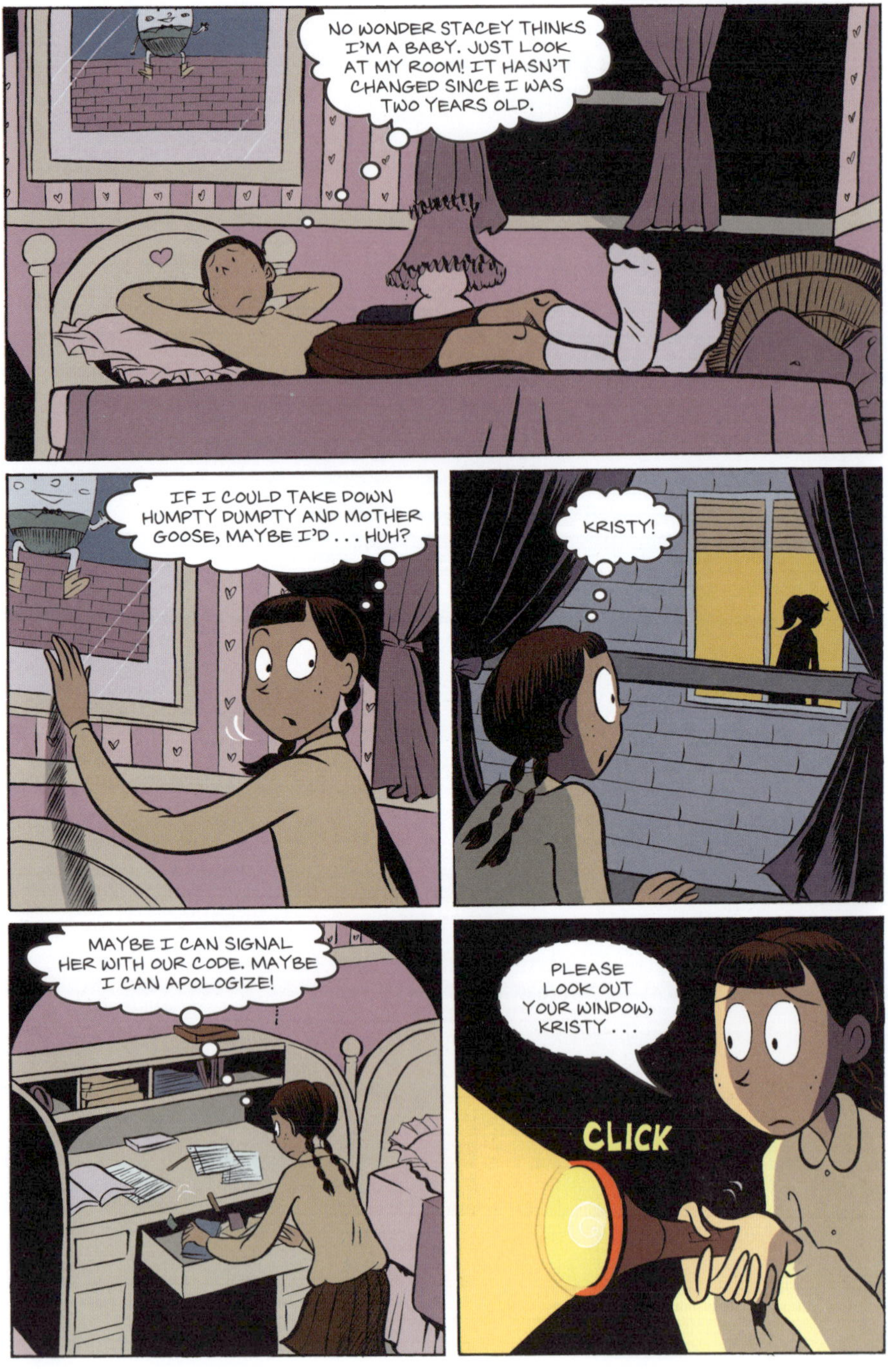
NO WONDER STACEY THINKS I'M A BABY. JUST LOOK AT MY ROOM! IT HASN'T CHANGED SINCE I WAS TWO YEARS OLD.
IF I COULD TAKE DOWN HUMPTY DUMPTY AND MOTHER GOOSE, MAYBE I'D . . . HUH?
KRISTY!
MAYBE I CAN SIGNAL HER WITH OUR CODE. MAYBE I CAN APOLOGIZE!
PLEASE LOOK OUT YOUR WINDOW, KRISTY . . .
CLICK

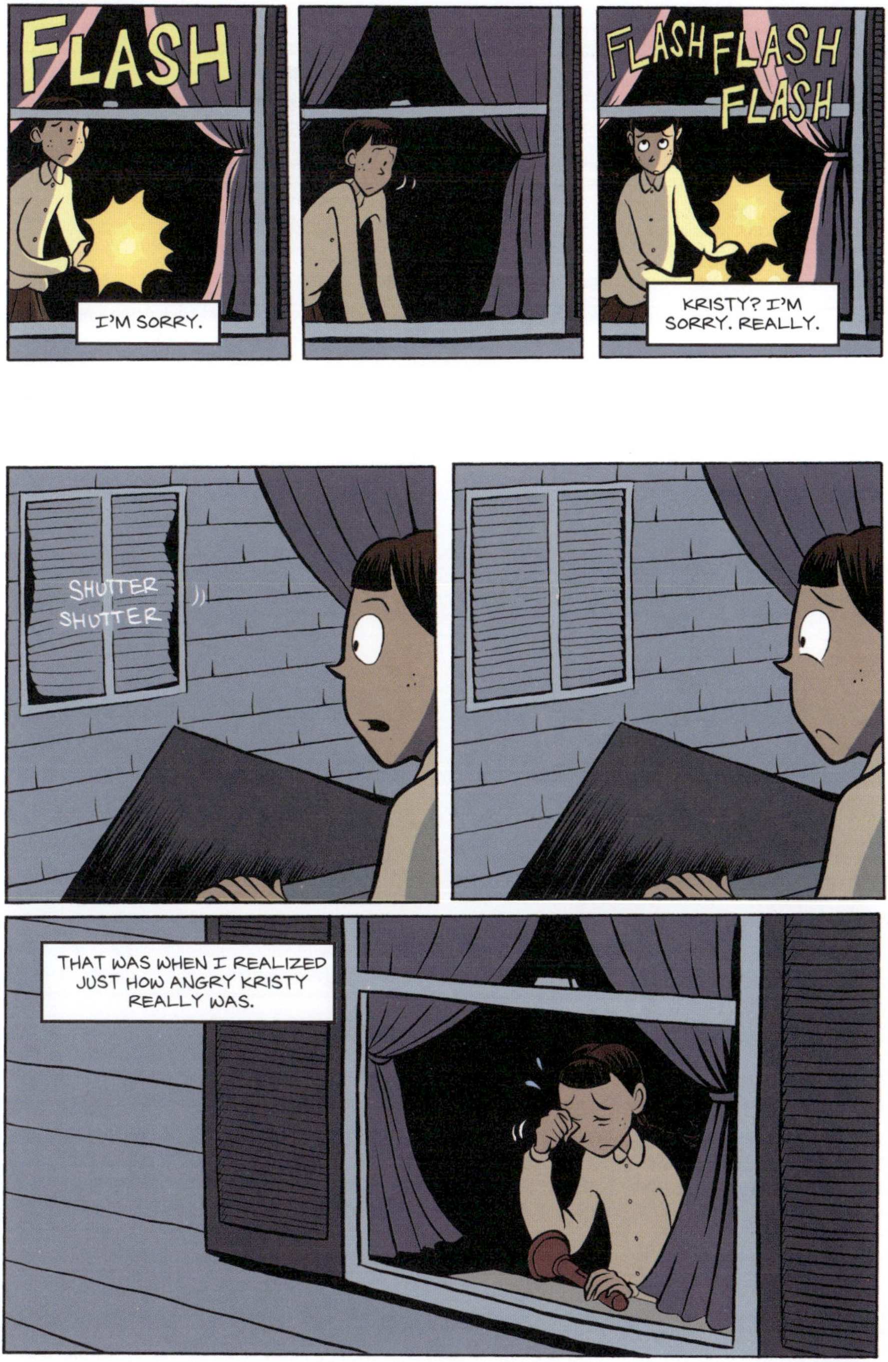
FLASH
I'M SORRY.
FLASH FLASH
FLASH
KRISTY? I'M SORRY. REALLY.
SHUTTER
SHUTTER
THAT WAS WHEN I REALIZED JUST HOW ANGRY KRISTY REALLY WAS.

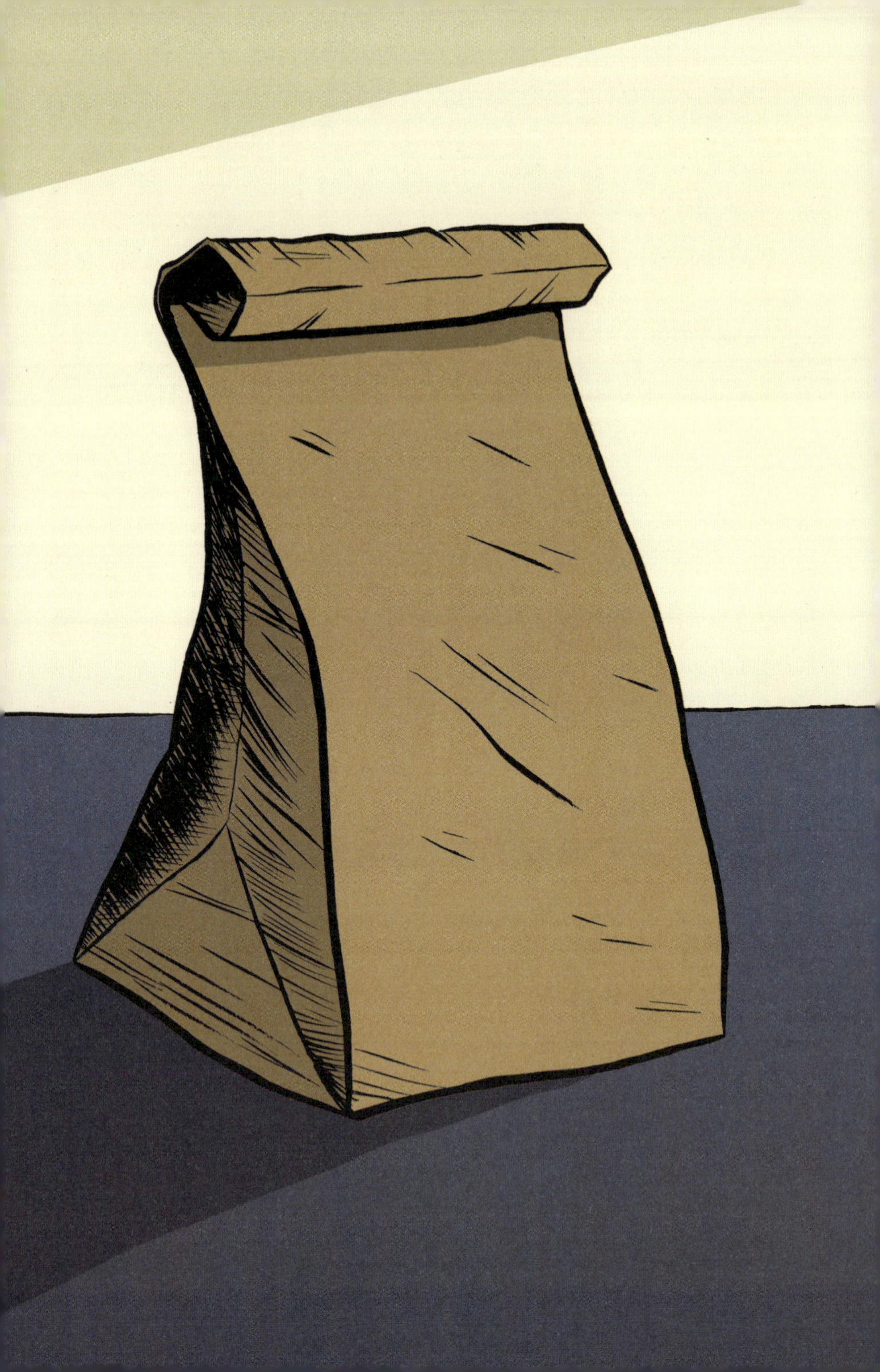

CHAPTER 3

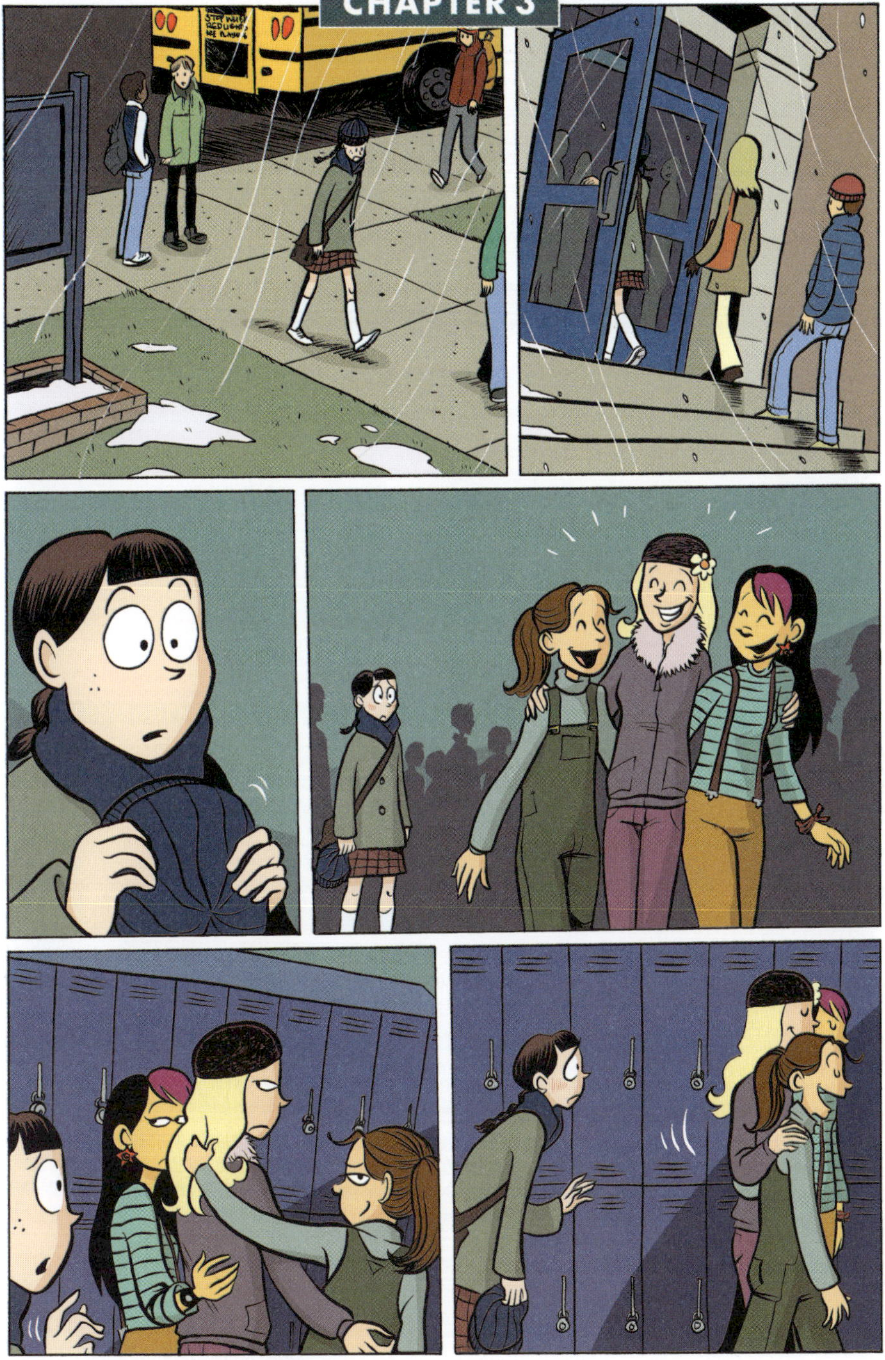

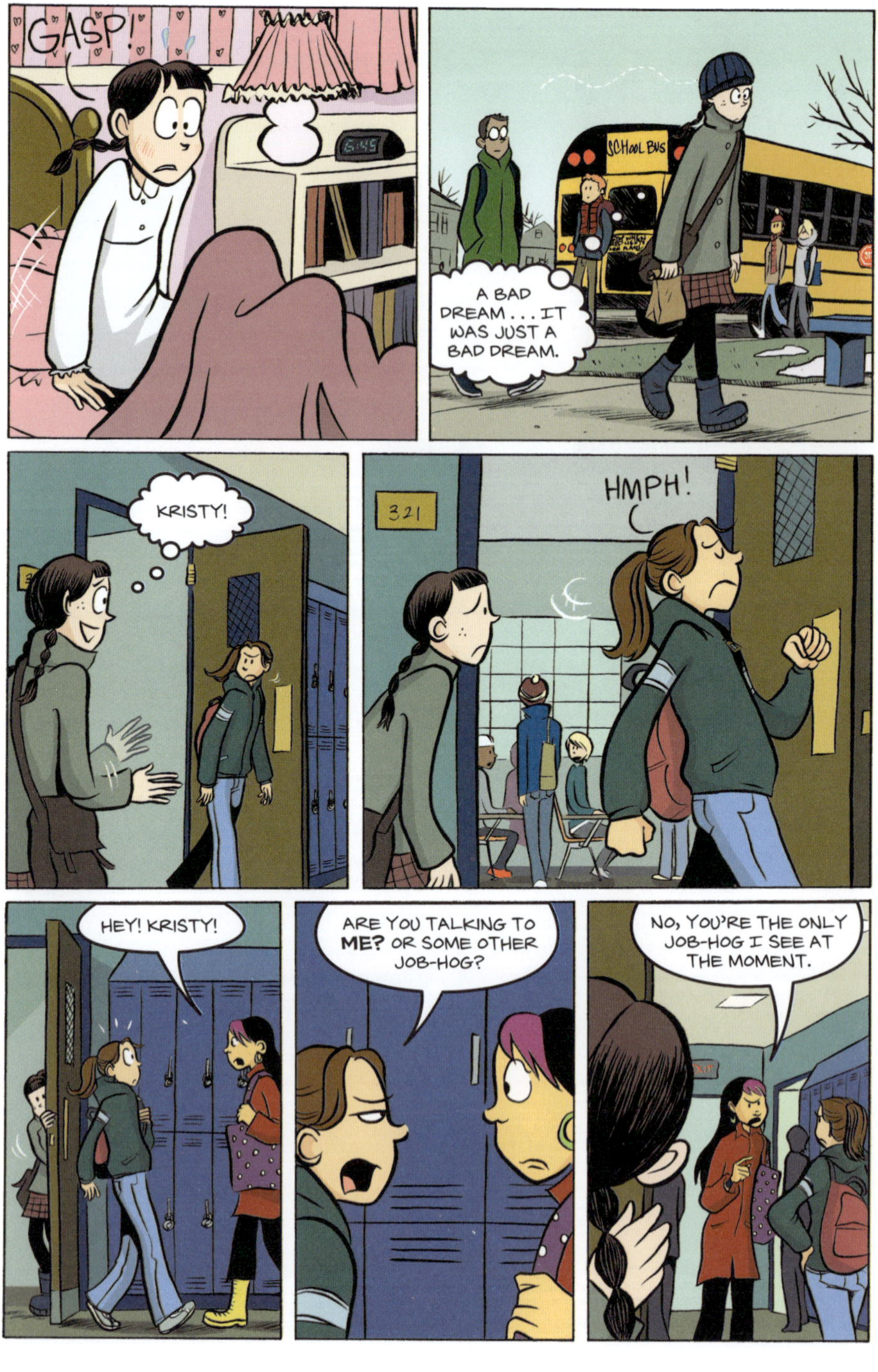
GASP!
A BAD DREAM . . . IT WAS JUST A BAD DREAM.
SCHOOL BUS
KRISTY!
321
HMPH!
HEY! KRISTY!
ARE YOU TALKING TO **ME?** OR SOME OTHER JOB-HOG?
NO, YOU'RE THE ONLY JOB-HOG I SEE AT THE MOMENT.

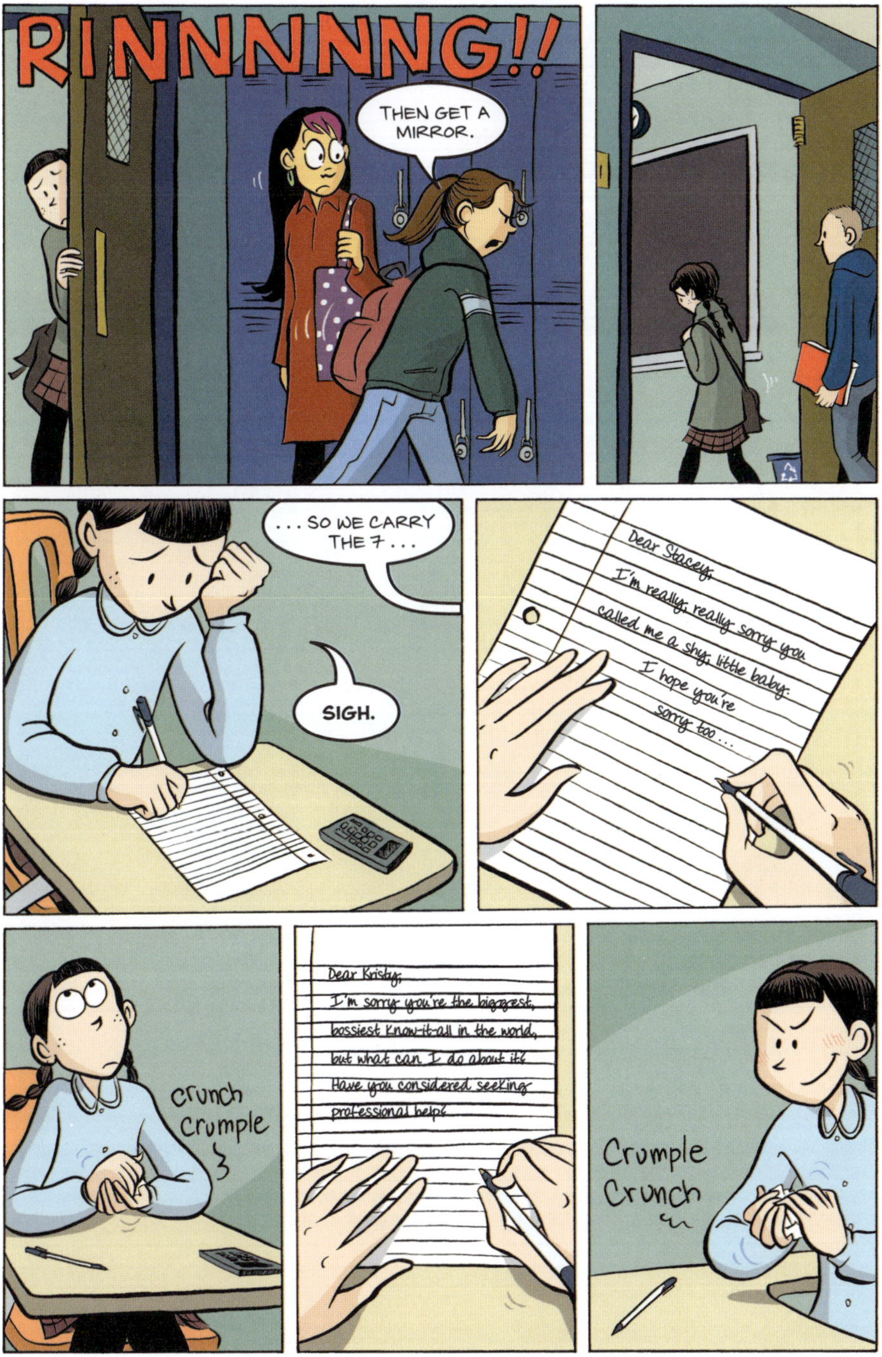
RINNNNG!!
THEN GET A MIRROR.
. . . SO WE CARRY THE 7 . . .
SIGH.
Dear Stacey,
I'm really, really sorry you called me a shy, little baby.
I hope you're sorry too . . .
crunch crumple
Dear Kristy,
I'm sorry you're the biggest, bossiest know-it-all in the world, but what can I do about it? Have you considered seeking professional help?
Crumple Crunch

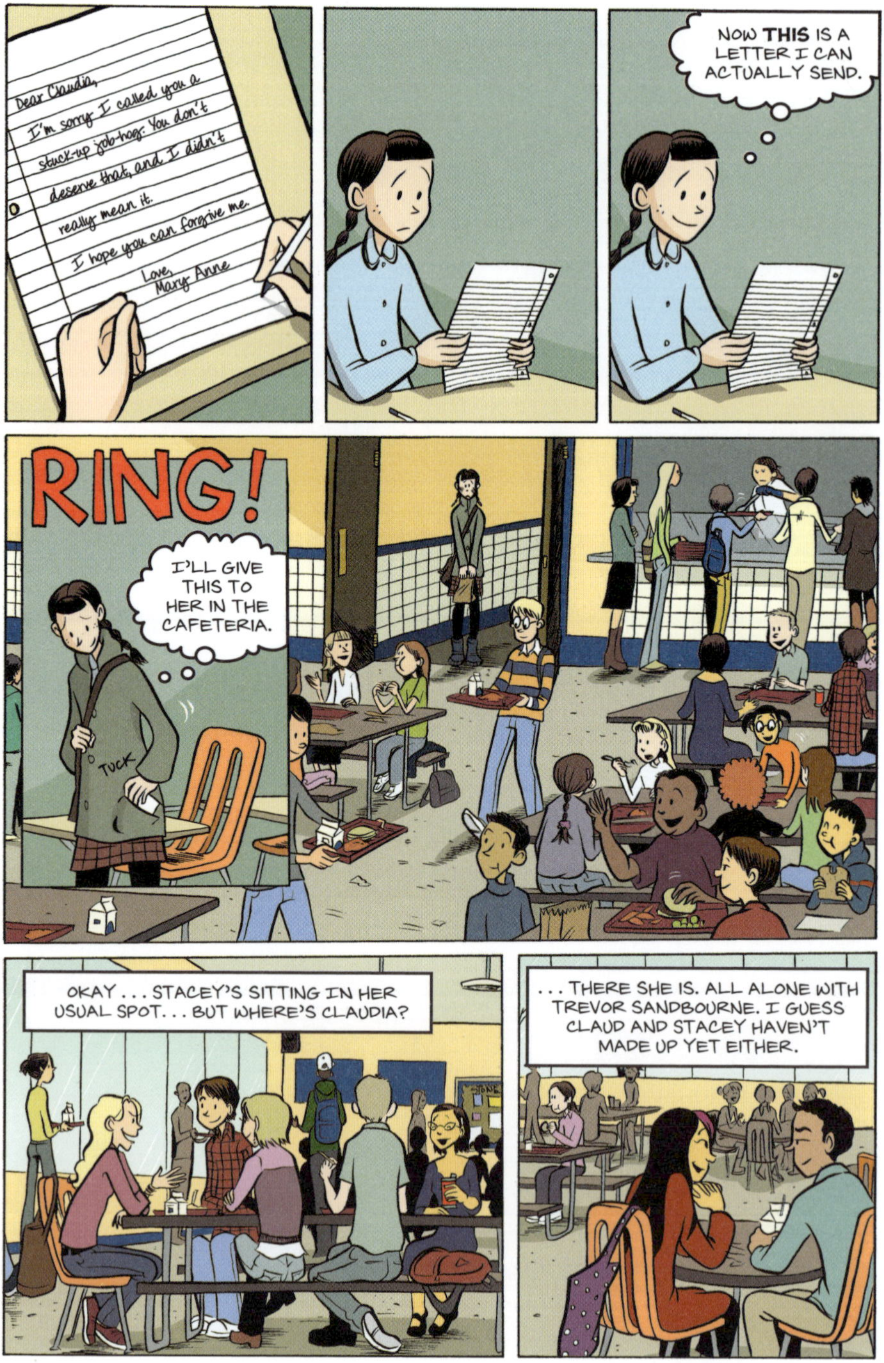
Dear Claudia,
I'm sorry I called you a stuck-up job-hog. You don't deserve that, and I didn't really mean it.
I hope you can forgive me.
Love, Mary Anne
NOW **THIS** IS A LETTER I CAN ACTUALLY SEND.
RING!
I'LL GIVE THIS TO HER IN THE CAFETERIA.
TUCK
OKAY . . . STACEY'S SITTING IN HER USUAL SPOT. . . BUT WHERE'S CLAUDIA?
. . . THERE SHE IS. ALL ALONE WITH TREVOR SANDBOURNE. I GUESS CLAUD AND STACEY HAVEN'T MADE UP YET EITHER.

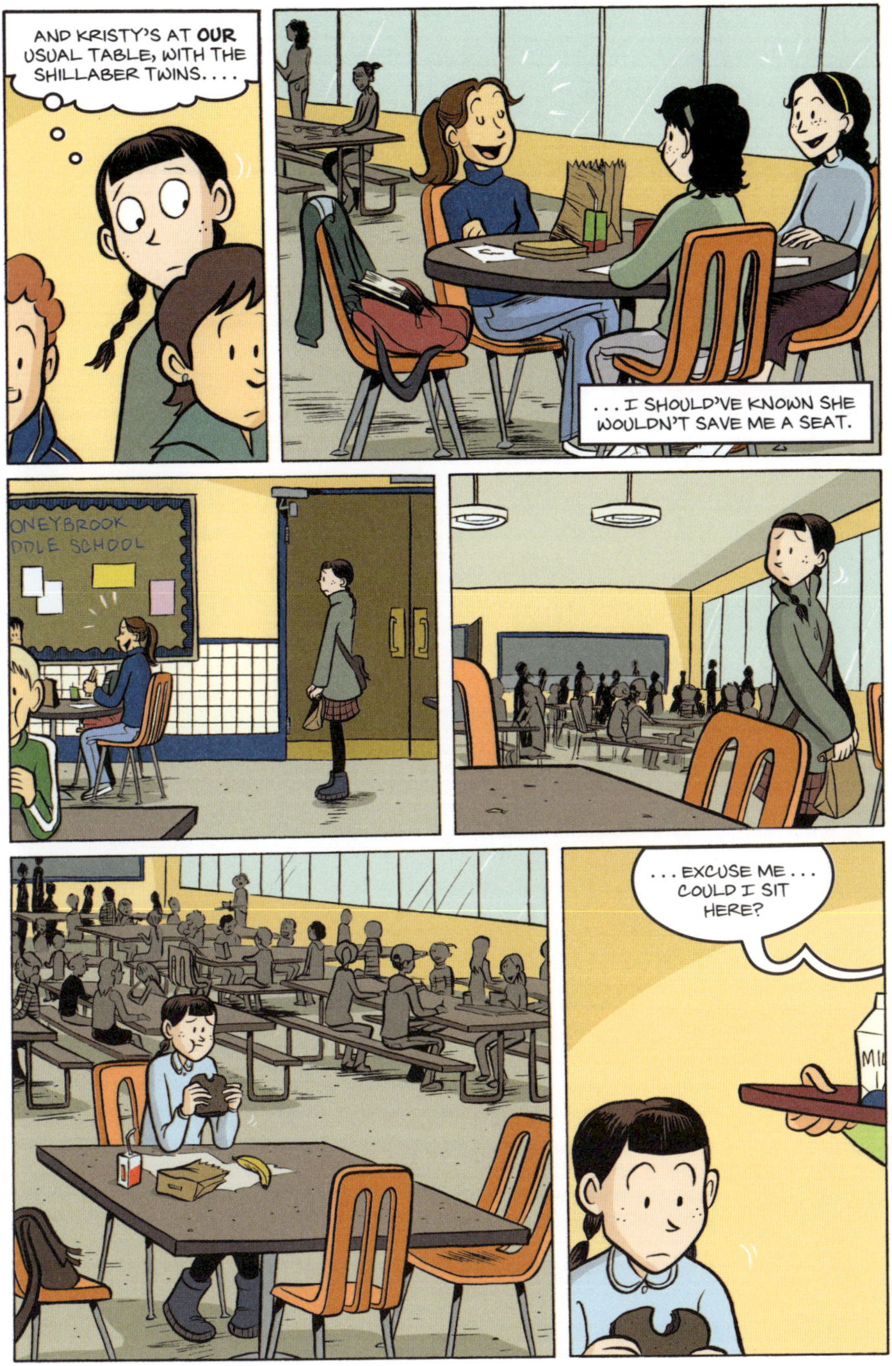
AND KRISTY'S AT **OUR** USUAL TABLE, WITH THE SHILLABER TWINS. . . .
. . . I SHOULD'VE KNOWN SHE WOULDN'T SAVE ME A SEAT.
ONEYBROOK
DDLE SCHOOL
. . . EXCUSE ME . . . COULD I SIT HERE?

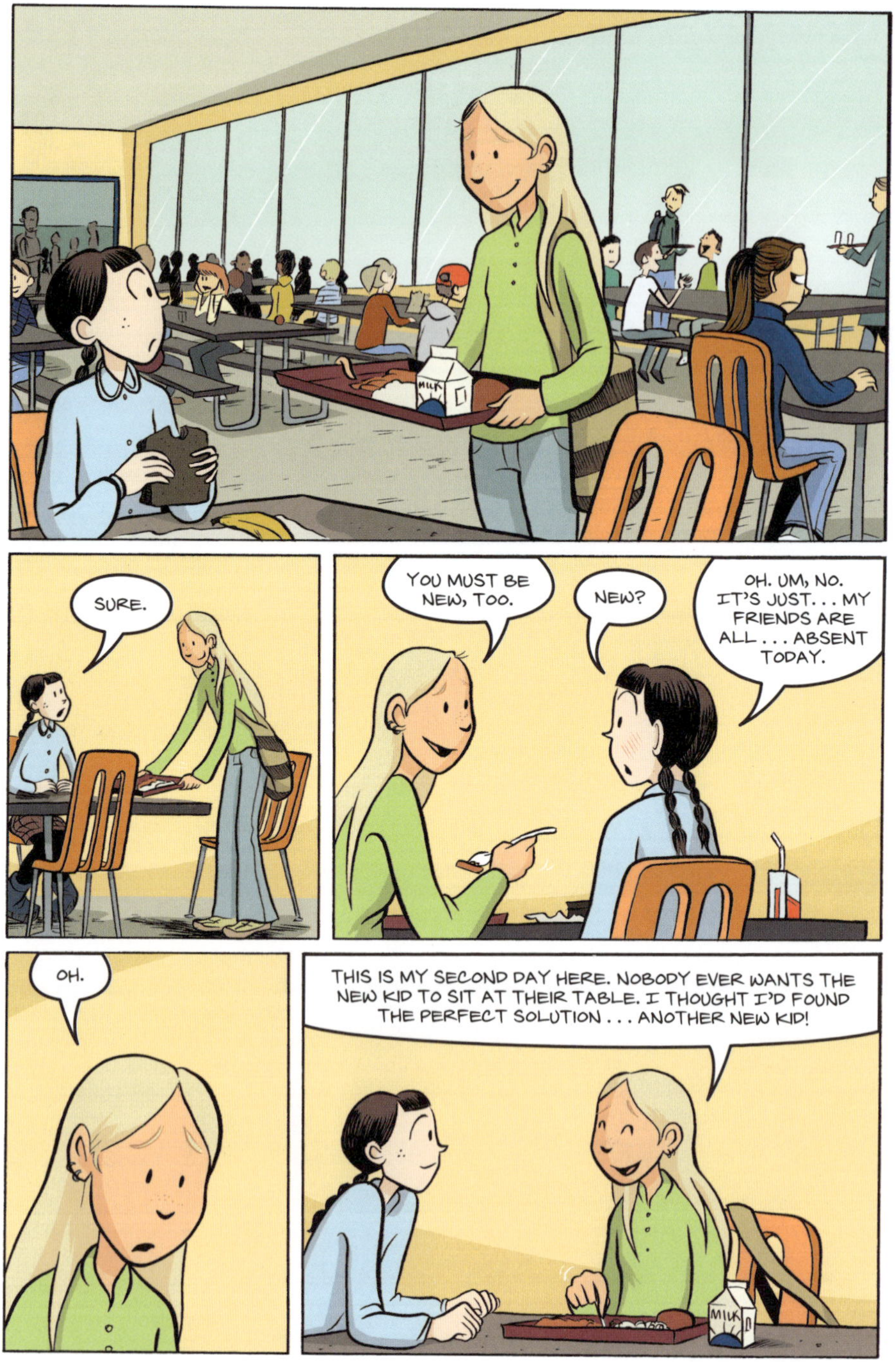
SURE.
YOU MUST BE NEW, TOO.
NEW?
OH. UM, NO. IT'S JUST . . . MY FRIENDS ARE ALL . . . ABSENT TODAY.
OH.
THIS IS MY SECOND DAY HERE. NOBODY EVER WANTS THE NEW KID TO SIT AT THEIR TABLE. I THOUGHT I'D FOUND THE PERFECT SOLUTION . . . ANOTHER NEW KID!

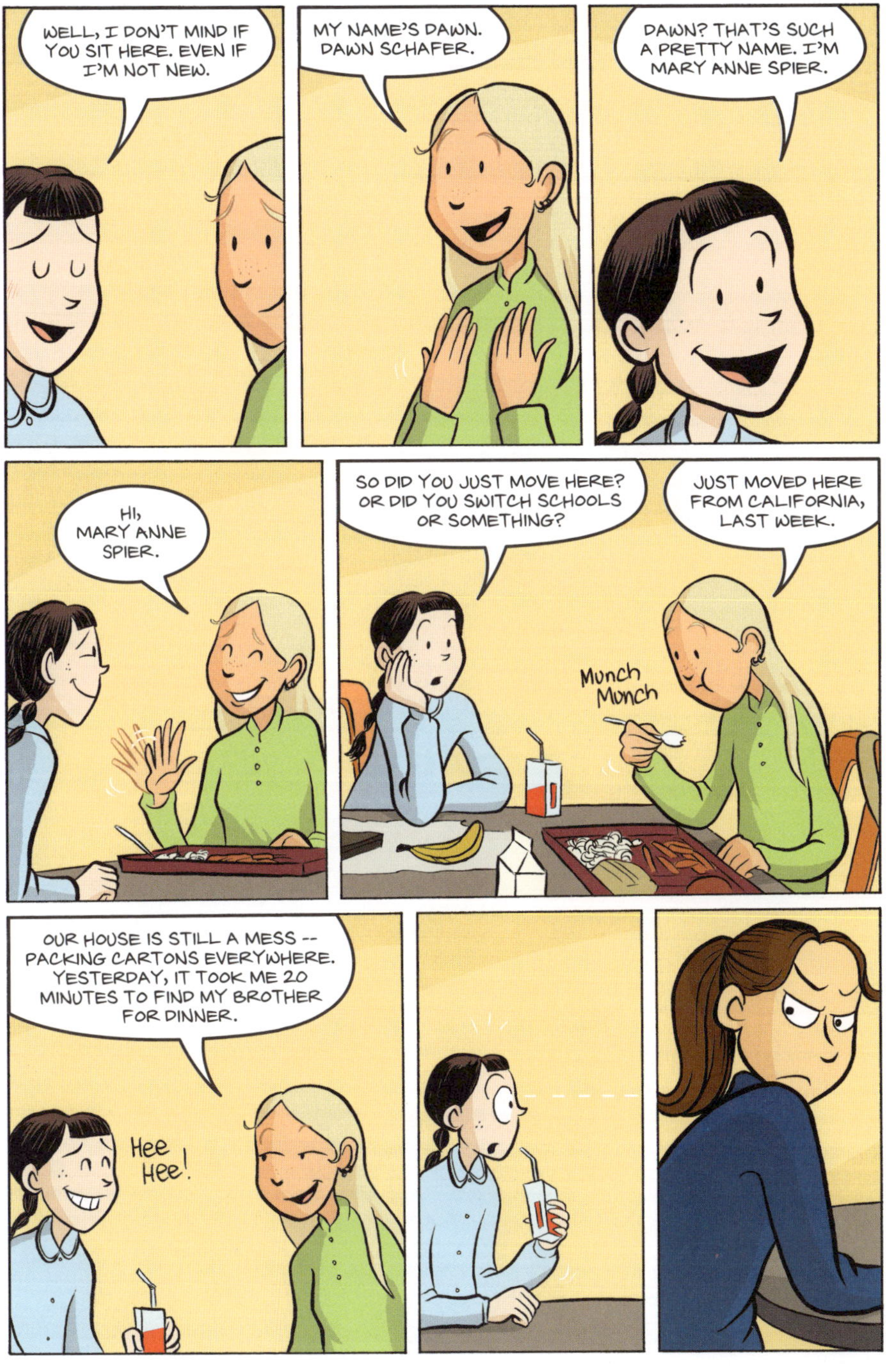
WELL, I DON'T MIND IF YOU SIT HERE. EVEN IF I'M NOT NEW.
MY NAME'S DAWN. DAWN SCHAFER.
DAWN? THAT'S SUCH A PRETTY NAME. I'M MARY ANNE SPIER.
HI, MARY ANNE SPIER.
SO DID YOU JUST MOVE HERE? OR DID YOU SWITCH SCHOOLS OR SOMETHING?
JUST MOVED HERE FROM CALIFORNIA, LAST WEEK.
Munch Munch
OUR HOUSE IS STILL A MESS -- PACKING CARTONS EVERYWHERE. YESTERDAY, IT TOOK ME 20 MINUTES TO FIND MY BROTHER FOR DINNER.
Hee Hee!

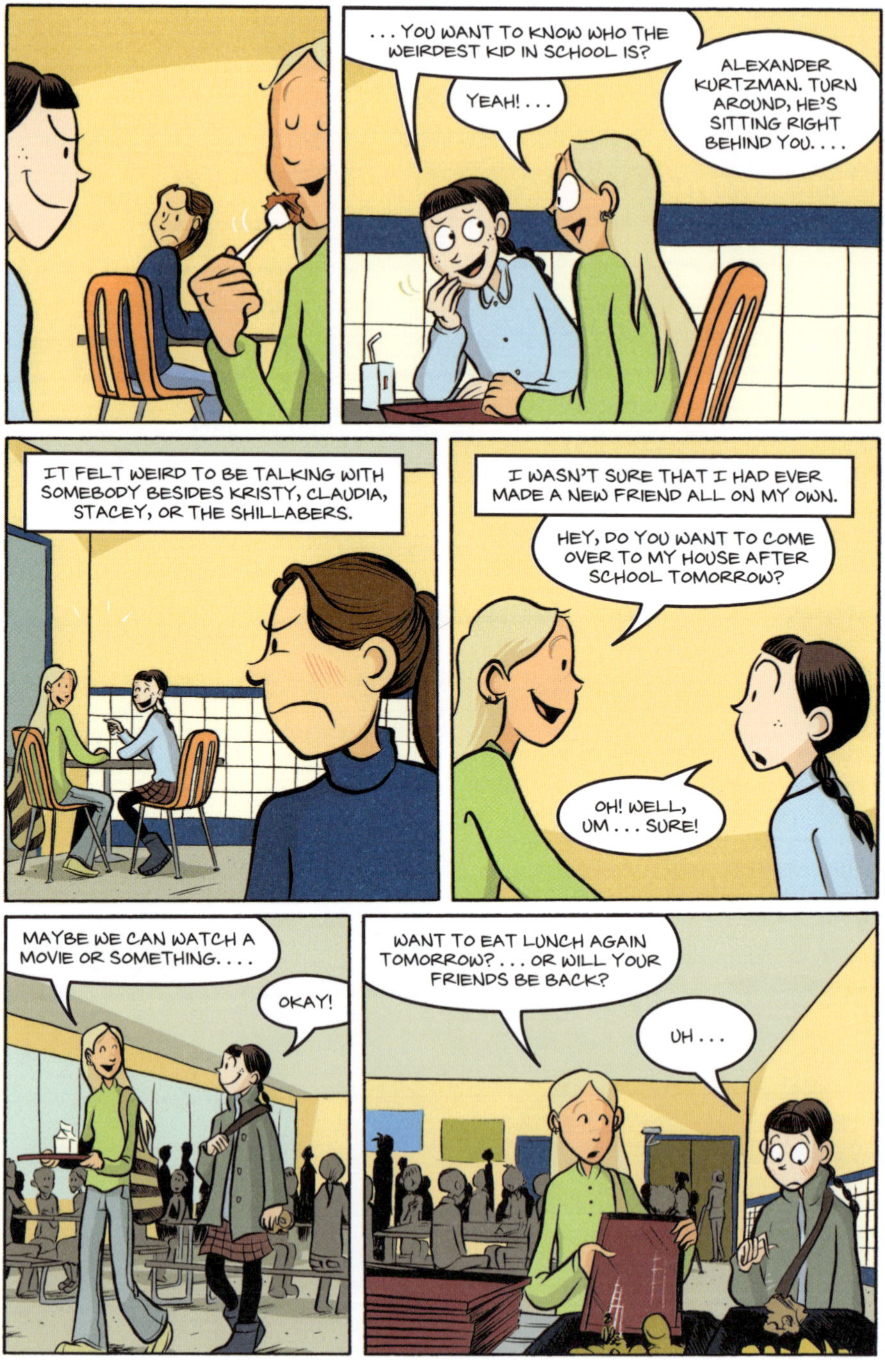

. . . YOU WANT TO KNOW WHO THE WEIRDEST KID IN SCHOOL IS?
YEAH! . . .
ALEXANDER KURTZMAN. TURN AROUND, HE'S SITTING RIGHT BEHIND YOU. . . .
IT FELT WEIRD TO BE TALKING WITH SOMEBODY BESIDES KRISTY, CLAUDIA, STACEY, OR THE SHILLABERS.
I WASN'T SURE THAT I HAD EVER MADE A NEW FRIEND ALL ON MY OWN.
HEY, DO YOU WANT TO COME OVER TO MY HOUSE AFTER SCHOOL TOMORROW?
OH! WELL, UM . . . SURE!
MAYBE WE CAN WATCH A MOVIE OR SOMETHING. . . .
OKAY!
WANT TO EAT LUNCH AGAIN TOMORROW? . . . OR WILL YOUR FRIENDS BE BACK?
UH . . .

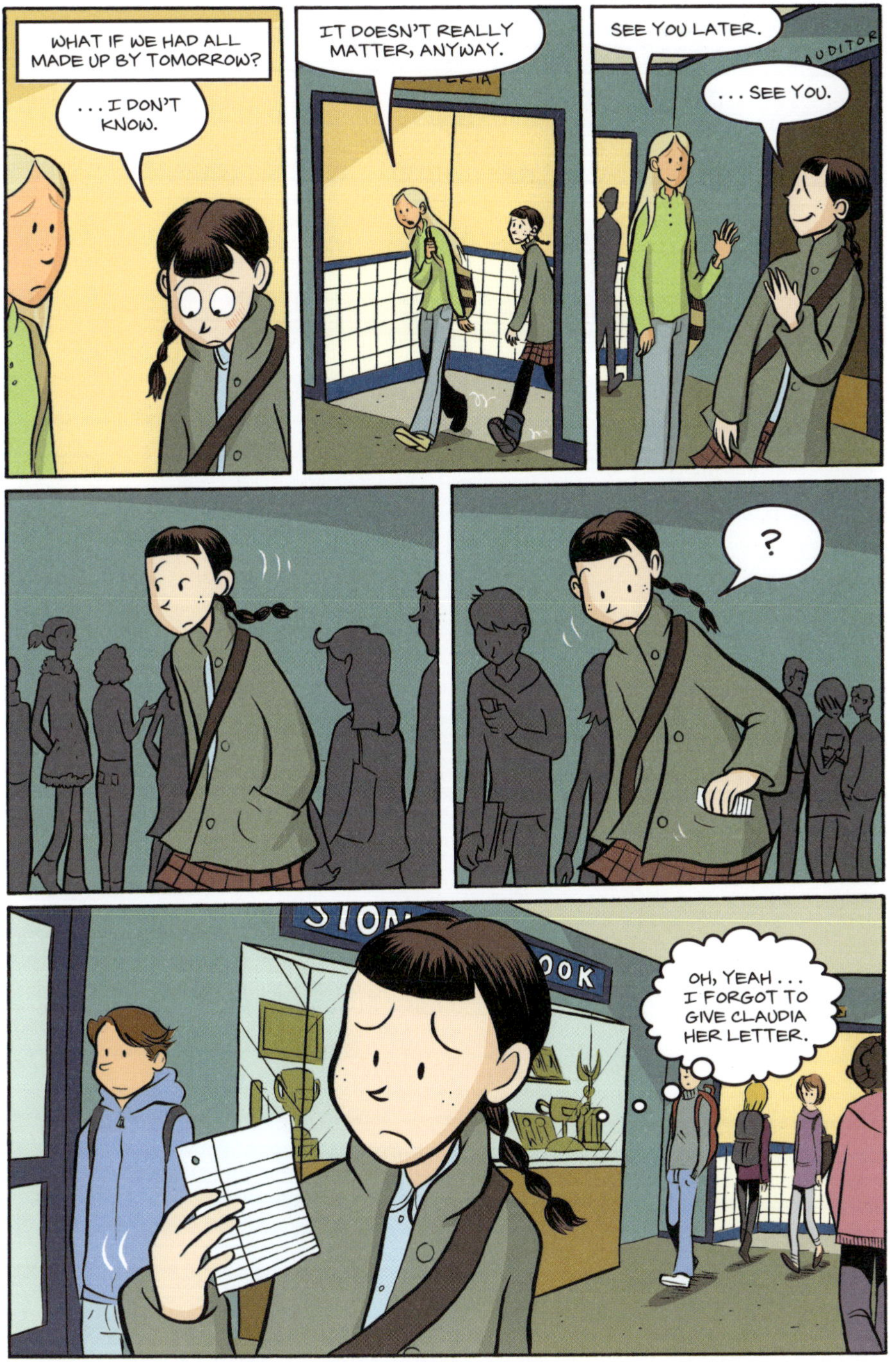
WHAT IF WE HAD ALL MADE UP BY TOMORROW?
. . . I DON'T KNOW.
IT DOESN'T REALLY MATTER, ANYWAY.
SEE YOU LATER.
. . . SEE YOU.
AUDITOR
?
OH, YEAH . . . I FORGOT TO GIVE CLAUDIA HER LETTER.

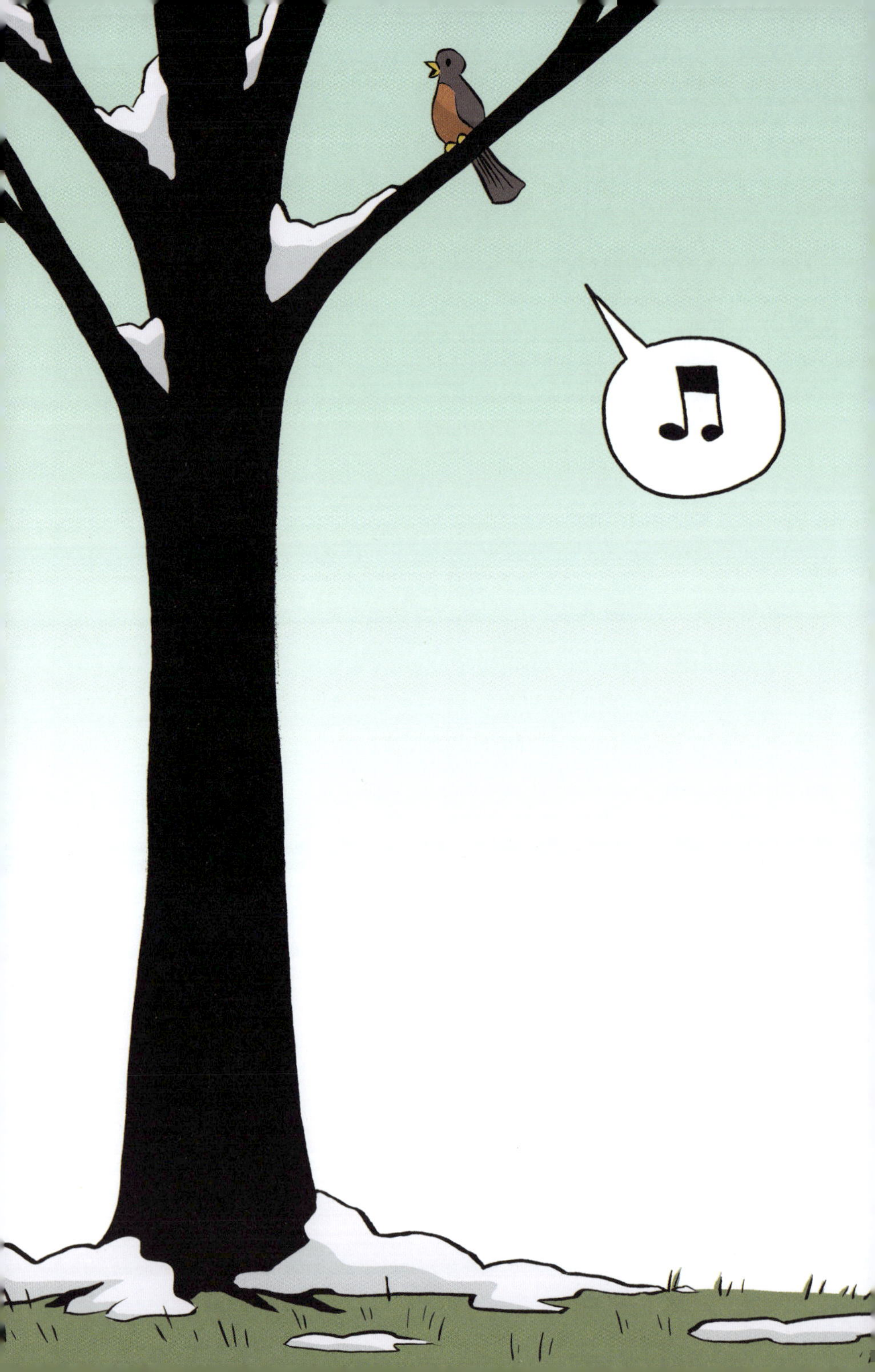

CHAPTER 4

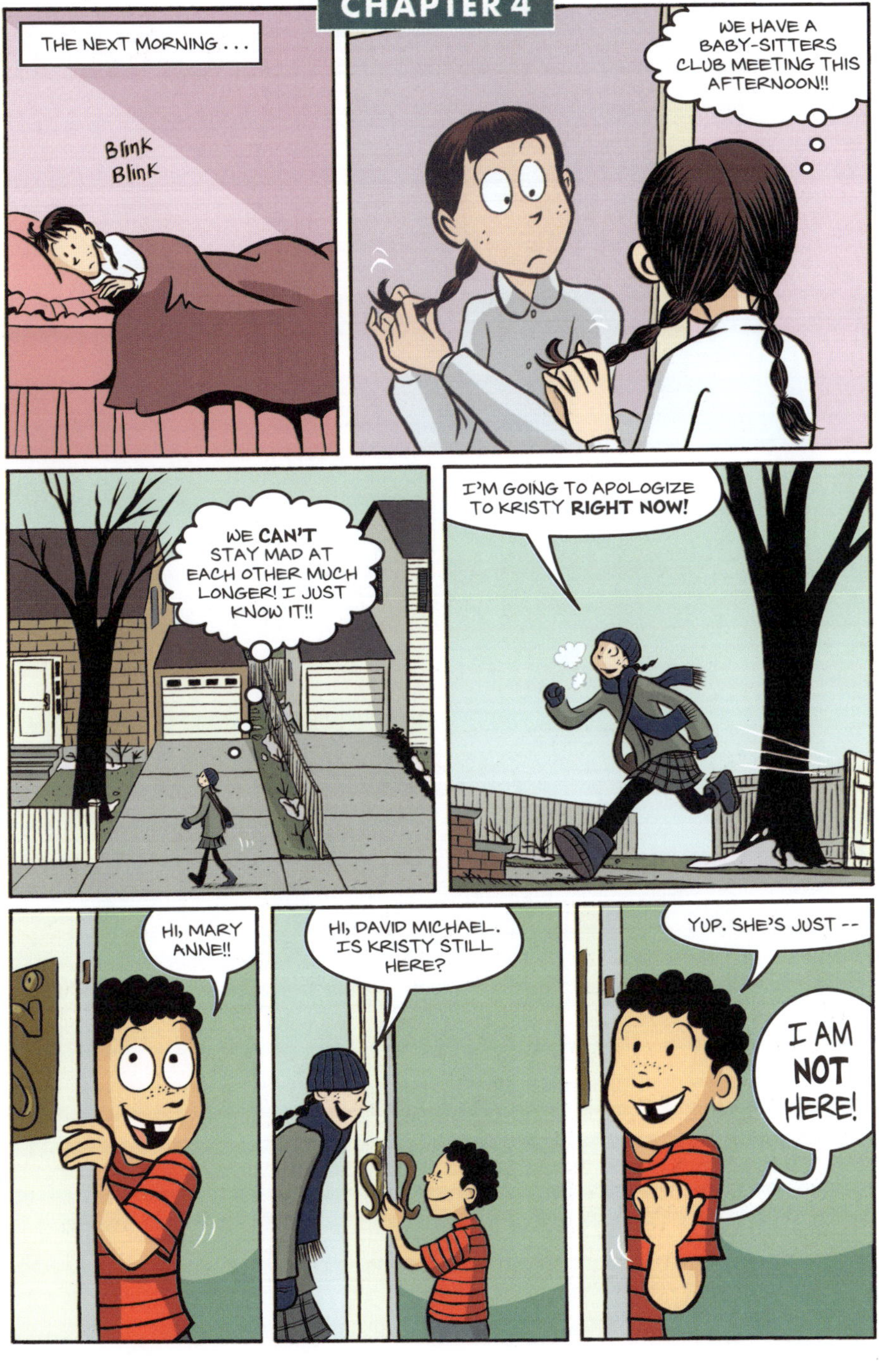
THE NEXT MORNING . . .
Blink
Blink
WE HAVE A BABY-SITTERS CLUB MEETING THIS AFTERNOON!!
WE **CAN'T** STAY MAD AT EACH OTHER MUCH LONGER! I JUST KNOW IT!!
I'M GOING TO APOLOGIZE TO KRISTY **RIGHT NOW!**
HI, MARY ANNE!!
HI, DAVID MICHAEL. IS KRISTY STILL HERE?
YUP. SHE'S JUST --
I AM **NOT** HERE!

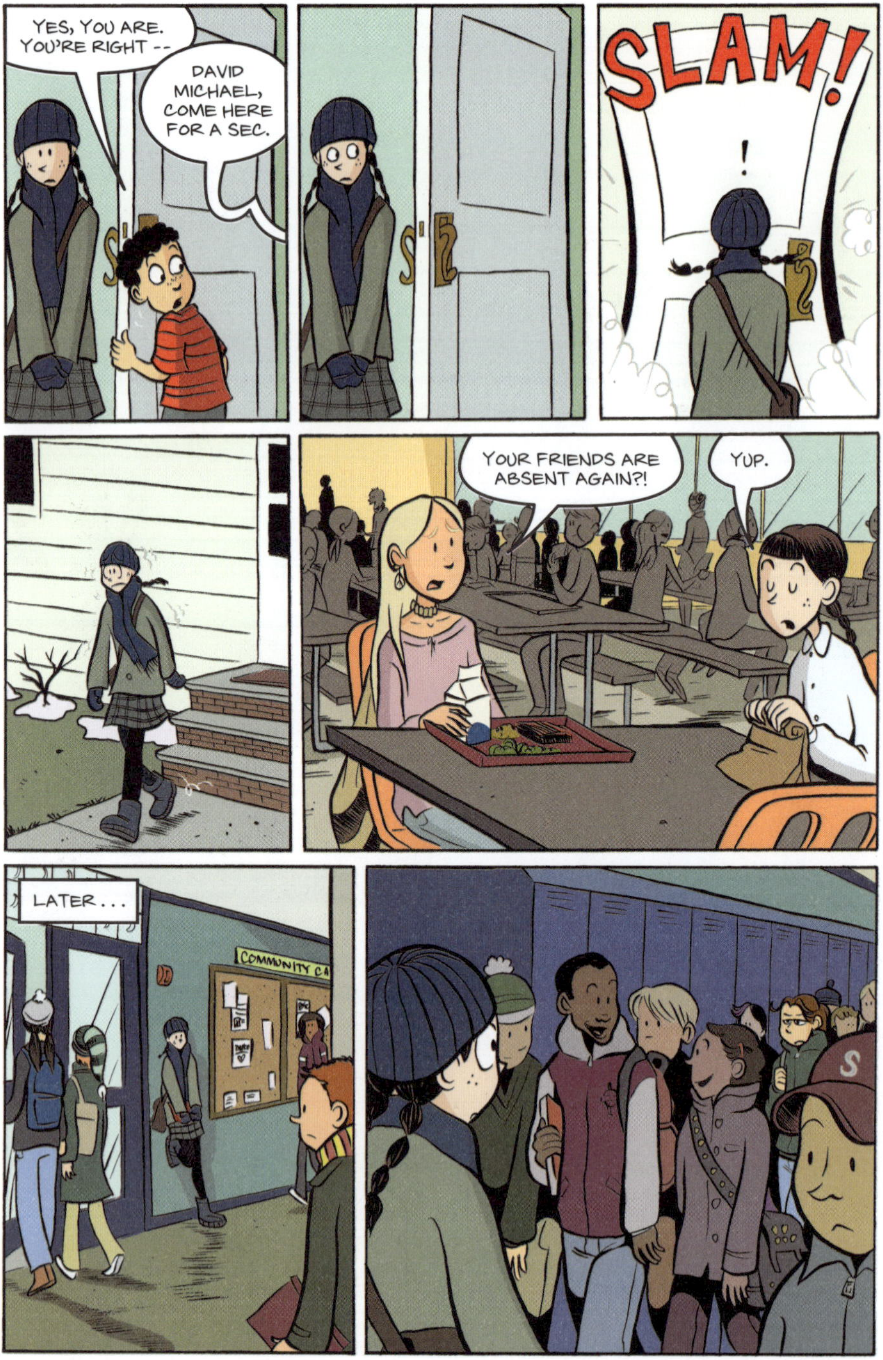
YES, YOU ARE. YOU'RE RIGHT --
DAVID MICHAEL, COME HERE FOR A SEC.
SLAM!
!
YOUR FRIENDS ARE ABSENT AGAIN?!
YUP.
LATER...
COMMUNITY CA

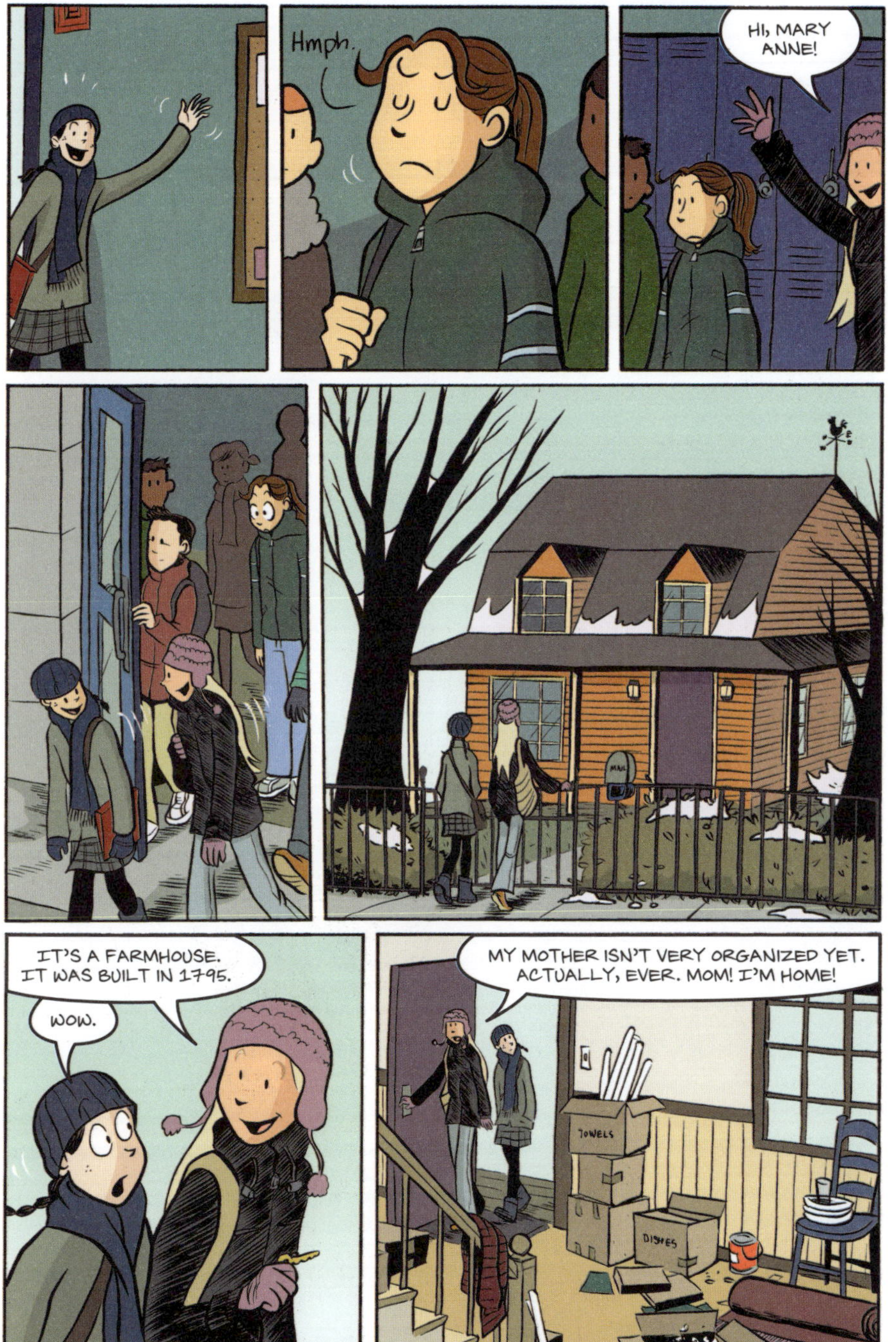
Hmph.
HI, MARY ANNE!
MAIL
IT'S A FARMHOUSE. IT WAS BUILT IN 1795.
WOW.
MY MOTHER ISN'T VERY ORGANIZED YET. ACTUALLY, EVER. MOM! I'M HOME!
TOWELS
DISHES

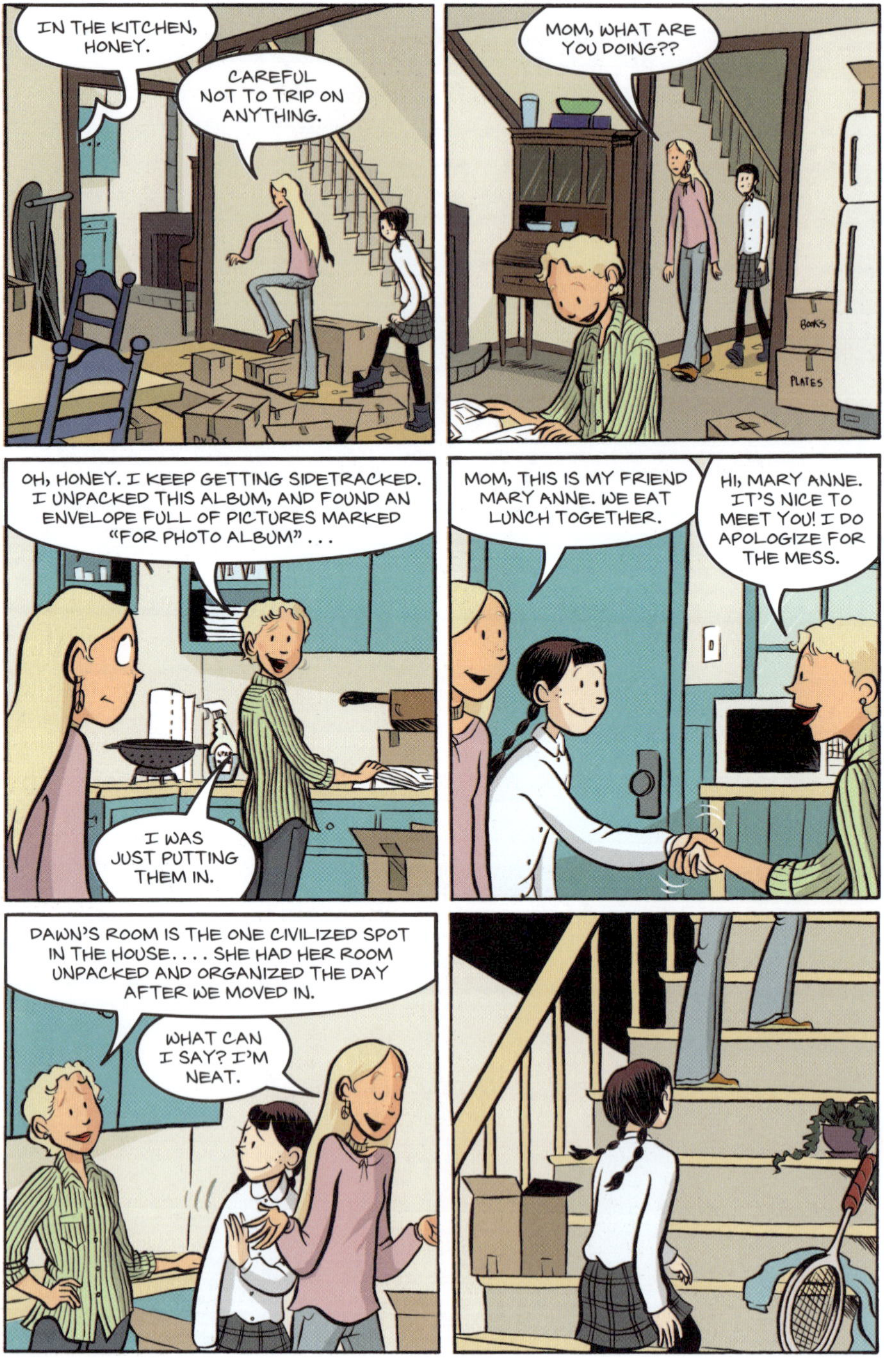
IN THE KITCHEN, HONEY.
CAREFUL NOT TO TRIP ON ANYTHING.
MOM, WHAT ARE YOU DOING??
BOOKS
PLATES
OH, HONEY. I KEEP GETTING SIDETRACKED. I UNPACKED THIS ALBUM, AND FOUND AN ENVELOPE FULL OF PICTURES MARKED "FOR PHOTO ALBUM" . . .
I WAS JUST PUTTING THEM IN.
MOM, THIS IS MY FRIEND MARY ANNE. WE EAT LUNCH TOGETHER.
HI, MARY ANNE. IT'S NICE TO MEET YOU! I DO APOLOGIZE FOR THE MESS.
DAWN'S ROOM IS THE ONE CIVILIZED SPOT IN THE HOUSE. . . . SHE HAD HER ROOM UNPACKED AND ORGANIZED THE DAY AFTER WE MOVED IN.
WHAT CAN I SAY? I'M NEAT.

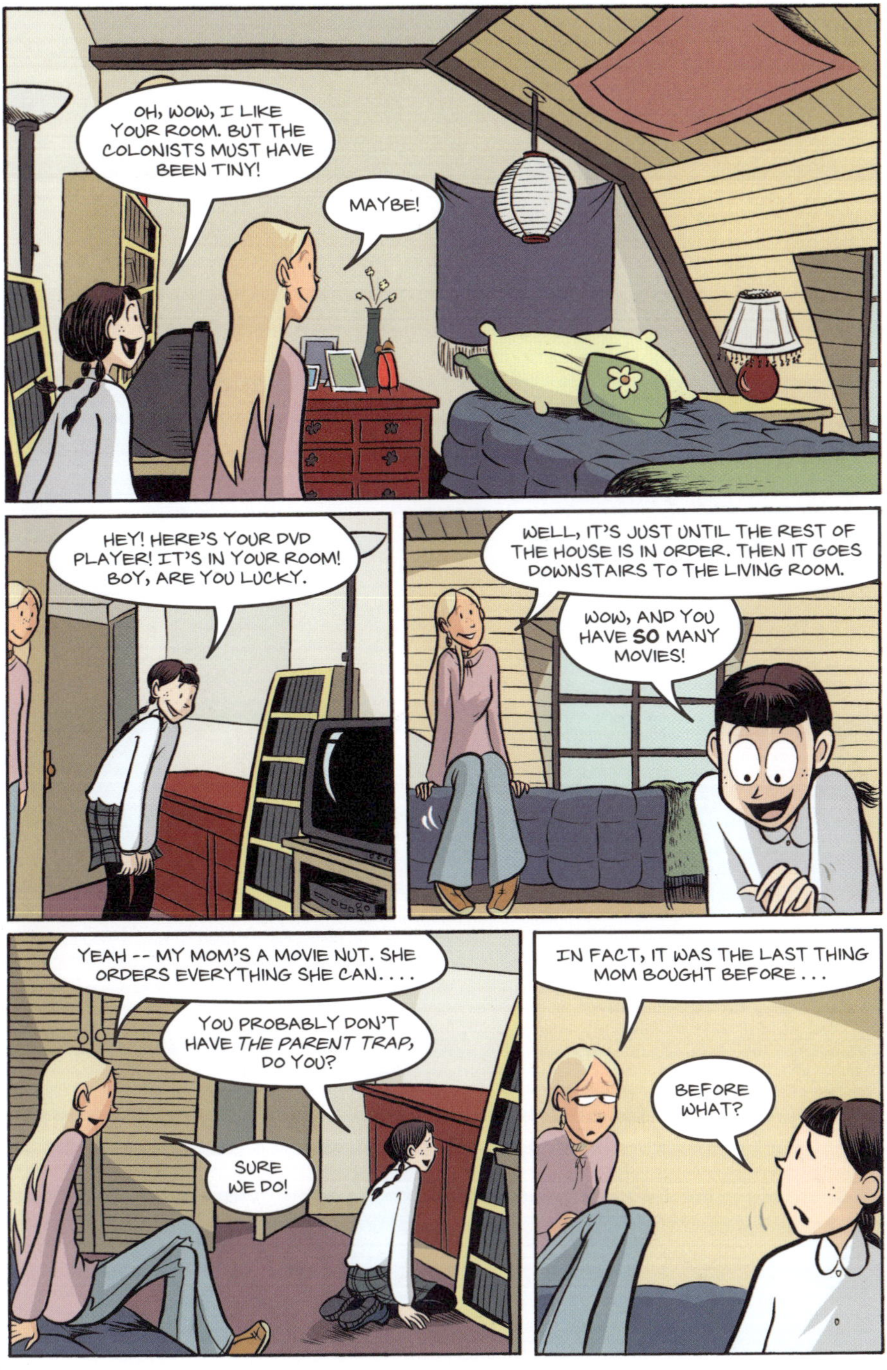
OH, WOW, I LIKE YOUR ROOM. BUT THE COLONISTS MUST HAVE BEEN TINY!
MAYBE!
HEY! HERE'S YOUR DVD PLAYER! IT'S IN YOUR ROOM! BOY, ARE YOU LUCKY.
WELL, IT'S JUST UNTIL THE REST OF THE HOUSE IS IN ORDER. THEN IT GOES DOWNSTAIRS TO THE LIVING ROOM.
WOW, AND YOU HAVE **SO** MANY MOVIES!
YEAH -- MY MOM'S A MOVIE NUT. SHE ORDERS EVERYTHING SHE CAN. . . .
YOU PROBABLY DON'T HAVE *THE PARENT TRAP*, DO YOU?
SURE WE DO!
IN FACT, IT WAS THE LAST THING MOM BOUGHT BEFORE . . .
BEFORE WHAT?

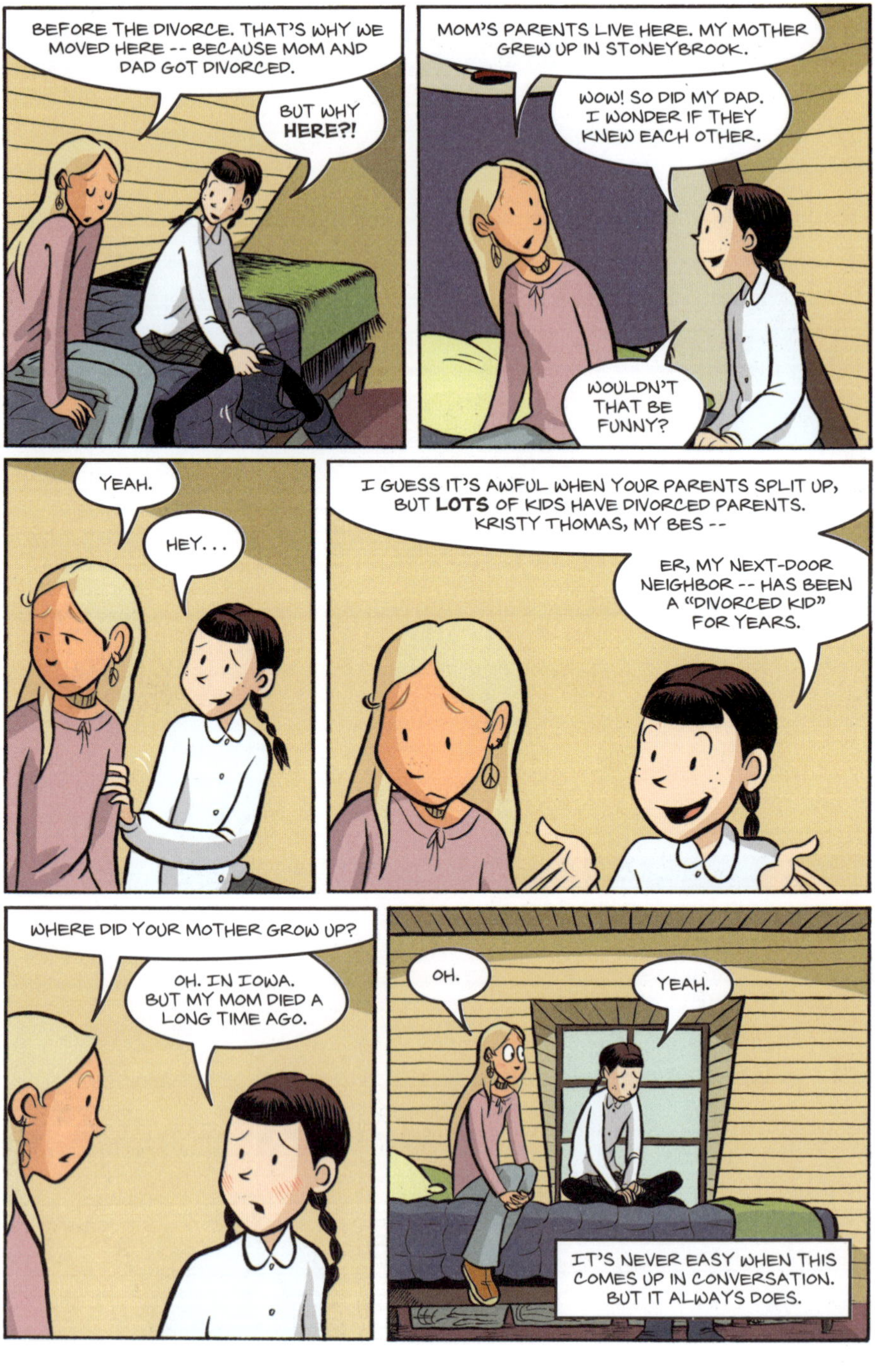
BEFORE THE DIVORCE. THAT'S WHY WE MOVED HERE -- BECAUSE MOM AND DAD GOT DIVORCED.
BUT WHY **HERE?!**
MOM'S PARENTS LIVE HERE. MY MOTHER GREW UP IN STONEYBROOK.
WOW! SO DID MY DAD. I WONDER IF THEY KNEW EACH OTHER.
WOULDN'T THAT BE FUNNY?
YEAH.
HEY...
I GUESS IT'S AWFUL WHEN YOUR PARENTS SPLIT UP, BUT **LOTS** OF KIDS HAVE DIVORCED PARENTS. KRISTY THOMAS, MY BES --
ER, MY NEXT-DOOR NEIGHBOR -- HAS BEEN A "DIVORCED KID" FOR YEARS.
WHERE DID YOUR MOTHER GROW UP?
OH. IN IOWA. BUT MY MOM DIED A LONG TIME AGO.
OH.
YEAH.
IT'S NEVER EASY WHEN THIS COMES UP IN CONVERSATION. BUT IT ALWAYS DOES.

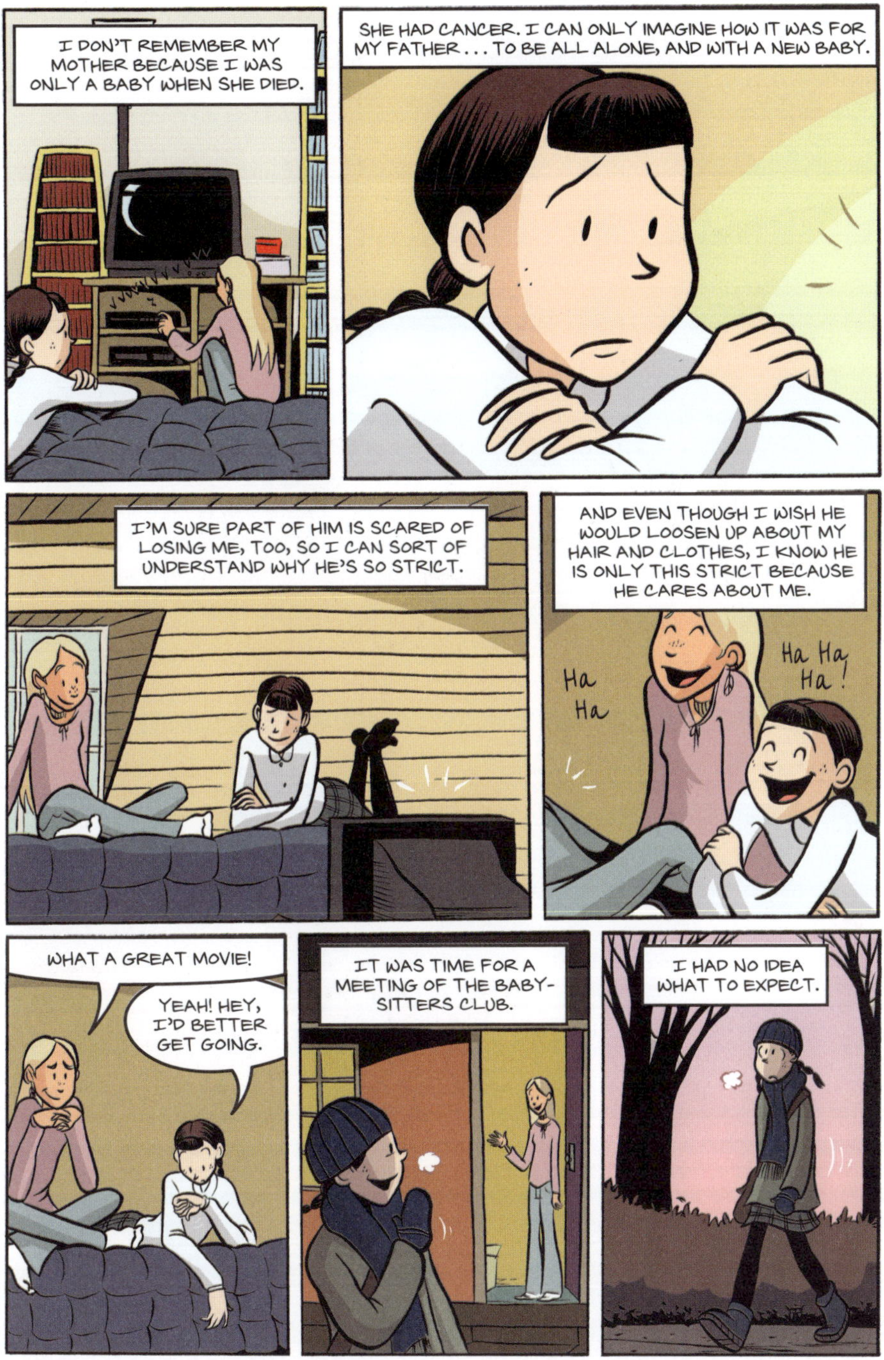
I DON'T REMEMBER MY MOTHER BECAUSE I WAS ONLY A BABY WHEN SHE DIED.
SHE HAD CANCER. I CAN ONLY IMAGINE HOW IT WAS FOR MY FATHER . . . TO BE ALL ALONE, AND WITH A NEW BABY.
I'M SURE PART OF HIM IS SCARED OF LOSING ME, TOO, SO I CAN SORT OF UNDERSTAND WHY HE'S SO STRICT.
AND EVEN THOUGH I WISH HE WOULD LOOSEN UP ABOUT MY HAIR AND CLOTHES, I KNOW HE IS ONLY THIS STRICT BECAUSE HE CARES ABOUT ME.
Ha Ha
Ha Ha Ha!
WHAT A GREAT MOVIE!
YEAH! HEY, I'D BETTER GET GOING.
IT WAS TIME FOR A MEETING OF THE BABY-SITTERS CLUB.
I HAD NO IDEA WHAT TO EXPECT.

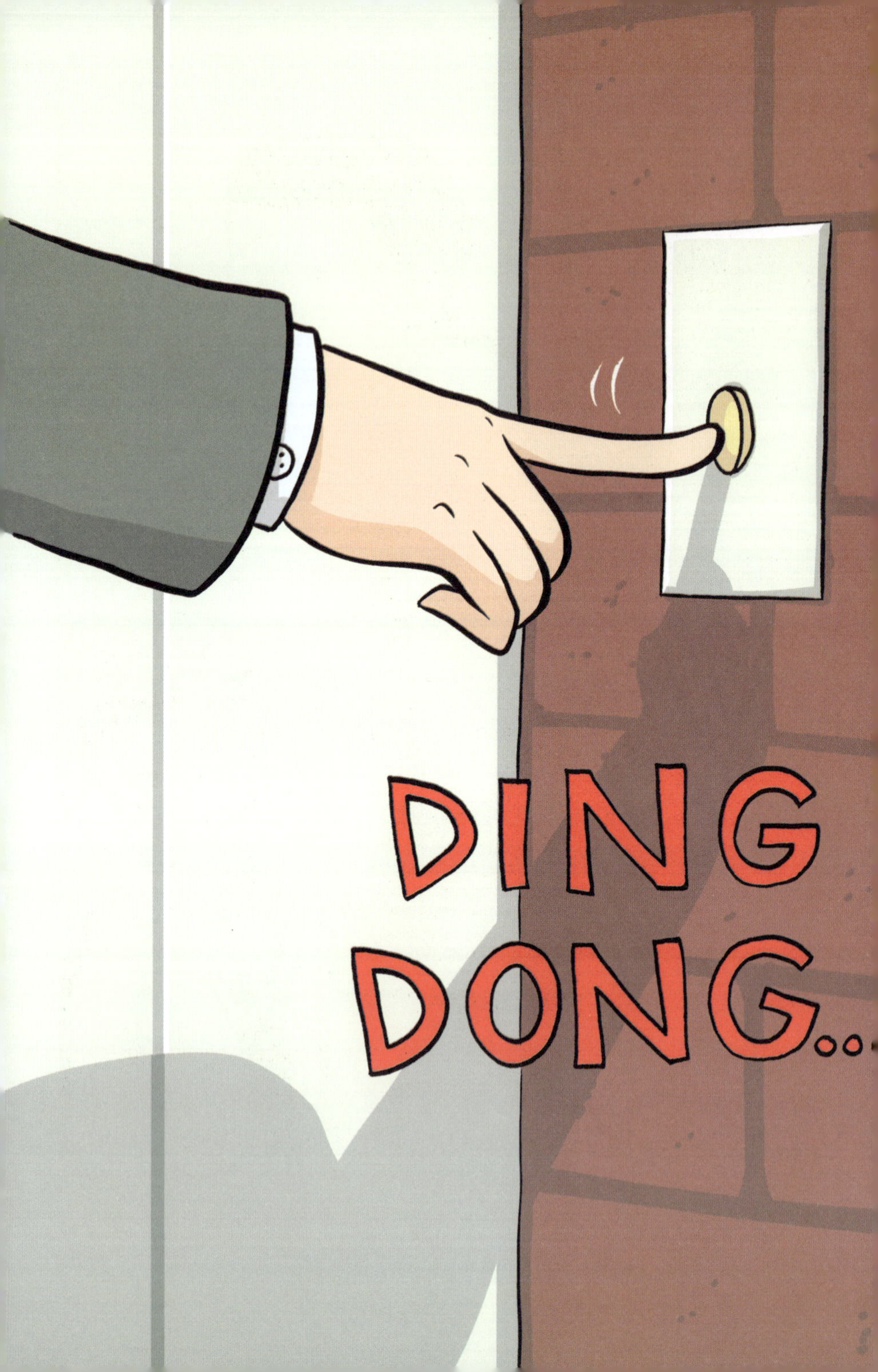
DING DONG...

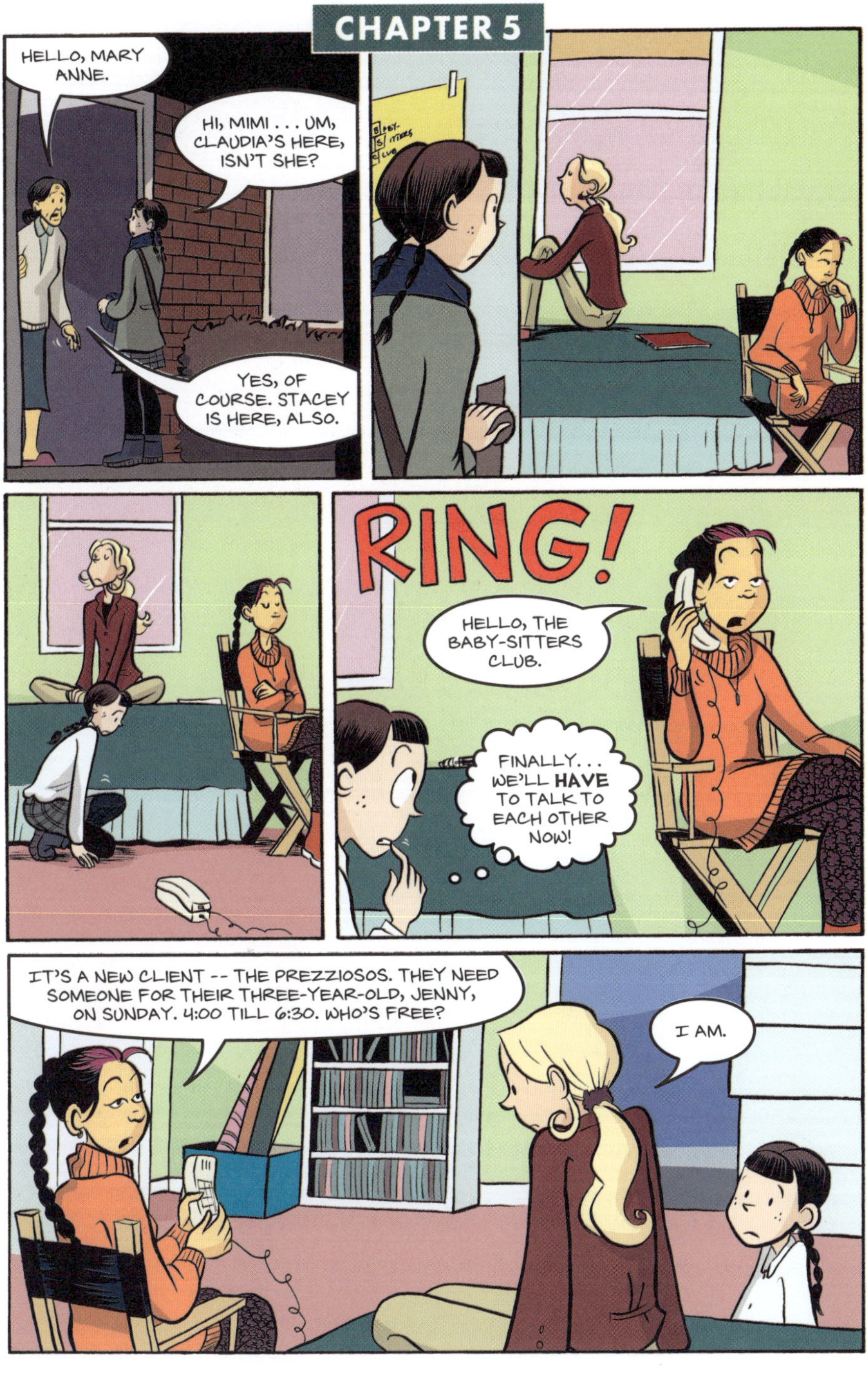
CHAPTER 5
HELLO, MARY ANNE.
HI, MIMI . . . UM, CLAUDIA'S HERE, ISN'T SHE?
YES, OF COURSE. STACEY IS HERE, ALSO.
RING!
HELLO, THE BABY-SITTERS CLUB.
FINALLY. . . WE'LL **HAVE** TO TALK TO EACH OTHER NOW!
IT'S A NEW CLIENT -- THE PREZZIOSOS. THEY NEED SOMEONE FOR THEIR THREE-YEAR-OLD, JENNY, ON SUNDAY. 4:00 TILL 6:30. WHO'S FREE?
I AM.

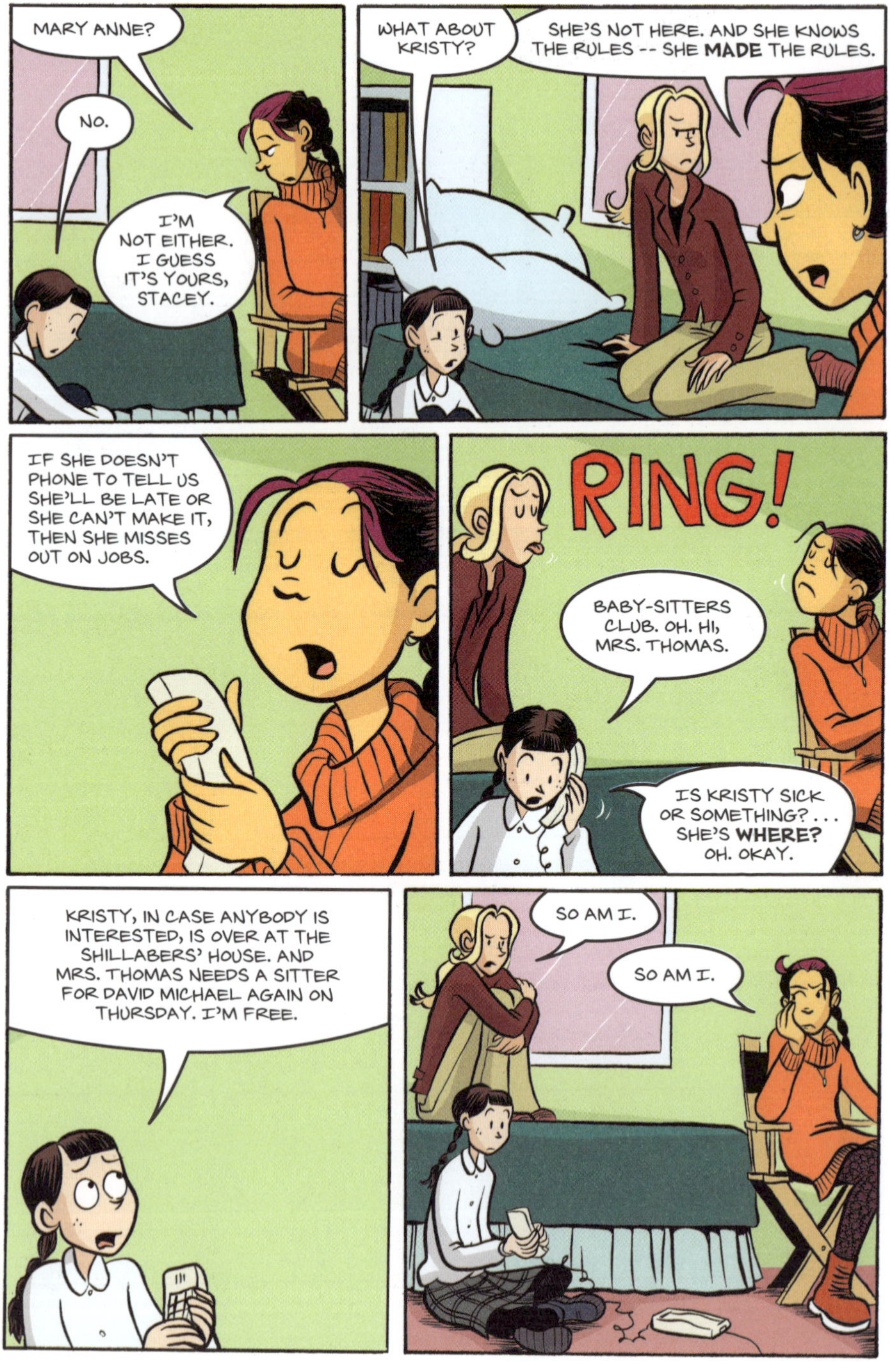
MARY ANNE?
NO.
I'M NOT EITHER. I GUESS IT'S YOURS, STACEY.
WHAT ABOUT KRISTY?
SHE'S NOT HERE. AND SHE KNOWS THE RULES -- SHE **MADE** THE RULES.
IF SHE DOESN'T PHONE TO TELL US SHE'LL BE LATE OR SHE CAN'T MAKE IT, THEN SHE MISSES OUT ON JOBS.
RING!
BABY-SITTERS CLUB. OH. HI, MRS. THOMAS.
IS KRISTY SICK OR SOMETHING? . . . SHE'S **WHERE?** OH. OKAY.
KRISTY, IN CASE ANYBODY IS INTERESTED, IS OVER AT THE SHILLABERS' HOUSE. AND MRS. THOMAS NEEDS A SITTER FOR DAVID MICHAEL AGAIN ON THURSDAY. I'M FREE.
SO AM I.
SO AM I.

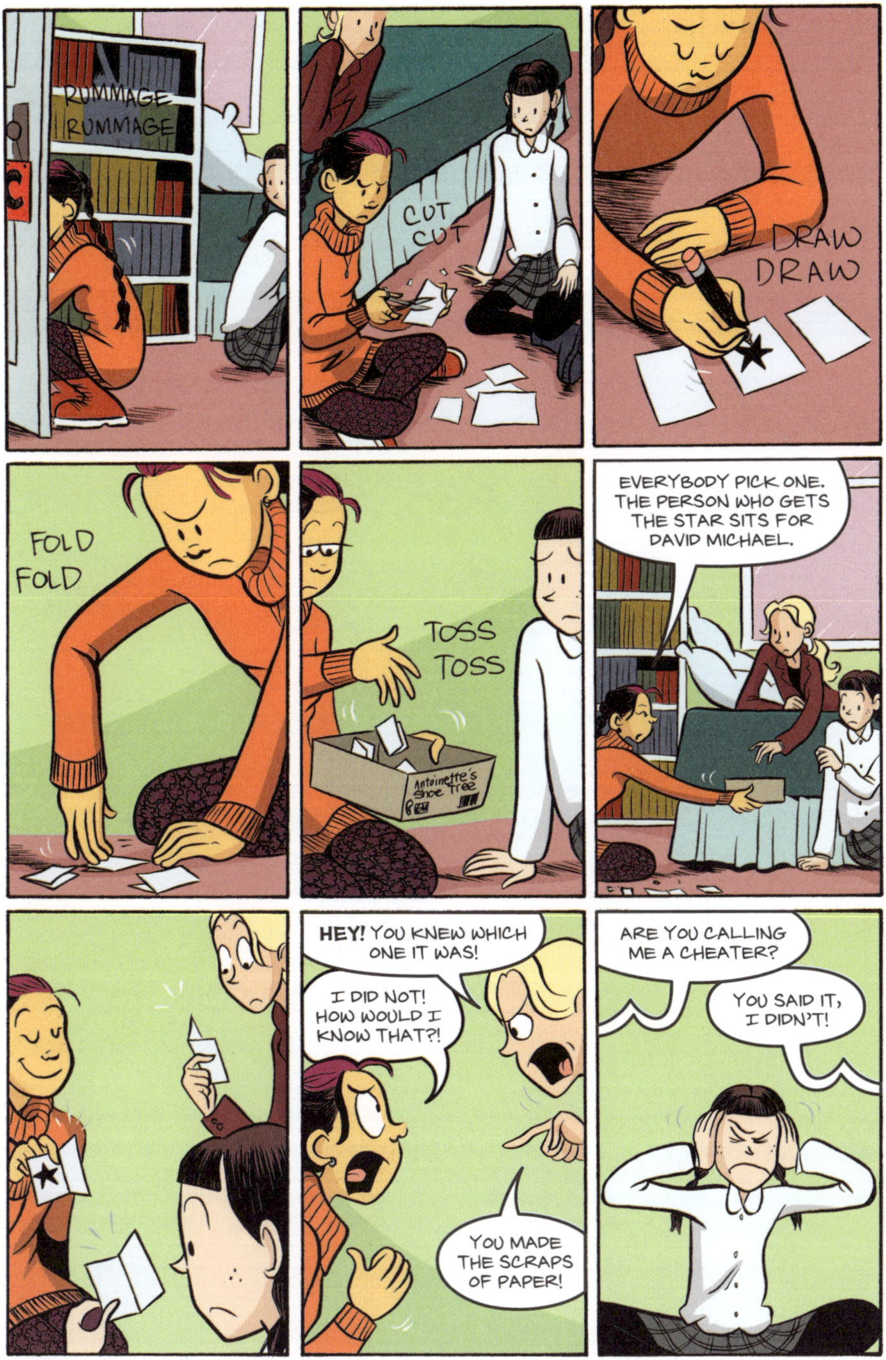
RUMMAGE
RUMMAGE
CUT
CUT
DRAW
DRAW
FOLD
FOLD
TOSS
TOSS
Antoinette's Shoe Tree
EVERYBODY PICK ONE. THE PERSON WHO GETS THE STAR SITS FOR DAVID MICHAEL.
HEY! YOU KNEW WHICH ONE IT WAS!
I DID NOT! HOW WOULD I KNOW THAT?!
YOU MADE THE SCRAPS OF PAPER!
ARE YOU CALLING ME A CHEATER?
YOU SAID IT, I DIDN'T!

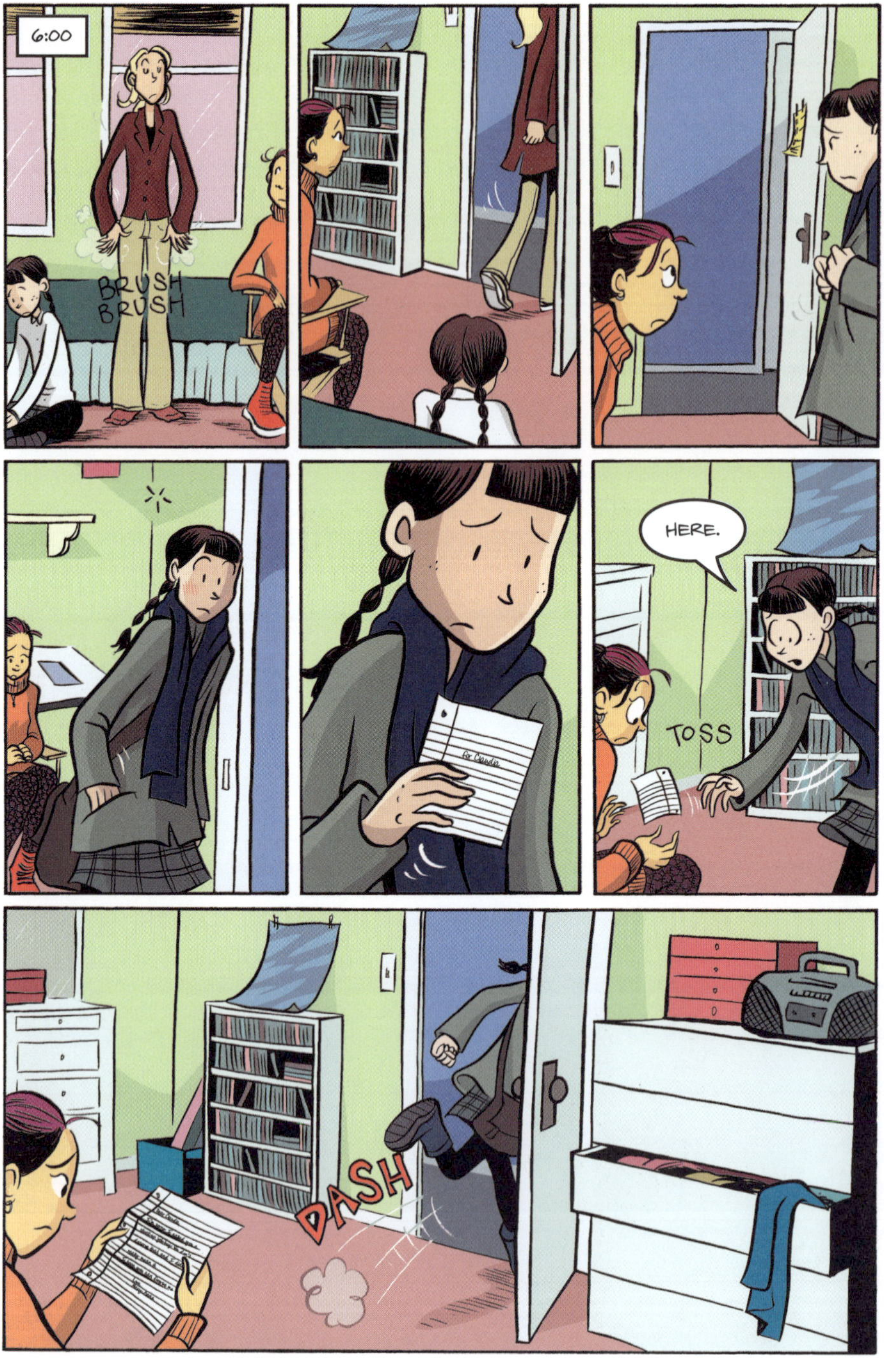
6:00
BRUSH BRUSH
HERE.
TOSS
DASH

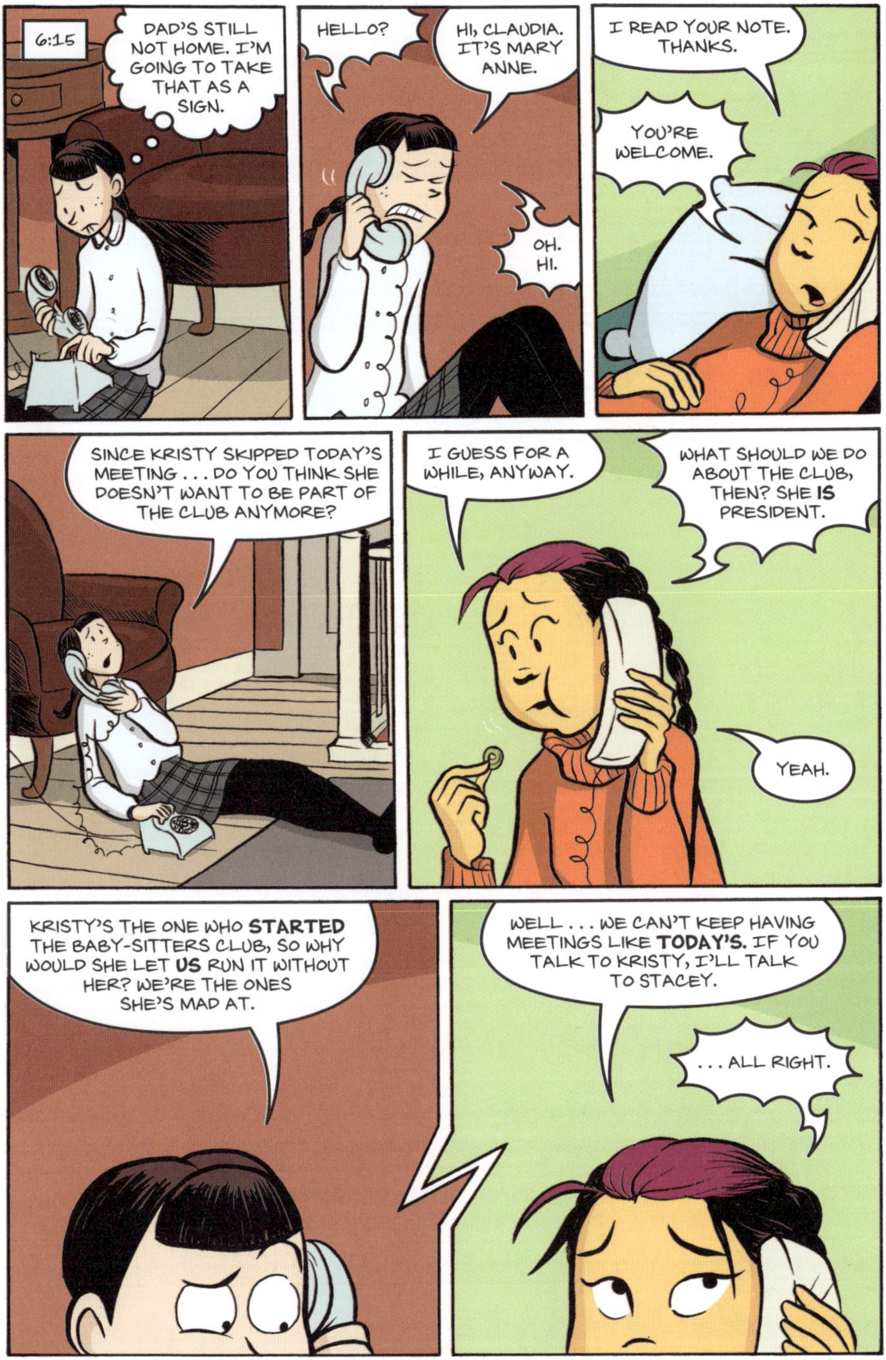
6:15
DAD'S STILL NOT HOME. I'M GOING TO TAKE THAT AS A SIGN.
HELLO?
HI, CLAUDIA. IT'S MARY ANNE.
OH. HI.
I READ YOUR NOTE. THANKS.
YOU'RE WELCOME.
SINCE KRISTY SKIPPED TODAY'S MEETING . . . DO YOU THINK SHE DOESN'T WANT TO BE PART OF THE CLUB ANYMORE?
I GUESS FOR A WHILE, ANYWAY.
WHAT SHOULD WE DO ABOUT THE CLUB, THEN? SHE **IS** PRESIDENT.
YEAH.
KRISTY'S THE ONE WHO **STARTED** THE BABY-SITTERS CLUB, SO WHY WOULD SHE LET **US** RUN IT WITHOUT HER? WE'RE THE ONES SHE'S MAD AT.
WELL . . . WE CAN'T KEEP HAVING MEETINGS LIKE **TODAY'S.** IF YOU TALK TO KRISTY, I'LL TALK TO STACEY.
. . . ALL RIGHT.

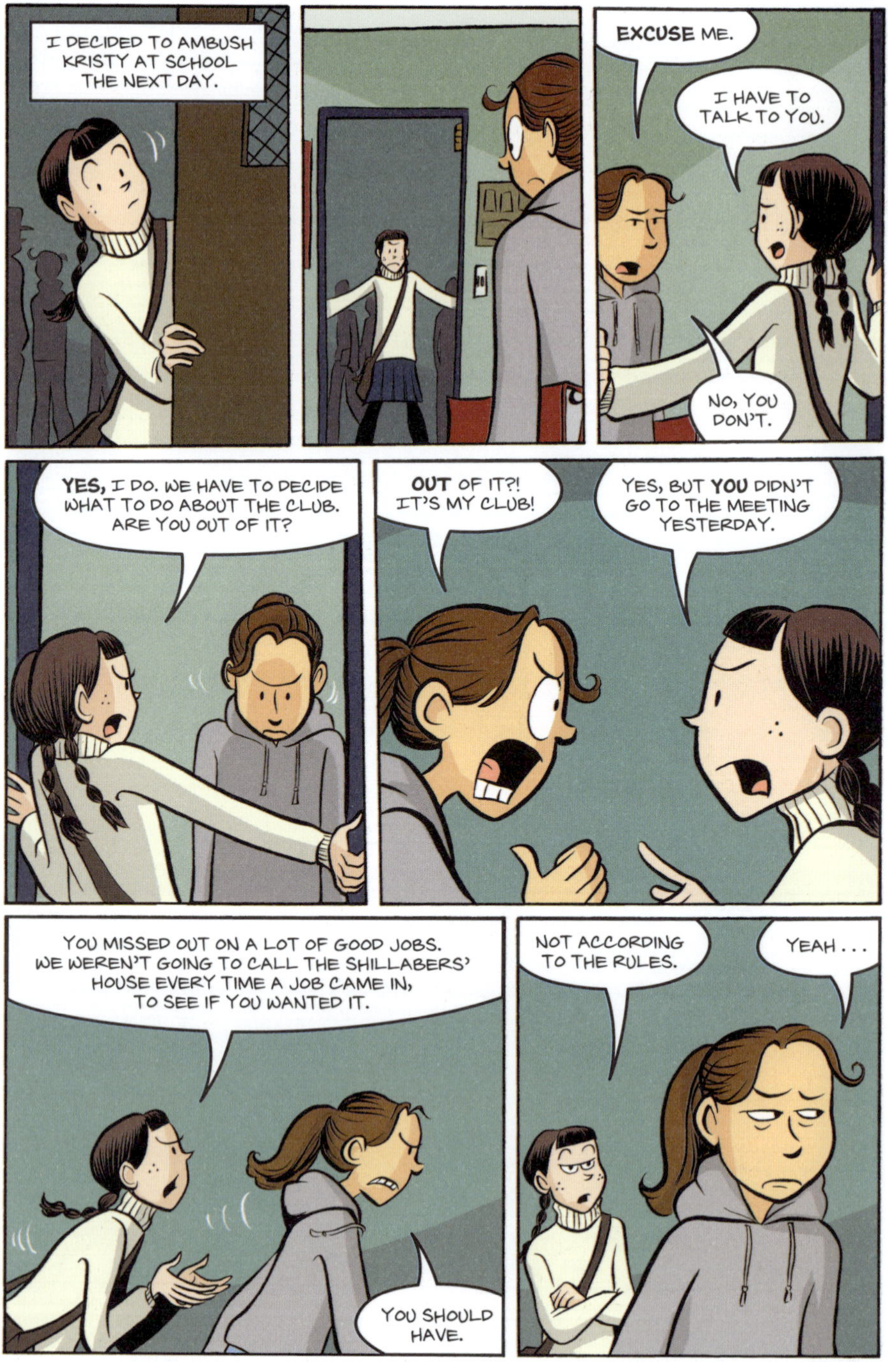
I DECIDED TO AMBUSH KRISTY AT SCHOOL THE NEXT DAY.
EXCUSE ME.
I HAVE TO TALK TO YOU.
NO, YOU DON'T.
YES, I DO. WE HAVE TO DECIDE WHAT TO DO ABOUT THE CLUB. ARE YOU OUT OF IT?
OUT OF IT?! IT'S MY CLUB!
YES, BUT YOU DIDN'T GO TO THE MEETING YESTERDAY.
YOU MISSED OUT ON A LOT OF GOOD JOBS. WE WEREN'T GOING TO CALL THE SHILLABERS' HOUSE EVERY TIME A JOB CAME IN, TO SEE IF YOU WANTED IT.
YOU SHOULD HAVE.
NOT ACCORDING TO THE RULES.
YEAH . . .

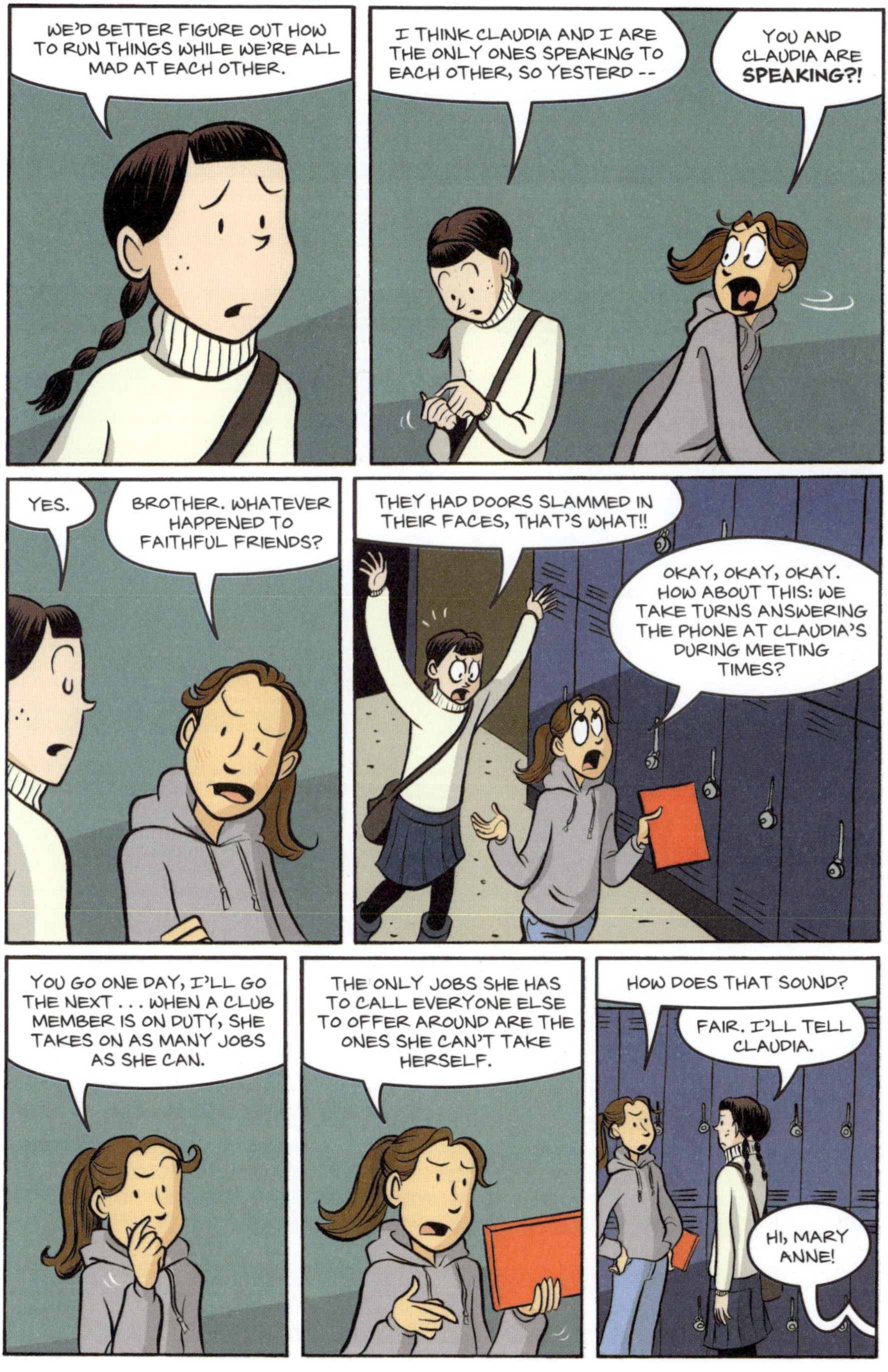

WE'D BETTER FIGURE OUT HOW TO RUN THINGS WHILE WE'RE ALL MAD AT EACH OTHER.
I THINK CLAUDIA AND I ARE THE ONLY ONES SPEAKING TO EACH OTHER, SO YESTERD --
YOU AND CLAUDIA ARE **SPEAKING?!**
YES.
BROTHER. WHATEVER HAPPENED TO FAITHFUL FRIENDS?
THEY HAD DOORS SLAMMED IN THEIR FACES, THAT'S WHAT!!
OKAY, OKAY, OKAY. HOW ABOUT THIS: WE TAKE TURNS ANSWERING THE PHONE AT CLAUDIA'S DURING MEETING TIMES?
YOU GO ONE DAY, I'LL GO THE NEXT . . . WHEN A CLUB MEMBER IS ON DUTY, SHE TAKES ON AS MANY JOBS AS SHE CAN.
THE ONLY JOBS SHE HAS TO CALL EVERYONE ELSE TO OFFER AROUND ARE THE ONES SHE CAN'T TAKE HERSELF.
HOW DOES THAT SOUND?
FAIR. I'LL TELL CLAUDIA.
HI, MARY ANNE!

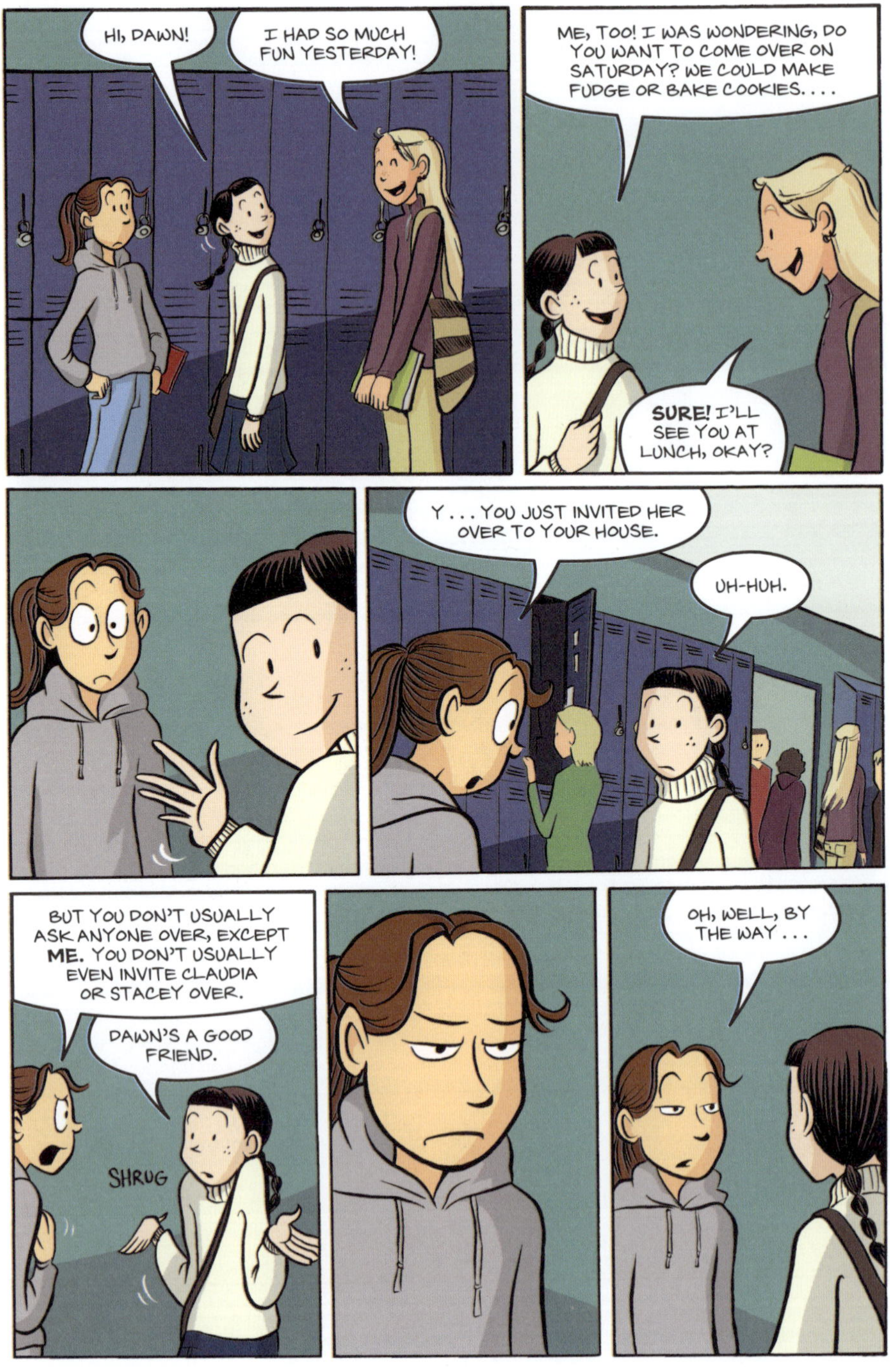
HI, DAWN!
I HAD SO MUCH FUN YESTERDAY!
ME, TOO! I WAS WONDERING, DO YOU WANT TO COME OVER ON SATURDAY? WE COULD MAKE FUDGE OR BAKE COOKIES. . . .
SURE! I'LL SEE YOU AT LUNCH, OKAY?
Y . . . YOU JUST INVITED HER OVER TO YOUR HOUSE.
UH-HUH.
BUT YOU DON'T USUALLY ASK ANYONE OVER, EXCEPT **ME.** YOU DON'T USUALLY EVEN INVITE CLAUDIA OR STACEY OVER.
DAWN'S A GOOD FRIEND.
SHRUG
OH, WELL, BY THE WAY . . .

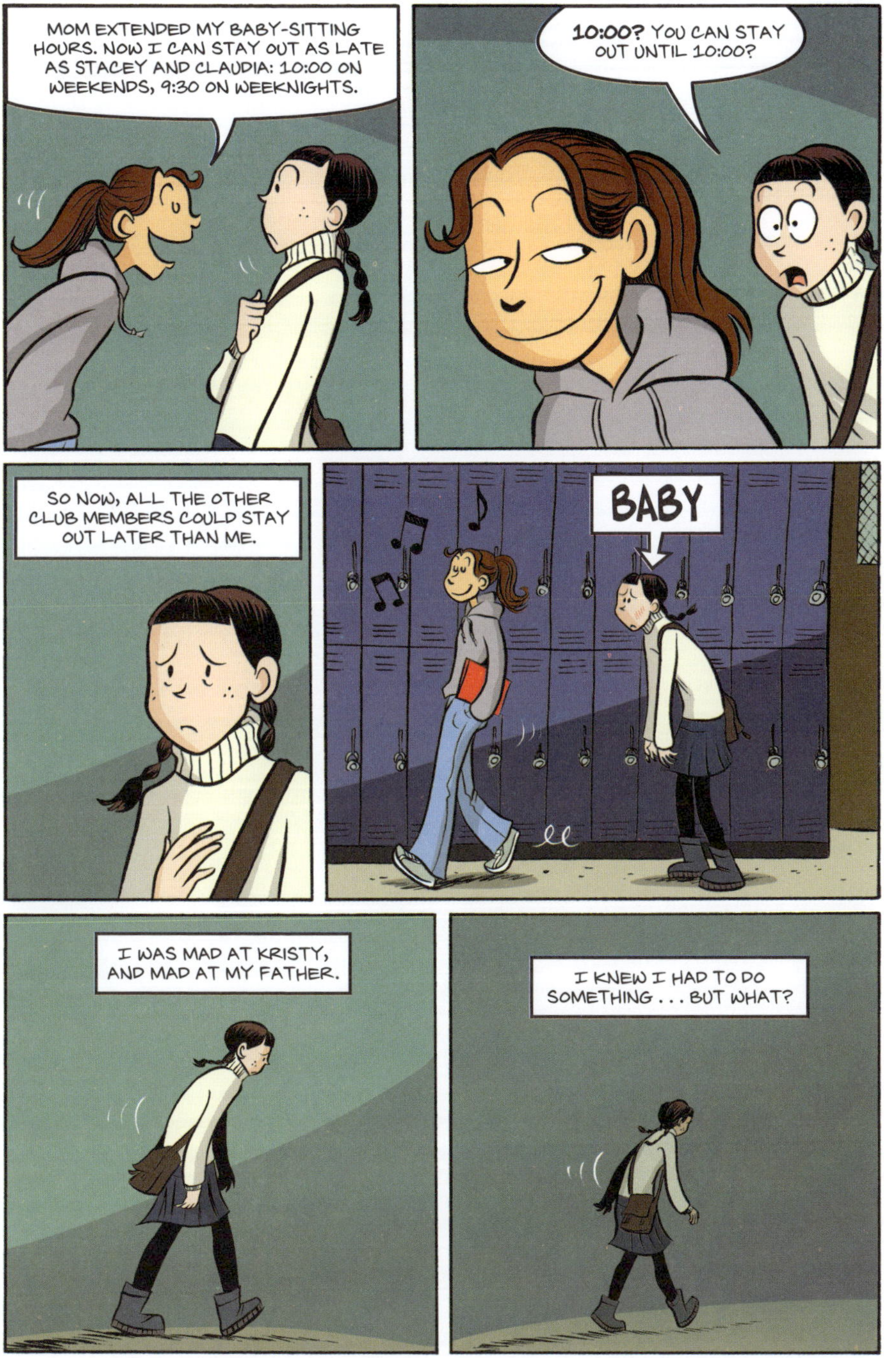
MOM EXTENDED MY BABY-SITTING HOURS. NOW I CAN STAY OUT AS LATE AS STACEY AND CLAUDIA: 10:00 ON WEEKENDS, 9:30 ON WEEKNIGHTS.
10:00? YOU CAN STAY OUT UNTIL 10:00?
SO NOW, ALL THE OTHER CLUB MEMBERS COULD STAY OUT LATER THAN ME.
BABY
I WAS MAD AT KRISTY, AND MAD AT MY FATHER.
I KNEW I HAD TO DO SOMETHING . . . BUT WHAT?

Sunday, January 11

    This afternoon, I sat for Jenny Prezzioso. Jenny is three. She's the Pikes' neighbor, so I had met her a few times before today. She and her parents both look very prim and proper but Mrs. Prezzioso is the only one who acts that way. She looks like she just stepped out of the pages of a magazine. And she dresses Jenny as if every day were Easter Sunday: frilly dresses, lacy socks, and ribbons in her hair. Mrs. P probably thinks "jeans" is a dirty word.

    Mr. P, on the other hand, looks like he'd rather be dozing in front of the TV in sweats, a T-shirt, and mismatched socks. And Jenny tries hard, but she just isn't what her mother wants her to be. . . .

                                         Stacey

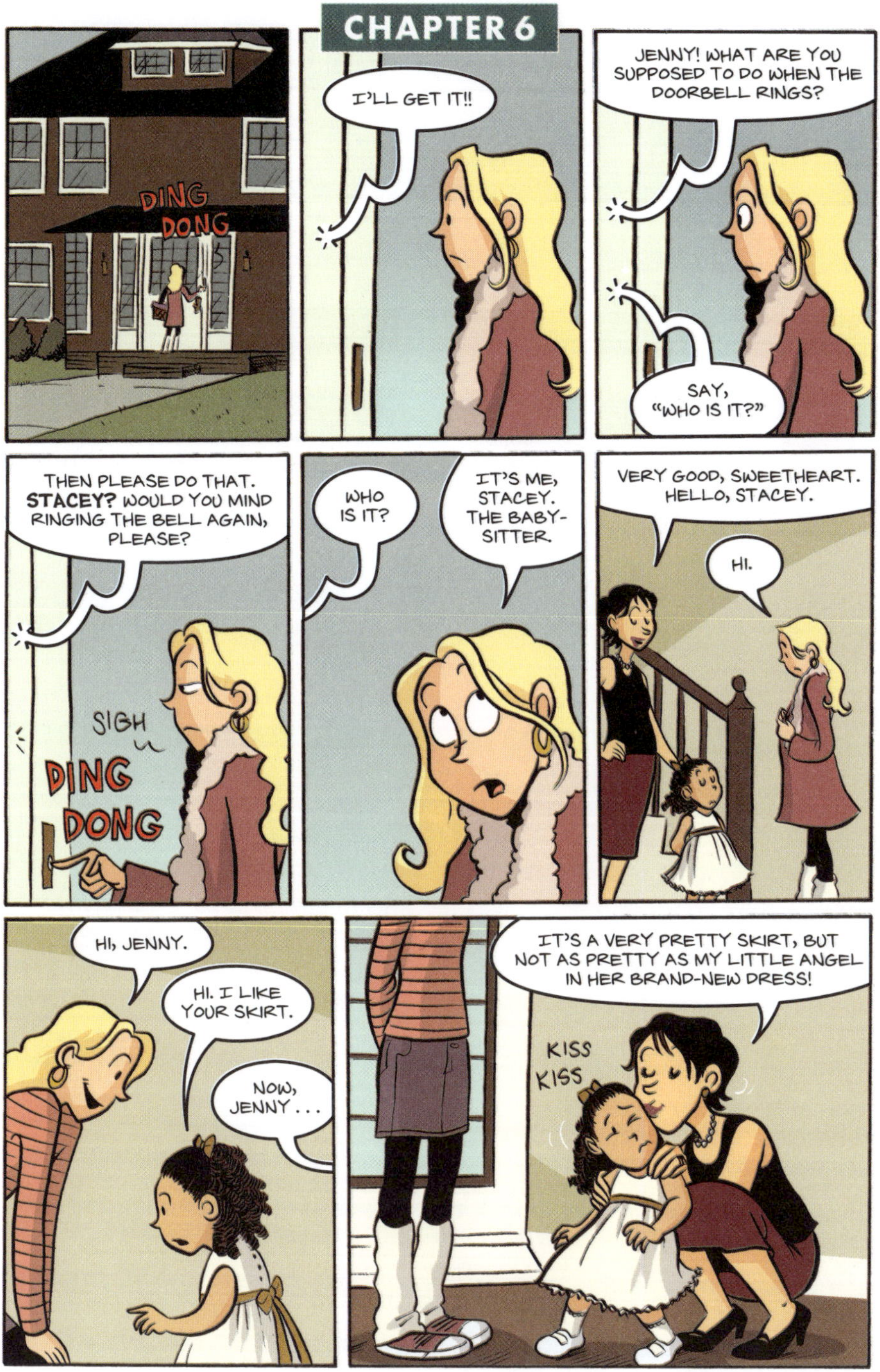
CHAPTER 6
DING DONG
I'LL GET IT!!
JENNY! WHAT ARE YOU SUPPOSED TO DO WHEN THE DOORBELL RINGS?
SAY, "WHO IS IT?"
THEN PLEASE DO THAT. STACEY? WOULD YOU MIND RINGING THE BELL AGAIN, PLEASE?
SIGH
DING DONG
WHO IS IT?
IT'S ME, STACEY. THE BABY-SITTER.
VERY GOOD, SWEETHEART. HELLO, STACEY.
HI.
HI, JENNY.
HI. I LIKE YOUR SKIRT.
NOW, JENNY . . .
IT'S A VERY PRETTY SKIRT, BUT NOT AS PRETTY AS MY LITTLE ANGEL IN HER BRAND-NEW DRESS!
KISS KISS

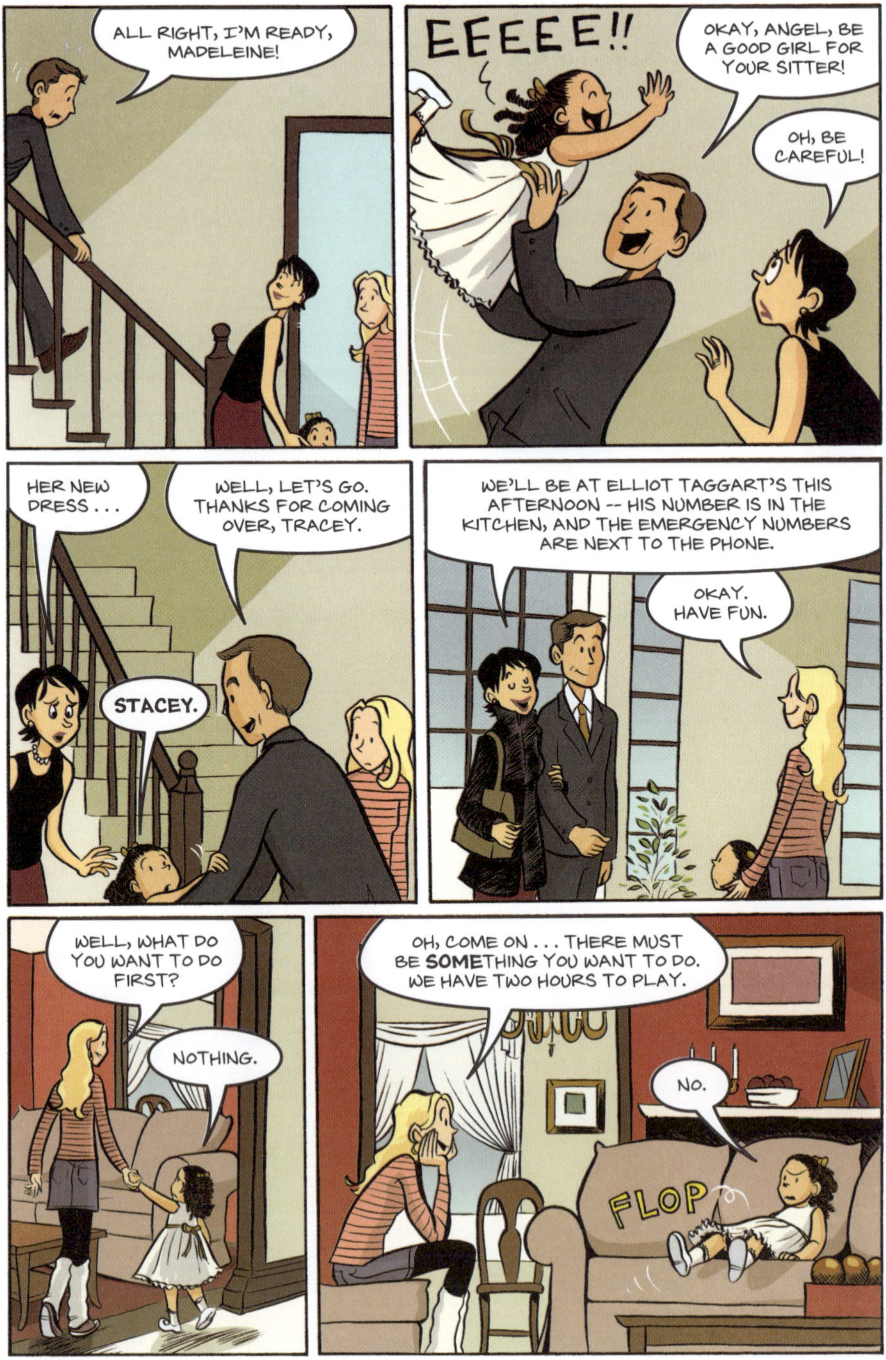
ALL RIGHT, I'M READY, MADELEINE!
EEEEE!!
OKAY, ANGEL, BE A GOOD GIRL FOR YOUR SITTER!
OH, BE CAREFUL!
HER NEW DRESS . . .
WELL, LET'S GO. THANKS FOR COMING OVER, TRACEY.
STACEY.
WE'LL BE AT ELLIOT TAGGART'S THIS AFTERNOON -- HIS NUMBER IS IN THE KITCHEN, AND THE EMERGENCY NUMBERS ARE NEXT TO THE PHONE.
OKAY. HAVE FUN.
WELL, WHAT DO YOU WANT TO DO FIRST?
NOTHING.
OH, COME ON . . . THERE MUST BE **SOME**THING YOU WANT TO DO. WE HAVE TWO HOURS TO PLAY.
NO.
FLOP

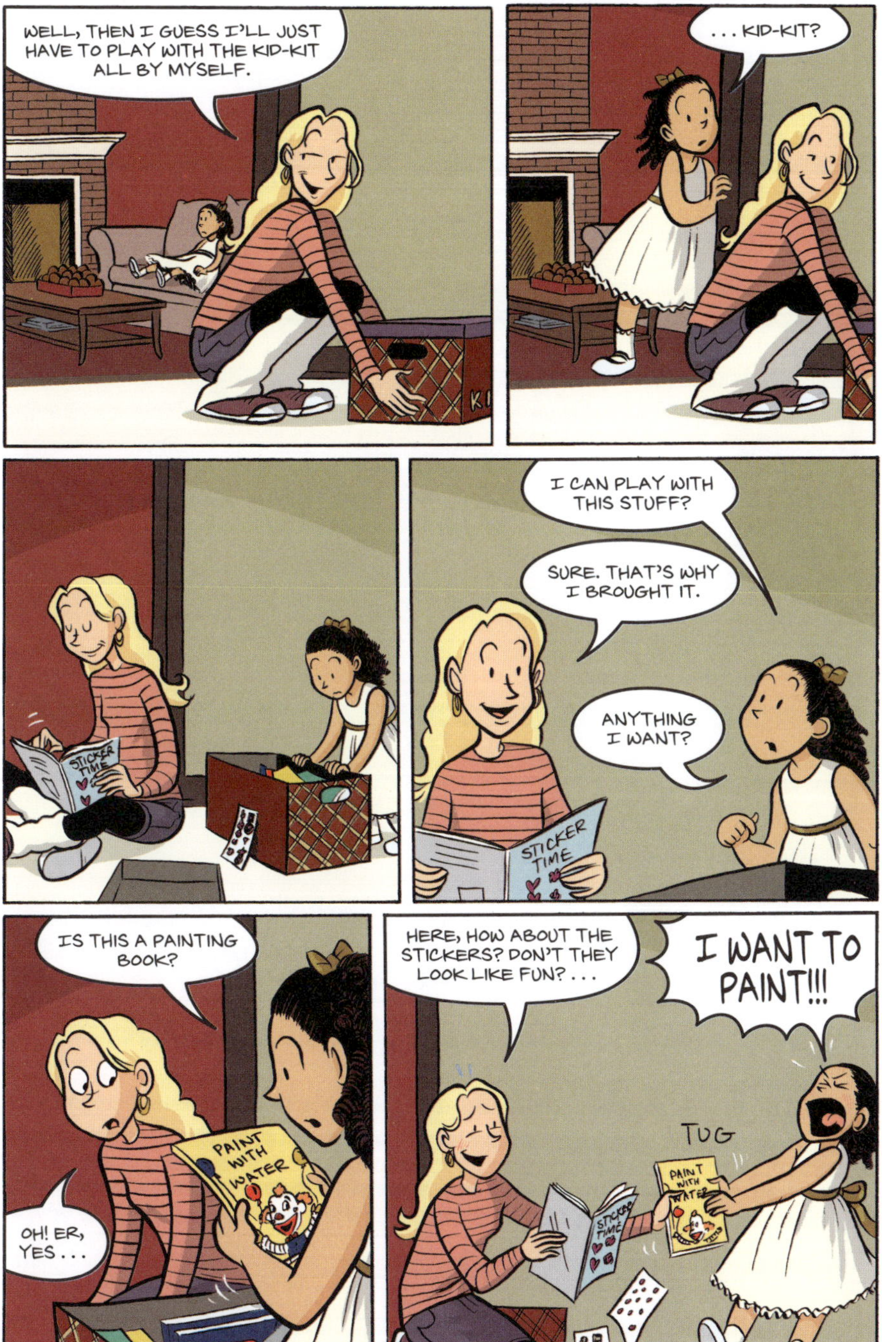
WELL, THEN I GUESS I'LL JUST HAVE TO PLAY WITH THE KID-KIT ALL BY MYSELF.
. . . KID-KIT?
I CAN PLAY WITH THIS STUFF?
SURE. THAT'S WHY I BROUGHT IT.
ANYTHING I WANT?
STICKER TIME
IS THIS A PAINTING BOOK?
OH! ER, YES . . .
PAINT WITH WATER
HERE, HOW ABOUT THE STICKERS? DON'T THEY LOOK LIKE FUN? . . .
I WANT TO PAINT!!!
TUG

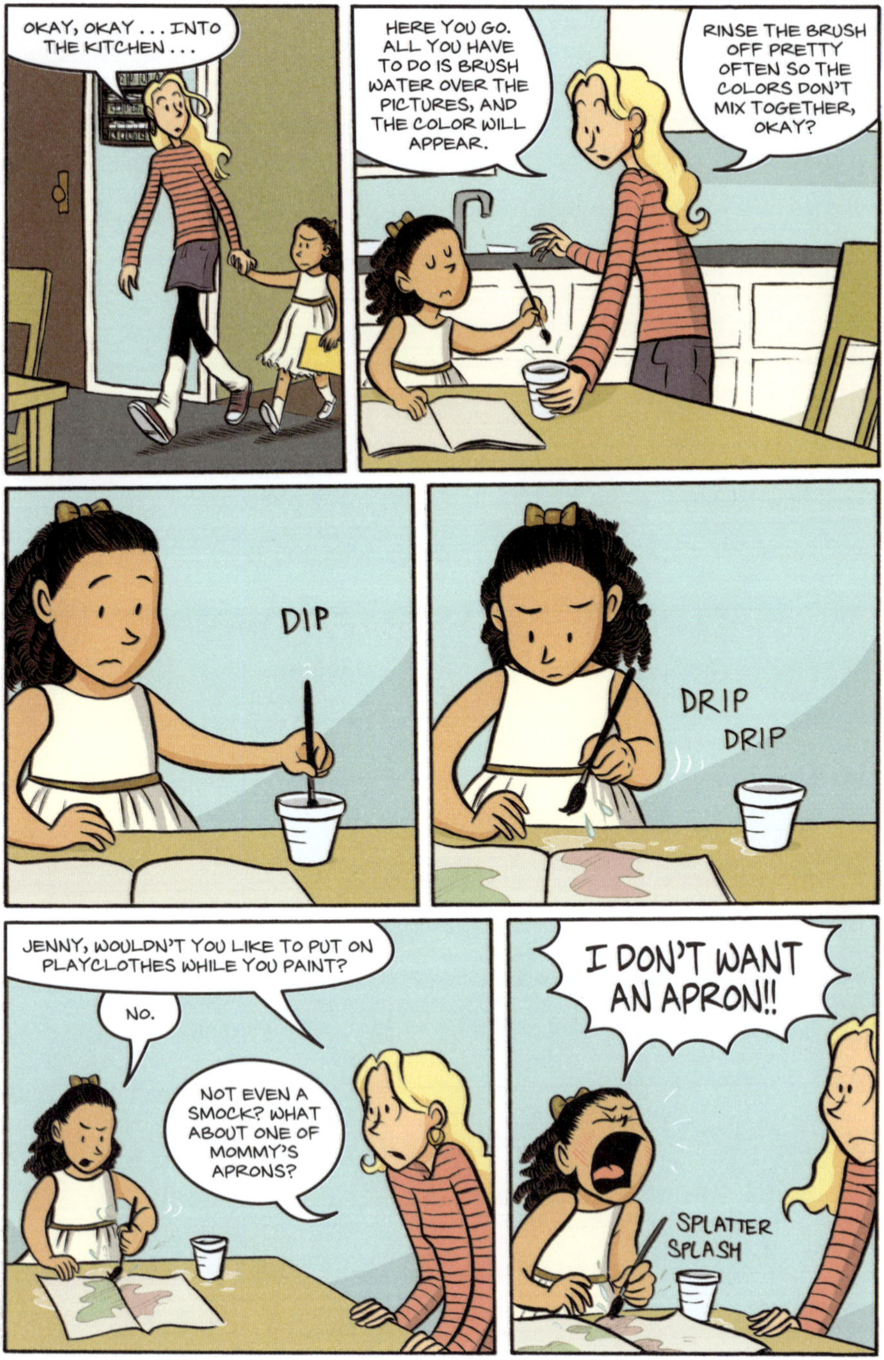
OKAY, OKAY . . . INTO THE KITCHEN . . .
HERE YOU GO. ALL YOU HAVE TO DO IS BRUSH WATER OVER THE PICTURES, AND THE COLOR WILL APPEAR.
RINSE THE BRUSH OFF PRETTY OFTEN SO THE COLORS DON'T MIX TOGETHER, OKAY?
DIP
DRIP
DRIP
JENNY, WOULDN'T YOU LIKE TO PUT ON PLAYCLOTHES WHILE YOU PAINT?
NO.
NOT EVEN A SMOCK? WHAT ABOUT ONE OF MOMMY'S APRONS?
I DON'T WANT AN APRON!!
SPLATTER
SPLASH

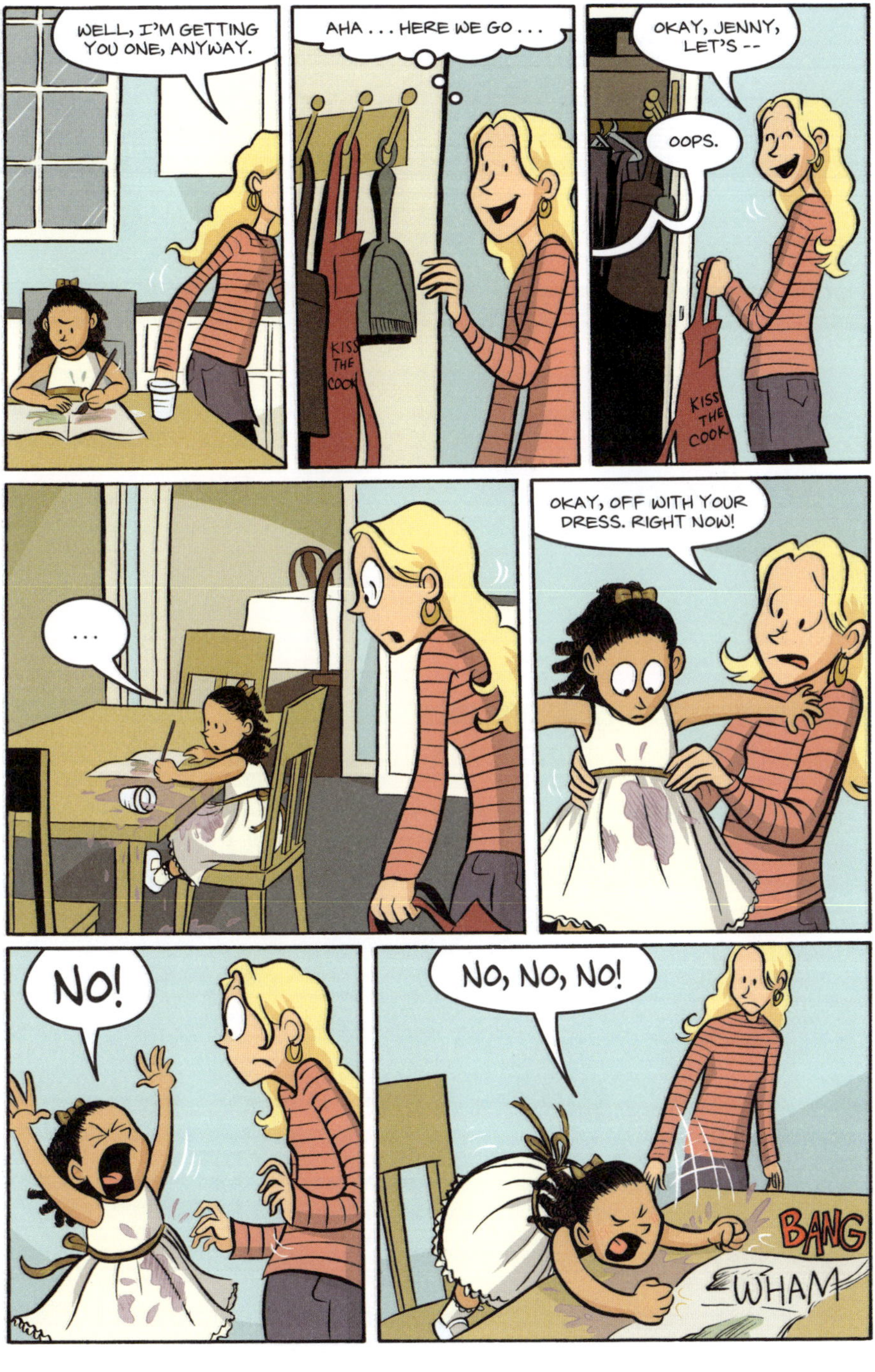
WELL, I'M GETTING YOU ONE, ANYWAY.
AHA . . . HERE WE GO . . .
KISS THE COOK
OKAY, JENNY, LET'S --
OOPS.
KISS THE COOK
. . .
OKAY, OFF WITH YOUR DRESS. RIGHT NOW!
NO!
NO, NO, NO!
BANG
WHAM

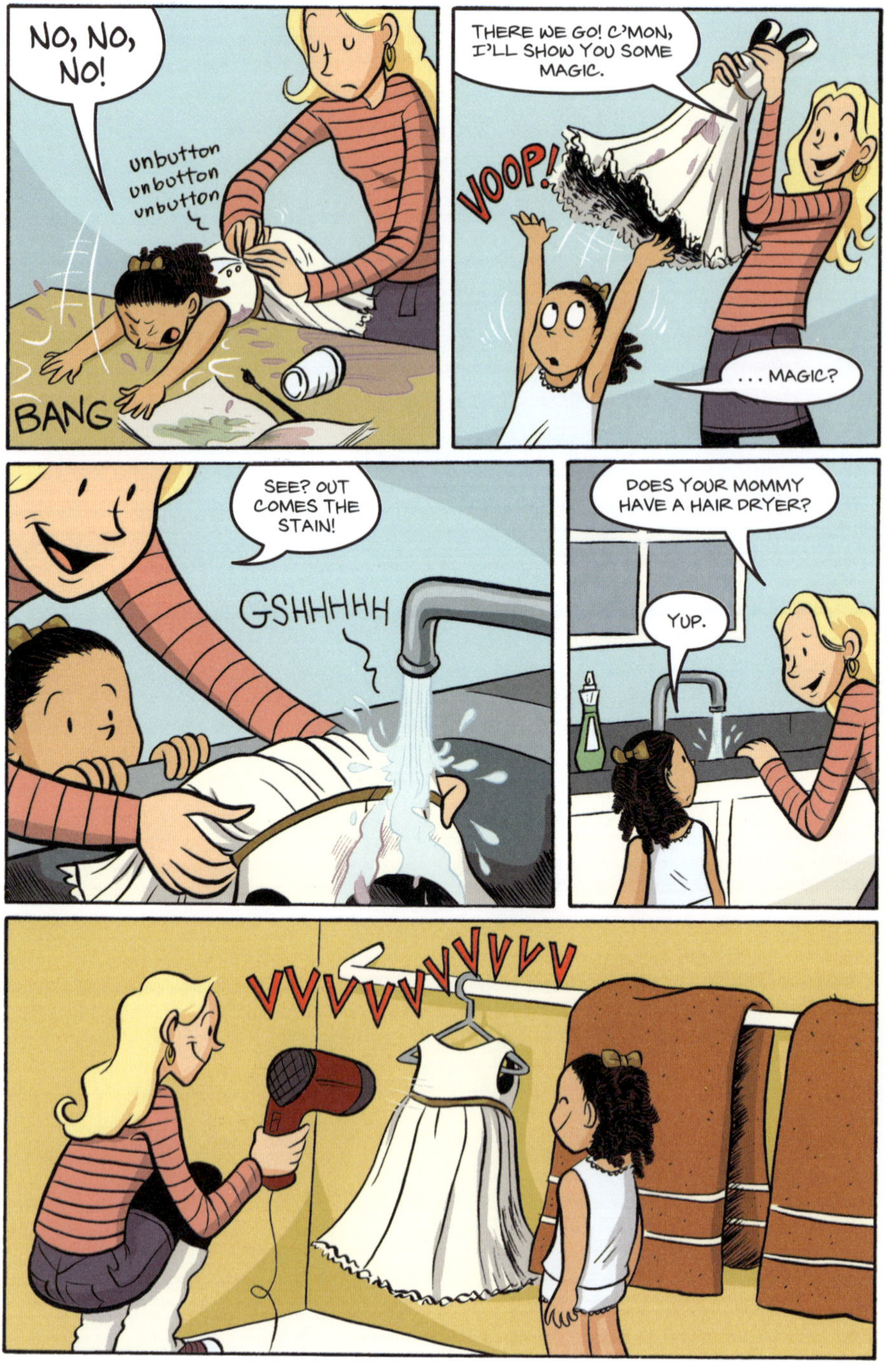
NO, NO, NO!
unbutton unbutton unbutton
BANG
THERE WE GO! C'MON, I'LL SHOW YOU SOME MAGIC.
VOOP!
. . . MAGIC?
SEE? OUT COMES THE STAIN!
GSHHHHH
DOES YOUR MOMMY HAVE A HAIR DRYER?
YUP.
VVVVVVVVVVVV

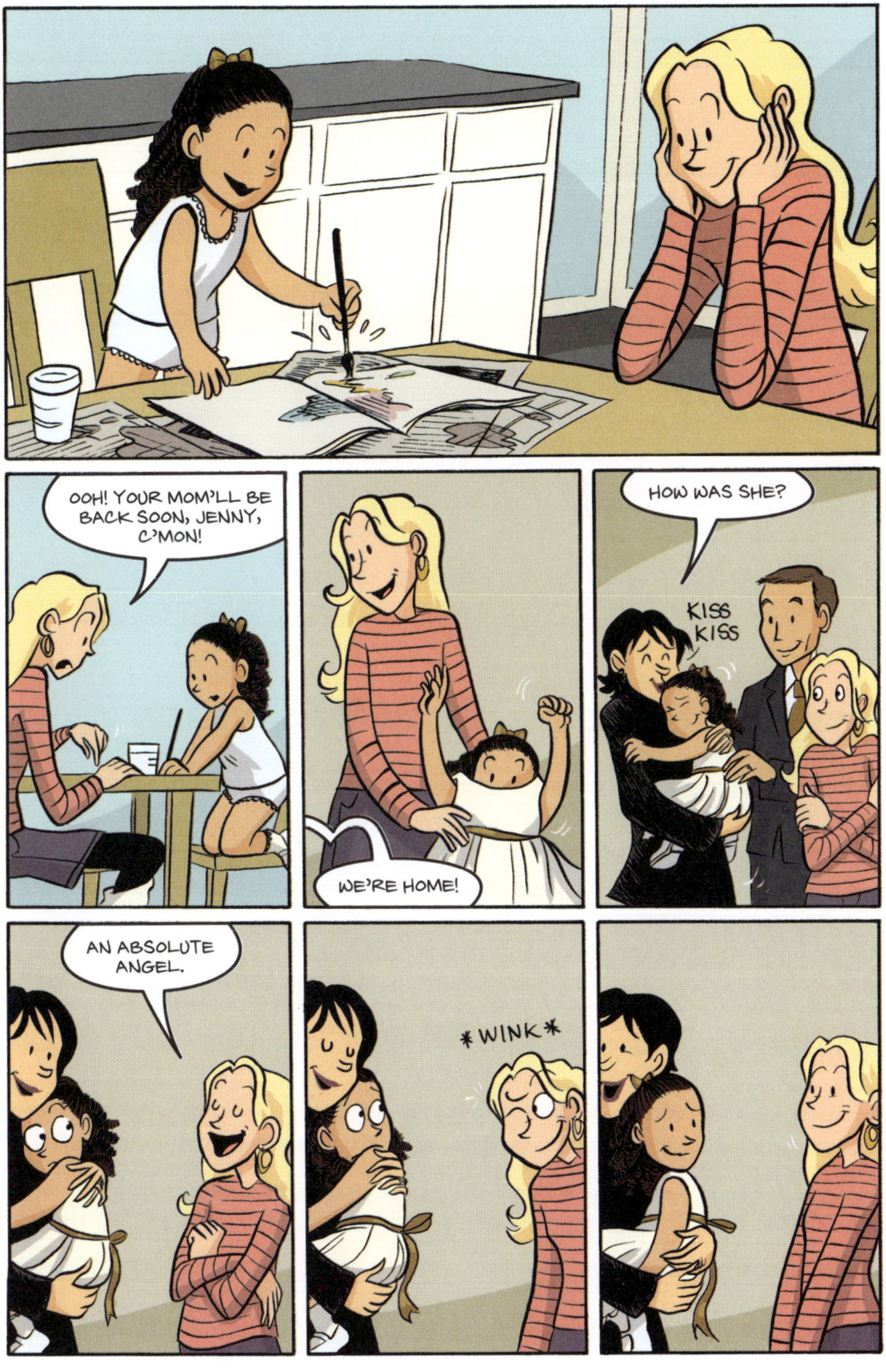
OOH! YOUR MOM'LL BE BACK SOON, JENNY, C'MON!
WE'RE HOME!
HOW WAS SHE?
KISS KISS
AN ABSOLUTE ANGEL.
WINK

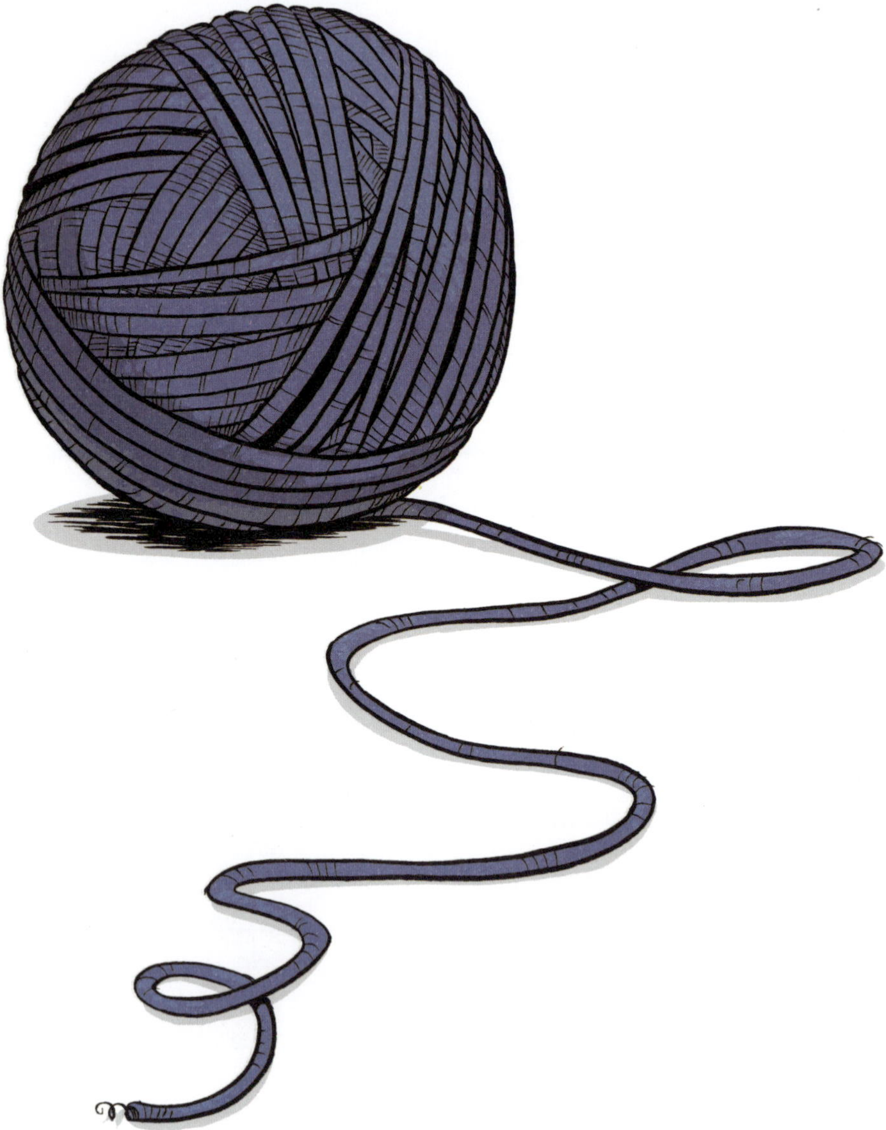

CHAPTER 7

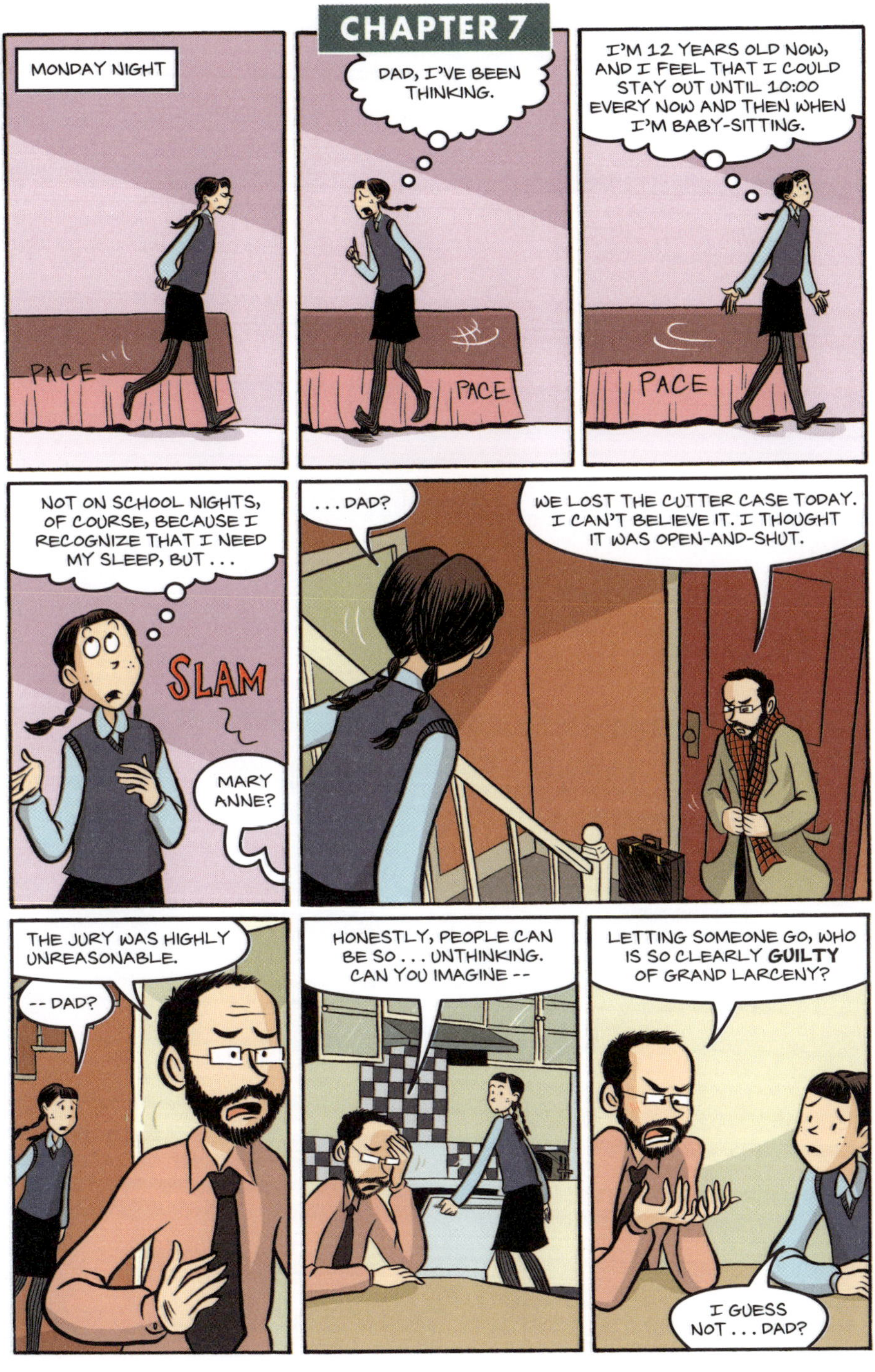
MONDAY NIGHT
PACE
DAD, I'VE BEEN THINKING.
PACE
I'M 12 YEARS OLD NOW, AND I FEEL THAT I COULD STAY OUT UNTIL 10:00 EVERY NOW AND THEN WHEN I'M BABY-SITTING.
PACE
NOT ON SCHOOL NIGHTS, OF COURSE, BECAUSE I RECOGNIZE THAT I NEED MY SLEEP, BUT . . .
SLAM
MARY ANNE?
. . . DAD?
WE LOST THE CUTTER CASE TODAY. I CAN'T BELIEVE IT. I THOUGHT IT WAS OPEN-AND-SHUT.
THE JURY WAS HIGHLY UNREASONABLE.
-- DAD?
HONESTLY, PEOPLE CAN BE SO . . . UNTHINKING. CAN YOU IMAGINE --
LETTING SOMEONE GO, WHO IS SO CLEARLY **GUILTY** OF GRAND LARCENY?
I GUESS NOT . . . DAD?

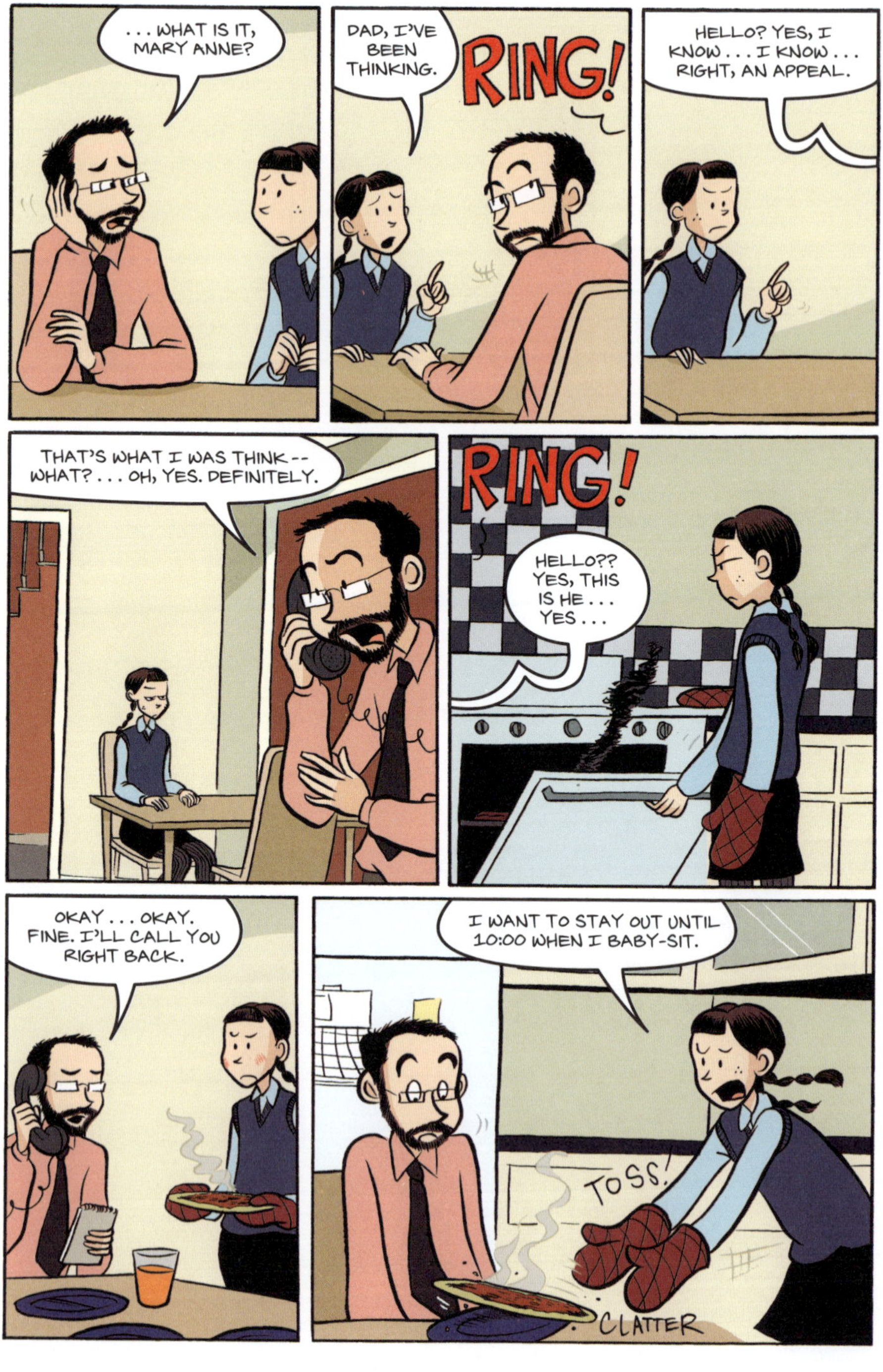
. . . WHAT IS IT, MARY ANNE?
DAD, I'VE BEEN THINKING.
RING!
HELLO? YES, I KNOW . . . I KNOW . . . RIGHT, AN APPEAL.
THAT'S WHAT I WAS THINK-- WHAT? . . . OH, YES. DEFINITELY.
RING!
HELLO?? YES, THIS IS HE . . . YES . . .
OKAY . . . OKAY. FINE. I'LL CALL YOU RIGHT BACK.
I WANT TO STAY OUT UNTIL 10:00 WHEN I BABY-SIT.
TOSS!
CLATTER

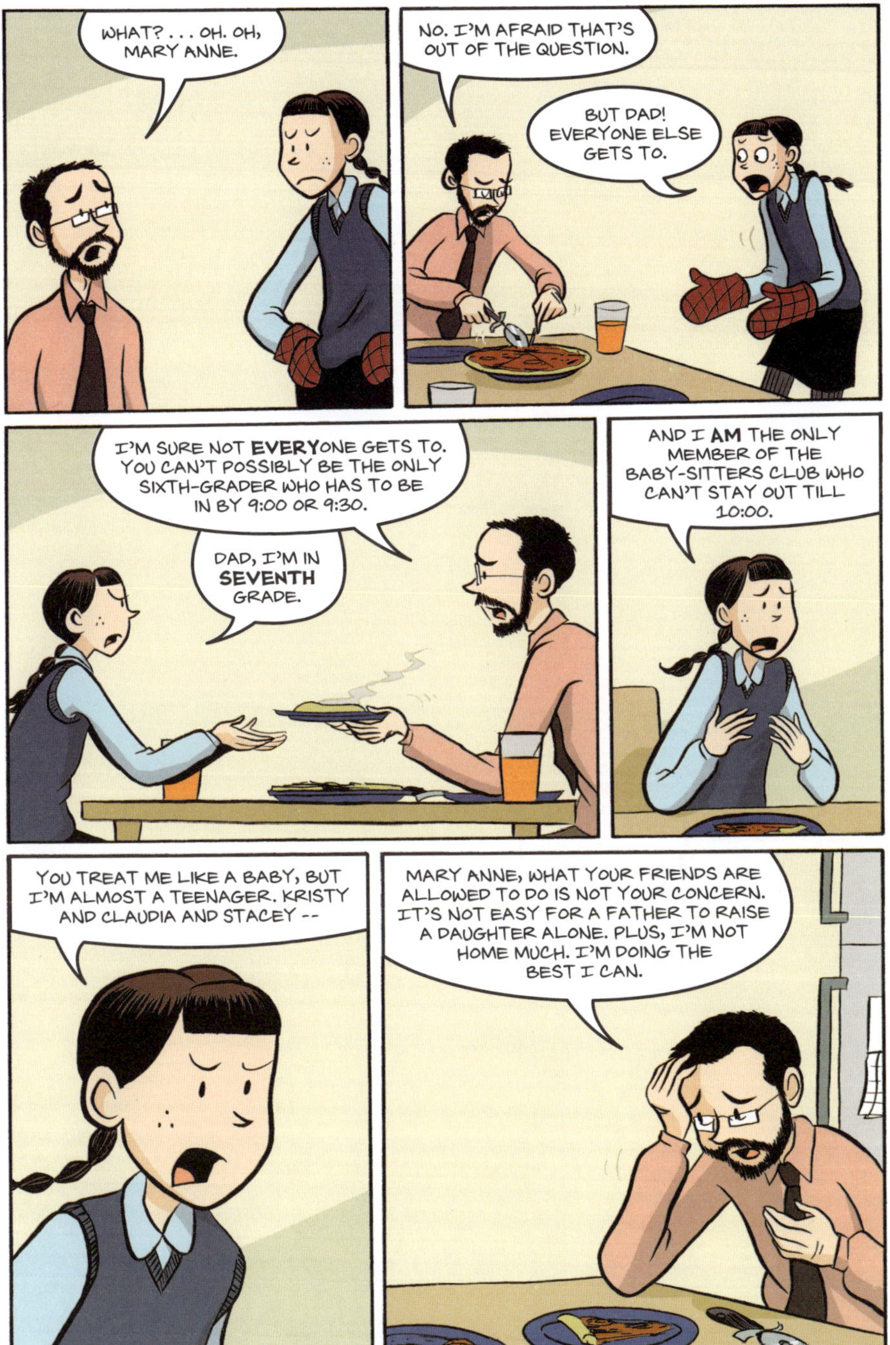
WHAT? . . . OH. OH, MARY ANNE.
NO. I'M AFRAID THAT'S OUT OF THE QUESTION.
BUT DAD! EVERYONE ELSE GETS TO.
I'M SURE NOT **EVERY**ONE GETS TO. YOU CAN'T POSSIBLY BE THE ONLY SIXTH-GRADER WHO HAS TO BE IN BY 9:00 OR 9:30.
DAD, I'M IN **SEVENTH** GRADE.
AND I **AM** THE ONLY MEMBER OF THE BABY-SITTERS CLUB WHO CAN'T STAY OUT TILL 10:00.
YOU TREAT ME LIKE A BABY, BUT I'M ALMOST A TEENAGER. KRISTY AND CLAUDIA AND STACEY --
MARY ANNE, WHAT YOUR FRIENDS ARE ALLOWED TO DO IS NOT YOUR CONCERN. IT'S NOT EASY FOR A FATHER TO RAISE A DAUGHTER ALONE. PLUS, I'M NOT HOME MUCH. I'M DOING THE BEST I CAN.

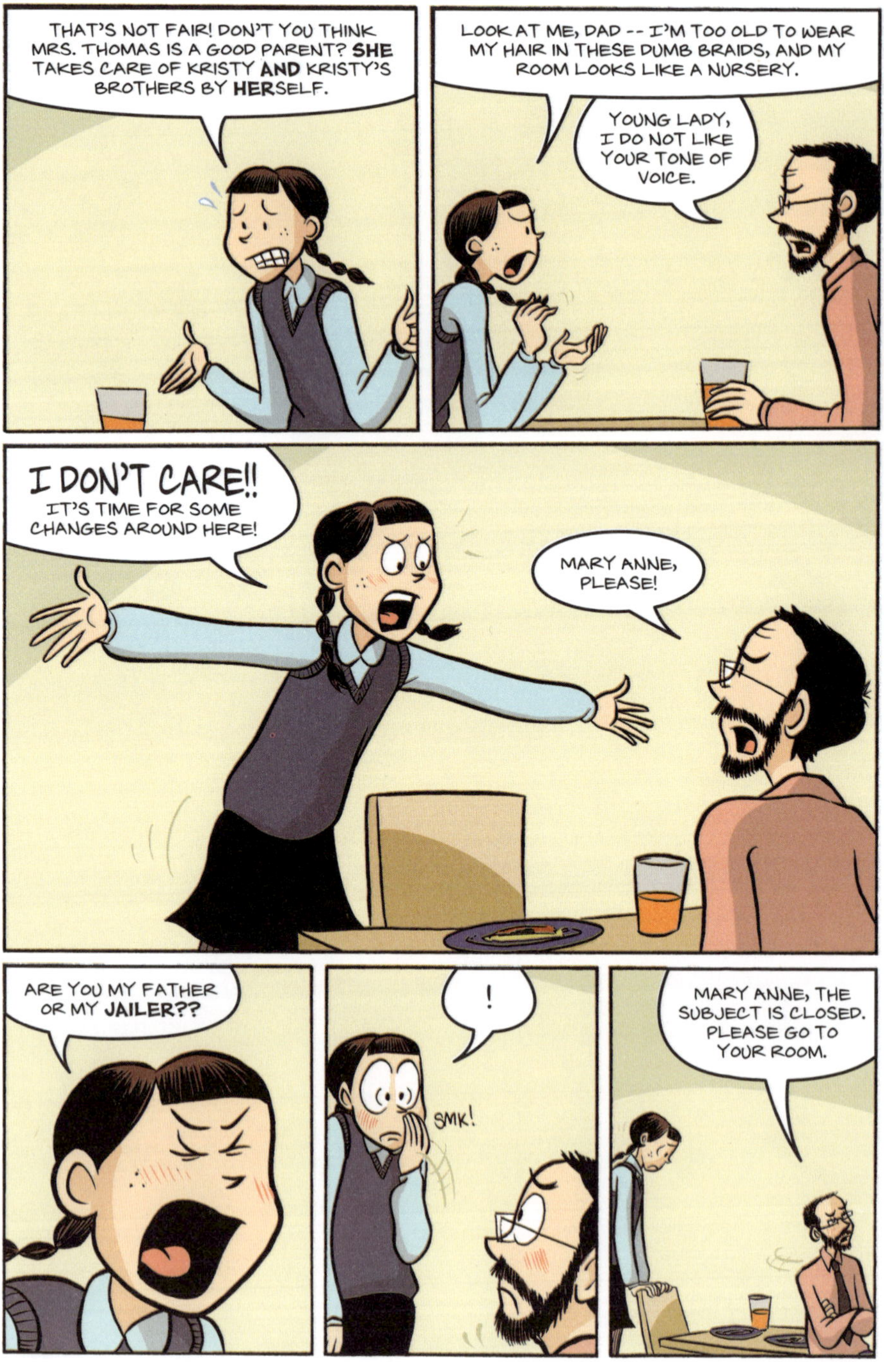
THAT'S NOT FAIR! DON'T YOU THINK MRS. THOMAS IS A GOOD PARENT? SHE TAKES CARE OF KRISTY AND KRISTY'S BROTHERS BY HERSELF.
LOOK AT ME, DAD -- I'M TOO OLD TO WEAR MY HAIR IN THESE DUMB BRAIDS, AND MY ROOM LOOKS LIKE A NURSERY.
YOUNG LADY, I DO NOT LIKE YOUR TONE OF VOICE.
I DON'T CARE!! IT'S TIME FOR SOME CHANGES AROUND HERE!
MARY ANNE, PLEASE!
ARE YOU MY FATHER OR MY JAILER??
!
SMK!
MARY ANNE, THE SUBJECT IS CLOSED. PLEASE GO TO YOUR ROOM.

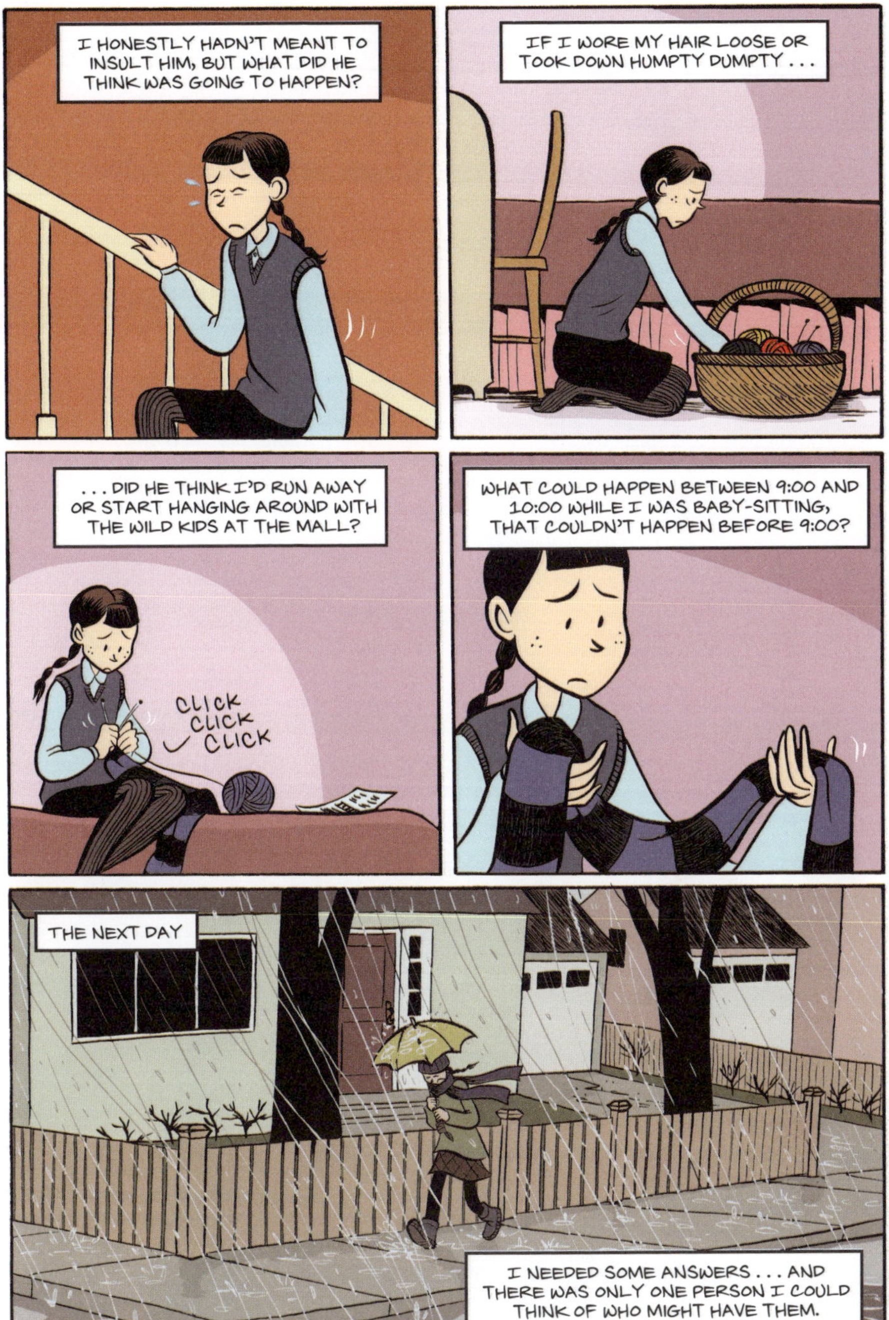
I HONESTLY HADN'T MEANT TO INSULT HIM, BUT WHAT DID HE THINK WAS GOING TO HAPPEN?
IF I WORE MY HAIR LOOSE OR TOOK DOWN HUMPTY DUMPTY . . .
. . . DID HE THINK I'D RUN AWAY OR START HANGING AROUND WITH THE WILD KIDS AT THE MALL?
CLICK CLICK CLICK
WHAT COULD HAPPEN BETWEEN 9:00 AND 10:00 WHILE I WAS BABY-SITTING, THAT COULDN'T HAPPEN BEFORE 9:00?
THE NEXT DAY
I NEEDED SOME ANSWERS . . . AND THERE WAS ONLY ONE PERSON I COULD THINK OF WHO MIGHT HAVE THEM.

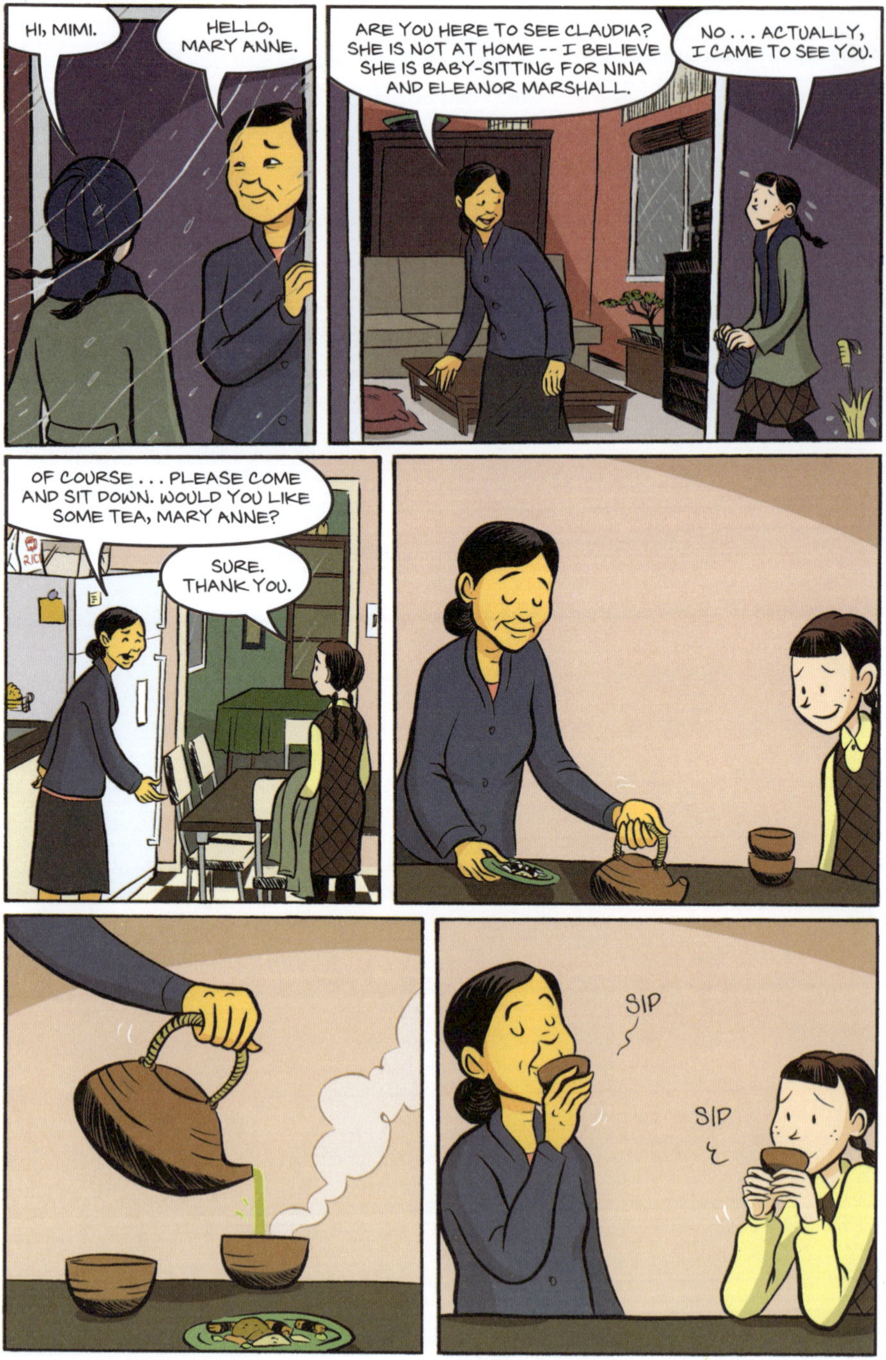
HI, MIMI.
HELLO, MARY ANNE.
ARE YOU HERE TO SEE CLAUDIA? SHE IS NOT AT HOME -- I BELIEVE SHE IS BABY-SITTING FOR NINA AND ELEANOR MARSHALL.
NO . . . ACTUALLY, I CAME TO SEE YOU.
OF COURSE . . . PLEASE COME AND SIT DOWN. WOULD YOU LIKE SOME TEA, MARY ANNE?
SURE. THANK YOU.
SIP
SIP

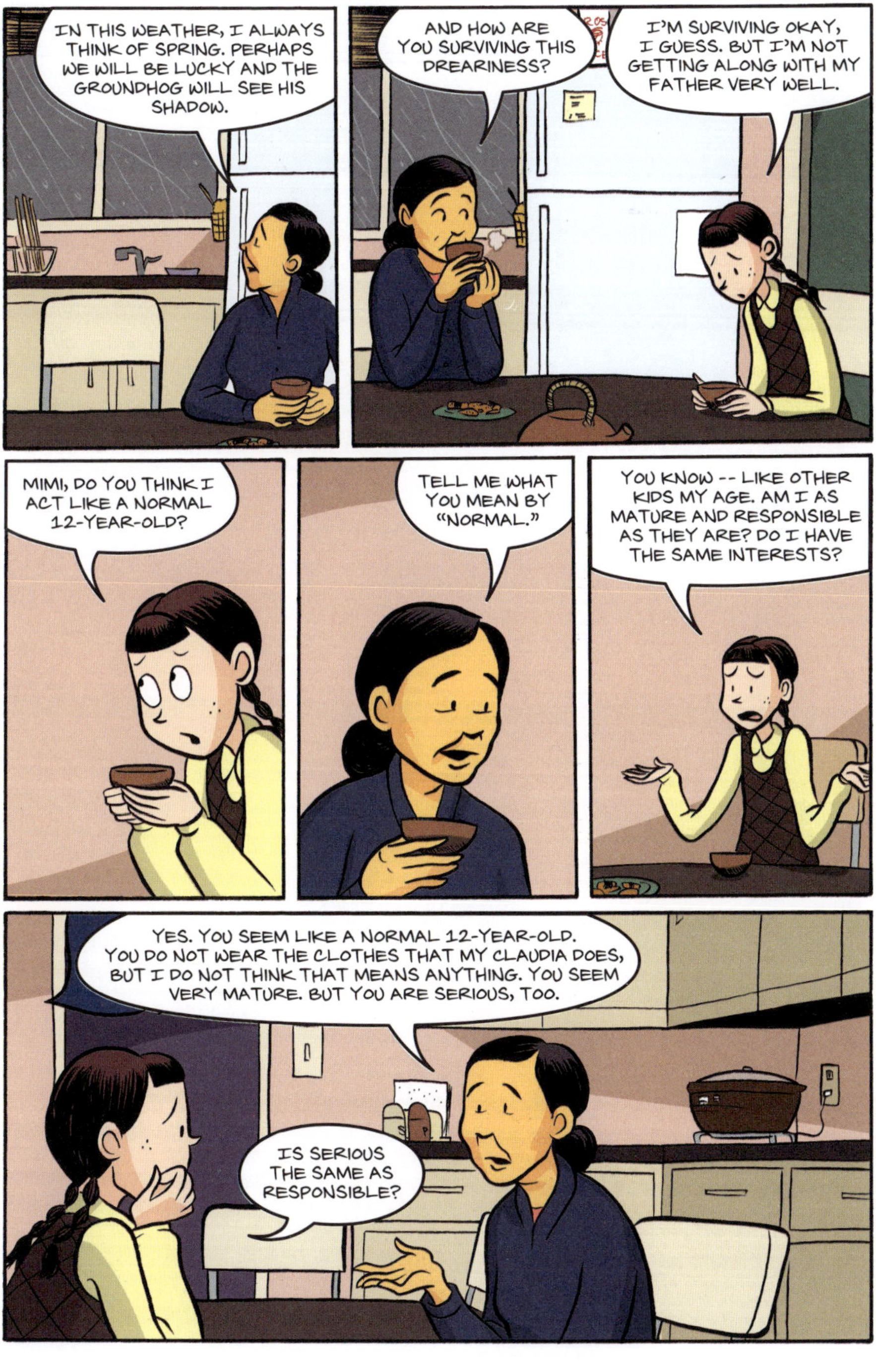
IN THIS WEATHER, I ALWAYS THINK OF SPRING. PERHAPS WE WILL BE LUCKY AND THE GROUNDHOG WILL SEE HIS SHADOW.
AND HOW ARE YOU SURVIVING THIS DREARINESS?
I'M SURVIVING OKAY, I GUESS. BUT I'M NOT GETTING ALONG WITH MY FATHER VERY WELL.
MIMI, DO YOU THINK I ACT LIKE A NORMAL 12-YEAR-OLD?
TELL ME WHAT YOU MEAN BY "NORMAL."
YOU KNOW -- LIKE OTHER KIDS MY AGE. AM I AS MATURE AND RESPONSIBLE AS THEY ARE? DO I HAVE THE SAME INTERESTS?
YES. YOU SEEM LIKE A NORMAL 12-YEAR-OLD. YOU DO NOT WEAR THE CLOTHES THAT MY CLAUDIA DOES, BUT I DO NOT THINK THAT MEANS ANYTHING. YOU SEEM VERY MATURE. BUT YOU ARE SERIOUS, TOO.
IS SERIOUS THE SAME AS RESPONSIBLE?

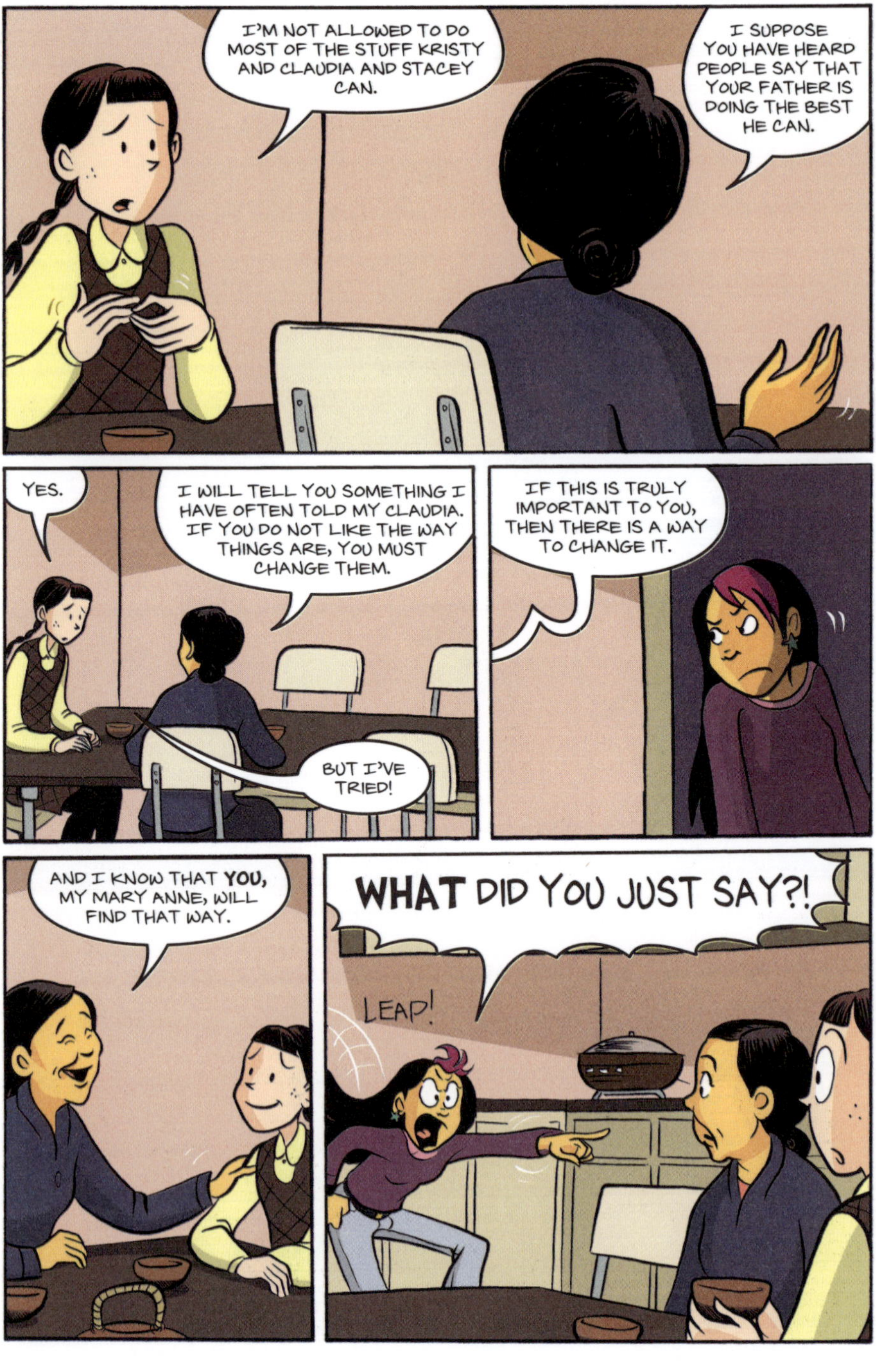
I'M NOT ALLOWED TO DO MOST OF THE STUFF KRISTY AND CLAUDIA AND STACEY CAN.
I SUPPOSE YOU HAVE HEARD PEOPLE SAY THAT YOUR FATHER IS DOING THE BEST HE CAN.
YES.
I WILL TELL YOU SOMETHING I HAVE OFTEN TOLD MY CLAUDIA. IF YOU DO NOT LIKE THE WAY THINGS ARE, YOU MUST CHANGE THEM.
BUT I'VE TRIED!
IF THIS IS TRULY IMPORTANT TO YOU, THEN THERE IS A WAY TO CHANGE IT.
AND I KNOW THAT **YOU**, MY MARY ANNE, WILL FIND THAT WAY.
WHAT DID YOU JUST SAY?!
LEAP!

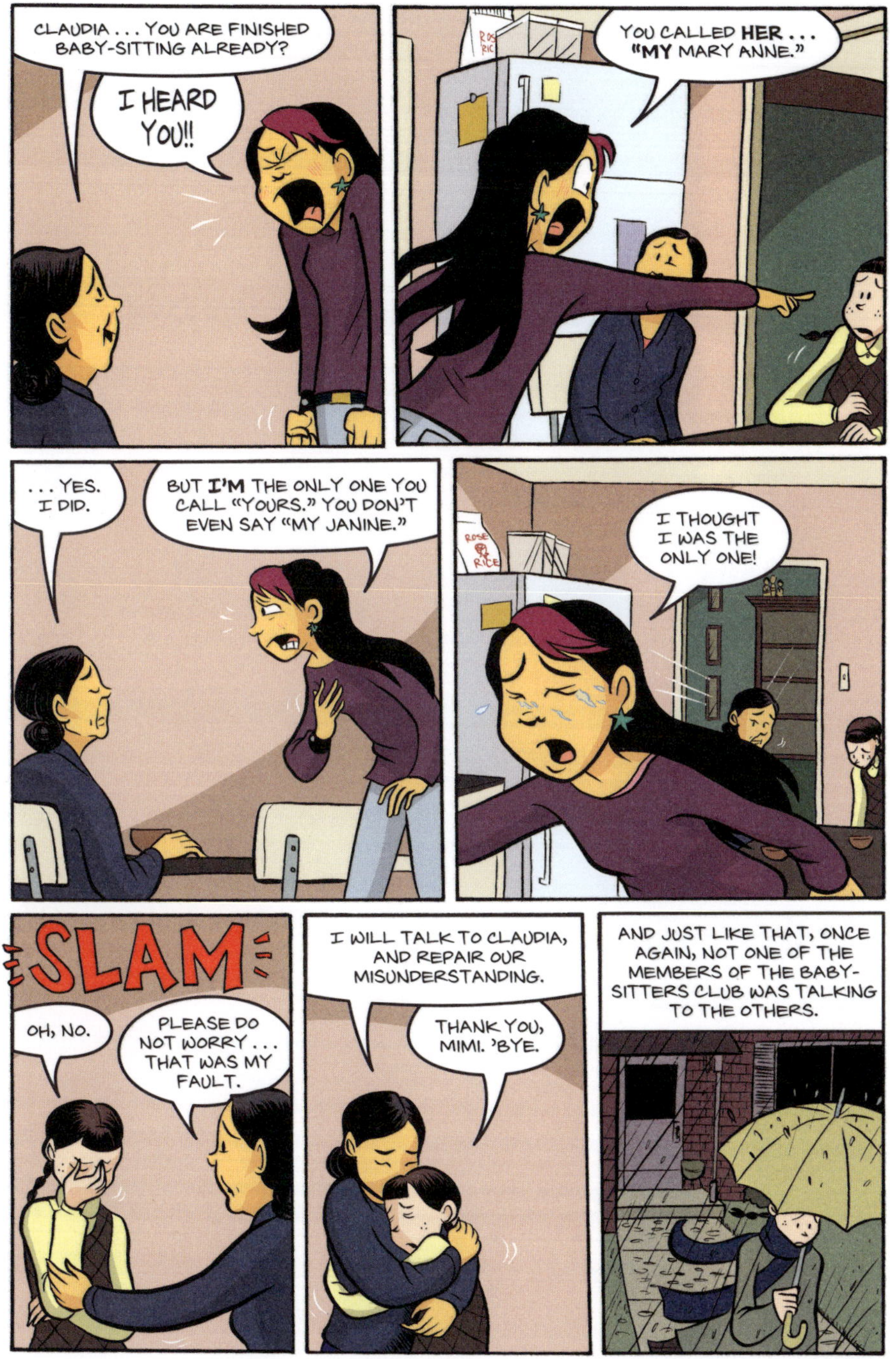
CLAUDIA . . . YOU ARE FINISHED BABY-SITTING ALREADY?
I HEARD YOU!!
YOU CALLED **HER . . . "MY** MARY ANNE."
. . . YES. I DID.
BUT **I'M** THE ONLY ONE YOU CALL "YOURS." YOU DON'T EVEN SAY "MY JANINE."
I THOUGHT I WAS THE ONLY ONE!
SLAM
OH, NO.
PLEASE DO NOT WORRY . . . THAT WAS MY FAULT.
I WILL TALK TO CLAUDIA, AND REPAIR OUR MISUNDERSTANDING.
THANK YOU, MIMI. 'BYE.
AND JUST LIKE THAT, ONCE AGAIN, NOT ONE OF THE MEMBERS OF THE BABY-SITTERS CLUB WAS TALKING TO THE OTHERS.

Teusday, January 20

I am so made! I know this notebook is for writing our siting jobs so we can keep track of club problems. Well, this is not a sitting job, but I have a club probleme. Her name is Mary Anne Spier or as she is otherwise known **MY MARY ANNE**. Where does Mary Anne get off being so chummy with Mimi? It isn't fair. It's one thing for Mimi to help her with her ~~niting~~ knitting but today they were sharing tea in the special cups and Mimi called her My Mary Anne. <u>NO FAIR.</u> So there.

Claudia

CHAPTER 8

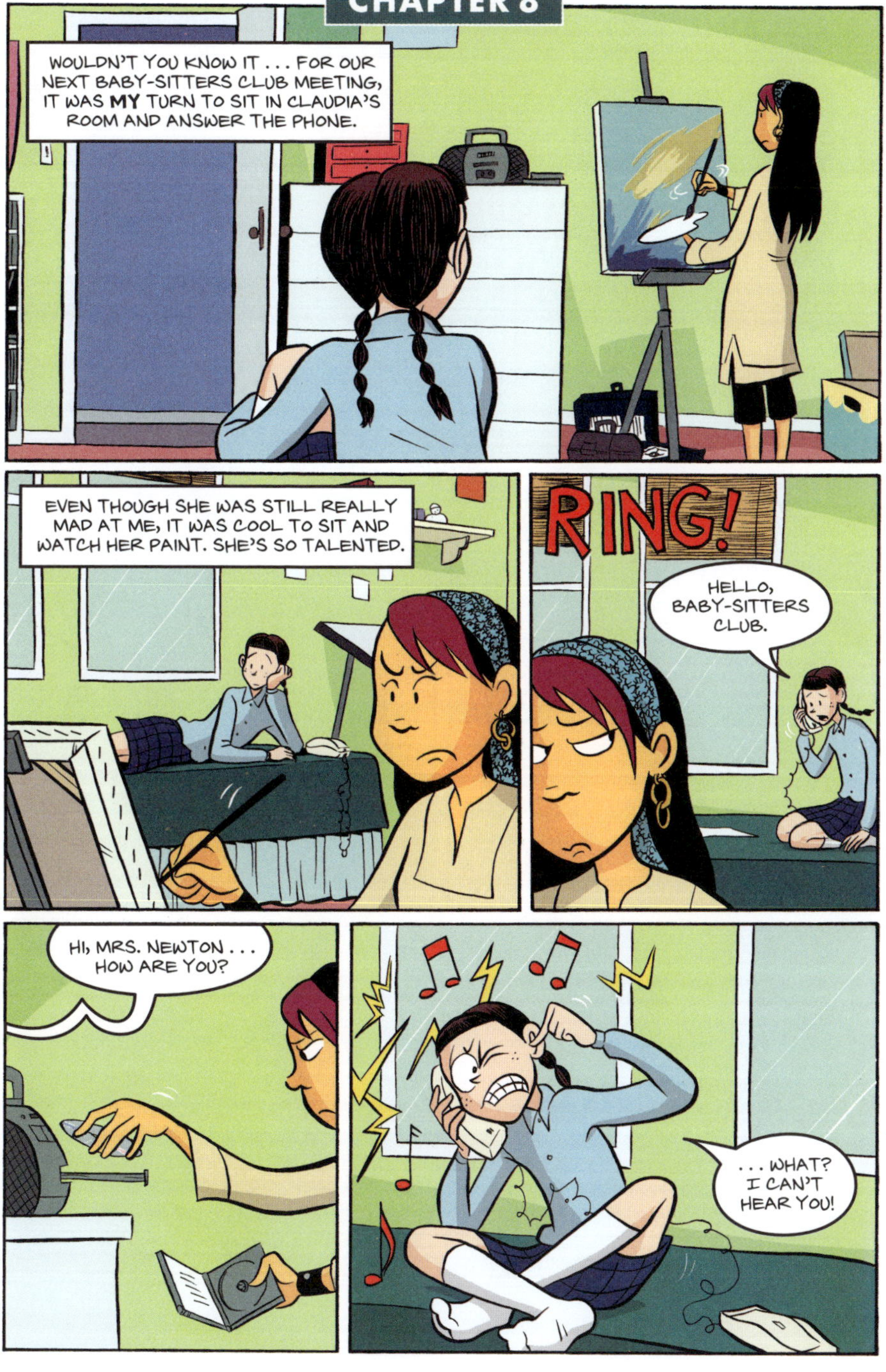
WOULDN'T YOU KNOW IT . . . FOR OUR NEXT BABY-SITTERS CLUB MEETING, IT WAS **MY** TURN TO SIT IN CLAUDIA'S ROOM AND ANSWER THE PHONE.
EVEN THOUGH SHE WAS STILL REALLY MAD AT ME, IT WAS COOL TO SIT AND WATCH HER PAINT. SHE'S SO TALENTED.
RING!
HELLO, BABY-SITTERS CLUB.
HI, MRS. NEWTON . . . HOW ARE YOU?
. . . WHAT? I CAN'T HEAR YOU!

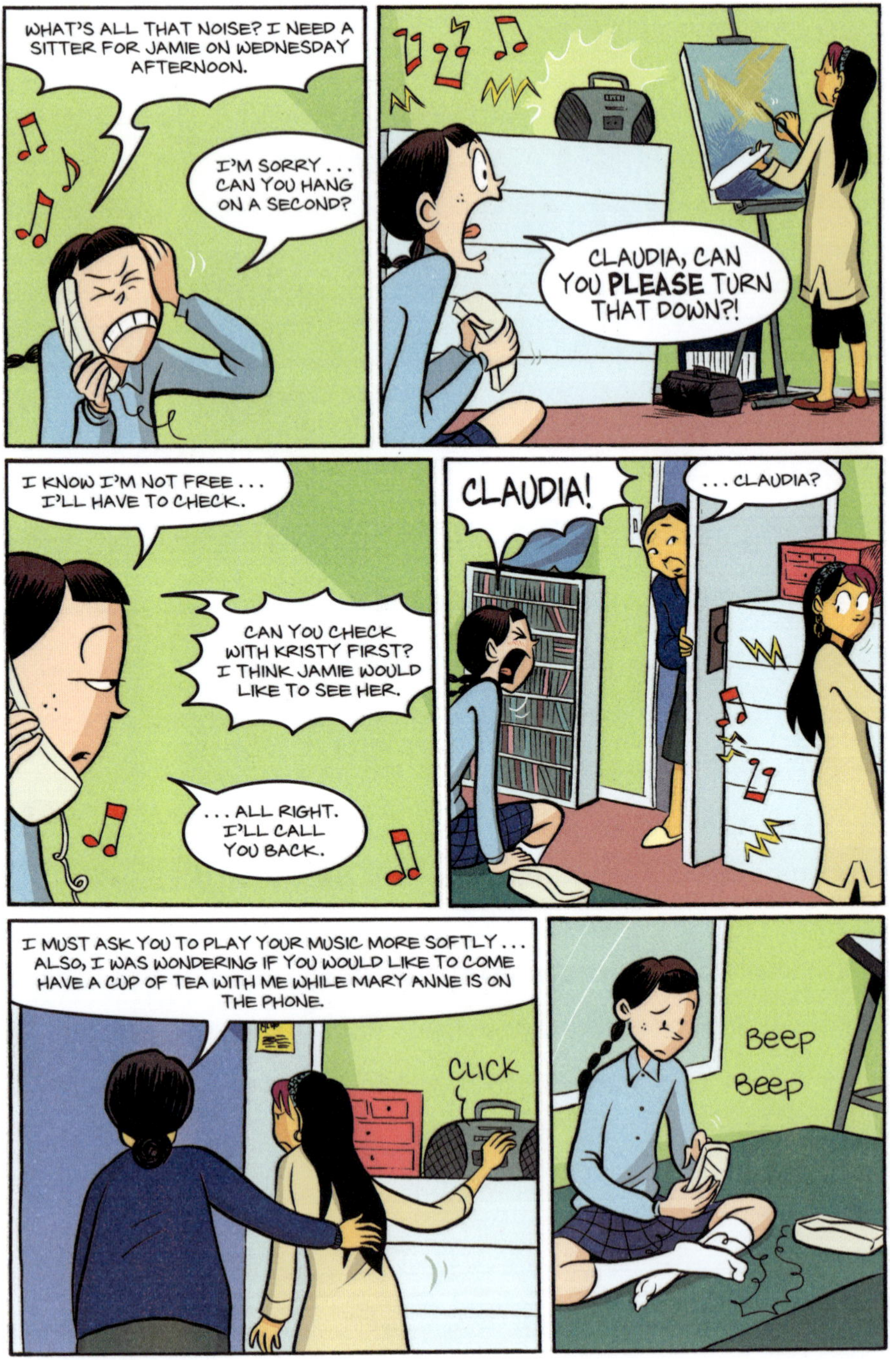
WHAT'S ALL THAT NOISE? I NEED A SITTER FOR JAMIE ON WEDNESDAY AFTERNOON.
I'M SORRY . . . CAN YOU HANG ON A SECOND?
CLAUDIA, CAN YOU PLEASE TURN THAT DOWN?!
I KNOW I'M NOT FREE . . . I'LL HAVE TO CHECK.
CAN YOU CHECK WITH KRISTY FIRST? I THINK JAMIE WOULD LIKE TO SEE HER.
. . . ALL RIGHT. I'LL CALL YOU BACK.
CLAUDIA!
. . . CLAUDIA?
I MUST ASK YOU TO PLAY YOUR MUSIC MORE SOFTLY . . . ALSO, I WAS WONDERING IF YOU WOULD LIKE TO COME HAVE A CUP OF TEA WITH ME WHILE MARY ANNE IS ON THE PHONE.
CLICK
Beep
Beep

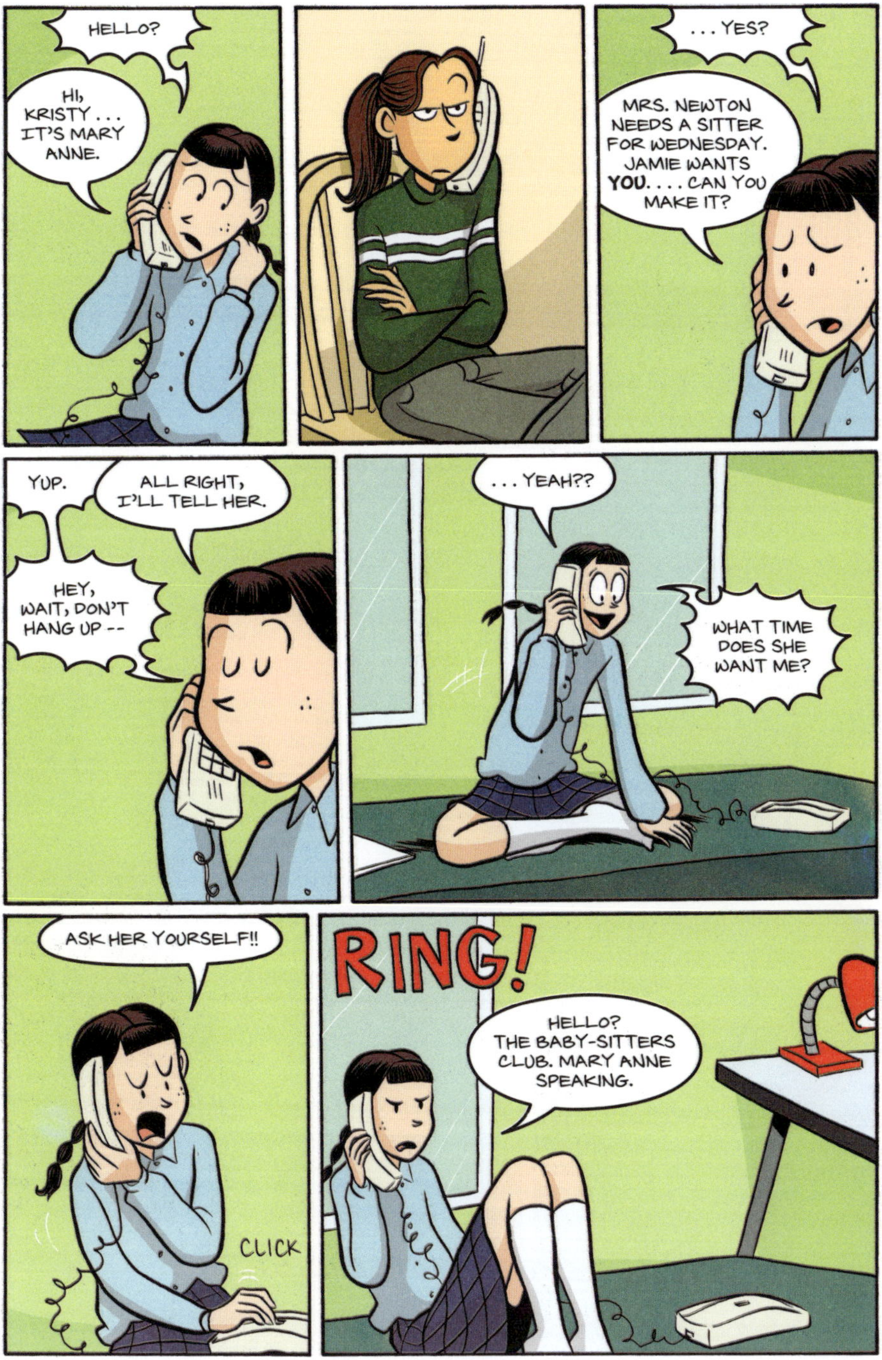
HELLO?
HI, KRISTY . . . IT'S MARY ANNE.
. . . YES?
MRS. NEWTON NEEDS A SITTER FOR WEDNESDAY. JAMIE WANTS YOU. . . . CAN YOU MAKE IT?
YUP.
ALL RIGHT, I'LL TELL HER.
HEY, WAIT, DON'T HANG UP --
. . . YEAH??
WHAT TIME DOES SHE WANT ME?
ASK HER YOURSELF!!
CLICK
RING!
HELLO? THE BABY-SITTERS CLUB. MARY ANNE SPEAKING.

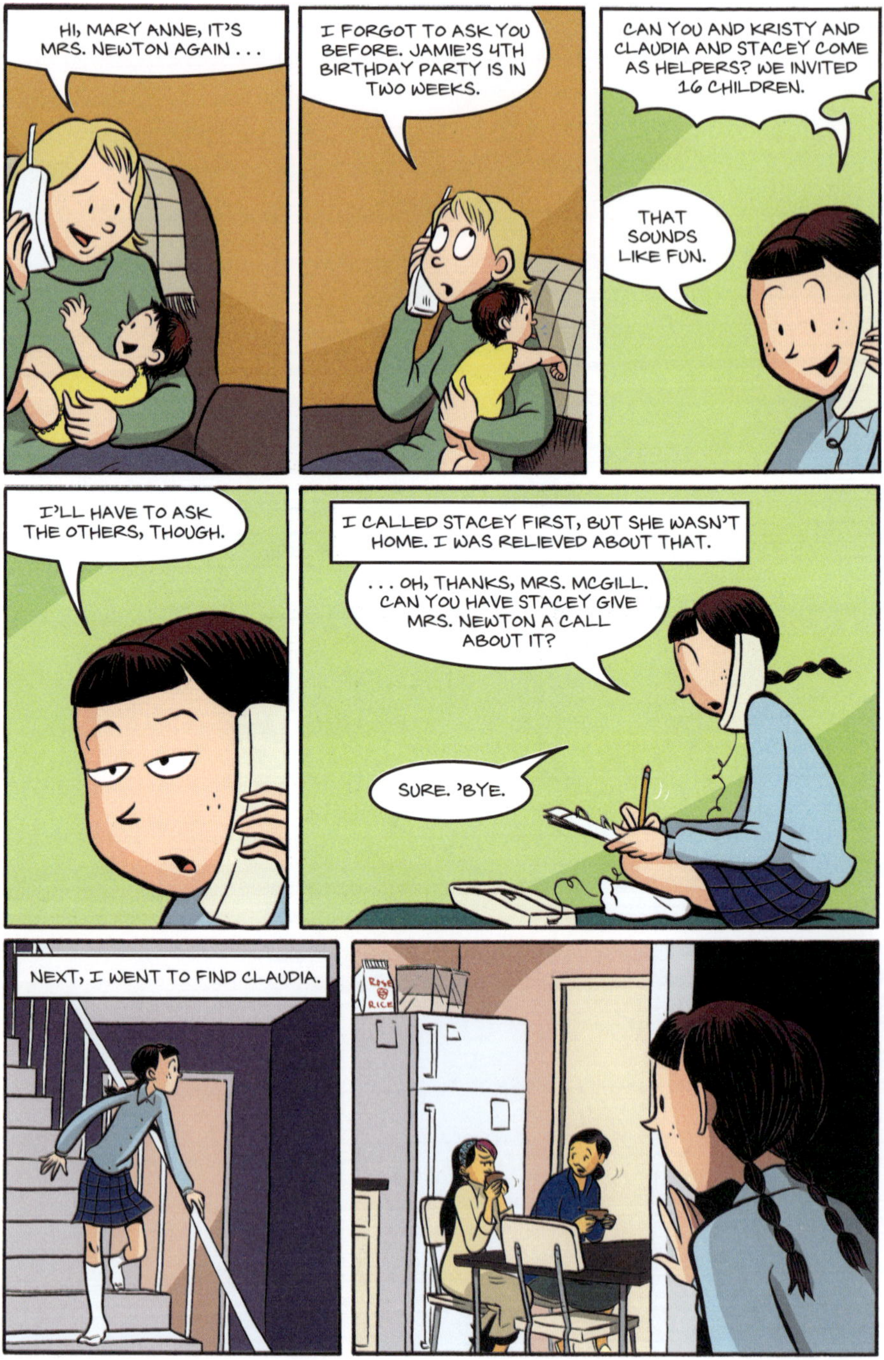
HI, MARY ANNE, IT'S MRS. NEWTON AGAIN . . .
I FORGOT TO ASK YOU BEFORE. JAMIE'S 4TH BIRTHDAY PARTY IS IN TWO WEEKS.
CAN YOU AND KRISTY AND CLAUDIA AND STACEY COME AS HELPERS? WE INVITED 16 CHILDREN.
THAT SOUNDS LIKE FUN.
I'LL HAVE TO ASK THE OTHERS, THOUGH.
I CALLED STACEY FIRST, BUT SHE WASN'T HOME. I WAS RELIEVED ABOUT THAT.
. . . OH, THANKS, MRS. MCGILL. CAN YOU HAVE STACEY GIVE MRS. NEWTON A CALL ABOUT IT?
SURE. 'BYE.
NEXT, I WENT TO FIND CLAUDIA.
ROSE RICE

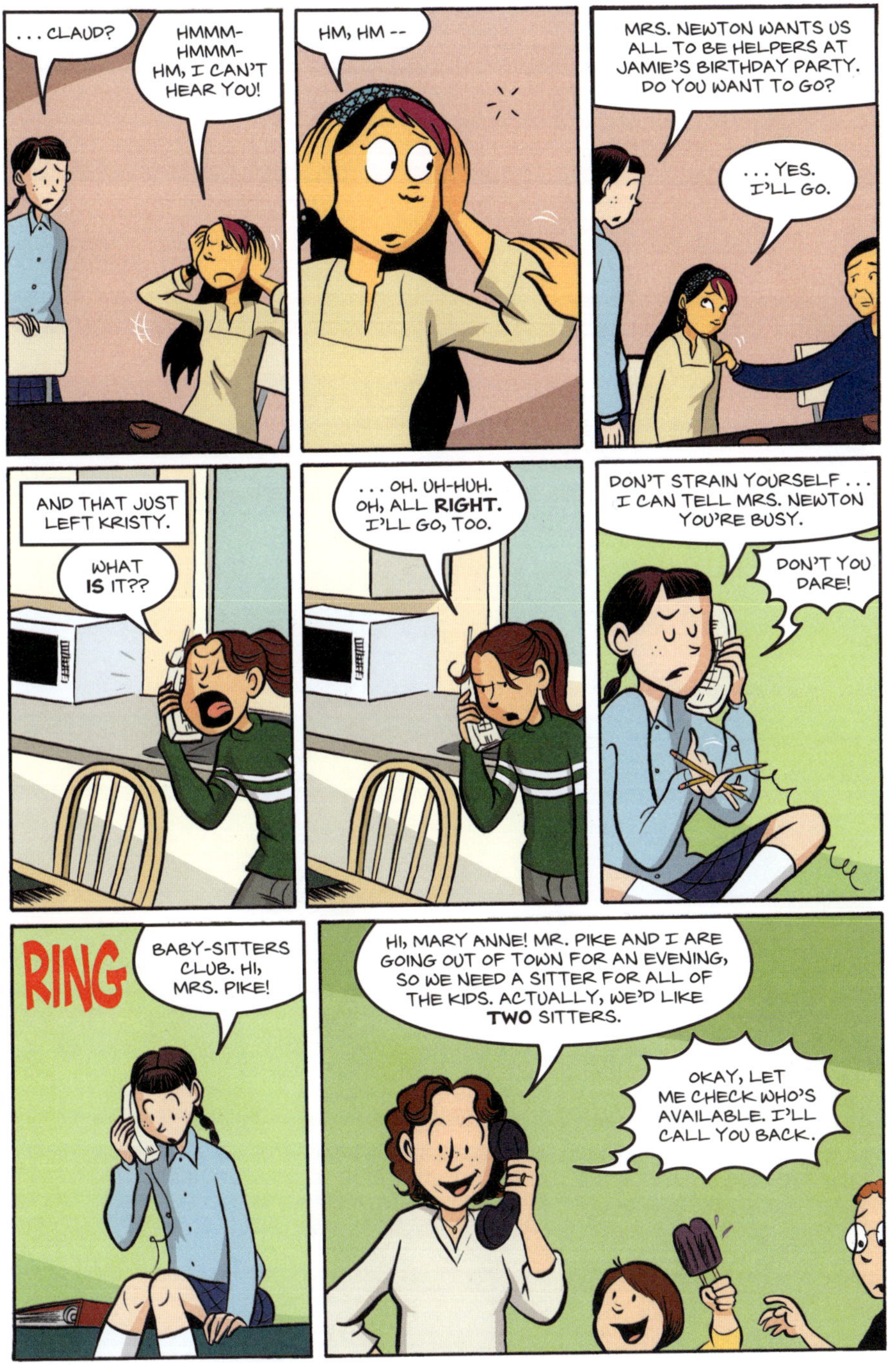

. . . CLAUD?
HMMM-HMMM-HM, I CAN'T HEAR YOU!
HM, HM --
MRS. NEWTON WANTS US ALL TO BE HELPERS AT JAMIE'S BIRTHDAY PARTY. DO YOU WANT TO GO?
. . . YES. I'LL GO.
AND THAT JUST LEFT KRISTY.
WHAT **IS** IT??
. . . OH. UH-HUH. OH, ALL **RIGHT.** I'LL GO, TOO.
DON'T STRAIN YOURSELF . . . I CAN TELL MRS. NEWTON YOU'RE BUSY.
DON'T YOU DARE!
RING
BABY-SITTERS CLUB. HI, MRS. PIKE!
HI, MARY ANNE! MR. PIKE AND I ARE GOING OUT OF TOWN FOR AN EVENING, SO WE NEED A SITTER FOR ALL OF THE KIDS. ACTUALLY, WE'D LIKE **TWO** SITTERS.
OKAY, LET ME CHECK WHO'S AVAILABLE. I'LL CALL YOU BACK.

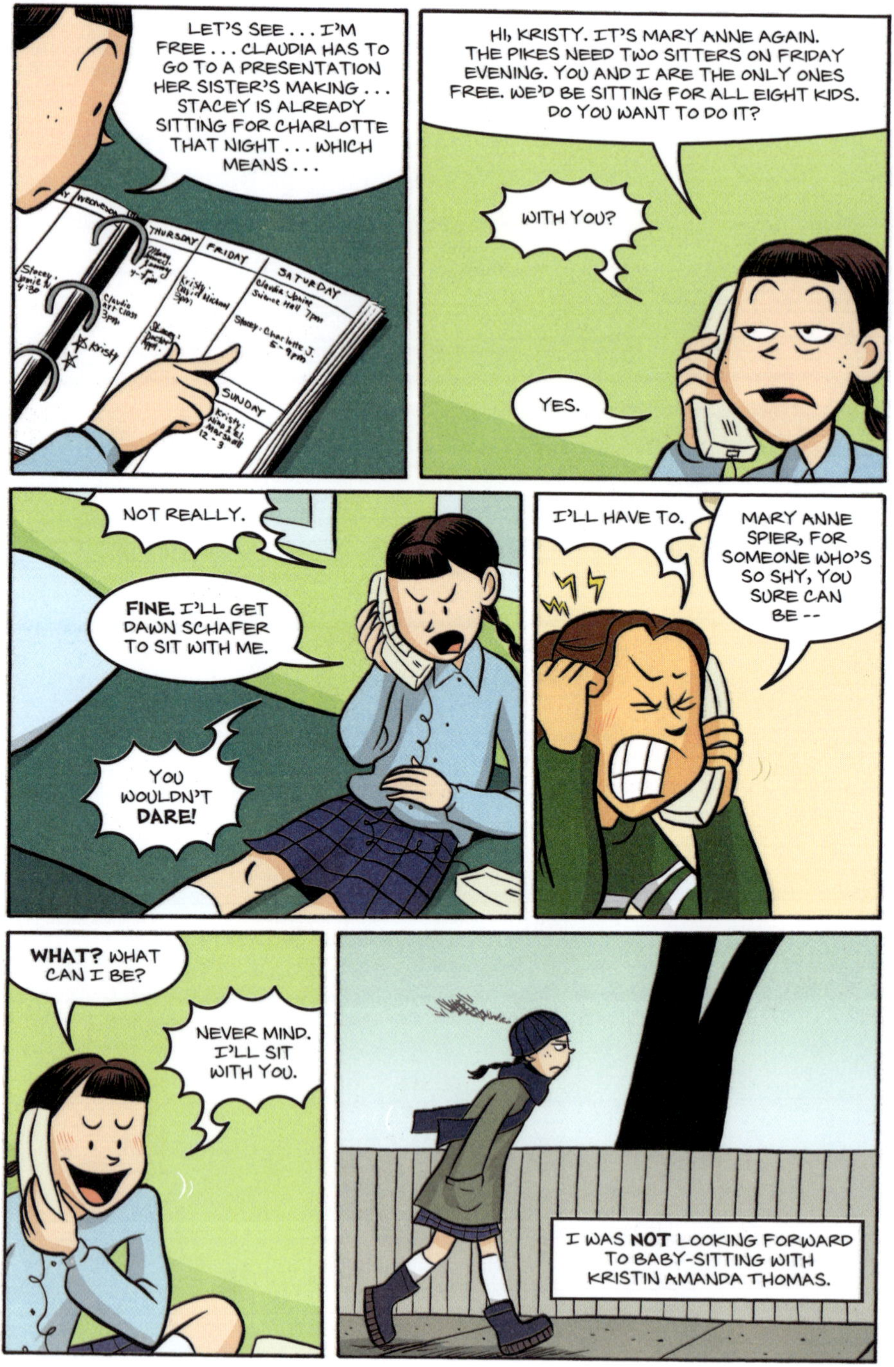
LET'S SEE . . . I'M FREE . . . CLAUDIA HAS TO GO TO A PRESENTATION HER SISTER'S MAKING . . . STACEY IS ALREADY SITTING FOR CHARLOTTE THAT NIGHT . . . WHICH MEANS . . .
THURSDAY
FRIDAY
SATURDAY
SUNDAY
HI, KRISTY. IT'S MARY ANNE AGAIN. THE PIKES NEED TWO SITTERS ON FRIDAY EVENING. YOU AND I ARE THE ONLY ONES FREE. WE'D BE SITTING FOR ALL EIGHT KIDS. DO YOU WANT TO DO IT?
WITH YOU?
YES.
NOT REALLY.
FINE. I'LL GET DAWN SCHAFER TO SIT WITH ME.
YOU WOULDN'T **DARE!**
I'LL HAVE TO.
MARY ANNE SPIER, FOR SOMEONE WHO'S SO SHY, YOU SURE CAN BE --
WHAT? WHAT CAN I BE?
NEVER MIND. I'LL SIT WITH YOU.
I WAS **NOT** LOOKING FORWARD TO BABY-SITTING WITH KRISTIN AMANDA THOMAS.

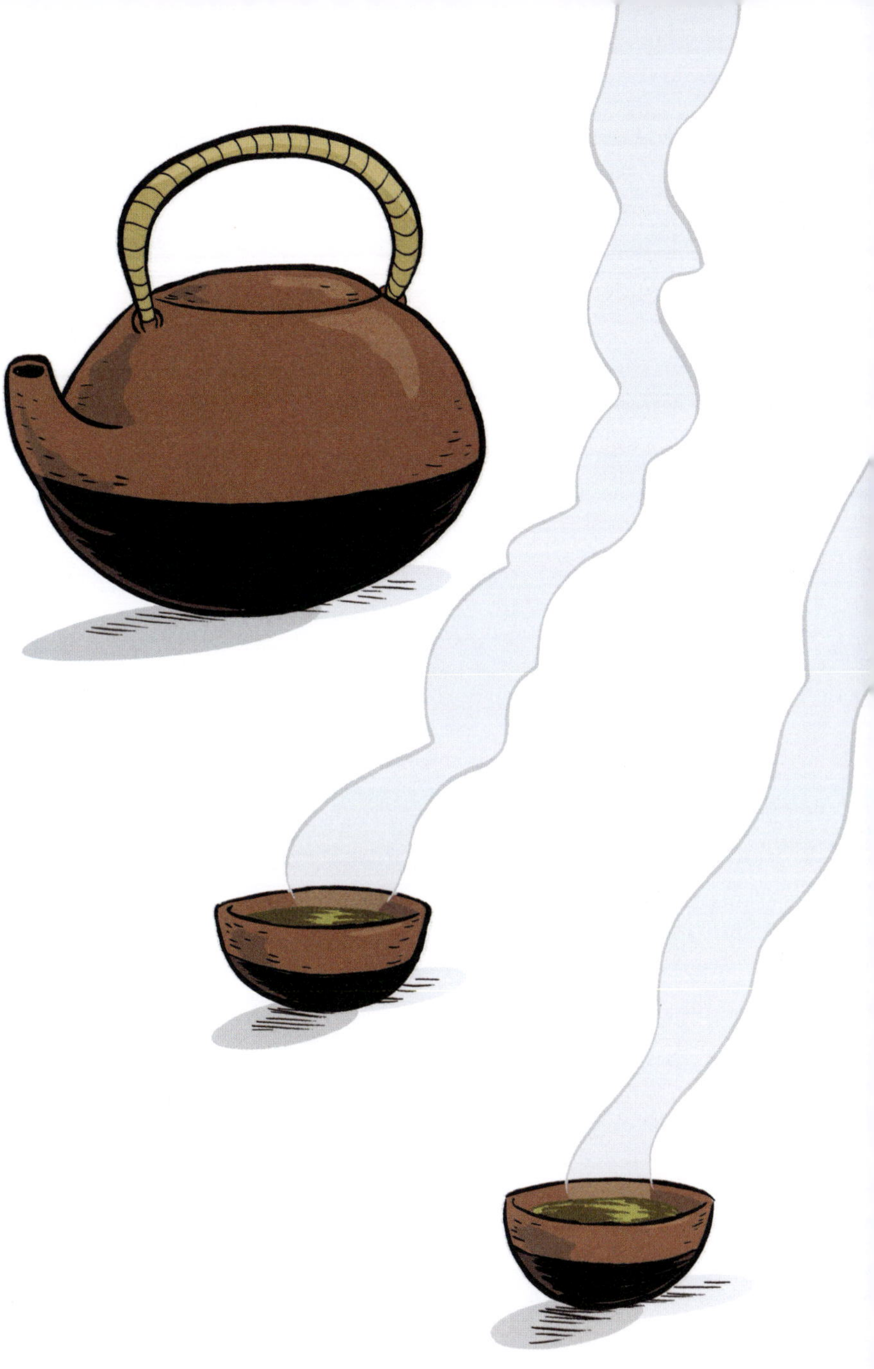

Saturday, January 31

Yesterday, Mary Anne and I baby-sat for the Pikes. I'm really surprised that we were able to pull it off. Hereby let it be known that it is possible:

1. For two people to baby-sit for eight kids without losing their sanity (the sitters' OR the kids'), and

2. for the baby-sitters to accomplish this without ever speaking to each other.

There should be a Baby-sitters' Hall of Fame where experiences like ours could be recorded and preserved for all to read about. To do what we did takes a lot of imagination.

... And a really good fight, I guess.

— Kristy

CHAPTER 9

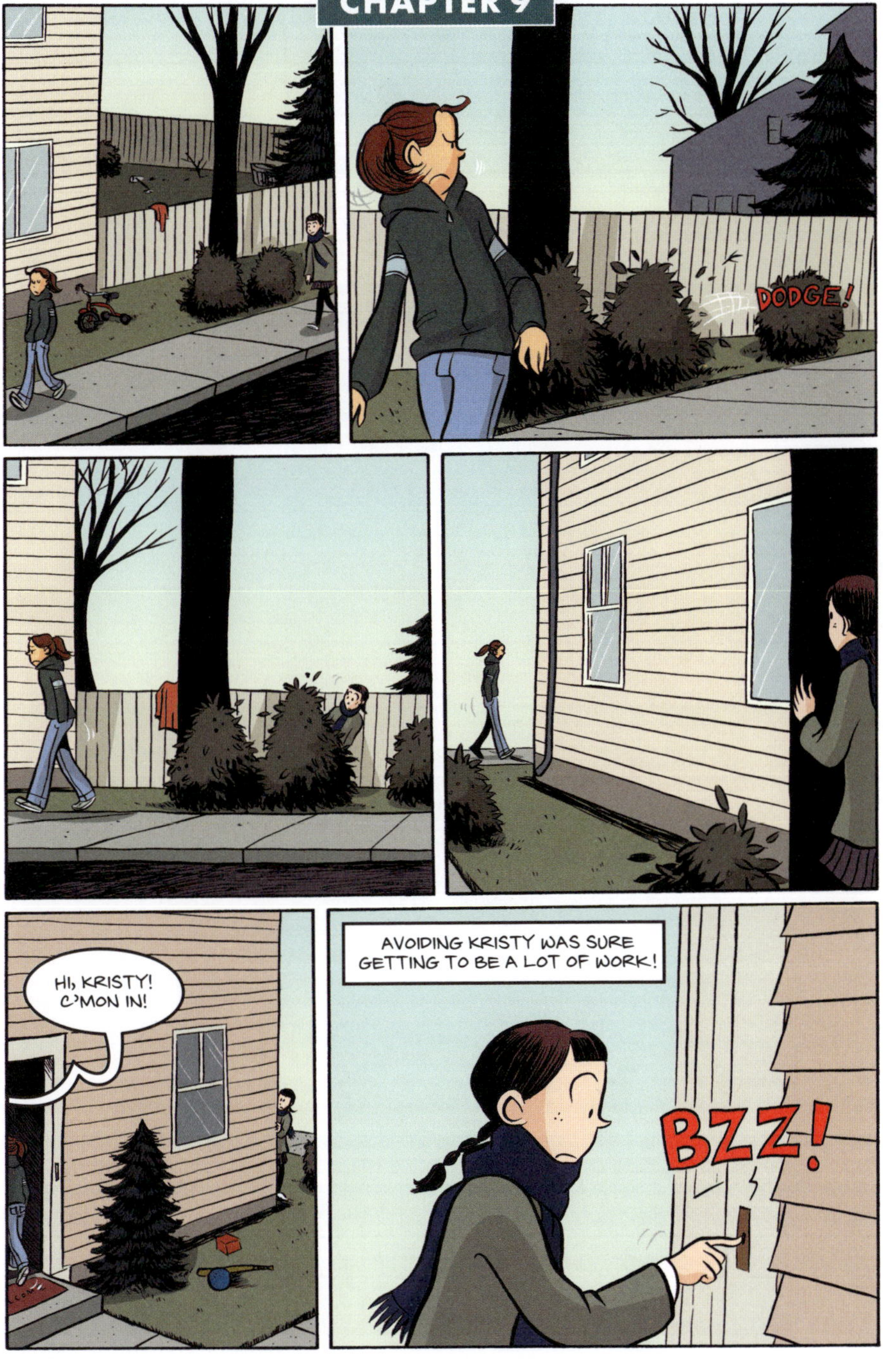
DODGE!
HI, KRISTY! C'MON IN!
AVOIDING KRISTY WAS SURE GETTING TO BE A LOT OF WORK!
BZZ!

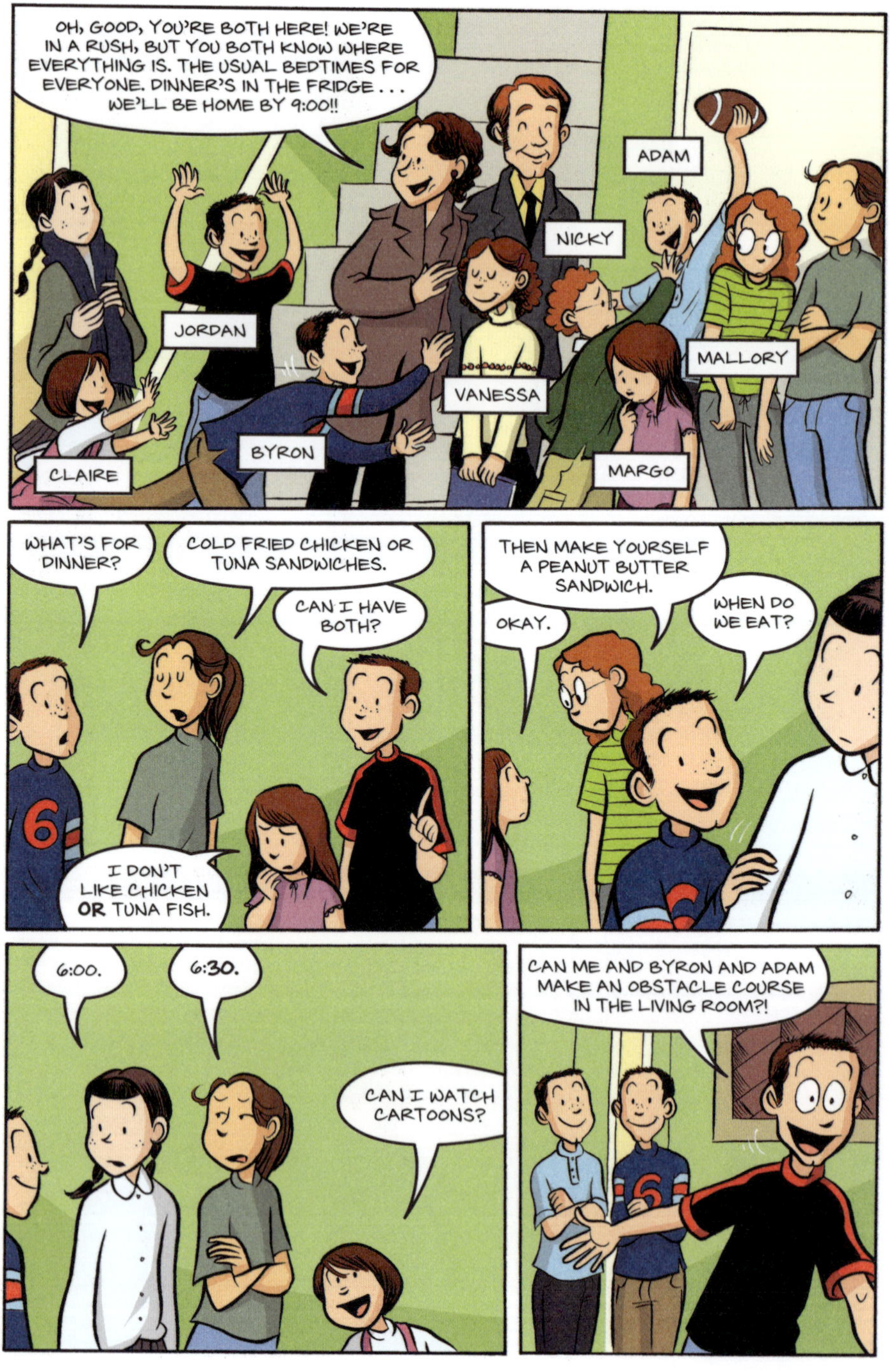
OH, GOOD, YOU'RE BOTH HERE! WE'RE IN A RUSH, BUT YOU BOTH KNOW WHERE EVERYTHING IS. THE USUAL BEDTIMES FOR EVERYONE. DINNER'S IN THE FRIDGE . . . WE'LL BE HOME BY 9:00!!
ADAM
NICKY
JORDAN
MALLORY
VANESSA
BYRON
MARGO
CLAIRE
WHAT'S FOR DINNER?
COLD FRIED CHICKEN OR TUNA SANDWICHES.
CAN I HAVE BOTH?
I DON'T LIKE CHICKEN **OR** TUNA FISH.
THEN MAKE YOURSELF A PEANUT BUTTER SANDWICH.
OKAY.
WHEN DO WE EAT?
6:00.
6:**30**.
CAN I WATCH CARTOONS?
CAN ME AND BYRON AND ADAM MAKE AN OBSTACLE COURSE IN THE LIVING ROOM?!

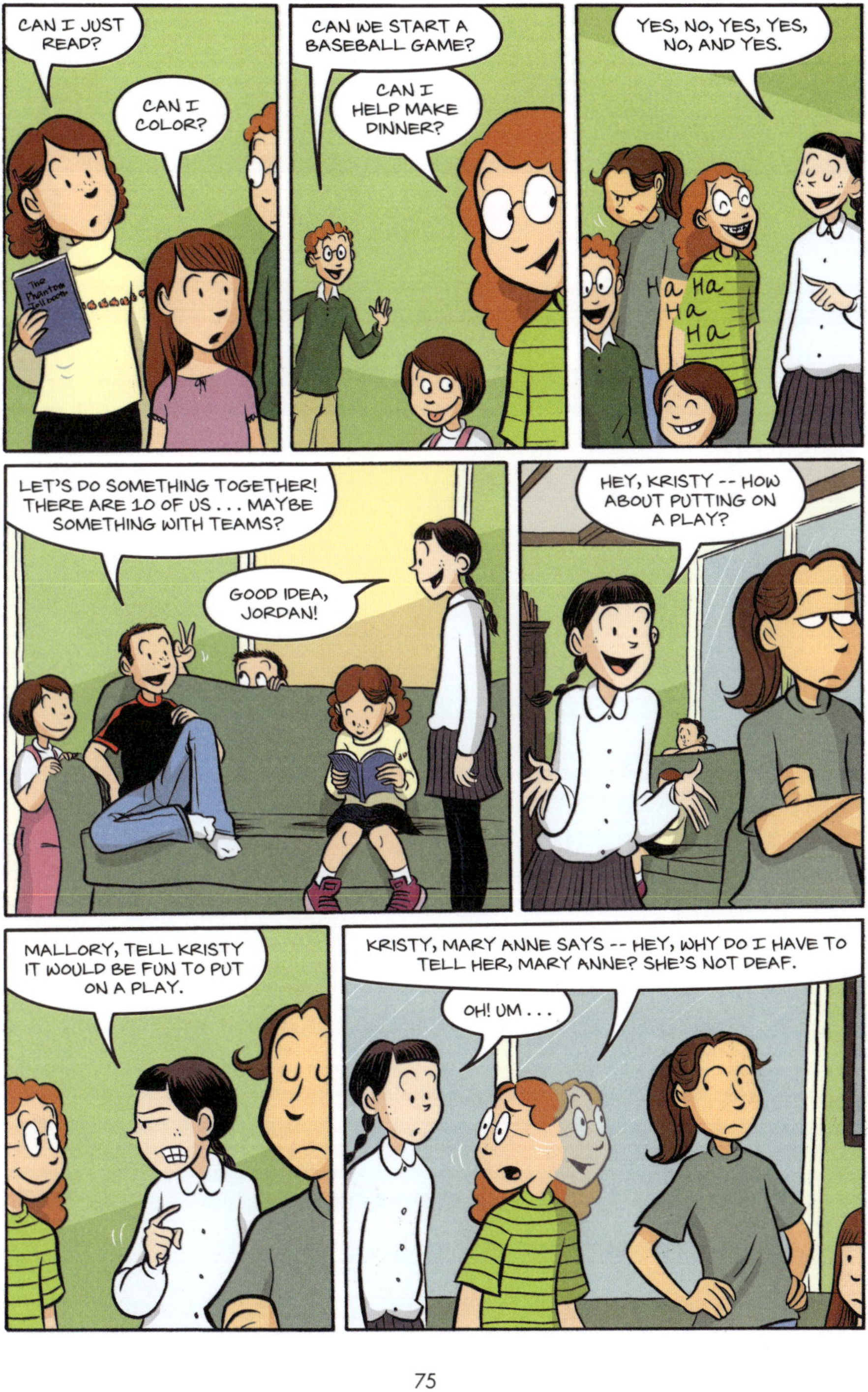
CAN I JUST READ?
CAN I COLOR?
CAN WE START A BASEBALL GAME?
CAN I HELP MAKE DINNER?
YES, NO, YES, YES, NO, AND YES.
The Phantom Tollbooth
Ha Ha
Ha
Ha
LET'S DO SOMETHING TOGETHER! THERE ARE 10 OF US . . . MAYBE SOMETHING WITH TEAMS?
GOOD IDEA, JORDAN!
HEY, KRISTY -- HOW ABOUT PUTTING ON A PLAY?
MALLORY, TELL KRISTY IT WOULD BE FUN TO PUT ON A PLAY.
KRISTY, MARY ANNE SAYS -- HEY, WHY DO I HAVE TO TELL HER, MARY ANNE? SHE'S NOT DEAF.
OH! UM . . .

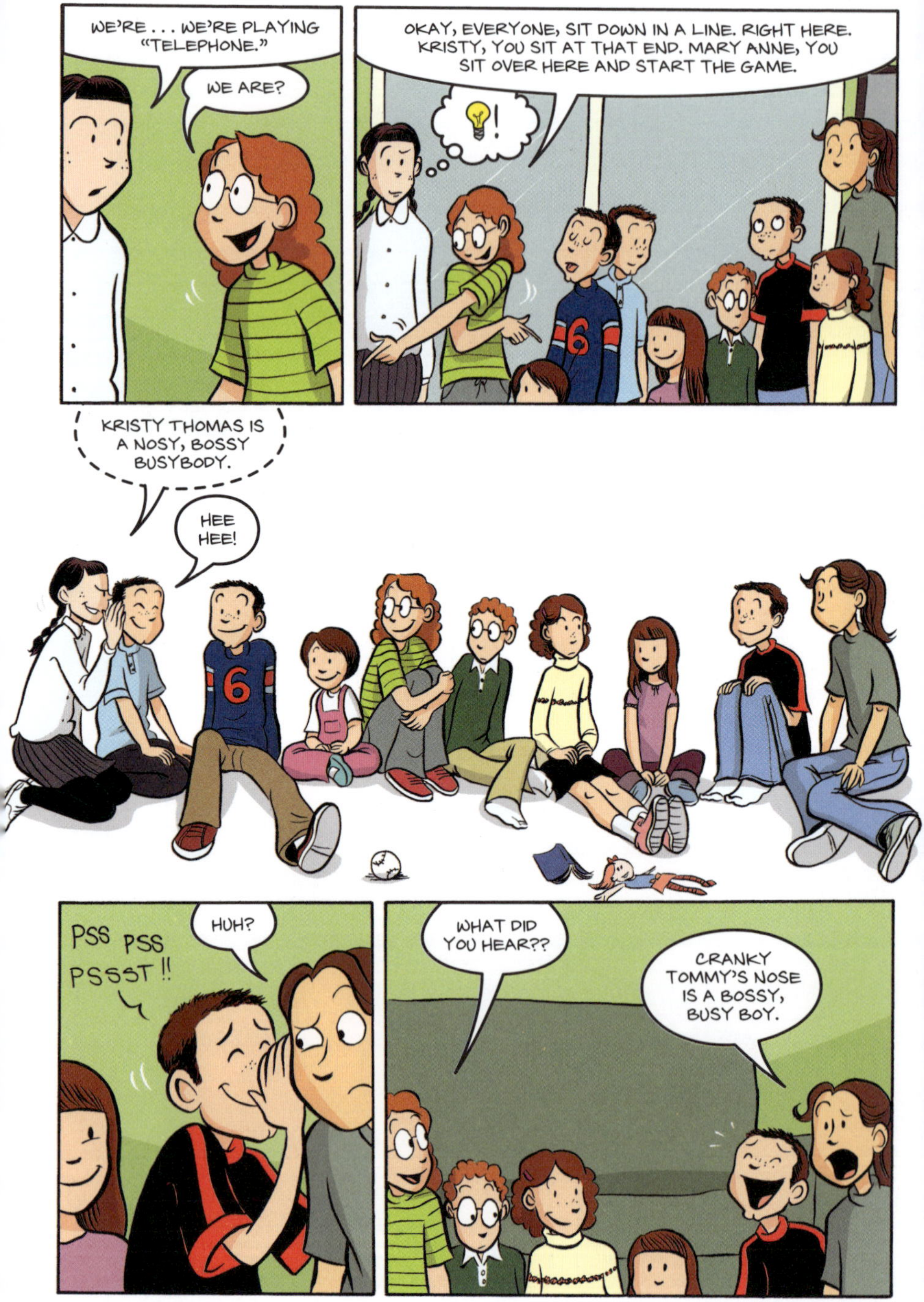
WE'RE . . . WE'RE PLAYING "TELEPHONE."
WE ARE?
OKAY, EVERYONE, SIT DOWN IN A LINE. RIGHT HERE. KRISTY, YOU SIT AT THAT END. MARY ANNE, YOU SIT OVER HERE AND START THE GAME.
!
KRISTY THOMAS IS A NOSY, BOSSY BUSYBODY.
HEE HEE!
PSS PSS PSSST !!
HUH?
WHAT DID YOU HEAR??
CRANKY TOMMY'S NOSE IS A BOSSY, BUSY BOY.

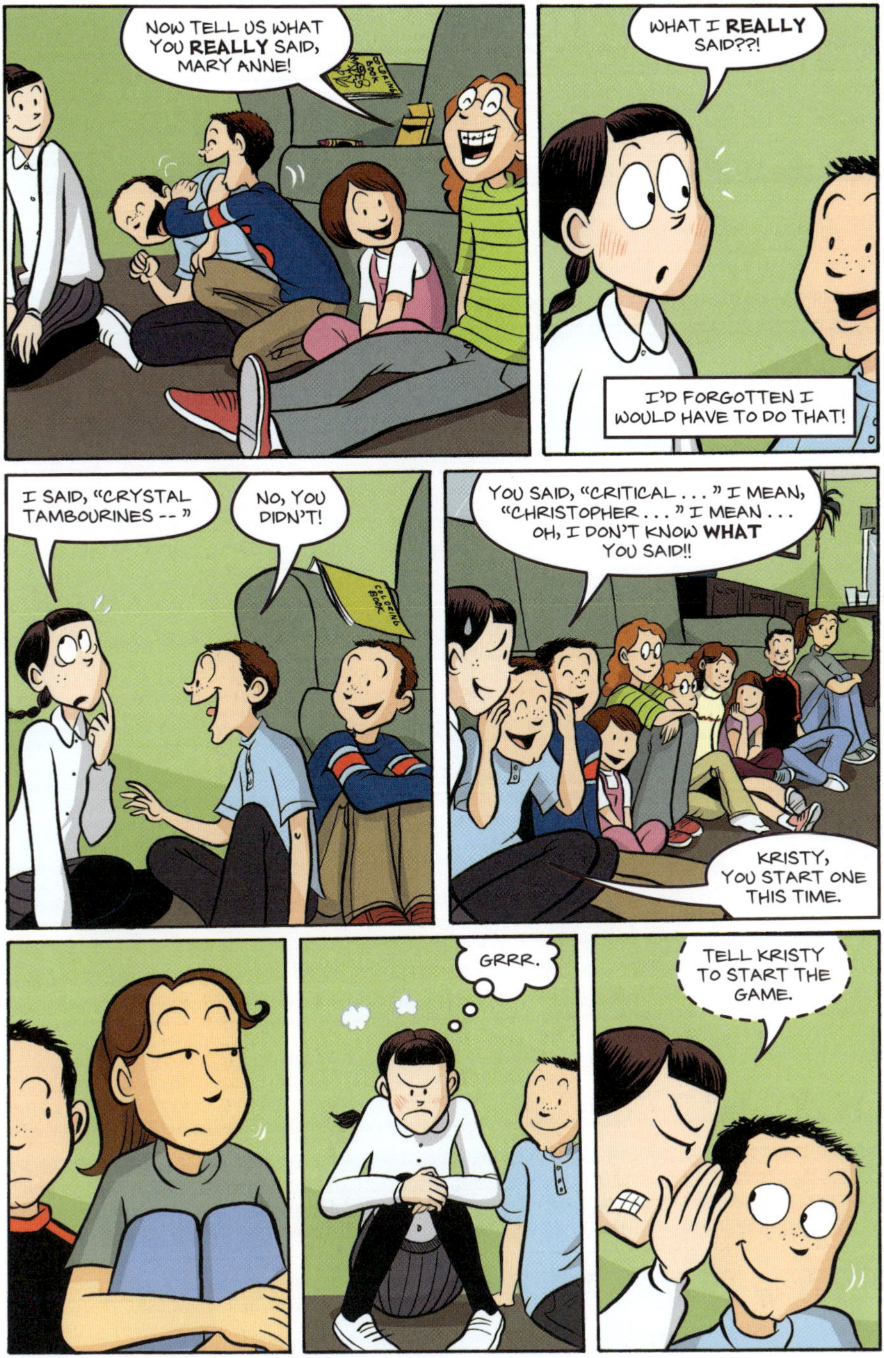

NOW TELL US WHAT YOU **REALLY** SAID, MARY ANNE!
COLORING BOOK
WHAT I **REALLY** SAID??!
I'D FORGOTTEN I WOULD HAVE TO DO THAT!
I SAID, "CRYSTAL TAMBOURINES --"
NO, YOU DIDN'T!
COLORING BOOK
YOU SAID, "CRITICAL . . ." I MEAN, "CHRISTOPHER . . ." I MEAN . . . OH, I DON'T KNOW **WHAT** YOU SAID!!
KRISTY, YOU START ONE THIS TIME.
GRRR.
TELL KRISTY TO START THE GAME.

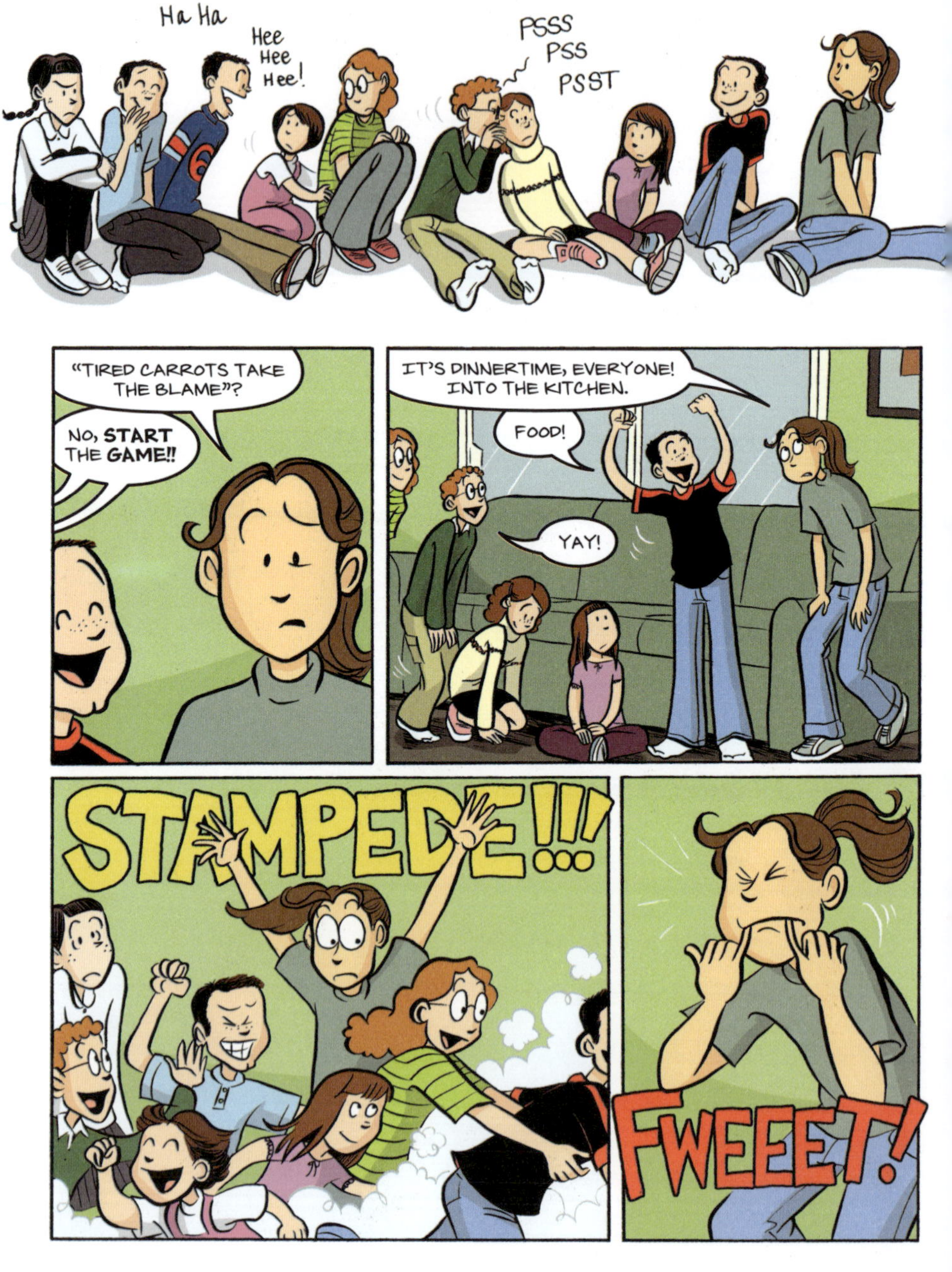
Ha Ha
Hee Hee Hee!
PSSS PSS PSST
"TIRED CARROTS TAKE THE BLAME"?
NO, START THE GAME!!
IT'S DINNERTIME, EVERYONE! INTO THE KITCHEN.
FOOD!
YAY!
STAMPEDE!!!
FWEEET!

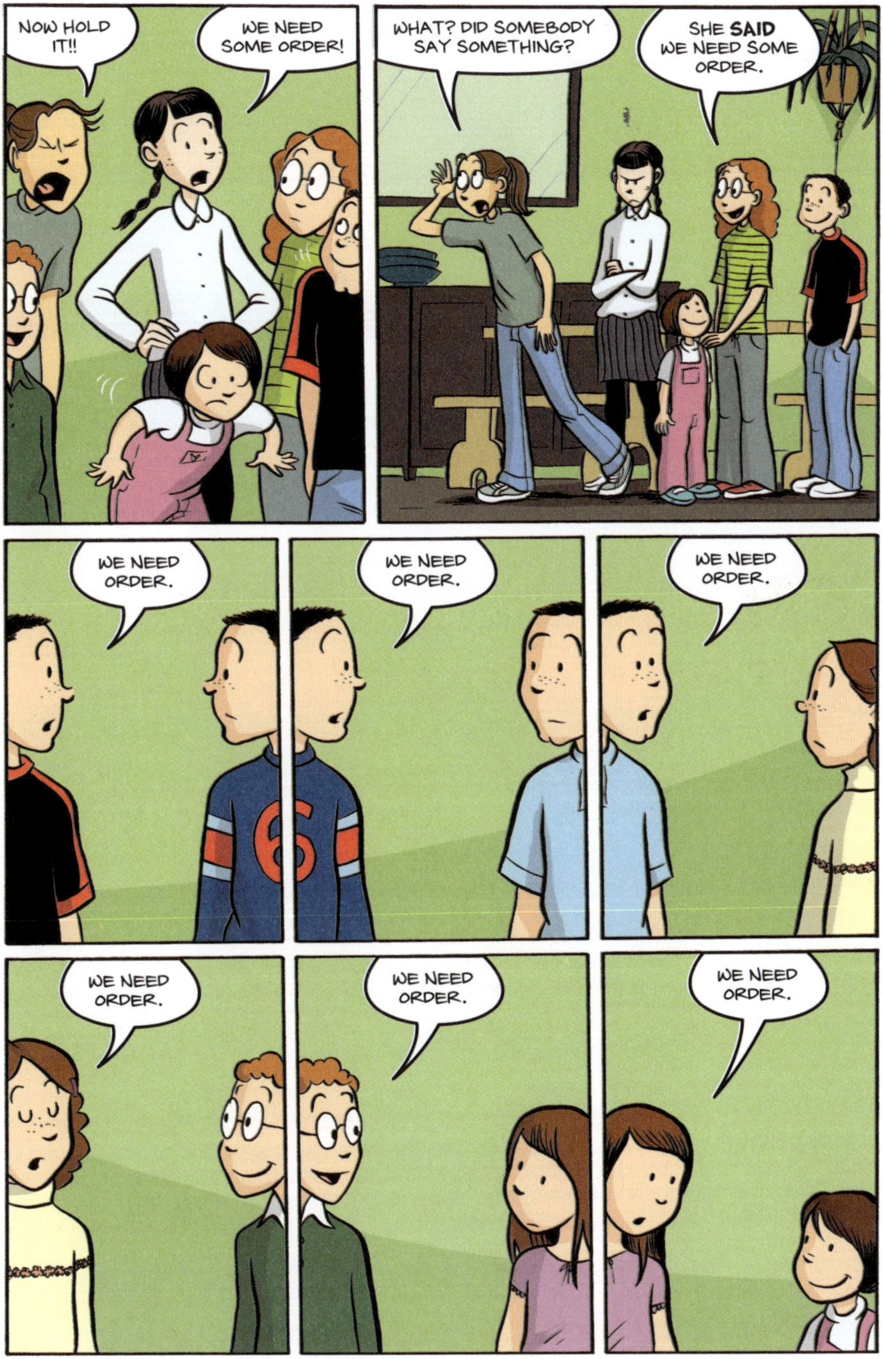
NOW HOLD IT!!
WE NEED SOME ORDER!
WHAT? DID SOMEBODY SAY SOMETHING?
SHE **SAID** WE NEED SOME ORDER.
WE NEED ORDER.
WE NEED ORDER.
WE NEED ORDER.
WE NEED ORDER.
WE NEED ORDER.
WE NEED ORDER.

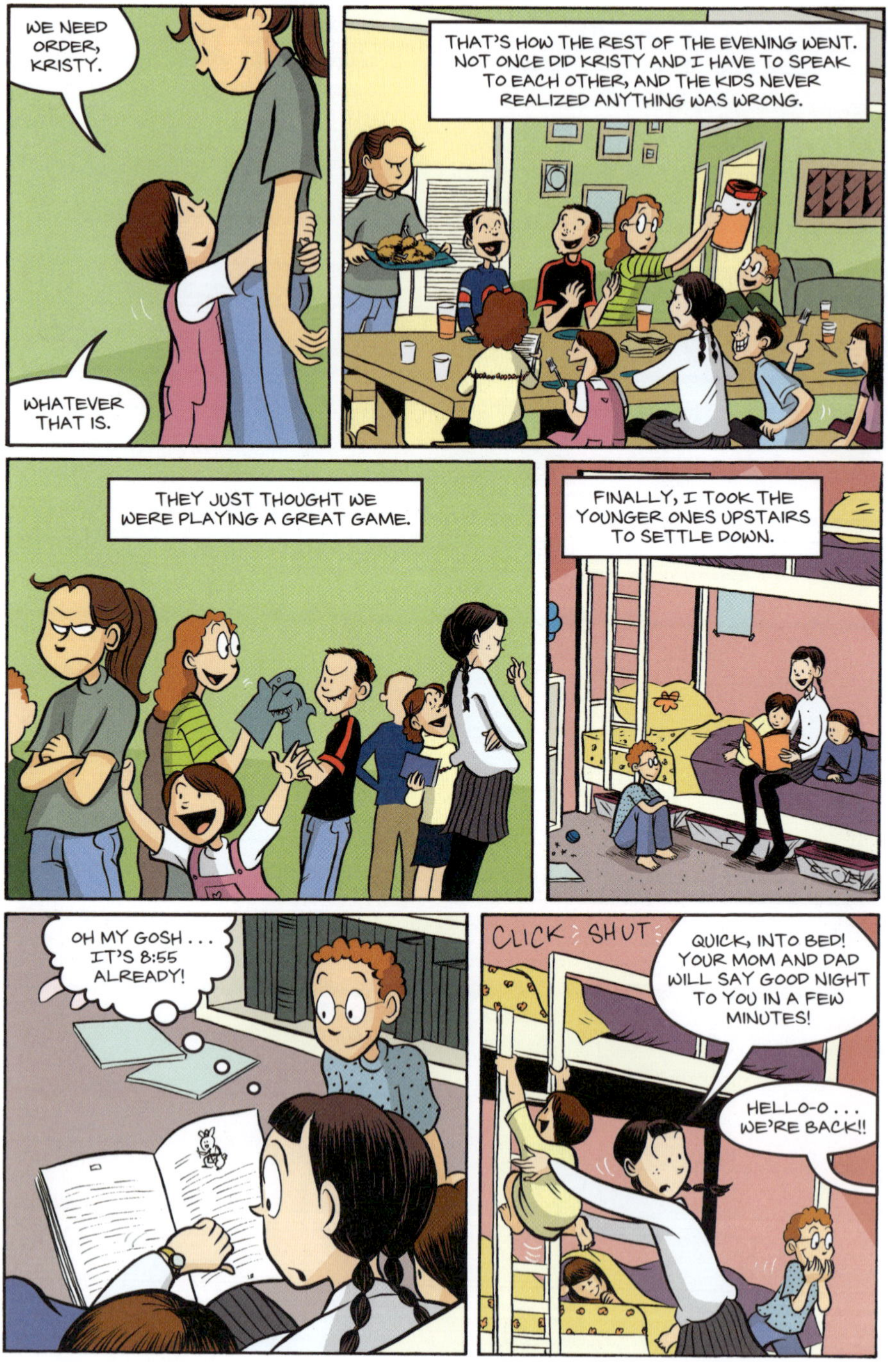
WE NEED ORDER, KRISTY.
WHATEVER THAT IS.
THAT'S HOW THE REST OF THE EVENING WENT. NOT ONCE DID KRISTY AND I HAVE TO SPEAK TO EACH OTHER, AND THE KIDS NEVER REALIZED ANYTHING WAS WRONG.
THEY JUST THOUGHT WE WERE PLAYING A GREAT GAME.
FINALLY, I TOOK THE YOUNGER ONES UPSTAIRS TO SETTLE DOWN.
OH MY GOSH . . . IT'S 8:55 ALREADY!
CLICK
SHUT
QUICK, INTO BED! YOUR MOM AND DAD WILL SAY GOOD NIGHT TO YOU IN A FEW MINUTES!
HELLO-O . . . WE'RE BACK!!

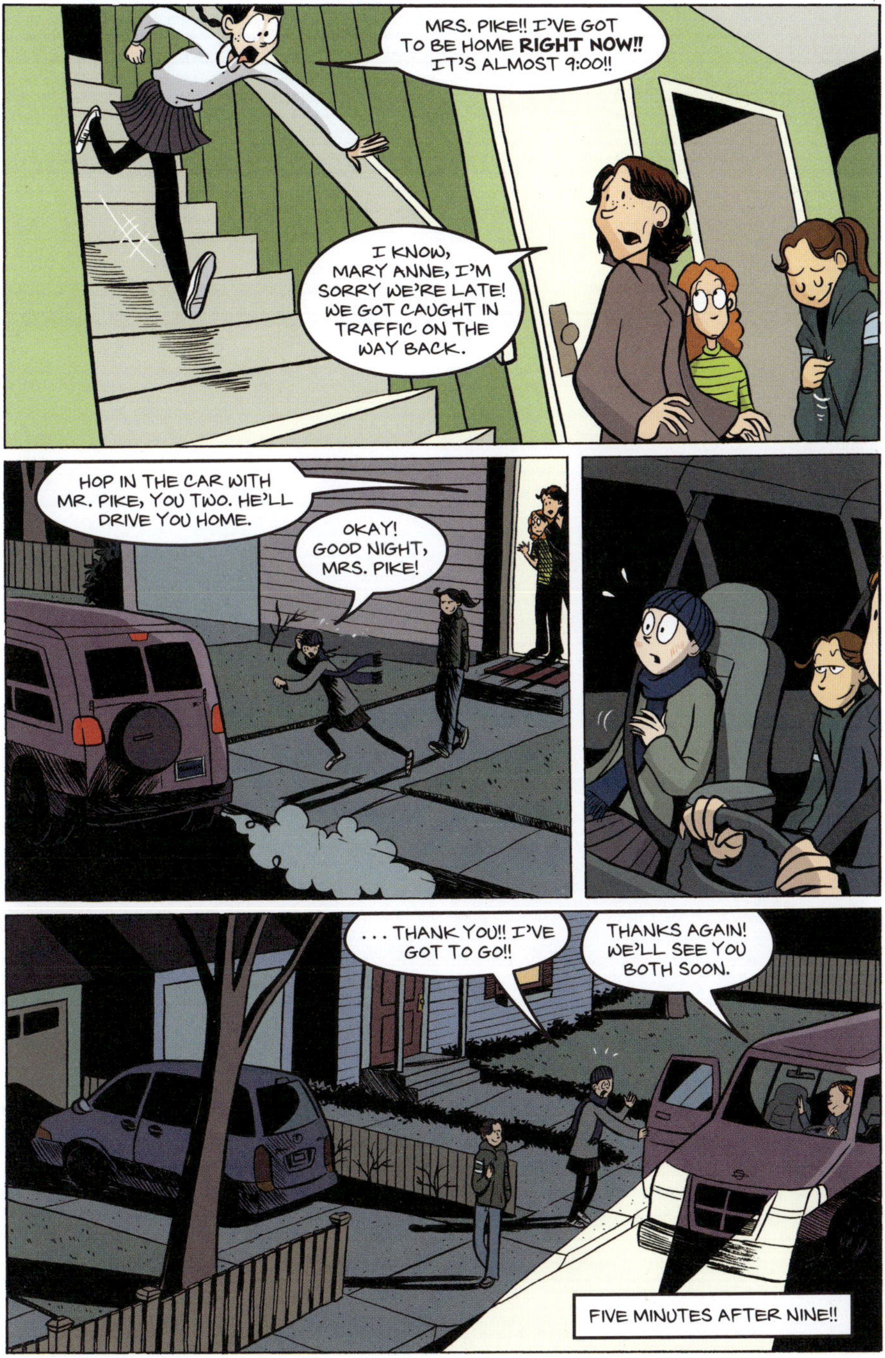
MRS. PIKE!! I'VE GOT TO BE HOME **RIGHT NOW!!** IT'S ALMOST 9:00!!
I KNOW, MARY ANNE, I'M SORRY WE'RE LATE! WE GOT CAUGHT IN TRAFFIC ON THE WAY BACK.
HOP IN THE CAR WITH MR. PIKE, YOU TWO. HE'LL DRIVE YOU HOME.
OKAY! GOOD NIGHT, MRS. PIKE!
. . . THANK YOU!! I'VE GOT TO GO!!
THANKS AGAIN! WE'LL SEE YOU BOTH SOON.
FIVE MINUTES AFTER NINE!!

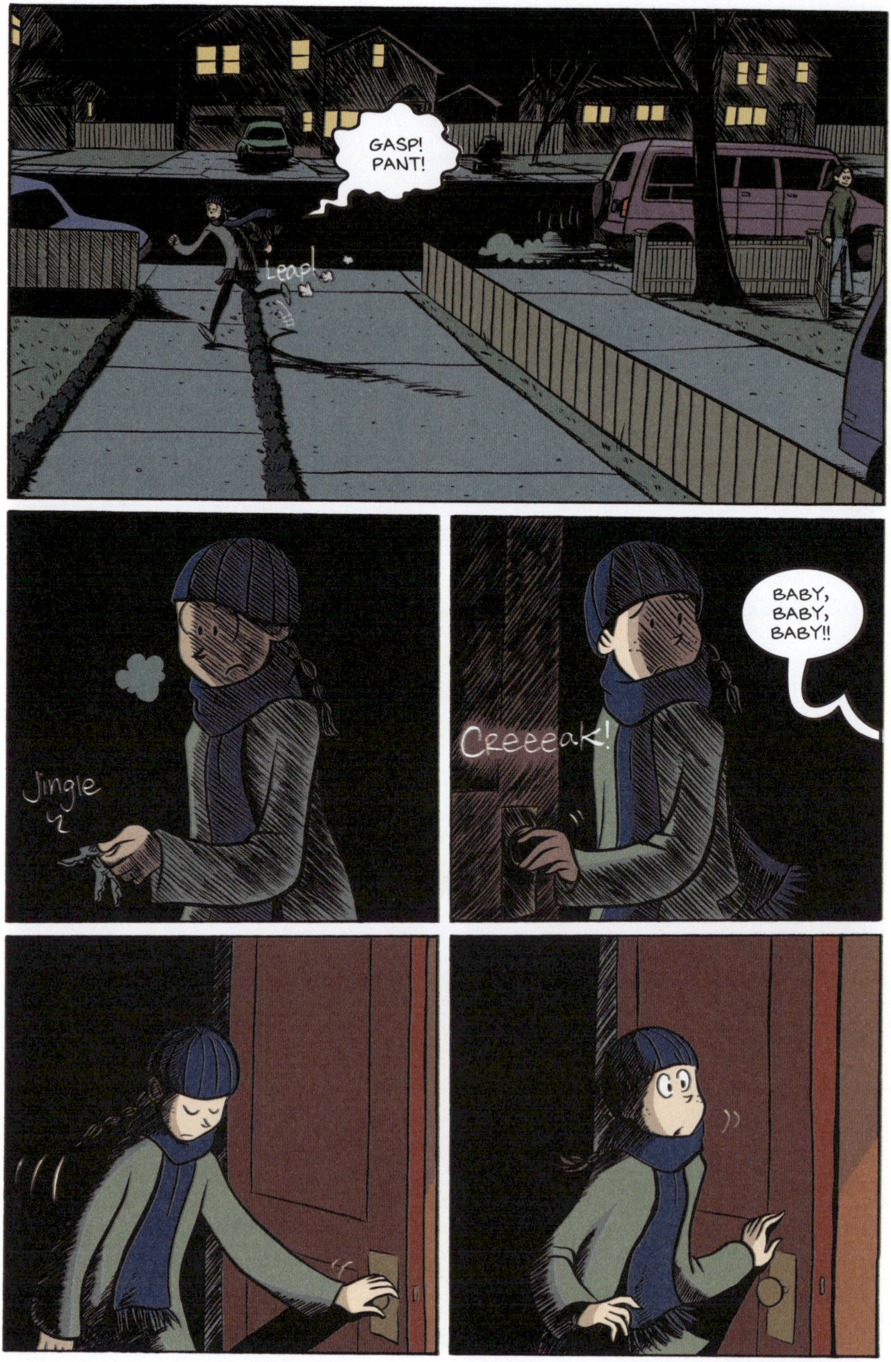
GASP! PANT!
Leap!
Jingle
Creeeak!
BABY, BABY, BABY!!

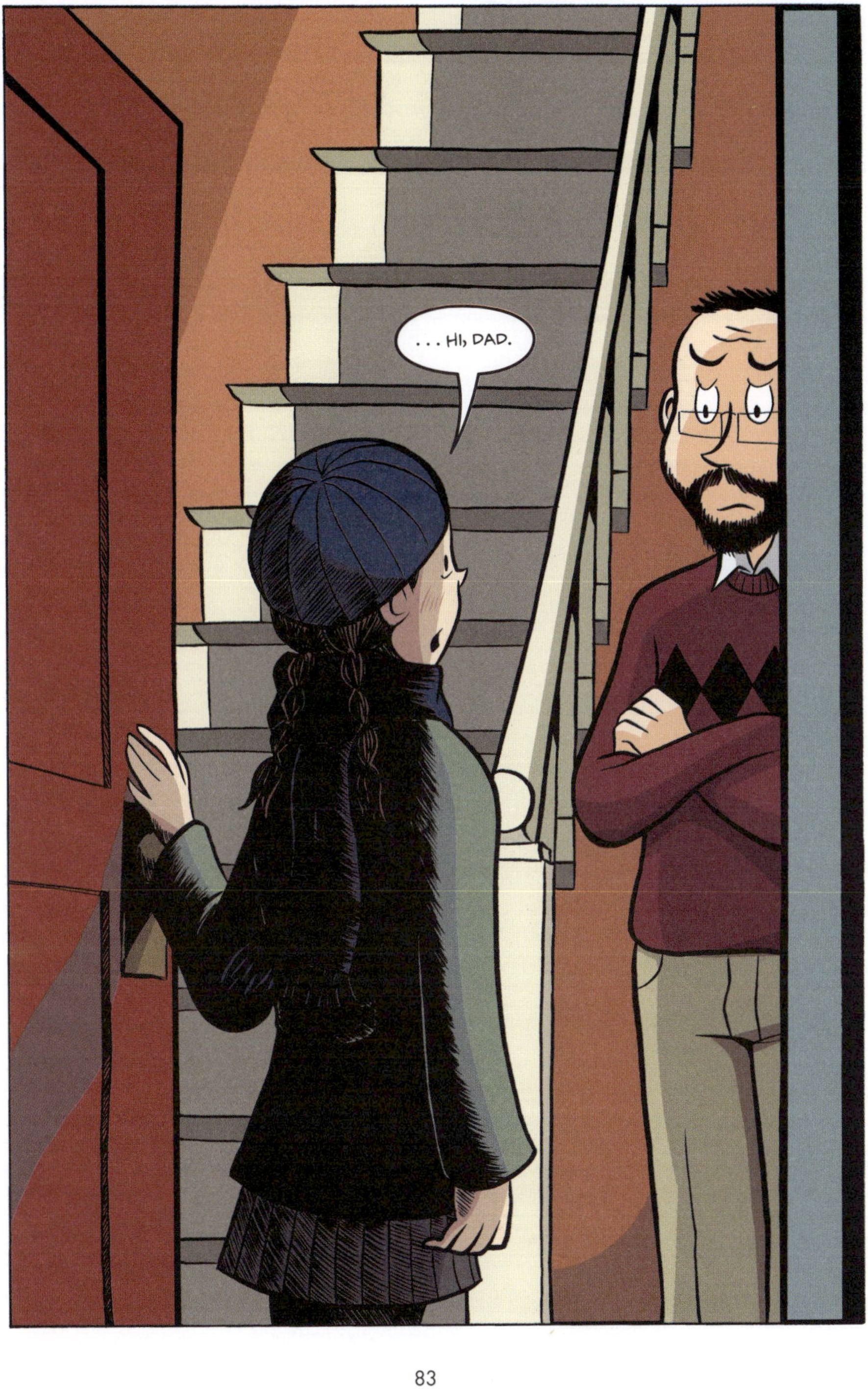
. . . HI, DAD.

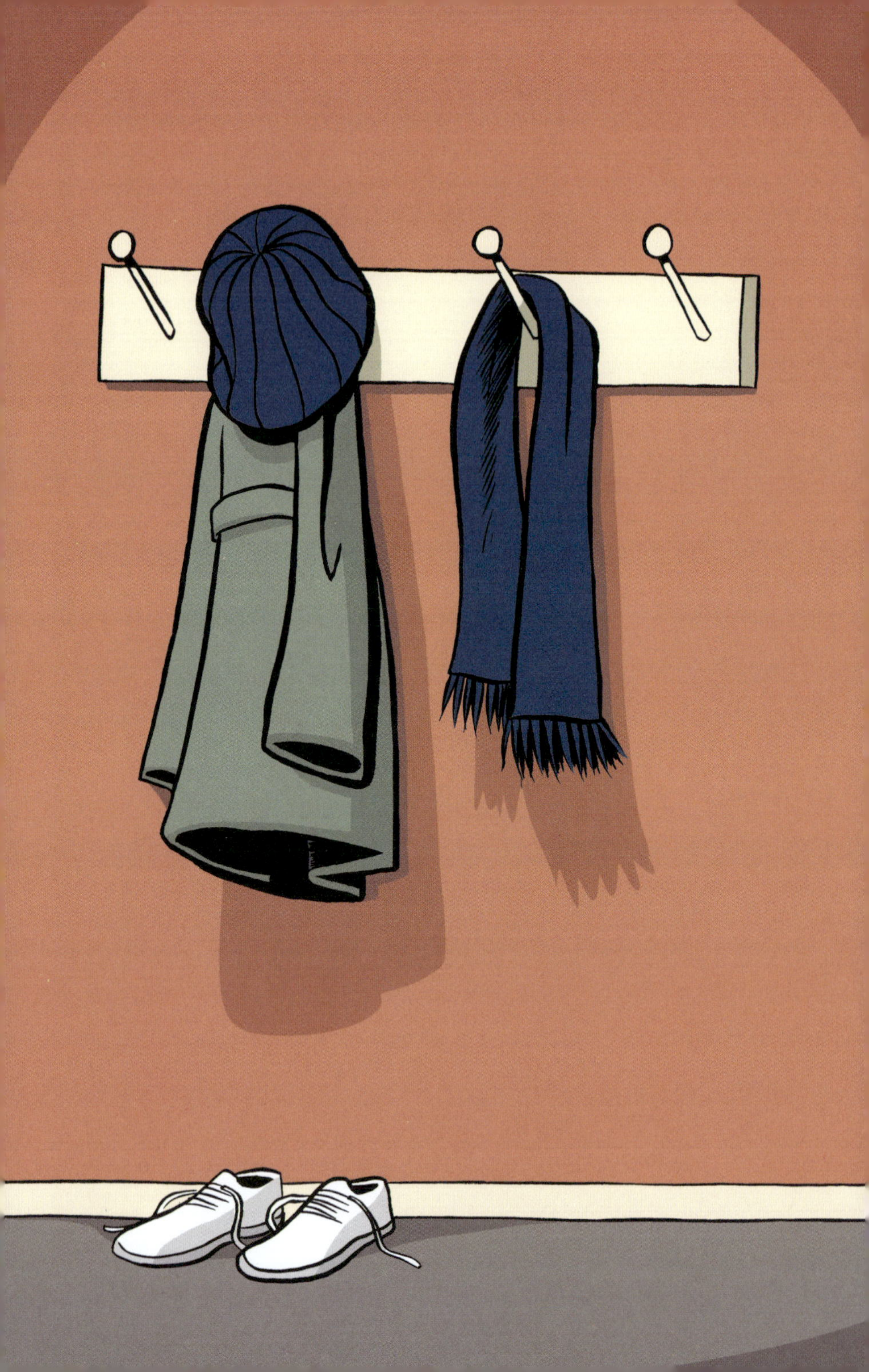

CHAPTER 10

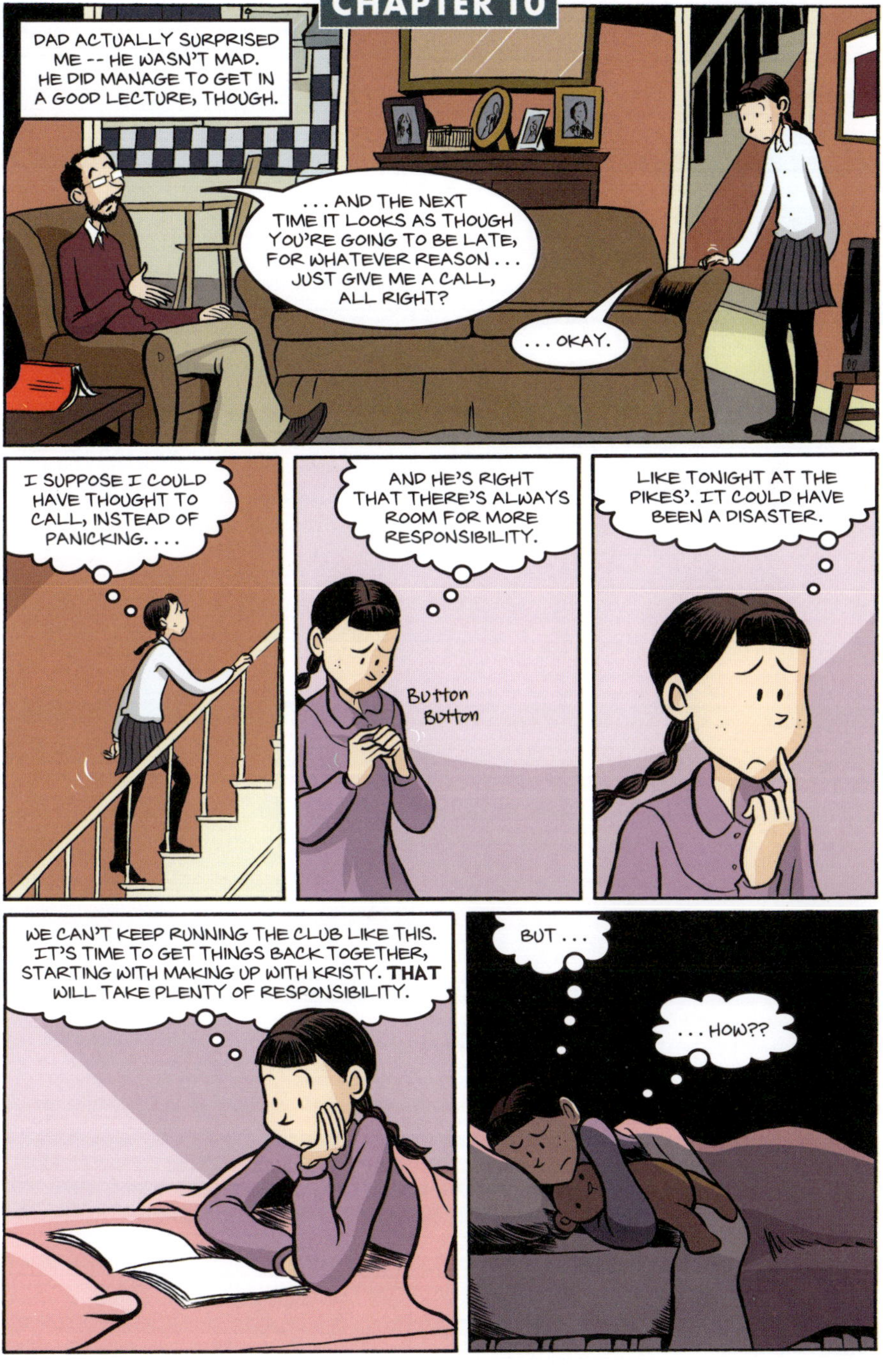
DAD ACTUALLY SURPRISED ME -- HE WASN'T MAD. HE DID MANAGE TO GET IN A GOOD LECTURE, THOUGH.
. . . AND THE NEXT TIME IT LOOKS AS THOUGH YOU'RE GOING TO BE LATE, FOR WHATEVER REASON . . . JUST GIVE ME A CALL, ALL RIGHT?
. . . OKAY.
I SUPPOSE I COULD HAVE THOUGHT TO CALL, INSTEAD OF PANICKING. . . .
AND HE'S RIGHT THAT THERE'S ALWAYS ROOM FOR MORE RESPONSIBILITY.
Button Button
LIKE TONIGHT AT THE PIKES'. IT COULD HAVE BEEN A DISASTER.
WE CAN'T KEEP RUNNING THE CLUB LIKE THIS. IT'S TIME TO GET THINGS BACK TOGETHER, STARTING WITH MAKING UP WITH KRISTY. **THAT** WILL TAKE PLENTY OF RESPONSIBILITY.
BUT . . .
. . . HOW??

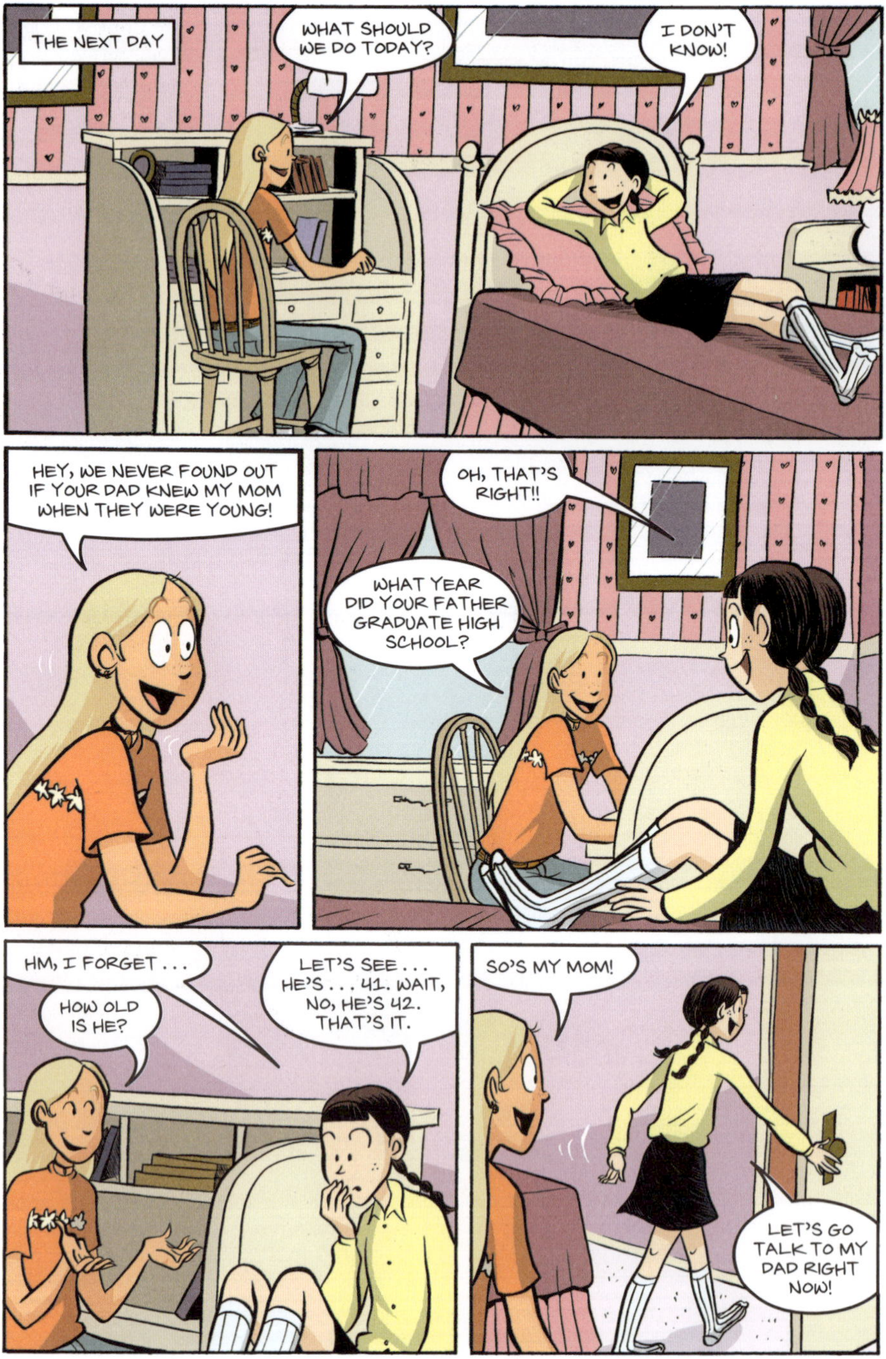
THE NEXT DAY
WHAT SHOULD WE DO TODAY?
I DON'T KNOW!
HEY, WE NEVER FOUND OUT IF YOUR DAD KNEW MY MOM WHEN THEY WERE YOUNG!
OH, THAT'S RIGHT!!
WHAT YEAR DID YOUR FATHER GRADUATE HIGH SCHOOL?
HM, I FORGET . . .
HOW OLD IS HE?
LET'S SEE . . . HE'S . . . 41. WAIT, NO, HE'S 42. THAT'S IT.
SO'S MY MOM!
LET'S GO TALK TO MY DAD RIGHT NOW!

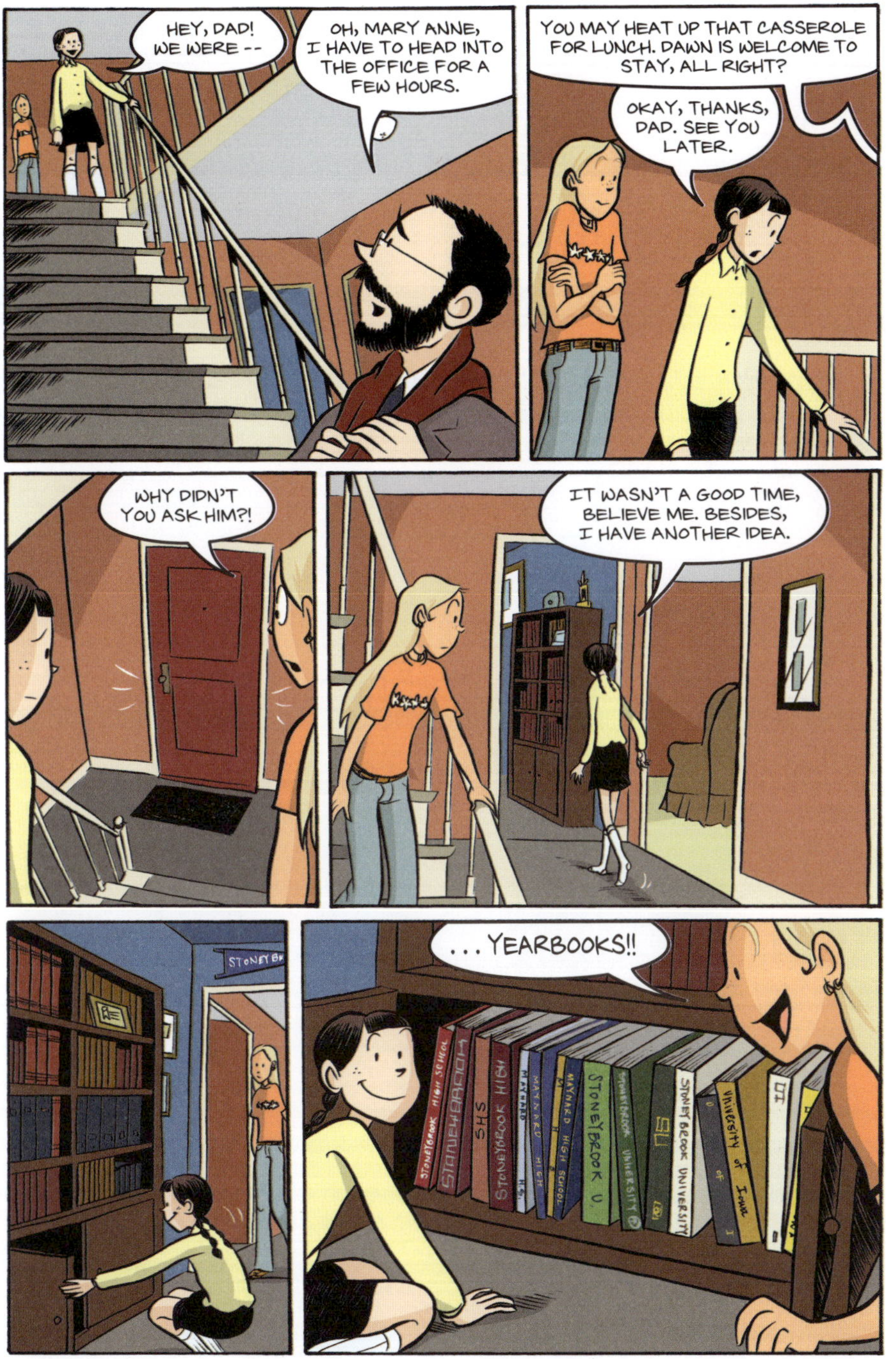
HEY, DAD! WE WERE --
OH, MARY ANNE, I HAVE TO HEAD INTO THE OFFICE FOR A FEW HOURS.
YOU MAY HEAT UP THAT CASSEROLE FOR LUNCH. DAWN IS WELCOME TO STAY, ALL RIGHT?
OKAY, THANKS, DAD. SEE YOU LATER.
WHY DIDN'T YOU ASK HIM?!
IT WASN'T A GOOD TIME, BELIEVE ME. BESIDES, I HAVE ANOTHER IDEA.
. . . YEARBOOKS!!

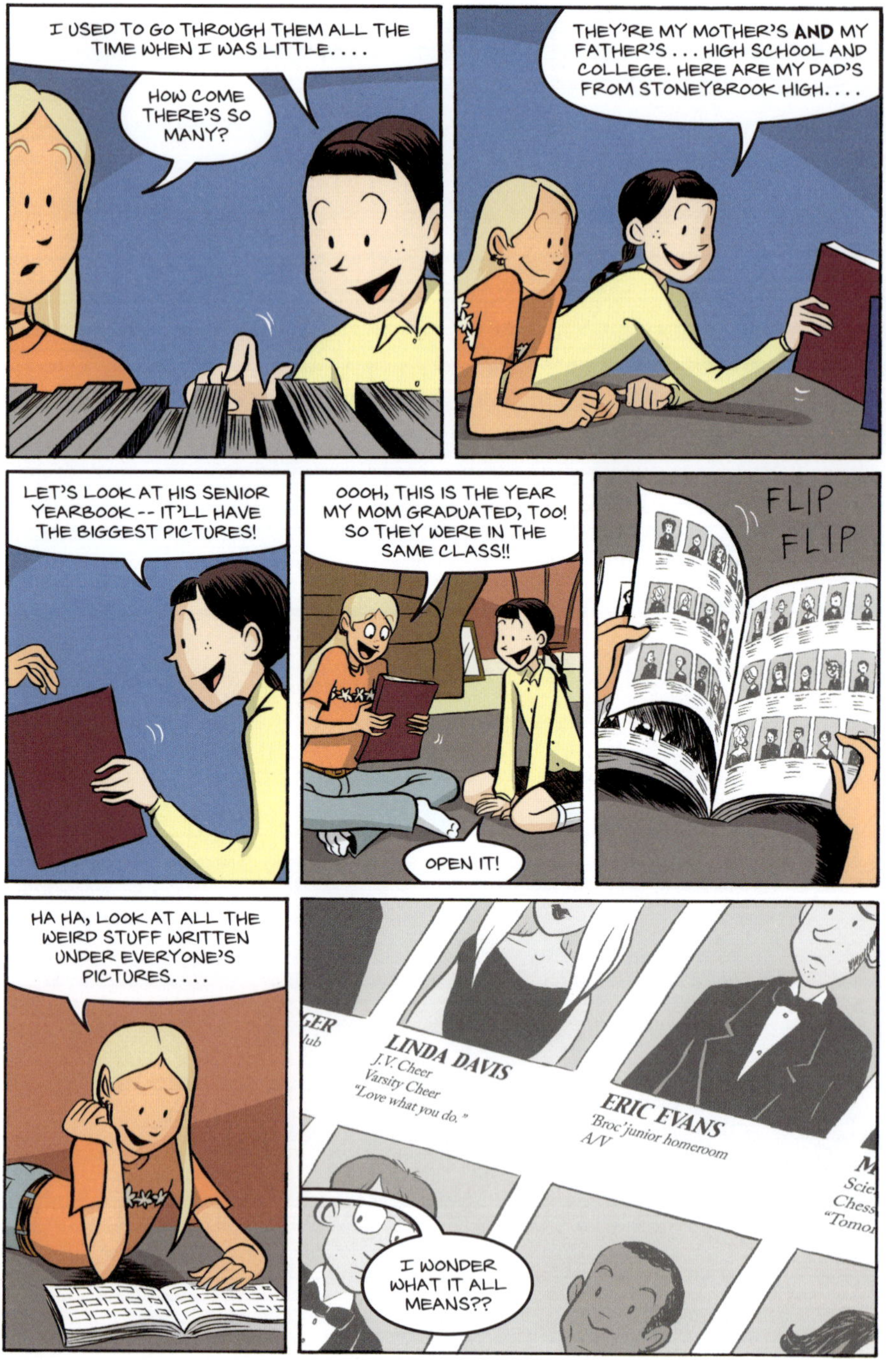
I USED TO GO THROUGH THEM ALL THE TIME WHEN I WAS LITTLE. . . .
HOW COME THERE'S SO MANY?
THEY'RE MY MOTHER'S AND MY FATHER'S . . . HIGH SCHOOL AND COLLEGE. HERE ARE MY DAD'S FROM STONEYBROOK HIGH. . . .
LET'S LOOK AT HIS SENIOR YEARBOOK -- IT'LL HAVE THE BIGGEST PICTURES!
OOOH, THIS IS THE YEAR MY MOM GRADUATED, TOO! SO THEY WERE IN THE SAME CLASS!!
OPEN IT!
FLIP
FLIP
HA HA, LOOK AT ALL THE WEIRD STUFF WRITTEN UNDER EVERYONE'S PICTURES. . . .
LINDA DAVIS
J.V. Cheer
Varsity Cheer
"Love what you do."
ERIC EVANS
Broc'junior homeroom
A/V
I WONDER WHAT IT ALL MEANS??

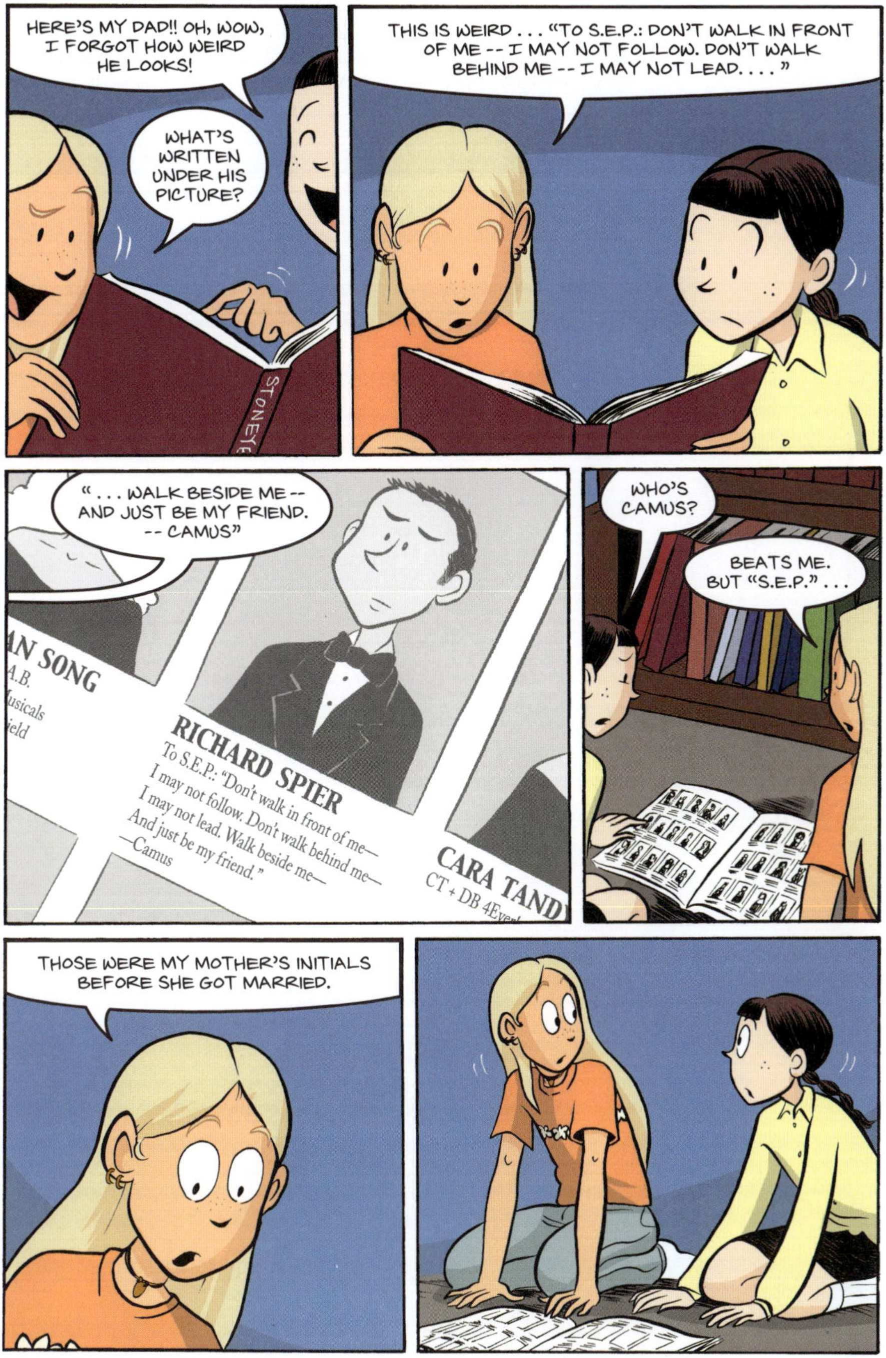
HERE'S MY DAD!! OH, WOW, I FORGOT HOW WEIRD HE LOOKS!
WHAT'S WRITTEN UNDER HIS PICTURE?
STONEYE
THIS IS WEIRD . . . "TO S.E.P.: DON'T WALK IN FRONT OF ME -- I MAY NOT FOLLOW. DON'T WALK BEHIND ME -- I MAY NOT LEAD. . . . "
" . . . WALK BESIDE ME -- AND JUST BE MY FRIEND. -- CAMUS"
RICHARD SPIER
To S.E.P.: "Don't walk in front of me— I may not follow. Don't walk behind me— I may not lead. Walk beside me— And just be my friend."
—Camus
CARA TAND
CT + DB 4Ever
WHO'S CAMUS?
BEATS ME. BUT "S.E.P." . . .
THOSE WERE MY MOTHER'S INITIALS BEFORE SHE GOT MARRIED.

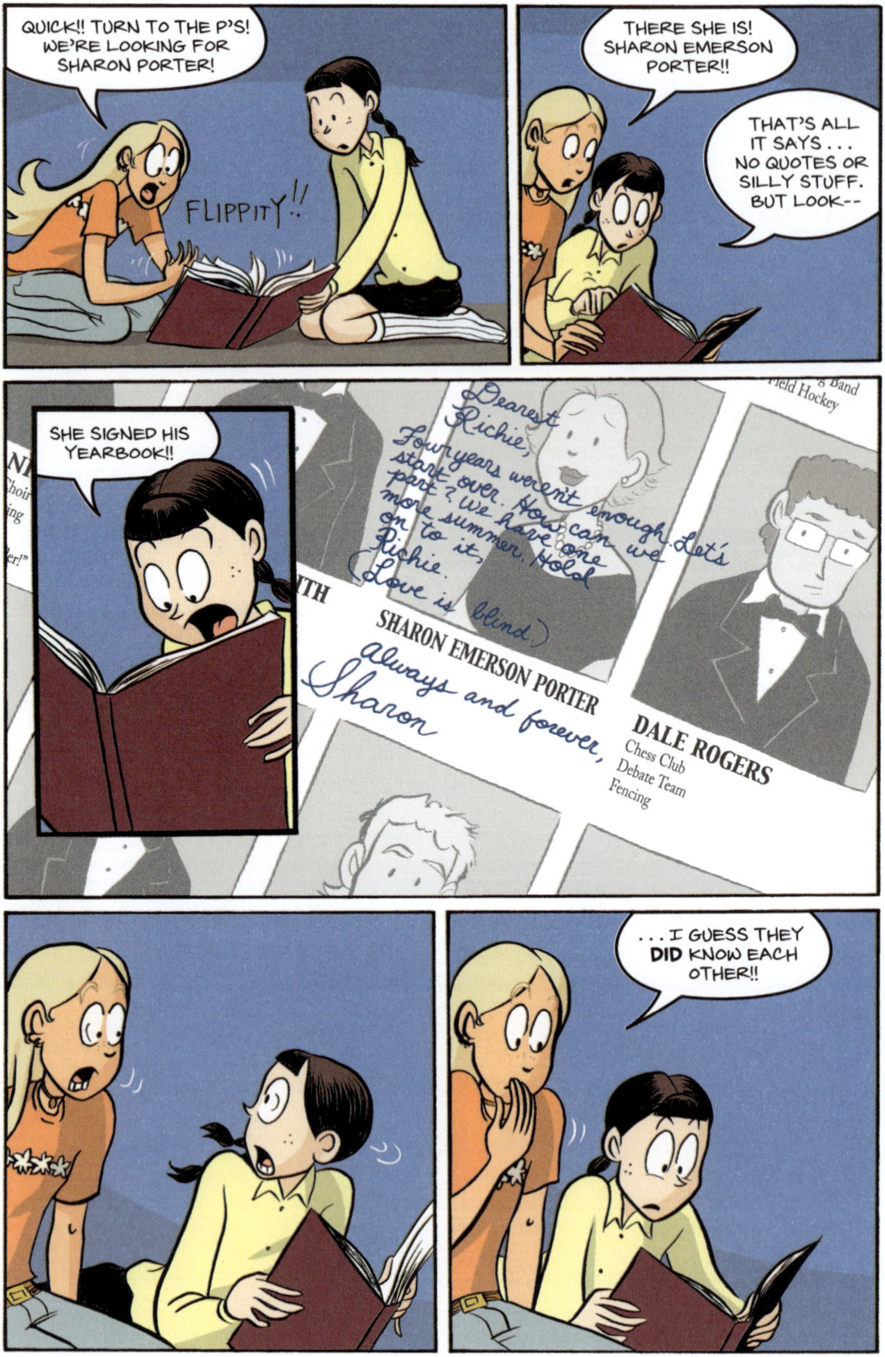

QUICK!! TURN TO THE P'S! WE'RE LOOKING FOR SHARON PORTER!
FLIPPITY!!
THERE SHE IS! SHARON EMERSON PORTER!!
THAT'S ALL IT SAYS . . . NO QUOTES OR SILLY STUFF. BUT LOOK--
SHE SIGNED HIS YEARBOOK!!
Field Hockey
Dearest Richie,
Four years weren't enough. Let's start over. How can we part? We have one more summer. Hold on to it, Richie.
(Love is blind.)
SHARON EMERSON PORTER
Always and forever,
Sharon
DALE ROGERS
Chess Club
Debate Team
Fencing
. . . I GUESS THEY **DID** KNOW EACH OTHER!!

CHAPTER 11

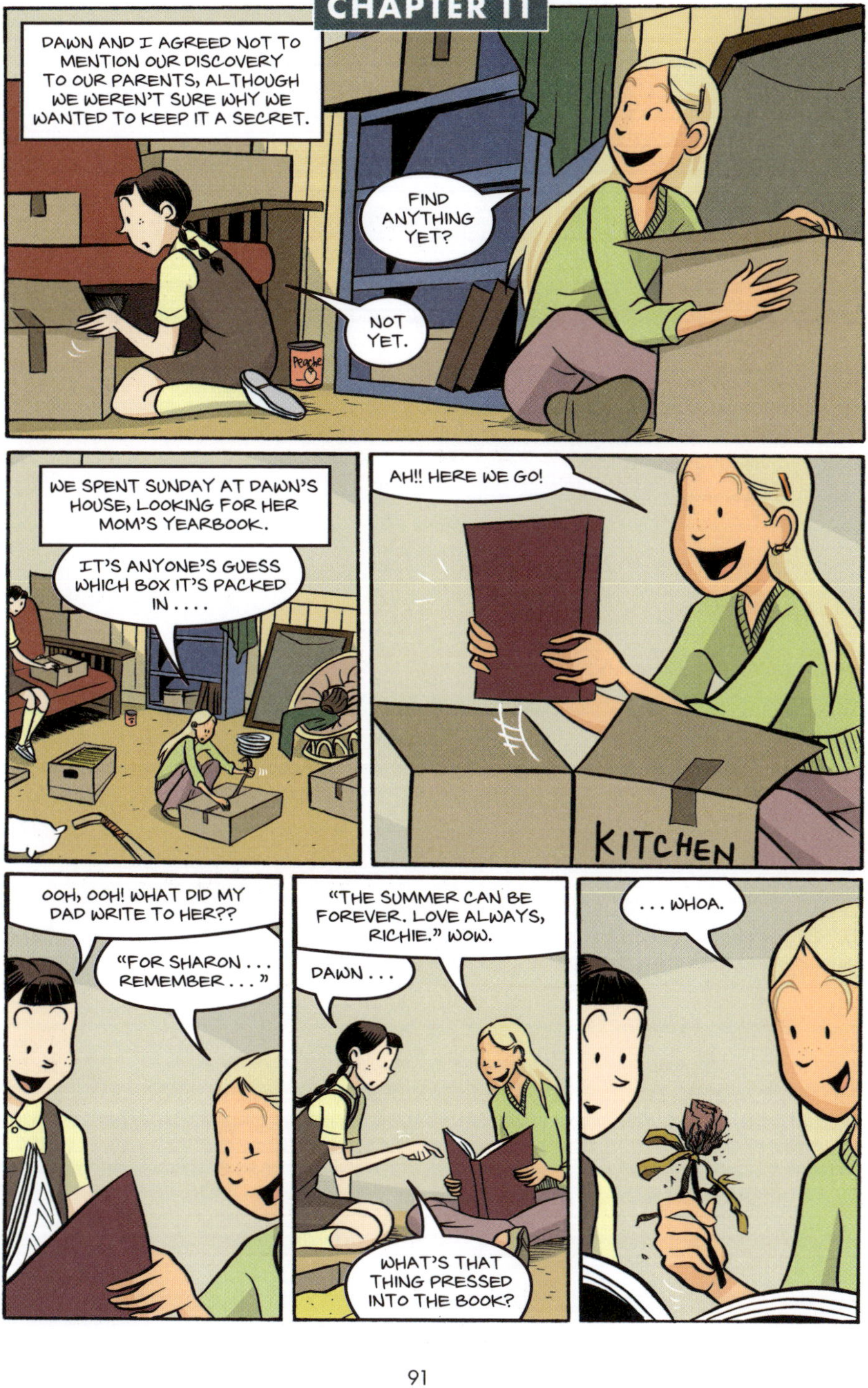
DAWN AND I AGREED NOT TO MENTION OUR DISCOVERY TO OUR PARENTS, ALTHOUGH WE WEREN'T SURE WHY WE WANTED TO KEEP IT A SECRET.
FIND ANYTHING YET?
NOT YET.
PEACHES
WE SPENT SUNDAY AT DAWN'S HOUSE, LOOKING FOR HER MOM'S YEARBOOK.
IT'S ANYONE'S GUESS WHICH BOX IT'S PACKED IN....
AH!! HERE WE GO!
KITCHEN
OOH, OOH! WHAT DID MY DAD WRITE TO HER??
"FOR SHARON... REMEMBER..."
"THE SUMMER CAN BE FOREVER. LOVE ALWAYS, RICHIE." WOW.
DAWN...
WHAT'S THAT THING PRESSED INTO THE BOOK?
...WHOA.

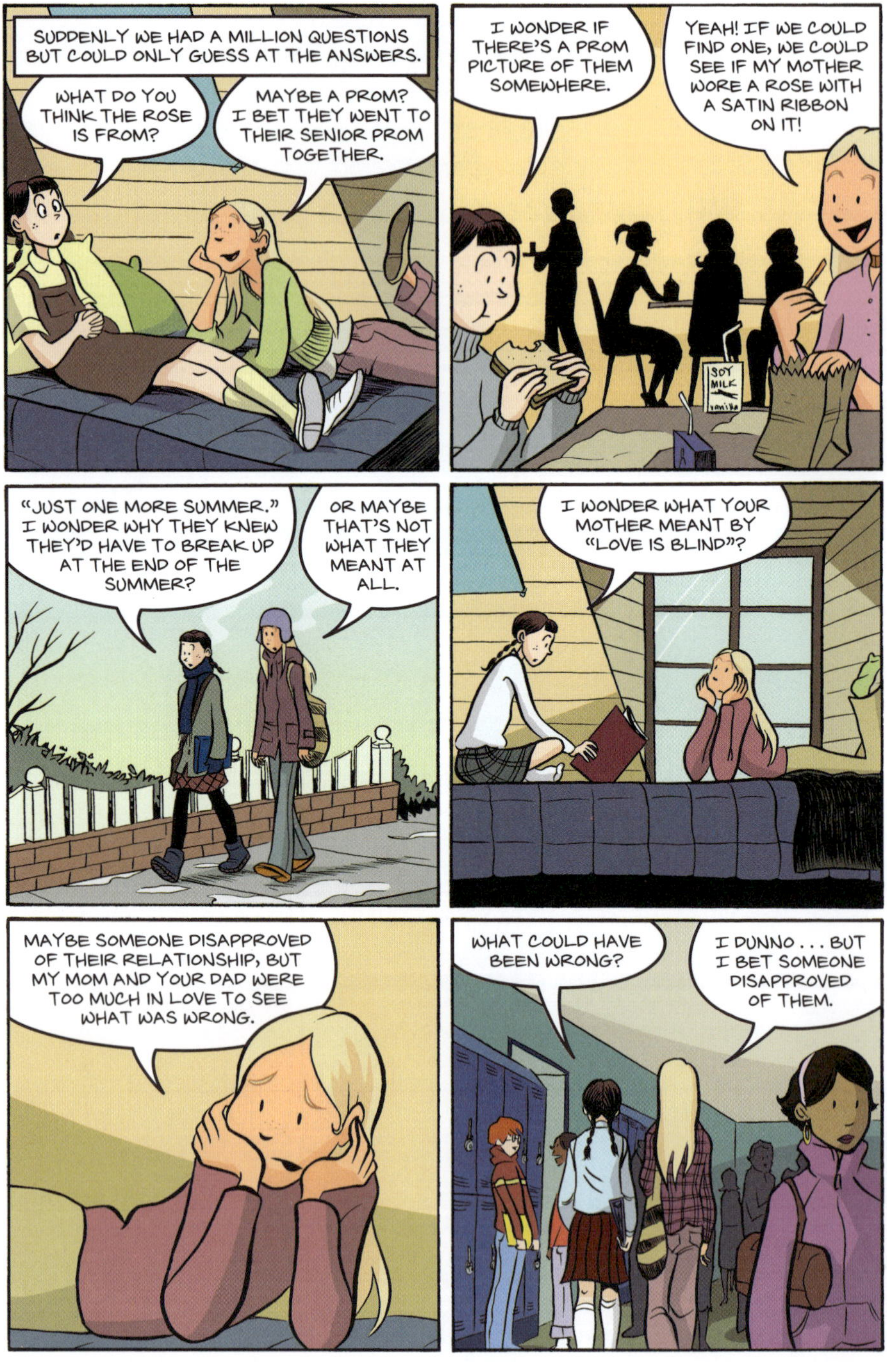
SUDDENLY WE HAD A MILLION QUESTIONS BUT COULD ONLY GUESS AT THE ANSWERS.
WHAT DO YOU THINK THE ROSE IS FROM?
MAYBE A PROM? I BET THEY WENT TO THEIR SENIOR PROM TOGETHER.
I WONDER IF THERE'S A PROM PICTURE OF THEM SOMEWHERE.
YEAH! IF WE COULD FIND ONE, WE COULD SEE IF MY MOTHER WORE A ROSE WITH A SATIN RIBBON ON IT!
SOY MILK
vanilla
"JUST ONE MORE SUMMER." I WONDER WHY THEY KNEW THEY'D HAVE TO BREAK UP AT THE END OF THE SUMMER?
OR MAYBE THAT'S NOT WHAT THEY MEANT AT ALL.
I WONDER WHAT YOUR MOTHER MEANT BY "LOVE IS BLIND"?
MAYBE SOMEONE DISAPPROVED OF THEIR RELATIONSHIP, BUT MY MOM AND YOUR DAD WERE TOO MUCH IN LOVE TO SEE WHAT WAS WRONG.
WHAT COULD HAVE BEEN WRONG?
I DUNNO . . . BUT I BET SOMEONE DISAPPROVED OF THEM.

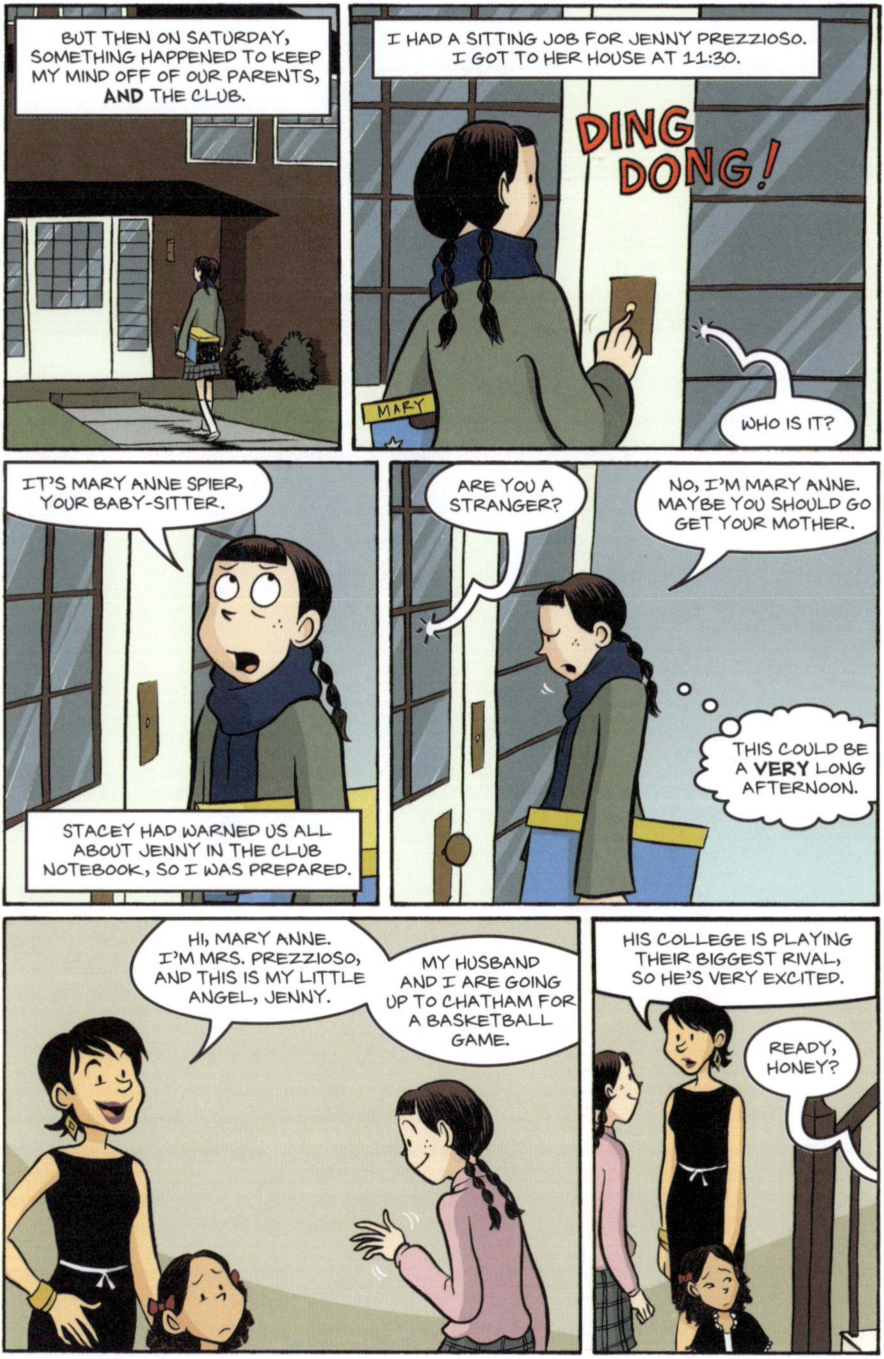
BUT THEN ON SATURDAY, SOMETHING HAPPENED TO KEEP MY MIND OFF OF OUR PARENTS, **AND** THE CLUB.
I HAD A SITTING JOB FOR JENNY PREZZIOSO. I GOT TO HER HOUSE AT 11:30.
DING DONG!
MARY
WHO IS IT?
IT'S MARY ANNE SPIER, YOUR BABY-SITTER.
STACEY HAD WARNED US ALL ABOUT JENNY IN THE CLUB NOTEBOOK, SO I WAS PREPARED.
ARE YOU A STRANGER?
NO, I'M MARY ANNE. MAYBE YOU SHOULD GO GET YOUR MOTHER.
THIS COULD BE A **VERY** LONG AFTERNOON.
HI, MARY ANNE. I'M MRS. PREZZIOSO, AND THIS IS MY LITTLE ANGEL, JENNY.
MY HUSBAND AND I ARE GOING UP TO CHATHAM FOR A BASKETBALL GAME.
HIS COLLEGE IS PLAYING THEIR BIGGEST RIVAL, SO HE'S VERY EXCITED.
READY, HONEY?

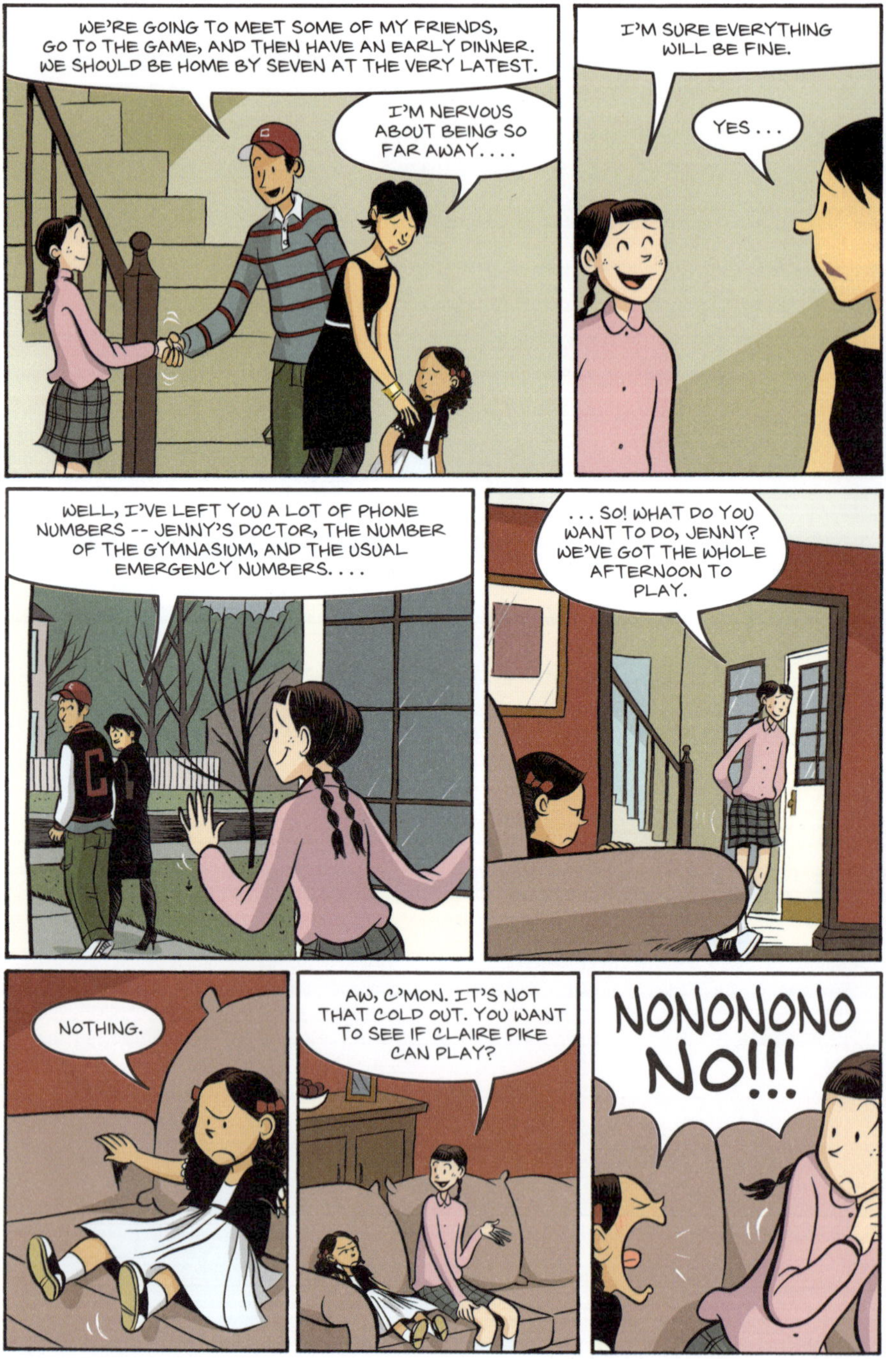
WE'RE GOING TO MEET SOME OF MY FRIENDS, GO TO THE GAME, AND THEN HAVE AN EARLY DINNER. WE SHOULD BE HOME BY SEVEN AT THE VERY LATEST.
I'M NERVOUS ABOUT BEING SO FAR AWAY. . . .
I'M SURE EVERYTHING WILL BE FINE.
YES . . .
WELL, I'VE LEFT YOU A LOT OF PHONE NUMBERS -- JENNY'S DOCTOR, THE NUMBER OF THE GYMNASIUM, AND THE USUAL EMERGENCY NUMBERS. . . .
. . . SO! WHAT DO YOU WANT TO DO, JENNY? WE'VE GOT THE WHOLE AFTERNOON TO PLAY.
NOTHING.
AW, C'MON. IT'S NOT THAT COLD OUT. YOU WANT TO SEE IF CLAIRE PIKE CAN PLAY?
NONONONO NO!!!

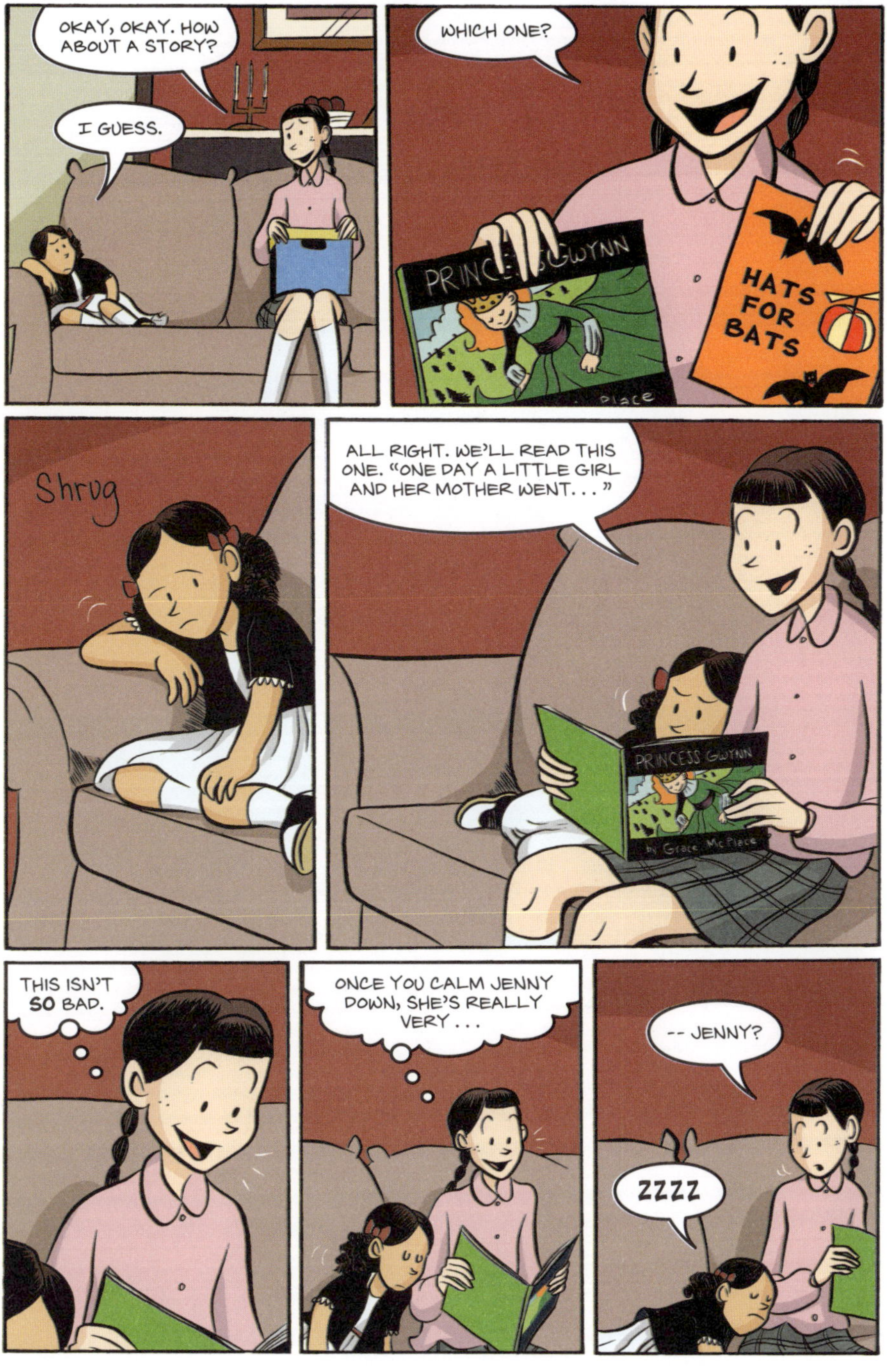
OKAY, OKAY. HOW ABOUT A STORY?
I GUESS.
WHICH ONE?
PRINCESS GWYNN
HATS FOR BATS
Shrug
ALL RIGHT. WE'LL READ THIS ONE. "ONE DAY A LITTLE GIRL AND HER MOTHER WENT. . . "
PRINCESS GWYNN
by Grace McPlace
THIS ISN'T **SO** BAD.
ONCE YOU CALM JENNY DOWN, SHE'S REALLY VERY . . .
-- JENNY?
ZZZZ

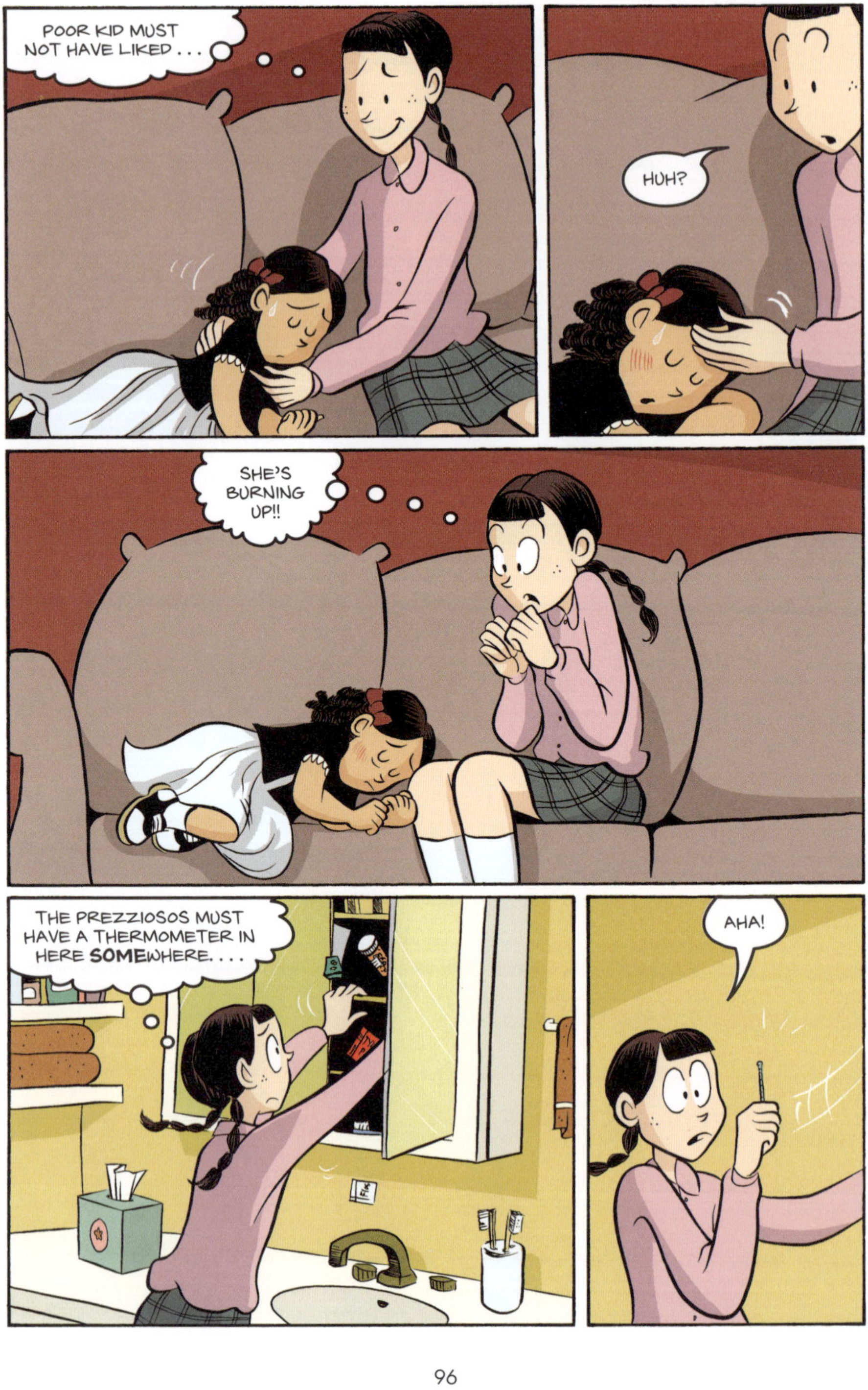
POOR KID MUST NOT HAVE LIKED . . .
HUH?
SHE'S BURNING UP!!
THE PREZZIOSOS MUST HAVE A THERMOMETER IN HERE **SOME**WHERE. . . .
AHA!

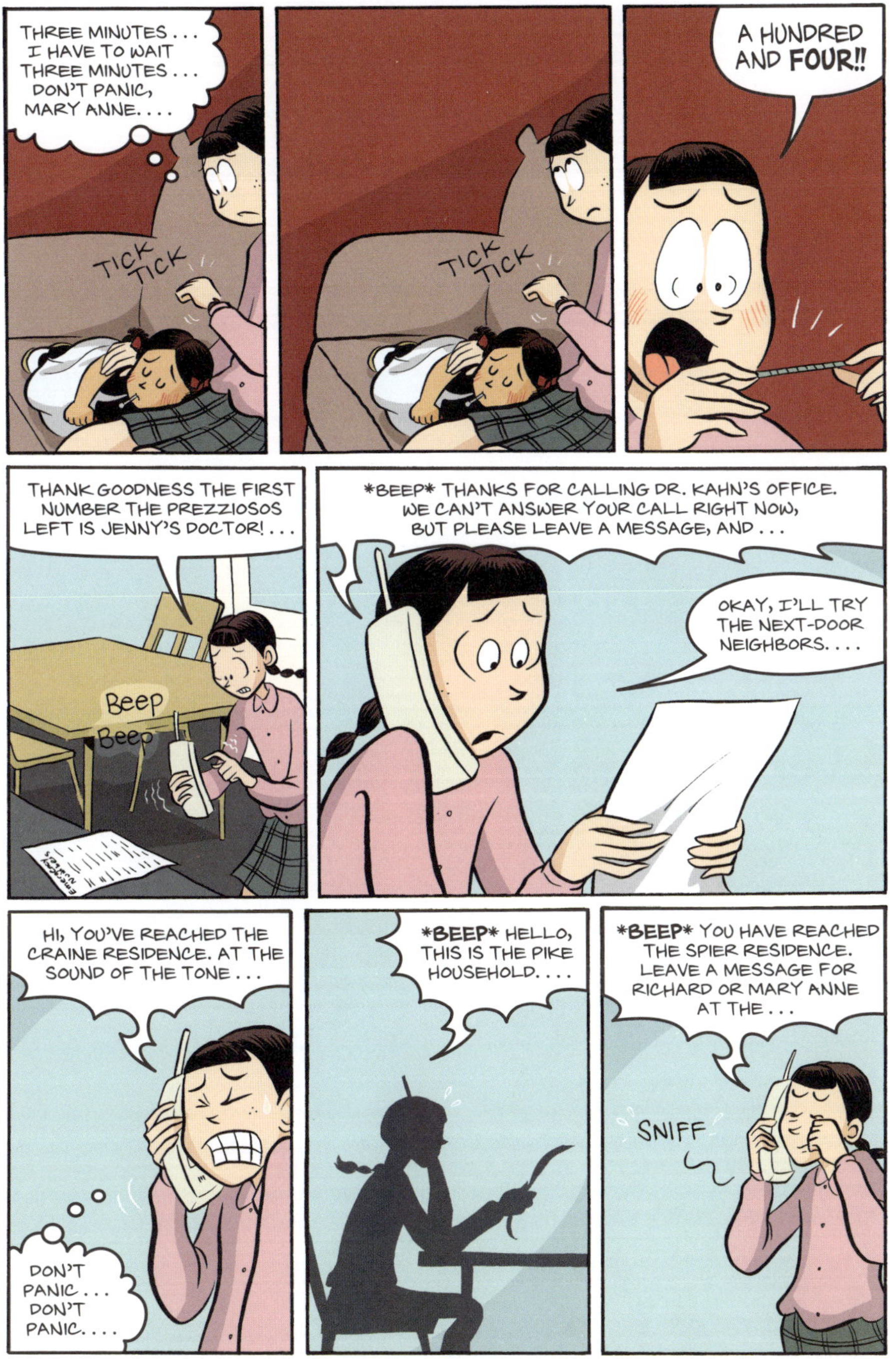
THREE MINUTES . . . I HAVE TO WAIT THREE MINUTES . . . DON'T PANIC, MARY ANNE. . . .
TICK TICK
TICK TICK
A HUNDRED AND **FOUR!!**
THANK GOODNESS THE FIRST NUMBER THE PREZZIOSOS LEFT IS JENNY'S DOCTOR! . . .
Beep
Beep
BEEP THANKS FOR CALLING DR. KAHN'S OFFICE. WE CAN'T ANSWER YOUR CALL RIGHT NOW, BUT PLEASE LEAVE A MESSAGE, AND . . .
OKAY, I'LL TRY THE NEXT-DOOR NEIGHBORS. . . .
HI, YOU'VE REACHED THE CRAINE RESIDENCE. AT THE SOUND OF THE TONE . . .
DON'T PANIC . . . DON'T PANIC. . . .
BEEP HELLO, THIS IS THE PIKE HOUSEHOLD. . . .
BEEP YOU HAVE REACHED THE SPIER RESIDENCE. LEAVE A MESSAGE FOR RICHARD OR MARY ANNE AT THE . . .
SNIFF

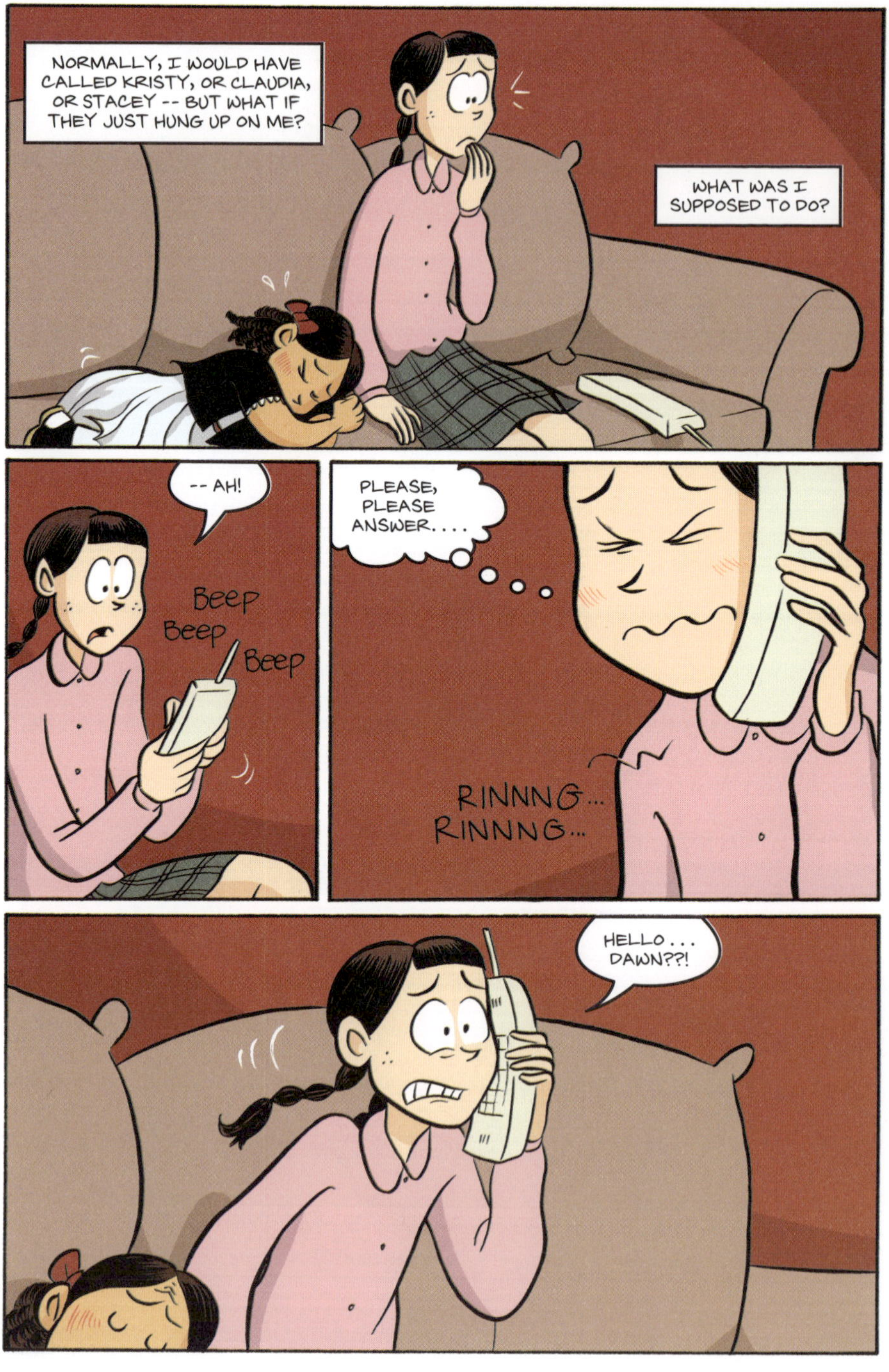
NORMALLY, I WOULD HAVE CALLED KRISTY, OR CLAUDIA, OR STACEY -- BUT WHAT IF THEY JUST HUNG UP ON ME?
WHAT WAS I SUPPOSED TO DO?
-- AH!
Beep
Beep
Beep
PLEASE, PLEASE ANSWER....
RINNNG...
RINNNG...
HELLO... DAWN??!

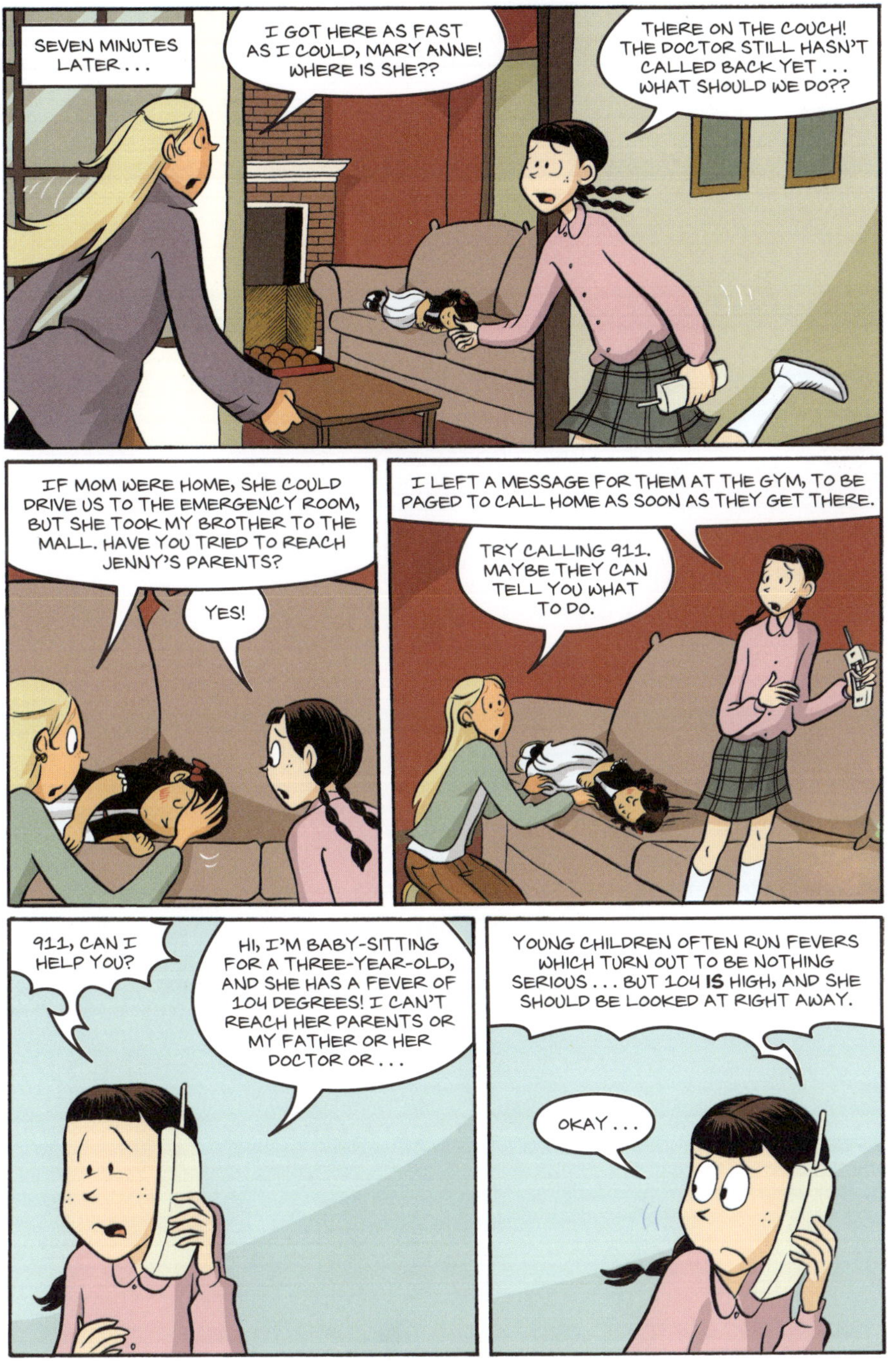
SEVEN MINUTES LATER . . .
I GOT HERE AS FAST AS I COULD, MARY ANNE! WHERE IS SHE??
THERE ON THE COUCH! THE DOCTOR STILL HASN'T CALLED BACK YET . . . WHAT SHOULD WE DO??
IF MOM WERE HOME, SHE COULD DRIVE US TO THE EMERGENCY ROOM, BUT SHE TOOK MY BROTHER TO THE MALL. HAVE YOU TRIED TO REACH JENNY'S PARENTS?
YES!
I LEFT A MESSAGE FOR THEM AT THE GYM, TO BE PAGED TO CALL HOME AS SOON AS THEY GET THERE.
TRY CALLING 911. MAYBE THEY CAN TELL YOU WHAT TO DO.
911, CAN I HELP YOU?
HI, I'M BABY-SITTING FOR A THREE-YEAR-OLD, AND SHE HAS A FEVER OF 104 DEGREES! I CAN'T REACH HER PARENTS OR MY FATHER OR HER DOCTOR OR . . .
YOUNG CHILDREN OFTEN RUN FEVERS WHICH TURN OUT TO BE NOTHING SERIOUS . . . BUT 104 **IS** HIGH, AND SHE SHOULD BE LOOKED AT RIGHT AWAY.
OKAY . . .

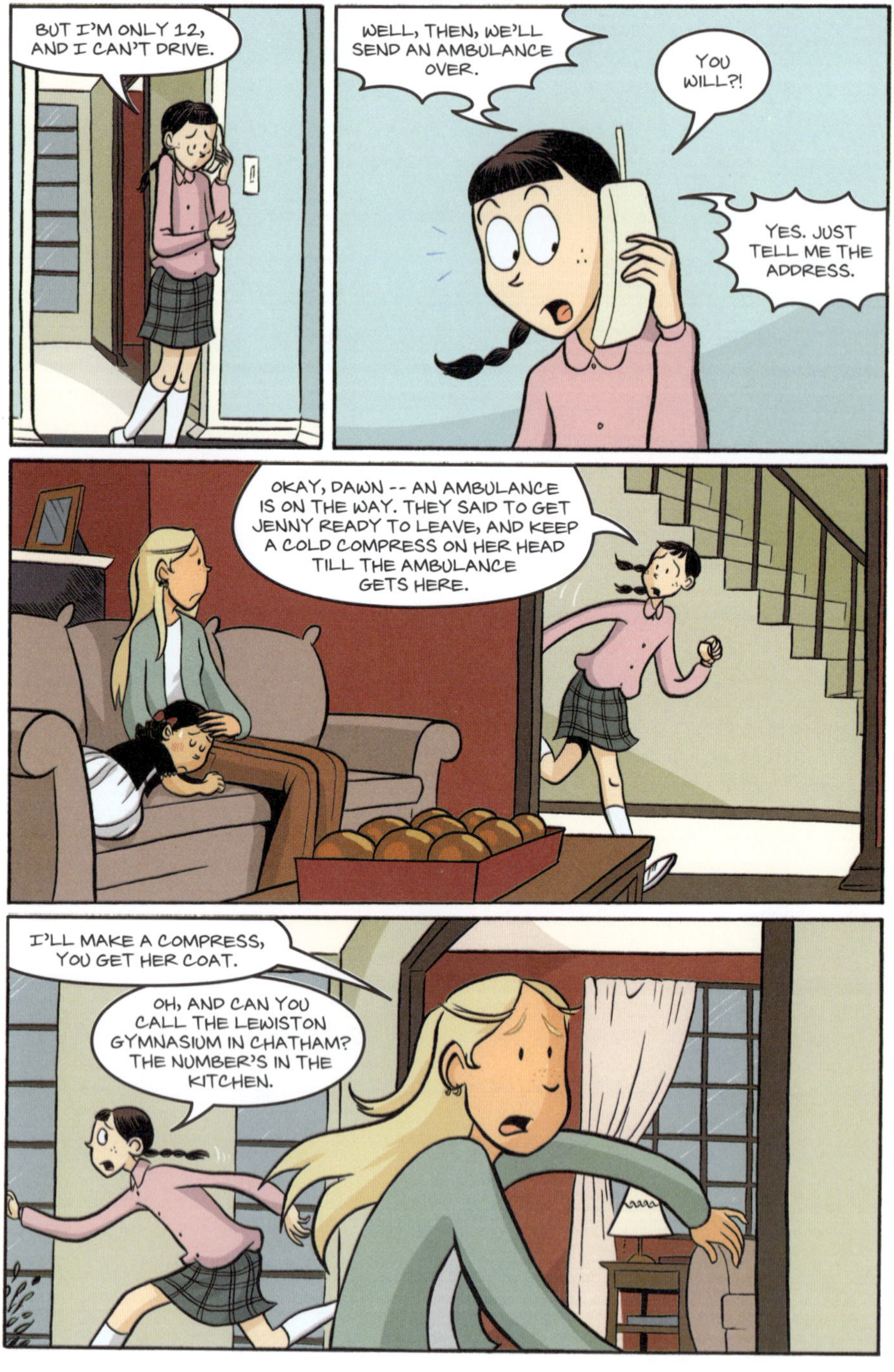
BUT I'M ONLY 12, AND I CAN'T DRIVE.
WELL, THEN, WE'LL SEND AN AMBULANCE OVER.
YOU WILL?!
YES. JUST TELL ME THE ADDRESS.
OKAY, DAWN -- AN AMBULANCE IS ON THE WAY. THEY SAID TO GET JENNY READY TO LEAVE, AND KEEP A COLD COMPRESS ON HER HEAD TILL THE AMBULANCE GETS HERE.
I'LL MAKE A COMPRESS, YOU GET HER COAT.
OH, AND CAN YOU CALL THE LEWISTON GYMNASIUM IN CHATHAM? THE NUMBER'S IN THE KITCHEN.

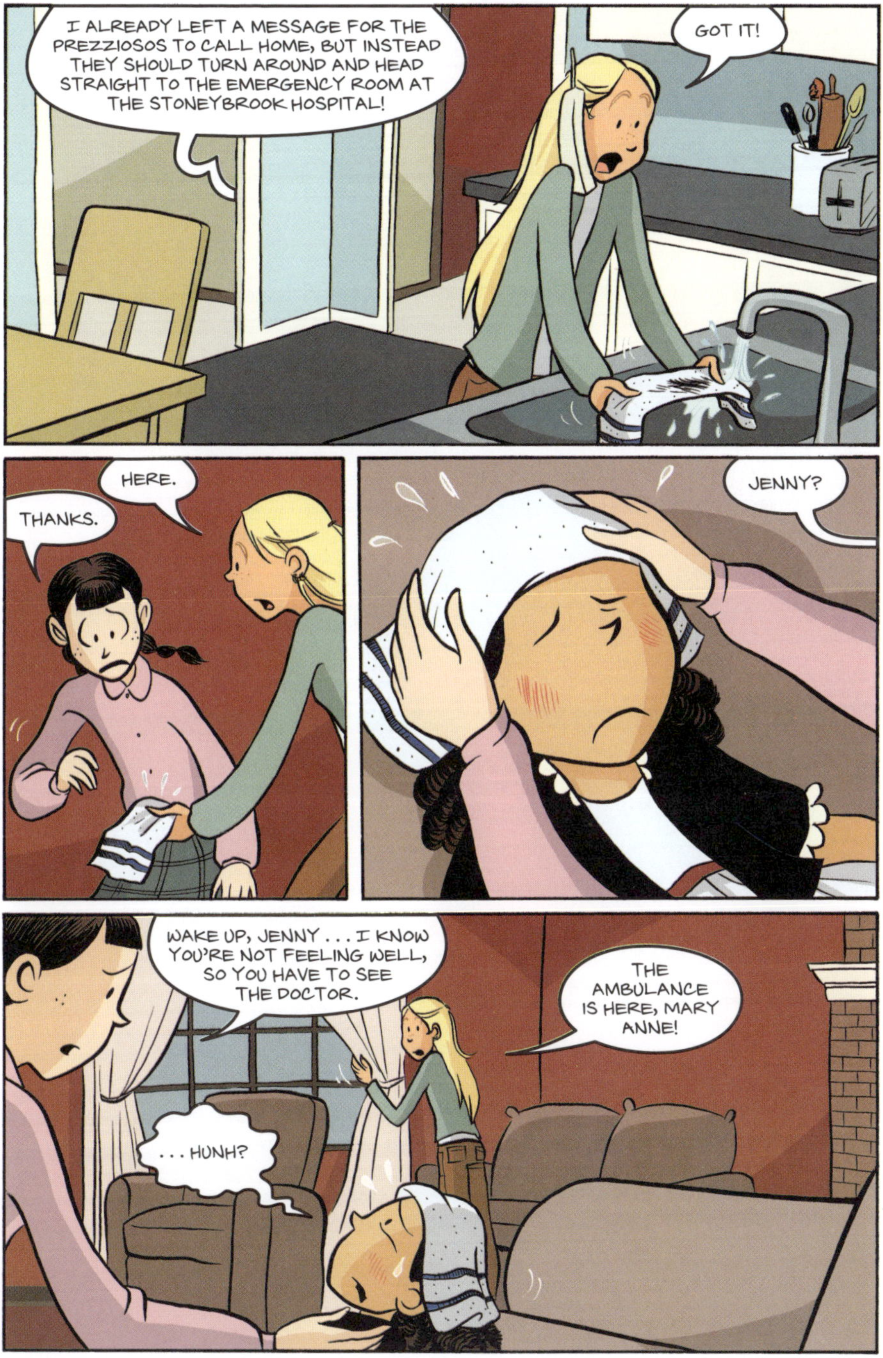
I ALREADY LEFT A MESSAGE FOR THE PREZZIOSOS TO CALL HOME, BUT INSTEAD THEY SHOULD TURN AROUND AND HEAD STRAIGHT TO THE EMERGENCY ROOM AT THE STONEYBROOK HOSPITAL!
GOT IT!
HERE.
THANKS.
JENNY?
WAKE UP, JENNY . . . I KNOW YOU'RE NOT FEELING WELL, SO YOU HAVE TO SEE THE DOCTOR.
THE AMBULANCE IS HERE, MARY ANNE!
. . . HUNH?

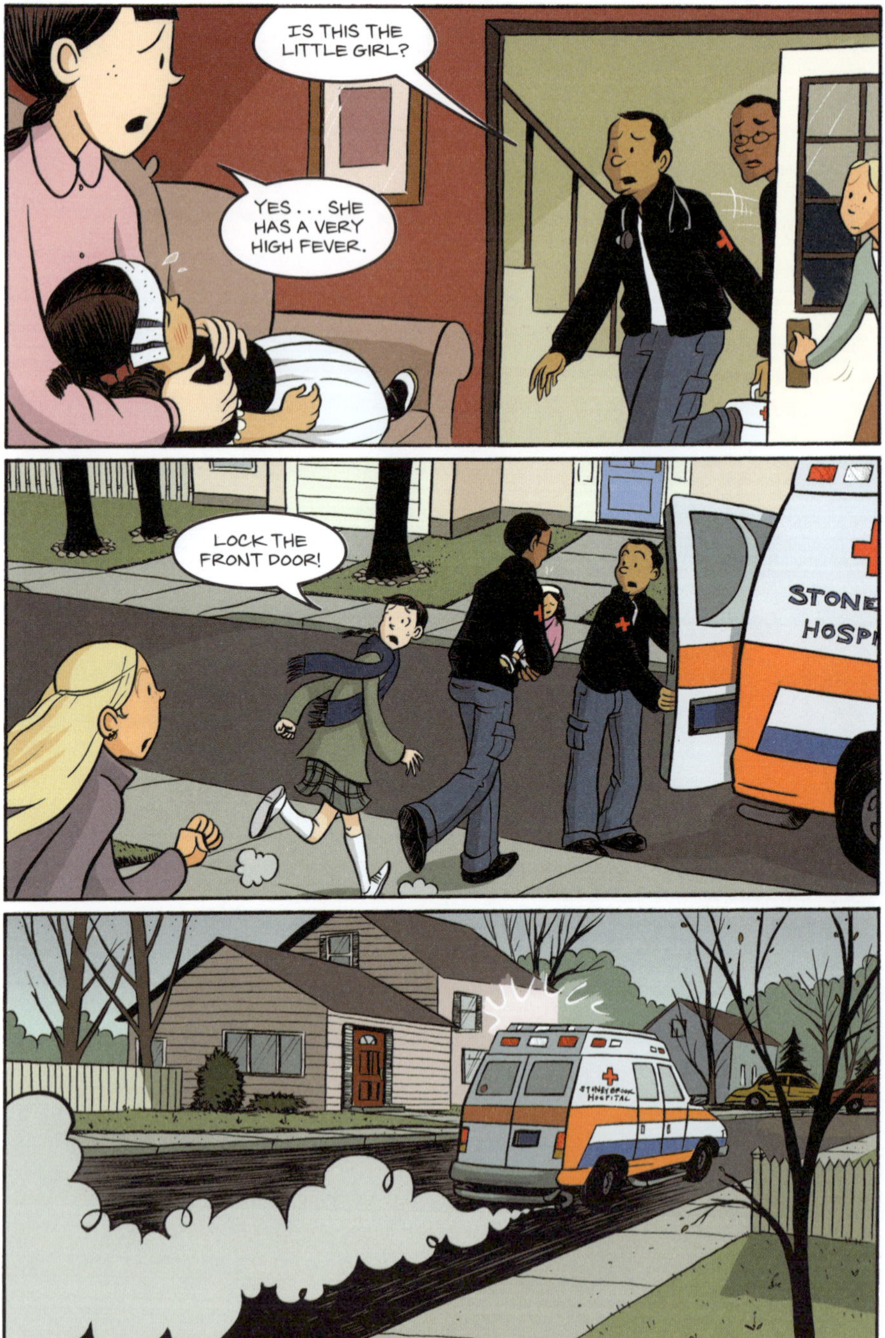
IS THIS THE LITTLE GIRL?
YES . . . SHE HAS A VERY HIGH FEVER.
LOCK THE FRONT DOOR!
STONE
HOSP
STONEY BROOK HOSPITAL

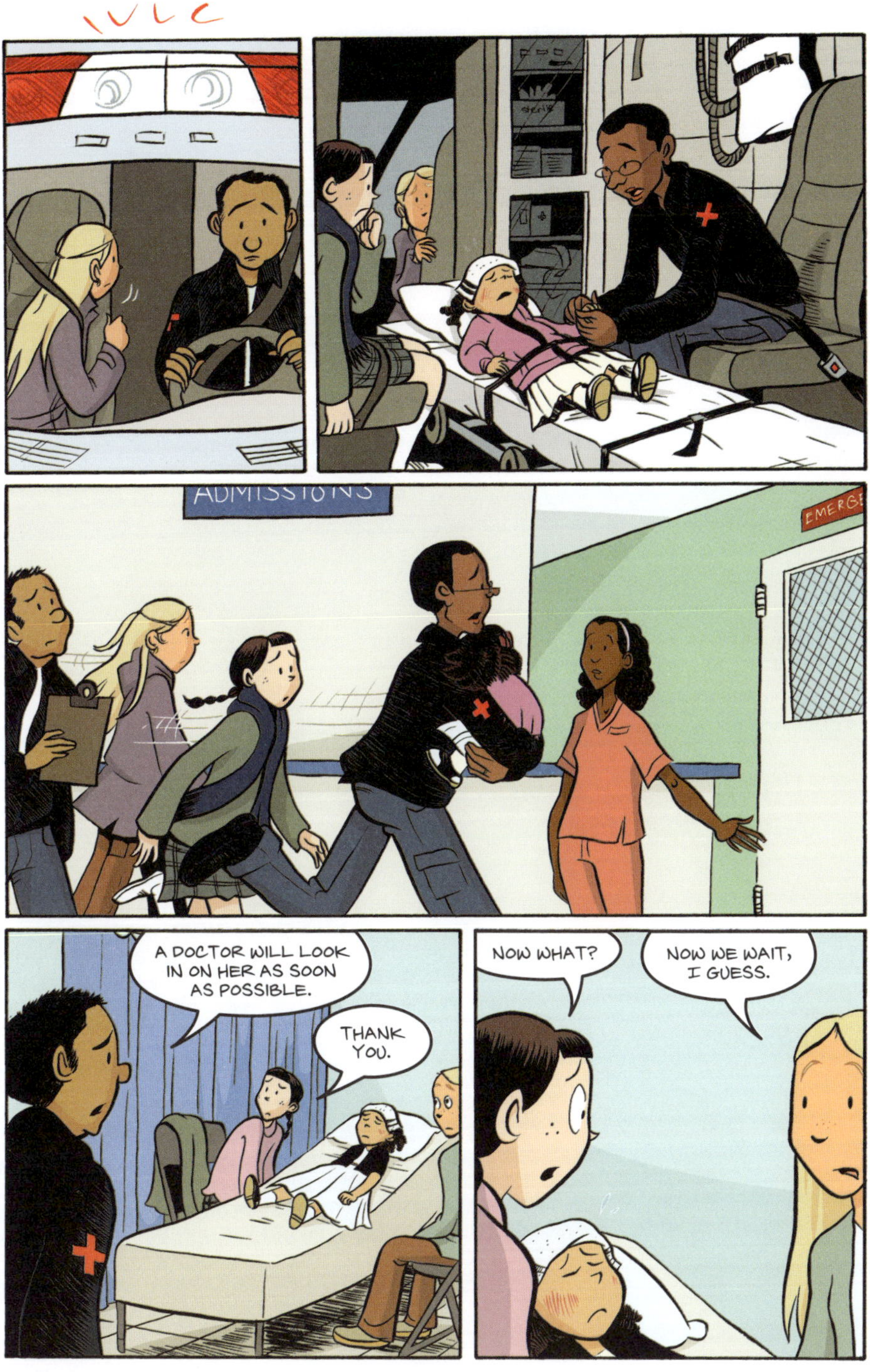

ADMISSIONS
EMERGE
A DOCTOR WILL LOOK IN ON HER AS SOON AS POSSIBLE.
THANK YOU.
NOW WHAT?
NOW WE WAIT, I GUESS.

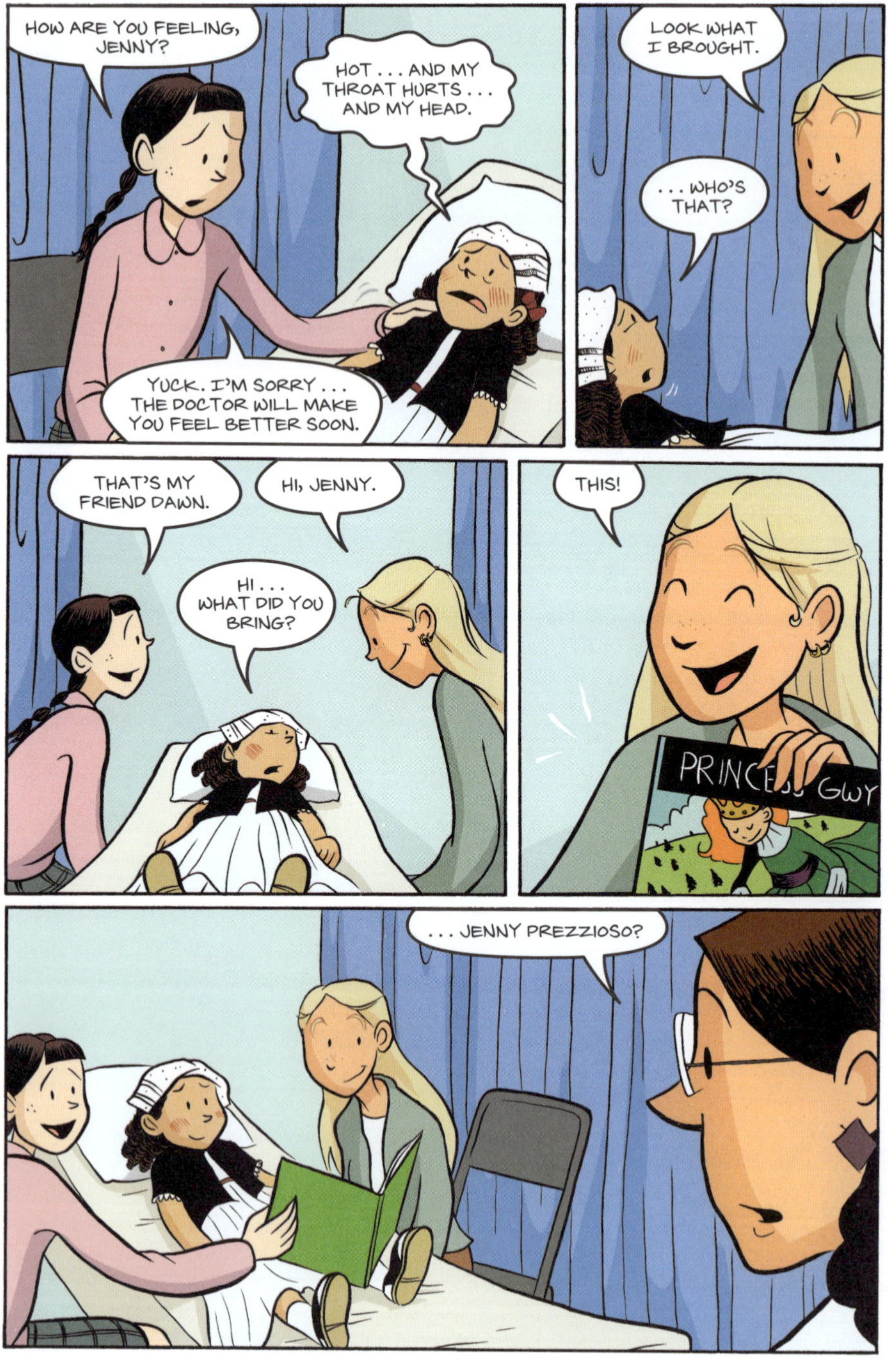
HOW ARE YOU FEELING, JENNY?
HOT . . . AND MY THROAT HURTS . . . AND MY HEAD.
YUCK. I'M SORRY . . . THE DOCTOR WILL MAKE YOU FEEL BETTER SOON.
LOOK WHAT I BROUGHT.
. . . WHO'S THAT?
THAT'S MY FRIEND DAWN.
HI, JENNY.
HI . . . WHAT DID YOU BRING?
THIS!
. . . JENNY PREZZIOSO?

GAG!
IT LOOKS LIKE A NICE CASE OF STREP THROAT. NOTHING TOO SERIOUS.
OH! THANK YOU SO MUCH!
WHERE ARE HER PARENTS?
HOPEFULLY ON THEIR WAY HERE, FROM CHATHAM.
OKAY. SHE CAN STAY HERE WHILE WE'RE RUNNING SOME TESTS. . . . I'D LIKE TO TALK TO THE PREZZIOSOS BEFORE JENNY LEAVES.
JUST A LITTLE LONGER TO WAIT . . . OKAY, JENNY?
NONONONONO!!!
. . . SHE'S ALREADY ON THE MEND!

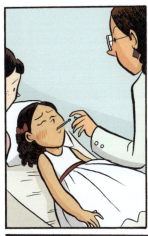

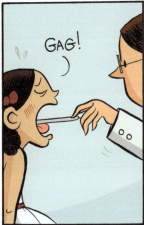

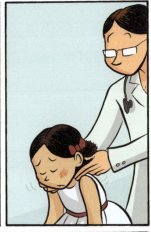

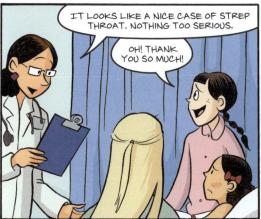

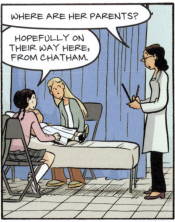

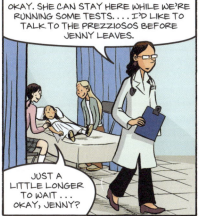

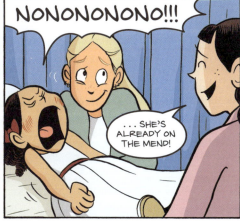

CHAPTER 12

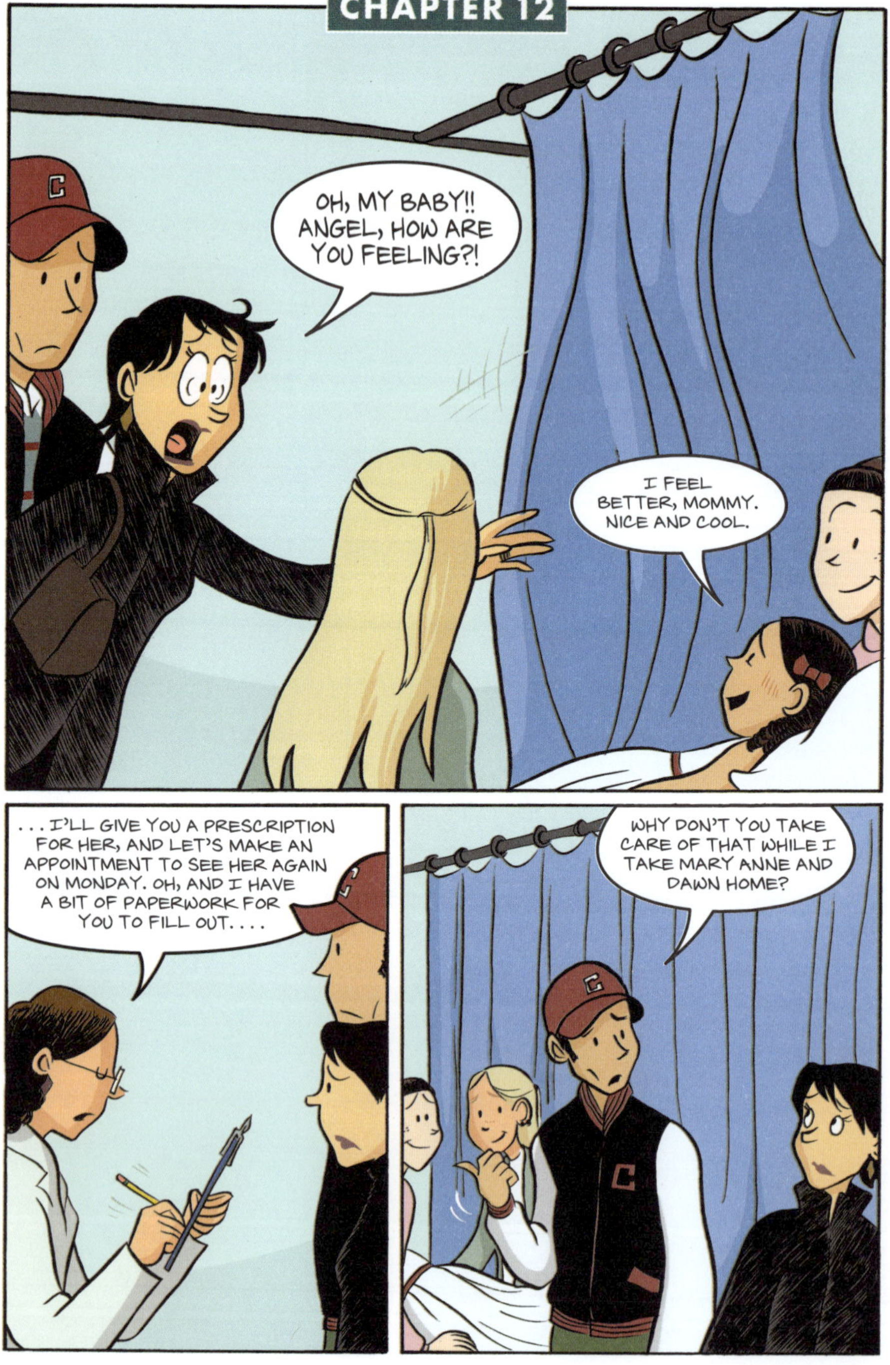
OH, MY BABY!! ANGEL, HOW ARE YOU FEELING?!
I FEEL BETTER, MOMMY. NICE AND COOL.
...I'LL GIVE YOU A PRESCRIPTION FOR HER, AND LET'S MAKE AN APPOINTMENT TO SEE HER AGAIN ON MONDAY. OH, AND I HAVE A BIT OF PAPERWORK FOR YOU TO FILL OUT....
WHY DON'T YOU TAKE CARE OF THAT WHILE I TAKE MARY ANNE AND DAWN HOME?

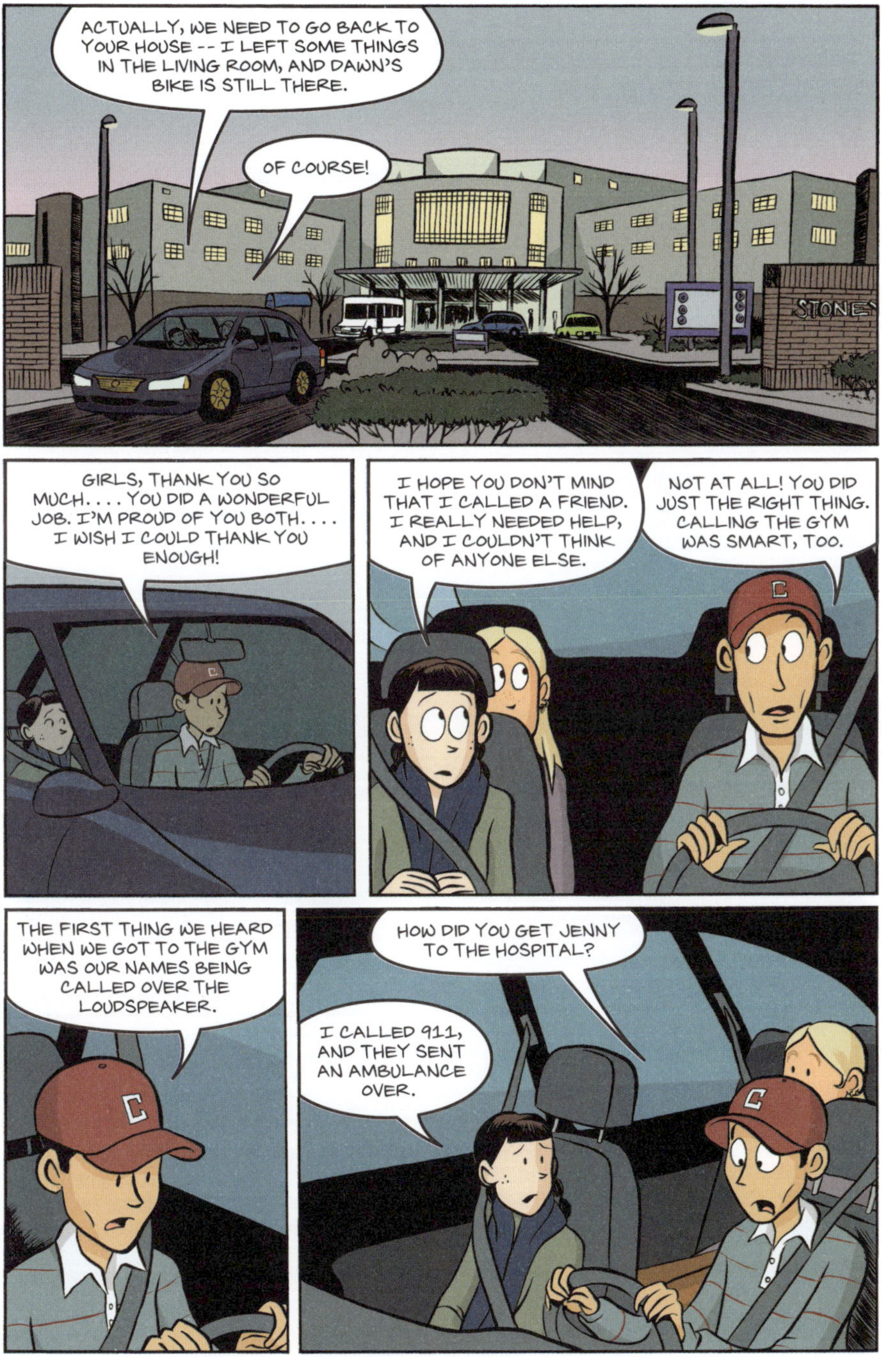
ACTUALLY, WE NEED TO GO BACK TO YOUR HOUSE -- I LEFT SOME THINGS IN THE LIVING ROOM, AND DAWN'S BIKE IS STILL THERE.
OF COURSE!
STONE
GIRLS, THANK YOU SO MUCH. . . . YOU DID A WONDERFUL JOB. I'M PROUD OF YOU BOTH. . . . I WISH I COULD THANK YOU ENOUGH!
I HOPE YOU DON'T MIND THAT I CALLED A FRIEND. I REALLY NEEDED HELP, AND I COULDN'T THINK OF ANYONE ELSE.
NOT AT ALL! YOU DID JUST THE RIGHT THING. CALLING THE GYM WAS SMART, TOO.
THE FIRST THING WE HEARD WHEN WE GOT TO THE GYM WAS OUR NAMES BEING CALLED OVER THE LOUDSPEAKER.
HOW DID YOU GET JENNY TO THE HOSPITAL?
I CALLED 911, AND THEY SENT AN AMBULANCE OVER.

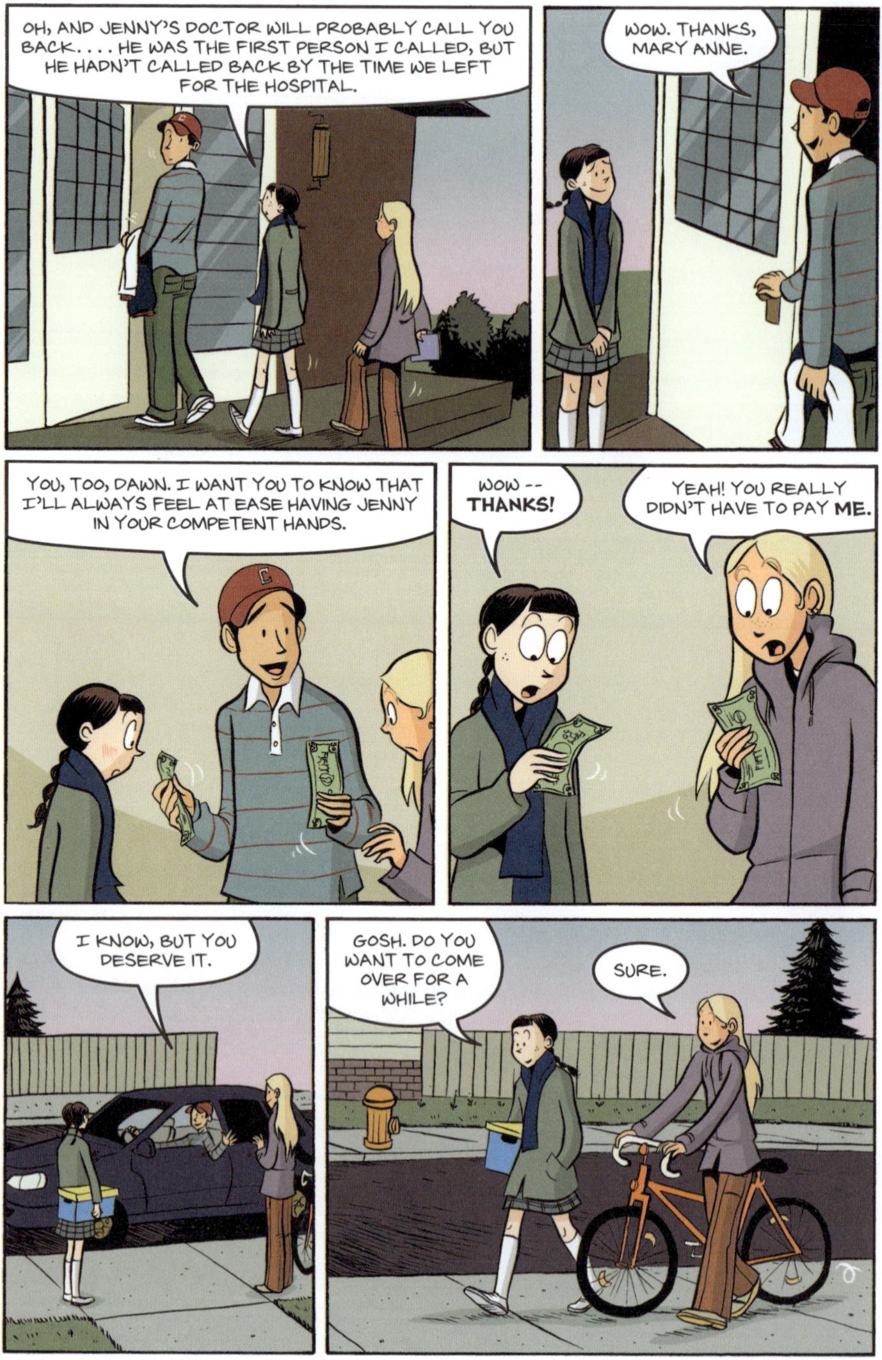
OH, AND JENNY'S DOCTOR WILL PROBABLY CALL YOU BACK. . . . HE WAS THE FIRST PERSON I CALLED, BUT HE HADN'T CALLED BACK BY THE TIME WE LEFT FOR THE HOSPITAL.
WOW. THANKS, MARY ANNE.
YOU, TOO, DAWN. I WANT YOU TO KNOW THAT I'LL ALWAYS FEEL AT EASE HAVING JENNY IN YOUR COMPETENT HANDS.
WOW -- **THANKS!**
YEAH! YOU REALLY DIDN'T HAVE TO PAY **ME.**
I KNOW, BUT YOU DESERVE IT.
GOSH. DO YOU WANT TO COME OVER FOR A WHILE?
SURE.

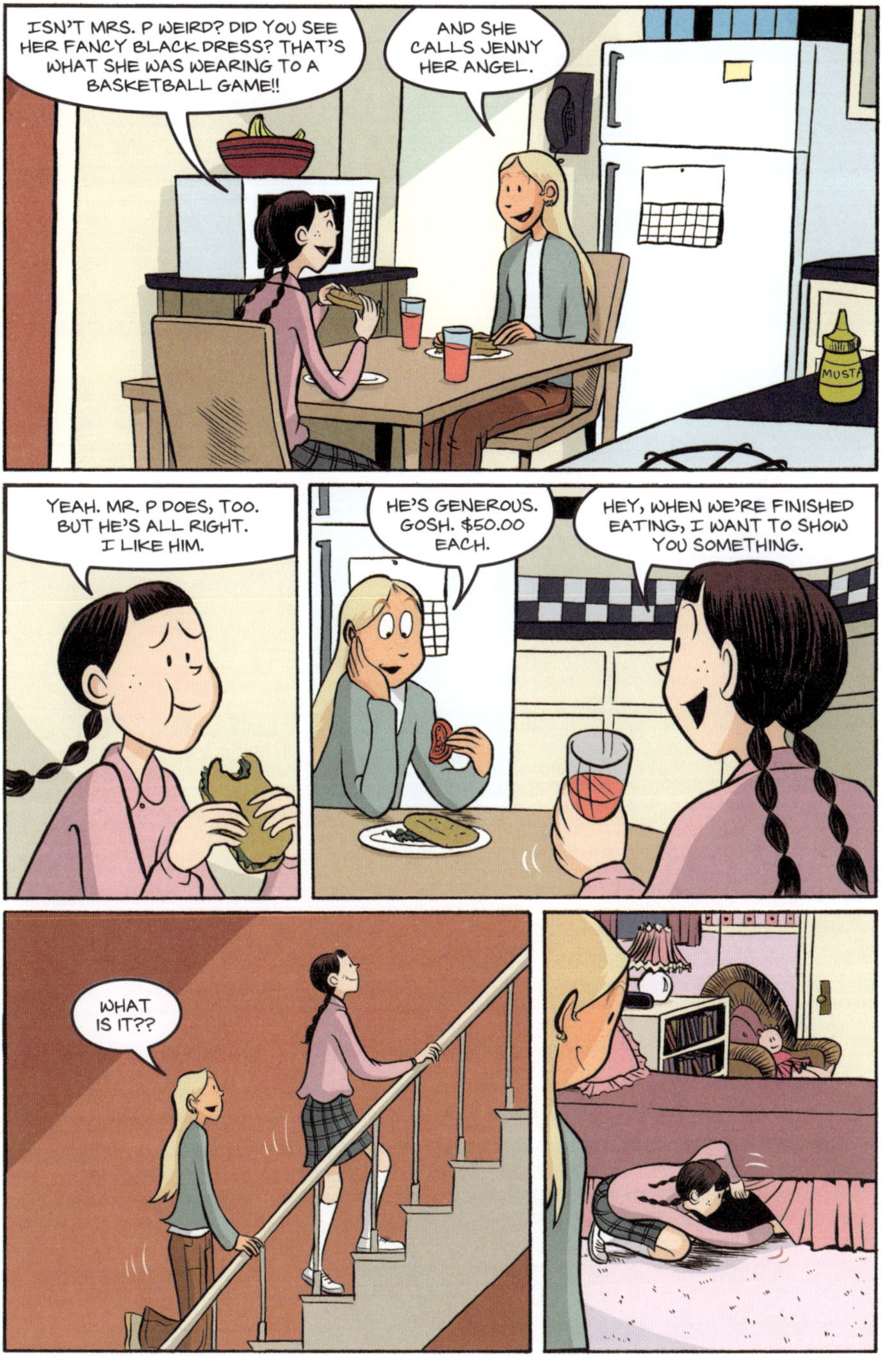
ISN'T MRS. P WEIRD? DID YOU SEE HER FANCY BLACK DRESS? THAT'S WHAT SHE WAS WEARING TO A BASKETBALL GAME!!
AND SHE CALLS JENNY HER ANGEL.
YEAH. MR. P DOES, TOO. BUT HE'S ALL RIGHT. I LIKE HIM.
HE'S GENEROUS. GOSH. $50.00 EACH.
HEY, WHEN WE'RE FINISHED EATING, I WANT TO SHOW YOU SOMETHING.
WHAT IS IT??

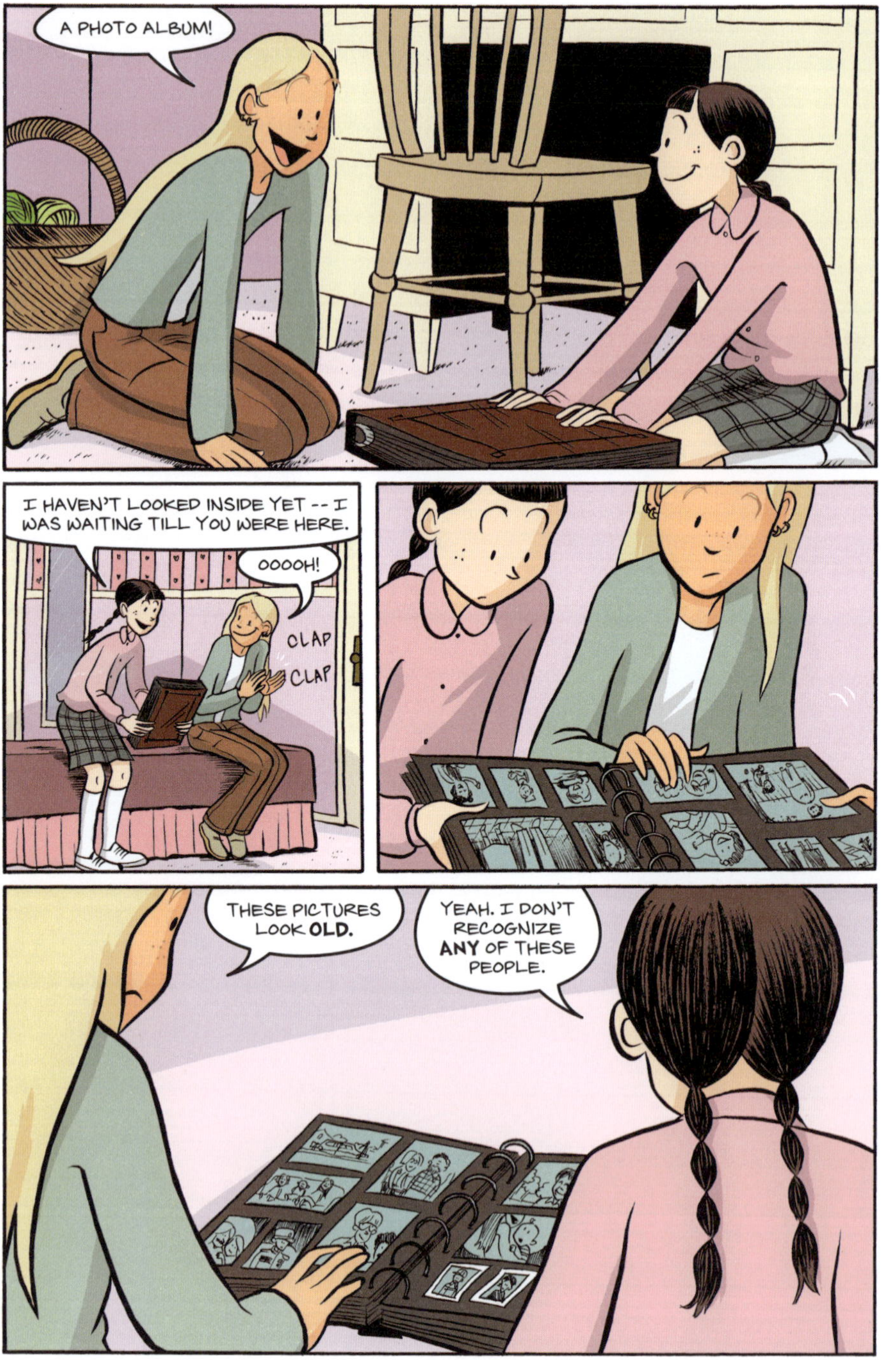
A PHOTO ALBUM!
I HAVEN'T LOOKED INSIDE YET -- I WAS WAITING TILL YOU WERE HERE.
OOOOH!
CLAP
CLAP
THESE PICTURES LOOK **OLD.**
YEAH. I DON'T RECOGNIZE **ANY** OF THESE PEOPLE.

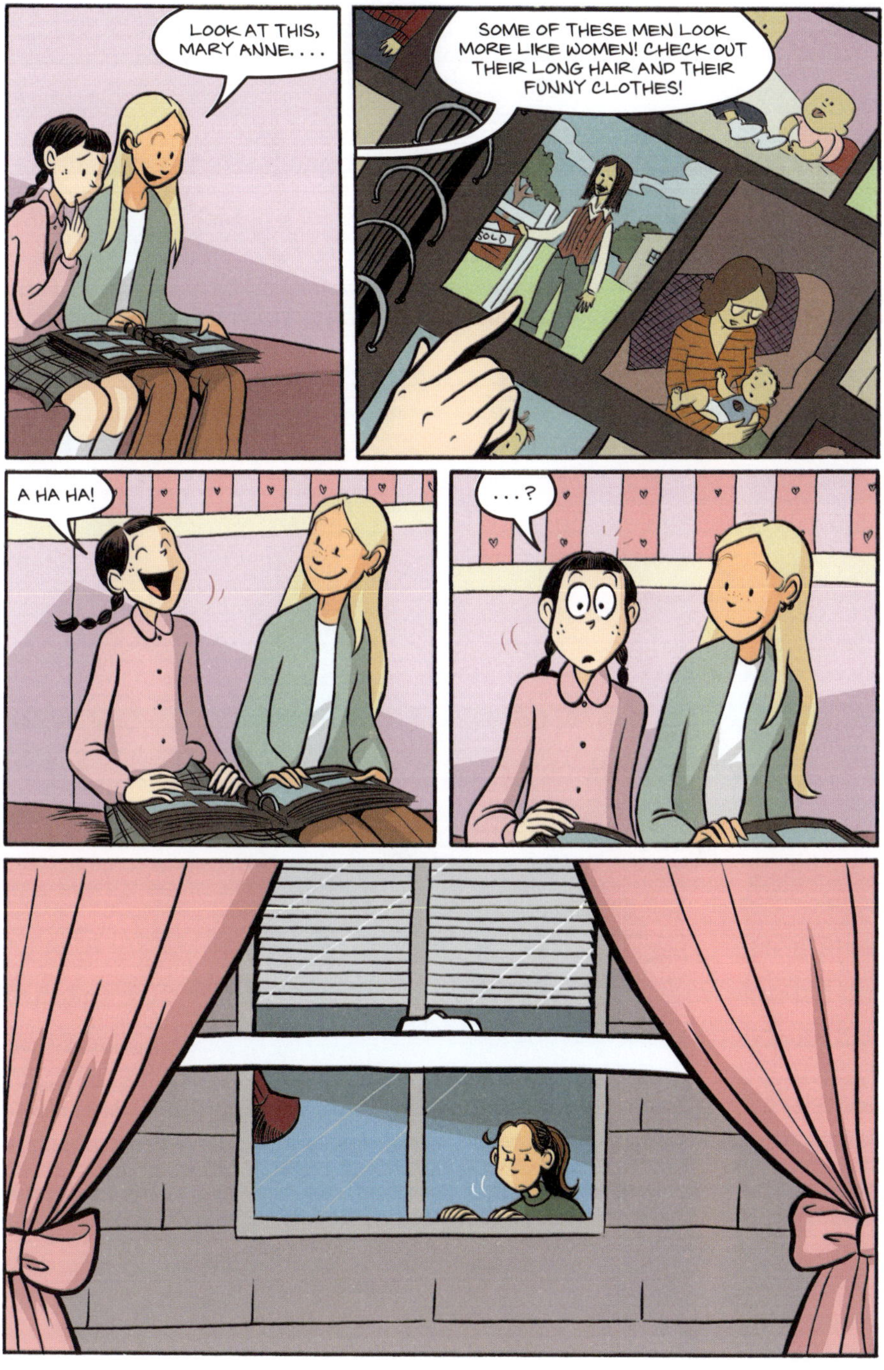
LOOK AT THIS, MARY ANNE. . . .
SOME OF THESE MEN LOOK MORE LIKE WOMEN! CHECK OUT THEIR LONG HAIR AND THEIR FUNNY CLOTHES!
SOLD
A HA HA!
. . . ?

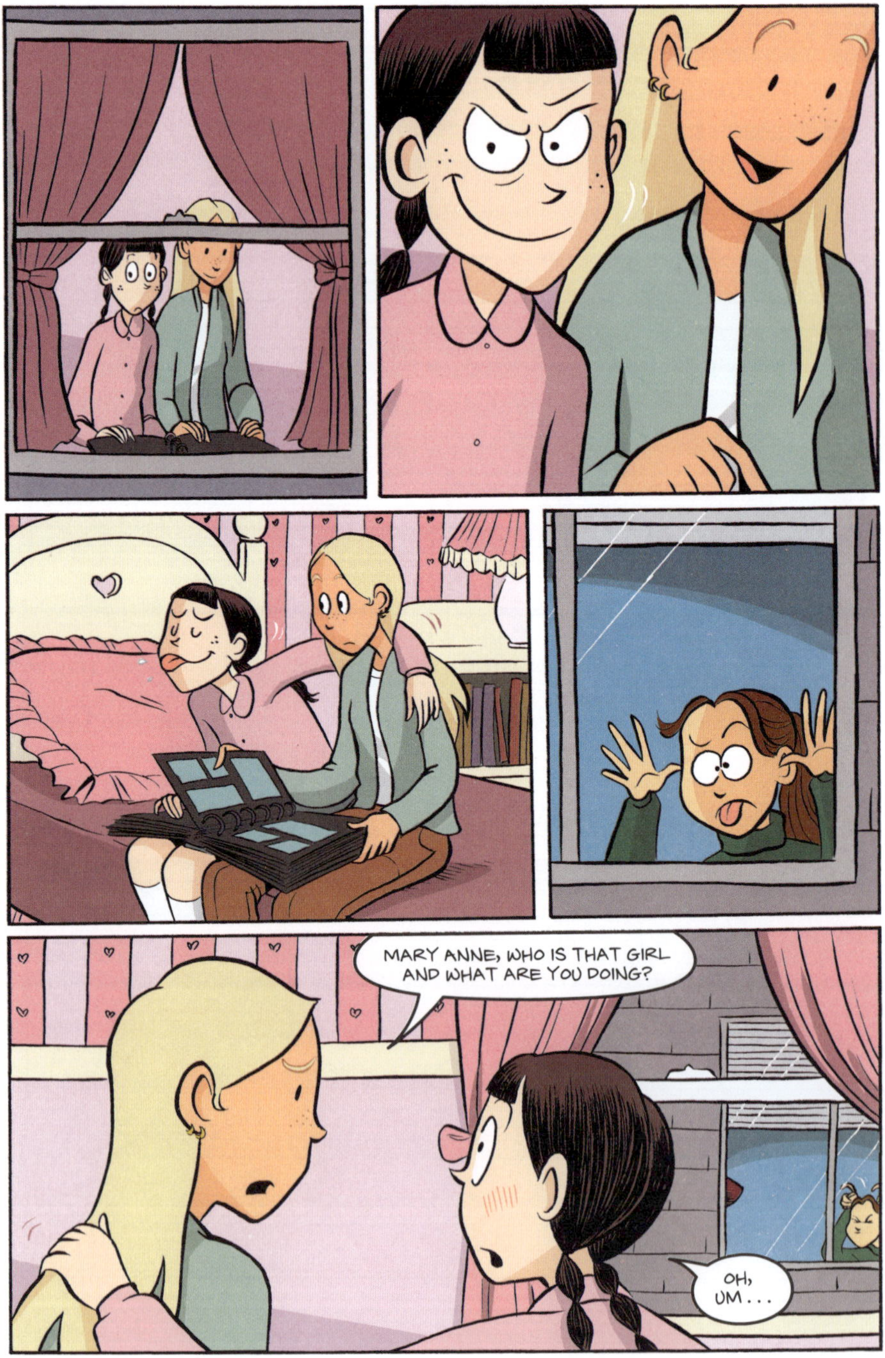
MARY ANNE, WHO IS THAT GIRL AND WHAT ARE YOU DOING?
OH, UM . . .

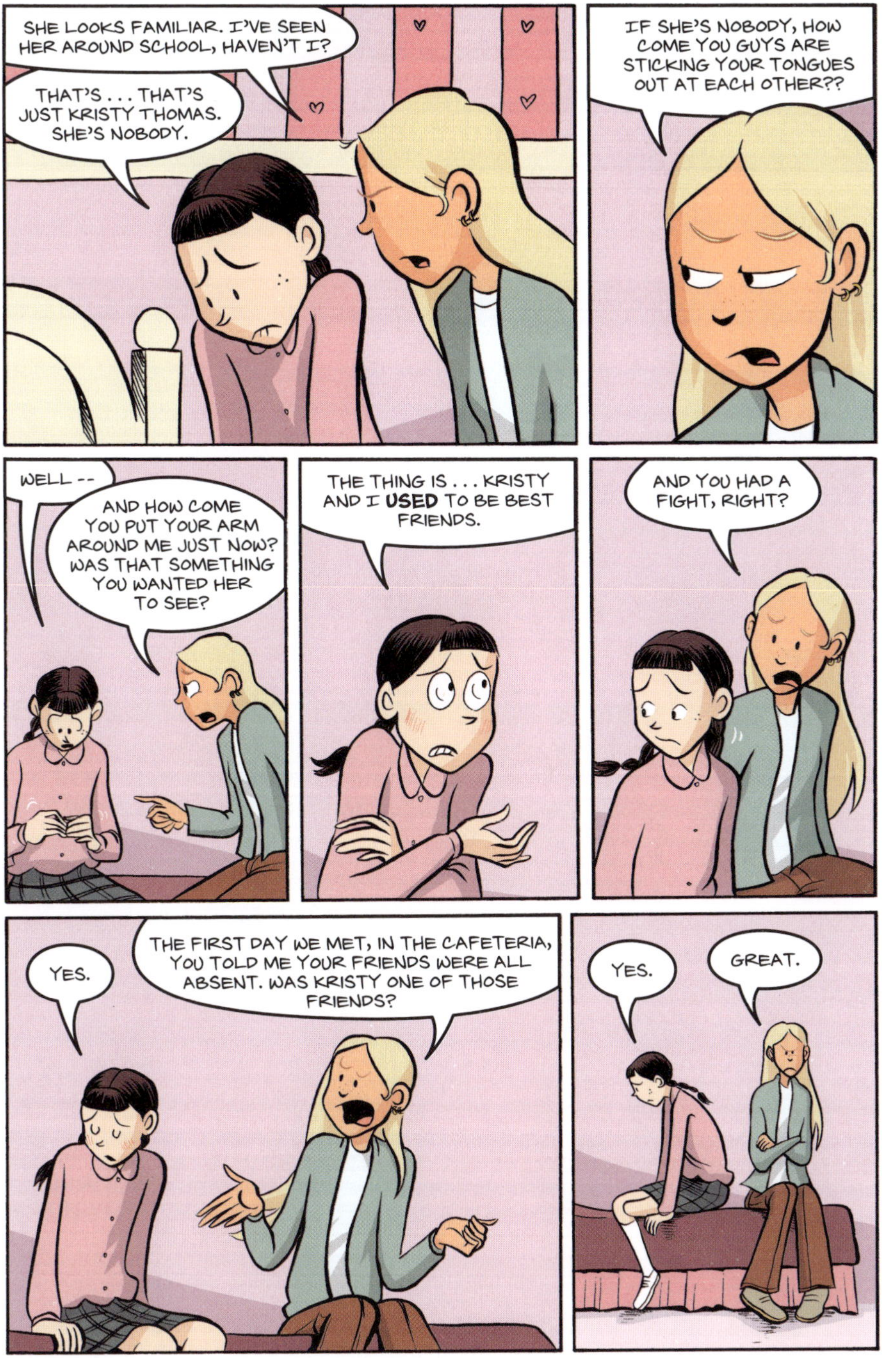
SHE LOOKS FAMILIAR. I'VE SEEN HER AROUND SCHOOL, HAVEN'T I?
THAT'S . . . THAT'S JUST KRISTY THOMAS. SHE'S NOBODY.
IF SHE'S NOBODY, HOW COME YOU GUYS ARE STICKING YOUR TONGUES OUT AT EACH OTHER??
WELL --
AND HOW COME YOU PUT YOUR ARM AROUND ME JUST NOW? WAS THAT SOMETHING YOU WANTED HER TO SEE?
THE THING IS . . . KRISTY AND I **USED** TO BE BEST FRIENDS.
AND YOU HAD A FIGHT, RIGHT?
YES.
THE FIRST DAY WE MET, IN THE CAFETERIA, YOU TOLD ME YOUR FRIENDS WERE ALL ABSENT. WAS KRISTY ONE OF THOSE FRIENDS?
YES.
GREAT.

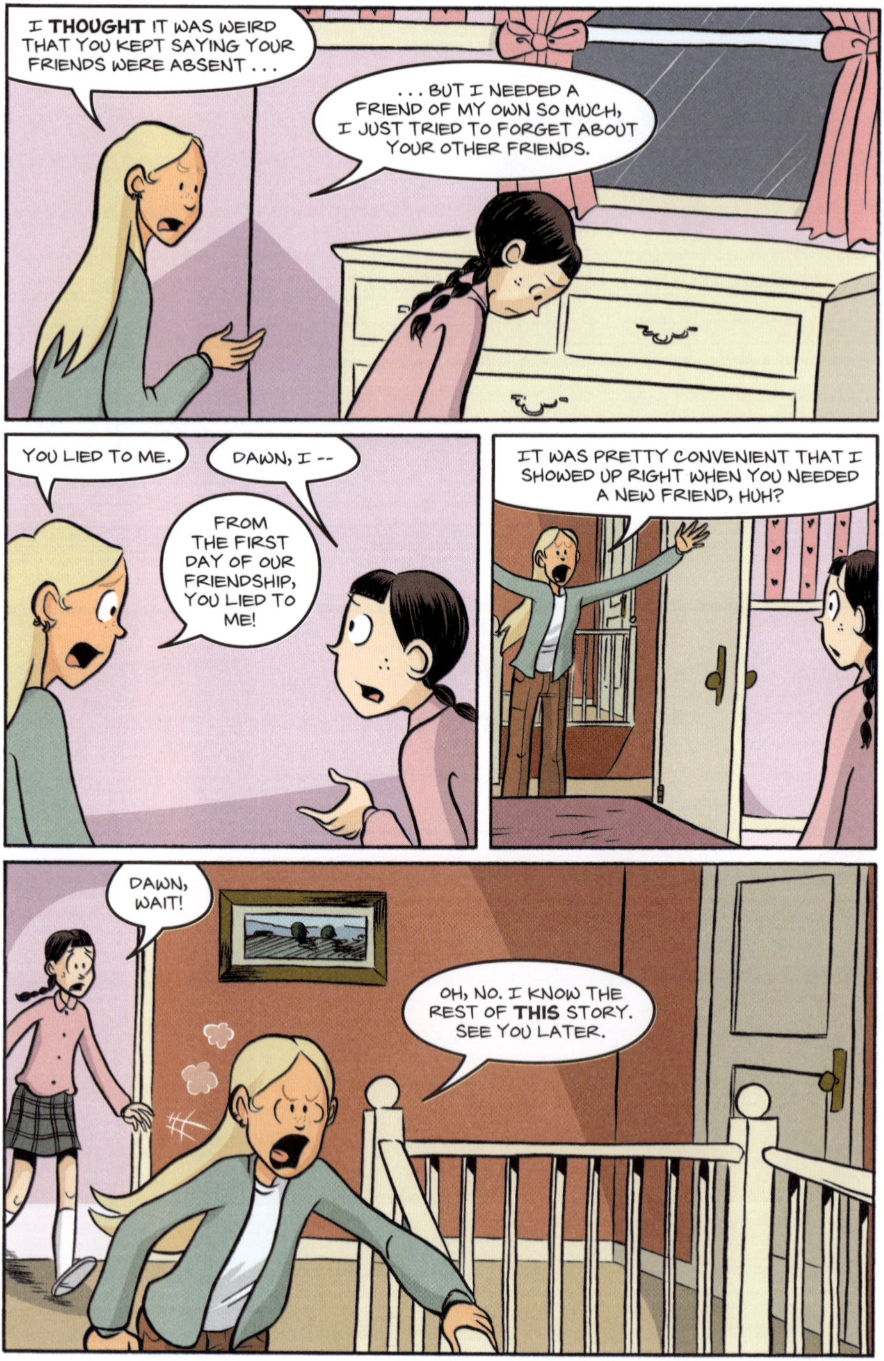
I **THOUGHT** IT WAS WEIRD THAT YOU KEPT SAYING YOUR FRIENDS WERE ABSENT . . .
. . . BUT I NEEDED A FRIEND OF MY OWN SO MUCH, I JUST TRIED TO FORGET ABOUT YOUR OTHER FRIENDS.
YOU LIED TO ME.
DAWN, I --
FROM THE FIRST DAY OF OUR FRIENDSHIP, YOU LIED TO ME!
IT WAS PRETTY CONVENIENT THAT I SHOWED UP RIGHT WHEN YOU NEEDED A NEW FRIEND, HUH?
DAWN, WAIT!
OH, NO. I KNOW THE REST OF **THIS** STORY. SEE YOU LATER.

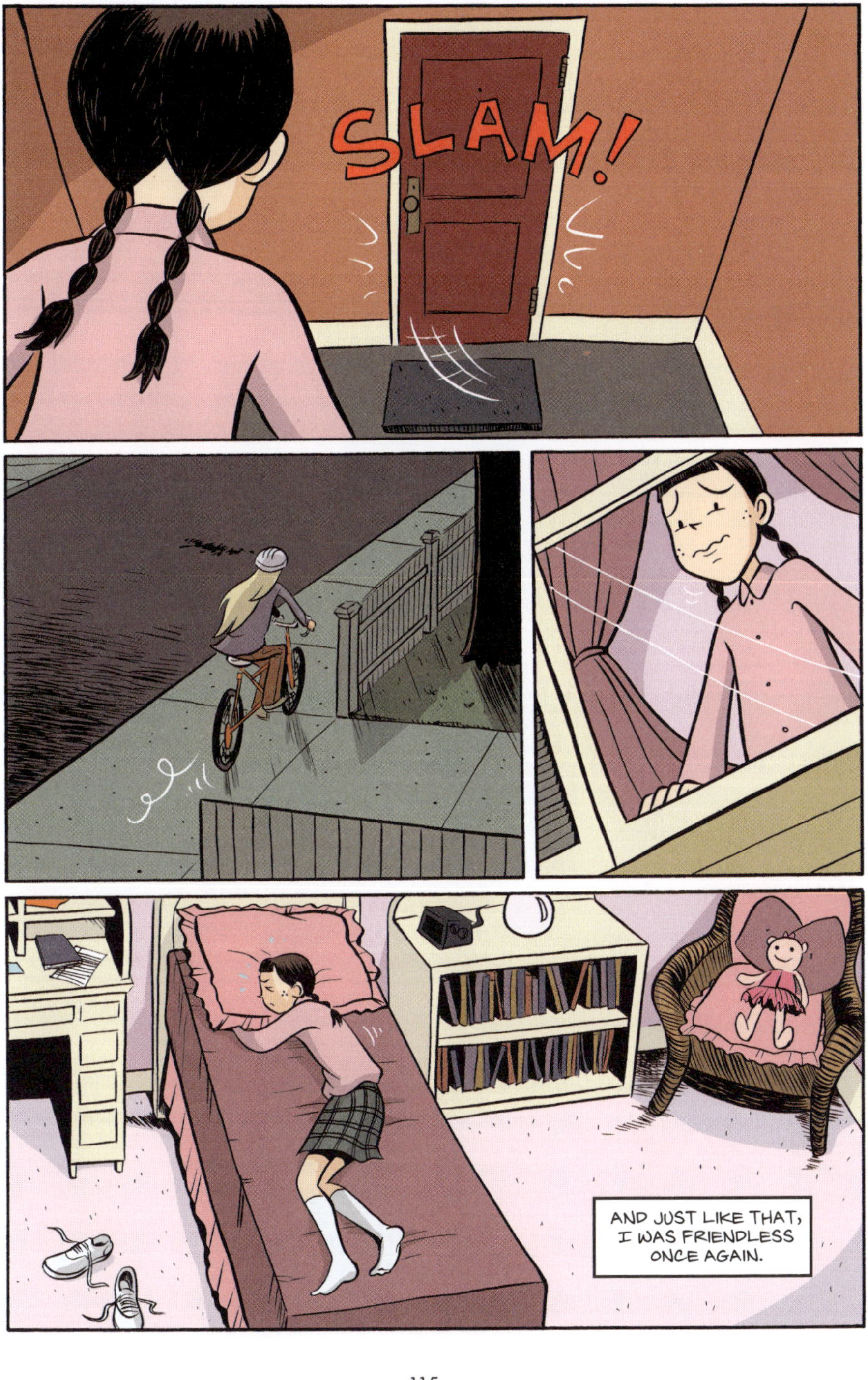
SLAM!
AND JUST LIKE THAT, I WAS FRIENDLESS ONCE AGAIN.

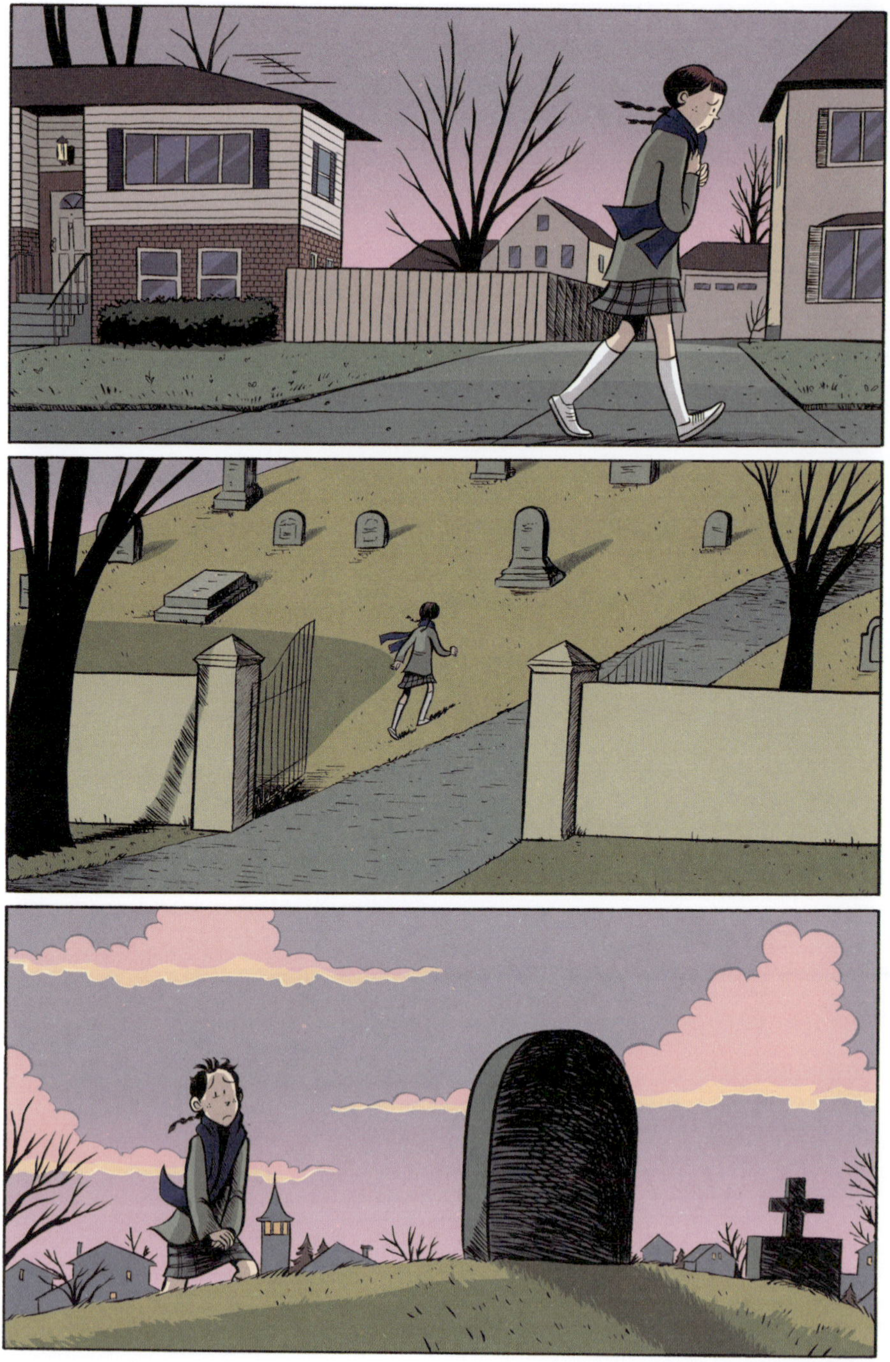

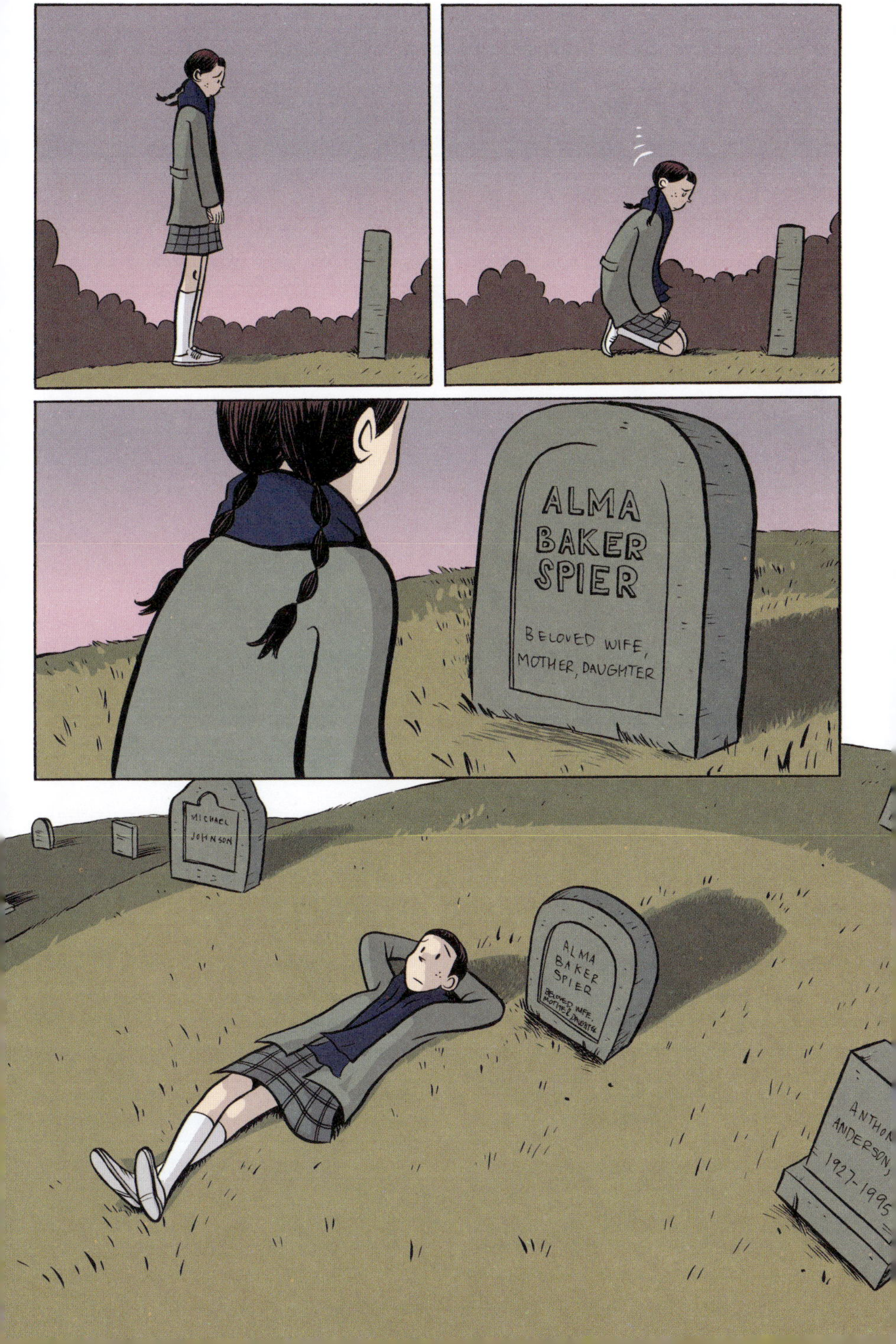
ALMA BAKER SPIER
BELOVED WIFE, MOTHER, DAUGHTER
MICHAEL JOHNSON
ALMA BAKER SPIER
ANDERSON,
1927-1995

CHAPTER 13

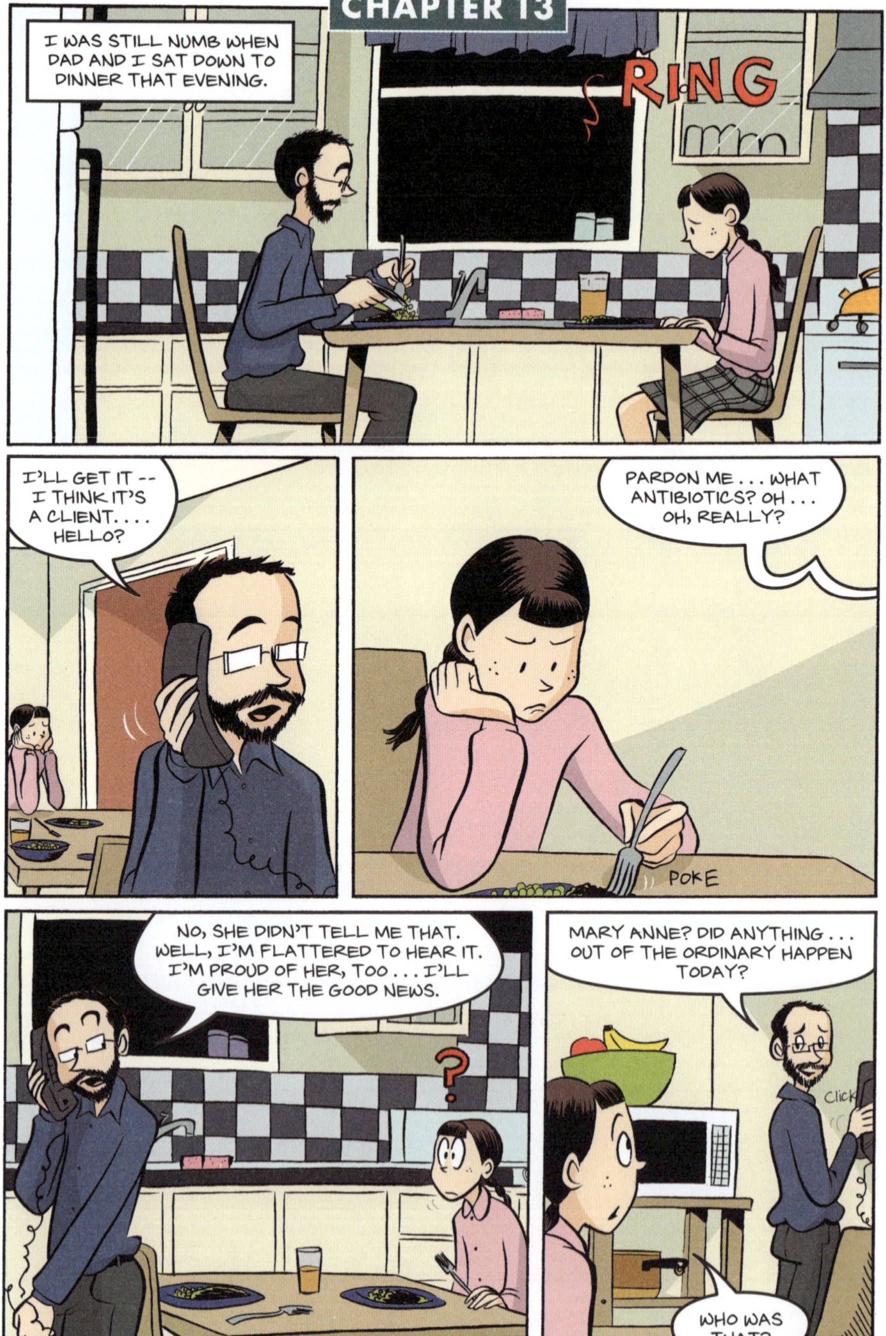

I WAS STILL NUMB WHEN DAD AND I SAT DOWN TO DINNER THAT EVENING.
RING
I'LL GET IT -- I THINK IT'S A CLIENT. . . . HELLO?
PARDON ME . . . WHAT ANTIBIOTICS? OH . . . OH, REALLY?
POKE
NO, SHE DIDN'T TELL ME THAT. WELL, I'M FLATTERED TO HEAR IT. I'M PROUD OF HER, TOO . . . I'LL GIVE HER THE GOOD NEWS.
?
MARY ANNE? DID ANYTHING . . . OUT OF THE ORDINARY HAPPEN TODAY?
CLICK
WHO WAS THAT?

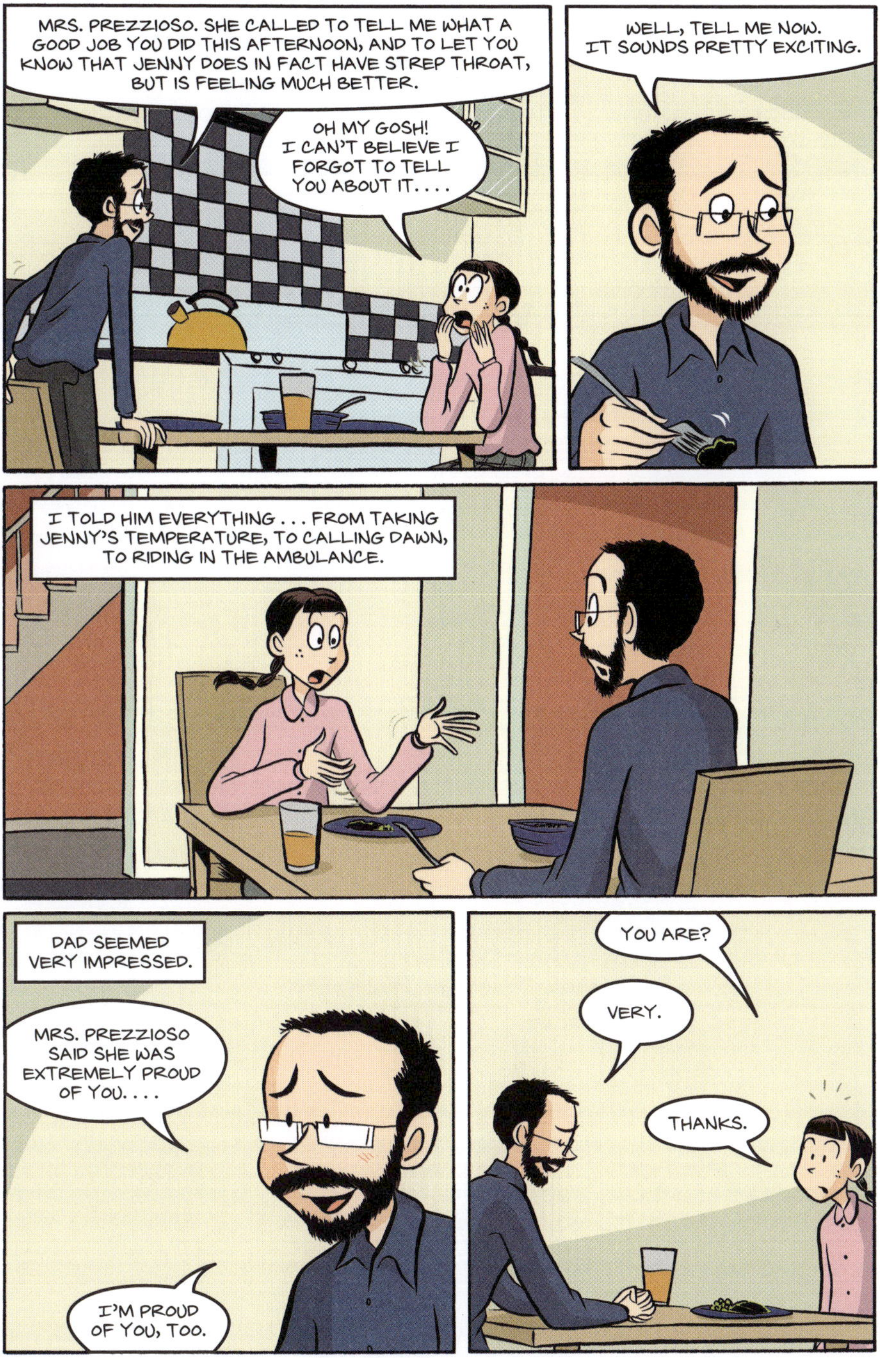
MRS. PREZZIOSO. SHE CALLED TO TELL ME WHAT A GOOD JOB YOU DID THIS AFTERNOON, AND TO LET YOU KNOW THAT JENNY DOES IN FACT HAVE STREP THROAT, BUT IS FEELING MUCH BETTER.
OH MY GOSH! I CAN'T BELIEVE I FORGOT TO TELL YOU ABOUT IT. . . .
WELL, TELL ME NOW. IT SOUNDS PRETTY EXCITING.
I TOLD HIM EVERYTHING . . . FROM TAKING JENNY'S TEMPERATURE, TO CALLING DAWN, TO RIDING IN THE AMBULANCE.
DAD SEEMED VERY IMPRESSED.
MRS. PREZZIOSO SAID SHE WAS EXTREMELY PROUD OF YOU. . . .
I'M PROUD OF YOU, TOO.
YOU ARE?
VERY.
THANKS.

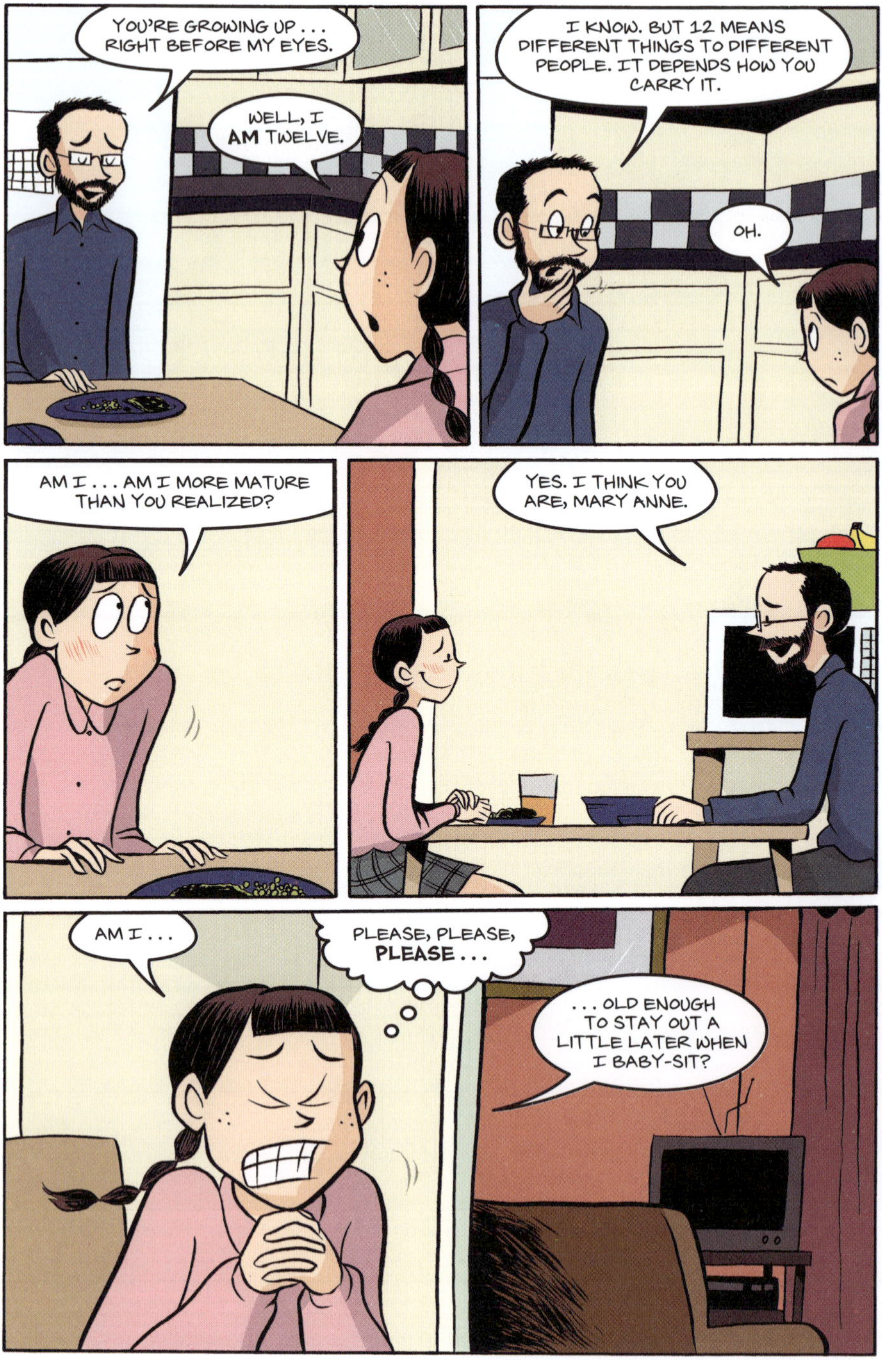
YOU'RE GROWING UP . . .
RIGHT BEFORE MY EYES.
WELL, I **AM** TWELVE.
I KNOW. BUT 12 MEANS DIFFERENT THINGS TO DIFFERENT PEOPLE. IT DEPENDS HOW YOU CARRY IT.
OH.
AM I . . . AM I MORE MATURE THAN YOU REALIZED?
YES. I THINK YOU ARE, MARY ANNE.
AM I . . .
PLEASE, PLEASE, **PLEASE . . .**
. . . OLD ENOUGH TO STAY OUT A LITTLE LATER WHEN I BABY-SIT?

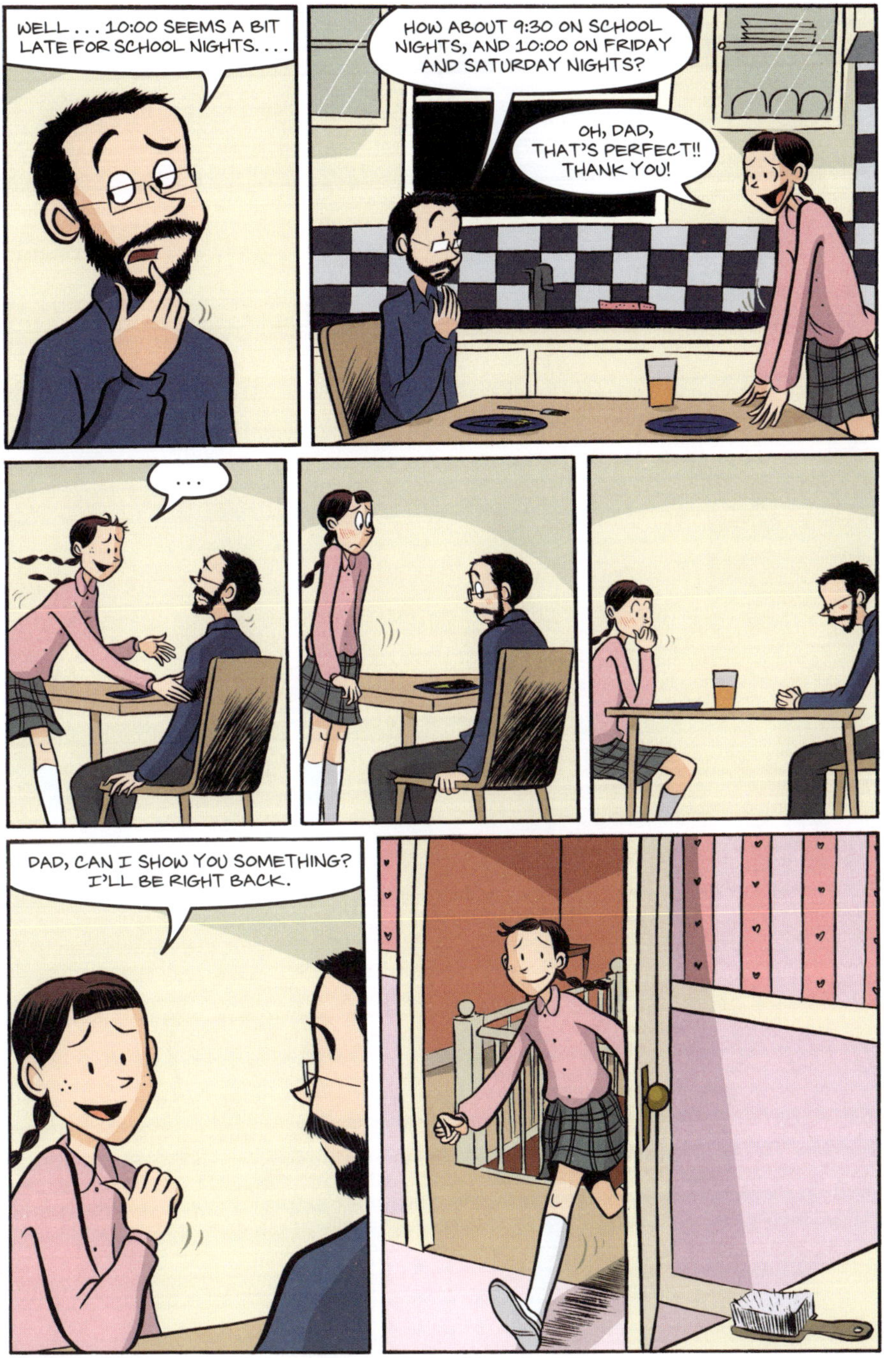
WELL . . . 10:00 SEEMS A BIT LATE FOR SCHOOL NIGHTS. . . .
HOW ABOUT 9:30 ON SCHOOL NIGHTS, AND 10:00 ON FRIDAY AND SATURDAY NIGHTS?
OH, DAD, THAT'S PERFECT!! THANK YOU!
. . .
DAD, CAN I SHOW YOU SOMETHING? I'LL BE RIGHT BACK.

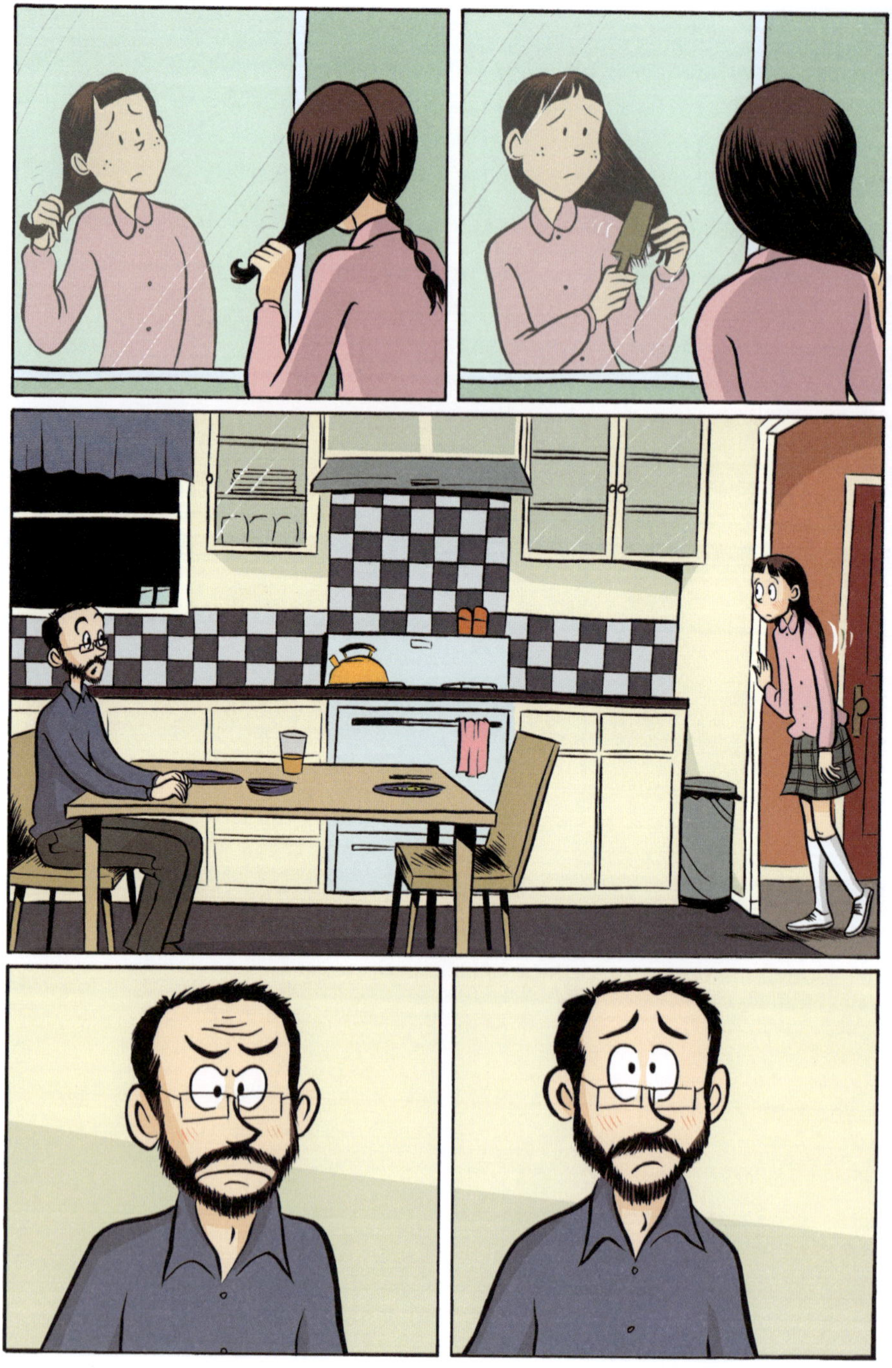

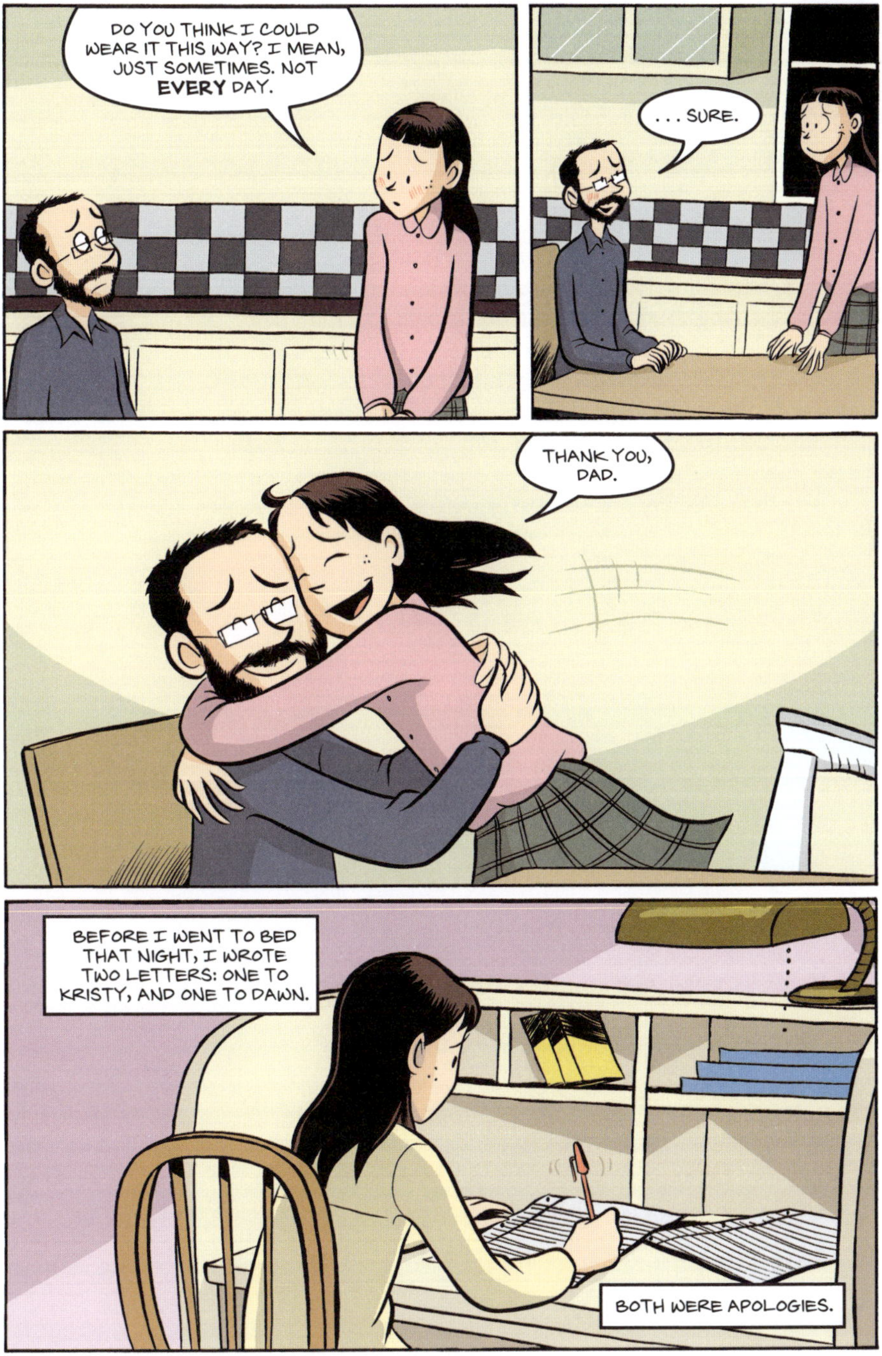
DO YOU THINK I COULD WEAR IT THIS WAY? I MEAN, JUST SOMETIMES. NOT **EVERY** DAY.
. . . SURE.
THANK YOU, DAD.
BEFORE I WENT TO BED THAT NIGHT, I WROTE TWO LETTERS: ONE TO KRISTY, AND ONE TO DAWN.
BOTH WERE APOLOGIES.

Sunday, February 8

   The members of The Baby-sitters Club have been enemies for almost a month now. I can't believe it. Claudia, Kristy, and Mary Anne — I hope you all read what I'm writing, because I think our fight is dumb, and you should know that. I thought you guys were my friends, but I guess not.

I'm writing this because tomorrow the four of us have to help out at Jamie Newton's birthday party, and I think it's going to be a disaster. I hope you read this before then because I think we should be prepared for the worst.

P.S. If anybody wants to make up, I'm ready.

Stacey

CHAPTER 14

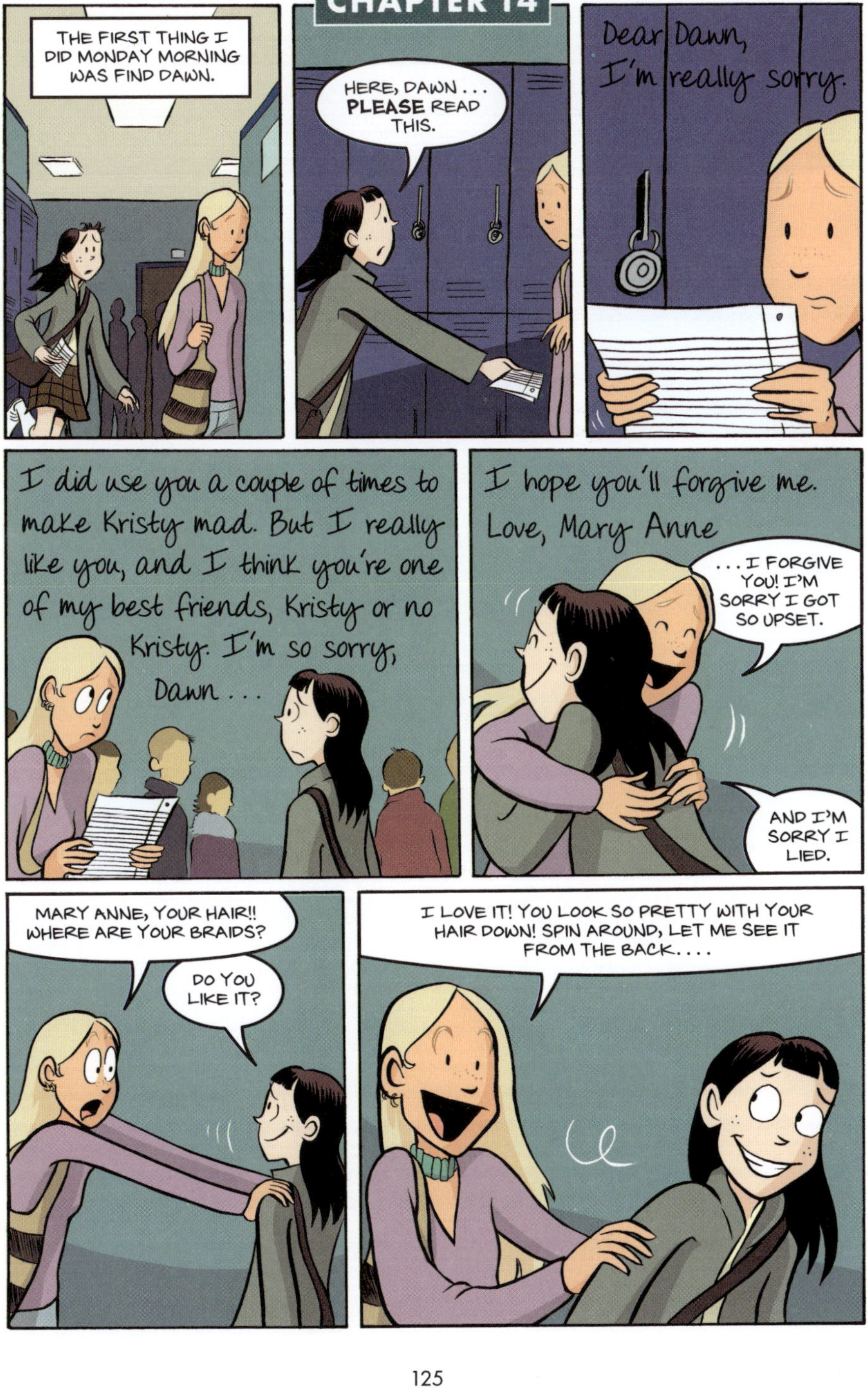
THE FIRST THING I DID MONDAY MORNING WAS FIND DAWN.
HERE, DAWN . . . PLEASE READ THIS.
Dear Dawn,
I'm really sorry.
I did use you a couple of times to make Kristy mad. But I really like you, and I think you're one of my best friends, Kristy or no Kristy. I'm so sorry, Dawn . . .
I hope you'll forgive me.
Love, Mary Anne
. . . I FORGIVE YOU! I'M SORRY I GOT SO UPSET.
AND I'M SORRY I LIED.
MARY ANNE, YOUR HAIR!! WHERE ARE YOUR BRAIDS?
DO YOU LIKE IT?
I LOVE IT! YOU LOOK SO PRETTY WITH YOUR HAIR DOWN! SPIN AROUND, LET ME SEE IT FROM THE BACK. . . .

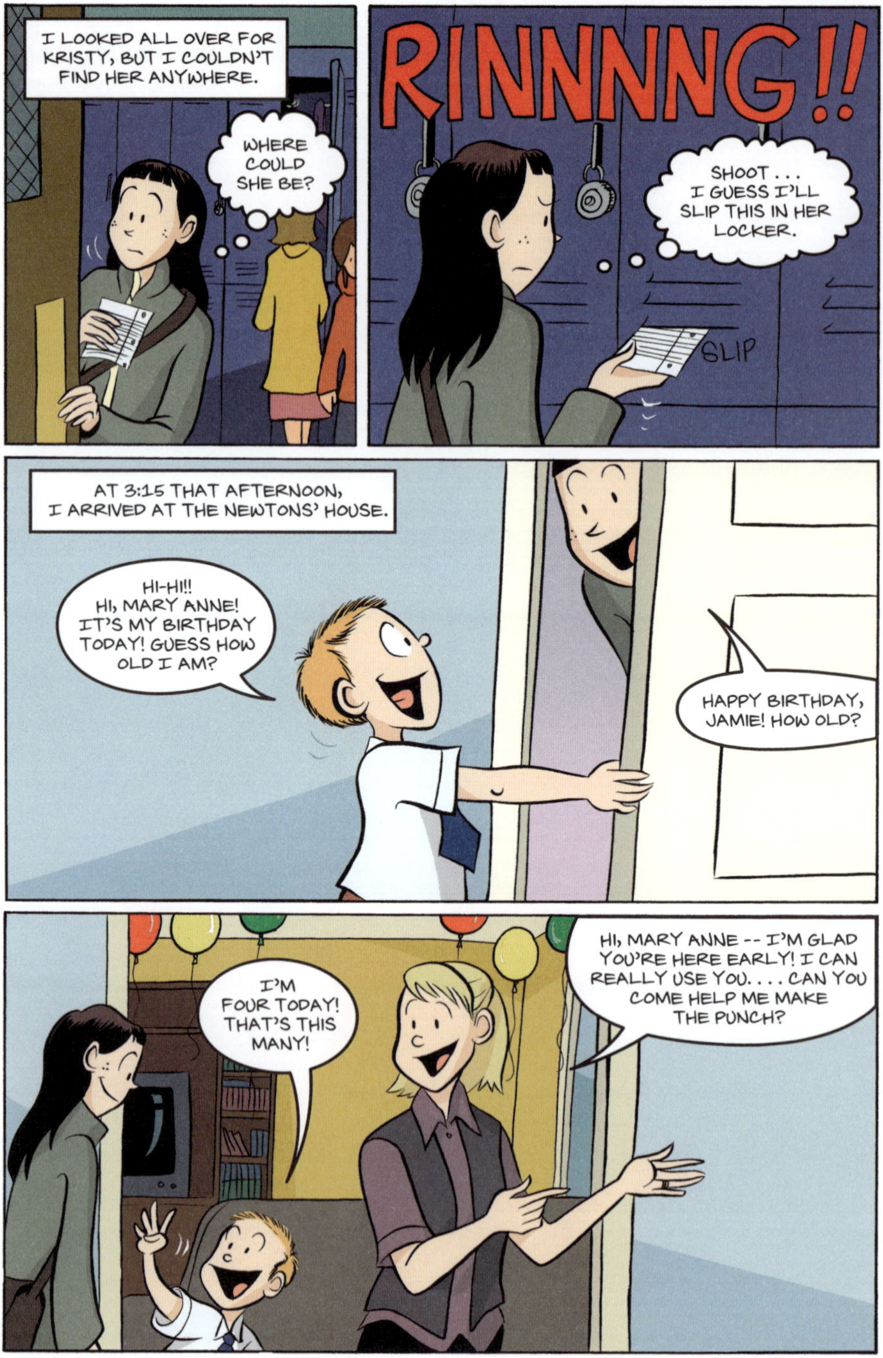
I LOOKED ALL OVER FOR KRISTY, BUT I COULDN'T FIND HER ANYWHERE.
WHERE COULD SHE BE?
RINNNNG!!
SHOOT . . . I GUESS I'LL SLIP THIS IN HER LOCKER.
SLIP
AT 3:15 THAT AFTERNOON, I ARRIVED AT THE NEWTONS' HOUSE.
HI-HI!! HI, MARY ANNE! IT'S MY BIRTHDAY TODAY! GUESS HOW OLD I AM?
HAPPY BIRTHDAY, JAMIE! HOW OLD?
I'M FOUR TODAY! THAT'S THIS MANY!
HI, MARY ANNE -- I'M GLAD YOU'RE HERE EARLY! I CAN REALLY USE YOU. . . . CAN YOU COME HELP ME MAKE THE PUNCH?

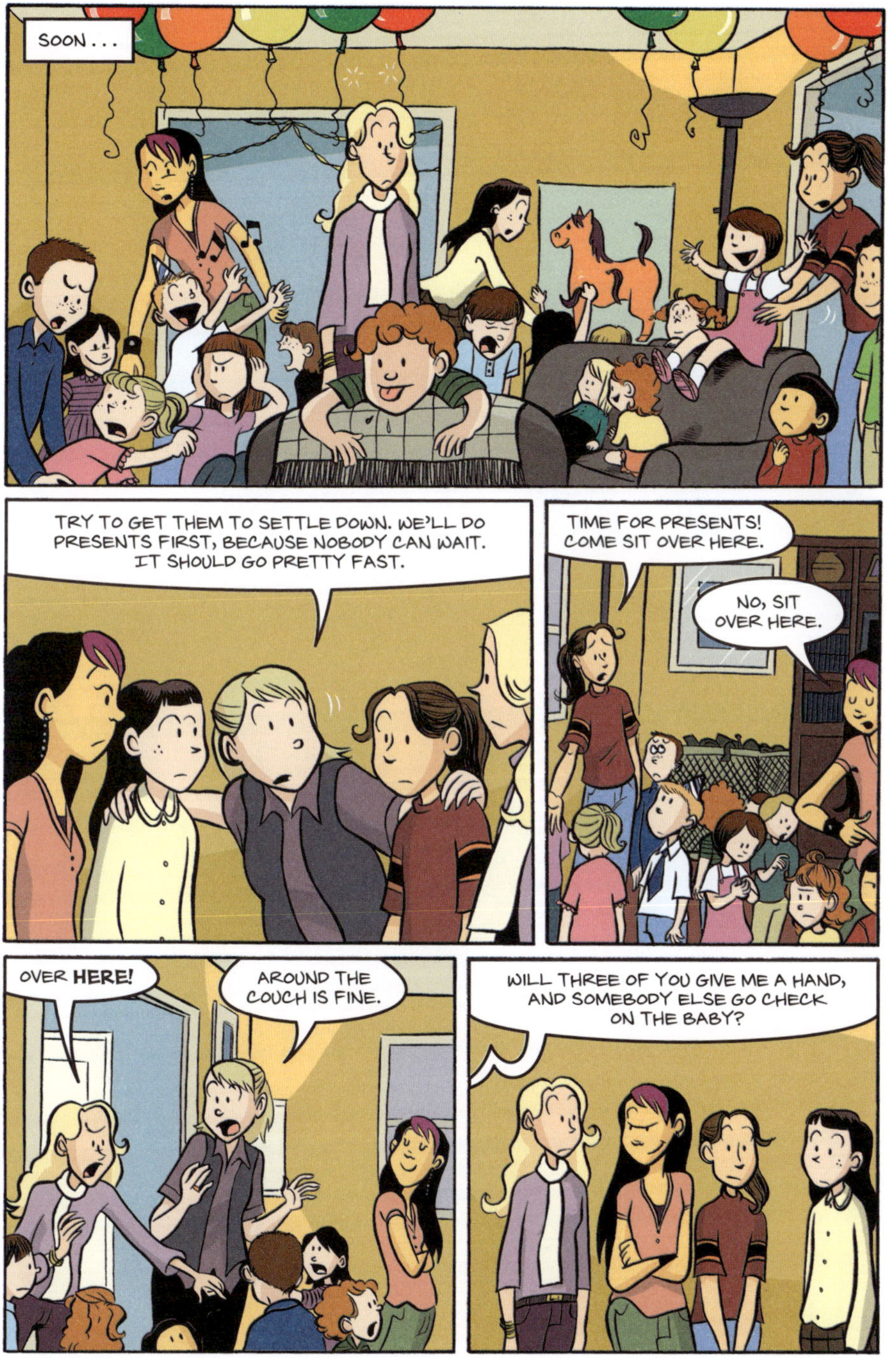
SOON . . .
TRY TO GET THEM TO SETTLE DOWN. WE'LL DO PRESENTS FIRST, BECAUSE NOBODY CAN WAIT. IT SHOULD GO PRETTY FAST.
TIME FOR PRESENTS! COME SIT OVER HERE.
NO, SIT OVER HERE.
OVER **HERE!**
AROUND THE COUCH IS FINE.
WILL THREE OF YOU GIVE ME A HAND, AND SOMEBODY ELSE GO CHECK ON THE BABY?

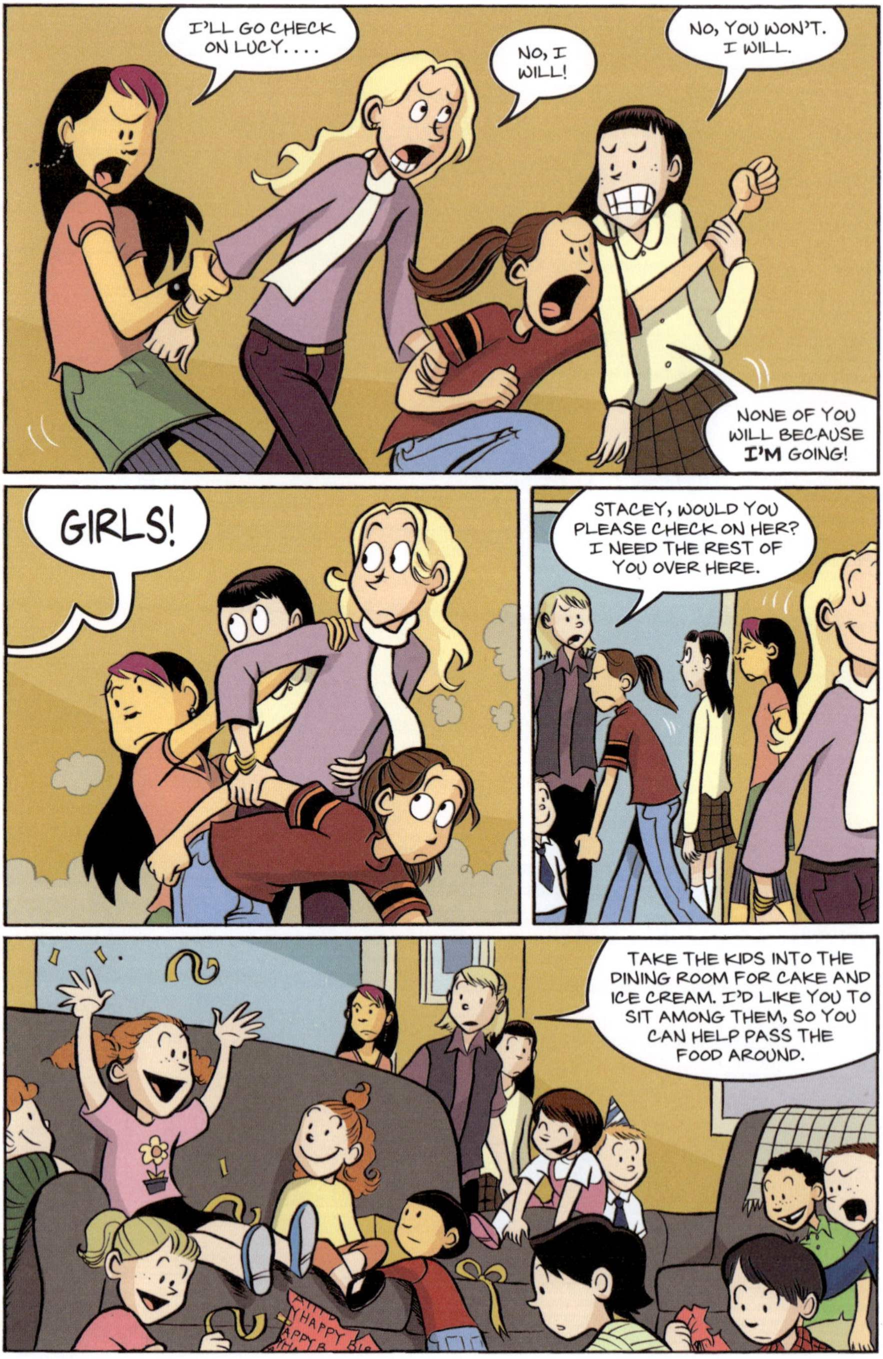
I'LL GO CHECK ON LUCY....
NO, I WILL!
NO, YOU WON'T. I WILL.
NONE OF YOU WILL BECAUSE **I'M** GOING!
GIRLS!
STACEY, WOULD YOU PLEASE CHECK ON HER? I NEED THE REST OF YOU OVER HERE.
TAKE THE KIDS INTO THE DINING ROOM FOR CAKE AND ICE CREAM. I'D LIKE YOU TO SIT AMONG THEM, SO YOU CAN HELP PASS THE FOOD AROUND.

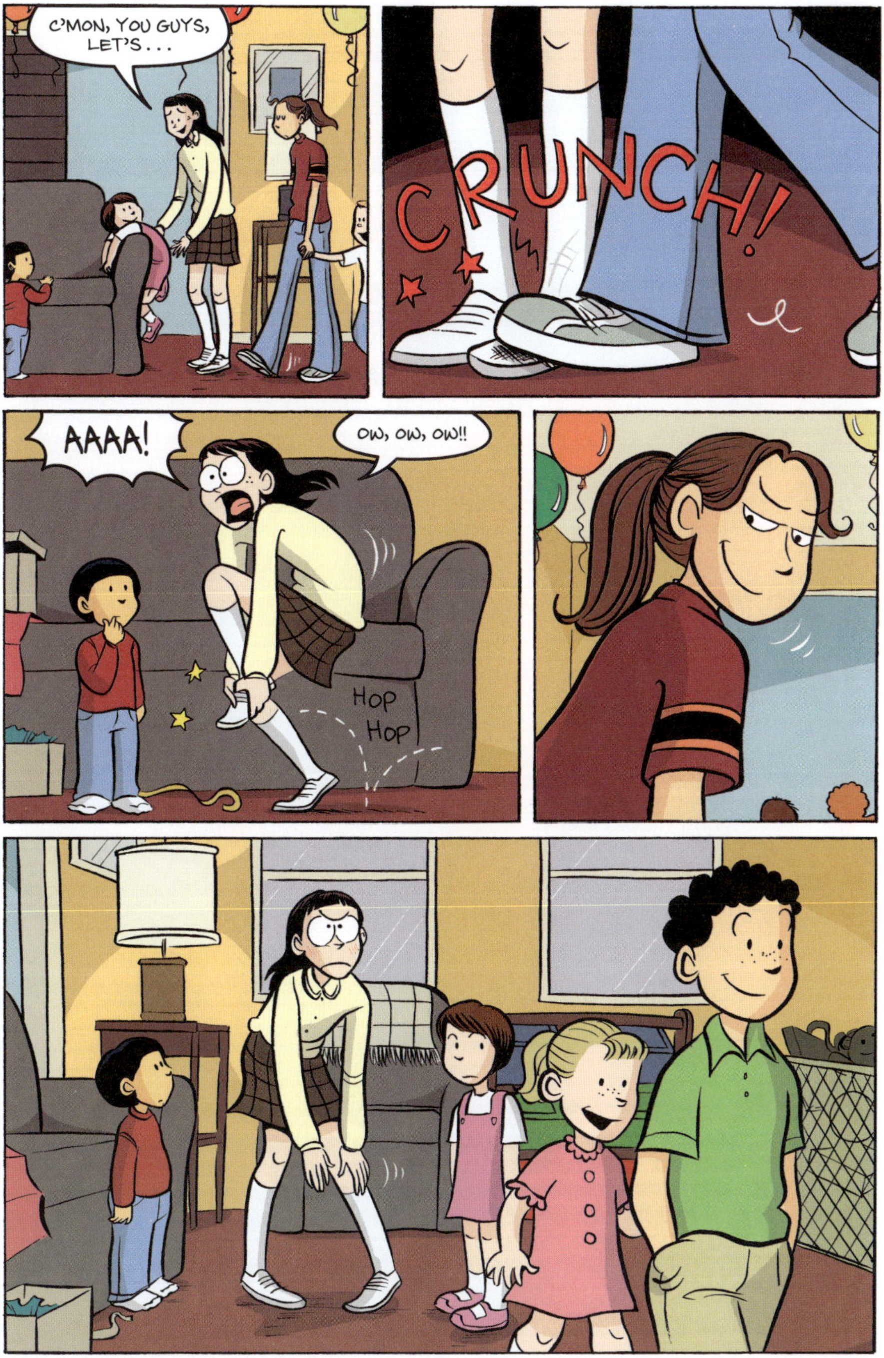
C'MON, YOU GUYS, LET'S...
CRUNCH!
AAAA!
OW, OW, OW!!
HOP
HOP

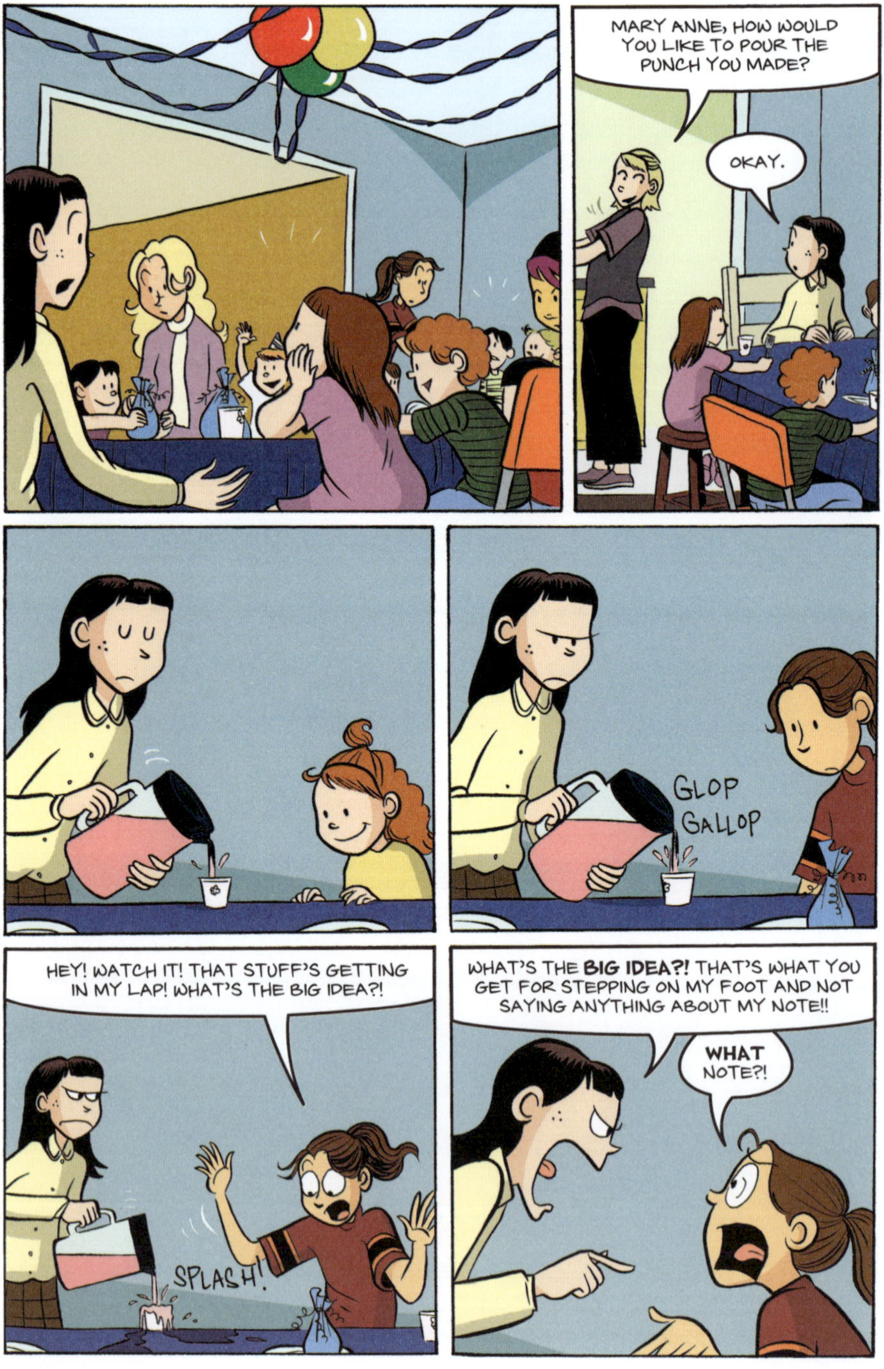
MARY ANNE, HOW WOULD YOU LIKE TO POUR THE PUNCH YOU MADE?
OKAY.
GLOP
GALLOP
HEY! WATCH IT! THAT STUFF'S GETTING IN MY LAP! WHAT'S THE BIG IDEA?!
SPLASH!
WHAT'S THE **BIG IDEA?!** THAT'S WHAT YOU GET FOR STEPPING ON MY FOOT AND NOT SAYING ANYTHING ABOUT MY NOTE!!
WHAT NOTE?!

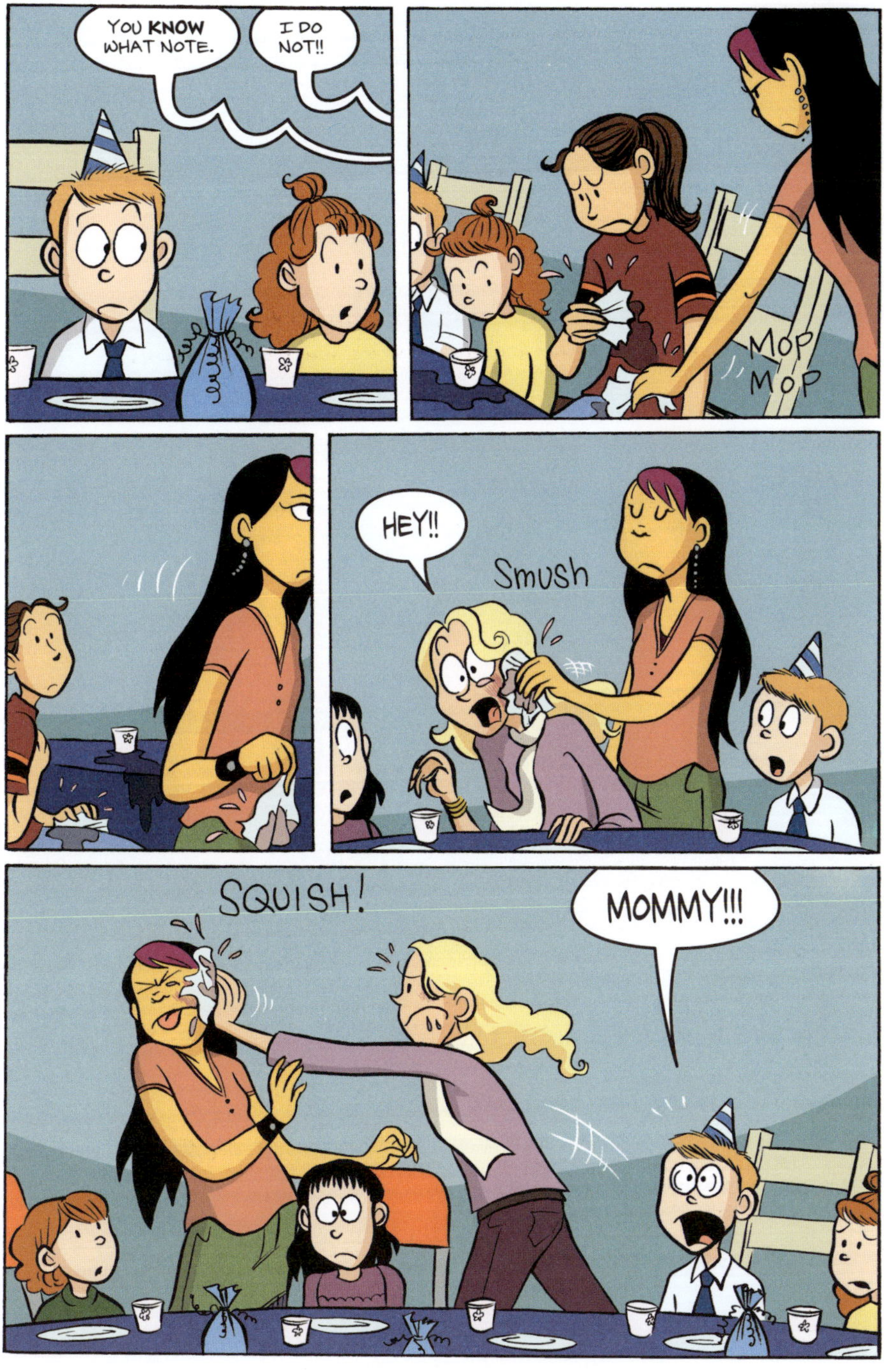
YOU KNOW WHAT NOTE.
I DO NOT!!
MOP MOP
HEY!!
Smush
SQUISH!
MOMMY!!!

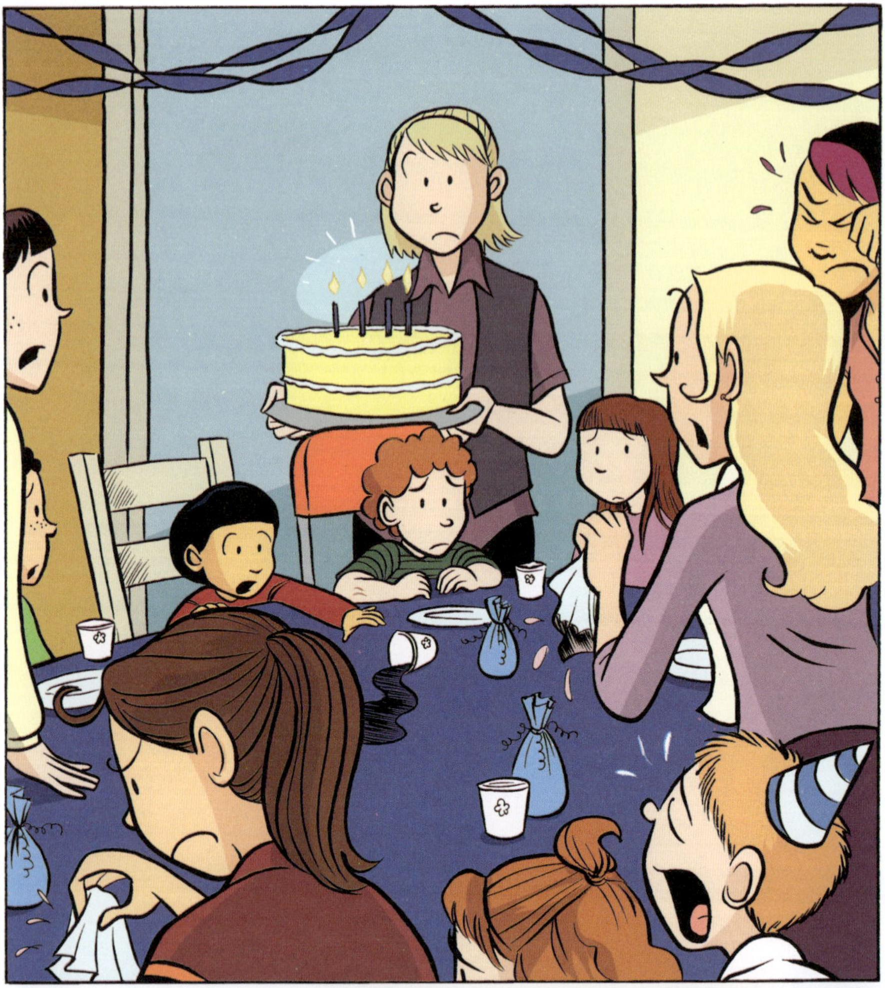

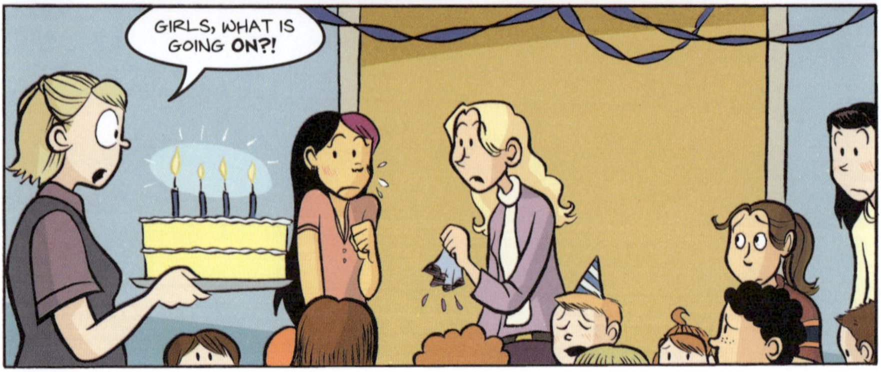
GIRLS, WHAT IS GOING **ON?!**

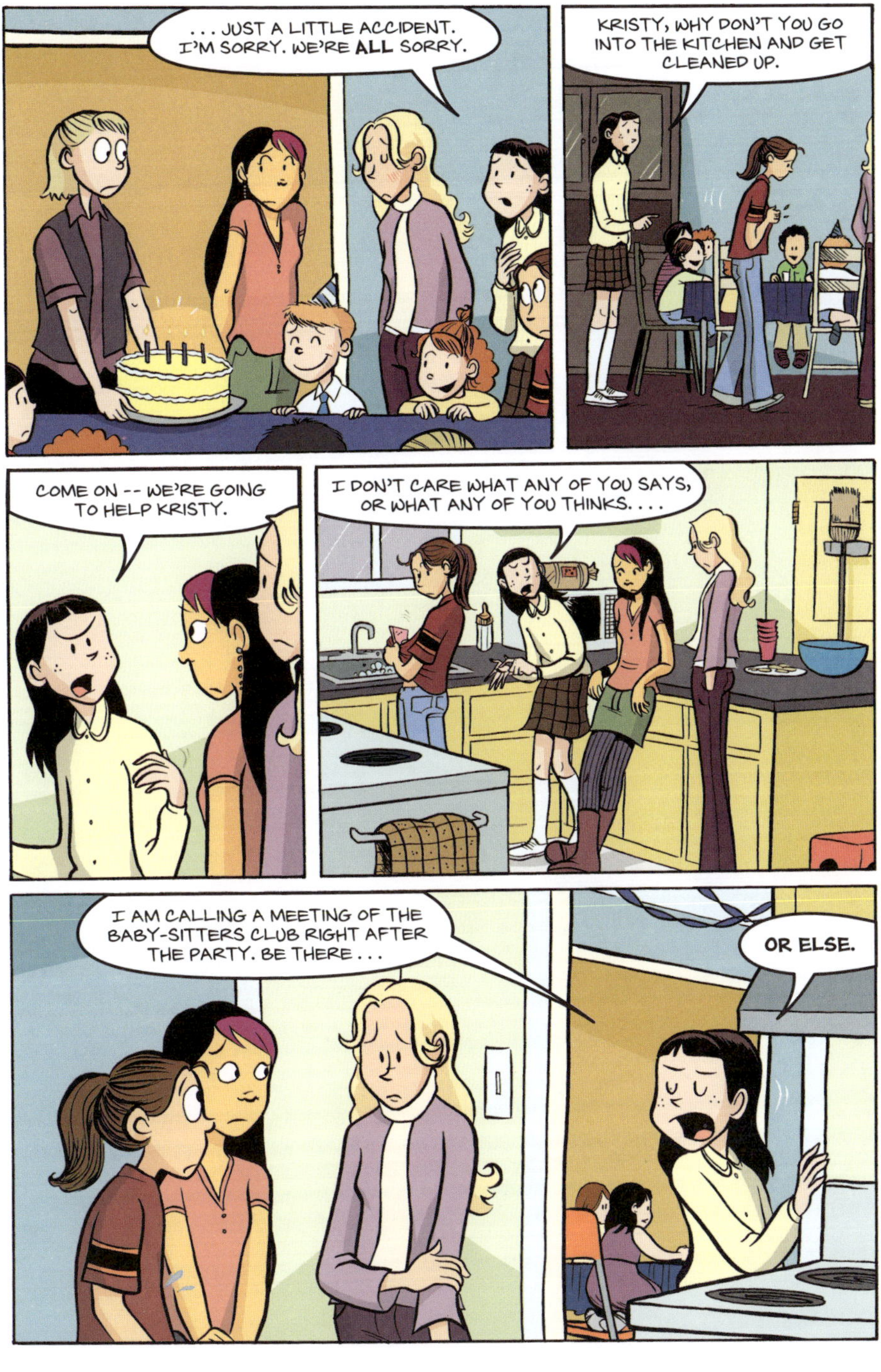

. . . JUST A LITTLE ACCIDENT. I'M SORRY. WE'RE **ALL** SORRY.
KRISTY, WHY DON'T YOU GO INTO THE KITCHEN AND GET CLEANED UP.
COME ON -- WE'RE GOING TO HELP KRISTY.
I DON'T CARE WHAT ANY OF YOU SAYS, OR WHAT ANY OF YOU THINKS. . . .
I AM CALLING A MEETING OF THE BABY-SITTERS CLUB RIGHT AFTER THE PARTY. BE THERE . . .
OR ELSE.

CHAPTER 15

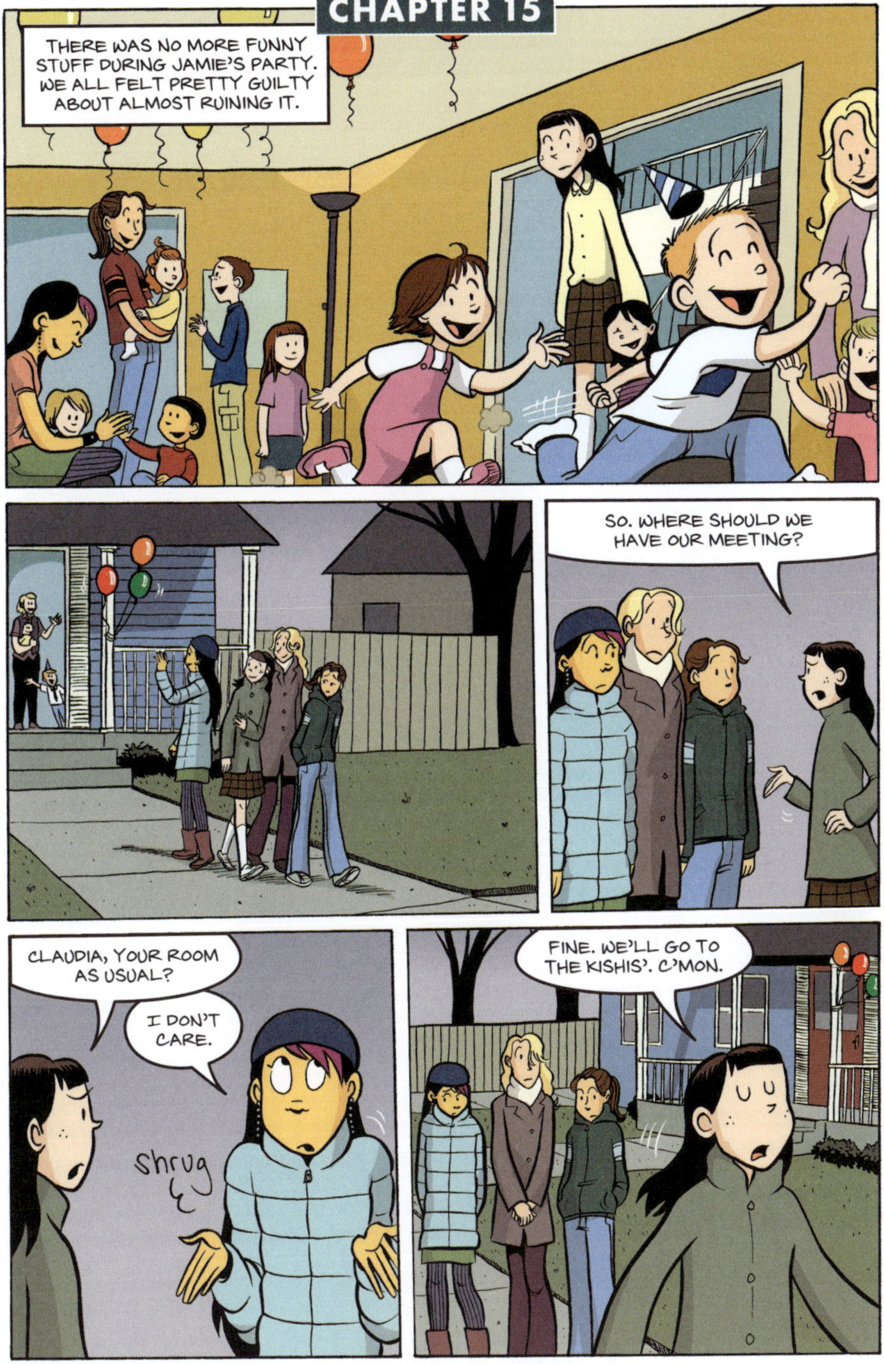

THERE WAS NO MORE FUNNY STUFF DURING JAMIE'S PARTY. WE ALL FELT PRETTY GUILTY ABOUT ALMOST RUINING IT.
SO. WHERE SHOULD WE HAVE OUR MEETING?
CLAUDIA, YOUR ROOM AS USUAL?
I DON'T CARE.
shrug
FINE. WE'LL GO TO THE KISHIS'. C'MON.

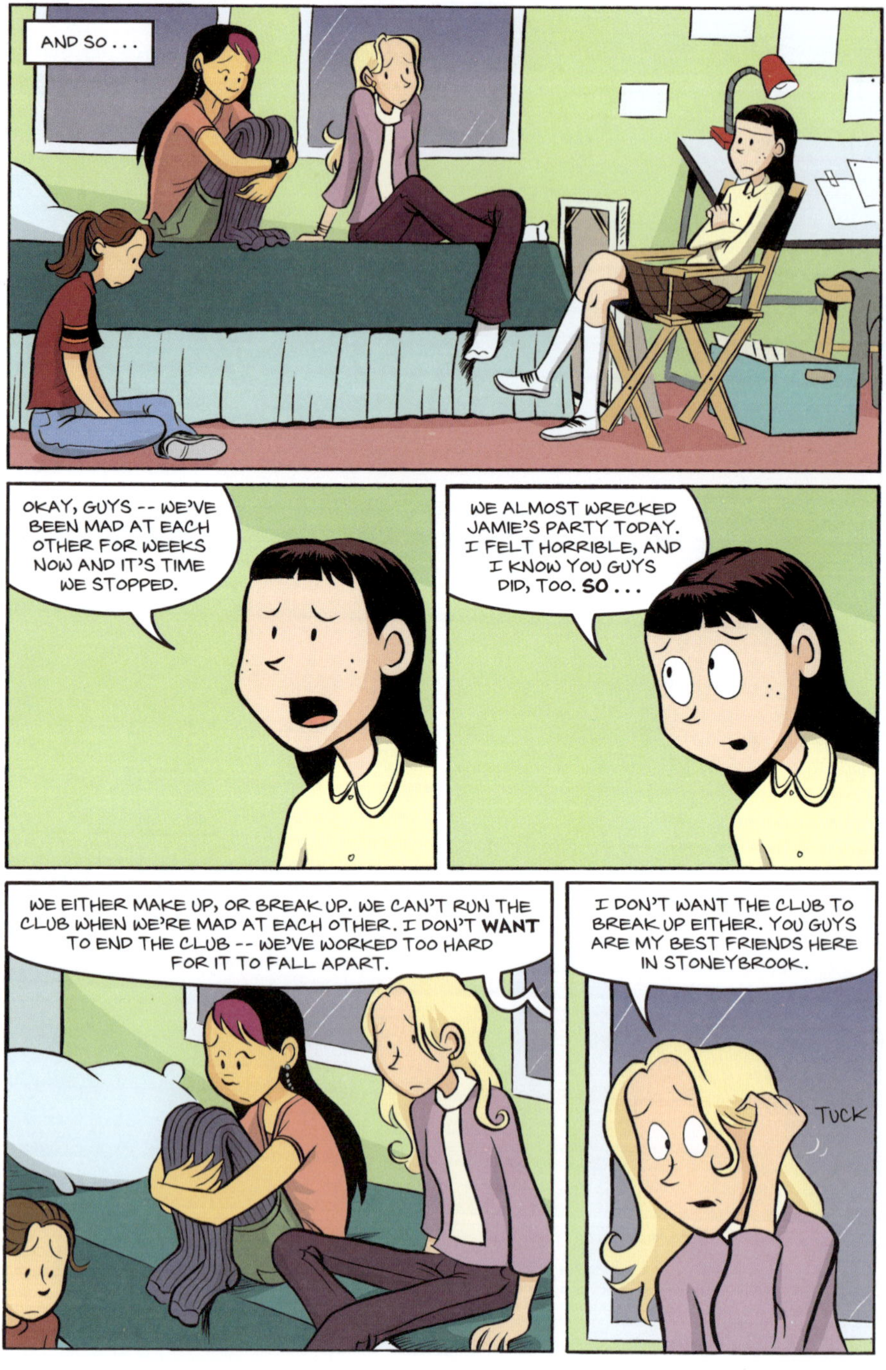
AND SO . . .
OKAY, GUYS -- WE'VE BEEN MAD AT EACH OTHER FOR WEEKS NOW AND IT'S TIME WE STOPPED.
WE ALMOST WRECKED JAMIE'S PARTY TODAY. I FELT HORRIBLE, AND I KNOW YOU GUYS DID, TOO. **SO . . .**
WE EITHER MAKE UP, OR BREAK UP. WE CAN'T RUN THE CLUB WHEN WE'RE MAD AT EACH OTHER. I DON'T **WANT** TO END THE CLUB -- WE'VE WORKED TOO HARD FOR IT TO FALL APART.
I DON'T WANT THE CLUB TO BREAK UP EITHER. YOU GUYS ARE MY BEST FRIENDS HERE IN STONEYBROOK.
TUCK

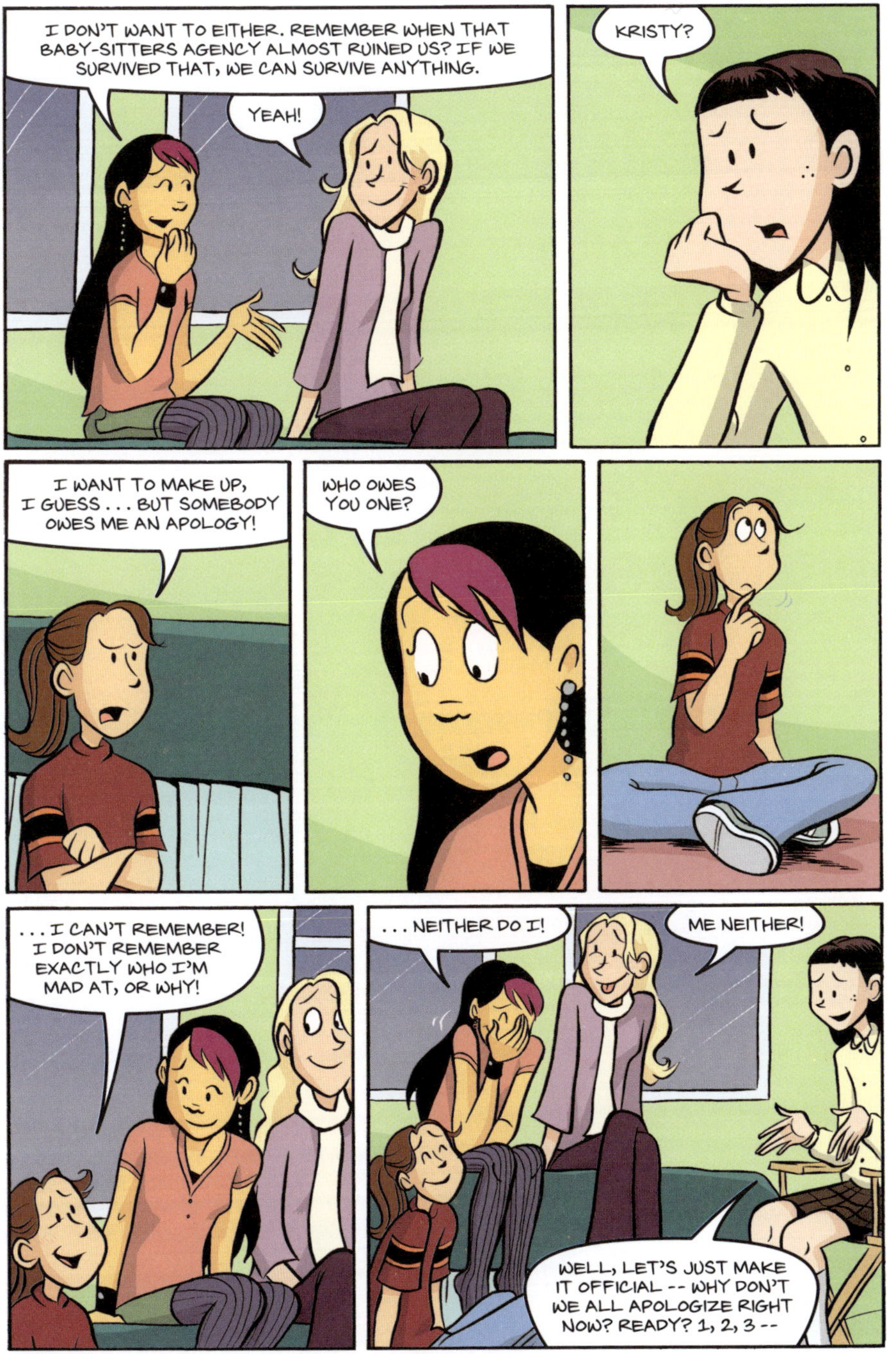
I DON'T WANT TO EITHER. REMEMBER WHEN THAT BABY-SITTERS AGENCY ALMOST RUINED US? IF WE SURVIVED THAT, WE CAN SURVIVE ANYTHING.
YEAH!
KRISTY?
I WANT TO MAKE UP, I GUESS . . . BUT SOMEBODY OWES ME AN APOLOGY!
WHO OWES YOU ONE?
. . . I CAN'T REMEMBER! I DON'T REMEMBER EXACTLY WHO I'M MAD AT, OR WHY!
. . . NEITHER DO I!
ME NEITHER!
WELL, LET'S JUST MAKE IT OFFICIAL -- WHY DON'T WE ALL APOLOGIZE RIGHT NOW? READY? 1, 2, 3 --

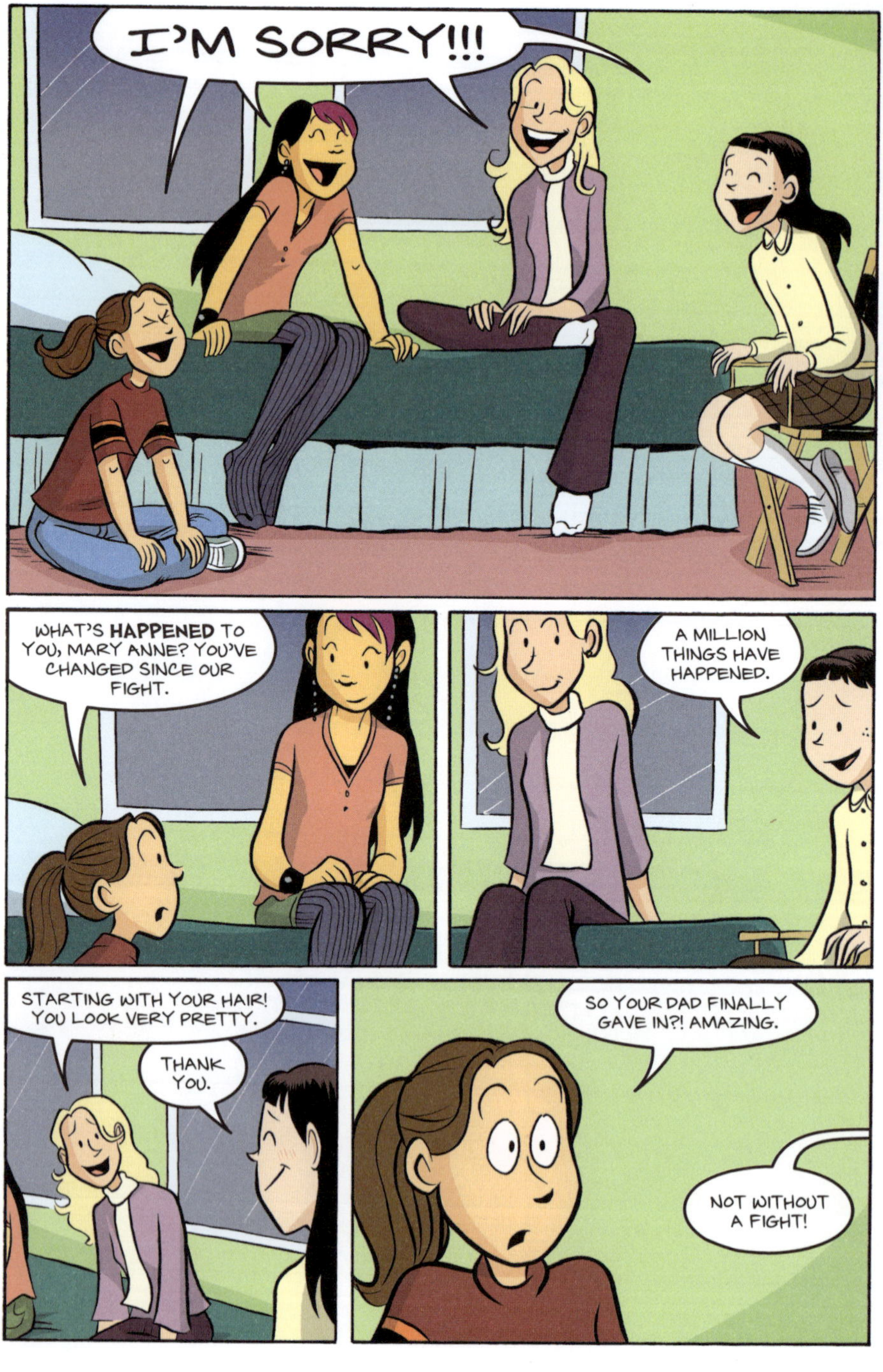
I'M SORRY!!!
WHAT'S **HAPPENED** TO YOU, MARY ANNE? YOU'VE CHANGED SINCE OUR FIGHT.
A MILLION THINGS HAVE HAPPENED.
STARTING WITH YOUR HAIR! YOU LOOK VERY PRETTY.
THANK YOU.
SO YOUR DAD FINALLY GAVE IN?! AMAZING.
NOT WITHOUT A FIGHT!

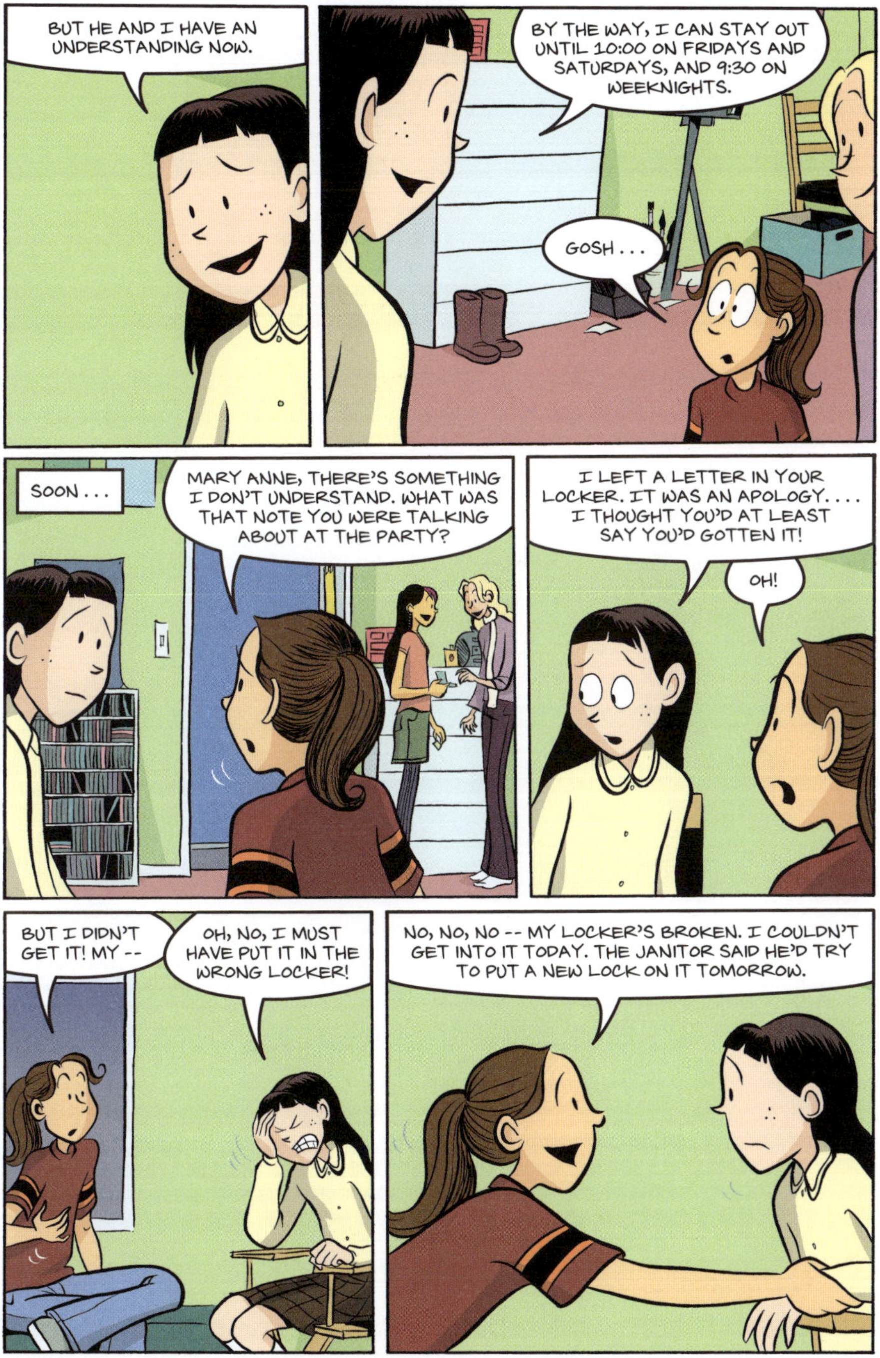
BUT HE AND I HAVE AN UNDERSTANDING NOW.
BY THE WAY, I CAN STAY OUT UNTIL 10:00 ON FRIDAYS AND SATURDAYS, AND 9:30 ON WEEKNIGHTS.
GOSH . . .
SOON . . .
MARY ANNE, THERE'S SOMETHING I DON'T UNDERSTAND. WHAT WAS THAT NOTE YOU WERE TALKING ABOUT AT THE PARTY?
I LEFT A LETTER IN YOUR LOCKER. IT WAS AN APOLOGY. . . . I THOUGHT YOU'D AT LEAST SAY YOU'D GOTTEN IT!
OH!
BUT I DIDN'T GET IT! MY --
OH, NO, I MUST HAVE PUT IT IN THE WRONG LOCKER!
NO, NO, NO -- MY LOCKER'S BROKEN. I COULDN'T GET INTO IT TODAY. THE JANITOR SAID HE'D TRY TO PUT A NEW LOCK ON IT TOMORROW.

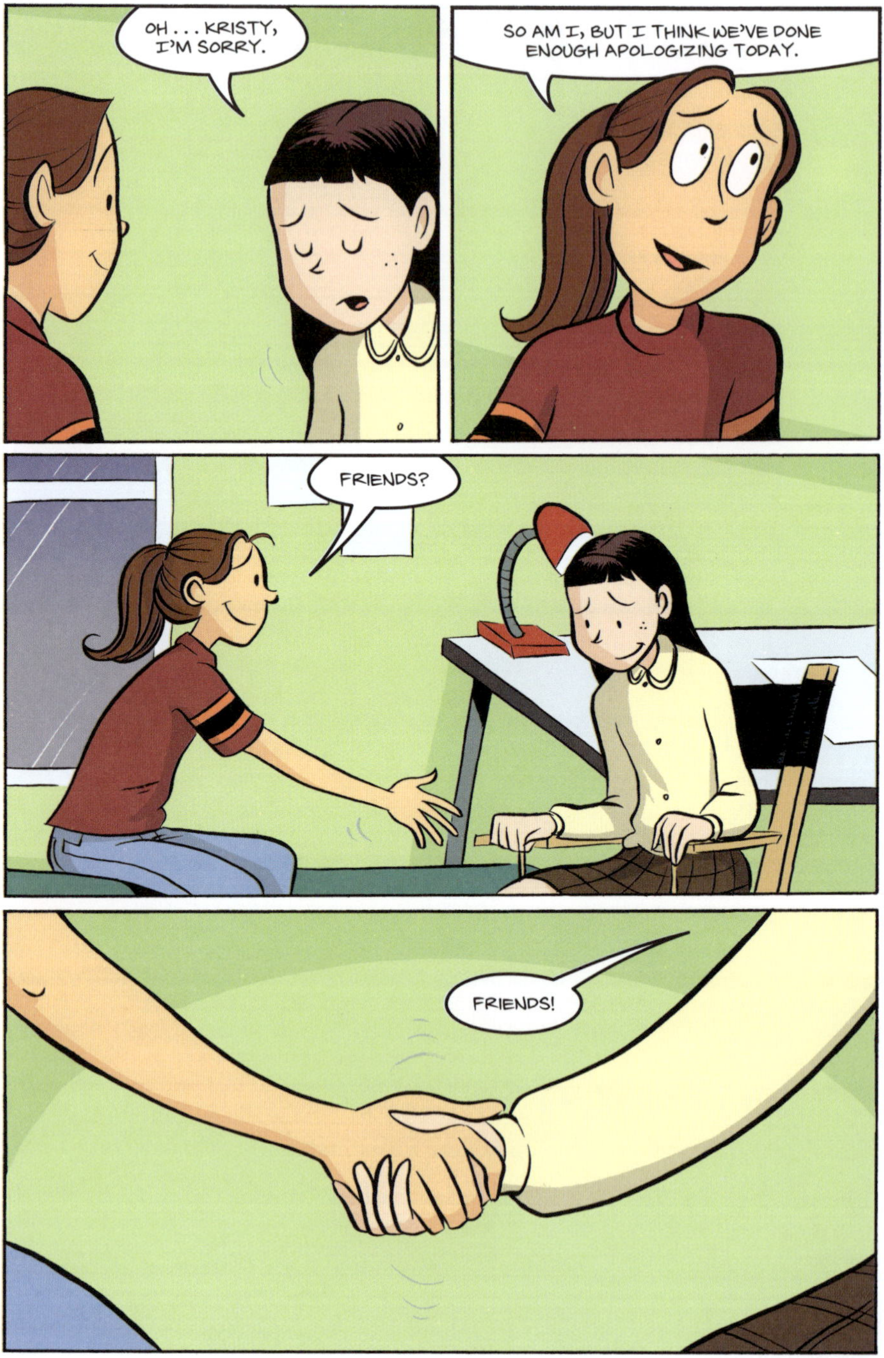
OH . . . KRISTY, I'M SORRY.
SO AM I, BUT I THINK WE'VE DONE ENOUGH APOLOGIZING TODAY.
FRIENDS?
FRIENDS!

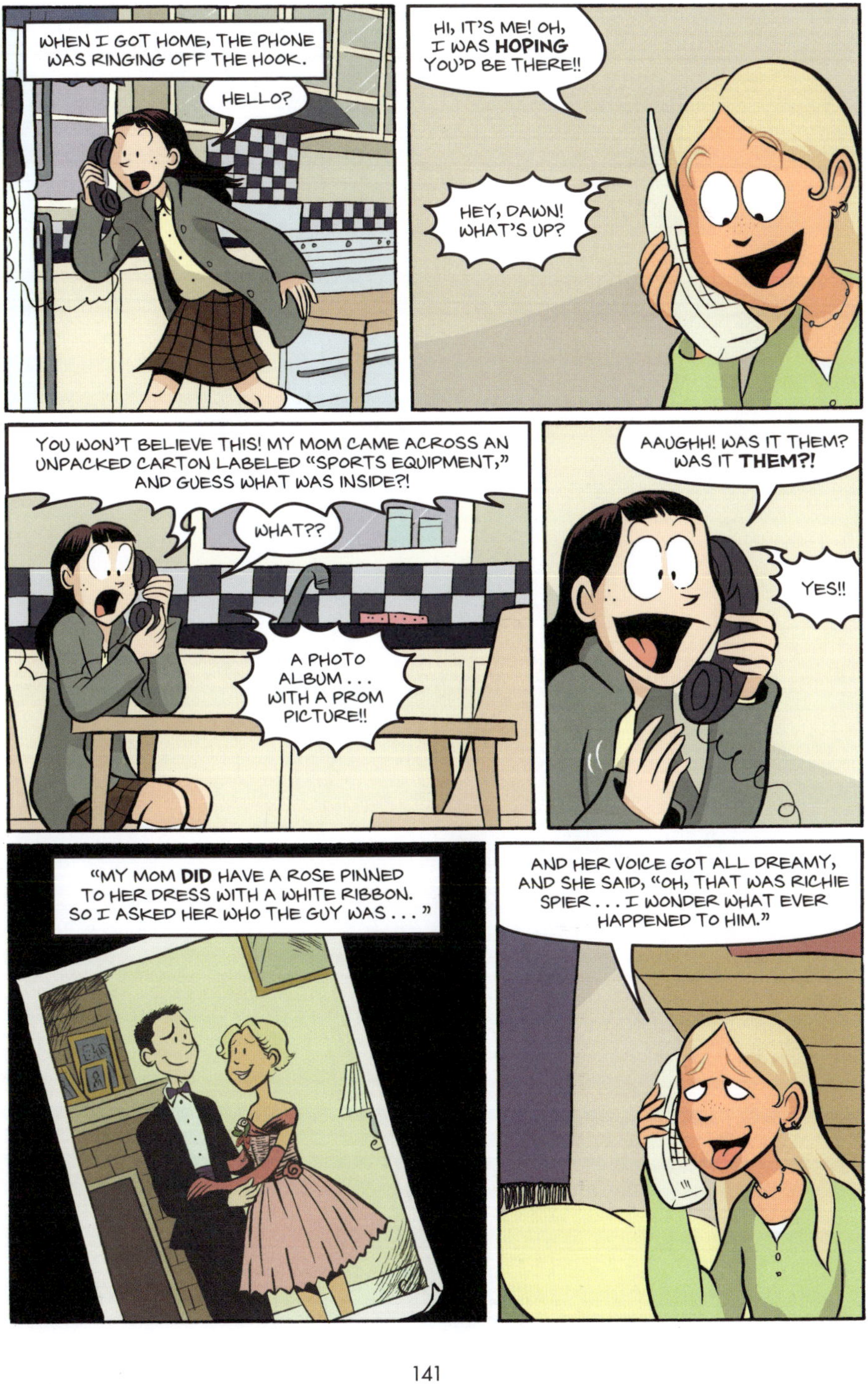
WHEN I GOT HOME, THE PHONE WAS RINGING OFF THE HOOK.
HELLO?
HI, IT'S ME! OH, I WAS **HOPING** YOU'D BE THERE!!
HEY, DAWN! WHAT'S UP?
YOU WON'T BELIEVE THIS! MY MOM CAME ACROSS AN UNPACKED CARTON LABELED "SPORTS EQUIPMENT," AND GUESS WHAT WAS INSIDE?!
WHAT??
A PHOTO ALBUM . . . WITH A PROM PICTURE!!
AAUGHH! WAS IT THEM? WAS IT **THEM?!**
YES!!
"MY MOM **DID** HAVE A ROSE PINNED TO HER DRESS WITH A WHITE RIBBON. SO I ASKED HER WHO THE GUY WAS . . . "
AND HER VOICE GOT ALL DREAMY, AND SHE SAID, "OH, THAT WAS RICHIE SPIER . . . I WONDER WHAT EVER HAPPENED TO HIM."

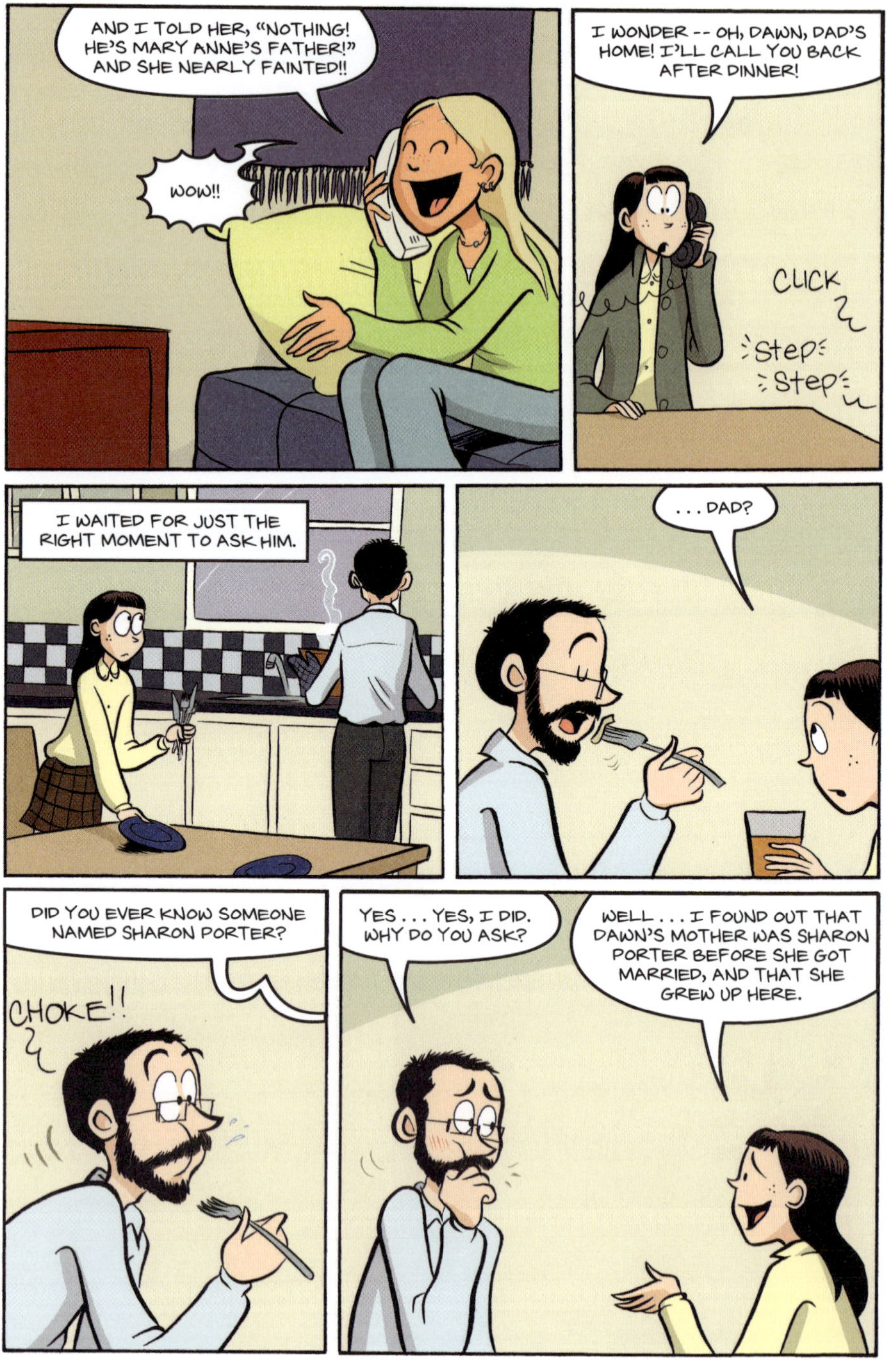
AND I TOLD HER, "NOTHING! HE'S MARY ANNE'S FATHER!" AND SHE NEARLY FAINTED!!
WOW!!
I WONDER -- OH, DAWN, DAD'S HOME! I'LL CALL YOU BACK AFTER DINNER!
CLICK
Step
Step
I WAITED FOR JUST THE RIGHT MOMENT TO ASK HIM.
. . . DAD?
DID YOU EVER KNOW SOMEONE NAMED SHARON PORTER?
CHOKE!!
YES . . . YES, I DID. WHY DO YOU ASK?
WELL . . . I FOUND OUT THAT DAWN'S MOTHER WAS SHARON PORTER BEFORE SHE GOT MARRIED, AND THAT SHE GREW UP HERE.

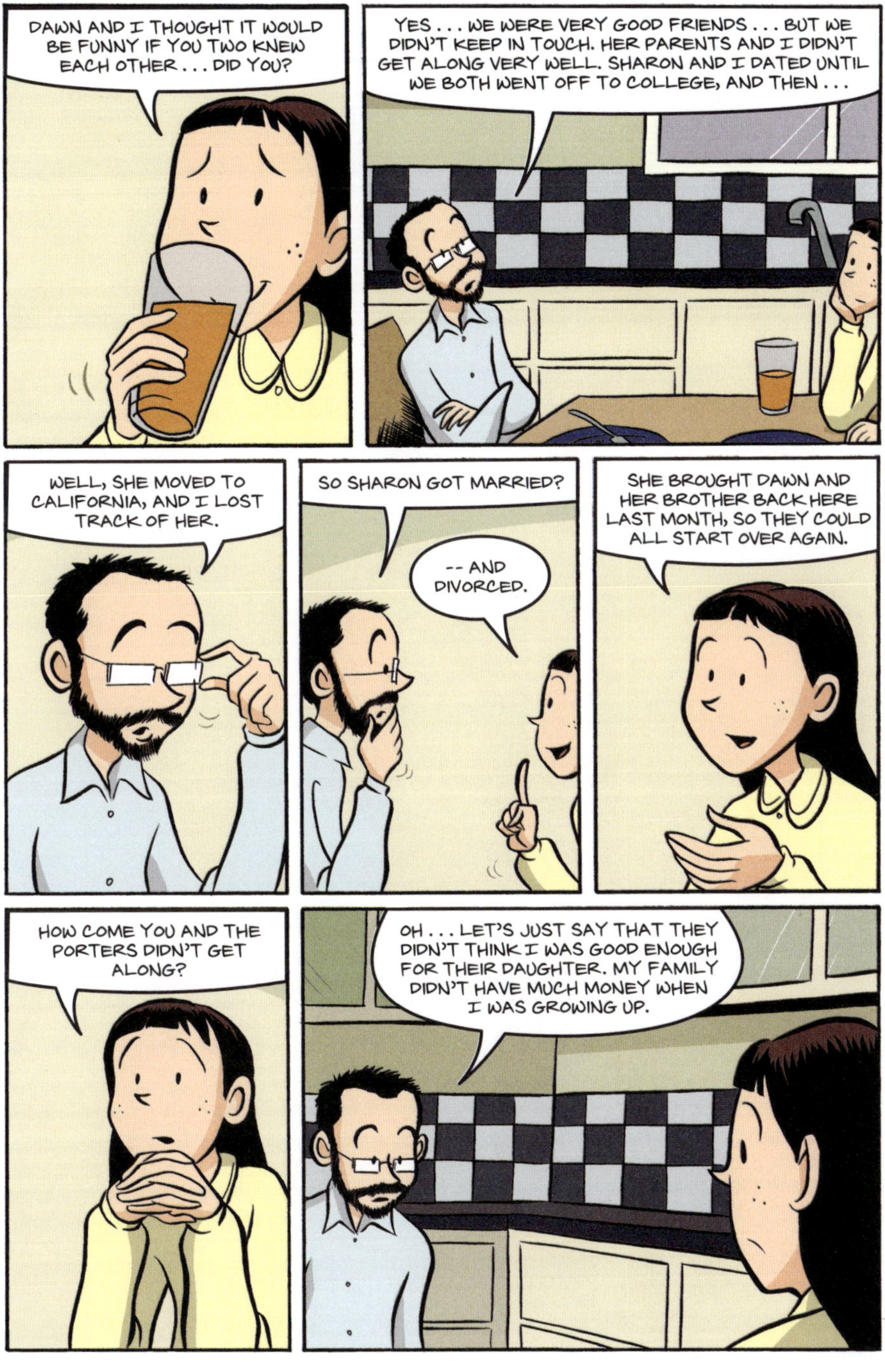
DAWN AND I THOUGHT IT WOULD BE FUNNY IF YOU TWO KNEW EACH OTHER . . . DID YOU?
YES . . . WE WERE VERY GOOD FRIENDS . . . BUT WE DIDN'T KEEP IN TOUCH. HER PARENTS AND I DIDN'T GET ALONG VERY WELL. SHARON AND I DATED UNTIL WE BOTH WENT OFF TO COLLEGE, AND THEN . . .
WELL, SHE MOVED TO CALIFORNIA, AND I LOST TRACK OF HER.
SO SHARON GOT MARRIED?
-- AND DIVORCED.
SHE BROUGHT DAWN AND HER BROTHER BACK HERE LAST MONTH, SO THEY COULD ALL START OVER AGAIN.
HOW COME YOU AND THE PORTERS DIDN'T GET ALONG?
OH . . . LET'S JUST SAY THAT THEY DIDN'T THINK I WAS GOOD ENOUGH FOR THEIR DAUGHTER. MY FAMILY DIDN'T HAVE MUCH MONEY WHEN I WAS GROWING UP.

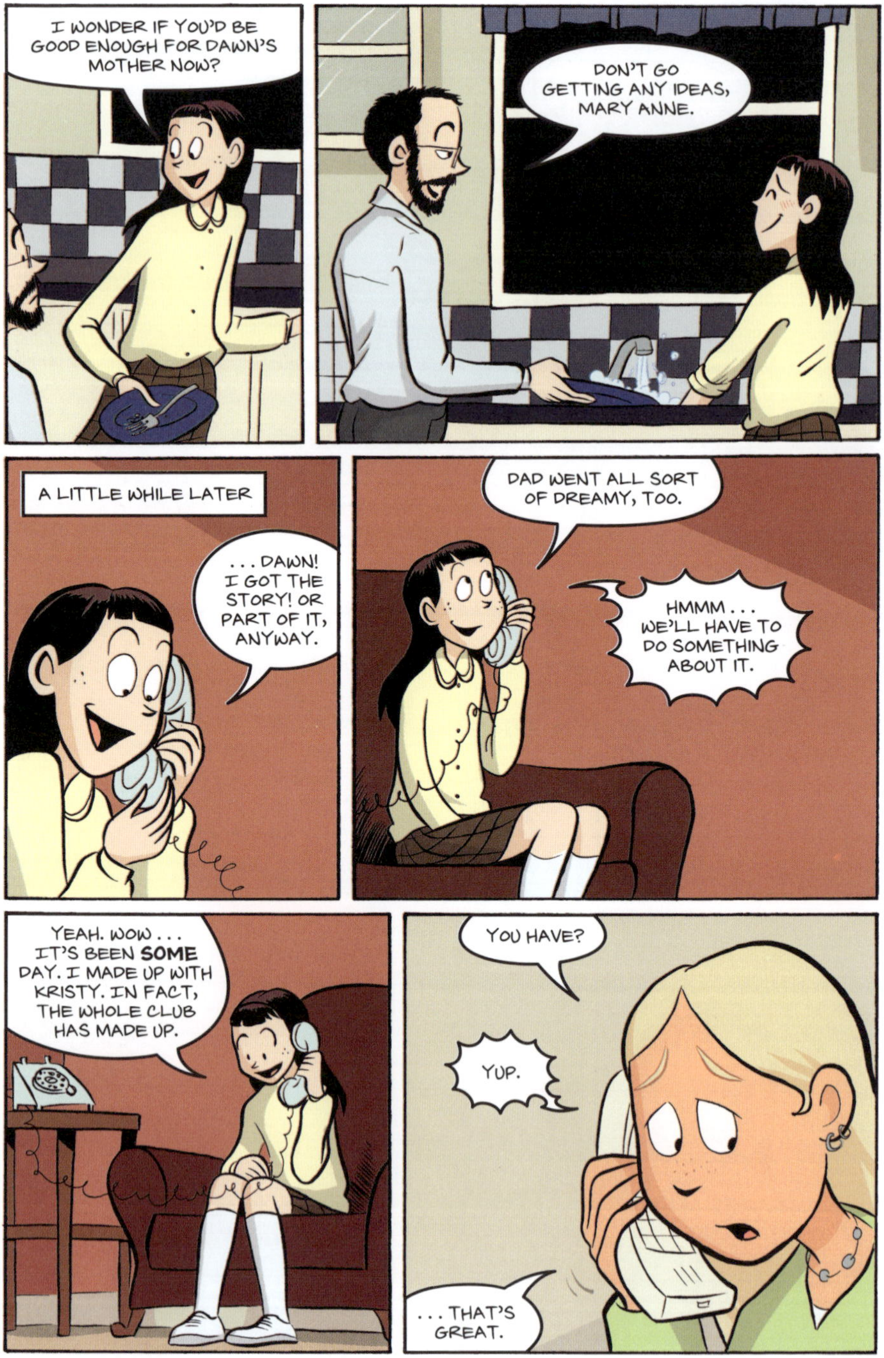
I WONDER IF YOU'D BE GOOD ENOUGH FOR DAWN'S MOTHER NOW?
DON'T GO GETTING ANY IDEAS, MARY ANNE.
A LITTLE WHILE LATER
. . . DAWN! I GOT THE STORY! OR PART OF IT, ANYWAY.
DAD WENT ALL SORT OF DREAMY, TOO.
HMMM . . . WE'LL HAVE TO DO SOMETHING ABOUT IT.
YEAH. WOW . . . IT'S BEEN **SOME** DAY. I MADE UP WITH KRISTY. IN FACT, THE WHOLE CLUB HAS MADE UP.
YOU HAVE?
YUP.
. . . THAT'S GREAT.

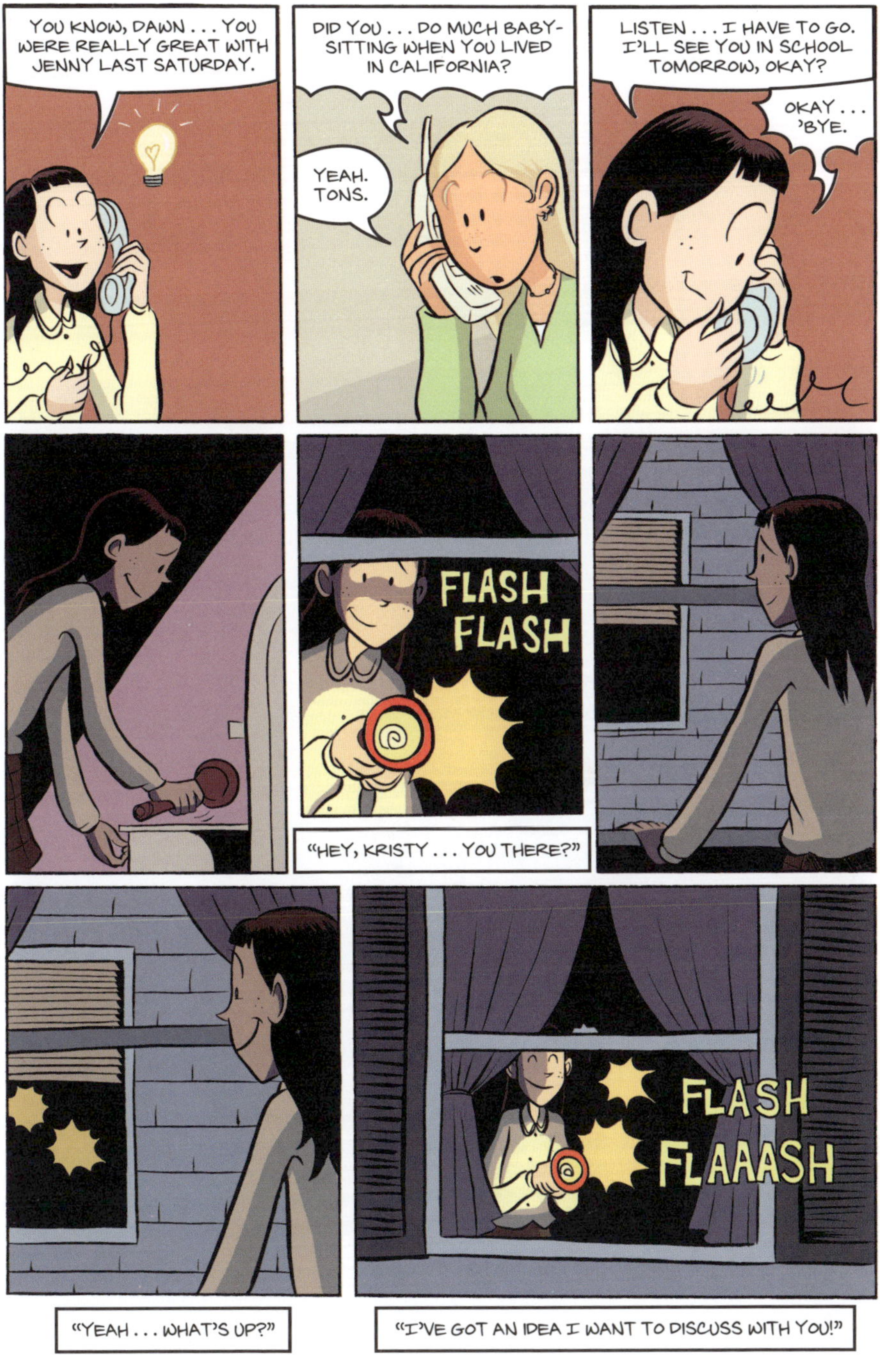
YOU KNOW, DAWN . . . YOU WERE REALLY GREAT WITH JENNY LAST SATURDAY.
DID YOU . . . DO MUCH BABY-SITTING WHEN YOU LIVED IN CALIFORNIA?
YEAH. TONS.
LISTEN . . . I HAVE TO GO. I'LL SEE YOU IN SCHOOL TOMORROW, OKAY?
OKAY . . . 'BYE.
FLASH
FLASH
"HEY, KRISTY . . . YOU THERE?"
"YEAH . . . WHAT'S UP?"
FLASH
FLAAASH
"I'VE GOT AN IDEA I WANT TO DISCUSS WITH YOU!"

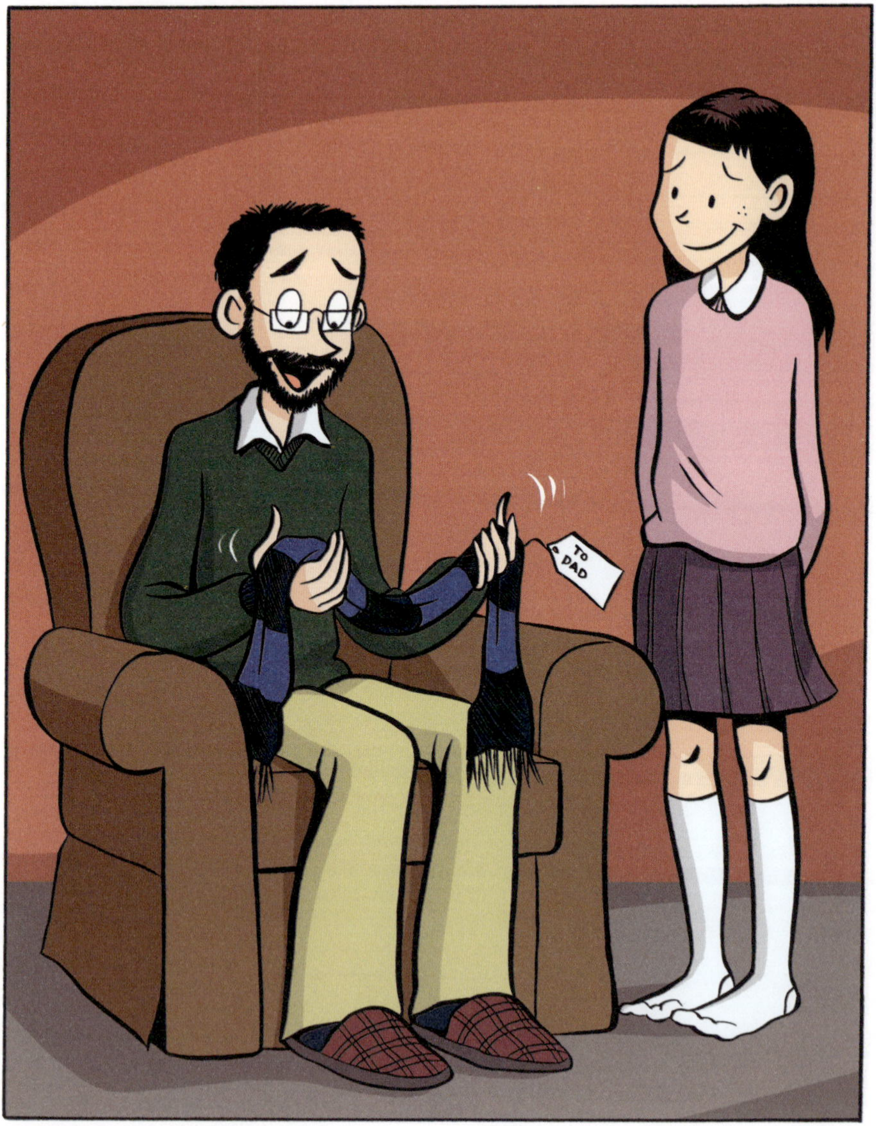
TO DAD

CHAPTER 16

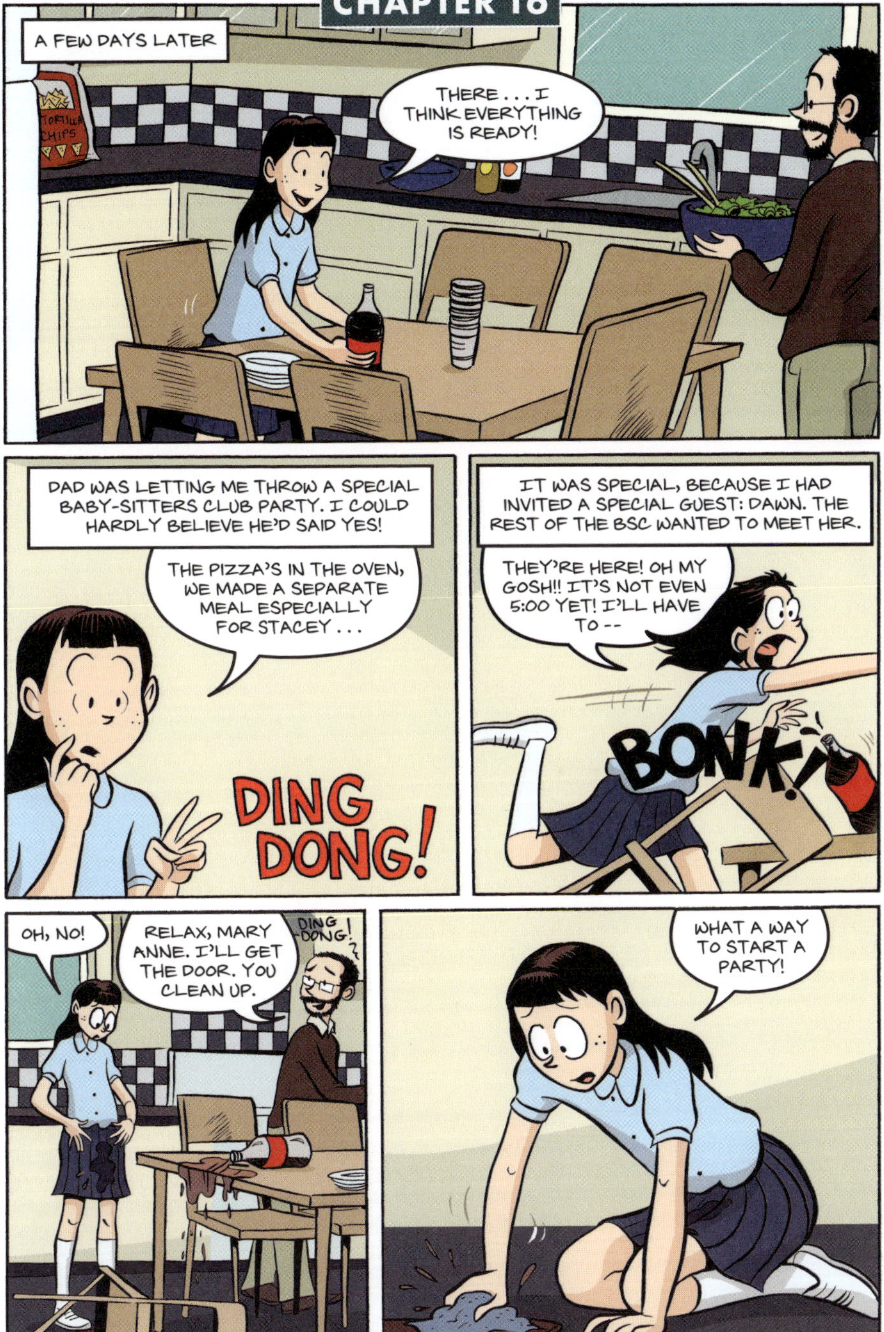

A FEW DAYS LATER
TORTILLA CHIPS
THERE . . . I THINK EVERYTHING IS READY!
DAD WAS LETTING ME THROW A SPECIAL BABY-SITTERS CLUB PARTY. I COULD HARDLY BELIEVE HE'D SAID YES!
THE PIZZA'S IN THE OVEN, WE MADE A SEPARATE MEAL ESPECIALLY FOR STACEY . . .
DING DONG!
IT WAS SPECIAL, BECAUSE I HAD INVITED A SPECIAL GUEST: DAWN. THE REST OF THE BSC WANTED TO MEET HER.
THEY'RE HERE! OH MY GOSH!! IT'S NOT EVEN 5:00 YET! I'LL HAVE TO --
BONK!
OH, NO!
RELAX, MARY ANNE. I'LL GET THE DOOR. YOU CLEAN UP.
DING DONG!
WHAT A WAY TO START A PARTY!

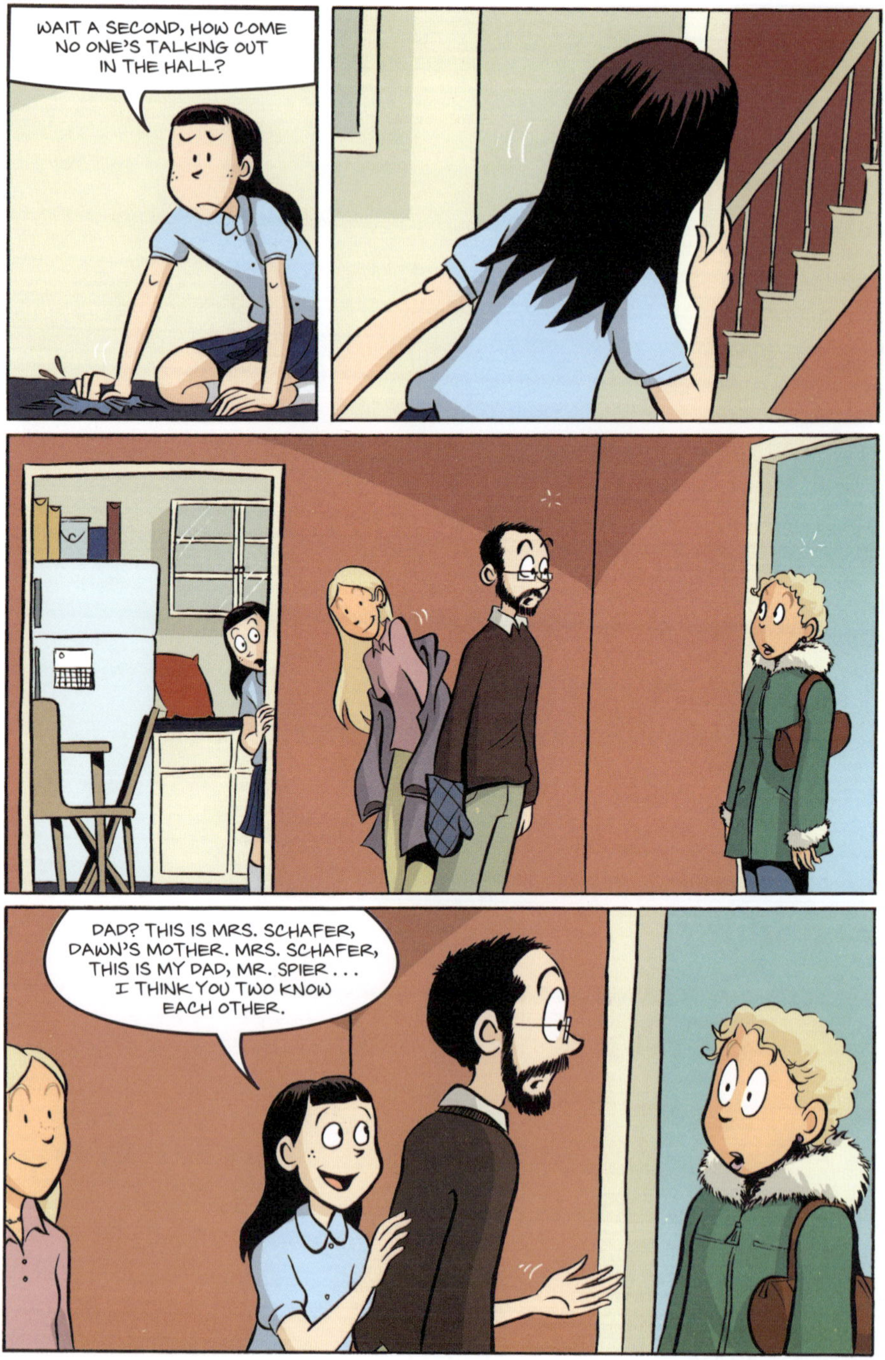
WAIT A SECOND, HOW COME NO ONE'S TALKING OUT IN THE HALL?
DAD? THIS IS MRS. SCHAFER, DAWN'S MOTHER. MRS. SCHAFER, THIS IS MY DAD, MR. SPIER . . . I THINK YOU TWO KNOW EACH OTHER.

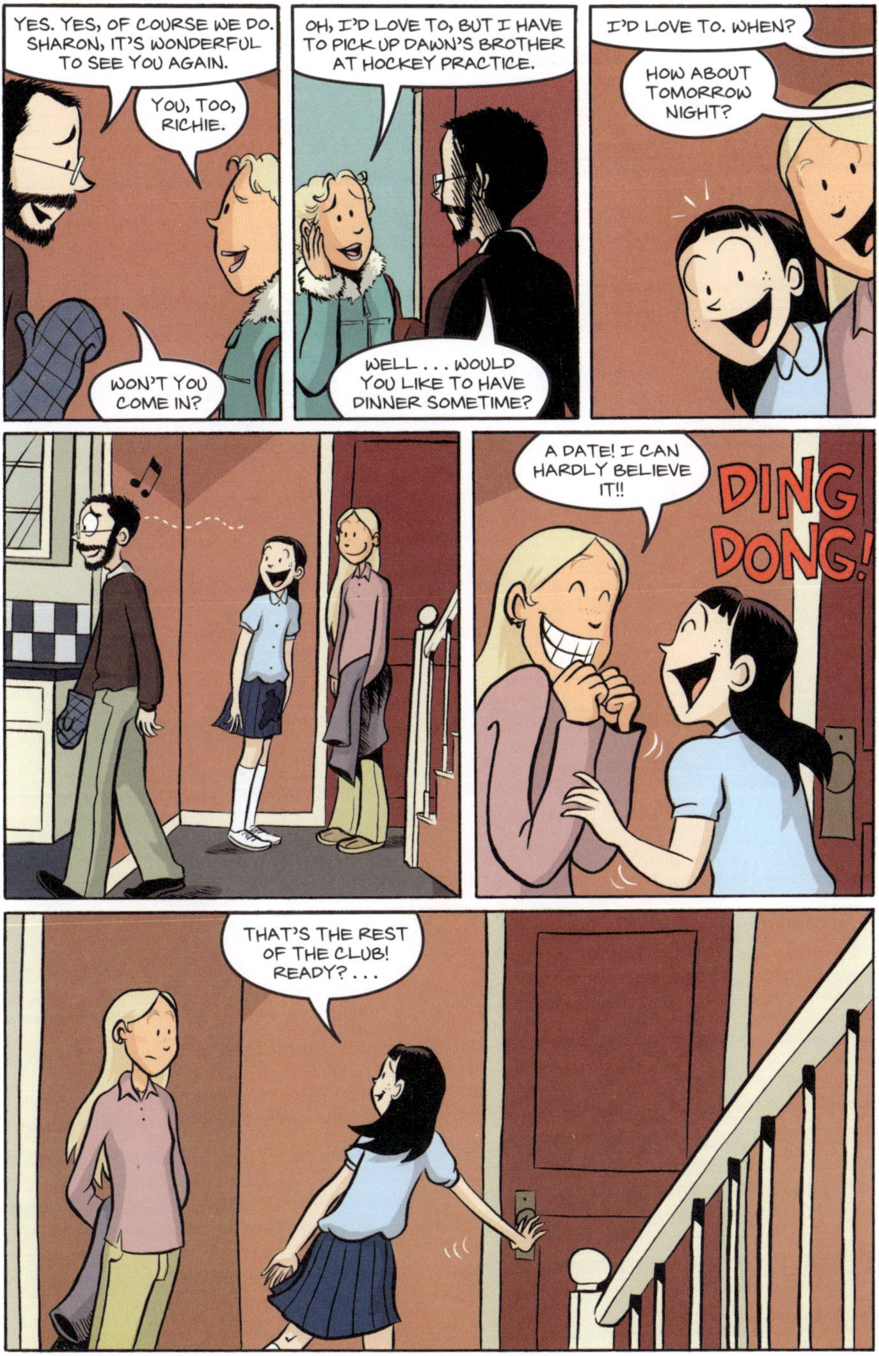
YES. YES, OF COURSE WE DO. SHARON, IT'S WONDERFUL TO SEE YOU AGAIN.
YOU, TOO, RICHIE.
WON'T YOU COME IN?
OH, I'D LOVE TO, BUT I HAVE TO PICK UP DAWN'S BROTHER AT HOCKEY PRACTICE.
WELL . . . WOULD YOU LIKE TO HAVE DINNER SOMETIME?
I'D LOVE TO. WHEN?
HOW ABOUT TOMORROW NIGHT?
A DATE! I CAN HARDLY BELIEVE IT!!
DING DONG!
THAT'S THE REST OF THE CLUB! READY? . . .

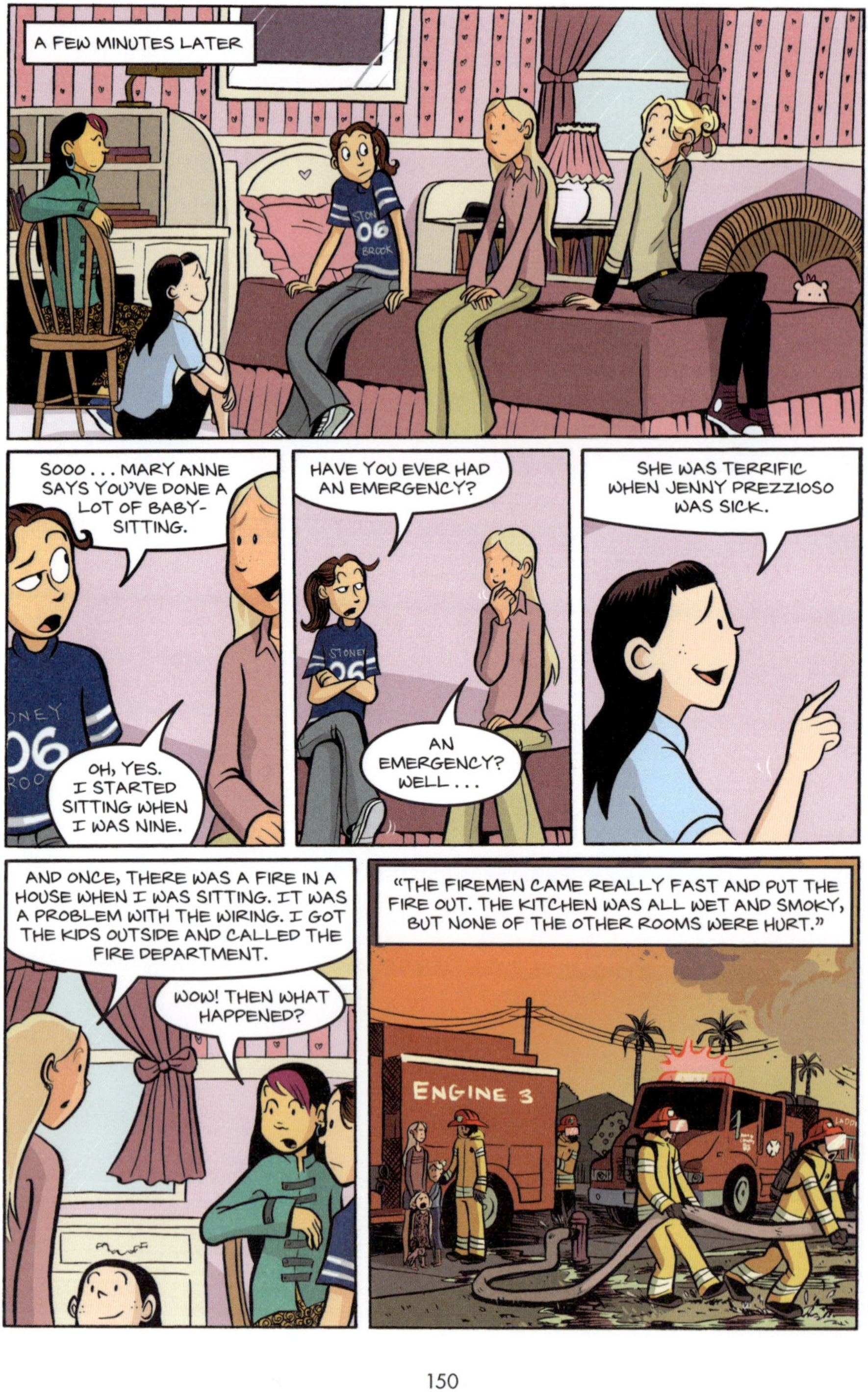
A FEW MINUTES LATER
SOOO . . . MARY ANNE SAYS YOU'VE DONE A LOT OF BABY-SITTING.
OH, YES. I STARTED SITTING WHEN I WAS NINE.
HAVE YOU EVER HAD AN EMERGENCY?
AN EMERGENCY? WELL . . .
SHE WAS TERRIFIC WHEN JENNY PREZZIOSO WAS SICK.
AND ONCE, THERE WAS A FIRE IN A HOUSE WHEN I WAS SITTING. IT WAS A PROBLEM WITH THE WIRING. I GOT THE KIDS OUTSIDE AND CALLED THE FIRE DEPARTMENT.
WOW! THEN WHAT HAPPENED?
"THE FIREMEN CAME REALLY FAST AND PUT THE FIRE OUT. THE KITCHEN WAS ALL WET AND SMOKY, BUT NONE OF THE OTHER ROOMS WERE HURT."
ENGINE 3

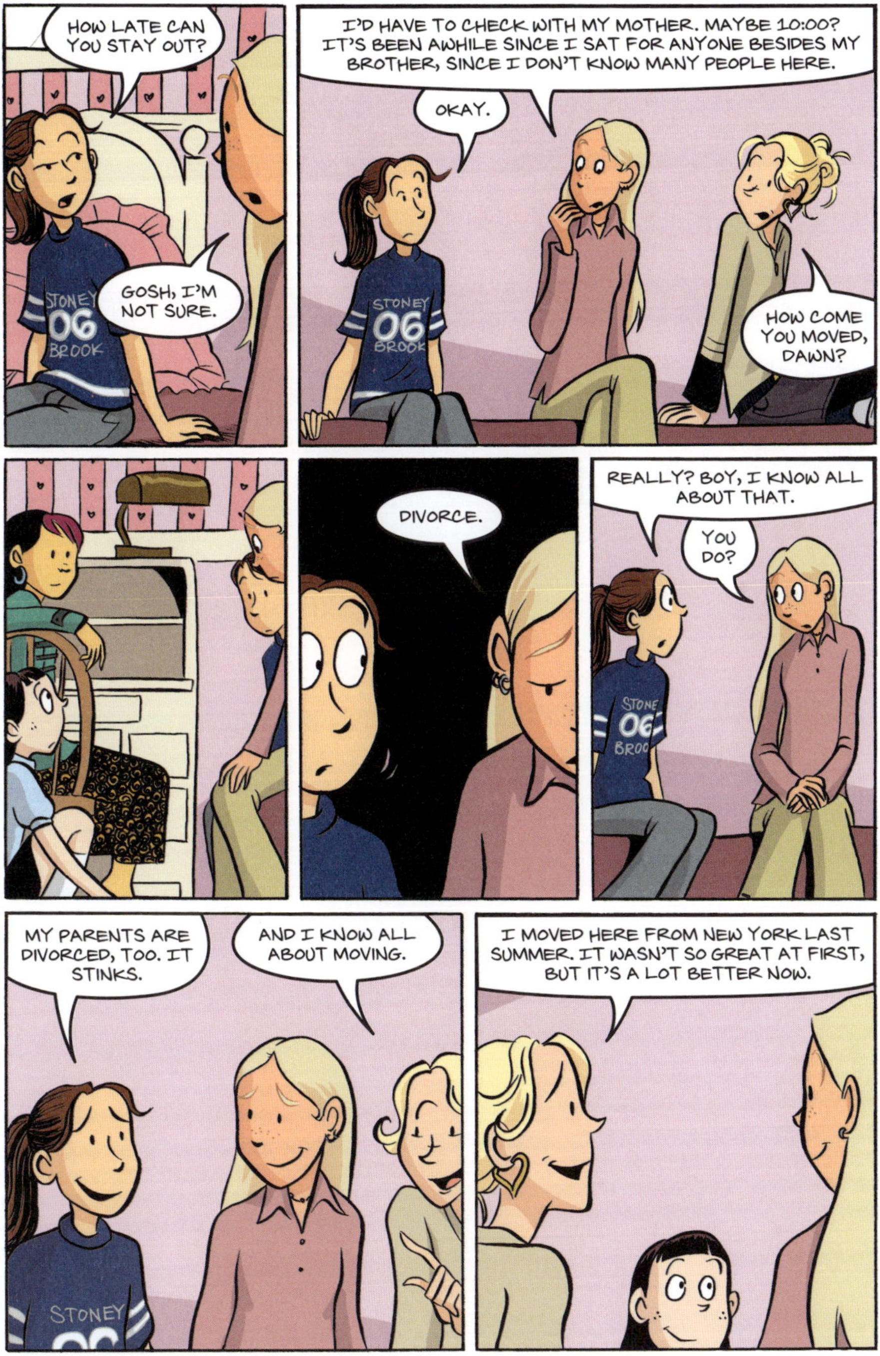
HOW LATE CAN YOU STAY OUT?
GOSH, I'M NOT SURE.
I'D HAVE TO CHECK WITH MY MOTHER. MAYBE 10:00? IT'S BEEN AWHILE SINCE I SAT FOR ANYONE BESIDES MY BROTHER, SINCE I DON'T KNOW MANY PEOPLE HERE.
OKAY.
HOW COME YOU MOVED, DAWN?
DIVORCE.
REALLY? BOY, I KNOW ALL ABOUT THAT.
YOU DO?
MY PARENTS ARE DIVORCED, TOO. IT STINKS.
AND I KNOW ALL ABOUT MOVING.
I MOVED HERE FROM NEW YORK LAST SUMMER. IT WASN'T SO GREAT AT FIRST, BUT IT'S A LOT BETTER NOW.

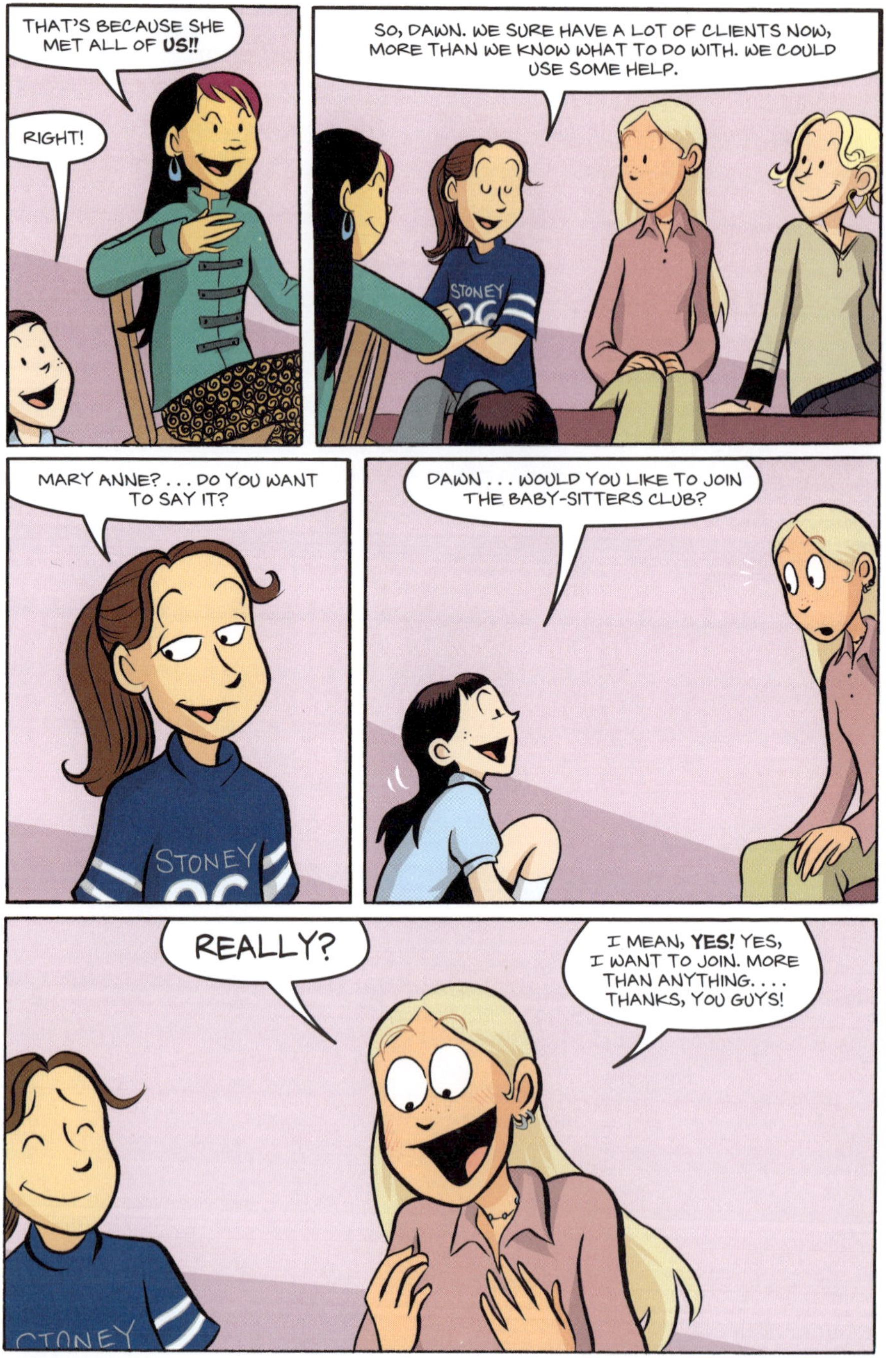
THAT'S BECAUSE SHE MET ALL OF **US!!**
RIGHT!
SO, DAWN. WE SURE HAVE A LOT OF CLIENTS NOW, MORE THAN WE KNOW WHAT TO DO WITH. WE COULD USE SOME HELP.
STONEY
MARY ANNE? . . . DO YOU WANT TO SAY IT?
STONEY
DAWN . . . WOULD YOU LIKE TO JOIN THE BABY-SITTERS CLUB?
REALLY?
I MEAN, **YES!** YES, I WANT TO JOIN. MORE THAN ANYTHING. . . . THANKS, YOU GUYS!

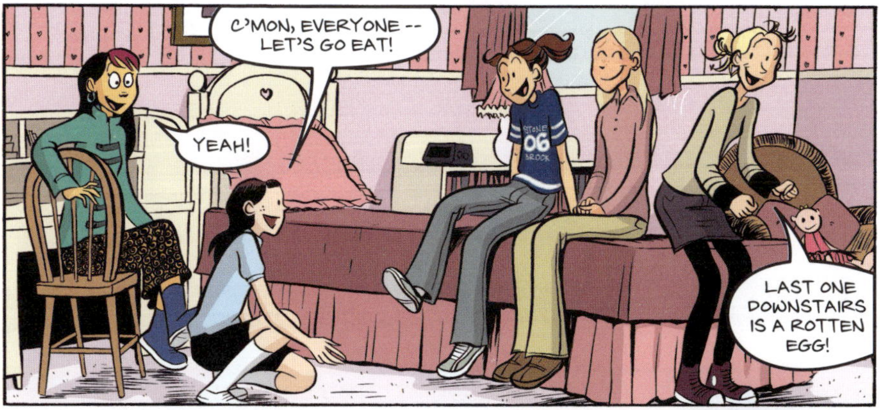
C'MON, EVERYONE -- LET'S GO EAT!
YEAH!
LAST ONE DOWNSTAIRS IS A ROTTEN EGG!

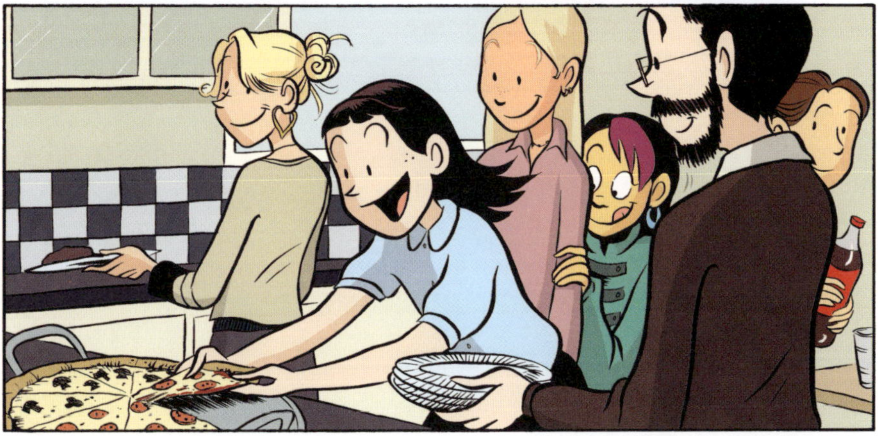

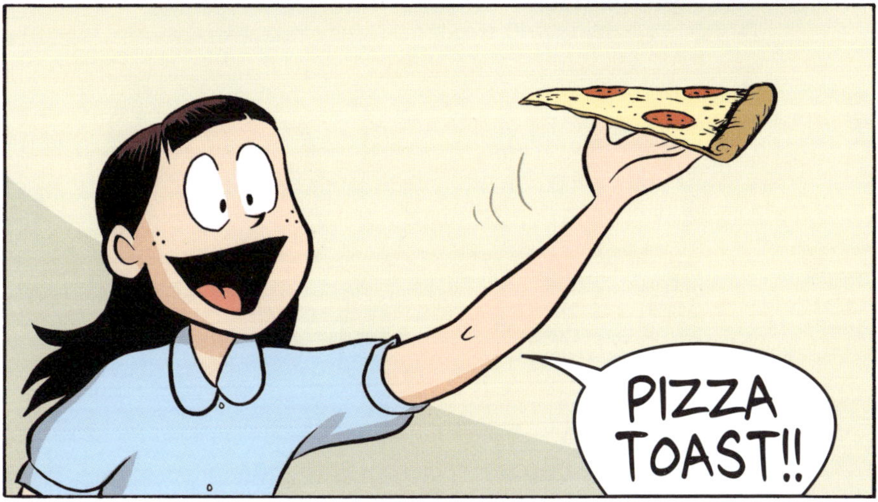
PIZZA TOAST!!

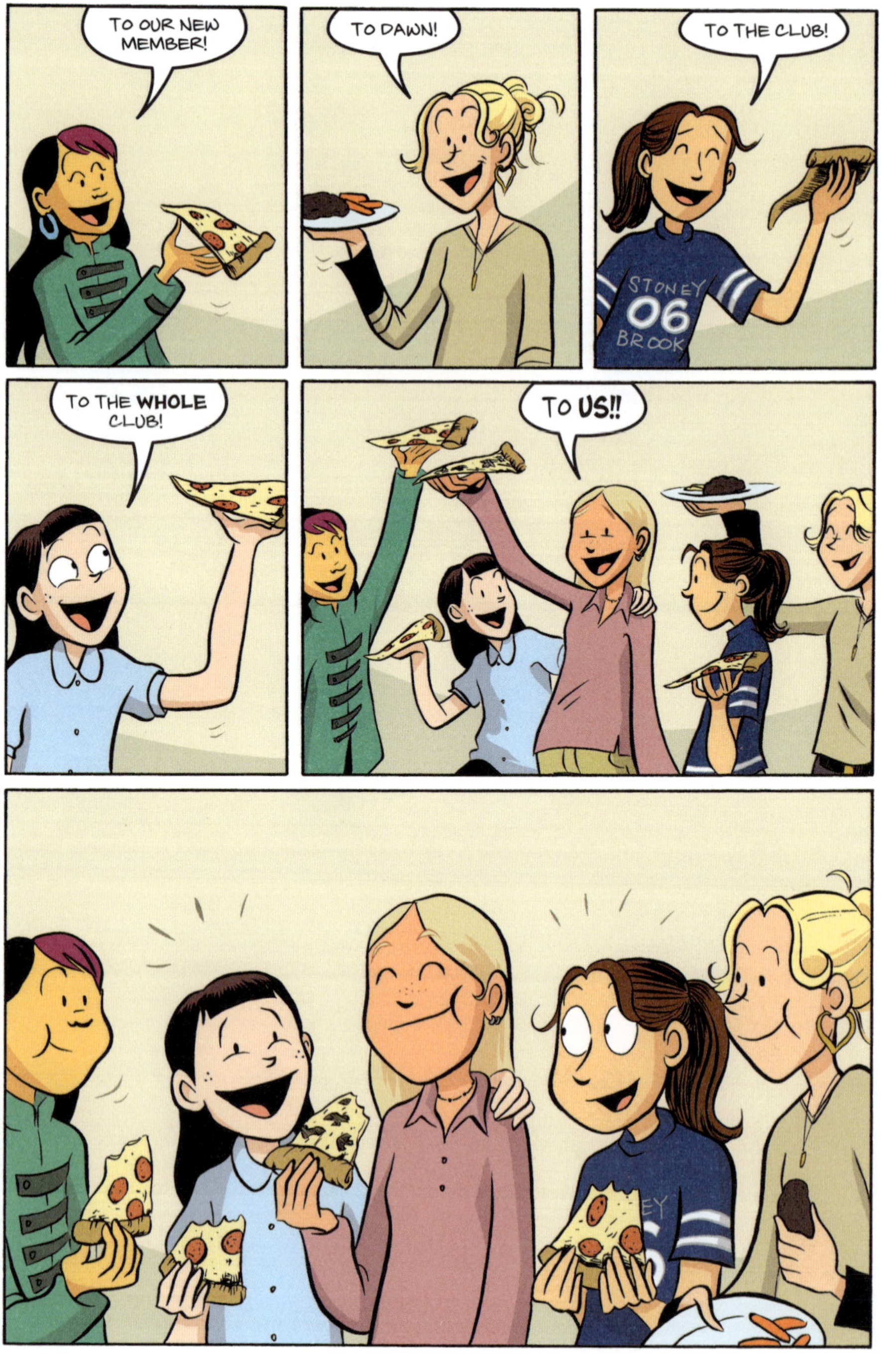
TO OUR NEW MEMBER!
TO DAWN!
TO THE CLUB!
STONEY 06 BROOK
TO THE WHOLE CLUB!
TO US!!

ANN M. MARTIN'S The Baby-sitters Club is one of the most popular series in the history of publishing — with more than 190 million books in print worldwide — and inspired a generation of young readers. Her novels include *Belle Teal*, *A Corner of the Universe* (a Newbery Honor book), *Here Today*, *A Dog's Life*, and *On Christmas Eve*, as well as the much-loved collaborations, *P.S. Longer Letter Later* and *Snail Mail No More*, with Paula Danziger, and *The Doll People* and *The Meanest Doll in the World*, written with Laura Godwin and illustrated by Brian Selznick. Ann lives in upstate New York.

RAINA TELGEMEIER is the #1 *New York Times* bestselling, multiple Eisner Award–winning creator of *Smile*, *Sisters*, and *Guts*, which are all graphic memoirs based on her childhood. She is also the creator of *Drama* and *Ghosts*, and is the adapter and illustrator of the first four Baby-sitters Club graphic novels. Raina lives in the San Francisco Bay Area. To learn more, visit her online at goraina.com.

DON'T MISS THE OTHER BABY-SITTERS CLUB GRAPHIC NOVELS!

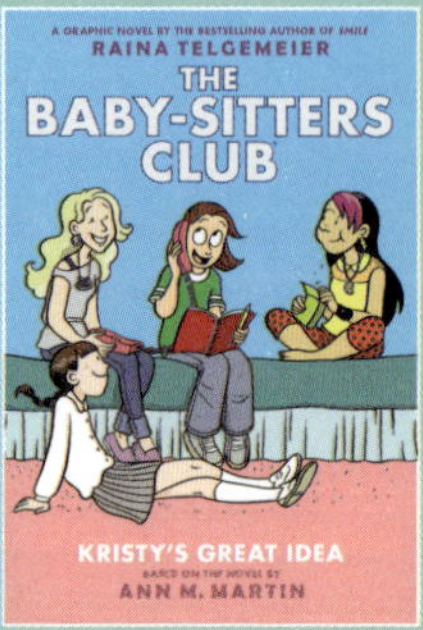
A GRAPHIC NOVEL BY THE BESTSELLING AUTHOR OF SMILE
RAINA TELGEMEIER
THE BABY-SITTERS CLUB
KRISTY'S GREAT IDEA
BASED ON THE NOVEL BY
ANN M. MARTIN

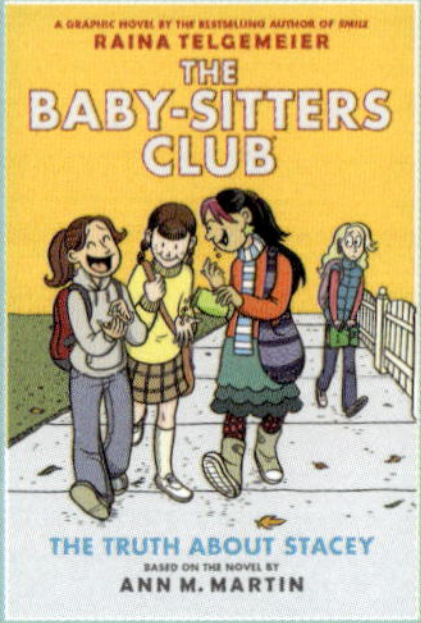
A GRAPHIC NOVEL BY THE BESTSELLING AUTHOR OF SMILE
RAINA TELGEMEIER
THE BABY-SITTERS CLUB
THE TRUTH ABOUT STACEY
BASED ON THE NOVEL BY
ANN M. MARTIN

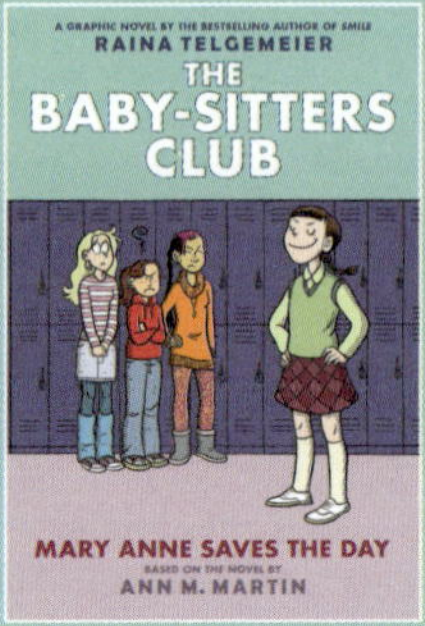
A GRAPHIC NOVEL BY THE BESTSELLING AUTHOR OF SMILE
RAINA TELGEMEIER
THE BABY-SITTERS CLUB
MARY ANNE SAVES THE DAY
BASED ON THE NOVEL BY
ANN M. MARTIN

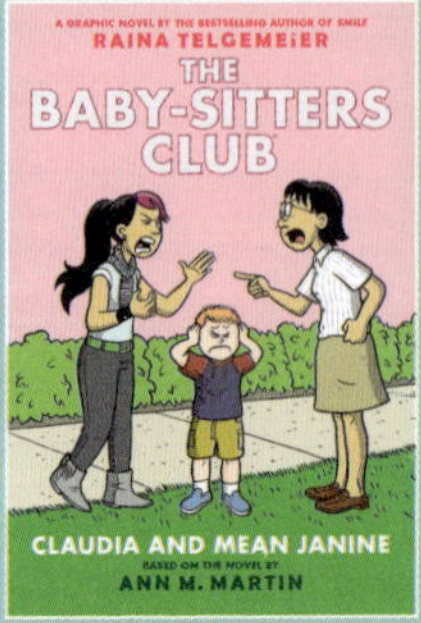
A GRAPHIC NOVEL BY THE BESTSELLING AUTHOR OF SMILE
RAINA TELGEMEIER
THE BABY-SITTERS CLUB
CLAUDIA AND MEAN JANINE
BASED ON THE NOVEL BY
ANN M. MARTIN

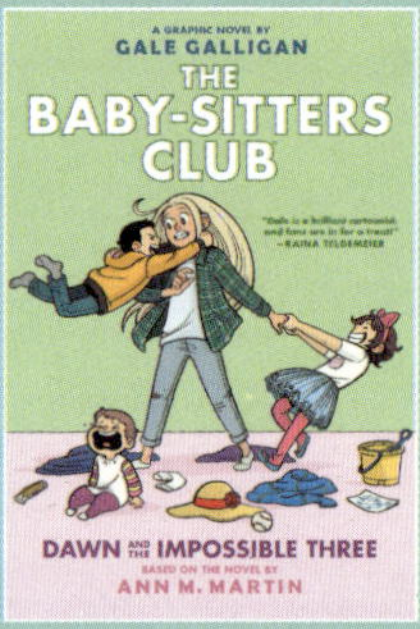
A GRAPHIC NOVEL BY
GALE GALLIGAN
THE BABY-SITTERS CLUB
DAWN AND THE IMPOSSIBLE THREE
BASED ON THE NOVEL BY
ANN M. MARTIN

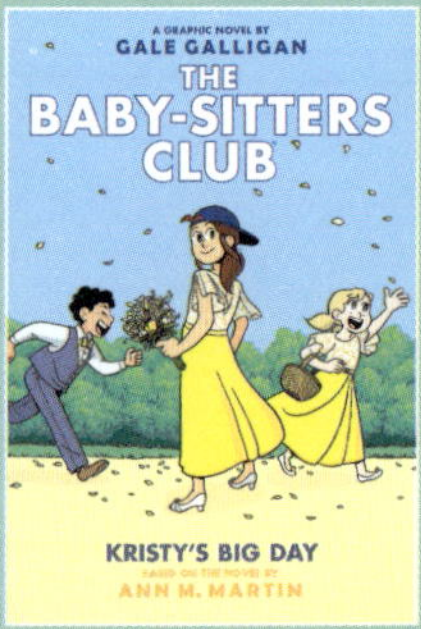
A GRAPHIC NOVEL BY
GALE GALLIGAN
THE BABY-SITTERS CLUB
KRISTY'S BIG DAY
BASED ON THE NOVEL BY
ANN M. MARTIN

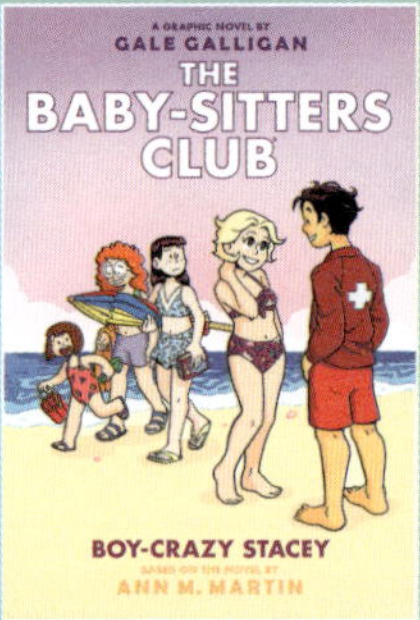
A GRAPHIC NOVEL BY
GALE GALLIGAN
THE BABY-SITTERS CLUB
BOY-CRAZY STACEY
BASED ON THE NOVEL BY
ANN M. MARTIN

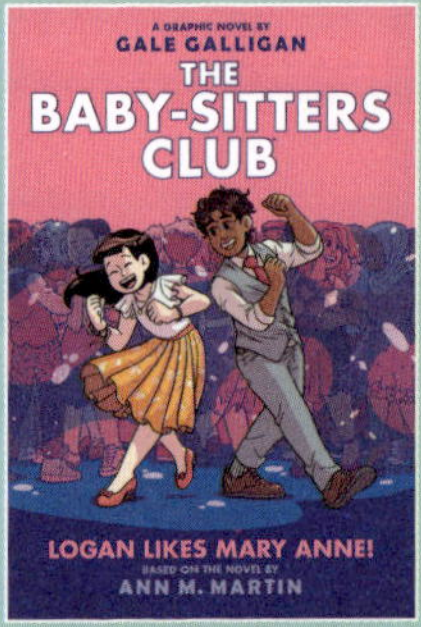
A GRAPHIC NOVEL BY
GALE GALLIGAN
THE BABY-SITTERS CLUB
LOGAN LIKES MARY ANNE!
BASED ON THE NOVEL BY
ANN M. MARTIN

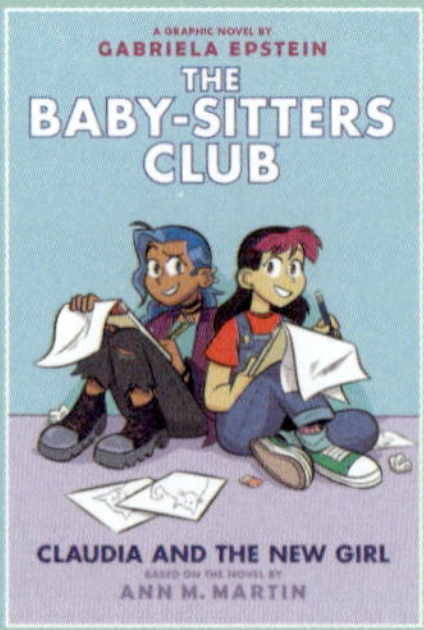
A GRAPHIC NOVEL BY
GABRIELA EPSTEIN
THE BABY-SITTERS CLUB
CLAUDIA AND THE NEW GIRL
BASED ON THE NOVEL BY
ANN M. MARTIN

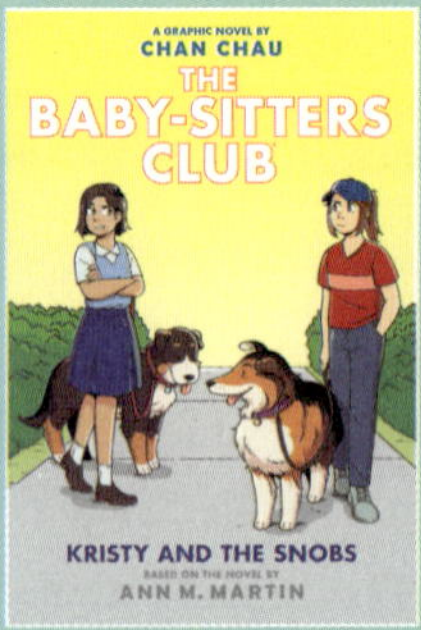
A GRAPHIC NOVEL BY
CHAN CHAU
THE BABY-SITTERS CLUB
KRISTY AND THE SNOBS
BASED ON THE NOVEL BY
ANN M. MARTIN

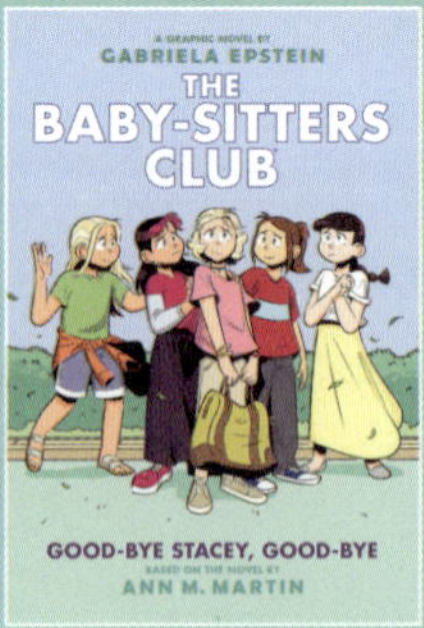
A GRAPHIC NOVEL BY
GABRIELA EPSTEIN
THE BABY-SITTERS CLUB
GOOD-BYE STACEY, GOOD-BYE
BASED ON THE NOVEL BY
ANN M. MARTIN

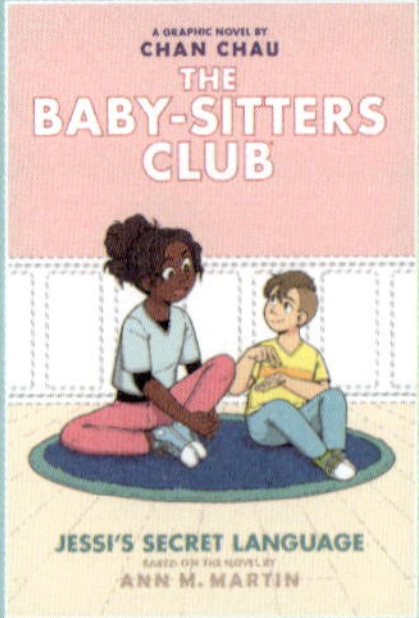
A GRAPHIC NOVEL BY
CHAN CHAU
THE BABY-SITTERS CLUB
JESSI'S SECRET LANGUAGE
BASED ON THE NOVEL BY
ANN M. MARTIN

THE BABY-SITTERS CLUB

CLAUDIA AND MEAN JANINE

**DON'T MISS THE OTHER
BABY-SITTERS CLUB GRAPHIC NOVELS!**

KRISTY'S GREAT IDEA

THE TRUTH ABOUT STACEY

MARY ANNE SAVES THE DAY

DAWN AND THE IMPOSSIBLE THREE

ANN M. MARTIN

THE BABY-SITTERS CLUB®

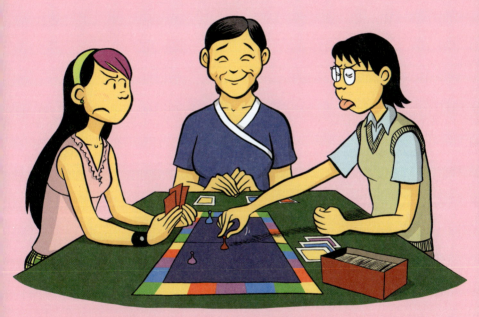

CLAUDIA AND MEAN JANINE

A GRAPHIC NOVEL BY

RAINA TELGEMEIER

WITH COLOR BY BRADEN LAMB

graphix

An Imprint of

SCHOLASTIC

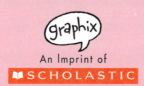

Text copyright © 2008, 2016 by Ann M. Martin
Art copyright © 2008, 2016 by Raina Telgemeier

All rights reserved. Published by Graphix, an imprint of Scholastic Inc., *Publishers since 1920*. SCHOLASTIC, GRAPHIX, THE BABY-SITTERS CLUB, and associated logos are trademarks and/or registered trademarks of Scholastic Inc.

The publisher does not have any control over and does not assume any responsibility for author or third-party websites or their content.

No part of this publication may be reproduced, stored in a retrieval system, or transmitted in any form or by any means, electronic, mechanical, photocopying, recording, or otherwise, without written permission of the publisher. For information regarding permission, write to Scholastic Inc., Attention: Permissions Department, 557 Broadway, New York, NY 10012.

This book is a work of fiction. Names, characters, places, and incidents are either the product of the author's imagination or are used fictitiously, and any resemblance to actual persons, living or dead, business establishments, events, or locales is entirely coincidental.

Library of Congress Control Number: 2015935840

ISBN 978-0-545-88623-9 (hardcover)
ISBN 978-1-338-88826-3 (paperback)

10 9 8 7 6 5 4   24 25 26 27

Printed in China   62
This edition first printing, April 2023

Lettering by John Green
Edited by Cassandra Pelham Fulton, Sheila Keenan, and David Levithan
Book design by Phil Falco
Creative Director: David Saylor

For Aunt Adele and Uncle Paul
A. M. M.

Thanks to everyone who has helped make this project a reality! Dave Roman, Marion Vitus, John Green, Ashley Button, Janna Morishima, David Saylor, David Levithan, Cassandra Pelham, Ellie Berger, Sheila Keenan, Kristina Albertson, Phil Falco, Vera Brosgol, Dr. Laurie Kane, the Green family: Bill, Martha, and MarMar, and most especially, Ann M. Martin.
R. T.

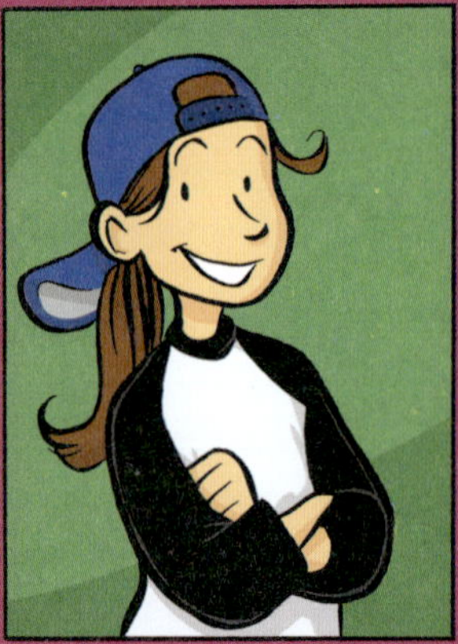

KRISTY THOMAS
PRESIDENT

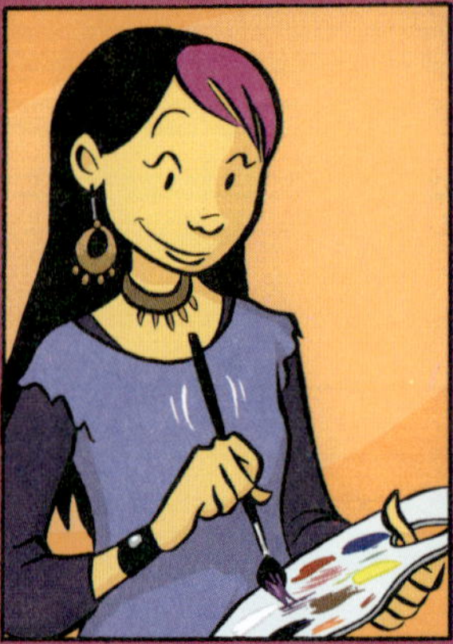

CLAUDIA KISHI
VICE PRESIDENT

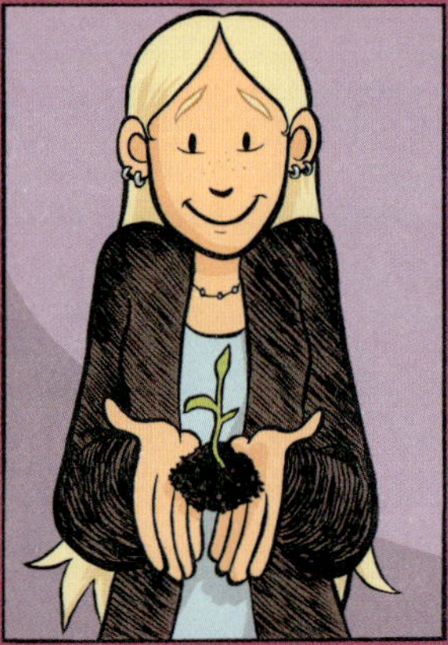

DAWN SCHAFER

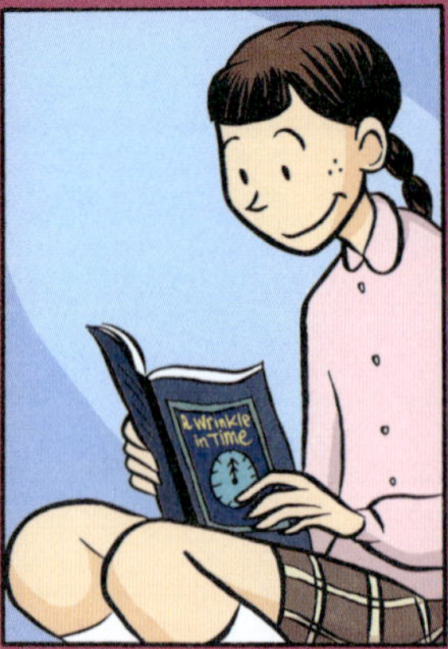
A Wrinkle in Time

MARY ANNE SPIER
SECRETARY

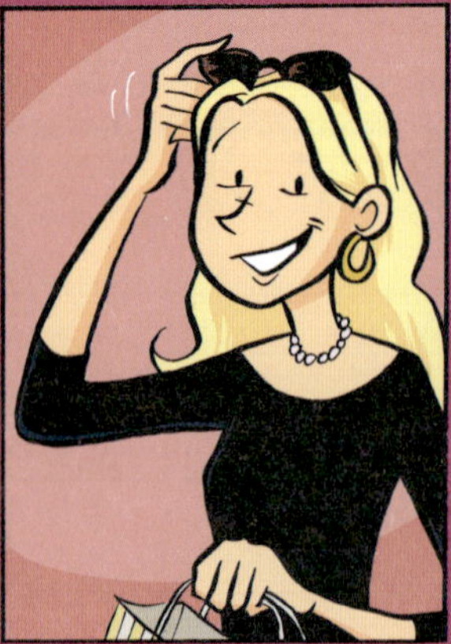

STACEY MCGILL
TREASURER

CHAPTER 1

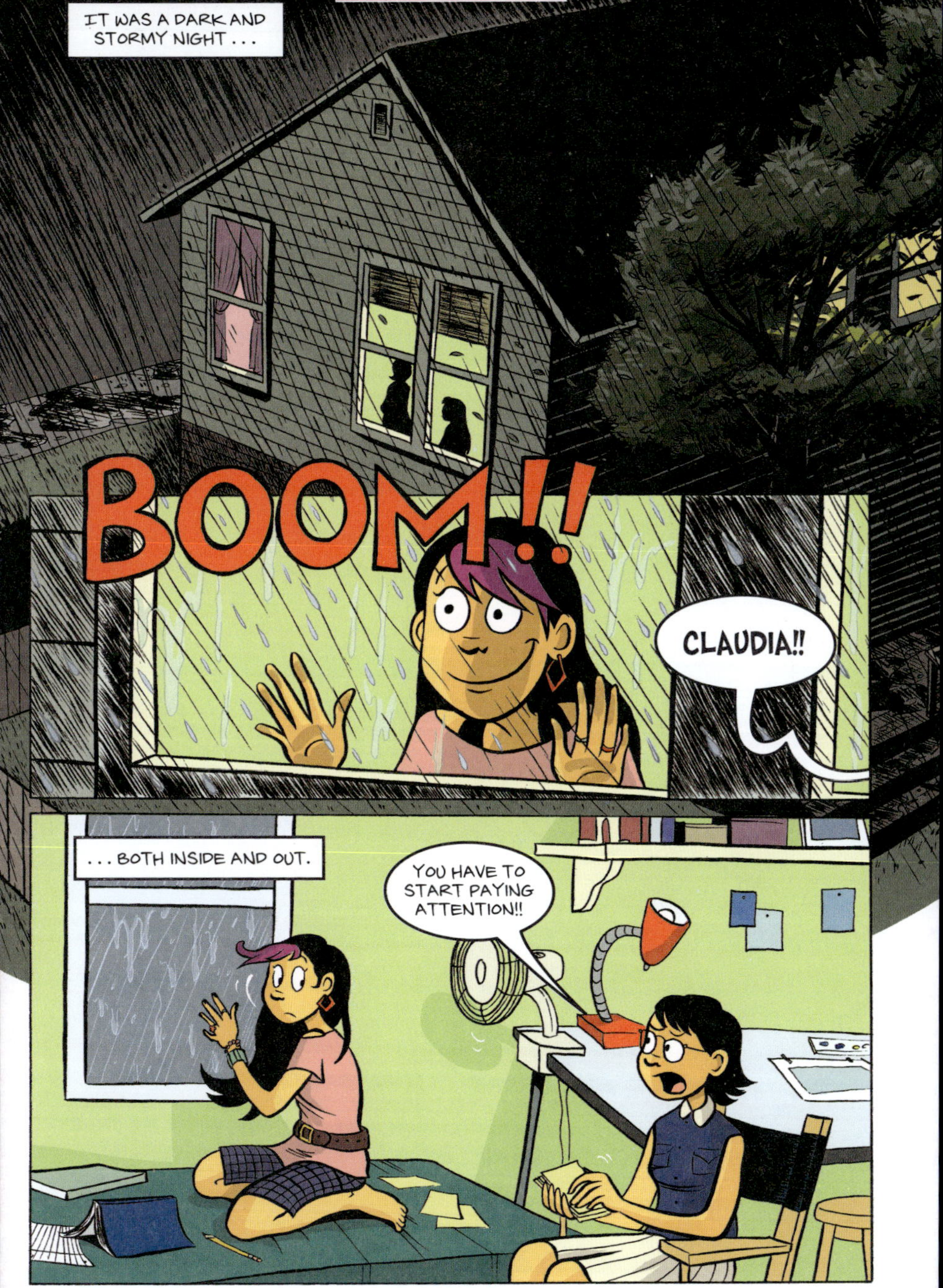
IT WAS A DARK AND STORMY NIGHT . . .
BOOM!!
CLAUDIA!!
. . . BOTH INSIDE AND OUT.
YOU HAVE TO START PAYING ATTENTION!!

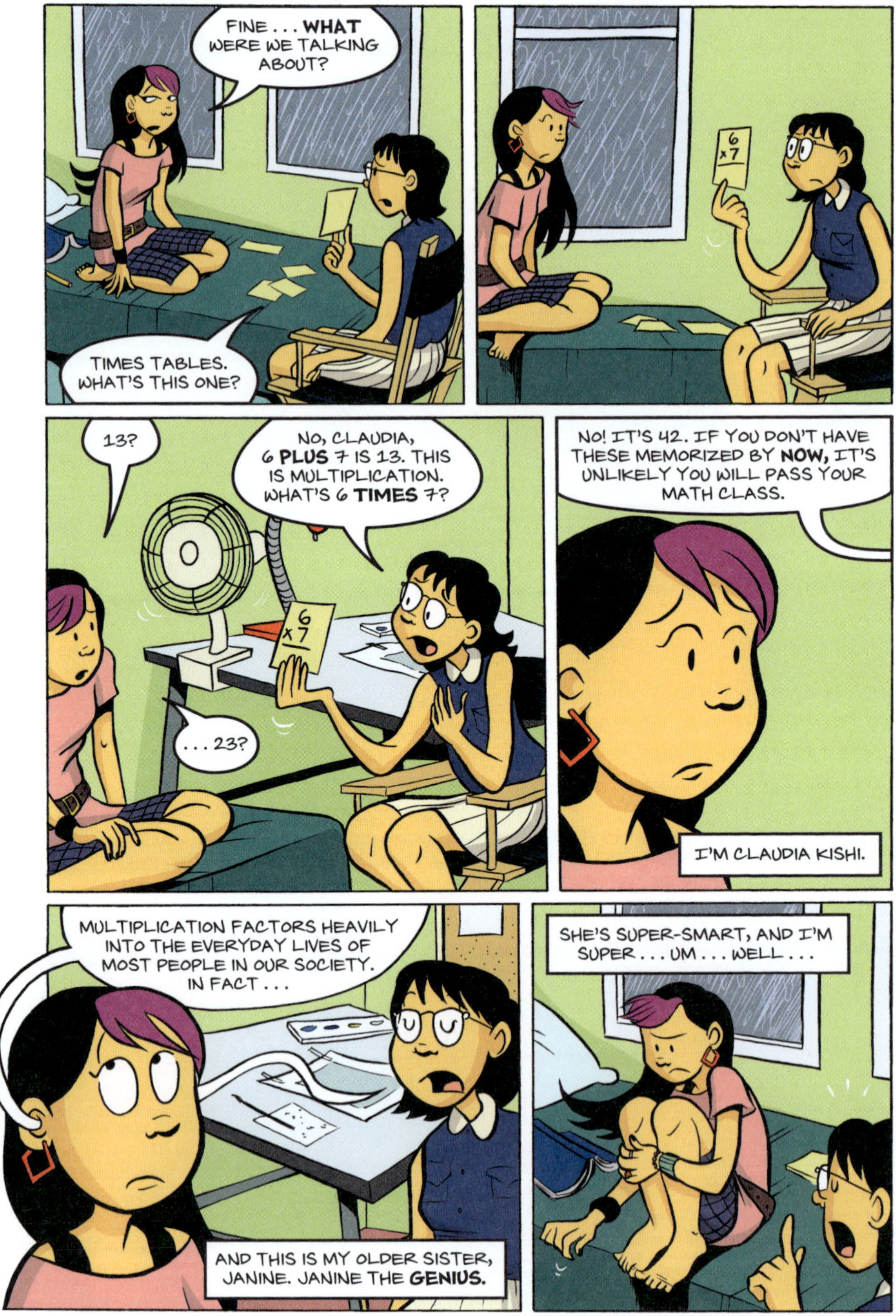

FINE . . . WHAT WERE WE TALKING ABOUT?
TIMES TABLES. WHAT'S THIS ONE?
6 x 7
13?
NO, CLAUDIA, 6 PLUS 7 IS 13. THIS IS MULTIPLICATION. WHAT'S 6 TIMES 7?
6 x 7
. . . 23?
NO! IT'S 42. IF YOU DON'T HAVE THESE MEMORIZED BY NOW, IT'S UNLIKELY YOU WILL PASS YOUR MATH CLASS.
I'M CLAUDIA KISHI.
MULTIPLICATION FACTORS HEAVILY INTO THE EVERYDAY LIVES OF MOST PEOPLE IN OUR SOCIETY. IN FACT . . .
AND THIS IS MY OLDER SISTER, JANINE. JANINE THE GENIUS.
SHE'S SUPER-SMART, AND I'M SUPER . . . UM . . . WELL . . .

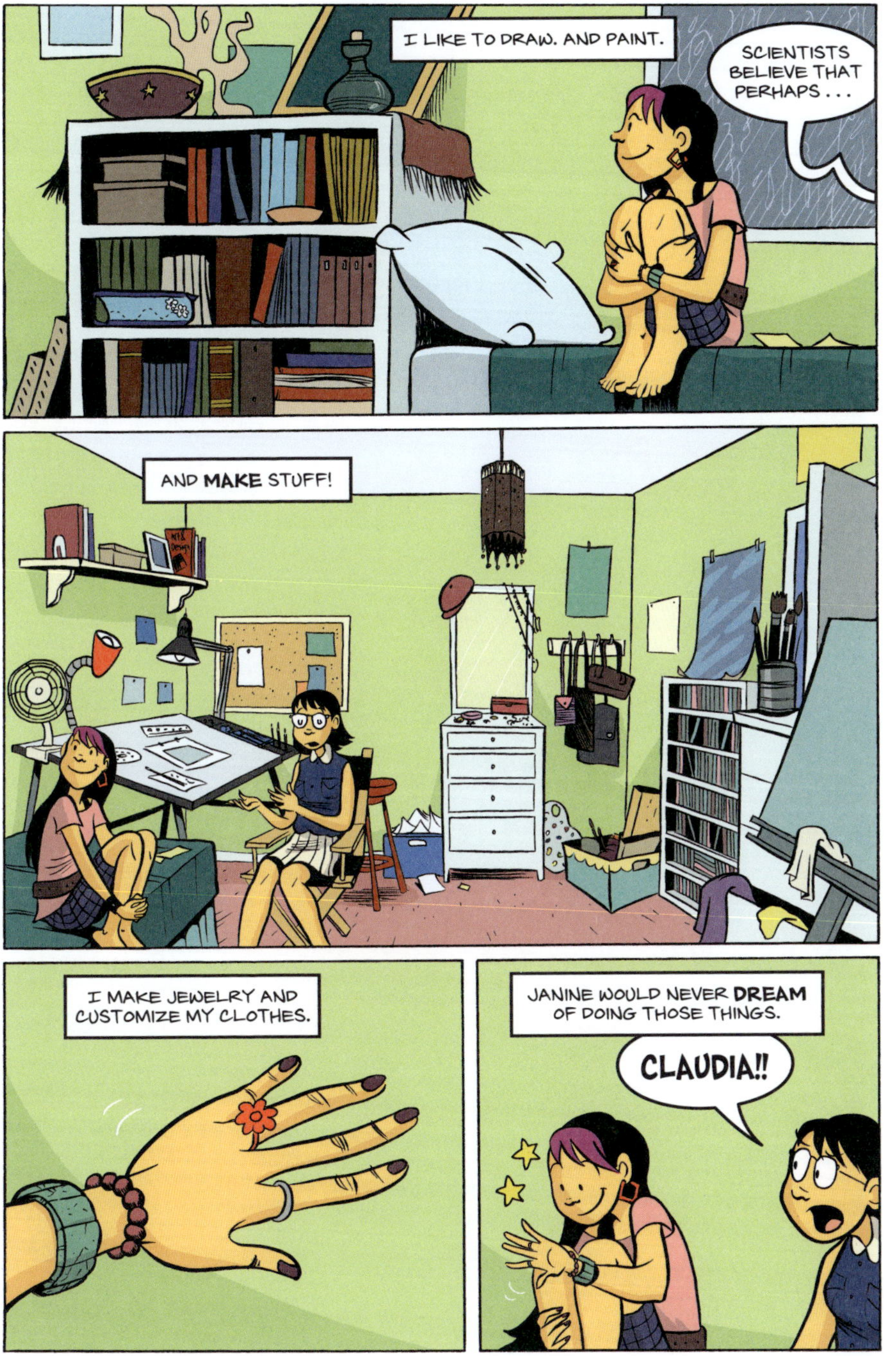
I LIKE TO DRAW. AND PAINT.
SCIENTISTS BELIEVE THAT PERHAPS . . .
AND **MAKE** STUFF!
I MAKE JEWELRY AND CUSTOMIZE MY CLOTHES.
JANINE WOULD NEVER **DREAM** OF DOING THOSE THINGS.
CLAUDIA!!

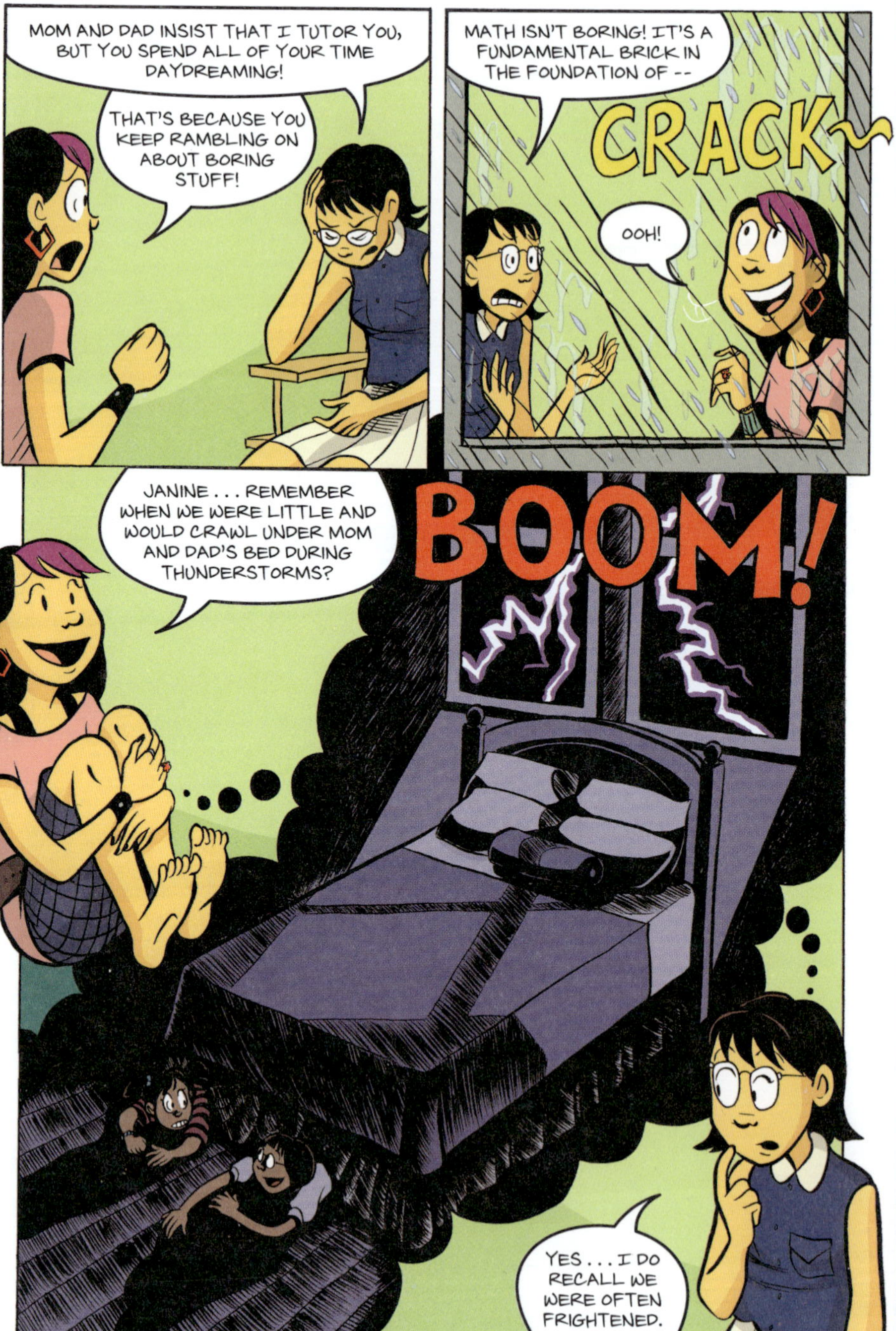
MOM AND DAD INSIST THAT I TUTOR YOU, BUT YOU SPEND ALL OF YOUR TIME DAYDREAMING!
THAT'S BECAUSE YOU KEEP RAMBLING ON ABOUT BORING STUFF!
MATH ISN'T BORING! IT'S A FUNDAMENTAL BRICK IN THE FOUNDATION OF --
CRACK
OOH!
JANINE . . . REMEMBER WHEN WE WERE LITTLE AND WOULD CRAWL UNDER MOM AND DAD'S BED DURING THUNDERSTORMS?
BOOM!
YES . . . I DO RECALL WE WERE OFTEN FRIGHTENED.

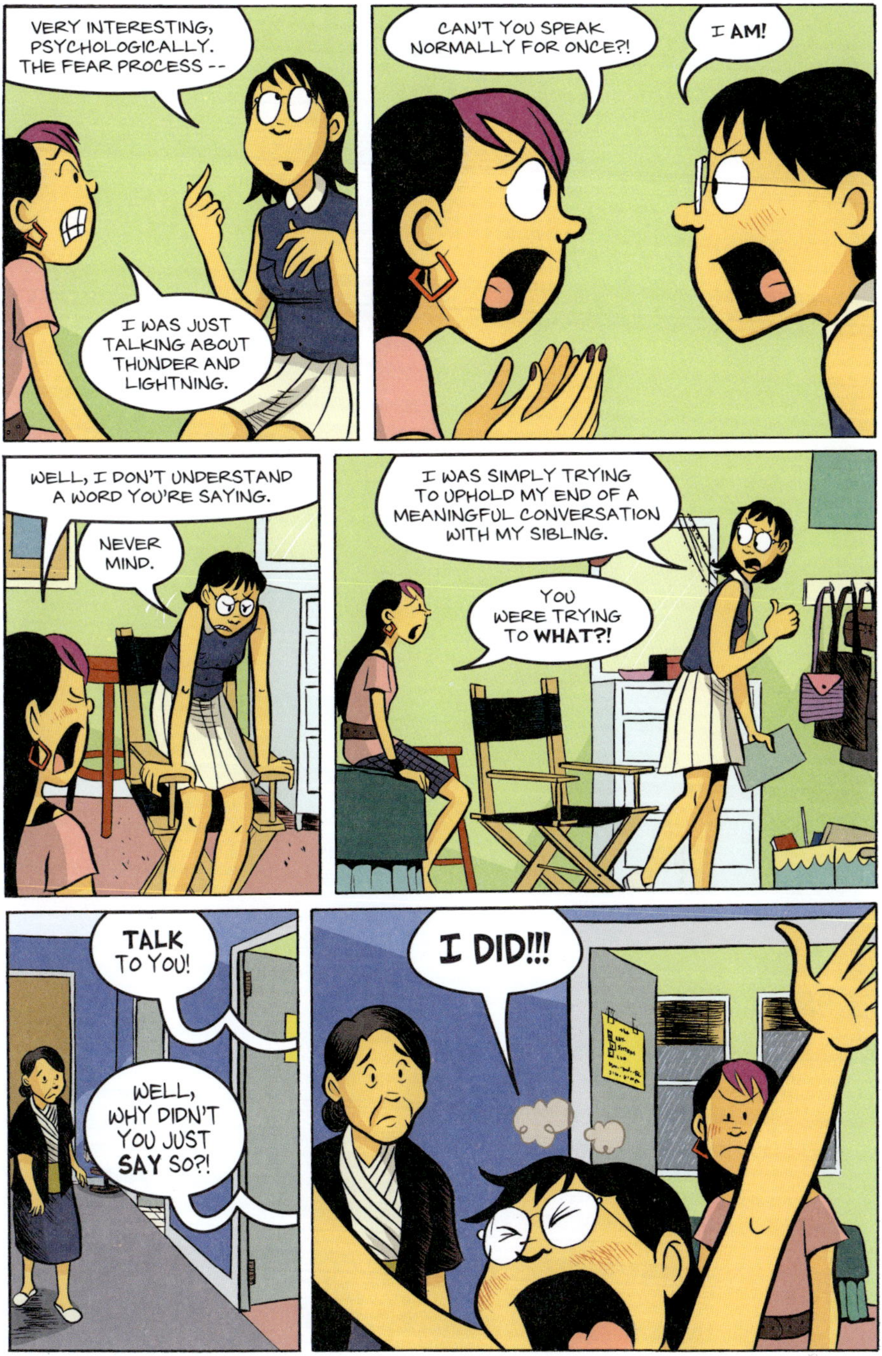
VERY INTERESTING, PSYCHOLOGICALLY. THE FEAR PROCESS --
I WAS JUST TALKING ABOUT THUNDER AND LIGHTNING.
CAN'T YOU SPEAK NORMALLY FOR ONCE?!
I AM!
WELL, I DON'T UNDERSTAND A WORD YOU'RE SAYING.
NEVER MIND.
I WAS SIMPLY TRYING TO UPHOLD MY END OF A MEANINGFUL CONVERSATION WITH MY SIBLING.
YOU WERE TRYING TO WHAT?!
TALK TO YOU!
WELL, WHY DIDN'T YOU JUST SAY SO?!
I DID!!!

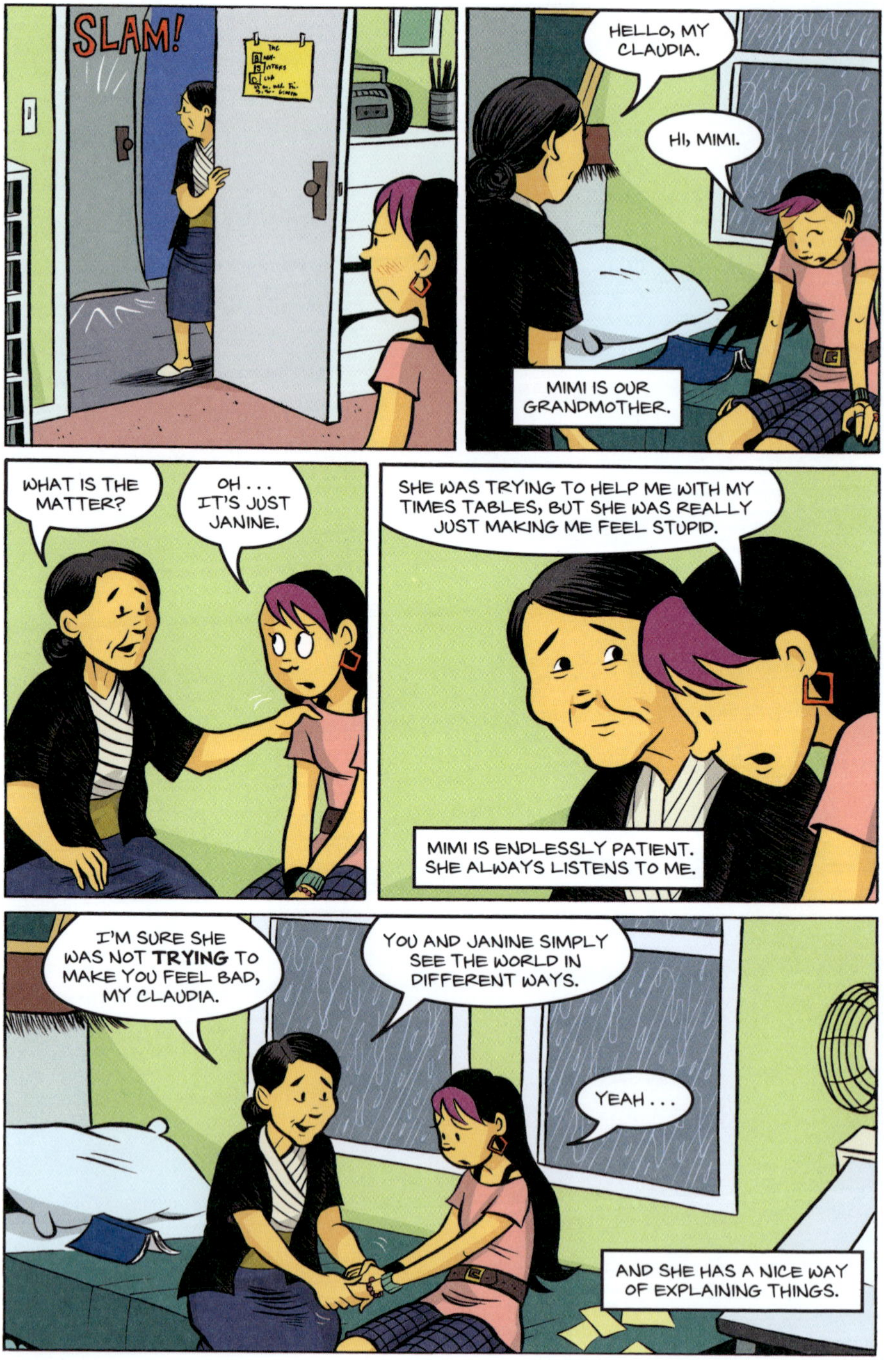
SLAM!
HELLO, MY CLAUDIA.
HI, MIMI.
MIMI IS OUR GRANDMOTHER.
WHAT IS THE MATTER?
OH . . . IT'S JUST JANINE.
SHE WAS TRYING TO HELP ME WITH MY TIMES TABLES, BUT SHE WAS REALLY JUST MAKING ME FEEL STUPID.
MIMI IS ENDLESSLY PATIENT. SHE ALWAYS LISTENS TO ME.
I'M SURE SHE WAS NOT **TRYING** TO MAKE YOU FEEL BAD, MY CLAUDIA.
YOU AND JANINE SIMPLY SEE THE WORLD IN DIFFERENT WAYS.
YEAH . . .
AND SHE HAS A NICE WAY OF EXPLAINING THINGS.

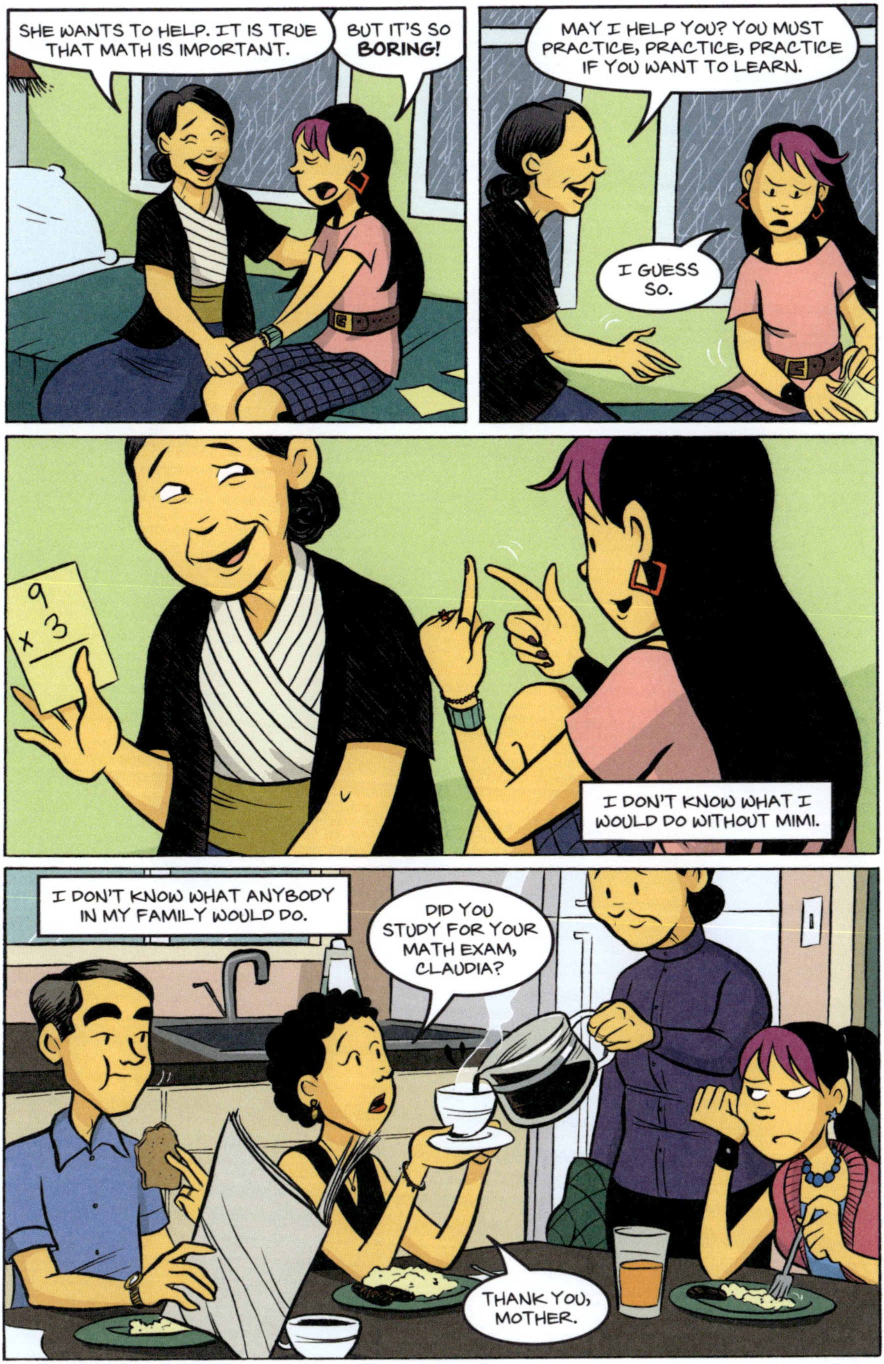
SHE WANTS TO HELP. IT IS TRUE THAT MATH IS IMPORTANT.
BUT IT'S SO **BORING!**
MAY I HELP YOU? YOU MUST PRACTICE, PRACTICE, PRACTICE IF YOU WANT TO LEARN.
I GUESS SO.
9 x 3
I DON'T KNOW WHAT I WOULD DO WITHOUT MIMI.
I DON'T KNOW WHAT ANYBODY IN MY FAMILY WOULD DO.
DID YOU STUDY FOR YOUR MATH EXAM, CLAUDIA?
THANK YOU, MOTHER.

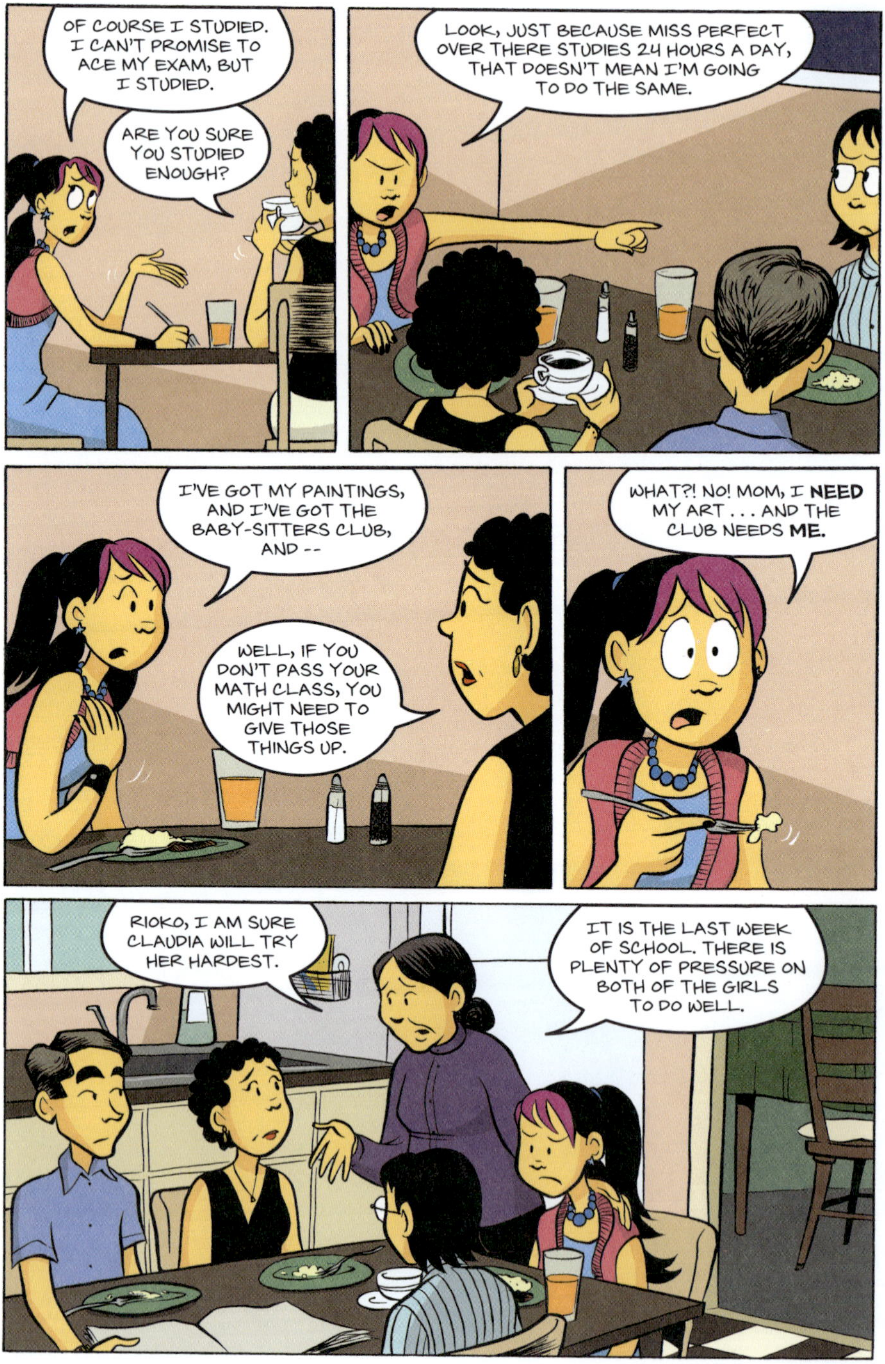
OF COURSE I STUDIED. I CAN'T PROMISE TO ACE MY EXAM, BUT I STUDIED.
ARE YOU SURE YOU STUDIED ENOUGH?
LOOK, JUST BECAUSE MISS PERFECT OVER THERE STUDIES 24 HOURS A DAY, THAT DOESN'T MEAN I'M GOING TO DO THE SAME.
I'VE GOT MY PAINTINGS, AND I'VE GOT THE BABY-SITTERS CLUB, AND --
WELL, IF YOU DON'T PASS YOUR MATH CLASS, YOU MIGHT NEED TO GIVE THOSE THINGS UP.
WHAT?! NO! MOM, I **NEED** MY ART . . . AND THE CLUB NEEDS **ME.**
RIOKO, I AM SURE CLAUDIA WILL TRY HER HARDEST.
IT IS THE LAST WEEK OF SCHOOL. THERE IS PLENTY OF PRESSURE ON BOTH OF THE GIRLS TO DO WELL.

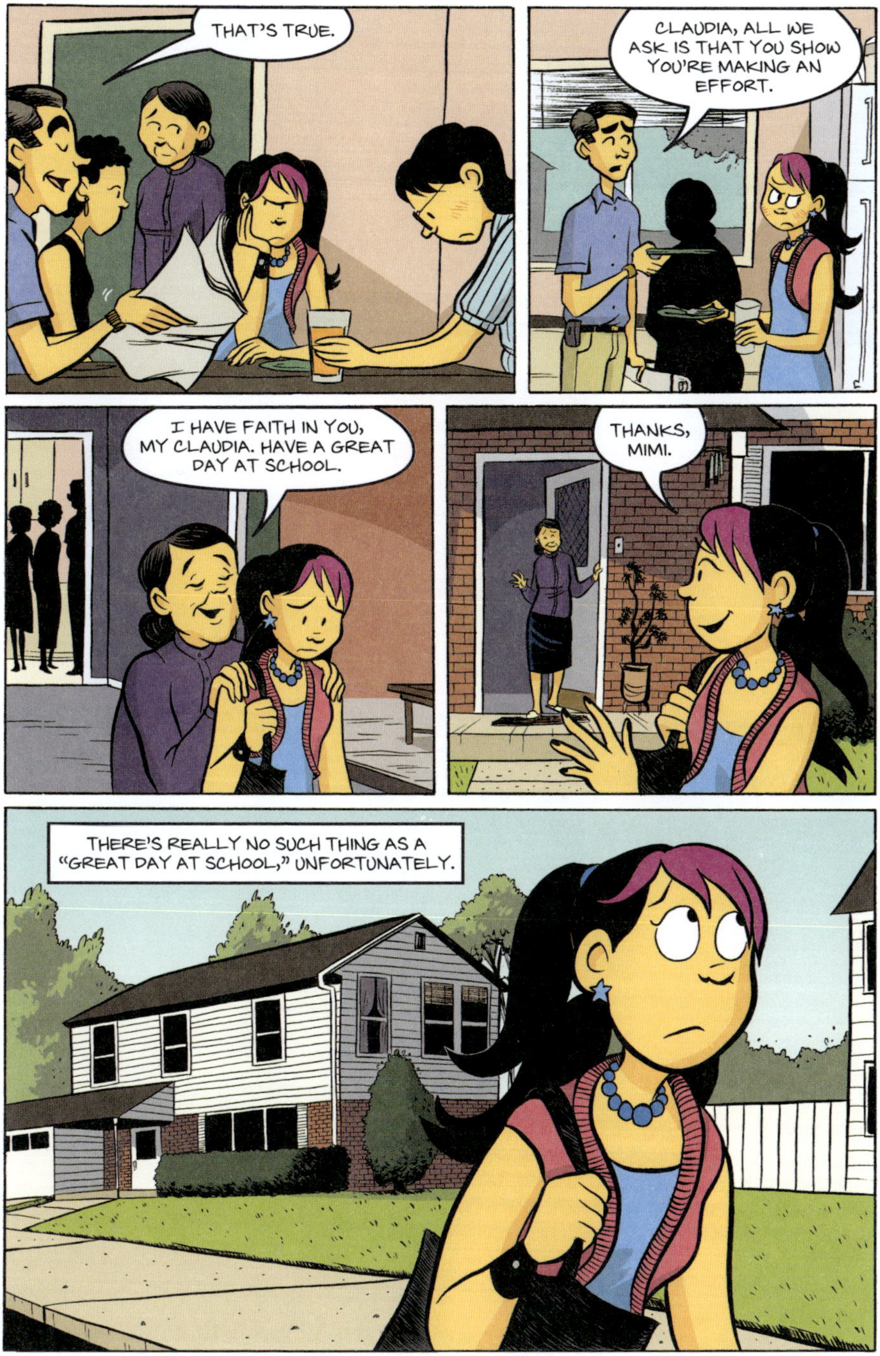
THAT'S TRUE.
CLAUDIA, ALL WE ASK IS THAT YOU SHOW YOU'RE MAKING AN EFFORT.
I HAVE FAITH IN YOU, MY CLAUDIA. HAVE A GREAT DAY AT SCHOOL.
THANKS, MIMI.
THERE'S REALLY NO SUCH THING AS A "GREAT DAY AT SCHOOL," UNFORTUNATELY.

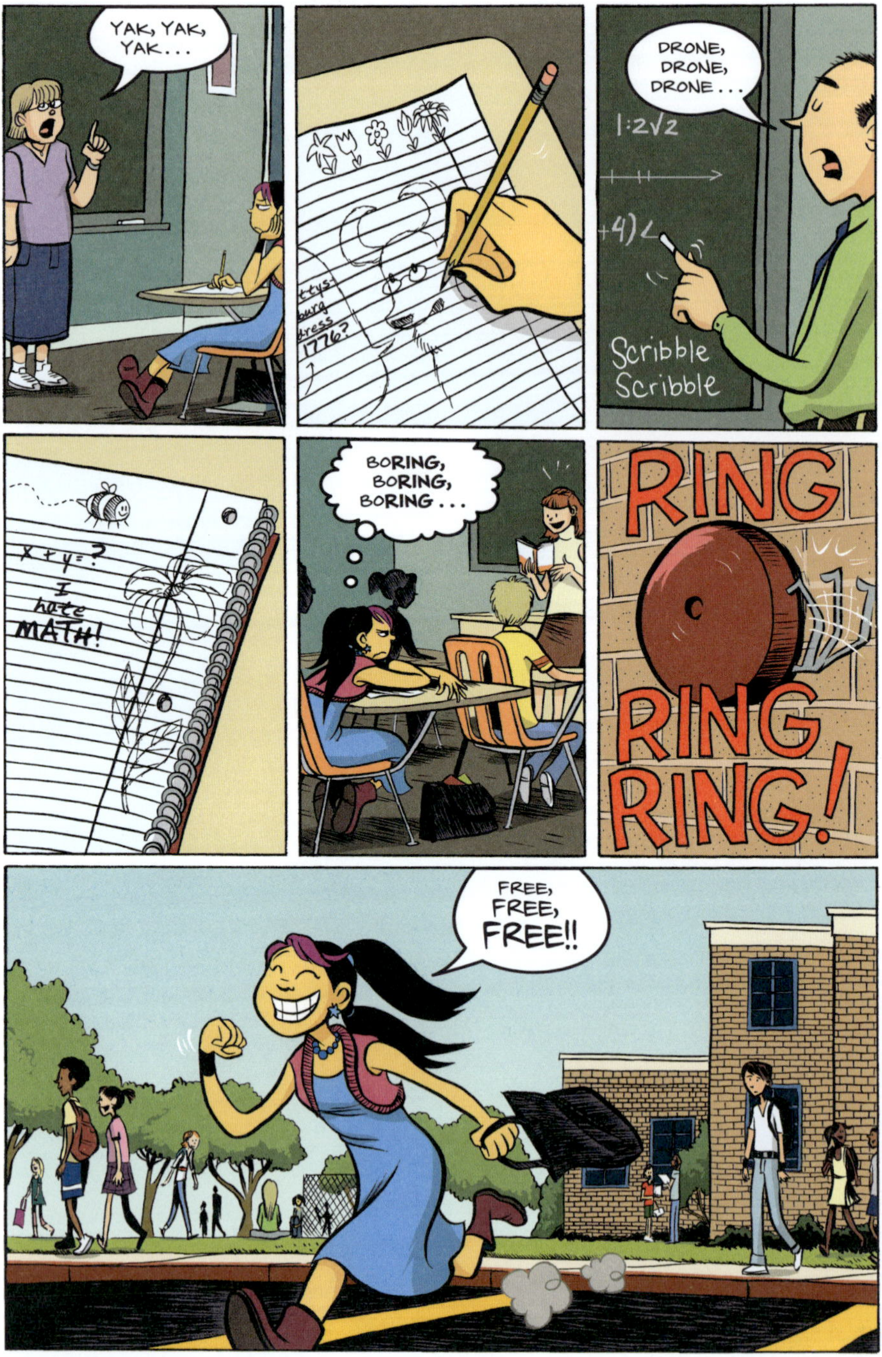
YAK, YAK, YAK . . .
DRONE, DRONE, DRONE . . .
1:2√2
Scribble Scribble
x + y = ?
I hate MATH!
BORING, BORING, BORING . . .
RING RING RING!
FREE, FREE, FREE!!

CHAPTER 2

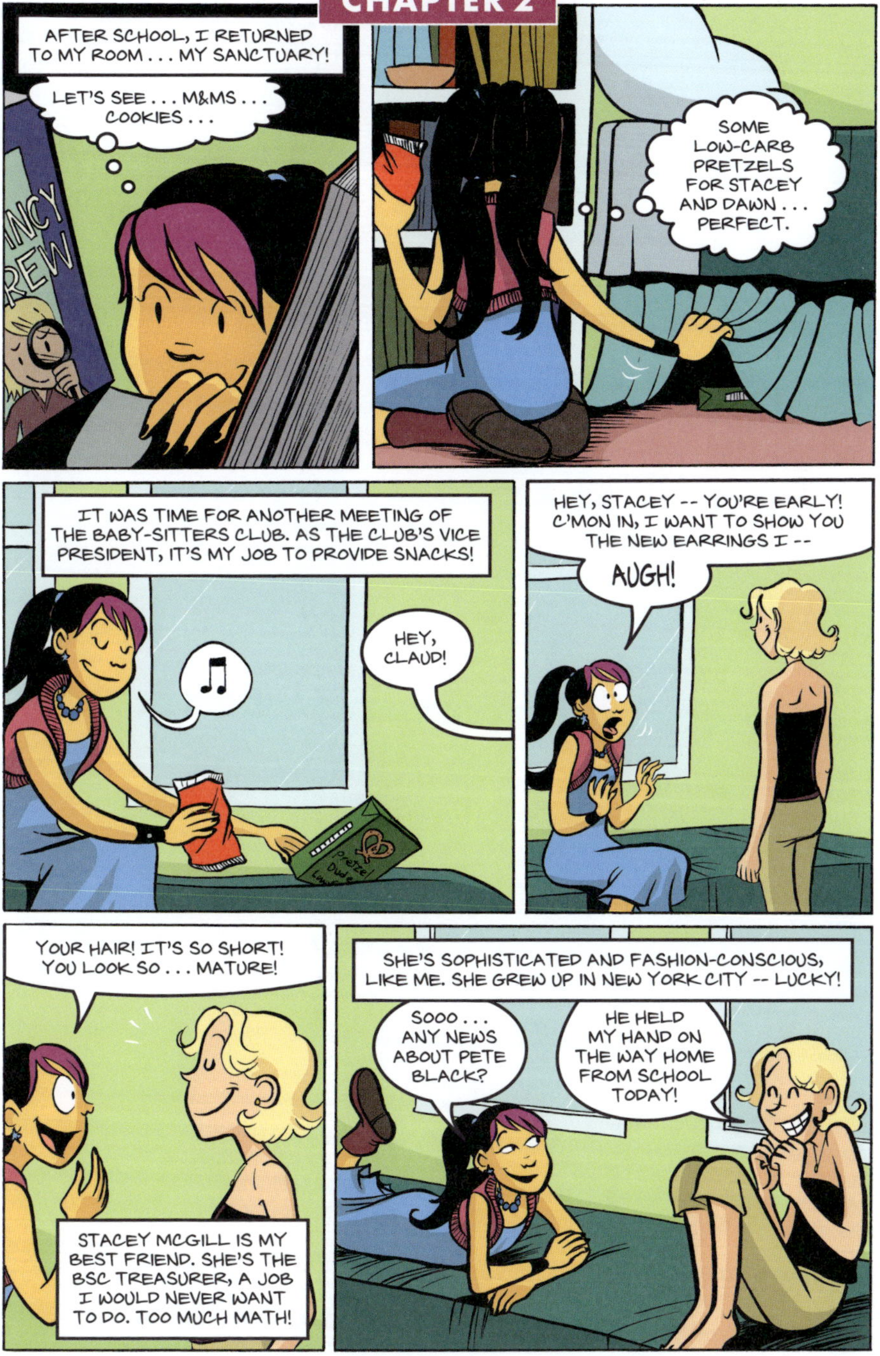

AFTER SCHOOL, I RETURNED TO MY ROOM . . . MY SANCTUARY!
LET'S SEE . . . M&MS . . . COOKIES . . .
SOME LOW-CARB PRETZELS FOR STACEY AND DAWN . . . PERFECT.
IT WAS TIME FOR ANOTHER MEETING OF THE BABY-SITTERS CLUB. AS THE CLUB'S VICE PRESIDENT, IT'S MY JOB TO PROVIDE SNACKS!
♫
HEY, CLAUD!
HEY, STACEY -- YOU'RE EARLY! C'MON IN, I WANT TO SHOW YOU THE NEW EARRINGS I --
AUGH!
YOUR HAIR! IT'S SO SHORT! YOU LOOK SO . . . MATURE!
STACEY MCGILL IS MY BEST FRIEND. SHE'S THE BSC TREASURER, A JOB I WOULD NEVER WANT TO DO. TOO MUCH MATH!
SHE'S SOPHISTICATED AND FASHION-CONSCIOUS, LIKE ME. SHE GREW UP IN NEW YORK CITY -- LUCKY!
SOOO . . . ANY NEWS ABOUT PETE BLACK?
HE HELD MY HAND ON THE WAY HOME FROM SCHOOL TODAY!

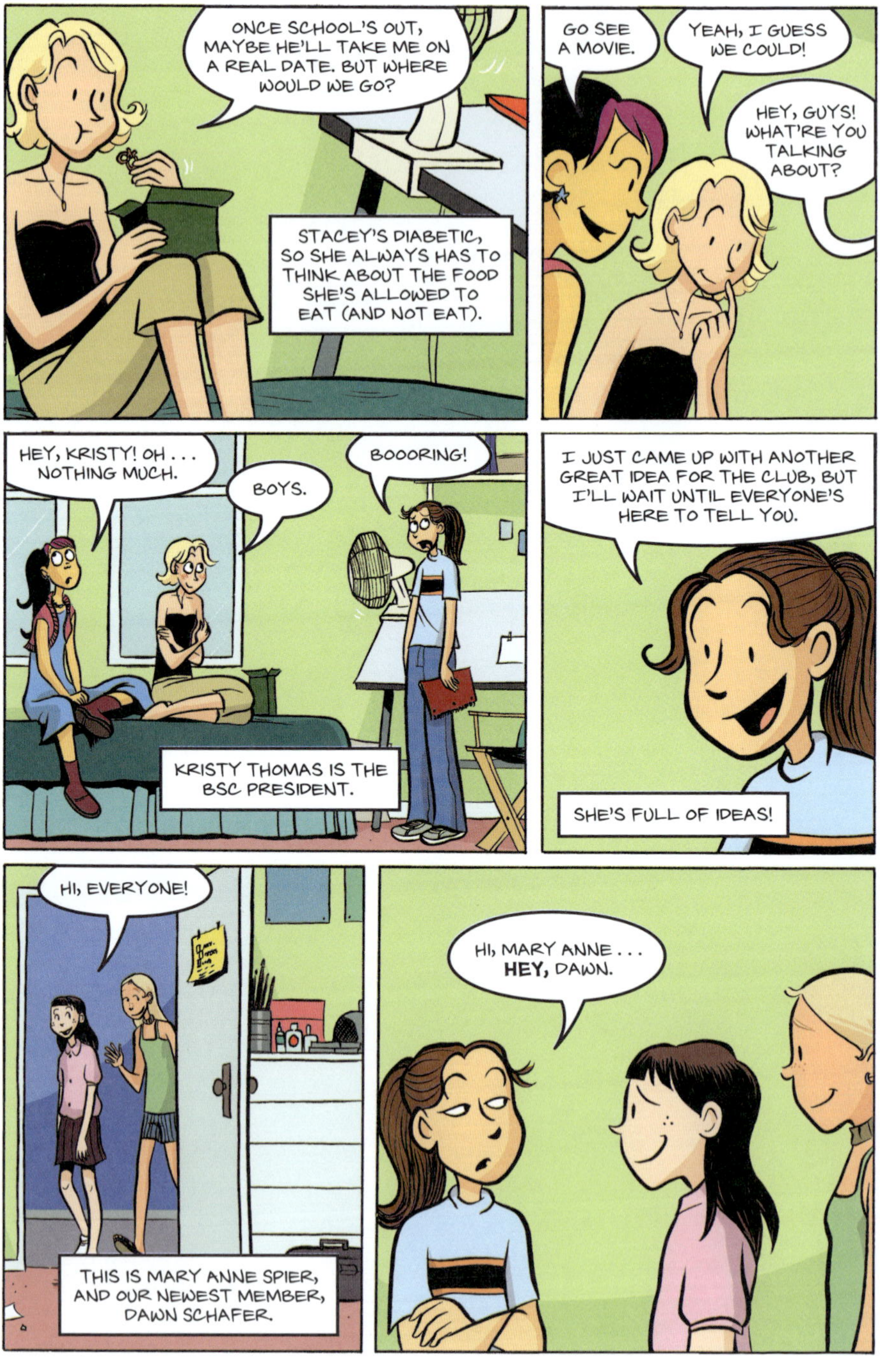
ONCE SCHOOL'S OUT, MAYBE HE'LL TAKE ME ON A REAL DATE. BUT WHERE WOULD WE GO?
STACEY'S DIABETIC, SO SHE ALWAYS HAS TO THINK ABOUT THE FOOD SHE'S ALLOWED TO EAT (AND NOT EAT).
GO SEE A MOVIE.
YEAH, I GUESS WE COULD!
HEY, GUYS! WHAT'RE YOU TALKING ABOUT?
HEY, KRISTY! OH . . . NOTHING MUCH.
BOYS.
BOOORING!
KRISTY THOMAS IS THE BSC PRESIDENT.
I JUST CAME UP WITH ANOTHER GREAT IDEA FOR THE CLUB, BUT I'LL WAIT UNTIL EVERYONE'S HERE TO TELL YOU.
SHE'S FULL OF IDEAS!
HI, EVERYONE!
THIS IS MARY ANNE SPIER, AND OUR NEWEST MEMBER, DAWN SCHAFER.
HI, MARY ANNE . . . **HEY,** DAWN.

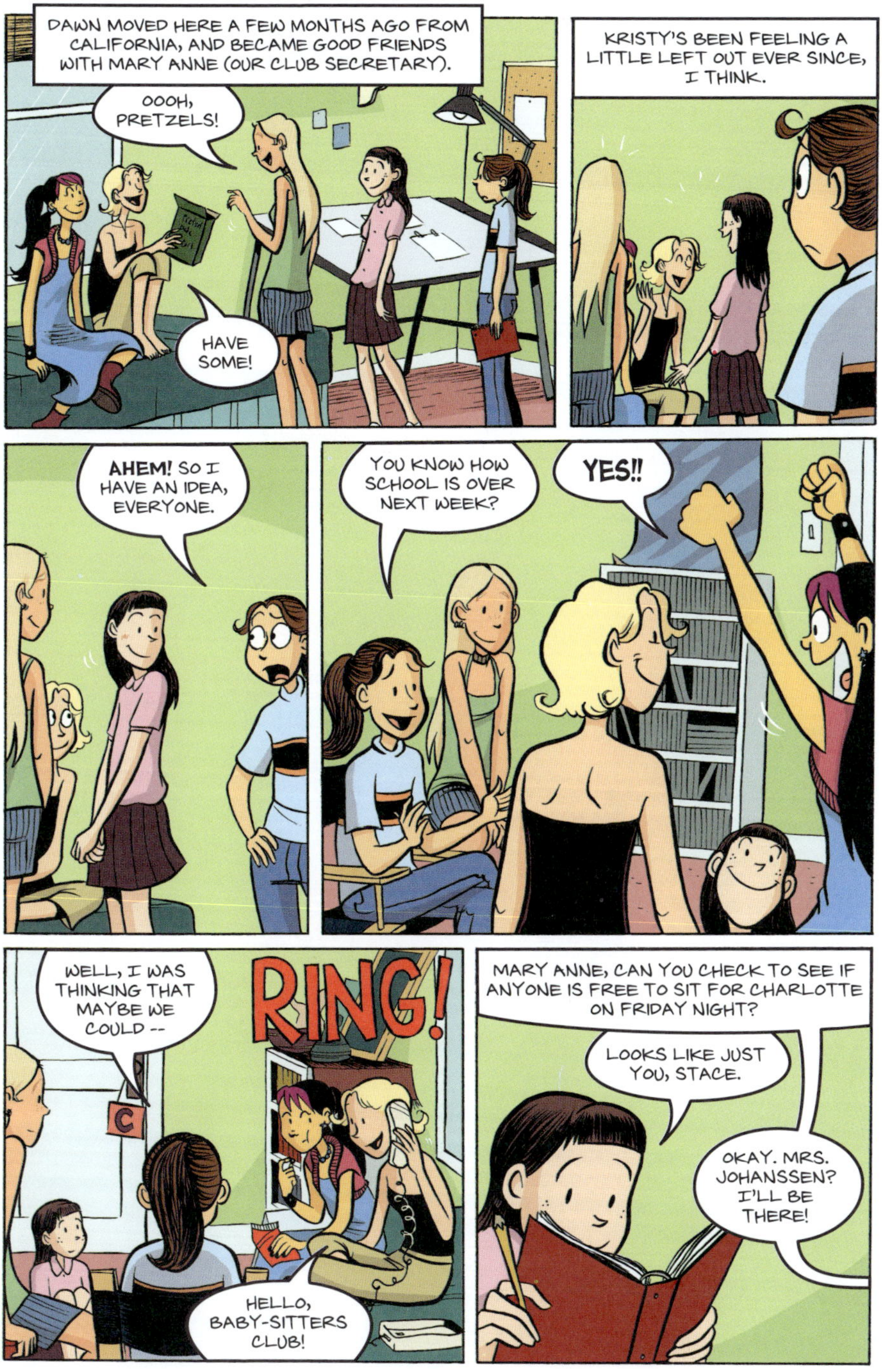
DAWN MOVED HERE A FEW MONTHS AGO FROM CALIFORNIA, AND BECAME GOOD FRIENDS WITH MARY ANNE (OUR CLUB SECRETARY).
OOOH, PRETZELS!
HAVE SOME!
KRISTY'S BEEN FEELING A LITTLE LEFT OUT EVER SINCE, I THINK.
AHEM! SO I HAVE AN IDEA, EVERYONE.
YOU KNOW HOW SCHOOL IS OVER NEXT WEEK?
YES!!
WELL, I WAS THINKING THAT MAYBE WE COULD --
RING!
HELLO, BABY-SITTERS CLUB!
MARY ANNE, CAN YOU CHECK TO SEE IF ANYONE IS FREE TO SIT FOR CHARLOTTE ON FRIDAY NIGHT?
LOOKS LIKE JUST YOU, STACE.
OKAY. MRS. JOHANSSEN? I'LL BE THERE!

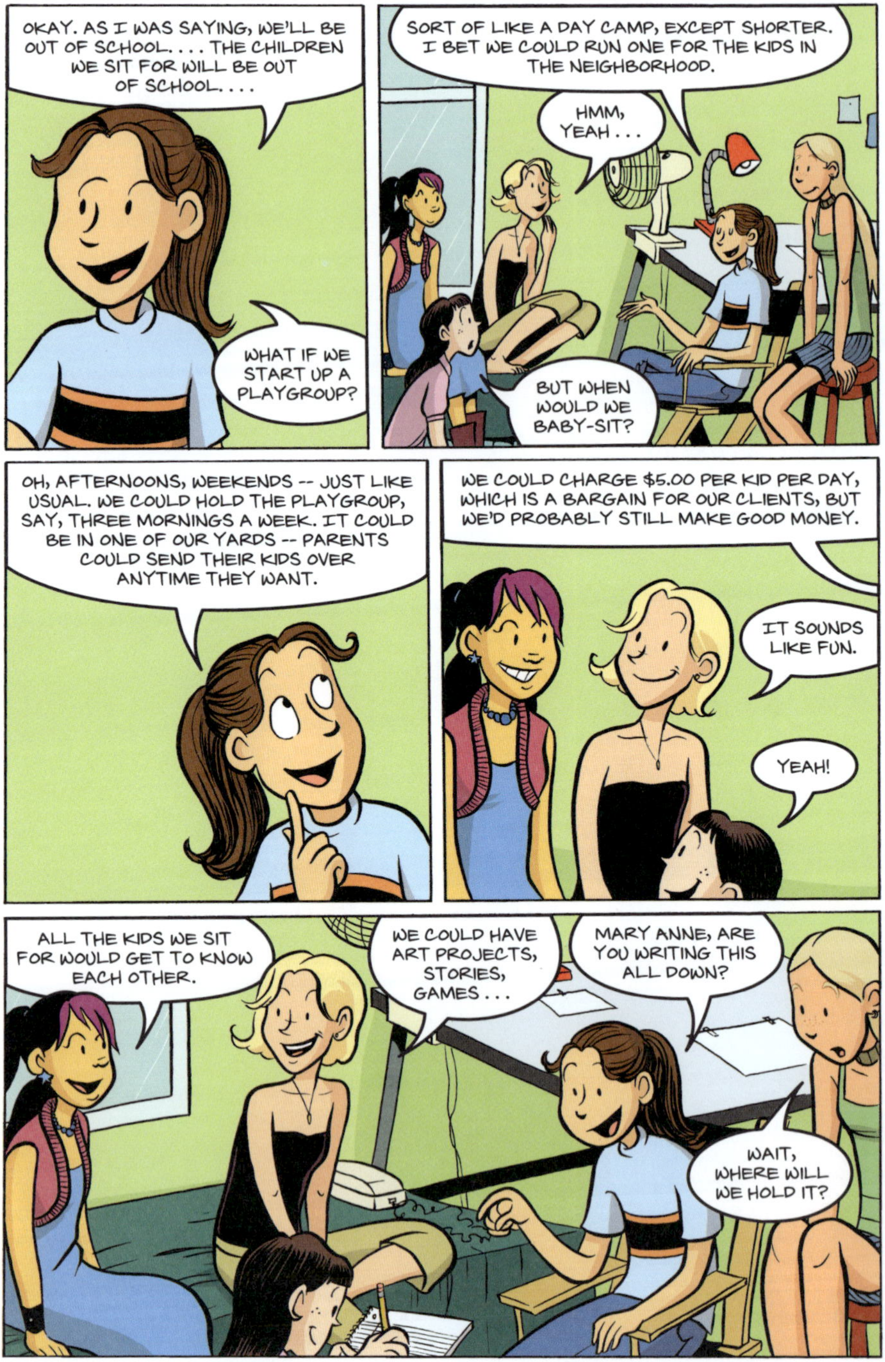
OKAY. AS I WAS SAYING, WE'LL BE OUT OF SCHOOL. . . . THE CHILDREN WE SIT FOR WILL BE OUT OF SCHOOL. . . .
WHAT IF WE START UP A PLAYGROUP?
SORT OF LIKE A DAY CAMP, EXCEPT SHORTER. I BET WE COULD RUN ONE FOR THE KIDS IN THE NEIGHBORHOOD.
HMM, YEAH . . .
BUT WHEN WOULD WE BABY-SIT?
OH, AFTERNOONS, WEEKENDS -- JUST LIKE USUAL. WE COULD HOLD THE PLAYGROUP, SAY, THREE MORNINGS A WEEK. IT COULD BE IN ONE OF OUR YARDS -- PARENTS COULD SEND THEIR KIDS OVER ANYTIME THEY WANT.
WE COULD CHARGE $5.00 PER KID PER DAY, WHICH IS A BARGAIN FOR OUR CLIENTS, BUT WE'D PROBABLY STILL MAKE GOOD MONEY.
IT SOUNDS LIKE FUN.
YEAH!
ALL THE KIDS WE SIT FOR WOULD GET TO KNOW EACH OTHER.
WE COULD HAVE ART PROJECTS, STORIES, GAMES . . .
MARY ANNE, ARE YOU WRITING THIS ALL DOWN?
WAIT, WHERE WILL WE HOLD IT?

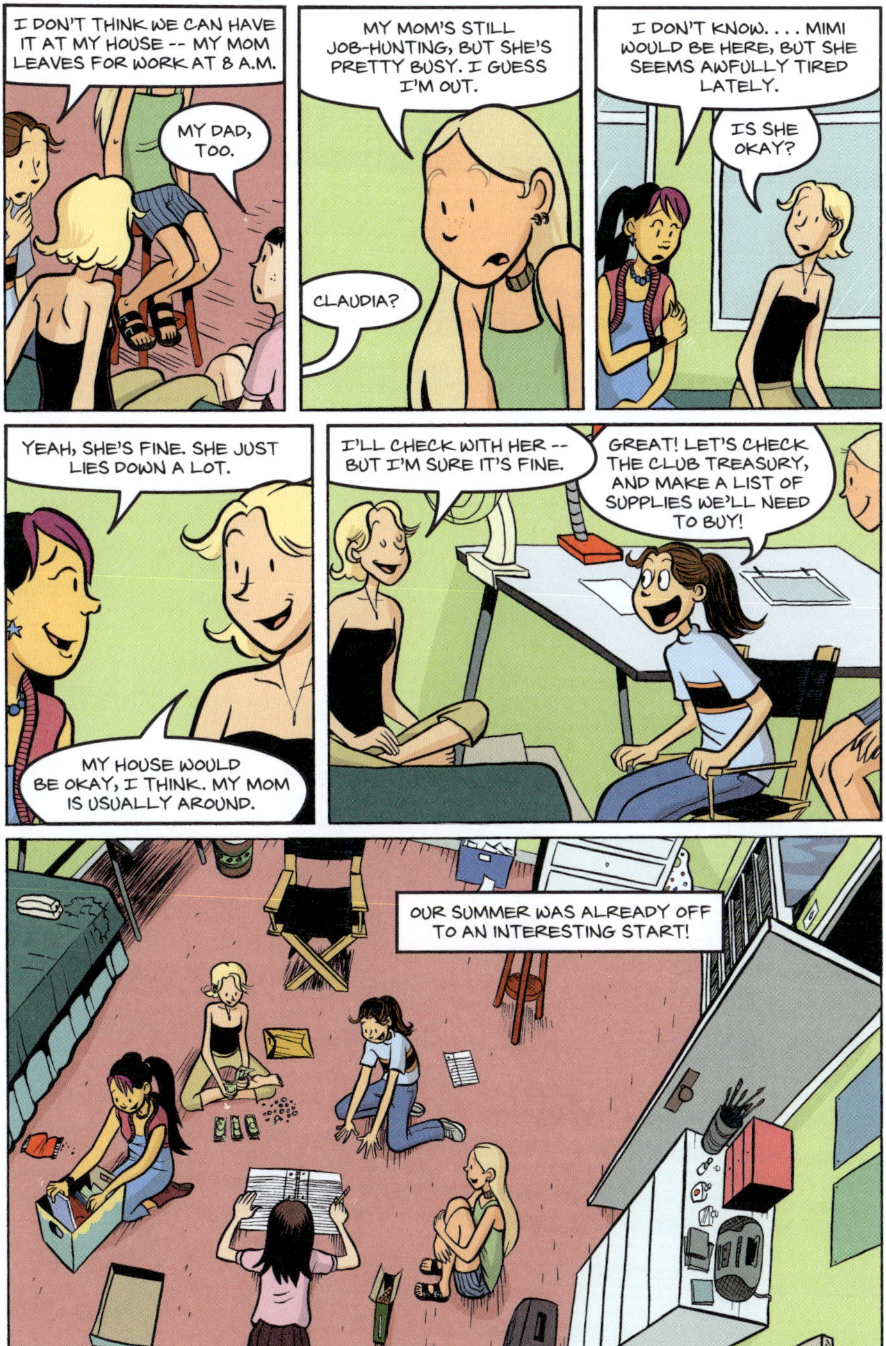

I DON'T THINK WE CAN HAVE IT AT MY HOUSE -- MY MOM LEAVES FOR WORK AT 8 A.M.
MY DAD, TOO.
MY MOM'S STILL JOB-HUNTING, BUT SHE'S PRETTY BUSY. I GUESS I'M OUT.
CLAUDIA?
I DON'T KNOW. . . . MIMI WOULD BE HERE, BUT SHE SEEMS AWFULLY TIRED LATELY.
IS SHE OKAY?
YEAH, SHE'S FINE. SHE JUST LIES DOWN A LOT.
MY HOUSE WOULD BE OKAY, I THINK. MY MOM IS USUALLY AROUND.
I'LL CHECK WITH HER -- BUT I'M SURE IT'S FINE.
GREAT! LET'S CHECK THE CLUB TREASURY, AND MAKE A LIST OF SUPPLIES WE'LL NEED TO BUY!
OUR SUMMER WAS ALREADY OFF TO AN INTERESTING START!

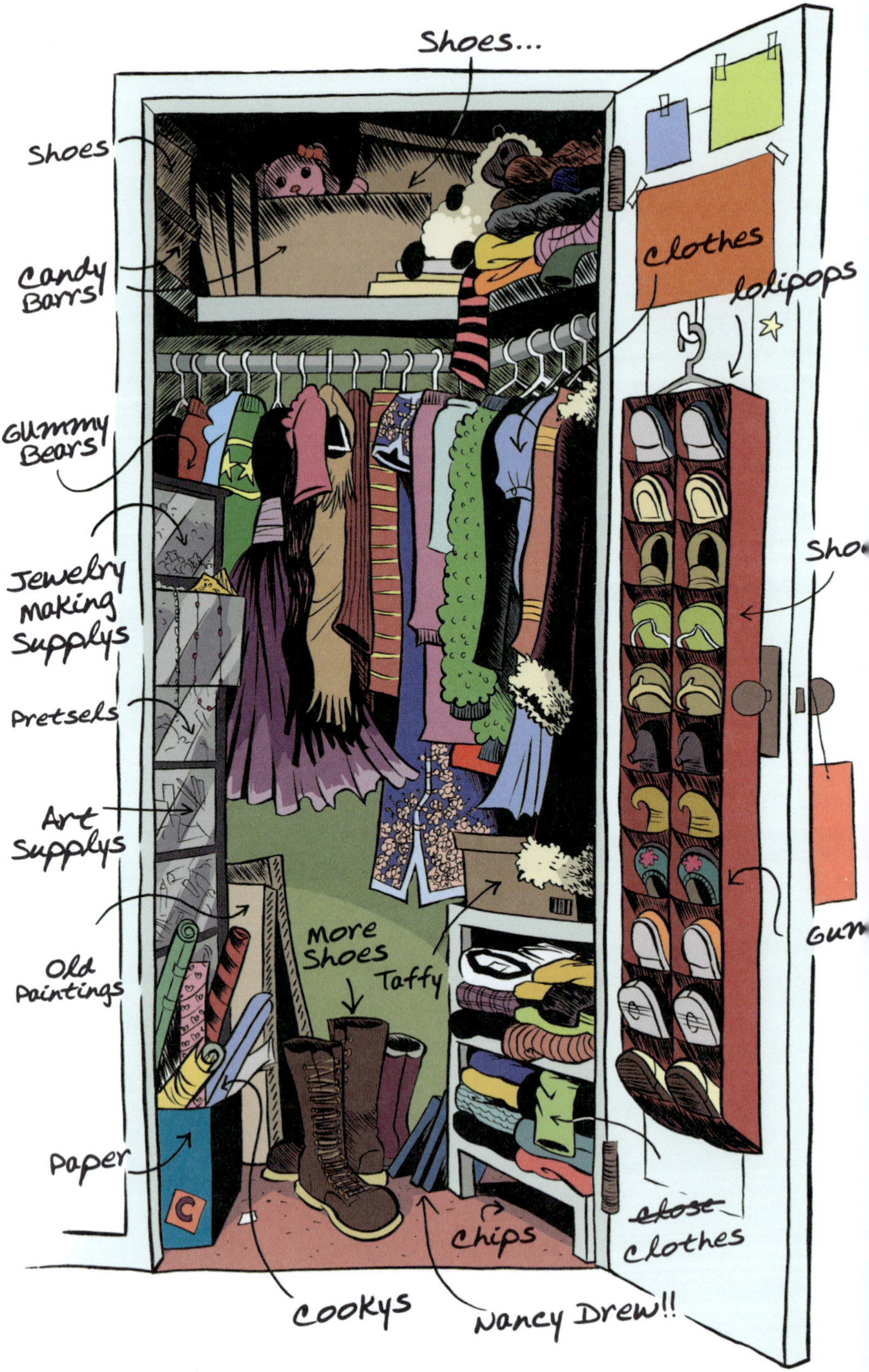
Shoes...
Shoes
Candy Barrs
Clothes
lolipops
Gummy Bears
Jewelry making supplys
Sho
Pretsels
Art supplys
Gum
Old Paintings
More Shoes
Taffy
Paper
close
clothes
chips
cookys
Nancy Drew!!

CHAPTER 3

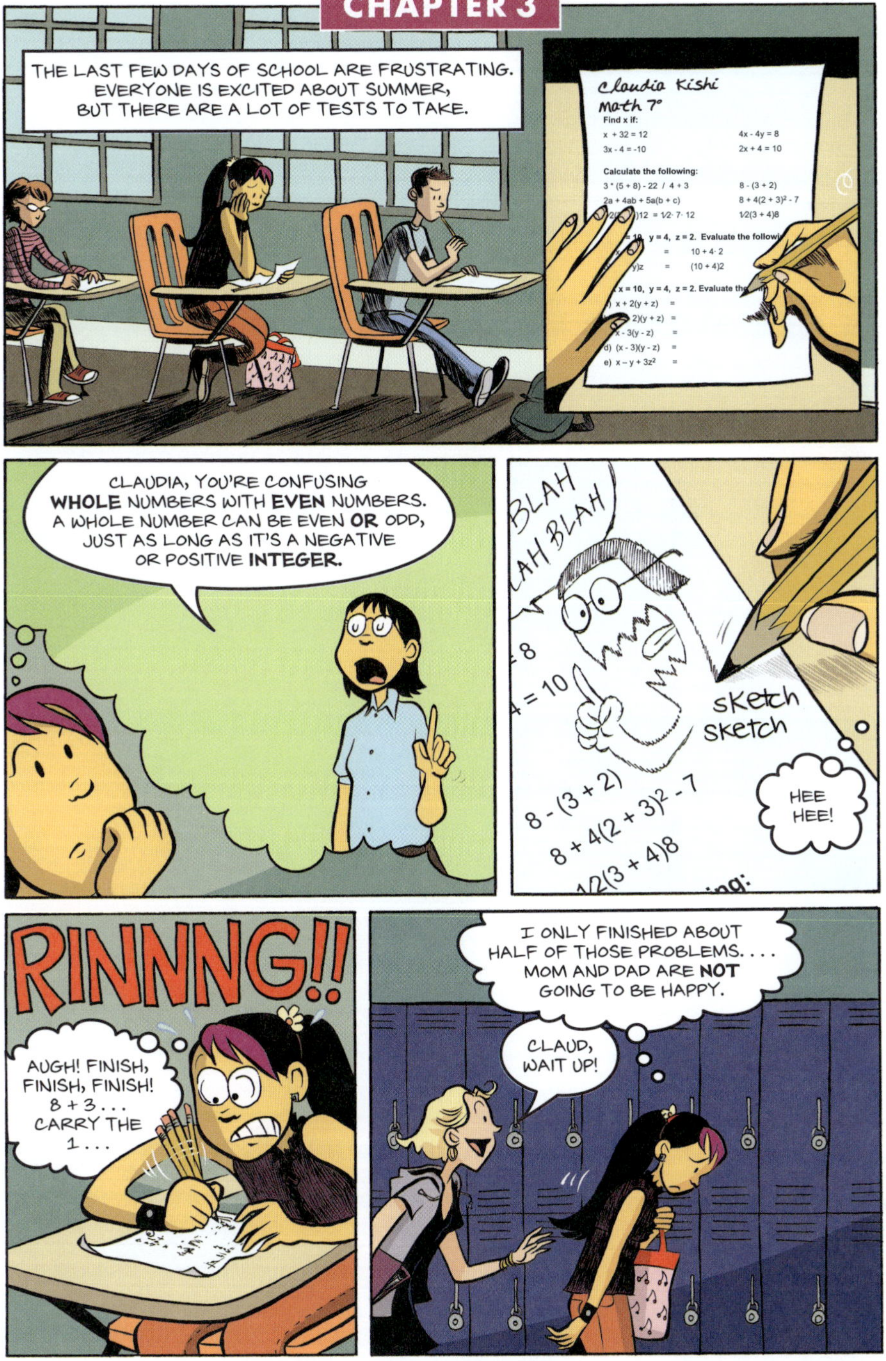
THE LAST FEW DAYS OF SCHOOL ARE FRUSTRATING. EVERYONE IS EXCITED ABOUT SUMMER, BUT THERE ARE A LOT OF TESTS TO TAKE.
Claudia Kishi
Math 7°
Find x if:
x + 32 = 12
4x - 4y = 8
3x - 4 = -10
2x + 4 = 10
Calculate the following:
3 * (5 + 8) - 22 / 4 + 3
8 - (3 + 2)
2a + 4ab + 5a(b + c)
8 + 4(2 + 3)² - 7
1/2(3 + 4)8
10 + 4· 2
(10 + 4)2
x + 2(y + z) =
x - 3(y - z) =
d) (x - 3)(y - z) =
e) x – y + 3z² =
CLAUDIA, YOU'RE CONFUSING **WHOLE** NUMBERS WITH **EVEN** NUMBERS. A WHOLE NUMBER CAN BE EVEN **OR** ODD, JUST AS LONG AS IT'S A NEGATIVE OR POSITIVE **INTEGER.**
BLAH
BLAH BLAH
sketch sketch
HEE HEE!
8 - (3 + 2)
8 + 4(2 + 3)² - 7
1/2(3 + 4)8
RINNNG!!
AUGH! FINISH, FINISH, FINISH! 8 + 3 . . . CARRY THE 1 . . .
I ONLY FINISHED ABOUT HALF OF THOSE PROBLEMS. . . . MOM AND DAD ARE **NOT** GOING TO BE HAPPY.
CLAUD, WAIT UP!

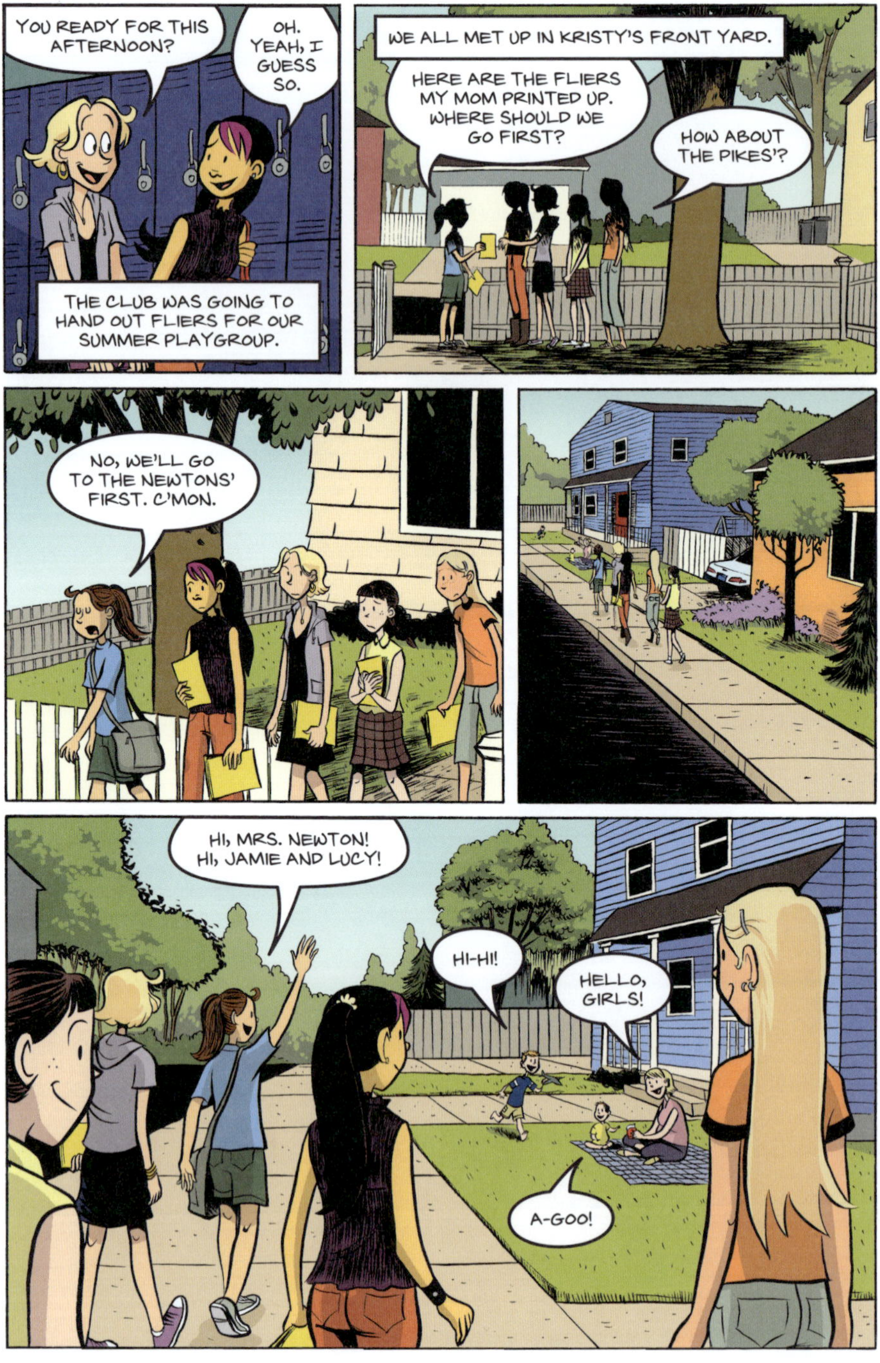
YOU READY FOR THIS AFTERNOON?
OH. YEAH, I GUESS SO.
THE CLUB WAS GOING TO HAND OUT FLIERS FOR OUR SUMMER PLAYGROUP.
WE ALL MET UP IN KRISTY'S FRONT YARD.
HERE ARE THE FLIERS MY MOM PRINTED UP. WHERE SHOULD WE GO FIRST?
HOW ABOUT THE PIKES'?
NO, WE'LL GO TO THE NEWTONS' FIRST. C'MON.
HI, MRS. NEWTON! HI, JAMIE AND LUCY!
HI-HI!
HELLO, GIRLS!
A-GOO!

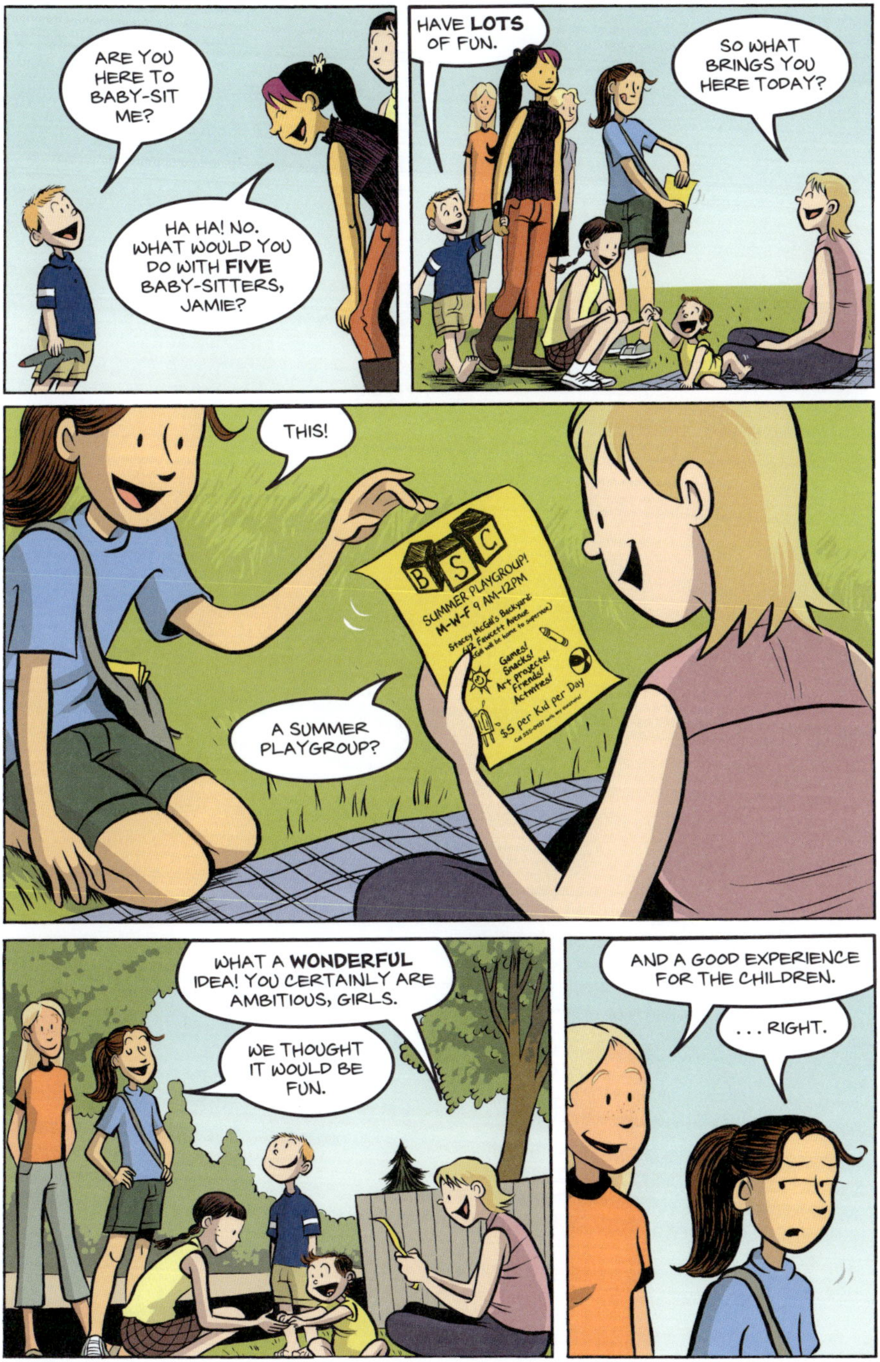
ARE YOU HERE TO BABY-SIT ME?
HA HA! NO. WHAT WOULD YOU DO WITH **FIVE** BABY-SITTERS, JAMIE?
HAVE **LOTS** OF FUN.
SO WHAT BRINGS YOU HERE TODAY?
THIS!
BSC
SUMMER PLAYGROUP!
M-W-F 9 AM-12PM
Stacey McGill's Backyard:
612 Fawcett Avenue
Games!
Snacks!
Art projects!
Friends!
Activities!
$5 per Kid per Day
A SUMMER PLAYGROUP?
WHAT A **WONDERFUL** IDEA! YOU CERTAINLY ARE AMBITIOUS, GIRLS.
WE THOUGHT IT WOULD BE FUN.
AND A GOOD EXPERIENCE FOR THE CHILDREN.
. . . RIGHT.

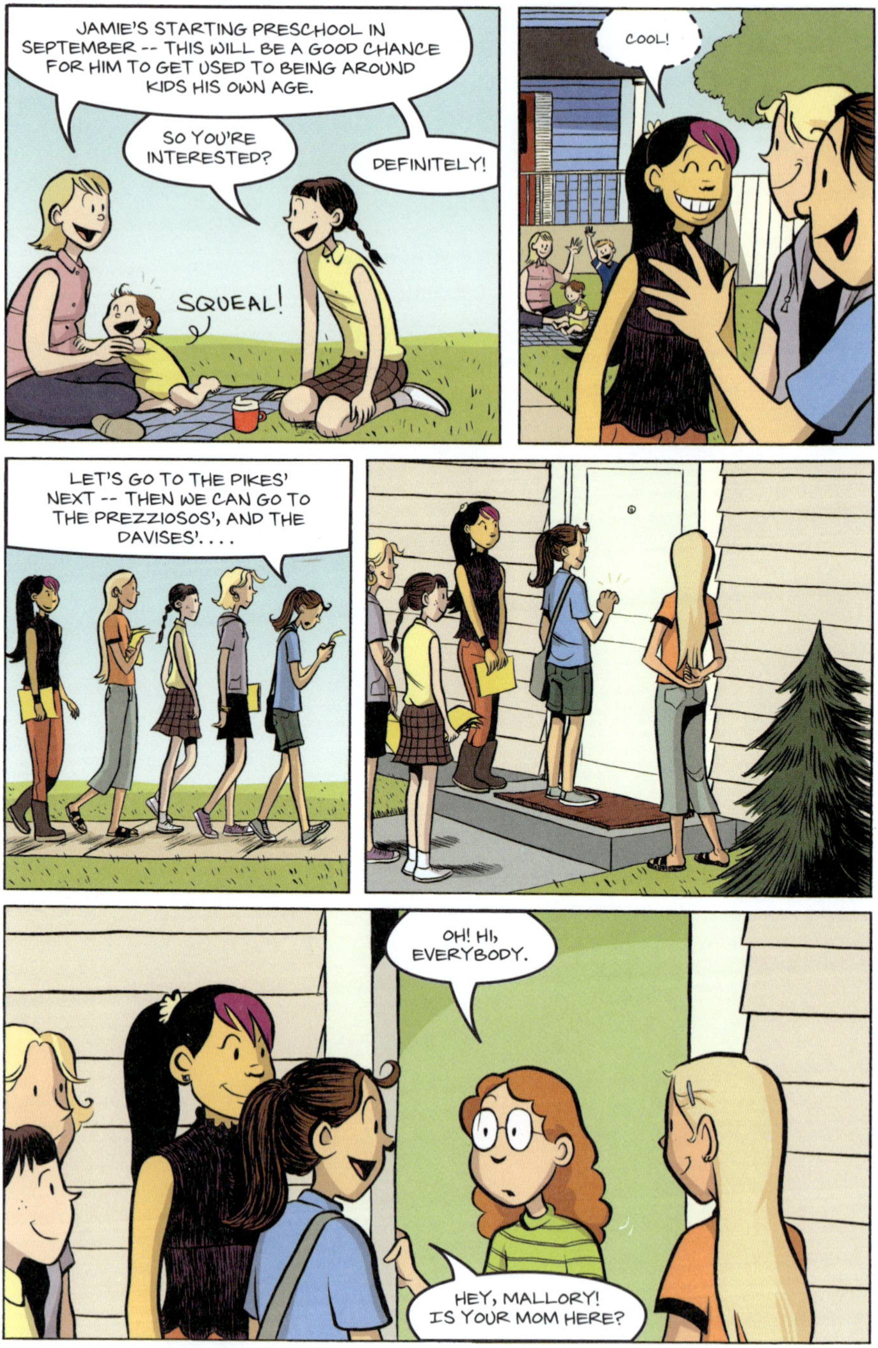
JAMIE'S STARTING PRESCHOOL IN SEPTEMBER -- THIS WILL BE A GOOD CHANCE FOR HIM TO GET USED TO BEING AROUND KIDS HIS OWN AGE.
SO YOU'RE INTERESTED?
DEFINITELY!
SQUEAL!
COOL!
LET'S GO TO THE PIKES' NEXT -- THEN WE CAN GO TO THE PREZZIOSOS', AND THE DAVISES'. . . .
OH! HI, EVERYBODY.
HEY, MALLORY! IS YOUR MOM HERE?

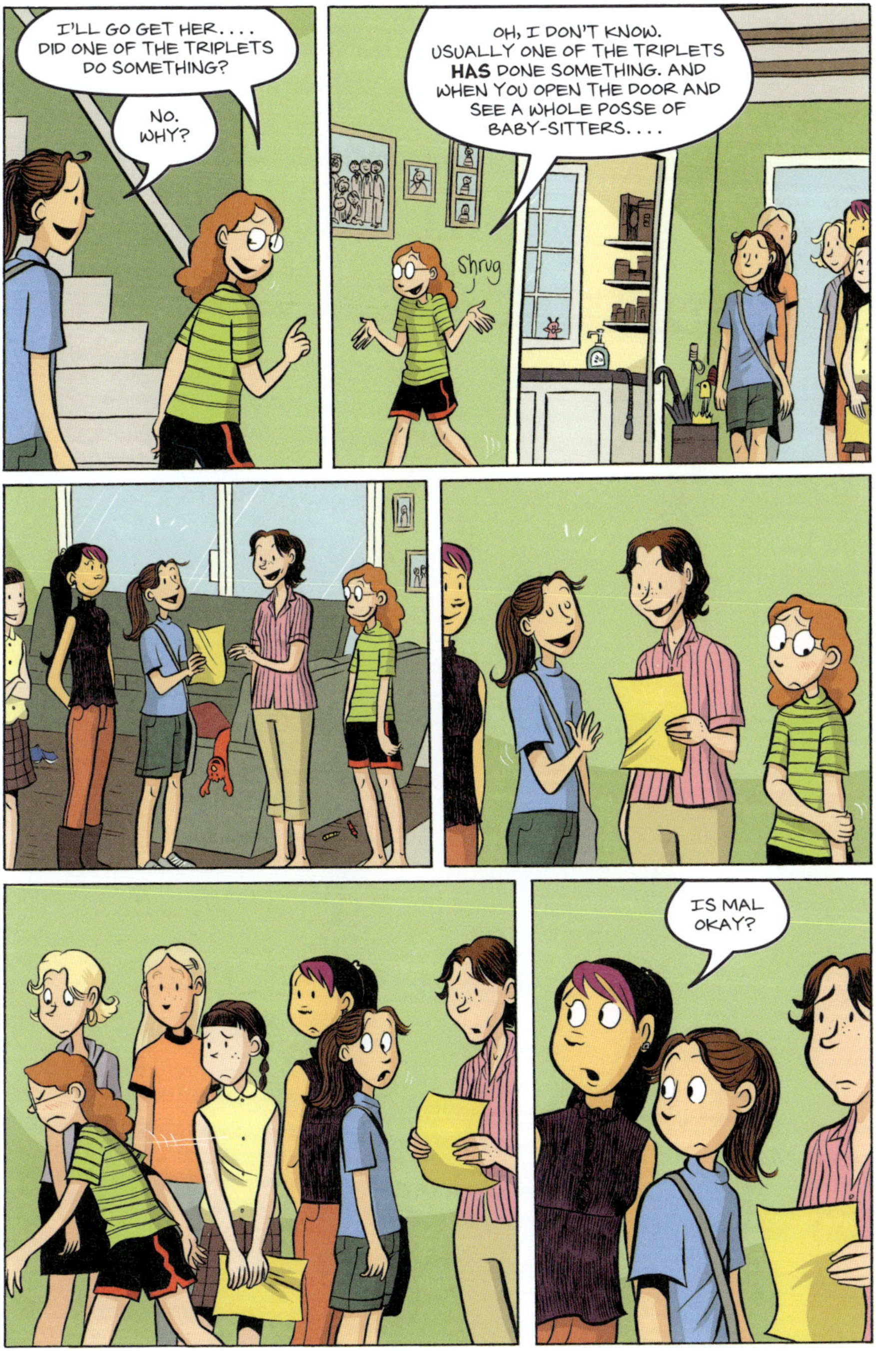
I'LL GO GET HER.... DID ONE OF THE TRIPLETS DO SOMETHING?
NO. WHY?
OH, I DON'T KNOW. USUALLY ONE OF THE TRIPLETS **HAS** DONE SOMETHING. AND WHEN YOU OPEN THE DOOR AND SEE A WHOLE POSSE OF BABY-SITTERS....
Shrug
IS MAL OKAY?

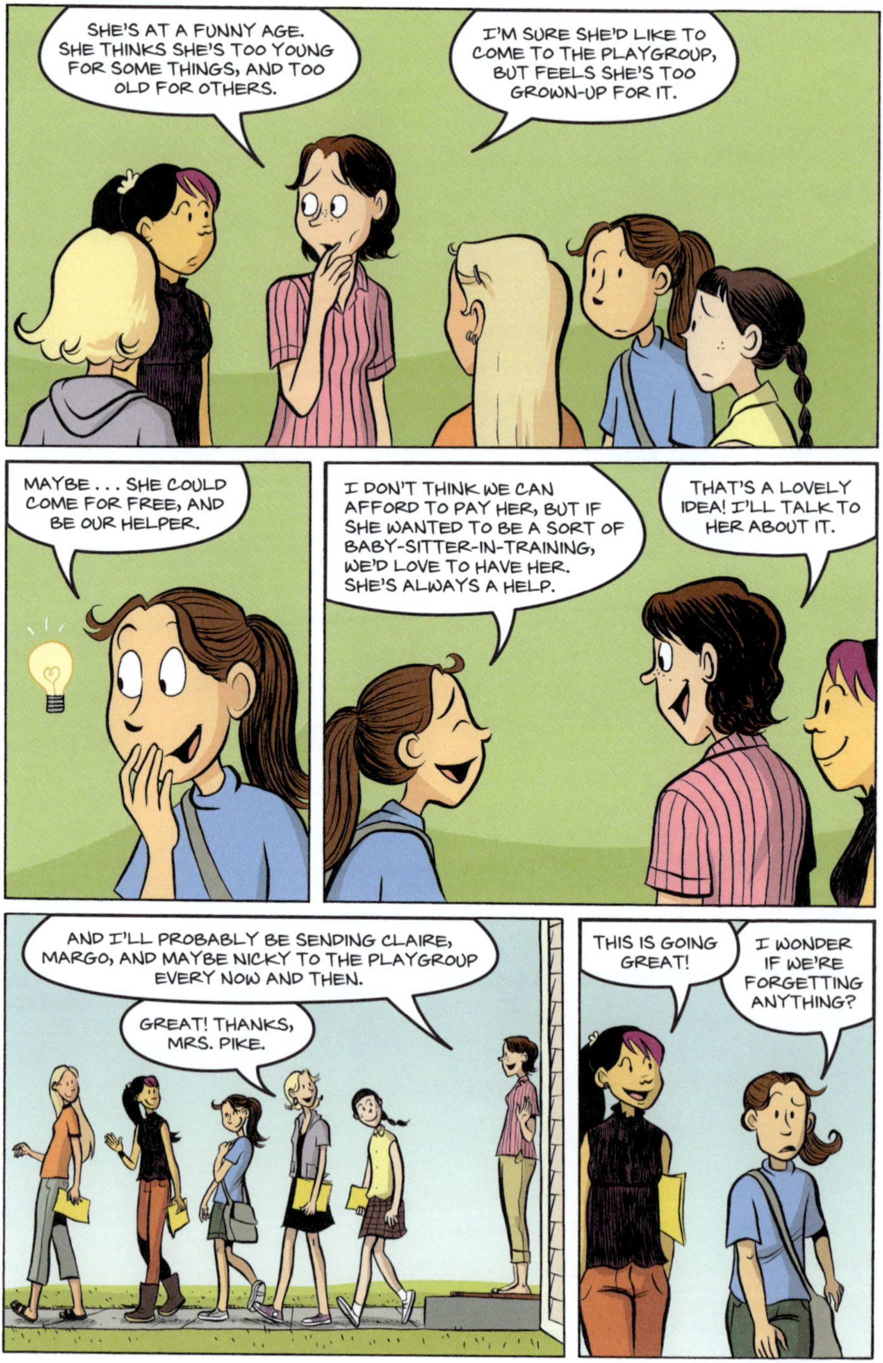
SHE'S AT A FUNNY AGE. SHE THINKS SHE'S TOO YOUNG FOR SOME THINGS, AND TOO OLD FOR OTHERS.
I'M SURE SHE'D LIKE TO COME TO THE PLAYGROUP, BUT FEELS SHE'S TOO GROWN-UP FOR IT.
MAYBE . . . SHE COULD COME FOR FREE, AND BE OUR HELPER.
I DON'T THINK WE CAN AFFORD TO PAY HER, BUT IF SHE WANTED TO BE A SORT OF BABY-SITTER-IN-TRAINING, WE'D LOVE TO HAVE HER. SHE'S ALWAYS A HELP.
THAT'S A LOVELY IDEA! I'LL TALK TO HER ABOUT IT.
AND I'LL PROBABLY BE SENDING CLAIRE, MARGO, AND MAYBE NICKY TO THE PLAYGROUP EVERY NOW AND THEN.
GREAT! THANKS, MRS. PIKE.
THIS IS GOING GREAT!
I WONDER IF WE'RE FORGETTING ANYTHING?

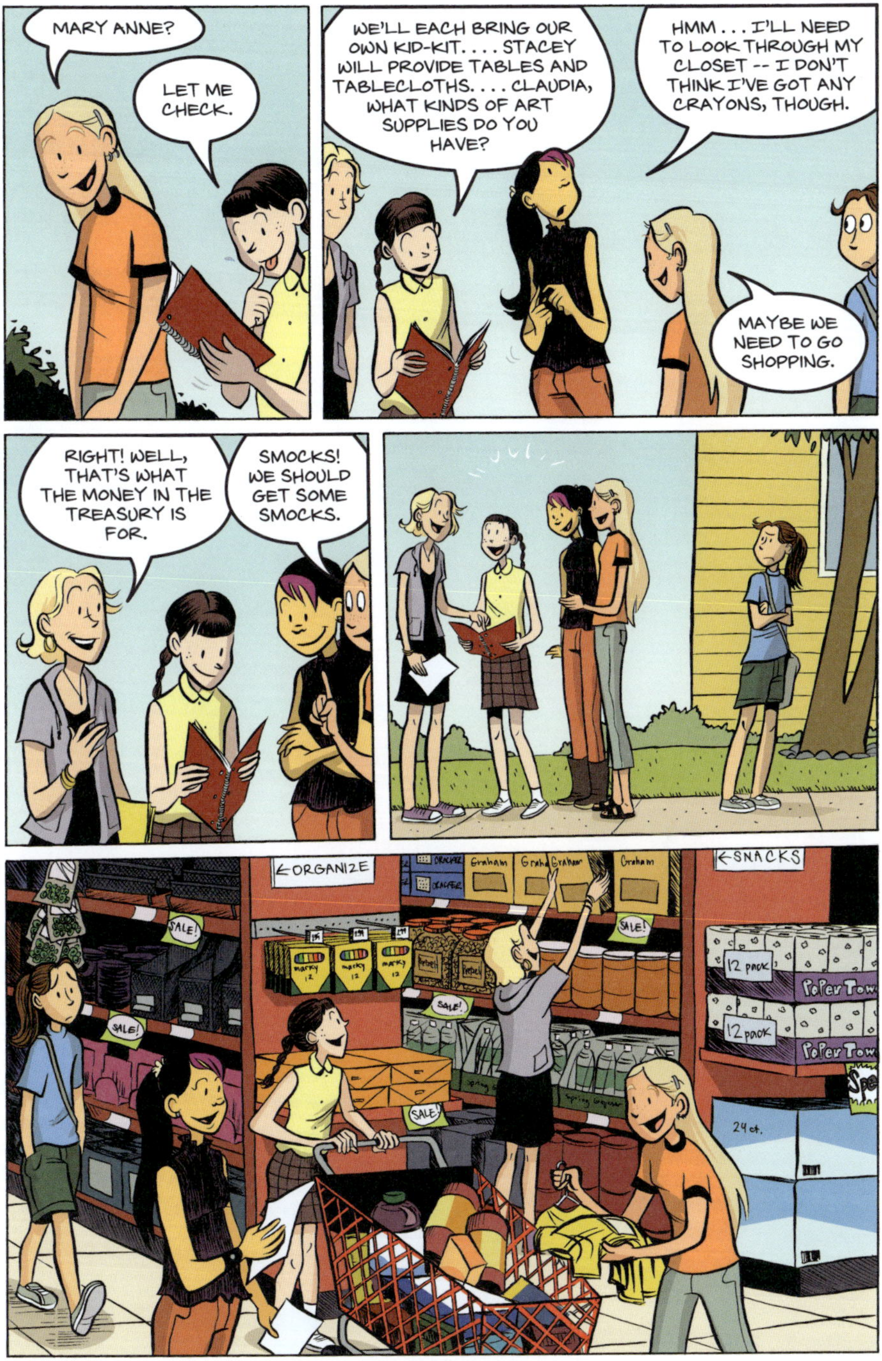
MARY ANNE?
LET ME CHECK.
WE'LL EACH BRING OUR OWN KID-KIT. . . . STACEY WILL PROVIDE TABLES AND TABLECLOTHS. . . . CLAUDIA, WHAT KINDS OF ART SUPPLIES DO YOU HAVE?
HMM . . . I'LL NEED TO LOOK THROUGH MY CLOSET -- I DON'T THINK I'VE GOT ANY CRAYONS, THOUGH.
MAYBE WE NEED TO GO SHOPPING.
RIGHT! WELL, THAT'S WHAT THE MONEY IN THE TREASURY IS FOR.
SMOCKS! WE SHOULD GET SOME SMOCKS.
←ORGANIZE
Graham
←SNACKS
SALE!
12 pack
Paper Towels
24 ct.

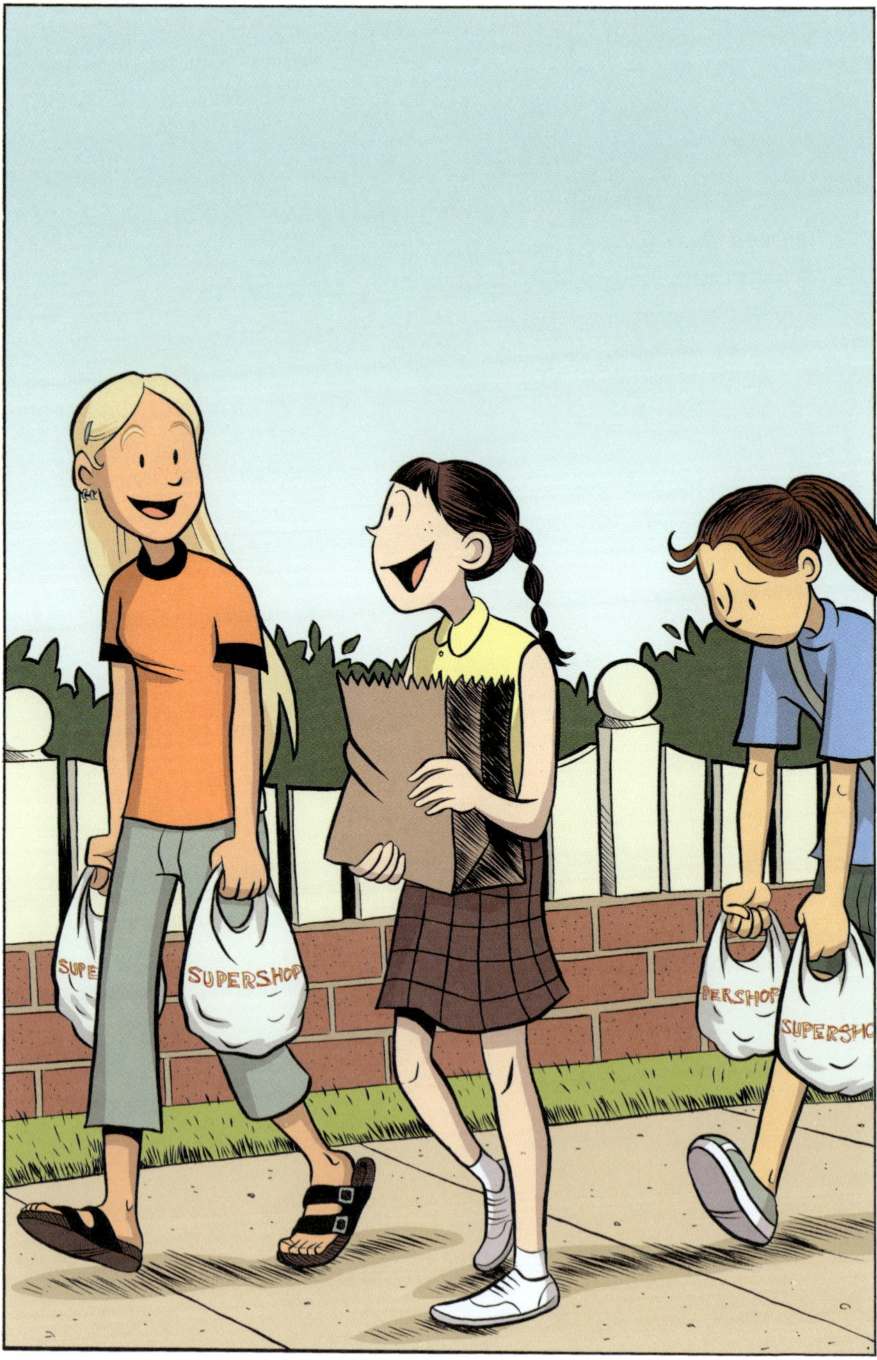
SUPE
SUPERSHOP
PERSHOP
SUPERSHO

CHAPTER 4

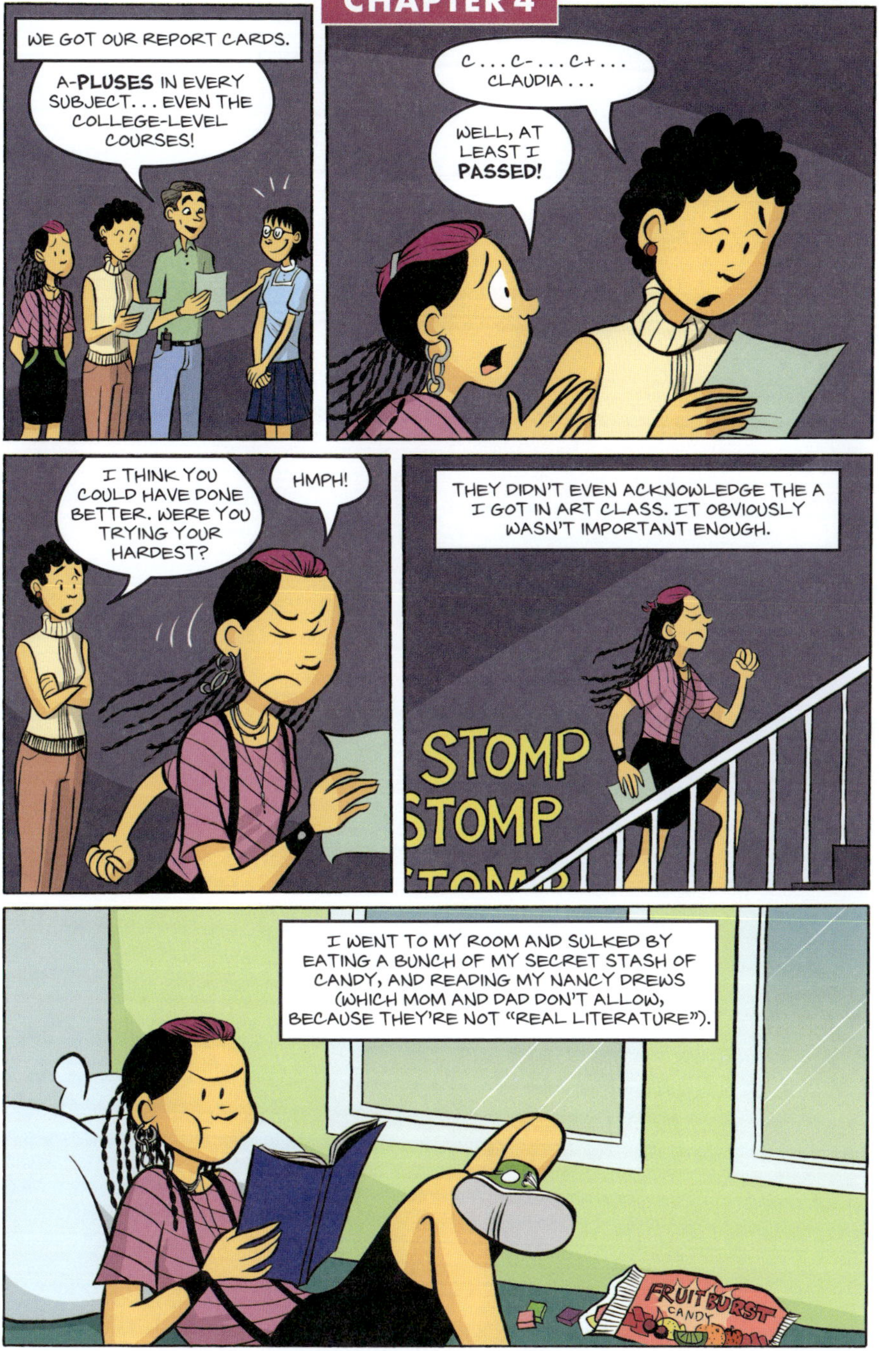

WE GOT OUR REPORT CARDS.
A-**PLUSES** IN EVERY SUBJECT. . . EVEN THE COLLEGE-LEVEL COURSES!
C . . . C- . . . C+ . . . CLAUDIA . . .
WELL, AT LEAST I **PASSED!**
I THINK YOU COULD HAVE DONE BETTER. WERE YOU TRYING YOUR HARDEST?
HMPH!
THEY DIDN'T EVEN ACKNOWLEDGE THE A I GOT IN ART CLASS. IT OBVIOUSLY WASN'T IMPORTANT ENOUGH.
STOMP
STOMP
I WENT TO MY ROOM AND SULKED BY EATING A BUNCH OF MY SECRET STASH OF CANDY, AND READING MY NANCY DREWS (WHICH MOM AND DAD DON'T ALLOW, BECAUSE THEY'RE NOT "REAL LITERATURE").
FRUITBURST CANDY

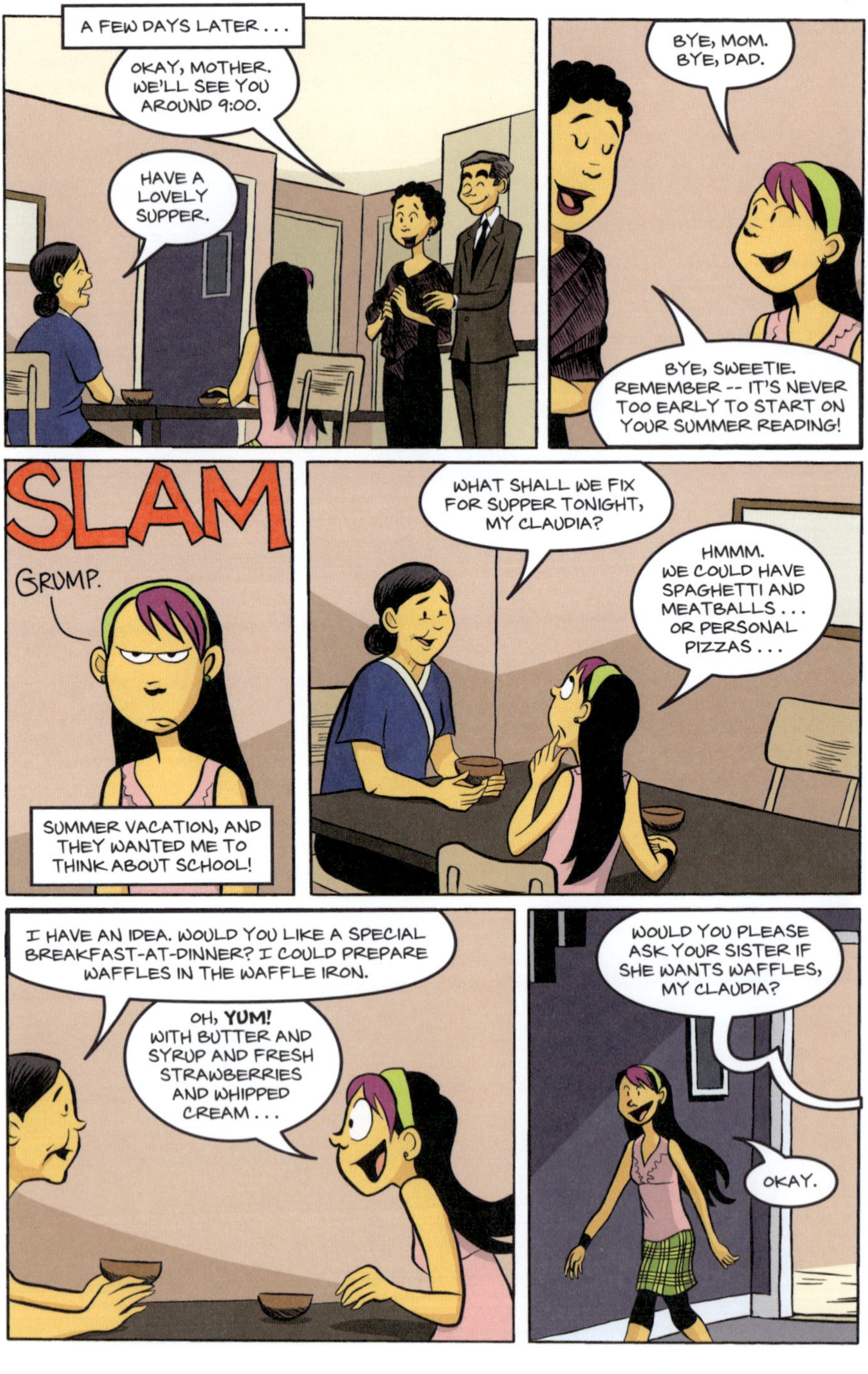
A FEW DAYS LATER . . .
OKAY, MOTHER. WE'LL SEE YOU AROUND 9:00.
HAVE A LOVELY SUPPER.
BYE, MOM. BYE, DAD.
BYE, SWEETIE. REMEMBER -- IT'S NEVER TOO EARLY TO START ON YOUR SUMMER READING!
SLAM
GRUMP.
SUMMER VACATION, AND THEY WANTED ME TO THINK ABOUT SCHOOL!
WHAT SHALL WE FIX FOR SUPPER TONIGHT, MY CLAUDIA?
HMMM. WE COULD HAVE SPAGHETTI AND MEATBALLS . . . OR PERSONAL PIZZAS . . .
I HAVE AN IDEA. WOULD YOU LIKE A SPECIAL BREAKFAST-AT-DINNER? I COULD PREPARE WAFFLES IN THE WAFFLE IRON.
OH, YUM! WITH BUTTER AND SYRUP AND FRESH STRAWBERRIES AND WHIPPED CREAM . . .
WOULD YOU PLEASE ASK YOUR SISTER IF SHE WANTS WAFFLES, MY CLAUDIA?
OKAY.

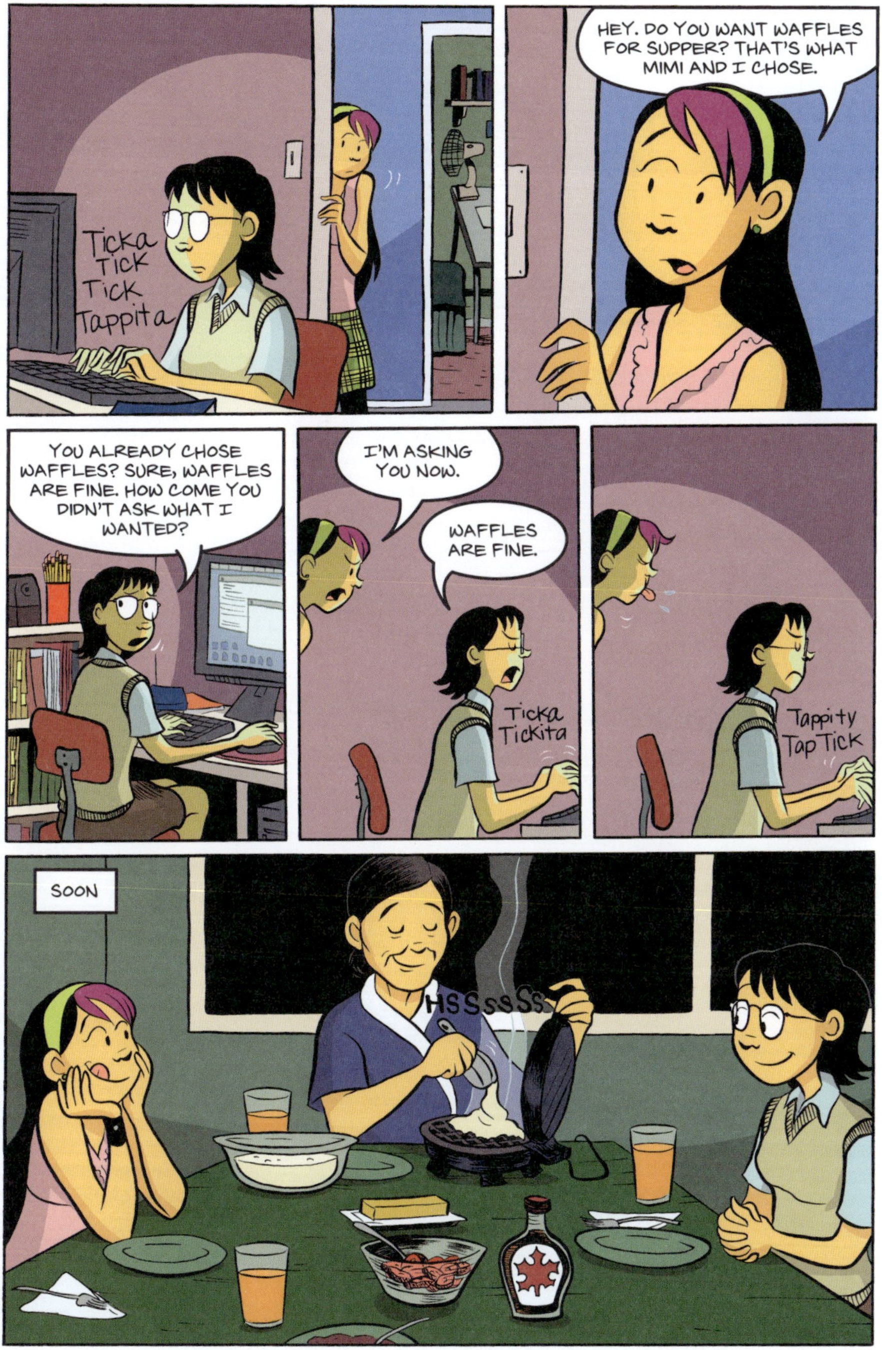

Ticka Tick Tick Tappita
HEY. DO YOU WANT WAFFLES FOR SUPPER? THAT'S WHAT MIMI AND I CHOSE.
YOU ALREADY CHOSE WAFFLES? SURE, WAFFLES ARE FINE. HOW COME YOU DIDN'T ASK WHAT I WANTED?
I'M ASKING YOU NOW.
WAFFLES ARE FINE.
Ticka Tickita
Tappity Tap Tick
SOON
HSSssSs

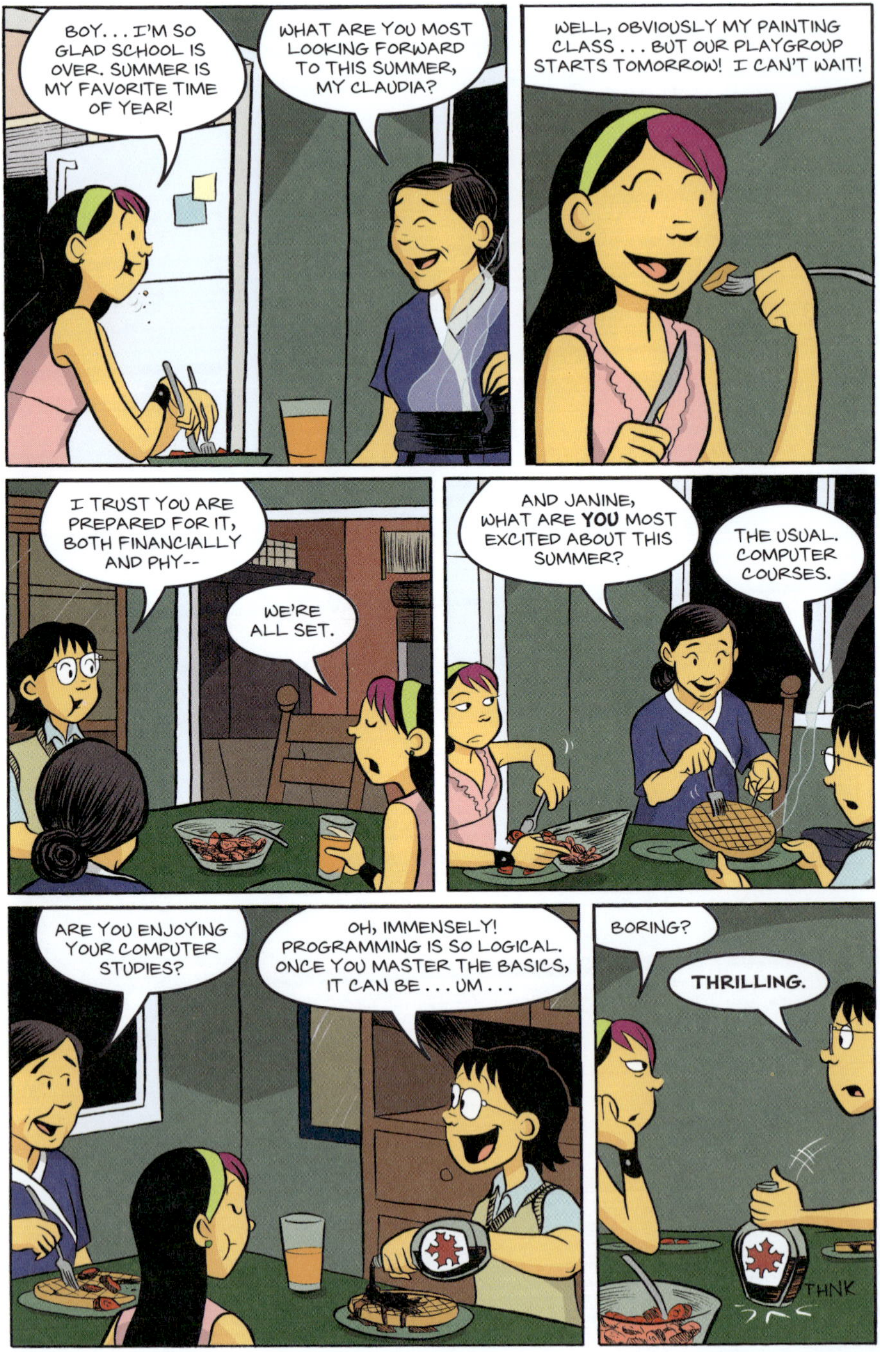
BOY... I'M SO GLAD SCHOOL IS OVER. SUMMER IS MY FAVORITE TIME OF YEAR!
WHAT ARE YOU MOST LOOKING FORWARD TO THIS SUMMER, MY CLAUDIA?
WELL, OBVIOUSLY MY PAINTING CLASS... BUT OUR PLAYGROUP STARTS TOMORROW! I CAN'T WAIT!
I TRUST YOU ARE PREPARED FOR IT, BOTH FINANCIALLY AND PHY--
WE'RE ALL SET.
AND JANINE, WHAT ARE **YOU** MOST EXCITED ABOUT THIS SUMMER?
THE USUAL. COMPUTER COURSES.
ARE YOU ENJOYING YOUR COMPUTER STUDIES?
OH, IMMENSELY! PROGRAMMING IS SO LOGICAL. ONCE YOU MASTER THE BASICS, IT CAN BE... UM...
BORING?
THRILLING.
THNK

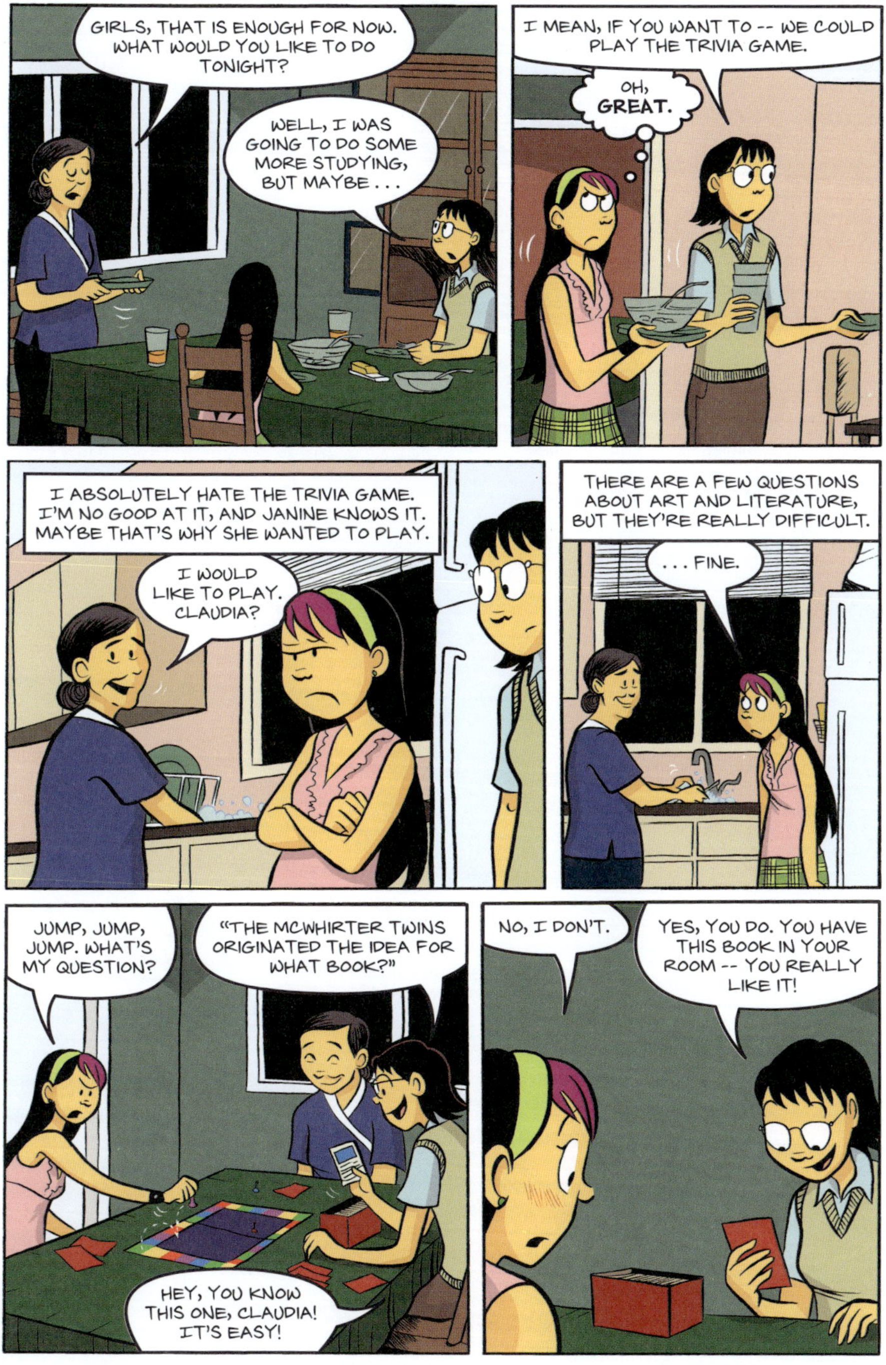
GIRLS, THAT IS ENOUGH FOR NOW. WHAT WOULD YOU LIKE TO DO TONIGHT?
WELL, I WAS GOING TO DO SOME MORE STUDYING, BUT MAYBE . . .
I MEAN, IF YOU WANT TO -- WE COULD PLAY THE TRIVIA GAME.
OH, GREAT.
I ABSOLUTELY HATE THE TRIVIA GAME. I'M NO GOOD AT IT, AND JANINE KNOWS IT. MAYBE THAT'S WHY SHE WANTED TO PLAY.
I WOULD LIKE TO PLAY. CLAUDIA?
THERE ARE A FEW QUESTIONS ABOUT ART AND LITERATURE, BUT THEY'RE REALLY DIFFICULT.
. . . FINE.
JUMP, JUMP, JUMP. WHAT'S MY QUESTION?
"THE MCWHIRTER TWINS ORIGINATED THE IDEA FOR WHAT BOOK?"
HEY, YOU KNOW THIS ONE, CLAUDIA! IT'S EASY!
NO, I DON'T.
YES, YOU DO. YOU HAVE THIS BOOK IN YOUR ROOM -- YOU REALLY LIKE IT!

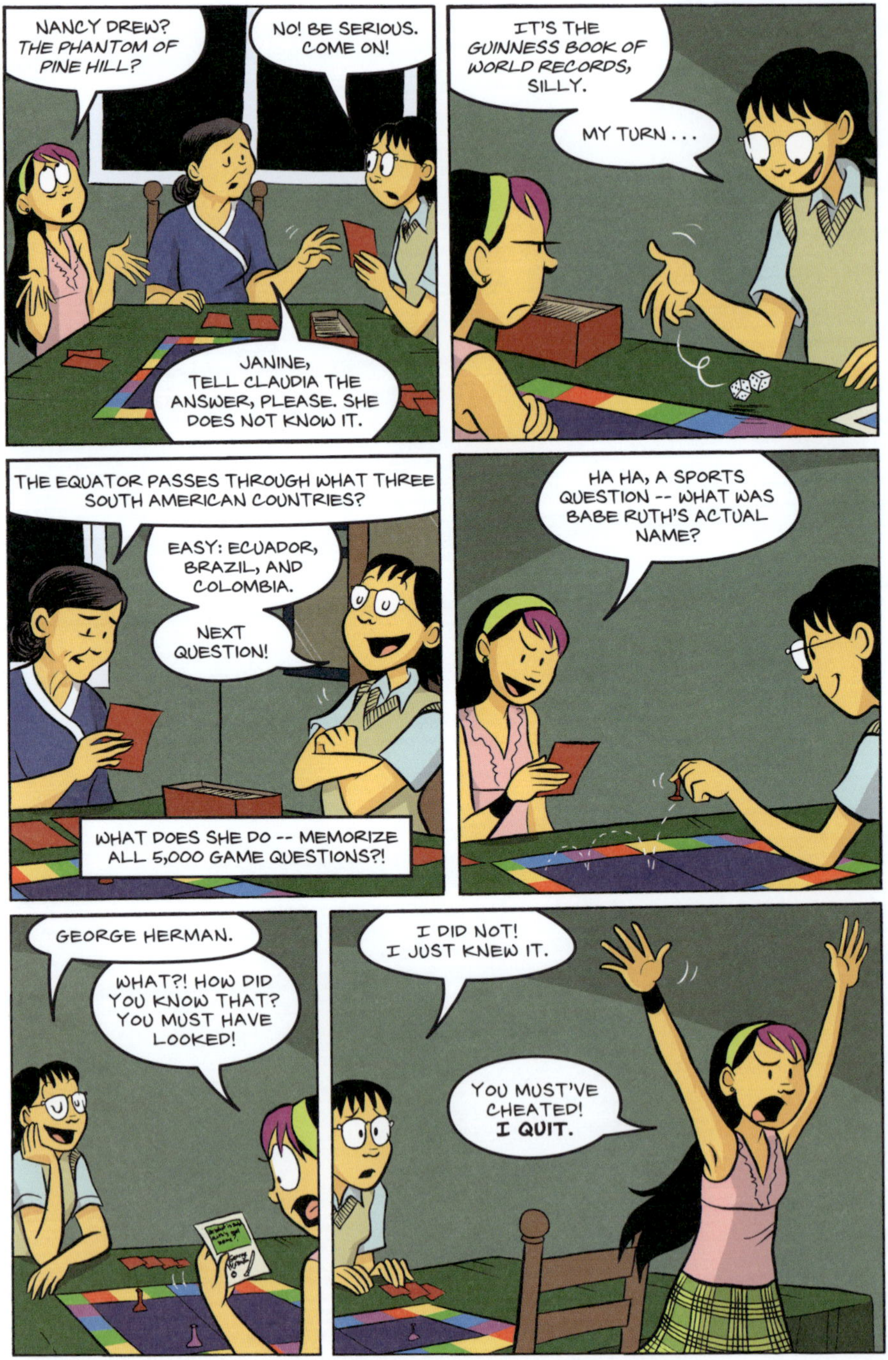
NANCY DREW? THE PHANTOM OF PINE HILL?
NO! BE SERIOUS. COME ON!
JANINE, TELL CLAUDIA THE ANSWER, PLEASE. SHE DOES NOT KNOW IT.
IT'S THE GUINNESS BOOK OF WORLD RECORDS, SILLY.
MY TURN . . .
THE EQUATOR PASSES THROUGH WHAT THREE SOUTH AMERICAN COUNTRIES?
EASY: ECUADOR, BRAZIL, AND COLOMBIA.
NEXT QUESTION!
WHAT DOES SHE DO -- MEMORIZE ALL 5,000 GAME QUESTIONS?!
HA HA, A SPORTS QUESTION -- WHAT WAS BABE RUTH'S ACTUAL NAME?
GEORGE HERMAN.
WHAT?! HOW DID YOU KNOW THAT? YOU MUST HAVE LOOKED!
I DID NOT! I JUST KNEW IT.
YOU MUST'VE CHEATED! **I QUIT.**

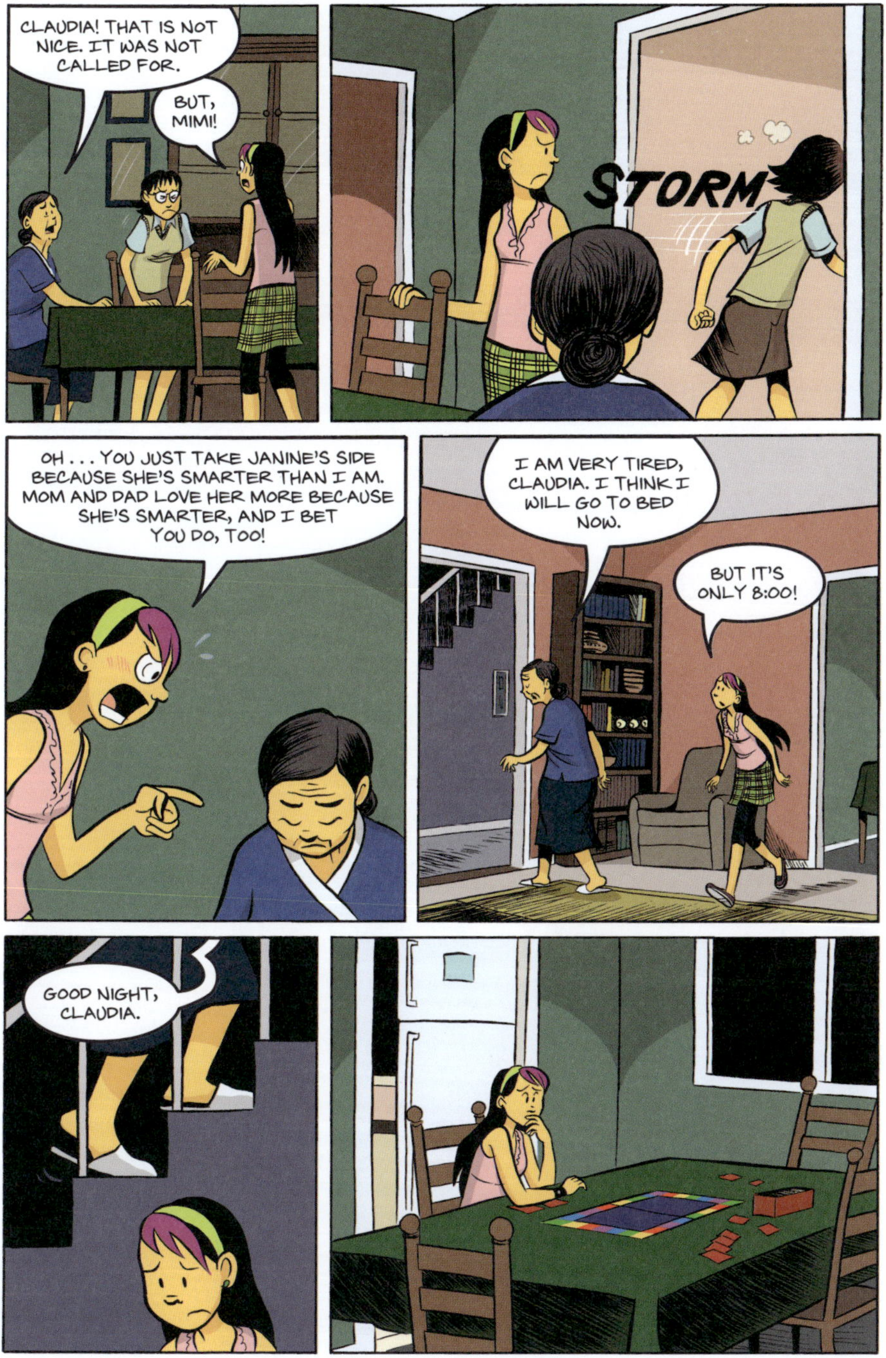
CLAUDIA! THAT IS NOT NICE. IT WAS NOT CALLED FOR.
BUT, MIMI!
STORM
OH . . . YOU JUST TAKE JANINE'S SIDE BECAUSE SHE'S SMARTER THAN I AM. MOM AND DAD LOVE HER MORE BECAUSE SHE'S SMARTER, AND I BET YOU DO, TOO!
I AM VERY TIRED, CLAUDIA. I THINK I WILL GO TO BED NOW.
BUT IT'S ONLY 8:00!
GOOD NIGHT, CLAUDIA.

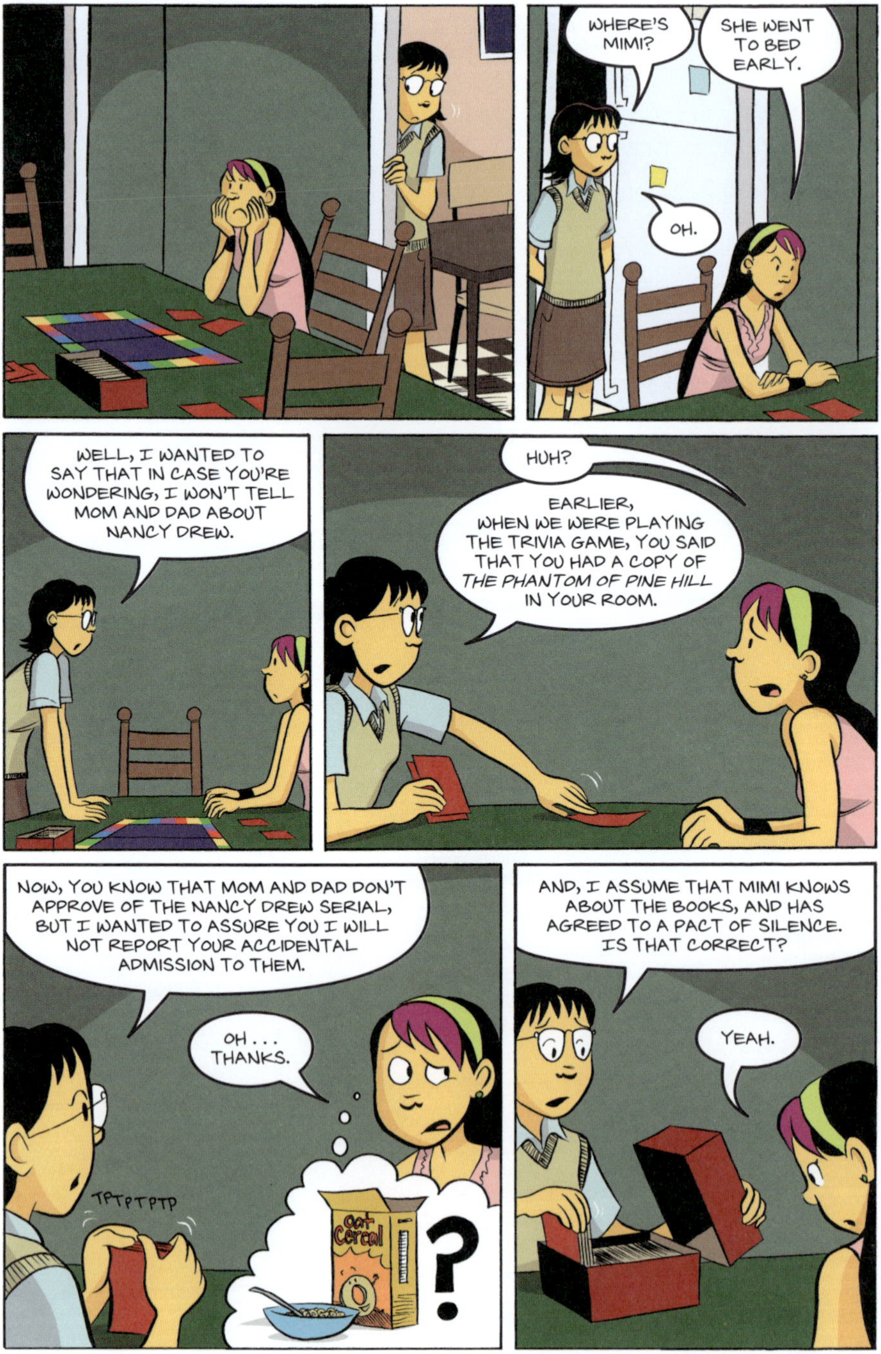
WHERE'S MIMI?
SHE WENT TO BED EARLY.
OH.
WELL, I WANTED TO SAY THAT IN CASE YOU'RE WONDERING, I WON'T TELL MOM AND DAD ABOUT NANCY DREW.
HUH?
EARLIER, WHEN WE WERE PLAYING THE TRIVIA GAME, YOU SAID THAT YOU HAD A COPY OF *THE PHANTOM OF PINE HILL* IN YOUR ROOM.
NOW, YOU KNOW THAT MOM AND DAD DON'T APPROVE OF THE NANCY DREW SERIAL, BUT I WANTED TO ASSURE YOU I WILL NOT REPORT YOUR ACCIDENTAL ADMISSION TO THEM.
OH . . . THANKS.
TPTPTPTP
Oat Cereal
?
AND, I ASSUME THAT MIMI KNOWS ABOUT THE BOOKS, AND HAS AGREED TO A PACT OF SILENCE. IS THAT CORRECT?
YEAH.

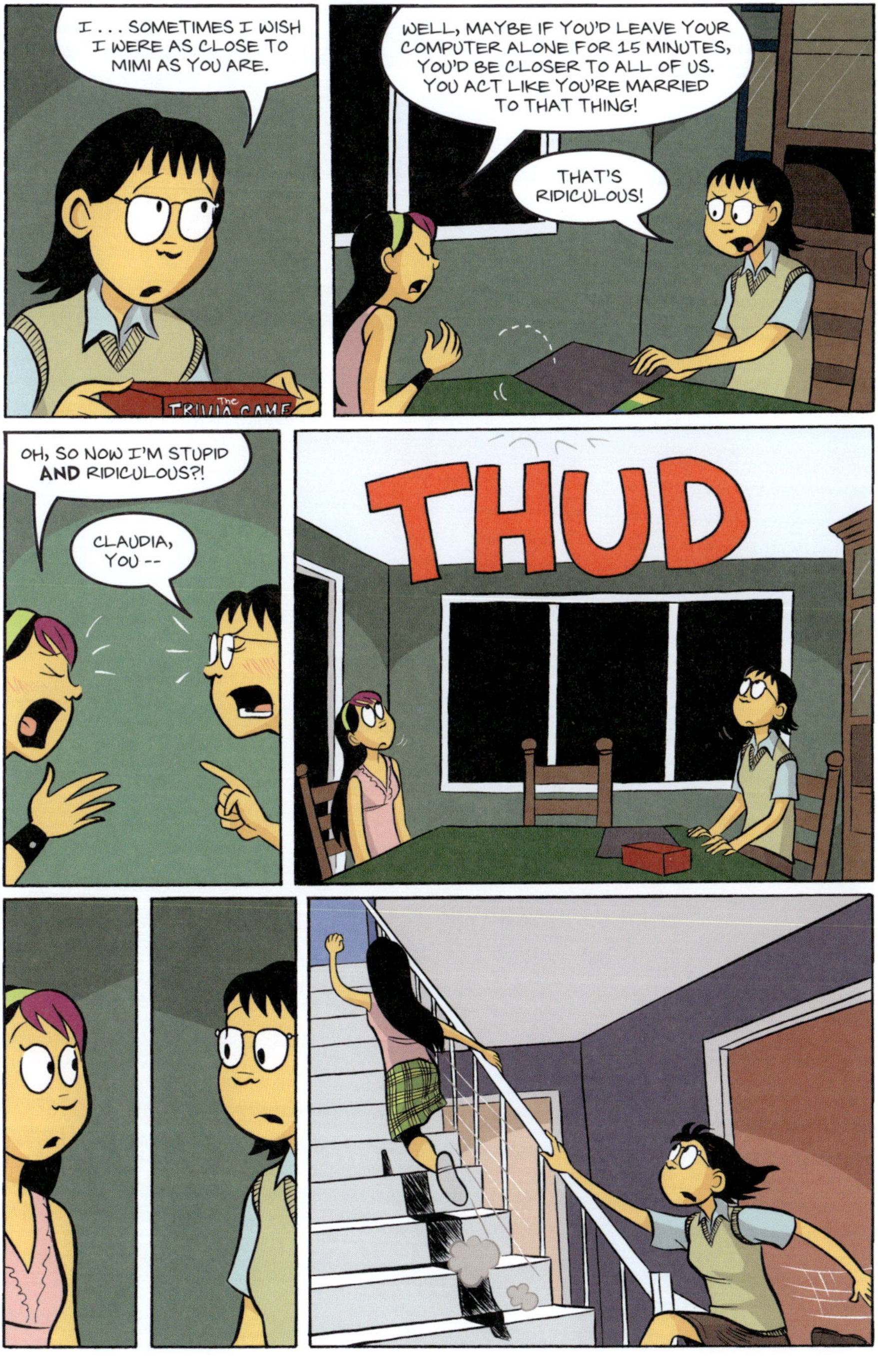
I . . . SOMETIMES I WISH I WERE AS CLOSE TO MIMI AS YOU ARE.
The TRIVIA GAME
WELL, MAYBE IF YOU'D LEAVE YOUR COMPUTER ALONE FOR 15 MINUTES, YOU'D BE CLOSER TO ALL OF US. YOU ACT LIKE YOU'RE MARRIED TO THAT THING!
THAT'S RIDICULOUS!
OH, SO NOW I'M STUPID **AND** RIDICULOUS?!
CLAUDIA, YOU --
THUD

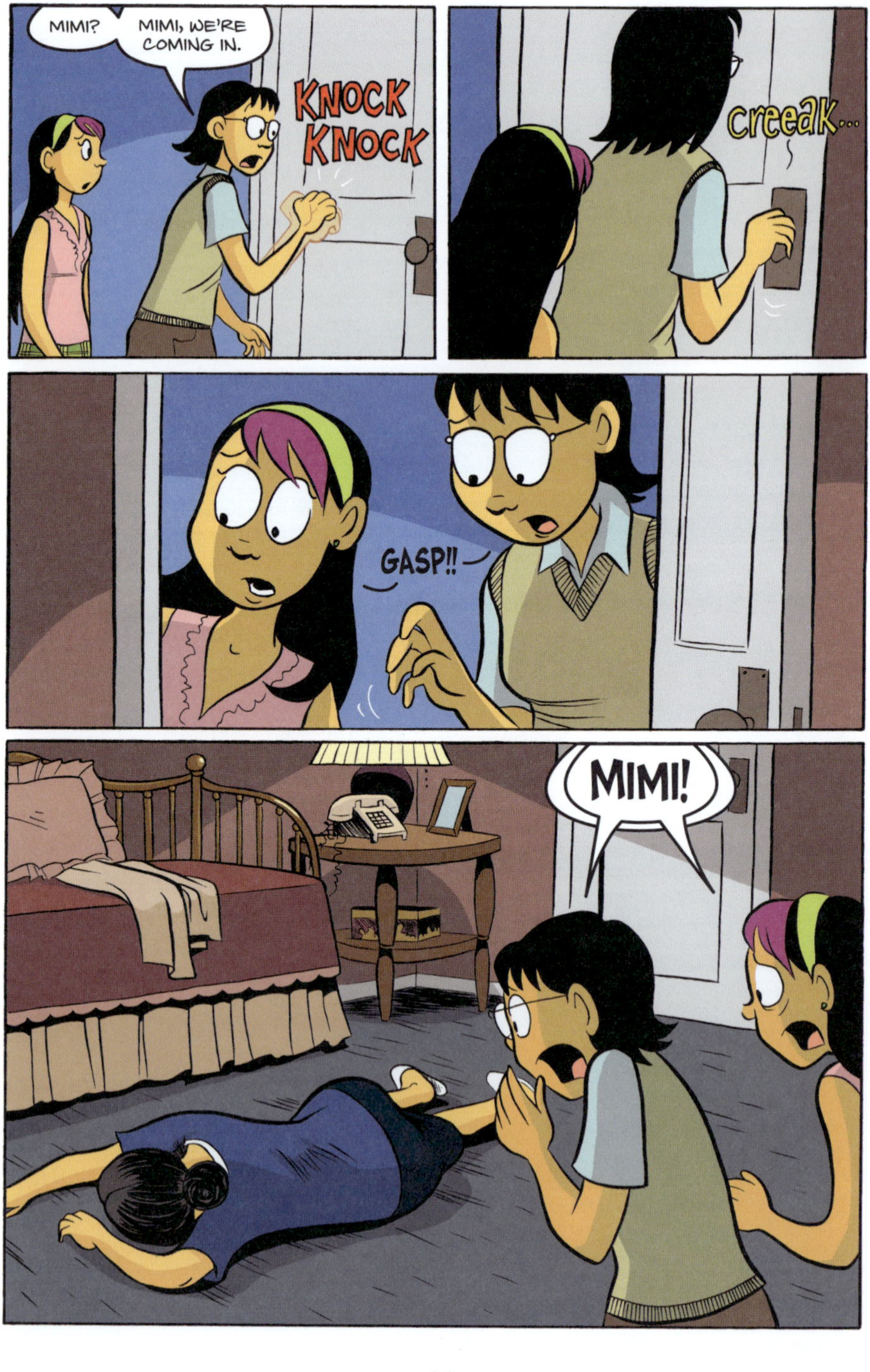
MIMI?
MIMI, WE'RE COMING IN.
KNOCK KNOCK
creeak...
GASP!!
MIMI!

CHAPTER 5

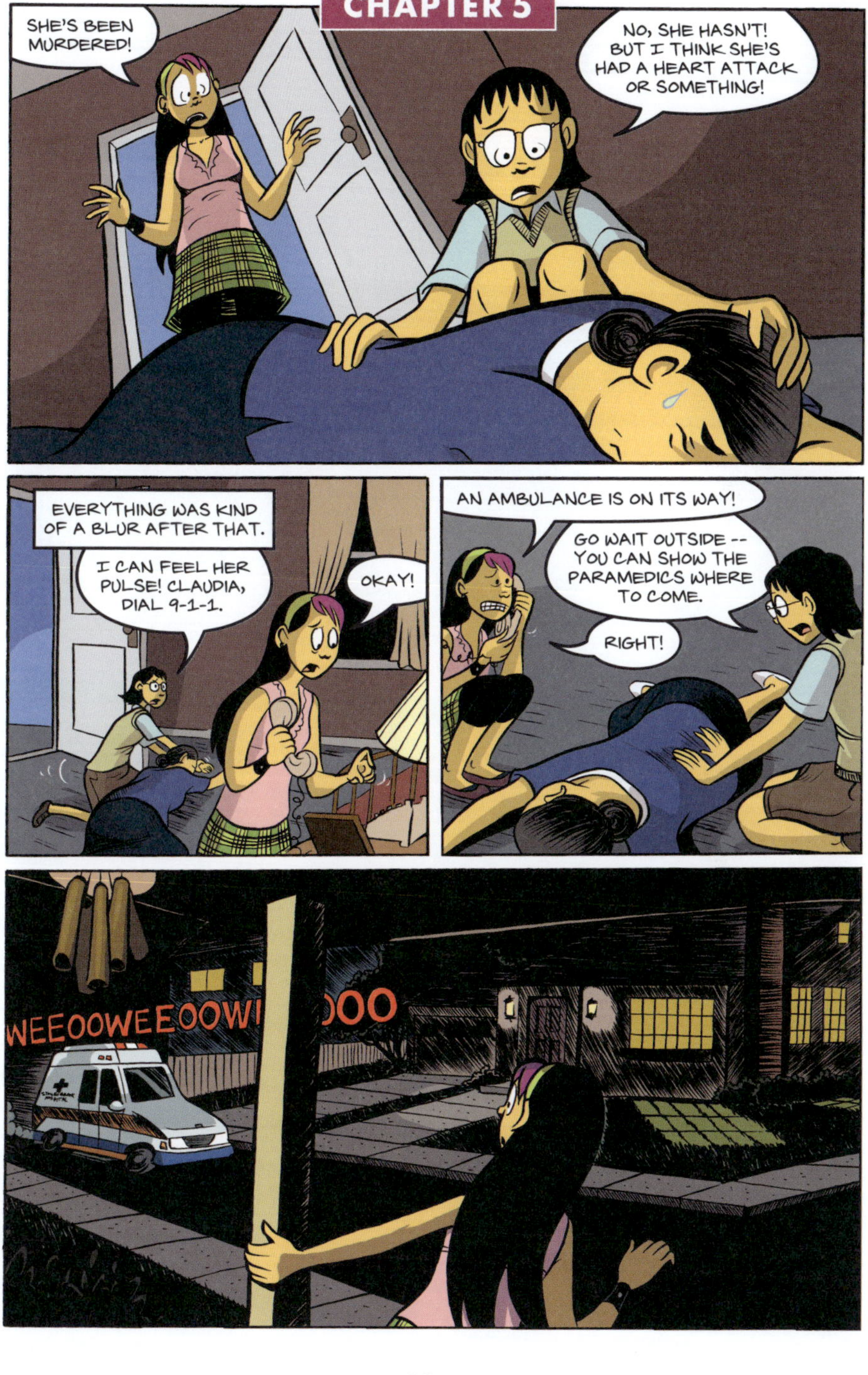
SHE'S BEEN MURDERED!
NO, SHE HASN'T! BUT I THINK SHE'S HAD A HEART ATTACK OR SOMETHING!
EVERYTHING WAS KIND OF A BLUR AFTER THAT.
I CAN FEEL HER PULSE! CLAUDIA, DIAL 9-1-1.
OKAY!
AN AMBULANCE IS ON ITS WAY!
GO WAIT OUTSIDE -- YOU CAN SHOW THE PARAMEDICS WHERE TO COME.
RIGHT!
WEEOOWEEOOWI OOO

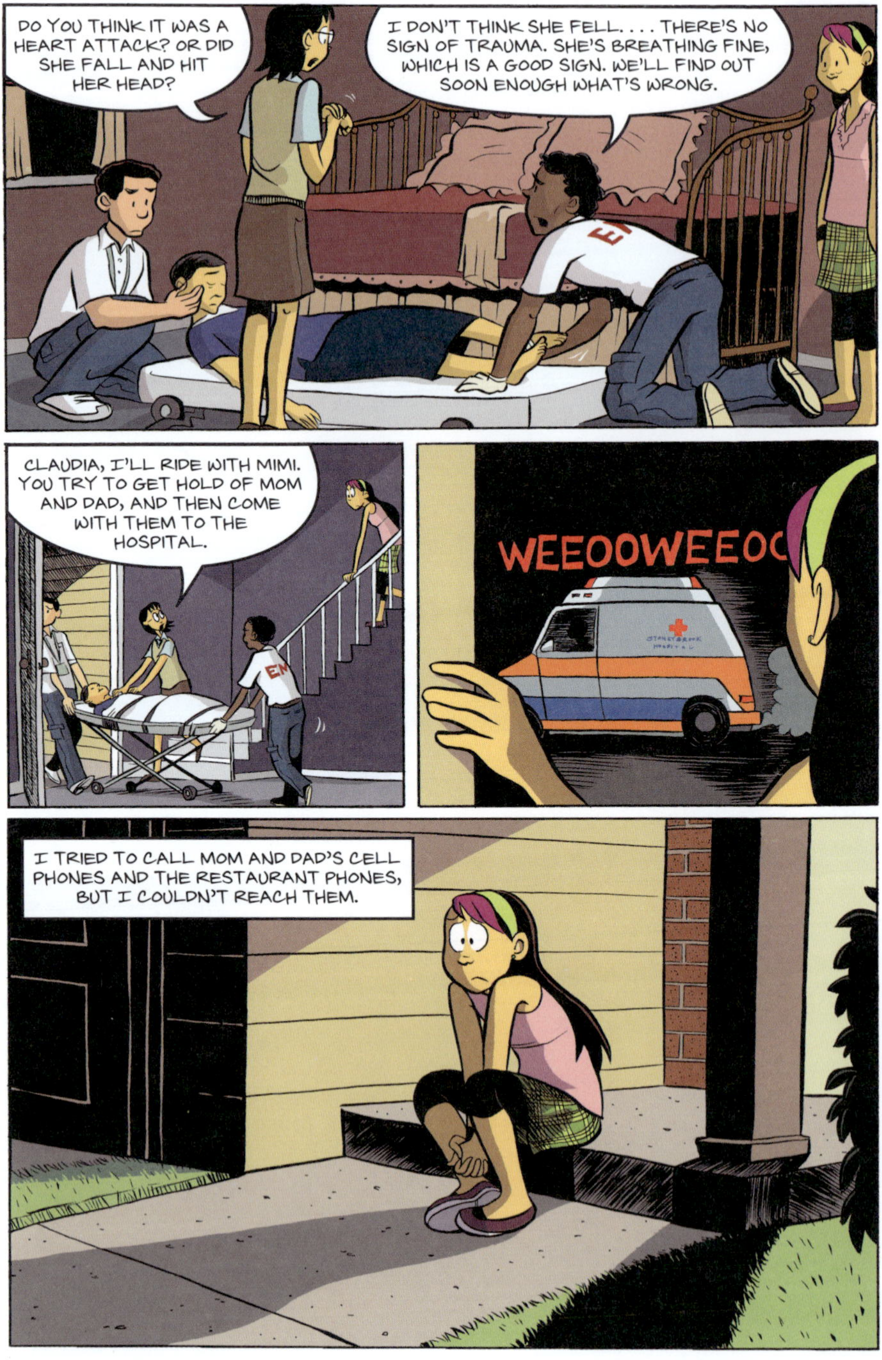
DO YOU THINK IT WAS A HEART ATTACK? OR DID SHE FALL AND HIT HER HEAD?
I DON'T THINK SHE FELL. . . . THERE'S NO SIGN OF TRAUMA. SHE'S BREATHING FINE, WHICH IS A GOOD SIGN. WE'LL FIND OUT SOON ENOUGH WHAT'S WRONG.
CLAUDIA, I'LL RIDE WITH MIMI. YOU TRY TO GET HOLD OF MOM AND DAD, AND THEN COME WITH THEM TO THE HOSPITAL.
WEEOOWEEOO
I TRIED TO CALL MOM AND DAD'S CELL PHONES AND THE RESTAURANT PHONES, BUT I COULDN'T REACH THEM.

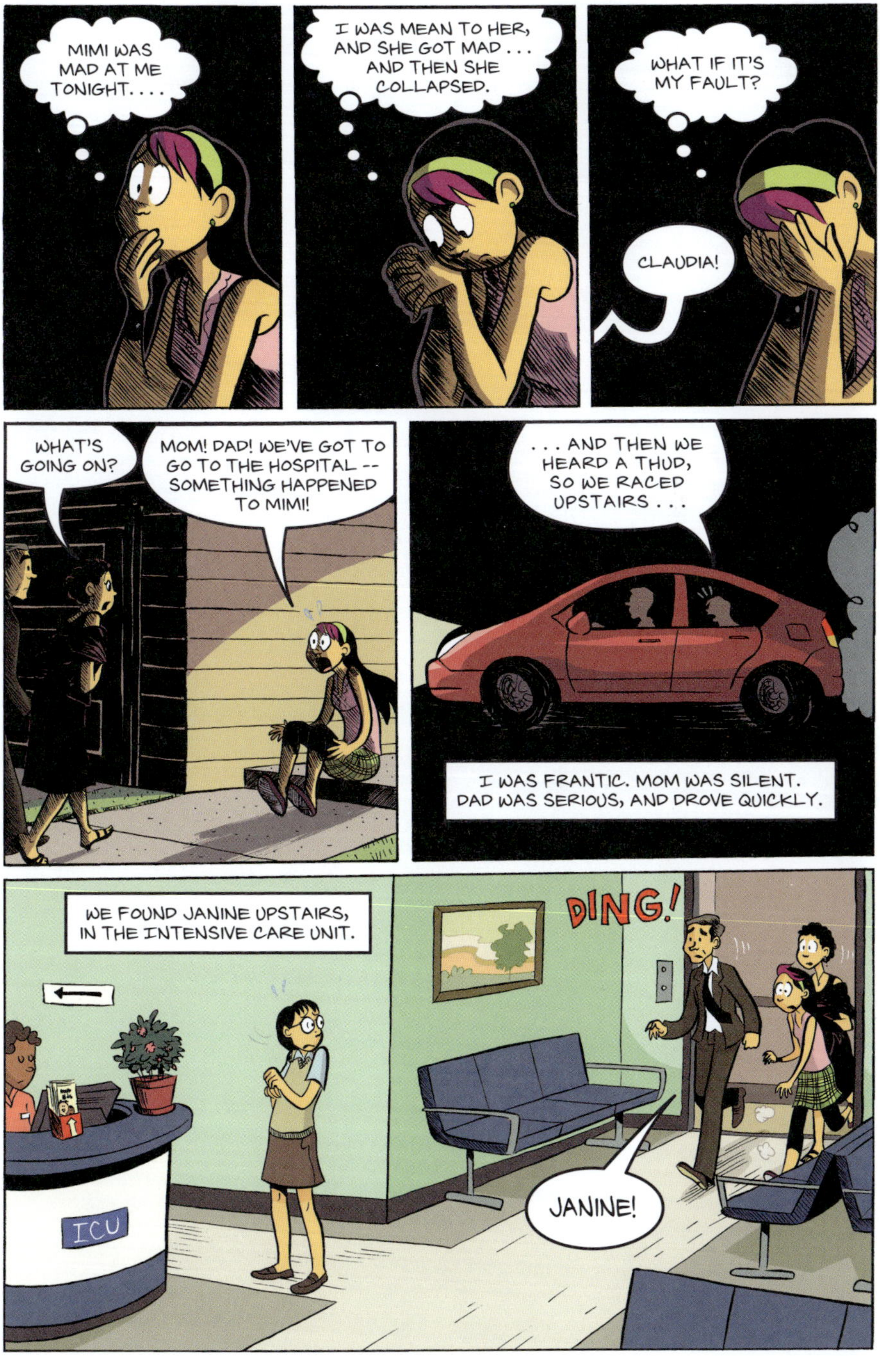
MIMI WAS MAD AT ME TONIGHT. . . .
I WAS MEAN TO HER, AND SHE GOT MAD . . . AND THEN SHE COLLAPSED.
WHAT IF IT'S MY FAULT?
CLAUDIA!
WHAT'S GOING ON?
MOM! DAD! WE'VE GOT TO GO TO THE HOSPITAL -- SOMETHING HAPPENED TO MIMI!
. . . AND THEN WE HEARD A THUD, SO WE RACED UPSTAIRS . . .
I WAS FRANTIC. MOM WAS SILENT. DAD WAS SERIOUS, AND DROVE QUICKLY.
WE FOUND JANINE UPSTAIRS, IN THE INTENSIVE CARE UNIT.
DING!
ICU
JANINE!

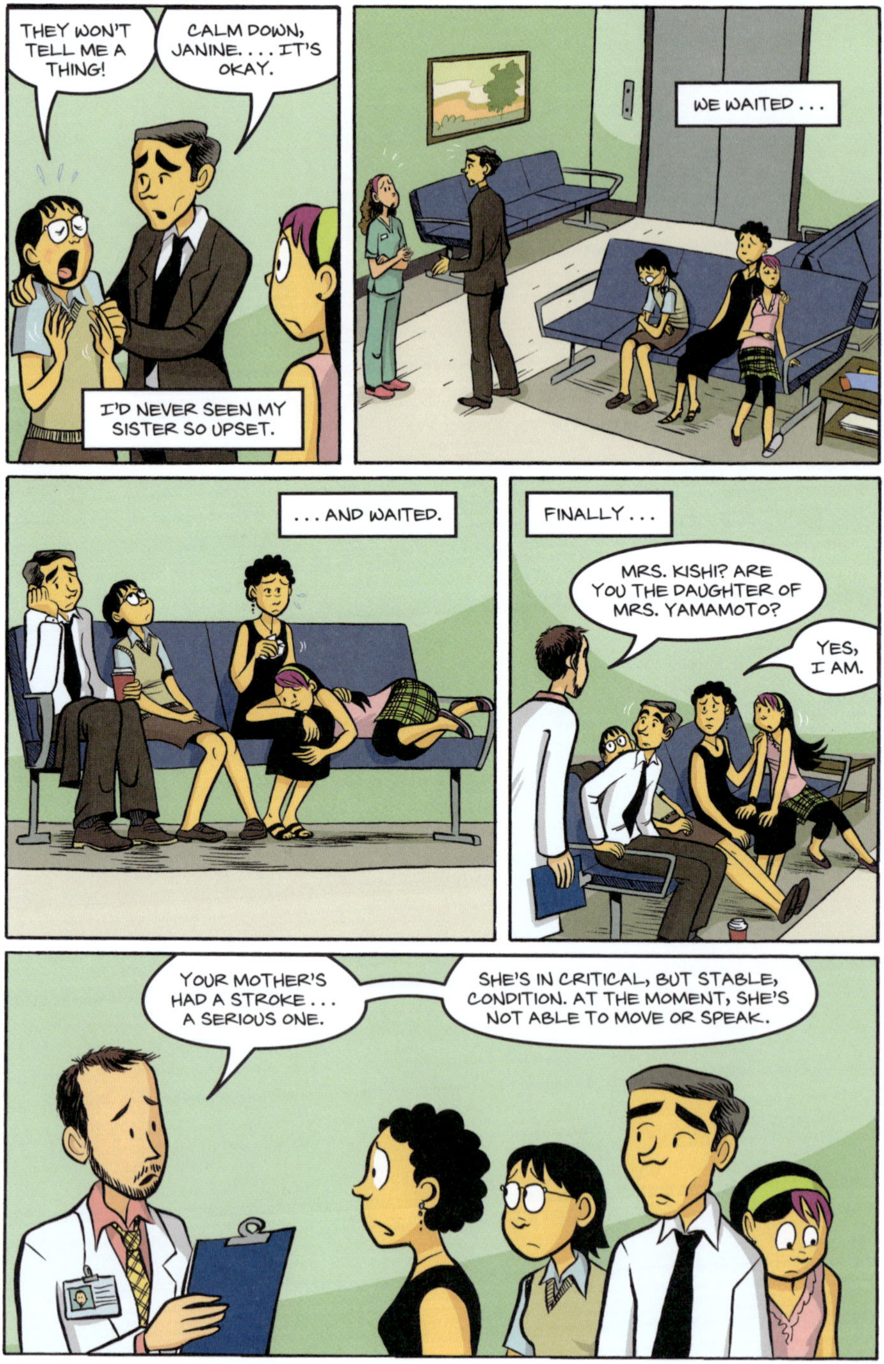
THEY WON'T TELL ME A THING!
CALM DOWN, JANINE. . . . IT'S OKAY.
I'D NEVER SEEN MY SISTER SO UPSET.
WE WAITED . . .
. . . AND WAITED.
FINALLY . . .
MRS. KISHI? ARE YOU THE DAUGHTER OF MRS. YAMAMOTO?
YES, I AM.
YOUR MOTHER'S HAD A STROKE . . . A SERIOUS ONE.
SHE'S IN CRITICAL, BUT STABLE, CONDITION. AT THE MOMENT, SHE'S NOT ABLE TO MOVE OR SPEAK.

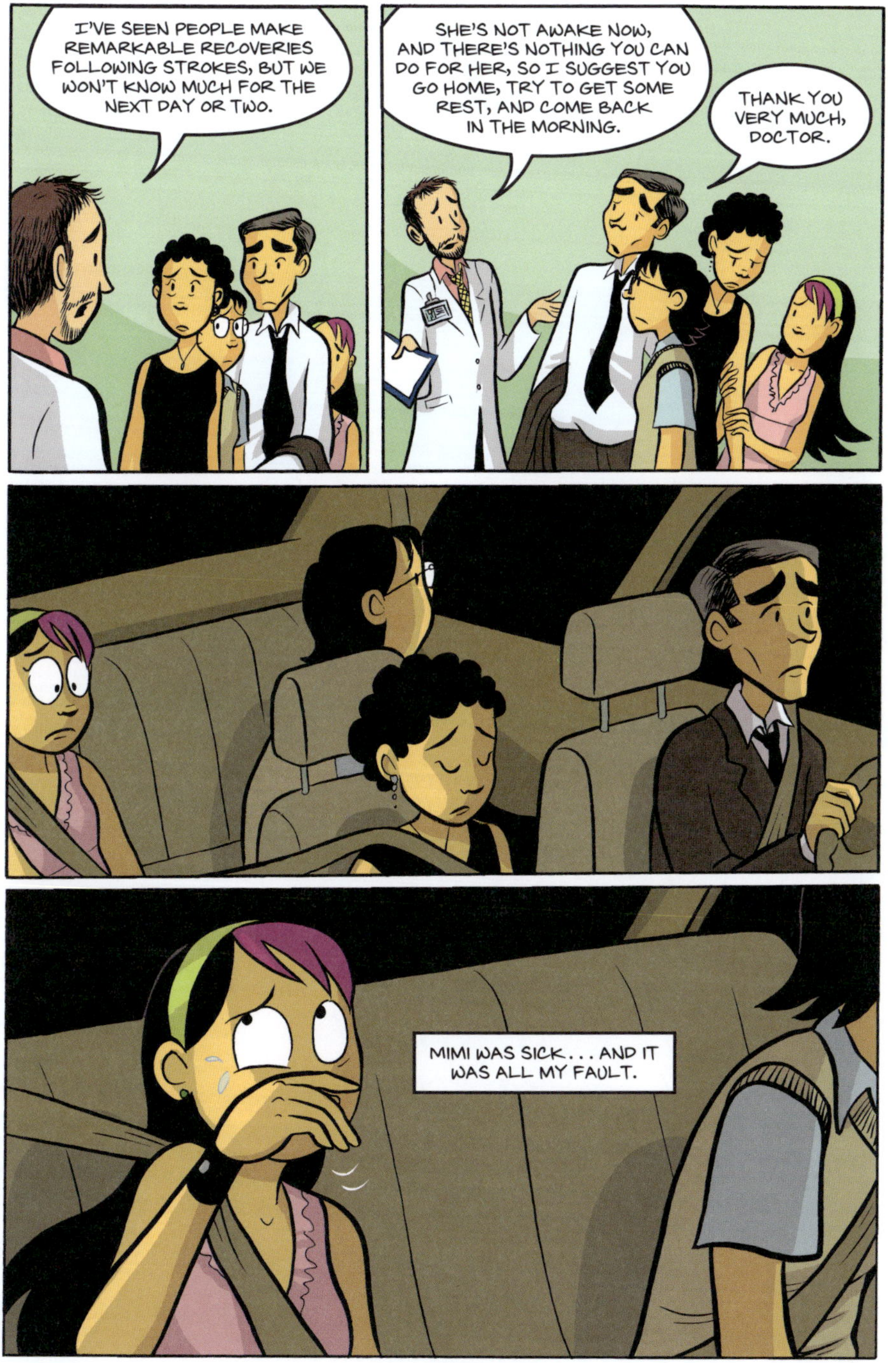
I'VE SEEN PEOPLE MAKE REMARKABLE RECOVERIES FOLLOWING STROKES, BUT WE WON'T KNOW MUCH FOR THE NEXT DAY OR TWO.
SHE'S NOT AWAKE NOW, AND THERE'S NOTHING YOU CAN DO FOR HER, SO I SUGGEST YOU GO HOME, TRY TO GET SOME REST, AND COME BACK IN THE MORNING.
THANK YOU VERY MUCH, DOCTOR.
MIMI WAS SICK . . . AND IT WAS ALL MY FAULT.

Monday, June 16

Today was a good news-bad news day for us baby-sitters. The good news was that nine children came to the first session of our playgroup and it went really well. David Michael, Nicky, and Marcus are kind of wild when they get together, but they're manageable. And we're going to have to do something about Jenny Prezzioso... she's a pain. Got any ideas, Mary Anne?

The bad news was about Claudia's grandmother, Mimi. It turns out that she had a stroke last night and is in the hospital. The news kind of upset us, but we were able to put our worries aside and run the playgroup okay, which I guess proves we're professionals.
— Dawn

CHAPTER 6

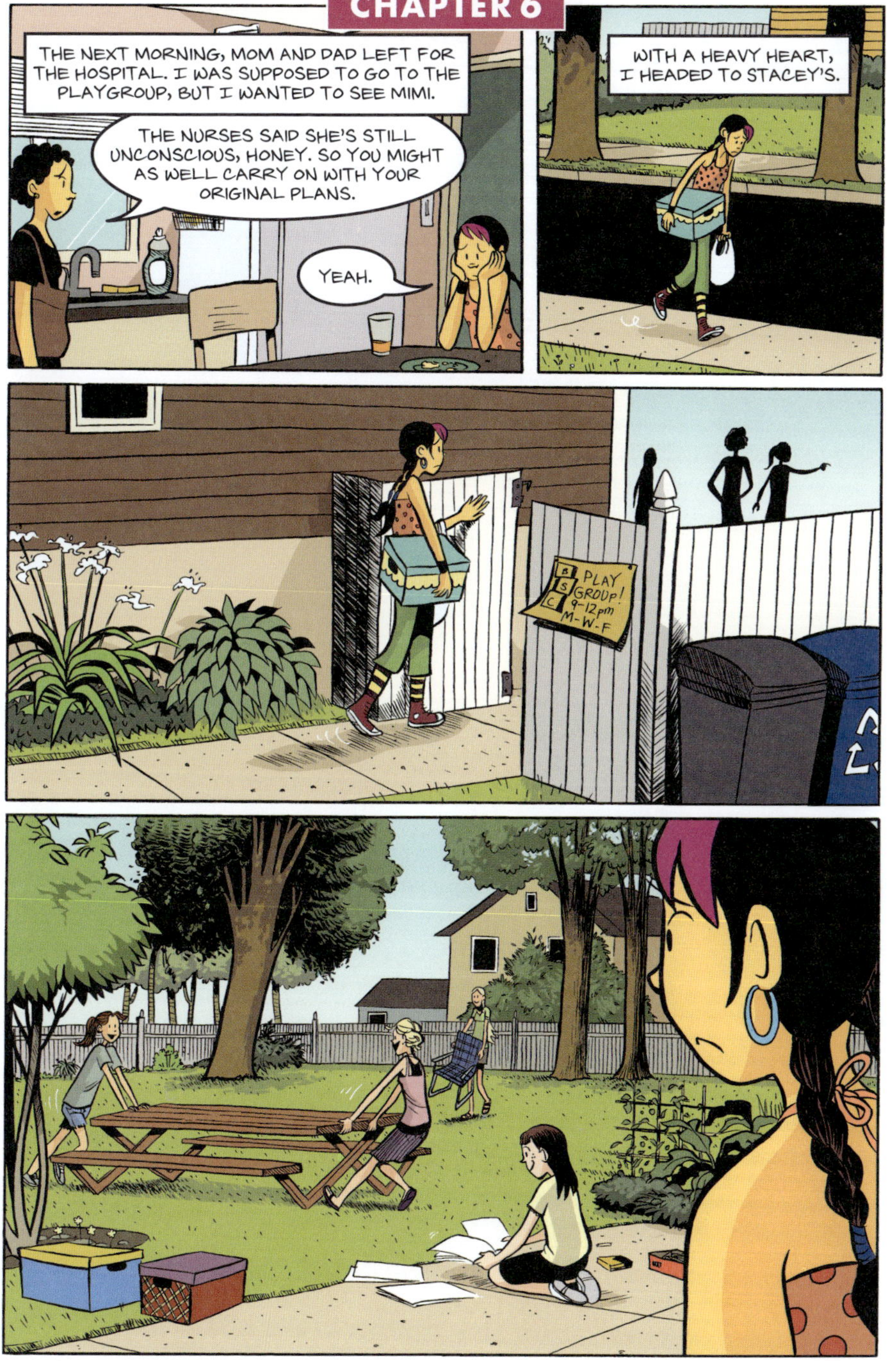
THE NEXT MORNING, MOM AND DAD LEFT FOR THE HOSPITAL. I WAS SUPPOSED TO GO TO THE PLAYGROUP, BUT I WANTED TO SEE MIMI.
THE NURSES SAID SHE'S STILL UNCONSCIOUS, HONEY. SO YOU MIGHT AS WELL CARRY ON WITH YOUR ORIGINAL PLANS.
YEAH.
WITH A HEAVY HEART, I HEADED TO STACEY'S.
BSC PLAY GROUP! 9-12pm M-W-F

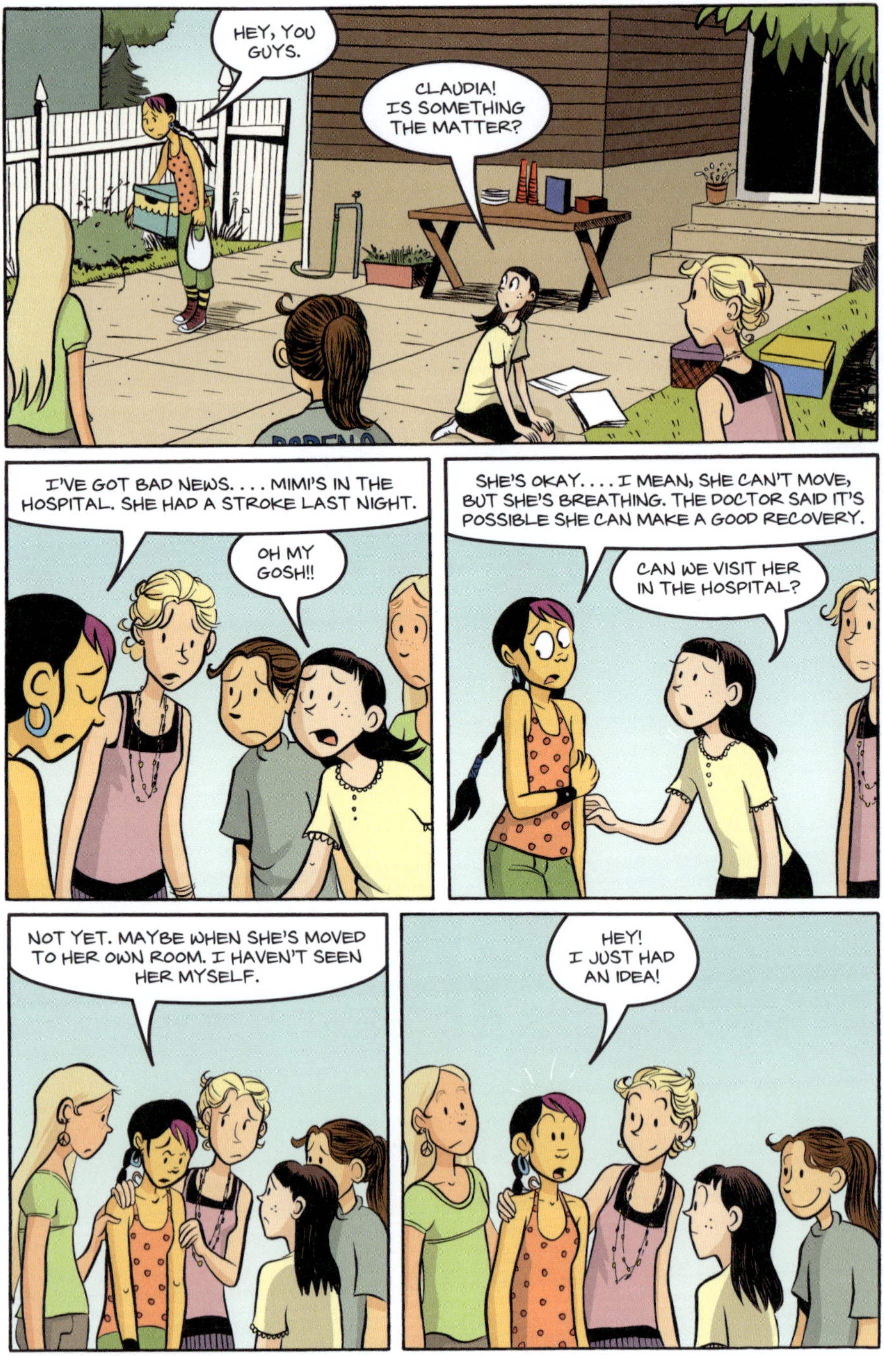
HEY, YOU GUYS.
CLAUDIA! IS SOMETHING THE MATTER?
I'VE GOT BAD NEWS. . . . MIMI'S IN THE HOSPITAL. SHE HAD A STROKE LAST NIGHT.
OH MY GOSH!!
SHE'S OKAY. . . . I MEAN, SHE CAN'T MOVE, BUT SHE'S BREATHING. THE DOCTOR SAID IT'S POSSIBLE SHE CAN MAKE A GOOD RECOVERY.
CAN WE VISIT HER IN THE HOSPITAL?
NOT YET. MAYBE WHEN SHE'S MOVED TO HER OWN ROOM. I HAVEN'T SEEN HER MYSELF.
HEY! I JUST HAD AN IDEA!

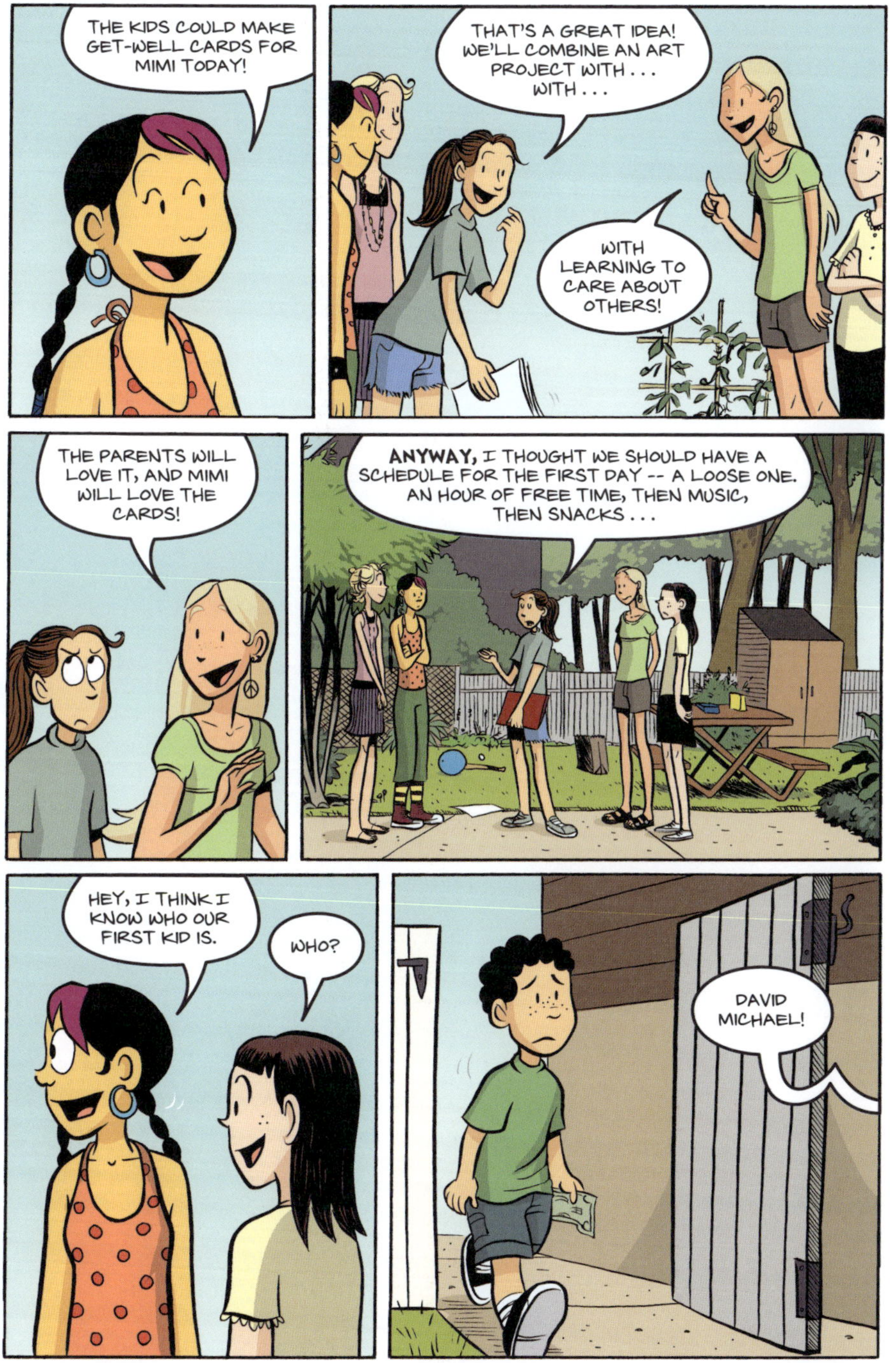
THE KIDS COULD MAKE GET-WELL CARDS FOR MIMI TODAY!
THAT'S A GREAT IDEA! WE'LL COMBINE AN ART PROJECT WITH . . . WITH . . .
WITH LEARNING TO CARE ABOUT OTHERS!
THE PARENTS WILL LOVE IT, AND MIMI WILL LOVE THE CARDS!
ANYWAY, I THOUGHT WE SHOULD HAVE A SCHEDULE FOR THE FIRST DAY -- A LOOSE ONE. AN HOUR OF FREE TIME, THEN MUSIC, THEN SNACKS . . .
HEY, I THINK I KNOW WHO OUR FIRST KID IS.
WHO?
DAVID MICHAEL!

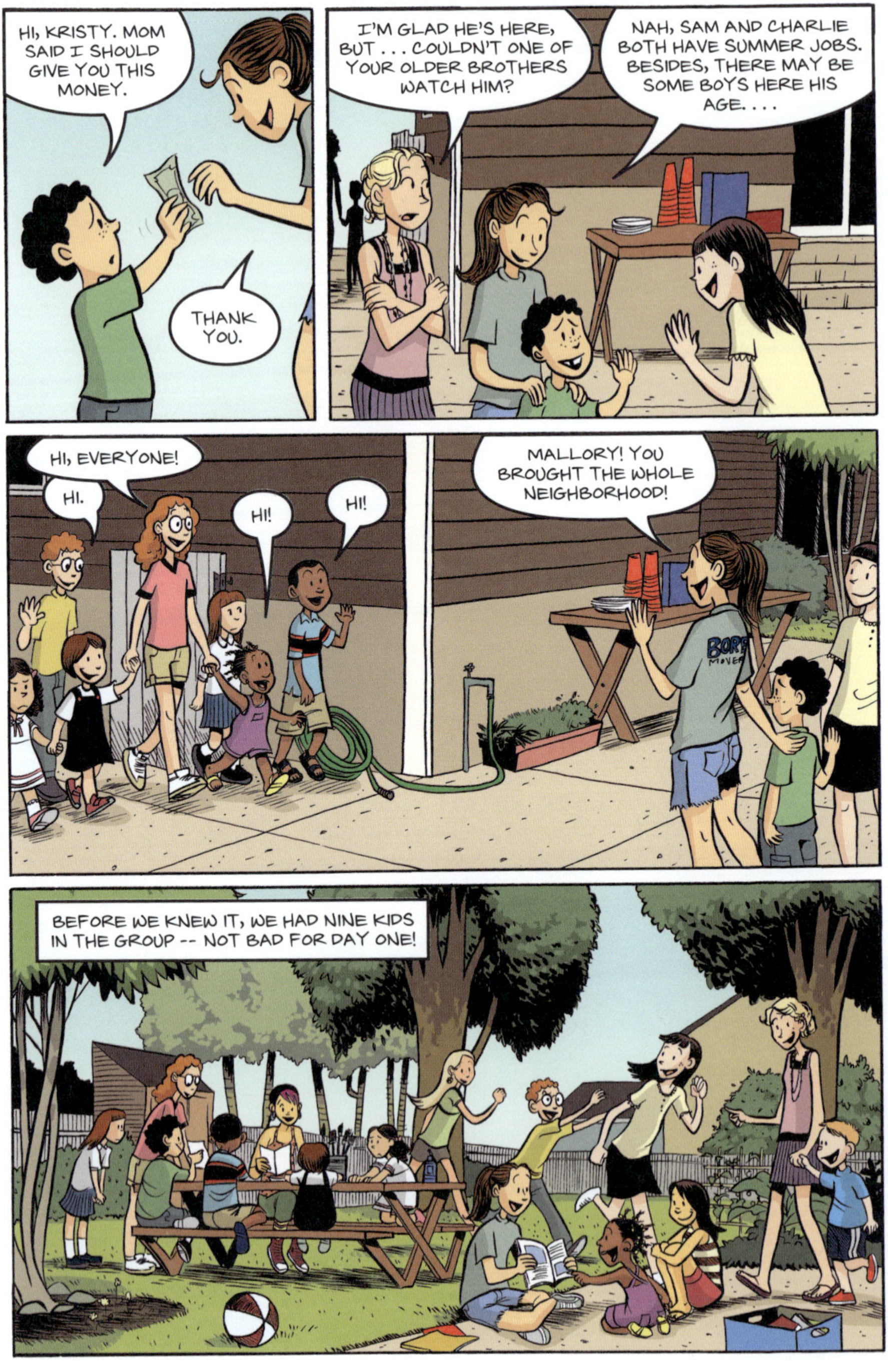
HI, KRISTY. MOM SAID I SHOULD GIVE YOU THIS MONEY.
THANK YOU.
I'M GLAD HE'S HERE, BUT . . . COULDN'T ONE OF YOUR OLDER BROTHERS WATCH HIM?
NAH, SAM AND CHARLIE BOTH HAVE SUMMER JOBS. BESIDES, THERE MAY BE SOME BOYS HERE HIS AGE. . . .
HI, EVERYONE!
HI.
HI!
HI!
MALLORY! YOU BROUGHT THE WHOLE NEIGHBORHOOD!
BEFORE WE KNEW IT, WE HAD NINE KIDS IN THE GROUP -- NOT BAD FOR DAY ONE!

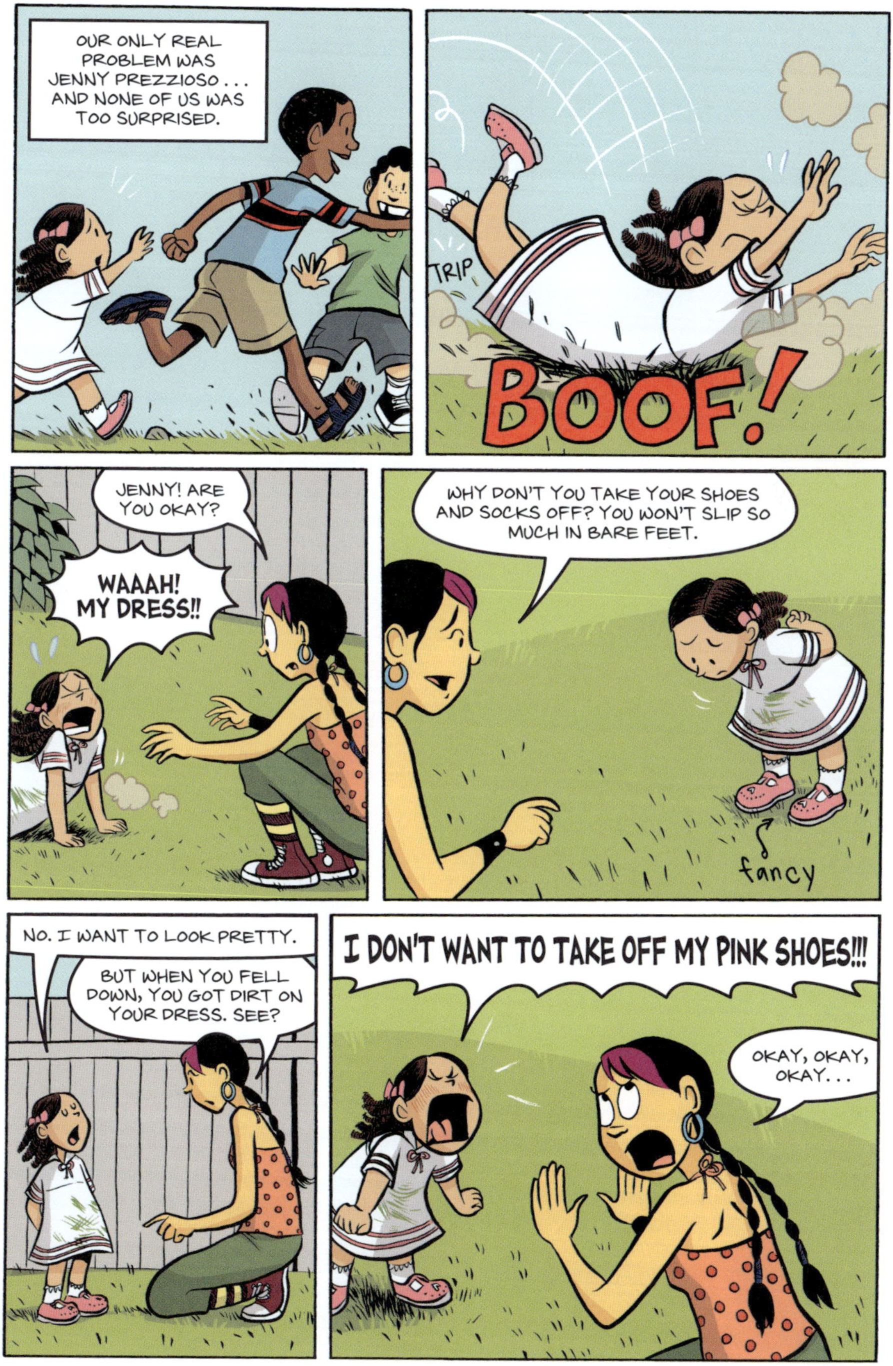
OUR ONLY REAL PROBLEM WAS JENNY PREZZIOSO . . . AND NONE OF US WAS TOO SURPRISED.
TRIP
BOOF!
JENNY! ARE YOU OKAY?
WAAAH! MY DRESS!!
WHY DON'T YOU TAKE YOUR SHOES AND SOCKS OFF? YOU WON'T SLIP SO MUCH IN BARE FEET.
fancy
NO. I WANT TO LOOK PRETTY.
BUT WHEN YOU FELL DOWN, YOU GOT DIRT ON YOUR DRESS. SEE?
I DON'T WANT TO TAKE OFF MY PINK SHOES!!!
OKAY, OKAY, OKAY...

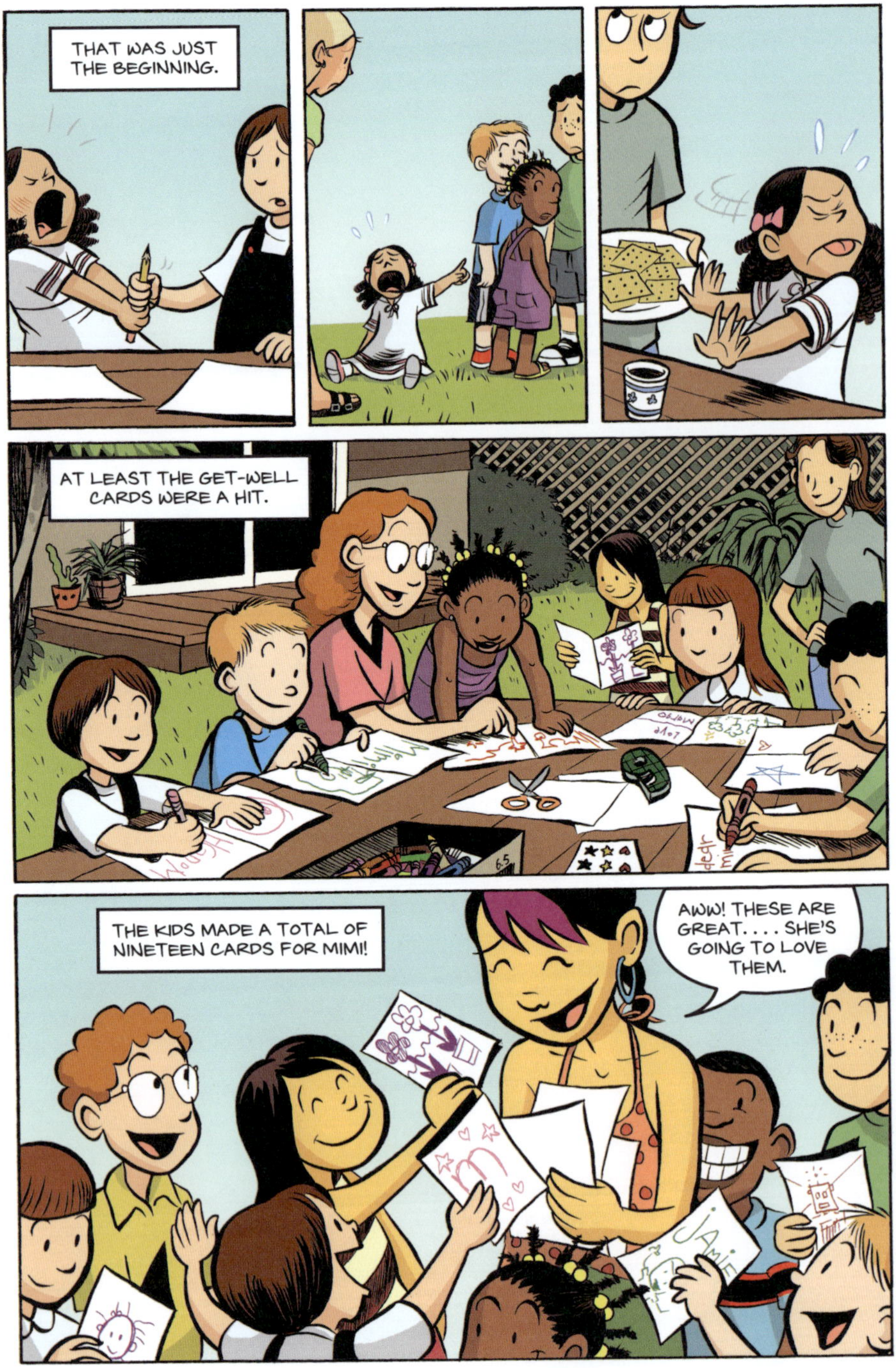
THAT WAS JUST THE BEGINNING.
AT LEAST THE GET-WELL CARDS WERE A HIT.
THE KIDS MADE A TOTAL OF NINETEEN CARDS FOR MIMI!
AWW! THESE ARE GREAT. . . . SHE'S GOING TO LOVE THEM.
JAMIE

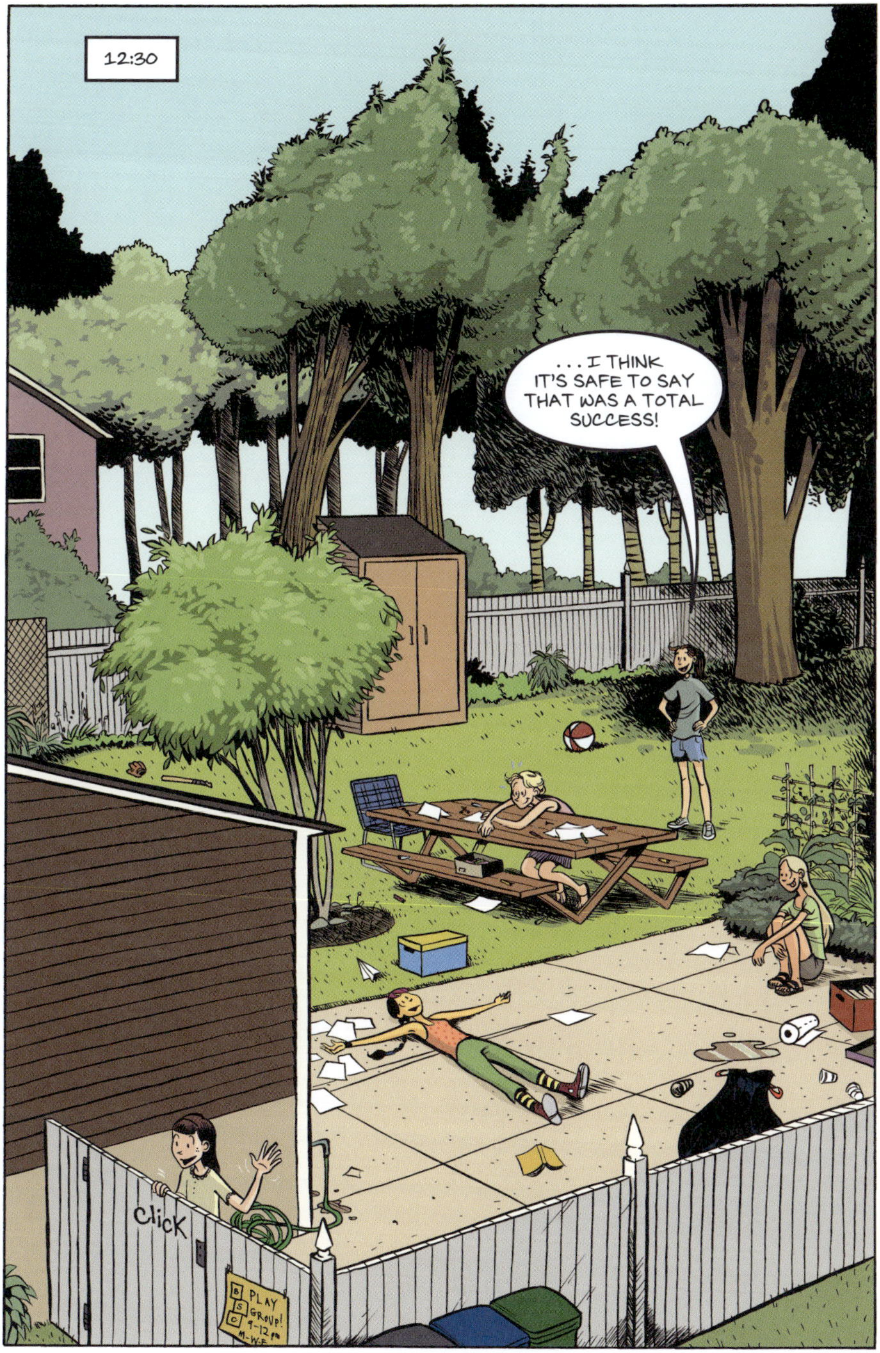
12:30
. . . I THINK IT'S SAFE TO SAY THAT WAS A TOTAL SUCCESS!
CLICK

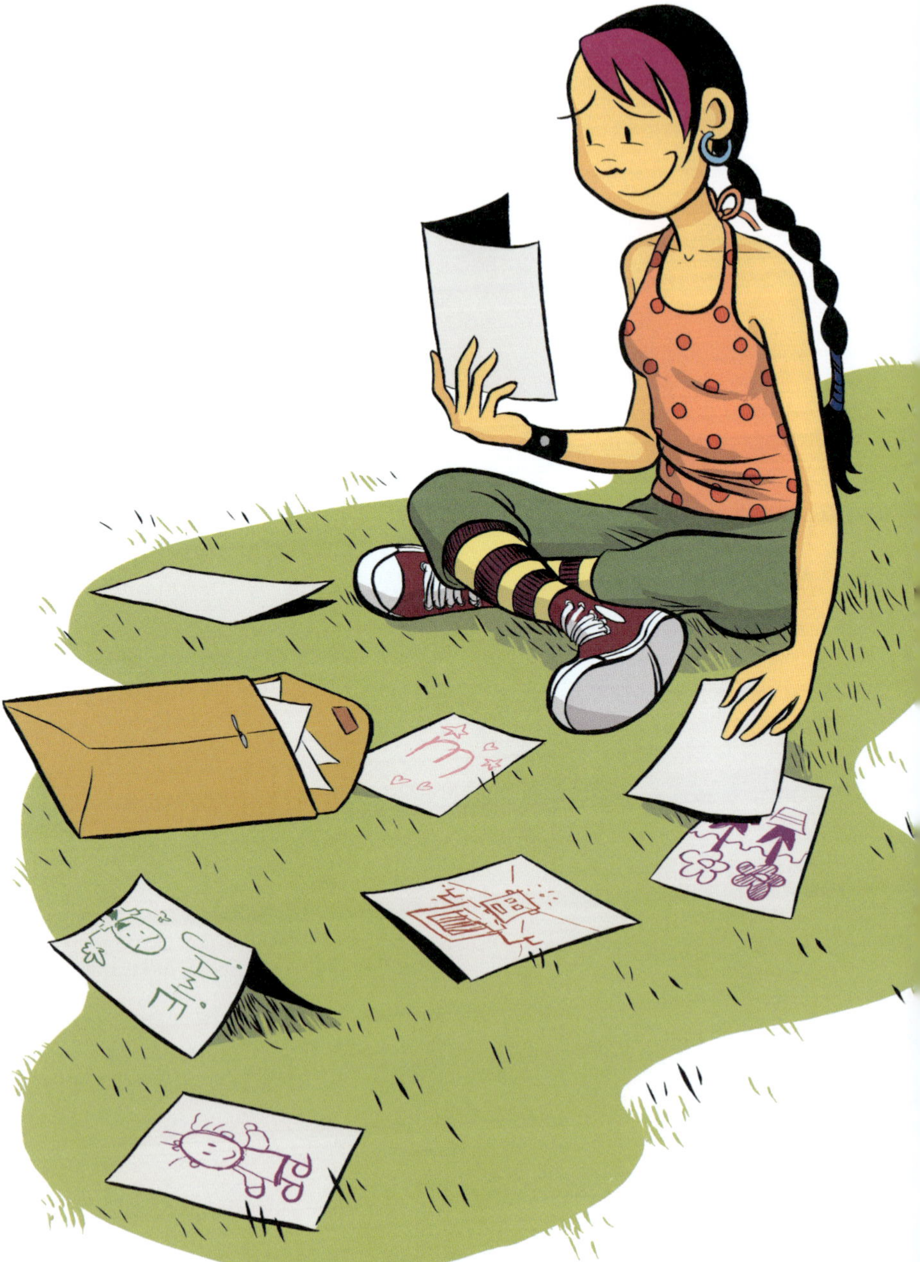
JAMIE

CHAPTER 7

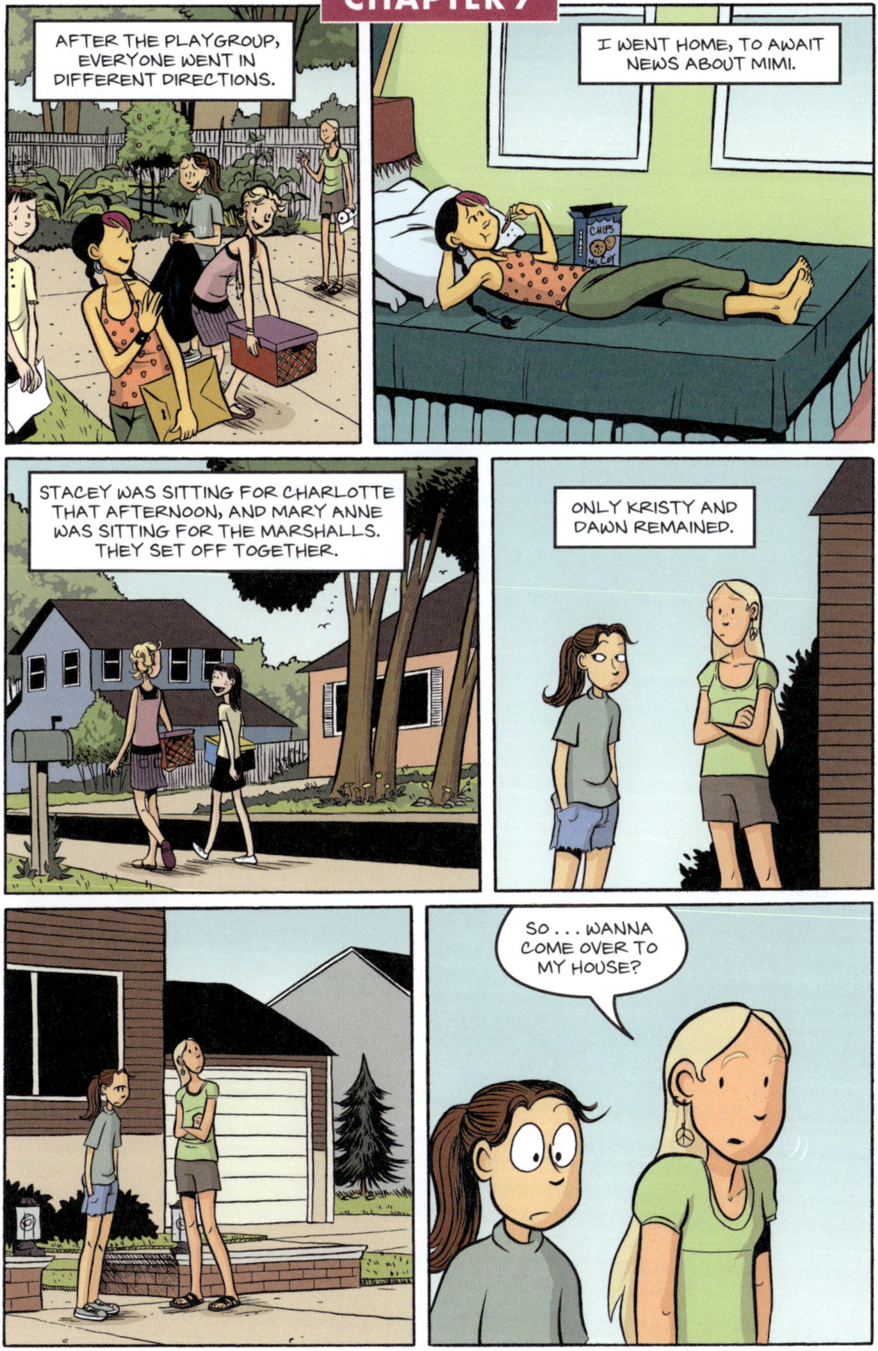
AFTER THE PLAYGROUP, EVERYONE WENT IN DIFFERENT DIRECTIONS.
I WENT HOME, TO AWAIT NEWS ABOUT MIMI.
STACEY WAS SITTING FOR CHARLOTTE THAT AFTERNOON, AND MARY ANNE WAS SITTING FOR THE MARSHALLS. THEY SET OFF TOGETHER.
ONLY KRISTY AND DAWN REMAINED.
SO . . . WANNA COME OVER TO MY HOUSE?

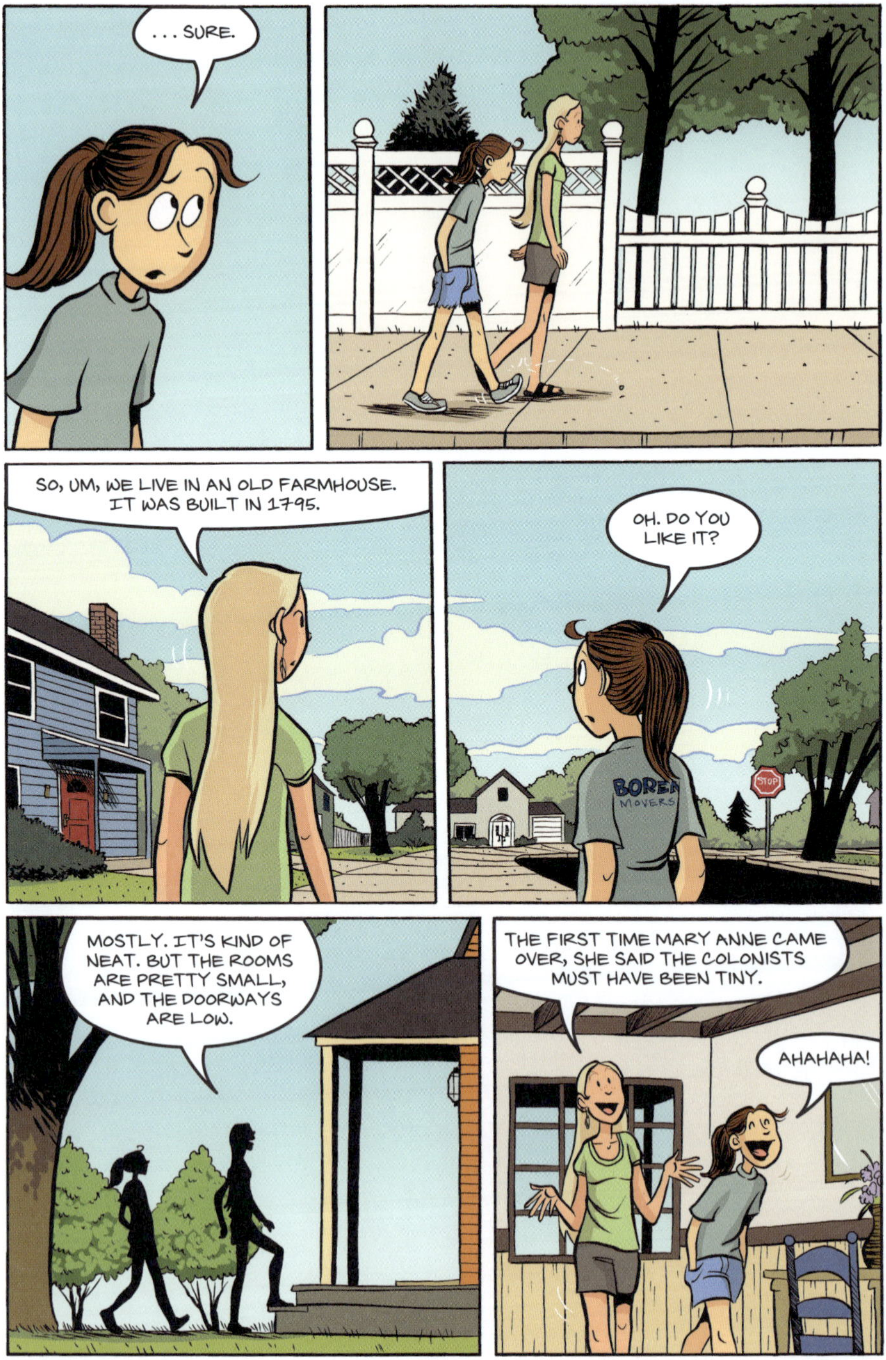
. . . SURE.
SO, UM, WE LIVE IN AN OLD FARMHOUSE. IT WAS BUILT IN 1795.
OH. DO YOU LIKE IT?
BOREN MOVERS
STOP
MOSTLY. IT'S KIND OF NEAT. BUT THE ROOMS ARE PRETTY SMALL, AND THE DOORWAYS ARE LOW.
THE FIRST TIME MARY ANNE CAME OVER, SHE SAID THE COLONISTS MUST HAVE BEEN TINY.
AHAHAHA!

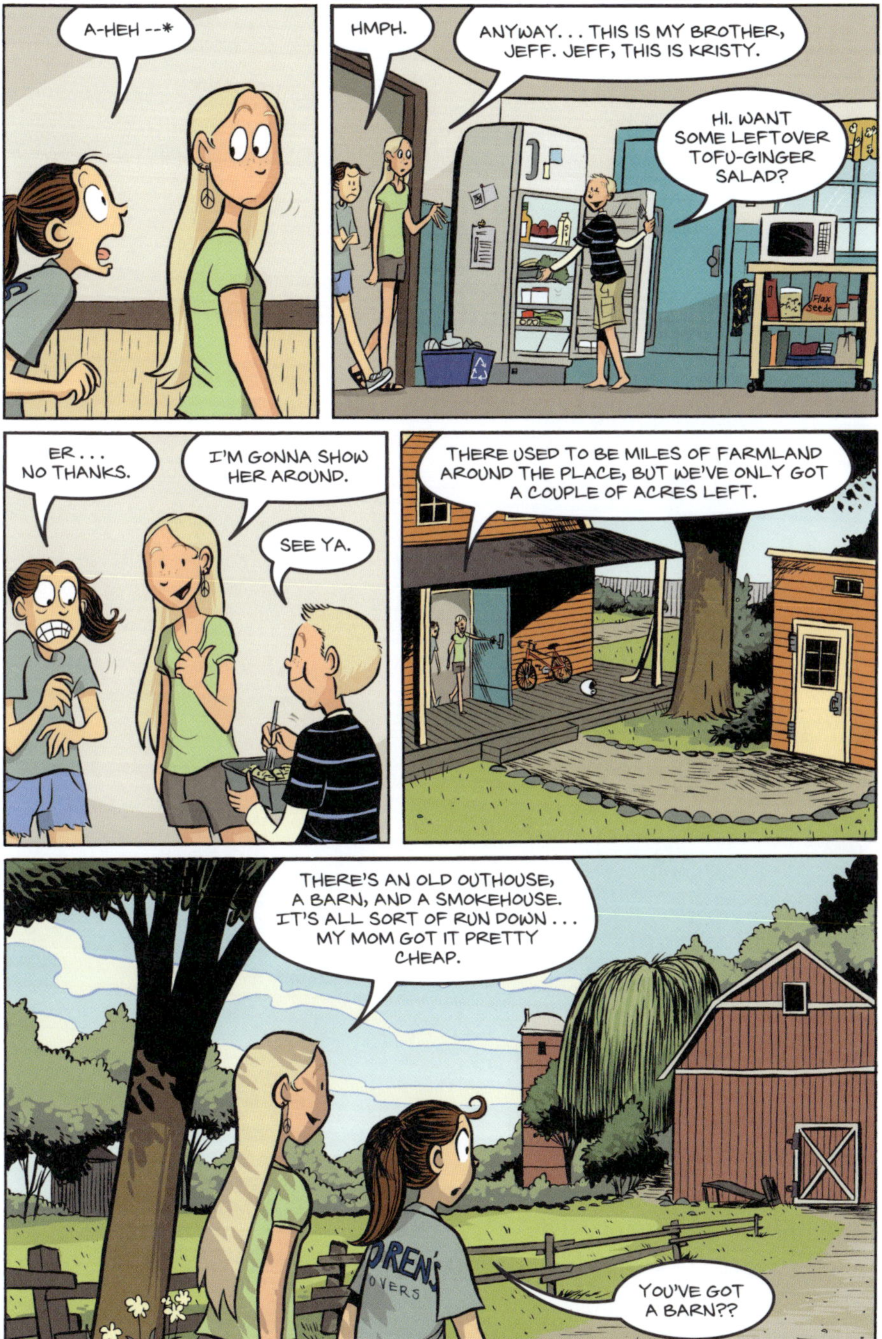
A-HEH --*
HMPH.
ANYWAY... THIS IS MY BROTHER, JEFF. JEFF, THIS IS KRISTY.
HI. WANT SOME LEFTOVER TOFU-GINGER SALAD?
Flax Seeds
ER... NO THANKS.
I'M GONNA SHOW HER AROUND.
SEE YA.
THERE USED TO BE MILES OF FARMLAND AROUND THE PLACE, BUT WE'VE ONLY GOT A COUPLE OF ACRES LEFT.
THERE'S AN OLD OUTHOUSE, A BARN, AND A SMOKEHOUSE. IT'S ALL SORT OF RUN DOWN... MY MOM GOT IT PRETTY CHEAP.
YOU'VE GOT A BARN??

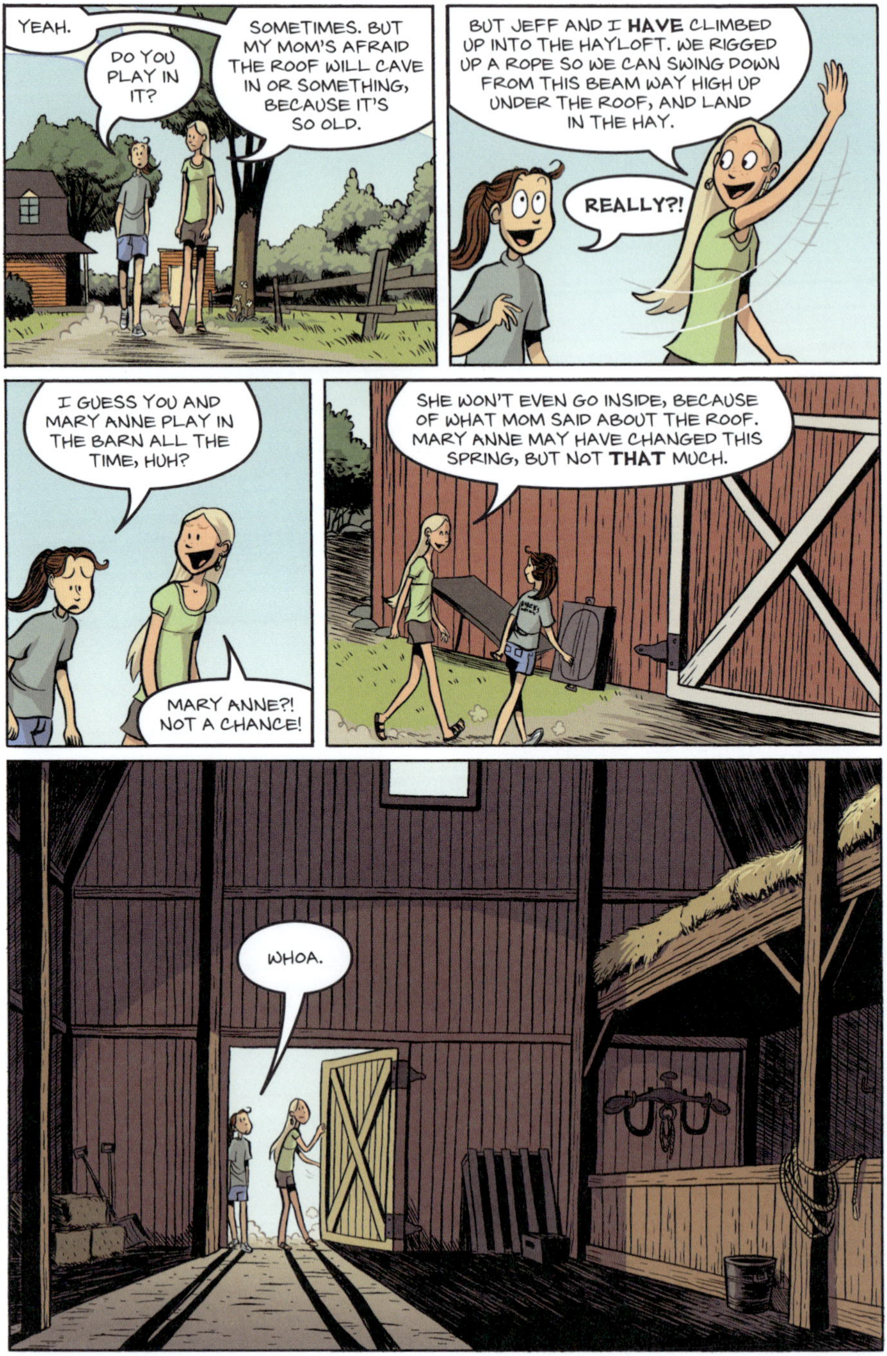
YEAH.
DO YOU PLAY IN IT?
SOMETIMES. BUT MY MOM'S AFRAID THE ROOF WILL CAVE IN OR SOMETHING, BECAUSE IT'S SO OLD.
BUT JEFF AND I **HAVE** CLIMBED UP INTO THE HAYLOFT. WE RIGGED UP A ROPE SO WE CAN SWING DOWN FROM THIS BEAM WAY HIGH UP UNDER THE ROOF, AND LAND IN THE HAY.
REALLY?!
I GUESS YOU AND MARY ANNE PLAY IN THE BARN ALL THE TIME, HUH?
MARY ANNE?! NOT A CHANCE!
SHE WON'T EVEN GO INSIDE, BECAUSE OF WHAT MOM SAID ABOUT THE ROOF. MARY ANNE MAY HAVE CHANGED THIS SPRING, BUT NOT **THAT** MUCH.
WHOA.

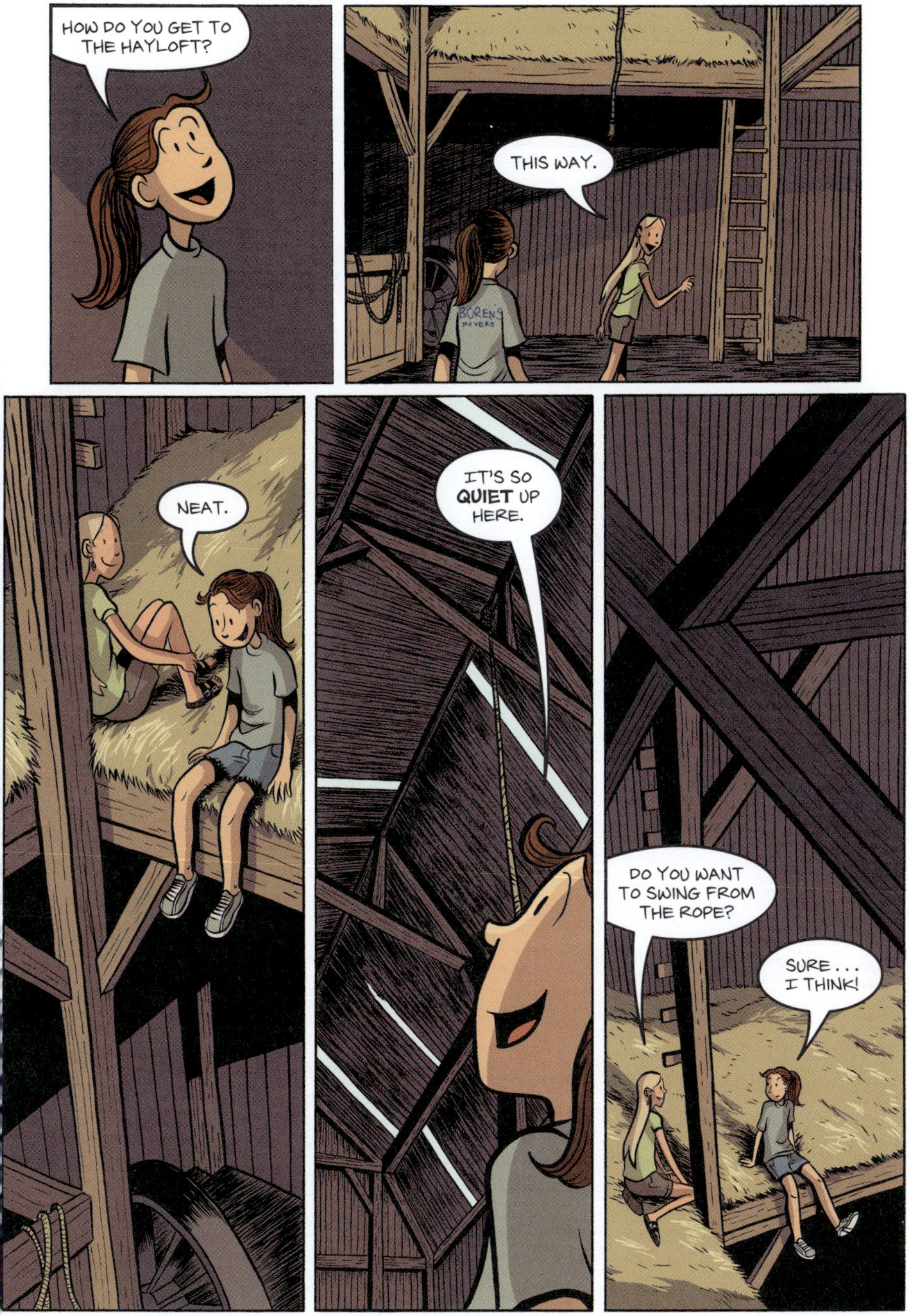
HOW DO YOU GET TO THE HAYLOFT?
THIS WAY.
BOREN'S MOVERS
NEAT.
IT'S SO **QUIET** UP HERE.
DO YOU WANT TO SWING FROM THE ROPE?
SURE . . . I THINK!

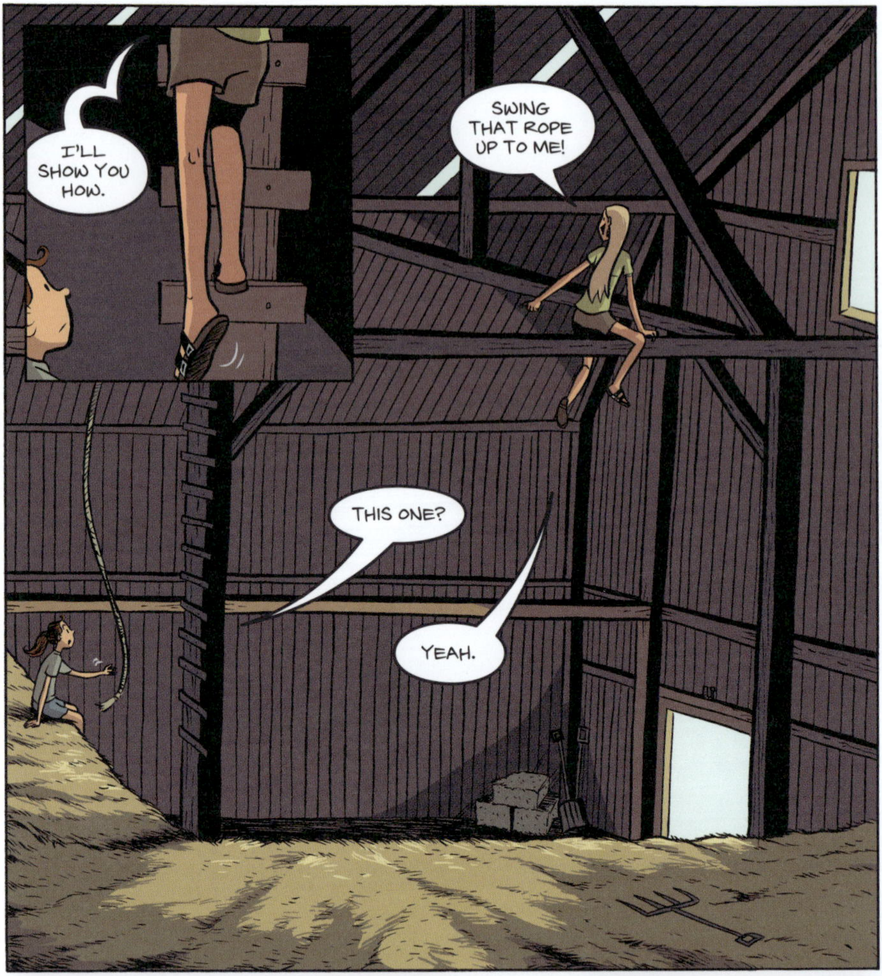
I'LL SHOW YOU HOW.
SWING THAT ROPE UP TO ME!
THIS ONE?
YEAH.

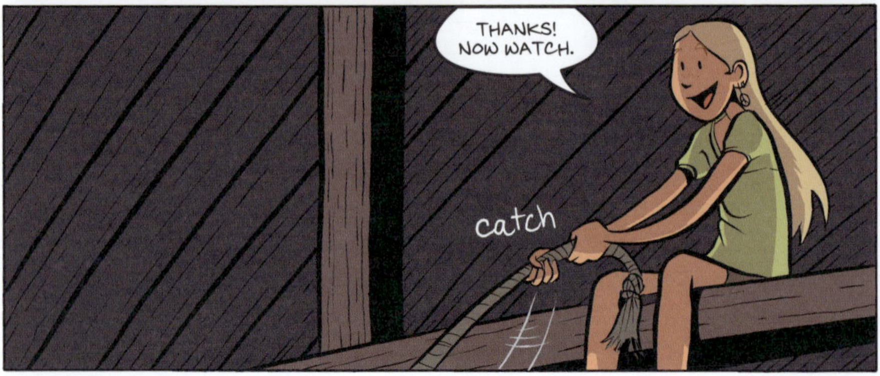
THANKS! NOW WATCH.
catch

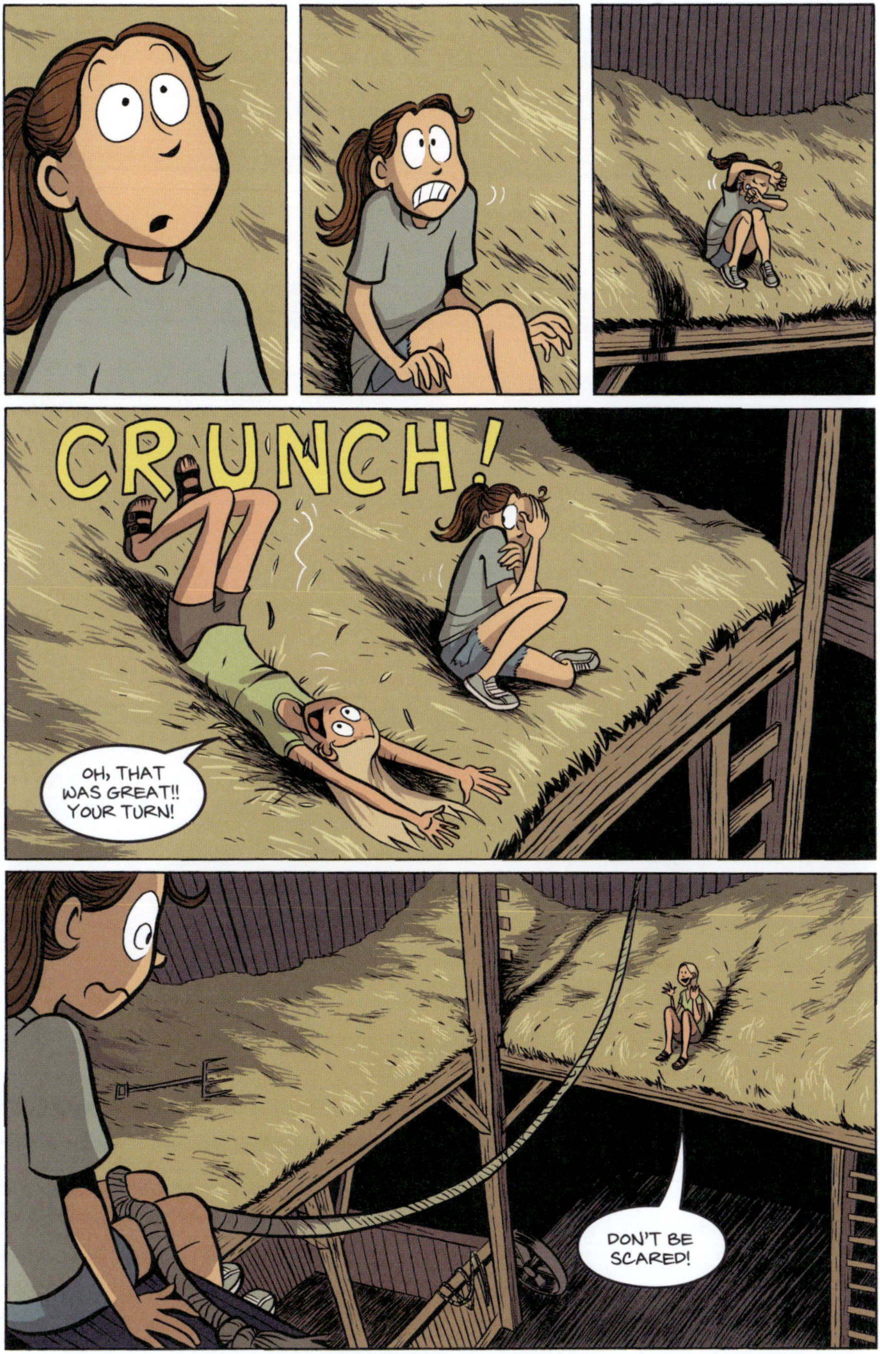
CRUNCH!
OH, THAT WAS GREAT!! YOUR TURN!
DON'T BE SCARED!

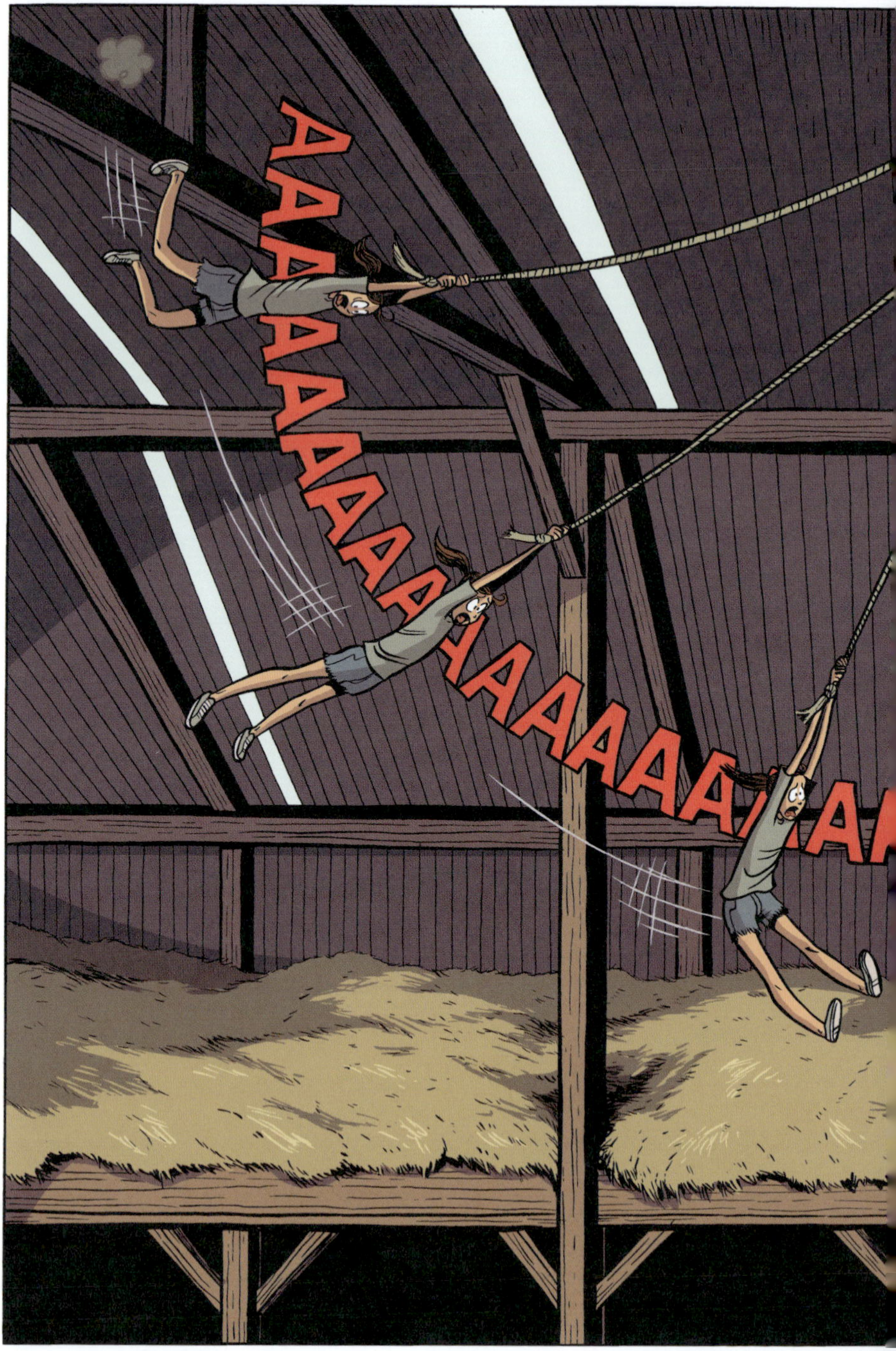
AAAAAAAAAAAAAAAAA

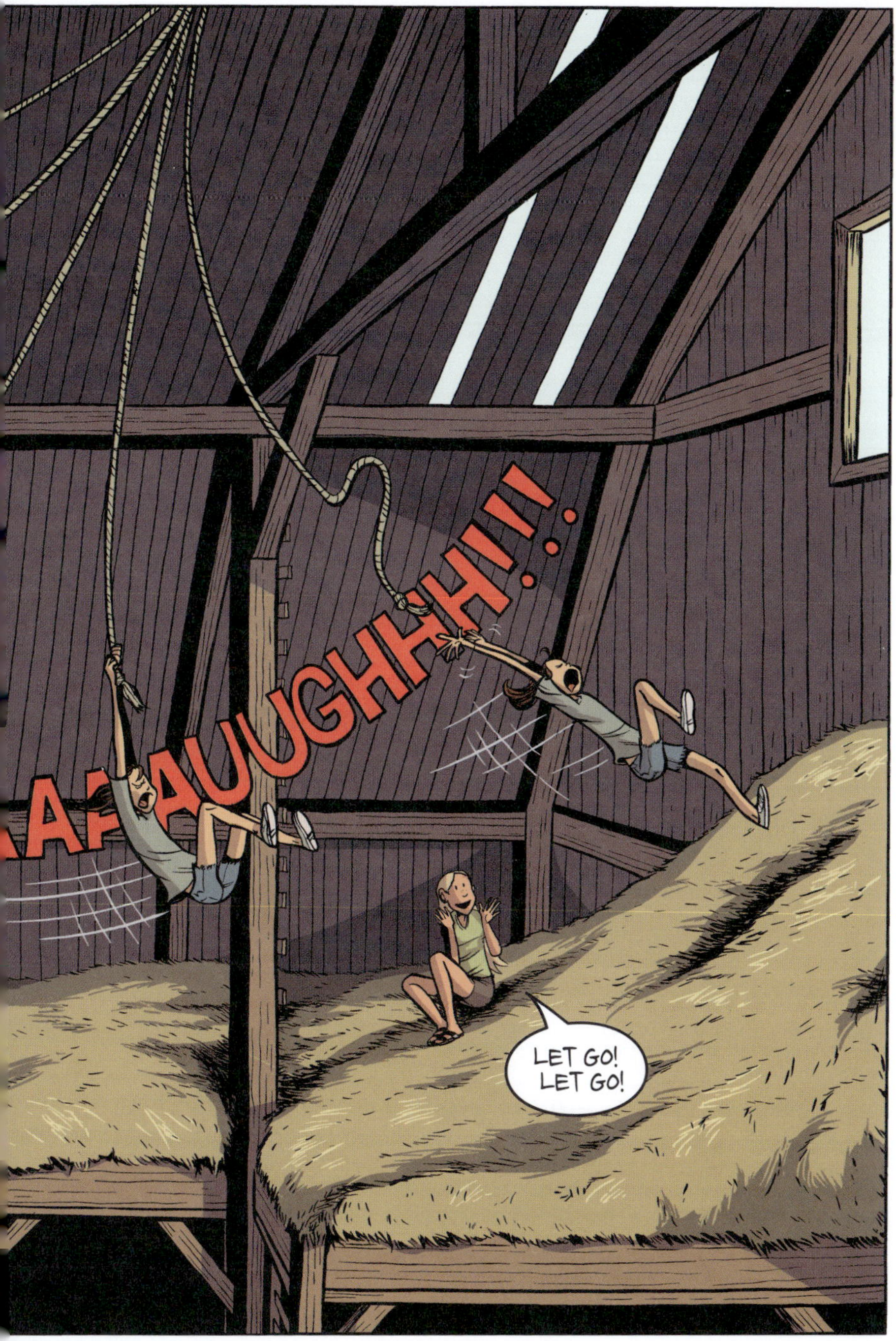
AAAUUGHHH!!!
LET GO! LET GO!

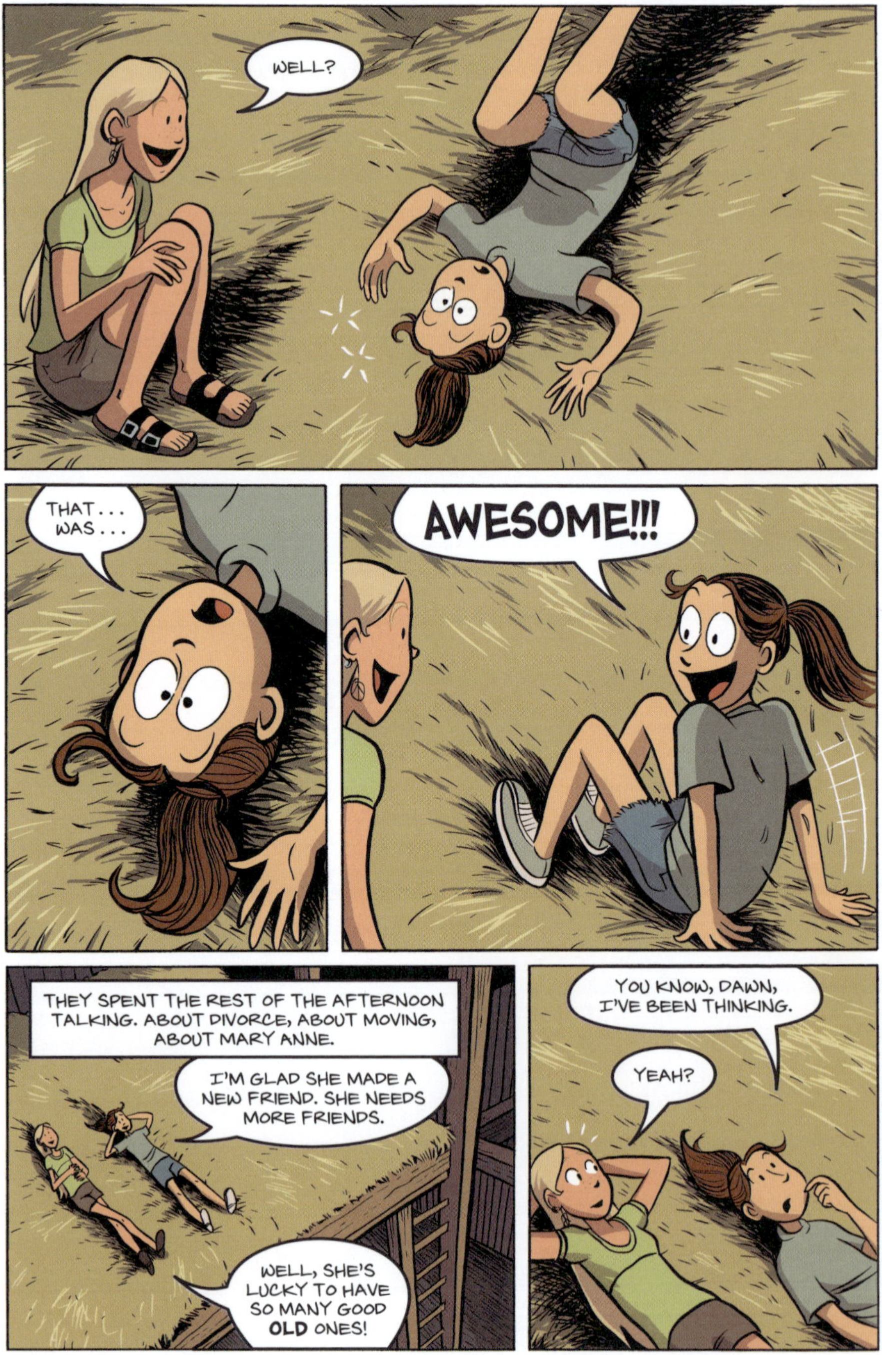
WELL?
THAT... WAS...
AWESOME!!!
THEY SPENT THE REST OF THE AFTERNOON TALKING. ABOUT DIVORCE, ABOUT MOVING, ABOUT MARY ANNE.
I'M GLAD SHE MADE A NEW FRIEND. SHE NEEDS MORE FRIENDS.
WELL, SHE'S LUCKY TO HAVE SO MANY GOOD **OLD** ONES!
YOU KNOW, DAWN, I'VE BEEN THINKING.
YEAH?

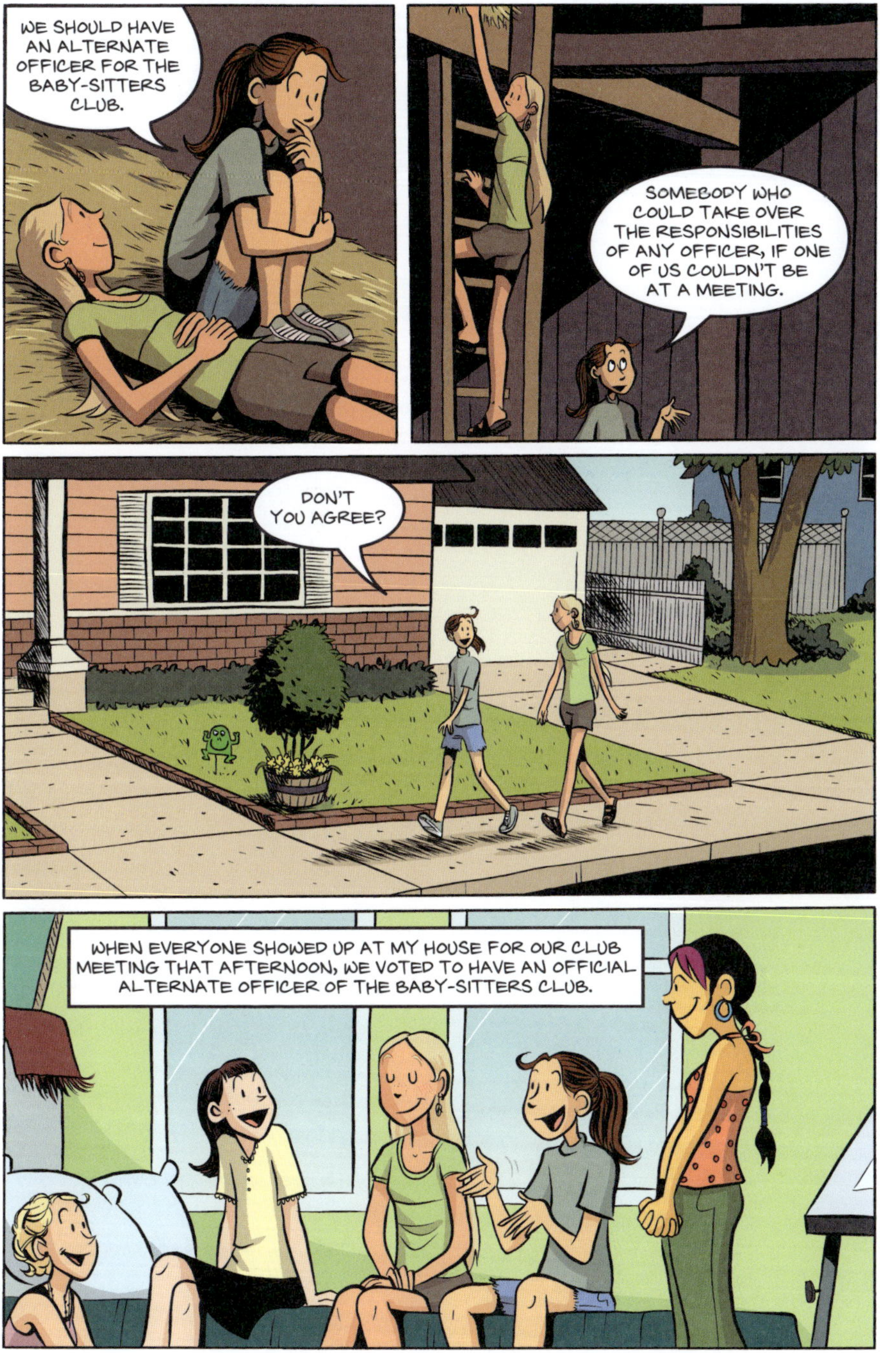
WE SHOULD HAVE AN ALTERNATE OFFICER FOR THE BABY-SITTERS CLUB.
SOMEBODY WHO COULD TAKE OVER THE RESPONSIBILITIES OF ANY OFFICER, IF ONE OF US COULDN'T BE AT A MEETING.
DON'T YOU AGREE?
WHEN EVERYONE SHOWED UP AT MY HOUSE FOR OUR CLUB MEETING THAT AFTERNOON, WE VOTED TO HAVE AN OFFICIAL ALTERNATE OFFICER OF THE BABY-SITTERS CLUB.

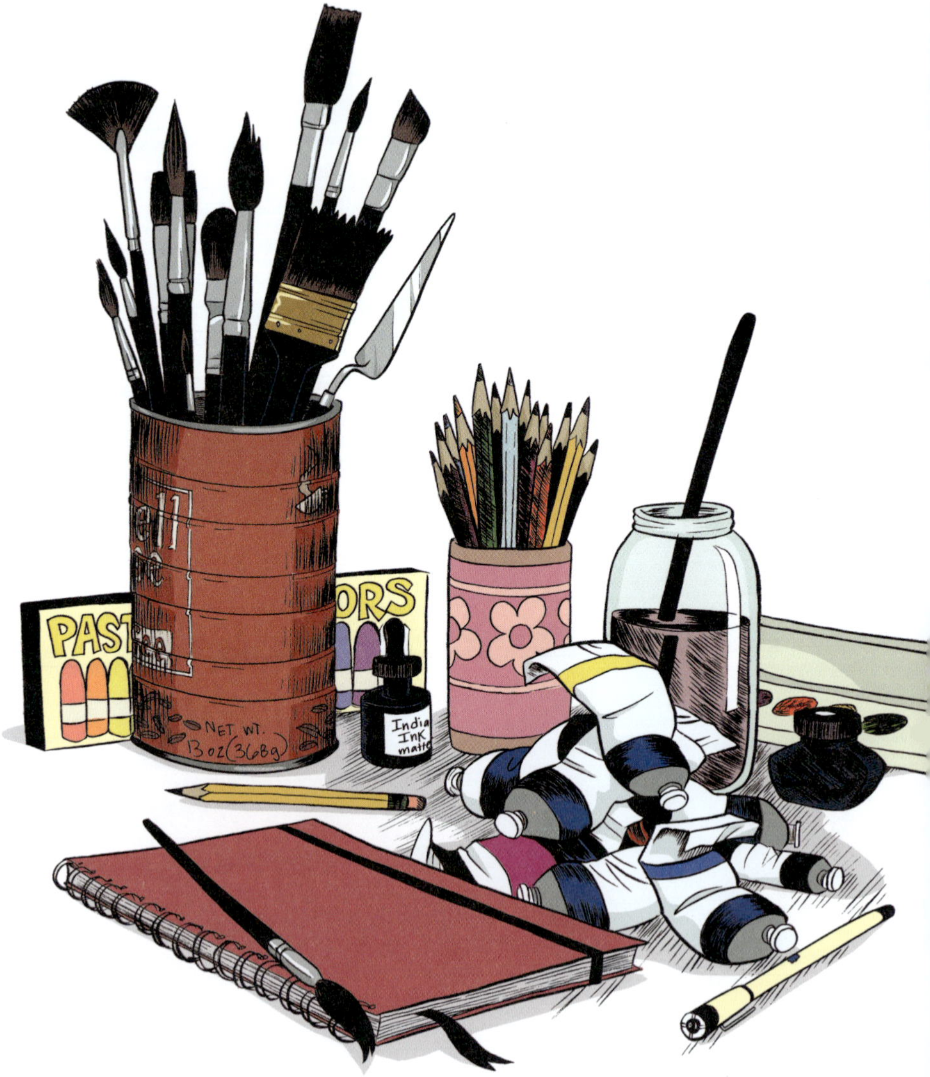
PAST
ORS
India INK matte
NET WT. 13 oz (368g)

CHAPTER 8

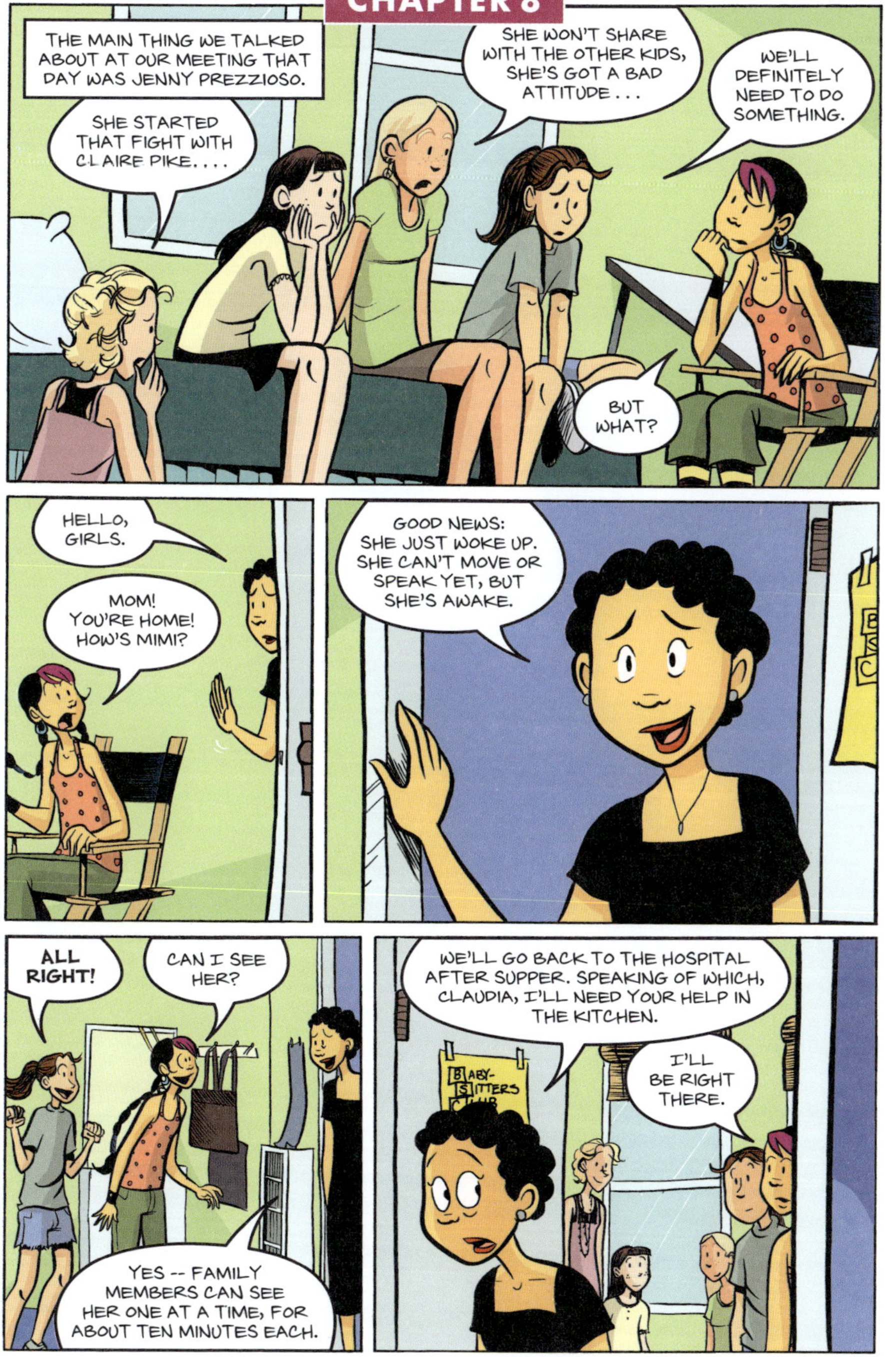
THE MAIN THING WE TALKED ABOUT AT OUR MEETING THAT DAY WAS JENNY PREZZIOSO.
SHE STARTED THAT FIGHT WITH CLAIRE PIKE....
SHE WON'T SHARE WITH THE OTHER KIDS, SHE'S GOT A BAD ATTITUDE...
WE'LL DEFINITELY NEED TO DO SOMETHING.
BUT WHAT?
HELLO, GIRLS.
MOM! YOU'RE HOME! HOW'S MIMI?
GOOD NEWS: SHE JUST WOKE UP. SHE CAN'T MOVE OR SPEAK YET, BUT SHE'S AWAKE.
ALL RIGHT!
CAN I SEE HER?
YES -- FAMILY MEMBERS CAN SEE HER ONE AT A TIME, FOR ABOUT TEN MINUTES EACH.
WE'LL GO BACK TO THE HOSPITAL AFTER SUPPER. SPEAKING OF WHICH, CLAUDIA, I'LL NEED YOUR HELP IN THE KITCHEN.
I'LL BE RIGHT THERE.

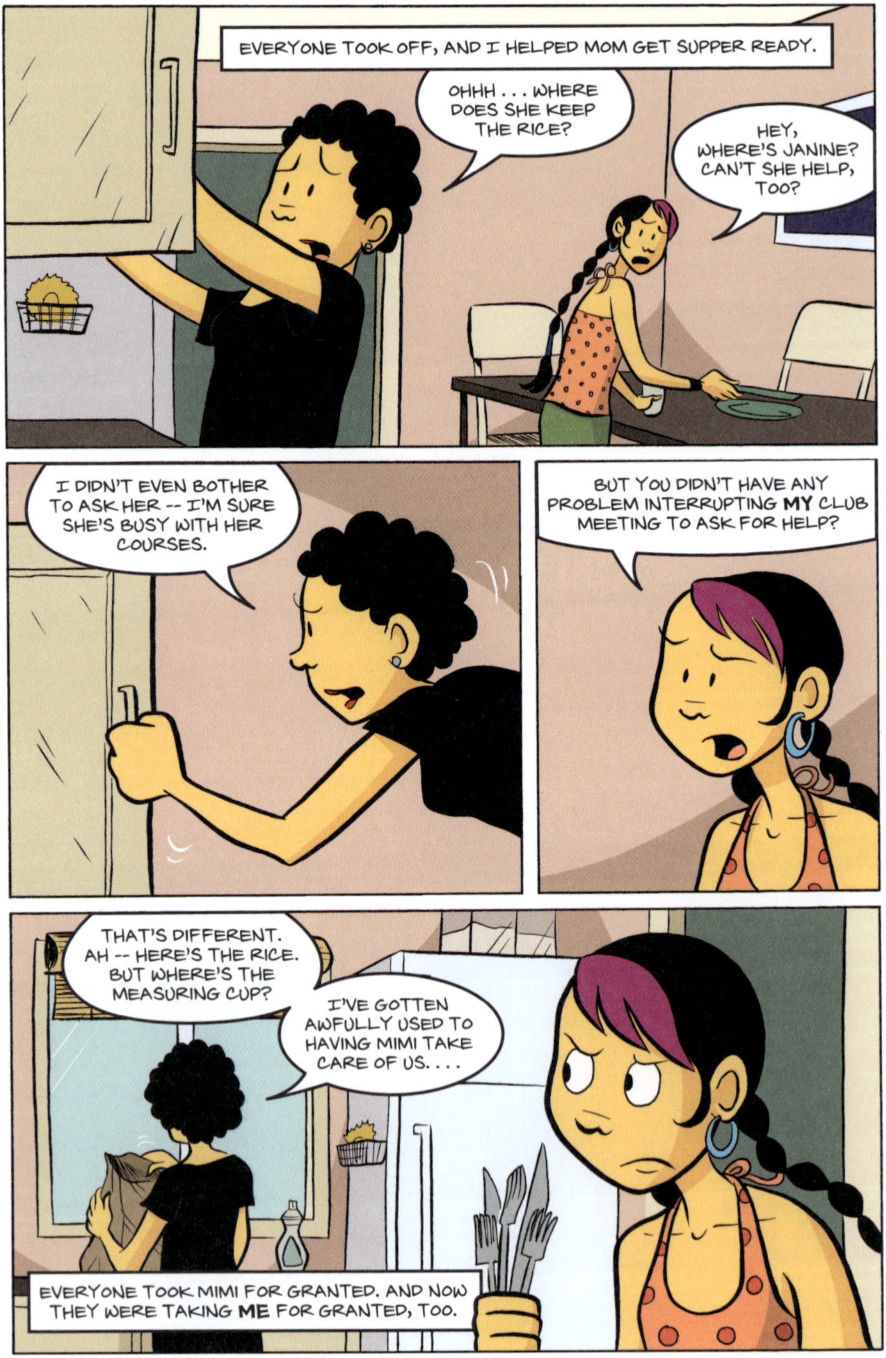
EVERYONE TOOK OFF, AND I HELPED MOM GET SUPPER READY.
OHHH . . . WHERE DOES SHE KEEP THE RICE?
HEY, WHERE'S JANINE? CAN'T SHE HELP, TOO?
I DIDN'T EVEN BOTHER TO ASK HER -- I'M SURE SHE'S BUSY WITH HER COURSES.
BUT YOU DIDN'T HAVE ANY PROBLEM INTERRUPTING **MY** CLUB MEETING TO ASK FOR HELP?
THAT'S DIFFERENT. AH -- HERE'S THE RICE. BUT WHERE'S THE MEASURING CUP?
I'VE GOTTEN AWFULLY USED TO HAVING MIMI TAKE CARE OF US. . . .
EVERYONE TOOK MIMI FOR GRANTED. AND NOW THEY WERE TAKING **ME** FOR GRANTED, TOO.

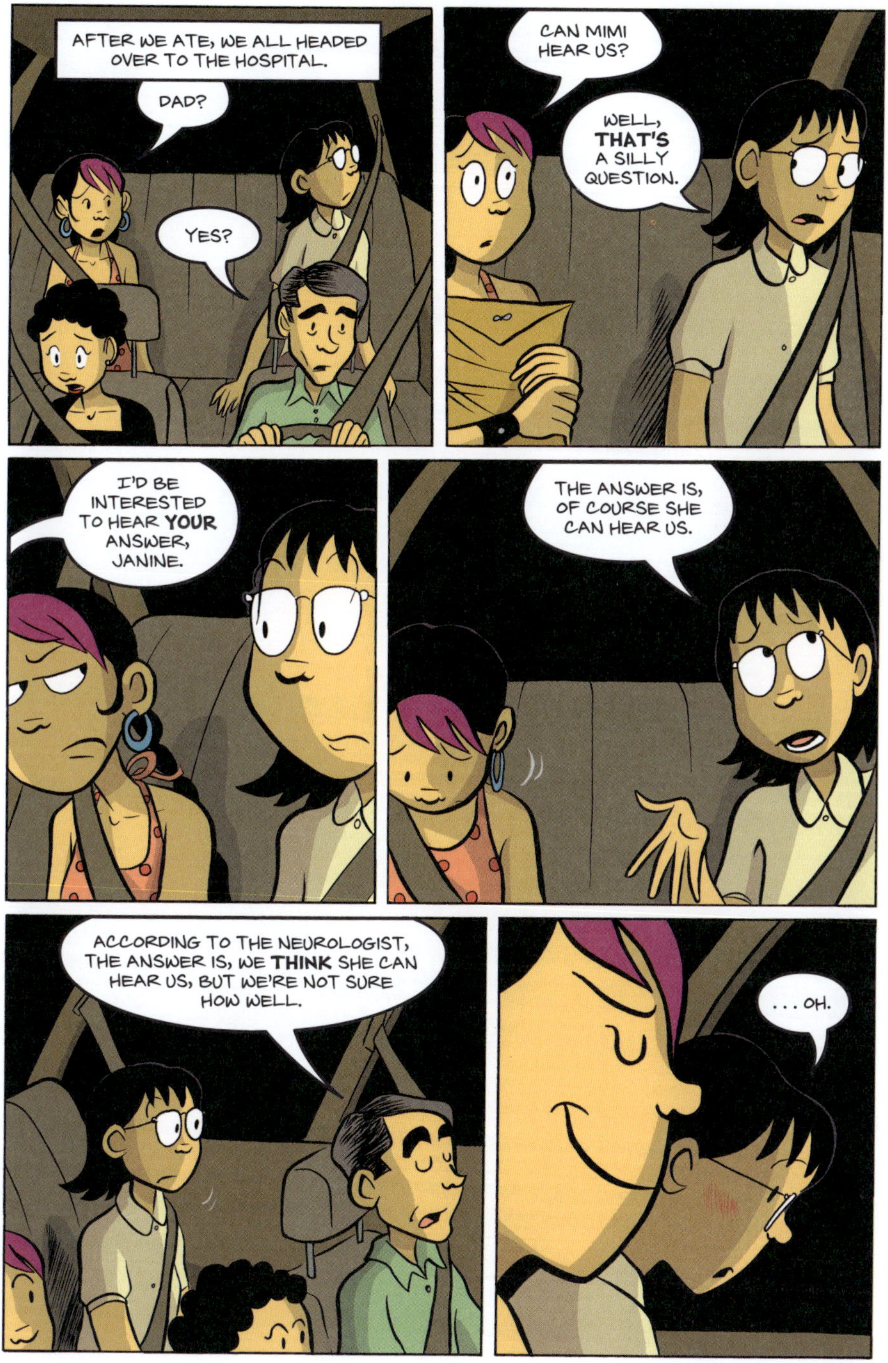
AFTER WE ATE, WE ALL HEADED OVER TO THE HOSPITAL.
DAD?
YES?
CAN MIMI HEAR US?
WELL, **THAT'S** A SILLY QUESTION.
I'D BE INTERESTED TO HEAR **YOUR** ANSWER, JANINE.
THE ANSWER IS, OF COURSE SHE CAN HEAR US.
ACCORDING TO THE NEUROLOGIST, THE ANSWER IS, WE **THINK** SHE CAN HEAR US, BUT WE'RE NOT SURE HOW WELL.
. . . OH.

EXIT
CAN I SEE HER FIRST?
SURE -- JUST KEEP TRACK OF THE TIME.
Yamamoto
307
AND DON'T BE FRIGHTENED . . . THERE'S A LOT OF EQUIPMENT IN THE ROOM. JUST REMEMBER THAT IT'S THERE TO HELP MIMI.
OKAY.
Beep... Beep... Beep...
drip

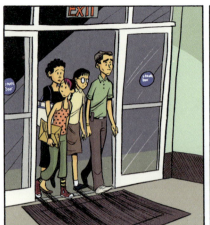

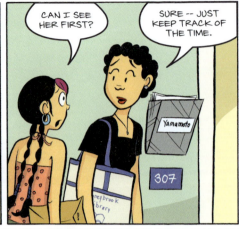

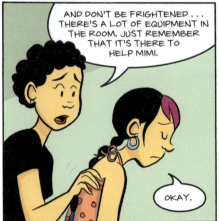

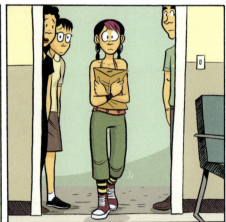

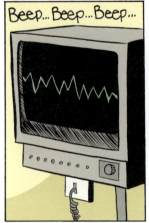

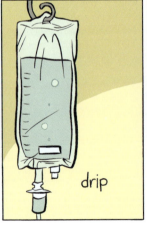

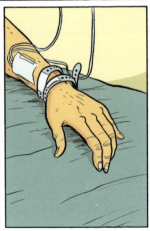

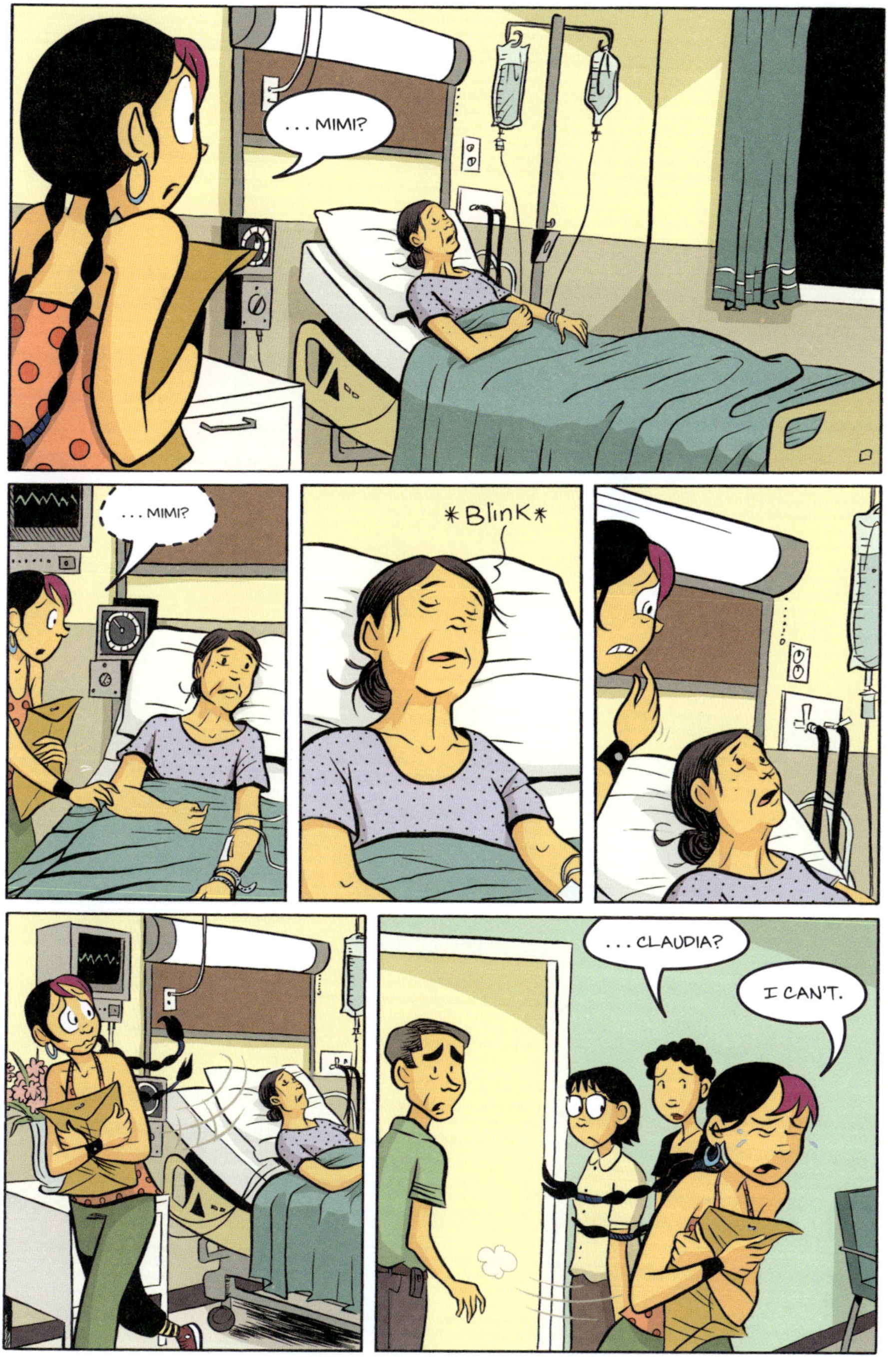
. . . MIMI?
. . . MIMI?
Blink
. . . CLAUDIA?
I CAN'T.

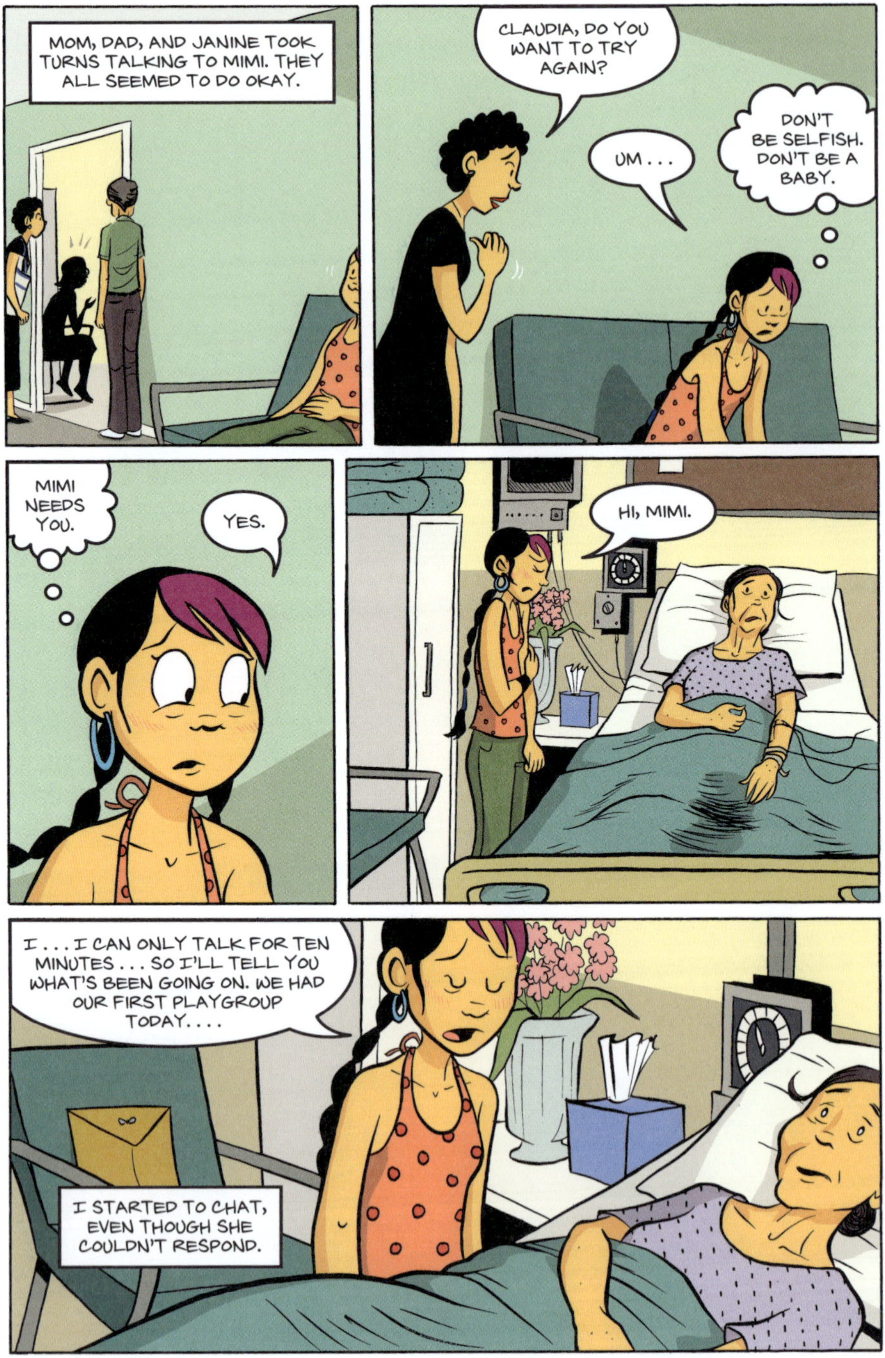
MOM, DAD, AND JANINE TOOK TURNS TALKING TO MIMI. THEY ALL SEEMED TO DO OKAY.
CLAUDIA, DO YOU WANT TO TRY AGAIN?
UM . . .
DON'T BE SELFISH. DON'T BE A BABY.
MIMI NEEDS YOU.
YES.
HI, MIMI.
I . . . I CAN ONLY TALK FOR TEN MINUTES . . . SO I'LL TELL YOU WHAT'S BEEN GOING ON. WE HAD OUR FIRST PLAYGROUP TODAY. . . .
I STARTED TO CHAT, EVEN THOUGH SHE COULDN'T RESPOND.

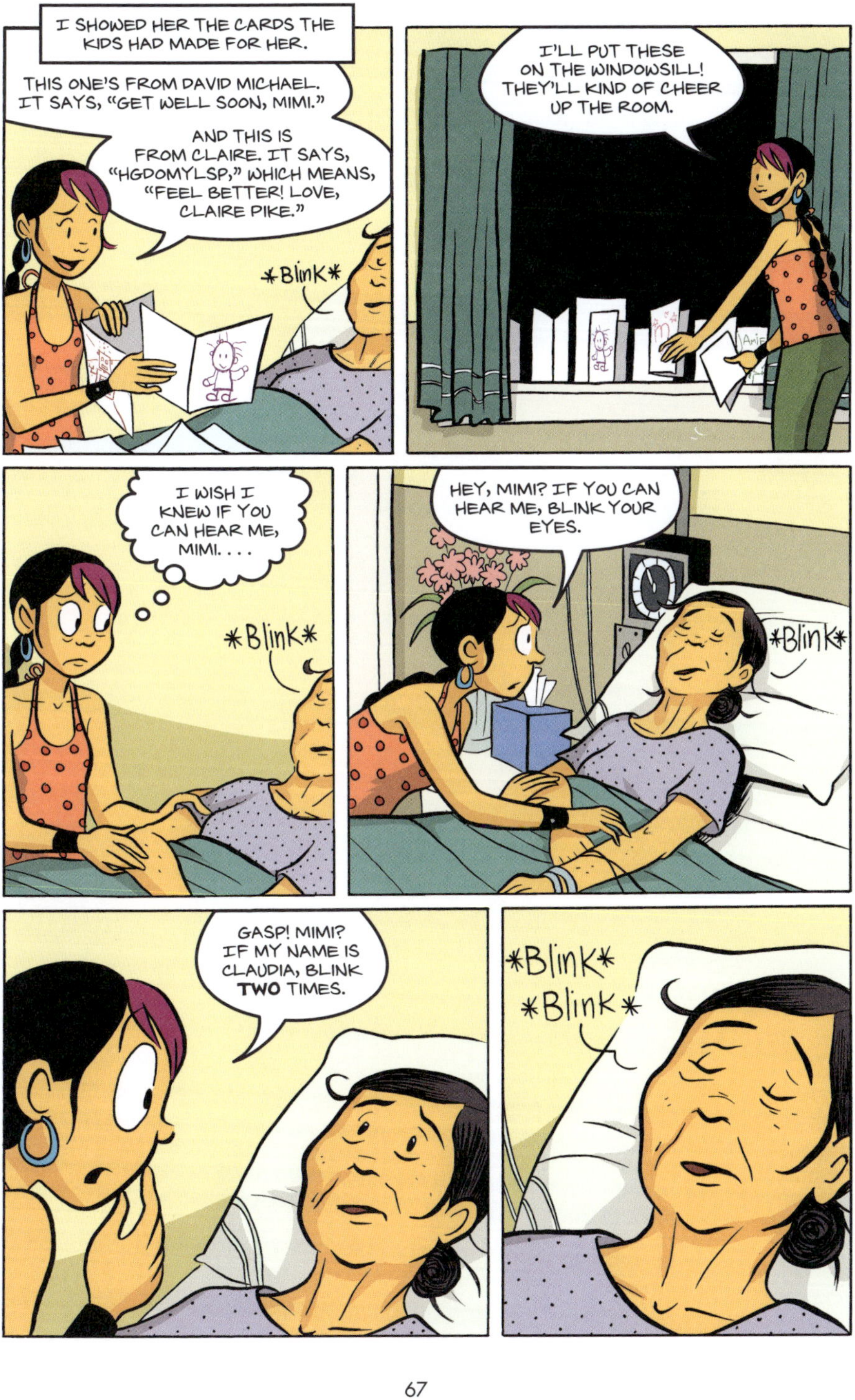
I SHOWED HER THE CARDS THE KIDS HAD MADE FOR HER.
THIS ONE'S FROM DAVID MICHAEL. IT SAYS, "GET WELL SOON, MIMI."
AND THIS IS FROM CLAIRE. IT SAYS, "HGDOMYLSP," WHICH MEANS, "FEEL BETTER! LOVE, CLAIRE PIKE."
Blink
I'LL PUT THESE ON THE WINDOWSILL! THEY'LL KIND OF CHEER UP THE ROOM.
I WISH I KNEW IF YOU CAN HEAR ME, MIMI. . . .
Blink
HEY, MIMI? IF YOU CAN HEAR ME, BLINK YOUR EYES.
Blink
GASP! MIMI? IF MY NAME IS CLAUDIA, BLINK **TWO** TIMES.
Blink
Blink

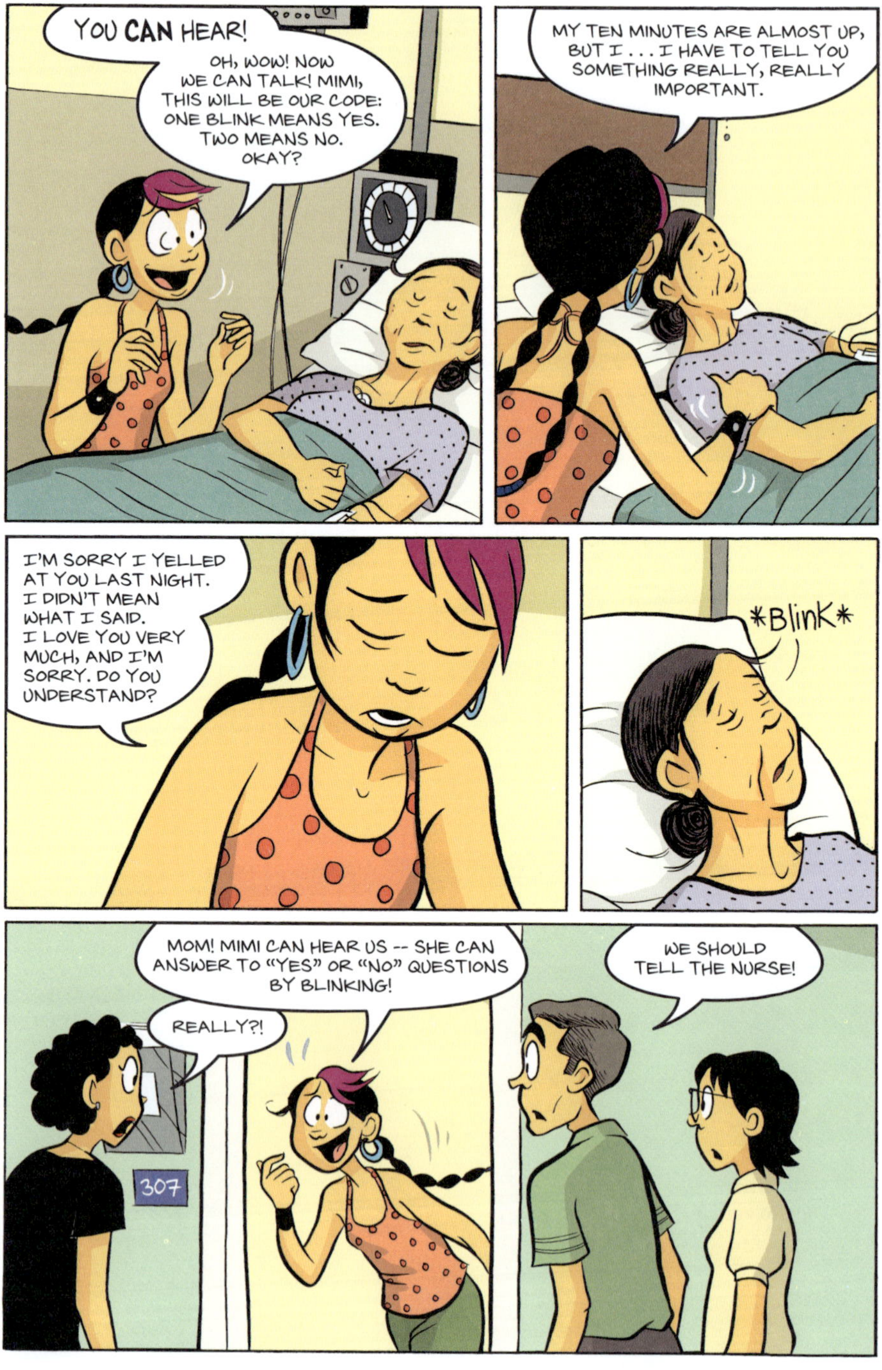
YOU CAN HEAR!
OH, WOW! NOW WE CAN TALK! MIMI, THIS WILL BE OUR CODE: ONE BLINK MEANS YES. TWO MEANS NO. OKAY?
MY TEN MINUTES ARE ALMOST UP, BUT I . . . I HAVE TO TELL YOU SOMETHING REALLY, REALLY IMPORTANT.
I'M SORRY I YELLED AT YOU LAST NIGHT. I DIDN'T MEAN WHAT I SAID. I LOVE YOU VERY MUCH, AND I'M SORRY. DO YOU UNDERSTAND?
Blink
MOM! MIMI CAN HEAR US -- SHE CAN ANSWER TO "YES" OR "NO" QUESTIONS BY BLINKING!
REALLY?!
307
WE SHOULD TELL THE NURSE!

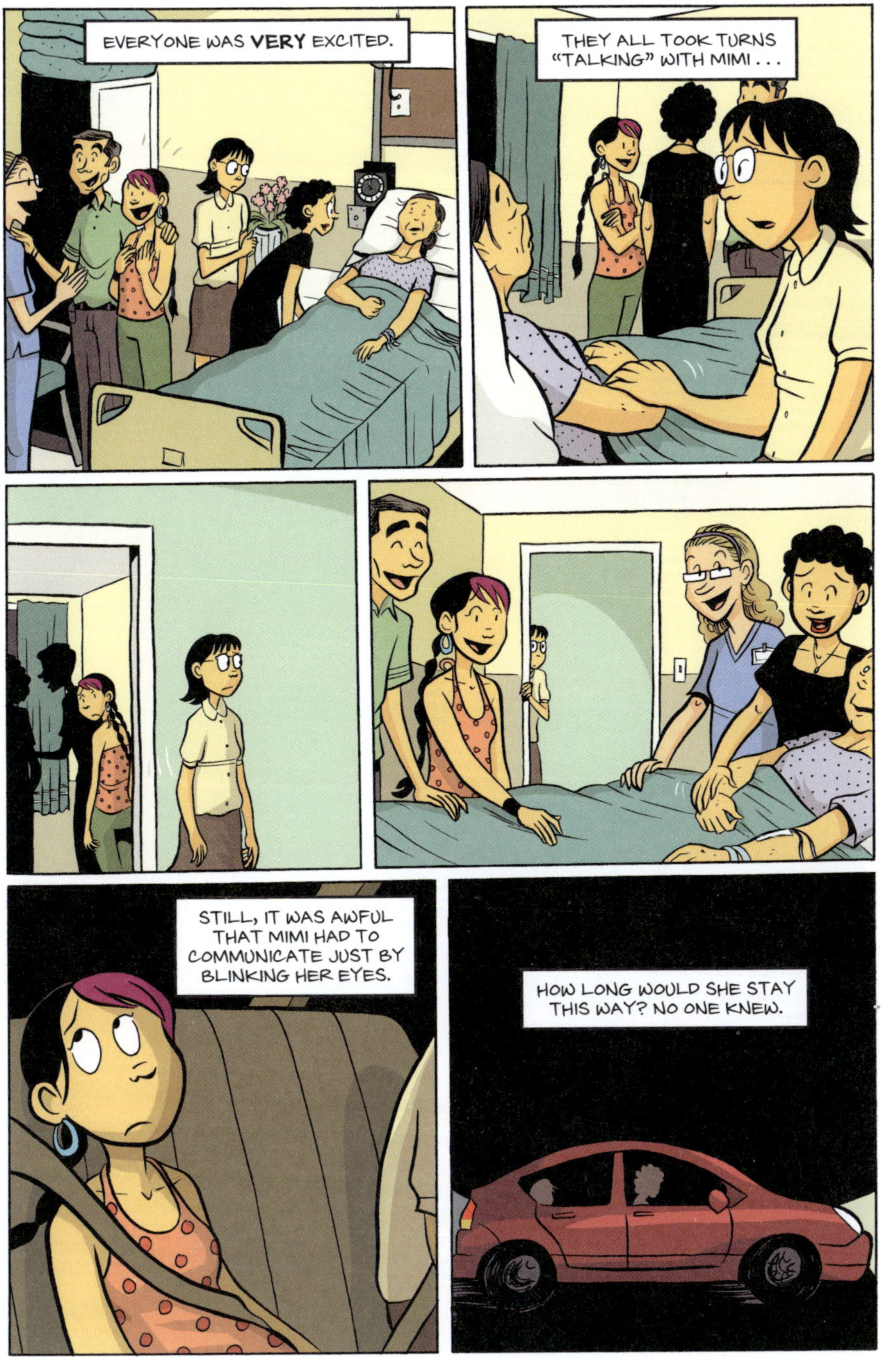
EVERYONE WAS **VERY** EXCITED.
THEY ALL TOOK TURNS "TALKING" WITH MIMI . . .
STILL, IT WAS AWFUL THAT MIMI HAD TO COMMUNICATE JUST BY BLINKING HER EYES.
HOW LONG WOULD SHE STAY THIS WAY? NO ONE KNEW.

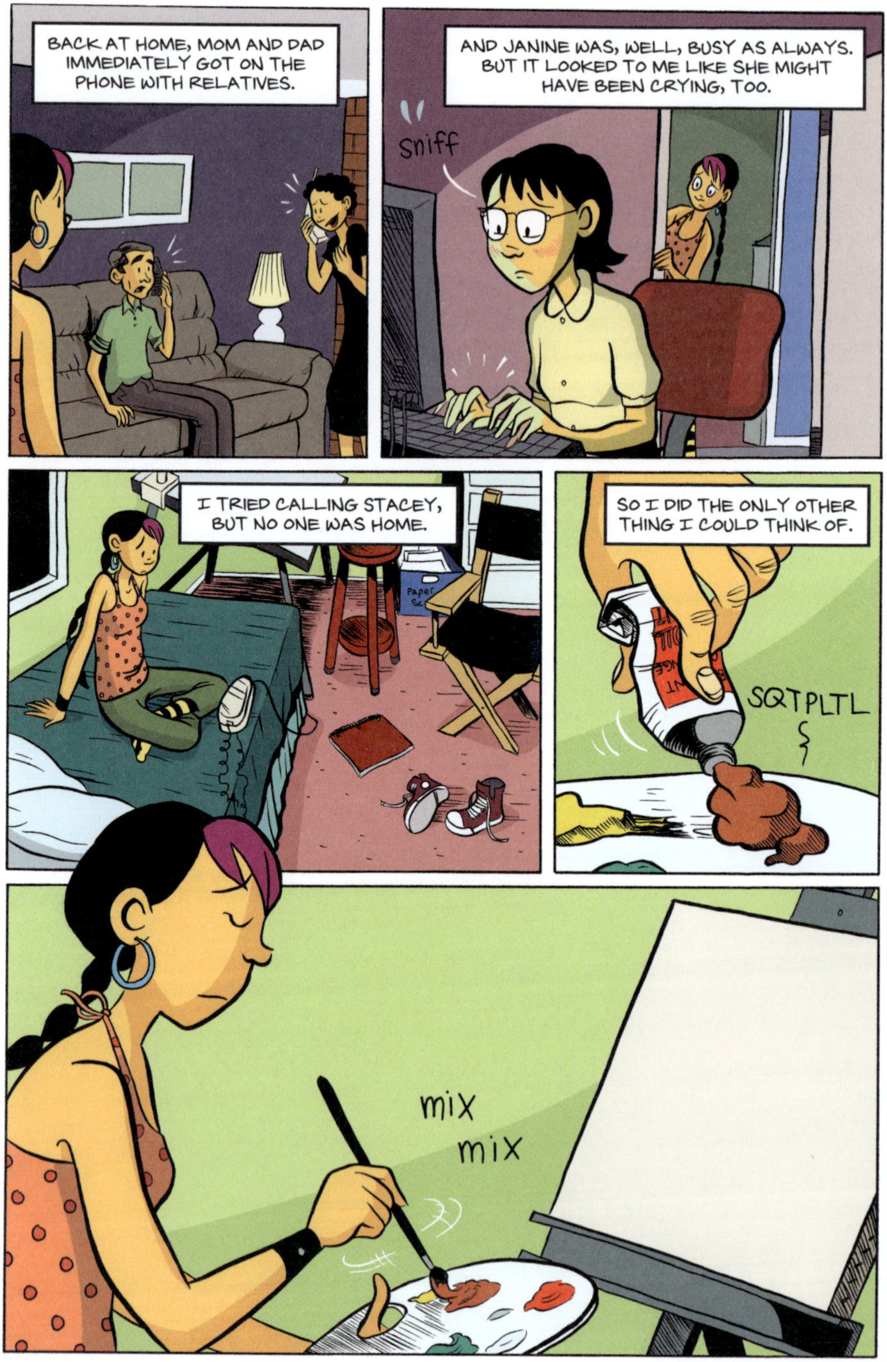

BACK AT HOME, MOM AND DAD IMMEDIATELY GOT ON THE PHONE WITH RELATIVES.
AND JANINE WAS, WELL, BUSY AS ALWAYS. BUT IT LOOKED TO ME LIKE SHE MIGHT HAVE BEEN CRYING, TOO.
sniff
I TRIED CALLING STACEY, BUT NO ONE WAS HOME.
SO I DID THE ONLY OTHER THING I COULD THINK OF.
SQTPLTL
mix
mix

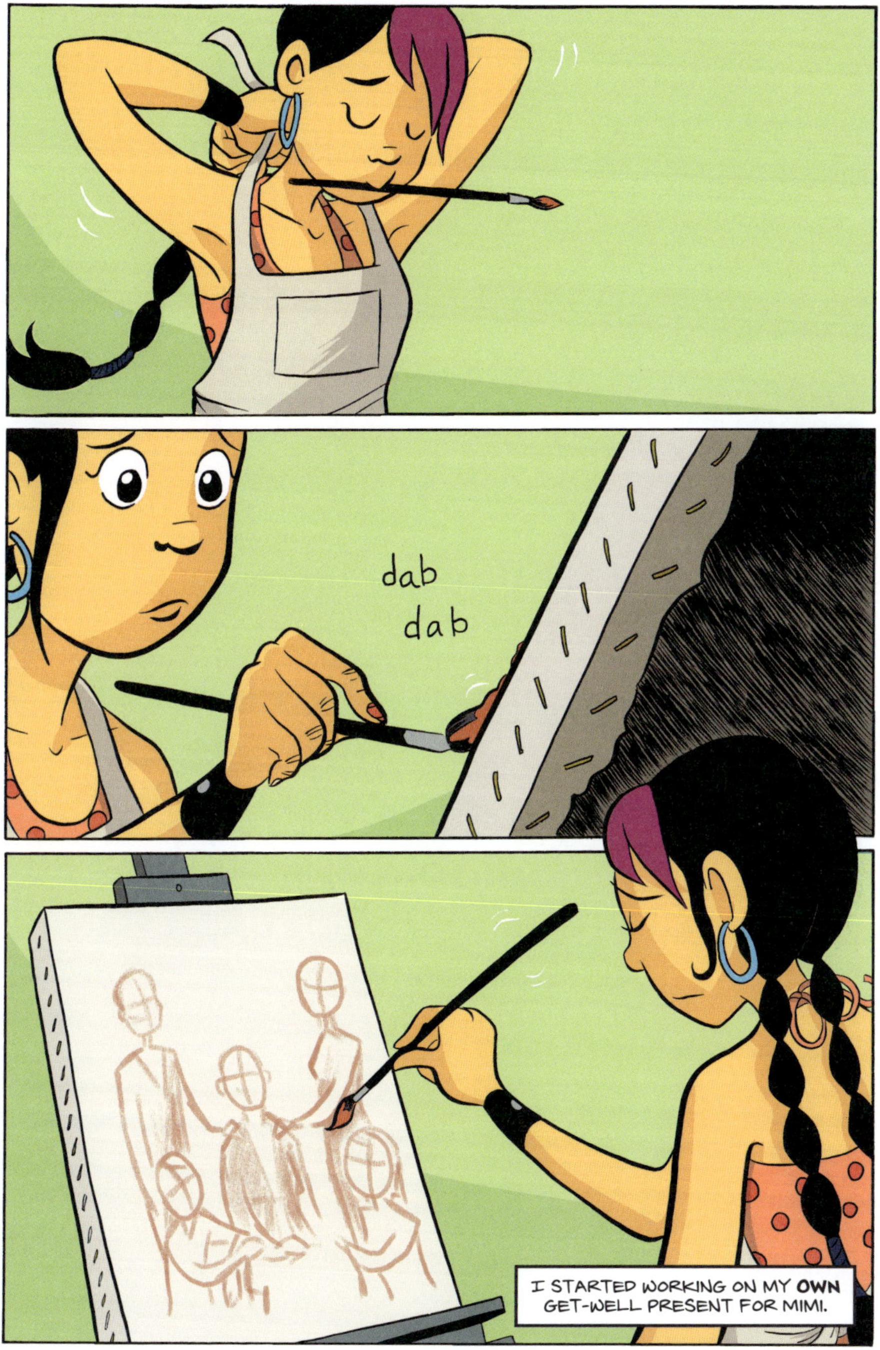
dab
dab
I STARTED WORKING ON MY **OWN** GET-WELL PRESENT FOR MIMI.

Wednesday, June 18

Well, Karen Brewer strikes again. When she's around, things are never dull. Today was the second session of our playgroup and Andrew and Karen came to it. Watson's ex-wife needed a last-minute sitter for them, so she called Watson and he decided to drop them off at Stacey's.

In the past, Karen has scared other kids with stories of witches, ghosts, and Martians. Today, she had a new one — a monster tale. But it was a monster tale with a twist, as you guys know. I'm not sure there's anything we can do about Karen. The thing is, she usually doesn't mean to scare people. She just has a wild imagination.

But, oh boy, when Karen and Jenny got together . . .
— Kristy

CHAPTER 9

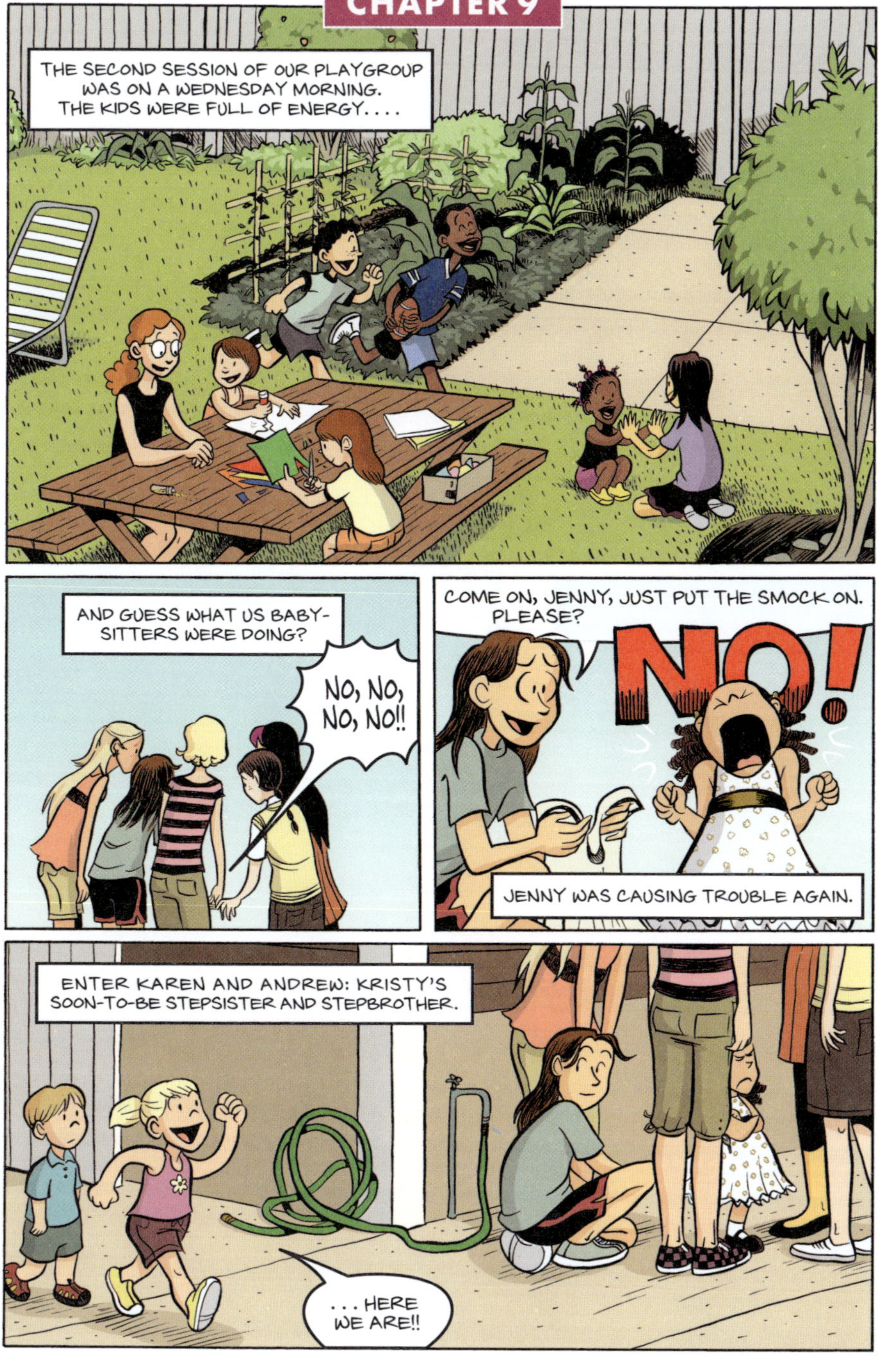
THE SECOND SESSION OF OUR PLAYGROUP WAS ON A WEDNESDAY MORNING. THE KIDS WERE FULL OF ENERGY....
AND GUESS WHAT US BABY-SITTERS WERE DOING?
NO, NO, NO, NO!!
COME ON, JENNY, JUST PUT THE SMOCK ON. PLEASE?
NO!
JENNY WAS CAUSING TROUBLE AGAIN.
ENTER KAREN AND ANDREW: KRISTY'S SOON-TO-BE STEPSISTER AND STEPBROTHER.
...HERE WE ARE!!

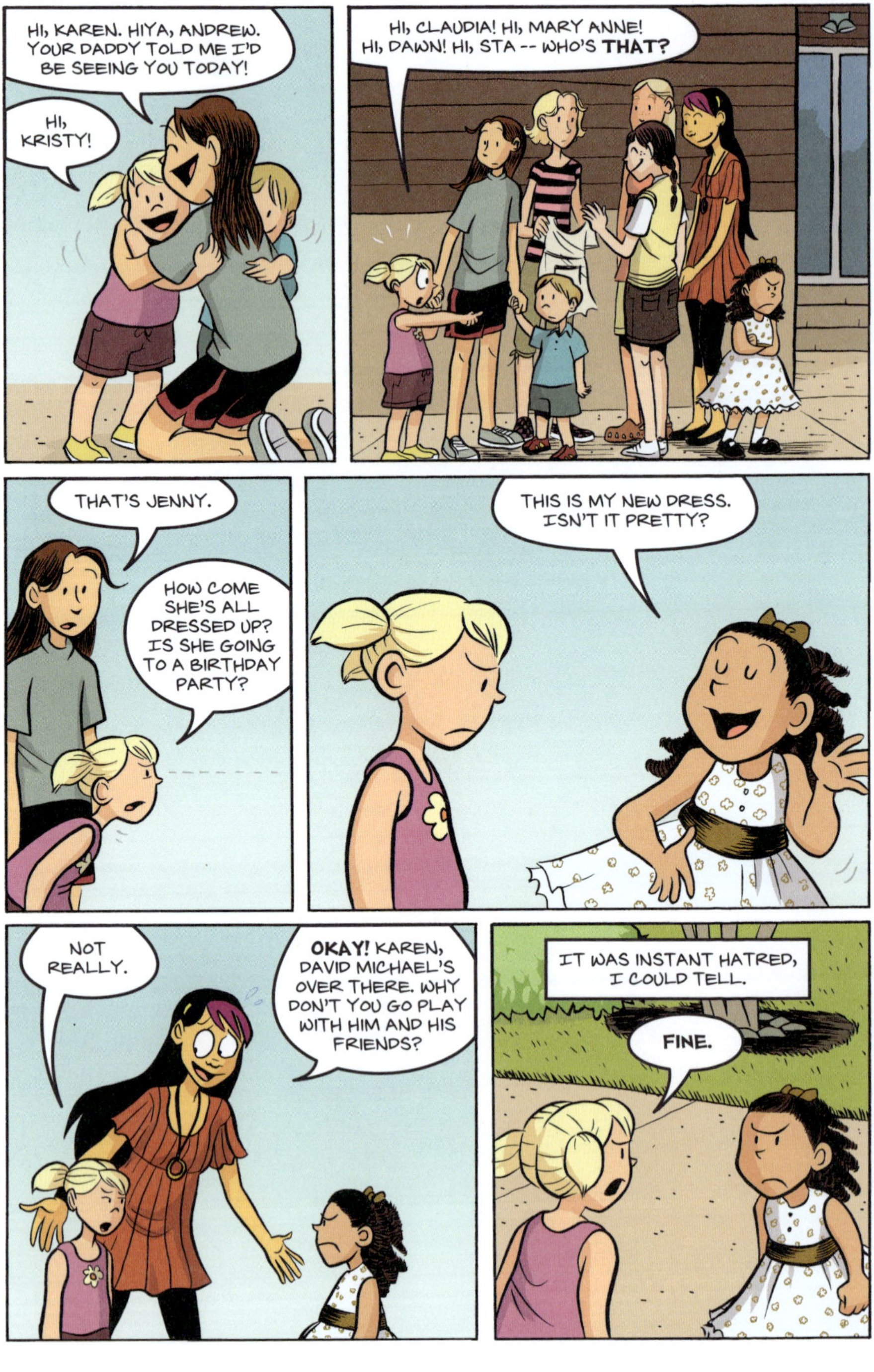
HI, KAREN. HIYA, ANDREW. YOUR DADDY TOLD ME I'D BE SEEING YOU TODAY!
HI, KRISTY!
HI, CLAUDIA! HI, MARY ANNE! HI, DAWN! HI, STA -- WHO'S **THAT?**
THAT'S JENNY.
HOW COME SHE'S ALL DRESSED UP? IS SHE GOING TO A BIRTHDAY PARTY?
THIS IS MY NEW DRESS. ISN'T IT PRETTY?
NOT REALLY.
OKAY! KAREN, DAVID MICHAEL'S OVER THERE. WHY DON'T YOU GO PLAY WITH HIM AND HIS FRIENDS?
IT WAS INSTANT HATRED, I COULD TELL.
FINE.

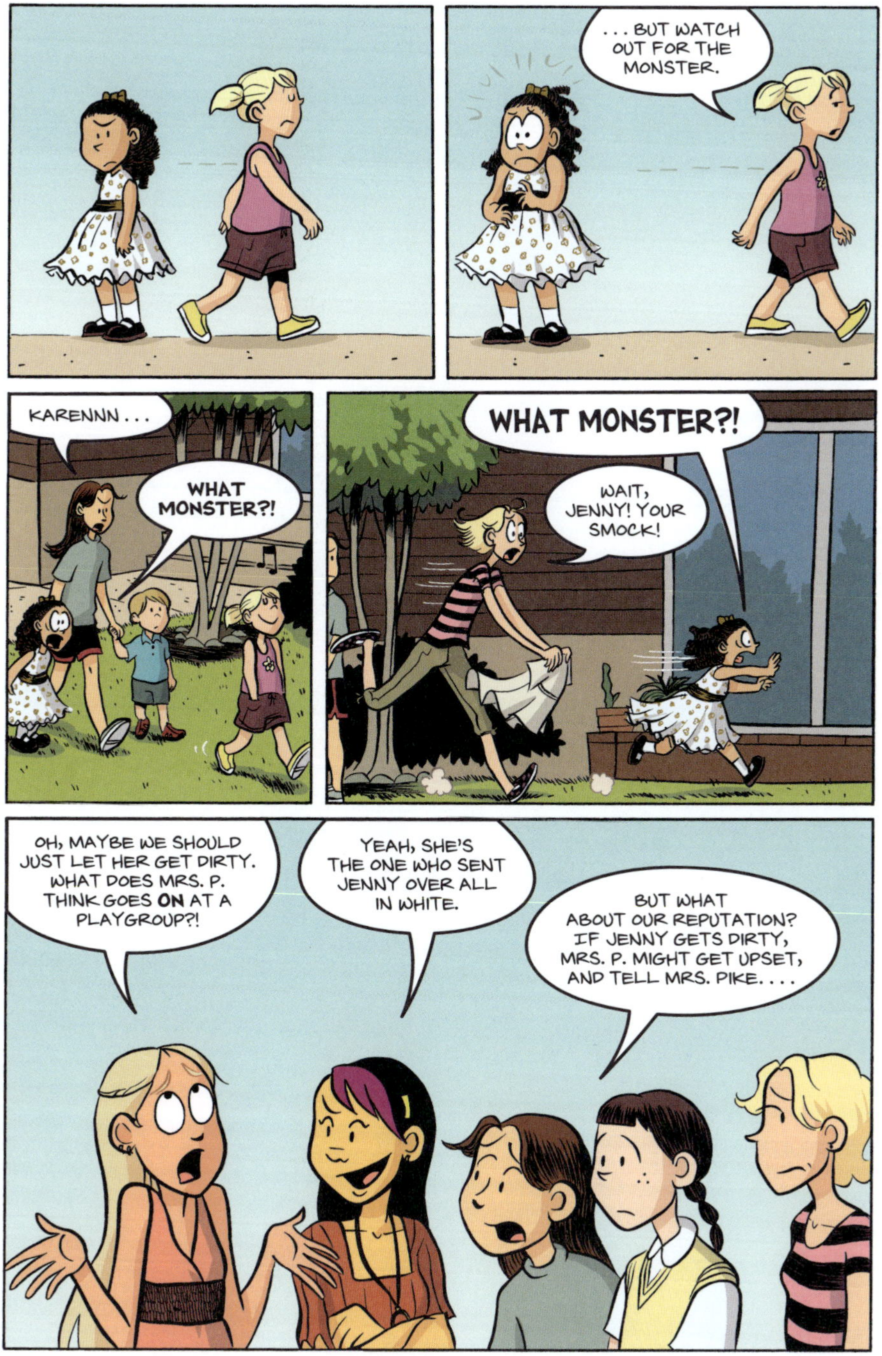
. . . BUT WATCH OUT FOR THE MONSTER.
KARENNN . . .
WHAT MONSTER?!
WHAT MONSTER?!
WAIT, JENNY! YOUR SMOCK!
OH, MAYBE WE SHOULD JUST LET HER GET DIRTY. WHAT DOES MRS. P. THINK GOES **ON** AT A PLAYGROUP?!
YEAH, SHE'S THE ONE WHO SENT JENNY OVER ALL IN WHITE.
BUT WHAT ABOUT OUR REPUTATION? IF JENNY GETS DIRTY, MRS. P. MIGHT GET UPSET, AND TELL MRS. PIKE. . . .

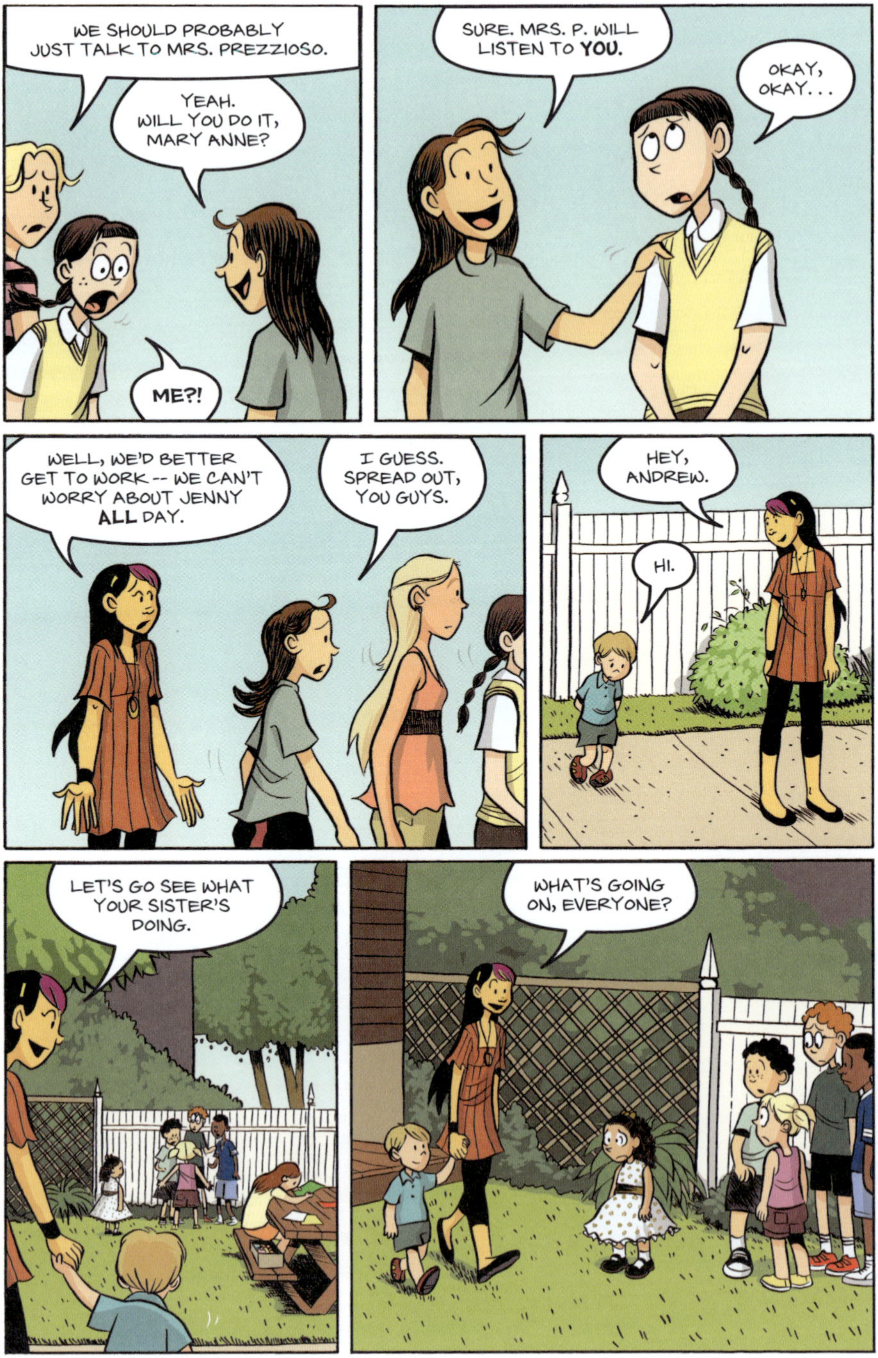
WE SHOULD PROBABLY JUST TALK TO MRS. PREZZIOSO.
YEAH. WILL YOU DO IT, MARY ANNE?
ME?!
SURE. MRS. P. WILL LISTEN TO **YOU.**
OKAY, OKAY. . .
WELL, WE'D BETTER GET TO WORK -- WE CAN'T WORRY ABOUT JENNY **ALL** DAY.
I GUESS. SPREAD OUT, YOU GUYS.
HEY, ANDREW.
HI.
LET'S GO SEE WHAT YOUR SISTER'S DOING.
WHAT'S GOING ON, EVERYONE?

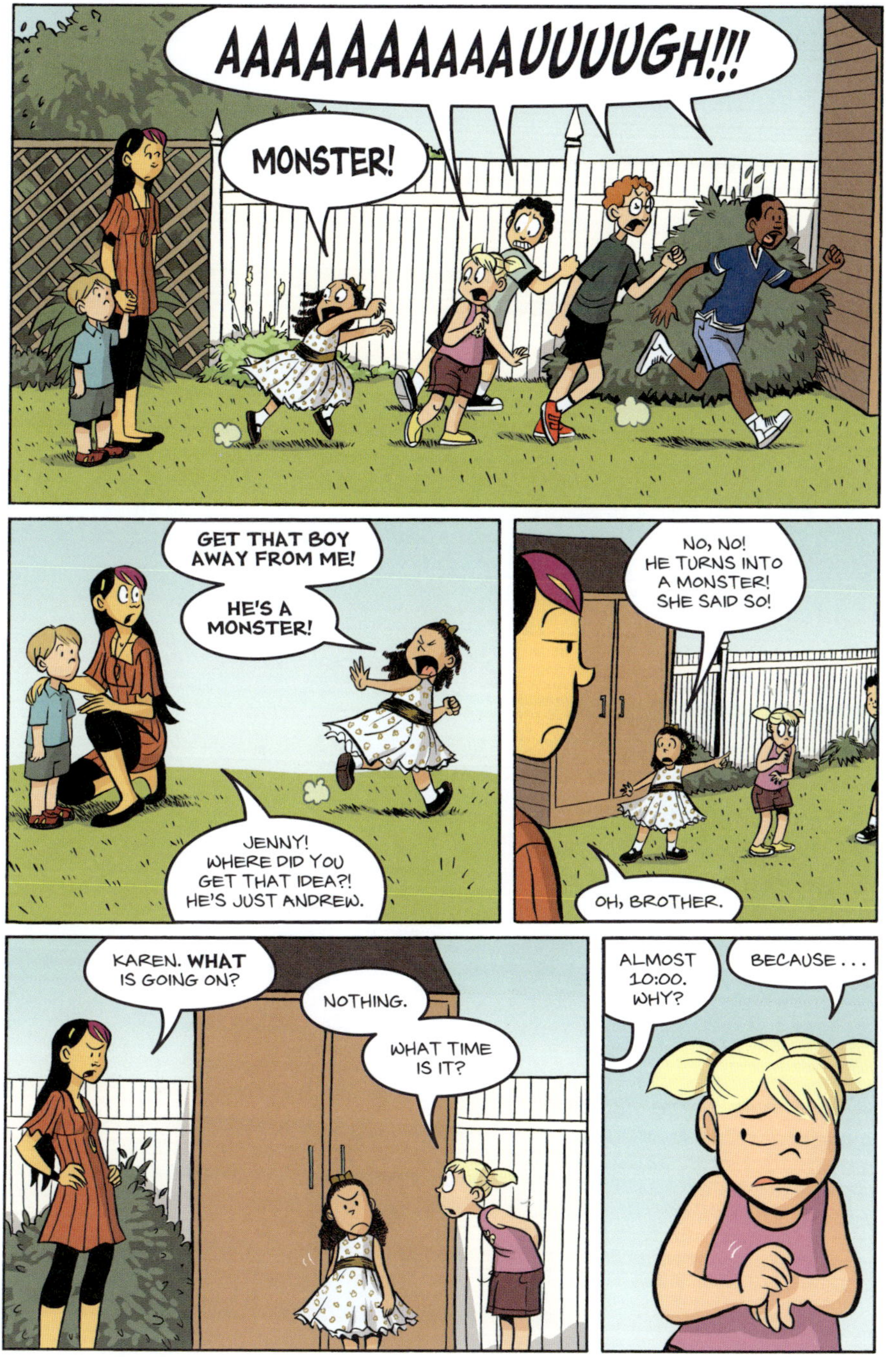
AAAAAAAAAAUUUUGH!!!
MONSTER!
GET THAT BOY AWAY FROM ME!
HE'S A MONSTER!
JENNY! WHERE DID YOU GET THAT IDEA?! HE'S JUST ANDREW.
NO, NO! HE TURNS INTO A MONSTER! SHE SAID SO!
OH, BROTHER.
KAREN. WHAT IS GOING ON?
NOTHING.
WHAT TIME IS IT?
ALMOST 10:00. WHY?
BECAUSE . . .

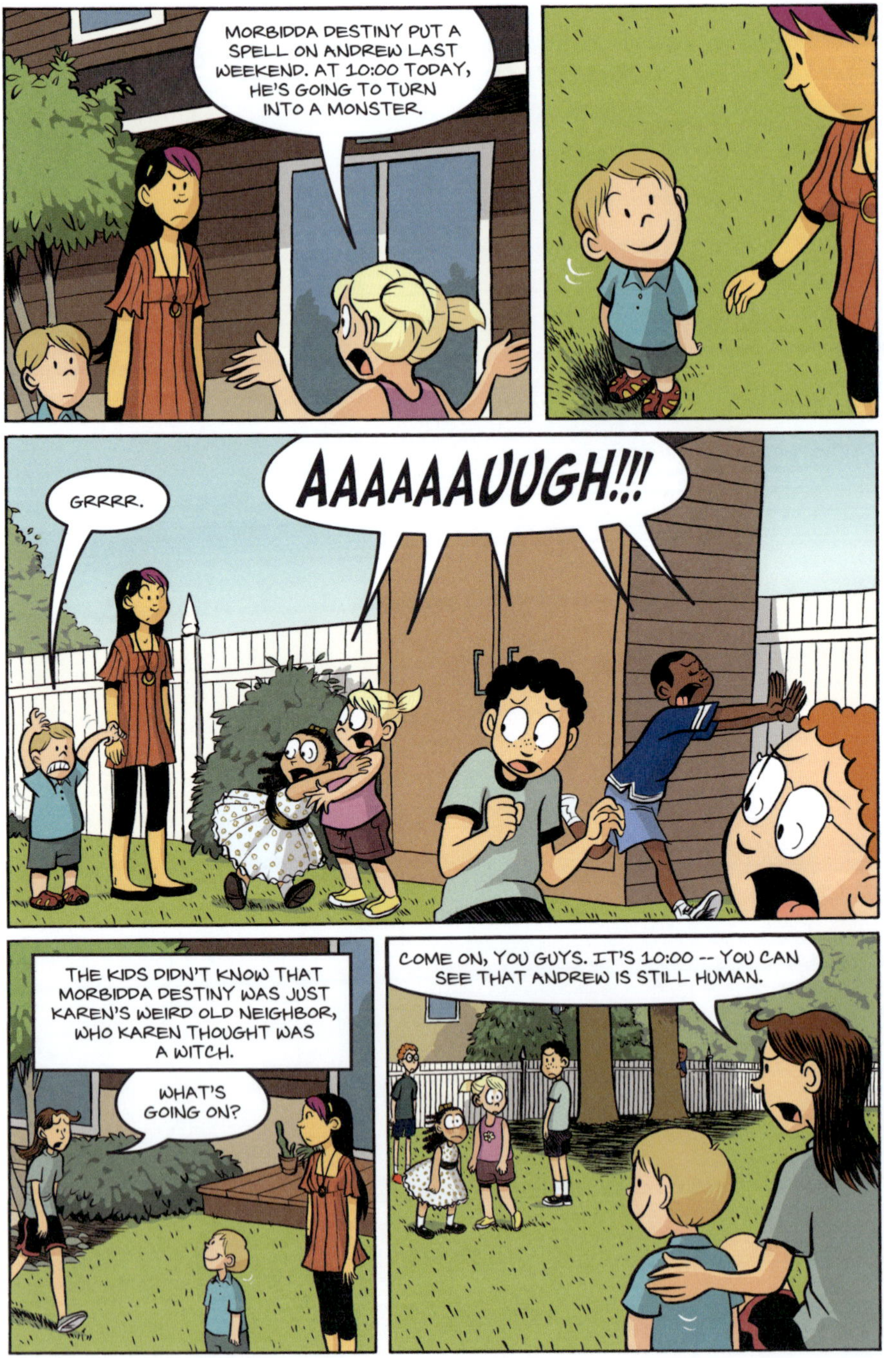
MORBIDDA DESTINY PUT A SPELL ON ANDREW LAST WEEKEND. AT 10:00 TODAY, HE'S GOING TO TURN INTO A MONSTER.
GRRRR.
AAAAAAUUGH!!!
THE KIDS DIDN'T KNOW THAT MORBIDDA DESTINY WAS JUST KAREN'S WEIRD OLD NEIGHBOR, WHO KAREN THOUGHT WAS A WITCH.
WHAT'S GOING ON?
COME ON, YOU GUYS. IT'S 10:00 -- YOU CAN SEE THAT ANDREW IS STILL HUMAN.

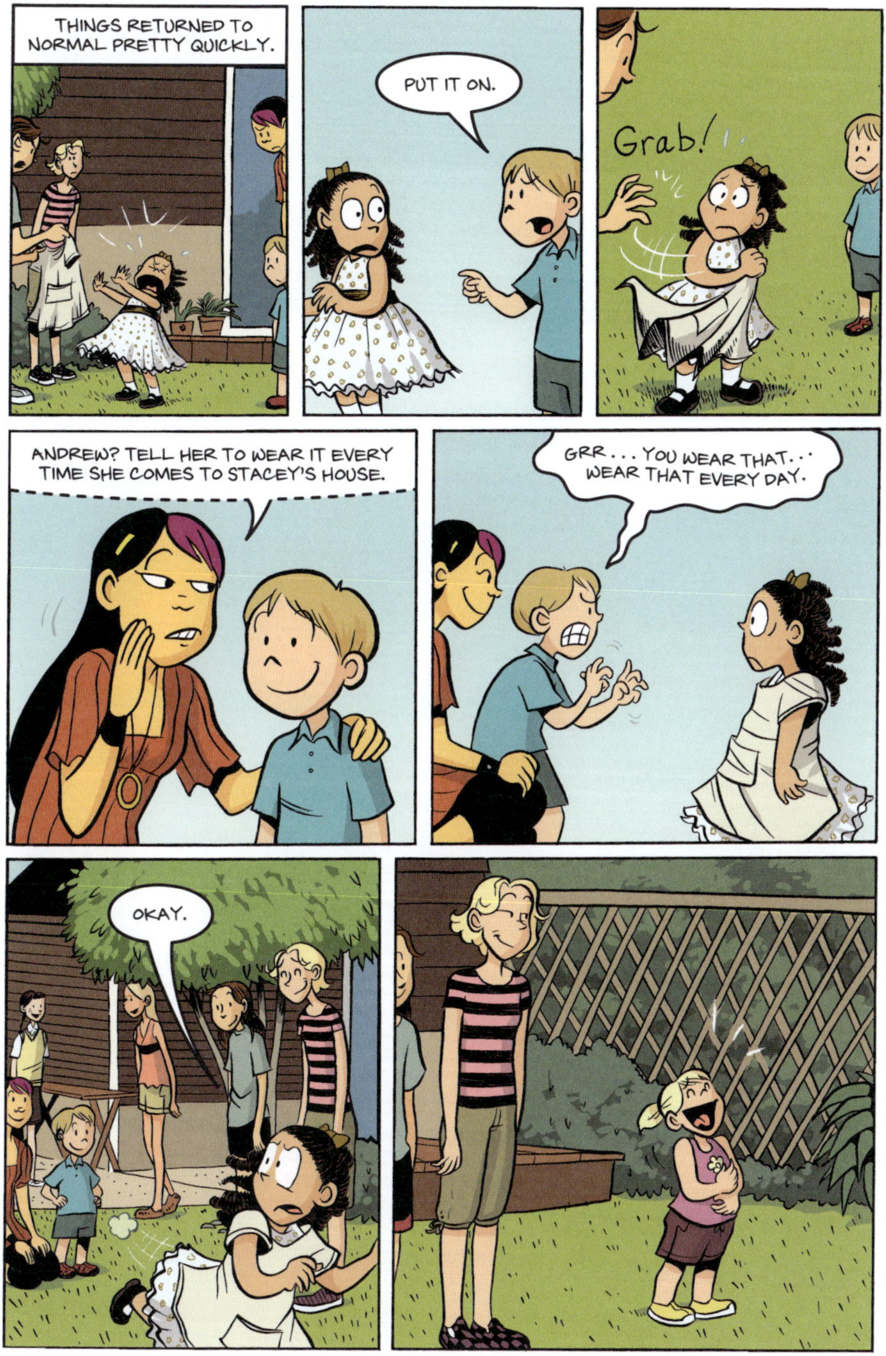
THINGS RETURNED TO NORMAL PRETTY QUICKLY.
PUT IT ON.
Grab!
ANDREW? TELL HER TO WEAR IT EVERY TIME SHE COMES TO STACEY'S HOUSE.
GRR... YOU WEAR THAT... WEAR THAT EVERY DAY.
OKAY.

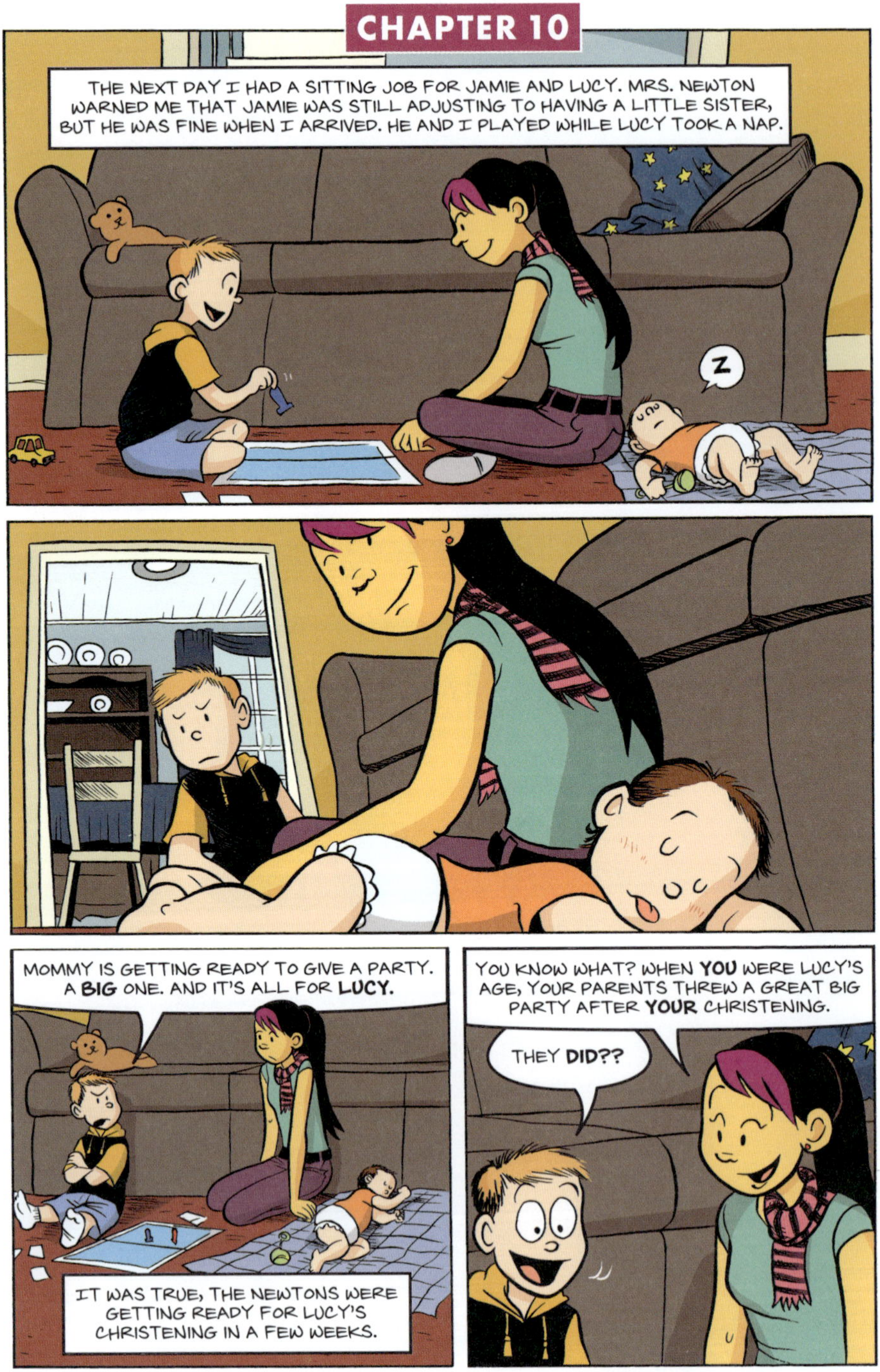
CHAPTER 10
THE NEXT DAY I HAD A SITTING JOB FOR JAMIE AND LUCY. MRS. NEWTON WARNED ME THAT JAMIE WAS STILL ADJUSTING TO HAVING A LITTLE SISTER, BUT HE WAS FINE WHEN I ARRIVED. HE AND I PLAYED WHILE LUCY TOOK A NAP.
Z
MOMMY IS GETTING READY TO GIVE A PARTY. A **BIG** ONE. AND IT'S ALL FOR **LUCY.**
IT WAS TRUE, THE NEWTONS WERE GETTING READY FOR LUCY'S CHRISTENING IN A FEW WEEKS.
YOU KNOW WHAT? WHEN **YOU** WERE LUCY'S AGE, YOUR PARENTS THREW A GREAT BIG PARTY AFTER **YOUR** CHRISTENING.
THEY **DID??**

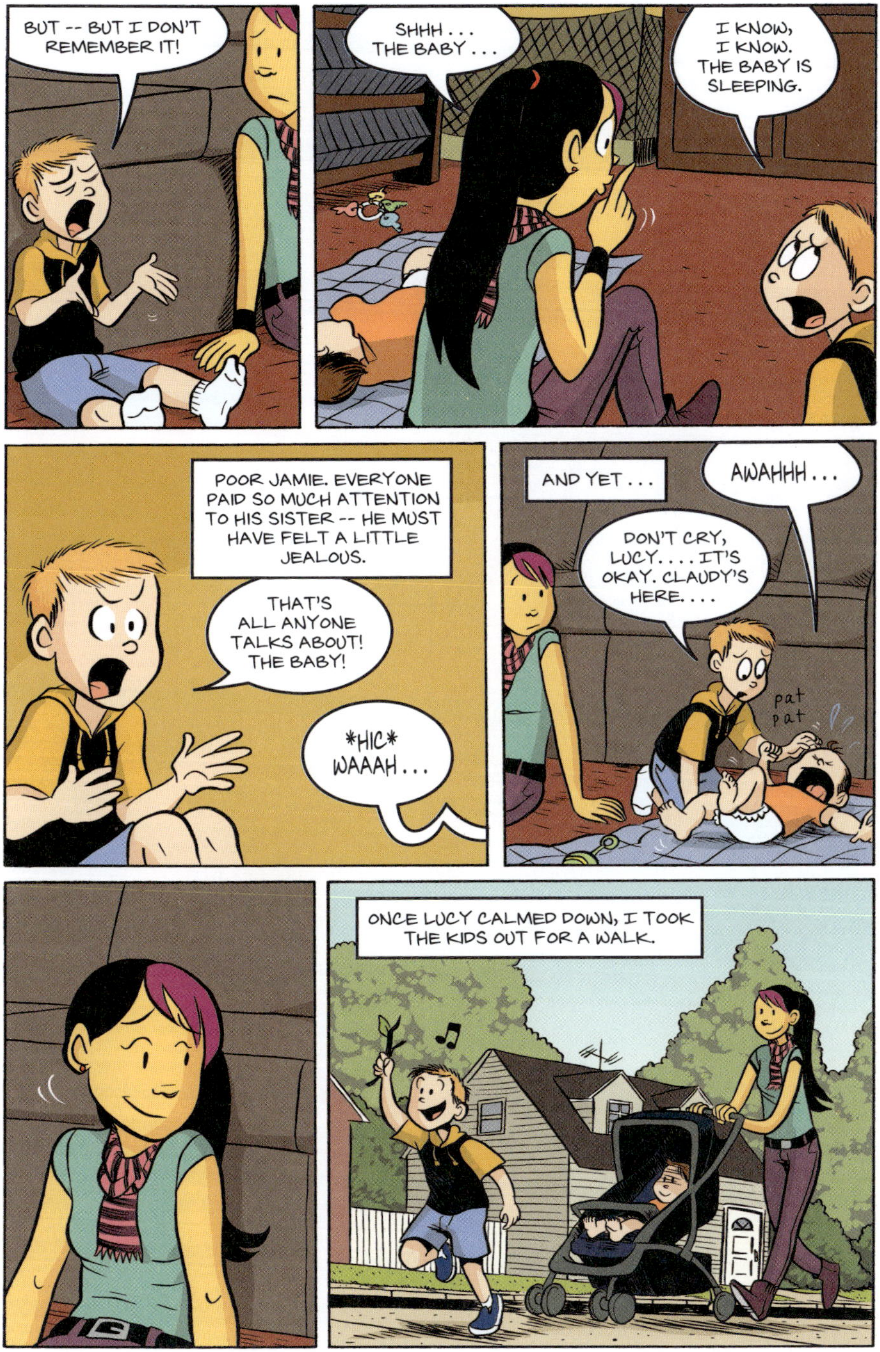
BUT -- BUT I DON'T REMEMBER IT!
SHHH . . . THE BABY . . .
I KNOW, I KNOW. THE BABY IS SLEEPING.
POOR JAMIE. EVERYONE PAID SO MUCH ATTENTION TO HIS SISTER -- HE MUST HAVE FELT A LITTLE JEALOUS.
THAT'S ALL ANYONE TALKS ABOUT! THE BABY!
HIC WAAAH . . .
AND YET . . .
AWAHHH . . .
DON'T CRY, LUCY. . . . IT'S OKAY. CLAUDY'S HERE. . . .
pat pat
ONCE LUCY CALMED DOWN, I TOOK THE KIDS OUT FOR A WALK.

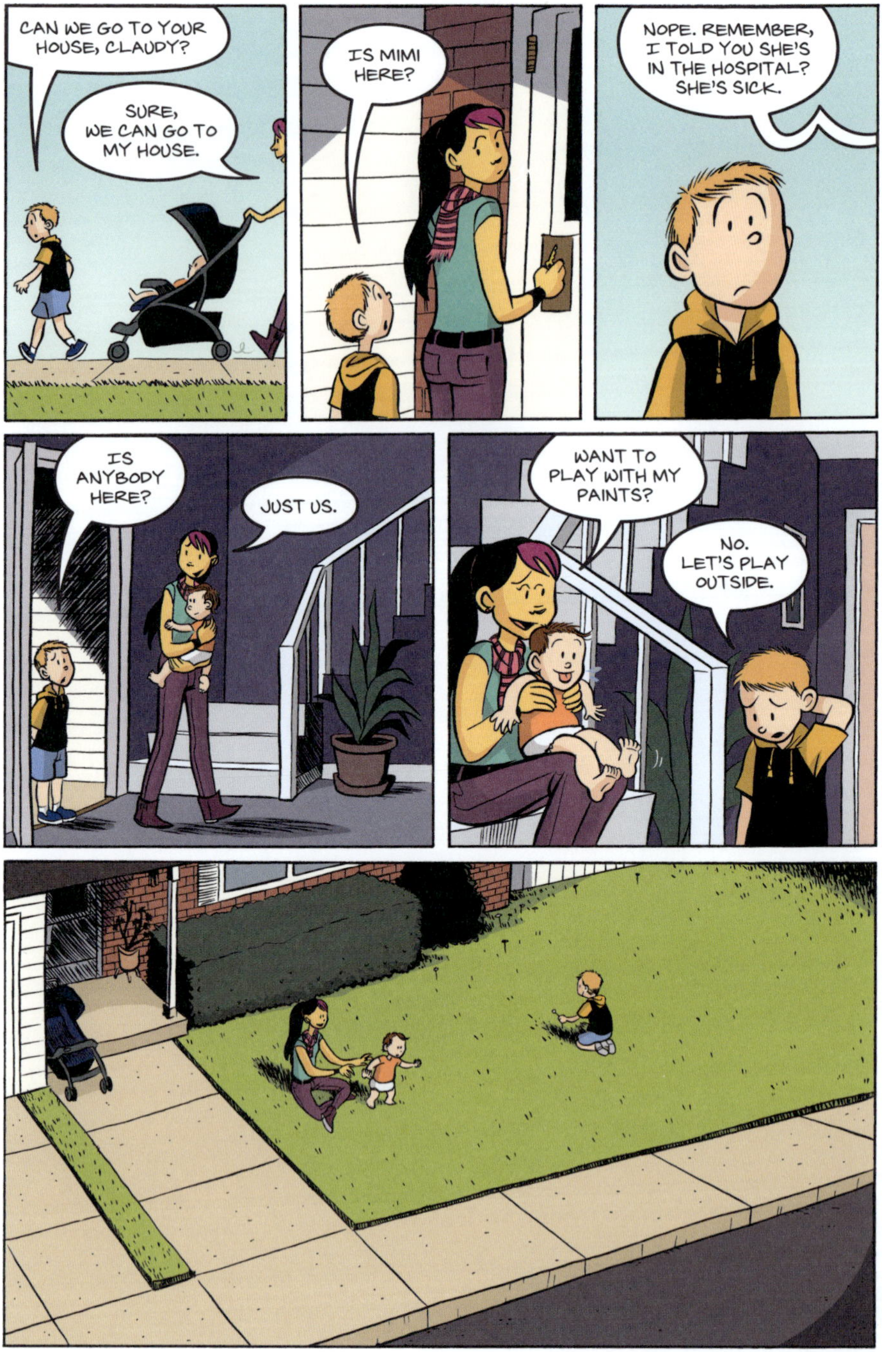
CAN WE GO TO YOUR HOUSE, CLAUDY?
SURE, WE CAN GO TO MY HOUSE.
IS MIMI HERE?
NOPE. REMEMBER, I TOLD YOU SHE'S IN THE HOSPITAL? SHE'S SICK.
IS ANYBODY HERE?
JUST US.
WANT TO PLAY WITH MY PAINTS?
NO. LET'S PLAY OUTSIDE.

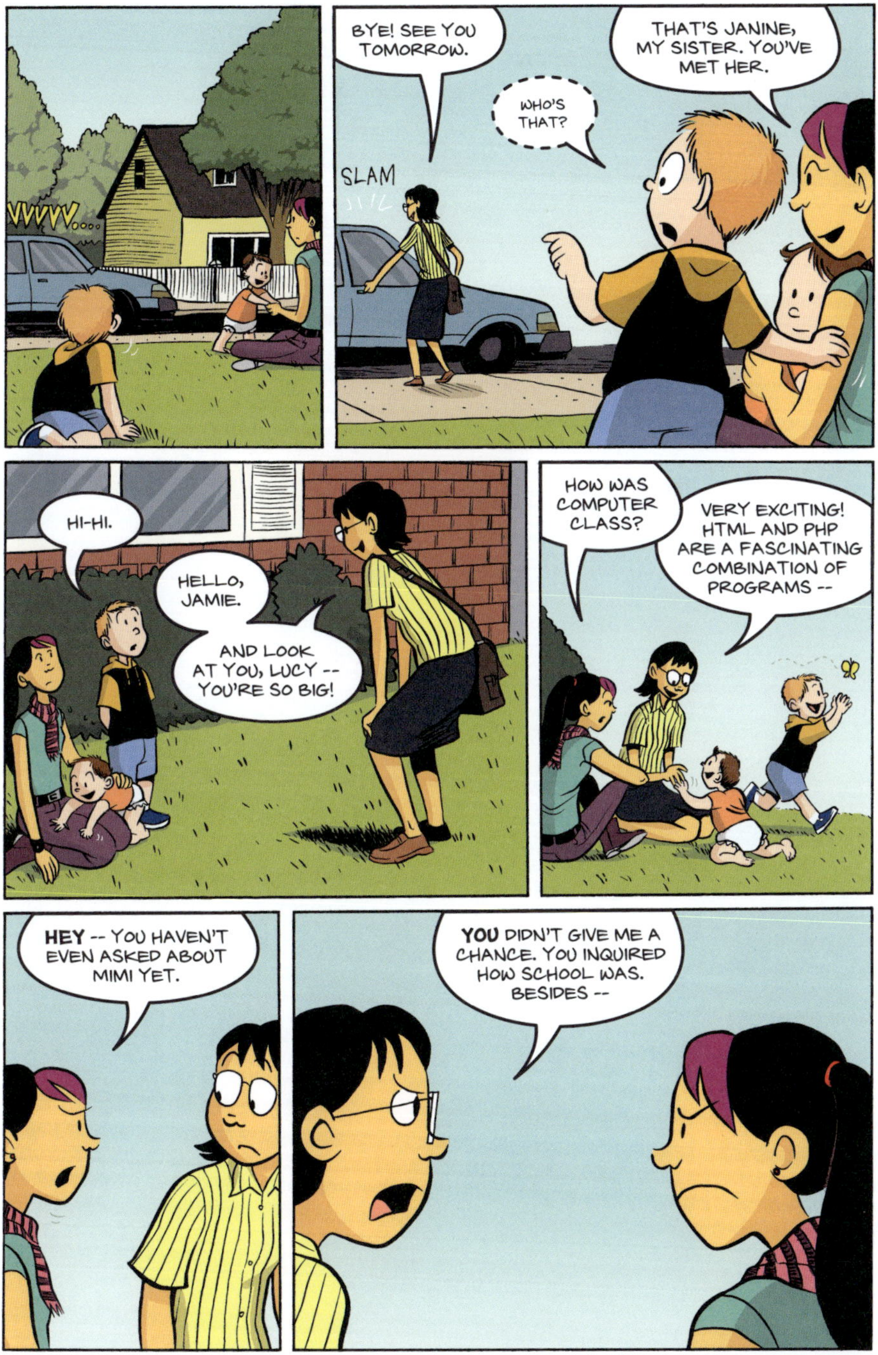
VVVVV...
BYE! SEE YOU TOMORROW.
SLAM
WHO'S THAT?
THAT'S JANINE, MY SISTER. YOU'VE MET HER.
HI-HI.
HELLO, JAMIE.
AND LOOK AT YOU, LUCY -- YOU'RE SO BIG!
HOW WAS COMPUTER CLASS?
VERY EXCITING! HTML AND PHP ARE A FASCINATING COMBINATION OF PROGRAMS --
HEY -- YOU HAVEN'T EVEN ASKED ABOUT MIMI YET.
YOU DIDN'T GIVE ME A CHANCE. YOU INQUIRED HOW SCHOOL WAS. BESIDES --

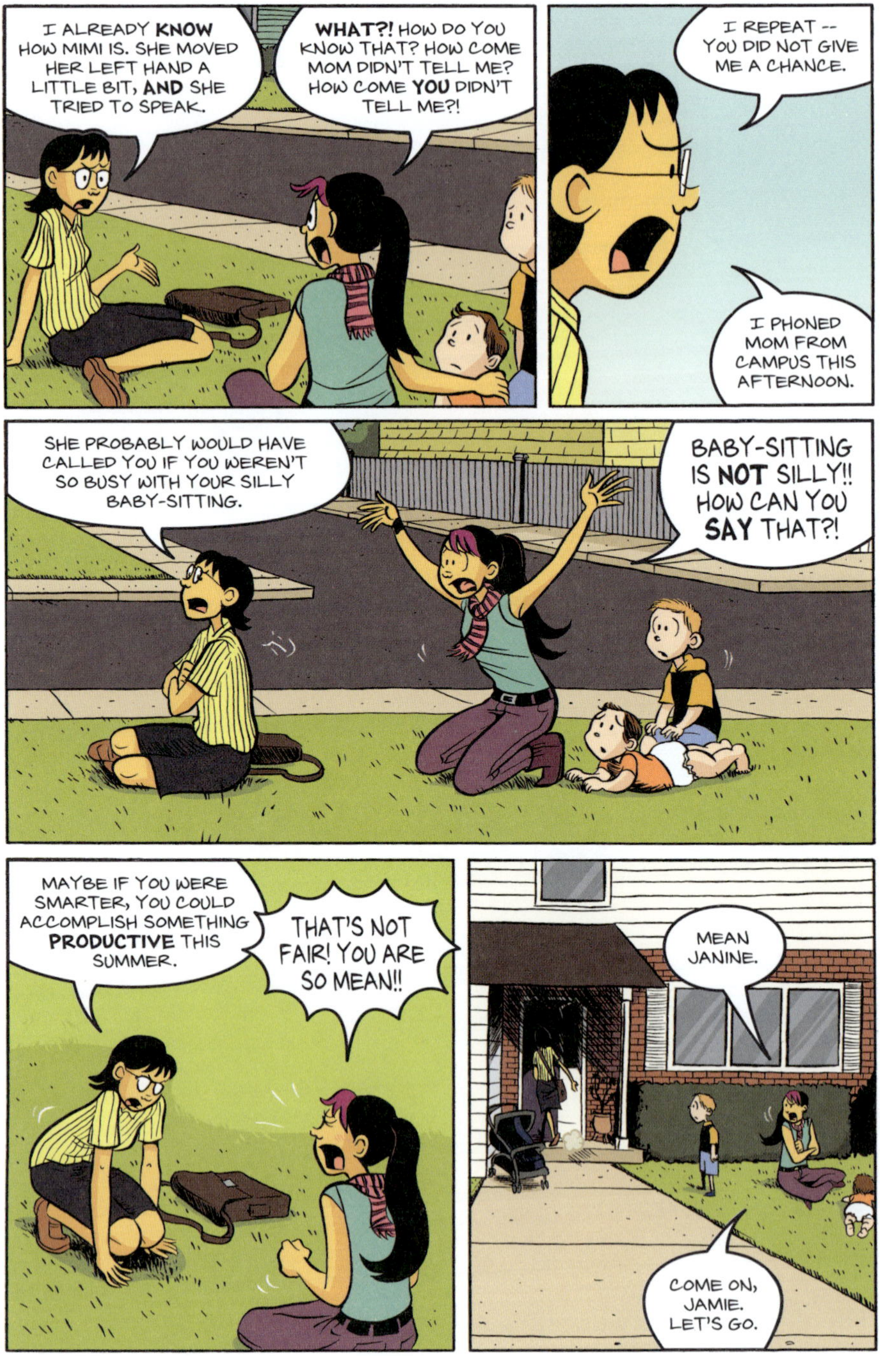
I ALREADY **KNOW** HOW MIMI IS. SHE MOVED HER LEFT HAND A LITTLE BIT, **AND** SHE TRIED TO SPEAK.
WHAT?! HOW DO YOU KNOW THAT? HOW COME MOM DIDN'T TELL ME? HOW COME **YOU** DIDN'T TELL ME?!
I REPEAT -- YOU DID NOT GIVE ME A CHANCE.
I PHONED MOM FROM CAMPUS THIS AFTERNOON.
SHE PROBABLY WOULD HAVE CALLED YOU IF YOU WEREN'T SO BUSY WITH YOUR SILLY BABY-SITTING.
BABY-SITTING IS **NOT** SILLY!! HOW CAN YOU **SAY** THAT?!
MAYBE IF YOU WERE SMARTER, YOU COULD ACCOMPLISH SOMETHING **PRODUCTIVE** THIS SUMMER.
THAT'S NOT FAIR! YOU ARE SO MEAN!!
MEAN JANINE.
COME ON, JAMIE. LET'S GO.

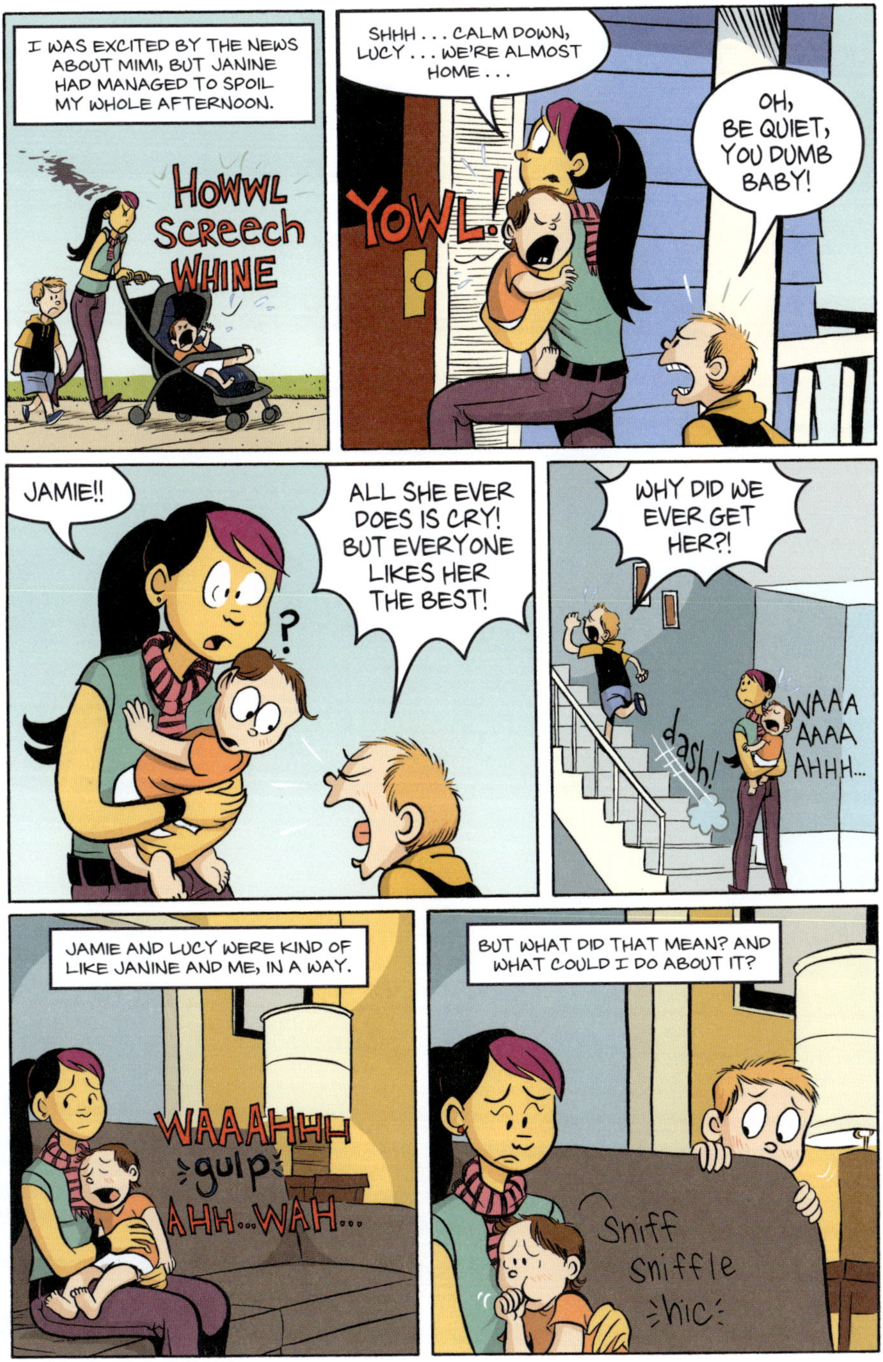
I WAS EXCITED BY THE NEWS ABOUT MIMI, BUT JANINE HAD MANAGED TO SPOIL MY WHOLE AFTERNOON.
HOWWL
SCREECH
WHINE
SHHH . . . CALM DOWN, LUCY . . . WE'RE ALMOST HOME . . .
YOWL!
OH, BE QUIET, YOU DUMB BABY!
JAMIE!!
?
ALL SHE EVER DOES IS CRY! BUT EVERYONE LIKES HER THE BEST!
WHY DID WE EVER GET HER?!
dash!
WAAA AAAA AHHH...
JAMIE AND LUCY WERE KIND OF LIKE JANINE AND ME, IN A WAY.
WAAAHHH
gulp
AHH...WAH...
BUT WHAT DID THAT MEAN? AND WHAT COULD I DO ABOUT IT?
Sniff
sniffle
hic

CHAPTER 11

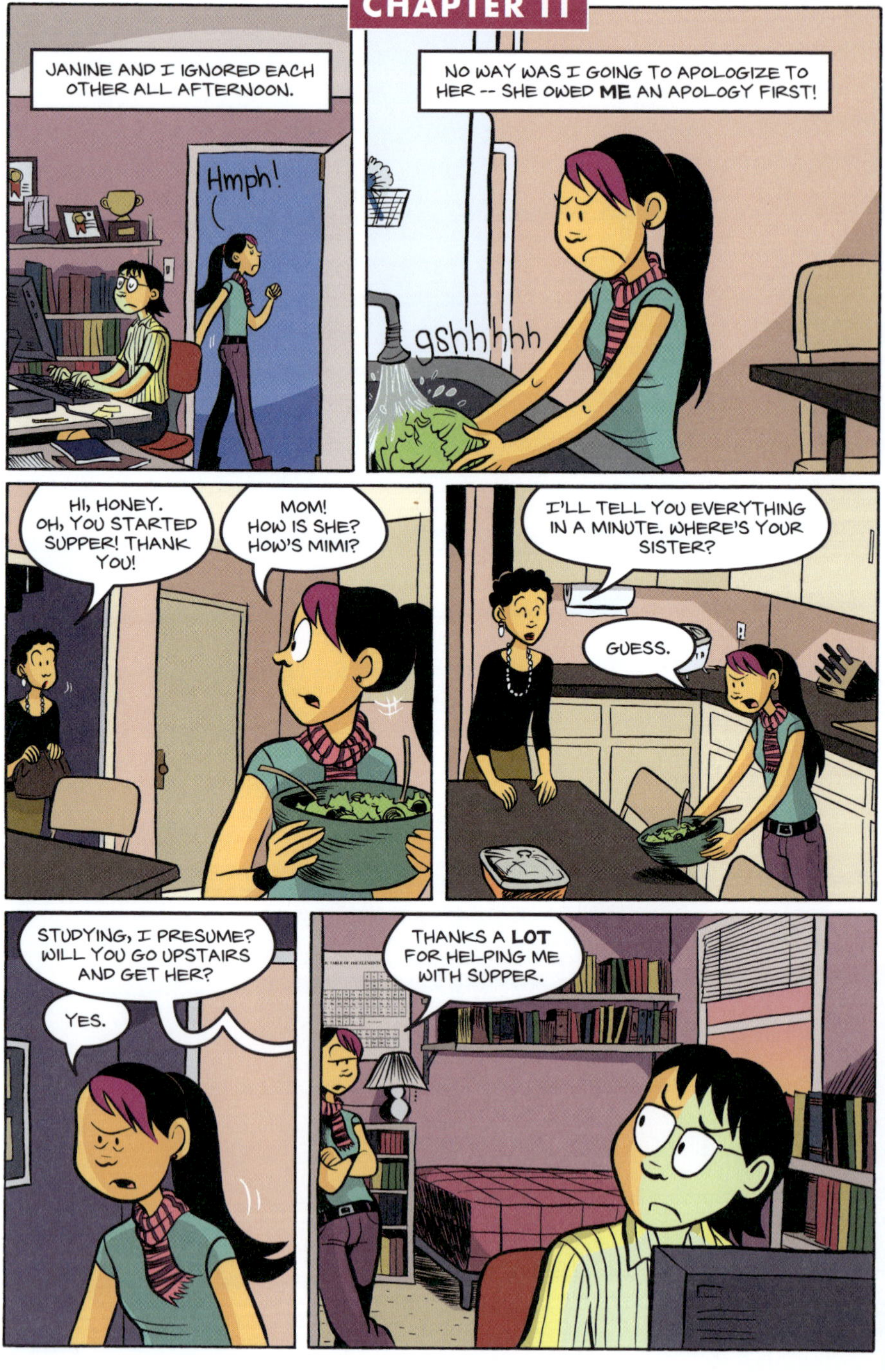

JANINE AND I IGNORED EACH OTHER ALL AFTERNOON.
Hmph!
NO WAY WAS I GOING TO APOLOGIZE TO HER -- SHE OWED **ME** AN APOLOGY FIRST!
gshh'hhh
HI, HONEY. OH, YOU STARTED SUPPER! THANK YOU!
MOM! HOW IS SHE? HOW'S MIMI?
I'LL TELL YOU EVERYTHING IN A MINUTE. WHERE'S YOUR SISTER?
GUESS.
STUDYING, I PRESUME? WILL YOU GO UPSTAIRS AND GET HER?
YES.
THANKS A **LOT** FOR HELPING ME WITH SUPPER.

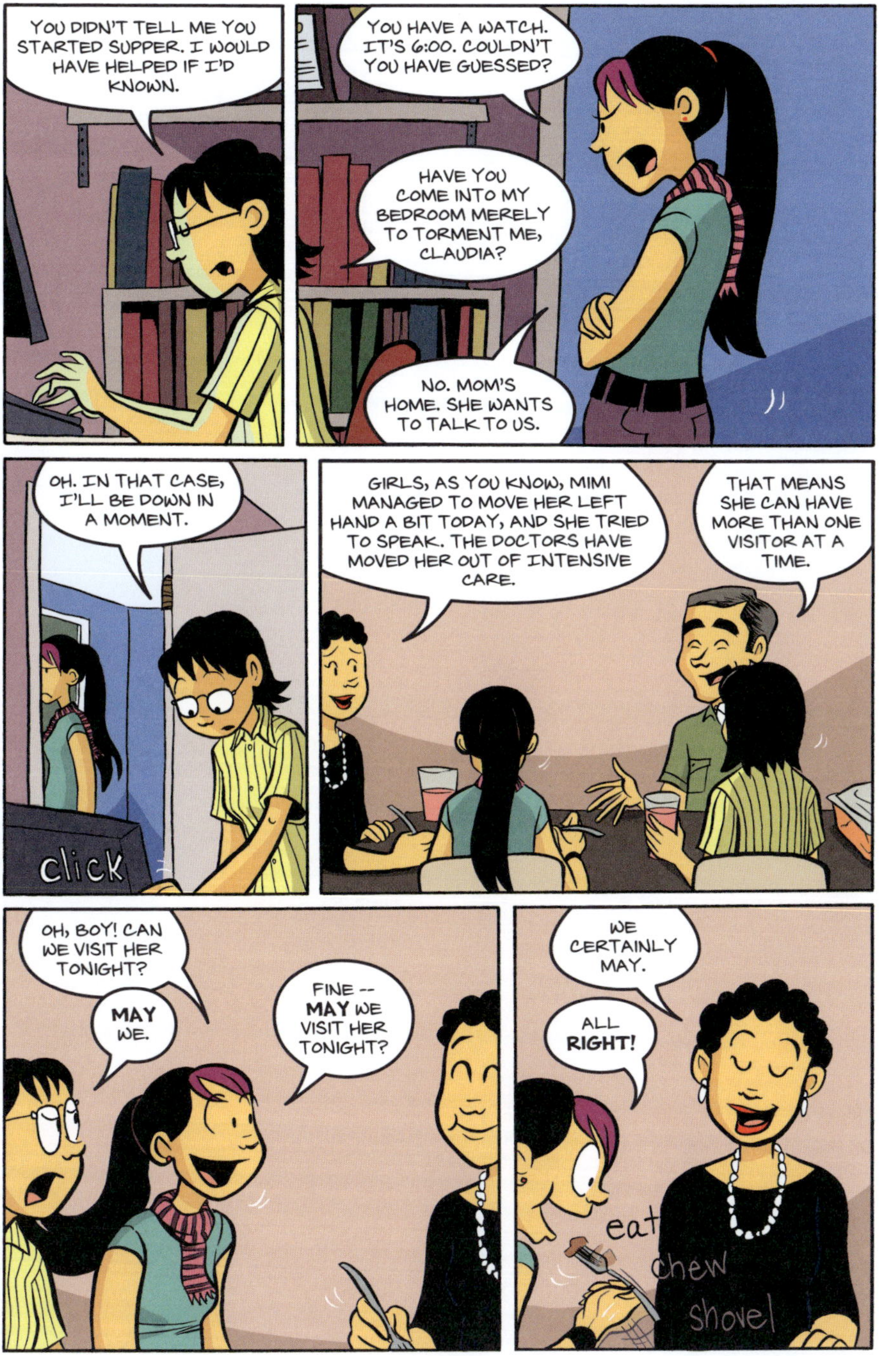
YOU DIDN'T TELL ME YOU STARTED SUPPER. I WOULD HAVE HELPED IF I'D KNOWN.
YOU HAVE A WATCH. IT'S 6:00. COULDN'T YOU HAVE GUESSED?
HAVE YOU COME INTO MY BEDROOM MERELY TO TORMENT ME, CLAUDIA?
NO. MOM'S HOME. SHE WANTS TO TALK TO US.
OH. IN THAT CASE, I'LL BE DOWN IN A MOMENT.
click
GIRLS, AS YOU KNOW, MIMI MANAGED TO MOVE HER LEFT HAND A BIT TODAY, AND SHE TRIED TO SPEAK. THE DOCTORS HAVE MOVED HER OUT OF INTENSIVE CARE.
THAT MEANS SHE CAN HAVE MORE THAN ONE VISITOR AT A TIME.
OH, BOY! CAN WE VISIT HER TONIGHT?
MAY WE.
FINE -- MAY WE VISIT HER TONIGHT?
WE CERTAINLY MAY.
ALL RIGHT!
eat
chew
shovel

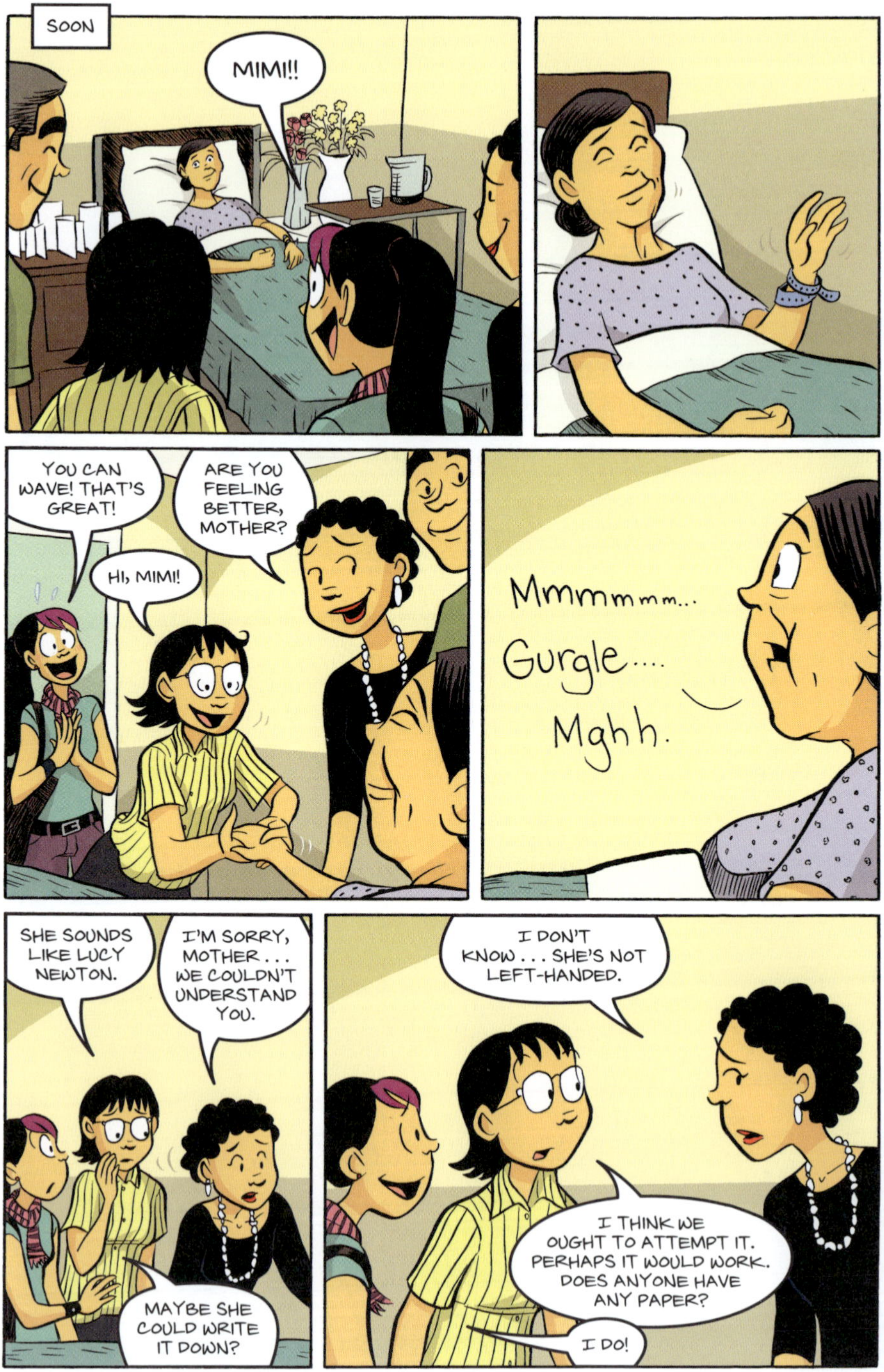
SOON
MIMI!!
YOU CAN WAVE! THAT'S GREAT!
ARE YOU FEELING BETTER, MOTHER?
HI, MIMI!
Mmmmmm...
Gurgle....
Mghh.
SHE SOUNDS LIKE LUCY NEWTON.
I'M SORRY, MOTHER . . . WE COULDN'T UNDERSTAND YOU.
MAYBE SHE COULD WRITE IT DOWN?
I DON'T KNOW . . . SHE'S NOT LEFT-HANDED.
I THINK WE OUGHT TO ATTEMPT IT. PERHAPS IT WOULD WORK. DOES ANYONE HAVE ANY PAPER?
I DO!

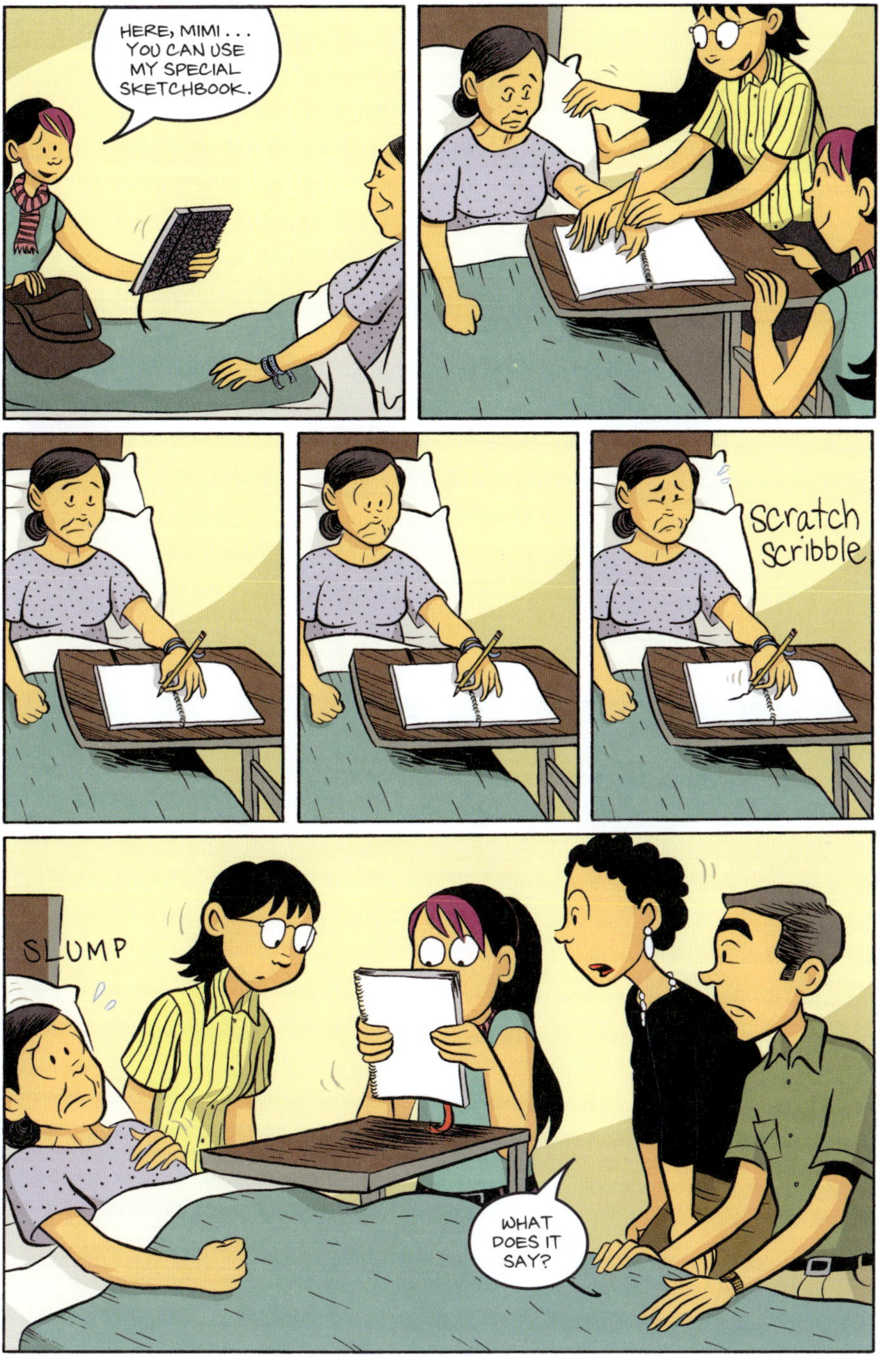
HERE, MIMI . . . YOU CAN USE MY SPECIAL SKETCHBOOK.
Scratch
Scribble
SLUMP
WHAT DOES IT SAY?

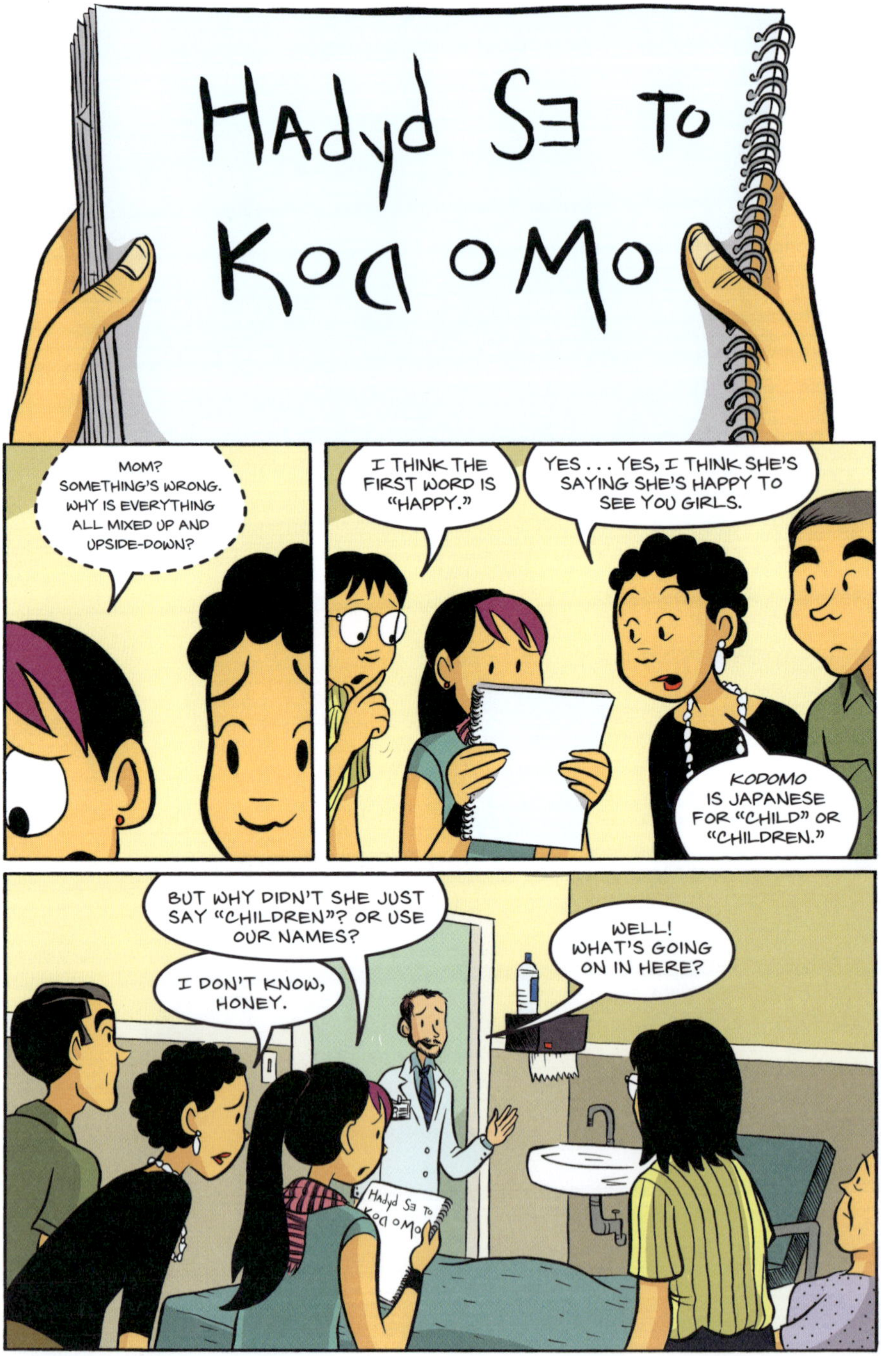
Hadyd S3 To
KoDoMo
MOM? SOMETHING'S WRONG. WHY IS EVERYTHING ALL MIXED UP AND UPSIDE-DOWN?
I THINK THE FIRST WORD IS "HAPPY."
YES . . . YES, I THINK SHE'S SAYING SHE'S HAPPY TO SEE YOU GIRLS.
KODOMO IS JAPANESE FOR "CHILD" OR "CHILDREN."
BUT WHY DIDN'T SHE JUST SAY "CHILDREN"? OR USE OUR NAMES?
I DON'T KNOW, HONEY.
WELL! WHAT'S GOING ON IN HERE?

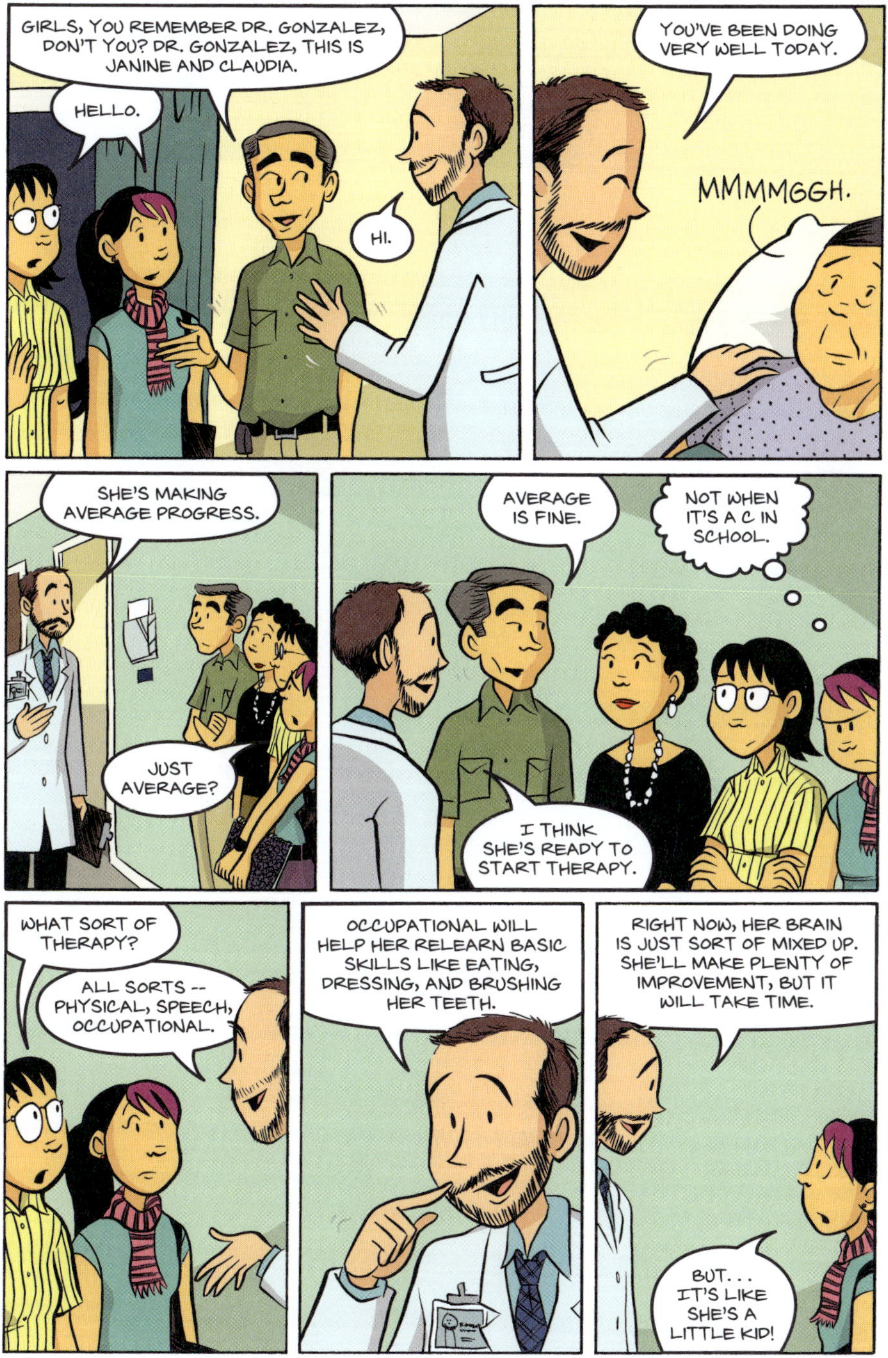
GIRLS, YOU REMEMBER DR. GONZALEZ, DON'T YOU? DR. GONZALEZ, THIS IS JANINE AND CLAUDIA.
HELLO.
HI.
YOU'VE BEEN DOING VERY WELL TODAY.
MMMMGGH.
SHE'S MAKING AVERAGE PROGRESS.
JUST AVERAGE?
AVERAGE IS FINE.
NOT WHEN IT'S A C IN SCHOOL.
I THINK SHE'S READY TO START THERAPY.
WHAT SORT OF THERAPY?
ALL SORTS -- PHYSICAL, SPEECH, OCCUPATIONAL.
OCCUPATIONAL WILL HELP HER RELEARN BASIC SKILLS LIKE EATING, DRESSING, AND BRUSHING HER TEETH.
RIGHT NOW, HER BRAIN IS JUST SORT OF MIXED UP. SHE'LL MAKE PLENTY OF IMPROVEMENT, BUT IT WILL TAKE TIME.
BUT. . . IT'S LIKE SHE'S A LITTLE KID!

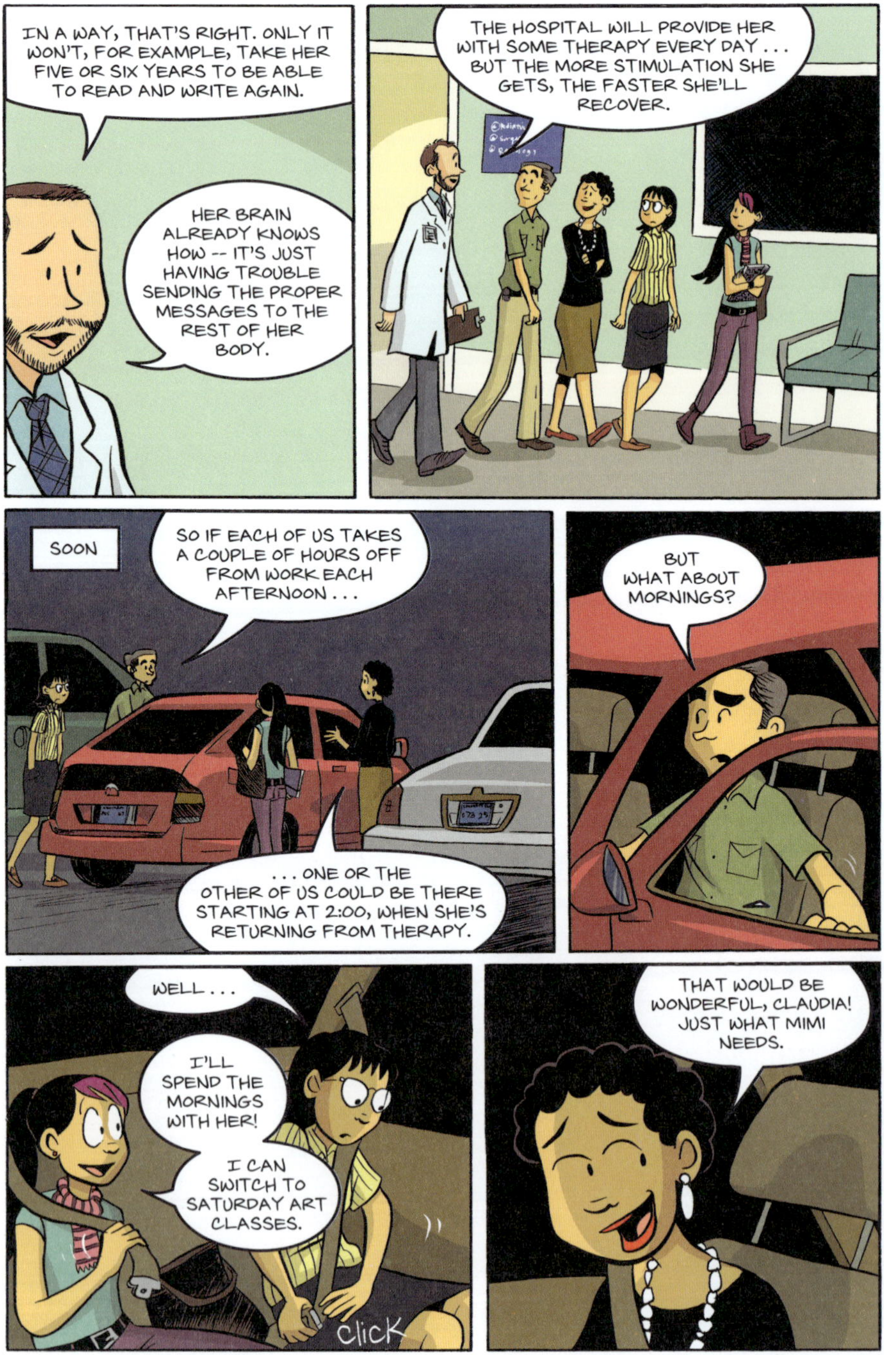
IN A WAY, THAT'S RIGHT. ONLY IT WON'T, FOR EXAMPLE, TAKE HER FIVE OR SIX YEARS TO BE ABLE TO READ AND WRITE AGAIN.
HER BRAIN ALREADY KNOWS HOW -- IT'S JUST HAVING TROUBLE SENDING THE PROPER MESSAGES TO THE REST OF HER BODY.
THE HOSPITAL WILL PROVIDE HER WITH SOME THERAPY EVERY DAY . . . BUT THE MORE STIMULATION SHE GETS, THE FASTER SHE'LL RECOVER.
SOON
SO IF EACH OF US TAKES A COUPLE OF HOURS OFF FROM WORK EACH AFTERNOON . . .
. . . ONE OR THE OTHER OF US COULD BE THERE STARTING AT 2:00, WHEN SHE'S RETURNING FROM THERAPY.
BUT WHAT ABOUT MORNINGS?
WELL . . .
I'LL SPEND THE MORNINGS WITH HER!
I CAN SWITCH TO SATURDAY ART CLASSES.
CLICK
THAT WOULD BE WONDERFUL, CLAUDIA! JUST WHAT MIMI NEEDS.

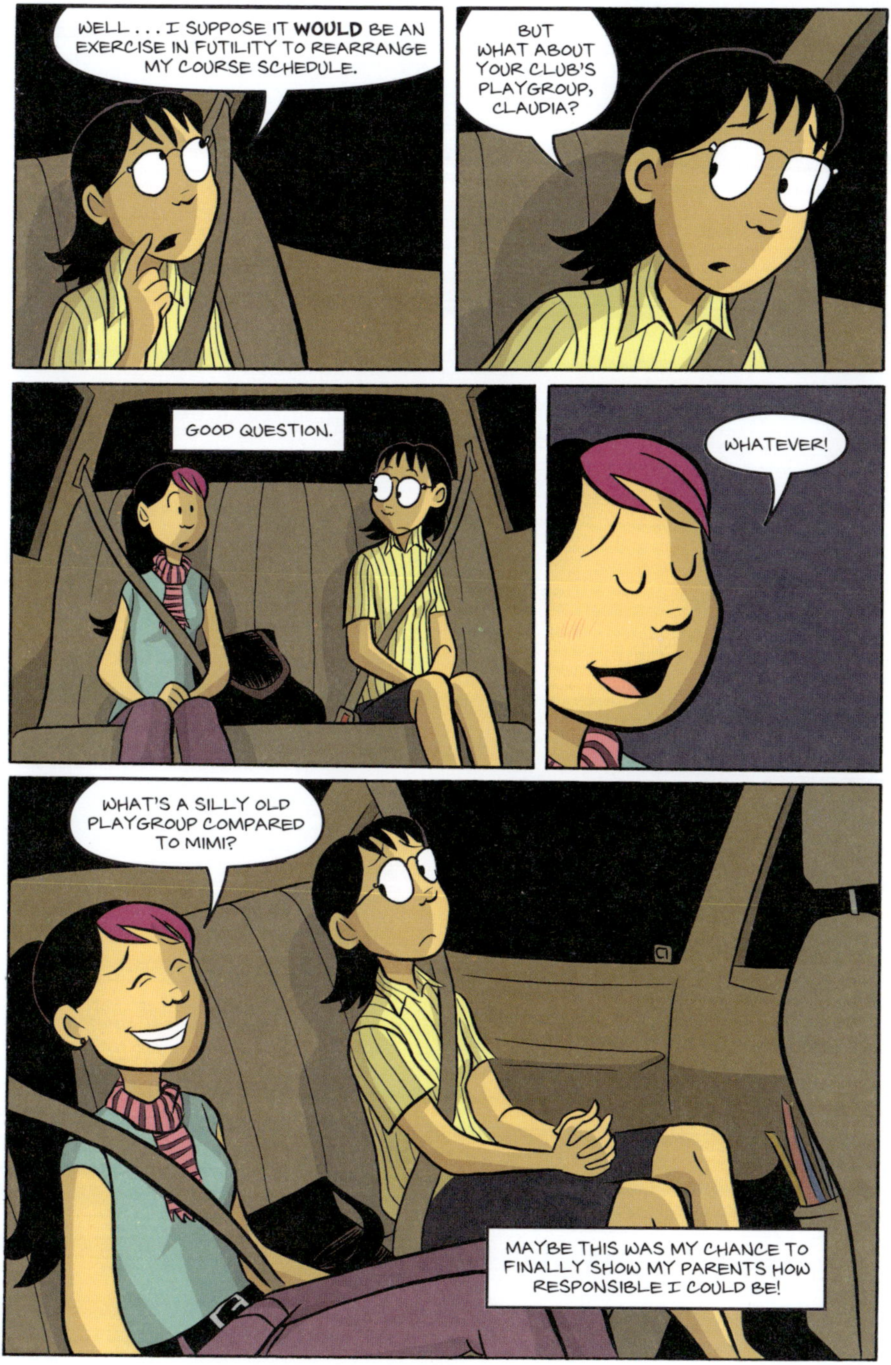
WELL . . . I SUPPOSE IT **WOULD** BE AN EXERCISE IN FUTILITY TO REARRANGE MY COURSE SCHEDULE.
BUT WHAT ABOUT YOUR CLUB'S PLAYGROUP, CLAUDIA?
GOOD QUESTION.
WHATEVER!
WHAT'S A SILLY OLD PLAYGROUP COMPARED TO MIMI?
MAYBE THIS WAS MY CHANCE TO FINALLY SHOW MY PARENTS HOW RESPONSIBLE I COULD BE!

Wednesday, June 23

   Today's playgroup ended hours ago and I'm still laughing about what went on. Now this is an example of something hilarious that probably could never have happened in New York City.... It started when David Michael brought Louie to the playgroup. Just to set things off on the wrong foot, it turns out that Jenny is afraid (and I mean terrified) of dogs. Remember that for the future, you guys.

Then Kristy decided we needed to give Louie a bath. That's when the trouble really began. When the morning was over, Louie was the only one who was both clean and dry. Thank goodness Jenny was wearing her smock.

   Claudia — we miss you!

                                        Stacey

CHAPTER 12

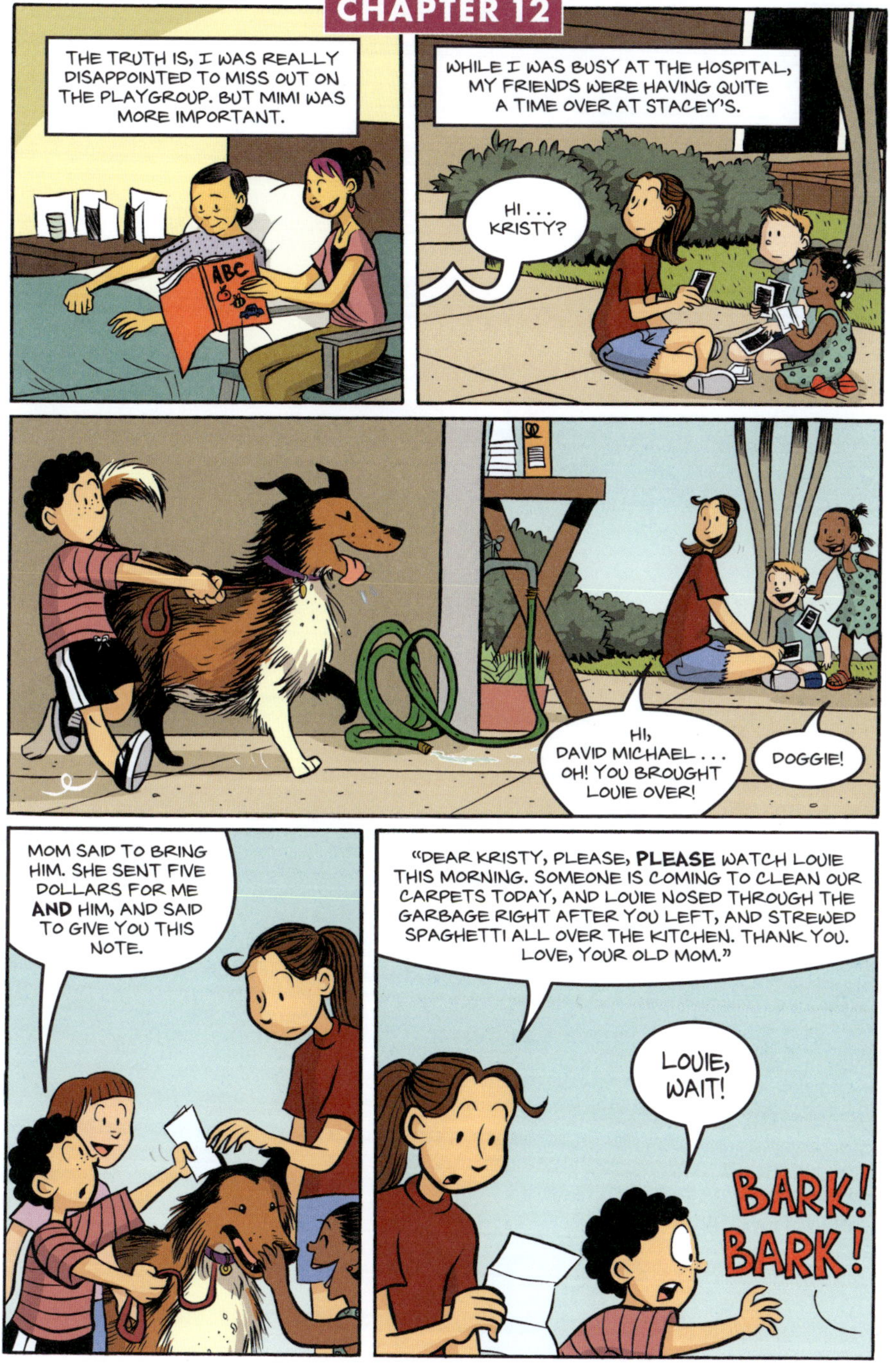
THE TRUTH IS, I WAS REALLY DISAPPOINTED TO MISS OUT ON THE PLAYGROUP. BUT MIMI WAS MORE IMPORTANT.
ABC
WHILE I WAS BUSY AT THE HOSPITAL, MY FRIENDS WERE HAVING QUITE A TIME OVER AT STACEY'S.
HI . . . KRISTY?
HI, DAVID MICHAEL . . . OH! YOU BROUGHT LOUIE OVER!
DOGGIE!
MOM SAID TO BRING HIM. SHE SENT FIVE DOLLARS FOR ME **AND** HIM, AND SAID TO GIVE YOU THIS NOTE.
"DEAR KRISTY, PLEASE, **PLEASE** WATCH LOUIE THIS MORNING. SOMEONE IS COMING TO CLEAN OUR CARPETS TODAY, AND LOUIE NOSED THROUGH THE GARBAGE RIGHT AFTER YOU LEFT, AND STREWED SPAGHETTI ALL OVER THE KITCHEN. THANK YOU. LOVE, YOUR OLD MOM."
LOUIE, WAIT!
BARK! BARK!

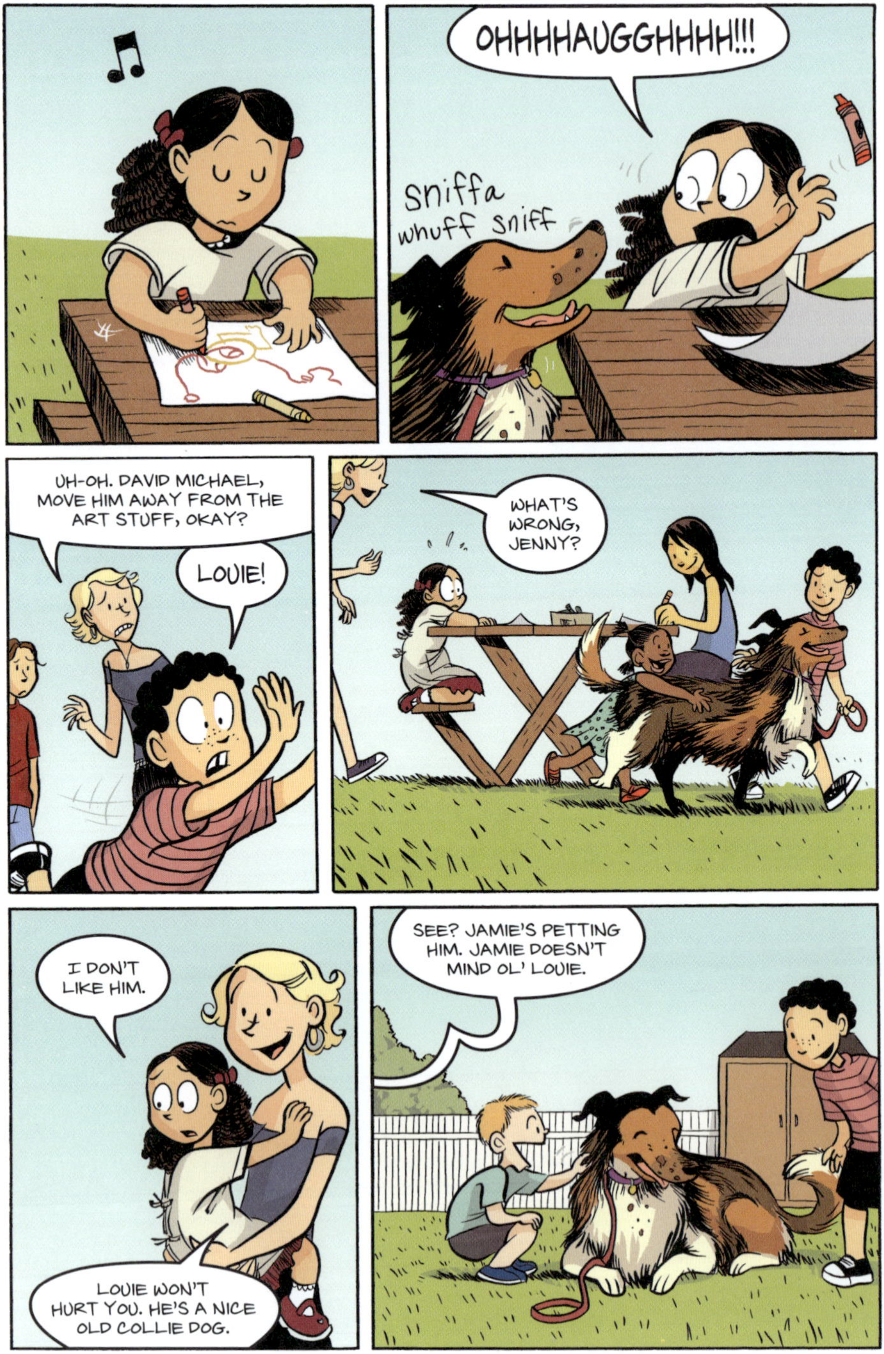
OHHHHAUGGHHHH!!!
sniffa
whuff sniff
UH-OH. DAVID MICHAEL, MOVE HIM AWAY FROM THE ART STUFF, OKAY?
LOUIE!
WHAT'S WRONG, JENNY?
I DON'T LIKE HIM.
LOUIE WON'T HURT YOU. HE'S A NICE OLD COLLIE DOG.
SEE? JAMIE'S PETTING HIM. JAMIE DOESN'T MIND OL' LOUIE.

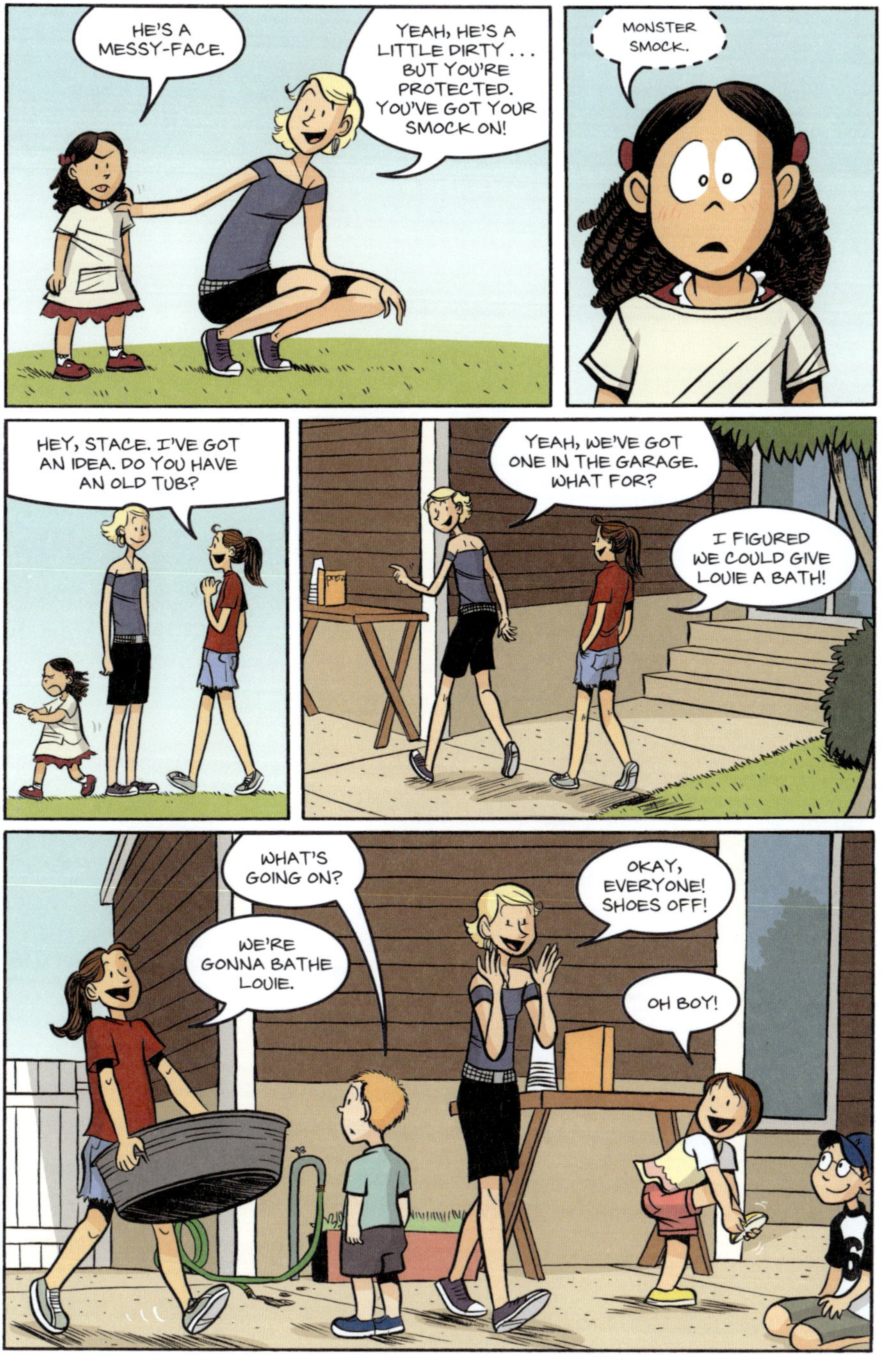
HE'S A MESSY-FACE.
YEAH, HE'S A LITTLE DIRTY . . . BUT YOU'RE PROTECTED. YOU'VE GOT YOUR SMOCK ON!
MONSTER SMOCK.
HEY, STACE. I'VE GOT AN IDEA. DO YOU HAVE AN OLD TUB?
YEAH, WE'VE GOT ONE IN THE GARAGE. WHAT FOR?
I FIGURED WE COULD GIVE LOUIE A BATH!
WHAT'S GOING ON?
WE'RE GONNA BATHE LOUIE.
OKAY, EVERYONE! SHOES OFF!
OH BOY!

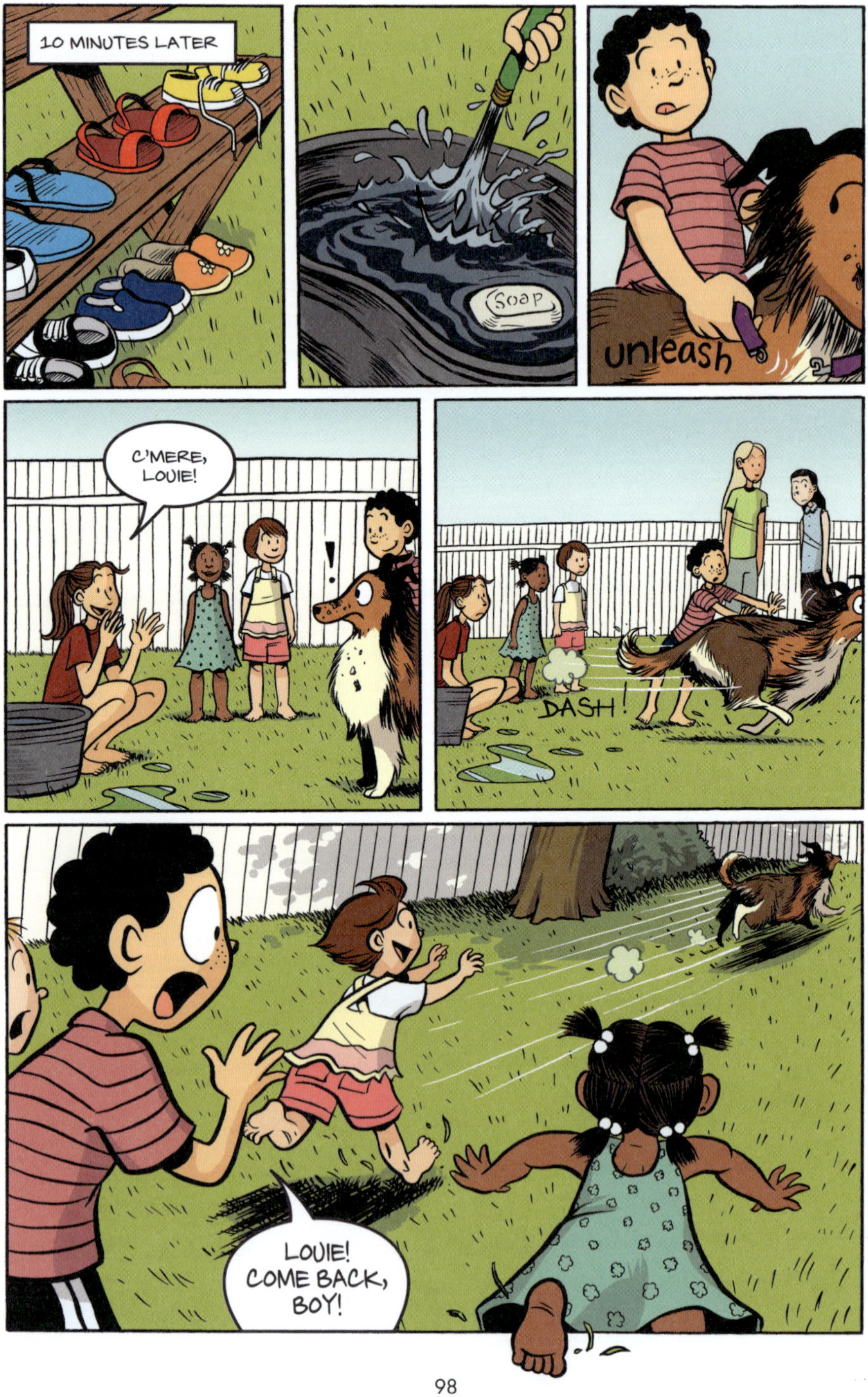
10 MINUTES LATER
Soap
unleash
C'MERE, LOUIE!
!
DASH!
LOUIE! COME BACK, BOY!

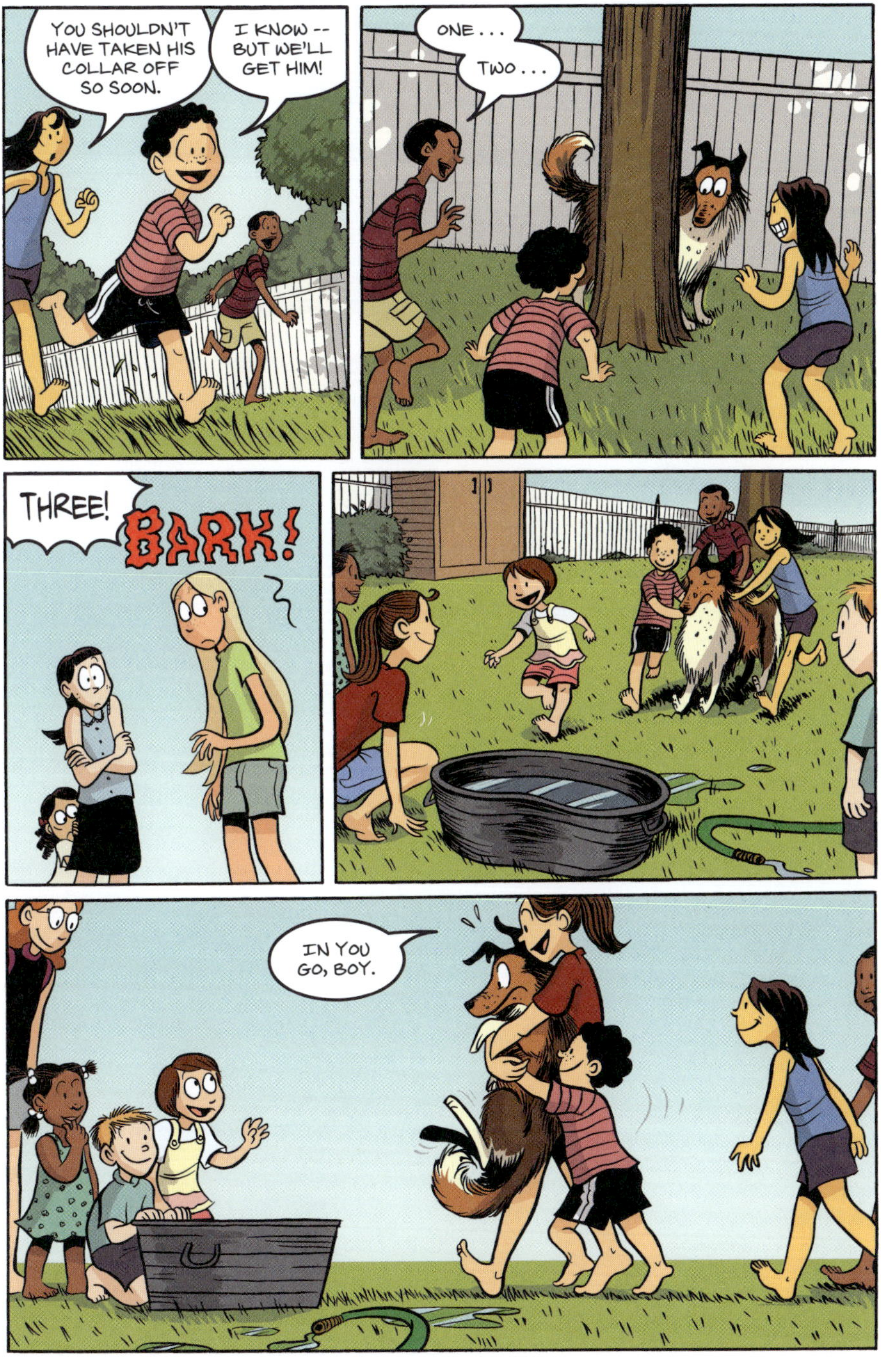
YOU SHOULDN'T HAVE TAKEN HIS COLLAR OFF SO SOON.
I KNOW -- BUT WE'LL GET HIM!
ONE . . .
TWO . . .
THREE!
BARK!
IN YOU GO, BOY.

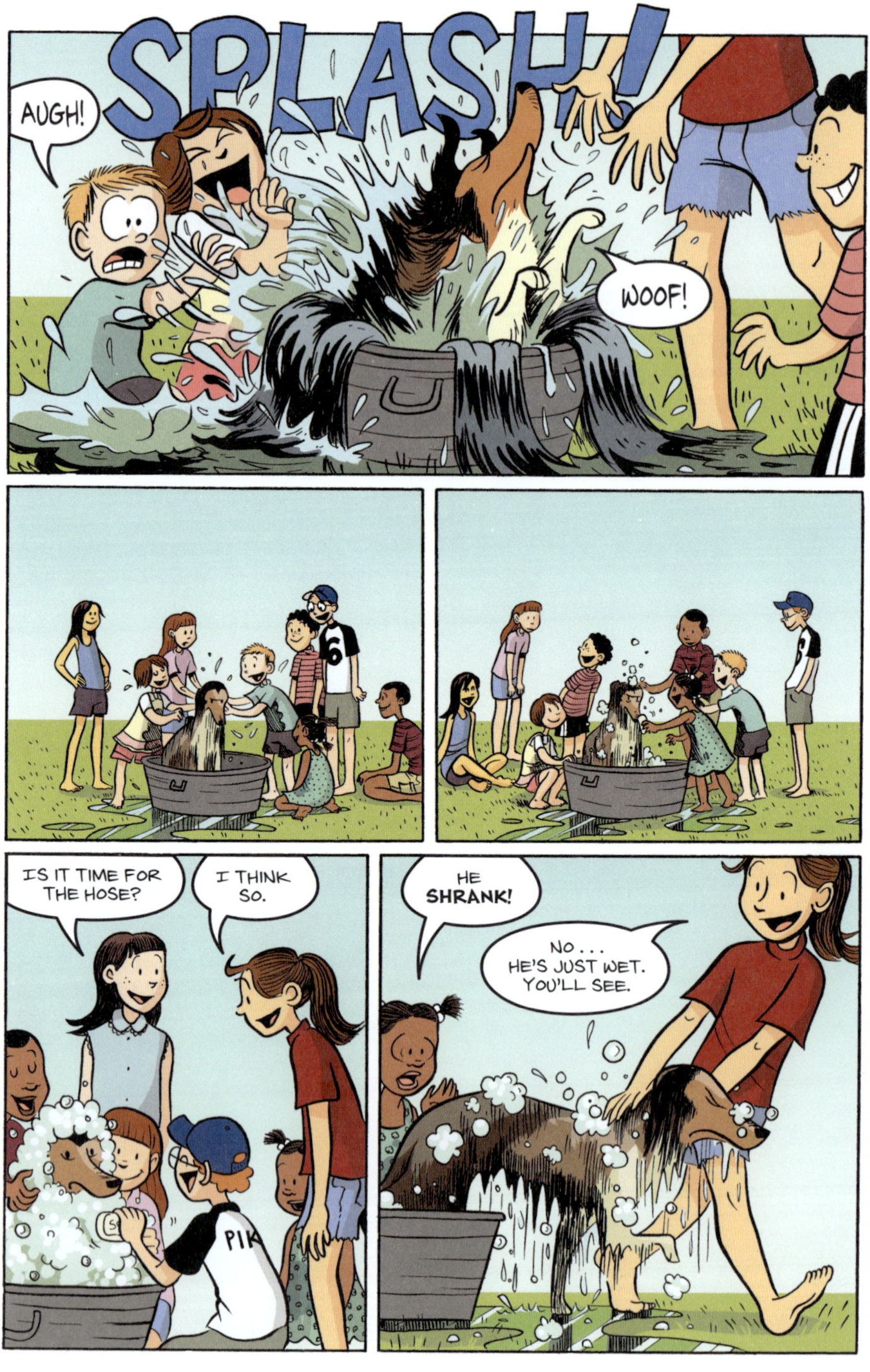
SPLASH!
AUGH!
WOOF!
IS IT TIME FOR THE HOSE?
I THINK SO.
HE SHRANK!
NO . . . HE'S JUST WET. YOU'LL SEE.

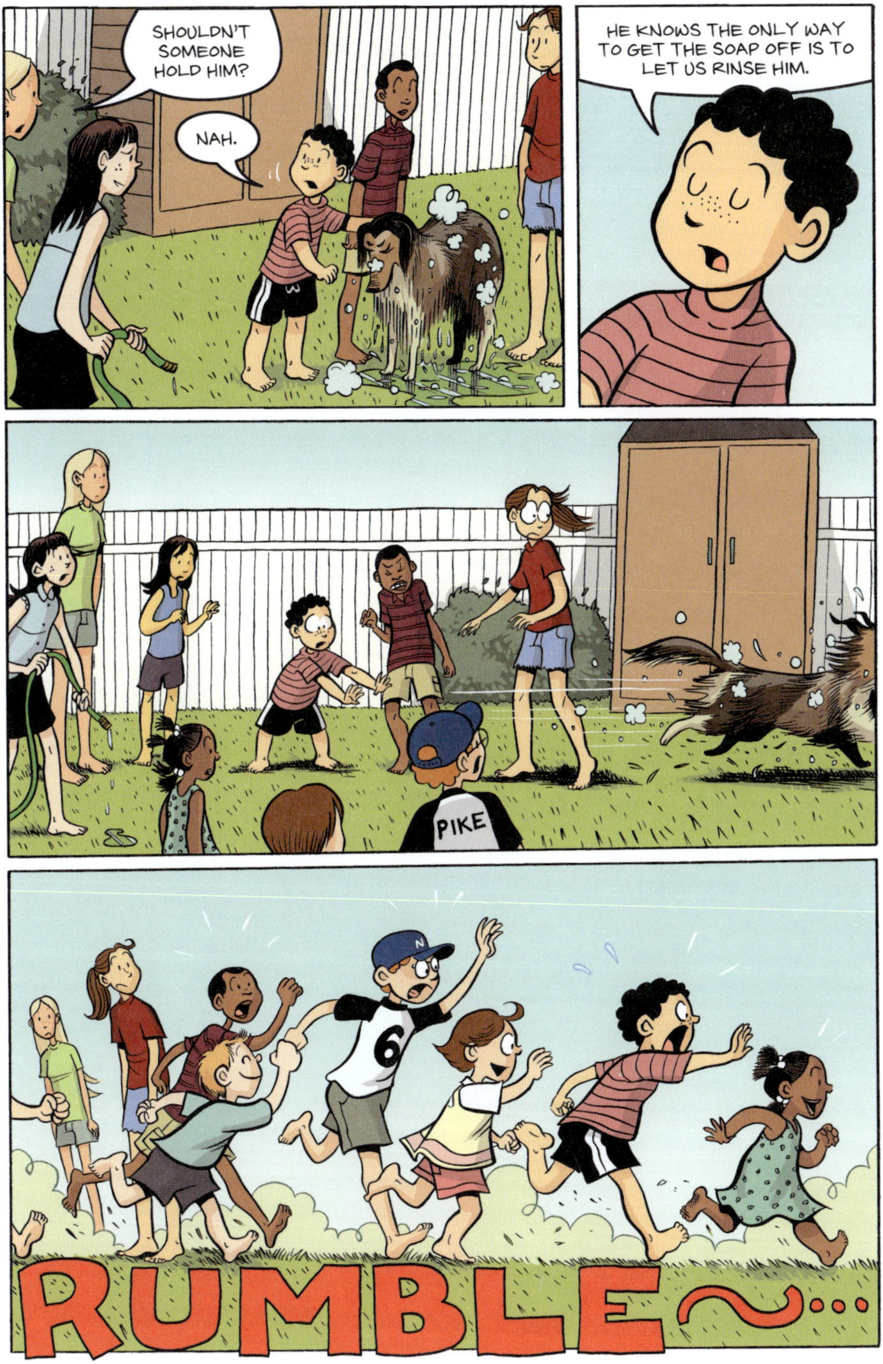
SHOULDN'T SOMEONE HOLD HIM?
NAH.
HE KNOWS THE ONLY WAY TO GET THE SOAP OFF IS TO LET US RINSE HIM.
PIKE
RUMBLE~...

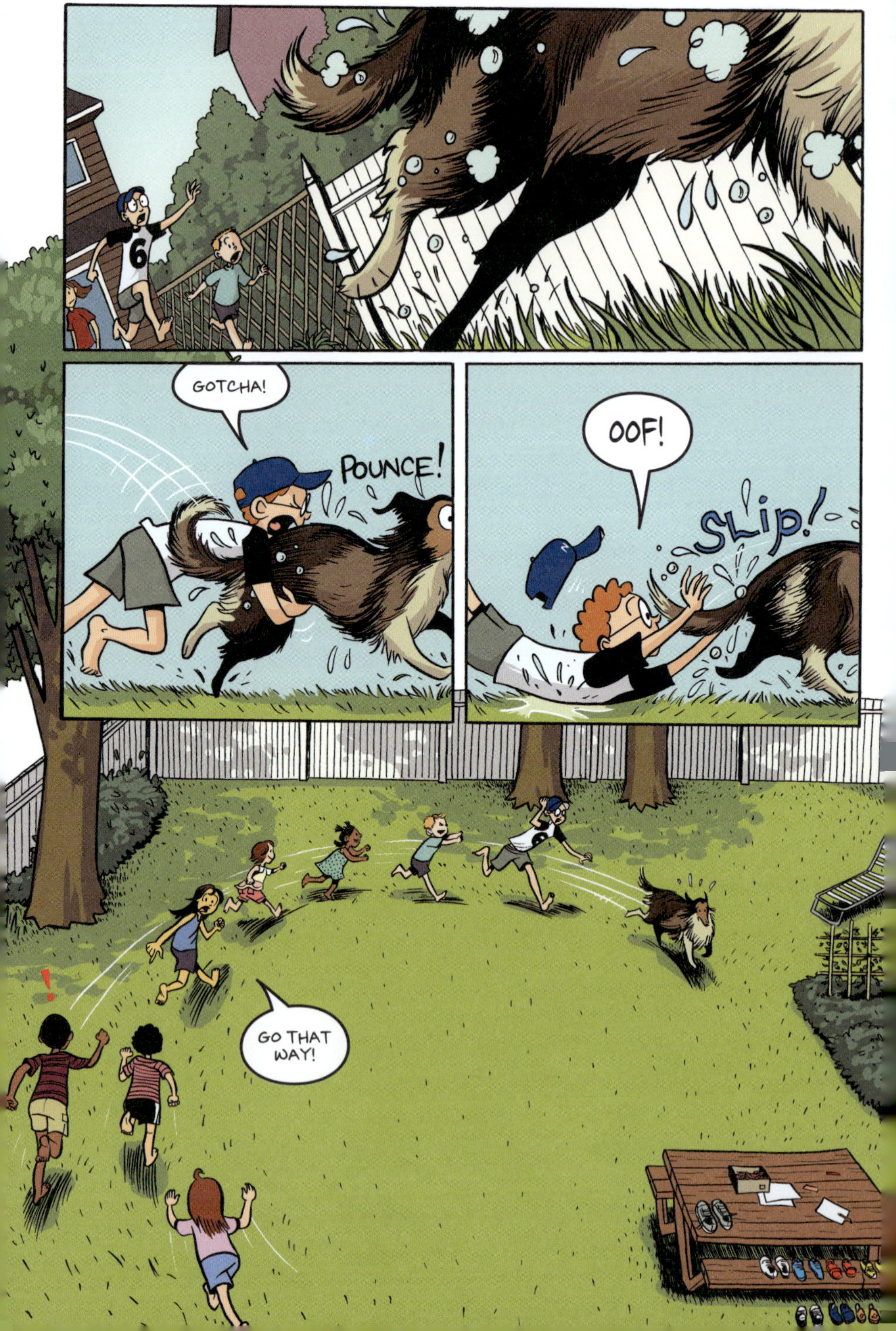
GOTCHA!
POUNCE!
OOF!
SLIP!
GO THAT WAY!

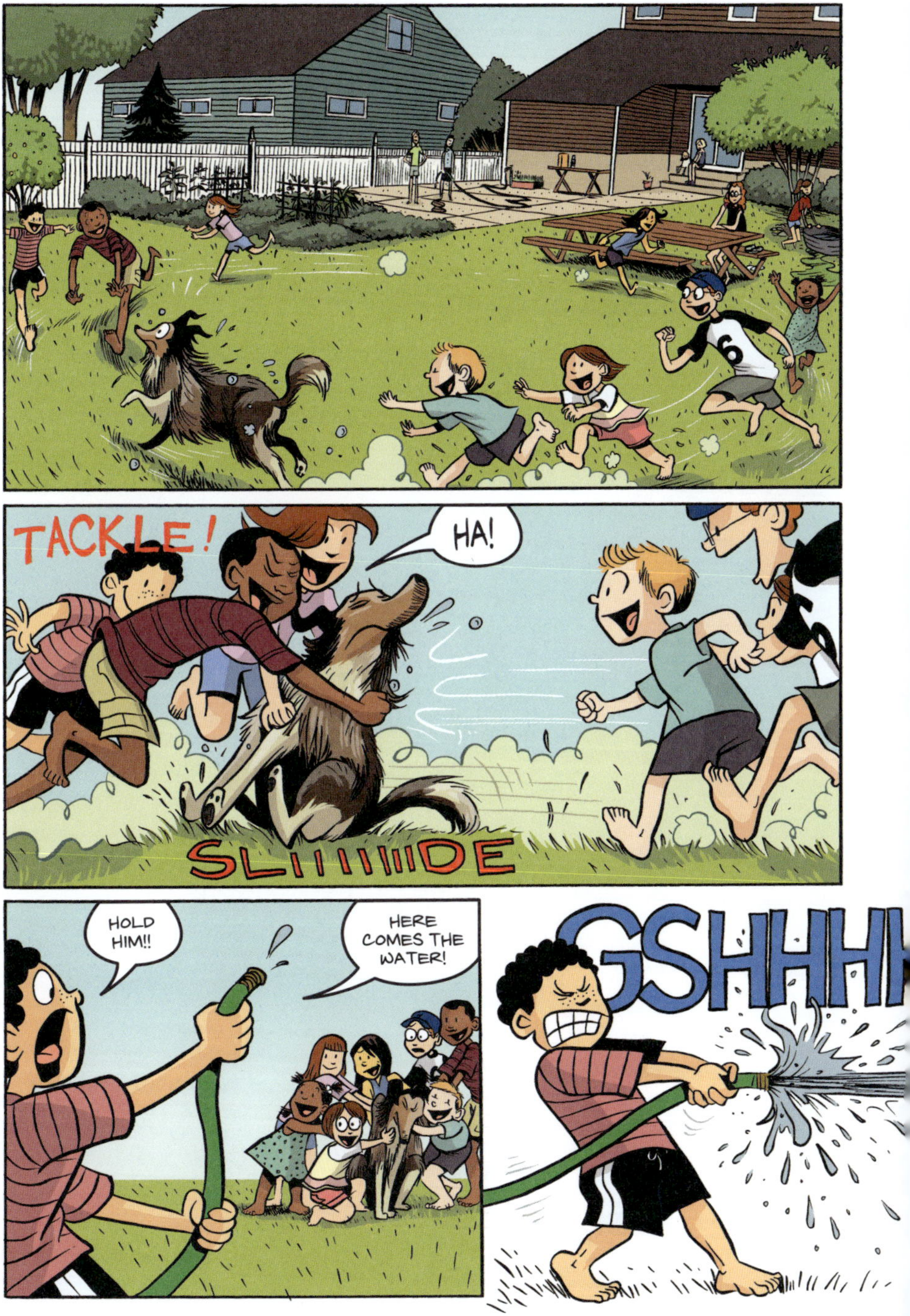
TACKLE!
HA!
SLIIIIIIIDE
HOLD HIM!!
HERE COMES THE WATER!
GSHHH

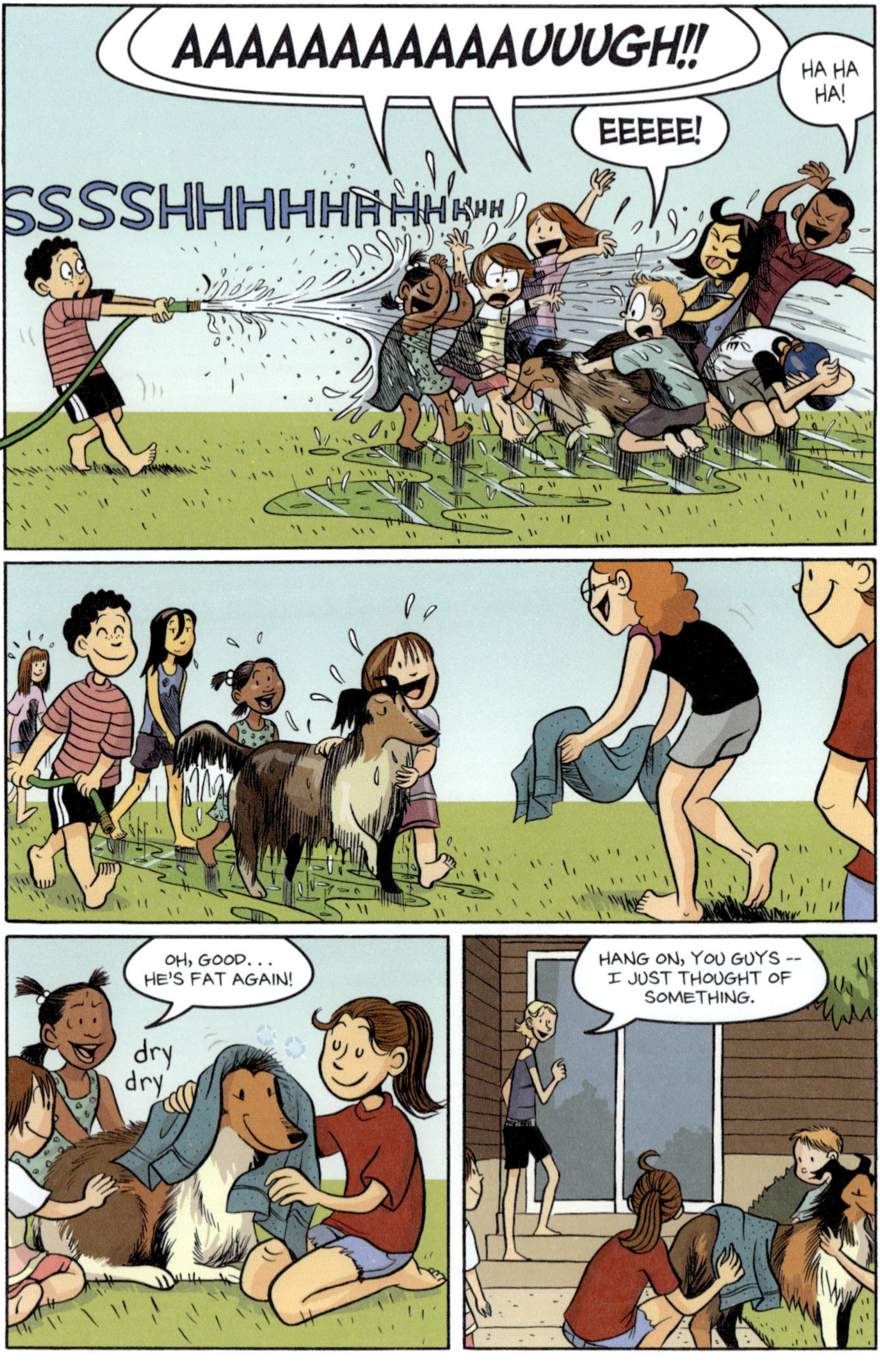
AAAAAAAAAAAAUUUGH!!
HA HA HA!
EEEEE!
SSSSHHHHHHHHHHHH
OH, GOOD. . . HE'S FAT AGAIN!
dry dry
HANG ON, YOU GUYS -- I JUST THOUGHT OF SOMETHING.

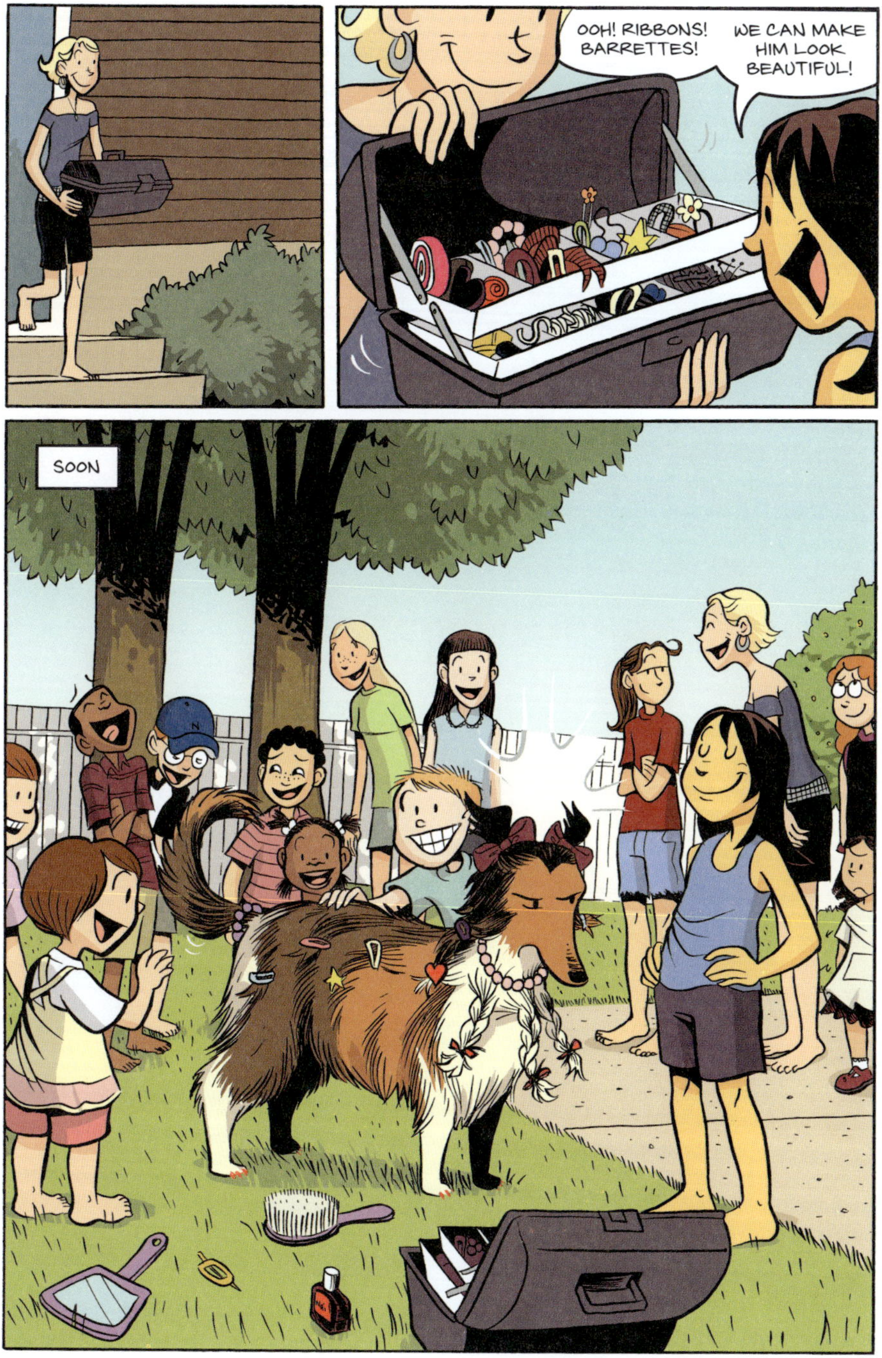
OOH! RIBBONS! BARRETTES!
WE CAN MAKE HIM LOOK BEAUTIFUL!
SOON

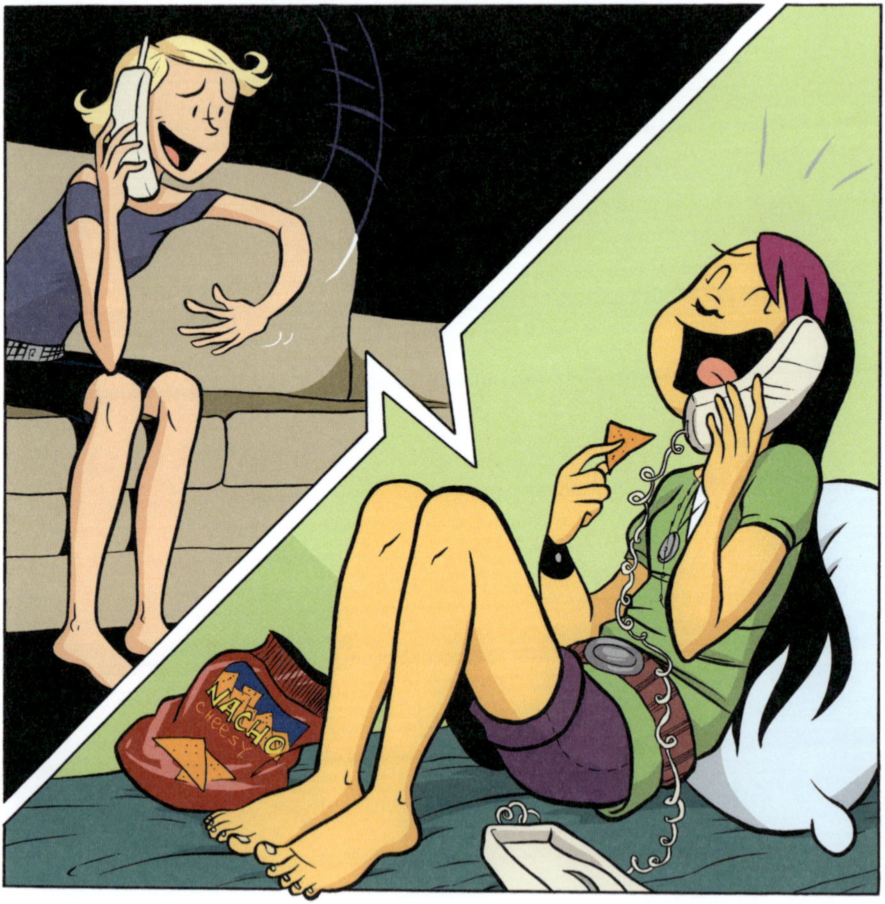
NACHO
CHEESY

CHAPTER 13

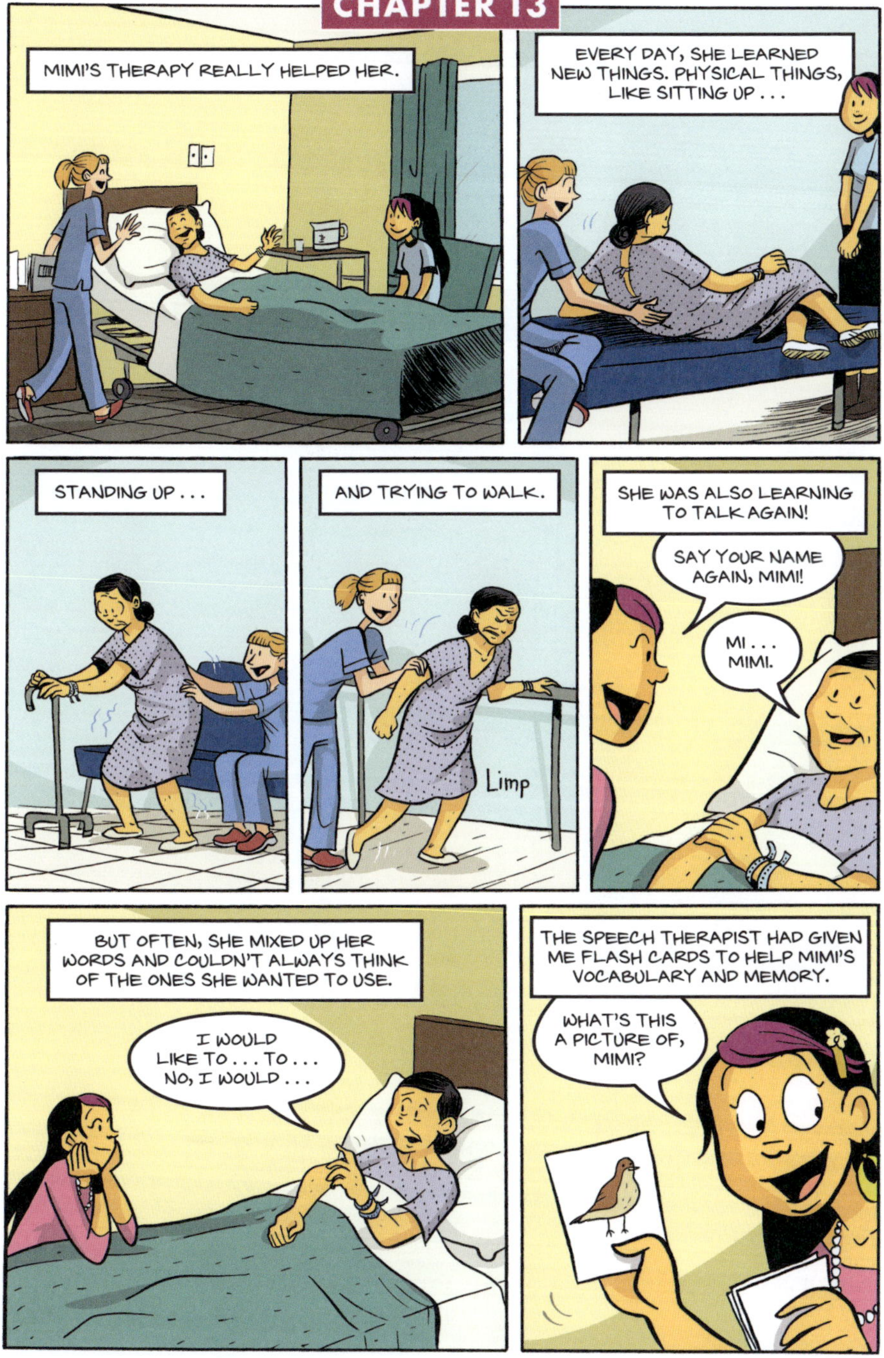

MIMI'S THERAPY REALLY HELPED HER.
EVERY DAY, SHE LEARNED NEW THINGS. PHYSICAL THINGS, LIKE SITTING UP . . .
STANDING UP . . .
AND TRYING TO WALK.
Limp
SHE WAS ALSO LEARNING TO TALK AGAIN!
SAY YOUR NAME AGAIN, MIMI!
MI . . . MIMI.
BUT OFTEN, SHE MIXED UP HER WORDS AND COULDN'T ALWAYS THINK OF THE ONES SHE WANTED TO USE.
I WOULD LIKE TO . . . TO . . . NO, I WOULD . . .
THE SPEECH THERAPIST HAD GIVEN ME FLASH CARDS TO HELP MIMI'S VOCABULARY AND MEMORY.
WHAT'S THIS A PICTURE OF, MIMI?

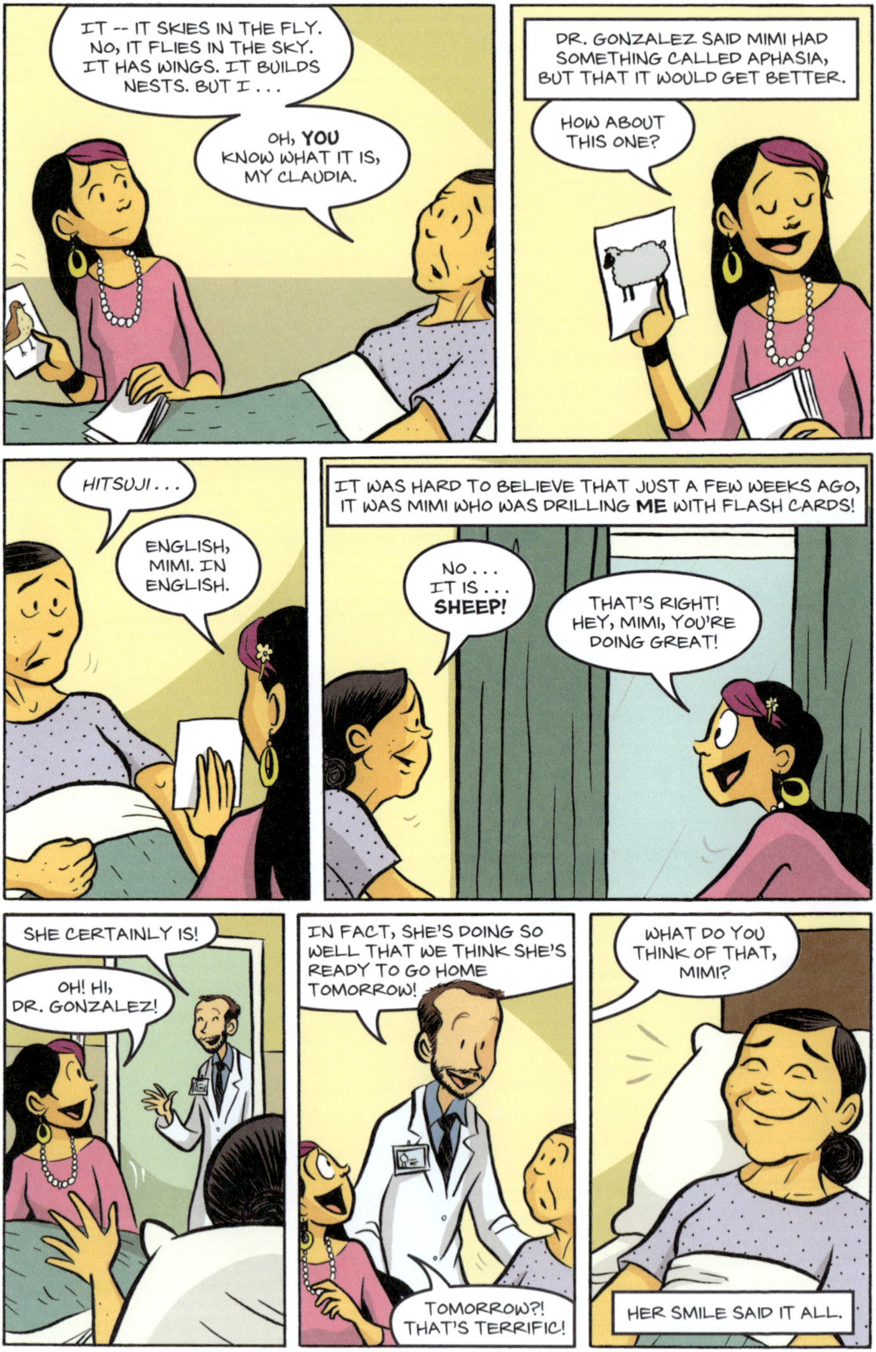
IT -- IT SKIES IN THE FLY. NO, IT FLIES IN THE SKY. IT HAS WINGS. IT BUILDS NESTS. BUT I . . .
OH, **YOU** KNOW WHAT IT IS, MY CLAUDIA.
DR. GONZALEZ SAID MIMI HAD SOMETHING CALLED APHASIA, BUT THAT IT WOULD GET BETTER.
HOW ABOUT THIS ONE?
HITSUJI . . .
ENGLISH, MIMI. IN ENGLISH.
IT WAS HARD TO BELIEVE THAT JUST A FEW WEEKS AGO, IT WAS MIMI WHO WAS DRILLING **ME** WITH FLASH CARDS!
NO . . . IT IS . . . **SHEEP!**
THAT'S RIGHT! HEY, MIMI, YOU'RE DOING GREAT!
SHE CERTAINLY IS!
OH! HI, DR. GONZALEZ!
IN FACT, SHE'S DOING SO WELL THAT WE THINK SHE'S READY TO GO HOME TOMORROW!
TOMORROW?! THAT'S TERRIFIC!
WHAT DO YOU THINK OF THAT, MIMI?
HER SMILE SAID IT ALL.

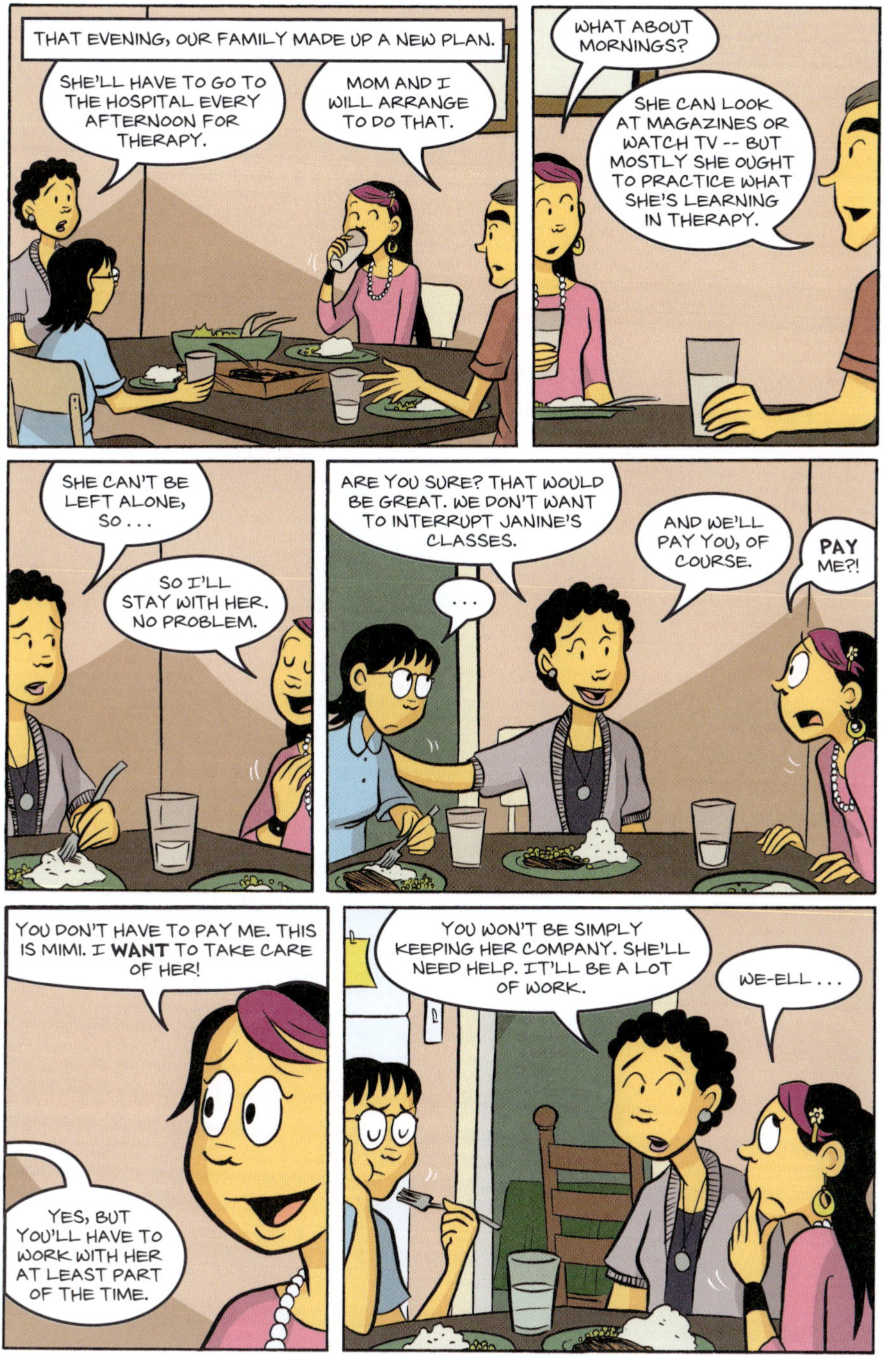
THAT EVENING, OUR FAMILY MADE UP A NEW PLAN.
SHE'LL HAVE TO GO TO THE HOSPITAL EVERY AFTERNOON FOR THERAPY.
MOM AND I WILL ARRANGE TO DO THAT.
WHAT ABOUT MORNINGS?
SHE CAN LOOK AT MAGAZINES OR WATCH TV -- BUT MOSTLY SHE OUGHT TO PRACTICE WHAT SHE'S LEARNING IN THERAPY.
SHE CAN'T BE LEFT ALONE, SO . . .
SO I'LL STAY WITH HER. NO PROBLEM.
ARE YOU SURE? THAT WOULD BE GREAT. WE DON'T WANT TO INTERRUPT JANINE'S CLASSES.
. . .
AND WE'LL PAY YOU, OF COURSE.
PAY ME?!
YOU DON'T HAVE TO PAY ME. THIS IS MIMI. I **WANT** TO TAKE CARE OF HER!
YES, BUT YOU'LL HAVE TO WORK WITH HER AT LEAST PART OF THE TIME.
YOU WON'T BE SIMPLY KEEPING HER COMPANY. SHE'LL NEED HELP. IT'LL BE A LOT OF WORK.
WE-ELL . . .

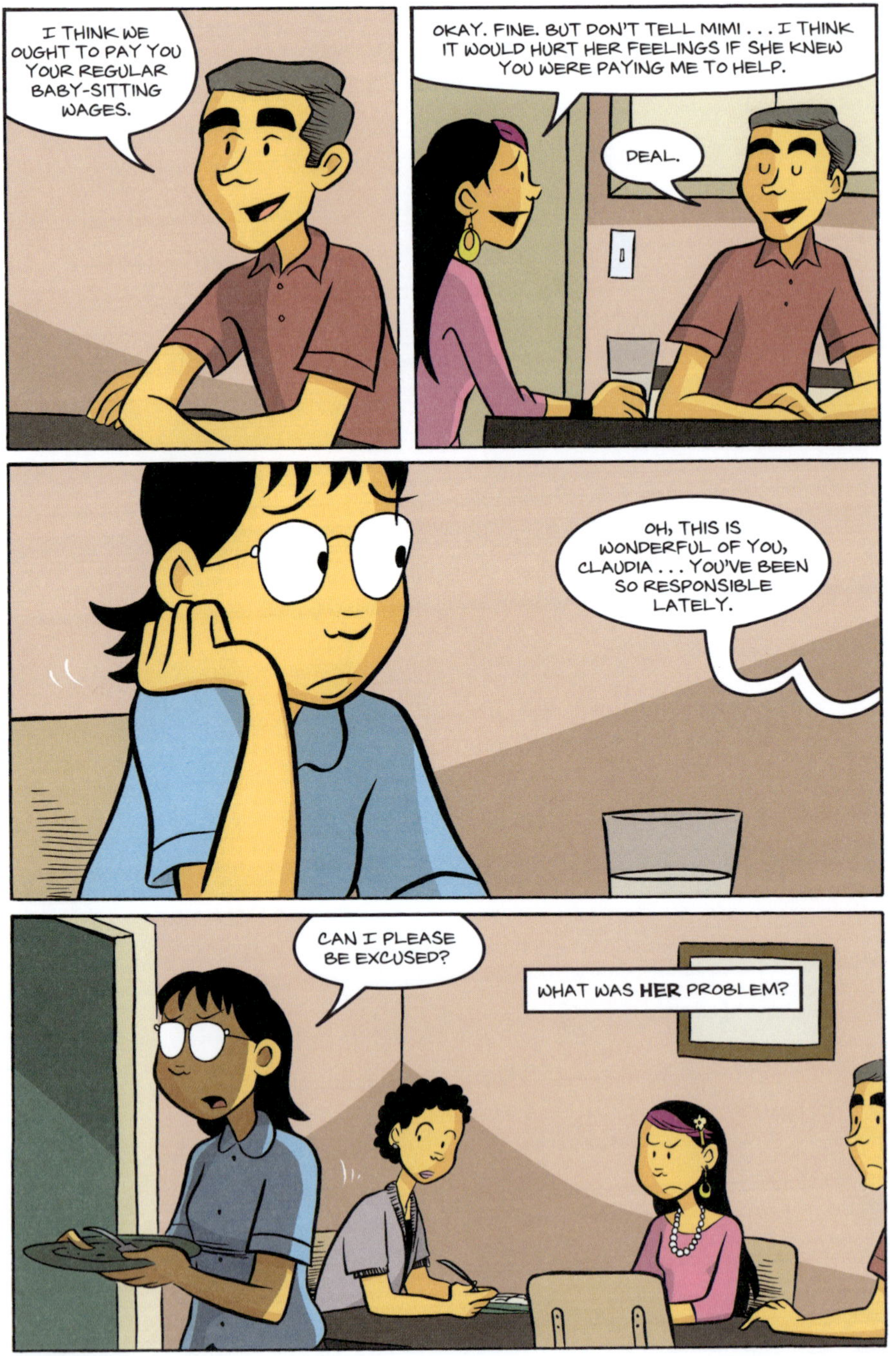
I THINK WE OUGHT TO PAY YOU YOUR REGULAR BABY-SITTING WAGES.
OKAY. FINE. BUT DON'T TELL MIMI . . . I THINK IT WOULD HURT HER FEELINGS IF SHE KNEW YOU WERE PAYING ME TO HELP.
DEAL.
OH, THIS IS WONDERFUL OF YOU, CLAUDIA . . . YOU'VE BEEN SO RESPONSIBLE LATELY.
CAN I PLEASE BE EXCUSED?
WHAT WAS **HER** PROBLEM?

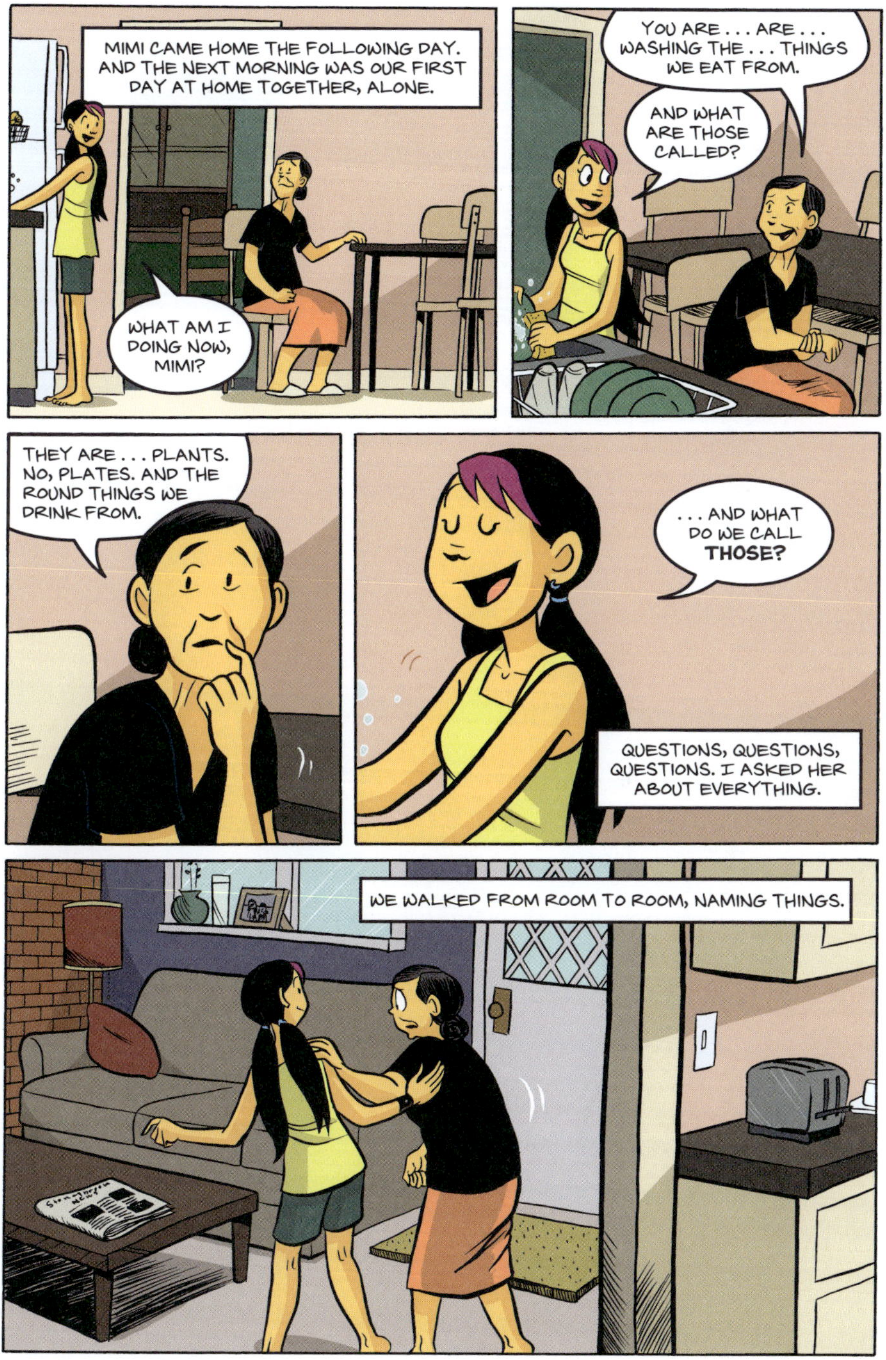
MIMI CAME HOME THE FOLLOWING DAY. AND THE NEXT MORNING WAS OUR FIRST DAY AT HOME TOGETHER, ALONE.
WHAT AM I DOING NOW, MIMI?
YOU ARE . . . ARE . . . WASHING THE . . . THINGS WE EAT FROM.
AND WHAT ARE THOSE CALLED?
THEY ARE . . . PLANTS. NO, PLATES. AND THE ROUND THINGS WE DRINK FROM.
. . . AND WHAT DO WE CALL **THOSE?**
QUESTIONS, QUESTIONS, QUESTIONS. I ASKED HER ABOUT EVERYTHING.
WE WALKED FROM ROOM TO ROOM, NAMING THINGS.

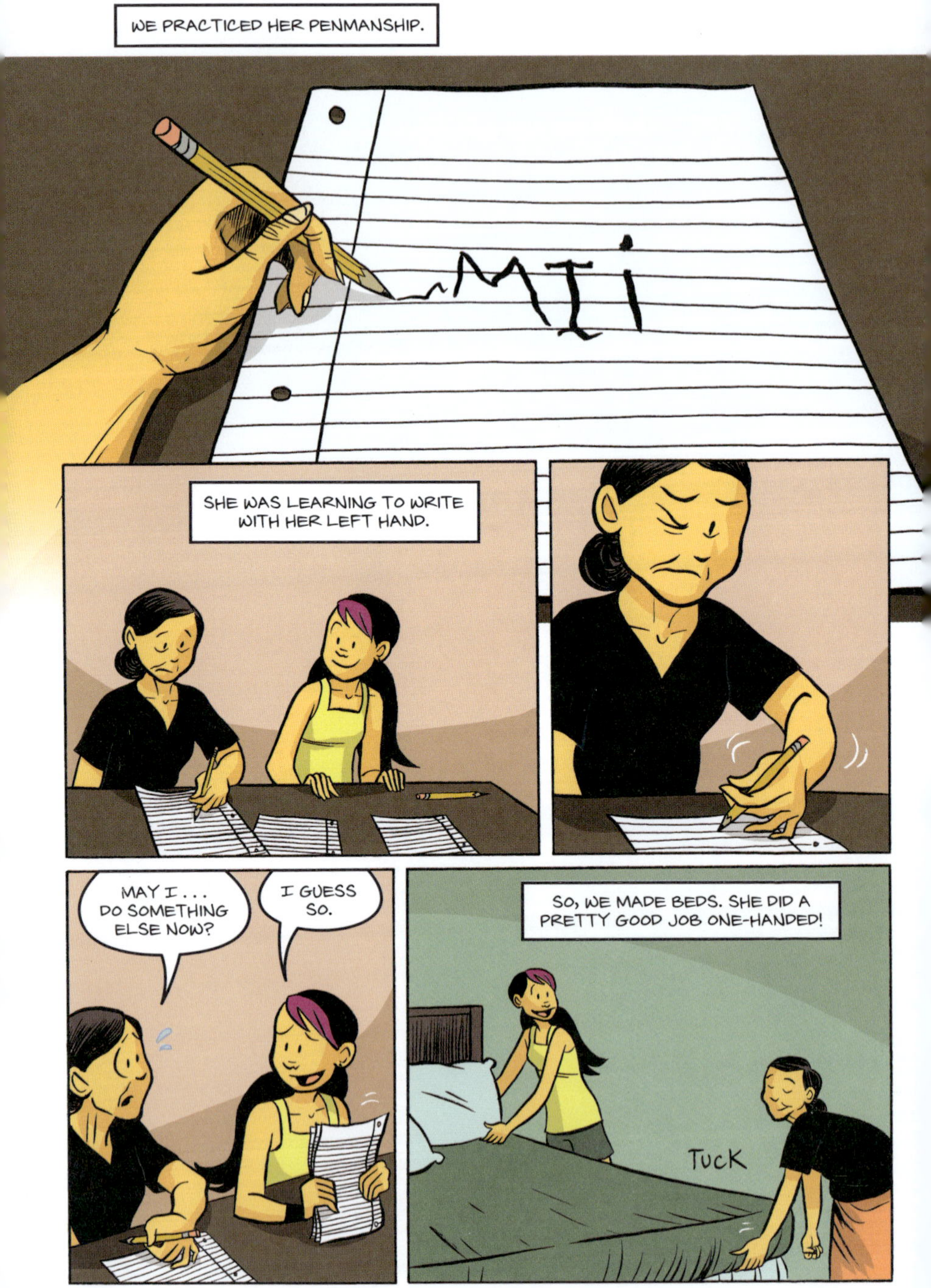

WE PRACTICED HER PENMANSHIP.
MII
SHE WAS LEARNING TO WRITE WITH HER LEFT HAND.
MAY I . . . DO SOMETHING ELSE NOW?
I GUESS SO.
SO, WE MADE BEDS. SHE DID A PRETTY GOOD JOB ONE-HANDED!
TUCK

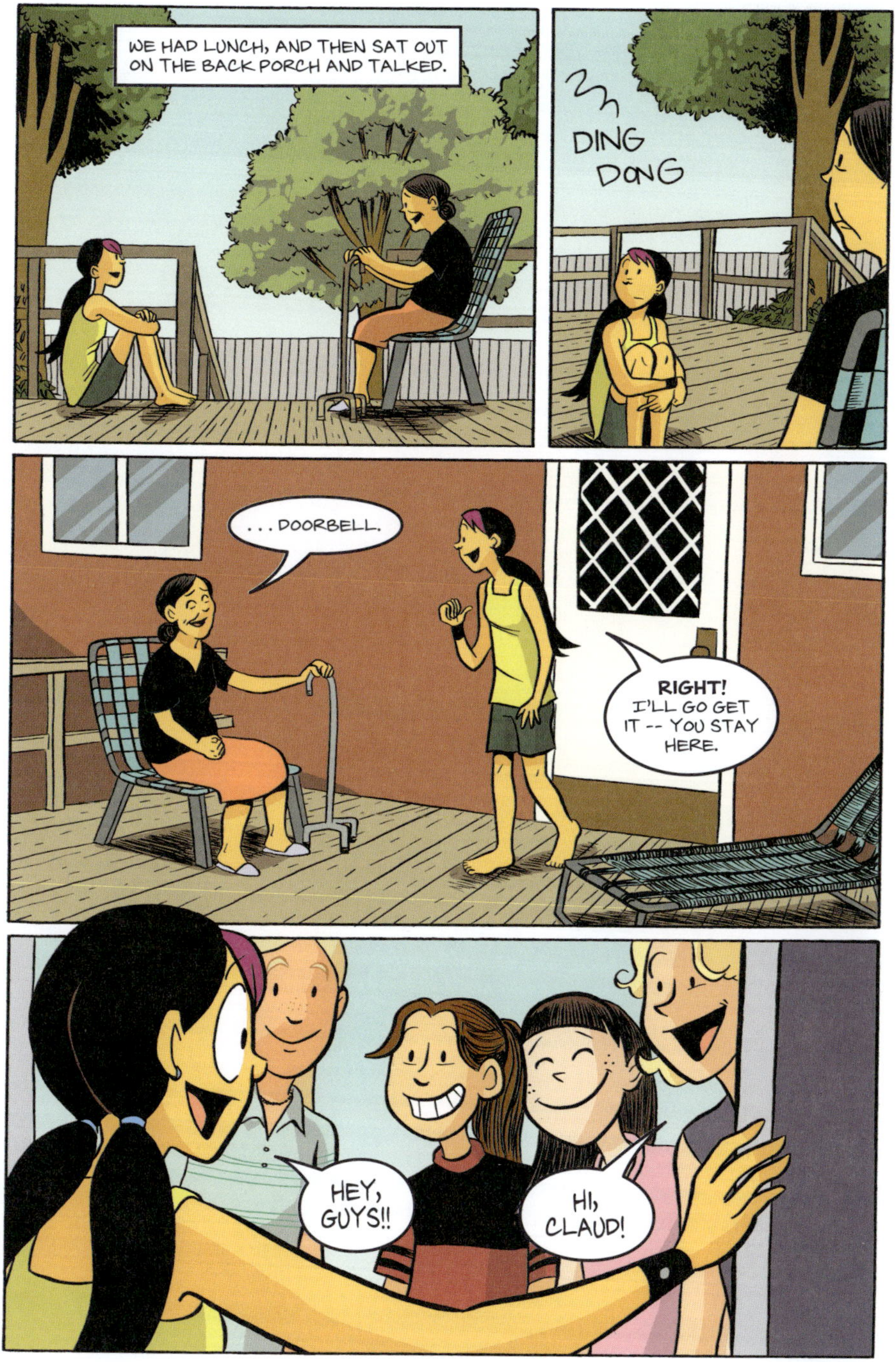
WE HAD LUNCH, AND THEN SAT OUT ON THE BACK PORCH AND TALKED.
DING DONG
...DOORBELL.
RIGHT! I'LL GO GET IT -- YOU STAY HERE.
HEY, GUYS!!
HI, CLAUD!

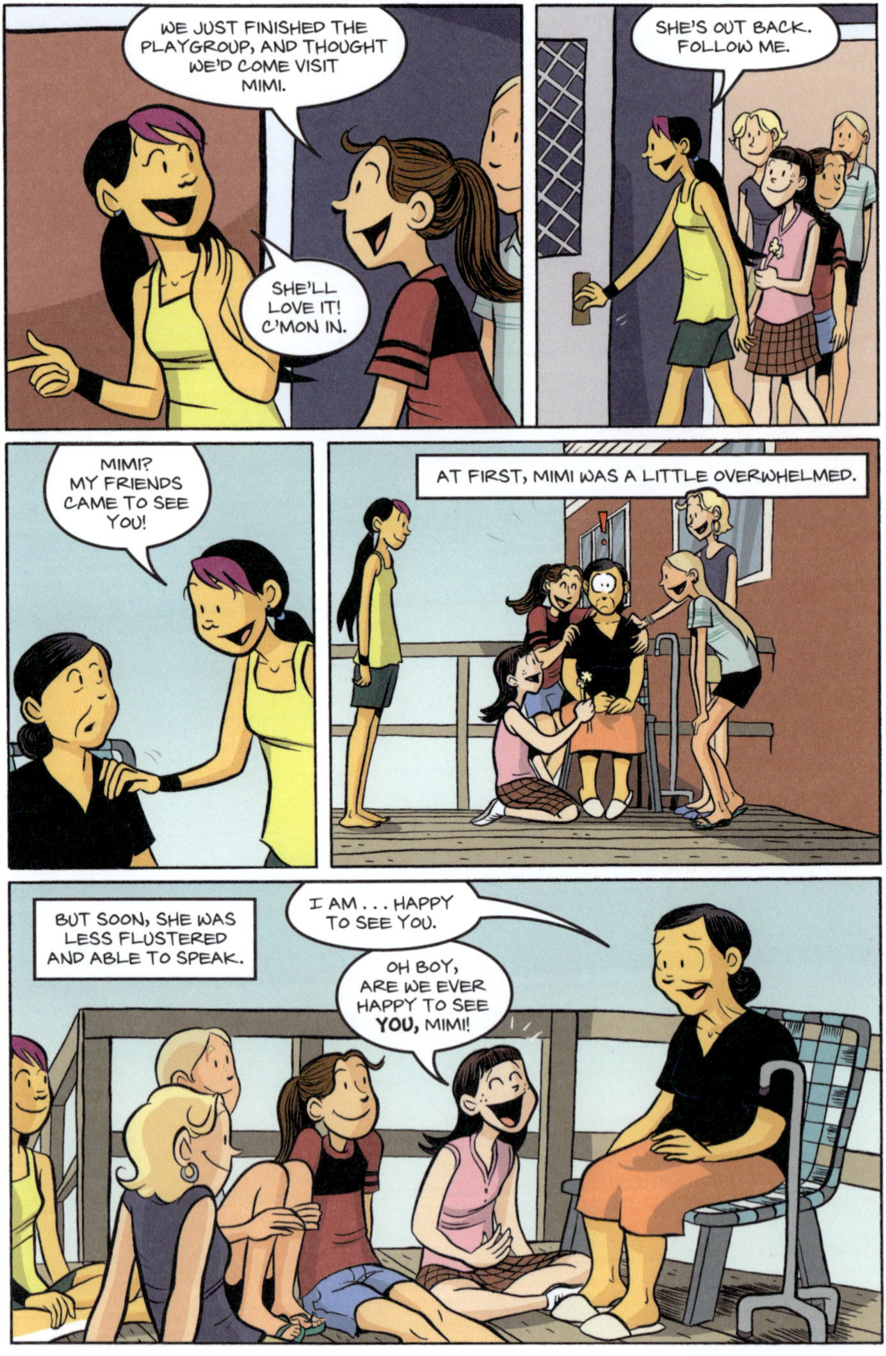
WE JUST FINISHED THE PLAYGROUP, AND THOUGHT WE'D COME VISIT MIMI.
SHE'LL LOVE IT! C'MON IN.
SHE'S OUT BACK. FOLLOW ME.
MIMI? MY FRIENDS CAME TO SEE YOU!
AT FIRST, MIMI WAS A LITTLE OVERWHELMED.
BUT SOON, SHE WAS LESS FLUSTERED AND ABLE TO SPEAK.
I AM . . . HAPPY TO SEE YOU.
OH BOY, ARE WE EVER HAPPY TO SEE **YOU,** MIMI!

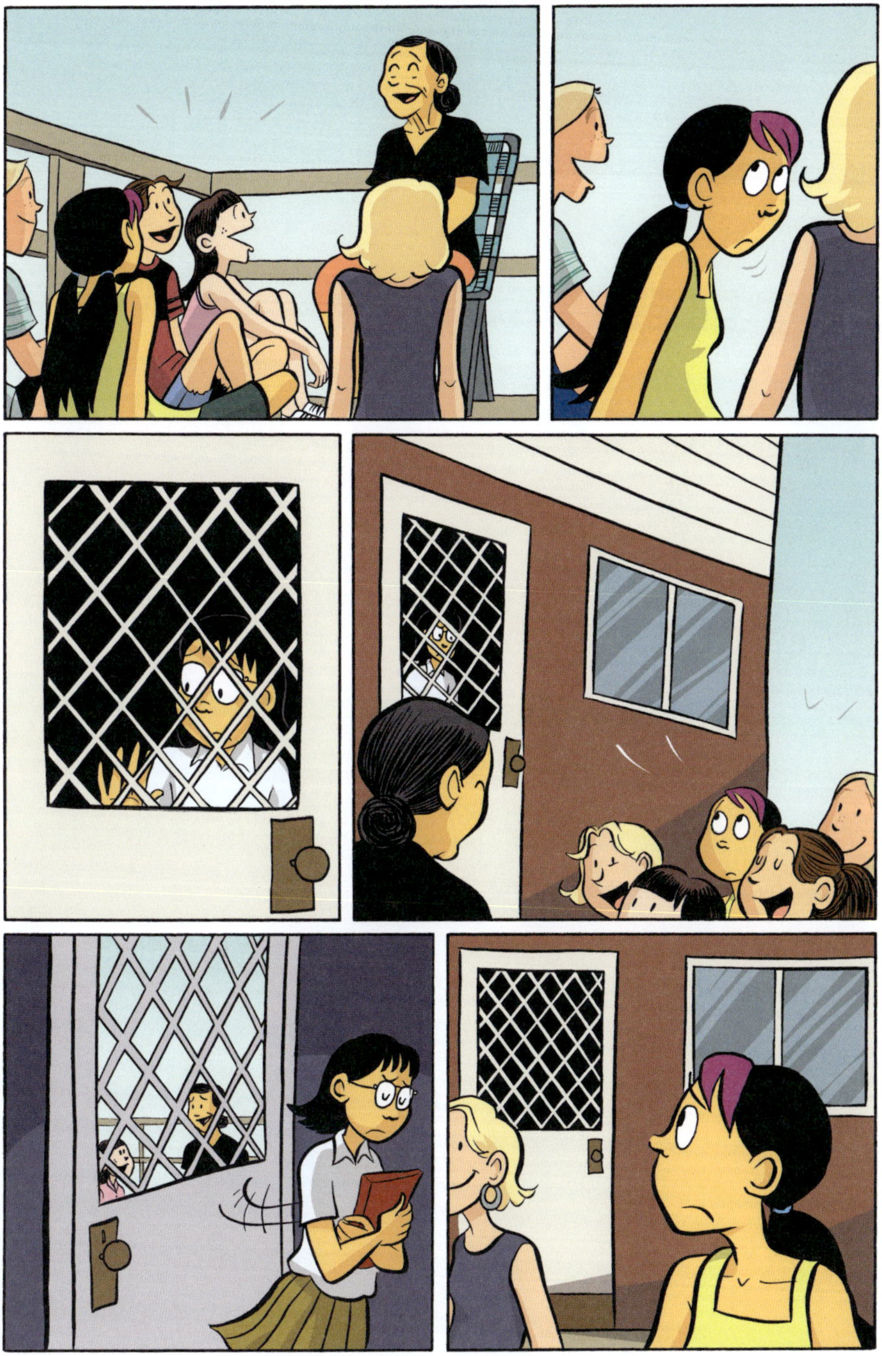

Friday, July 18

This morning I didn't baby-sit...
<u>I Mimi-sat!</u>

Claudia was helping out at the Newtons' all day, so Mrs. Kishi asked if I could stay with Mimi. I was happy to, of course, but I wasn't expecting Mimi to be so different. She can't even remember the simplest things sometimes.

In case any of you stays with Mimi while she's getting better, you should know that she gets upset easily. Frustrated, I guess. She yelled at me and Mimi has never, ever yelled at me. In fact, Claudia told me later that Mimi has never yelled at anyone in their family, so I assume Mimi was embarrassed about needing a sitter in the first place.

       Mary Anne

CHAPTER 14

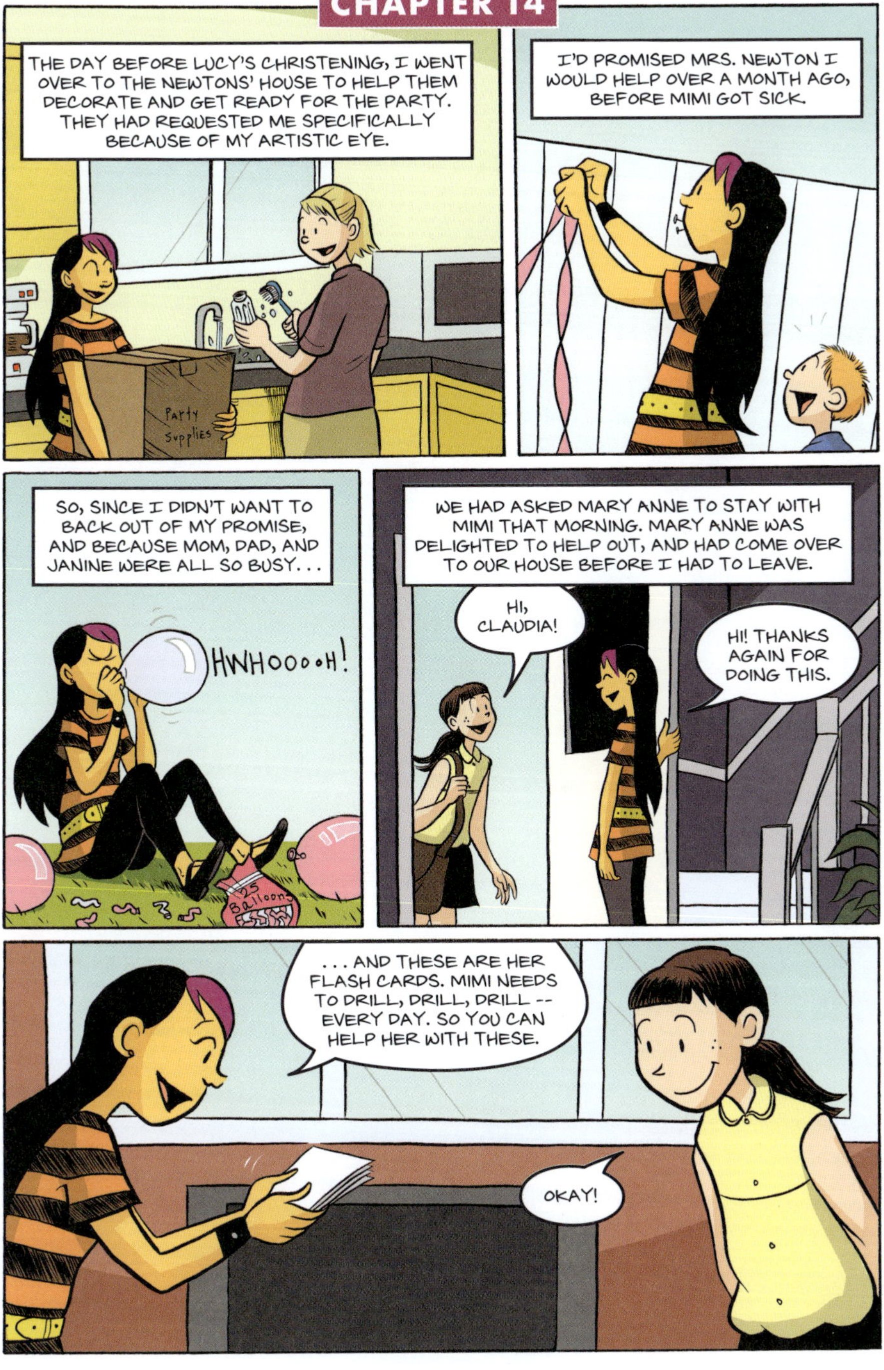

THE DAY BEFORE LUCY'S CHRISTENING, I WENT OVER TO THE NEWTONS' HOUSE TO HELP THEM DECORATE AND GET READY FOR THE PARTY. THEY HAD REQUESTED ME SPECIFICALLY BECAUSE OF MY ARTISTIC EYE.
Party Supplies
I'D PROMISED MRS. NEWTON I WOULD HELP OVER A MONTH AGO, BEFORE MIMI GOT SICK.
SO, SINCE I DIDN'T WANT TO BACK OUT OF MY PROMISE, AND BECAUSE MOM, DAD, AND JANINE WERE ALL SO BUSY...
HWHOOOOOH!
25 Balloons
WE HAD ASKED MARY ANNE TO STAY WITH MIMI THAT MORNING. MARY ANNE WAS DELIGHTED TO HELP OUT, AND HAD COME OVER TO OUR HOUSE BEFORE I HAD TO LEAVE.
HI, CLAUDIA!
HI! THANKS AGAIN FOR DOING THIS.
...AND THESE ARE HER FLASH CARDS. MIMI NEEDS TO DRILL, DRILL, DRILL -- EVERY DAY. SO YOU CAN HELP HER WITH THESE.
OKAY!

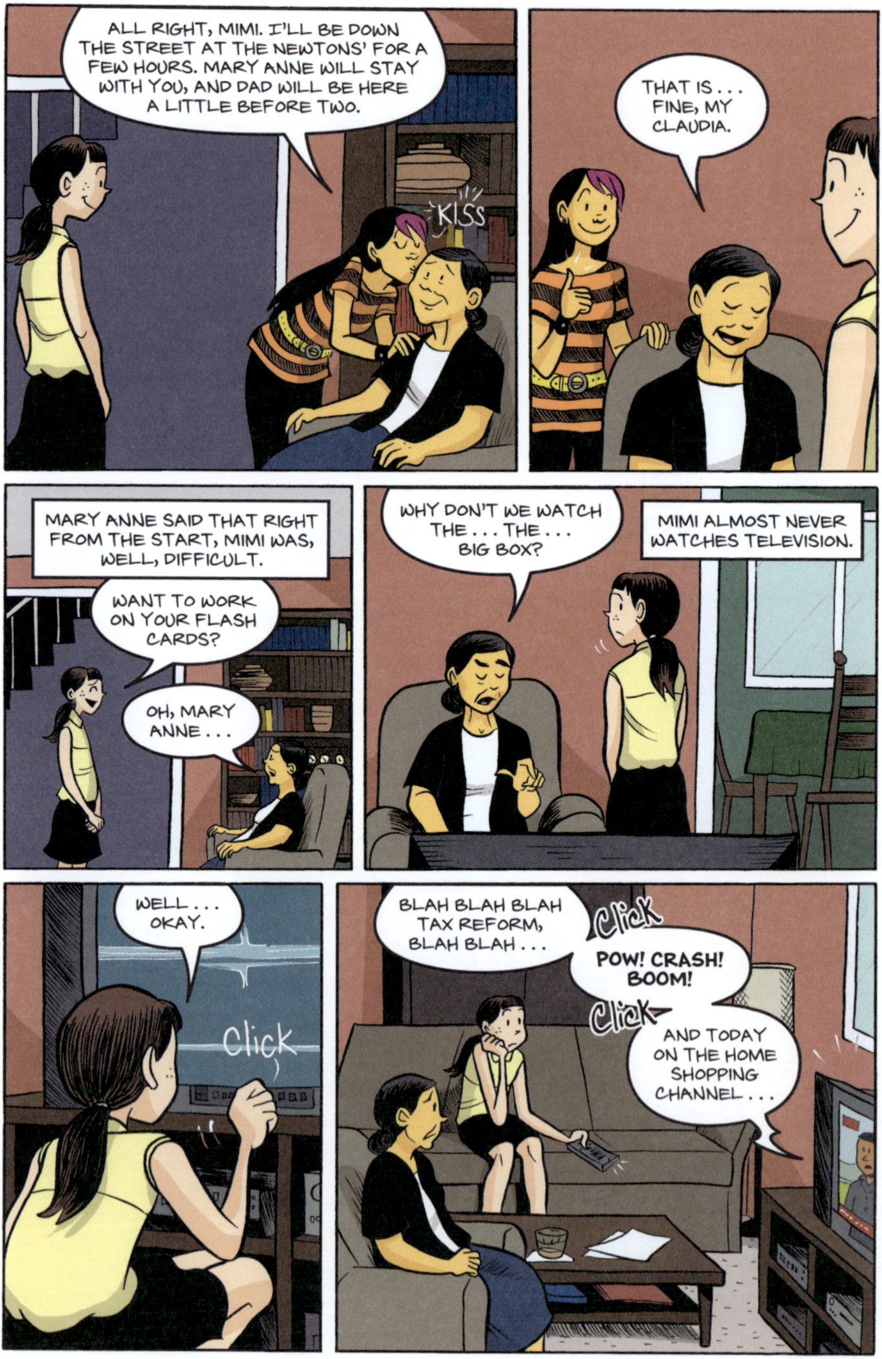
ALL RIGHT, MIMI. I'LL BE DOWN THE STREET AT THE NEWTONS' FOR A FEW HOURS. MARY ANNE WILL STAY WITH YOU, AND DAD WILL BE HERE A LITTLE BEFORE TWO.
KISS
THAT IS . . . FINE, MY CLAUDIA.
MARY ANNE SAID THAT RIGHT FROM THE START, MIMI WAS, WELL, DIFFICULT.
WANT TO WORK ON YOUR FLASH CARDS?
OH, MARY ANNE . . .
WHY DON'T WE WATCH THE . . . THE . . . BIG BOX?
MIMI ALMOST NEVER WATCHES TELEVISION.
WELL . . . OKAY.
CLICK
BLAH BLAH BLAH TAX REFORM, BLAH BLAH . . .
CLICK
POW! CRASH! BOOM!
CLICK
AND TODAY ON THE HOME SHOPPING CHANNEL . . .

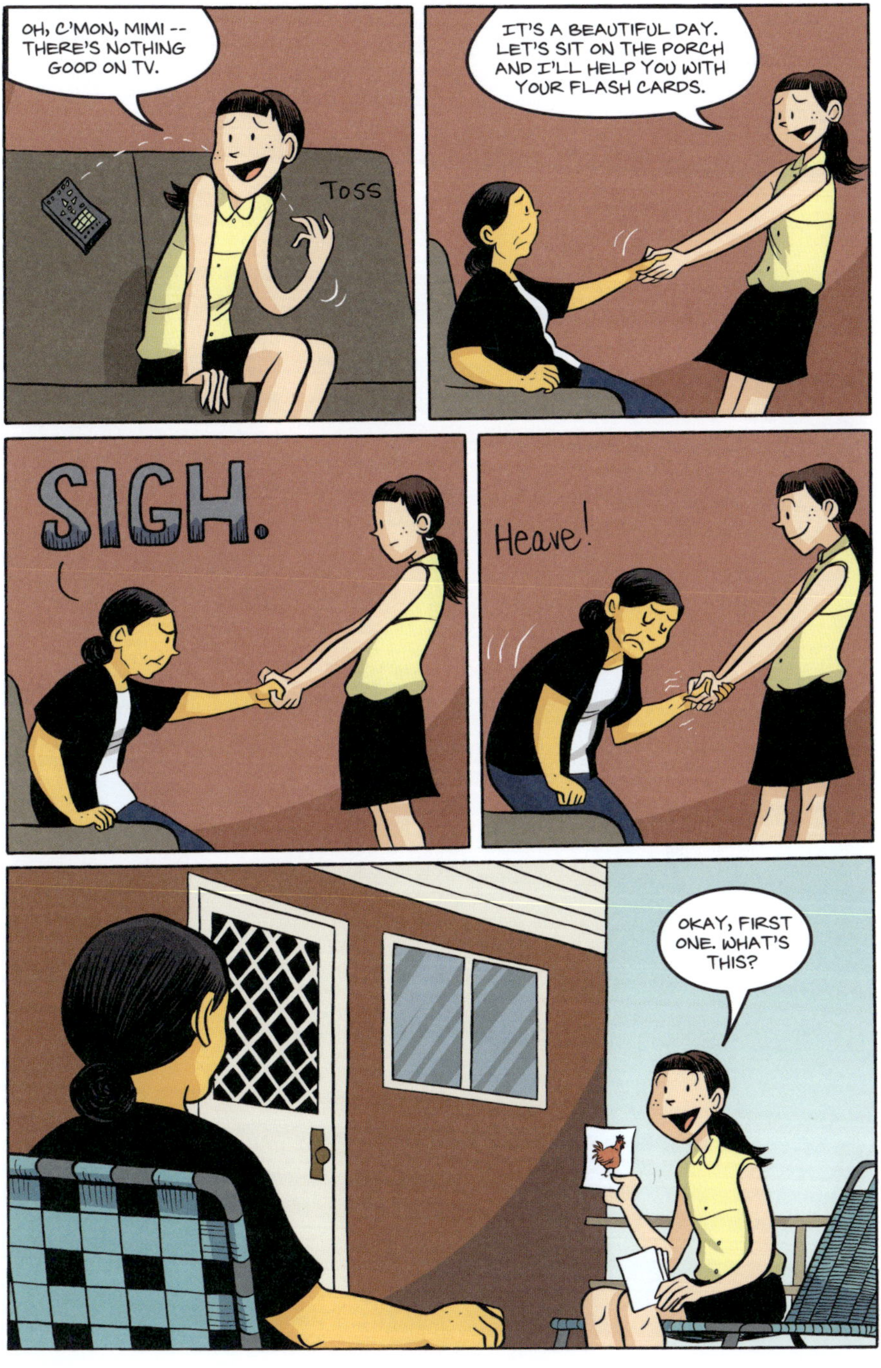
OH, C'MON, MIMI -- THERE'S NOTHING GOOD ON TV.
TOSS
IT'S A BEAUTIFUL DAY. LET'S SIT ON THE PORCH AND I'LL HELP YOU WITH YOUR FLASH CARDS.
SIGH.
Heave!
OKAY, FIRST ONE. WHAT'S THIS?

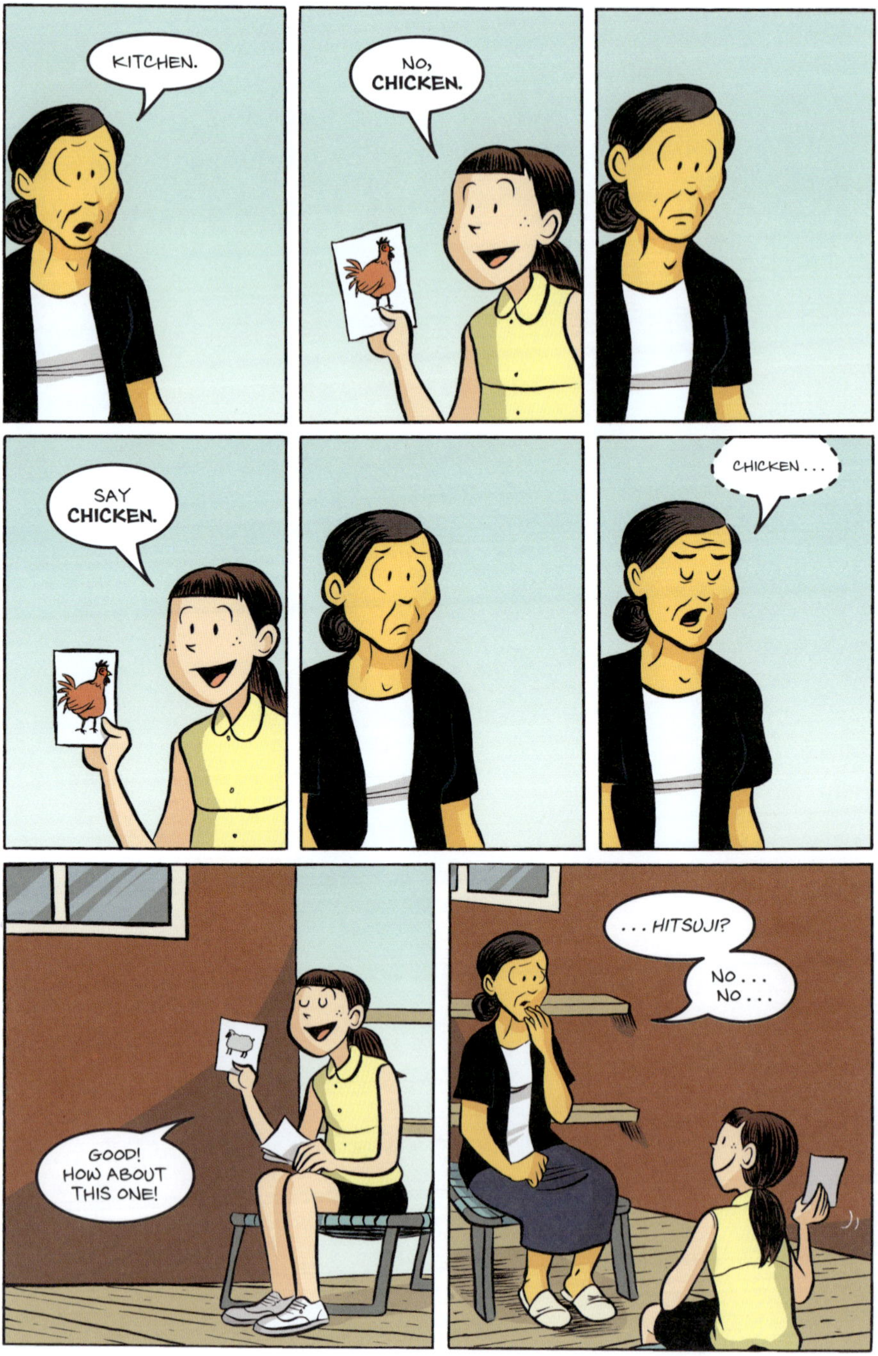
KITCHEN.
NO, CHICKEN.
SAY CHICKEN.
CHICKEN . . .
GOOD! HOW ABOUT THIS ONE!
. . . HITSUJI?
NO . . . NO . . .

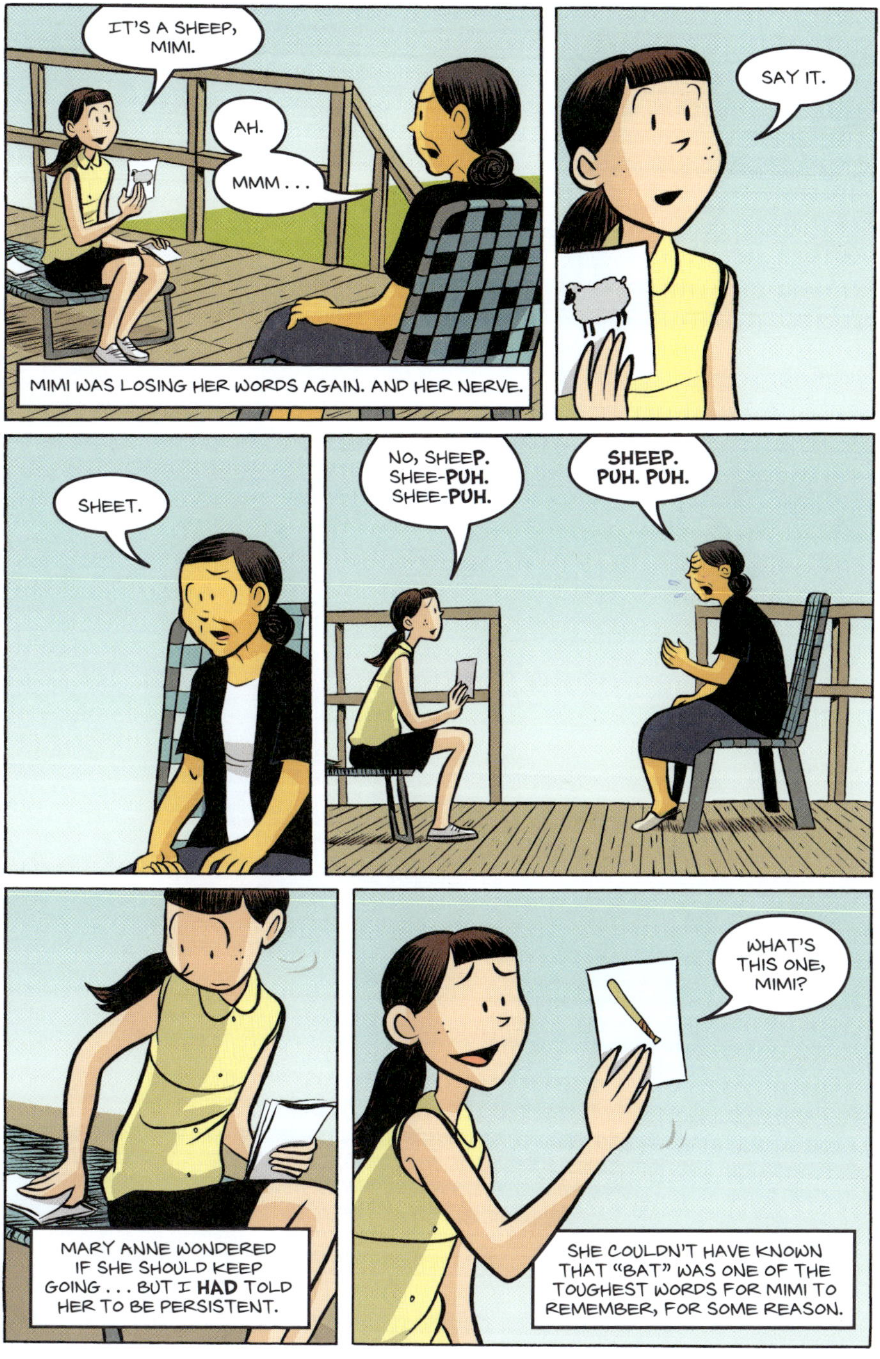
IT'S A SHEEP, MIMI.
AH.
MMM . . .
MIMI WAS LOSING HER WORDS AGAIN. AND HER NERVE.
SAY IT.
SHEET.
NO, SHEEP. SHEE-PUH. SHEE-PUH.
SHEEP. PUH. PUH.
MARY ANNE WONDERED IF SHE SHOULD KEEP GOING . . . BUT I HAD TOLD HER TO BE PERSISTENT.
WHAT'S THIS ONE, MIMI?
SHE COULDN'T HAVE KNOWN THAT "BAT" WAS ONE OF THE TOUGHEST WORDS FOR MIMI TO REMEMBER, FOR SOME REASON.

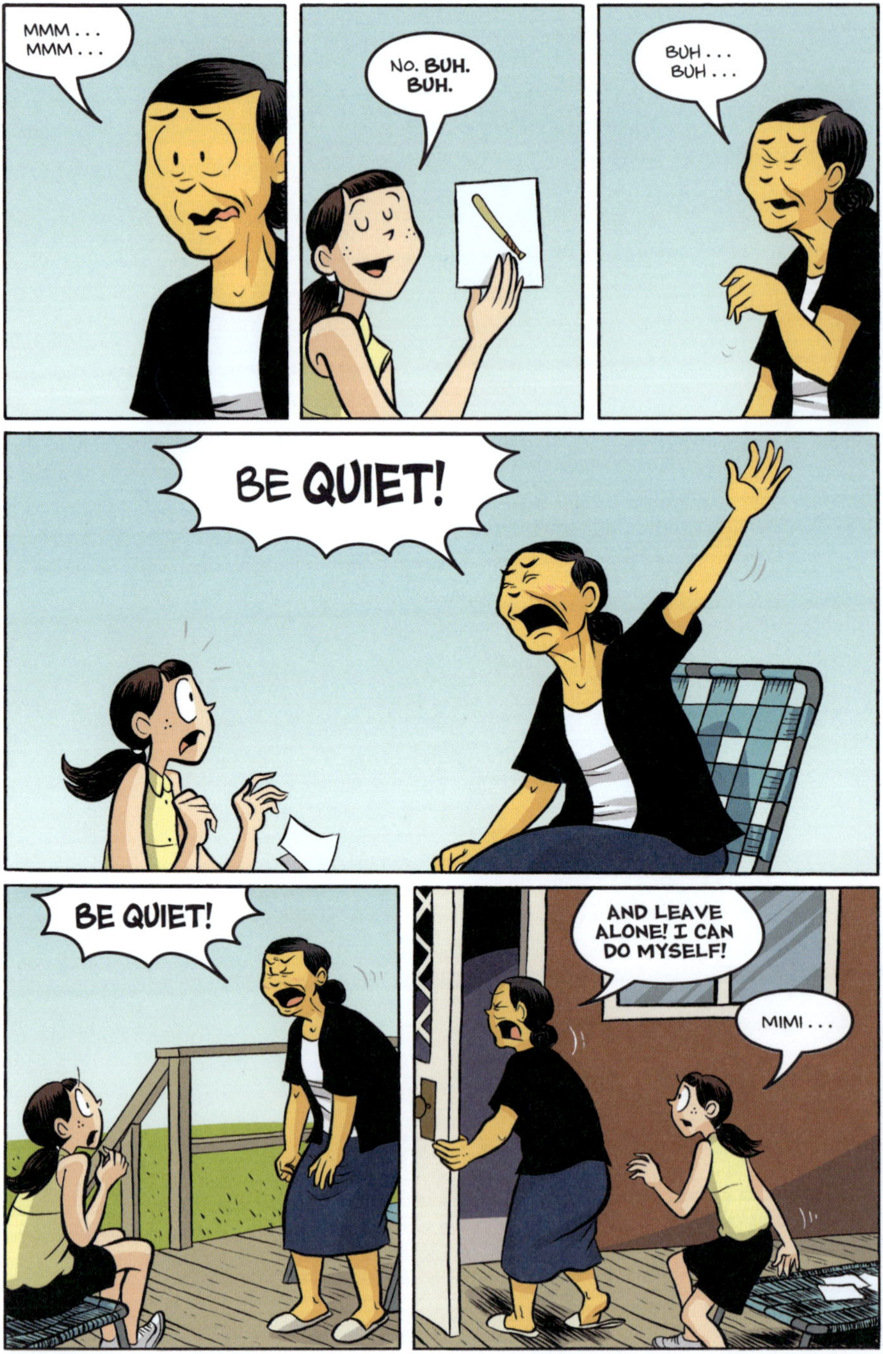
MMM . . .
MMM . . .
NO. BUH. BUH.
BUH . . .
BUH . . .
BE QUIET!
BE QUIET!
AND LEAVE ALONE! I CAN DO MYSELF!
MIMI . . .

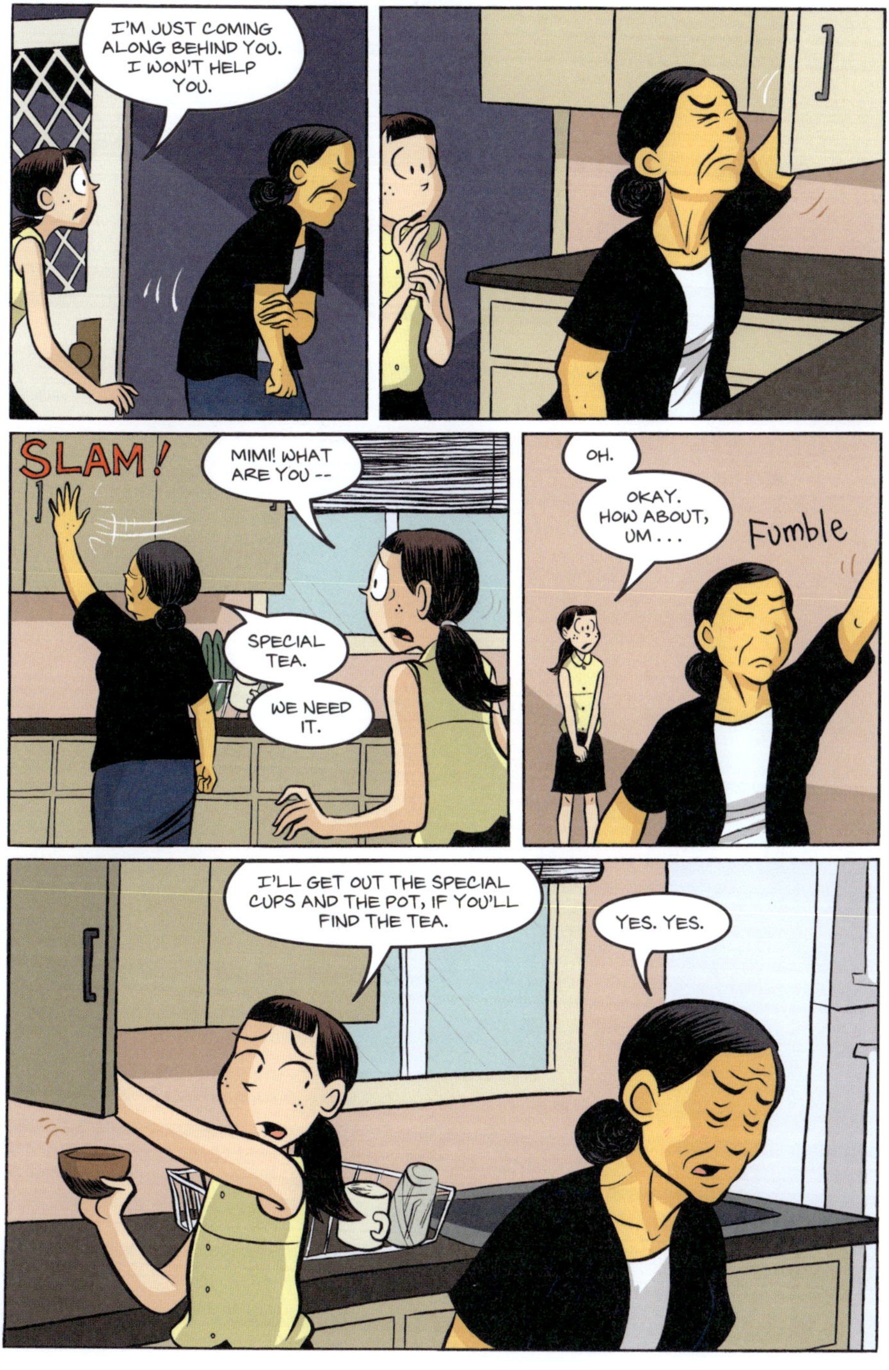
I'M JUST COMING ALONG BEHIND YOU. I WON'T HELP YOU.
SLAM!
MIMI! WHAT ARE YOU --
SPECIAL TEA.
WE NEED IT.
OH.
OKAY. HOW ABOUT, UM . . .
Fumble
I'LL GET OUT THE SPECIAL CUPS AND THE POT, IF YOU'LL FIND THE TEA.
YES. YES.

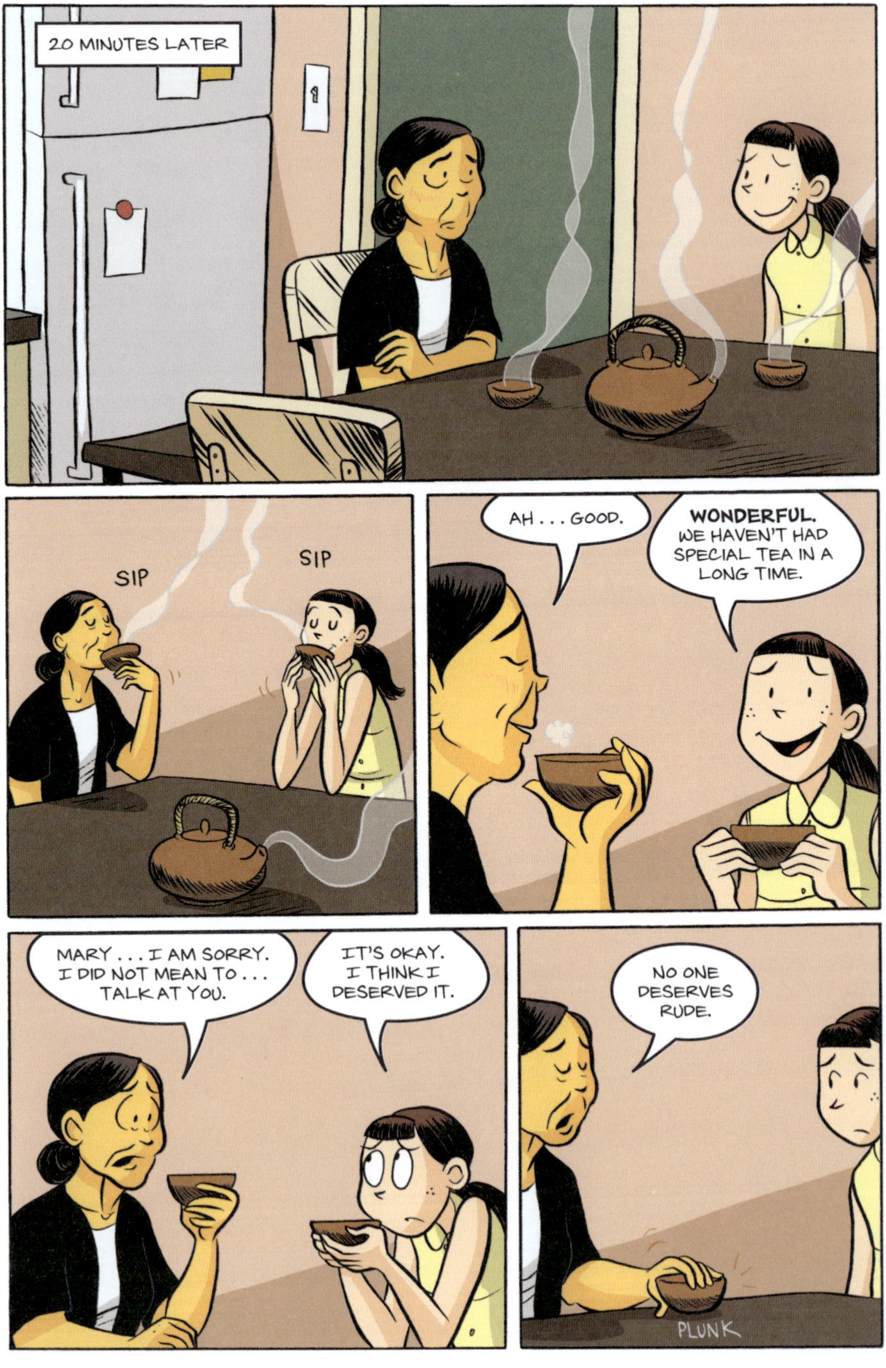
20 MINUTES LATER
SIP
SIP
AH . . . GOOD.
WONDERFUL. WE HAVEN'T HAD SPECIAL TEA IN A LONG TIME.
MARY . . . I AM SORRY. I DID NOT MEAN TO . . . TALK AT YOU.
IT'S OKAY. I THINK I DESERVED IT.
NO ONE DESERVES RUDE.
PLUNK

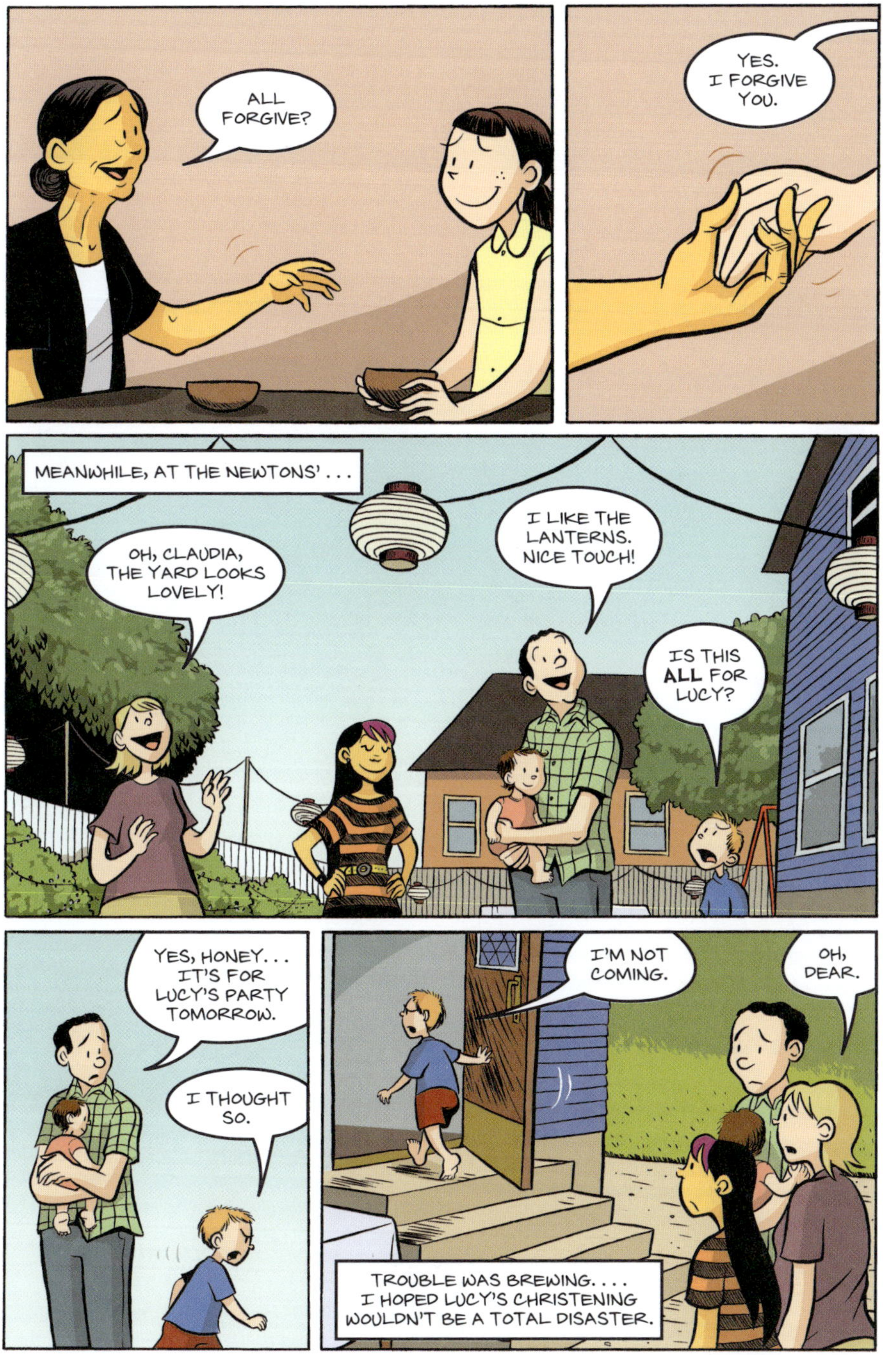
ALL FORGIVE?
YES. I FORGIVE YOU.
MEANWHILE, AT THE NEWTONS' . . .
OH, CLAUDIA, THE YARD LOOKS LOVELY!
I LIKE THE LANTERNS. NICE TOUCH!
IS THIS **ALL** FOR LUCY?
YES, HONEY. . . IT'S FOR LUCY'S PARTY TOMORROW.
I THOUGHT SO.
I'M NOT COMING.
OH, DEAR.
TROUBLE WAS BREWING. . . . I HOPED LUCY'S CHRISTENING WOULDN'T BE A TOTAL DISASTER.

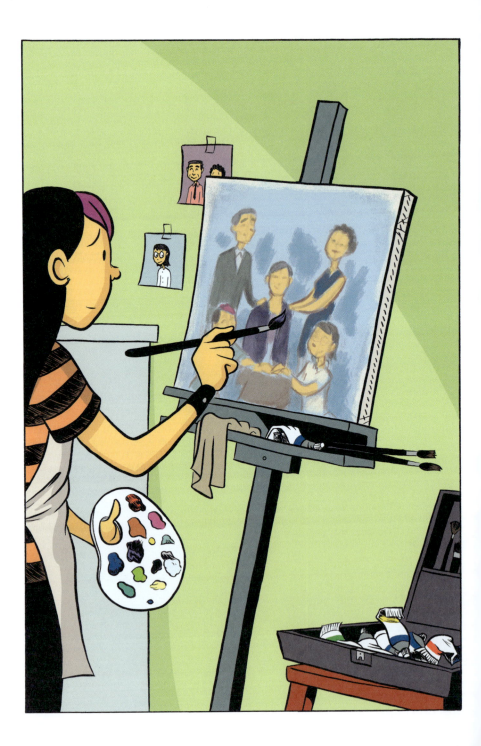

CHAPTER 15

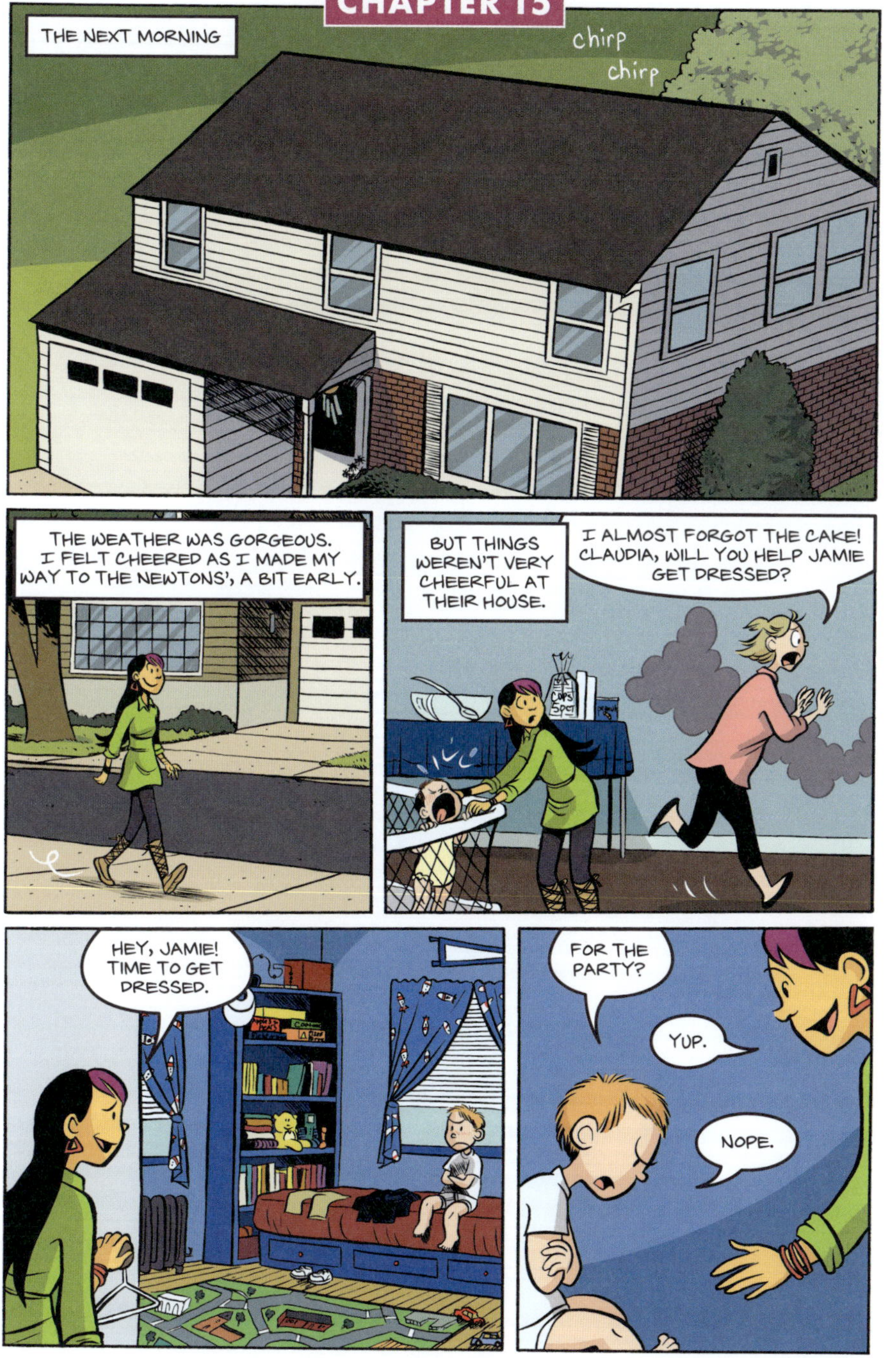
THE NEXT MORNING
chirp
chirp
THE WEATHER WAS GORGEOUS. I FELT CHEERED AS I MADE MY WAY TO THE NEWTONS', A BIT EARLY.
BUT THINGS WEREN'T VERY CHEERFUL AT THEIR HOUSE.
I ALMOST FORGOT THE CAKE! CLAUDIA, WILL YOU HELP JAMIE GET DRESSED?
HEY, JAMIE! TIME TO GET DRESSED.
FOR THE PARTY?
YUP.
NOPE.

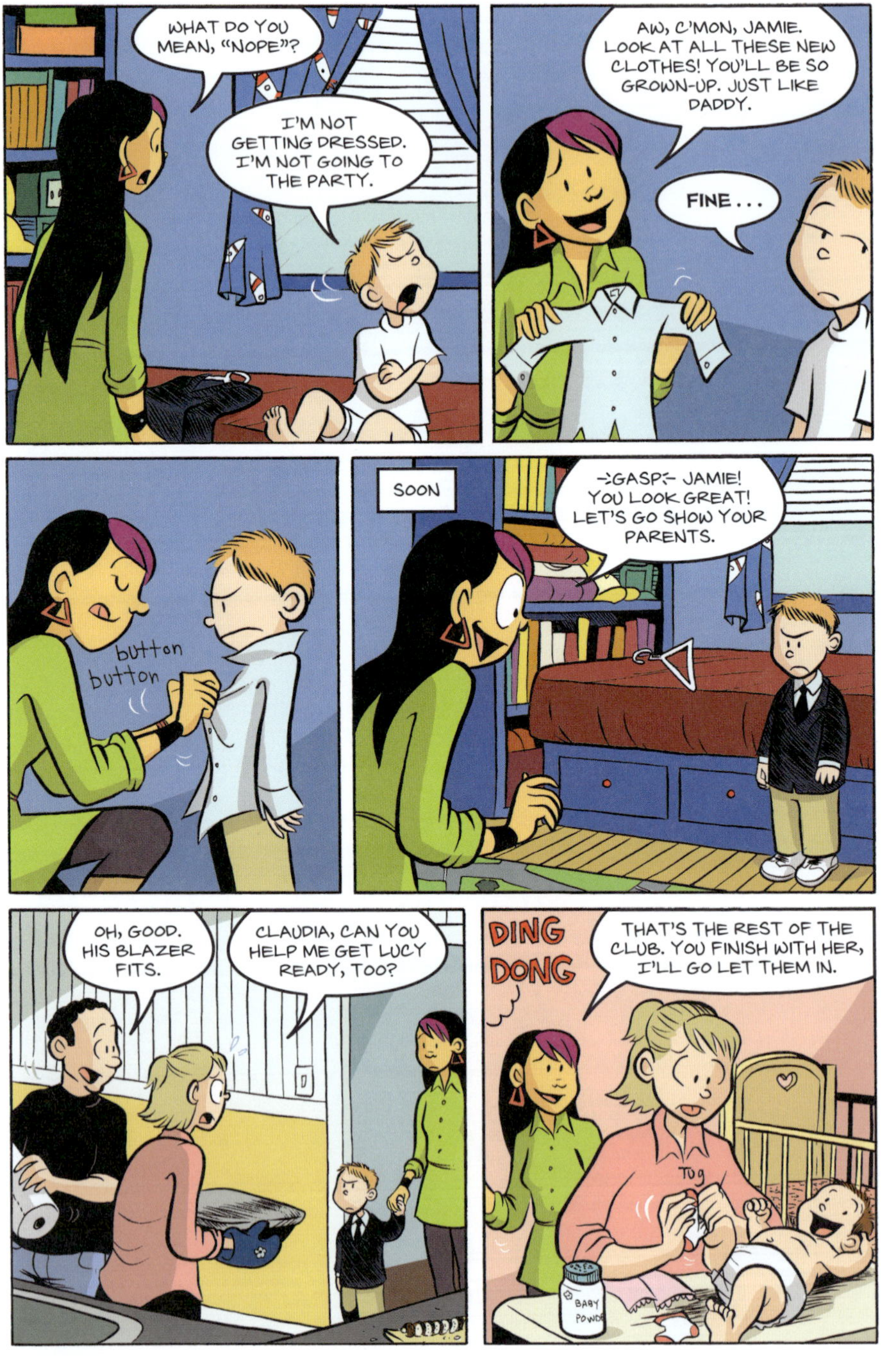
WHAT DO YOU MEAN, "NOPE"?
I'M NOT GETTING DRESSED. I'M NOT GOING TO THE PARTY.
AW, C'MON, JAMIE. LOOK AT ALL THESE NEW CLOTHES! YOU'LL BE SO GROWN-UP. JUST LIKE DADDY.
FINE . . .
button button
SOON
-GASP- JAMIE! YOU LOOK GREAT! LET'S GO SHOW YOUR PARENTS.
OH, GOOD. HIS BLAZER FITS.
CLAUDIA, CAN YOU HELP ME GET LUCY READY, TOO?
DING DONG
THAT'S THE REST OF THE CLUB. YOU FINISH WITH HER, I'LL GO LET THEM IN.
Tug
BABY POWD

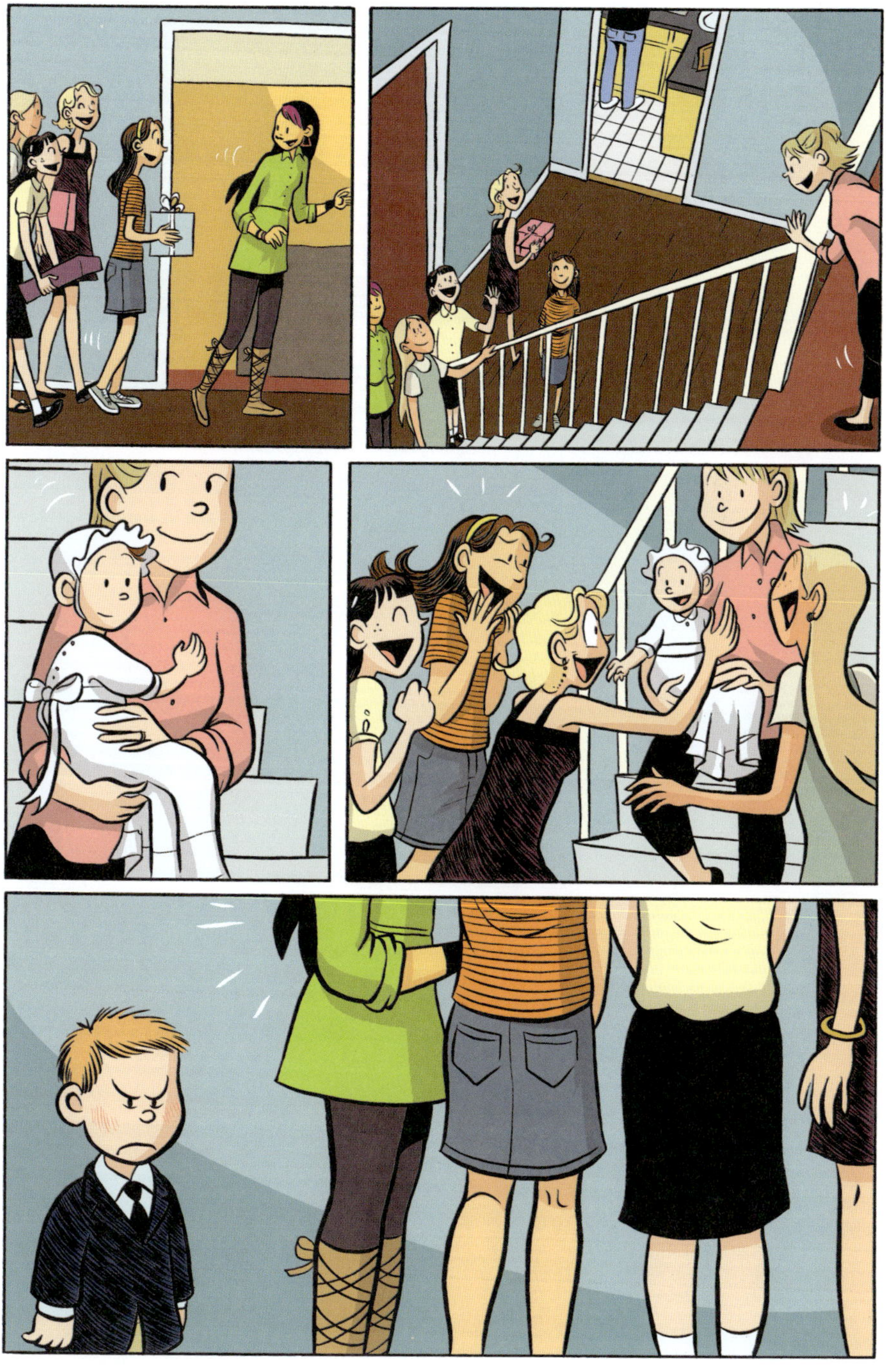

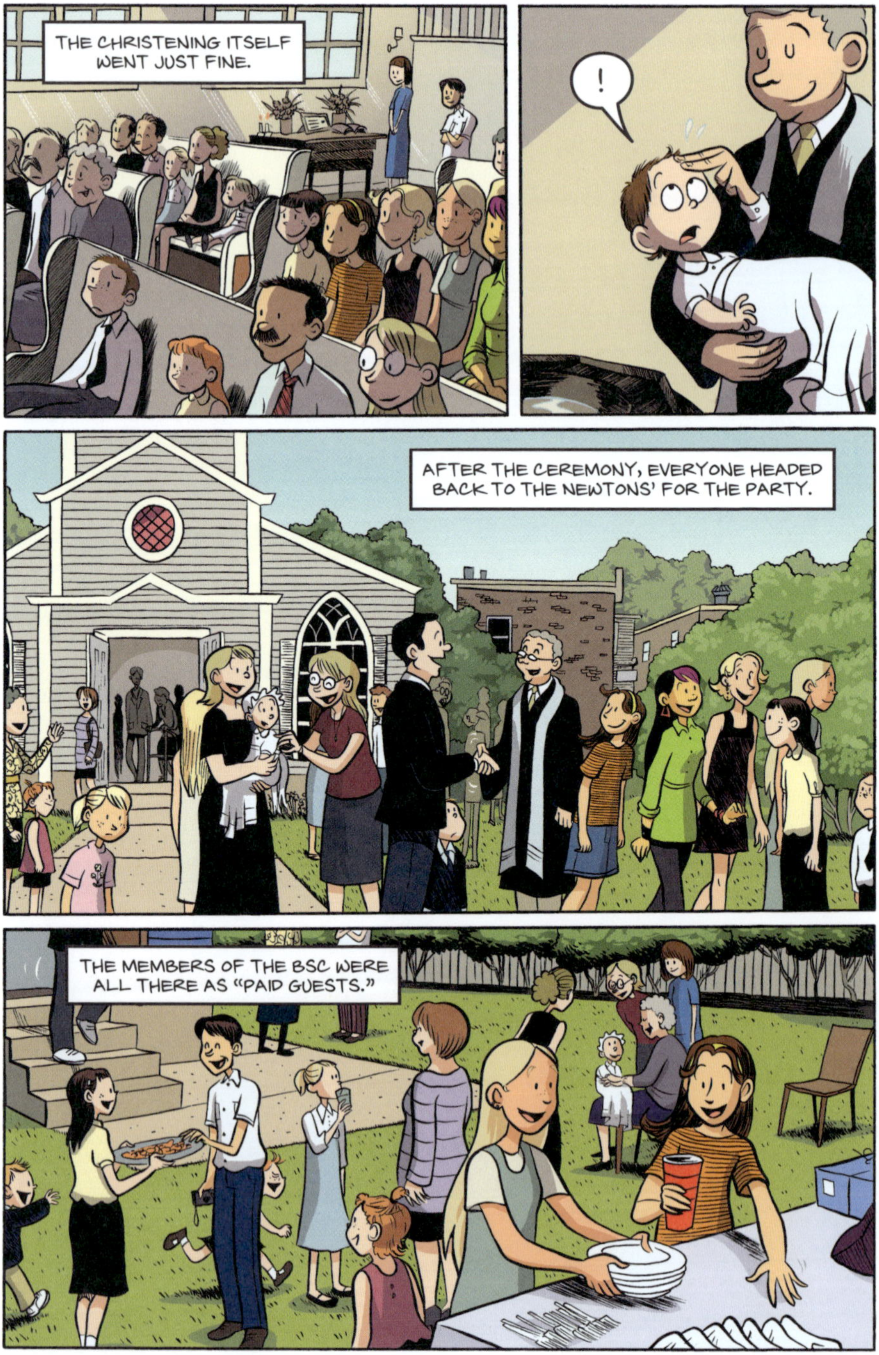
THE CHRISTENING ITSELF WENT JUST FINE.
!
AFTER THE CEREMONY, EVERYONE HEADED BACK TO THE NEWTONS' FOR THE PARTY.
THE MEMBERS OF THE BSC WERE ALL THERE AS "PAID GUESTS."

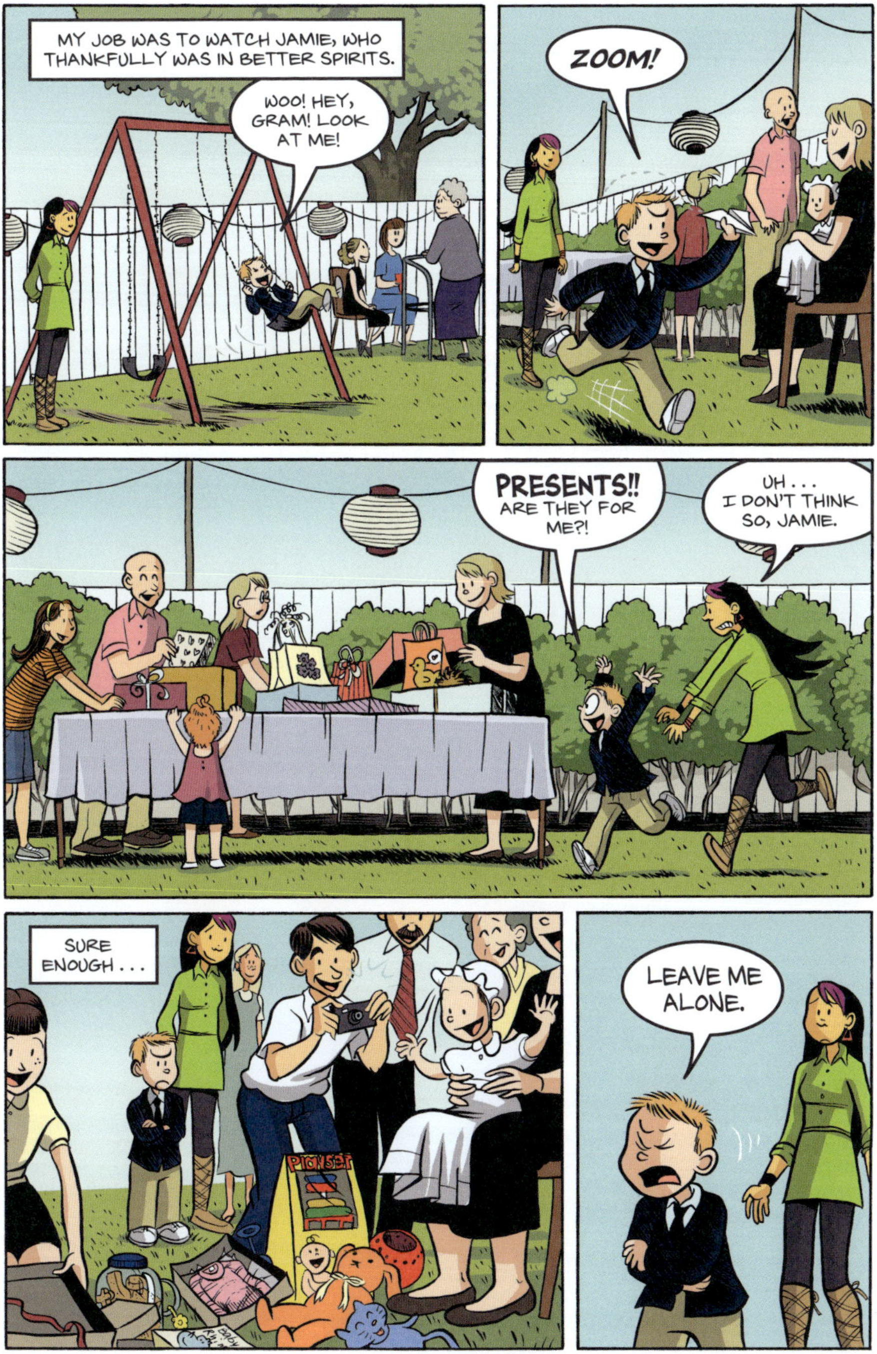
MY JOB WAS TO WATCH JAMIE, WHO THANKFULLY WAS IN BETTER SPIRITS.
WOO! HEY, GRAM! LOOK AT ME!
ZOOM!
PRESENTS!! ARE THEY FOR ME?!
UH . . . I DON'T THINK SO, JAMIE.
SURE ENOUGH . . .
PLAYSET
LEAVE ME ALONE.

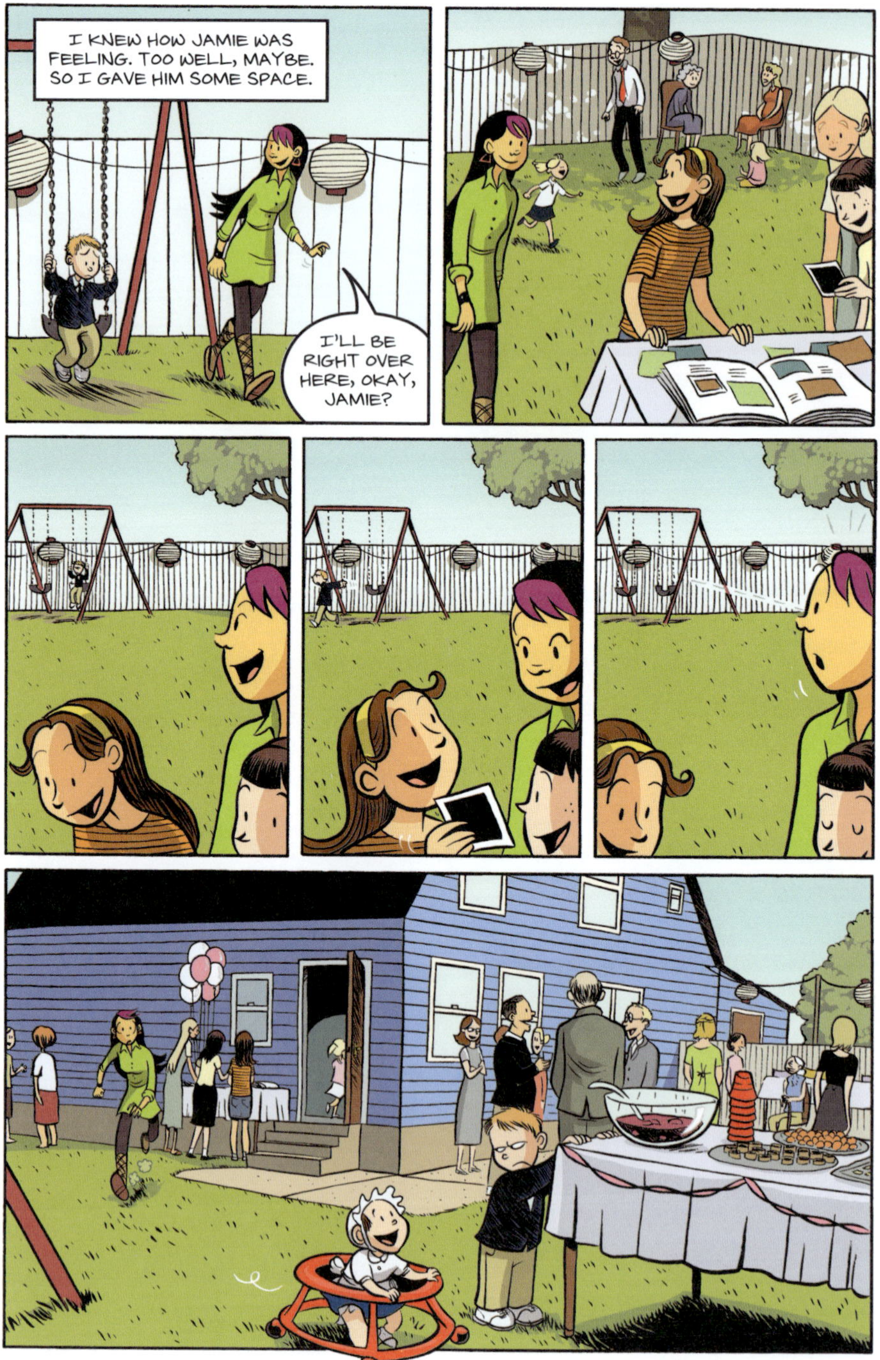
I KNEW HOW JAMIE WAS FEELING. TOO WELL, MAYBE. SO I GAVE HIM SOME SPACE.
I'LL BE RIGHT OVER HERE, OKAY, JAMIE?

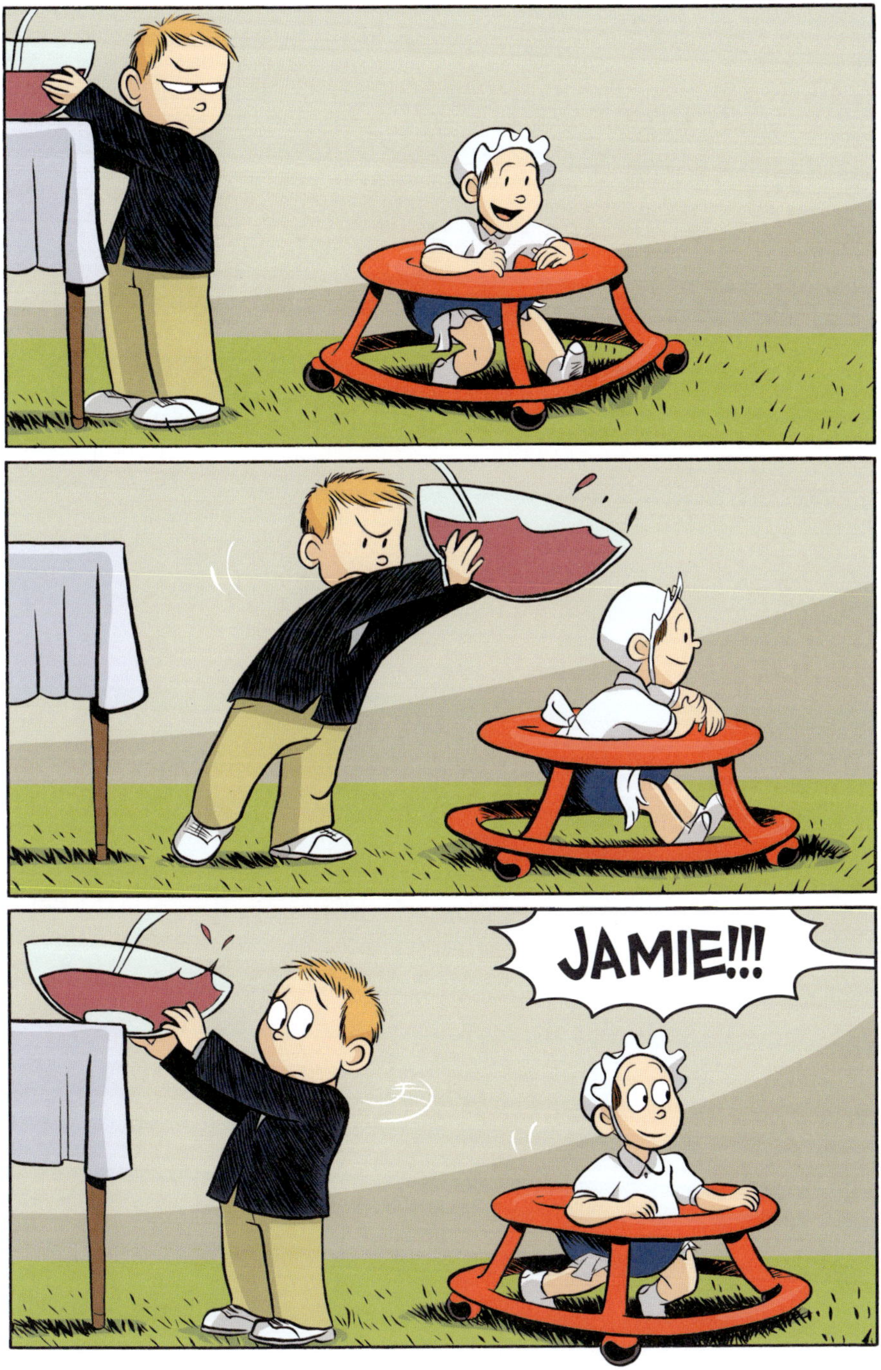
JAMIE!!!

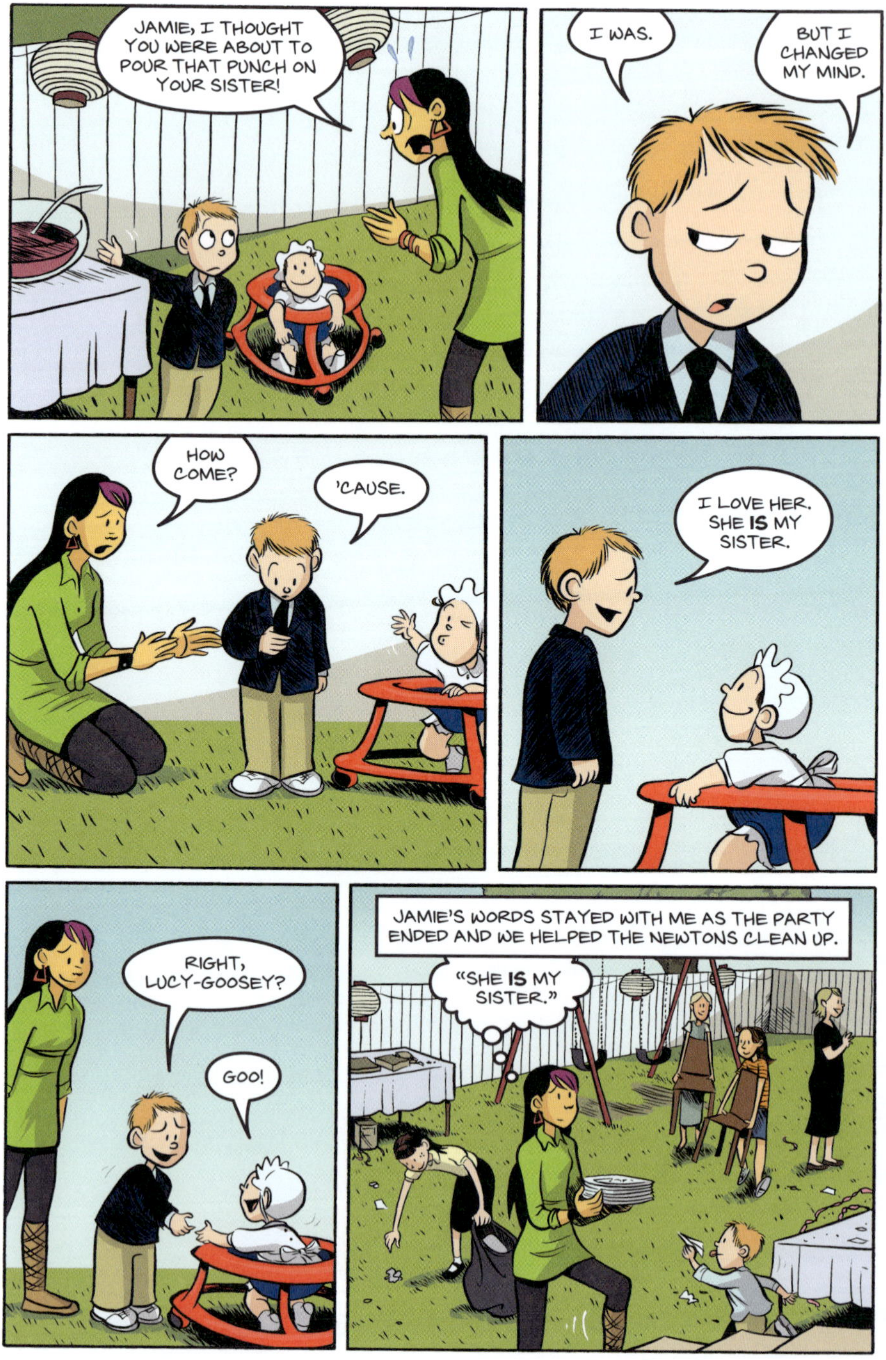
JAMIE, I THOUGHT YOU WERE ABOUT TO POUR THAT PUNCH ON YOUR SISTER!
I WAS.
BUT I CHANGED MY MIND.
HOW COME?
'CAUSE.
I LOVE HER. SHE **IS** MY SISTER.
RIGHT, LUCY-GOOSEY?
GOO!
JAMIE'S WORDS STAYED WITH ME AS THE PARTY ENDED AND WE HELPED THE NEWTONS CLEAN UP.
"SHE **IS** MY SISTER."

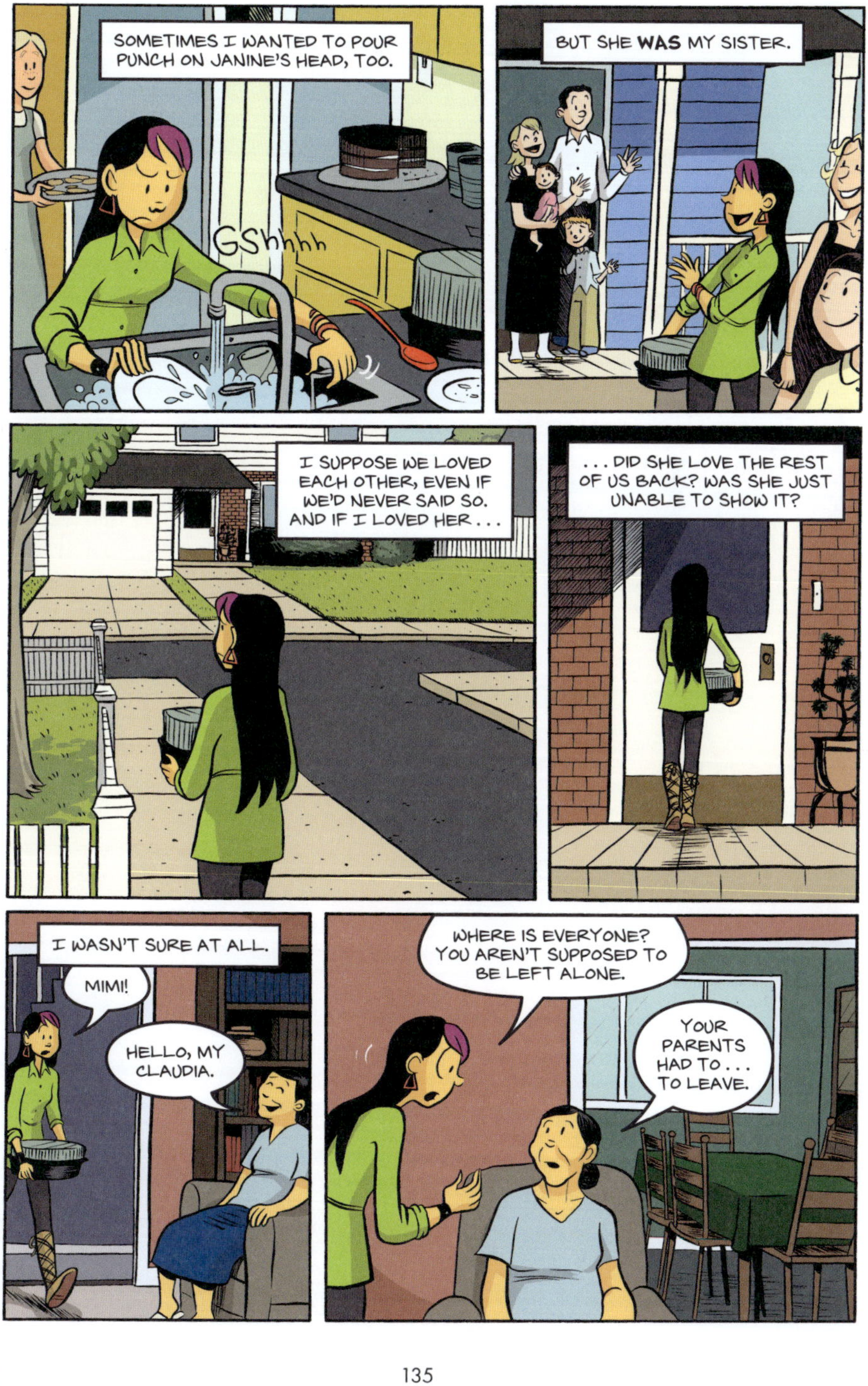
SOMETIMES I WANTED TO POUR PUNCH ON JANINE'S HEAD, TOO.
GShhhh
BUT SHE **WAS** MY SISTER.
I SUPPOSE WE LOVED EACH OTHER, EVEN IF WE'D NEVER SAID SO. AND IF I LOVED HER . . .
. . . DID SHE LOVE THE REST OF US BACK? WAS SHE JUST UNABLE TO SHOW IT?
I WASN'T SURE AT ALL.
MIMI!
HELLO, MY CLAUDIA.
WHERE IS EVERYONE? YOU AREN'T SUPPOSED TO BE LEFT ALONE.
YOUR PARENTS HAD TO . . . TO LEAVE.

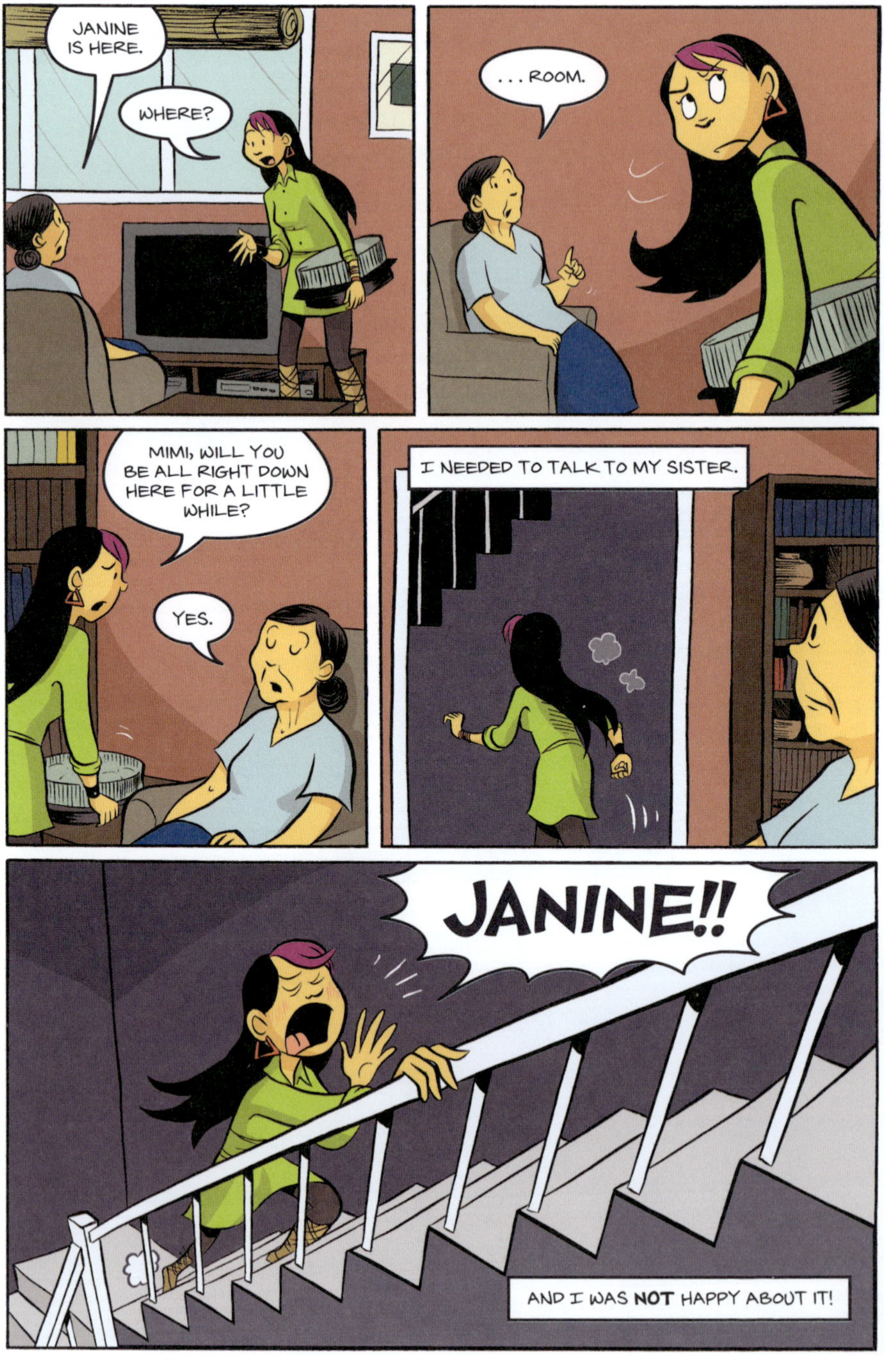
JANINE IS HERE.
WHERE?
. . . ROOM.
MIMI, WILL YOU BE ALL RIGHT DOWN HERE FOR A LITTLE WHILE?
YES.
I NEEDED TO TALK TO MY SISTER.
JANINE!!
AND I WAS NOT HAPPY ABOUT IT!

CHAPTER 16

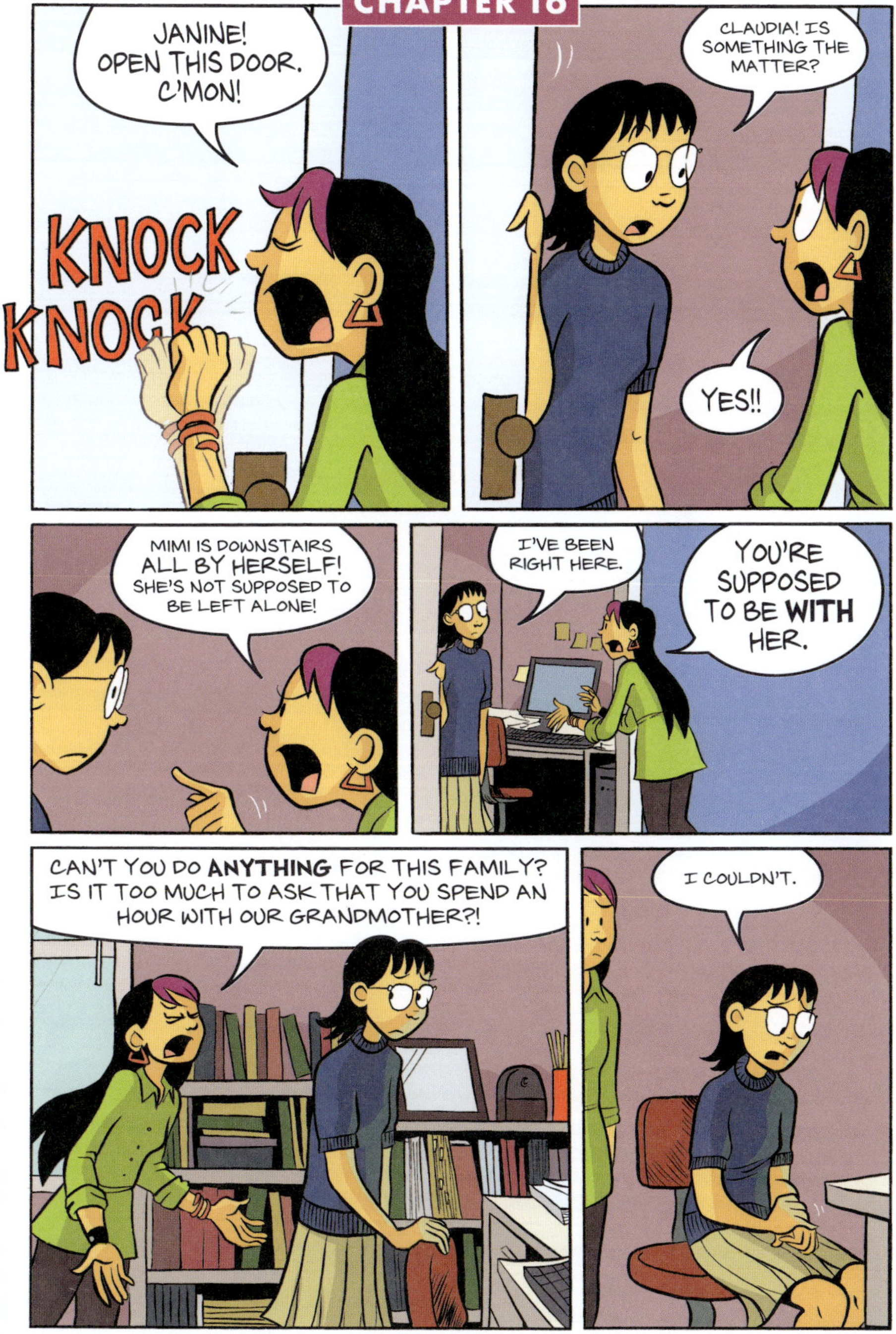

JANINE! OPEN THIS DOOR. C'MON!
KNOCK KNOCK
CLAUDIA! IS SOMETHING THE MATTER?
YES!!
MIMI IS DOWNSTAIRS ALL BY HERSELF! SHE'S NOT SUPPOSED TO BE LEFT ALONE!
I'VE BEEN RIGHT HERE.
YOU'RE SUPPOSED TO BE **WITH** HER.
CAN'T YOU DO **ANYTHING** FOR THIS FAMILY? IS IT TOO MUCH TO ASK THAT YOU SPEND AN HOUR WITH OUR GRANDMOTHER?!
I COULDN'T.

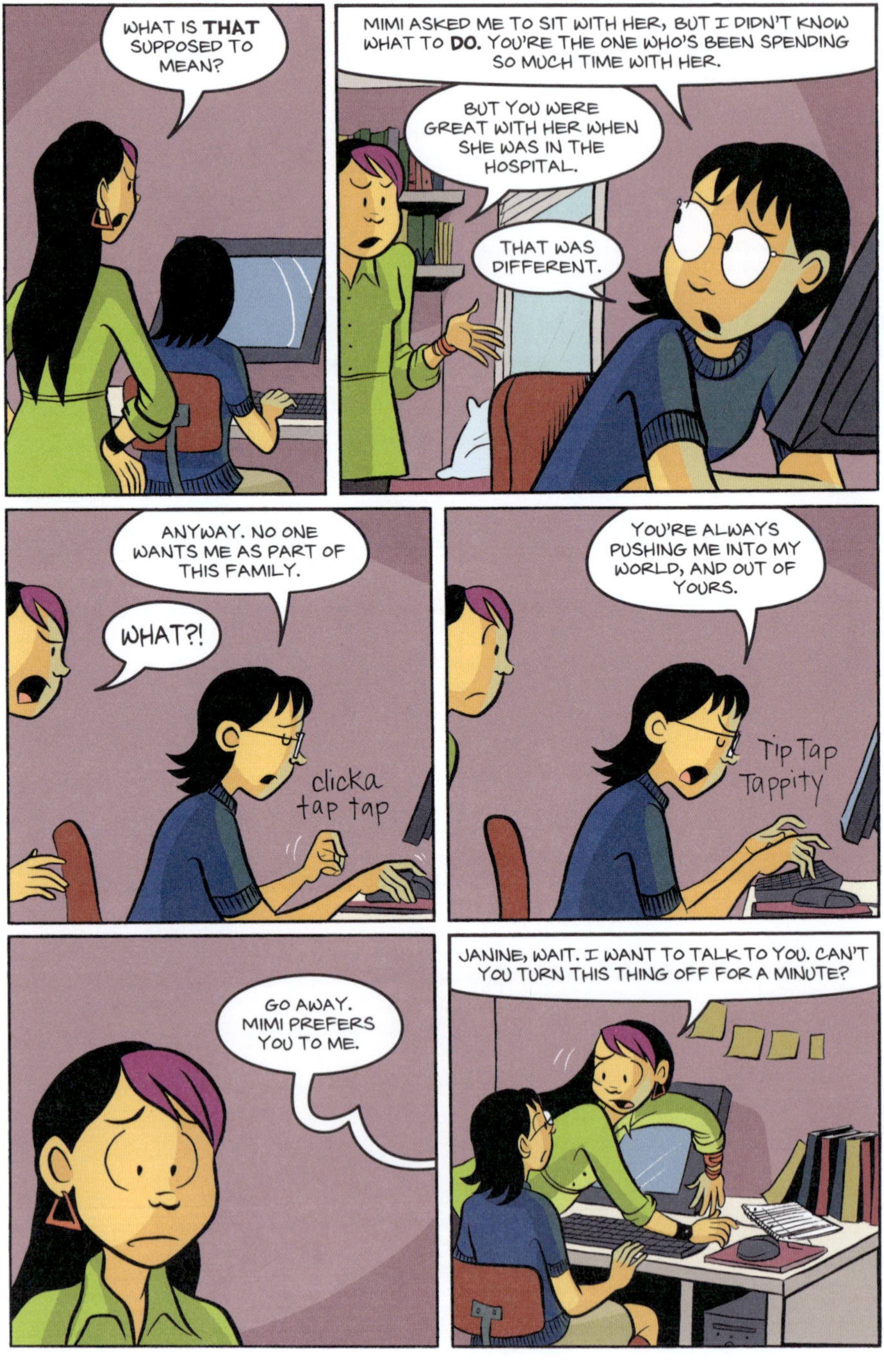
WHAT IS **THAT** SUPPOSED TO MEAN?
MIMI ASKED ME TO SIT WITH HER, BUT I DIDN'T KNOW WHAT TO **DO.** YOU'RE THE ONE WHO'S BEEN SPENDING SO MUCH TIME WITH HER.
BUT YOU WERE GREAT WITH HER WHEN SHE WAS IN THE HOSPITAL.
THAT WAS DIFFERENT.
ANYWAY. NO ONE WANTS ME AS PART OF THIS FAMILY.
WHAT?!
clicka tap tap
YOU'RE ALWAYS PUSHING ME INTO MY WORLD, AND OUT OF YOURS.
Tip Tap Tappity
GO AWAY. MIMI PREFERS YOU TO ME.
JANINE, WAIT. I WANT TO TALK TO YOU. CAN'T YOU TURN THIS THING OFF FOR A MINUTE?

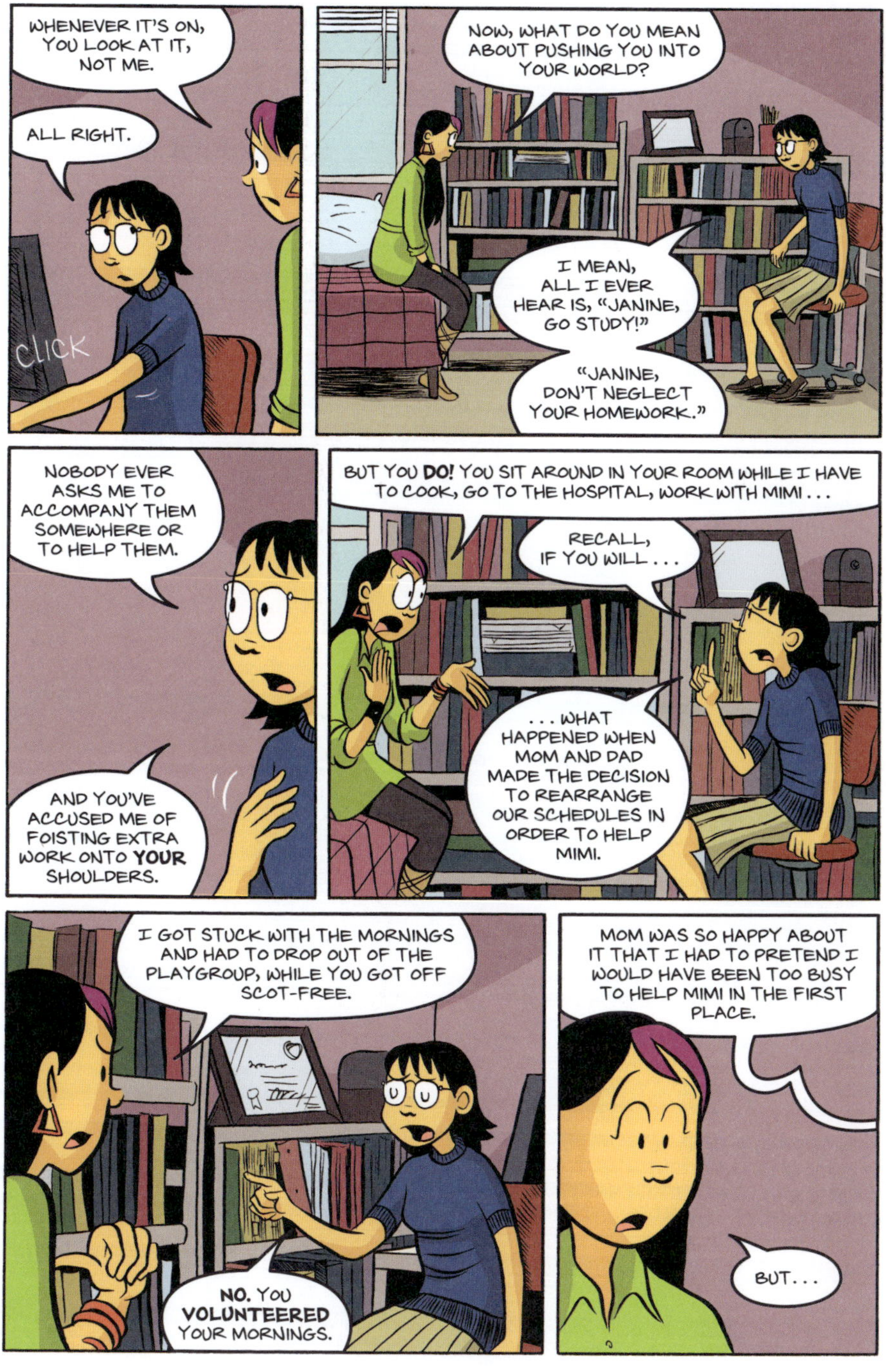
WHENEVER IT'S ON, YOU LOOK AT IT, NOT ME.
ALL RIGHT.
CLICK
NOW, WHAT DO YOU MEAN ABOUT PUSHING YOU INTO YOUR WORLD?
I MEAN, ALL I EVER HEAR IS, "JANINE, GO STUDY!"
"JANINE, DON'T NEGLECT YOUR HOMEWORK."
NOBODY EVER ASKS ME TO ACCOMPANY THEM SOMEWHERE OR TO HELP THEM.
AND YOU'VE ACCUSED ME OF FOISTING EXTRA WORK ONTO **YOUR** SHOULDERS.
BUT YOU **DO!** YOU SIT AROUND IN YOUR ROOM WHILE I HAVE TO COOK, GO TO THE HOSPITAL, WORK WITH MIMI . . .
RECALL, IF YOU WILL . . .
. . . WHAT HAPPENED WHEN MOM AND DAD MADE THE DECISION TO REARRANGE OUR SCHEDULES IN ORDER TO HELP MIMI.
I GOT STUCK WITH THE MORNINGS AND HAD TO DROP OUT OF THE PLAYGROUP, WHILE YOU GOT OFF SCOT-FREE.
NO. YOU **VOLUNTEERED** YOUR MORNINGS.
MOM WAS SO HAPPY ABOUT IT THAT I HAD TO PRETEND I WOULD HAVE BEEN TOO BUSY TO HELP MIMI IN THE FIRST PLACE.
BUT. . .

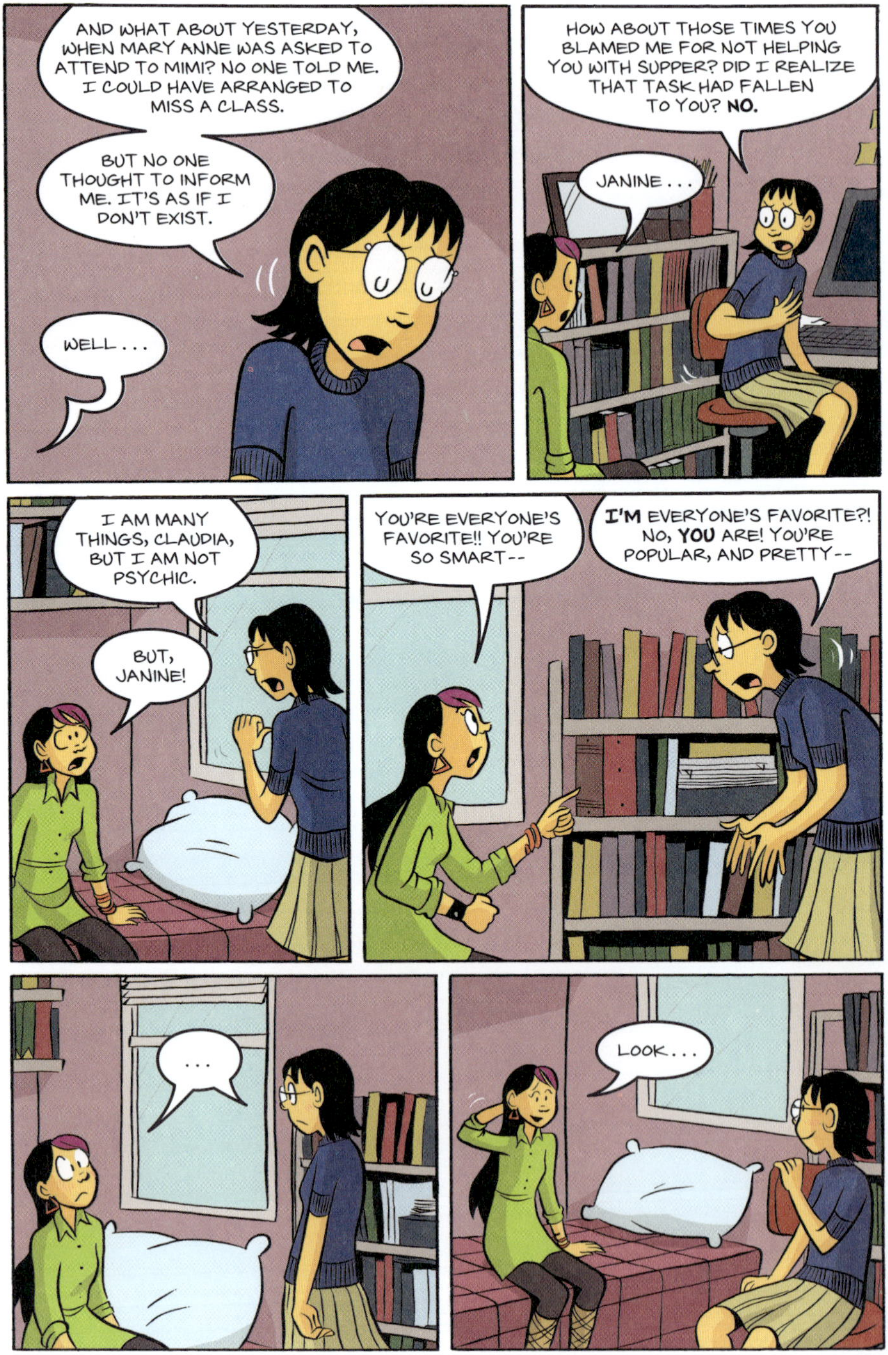
AND WHAT ABOUT YESTERDAY, WHEN MARY ANNE WAS ASKED TO ATTEND TO MIMI? NO ONE TOLD ME. I COULD HAVE ARRANGED TO MISS A CLASS.
BUT NO ONE THOUGHT TO INFORM ME. IT'S AS IF I DON'T EXIST.
WELL . . .
HOW ABOUT THOSE TIMES YOU BLAMED ME FOR NOT HELPING YOU WITH SUPPER? DID I REALIZE THAT TASK HAD FALLEN TO YOU? **NO.**
JANINE . . .
I AM MANY THINGS, CLAUDIA, BUT I AM NOT PSYCHIC.
BUT, JANINE!
YOU'RE EVERYONE'S FAVORITE!! YOU'RE SO SMART--
I'M EVERYONE'S FAVORITE?! NO, **YOU** ARE! YOU'RE POPULAR, AND PRETTY--
. . .
LOOK . . .

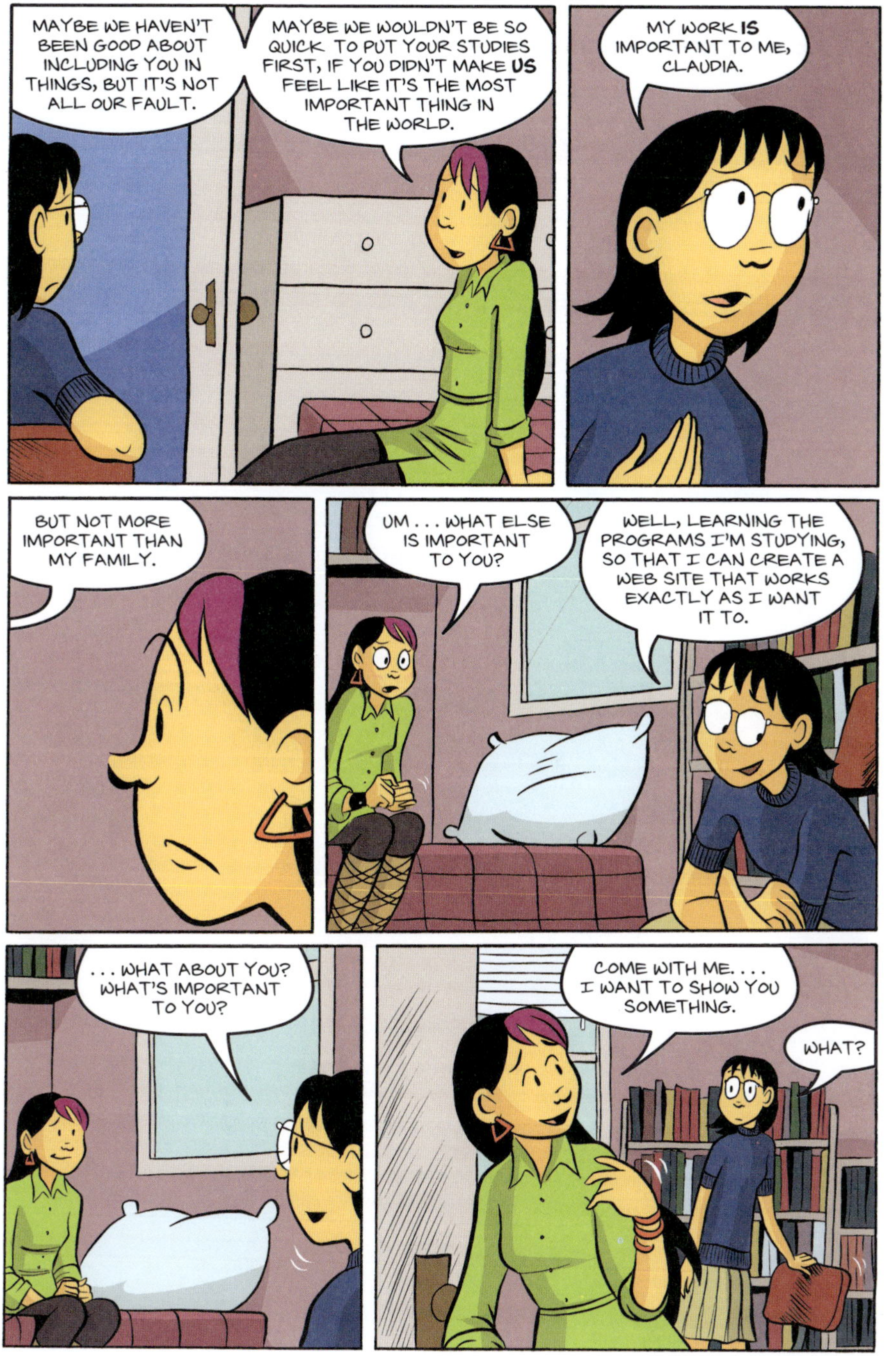
MAYBE WE HAVEN'T BEEN GOOD ABOUT INCLUDING YOU IN THINGS, BUT IT'S NOT ALL OUR FAULT.
MAYBE WE WOULDN'T BE SO QUICK TO PUT YOUR STUDIES FIRST, IF YOU DIDN'T MAKE **US** FEEL LIKE IT'S THE MOST IMPORTANT THING IN THE WORLD.
MY WORK **IS** IMPORTANT TO ME, CLAUDIA.
BUT NOT MORE IMPORTANT THAN MY FAMILY.
UM . . . WHAT ELSE IS IMPORTANT TO YOU?
WELL, LEARNING THE PROGRAMS I'M STUDYING, SO THAT I CAN CREATE A WEB SITE THAT WORKS EXACTLY AS I WANT IT TO.
. . . WHAT ABOUT YOU? WHAT'S IMPORTANT TO YOU?
COME WITH ME. . . . I WANT TO SHOW YOU SOMETHING.
WHAT?

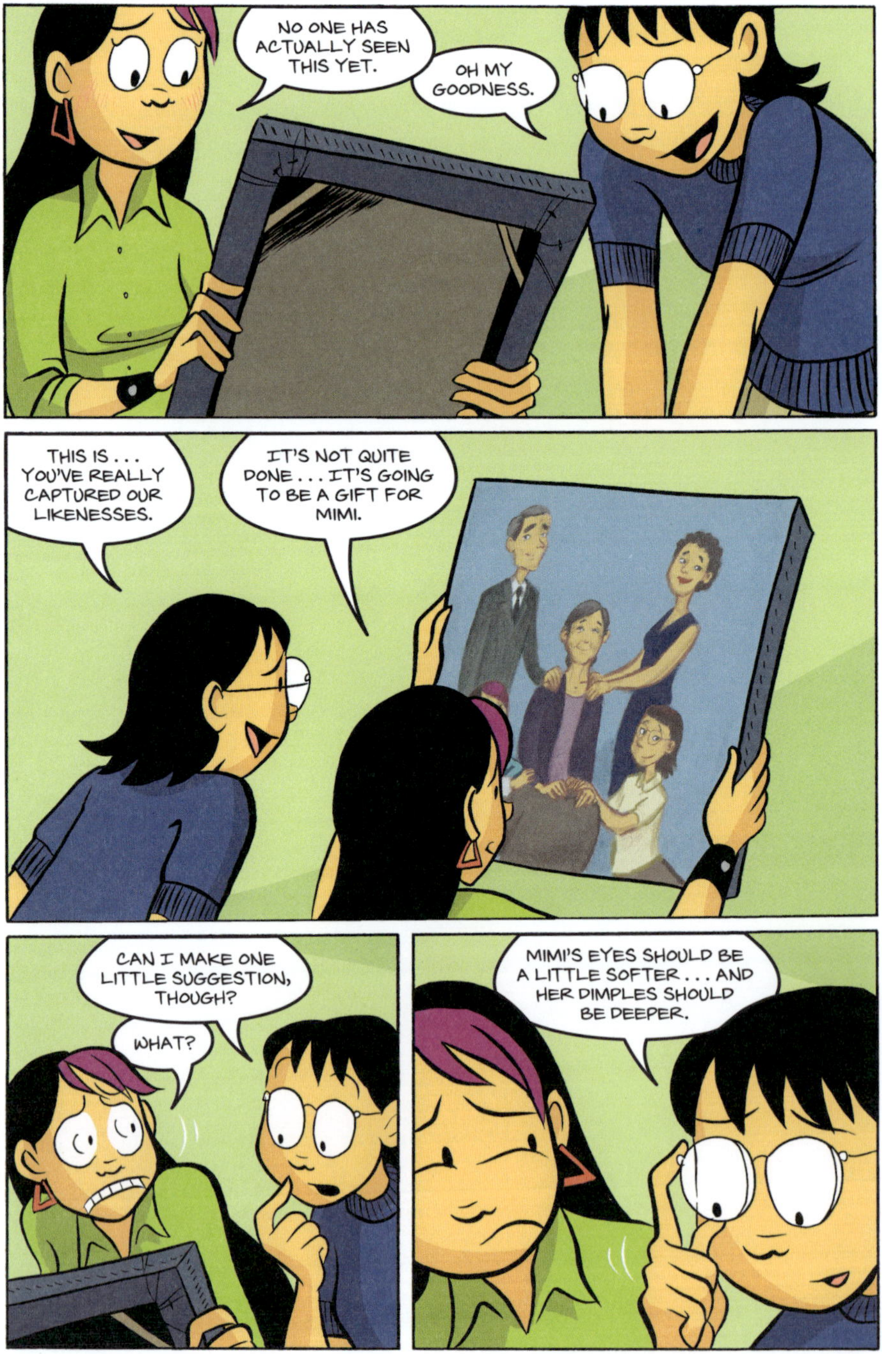
NO ONE HAS ACTUALLY SEEN THIS YET.
OH MY GOODNESS.
THIS IS . . . YOU'VE REALLY CAPTURED OUR LIKENESSES.
IT'S NOT QUITE DONE . . . IT'S GOING TO BE A GIFT FOR MIMI.
CAN I MAKE ONE LITTLE SUGGESTION, THOUGH?
WHAT?
MIMI'S EYES SHOULD BE A LITTLE SOFTER . . . AND HER DIMPLES SHOULD BE DEEPER.

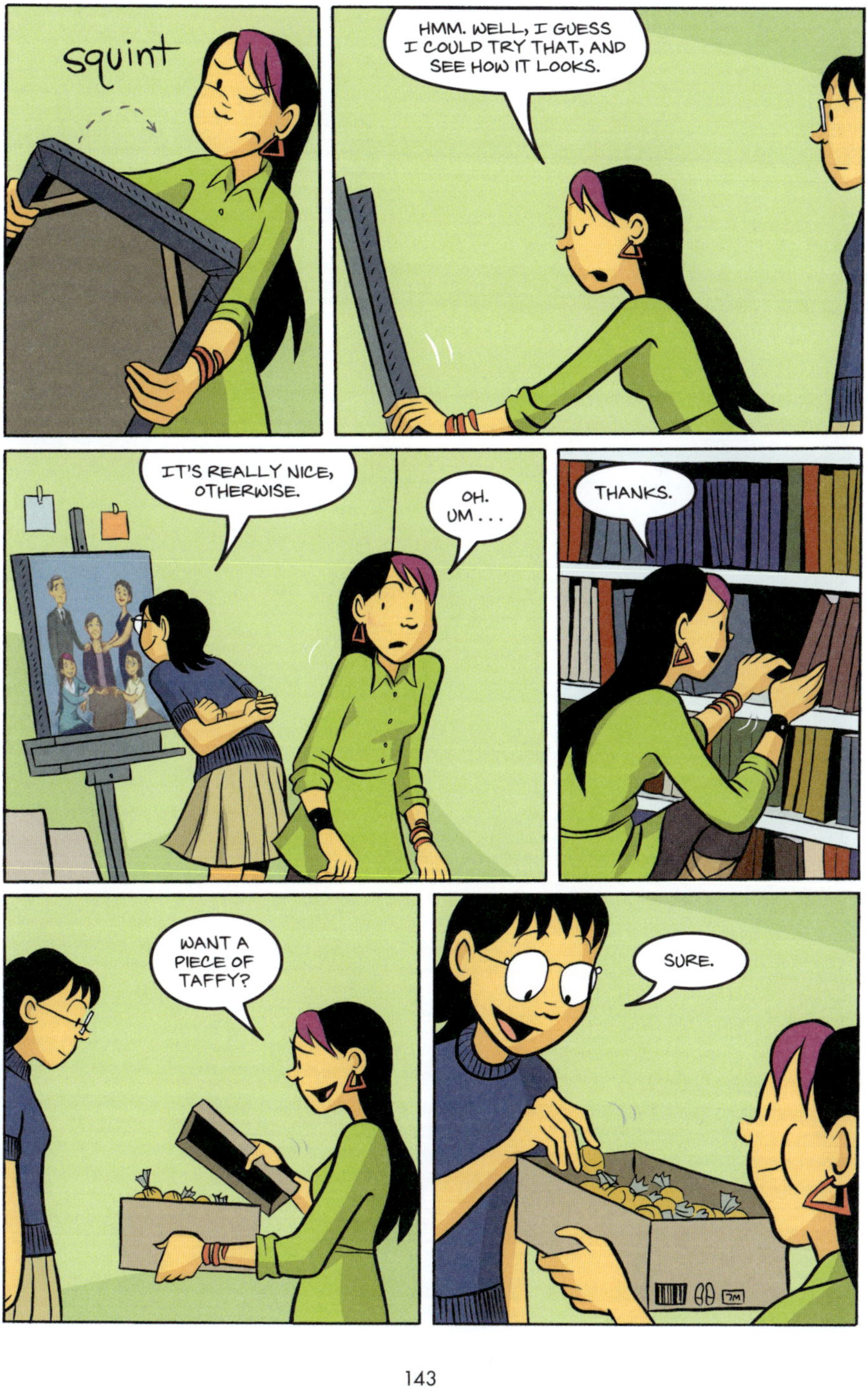
squint
HMM. WELL, I GUESS I COULD TRY THAT, AND SEE HOW IT LOOKS.
IT'S REALLY NICE, OTHERWISE.
OH. UM . . .
THANKS.
WANT A PIECE OF TAFFY?
SURE.

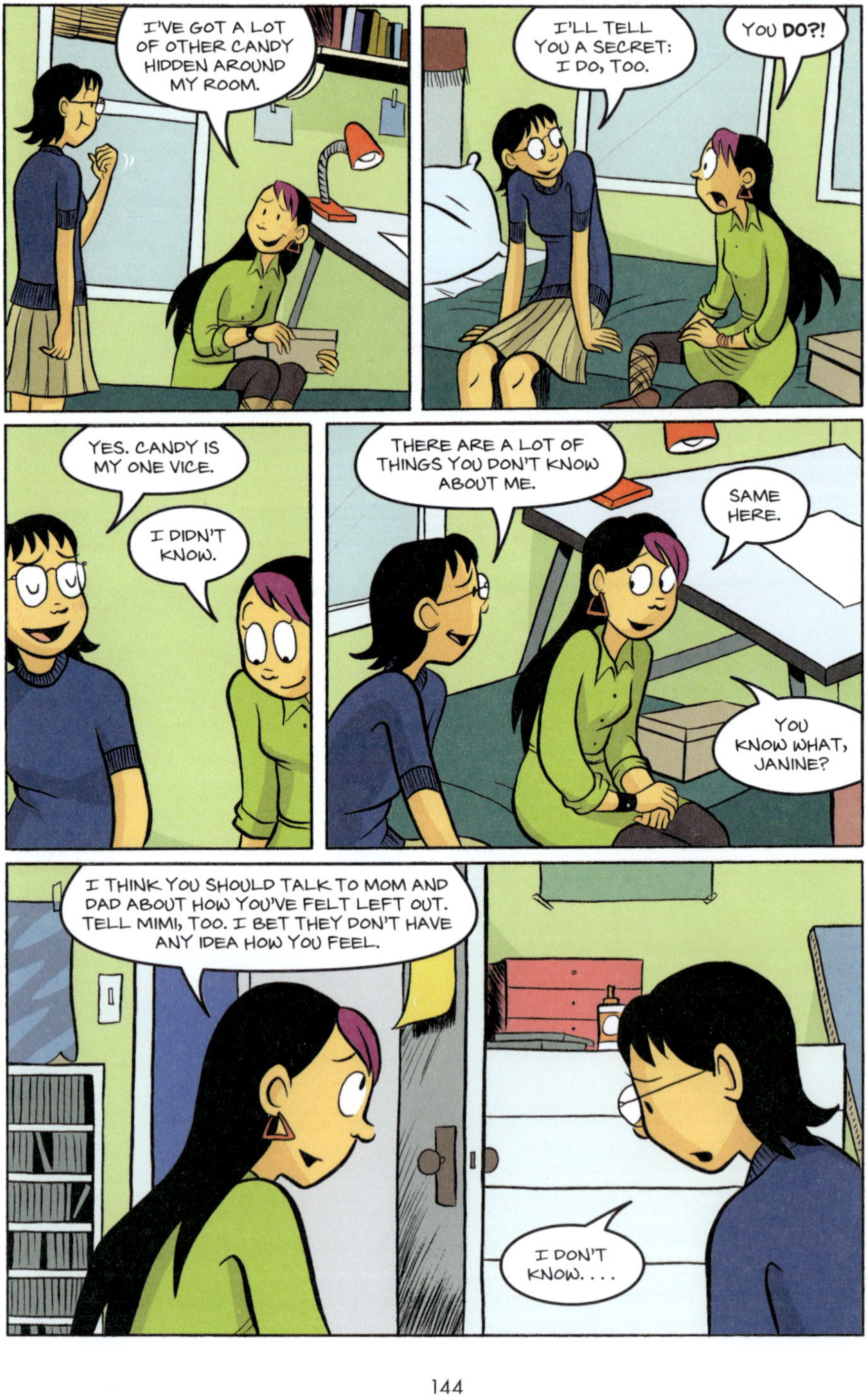
I'VE GOT A LOT OF OTHER CANDY HIDDEN AROUND MY ROOM.
I'LL TELL YOU A SECRET: I DO, TOO.
YOU **DO?!**
YES. CANDY IS MY ONE VICE.
I DIDN'T KNOW.
THERE ARE A LOT OF THINGS YOU DON'T KNOW ABOUT ME.
SAME HERE.
YOU KNOW WHAT, JANINE?
I THINK YOU SHOULD TALK TO MOM AND DAD ABOUT HOW YOU'VE FELT LEFT OUT. TELL MIMI, TOO. I BET THEY DON'T HAVE ANY IDEA HOW YOU FEEL.
I DON'T KNOW. . . .

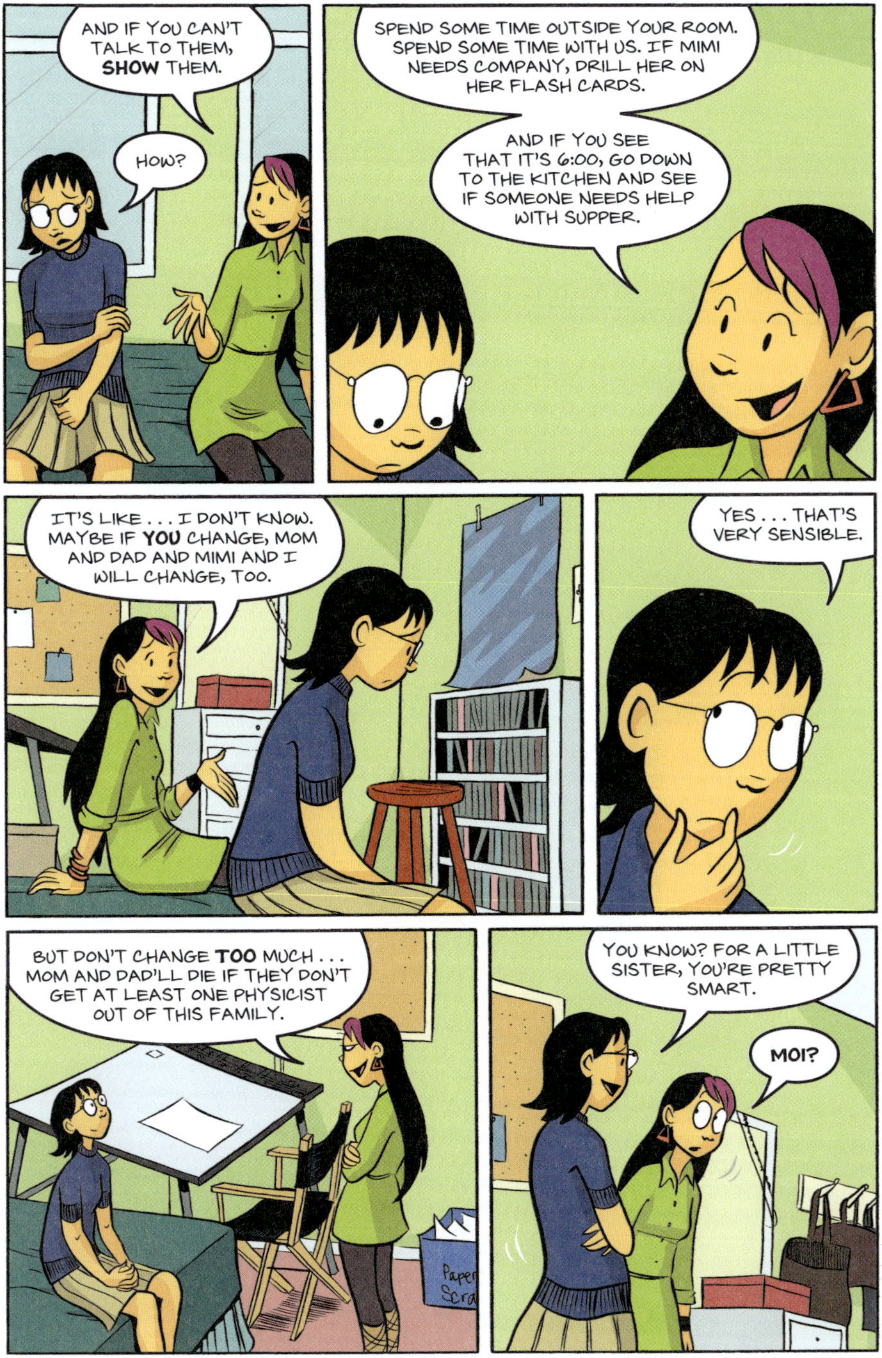
AND IF YOU CAN'T TALK TO THEM, **SHOW** THEM.
HOW?
SPEND SOME TIME OUTSIDE YOUR ROOM. SPEND SOME TIME WITH US. IF MIMI NEEDS COMPANY, DRILL HER ON HER FLASH CARDS.
AND IF YOU SEE THAT IT'S 6:00, GO DOWN TO THE KITCHEN AND SEE IF SOMEONE NEEDS HELP WITH SUPPER.
IT'S LIKE . . . I DON'T KNOW. MAYBE IF **YOU** CHANGE, MOM AND DAD AND MIMI AND I WILL CHANGE, TOO.
YES . . . THAT'S VERY SENSIBLE.
BUT DON'T CHANGE **TOO** MUCH . . . MOM AND DAD'LL DIE IF THEY DON'T GET AT LEAST ONE PHYSICIST OUT OF THIS FAMILY.
YOU KNOW? FOR A LITTLE SISTER, YOU'RE PRETTY SMART.
MOI?

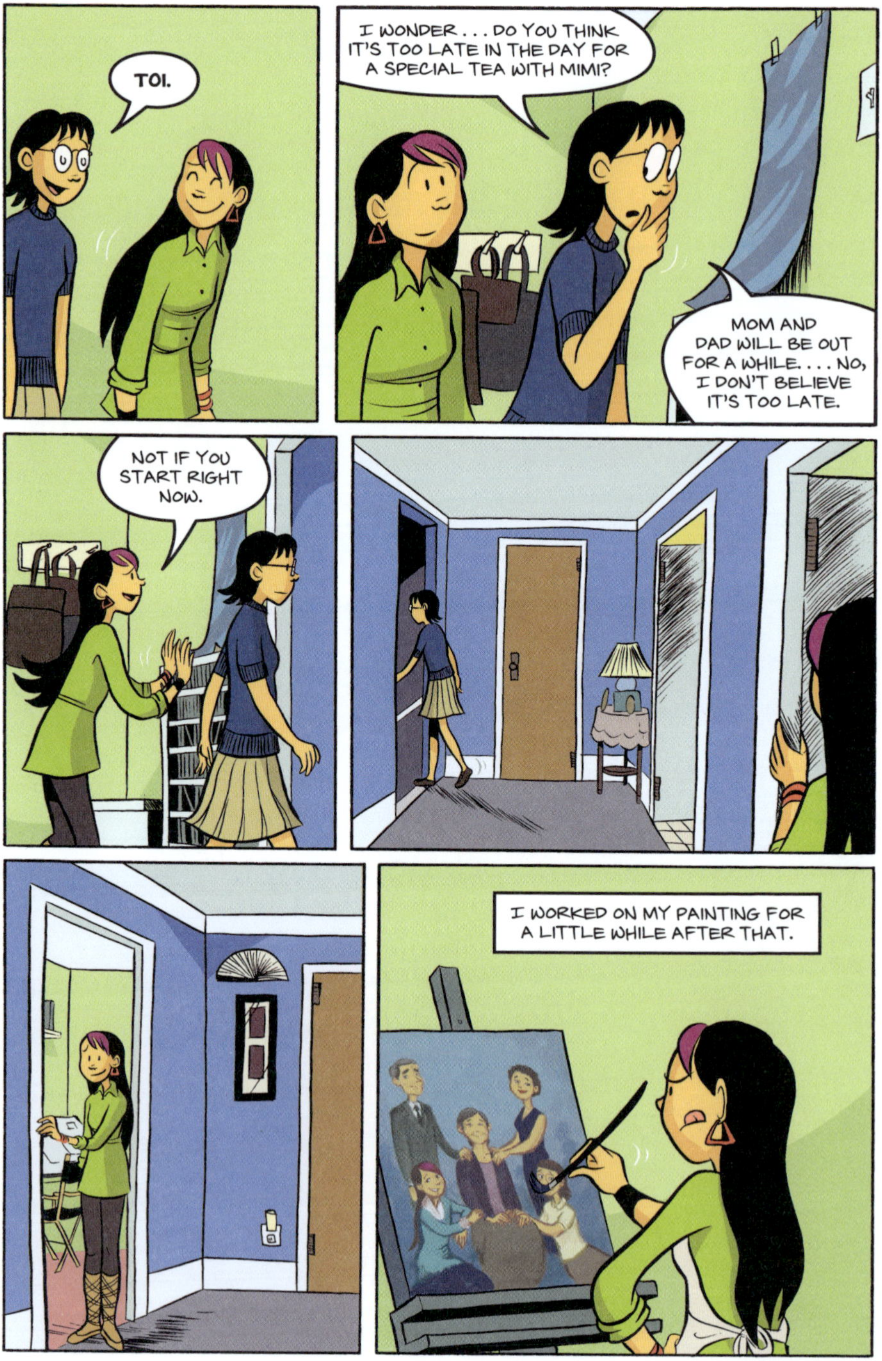
TOI.
I WONDER . . . DO YOU THINK IT'S TOO LATE IN THE DAY FOR A SPECIAL TEA WITH MIMI?
MOM AND DAD WILL BE OUT FOR A WHILE. . . . NO, I DON'T BELIEVE IT'S TOO LATE.
NOT IF YOU START RIGHT NOW.
I WORKED ON MY PAINTING FOR A LITTLE WHILE AFTER THAT.

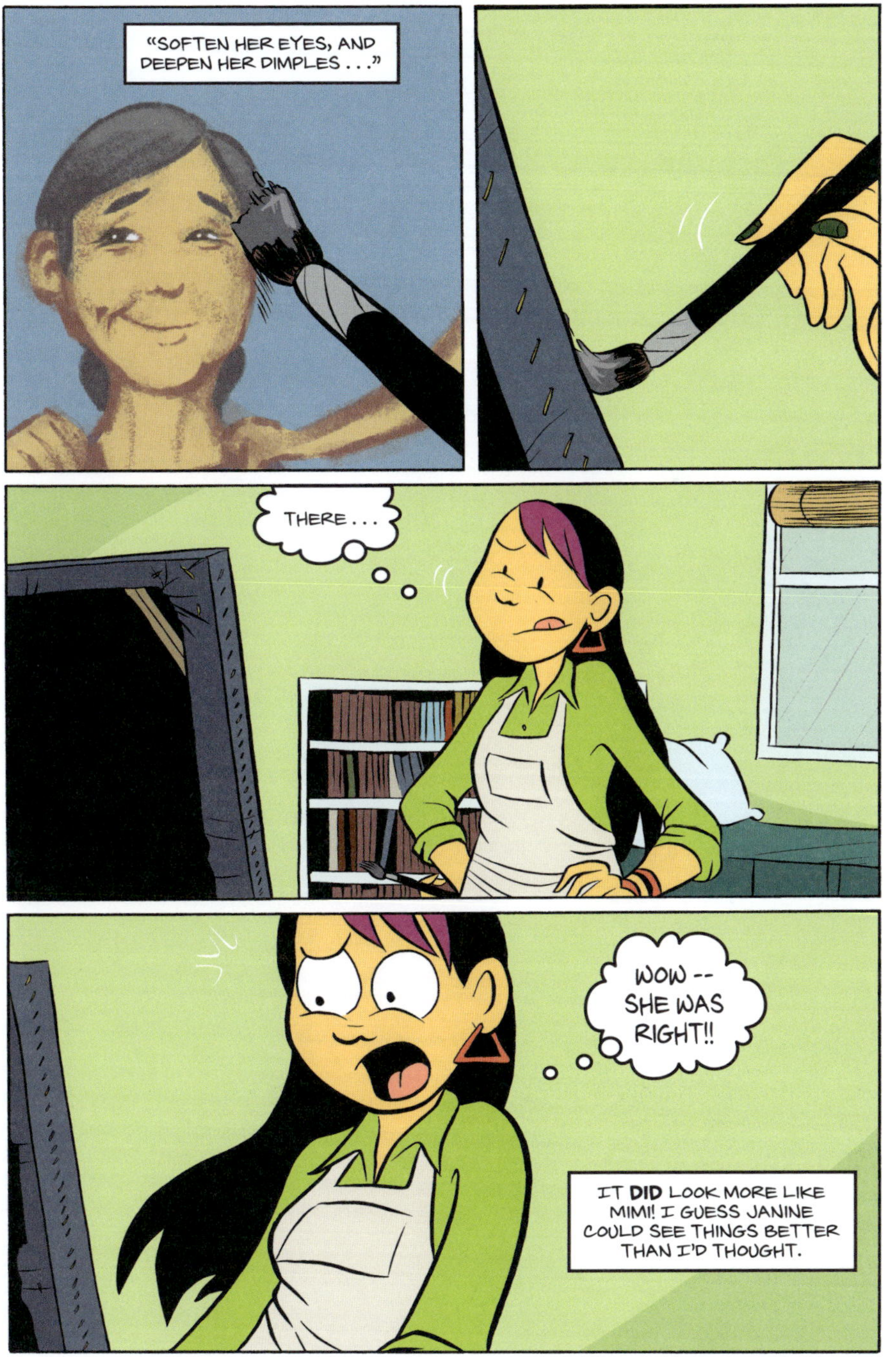
"SOFTEN HER EYES, AND DEEPEN HER DIMPLES . . ."
THERE . . .
WOW -- SHE WAS RIGHT!!
IT **DID** LOOK MORE LIKE MIMI! I GUESS JANINE COULD SEE THINGS BETTER THAN I'D THOUGHT.

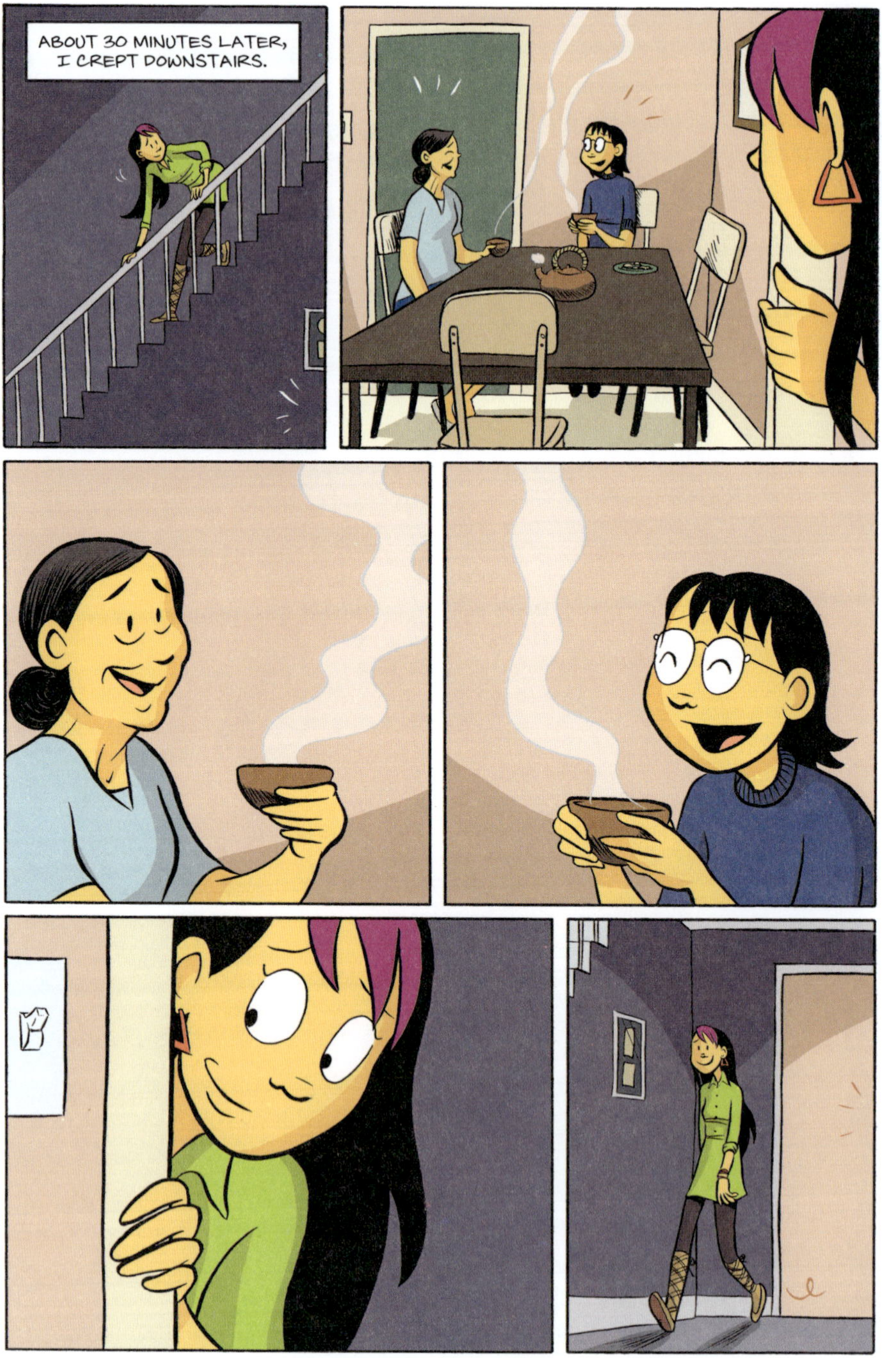
ABOUT 30 MINUTES LATER, I CREPT DOWNSTAIRS.

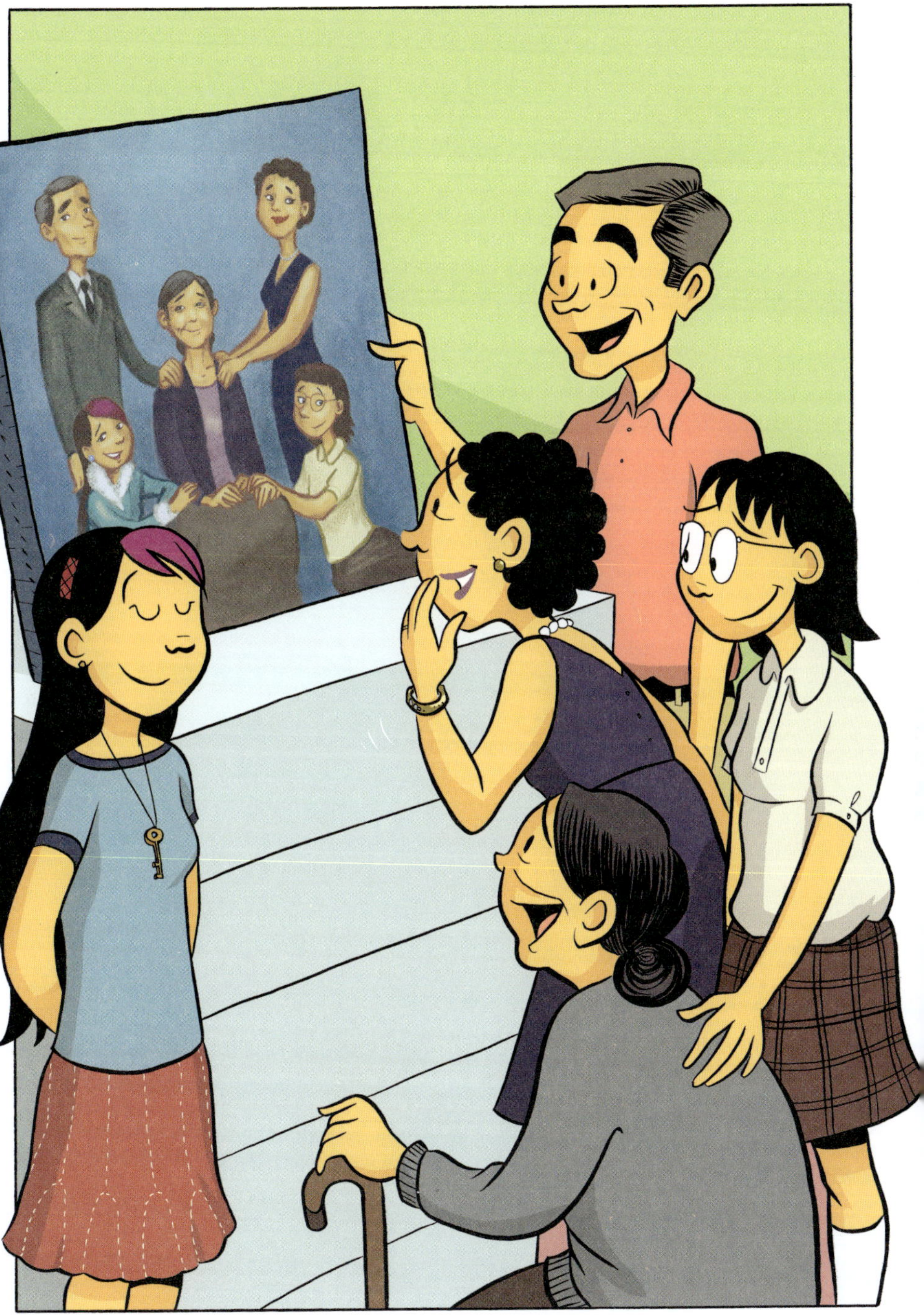

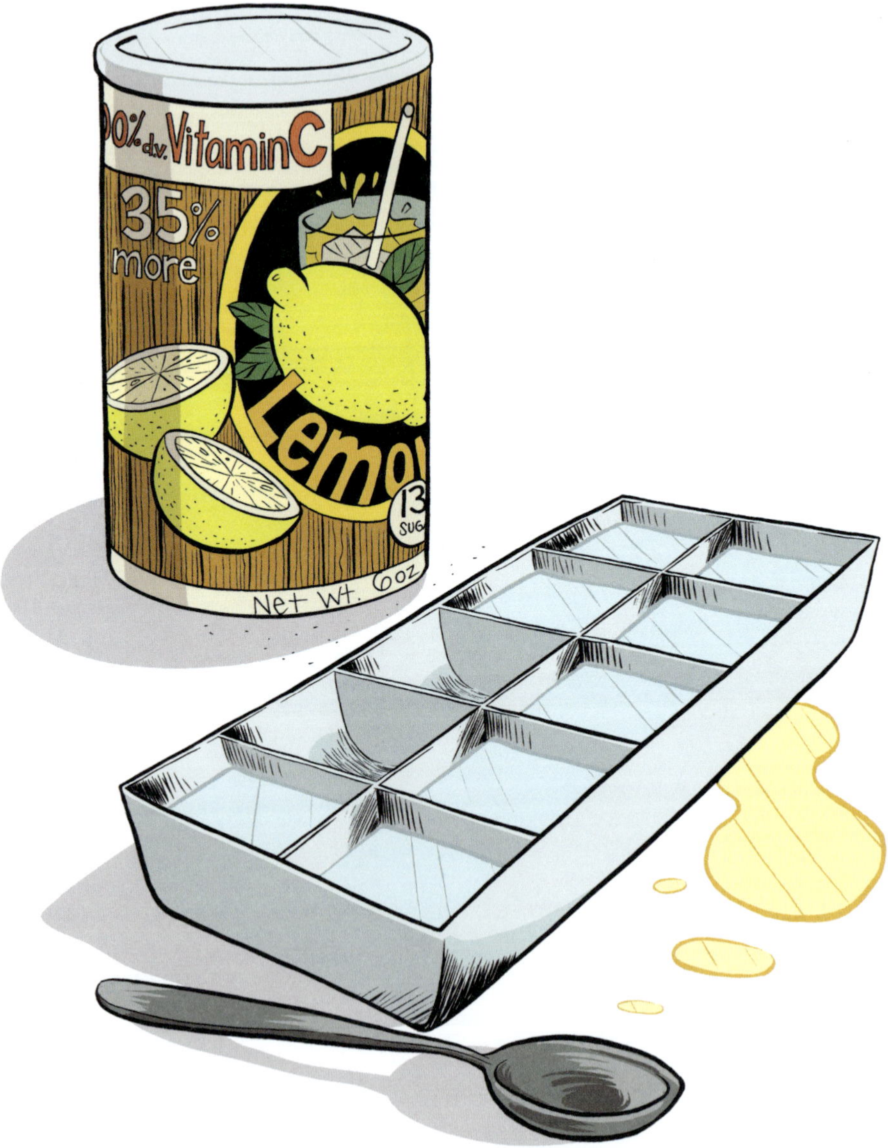
d.v. VitaminC
35%
more
Net Wt. 6oz

CHAPTER 17

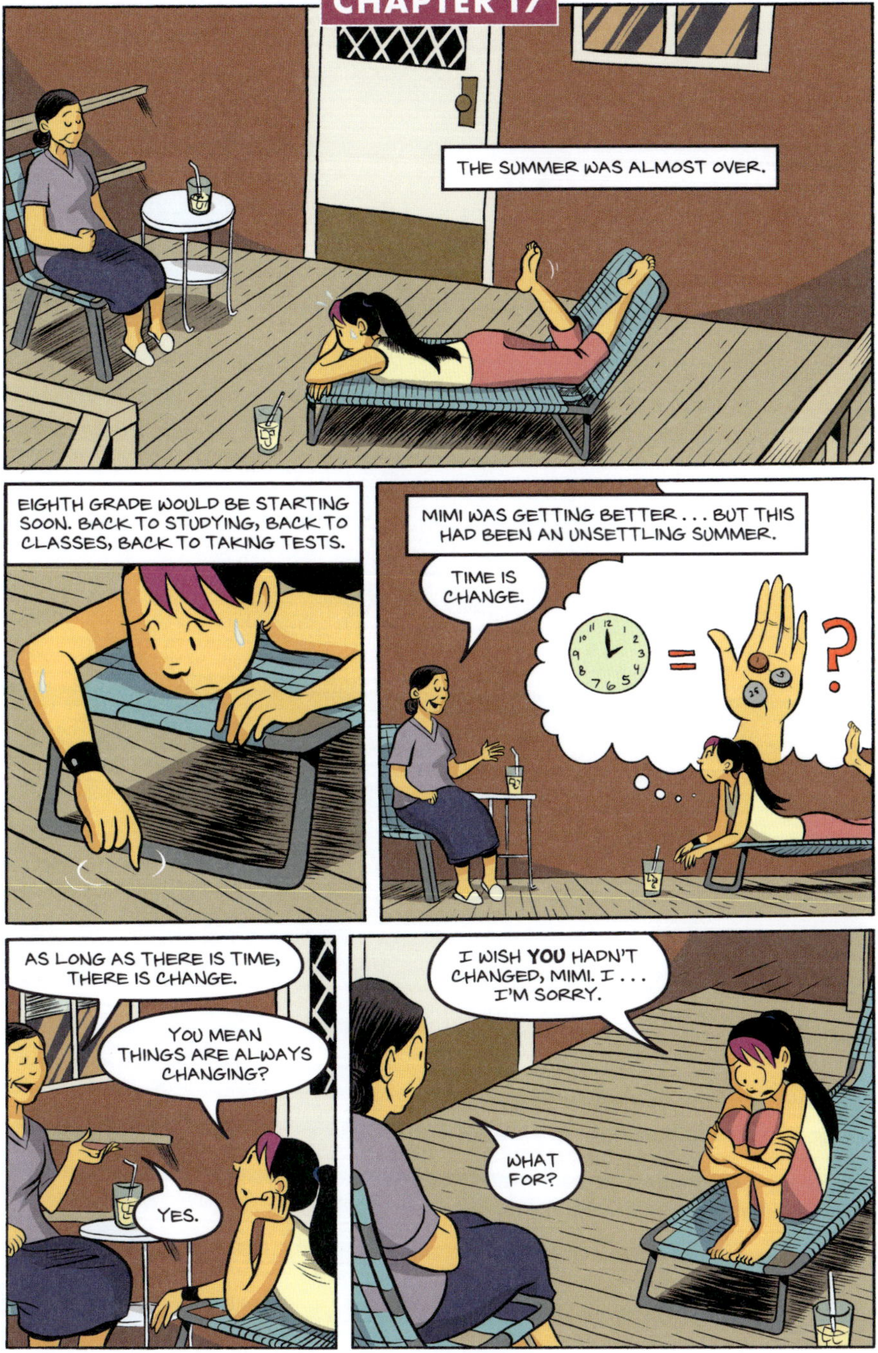
THE SUMMER WAS ALMOST OVER.
EIGHTH GRADE WOULD BE STARTING SOON. BACK TO STUDYING, BACK TO CLASSES, BACK TO TAKING TESTS.
MIMI WAS GETTING BETTER . . . BUT THIS HAD BEEN AN UNSETTLING SUMMER.
TIME IS CHANGE.
=
?
AS LONG AS THERE IS TIME, THERE IS CHANGE.
YOU MEAN THINGS ARE ALWAYS CHANGING?
YES.
I WISH **YOU** HADN'T CHANGED, MIMI. I . . . I'M SORRY.
WHAT FOR?

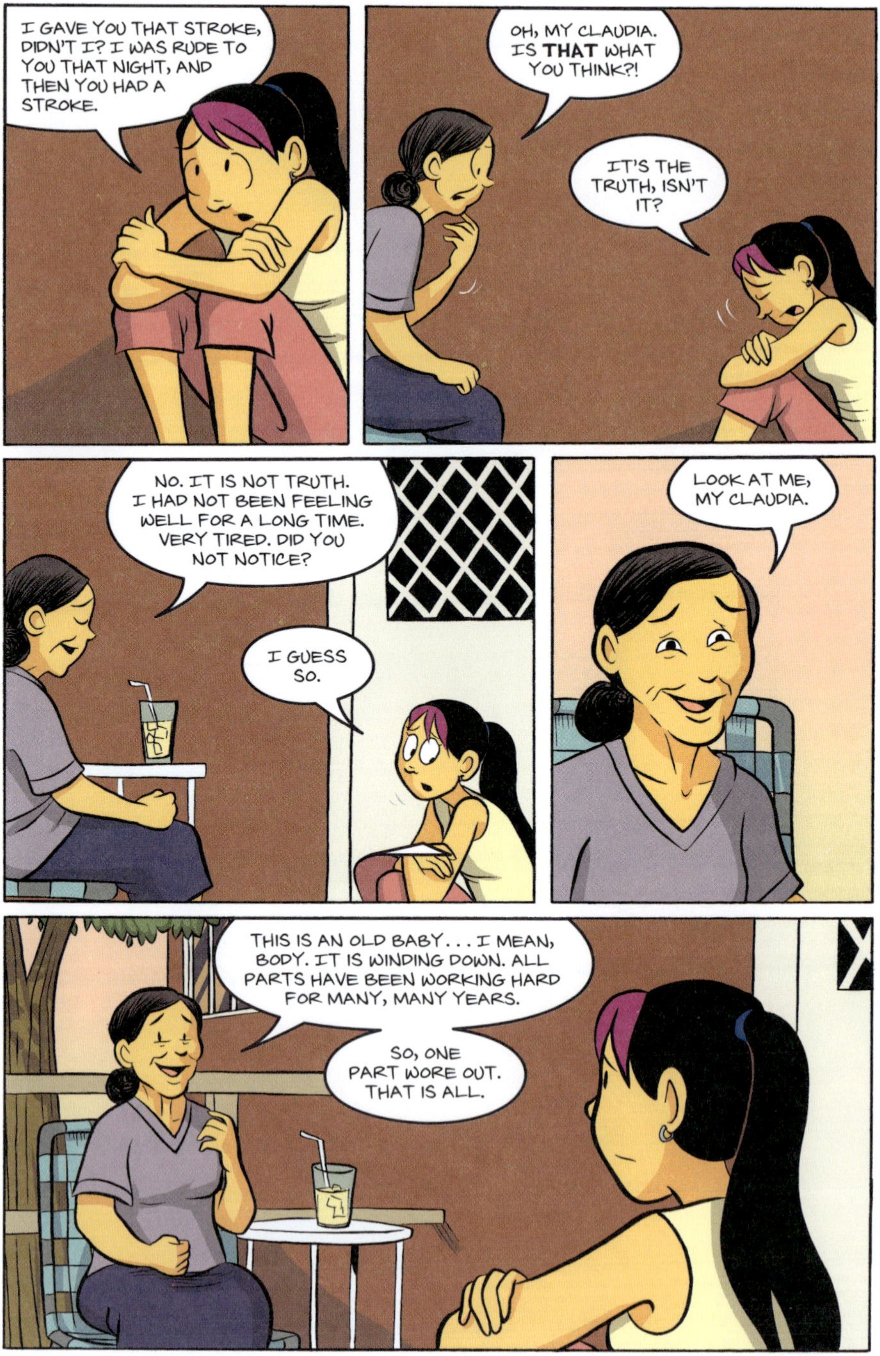
I GAVE YOU THAT STROKE, DIDN'T I? I WAS RUDE TO YOU THAT NIGHT, AND THEN YOU HAD A STROKE.
OH, MY CLAUDIA. IS **THAT** WHAT YOU THINK?!
IT'S THE TRUTH, ISN'T IT?
NO. IT IS NOT TRUTH. I HAD NOT BEEN FEELING WELL FOR A LONG TIME. VERY TIRED. DID YOU NOT NOTICE?
I GUESS SO.
LOOK AT ME, MY CLAUDIA.
THIS IS AN OLD BABY . . . I MEAN, BODY. IT IS WINDING DOWN. ALL PARTS HAVE BEEN WORKING HARD FOR MANY, MANY YEARS.
SO, ONE PART WORE OUT. THAT IS ALL.

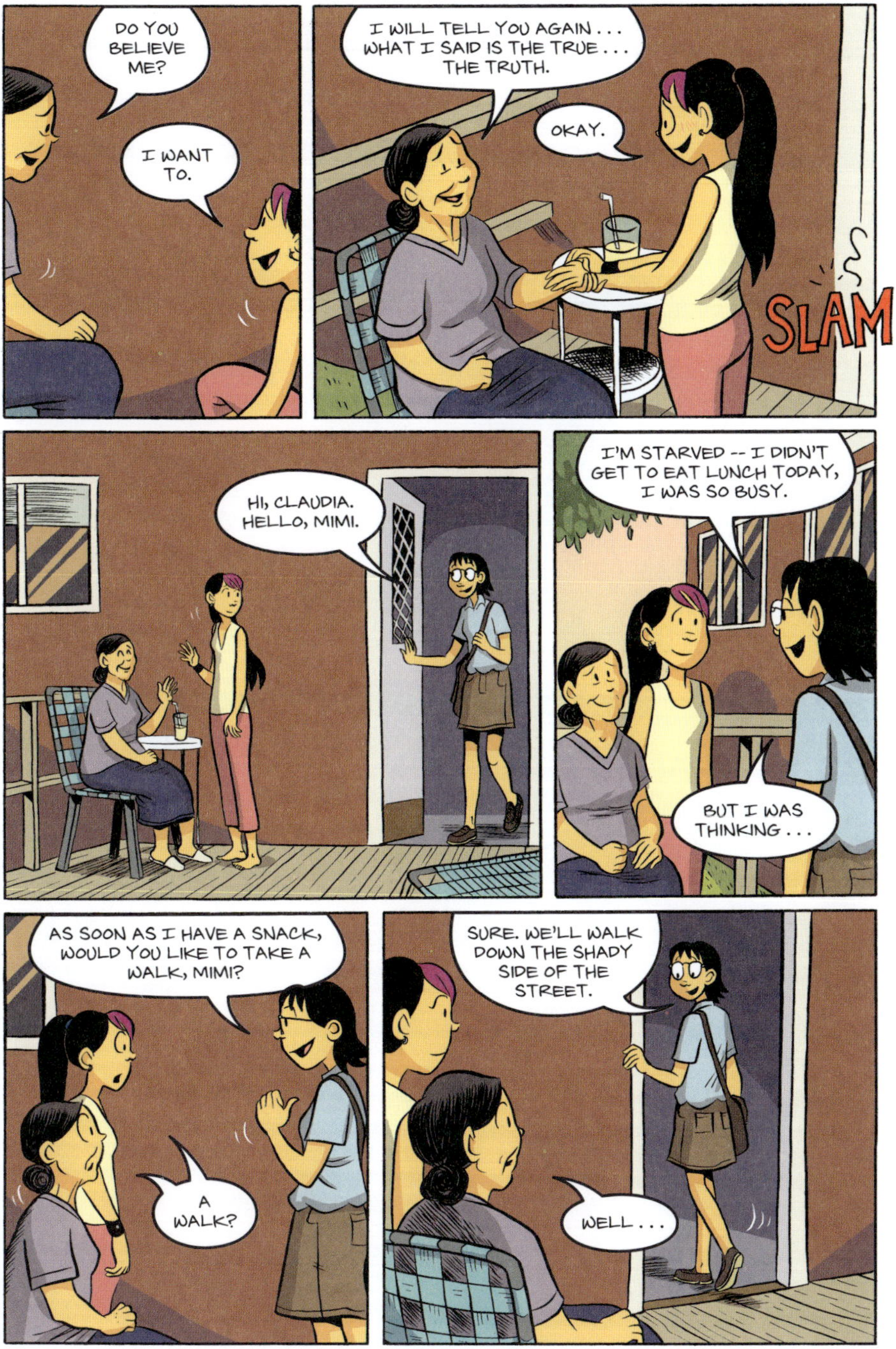
DO YOU BELIEVE ME?
I WANT TO.
I WILL TELL YOU AGAIN . . . WHAT I SAID IS THE TRUE . . . THE TRUTH.
OKAY.
SLAM
HI, CLAUDIA. HELLO, MIMI.
I'M STARVED -- I DIDN'T GET TO EAT LUNCH TODAY, I WAS SO BUSY.
BUT I WAS THINKING . . .
AS SOON AS I HAVE A SNACK, WOULD YOU LIKE TO TAKE A WALK, MIMI?
A WALK?
SURE. WE'LL WALK DOWN THE SHADY SIDE OF THE STREET.
WELL . . .

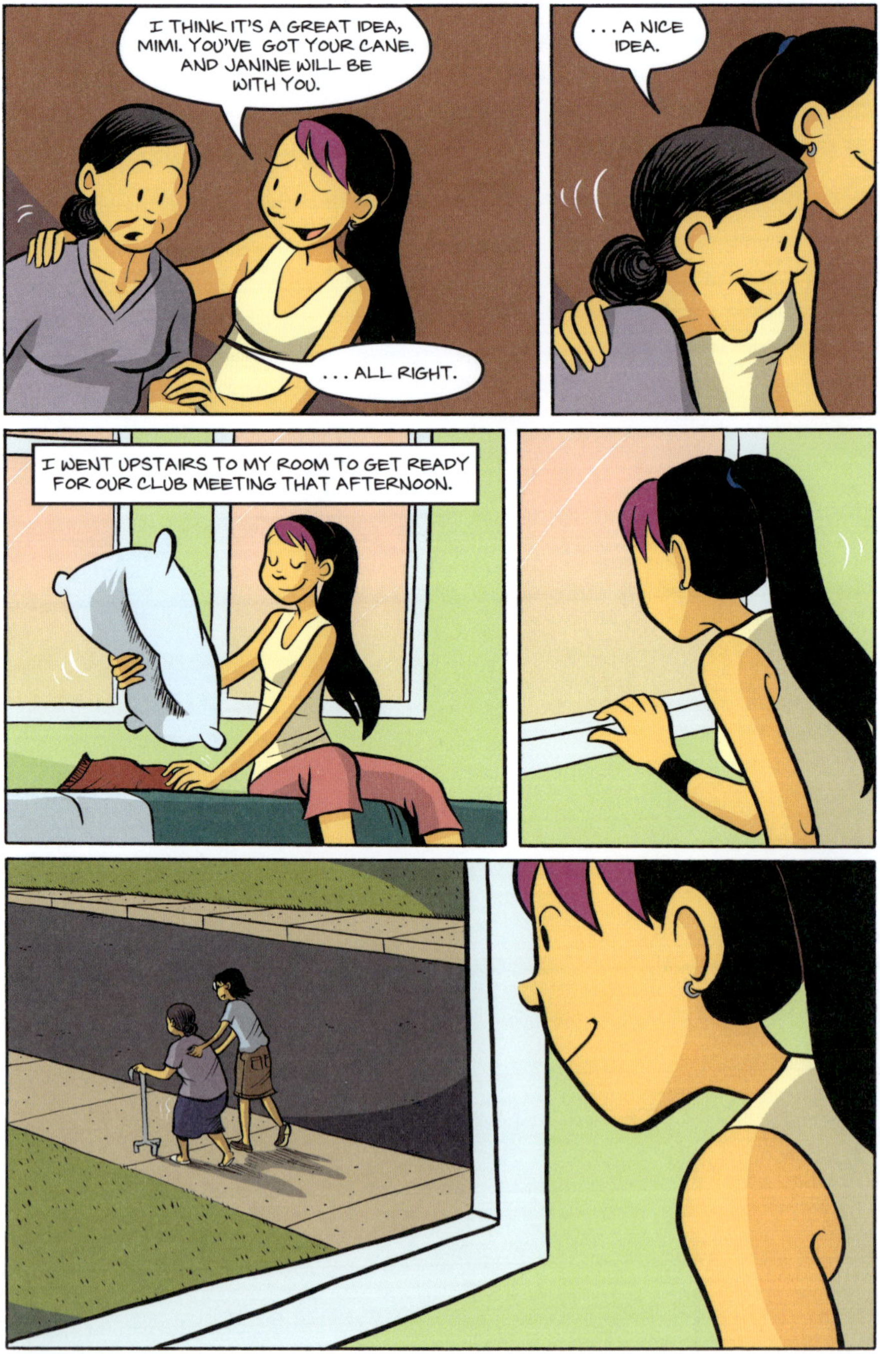
I THINK IT'S A GREAT IDEA, MIMI. YOU'VE GOT YOUR CANE. AND JANINE WILL BE WITH YOU.
. . . ALL RIGHT.
. . . A NICE IDEA.
I WENT UPSTAIRS TO MY ROOM TO GET READY FOR OUR CLUB MEETING THAT AFTERNOON.

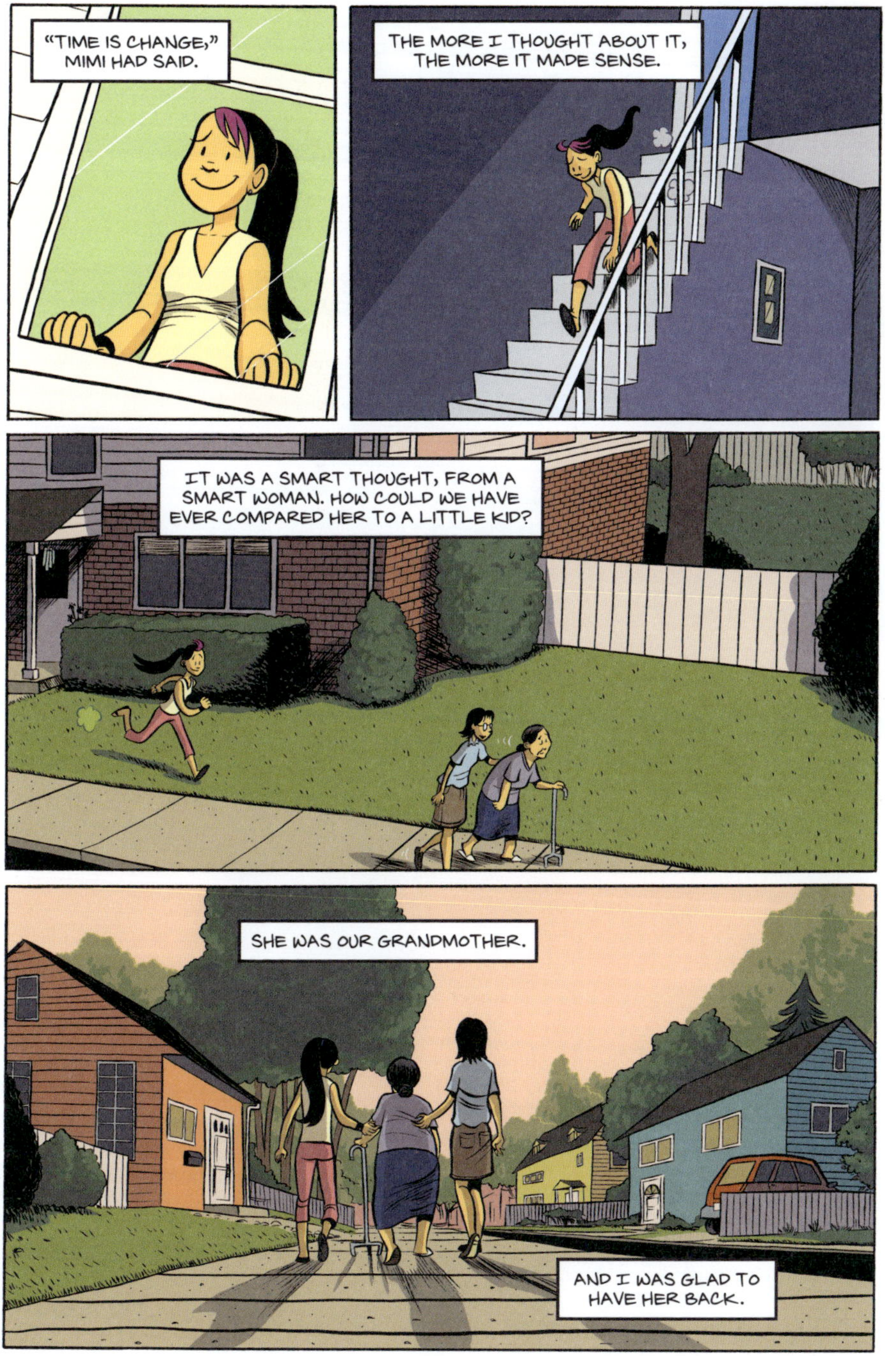
"TIME IS CHANGE,"
MIMI HAD SAID.
THE MORE I THOUGHT ABOUT IT, THE MORE IT MADE SENSE.
IT WAS A SMART THOUGHT, FROM A SMART WOMAN. HOW COULD WE HAVE EVER COMPARED HER TO A LITTLE KID?
SHE WAS OUR GRANDMOTHER.
AND I WAS GLAD TO HAVE HER BACK.

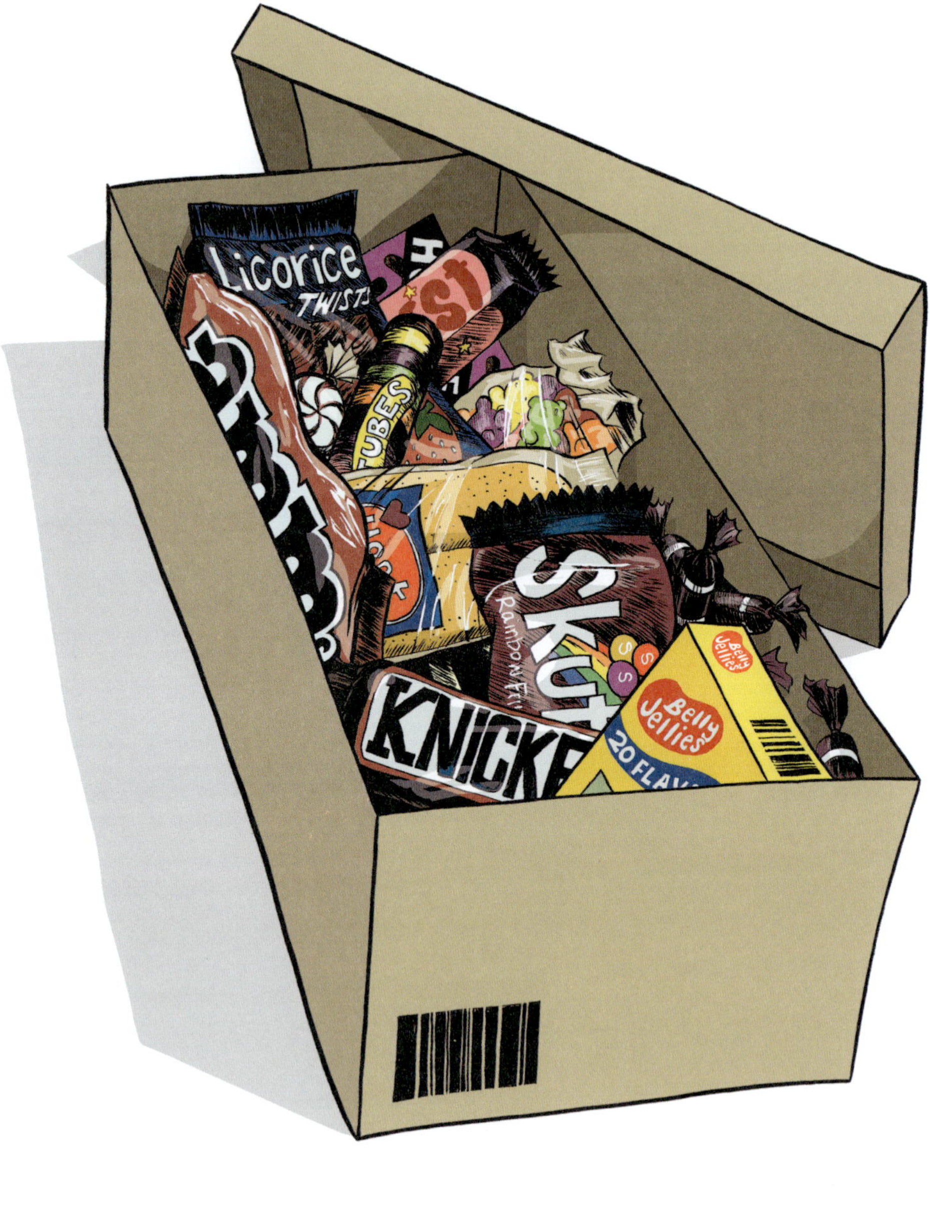
Licorice
TWISTS
TUBES
Belly Jellies
Belly Jellies

EPILOGUE

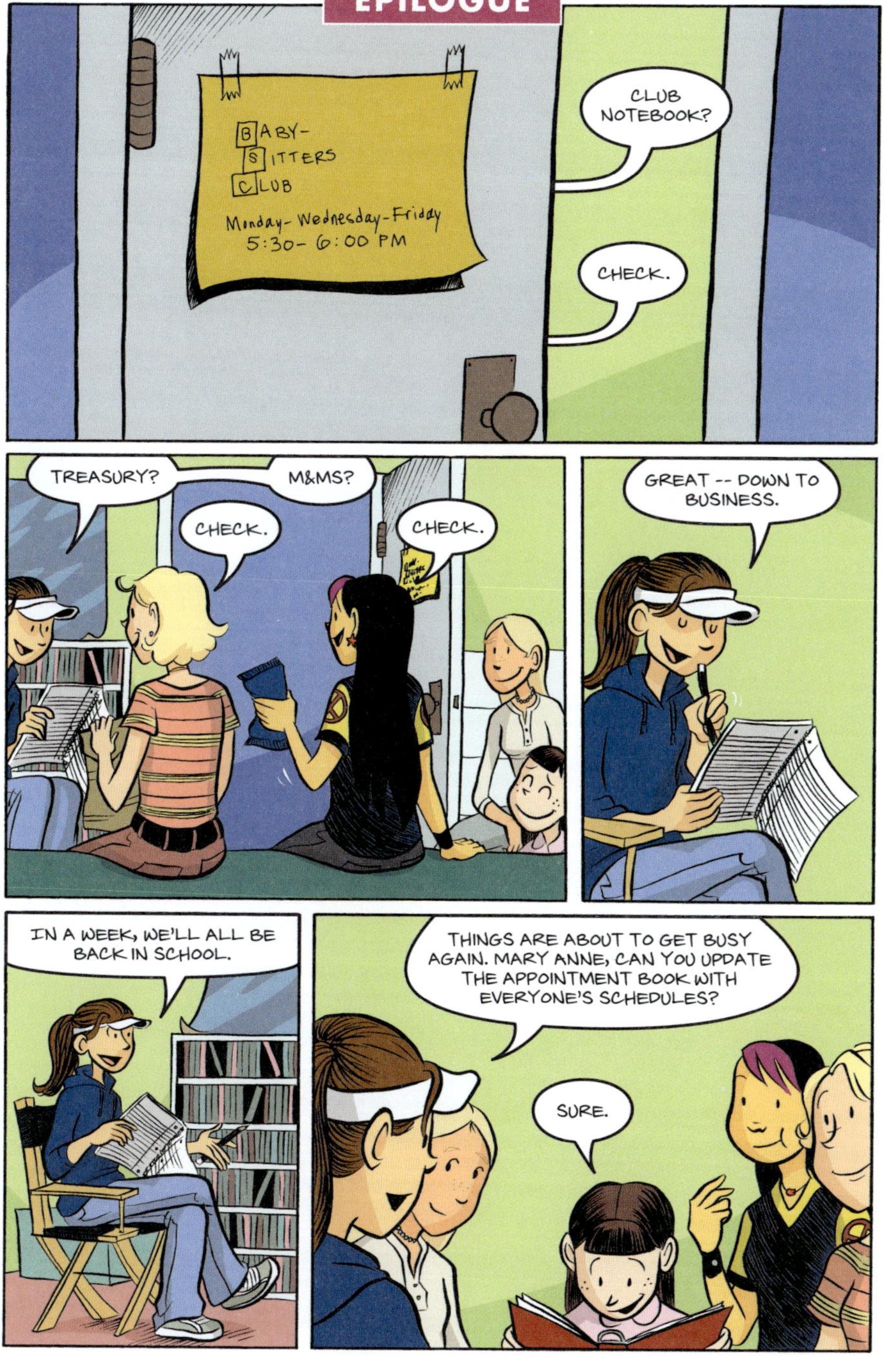

BABY-
SITTERS
CLUB
Monday-Wednesday-Friday
5:30-6:00 PM
CLUB NOTEBOOK?
CHECK.
TREASURY?
CHECK.
M&MS?
CHECK.
GREAT -- DOWN TO BUSINESS.
IN A WEEK, WE'LL ALL BE BACK IN SCHOOL.
THINGS ARE ABOUT TO GET BUSY AGAIN. MARY ANNE, CAN YOU UPDATE THE APPOINTMENT BOOK WITH EVERYONE'S SCHEDULES?
SURE.

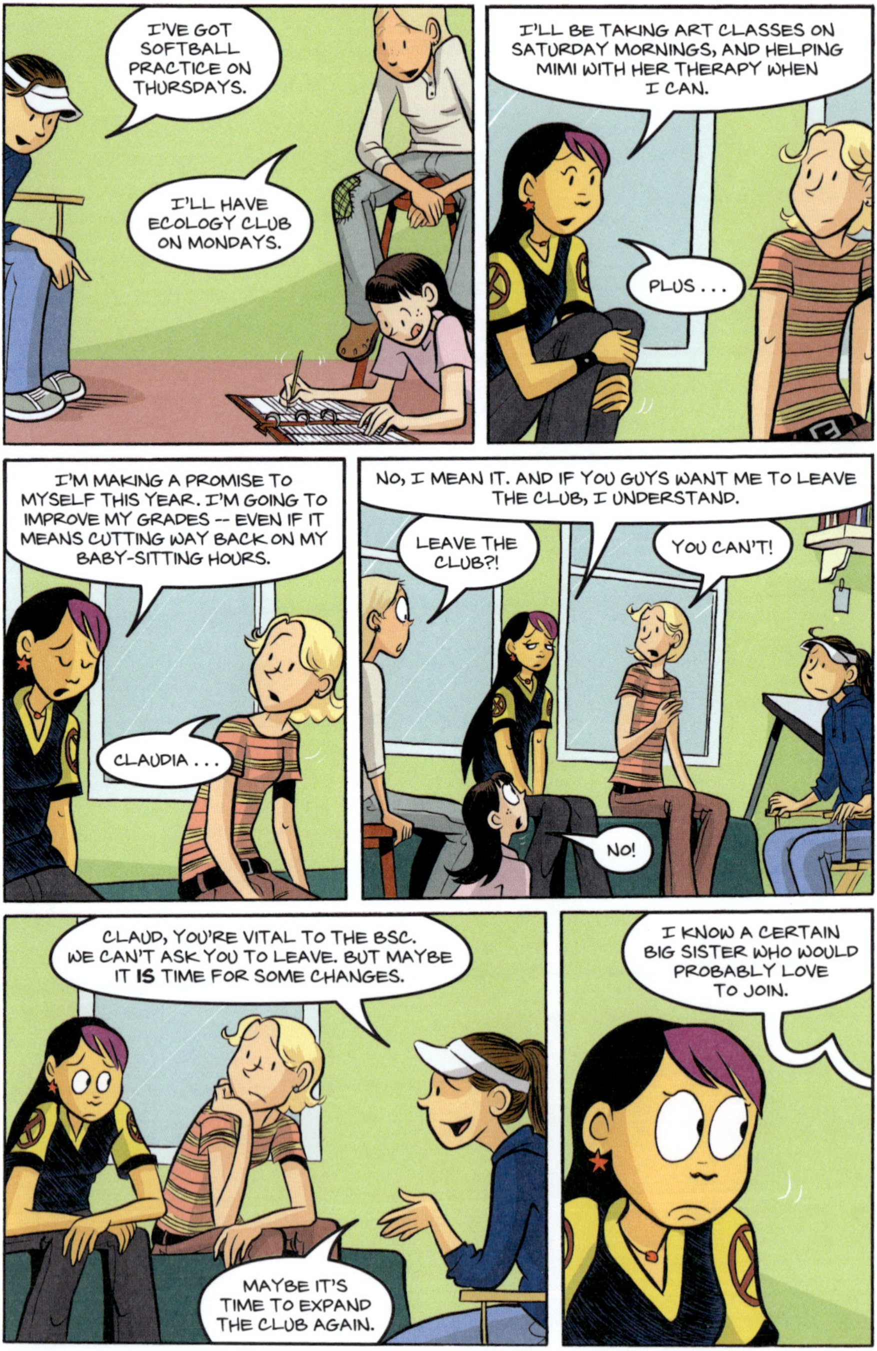
I'VE GOT SOFTBALL PRACTICE ON THURSDAYS.
I'LL HAVE ECOLOGY CLUB ON MONDAYS.
I'LL BE TAKING ART CLASSES ON SATURDAY MORNINGS, AND HELPING MIMI WITH HER THERAPY WHEN I CAN.
PLUS . . .
I'M MAKING A PROMISE TO MYSELF THIS YEAR. I'M GOING TO IMPROVE MY GRADES -- EVEN IF IT MEANS CUTTING WAY BACK ON MY BABY-SITTING HOURS.
CLAUDIA . . .
NO, I MEAN IT. AND IF YOU GUYS WANT ME TO LEAVE THE CLUB, I UNDERSTAND.
LEAVE THE CLUB?!
YOU CAN'T!
NO!
CLAUD, YOU'RE VITAL TO THE BSC. WE CAN'T ASK YOU TO LEAVE. BUT MAYBE IT **IS** TIME FOR SOME CHANGES.
MAYBE IT'S TIME TO EXPAND THE CLUB AGAIN.
I KNOW A CERTAIN BIG SISTER WHO WOULD PROBABLY LOVE TO JOIN.

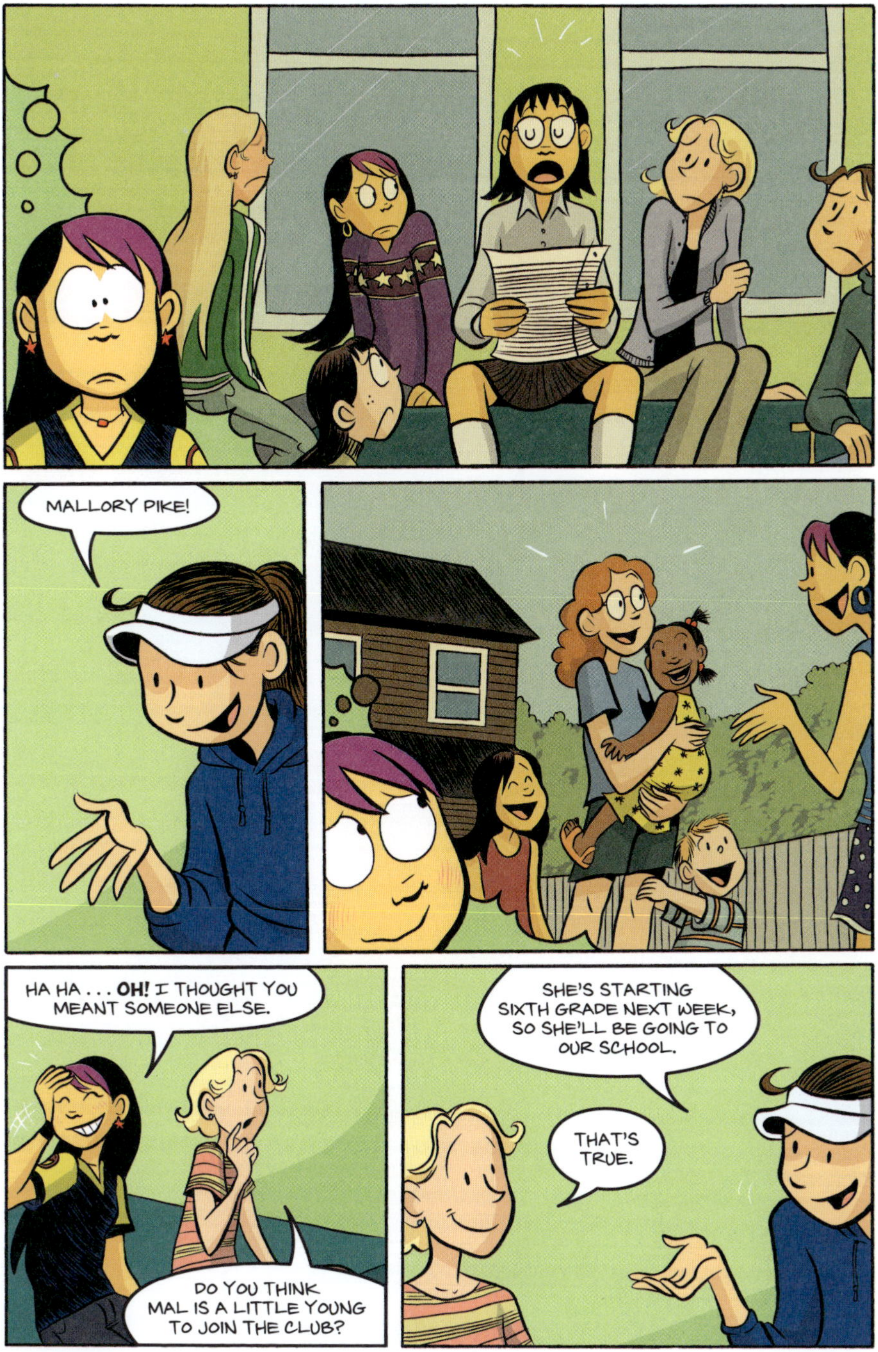
MALLORY PIKE!
HA HA . . . **OH!** I THOUGHT YOU MEANT SOMEONE ELSE.
DO YOU THINK MAL IS A LITTLE YOUNG TO JOIN THE CLUB?
SHE'S STARTING SIXTH GRADE NEXT WEEK, SO SHE'LL BE GOING TO OUR SCHOOL.
THAT'S TRUE.

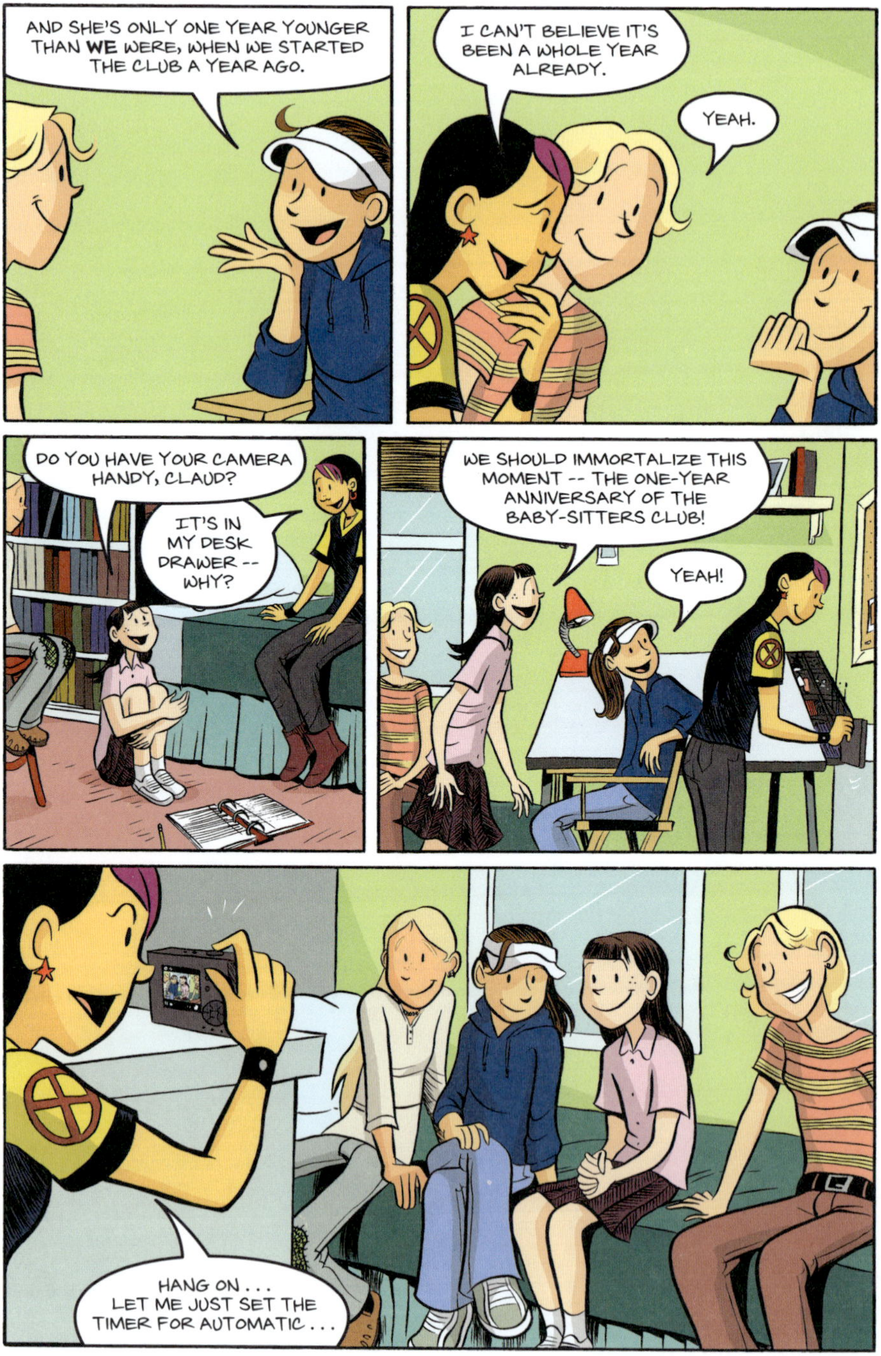
AND SHE'S ONLY ONE YEAR YOUNGER THAN **WE** WERE, WHEN WE STARTED THE CLUB A YEAR AGO.
I CAN'T BELIEVE IT'S BEEN A WHOLE YEAR ALREADY.
YEAH.
DO YOU HAVE YOUR CAMERA HANDY, CLAUD?
IT'S IN MY DESK DRAWER -- WHY?
WE SHOULD IMMORTALIZE THIS MOMENT -- THE ONE-YEAR ANNIVERSARY OF THE BABY-SITTERS CLUB!
YEAH!
HANG ON . . . LET ME JUST SET THE TIMER FOR AUTOMATIC . . .

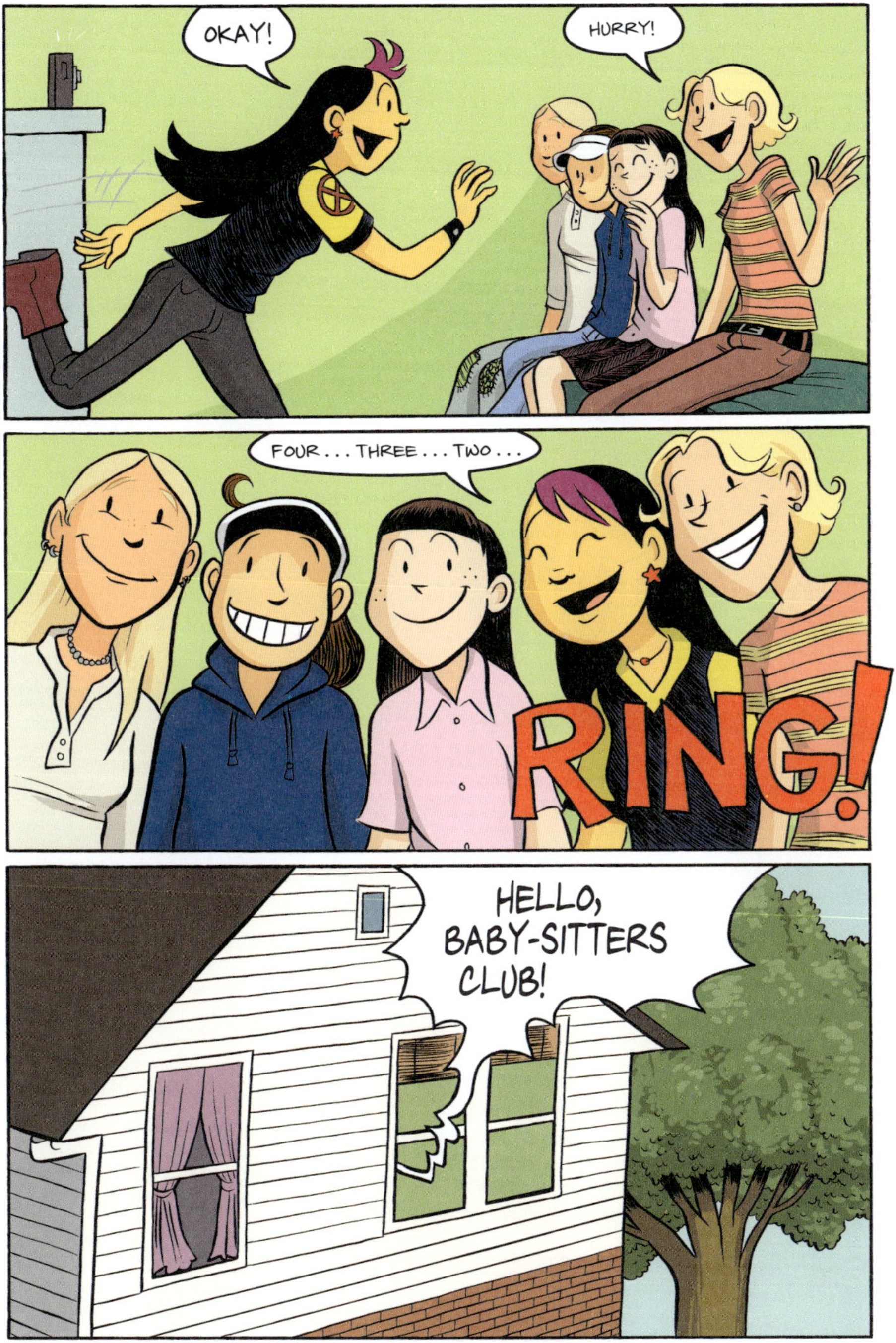
OKAY!
HURRY!
FOUR . . . THREE . . . TWO . . .
RING!
HELLO, BABY-SITTERS CLUB!

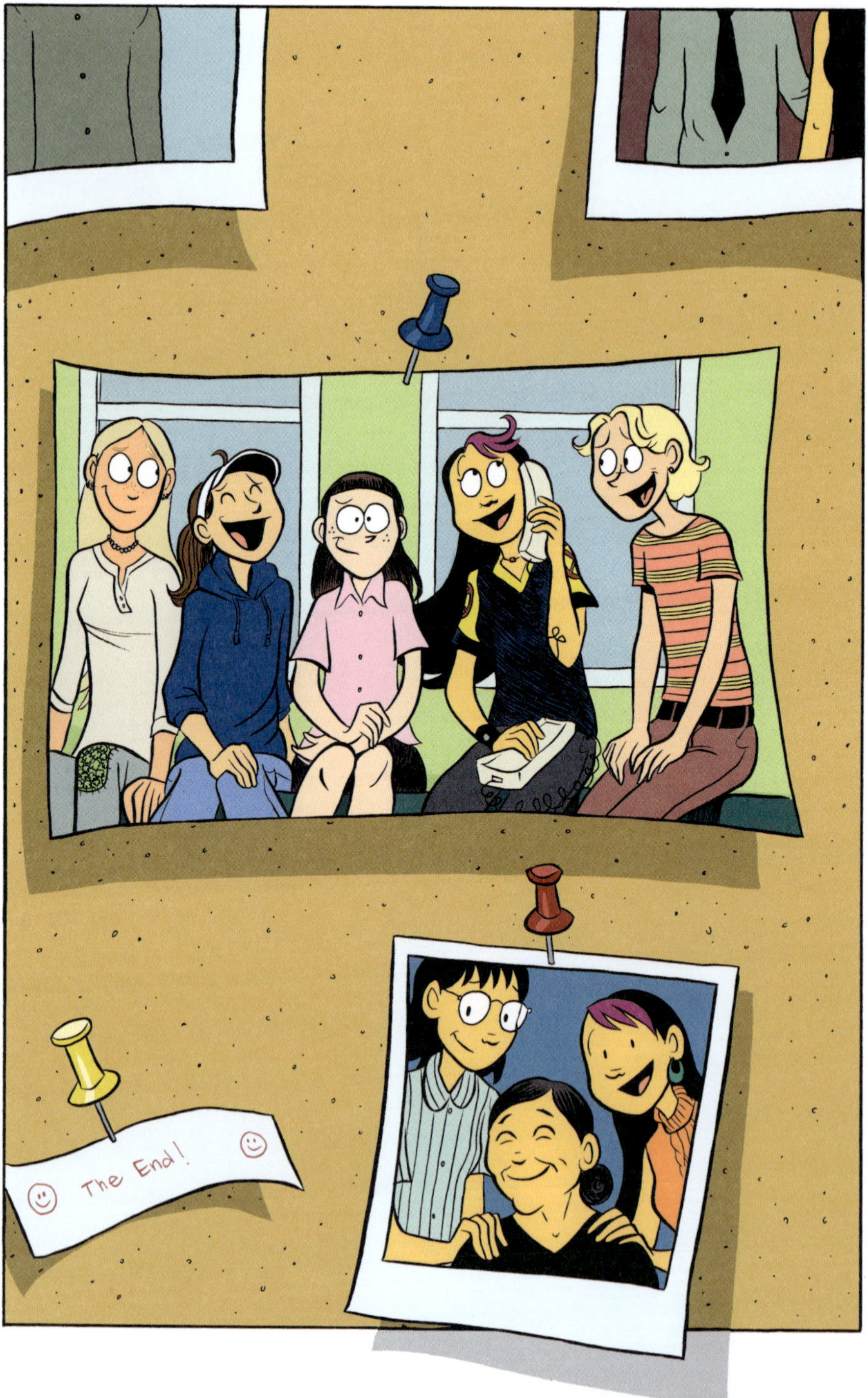
The End!

THE MAKING OF

THE BABY-SITTERS CLUB®

GRAPHIC NOVEL

STEP 1

Raina reads the original Baby-sitters Club book she is about to adapt several times before she starts working on the graphic novel. She underlines parts she especially likes, writes notes, and draws sketches of any new characters. Raina was a big fan of the BSC books when she was young, and often remembers things about the stories from the very first time she read them!

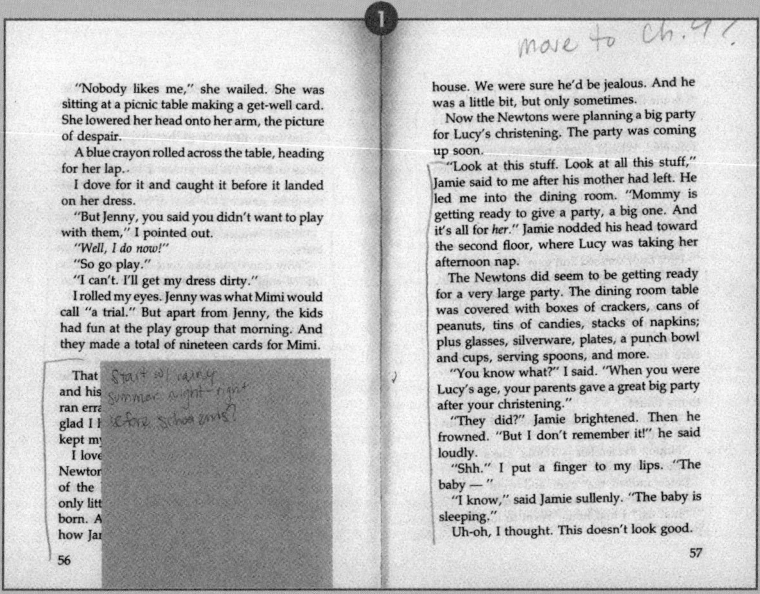
1

"Nobody likes me," she wailed. She was sitting at a picnic table making a get-well card. She lowered her head onto her arm, the picture of despair.

A blue crayon rolled across the table, heading for her lap.

I dove for it and caught it before it landed on her dress.

"But Jenny, you said you didn't want to play with them," I pointed out.

"Well, I do now!"

"So go play."

"I can't. I'll get my dress dirty."

I rolled my eyes. Jenny was what Mimi would call "a trial." But apart from Jenny, the kids had fun at the play group that morning. And they made a total of nineteen cards for Mimi.

That ... and his ... ran erra... glad I ... kept m...

I love... Newtor... of the ... only litt... born. A... how Jar...

56

Start w/ rainy summer night—right before school ends?

move to Ch. 4?

house. We were sure he'd be jealous. And he was a little bit, but only sometimes.

Now the Newtons were planning a big party for Lucy's christening. The party was coming up soon.

"Look at this stuff. Look at all this stuff," Jamie said to me after his mother had left. He led me into the dining room. "Mommy is getting ready to give a party, a big one. And it's all for *her*." Jamie nodded his head toward the second floor, where Lucy was taking her afternoon nap.

The Newtons did seem to be getting ready for a very large party. The dining room table was covered with boxes of crackers, cans of peanuts, tins of candies, stacks of napkins; plus glasses, silverware, plates, a punch bowl and cups, serving spoons, and more.

"You know what?" I said. "When you were Lucy's age, your parents gave a great big party after your christening."

"They did?" Jamie brightened. Then he frowned. "But I don't remember it!" he said loudly.

"Shh." I put a finger to my lips. "The baby —"

"I know," said Jamie sullenly. "The baby is sleeping."

Uh-oh, I thought. This doesn't look good.

57

STEP 2

Then, she begins to create thumbnails. These are small, simple, quick pages created on pieces of computer paper. Using a No. 2 pencil, Raina sketches out where the action and dialogue and drawings will appear on every page. She does this for the entire book, so she can see if the whole story works as well in comic form as it did in written form. It's easy to edit, shift things around, re-sketch, and rewrite at this stage. She also shows this to her editors and Ann M. Martin, the BSC's original author!

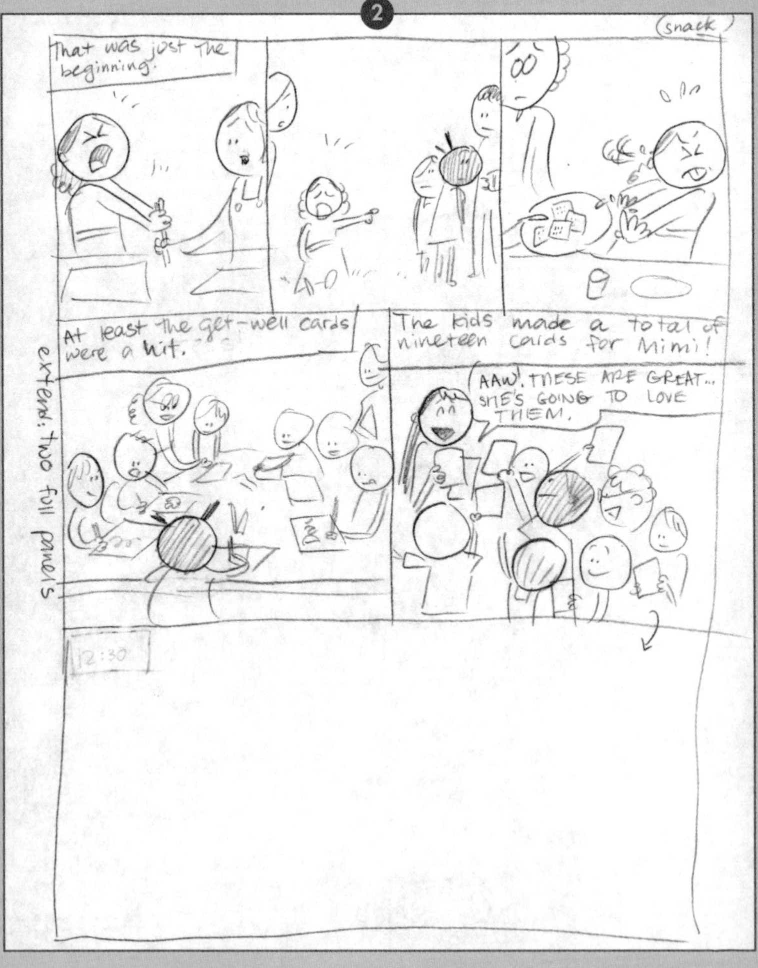
2
(snack)
That was just the beginning.
At least the get-well cards were a hit.
extend: two full panels
The kids made a total of nineteen cards for Mimi!
AAW! THESE ARE GREAT... SHE'S GOING TO LOVE THEM.
12:30

STEP 3

Once the thumbnails have been approved, Raina types up all the dialogue. This will be used when the book gets lettered (Step 8).

PAGE 46

PANEL 1
1. Caption: That was just the beginning.

PANEL 4
2. Caption: At least the get-well cards were a hit.

PANEL 5
3. Caption: The kids made a total of nineteen cards for Mimi!
4. Claudia: Aww! These are great. . . . She's going to love them.

STEP 4

Next, Raina uses a light blue pencil to do final layouts. She draws the panel borders and redraws her sketches onto large 11" x 14" Bristol board. It's a lot of work to redraw the sketches, even though they look very simple. This is where Raina works out perspective, composition, and general action in every panel. It also helps her see where the word balloons are going to go, so she can leave room for them. Being messy is no problem because blue pencil doesn't show up when the pages are scanned! See how this page changed between the thumbnail stage and the layout stage?

STEP 5

Now the real fun begins! Raina draws over her blue lines with a regular No. 2 pencil, this time going nice and slow and drawing in all the details. You can see how different the page is starting to look! The blue lines help guide the more finished art.

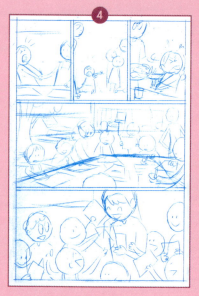

STEP 6

Raina's favorite stage is inking. She uses a Faber-Castell artist pen to draw the panel borders (using a ruler, of course!), and then a #2 Winsor & Newton watercolor brush and a bottle of waterproof India ink to ink the drawings. Little details like eyeballs and buttons are drawn with a tiny-tipped Micron pen, and are usually added last.

STEP 7

After the ink dries, Raina erases all the pencil lines. Each page is scanned into the computer at 64% its size, and then "cleaned up" in Photoshop. Instead of using Wite-Out, Raina just erases little mistakes digitally, which is faster. When each page file is clean, they are sent to the letterer!

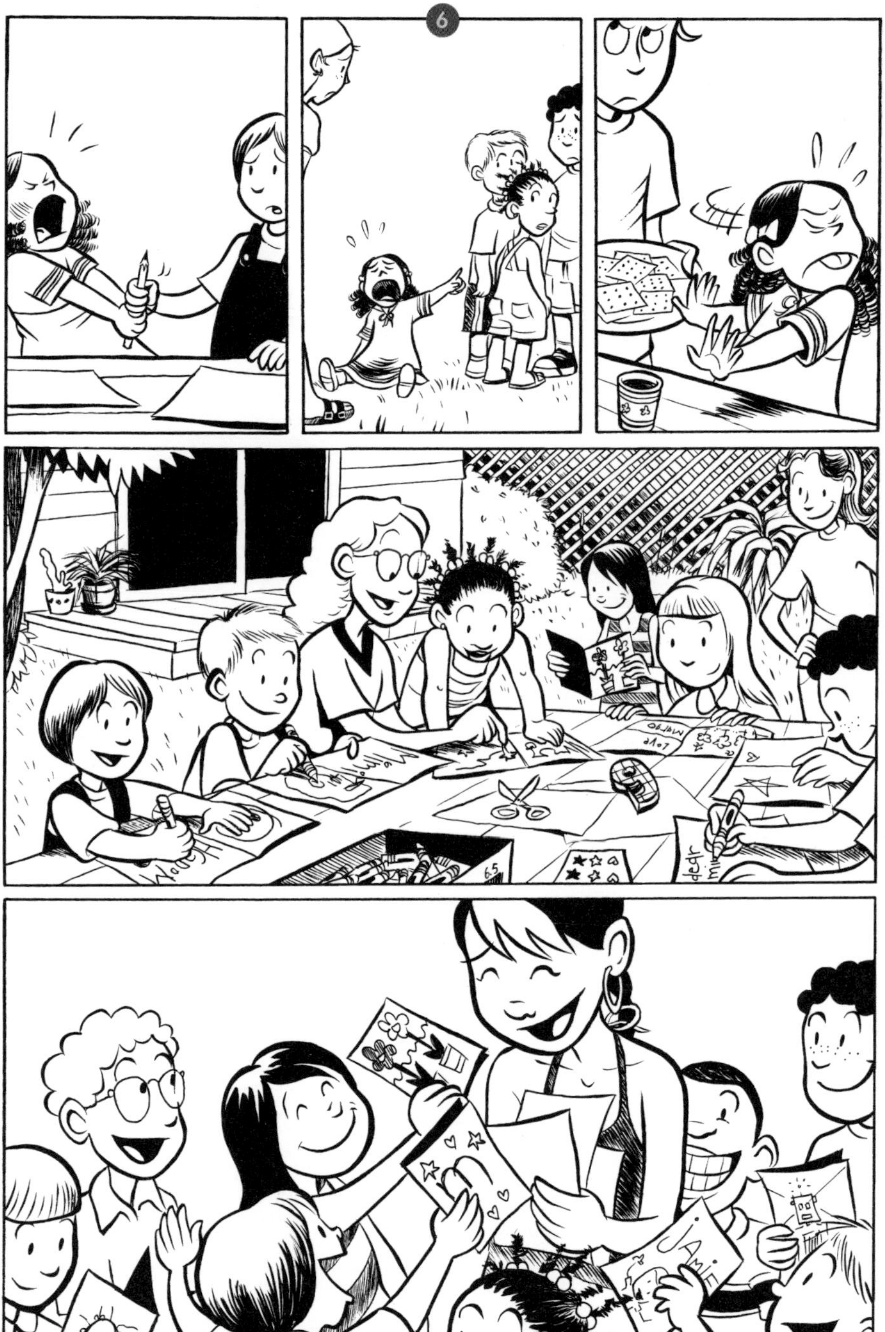
JAMIE

STEP 8

The letterer, John, creates word balloons in Adobe Illustrator, and then fills them in with the dialogue from the script that Raina typed up.

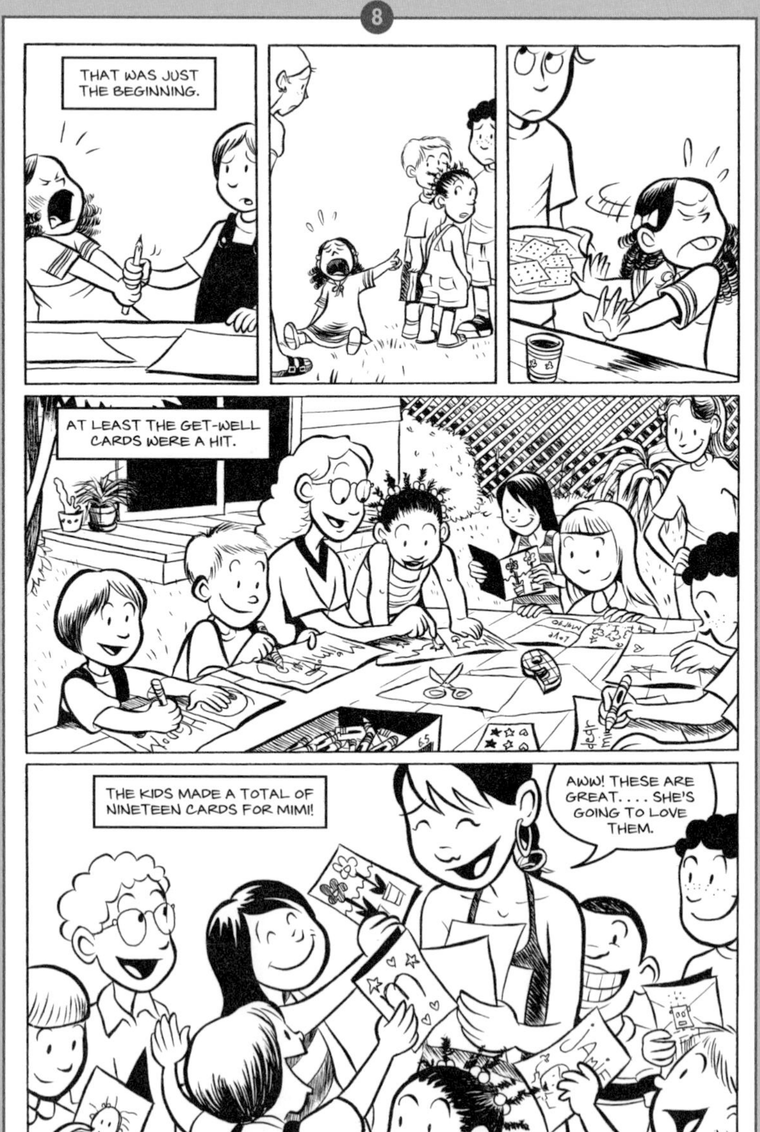
8
THAT WAS JUST THE BEGINNING.
AT LEAST THE GET-WELL CARDS WERE A HIT.
THE KIDS MADE A TOTAL OF NINETEEN CARDS FOR MIMI!
AWW! THESE ARE GREAT. . . . SHE'S GOING TO LOVE THEM.

STEP 9

In the final step, the colorist, Braden, uses Adobe Photoshop to add digital color to the black-and-white art. Now the finished pages are ready to go to the printer!

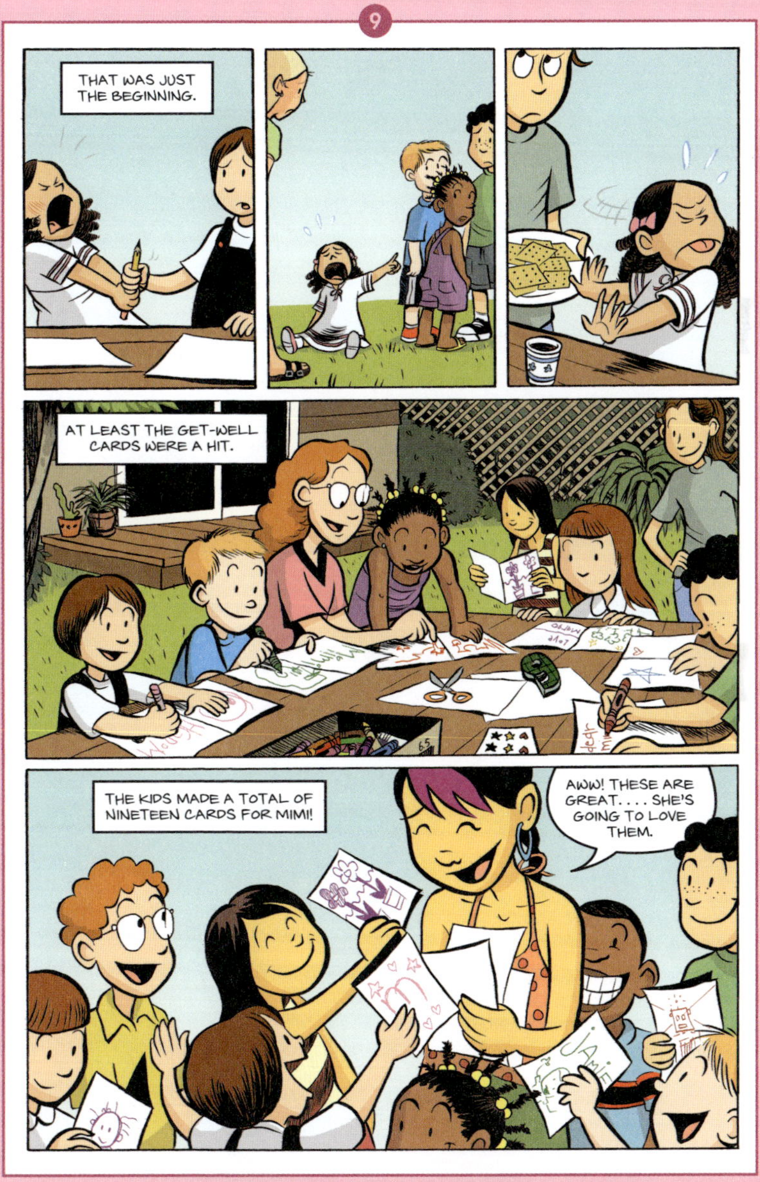

9
THAT WAS JUST THE BEGINNING.
AT LEAST THE GET-WELL CARDS WERE A HIT.
THE KIDS MADE A TOTAL OF NINETEEN CARDS FOR MIMI!
AWW! THESE ARE GREAT.... SHE'S GOING TO LOVE THEM.

ANN M. MARTIN'S The Baby-sitters Club is one of the most popular series in the history of publishing — with more than 190 million books in print worldwide — and inspired a generation of young readers. Her novels include *Belle Teal*, *A Corner of the Universe* (a Newbery Honor book), *Here Today*, *A Dog's Life*, and *On Christmas Eve*, as well as the much-loved collaborations, *P.S. Longer Letter Later* and *Snail Mail No More*, with Paula Danziger, and *The Doll People* and *The Meanest Doll in the World*, written with Laura Godwin and illustrated by Brian Selznick. Ann lives in upstate New York.

RAINA TELGEMEIER is the #1 *New York Times* bestselling, multiple Eisner Award–winning creator of *Smile*, *Sisters*, and *Guts*, which are all graphic memoirs based on her childhood. She is also the creator of *Drama* and *Ghosts*, and is the adapter and illustrator of the first four Baby-sitters Club graphic novels. Raina lives in the San Francisco Bay Area. To learn more, visit her online at goraina.com.